THE ROOKIE

Also by **Scott Sigler**

Infected
Contagious
Ancestor
Nocturnal

The Galactic Football League series (YA)

The Rookie
The Starter
The All-Pro
The MVP

The Galactic Football League novellas (YA)

The Reporter
The Detective
The Gangster (coming in 2013)
The Rider (coming in 2013)
Title Fight

The Color Series short story collections

Blood is Red
Bones are White
Fire is Orange (coming in 2013)

THE ROOKIE

Galactic Football League: Book One

Scot

Diversion Books
A Division of Diversion Publishing Corp.
80 Fifth Avenue, Suite 1101
New York, New York 10011
www.DiversionBooks.com

THE ROOKIE
(The Galactic Football League Series, Book I)

Published in the United States by
Dark Øverlord Paperback,
an imprint of Diversion Books.

For more information, email
info@diversionbooks.com
or media@scottsigler.com

Library of Congress Cataloging-in-Publication Data
Sigler, Scott
     The Rookie / Scott Sigler. — 1st ed.
     p. cm.
     1. Science Fiction—Fiction.   2. Sports—Fiction.
 ʼrary of Congress Control Number: 2009930686

 ᵀ: 978-1-938120-09-1

    design by Donna Mugavero at Sheer Brick Studio
    design by Scott E. Pond at Scott Pond Design Studio
    rt (figure) by Adrian Bogart at Punch Designs

    rsion Books edition AUGUST 2012

This book is dedicated to Coach Irv Sigler, my father, the greatest football coach and greatest man I have ever known.

This book is dedicated to the Junkies, the most rabid fans a writer could ever ask for. Let's go tailgatin'!

Acknowledgments

A team of talented friends made these paperback editions happen. Y'all are a world-class offensive line that make this journeyman quarterback look like an All-Pro:

Adrian "The Bruiser" Bogart at Punch Designs for cover illustration

A "Future Hall-of-Famer" Kovacs at Dark Øverlord Media for overall management

Donna "Chalkboard" Mugavero at Sheer Brick Studio for interior book design

Scott "Big Fish" Pond at Scott Pond Design Studios for cover design

Mary Cummings and Scott Waxman at Diversion Books for the brand new playing field

Special Thanks

Carol Sigler, who never missed a game. Go Chiefs! Go Redskins!

Jody Sigler, always subject to the first draft. Go Pack!

Scott Christian, for reading with a critical eye. Go Bama!

Shannon Fairlamb, for solid proofreading. Go Bears!

Rob Otto, talented commentator with a knack for stats. Go Titans (and Vikings, and Colts, and whoever else you've decided to root for this year because they happen to be winning this season)!

Irv Sigler III: The second-best football player among the Sigler Brothers (okay, that's a dirty lie, but it's my book, so I can say whatever the heck I want).

Looking forward to watching these guys play football

Tyler "Redneck" Sigler

Caden "The Crusher" Sigler

THE ROOKIE

BOOK ONE:
THE PNFL

TALENT SHOW

Semifinals of the Purist Nation Football League (PNFL)
Outland Fleet Corsairs (7-2) at Mining Colony VI Raiders (9-0)
Micovi Memorial Stadium
7:25 pm PNST
Coverage:
Holocast: Channel 15 Promised Land Sports Network
Translight Radio: 645.6 TL "The Fan"

Third and 7 on the defense's 41.

Micovi's three tiny moons hung in the evening sky like pitted purple grapes. Their reflected light diffused into the night's mist, making them glow with a fuzzy magnificence.

Smells of Human sweat, iron-rich mud and the saltwater-like odor of Carsengi Grass filled the frigid air. The endless hum of the atmosphere processor echoed through packed stands, but the players — and the crowd — had long since tuned out its ever-present droning.

Quentin Barnes slowly walked up behind the center, head sweeping from left to right as he took in every detail of the defense. Well, some would call it a "walk," most would call it a "swagger." A step left, a half bounce left, a step right, a half bounce right. He stood behind the center, his hands tapping out a quick left-right-left "ba-da-bap" on the center's ample behind.

From his crouch, the center smiled — the *ba-da-bap* was the kind of thing other players would tease you for — that is, unless your quarterback was Quentin Barnes. The center smiled because

Quentin only did that, did the *ba-da-bap*, when he saw a hole in the defense. And what Quentin saw, Quentin took.

Behind Quentin, the tailback and the fullback lined up an I-formation. Two wide receivers lined up on the left side, with a tight end on the right.

"Red, fifteen! Red, *fiftoooooon!*" Quentin's gravel and sandpaper voice barked out the audible. His breath shot out in a growing white cloud, which seemed to break into slow motion as the crystallized vapor rose almost imperceptibly into the windless night. Across the offensive and defensive lines, similar start-stop breaths filled the air like a thin fog of war, each puff illuminated by the powerful field lights.

"Watch that shucker!" the Corsairs' outside linebacker called as he pointed to the tight end. The tight end had caught six passes on the day, four of them in third-down situations, racking up 52 yards and a touchdown. And it wasn't even halfway through the third quarter. The linebacker's jersey, once blazing white with royal blue numbers, was now a torn mess of brown streaks, green smears and splotches of red fading to pink. The linebacker moved to line up directly over the tight end.

From his stance, the tight end smiled. Now he saw it, now he saw the same thing Quentin had seen almost the second they broke from the huddle.

"Huuut ... hut!"

The center snapped the ball into Quentin's wide hands. The linemen launched into their endless battle, huge cleated shoes kicking up clods of tortured grass and well-worked mud. Quentin dropped straight back as the fullback and tailback moved to the left and to the right, respectively, ready to block. The tight end shot off the line, big legs pumping and big arms swinging. The linebacker backpedaled, eyes wide and angry — he wasn't going to let the tight end beat him this time.

The linebacker watched Quentin's eyes as they locked onto the tight end. The tight end stepped to the right, like he was breaking outside, his head looking up and his shoulders turning out in an exaggerated move before he cut sharply left, to the inside, and curled up at eight yards from the line of scrimmage. Quentin's left arm reared back — the linebacker snarled as he jumped the rout: it was payback time, an easy interception.

Quentin's arm came forward as the linebacker closed on the tight end — but the ball never left the tall quarterback's hand. Pump fake. Quentin reared back again, lightning fast, and lofted a smooth, arching pass. The linebacker leapt, but the ball sailed just a few inches over his outstretched fingers to fall perfectly into the arms of the sprinting tailback, who had come out of the backfield on a delayed pattern. The tailback turned upfield, never breaking stride.

The tailback threw a head-and-shoulders juke on the free safety, who couldn't change direction quickly enough to catch the streaking runner. The tailback cut to the right, toward the sidelines, and turned on the jets — the strong safety had a good angle of pursuit, but there just wasn't enough field to catch up. The tailback strode into the dirty end zone standing up. The record crowd of 15,162 roared its approval.

Micovi Raiders 34, Purist Nation Outland Fleet Corsairs 3.

Quentin Barnes reached down and plucked a few blades of the tough Carsengi Grass from the muddy, cleat-torn field, then held them to his nose. He breathed deeply, smiled, then rolled his fingers, feeling the grass's rough texture before the blades scattered to the ground.

SMILES SEEMED LIMITLESS that day, particularly to players and fans of the black-and-silver Mining Colony Six Raiders. And for Stedmar Osborne, the Raiders' owner, the smile was so big it looked almost painful. He sat behind the smoked glass of his luxury box, enjoying an illegal Jack Daniel's on the rocks and smoking an illegal Tower Republic cigar. Normally he was down on the field, as any young owner should be, but this week he was entertaining a visitor — a Quyth Leader, forbidden both because of his rap sheet and his species. Not that it was legal for any species other than Humans to stand on Purist Nation soil. But out here on the fringe colonies, such things were often ignored if you had enough influence.

"What did I tell you, *Shamakath*," Stedmar said, respectfully using the Quyth word for "leader."

Gredok the Splithead nodded quickly, his three sets of foot-long black antennae bobbing like dreadlocks. Gredok had to look up — he was tall for a Quyth Leader, but at three feet, two inches, he was exactly half Stedmar's height.

Out of all the galaxy's known species, Humans and Quyth shared the most similar body plan. Most similar, which was actually not very similar at all. Both species had evolved from primitive quadrupeds into bipeds, giving them two legs and two arms. From that point on, however, any similarity broke down. The average Human stood at twice the height of an average Quyth Leader and weighed three times as much.

The Quyth Leader's body looked as if a sculptor had taken a Human child's arms and moved them down to just above the hips. Both arms and legs ended in three-pincered claws, which provided solid footing but were incapable of manipulating any tool. The proximity of legs and arms meant the Quyth could move with equal ease as a biped or a quadruped, although no respecting Quyth Leader would ever be caught walking on all-fours. Such behavior was fine for Warriors and Workers, but never for a Leader.

The trunk continued up from the arms, a long, smooth, furry body that ended in a head dominated by one softball-sized eye. A small, vertical mouth sat under the eye. A set of pedipalps extended from the sides of the Quyth's vertical mouth — what were once tools for killing and eating had evolved into long, dexterous appendages the Quyth used like Human hands.

"I don't know why he hasn't thrown deep more," Stedmar said. "With that kid's arm, they should be going for the bomb on every play, you know?"

Gredok looked back at the field and rolled his eye, marveling in Stedmar's idiocy. Gredok caught himself in the act, then stared straight ahead — rolling one's eye was an expression of derision he'd picked up from hanging around Humans for far too long.

Any neophyte could see that the quarterback had been setting that play up for at least the last two offensive series.

Gredok looked to his left, at Hokor the Hookchest, also a Quyth Leader. Hokor had forgotten more about football than Gredok would ever know. Hokor's single eye glowed slightly yellow with an internal light. The tips of his three sets of flexible, foot-long antennae spun in tiny circles — there was nothing Human about *that* expression. Hokor's stubby legs were the only things that stayed still: his tan-striped yellow fur raised and lowered with subconscious excitement, his tiny three-pincered hands flexed involuntarily, and his pedipalps twitched, as if they were searching for food to stuff into his small mouth. Gredok reached over and gently nudged Hokor. Hokor's antennae immediately stopped circling, and the yellow light faded until his big eye was perfectly clear.

Hokor was a great coach, but he had little of what the Humans called a "poker face." Gredok, on the other hand, remained calm and collected. His antennae and pedipalps sat perfectly still, while his own fur, silky-black and impeccably groomed, lay smooth and undisturbed.

It might have been a casual outing of three business acquaintances, not much different than what went on in the stadium's other luxury boxes save for the fact that there were probably no other non-Humans in the stadium, nor were they packed with lethal-looking bodyguards: four Humans, who belonged to Stedmar; and two thickly muscled, six-foot-tall Quyth Warriors, their furless, hard-shelled carapaces showing battle scars and the hand-painted emblems of combat tours and various war campaigns.

"Greedy, I've got to hand it to you on this football team stuff," Stedmar said as the kicker knocked through the extra point to make the score 35-3. "I had no idea how lucrative this could be, but you were right — I'm moving at least five hundred keys of smack every road game and coming back with a bus full of money. I never *dreamed* smuggling could be so easy. Local customs officials barely look at a team bus. Even the shucking bats don't bother."

"The Creterakians introduced football," Gredok said, noting how Stedmar still referred to the ruling race as "bats," a reference to some Human animal Gredok had never seen. "Football supposedly reduces interspecies violence. They don't want to rock the boat over a little thing like smuggling."

Stedmar lifted his glass. "Well, here's to interspecies cooperation," he said, then took a drink as the ice cubes rattled wetly.

"And you have a Tier Three team," Gredok said, "Imagine how valuable it becomes with a Tier Two team, and you're moving across entire systems, or even a Tier One team, and you've got complete immunity across all governments."

Stedmar nodded. "Tier Three is good enough for now. It's going to take me a few years to buy out a Tier Two team. But hey, if I can hold on to Barnes, I'll be competitive from the start."

"Don't be sure Barnes can carry your team," Gredok said. "There's a reason no Nationalite quarterback has ever led a team to a championship. It's one thing to be great in an all-Human league. It's a very different game when Barnes has to throw past eight-foot-tall Sklorno defensive backs and dodge 400-pound Quyth Warrior linebackers."

Stedmar shrugged. "The boy thinks he can handle it."

"The rest of your team can't. Your repressive government barely allows non-Human trade let alone bringing in other races to play football. In Tier Two ball, you need Quyth Warriors, Sklorno and Ki. It would be fun to watch your puny 400-pound linemen try and block a 600-pound Ki nose tackle."

"I'm working on it, *Shamakath*," Stedmar said. Stedmar did an admirable job of pronouncing the word correctly, no small feat considering his Human vocal cords were only half as versatile as the Quyth voice chamber. It was a clear sign of his respect toward the leader of his syndicate. Hokor genuinely liked Stedmar and had big plans for his lieutenant. Assuming, of course, that Stedmar lived to see the end of this game.

"Football is becoming too popular, even in the Purist Nation," Stedmar said. "You know how the Holy Men are, how much they hate the Planetary Union and the League of Planets. It drives the

Holy Men crazy to know those two heretic systems have fielded so many championship teams over the past twenty-five years."

"Heretic?" Gredok said. "Is that what you believe?"

Stedmar laughed. "How can you ask that? I don't follow this system's damned religion."

Gredok pointed to the infinity symbol tattooed on Stedmar's forehead. "You seem to have all the trappings of a Church member."

"The cost of doing business in this system. If you're not a confirmed member of the Church, you can't get near most of the business. Corruption abounds and is quite profitable."

Gredok let out a rapid *click-click-click* of disgust. "Still, the Purist Nation is not going to allow non-Human races inside its borders, and you need other races to win in the Galactic Football League. Governments have been working on that for three centuries — the GFL has only been around for twenty-three seasons, and three of those were suspended."

Stedmar shrugged again. "The bats have been here for forty years."

"That's different," Gredok said. "They conquered all the Human planets. Your people don't have a choice."

"The scriptures also say no non-Humans on any Purist Nation planet, but you know the Holy Men — when they want something, the Book is always full of loopholes. If it wasn't for out-system smuggling, the border colonies couldn't even survive. Our economy is a disaster and everyone knows it. Things are going to change, and soon."

"You forget I've been alive three times as long as you. I've always heard about 'coming changes' in your system, yet it's one fundamentalist coup after another. If it wasn't for the Creterakians, the Purist Nation would have torn itself apart long ago."

"Look at Buddha City," Stedmar said. "They've got every race in the galaxy on that station, and it orbits Allah, the very *seat* of the Purist Nation. But that's allowed because the aliens can't set foot on Allah itself. That policy has survived through the last three regimes because even the radicals know the economy can't sustain itself without at least some official out-system trade. There's even talk of allowing a limited non-Human presence on outlying food and research facilities, space stations and, you guessed it, mining colonies."

"And you think you'll still have Barnes when that happens?" Gredok leaned forward, the football game forgotten, his game, the power game, now fully under way.

Stedmar shrugged. "The Holy Men might not open things for another ten years, so who knows. Besides," Stedmar said as he turned to look straight into Gredok's big eye, "I've got offers on the table for Barnes' contract."

Gredok showed no emotion. He kept his antennae still, but inside he felt a combination of disappointment and a rush of excitement. Of course the Human knew why Gredok had come.

Gredok turned back to the game. The Corsairs were driving, using their fast-passing game to move forward five or ten yards at a crack. Both teams wore simple uniforms: pants with no stripe, jersey decorated with only the player's number, front and back in block-letter style, a helmet decorated only with the first letter of the team name. Every team in the Purist Nation Football League wore uniforms that were identical save for the team colors. The Raiders had silver-gray pants and helmets with black jerseys, while the Corsairs wore royal blue pants and helmets with white jerseys.

"Who would want Barnes?" Gredok said with disgust. "Purist Nation quarterbacks can't handle the Upper Tiers. It has been proven time and time again."

Stedmar's thin smile returned. "Kirani-Ah-Kollok."

This time, Gredok couldn't control his quivering antennae. Kirani-Ah-Kollok, *Shamakath* of the Ki Homeworld Syndicate. The very being that Gredok hoped to someday replace.

"Kollok? Why would he want Barnes when he's got Frank Zimmer at quarterback?"

"Zimmer's getting old," Stedmar said. "He's thirty-three. I know that's not much to you, *Shamakath*, but for a Human that means he's only got four or five good years left. Barnes is only nineteen. Kollok figures that by the time Zimmer starts to fade, Barnes will be in his mid-twenties, just hitting the peak of his abilities."

Few bosses were as ruthless and clever as Kollok, who was not only a shrewd businessman but also a great judge of football talent. Kollok's team, the To Pirates, had won the GFL championship in 2681 and followed up with a trip to last season's title game, where they lost to the current champions, the Jupiter Jacks.

On the field, the Corsairs' quarterback dropped back and threw deep downfield. The ball hung in the air for far too long, giving the Raiders' strong safety time to make a well-timed leap. His outstretched hands snagged the ball before the receiver dragged him down. The crowd roared in approval.

"That's the quarterback's fourth interception," Hokor said quietly. "He should be shot."

Stedmar laughed at what he thought was a joke, but Gredok knew it was no laughing matter. Hokor was a demanding coach, to say the least. Back in his days as a Tier Three coach in the Quyth Planetary League, he had executed more than one ineffectual player.

A flock of Creterakian soldiers flew over the field, moving from perches on one side of the stadium to the other. As their small shadows zipped across the near stands, then the field, then the far stands, the crowd noise fell to a hush. The tiny creatures always made their presence felt during football games, where radicals were fond of deadly terrorist acts. Each one of the twenty or so winged beings carried an entropic rifle, capable of killing a man with even a glancing shot. Like any other public gathering, even ones with only a hundred or so people, the local Creterakian garrison wanted to see and be seen.

"I *hate* those little shuckers," Stedmar said quietly. "They do those flyovers on purpose, you know, to make sure the crowd doesn't get too wild."

Over the years, Gredok had seen several "wild" crowds of repressed Purist Nation citizens. Just during the drive from the spaceport to the city center and the football field, he'd seen two minor riots and one lynch mob. The lynch mob ended when a flock of soldiers flew in to break it up, then some Purist genius started throwing rocks at the ugly little flying creatures: the lynching originally intended to kill one man for an unknown crime ended in at least twelve deaths when the Creterakians opened fire. Mining Colony VI, or "Micovi" as the locals liked to call it, was little more than a barely controlled, overpopulated border outpost of a Third World system.

The Raiders' offense ran onto the field, led by the swaggering Barnes. The crowd noise picked up once again as hometown fans cheered for their star player.

"He's awfully big for a quarterback," Gredok said.

"Seven feet even," Stedmar said. "Seven feet tall, 360 pounds."

So big, Gredok thought. Big enough, possibly, to stand up to the punishment that Upper Tier quarterbacks took week after week. Frank Zimmer was 6-foot-9, 310 pounds, and was one of the biggest quarterbacks in the league. "It's amazing how players keep getting larger and larger. Fifteen years ago a Human that size could have been a small tight end."

Barnes barked out the signals, looking up and down the line as he did. He paused, stood for a moment, and his hands did a *ba-da-bap* on the center's behind. Barnes screamed out an audible. Behind him, the tailback went in motion to the left, lining up in the slot between the tight end and the wide receiver.

"Here we go again," Stedmar said. "He sees something!"

Gredok and Hokor also leaned forward, although they knew what was coming — any fool could see the Corsairs' defensive backs were in man-to-man while the tailback's motion revealed that the linebackers were in a short zone. Barnes now had three targets to his left — the wide receiver, the tailback and the tight end.

"Roll out?" Gredok asked. Hokor nodded.

Barnes took the snap as the line erupted in the dirt-churning mini-war. He ran to his left, down the line, as the three left-side receivers sprinted straight downfield. But Hokor and Gredok weren't the only ones to see what Quentin had seen — the much-maligned linebacker tore up field, blitzing just inside the sprinting tight end. Quentin and the linebacker seemed to be on a direct collision course. The 360-pound linebacker closed in and launched himself, at which point Quentin calmly sidestepped toward the line of scrimmage. The linebacker sailed through the air, not even laying a finger on the deft quarterback.

The defensive end had separated from his block. Quentin's cut inside the linebacker took him right into the defensive end's reaching arms. Quentin cut back to the outside at the last second as the 400-pound end grabbed him with cannon-sized arms. The quarterback kept his feet pumping and pushed hard with his right arm. The end's feet chopped at the ground as he tried to keep up, but Quentin's stiffarm had knocked him off balance. The end fell, both hands wrapped in Quentin's jersey, pulling the smaller quarterback down. Quentin stumbled, leaned, then seemed to take a step toward the defensive end and twisted his shoulders as he pushed out with his right arm yet again. The end fell to the ground, his big hands slipping free of Quentin's jersey. Then the quarterback popped upright, like a stiff spring that had been bent to the ground then released.

So strong, Gredok thought. *I've never seen a Human quarterback so strong.*

Already moving upfield and now free of the clutching defensive end, Quentin tucked the ball and ran. The defense shifted from their pass coverage to come after him, but in the two seconds after his initial cut, he was already ten yards upfield and cutting to the outside.

"Hikkir," Hokor said quietly—the Quyth equivalent of "oh my."

The crowd roared as the cornerback streaked toward Quentin, but the defender came in too fast. Quentin juked to the right, to the inside, but in the same second was moving back to the left. The cornerback stumbled and started to fall — he reached out for Quentin, who slapped his hands away like an angry parent scolding a spoiled child.

"Hikkirapt," Hokor said, a little louder this time, the Quyth equivalent of "that's quite impressive."

Quentin sprinted down the sideline. The free safety closed with a good angle of pursuit. There was nowhere to cut this time, so Quentin lowered his right hand and brought it up hard just as the

free safety reached for the tackle. Quentin's thick forearm caught
the free safety under the chin, lifting him off his feet. The free
safety seemed to float for a second, moving downfield at the same
speed as Quentin, before crashing into the ground and skidding
clumsily across the torn Carsengi Grass.

"Juro jirri," Hokor said loudly. That loosely translated into
"You've got to be kidding me."

Stedmar jumped up and down and screamed nonsensical syllables, his drink spilling onto the floor. His bodyguards had lost
discipline, straying from their posts to get a glimpse of the sprinting quarterback. Hokor leaned forward so far his neon-bright yellow eye pressed against the luxury box's glass windows.

It boiled down to Quentin and the strong safety, who closed in
as the quarterback passed the 30-yard line. Quentin looked back
once, then turned his head upfield and seemed to *take off*, as if he
had booster rockets. Quentin strolled into the end zone for a 52-
yard touchdown run.

Raiders 41, Corsairs 3.

"Just how fast is he?" Gredok asked quietly.

"Yesterday in practice they timed him at 3.8 in the 40-yard
dash."

Gredok simply nodded. Of course. Why not? Why shouldn't
the *nineteen-year-old* huge quarterback, with a plasma rifle for an
arm, the eyes of an aerial predator and the mind of a general run a
3.8-second 40-yard dash? That was faster than most Human running backs and definitely faster than the typical 380-pound Human tight end. It wasn't nearly as fast as a Sklorno wide receiver
or defensive back, but it was about equal with a Quyth Warrior
linebacker. A *Tier One* linebacker — Quentin would leave most
Tier Two linebackers in the dust.

Hokor still leaned forward, his eye and both sets of his hands
pressed against the glass, his antennae quivering like drug-addled
snakes. Gredok poked him again — hard. Hokor looked up and
saw Gredok's eye clouding over with just a touch of black. Hokor
swept a pedipalp over his head, submissively pushing his antennae
back, then sat quietly in his seat.

Gredok stared at his coach. Hokor had come across a tape of Barnes and had instantly insisted the boy was Tier One material. Gredok had argued — there were reasons no Nationalite had ever quarterbacked a championship team. Most Nationalite quarterbacks, in fact, washed out within two seasons. Despite the boy's skills, he had *no* experience dealing with other races, let alone leading them. There was more to quarterbacking than pure football skill. Far more.

But Gredok believed in his coach. He'd already leveraged his entire organization's finances to create the team Hokor wanted, the team that would make the leap from Tier Two to the big time … to Tier One. Hokor wanted Barnes, but to get Barnes, Gredok needed to make a play that could have serious business consequences.

Gredok's wide eye asked an unspoken question: *Are you sure? Is this kid really worth it?*

Hokor stared back with an unspoken answer: *Absolutely.*

"I think Kollok is going to pay through the nose for this kid," Stedmar said quietly, a smug smile on his lips. "Don't you think he will, *Shamakath?*"

The time had come to formally open up the power game. Gredok wasn't taking any chances.

"Actually," Gredok said, "Barnes might do well on my team."

Stedmar raised his eyebrows in a Human expression for surprise. Gredok sensed Stedmar's body heat — very steady, only a hair above normal. Stedmar concealed his emotions very well, which was just one of the reasons Gredok liked him. Stedmar was also smart and ruthless. But for all his strong points, he should have known better than to play the game with Gredok the Splithead.

"You've got Don Pine," Stedmar said. "Why would you want anyone else?"

"Pine is not what he used to be."

Stedmar nodded. "But I've already got a considerable offer from Kollok."

"You should just give me Barnes's contract as tribute."

Stedmar smiled. "Now, come on, we both know tribute doesn't

cover something like this. You wouldn't want me in your organization if I'd do something as stupid as give up this kid for free."

Gredok thought for a second, then nodded. Stedmar played it smart: polite, respectful and logical. "What is Kollok's offer?"

Stedmar walked to the bar and poured himself another drink. "Well, Barnes's contract is negligible," he said. "I have him signed for another year at one million credits."

Such a low number for such talent, Gredok thought.

"That is impressive, Stedmar. Barnes is worth three times that amount, even for a Tier Three team. How did you manage it?"

Stedmar shrugged and smiled. "Technically, I don't have to pay him at all. He's an orphan, like about a million other Nationalite kids his age. Pogroms, coups, fundamentalist revolutions, power struggles — thousands of people die or just disappear every year. Quentin never even knew his parents. They disappeared when he was one, maybe younger. He had a brother, got hung for stealing food when Quentin was only five. That was all the family he had."

"How old was the brother?"

"Nine or ten, Quentin doesn't remember for sure. Anyway, in the Purist Nation, family members are responsible for crimes committed by other family members, up to three generations. Since Quentin was the only one left in his family, they put him to work in the forced-labor mines."

"A five-year-old Human, working in the Micovi mines?"

Stedmar nodded. "Happens all the time. Makes for a very cheap labor source."

"Slave labor is always the cheapest."

"The nice term is 'honor worker,' as in working in the forced-labor camps clears your family honor, you know? Only takes twenty years."

Gredok's antennae circled slowly. He didn't like Human systems to start with, and the Purist Nation was by far the worst of the lot. "So if he was an honor worker in a mine, how did you discover him?"

Stedmar laughed. "It was the craziest thing. I was driving out to the mines to conduct some business. So I'm driving by in my limo when the workers are on break. There's a crowd built up like it's a fight. Well, I love to watch a good fight, especially on this planet — did you know if you kill a man in a fair fight here, you don't go to jail?"

"Why am I not surprised?"

"Anyway, so people really go at it. So I pull up to see what's going on, only there's not a fight, everyone is laughing and clapping, looking at each other in amazement. There's this giant-sized shucker, must have been 425 pounds, built like an air-tank with legs, you know? Anyway, this guy looks pissed. He heaves back and chucks a rock, maybe the rock is a pound or two, chucks it about sixty yards, really impressive throw. Some guy runs the rock back, and that's when the workers start flashing money back and forth — they're making bets. Then this scrawny kid steps up, he's about six feet tall, but you can tell he's real young. The big guy has a look on his face like he could eat a bat whole, entropic rifle and all, you know? He's looking at this kid like he wants to kill him. And the kid is just laughing. The kid takes the rock, pretends like he's lining up under a center and actually barks out some signals. He's looking left, looking right, then takes a five-step drop like he's quarterbacking the Rodina Astronauts or something, and he *heaves* that rock. I mean the thing flew eighty-five, maybe ninety yards. I just about crapped myself."

Gredok nodded. He was always amazed by Stedmar's fascination with fecal euphemisms. "And that's why you signed him?"

"Partially. So this kid won the bet, obviously, the big guy hands him a wad of bills, and the kid starts doing this dance, really rubbing it in, you know? Well, the big guy, he just loses it. He throws a big sucker-punch that knocks the kid on his butt. The kid pops up like nothing happened, except he's not laughing now, he's pissed."

Gredok nodded again. Urine was also a key element of Stedmar's stories.

"So the big guy comes after this kid, and this kid lays into him. I mean he took this big guy apart. Three straight jabs and then a big left hook, and the guy goes down. But the kid isn't finished. He jumps on the guy and starts blasting him with big haymaker lefts, over and over again. There's blood all over the dirt, in a couple of seconds the guy's face looks like hamburger. The workers are laughing and having a grand time, but you know what I'm thinking to myself, *Shamakath*?"

"No."

"I'm thinking, 'What if that kid hurts his hands?' Swear to High One, that's what I'm thinking. So I send my Sammy and Dean and Frankie over there to pull the kid off. But he's like a wildcat — doesn't know who my boys are or what they want, so he lays Sammy out with that same left hook."

Stedmar turned to look at one of his bodyguards, a thick Human with a nose that looked as if it had been broken a dozen times.

"You remember that punch, Sammy?"

"Yeah, boss," Sammy said, laughing. "And he weighed about two hundred pounds less back then."

"I didn't want the kid hurt, but you can't expect the boys to take that, you know? But the more they hit him, the madder he gets, and he just won't stay down. Finally, Sammy gets up and he whips out a stun stick and puts the kid out. They drag him over to me. I ask the kid if he knows who I am. You know what he says to me?"

"No," Gredok said, patiently waiting for the end of the story. Humans always took so long to get to the point.

"Through a split lip, he says to me, 'You're the new owner of the Raiders.' Not 'You're Stedmar Osborne, notorious gangster,' or 'You're that guy that shakes down the mine owners' or anything like that. Just 'the owner of the Raiders.' That was it for me, I knew the kid lived and breathed football. So I ask him, 'How old are you?' And he tells me, 'Fifteen.' *Fifteen*. You know what I almost did?"

"Crapped yourself?" Gredok said.

"Yah! I almost crapped myself! I paid off the kid's family debt. That's why, technically, I don't have to pay him at all, I sort of *own* him. And just to let you know, a million a year is probably more than his entire family saw going back three generations, if not four or five. He thinks he's rich. So I signed the kid and put him on the team. He'd never played organized ball before, and the next year, at *sixteen years old*, he's the backup quarterback."

At this, Hokor looked away from the field and listened attentively. Gredok knew why — this quarterback already had four years of professional experience, albeit in the lowly PNFL.

"At *seventeen* he started for me," Stedmar said. "We went 5-4 that year, he won his last three games. The next year, this *eighteen-year-old* kid wins it all for me, 9-0, and two more wins in the playoffs to give me my first championship. This year, we're 9-0 again, we'll obviously win today, and that's 21 games in a row for him. Next week the championship game should be a cakewalk."

"All because you were driving by and happened to see him throw a rock."

Stedmar laughed. He obviously relished telling this story. "Yah! Crazy, isn't it?"

"You still haven't told me Kollok's offer."

"Kollok will hand me fifteen million," Stedmar said, that same self-confident smile on his lips. "Plus smuggling rights for any pyuli he wants to unload in Purist Nation space."

Gredok nodded, sensing Stedmar's body heat increase just a bit. He was lying about the fifteen million, but not about the Ki-grown narcotic pyuli, of which some Humans just couldn't get enough — a year's worth of rights to that stuff was worth far more than fifteen million. But Micovi belonged to Gredok. Most of it, anyway. Was this Kollok's first move to cut into Gredok's territory? Was Stedmar to be trusted?

"You should never take a deal with another syndicate without consulting me," Gredok said, the anger building within him.

Stedmar ran his left hand over his head, brushing his hair back — while he had no antennae, the motion perfectly mimicked the Quyth sign of fealty. Gredok felt his anger subside a little, an involuntary, instinctive reaction to the gesture. His lieutenant was very good at this game. Gredok would never again underestimate Stedmar Osborne.

"But I have not taken the deal, *Shamakath*, nor would I ever do so without your blessing."

"I will give you ten million for Barnes's contract," Gredok said. "Plus, I'll give you Muhammad Jorgensen's territory on Allah."

Stedmar's face wrinkled. "I suspect you were going to give me Muhammad's territory anyway. He's getting run over by the Giovanni syndicate — they want to expand their Purist Nation territory in a bad way."

Gredok nodded again. Stedmar was correct. And yet, the offer had been placed on the table — to change it now was a sign of weakness, and any *shamakath* could not admit weakness in front of his vassals. Stedmar had made his first mistake — instead of simply trying to add options, he insinuated that Gredok's offer was no good.

"I have offered you a deal," Gredok said quietly, his antennae pinning down flat against the back of his head, like a dog's ears just before an attack. "You will now accept."

Stedmar's eyes widened slightly when he saw the antennae go back, and his temperature spiked almost a full degree. He quickly glanced at Gredok's two bodyguards, who showed no sign of emotion.

Where Quyth Leaders were small and slight, Quyth Warriors were so much larger that they looked like a different species altogether. They shared the same body style of two legs, two arms with three-pincer hands and two pedipalps on either side of the vertical mouth. But while a Leader's pedipalps were two feet long and slender, a Warrior's were usually about three feet long, thick with muscle and heavily armored. Warriors did not have silky fur. Instead, thick chitin covered their bodies. The last difference was perhaps the most pronounced — a Leader's softball-sized eye glowed like a window to the soul's emotions, while the Warrior's cold eye was smaller, like a baseball, surrounded by a heavy ridge of chitin and hooded by a thick, tough, leathery eyelid.

Crazy red and orange designs — the marks of Quyth commandos — decorated the bodyguards' upper carapaces. Warriors wore pants, usually gray and devoid of color, but rarely wore anything that would cover their enameled markings. Stedmar's bodyguards, four densely muscled 400-pound Humans, tensed up, ready for action.

"*Shamakath*, please understand," Stedmar said calmly. "With all due respect, Kollok's deal is better. It's bad business not to take it."

"You will take my offer, Stedmar," Gredok said. "And you will take it now."

"Perhaps we could add some money to the offer—"

"The offer is tendered. There will be no changes."

Stedmar's eyes narrowed. He looked down at the diminutive Quyth Leader. "*Shamakath*, I respectfully invoke my right to decline Kollok's offer and therefore am not obligated to take your offer. Barnes will play for me next season."

Gredok's antennae rose slightly. Stedmar had quickly taken his only way out. By keeping Barnes and not selling his contract to anyone, Stedmar could turn down Gredok's offer without Gredok losing face.

But proper etiquette or no, Gredok *wanted* Barnes. And that was all that mattered.

Gredok clapped his pincers together and gestured to one of his bodyguards, who walked over as he reached into his belt. The Human bodyguards immediately went for their weapons, but Stedmar held up a hand to still them.

"Virak," Gredok said to his bodyguard. "Show Stedmar the screen."

The 375-pound Virak the Mean struck a rather imposing figure, but Stedmar never flinched. Despite the fact that everyone in the room knew Virak could kill Stedmar in the blink of an eye, the burly bodyguard looked at the Human and brushed back his one set of retractable antennae just before looking at Gredok and doing the same. He then produced a small holoprojector from his belt and switched it on.

The image flared to life. A dangerous stillness filled the luxury box. Stedmar looked at the image, eyes widening with rage. He glanced down to the stands, to the first row, then back again. Gredok sensed the skyrocketing stress level of the Human bodyguards. They reached for their weapons again, but Stedmar's curtly raised hand stopped them for the second time.

The holoscreen showed a smiling, blonde Human woman holding a baby, both warmly dressed against the evening's cold. They sat in the stadium's front row, the woman laughing with two other Human women, all of them surrounded by alert bodyguards. The image shook slightly, obviously due to a long range focus.

"Your mate and offspring," Gredok said.

Stedmar swallowed. "Where is this picture coming from?"

"From the scope of pulse cannon, manned by a sniper sitting in one of the atmosphere processors overlooking the stadium."

Stedmar looked across the field, up to the skyline, at the endless line of atmosphere processors that towered thirty stories high. The big machines were filled with platforms, grates, pipes, blocky compressors … there were a hundred places a sniper could hide unseen.

"I'm sure you're thinking you can kill me now and save your mate and offspring," Gredok said. "But if the sniper doesn't hear from me in the next five minutes, he'll fire. The pulse cannon will incinerate that entire section, killing everyone in a twenty-yard radius. So I suggest no sudden moves on her part — if she should rise to relieve herself, for example, she'll be the epicenter of a rather large crater."

"Frankie," Stedmar said to one of his bodyguards. "Call down to Stefan, tell him to make sure everyone stays put, *especially* Michelle."

"Very good," Gredok said. "The deal is tendered. You will take it now."

Stedmar nodded, his face a narrow-eyed visage of barely controlled rage. That disappointed Gredok — Stedmar would have to improve his self control if he wanted to move even farther in the syndicate's hierarchy.

Virak produced a contract box and handed it to Stedmar. The Human read through the contract, nodded, then placed his thumb in the slot on one end. Gredok placed his middle left pincer in the box's other slot. The machine quickly recorded their genetic makeup, linked up to the Intergalactic Business Database, verified their identities, then gave a low "beep" to indicate the transaction had been recorded.

Gredok's antennae rose to their normal angle. "Very good, Stedmar. I will now take my leave. Shall I remove Muhammad for you?"

"I'll take care of it," Stedmar said in a cold voice.

Gredok nodded, then left the luxury box, Hokor and his two bodyguards close behind.

QUENTIN

QUENTIN BARNES RAISED his face into the shower's steaming spray. The water trickled down his body to join the water cascading off of other players before it all slid down the drain. Streaks of brown and green and red diffused in the water rolling off the other players. Brown mud, green grass stains, red blood. Quentin's water, of course, carried nothing more than white soap — he'd barely even been touched. Tackled twice, no sacks. The only thing he had to wipe off was his own sweat.

Tattoos covered the arms and chests of his teammates, many designs denoting various Church rankings or religious accomplishments. Many were fully confirmed, with the curving infinity symbol inked on their foreheads. Church participation was expected of PNFL players — after all, their talents came courtesy of the High One. And weren't these men, who dominated Purist Nation pop culture along with soccer players, an example to all Purists? The government strongly encouraged players to be vocal proponents of the faith. There were even well-known incidents of players, *good* players, being blackballed from the league for not participating in the Church.

Quentin had tats as well, one on either side of his sternum. The one on his right, in neat block letters, simply said "SHUCK." The matching tat on his left said "YOU."

Ceiling vents greedily sucked up most of the steam, but twenty simultaneous showers still produced a light fog. Quentin walked through the haze as he left the shower, passing by his teammates, every last one of whom threw him a smile and a compliment.

"Way to do it, Quentin."

"The High One blessed you today, Quentin."

"Nice work, boss."

"They know who they played, right, Quentin?"

He smiled back at everyone, answered most of the comments with a simple nod of the head.

His teammates were civil enough in the locker room and on the field, but they weren't his friends. They knew it. They made sure *he* knew it. Most of the players came from privileged families, *Church* families. Only Church families sent their kids to school, and only in school could you play organized football.

For the lower classes, time in class or on the field was time away from the mines. They learned the basics: reading, writing, math, religion and how to kill the Satanic races. By seven or eight years old, lower-class kids had all the knowledge they would ever need, or so the logic went. Quentin never forgot how lucky he was that Stedmar happened to drive by that one day, four long years ago.

Every year a few poor players found a way into the PNFL, and they embraced the Church wholeheartedly. Some believed, some didn't, but for all, the Church was their only chance to achieve some kind of station in life. Every government job, the majority of private-sector jobs, anything that involved money, you had to be confirmed or at least well on your way. On Micovi, football was a ticket out of a hard existence of grinding manual labor and a lifespan of forty years. Fifty, if you were lucky.

But Quentin Barnes refused to embrace the Church. In fact, as far as he was concerned, the Church could take a flying leap.

His left tackle, Maynard Achmad, walked by, flashing Quentin a big smile.

"Great game, Q," he said. "We're going all the way!"

Quentin smiled and sat. Achmad stopped in front of Pete Oky-mayat's locker. He leaned and said something to the big linebacker, which made Pete throw his head back with laughter. He waved over Adrian Yellow, the kicker, and repeated Achmad's comment. Adrian laughed as well, reaching up to slap Pete on the shoulder. The men were happy they were going to the title game. They were happy, and they were sharing it, together.

Quentin looked around the locker room. Everywhere teammates sat or stood in groups, yelling, laughing and celebrating. There were *always* groups, groups that never included him. Word might get back to The Elders that the men regularly associated with someone from a known family of criminals. He felt a pang of loneliness, then chased the thought away. Shuck them all. He didn't need them. He didn't need anyone.

He turned back to face his locker and thought about Achmad's words. *We're going all the way*. All the way to *what*? The Purist Nation Football League championship? Next week the Raiders faced off against the Sigurd City Norsemen, the champs of the Homeworld Division. They'd kill the Norsemen, then stand atop the twelve-team PNFL.

The PNFL Championship. Big deal. Champions of a Tier Three league. And an *all-Human* Tier Three team at that. It was about as far away from the big time as you could get. But the road to galactic exposure had to start somewhere. The Tier Two teams couldn't ignore stats like his three-touchdown, 24-for-30, 310-yard passing performance against the Corsairs (with another 82 on the ground including a *sweet* 52-yard TD run, thank you very much). He was the best player in the PNFL, bar none, possibly the best Tier Three player in the galaxy.

He toweled off, rubbing dry his chest, then his face and hair. When he removed the towel, he saw the big tight end Shua Mullikin walking toward him. Quentin stood there, naked and fearless, calmly smiling and staring straight up into Shua's flaring eyes.

"I was open all day and you know it," Shua said.

"The guy throwing the ball might disagree with you, big fella."

Shua's eyes narrowed with rage. "That was the *semifinals*. Everyone in the Nation was watching that game, and I didn't catch a single pass."

Quentin shrugged, then sat on the bench in front of his locker and started dressing.

"This is because I argued with you in practice, isn't it," Shua said, a statement rather then a question. "I *dared* to contradict you in front of everyone else and you had to punish me."

Quentin didn't bother to look up as he answered. "It's my show, Shu. You know this. It's not like this is new information."

Quentin felt Shua's stare. Shua wanted to hit him, wanted it bad, but everyone knew that Quentin could kick the tar out of just about anyone on the team.

"You think you're so high and mighty," Shua said, his voice rising. "Someday you won't be playing football, and you'll go back to being the little *orphan* piece of garbage that you were before Stedmar found you."

A hush fell over the locker room. On some planets, calling someone a "retard" was a major insult. On Micovi, in the Nation, that major insult was "orphan." Even if it was true, it wasn't something you tossed about casually.

Quentin turned and looked into Shua's eyes. "I'm getting the impression you don't want to catch any passes in the championship game, either."

Shua's nostrils flared, his expression a combination of anger and anxiety. Sure, Shua hated him, but he also wanted his share of the limelight. Any hero of the PNFL Championship game was guaranteed to move high in the Church.

"Is that right, Shua?" Quentin said quietly. "You don't want to see the rock next week?"

Shua swallowed. "Of course, I want to."

Quentin nodded. "Okay, then apologize."

The big tight end's face screwed into a furious mask. "Apologize? You underclass piece of — "

Quentin turned away, facing back into his locker. The move stopped Shua in mid-sentence. Shua looked around the locker room, looking for support, but he found none. No one was going to back him up. Not now, not with the championship just one week away.

Quentin started to whistle as he put on his socks.

Shua's fists clenched and unclenched. "I'm ... sorry."

Quentin cupped his hand to his ear and looked up from the corner of his eye. "What? Sorry, man, I couldn't hear you."

This time it was loud enough for everyone to hear. "I said I'm sorry."

Quentin smiled graciously. "No problem, Shu. Apology accepted."

Shua turned and stormed away, his face red from rage and humiliation. The teammates looked at Quentin for a few more seconds, then turned back to their various groups and quietly resumed their conversations.

They hated the fact that he held so much power. Most of them treated underclass people like they were slaves. But on the field, in the locker room, they couldn't do that to Quentin Barnes. If they hated him because he wasn't like them, he made sure they at least respected his role as the team leader.

Quentin reached into the bottom of his locker and pulled out a can of Shokess Beer. He twisted the top, smiling in anticipation as the can instantly frosted up. He flipped the lid and took a long drink. It was the best beer the Purist Nation had to offer, which wasn't saying much — he'd had a can of Miller Lager once when playing at Buddha City Stadium. Now *that* was real beer. You could get almost anything you wanted in Buddha City. Beer, contraband, music, women ... he'd even heard some of his holier-than-thou teammates had slept with blue-skinned women from Satirli 6. Talk about a *sin*. It didn't get much worse than that, unless you debased yourself by sleeping with one of the Satanic species. Quentin had ignored sinful behavior, with the notable exception of beer.

Alcohol, of course, was basically forbidden in public places. Other players would have been severely punished for drinking in the locker room, but Stedmar had taught him that when you had something other people wanted, something they *needed*, the rules don't necessarily apply to you.

Theron Akbar, the team manager, walked up to Quentin, a big smile on his little face. His smile faded when he saw the beer.

"That's a sin, Quentin."

"It's also tasty," Quentin said, then chugged the remainder. He liked Akbar, who oddly enough was the only member of the organization with the balls to say something right to Quentin's face.

"Coach wants to see you, Quentin," Akbar said. "Right away."

Quentin set down the empty can and continued toweling off. "What's up?"

"Rumor is you've been bought."

The toweling stopped.

"Stedmar had some off-worlder in the luxury box. Right after the game he talked to the coach, now the coach wants to see you. You do the math. And the High One really blessed you tonight. Great game."

Akbar walked away. Quentin practically dove into his clothes. This was it — he was finally escaping the shucking rock he'd called home his entire life.

The universe awaited.

FULLY DRESSED, Quentin stepped through the open door into his coach's office.

"You wanted to see me, Coach?"

Coach Ezekiel Graber sat behind his desk. He wore a skullcap in Raider colors, black with a silver "R." The Raider logo wasn't much to look at, just a plain block letter, the same style used for all the PNFL teams. Graber wore a sweatshirt, a piece of clothing that had endured for centuries as fashion and style fluctuated across a dozen Human planets.

"Sit down, Barnes," Coach Graber said. He was smiling, but he didn't look happy. "You've got a decision to make."

The infinity symbol tattooed on Graber's forehead had faded in the twenty or so years since his confirmation at the age of thirty — what had once been a detailed, deep black was now a slightly fuzzy gray.

"Barnes, you've had one hell of a season."

"Thanks, Coach."

"Best I've ever coached, I'll tell you that. High One as my witness." Coach Graber paused. Quentin nodded once, smiled, and the coach continued.

"Quentin, there comes a time in every young man's life when he has to decide his path. Your time is now. Stedmar sold your contract."

Quentin's stomach dropped to nothingness, replaced by a tingly swarm of butterflies. This was *it*. He was *going*. "Who?" he said with a dry mouth.

"Ionath Krakens."

Quentin frowned. The Krakens ... a Tier Two team. He'd hoped for a Tier One franchise, like the up-and-coming Alimum Armada, or even his boyhood dream of the To Pirates.

"The Krakens? You're sure?"

Coach Graber nodded. "I've got the contract right here." He handed Quentin a messageboard. Quentin looked at the readout — it was a done deal, all right. All he had to do was put his thumbprint on it to make it official.

The Ionath Krakens. If that was his ticket out of the Purist Nation, that was good enough for him. And it was a team based in the Quyth system, where millions of Nationalites had fled during Butcher Smith's *cleansings*. He'd often prayed his parents weren't dead, but had actually fled to the Quyth system and couldn't return or contact him in any way. Maybe now he'd find out. Tier Two teams still enjoyed galactic broadcast coverage — even if his parents weren't in the Quyth system, there was a chance they'd see him play, see him and join him. He'd have a real family.

"Now Quentin, you know full well that's going to take you out of the system. You've still got the option of religious refusal."

"Yeah," Quentin said dryly. "I have that option."

"There's a lot of people in the Purist Nation, including me, my son, who hope that you stay in-system until your thirtieth birthday so you can be confirmed. A person with your fame could go far in the Church. You could be a Bishop, or even a Mullah, if you applied yourself."

Quentin nodded, only half listening. He loved it when people used the words "'my son." Someday, someone would use those words and it would *mean* something, something real. Right now, it meant jack.

He could take religious refusal, which would negate the contract. If he did that, a different Tier Two or Tier One team could pick him up — but only after the next PNFL season. League rules specified his contract could only be sold once per season, and if he refused that contract, that meant another year with the Raiders.

Another year of Tier Three ball. Another year of dirt and mud and the never-ending drone of the atmosphere processors.

"Coach, I've always wanted to play Upper Tier ball. To tell you the truth, I can't wait to get out of here."

"Then stop ignoring your religious calling. Get confirmed, see the galaxy as a missionary spreading the faith."

Quentin hated the Church with all his soul. He loved the High One, believed deeply in the High One, but he knew in his heart that the Church was rife with flaws, half-truths and outright lies, all designed to keep certain families in power and keep the majority of the population from questioning their lowly place in the Purist Nation. He would always believe, but would never preach the Gospel of Stewart.

"I'm no missionary, Coach. You know that."

"Someday you'll feel the calling. But you have to be careful about going out-system before your soul is prepared! Satan lives out there. We can see him on the news every day, he takes the shape of the Whitok, Ki, the Sklorno, the Quyth, and disguises himself in Human form in the Planetary Union, the League of Planets, the Tower —"

"Yeah, Coach, I got it. I've heard this speech before. In fact, I've heard it all my life, a few too many times from a few too many people."

Coach Graber's eyes narrowed. "It's a speech you need to *listen* to, son, not just *hear*."

"I'm not your son," Quentin said. "And I'm not part of your Church."

"Do you *dare* blaspheme against the High One?"

"I believe in the teachings of the High One," Quentin said. "I just don't believe in the Church. There's a big difference. The best football players are aliens, and I want to play against the best."

"Satan takes many forms, Quentin. Are you going to consort with crickets and salamanders and Satan's other minions?"

"I'm not going to *consort* with anyone, Coach. I don't have to associate with them, just win ball games with them. If Satan himself can run a post pattern, I'll hit him in stride for six."

Graber's breath shot out in a huff. "That's blasphemous! And besides, you're not ready to play Tier Two. You couldn't handle the speed."

"Shuck *that*. I'm going to rip Tier Two apart."

"Quentin, I think you just need another season or two to prepare yourself. You've only been playing the game for four years, my son. Imagine how much you can learn with just one more season!"

"One second I shouldn't go because it's sacrilegious, the next I shouldn't go because I'm not good enough yet? Maybe you just want me to stick around and win you a couple more PNFL championships, is that it?"

Graber leaned back, his eyes wide with hurt. "Quentin, you can't think that I have anything but your best interests at heart. I don't want Satan to swallow your soul, boy, and that's what will happen if you go out-system and mingle with the sub races."

"I'm not a boy."

"You are until you're thirty! You know the Scriptures!"

Quentin stood up. "You can toss your Scriptures into the Void. No one here gave a crap about me before I threw a football. You all talk of the glory of the Purist Nation and the purity of Humans, but all I see is a galaxy ruled by off-worlders. If the Purist Nation is so great, if we're the *chosen ones*, then why are we ruled by the bats? I'll win the PNFL championship for you next week, but then I'm out of here."

"You're not ready."

"Is that right, Coach?" Quentin held the message board inches from Graber's face, then slowly brought his left thumb toward the imprint spot. He stared into Graber's angry eyes as his thumb punched home his destiny. The board let out a small confirming *beep*.

"I'll be here for practice this week, and I'll win your stupid PNFL championship for you," Quentin said. "And as soon as that game is over, you can kiss my butt good-bye."

Coach Graber's shoulders sagged. "Your decision is made. May the High One have mercy on your soul."

Quentin laughed. "My soul? Coach, without me, you'd better be worried if the High One will have mercy on the Raiders."

Quentin walked out of the office, slamming the door shut behind him.

SEVEN DAYS AFTER SIGNING the Krakens' contract, Quentin Barnes walked out of the Raiders locker room for what he hoped was the last time. He'd left them with a 35-14 win over the Sigurd Norsemen, and another PNFL championship.

In his left hand he carried his duffel bag. In his right he carried the PNFL Championship MVP trophy. High One knew he'd earned it, with a record-setting 24-for-28, 363-yard performance. That and four TD passes. Not a bad day's work.

He walked outside, where the constant sound of the atmosphere processor greeted him. He hated that noise, and he hated this place. A hundred people waited for him, many of them wearing the blue tunics of the Church. Most of the others, and even some of the tunic-wearers, wore some kind of Raider gear — shirts, hats or banners. He looked out at a throng of silver and black, most of it from Raiders' jerseys marked with the number "10" — Quentin's number.

Once again his eyes searched for a certain face that he did not yet know. For a pair of eyes that looked like his. For a smile that only a parent could have for a child.

Once again, he saw nothing but strangers.

The crowd surrounded him. At seven feet tall, he towered over everyone. Kids thrust messageboards at him, begging for his thumbprint and maybe a few words.

"Oh, Elder Barnes, you're the greatest!"

"What a great game! Can you sign this 'To Anna'?"

"Elder Quentin, sign my pad, *please*!"

They called him "Elder," a term of respect, even though he was no more a part of the Church than the Creterakian occupiers. He didn't bother to correct them.

Stedmar Osborne was waiting for him, leaning against a jet-black limo, Sammy and Frankie and Dean his ever-present bodyguards.

Quentin signed quickly, but he signed every messageboard thrust his way. He didn't have time for personalized messages, so he pressed down thumbprints as fast as he could. The satisfied kids and their parents started to drift away as he kept signing. At the end, the weak children finally found their way to him. His heart sank as he looked at some of them — more than a few had Hiropt's Disease, all of them assuredly from Micovi's slums, where the roundbugs grew to the size of house cats. One of the boys, dressed in the blue tunic of a Church ward, was missing a leg.

"What happened to you?" Quentin asked the smiling boy.

"My family lived on an ore hauler over on the North Coast," the boy said, his eyes wide with hero worship. "One of the engines blew and I got hurt."

"You here with your family?"

"High One took them, Mr. Barnes," the boy said, a smile still on his face as if his family's tragedy was the most pleasant of conversations. "Died in the explosion. The Holy Men have told me it was part of the High One's plan. I'm in the Church now, someday I'll be confirmed."

Quentin smiled sadly at the boy. An orphan. Without a family sponsor, he had little or no chance of being confirmed. Not unless he could run a forty in 3.8 seconds and haul in passes with his one arm. This boy would spend the rest of his life in the mines. But at least the boy's parents hadn't abandoned him.

He shook away the thought. Who was he to question his own parents? Maybe they were out there, somewhere. Millions fled the planet during the cleansings, fled or died. Maybe they just couldn't find him ... right, couldn't find the most famous athlete in all of the Purist Nation.

He pressed his thumbprint to the boy's messageboard. Quentin opened his duffel bag and handed the boy his sweaty game jersey. The boy's eyes widened to white marbles dotted with flecks of blue.

"Take it," Quentin said. The boy dropped his messageboard as he grabbed the jersey with his one arm. He clutched the jersey to his chest, his face the very picture of joy.

"Let's go, Quentin," Stedmar called.

Quentin nodded at him and knelt to pick up his bag. He paused there, looking at the bag, then reached in and started passing out the contents. To each of the remaining kids, he gave something: shoes, game pants, a T-shirt, even the bag itself. When he had nothing left to give, he stood and walked past the clamoring children to the waiting limo.

Stedmar was laughing at him. "Traveling light, kid?"

Quentin shrugged. "Don't need that stuff anymore, sir." He had to look down to talk to Stedmar, who at six-foot-four was a full eight inches shorter than Quentin.

One of the bodyguards held the door. Quentin and Stedmar got in the back. The bodyguard drove the limo toward the spaceport, a mere five minutes away from the stadium.

"I'm surprised you didn't give away the trophy," Stedmar said with a smile.

Quentin held it out. "I saved that for you, Mr. Osborne."

The smile vanished from Stedmar's face. "Don't you mess with me, kid."

"No, sir," Quentin said. "Four years ago you found me and gave me a chance. I'm off this planet because of *you*."

Stedmar slowly took the trophy. He looked at it, a strange expression on his face, then looked back at Quentin.

"I made a pretty penny on you, Quentin. I won't lie to you about that. I was already underpaying you, and I sold that same contract to Tier Two, where it's not even close to what you're worth."

Quentin shrugged. "It doesn't matter. I'll be able to renegotiate next year."

"Sure, unless by some crazy fluke the Krakens make it to Tier One. Then you're a protected player for two years, and they can keep paying you what you're making now."

"I'll make the money back eventually, Mr. Osborne."

Stedmar nodded. "Somehow I know you will. But listen, kid, you're in for a lot of changes. Some people like the big time, some don't. I've seen a lot of Nationalites go out-system with big dreams, and most of them come running back. They can't handle being in the same cities with the aliens, being on the same busses, shuttles and transport tubes. I mean, have you ever *seen* a Sklorno up close?" Stedmar's face wrinkled with disgust. "You can see right through their skin. And they drool. It's a big adjustment."

"I'm not leaving to make friends," Quentin said. "I'm going to win a Tier One championship."

"And I hope you do, kid. Just remember that if you don't like the galaxy, you've always got a home here with the Raiders."

"And how do you think your Raiders will do next season?"

Stedmar looked out the window. "I don't think we'll be worth a dead roundbug. But you've still got something to learn, Quentin."

"You're not going to give me the Holy Man speech, are you? I got that from Coach Graber."

Stedmar laughed. "You know me better than that. I don't buy into the Church any more than you do. But what you've got to learn, Quentin, is that time always wins, and there's always someone to take your place. I won't be able to replace you next year, or the year after that, but you know what? Someone will line up at quarterback for the Raiders. The team won't shut down because you're gone. We won't win another championship next season, but eventually, we will. And when that happens, there will be some other quarterback coming out of that locker room, mobbed by kids wanting autographs."

Quentin smiled politely. Stedmar was the owner, after all, and deserved respect. He also had the power to have Quentin whacked anytime he saw fit, and that *definitely* deserved respect. But Stedmar clearly didn't understand football.

"Yes, sir, Mr. Osborne."

Stedmar grinned, as if he'd just passed on some great pearl of wisdom and now felt better of himself for the charity. "We'll have your things shipped to the Krakens' team bus. The league wants you to go straight to the *Combine*."

"Don't I get a chance to meet the team? The coaches?"

Stedmar shook his head. "That's not the way it works, kid. You've got to go to the *Combine* to make sure you're not using any disguising technology to hide gene modification, cybernetic implants or anything like that."

"But I haven't got any of that bush league garbage."

"Don't sweat it, kid, every rookie has to go through it. Besides, it's a chance for you to see the home planet of our beneficial *rulers*." Stedmar spat the last word out like it was a poisonous spider crawling around in his mouth.

"Creterak," Quentin said distantly. "What's the *Combine* like? I've heard a lot of stories."

"You mean the stories like how it used to be a prison station, how they take samples from all over your body, how they jack your brain into an A.I. mainframe to test your analytical powers, how they throw you in a cage with a live Grinkas mudsucker to test your reflexes in a life and death situation?"

Quentin looked out the window. "Yeah, stuff like that."

"I don't know, kid. It's probably all bull. The League doesn't want the merchandise damaged, if you get what I'm saying."

The red and yellow buildings of the city gave way to the wide open spaces of the spaceport tarmac. Disabled anti-orbital batteries dotted the landscape, rusted and pitted with forty years of neglect. The huge relics were once capable of taking out a dread-nought as far away as a light-year, or so the story went.

Quentin's stomach quivered. A chill filtered through his body. The anti-orbital batteries marked the edge of the spaceport — he'd soon be on the shuttle and, after that, the ship that would carry him to the *Combine*.

Quentin clasped his hands together to stop their shaking, but he couldn't hide his fear from Stedmar.

"Pre-flight jitters, kid?"

Quentin looked out the window and nodded. On the tarmac, a shuttle shot straight up, probably headed for the same ship he'd soon be on himself.

"I'll never get that," Stedmar said. "You go out on the field and those animals are trying to rip your head off, doesn't bother you at all, but you act like an old lady when it comes to simple space travel."

Quentin shrugged and kept looking out the window. Tier Two meant more flying, a *lot* more flying than his four or five yearly trips with the Raiders. He didn't have a choice.

The car slowed to a stop. One of Stedmar's bodyguards opened Quentin's door. Stedmar handed Quentin a mini-messageboard. "Your passport is in there. So is the Krakens' playbook. You need your thumbprint to access either file, but don't get careless with it — thumbprints can be faked, and plenty of people would love to get their hands on a GFL passport. Just mind your manners, Quentin, you've got no experience dealing with these other races, and sometimes they can find just about anything offensive. Watch more, talk less."

Quentin took the messageboard and slid out of the car. He leaned in to look at Stedmar. "As soon as they put a football in my hands, everything will be just fine, Mr. Osborne."

Stedmar smiled and nodded, an expression on his face that seemed both proud and slightly condescending. "Tear 'em up, kid."

Quentin turned and walked through the doors. He didn't bother looking back — there was nothing he wanted to see on this planet, and nothing he ever planned on seeing again.

Excerpt from "The GFL for Dummies," by Robert Otto

The GFL's three-tier system is often a source of confusion to neophyte fans. While most understand the concept of "Tier Three" as feeder teams, or what the Old Earth NFL used to call "minor leagues," the interaction between Tier Two and Tier One is a little more complicated.

Currently there are 280 registered Tier Three teams spread throughout the galaxy. These are official Galactic Football League franchises, registered with the Creterakian Empire and controlled by the Empire Bureau of Species Interaction (EBSI). In truth, the EBSI does little to control Tier Three other than to provide the same rules of play that govern the Upper Tiers and to provide licensed referees from the Referees Guild.

There are twenty-four Tier Three conferences. Most Tier Three conferences operate on a single planet. Some, like the Purist Nation Football League, feature inter-planetary play. Conferences have around ten teams and on average play a nine-game season, plus any conference playoffs or tournaments. The season culminates in the thirty-two-team Tier Three Tournament. Each conference champ is invited, as are eight at-large teams (note: due to religious preferences, the PNFL does not participate in the tournament). In this grueling tournament, a team plays every three days until a champion is crowned. The tournament is affectionately known as "The Two Weeks of Hell."

Tier Three is a individual entity, separate from the other two Tiers. Tier Two and Tier One, commonly called the "Upper Tiers," are actually two divisions of the same league. If Tier Three is considered the "minor leagues," the seventy-six Upper Tier teams constitute the "major leagues" of professional football.

Most fan attention, naturally, focuses on the twenty-two Tier One teams. Tier One teams are evenly divided into the Planet Division and the Solar Division. The top three teams from each division make the six-team Tier One playoff. The two teams with the best record have a bye, while the remaining four teams compete in the opening round. The winners of the opening-round games play the top teams, and the winners of those games meet in the GFL Championship.

But where there are winners, there are always losers, and that's where Tier Two comes into play. While the top Tier One teams compete for fortune and glory, the worst two teams are dropped from Tier One and must compete in Tier Two the following season.

There are six Tier Two conferences: the Human, the Tower, the Ki, the Harrah, the Sklorno and the Quyth Irradiated. The winners of each conference compete in the Tier Two Playoffs. The two teams that make it to the final game move up to Tier One the following year to replace the two demoted Tier One teams. This is the goal of every Tier Two team at the beginning of the season and is such a dramatic accomplishment that the actual Tier Two Championship game is almost an afterthought. The Tier Two Championship is more like a scrimmage, as neither team wants to incur injuries.

Why don't the teams want to risk injuries? Because the Tier One season begins two weeks after the Tier Two Championship game. Tier Two teams have only a brief respite from battle before they are thrust into the meat grinder that is Tier One.

This system successfully produces intense play all year long, particularly among the Tier One teams near the bottom of the standings. To drop into Tier Two costs a team untold billions in revenue from network coverage and merchandising.

BOOK TWO:
PRE-SEASON

HE WAITED for it.

Waited for the punch-out.

His pulse raced in a way it never did on the football field — a *panicky* way. He felt anxious, tried to control his breathing.

This is your fourteenth flight, everything went fine before.

The ship started to vibrate, just a little. A thin sheen of sweat covered his hands, which clutched tightly to his playbook messageboard. They were about to drop out of punch space and back into what people once called "reality."

This is the most statistically safe method of travel in the galaxy.

Statistics didn't stop newscasts, however, especially newscasts of passenger ships forever lost in punch-space, or the horrific remains of a ship that met some stray piece of debris during the punch-out back to relativistic speeds. They called it the "reality wave," the feeling that washed over the ship when it dropped out of punch-space and back into regular time.

You'll be fine, you'll be fine, you'll be —

His breath seized up, and he squeezed his eyes shut as the shudder hit. That sickening feeling of *splitting*, or *spreading*. He knew everything *blurred*, himself included. He'd seen that blurring the first time he'd flown — seeing it once was enough.

Oh High One oh High One oh no oh no ...

And then it was over. He forced himself to relax, forced open his tightly clenched teeth. He opened his eyes. The observation deck was still there. Quentin slowly let out a long-held breath. Everyone else on the deck looked relaxed. Everyone else always did. He liked to tell himself that they were just oblivious to the danger, rather than tell himself to stop being such a pansy.

Four seasons in the PNFL had taken him to every major city in the Purist Nation. He'd seen all four planets, Mason, Solomon, Allah and Stewart, as well as most of the colonies. Space travel was nothing new to Quentin, but this time it was different.

This was his first trip alone, without the familiarity of his teammates. But on this flight he certainly didn't suffer for lack of attention. On a ship full of Purist Nation businessmen, the league's MVP never went wanting for a drink or a dinner or some fat old fool looking to shake his hand.

One guy on the ship, Manny Sayed, followed him everywhere, trying to get Quentin to endorse his luxury yacht company. Quentin wasn't endorsing anything just yet — he didn't want to associate himself with one company before he signed with an advertising firm that could connect him to the hundreds of industries trying to cash in on the phenomenal marketing power of the GFL.

The distance of this trip also made it different. The Purist Nation was only twenty light-years across at its widest: most flights took only half a day. This time, however, he was at the edge of the Galactic Core, at Creterak — the end of a three-day journey of some forty-five light-years.

Quentin stared out the huge observation window, looking into space as the passenger liner gradually slowed to a halt some ways off the Creterakian orbital station Emperor Two. It was a huge construct, bigger than anything Quentin had ever seen. Hundreds of ships surrounded the station, all a respectful distance away. The tiny, flashing dots that were shuttles constantly flew back and forth from the ships to the station, like a glowing rainstorm simultaneously falling toward and away from mile-long piers that jutted from the station's equator.

He heard the rhythmic *clonk* of a now familiar footstep. Quentin grimaced, waiting for the fat voice to speak.

"You think this is big, you should see Emperor One," said Manny Sayed. "It's almost twice as big." He bore the forehead tattoo and the blue robe of a confirmed church man — a big robe to cover his wide girth. He also brandished a half-dozen rings fashioned from the rare metals of the galaxy and a Whopol necklace suffused with a glowing silvery light. Manny's left leg was missing just below the knee, yet he managed to turn even his handicap into a show of wealth: his platinum, jewel-studded prosthetic leg announced his presence wherever he walked.

Three days ago, the ostentatious show of wealth on a man wearing the blue took Quentin by surprise. The ship was full of such men ... businessmen who paid lip service to the tenets of the Church but also bore the trappings of a more powerful religion — commerce.

"I'm just taking in the scenery by myself, if you don't mind," Quentin said.

"Don't mind at all." Manny stood next to Quentin and looked out the bubble-like view port. "Hell of a sight."

Quentin shook his head and sighed.

"It's ironic," Manny said. "Creterak is somewhat like the Purist Nation — no non-Creterakians are allowed on the planet. All trans-galactic activity is handled on one of the five orbital stations. But while we do it for religious purposes, the Creterakians do it for reasons of defense."

"Why do they need to worry about that? They rule the whole freakin' galaxy."

Manny laughed. "If you add it up, there's two trillion Humans, Ki, Harrah, Sklorno and Leekee who'll do anything to end that rule. Patriots attack Creterakian garrisons all over the galaxy, every day. Imagine what they'd do if they could actually land on the Creterakian homeworld."

Quentin noticed Manny used the word "patriots" instead of "terrorists."

"They think all the other races are too warlike to be trusted. Don't forget your history, my son. They hid their sentience from the rest of the galaxy for over two centuries. They just sat there and listened to the rest of us killing each other."

"No offense, Mr. Sayed, but I've had my history lessons. I'd like to be by myself now."

"You're headed to the *Combine*, am I right?"

Quentin nodded.

Manny pointed to a bright star off the port side. "That's it right there."

Quentin leaned into the window and stared at his future. "What's it like?"

Manny shrugged. "Looks like any other station, really. Used to be a prison station, where the Creterakians shipped their prisoners of war during the Takeover."

"That's just a myth."

"'Fraid it's quite true, my son. From 2643 to 2659, the station that is now the *Combine* was one of the worst places to be in the entire Galaxy. They kept thousands of prisoners there. Not that many people made it out, and those that did were never the same."

"Why's that?"

"Torture, interrogation. The Creterakians wanted to learn everything they could about their new subjects, and they view prisoners of war as property. Creterakians breed in the billions, and they only live for ten or fifteen years, so life and death doesn't mean the same thing to them as they do to us."

"Great. So I'm headed to a former prison station that was used to torture and execute millions."

Manny smiled and reached up to clap Quentin on the shoulder. "Oh ,come on, my son, you're on your way to the GFL! Hell, if I made it out alive, a big kid like you will have no problems."

Quentin looked inquisitively at the fat man. "*You* were in the *Combine*?"

Manny's smile faded, and he shook his head. "Not the *Combine*. You might say I was an original tenant."

Quentin's eyes went wide with surprise. He hadn't met many veterans of the Takeover. The majority of soldiers who served in that short, failed war were long-since dead. Creterakians fought viciously and rarely left their enemies alive.

"Which planet did you fight on?" Quentin asked quietly.

"Allah." Manny stared out the view port. "The homeworld itself. They only managed to land four ships — our boys in the sky destroyed about four hundred others. We like to remember that we destroyed ninety-nine percent of the infidels, but that last one percent was all they needed. High One knows that was all they were planning for, with their strategy of victory through overwhelming numbers. The Creterakians packed one *million* soldiers into each landing vessel. Packed them in there like a gas, filling up every nook and cranny. And they came out like a gas, too. An endless cloud of them. We had a half-million soldiers on the ground — so just like that we were outnumbered ten-to-one."

Manny's voice trailed off, the memory etching a tired, sad expression on his face.

"What was it like?" Quentin asked. "The fighting, I mean."

Manny laughed, a dark, hopeless laugh. "Don't believe what the Holy Men write in the history books. It wasn't a fight, it was a slaughter. They moved so fast, flying in low, millions of them, so many you could barely make out an individual amongst the masses. You've seen the sparrows flocking on Allah?"

Quentin nodded.

"Well, think of that, except they're so thick they darken the sky, the entire horizon, and each one carries a little entropic rifle. I remember the first wave came flying over the hill, and we let them have it — sonic cannons, laser sweeps, shrapnel dust, you name it. We killed thousands of them, *tens* of thousands, but the rest just poured over us. I was hit in that first wave ..."

His voice trailed off. Quentin didn't want to look at Manny's leg, but he had to, then looked up again.

"The rifle take off your leg?"

Manny smiled, a sad smile with no humor as his eyes looked into some faraway memory.

"No, my son, I did that myself. I was hit in the shin. I don't know why I didn't go into shock, like most of my friends did when they were hit. I looked down and my leg was just *disintegrating*, down toward my foot and up my leg as well. Those entropic rifles, if you don't get to the wound fast, there's nothing left of you. I got out my hatchet and just swung it."

Quentin winced at the thought of such horror.

Manny's eyes refocused, and he looked at Quentin. "Well, anyway, we beat off that initial attack. My friends, the few that were left alive, managed to stabilize my wound. But the bats came again. There had to be at least 200,000 in that wave. I watched every one of my friends disintegrate within thirty seconds. That's how fast it was over. Thirty seconds. Did your history books tell you that?"

Quentin shook his head. "The history books tell us the fight went on for days."

"Right," Manny said. "Figures. It was over just like that. For some reason the High One spared me, and they just shot everyone around me while I stood there, firing away, killing a few, as they ignored me. The funny thing is when I got back home, all the Holy Men called my survival a *miracle*. They said the High One was watching over me. I guess there were only a few miracles to go around that — there weren't any available to all my friends, or the 490,000 men that died that day. When everyone else was gone, the bats surrounded me and told me to surrender or die. Regardless of what I'm told awaits me on the other side, I'm not that partial to dying. They drugged me up and shipped me off to what's now known as the *Combine*."

Quentin waited for more of the story, but Manny said nothing.

"What was it like," Quentin asked finally. "What did ... what did they do to you?"

Manny shook his head and forced a practiced businessman's smile. "I don't talk about that anymore, my son. High One saw fit to see me through. But don't you worry about it. It's a different world now. The Creterakians run everything, and they're very fond of the GFL, so they won't hurt the players. I know a lot of Nationalites think you're a race-traitor for leaving, but I hope you do well. Just try not to get killed in the first season. That's always embarrassing."

"I'll do my best."

A flock of five Creterakians flew onto the observation deck in a sudden blur of motion. Just as quickly, they perched on any available surface. Manny, Quentin and the three other Humans on the observation deck froze in place, a reaction bred from thousands of stories of Creterakians shooting anyone who moved too fast or in a threatening manner. The five-pound, winged creatures all wore the tiny silver vests that marked them as security forces, and each held a small entropic rifle. Manny started to sweat and the fat on his chin quivered — but he stayed perfectly still.

The Creterakian body consisted of, ironically, a football-shaped trunk, one end of which tapered off into a flat, two-foot-long tail — like the body of a tadpole, but with the tail flat on the horizontal plane instead of the vertical. Their bodies were different shades of red, some a solid color, some with splotchy patterns of pink or purple. Thin, short legs ended in feet with three thin, splayed toes that curled up around anything available. Two pair of foot-long arms reached out from either side of the body. The upper pair were webbed with membranous, patterned wings that ran from the tip of the arm to the base of the tail. The bottom pair looked just like the first, but without the membrane.

The bottom arms held the deadly entropic rifles.

Quentin had always found Creterakian heads rather revolting. Three pairs of eyes lined the round head: a pair looked straight ahead, a pair sat a bit below those and on the outside looking out to the left and right, and a pair that pointed straight down.

"Quentin Barnes," two of them said in unison, their brassy, high-pitched voices sounding almost as one. The other three simply sat, feet shuffling back-and-forth. "You will come with us."

Quentin let out a slow breath and tried to calm his heart rate. Not since he'd been a child of eleven had a bat actually spoken to him. There had been a riot at the mines. When the bats came to break it up, they killed fifteen men.

"Good luck, my son," Manny said as he bowed twice in the respectful manner of the Church. He handed Quentin a small plastic chip. "My card. I'll be at Emperor One for a week, so if you need anything give me a call. And think about my offer — you'd look very photogenic at the helm of a luxury yacht."

Quentin slipped the chip into his pocket. "Thanks," he mumbled, then walked out of the observation deck. The Creterakians whipped into a hovering formation around him, surrounding him like an honor guard.

An honor guard or a prison escort, Quentin thought. *I've got armed military guards leading me to a former prison station. Great, just great.*

Somehow, his introduction to the Galactic Football League wasn't quite as glamorous as he'd expected.

3

THE COMBINE

THE *COMBINE* WAS much smaller than Emperor Two. A feature-less gray orb devoid of any color, the *Combine* looked the part of a prison station. The shuttle docked, and the Creterakian escort led Quentin out. More Creterakians were waiting inside — many more. Quentin tried to count them, but they flew so quickly and were so numerous his eyes couldn't lock on. It was like being in the middle of a swarming flock of birds. He shuddered as he thought what it must have been like for Manny and the other Human ground forces that tried to fight the Creterakians some forty years ago.

Quentin walked down the hall. It seemed as if the small fly-ing creatures would slam into him at any moment, but they al-ways banked left or right at the last possible second, just missing him. He walked forward, trying to ignore the little creatures that seemed to fill the tight hallway like a gas.

He walked past a row of small pressure doors. His escort stopped in front of an open one. A Creterakian perched on the door frame, seemingly waiting for them.

"You are Quentin Barnes," it said, a statement more than a question.

"Yes."

"You are now number 113. You will answer to that number while you are at the *Combine*. Inside you will find Human clothes. Wear them. You have five minutes to prepare, then we will begin testing."

Quentin walked into the room. The door shut behind him. It took him only a second to realize he was in a prison cell. The only furnishing was a Human-length metal shelf that stuck out from the wall at waist level. A metal toilet hung from the back wall. On the floor next to the toilet was a two-foot-diameter circle of fine metal mesh. He recognized the mesh as a nannite shower — he'd used them at some of the opposing teams' locker rooms in stadiums that didn't have large water supplies like Micovi. On the shelf sat a yellow, form-fitting bodysuit labeled on the chest with the number "113."

Quentin looked on the back of the suit, expecting to see "Barnes" written in the typical block letters, but there was no name — just another "113." The suit seemed heavy. The material felt slightly lumpy, as if it were filled with micro-wires and various tiny electronic devices.

He sighed, wondering what he was in for, and started to strip.

A BUZZER SOUNDED from a hidden loudspeaker, making Quentin jump. The door to his cell opened. He looked out at the rush of Creterakians moving back and forth, so fast they were nothing more than a flash of silver uniforms and black wings.

A Creterakian flew into his cell. "Number 113, exit your room and wait for instructions."

Dressed in his yellow suit, a bare-footed Quentin stepped out and stood on the hallway's cold metal grille. There were even more bats now, but there were other Humans as well. In front of each door stood a man dressed in a yellow bodysuit identical to Quentin's.

It surprised him that he felt infinitely relieved to see other Humans. Three doors down and across the hall, he recognized Alonzo Castro, linebacker from Sigurd. Castro had led the PNFL in tackles and hit like the impact of an asteroid. At least that was the rumor — in the championship game, he hadn't been able to lay a glove on Quentin.

Alonzo caught his gaze and waved. "Quentin! What's up, champ?"

"Just doing my time in prison."

Alonzo laughed. "Yeah, I heard about this place."

The hallway filled with light conversation as men recognized each other from their on-field battles or from holocasts of the hundreds of Tier Three teams. It seemed strange, talking while countless Creterakians flew back and forth, but Quentin was already growing used to their presence.

"Who bought out your contract?" Alonzo asked.

"The Krakens. You?"

"Texas Earthlings. I'll be living in the Planetary Union, if you can believe that."

"No offense, but for a linebacker, aren't you a little ... well ..."

"Small?" Alonzo said, finishing Quentin's thought. His smile stayed, but the friendly expression faded from his eyes. "Yeah, well, they seem to think I've got what it takes. Hey, if we'z lucky, I'll see you in the playoffs."

Quentin thought for a second, then nodded. Alonzo was very fast and as strong as a Mason seabull. He'd given the Raiders' offensive line fits trying to block him. If he could overcome his small stature, he might be a real factor for the Earthlings.

"I hear we're in for a long day," Alonzo said.

"Why's that?"

"This testing crap goes on forever, I'm told."

The man to Quentin's right spoke up. "I was here last year. Today will be pure hell."

He was big, almost as big as a PNFL guard or tackle, yet he had that lean look of a man who could move — obviously a tight end. His pale blue skin marked his probable origin as the League of Planets, and his hair was electric blond.

"Why are you here *again*?" Quentin asked. "I thought you only had to do the *Combine* once, then you get individual testing after that."

The man nodded. "Yeah, if you make the team. My contract was picked up by the Parasites last year, but I didn't make the cut, so it was back to another season of Tier Three."

"How's the play there?"

"Tougher every year," the man said with a grimace. He offered his hand. "I'm Olaf Raunio."

Quentin looked at the blue-skinned hand for a second. To not shake it was an instant insult. To touch a blue skin, however, was to touch people who had been kicked off of Earth for consorting with Satan. The hand hung there awkwardly, for almost a second, before Quentin shook it, not quite able to hide his revulsion.

"I'm Quentin Barnes."

Olaf looked surprised. "The PNFL guy? Yeah, I watched that game on the 'net. You made Sigurd look like a bunch of pansies."

"Pansies?" Alonzo said from across the hall. His light-hearted tone had vanished, now there was nothing but malice in his deep voice. "Keep it up, blue-boy, and I'll show you a pansy."

Olaf bristled at the racial insult so frequently levied against people from the League of Planets.

"Never mind him," Quentin said. "He's still chapped from the spanking I gave him in the championship game."

The two men kept staring at each other for a few seconds, then Olaf laughed dismissively and turned back to Quentin. "I figured you'd go Tier One."

Quentin shrugged. "Me, too, but I'll get there soon enough."

Olaf smiled. "Hope so. You might find it's not as easy as you think."

"So you've been here before, where's all the aliens?"

"Each race has its own wing. This used to be a prison, and they kept the races separate to cut down on the violence."

"What's so tough about today?" Quentin asked. "What kind of tests?"

Olaf shrugged. "Can't tell you that. They tell you that any mention of what goes on here gets you kicked out of the league, but I suspect that if you talk about the inner workings of the *Combine*, you disappear for good."

A sudden, blaring buzzer sounded again, ending all conversation. A Creterakian in a blue uniform hovered at the end of the hall, his black wings nothing but a blur.

"This is the *Combine*," the little creature said, his voice amplified by the ship's speakers. "You will refer to me and any other you see in a blue suit as Boss. I am Boss One. If you do not follow instructions, you will be removed before you can complete the testing. If you do not complete the testing, you cannot play Upper Tier football."

The hallway fell deathly silent. Every man here would rather be dragged behind an Earth horse than go back for another season of Tier Three.

"The *Combine* tests purity," Boss One said. "Creterakian law makes it illegal for Humans or any other race to have biological modifications, cybernetic implants, strength- or performance-enhancing chemicals, mental accelerator chips or any other non-natural augmentation. The Galactic Football League is a showcase of cooperation amongst the races, and therefore, you must be pure to ensure fair competition."

The men nodded in agreement and understanding, but everyone knew the real reason for "purity." The Creterakians ruled by military strength. They did not allow any biological modifications that might make the subject races more effective warriors. Their post-war pogrom killed millions of soldiers: biotech-enhanced Human warriors, the cyborg Ki commandos, the Sklorno with carbon-titanium chitin genes for impermeable shells, Quyth Warriors with their hordes of implanted bio-repair nanocytes — all wiped out in a two-year-long purge designed to eliminate potential guerrilla fighters. Since that time, discovery of any bio-modification resulted in a prison sentence if it could be removed, or a death sentence if it could not.

"The yellow lines on the floor will lead you through the stations," Boss One said. "Follow the lines and follow all instructions. Failure to comply with a Boss's orders results in immediate dismissal. There is no talking. The testing begins immediately."

• • •

QUENTIN SHUFFLED ALONG on the yellow line, waiting for the 112 players ahead of him to enter the first station. Each man went in, the door closed and stayed closed for a few minutes, then the door opened for the next in line.

Finally it was his turn. The door closed behind him as he entered a room with racks of yellow jumpsuits. A large black machine with a gray, man-sized "X" dominated the back wall, complete with shackles at each end; two for hands and two for feet.

"Sit down, 113."

The voice came from the other end of the room, where a blue-suited boss perched on a table. A rail, hanging just two feet from the ceiling, ran the circumference of the room. Every last inch of that rail was packed with fidgeting, black-suited Creterakians.

"Sit down, 113," the boss repeated. A small metal stool sat in front of the table. Quentin walked to it and sat. The stool was just high enough that his feet didn't quite hit the floor. The stool's edges pushed the suit's micro-wires into the backs of his thighs.

"I am Boss Two. I am an official magistrate of the Creterakian Empire. To lie to me in any way is punishable by imprisonment." It was typical Creterakian communication — a statement without questions. They never said things that Human authority figures said, like "do you understand?" or "do I make myself clear?" A Creterakian spoke once and only once. If you didn't listen, or just plain didn't hear him, too bad for you.

Boss Two fluttered up from his perch and landed on Quentin's head. Quentin felt its sharp little claws and soft fleshy fingers on his scalp, and he instantly wondered if Boss Two carried an entropic pistol. His body prickled with heat, but he fought back the urge to swat Boss Two away like one might do to a pesky fly or one of those flying tarantulas from the planet To.

Is this part of the test? Quentin thought. *Just relax, be cool in the pocket.*

"I will now ask you questions. Get into the device at the end of this room."

Quentin looked suspiciously at the big X. He'd seen such devices in movies before — an interrogation table. The Purist Nation used such machines on prisoners, heretics and on the rare occasions someone actually prosecuted an organized crime figure.

"And if I don't get in it?"

"You will be dismissed."

Quentin walked to the X as Boss Two fluttered up to the perch rail. Quentin backed into it, putting his feet on the little platforms at the bottom. He gripped the hand holds at the top. He had time for one deep, ragged breath, then a dozen Creterakians flew down from their ceiling perches. They fluttered around him, working the controls. Restraining locks snapped in place around his wrists, legs and waist. The tight locks dug into his arms and shins.

Be calm, be calm, it's just like a linebacker blitz. Be calm and make the right decision.

"Recruit 113, have you ever had any kind of cybernetic implant?"

"No."

"Have you ever had any biotech modifications to your body?"

"No."

A pair of small mechanical arms dropped down from either side of his head. Each arm had a small screen — tiny, but when right in front of his eyes, they filled up his entire range of vision. Multi-colored static played on the screen. Quentin felt his heart rate increase.

"Have you ever taken performance-enhancing drugs?"

"No."

"Have you ever stolen?"

Quentin started to automatically say "no," then stopped himself. He'd stolen plenty of times as a kid. Could the Creterakians know about that? Did they have access to Purist Nation criminal files?

"Have you ever stolen, 113?"

The GFL demanded poster boy types from all races. If he admitted to stealing, would they kick him out? Would he be sent back to the PNFL to live out his career in the most backwater of football leagues?

"You will answer now, or you will be dismissed. Have you ever stolen?"

"Yes."

A stabbing, needle-like pain erupted from the small of his back.

"What's going on? What are you doing to me?"

"Have you ever taken the stimulants cocaine, esatrex, heroin, mesh or Kermiac bacterial extract?"

Another needle-like pain, this one from his shoulder. He grunted in pain and pulled at the restraints, but they held him fast. He tried to turn his head and look, but little screens moved with him, and he could see nothing but multi-colored static.

"Candidate 113, you will answer the question or be dismissed."

"I took bacterial extract once, but not the others. And when I get out of this thing, I'm going to twist your little shucking head right off your body."

Two more needle stings, one in each buttock.

"Do not threaten violence, 113, or you will be dismissed. You will now be asked five questions, and if you answer incorrectly, you will receive a shock."

A fifth needle-like sting, this time from his thigh, and much worse than the others. This one dug deep. Through the piercing agony, Quentin thought he felt the point punch into his femur.

"Is your name Quentin Barnes?"

"Yes."

"What is four times fifteen?"

"Sixty."

"What is the square root of 249?"

"What?"

A short, one-second blast of electricity ripped through his body. His back arched involuntarily, pushing his stomach hard against the waist restraint.

"What is the square root of 249?"

"How should I know?"

Another blast of electricity hit him, this one two seconds long and stronger than the first.

"The Void take you, let me out of this thing!"

"Do you wish to quit the test?"

Quentin fell silent. Quitting now meant he failed and would never reach Tier Two, let alone Tier One. He took a fast, deep breath, tried to block out the needle pain.

"No. I will continue."

"Who do you know in the Zoroastrian Guild?"

"The what?"

A third shock wave hit him, much harder than the last.

"Who do you know in the Zoroastrian Guild?"

"I don't know anyone in any guild!"

"If a shuttle leaves Buddha City at a speed of three light-years per day, and it is heading for the Planetary Union consulate on New Earth, which is at a distance of twelve light-years but moving away at a rate of two light-years per day, how long will it take the shuttle to reach the consulate?"

"A *story problem*? What does this have to do with football?"

A five-second blast of electricity ripped into him. His body shook and convulsed of its own accord. Primal urges took over, and Quentin pulled at his restraints with all his might. The restraints rattled with his efforts but did not give way.

"Answer the question."

"I don't know!"

Another five-second blast hit him, although it seemed as if it lasted for hours. He tasted blood in his mouth, hot and coppery and salty.

"Answer the question!"

Quentin took a breath and tried to think. He had to answer the question or they'd keep hitting him with shocks. "Give me a second, okay? You said ... what, three light-years per day?"

Suddenly the static screens went blank and the lights died, casting the room into blackness. Sparks erupted from the X-table, illuminating the room in brief strobe-light bursts. The smell of smoke filled the air, as did the high-pitched screeches of the two dozen Creterakians.

[MALFUNCTION, MALFUNCTION] droned a robotic voice. [SUS-

PECT IN DANGER OF ELECTRICAL OVERLOAD. SHUT DOWN INTERRO-
GATION TABLE IMMEDIATELY.]

The lights flickered back on at half strength, just in time for
Quentin to see the Creterakians abandon the room, flying out
through holes in the ceiling. In only two seconds he was alone,
trapped on the X-table. His heart whacked away inside his chest,
the strongest muscle in his body pumping panic through his limbs.

[WARNING, SUSPECT IN DANGER OF ELECTROCUTION]

Quentin pulled forward with all the strength in his arms. He
strained with effort, a small grunt escaping his lips. The smell of
sparks and smoke filled his nose. He pulled and pulled, muscles
bulging beneath his yellow bodysuit.

[WARNING, SUSPECT WILL RECEIVE FATAL SHOCK IN FIVE SECONDS]

What in High One's name is happening?

Quentin pulled harder, and the restraints started to give. He
threw the last of his strength — strength he didn't even know he
possessed — into the effort, and the arm restraints snapped free
with a metallic complaint. He reached down and ripped the restraints from first his left leg, then his right, then dove to the floor
just as the chair crackled and hummed with a huge burst of electricity.

A shudder ripped through the station, so strong Quentin
grabbed at the stool to keep his balance.

[WARNING, STATION DECOMPRESSION IMMINENT, EVACUATE IM-
MEDIATELY]

The door opposite the one he had entered slid open with a
hiss. He fought down panic — somehow he'd gone from a simple test to a sudden run for his life. Quentin looked above the
door. The orange circle — the universal symbol for a path to an
escape pod — emitted a welcoming glow. If he just followed doors
marked with that circle, the path would lead him to a way out.

He sprinted through the door, which led into a long hall. At the
end of the hall, he saw another orange circle. Strong legs pumped
beneath him, and he ate up the distance in seconds. At the end of
the second hall, the door slid open for him, and he jumped through.
This room looked like a medical bay, full of tables and cabinets.

The floor shifted below him, tilting to the left.

[DECOMPRESSION IMMINENT. MOVE TO THE NEAREST EVACUATION STATION.]

The lights started to flicker. Quentin had seen enough newscasts to know decompression wasn't a pretty sight. He scanned the three doors in the room — the one at the far end showed the welcome orange circle. Just as he ran forward, the room tilted steeply to the right. He kept his balance and kept moving forward, but the tables rolled into his path. He hopped backward as one rolled just in front of him and slammed against the wall. He took three steps forward before the room shifted again, this time hard to the left.

The tables rolled back across his path. He hurdled the first and kept moving forward, but the second table caught him on the hip. The solid metal surface dug into him and tossed him into the far wall. Quentin barely managed to stay on his feet. The floor shifted yet again, but this time he was ready for it, angling his body to the left to compensate.

[DECOMPRESSION IN FIFTEEN SECONDS]

The door opened, and he again looked down a hall, this one much shorter — and at the end sat an open airlock door leading into an escape pod. Inside the pod he saw the welcome sight of shock-webbing designed to hold him in place during the rough ejection process.

Quentin sprinted down the hall and launched himself through the door, slapping the "close" button in mid-air. The door hissed shut behind him as he flew into the shock-webbing. The webbing bent elastically under his weight, absorbing his momentum even as free strands of the pliable biomechanical material wrapped around his body, ready to hold him securely against the wild and unpredictable G-forces that accompanied any emergency escape.

He breathed hard from exertion, from stress and from fear. He waited for the sudden, jarring impact of jettison.

But none came.

Instead, one wall of the rounded pod smoothly lifted up. Quentin gasped in disbelief. The other side of that wall should have been nothing but the deepness of space. Instead, he looked into a large room filled with flying and fidgeting Creterakians, two blue-skinned Humans, a Quyth Leader and three huge Humans wearing silver security uniforms and holding shock-wands. They weren't moving toward him, but their stance made it quite clear what they would do if Quentin tried to get past them to the Quyth Leader beyond. More than a dozen holotanks hung on the walls. It only took a second to realize that the small three-dimensional images were of him during various stages of his frantic evacuation.

"Candidate 113, please rise," said one of the blue-boys. The shock-webbing slithered off him like a thing alive, gently lowering him to the ground, then returning to its dormant, hanging state. Quentin stood up, adrenaline still racing through his body, his muscles on fire with exertion. Sweat soaked his yellow bodysuit. His eyebrows knitted together in deep anger.

"This was all a test?"

The blue-boy nodded. "Yes, that is the first test of the *Combine*. While it is not the last, it is the most important because it tests to see if you're pure. If you're not pure, there is no point in the other tests. If you'll step to the staging area," the man said, gesturing to a yellow circle painted on the floor in the middle of the room, "we'll review your performance."

Quentin shook his head in amazement. He'd been fighting for his life, awash in near heart-attack panic, only to find it was all part of the *Combine*. *Well, la-de-da*. Someday he'd kick *someone's* rear for this. He didn't know who, and he didn't know when, but someday.

He walked to the circle. As he did, the hinged "escape pod" hissed shut behind him.

"You tested very high for your position."

"What did you test?"

"The stings you felt were bio-samples: skin, blood, muscle, bone. You have been tested for biomechanics, cybernetics, biotech, drugs and stimulants. You passed all those tests."

"Of course, I passed," Quentin spat, the fury flowing through him like molten magma. "You think I would have come here if I had any mods?"

The man simply nodded. "You are the 113th candidate. You'd be interested to know that twenty-seven of the candidates before you have already been dismissed."

"Twenty-seven ..." Quentin said in a surprised whisper. "That many?"

The man nodded again. "Yes. It is a statistically common amount. Some were eliminated immediately from the instant testing of the bio samples. Others were eliminated because of unnatural strength."

Quentin nodded slowly. "The restraints?"

"Yes, the restraints are sophisticated strength-measurement devices. Historically we find that only conditions of severe stress induce full-strength exertions."

"What about the run to the escape pod?"

"Again, severe stress tests the Human body to the utmost of its potential, be it natural or augmented. The computers recorded your strength, your speed, your mental acuity, your stress levels and your resistance to pain. The rolling tables, for example, let us test your reflexes and acceleration from a complete stop."

Quentin thought back to the long hallway. "Let me guess, the hallway is exactly 40 yards long?"

"Yes. And you set a position record for the *Combine* — a 3.6-second 40-yard dash."

Quentin's jaw dropped. He'd been timed at 4.0 before, but his fastest speed was a 3.8. A 3.6? That was fast for a *running back*, but he'd never even heard of a *quarterback* with such speed.

"Does everyone go through this?"

"The tests are different based on position," the man said. "With your record-setting performances in the PNFL, you were assigned the most demanding tests we have to offer."

Quentin swallowed, knowing his next question held the key to his fate. "But I passed, right? I qualified for Tier Two?"

The man nodded. "Yes, you qualified. You are finished for the day. Please exit out the blue door and follow the blue path back to your room. There will be more tests tomorrow, but rest assured, nothing as stressful as today."

Quentin let out a long breath. He still wanted to kick some-one's butt, and the blue-skinned League of Planets native would have done just as well as the next guy. The three giant men with the shock-sticks, however, stood between him and any of the test-monitoring staff.

The escape pod hissed open. Before Quentin left the room, he saw a new man — his suit numbered 114 — tangled in the shock-webbing. Quentin shook his head and walked out, following the blue path.

Excerpt from "A History of the Game: The rise, fall and rise of the GFL," by Robert Otto

The civilized galaxy consists of sixty-two populated planets, hundreds of colonies and thousands of intergalactic vessels with populations the size of small cities. With such diverse habitations, each with its own length of day, measurements of "weeks" and "months" or their cultural equivalents and completely differ-ent "seasons," deciding on a calendar-based GFL season seemed fraught with difficulty.

Demarkus Johanson, the League of Planets cultural scientist who invented the GFL in 2658, tried to adapt the "season" con-cept created by the National Football League of ancient Earth, just as he adapted the majority of rules, strategy and league organiza-tion. Based on Earth seasons, which were as random a choice as any other planet's orbital cycles, the GFL's first seventeen seasons involved a fixed 16-game schedule that began at the same time every year.

In 2665 Purist Nation officials seized the team bus for the New Rodina Astronauts and executed all non-Human players. Follow-ing that event, the Creterakians shut down the GFL. That shut-down created what League of Planets sociologist Clarissa Cho dubbed an "entertainment vacuum." Ki businessman Huichy-O-Wyl filled that vacuum with the creation of the Universal Football League.

While the caliber of UFL teams was far below that of the GFL, the new league had two distinct advantages. First, it had very few regulations regarding new franchises. Anyone with the money to afford a payroll, equipment and an interstellar-capable team bus could bring a new team into the league. Second, the UFL embraced the Creterakian calendar, a year of which is 241.25 Earth days. The UFL played a 12-game season with a two round playoff, allowing two "seasons" each Creterakian year.

This resulted in many new teams and a constant football presence. By 2668, the UFL boasted 32 teams and had crowned six champions. The "never-ending season" format worked so well and created so much fan interest, the Creterakians modified it when they forcibly disbanded the UFL and reinstated the GFL. The first half of the year is the Tier Two season. The second half is for Tier One. Tier Three runs constantly, with two seasons a year, the schedules of which match the Tier Two and Tier One seasons.

The result of this back-to-back scheduling is that rookies moving up from a Tier Three to an Upper Tier team have only two weeks before the season's first game. Rookies must be cleared through the *Combine* and can only be brought in for the roughly one week that remains of the preseason. After the preseason, teams can fill roster gaps only by grabbing free agents who have already played on a GFL roster.

THE SECOND DAY, the computer woke Quentin and told him to dress. He followed directions and didn't have to wait long before the door opened and something started to come through, to *float* through. Quentin jumped away from the door, his back hitting the small cell's wall.

It floated at chest height, a white, tapered, flattish creature about four feet across and six feet long. At the outer edges of the body, thick skin moved in undulating waves, like the long wings of a stingray or a skate. A row of six deep, black sensory pits lined the creature's curved front.

A Harrah.

"My goodness," the creature said. "Are you all right?"

The *creature* hadn't said it because Quentin didn't see movement from anything that might be a mouth. He realized that the words came from a small metal machine strapped to the creature's back.

He recognized the creature as a resident of one of the five gas giant planets that made up the Harrah Tribal Accord. He'd never seen one in person, just on holos as GFL refs. He'd also studied them in the classes that taught every Purist Nation child how to kill the sub-races. The common nursery rhyme jumped unbidden into his head:

> *A punch in the pit, any of them will do*
> *Grab the wings and pull down, so blessed are you*
> *Bring up your knee, oh so so so high*
> *Let this enemy of High One die.*

He remembered that kind of move put sudden compression on the Harrah's heart, causing it to rupture.

The Harrah's sensory pits combined to produce a kind of sonar that *let* them "see" everything via sound waves. A curled tentacle sat outside the leftmost and rightmost black pit — the Harrah equivalent of hands. It wore a pack of some kind on its back, an orange-and-black pack with many compartments and pockets.

Quentin stared for a second before he realized his hands were balled up into tight fists. "Who the hell are you?"

"I'm the Krakens' team doctor. You may call me Doc. Please relax, my good man. I'm here for your physical."

"I don't get a Human doctor?"

"Harrah make excellent doctors, I assure you. I've been studying multi-species sports medicine for fifty years. I realize that my appearance may be a bit startling to you, Quentin, but I pose no danger. Now, please, sit and relax."

Doc reached a tentacle into his backpack and came out with a bracelet done in a bluish metal.

"Please disrobe and hold out your wrist."

"I want a Human doctor."

"That's fine. But I'm the team doctor for the Ionath Krakens. If you want to play for the Krakens, I have to examine you. If you want to go back to the PNFL for another year so you can find a team with a Human doctor, that is your prerogative."

Quentin gritted his teeth. He wasn't waiting another year. He stripped out of his bodysuit and held out his hand.

Doc's tentacles shot to the long scar on Quentin's right arm. Quentin managed not to flinch as the alien examined the old wound.

"How did this happen?"

"Grinder accident when I was a kid, working in the mines. I almost lost my arm."

"But that scar ... did they use *stitches*? With a *needle* and *thread*?"

"It was a pretty bad injury. I think they did a great job. They grafted the bone together, repaired the muscle connections and stitched the whole thing up."

"Stitches and bone grafts," Doc said quietly. "Sheer barbarism."

Doc fastened the bracelet around his wrist.

"This device will check all of your vital signs. I already have a great deal of physical information on you from yesterday's test, so this is somewhat of a formality. Now I'm going to check your joints — machines can't always find what can be found by touch."

Quentin's lip curled involuntarily at the thought of that thing touching him. But he'd have to get used to aliens, so he might as well start now.

Doc's tentacles gripped his arm. They were warm and soft, not cold and clammy as he'd expected. Doc bent his arm at the elbow, then straightened it, pushing against the joint.

"Does it hurt when I do this?"

"No," Quentin said. Doc continued his examination, moving from joint to joint.

"PNFL doesn't give out medical records. What sports-related injuries have you sustained?"

"None."

Doc paused. "There's no use in lying, my good man. I'm going to find any injuries you've had."

"Search all you want," Quentin said.

The Harrah doctor continued looking. After five minutes of gentle poking, prodding and bending, he stopped. He pulled the device off Quentin's wrist, looked at it for a moment, then returned it to his backpack.

"How is it," Doc said, "that you played football for four years, yet you have no injuries?"

Quentin shrugged. "I don't get hit very much."

"Yes, well, I suppose you don't. Now we have just one more test, Quentin. We must check you for a hernia."

Quentin's heart sank. He'd forgotten about that most invasive part of the sports physical.

"I don't have one."

"I need to check. Please stand."

Quentin sighed.

Tentacles on my testicles, he thought. *I'm really moving up in the world.*

4

THE TEAM

QUENTIN SPENT two days at the *Combine*, but experienced nothing as arduous as the initial test or as disturbing as his exam with Doc. League officials continued to test his reflexes, his strength and his endurance. The initial exam created a baseline of his physical capabilities. Subsequent tests further developed that analysis and were combined with extensive measurements of intelligence, analytical thinking and mental reaction time. Meal trays slid through a slot in his cell walls, three times a day, the same time every day. The best of that food tasted like a bland nothing, the worst like some kind of rancid sawdust. He ate it anyway. Quentin wondered if the food would be like this on the Krakens' team bus — the thought made him shudder. He wanted some good old-fashioned Nationalite cooking.

After his last test, a holographic video game that had him slapping colored balls in a pre-described pattern as fast as his hands could move, Quentin returned to his cell to find new clothes laid out on his metal bunk. Loose-fitting sweatpants and a sweatshirt, new Nike football shoes and socks, all in the orange-and-black colors of the Ionath Krakens. A orange-and-black bag sat next to the clothes, containing a second set of sweats and the clothes he wore when he arrived at the *Combine*. The last item, the one that really caught his attention, was an Ionath Krakens jersey.

A jet-black jersey, it had an orange 10 with white trim on the front and the back. He was glad to see he'd keep his old number from the Raiders. Orange, black and white Krakens logo patches were sewn onto each shoulder. A "Kraken" was a huge oceanic predator native to Quyth, the Concordia's capital planet. As long as two hundred feet, with a twenty-foot-wide tail and six tentacles that ended in sharp, jagged hooks, the Kraken was a vicious hunter. Quentin thought it a fitting nickname for a football team, much better than, say, the scientific-based names of League of Planets teams like the Wilson 6 Physicists or the Satirli 6 Explorers.

This is it. I'm on my way. I'll be on every holotank in the freakin' galaxy. My parents will find me for sure.

A buzz sounded from the speakers, followed by the computer voice.

[ATTENTION PROSPECTS. GARB YOURSELVES IN THE CLOTHES PROVIDED, AND WHEN YOUR DOOR OPENS, CARRY YOUR BAG AND TAKE ONE STEP OUTSIDE. YOU WILL BE GUIDED TO YOUR TEAM REPRESENTATIVE AND TAKEN TO TRAINING CAMP.]

Quentin quickly removed the sweat-stained yellow bodysuit and stepped onto the mesh circle. A nearly invisible cloud of tiny machines flew up from the mesh like a hazy fog. He moved slowly, raising his arms, lifting his feet, letting the nannites reach his every nook and cranny. The tiny, tingling machines scoured his skin, gobbling up every piece of dirt and dust, scrubbing away sweat and grime. While effective, the nannites did not offer the pleasure of a steaming water shower.

In less than a minute, the cloud disappeared, fading back into the metal mesh. Quentin couldn't contain his excitement as he put on his new team clothes. Tier Two or not, he felt a surge of pride as he slipped on the orange and black. This was *his* team now, the team he would lead to victory.

The door to his cell hissed open. Quentin hurriedly pulled the sweatshirt on over his jersey, grabbed the bag and stepped outside. Up and down the hall stood smiling young men with similar clothes, but all in different colors — Alonzo in the red and blue of the Earthlings, Olaf in the gray-on-black stripes of the Klipthik Parasites, a player in the cherry-red dots of the Satah Air-Warriors and another in the multi-shaded purple of the Sky Demolition, a team in the Quyth Irradiated Conference along with the Krakens. There were far fewer players than Quentin had seen the first day. By his rough estimate, around thirty percent of them were gone. He wondered what fate awaited those men — either an ignoble ride home for a trivial offense, surgery and prison for any removable mods, or possibly they had already been executed.

Boss One fluttered through the hall. "You have all passed the *Combine*. You will now join your team representative. Be aware that other species may be joining you at this point. It is a crime under Creterakian law to use racial insults against other species, and species-based crimes such as assault result in far harsher penalties than the same crime against a member of your own species. Intolerance of other species is not allowed under Creterakian law."

Boss One fluttered to his perch.

The voice once again came over the loudspeaker. [TEXAS EARTHLING PROSPECTS, FOLLOW THE BLUE LINE]

A blue line glowed on the floor. Alonzo and a lanky blackskinned man, probably a quarterback, walked down the hall.

Alonzo waved. "Good luck, Quentin. I hope I see you in the playoffs."

[SHORAH CHIEFTAIN PROSPECTS, FOLLOW THE BLUE LINE]

Three men wearing green dots on black walked to the end of the hall. All three were obviously quarterbacks, and Quentin knew two of them would probably open their lockers in a week to find a ticket home — only one would make the cut.

[IONATH KRAKENS, FOLLOW THE BLUE LINE]

Quentin stepped out. For a second, he thought he was the only one in orange and black, but another man fell in line behind him. Quentin hadn't seen him during the *Combine* nor did he recognize the face. The man wore number 26.

Quentin followed the blue line, his new teammate right behind him. Two hallways later, an airlock hissed open, and he found himself on a empty deck in the landing bay. The deck had four doors — the eight-foot-high one that Quentin had just walked through, another just like it, a narrower one twelve feet high and one ten feet high and eight feet wide.

The view port showed that the deck's sealed airlock connected to a hundred-foot-long shuttle, an older model but neatly trimmed out in orange and black. Five Creterakian guards waited there, flittering about, first in the air, then hopping on the floor, then hanging from the ceiling, never staying still.

"I am Boss Seven," the lead Creterakian said. "Line up on the blue line." At his command, a blue line appeared on the deck, perpendicular to the airlock. Quentin did as he was told. He turned to number 26, his new teammate, a burly, thick-chested man with legs the size of sonic cannons. He had dark, yellowish skin and a curly beard that hung to his chest.

"Quentin Barnes," Quentin said, offering his hand.

"Yassoud Murphy," the man said, shaking Quentin's hand. Quentin finally recognized the man's face — Yassoud had broken the Tier Three rushing record in the Sklorno league and led his team to the championship of the Tier Three tournament.

"Glad to have you aboard," Quentin said. "I saw highlights of your performance in the finals."

Yassoud nodded. "Yeah, thanks. That was a pretty good game. I cleaned up on the point spread on that one."

Quentin's eyes narrowed in disbelief. "You bet on your own game?"

"Oh, yep," Yassoud said. "Everyone bets in the Sklorno leagues. What, you never bet on your own game?"

"Not on your life."

"Well, you should," Yassoud said. "There's money to be made if you know the odds. There's bets for everything in the GFL, man. Take me, for example. Did you know the odds of me making it through the season without serious injury are three-to-five?"

"That's not very good."

"Not very good? Are you crazy? Three-to-five is *great* for a rookie. I'm only here because the Krakens third running back caught Fenkel Fever from some girl on Earth. He's out for the season. That means I'm third string, so I won't see a whole lot of action playing behind Mitchell Fayed and Paul Pierson. But then again, you know how frequently running backs get hurt in this league. Everyone except Fayed, anyway — that guy can take more hits than a battle cruiser. They don't call him 'The Machine' for nothing."

"What are my odds to start, about even?"

Yassoud laughed. "Start? Hardly. Odds are three-to-one that you don't even make it through the season before they ship you back to the Purist Nation."

Quentin felt anger instantly overtake him. "That's bull."

"Nope," Yassoud said. "It's not. Three-to-one."

"Why the hell is that?"

"You're a Nationalite," Yassoud said. "You've probably never met other species face to face, let alone played with them. Did you know that only twenty percent of Purist Nation rookies make it through their first season?"

Quentin shook his head. He'd had no idea his people held such a dismal success rate.

Yassoud continued. "It's true. You backwater jokers usually can't handle the inter-species dynamics. Hell, I've got a thousand on you dropping out before the season is half over."

Quentin paused a moment, trying to control his anger. "Then you made a big mistake."

Yassoud shrugged. "We'll see. You win some, you lose some."

Quentin started to speak when the twelve-foot-high airlock door hissed open. Two Sklorno stepped onto the deck. Quentin had seen them on the net before, but never in person. They were tall, probably nine feet apiece — twelve long feet, if you counted the tail that extended past their legs. Translucent chitin covered black skeletons and ghostly images of semi-translucent internal organs. They reminded Quentin of full-body Human X-rays he'd seen in his childhood schoolbooks. Coarse black fur jutted out at every joint.

Their legs practically screamed *speed* and *leaping*. Translucent two-foot segments, folded back like a grasshopper's legs, ended in a thick pad of a foot with five long, splayed toes.

The legs supported a slender body-stalk that curved backward like a bow. Two long arms — coils of translucent, boneless muscle three feet long — jutted out from three-quarters of the way up the trunk, in the approximate position where a Human female's breasts would be. Each Sklorno wore an orange-and-black jersey, with the numbers 81 and 82, respectively, on the trunks below their coiled arms.

Even though he'd seen Sklorno heads a few times on the Web, they still took some getting used to. Two curled raspers hung at the top of the body-stalk, just below the head, partially covered by a chitinous chin-plate. When unrolled, the raspers reached to the floor. Hundreds of tiny teeth coated each rasper — they could tear through most anything. Back in the wartimes, stories abounded that the Sklorno ate their enemies. Humans were supposed to be a particular favorite.

The head itself was nothing more than a softball-sized block of oily, coarse black hairs. Sklorno heads didn't require a lot of volume, as the brain was located in a long column on the back of the trunk. Four boneless eyestalks, each a pebbly, deep magenta, jutted from the furry black ball. The eyestalks moved independently, like intelligent snakes on the head of the mythical Medusa.

Boss Seven shouted something in the high-pitched click-and-squeal Sklorno language. The Sklorno walked up to the blue line, eyestalks waving as they examined every angle of the flight deck. Quentin fought down a wave of revulsion. He felt grateful the two wore jerseys — otherwise, there was no way to tell them apart.

Number 81 stood on Quentin's right side, and Number 82 stood to the right of Number 81. Number 81's raspers rolled out, wet with saliva. A thin strand of drool dangled from the left rasper, wetly swinging down the eight feet to the floor.

"You are Quentin Barnes?" Its voice sounded like a combination of bird whistles, but Quentin had no problem understanding the words. He nodded in acknowledgement. It lowered itself, rear legs folding up like a grasshopper's. In that position, it stood just under six feet tall and actually looked up at Quentin.

"I am Denver," the Sklorno said. It used its tentacle-arm to point at the other. "This is Milford." Another string of drool dripped down from Denver's left rasper. Quentin fought the urge to turn away.

"You are great thrower," Milford said. "The Sklorno people watch you on the 'net. I am looking forward to catching many passes thrown by you."

"No, *I* am looking forward to catching many passes thrown by you," Denver said. "*I* will catch the majority of passes."

Milford turned suddenly and stood tall, extending to a full nine feet. "No! *I* will catch the majority of his passes!"

Denver also stood, eyestalks waving wildly, tentacle-arms whirling in a threatening pattern. "No! *You* will be on the sidelines watching *me* catch passes!"

Milford's body began to shake, sending streamers of drool flying across the flight deck. The boneless arms stretched back, as if to strike at Denver, then suddenly five Creterakians brandishing entropic rifles flew between the two Sklorno.

"Cease hostilities!" Boss Seven said loudly. "Cease or you will be deported before you can report to your team."

As quickly as the flare-up started, it ceased. Denver and Milford sat down on their tails. They twitched and moved and squeaked, just a little, as if neither was capable of sitting perfectly still or remaining perfectly quiet. Their ever-moving eyestalks flittered in all directions.

"You must be one sexy guy," Yassoud said quietly. "The girls are fighting over you."

"Girls? They're females?"

Yassoud rolled his eyes. "Don't they teach you backwater Purist idiots anything? You never took basic multi-species biology?"

Another nursery rhyme jumped into his brain.

> *The crickets have eyes on top of their head*
> *Grab them and pull them they'll soon be dead.*

With Satan's soldiers don't ever be kind
They can't see to sin if they are made blind.

Quentin shrugged. "I know how to kill them. That's all the biology the Nation is concerned with."

Yassoud laughed. "Yeah, that's what I've heard. Sklorno females are the athletes, the soldiers. The males are these little two-foot-high things, kind of like a furry black ball."

Quentin's face wrinkled in surprise, remembering broadcasts showing the small creatures that seemed to throng around the tall Sklorno he now knew to be females. "Those things? There's hordes of those. Those are the males? I thought those were *pets.*"

Yassoud shook his head. "Ah, the wonderful education system of the Purist Nation."

Quentin again felt very stupid and hickish. The feeling made him want to hit someone. "Hey, wait a minute," he said. "I've heard the word *Denver*. Isn't that a city on Earth?"

"Yeah. The Sklorno are football crazy. Once they start playing the game, they take the name of an Earth city or region because Earth was the birthplace of football."

"I didn't know Sklorno could speak English."

"English is the language of football," Yassoud said. "You either understand it or you won't get to this level. The Sklorno players spend several hours a day working on it, but it's very difficult for them. Quyth have no problem, of course, and the Ki can understand it well enough even though they can't speak it for crap."

The ten-foot by eight-foot door hissed open, and a nightmare crawled out.

Like the Sklorno, Quentin had seen Ki only on the 'net. Ki were often cast in Purist Nation movies as blood-thirsty monsters or tricksters out to collect Human souls. With movie-making technology that could make any imagined creature as real as a Human, however, everything on the 'net took on a sense of fantasy. This Ki looked like the movie creatures, but a holocast simply didn't do the species justice.

Its twelve-foot-long, tube-shaped body bent upwards in the middle, giving it a six-foot-long horizontal piece and a six-foot-high vertical piece. Bright orange skin covered with small dots of reddish-brown enamel covered the body. Six legs stuck out from the sides of the horizontal segment, each leg thick and just over four feet long. Two more limbs protruded from each side of the vertical body — these were shorter but thicker, with muscle rippling under the pebbled skin. Each upper-body limb ended in four stubby fingers.

Five glossy black eyespots surrounded the vertical body's tapered point. Ki were well known for their 360-degree vision. At the very top of the tapered point was the vocal spout, a small cluster of wormlike tubes. Between the top sets of vertical arms was the thing that gave Quentin nightmares as a child — the Ki "mouth." The mouth consisted of six short, thick, sharp black hooks in a hexagonal pattern. Inside the hex was a pinkish hole lined with row after row of triangular black teeth. He'd seen many movies where the upper arms would drag Human prey to the mouth. The hexagonal hooks dug into the screaming victim, pulling it tight, while the triangular teeth ripped out chunk after chunk after chuck — bite, swallow, bite, swallow.

What do I do if a Ki should attack?
I get behind him with my foot in his back
I bend him hard, his back gives a crack
Because the High One loves me, and I love him back.

The Ki's orange-and-black, four-sleeved jersey ran from the bottom of the vertical body to just under the horrific mouth. There was just enough room for a small number 93 on the chest.

Quentin shuddered as he pictured the creature tearing through an offensive line, multi-jointed arms wrapping him up and taking him down. This Ki had to weigh at least 580 pounds. The smell of rotting meat filled Quentin's nose. His face wrinkled in disgust, and he waved his hand to clear away the odor.

"What is that *stench*?"

Yassoud laughed. "Better get used to it, that's how Ki smell."

Boss Seven barked out a command. The Ki language sounded hoarse, gravelly, guttural, and Quentin didn't understand a word of it. The hulking Ki scuttled toward the blue line, its horizontal legs moving like a cross between an insect's and the oars of an old Greek warship.

Yassoud nudged Quentin. "That's Mum-O-Killowe. He played in the Sklorno leagues. Had twenty-six sacks in a twelve-game season, another five in the playoffs."

"You played against him?"

Yassoud nodded. "Yeah. You can't imagine how hard that thing hits. And he has no concept of the difference between practice and a game, so don't get on his bad side."

Mum-O-Killowe stopped four feet from the blue line. He pointed his upper right arm straight at Quentin. The tubes of the vocal spout quivered as the nightmarish creature let out a long, barking sound. It then reared back and started lunging forward. Quentin had already taken two steps back before the Creterakian guards flew in front of Mum-O-Killowe, their entropic rifles aimed directly at his eyespots. The Ki stopped, turned his long body, and got on the blue line to the right of Milford.

"Too bad," Yassoud said. "Looks like you're already on his bad side."

"Did you understand what he said?"

"Some of it. It seems your fame precedes you. He said something to the effect that he saw your championship game, and he prayed to the Ki gods that you were on another Tier Two team so he could cripple you."

"Cripple me?"

"The Ki consider it a high point of honor to knock someone out of the game — maiming, dismembering and death are all acceptable methods. Now that you're on the same team, and he'll see you every day in practice, he figures he'll cripple you for sure."

"Oh, this is just *great*."

Yassoud laughed. "You know, if you want to put some money down that you won't make it through training camp, I can put you in touch with my bookie."

"Screw you."

"Hey, I'm just saying you might as well come out of this with some money, if only to pay your prolonged hospital bills."

Quentin turned and raised his fist, but Yassoud raised his hands, palms out in a defensive posture. His eyebrows rose high in mock surprise. "Hey, now! Take it easy," he said. "I'm just riding you — and if you throw that punch, you're on the next ship back to the Purist Nation."

Quentin lowered the fist and stared straight out from the blue line. "Just keep talking," he said quietly. "You'll get yours soon enough."

The main airlock door, the one connected to the orange-and-black shuttle, hissed open. A pair of furry Quyth Leaders scurried out, one with jet-black fur that glistened under the landing deck lights, the other with unkempt yellow fur mottled with irregular brown stripes.

Two dangerous-looking Quyth Warriors followed the Leaders, one about 300 pounds, the other a good-sized 375. Their carapaces were both painted in the wild reds and oranges of Quyth commandos, and each carried a five-foot-long stun-stick. Quentin had read about Quyth Warriors in his history classes. They were one of the deadliest creatures in the galaxy: fast, strong and vicious. One-on-one, they were no match for trained Purist Nation soldiers, of course. At least that's what the history books said. Standing this close to one, Quentin suddenly found himself wondering if his history books were more than a little bit colored by Holy Men's propaganda.

The big warrior, Quentin was surprised to see, wore a Krakens jersey with the number 58 on the chest.

A Creterakian dressed in a blue vest inlaid with tiny, tinkling silver bells flew out of the airlock, did a pair of 360-degree circles, then fluttered in front of Mum-O-Killowe. The Creterakian barked something out in the Ki language, the Ki answered, and the Creterakian settled down on top of the bigger creature's head.

Quentin leaned over to Yassoud. "What the heck was that all about?"

"Most Ki can't speak Human or Quyth," Yassoud said. "Creterakians can speak all languages, so they frequently act as interpreters."

"Why is it dressed like that?" Quentin asked. "Is that some kind of an interpreter's uniform?"

Yassoud chuckled softly. "He's a civilian."

"A ... civilian? You mean it's not in the military?"

"Let me guess, the Holy Men taught you that all Creterakians are mindless soldiers bent on exterminating all the other races?"

His hickish feeling cranked up another notch. "Well ... yeah, that's about right."

Yassoud shook his head. "It's amazing that such a backwater place can even function. Creterakians are just like everybody else. They've got a mostly civilian population along with the military."

"Well, I'll be."

"Just don't trust them," Yassoud said. "All the Creterakians that deal with Tier Two and Tier One are con men, or so I'm told."

Quentin started to ask another question but fell silent when the black-furred Quyth Leader stepped forward.

"I am Gredok the Splithead. You are all now my property. You are rookies, you are nothing of importance. I own your contracts for this season and have the final say on if you make the team or not." He gestured to the yellow-furred Leader. "This is Hokor the Hookchest, coach of the Ionath Krakens. You will follow his instructions to the letter."

Hokor stepped forward, his antennae plastered back flat against his skull.

"Training camp begins immediately. This shuttle will take you to the *Touchback*, our team bus, which is your home as long as you are with the Krakens. You will stow your gear, then report to position meetings, where you will be given your study assignments. Once you have been shown how to operate the Kriegs-Ballok Virtual Practice System, you will report to the field for practice."

Mum-O-Killowe barked out something unintelligible.

 Want to learn more about the basics of American football? Hear the author give you info that will add to your enjoyment of **The Rookie**, at http://www.scottsigler.com/football101.

"Shizzle, what does he want?" Hokor asked the blue-suited Creterakian.

Shizzle swooped down, his silver bells tinkling in time with each flap. "The great Mum-O-Killowe wants to know when he can begin to hit the Human Quentin Barnes."

Quentin's eyes widened with surprise. This giant Ki wanted to tear his head off.

"Tell him to shut up," Hokor said. "And tell him he'll only be told once."

Shizzle relayed the command, then Mum-O-Killowe turned and strode toward Quentin, roaring sounds that rang obscene despite the language barrier.

Quentin turned to face him and crouched, mind instantly switching to game mode, looking for the best place to hit the 580-pound, 6-legged, 4-armed nightmare. The nursery rhyme said to go for its back, but he didn't see a way around the long, muscular arms.

Quentin barely saw movement before the two Quyth Warriors were on Mum-O-Killowe. They both jabbed him with their staffs, resulting in a loud crackling sound and flickers of blue-white light. Mum-O-Killowe roared in pain. He turned and grabbed for the Quyth Warrior wearing the Krakens' jersey, but the smaller creature danced back, effortlessly avoiding the wild grab, then jabbed the stun-stick into Mum-O-Killowe's chest. Mum-O-Killowe sagged, then fell to the ground, a twelve-foot-long motionless blob.

The rookies stood in silence. The smell of ozone filled Quentin's nostrils. The Quyth Warriors each grabbed one of Mum-O-Killowe arms and labored to drag him into the shuttle.

"Normally, we'd kick him off the team," Hokor said, "but we're short on defensive linemen and the season is only a week away. We're not, however, short on wide receivers, running backs or quarterbacks."

Hokor walked down the blue line until he stood in front of Quentin. "Kneel down, Human, I want to look you in the eye."

Quentin quickly looked at Yassoud, who nodded nervously. Quentin got on one knee and still had to lean down to look straight into Hokor's one big eye. He'd never seen a Quyth Leader — or any other alien, for that matter — this close up. Hokor's eye wasn't really clear, but a translucent light blue, filled with hundreds of green disks in a tight geometrical pattern. His fur was thick, each strand much thicker than a Human hair. The most disturbing physical aspect was the pedipalps, quivering things on either side of the mouth, as coordinated and well-developed as a Human arm. Quentin kept his cool, but it surprised him to feel the grip of a lifetime of Purist Nation teachings. Most of his people would be screaming right now, either with pure terror or righteous, murderous rage. He mostly viewed those people with contempt, so it shocked Quentin that he felt *both* emotions stirring up from somewhere so deep in his subconscious he hadn't even known they existed.

But Quentin was on a mission. And his pure, unstoppable desire to play football at the highest levels ran far stronger than programmed ideology.

"As soon as practice starts, nobody is going to be there to stop him," Hokor said. "You had better be ready to complete the offensive play when *three* of those things are coming at you, hoping to maim you or, if they get in a good shot, just kill you outright."

Quentin smiled. "Just give me the ball, Coach."

Hokor's antennae quivered once, then fell flat. "We'll see, rookie." He walked to the airlock door. "Krakens rookies, come aboard."

Transcript from "the Galaxy's Greatest Damn Sports Show with Dan & Akbar & Tarat the Smasher."

DAN: Welcome back, sports fans, Dan Gianni here with Akbar Smith and our own football-legend-in-residence, Tarat the Smasher.

TARAT: Thanks, Dan.

DAN: So what are we going to talk about today?

AKBAR: As if there's any question.

DAN: Baseball season is almost over, and to tell you the truth, with four player strikes in the past ten seasons, I really don't think anyone gives a damn. It's so boring!

AKBAR: I still like baseball.

DAN: Like I said, no one gives a damn. Intergalactic Soccer Association season is coming up, but that's a little boring as well.

TARAT: Good sport, but the Sklorno have completely taken it over.

AKBAR: There are 1,012 players in that league, and all of them are Sklorno.

DAN: You can't fight speed, not in soccer. But we all know one sport that caters to all species, and that's only one week away.

TARAT: Nothing like finishing up Tier One football and rolling right into Tier Two.

DAN: That's right, sports fans, we're talking Tier Two football. The Jupiter Jacks captured the Tier One crown last week, with a thrilling 21-20 Galaxy Bowl win over the To Pirates. Don't the rookies arrive in camp today?

AKBAR: That's right, Dan. You know how I hate this system — the rookies only have one week in camp before the first game.

TARAT: But there is no way around that.

DAN: I know there's no way around it, but it still sucks. I mean, some of these guys were playing in championship games only a few days ago!

TARAT: Trust me, not one of them is complaining.

DAN: Sure, no argument there, but take Quentin Barnes, for example, the quarterback of the Micovi Raiders of the PNFL. I mean he played the PNFL championship only a week ago, and in seven days he'll line up for his first Tier Two game with the Ionath Krakens. That's crazy!

AKBAR: What makes you think he'll play a down? He'll ride the bench for the first half of the season like most of the rookies.

DAN: You think? The Krakens have to get someone at quarterback who can win games.

AKBAR: Were you dropped on your head repeatedly as a child? Have you ever heard of the Krakens' quarterback, some guy named Donald Pine?

DAN: He's all washed up. He can't win the big games.

AKBAR: He won two Galaxy Bowls!

DAN: Ancient history. He has choked in every big game in the past three seasons for the Krakens.

AKBAR: And you think some rookie is the answer?

DAN: Probably not, we all know quarterbacks from the Purist Nation don't last. But Barnes probably doesn't have to do much to be better than Donald Pine is right now.

AKBAR: You've *got* to be kidding me.

DAN: Look at the games, will ya? Last year the Krakens went 6-3 and missed the playoffs with a week-nine loss to Orbiting Death. Pine throws four interceptions. He gets pulled, and the number-two quarterback, Tre Peterson, dies four plays later. Pine goes back in and throws another interception.

AKBAR: Okay, so that's one game.

DAN: What about two seasons ago? Krakens kill eventual league champ Sala Intrigue 48-24. But they drop four games to teams with a combined record of 13-23. All of those games were upsets — Pine couldn't win the games he's supposed to win.

AKBAR: He's not the only guy on the field, Dan.

DAN: Of course not. But look at Pine's record since he won that last Galaxy Bowl back in 2676. You know how this game works — the blame falls on the quarterback. If it wasn't for Mitchell Fayed, the Krakens would be nothing.

TARAT: I played against Fayed before I retired. That is the toughest Human I've ever seen. You hit him and hit him, and he just gets up and smiles.

DAN: That's why they call him *The Machine*. Number forty-seven just keeps on running.

AKBAR: Can we get back on the subject of Donald Pine?

DAN: Look, Pine's still a great quarterback, but in some games he just flat-out chokes.

AKBAR: So again, you're going on record saying Quentin Barnes is the answer?

DAN: I didn't say that. He's a rookie. And a Purist Nation rookie at that. He's never been hit by a Ki lineman and never faced a blitz from a Quyth Warrior. If he lasts one season I'll be surprised. Pine will start, as usual, Pine will lose the big games, as usual, and the Krakens will flail about in the middle of the pack, as usual.

THE SHUTTLE DISENGAGED from the airlock and shot away from the *Combine*. It felt cramped inside the small vehicle, which probably would have seated twelve Humans comfortably. The prone form of Mum-O-Killowe took up half the floor. The rest of the rookies took whatever seats they could find.

Within minutes, they approached the *Touchback*. It was only half the size of the starliner that had brought him from Micovi, yet much larger than Quentin had thought it would be. Perhaps an eighth of a mile long, over half the ship consisted of a clear dome covering a full-sized practice field, 100 yards long with 10-yard end zones, one painted orange, one painted black. Eighteen decks rose up all around the field, as if engineers had scooped out a large section of ship, put down the field, then sealed everything off with the clear dome. It seemed that from every deck, one would be only a short walk from a view of the practice field.

A large engine assembly sat behind the black end zone. The passenger decks, bridge and other ship constructs were on the opposite side, behind the orange end zone. Instead of the sleek, eye-pleasing lines of a passenger liner, the *Touchback* bore the blocky profile of a distinctly military vehicle. As the shuttle drew closer, Quentin recognized the tell-tale mounted spheres of weapon assemblies.

"High One ... Are those *gun* mounts?"

Yassoud nodded. "Looks like a converted frigate. Couldn't tell you what kind, though — I've never actually seen a warship, except in the movies."

The sudden sound of rapidly tinkling bells accompanied by the heavy fluttering of wings erupted near their heads. Quentin instinctively ducked down to one knee, while Yassoud simply turned. Shizzle hovered, resplendent in his blue and silver suit.

"The *Touchback* is a converted Planetary Union Achmed-

Class heavy-weapons platform," the flying creature said in a tone as smooth as the voice-over for an intoxicant commercial. "Formerly known as the Baghavad-Rodina, a component of the famed Blue Fleet. Taken by Creterakian boarding parties in the battles of 2640. Temporarily used as a patrol craft. Mothballed in 2644. Purchased by Gredok the Splithead in 2665 under special license from the Creterakian Empire when he acquired the Ionath Krakens franchise."

Quentin stood, feeling foolish for having ducked like a frightened child. The two Quyth Warriors stared at him, stock-still save for their pedipalps, which quivered in a sickening fashion. The two Sklornos, Denver and Milford, also stared at him but seemed emotionless. He looked at Hokor and Gredok — he didn't know much about Quyth Leaders, but he felt quite sure they were laughing at him.

"What's the matter, Human?" Gredok asked, his pedipalps quivering. "Haven't spent much time around Creterakians?"

Quentin felt his face flushing red. The Quyth Warriors weren't moving, but their pedipalps quivered just like the Leaders' — they were *all* laughing at him.

"Don't sweat it," Yassoud. "You get used to it. The Creterakian civilians love the game, you'll see them all the time."

"I am not used to beings being frightened of me," Swizzle said. "Especially one that's thirty times my mass."

"I'm not afraid of you," Quentin said quickly. "You just startled me, that's all." He felt eager to change the subject. "I thought weapons were illegal on anything but System Police vessels and Creterakian military ships."

Gredok stood and walked over, emanating confidence and control despite the fact that Quentin towered over him. "I don't know what kind of news they show you in the 'Nation, but piracy is still a major problem. The SP forces have cut it down quite a bit since they were implemented in '54, but it's still out there. Since the league started in '59, five team busses have been destroyed by pirates — that's an entire franchise, players, coaching staff, everything, instantly wiped out. Wreaks havoc on a league schedule. So

GFL ships are allowed limited defensive weaponry. Nothing that would be a match for a Creterakian frigate, mind you, but it's usually enough to fend off pirates.

The *Touchback* loomed large outside the view port. The shuttle banked sharply — Quentin and Yassoud each had to place a hand on the bulkhead to keep their balance. Quentin noticed that the Quyths, both Leaders and Warriors alike, instantly adjusted their weight and barely seemed to notice the sharp bank.

The shuttle slowed and docked. Quentin's ears popped as the airlock hissed open. Gredok and Hokor led the rookies out, followed by the Warriors who dragged the still-unconscious Mum-O-Killowe by his front arms.

The airlock opened into an expansive landing bay covered by a fifty-foot-high domed ceiling. The place looked fairly empty save for orderly rows of equipment and stacked metal crates. A handful of Humans, Sklorno, Ki, Quyth Leaders and Quyth Warriors walked forward to greet the rookies. A babble of strange languages filled the landing bay.

A huge, glowing hologram hung in the middle of the bay. It read: THE IONATH KRAKENS ARE ON A COLLISION COURSE WITH A TIER ONE BERTH. THE ONLY VARIABLE IS TIME.

A tall man eased out of the crowd and walked up to Quentin.

"Praise the High One for blessing your journey," the man said in a traditional Purist greeting. "Welcome. I'm Rick Warburg, tight end."

Warburg extended his hand, and Quentin shook it. He hadn't expected to feel homesick, but he did, just a little, and he was surprised to feel relief at the sight of one of his countrymen. Warburg was tall, an even seven feet, and looked to weigh around 365 pounds. He had curly, deep black hair, light brown skin and the infinity forehead tattoo of a confirmed church member.

"Quentin Barnes, praise to the High One for bringing us together," Quentin said in the traditional answer to Warburg's welcome.

Warburg was nothing short of a national hero to the Purist Nation. He was one of twenty-nine Purist players among the top two Tiers, and all of them were quite famous within Nation space.

When Quentin had been a child, twenty-odd Purist Nation players in the league sounded like a lot. Other than reporting scores, the only feature stories and highlights broadcast over the government network concerned Nation players, so Quentin had thought his Purist Nation heroes ruled the GFL. The truth, however, was that with 76 teams, each with a roster of 44, there were 3,344 players in the league. That meant that Purist Nation players took up less than one percent of league roster spots.

"It's so good to see a Nationalite here," Warburg said with a warm grin. "These sub-races can challenge the will of any man."

"Uh-oh, there we go again with the *sub-races* chat." A smiling, 6-foot-6 blue-skinned Human pushed through the crowd and extended his hand to Quentin. Despite the Nation's limited GFL coverage, Quentin had no problem recognizing the man — Donald Pine, quarterback for the GFL Champion Jupiter Jacks in '75 and '76. Quentin found himself caught between a burst of hero worship and a sense of revulsion at touching blue skin. But that wasn't who he was anymore — he shook Pine's hand.

Pine smiled, his teeth a sharply white contrast against his blue skin and darker blue lips. "Warburg, you've always got such a friendly outlook on things."

"The truth should never be blurred over, eh, Pine?" Warburg said. He was also smiling, but there was nothing happy about it. "You were born this way, you know I don't hold it against you."

Pine laughed. "Well, let's just hope that Quentin doesn't hold it against me, either. I see he's not wearing forehead makeup, so maybe he doesn't think quite like you, eh?"

Warburg's smile disappeared. "I've told you before, blue-boy, it's not makeup, it's a holy mark."

"Oh, that's right." Pine said. "Yeah, you *did* tell me that. So sorry, your Holy Holiness."

Warburg nodded, his features melting into a dark, dangerous scowl. "One of these days, blue-boy, you won't be the starter anymore." Warburg tilted his head to indicate Quentin. "And that's going to happen sooner than you think. And when it does, you and I are going to settle up. Quentin, I'll see you at dinner."

Warburg walked away.

"Charming fellow," Pine said. "Not entirely indicative of all the Nationalites I've met, but not far from it, either."

"He's confirmed," Quentin said, not sure if Pine's comments were a slam on Warburg or on all Nationalites. "Confirmed church members are rather set in their ways."

Donald Pine nodded. "And I see you're *not* confirmed. Does that mean you've got that ever-so-rare Purist Nation resource known as an open mind?"

Quentin shrugged. "I'm set in my ways, too. They might not be the same ways as Warburg."

"Well, that's a start," Pine said with a smile. "It's my duty to show you around the ship and get you ready for practice, give you any help you might need."

As a teenager, Quentin had idolized Pine, watching pirated broadcasts of the Jupiter Jacks' games, marveling in the man's effortless skill. All Pine needed was enough time and he could dissect any secondary. But that was in the mid-'70s — recently, Pine's star had fallen and fallen fast. After three straight losing seasons, the Jacks traded Pine to the Bord Brigands in 2680. He lasted only one season there before the Krakens picked him up, hoping he would lead them back to Tier One. The Krakens were still hoping. Considering they had picked up a certain Quentin Barnes, that hope no longer seemed to hinge solely on Donald Pine.

"I don't need any help," Quentin said coldly. "I've learned to figure things out for myself."

Pine's smile faded, just a little, then returned as he shrugged. He waved another man over. "Suit yourself. Let me introduce you to another Krakens' QB, Yitzhak Goldman."

Yitzhak stepped forward and shook Quentin's hand. At 6-foot-4, he was very short for a quarterback. He had the bleach-white skin of a Tower Republic native of the planet Fortress, along with equally white hair and eyebrows. The only things of any color were his deep black eyes. The irises were just as black as the pupils, giving the man an eerie, haunting stare.

"Welcome aboard," Yitzhak said.

Quentin simply nodded. He'd seen Yitzhak play last year when Pine was out two weeks for knee replacement. Quentin had been less than impressed.

Through the flurry of meet-and-greet, a strange creature crawled forward. Quentin couldn't help but take a step back — he'd never seen the like before. It resembled a Quyth Leader, or Warrior, or at four feet tall maybe something in-between. It had only one eye, which was much smaller than a Leader's or a Warrior's. The creature's pedipalps were long, almost three feet long, and so thick they seemed like Human arms. It smelled like onions.

The creature reached out with one of the pedipalps and gently tried to take Quentin's bag. Quentin turned his shoulder, pulling the bag slightly away. The demonic-looking creature made his skin crawl, but he concentrated on staying his ground, dead-set against repeating the embarrassment he'd felt when he hit the deck at the sound of Swizzle's flapping wings.

"What's the matter?" Pine asked. "Pilkie here will take your bag for you."

"Pilkie?" Quentin said, never taking his eyes of the creature.

"It's okay, Quentin," Yitzhak said. "You look tense."

Quentin looked at Yitzhak, then at Pine, then lifted the bag-strap off his shoulder and set it down on the deck. Without a sound, Pilkie grabbed the bag and walked toward a door at the edge of the landing bay.

Pine laughed. "You okay, boy? You act like you've never seen a Quyth Worker before."

Quentin shrugged. "I haven't."

Pine and Yitzhak laughed, then stopped when they realized that Quentin wasn't kidding.

"Sorry about that, Quentin," Pine said, clapping Quentin on the shoulder. "I forgot you're fresh off the Purist Nation. Come on, we've got a position meeting in twenty minutes. Hokor handles the quarterback meetings, and trust me, you do not want to be late."

"So are there any other kinds of Quyth?" Quentin asked. "I'm getting kind of tired of surprises."

"Just the females," Yitzhak said. "But there's none of those onboard. Females are sacred in Quyth culture. No non-Quyth are even supposed to lay eyes on them. Females never leave their home planets."

"Can we see the field?" Quentin asked.

Pine nodded. "Right this way, kid."

A central tunnel, large enough for heavy equipment, ran from the flight deck all the way to the other end of the ship. The tunnel, with its arched ceiling and curved walls, acted like a main highway — every thirty feet or so, smaller tunnels branched off at right angles, leading into the ship's numerous sections. Quentin followed Pine straight down the main tunnel, until it opened up into the huge space that was the Krakens' practice field.

The clear dome revealed the black expanse of space. Thousands of bright sparks glittered; the stars of the Milky Way Galaxy. Ten yards or so past the end zones and sidelines, the ship's decks rose up eighteen levels high.

They walked onto the field, entering at the orange end zone. The surface had some give and felt a lot like the Carsengi Grass that covered most Purist Nation fields, but he could tell this was artificial. Hundreds of flat, circular, white creatures, each the size of a pancake, moved around the field. They moved slowly but quickly scooted out of the way of approaching feet.

"I think you guys need to call an exterminator," Quentin said.

"Those are clippers," Yitzhak said. "This is nanograss, self-replicating mechanical cells that grow constantly to give us a good practice surface. The clippers are little robots that keep the nanograss at a constant height."

"They ever get underfoot?"

Yitzhak shook his head. "Naw, they steer clear of anything that moves."

As they walked past the 50-yard line, Quentin noticed that the white disks cleared out in front of them, then closed in behind as the Humans passed by. He looked around, trying to take it all in — this is where his destiny would start.

Just past the black end zone, the three men stepped aboard a lift. Pine pressed a button, and the lift rose swiftly to deck eighteen.

Quentin followed Pine down the hall. The orange walls complemented the white and black carpet. Most of the diverse furnishings — two seats each for the varying body styles of Quyth, Ki, Sklorno and Human — were also done in orange-and-black. The high ceiling allowed Human and Sklorno alike to pass in comfort. Holoframes covered the walls, showing great players from the 23-year history of the Ionath Krakens. Most holoframes, of course, depicted players or scenes from the Krakens' Tier One Championship of 2665.

That had been the franchise's heyday, back when quarterback Bobby "Orbital Assault" Adrojnik put together three fantastic seasons, culminating in the '65 title, a 23-21 thriller over the Wabash Wall. After that game, Adrojnik died in a bar fight under conditions most called "suspicious." Krakens fans blamed Wabash supporters, or possibly even the Wabash owner herself. Gloria Ogawa, who had founded the Wall in the GFL's inaugural season of 2659, was a known gangland figure in the Tower Republic and had not taken the loss well.

"This deck holds the Krakens' corporate offices," Pine said. "Communications with the league, archiving, marketing, network relations, stuff like that." Pine looked at the famous holoframe of the smiling Adrojnik, held aloft by two Ki linemen, raising the Championship trophy high in one hand.

"Is that what you're going to be kid?" Pine said quietly. "The next Adrojnik? The future of this franchise?"

Quentin shrugged. He'd never seen Adrojnik play. Sometimes you could score pirated games on Micovi, or on Buddha City, but for the most part the old historical GFL stuff just wasn't available.

Pine grinned, looked at Quentin and continued down the hall. "Yep, you could be the savior. What are you kid, twenty-one? twenty-two?"

"Nineteen," Quentin said.

Pine's eyebrows rose up. He looked at Yitzhak, who let out a low whistle and shook his head.

"Nineteen," Pine said. "Kid, you play your cards right and you could have a great career ahead of you."

"Of course, that's what the press said about Timmy Hammersmith in 2678," Yitzhak said. "And Crane McSweeney in 2681, after Hammersmith washed out in just two seasons."

Pine smiled and nodded, looking at Quentin the whole time. "Yeah, that's right! But McSweeney didn't last much longer. He might have developed into something big if he hadn't died during that game against the Wallcrawlers in 2680. Rookie QBs just don't seem to fare too well around here."

"It seems veterans don't fare too well, either," Quentin said. He wasn't going to put up with this *rookie* bull — he was no normal rookie, something they'd all find out soon enough. "They brought you in to finish the 2680 season, didn't they, Pine? Two and a half seasons at the helm, and the Krakens are still Tier Two."

Yitzhak stopped and turned to face Quentin. "Hey, now, you'd better watch yourself, rookie, you don't —"

Pine held up his left hand to stop Yitzhak, cutting the shorter man off in mid-sentence. Pine's smile was no longer friendly, but that of someone who looks down on another.

"That's a good point, Quentin," Pine said. He held up his right hand. On his ring and index finger were two thick, golden rings, each set with dozens of sparkling rubies. Championship rings from 2675 and 2676. At the sight of the rings, Quentin felt his soul roil with pure envy, greed and flat-out desire.

"You can have all the good points you want, *rookie*," Pine said. "But until you prove it out on the field, it's all talk. Until you've got one of *these* —" Pine wiggled his fingers, letting the rubies catch the hall's light — "I suggest you keep those good points to yourself."

Quentin smiled graciously, flourished, and gave a half-bow. "Whatever you say, pops."

Pine's smile briefly faded to a glare, then he continued down the hall. Quentin felt the competitive fire building inside his brain. He couldn't wait to get out on the field. He was the future of the Krakens, not this washed-up has-been. He'd learn what he could from this old man in the next week, before the old man got used to his new position: benchwarmer.

They turned into a large room, about fifty yards in diameter, with a clear dome open to the star-speckled blackness of space. The floor consisted of a silvery grid of small hexes, each only a centimeter or so wide. Just inside the door sat a long rack of footballs, built on a tilt so the balls would roll down and stop at a catch at the end.

"What is this?" Quentin bounced on his toes, feeling the hexes give slightly under his feet.

"This is the sim-room," Pine said. "State-of-the-art in football technology." He walked to the end of the rack and picked up a football. The other footballs rolled down the rack to fill the space.

"The Kriegs-Ballok Virtual Practice System," Yitzhak said. "Gredok had it installed during the off-season."

"Ship," Pine called. "Grontak Stadium, night game."

The clear dome shimmered with flashes of blue and silver, then it was gone, instantly replaced by a bright purple sky arching over a massive stadium. The room's sound went from echoing silence to the sudden cacophony of 165,000 fans, mostly Quyth, screeching in their spine-rippling equivalent of a Human cheer.

Quentin spun around, suddenly disoriented by the purple sky, the thousands of fans swinging black, teal and white banners and flags, the steady, subdued roar of a crowd waiting between plays. A blazing sun hung almost directly over head, and a blue moon ringed with light red hung suspended in the southern sky. It was all so real. The floor shimmered as well, and then the hexes were gone, replaced with millions of the flat blue plants that made up a Quyth playing field, complete with white yard markers.

"Krakens, first-and-ten," Pine said. "Boss-right set, split left, double-hook and post."

More blue and silver shimmers flashed in the air, this time only ten feet from where the three men stood. Ten players dressed in Krakens uniforms materialized and moved to the line of scrimmage: the scurrying waddle of huge Ki linemen, the loping, graceful strides of three Sklorno receivers, the natural gait of the Human tailback and right end. The players moved like the real thing, although they were all slightly translucent. Their uniform colors seemed blurred by a slight blue haze.

A computer voice echoed through the chamber.

[DEFENSIVE SELECTION, PLEASE]

"Random," Pine said as he walked up to the line, crouched and held the ball in front of him as though he were ready to take a snap.

Another flash preceded the sudden appearance of players clad in the black, teal and blue colors of the Glory Warpigs. Quentin's awe over the technology faded away. His strategic mind took over as he watched the holographic Warpigs players line up in a 3-4 with man-to-man coverage.

"Red fifteen, red fifteen," Pine called out, barking out the signals so he could be heard over the crowd. Quentin felt his heart rate increase and the rush of adrenaline pump into his veins — he'd never seen anything like this. He could feel the stadium shake as the crowd's intensity increased.

"Hut …. HUT!"

Pine dropped back five steps, then planted and bounced a half step forward. He stood tall, looking downfield as his Sklorno receivers darted out, tightly covered by the Warpigs defensive backs. Pine threw the ball a split second before the right wide receiver suddenly cut back toward the line — a timing pattern. The receiver raised her long arms to catch the ball — it went right through the hologram, skipping and rolling down the field. The players vanished, although the crowd and the crowd noise remained.

[PASS COMPLETE. A GAIN OF SIX YARDS. SECOND AND FOUR]

Pine walked back to Quentin, who couldn't stop himself from constantly looking around. "What do you think, rookie?"

"This is incredible. Is this where we practice?"

Pine shook his head. "No, we practice on the main field. But this is where you do your position work and drill for each week's game. This way you can practice sets over and over again against holographs that are just as fast as the opposition's defensive backs. Practice squad players aren't as much of a challenge."

"Can I give it a try?"

Pine grabbed a football and tossed it to Quentin. "Be my guest. Let me set it up for you. It's second-and-four, what do you want to run?"

Quentin smiled. "I want to go deep."

Pine smiled — that condescending smile again — and nodded. "Wide set, snake package, double post. On two. Defense, cover two with woman-to-woman under."

"You mean man-to-man."

"The Sklorno are females, remember? Woman-to-woman. There you go, kid, I made it easy for you."

The players materialized and ran to the line. Quentin walked forward, eyes wide with wonder. He crouched below the center as his eyes scanned the defense. The reality was such that he recognized Warburg at tight end, Scarborough at wide receiver, Hawick in the slot, two yards in and one yard back from Scarborough. He didn't bother to look, but he knew a life-like image of number 47, tailback Mitchell Fayed, would be right behind him.

"Hut ... hut!" The line surged forward. It almost sounded similar to a real line crash but was just a bit stale and echoey. Quentin dropped back five steps, planted and eased into his standup, ball at the ready.

He watched the holo-Scarborough streak down the right sideline. The man-to-man (woman-to-woman, that is) coverage quickly fell behind. Just as the safety started to pick up the route, Quentin reared back and let the ball fly. It sailed through the air in a perfect, arching spiral, a brown missile framed against a bright purple sky. The ball looked on the money, but the safety moved faster than anything Quentin had ever seen on a football field.

"Damn it," Quentin whispered as the holo safety blurred in front of the holo-Scarborough, leapt twelve feet into the air, and reached for the ball. The ball continued down the field, bouncing off the flat leaves, but Quentin didn't need the computer to tell him the results.

[PASS INTERCEPTED]

"Why'd you guys have to rig this? Quentin said. "You think that's funny?"

"Rig it?" Pine said. "What are you talking about?"

"Oh, come on, you saw how fast that safety closed. Nothing moves that fast."

Pine and Yitzhak looked at each other, then started laughing.

"Welcome to the GFL, backwater," Yitzhak said. "You're going to love it here."

Quentin glared. If they wanted to play stupid games with him, he'd show them. "Let me try that again."

"Why, so you can *fail* again?" Hokor's voice caught him by surprise. He turned, an unexpected sense of trepidation in his chest, as if he were a teenage boy caught in the middle of masturbating.

"End simulation!" Hokor barked. The tiny Quyth Leader marched toward Quentin as the field, the fans, the stadium and the players vanished, replaced by the clear dome and the sparkling stars.

"Barnes, what in the name of your primitive, backwater gods was *that*?"

Hokor's fur seemed to stand on end, making him look thicker than normal. Quentin knew that was some instinctive reaction, evolutionarily designed to make Hokor look bigger, therefore more dangerous, but in reality it just made him look fuzzy, like a stuffed animal. Still, his voice had a tone of command Quentin's previous coaches had never possessed. Or, perhaps more accurately, had never *used*, at least not on him.

"That was an interception, Coach," Quentin said calmly.

"Why did you throw it?"

"Well, I thought I had Scarborough on the streak."

"You thought? You *thought*? Don't you know who the Warpigs' safety is?"

Quentin thought it was a rhetorical question, but Hokor seemed to wait for an answer. Quentin shrugged. "Nope."

Hokor's pedipalps quivered with anger. "You don't know who it is, but you threw the pass anyway? You didn't know that the Warpigs' picked up Keluang in free agency?"

"Keluang?" Quentin asked. "I thought he, I mean, *she*, played for the Hullwalkers, in Tier One."

"Well, *now*, she plays for the Warpigs!" Hokor's furry body shook with anger. "You stupid Human, you don't even know who you're playing against and you just blindly throw into coverage."

Quentin smiled. "Take it easy, Coach. How am I supposed to know who's on what team right now?" Quentin saw Pine and Yitzhak duck their heads in an effort to conceal their grins. Yitzhak hid his face in his hands and slowly shook his head.

"It's your *job* to know," Hokor said coldly. "You are a quarterback for the Ionath Krakens. We will not make it to the Tier Two tournament and therefore back into the glory of Tier One if my helpless quarterbacks don't know *everything* there is to know about the opposition. You must be punished for this error. You will report to me after practice. And by tomorrow, you will know the defensive roster of all nine teams in the Quyth Conference."

"By tomorrow? Come on, Coach — I figure that out on the field. Nobody knows all that stuff, nobody except sports reporters."

Hokor turned to face Pine. "Who is the second-string free safety for the Sheb Stalkers?"

"Fairmont," Pine answered instantly.

"What are her stats?

"Last recorded time in the 40 was a 3.2. She's seventeen years old, an eight-year veteran, tends to jump the short routes and give extra space on deep routes for passing situations. She comes in as nickel back but doesn't like to hit big tight ends head-on."

"Yitzhak, what is the strategy when playing her?"

"Passing situations, send tight ends on deep outs or deep curls. She doesn't pressure the tight end enough, usually allowing for a little extra time to make a well-placed throw. Shouldn't go deep on her if avoidable, but put the ball up high if you must because her vertical leap of twelve feet usually can't compete with our receivers."

Hokor turned back to Quentin. "*That* is why these men have been around the league for so long."

Quentin sneered. "With all due respect, Coach, just because you guys memorize one player doesn't mean anything. I may be young, but I wasn't born yesterday. You guys set that up just to impress me."

Hokor's fur rippled, and his pedipalps were a vibrating blur. "Pick a player."

"Huh?"

"Pick a player."

Quentin felt a sinking feeling. "From what team?"

"Any team in the Quyth Irradiated Division."

"Okay, how about this? The second-string weak-side linebacker for the Bigg Diggers."

"Ripok the Stonecutter," Pine and Yitzhak said simultaneously.

"Last recorded time of 3.9 in the 40," Pine said.

"Five-year veteran, the last three with the Diggers," Yitzhak added.

"Very disciplined," Pine said. "Plays excellent zone, makes excellent reads, but poor lateral movement due to leg-replacement surgery in 2671."

"Use quick tight end out patterns," Yitzhak said. "Or, bring wide receivers on crossing patterns and throw when they are equal to Ripok because he can't break on the ball as fast as they can."

Quentin just stared. He didn't know that much information about his own linebackers for the Raiders, let alone for another team. And these guys had ripped off the info without a second thought.

"Now, are you impressed?" Hokor asked.

Quentin nodded dumbly.

"By tomorrow," Hokor said, "know every player on the rosters. We will work on stats and tendencies throughout this week. Let us commence with our position meeting. We are six days from the season opener against the Woo Wallcrawlers. It will take us four days to reach Ionath. We will practice on the *Touchback* until we reach Ionath, then shuttle down to the field facility for on-field practices."

• • •

BY THE TIME the position meeting ended, Quentin felt thoroughly annoyed. He had several days of busy work lined up — rote memorization of defensive players and schemes in addition to his offensive studies. And the real annoyance was that none of it really mattered. When he took the field, that's when all this garbage would fade away, once Hokor saw what he could do.

After the position meeting, Quentin followed Pine and Yitzhak onto the dining deck. He had an uneasy feeling he couldn't quite explain. He'd never done "team functions" with the Raiders, he'd always done his own thing. Here, he gathered, he was expected to dine with the team. The brightly lit room held over twenty tables, each surrounded by a variety of chairs designed for the different body types of Humans, Sklorno, Quyth Warrior and Quyth Leader. Unlike the corporate offices, there were none of the six-foot-long, table-like chairs made for Ki.

"We have to eat with the sub … I mean, the *other* races?"

Pine stared at him. "What, you can play a game with them, but you can't eat with them?"

"You have to have the different races to win the game," Quentin said. "But that doesn't mean you have to *eat* with them, for High One's sake."

"It's a league rule," Yitzhak said. "All species must use the same dining facilities. Remember the Creterakians' whole point of this league is to create a sense of ambassadorship amongst the races."

"Are the Ki an exception, then?" Quentin didn't see any of the monstrous creatures in the dining hall.

Yitzhak shuddered before he answered. "Their eating habits are a little, er, *messy* compared to the other races. They eat alone."

"What do you mean, *messy*?"

"They butcher their food at the table," Pine answered. "They eat it raw."

Quentin looked at both men. "You're kidding me, right?"

They shook their heads.

"It's horrific," Yitzhak said. "They kill the animal right there on the table. The table is even designed to catch all the blood so they can drink that, too."

"That's disgusting."

"That's not the worst of it," Yitzhak said. "That's just the ones from the Ki Empire planets. The ones that come from the Ki Rebel Establishment planets, they don't even bother to kill the animal before they start eating."

Quentin stared dumbly. "You mean they eat it *live?*"

Yitzhak nodded.

"High One," Quentin said. "They *are* demons."

"Oh, take your morality and vent it, Barnes," Pine said. "They're not *demons*, they're *different* from Humans, that's all. Meals are a major ritual for the Ki. It's part of their culture, how they bond and crap like that."

"But to eat a *live* animal? Only a mongrel race could do that!"

Yitzhak laughed. "Well then, I guess Pine here is a mongrel."

Pine smiled, but Quentin just stared, dumbfounded at the evil surrounding him. "You've broken bread with creatures that eat their food alive?"

Pine simply nodded.

Quentin felt his stomach churning at the thought and suddenly found Pine's blue skin more repulsive than ever. "What *are* you, blue-boy, some kind of Satanist?"

"And there it is," Pine said with a knowing nod. "See, you *are* just like Warburg. Just another Purist racist. I'm a *leader*, Barnes. Ki don't really accept you until you eat with them, until you fight and bleed with them. I do whatever it takes to make this team play as a whole. That's something you'll either figure out and succeed, or won't figure out, and you'll be gone."

Quentin turned to Yitzhak. "And I suppose *you've* eaten living flesh, too?"

Yitzhak shuddered. "Couldn't quite bring myself to do that, but I managed to sit through the whole thing and drank some blood. You've got to see it to believe it — it's worse than any horror holo you've ever seen."

Quentin shook his head, then turned and walked away. Position meetings were over, and he didn't have to spend any more time with these two barbarians. He spotted Warburg, sitting alone, a huge tray of food in front of him.

"Quentin," Warburg called out. "Come let us break bread."

Quentin walked up to the table and stared at the food. With all the activity, he hadn't eaten and suddenly realized that he was famished.

"Where's the chow?"

Warburg stuffed some potatoes into his mouth as he gestured to the back wall. A glass-enclosed counter ran the entire length, all fifty feet of it. Under the glass sat every kind of food Quentin could imagine. The counter was divided into sections, each about two feet in length. Above each section glowed a holographic symbol of a planet or system. Quentin didn't recognize half the symbols, but the Purist Nation infinity symbol glowed a warm welcome. He grabbed a tray from an overhead shelf and started loading up: the mint mashed potatoes he'd seen Warburg eating, chicken breasts smothered in curry paste, pita bread and Mason gravy, multi-colored broccoli, which grew only on the planet Stewart, and a thick piece of chocolate cake.

Just to his right was the flag of the Planetary Union. The dishes looked somewhat familiar but were all things he'd never before tried. One of the dishes seemed to be some kind halved shell, with a raw, glisteny, grayish mass sitting inside. Raw food — typical blasphemy of non-Nation races. Quentin didn't exactly say his twenty Praise High Ones each night, but that didn't mean he was so sinful he'd eat raw food.

Just to his left was the glowing Five Star Circle of the Quyth Concordia. His lip wrinkled involuntarily in disgust at the brownish selections, many of which had more spindly legs than any insect he'd ever seen.

Quentin turned away from the strange foods and walked back to the table, rejoicing in the smells that drifted up from his plate.

"Did you see that disgusting garbage the Quyth eat?" Warburg asked as Quentin sat.

"Yes, what is that crap, bugs?"

Warburg shrugged. "I don't know and I don't care to know. High One knows it's something unblessed and blasphemous. We'll see what they eat when they're burning in Hell."

Quentin cut a big piece of chicken breast and bit into it — his eyes closed in pleasure at the taste.

"Food's gotten pretty good since Gredok picked you up," Warburg said with a smile.

"It wasn't good before?"

Warburg shrugged. "It wasn't bad. The cooks would try to make Nation dishes out of whatever Planetary Union or League of Planets crap they had laying around. Ever since they signed you, though, they've been bringing in the real deal from Nation freighters or whatever. Seems like Gredok and Hokor want to make you right at home."

Quentin shoveled in some potatoes, marveling at the succulent taste. "I'm glad they feel that way. I haven't had decent food since I got to the *Combine*."

"I hope they start you right away," Warburg said. "I can't stand that shucking blue-boy Pine."

Quentin nodded. "You know he told me he's eaten raw flesh with the Ki?"

"What do you mean, *eaten*? That's past tense. He does it every week. Low One take him, look at him now."

Warburg gestured to the far end of the hall. Most of the tables held members of only one race, either Human, Quyth or Sklorno. But Pine sat at a table of Quyth Warriors, laughing, smiling and stuffing some limp, brown, multi-legged creature into his mouth.

"I hope he likes the heat, considering where the High One will place him on Judgment Day," Warburg said. "I mean, it's one thing to have to talk to these demons, that's just the nature of the game, but to *sit down* with them, to *eat* with them and eat their *barbaric* food. It's unforgivable."

Quentin nodded and turned back to his plate. The sight of Pine chewing that brown thing had killed his appetite, but he kept eating anyway. Tomorrow was the first practice, and he'd need all of his strength if he was going to win the starting QB slot.

PRACTICE

AS INSTRUCTED, his room lights flickered on at 6 a.m., one hour before the position meeting. His room filled with the loud sounds of the band Trench Warfare. He stretched as he listened to the seductive but strong vocals of Trench's lead singer, Somalia Midori. Their music was banned back on Micovi, but Quentin had managed to get his hands on a few pirated broadcasts. As a kid, he didn't know it was even possible to circumvent the laws of the Holy Men. The more games he won, however, the easier it became to obtain contraband items like erotic pictures, recorded GFL broadcasts or out-of-system books and music.

When he entered his sparse room for the first time the night before, he'd asked the computer if it could play any Trench Warfare for his wake-up call. The shocking answer — the computer had access to not only every Trench album, but most of the band's live performances from the last five years. He could watch holo or just listen to audio. He'd had time for one holo before going to bed and had watched in amazement at the four musicians performing on stage to a jumping, gyrating crowd of Humans. He'd been shocked to see that Somalia bore the blue skin of a Satirli 6 native.

He thought she was beautiful, but just for a second, then asked the computer for sound only.

Discovering an endless library of music had been a surprise pleasure, but nothing compared to the well-nigh religious experience that came when he asked the computer if there were any archived GFL games.

[WHAT TEAM AND WHAT YEAR?] The computer had asked.

"How far back do the games go?"

[TO THE BEGINNING]

"What, the very first GFL games?"

[TO THE BEGINNING OF FOOTBALL]

"What do you mean, to the beginning of football? What's the oldest game you've got?"

[FORDHAM COLLEGE, EARTH, VERSUS WAYNESBURG COLLEGE, EARTH, 1939]

"But, but that's seven hundred years ago!"

[SEVEN HUNDRED AND FORTY-THREE YEARS AGO] the computer corrected. [WOULD YOU LIKE TO SEE?]

"Yes!"

Quentin turned to the holotank. A picture flashed in the tank, but it looked very strange. He could make out football players, but they were tiny and far away, without color, and they were ... flat, like a printed picture.

"What's wrong with it? It looks broken."

[THIS WAS CALLED "TELEVISION," A TWO-DIMENSIONAL ELECTRONIC REPRESENTATION OF ACTUAL EVENTS.]

"Do you have more of these television broadcasts?"

[GALACTIC FREE ARCHIVE HAS EVERY GAME EVER BROADCAST VIA TELEVISION, RADIO AND HOLOCAST]

Quentin watched a play, in which the quarterback took the snap, turned almost 360 degrees and followed a wall of blockers into a wall of defenders. His heart raced — to think he was watching the beginnings of his sport, a game played almost 750 years ago! He could watch any game ever recorded, all of the To Pirates games, even games from the archaic NFL.

One of those games played now in his holotank, between

teams called the "Kansas City Chiefs" and the "Chicago Bears." He'd instructed the computer to wake him with not only music, but also a random football broadcast at least 500 years old or older.

As the music's heavy beat pounded through his small quarters, he dragged himself out of bed and started stretching. He had plans today — he'd show them all just what kind of a player he was.

He walked through the ship's empty corridors, descended to field level and entered the central locker room. A circular area, the central locker room was built around a holoboard. Four doors lined the circular room. A small icon hung on each door: a Human, a Ki, a Sklorno and a Quyth Warrior. A huge, realistic mural dominated the other side of the circular room. Quentin stared at the brightly colored, six-tentacled monster, rising up from the depths in a spray of deep-red water. Rows of long, backward-curved teeth lined a cavernous mouth. One large eye glowed an eerie green. He nodded to the picture.

He entered the Human door and found his own space.

Barnes, #10 it read above the locker.

Get used to that number, galaxy. You're going to be hearing it a lot.

He opened the locker. The first thing he took out was his practice jersey. He stared at the number 10 on the chest. He felt the texture of the black Kevlar fabric. This was only a practice jersey, and it was of a far higher quality than anything he'd worn in the PNFL.

He set the jersey flat on the ground.

He smiled as he pulled out a Kool Products body-control suit, designed to regulate his temperature on the field. Coolant fluid constantly circulated through microtubules in the suit's thin, rubbery fabric. He slid into the suit, which automatically adjusted itself to conform perfectly to his body.

Next he pulled out his arm-and-shoulder armor. Rawlings Null-Contact™ inertia-dampening system. State of the art. Supposedly the armor could stop a bullet, absorbing the velocity into the hard shell instead of transmitting it to the wearer.

He slid it on. Like the Kool suit, the armor's micro-sensor circuits automatically adjusted for a tailored fit. The armor was thinner on his left arm, his throwing arm, to allow maximum flexibility.

Next came the matching lower-torso armor, which would protect his ribs, stomach, kidneys and lower back. He wrapped it around his waist — the micro-sensors contracted and expanded, locking it in precisely with the shoulder armor.

Groin and leg armor were more of the same. The knee joints were made of an interstellar-caliber alloy, designed to allow normal flexibility but locking out any possible hyperextension. He slid his feet into the armored boots, which locked in perfectly with the leg armor.

With all this protection, it seemed a wonder that any being got hurt at all. And yet they did get hurt — frequently and badly. Football players were just too big, too strong, too fast and too violent. Quentin wondered what kind of injuries might occur were it not for this high-tech armor.

He moved around, feeling the armor move with him, a perfect fit that didn't seem to hinder his range of motion. He pulled on the jersey, then grabbed his helmet. The shiny black Riddell helmet was lighter than anything he'd used before, but probably ten times stronger than what he'd worn on Micovi. A patch of bright orange decorated the front of the helmet, from temple to temple. Six white stripes stretched out from the orange patch, like the arms of a stylized sunrise. There were three white stripes on each side: one curving above the ear hole, one halfway up the curving side and one higher up on each side of the helmet's center. The stripes represented the six tentacles of the Quyth creature for which the Krakens were named.

A recessed button sat under the right ear-hole. Quentin pushed it: a holographic test pattern hovered just in front of the facemask. Once again, state of the art — he'd tried to talk Stedmar into springing for the in-helmet holo display, but Stedmar balked at the half-million-credit price tag. The display would let a quarterback see the playbook, live statistics and the coach in case coaches used hand signals, lip-reading or some other secretive play-calling method. He pushed the button again, and the test pattern disappeared.

Quentin headed for the sim-room, cleats clacking against the metal floor. The lights blinked on as he walked in. As he'd suspected, the place was empty. Everyone else was still sleeping.

"Ship," Quentin called as he walked to the center of the room. "Do you have a sim for the Krakens' practice field?"

The dome flickered briefly, then Quentin found himself in a dead-on simulacrum of the practice field.

"Ship, give me first-string defense for the Grontak Hydras."

The semi-translucent players appeared out of nowhere, a combination of Human and other species, all dressed in the red-and-yellow checkerboard Hydra jerseys.

"Ship, call out the names of each defensive player before each play. Give me X-right formation, double-streak left, Y-right."

Krakens players materialized. The Ki linemen scurried up to the line and lowered themselves for the snap. The computer started calling out the names of the defense as Quentin approached the line. He'd practice and study at the same time and would show them all what the Purist Nation had to offer.

THE 7 A.M. POSITION MEETING didn't take more than ten minutes, just enough time for Hokor to outline the day's practice. They would focus on route passing: no offensive line and no defense. The three quarterbacks walked to the lift.

In the center of the field stood seven Sklorno receivers dressed in orange practice jerseys. Sklorno's orange leg armor was thin and light so as not to hamper their speed. For the upper body, they wore a black, metal-mesh armor that protected but also allowed for the full range of motion needed by boneless tentacles and the flexible eyestalks. The black helmet with the orange patch and the white stripes looked like a small bowling ball, with four finger-holes on top, one for each armored eyestalk and a gap in front that let their raspers hang free.

Even before the lift reached the field, the Sklorno looked up at the oncoming Humans and began to visibly tremble.

Their raspers rolled out, almost to the ground, and each of them began to shout various Sklorno words, all of which sounded like gibberish.

"What's their problem?" Quentin asked. "They afraid of Coach or something?"

Pine shook his head, and Yitzhak laughed.

"Not exactly," Yitzhak said. "The Righteous Brother Pine here is somewhat of a religious figure in the Sklorno culture."

"Religious? What, like he's a preacher or something?"

Yitzhak laughed louder. "No, not exactly."

"Oh, give it a rest," Pine said, his blue-skinned face turning a strange shade of purple.

Yitzhak put his hand to his chest, his expression that of mock pain. "Oh, forgive me, Great One. Don't strike me down with your Godly quarterback powers."

Quentin looked back to the Sklorno receivers — the closer the Humans got, the more the Sklorno shook. It reminded him of the truly devout back home during noonday prayers, how they would shudder and shake, their blue robes rustling with sudden movements, oftentimes speaking in tongues, their eyes rolling back into their heads. As a child, such behavior had scared the crap out of him. When he grew older, he learned that those people were supposedly in deep communion with the High One.

The similarities clicked home.

"They *worship* Pine? You mean like a god or something?"

Yitzhak nodded. "Something like that. As a Human it's kind of difficult to understand, but from what we hear, there are at least thirty-two confirmed houses of worship dedicated to The Great Pine spread throughout Sklorno space."

"Cut it out," Pine said. "It's not like I encourage this."

"There's actually a statue of The Great and Glorious Pine on the Sklorno's capital planet. How tall is it again, Pine, 100 feet or so?"

"Get lost, Yitzhak."

"Why do they worship him?" Quentin asked.

Yitzhak shrugged. "Something about the quarterback position, that and great coaches, strikes a chord with their culture. Sklorno aren't as independent as Humans, they tend to blindly follow their leaders. Coaches and quarterbacks get the most media attention in football, and the Sklorno are *insane* football fans. The nature of the game and their culture just kind of combine. Who knows, Quentin — you put together a couple of good seasons, and there might be a church or two in your name."

Quentin felt his own face turning red. The idea of someone worshiping him, not as a fan-to-player, but as a subject-to-God, made him deeply uncomfortable. He felt sacrilegious just *thinking* about it.

They reached midfield. Quentin heard the burble of a small anti-grav engine, and he looked up to see Hokor flying toward them in a hovercart, the kind people used to move around on a golf course.

"What the hell is that? Coach can't walk all of a sudden?"

Pine laughed. "Hokor likes to watch from above, get a full view of the field, but he wants to come down to offer his own special brand of encouragement."

The hovercart slowed and floated about ten feet off the field.

"I hate that damn golf cart," Yitzhak said quietly. "Just wait, you'll see — he's got a loudspeaker in it and everything."

As if on cue, Hokor's amplified voice bellowed across the field.

"Okay, that's enough of that crap," the yellow-furred coach said. "You will cease this shivering thing immediately!"

As a unit, the Sklorno instantly stopped shaking, raspers quickly rolling back up under their chin plates. They stood as still as they could, but kept twitching, little chirps escaping them every few seconds.

"That's better," Hokor said. "Pine, line them up and run hook routes."

They all stood on the 50-yard line, the eight Sklorno 15 yards to the right of the Human quarterbacks. It surprised Quentin that he immediately recognized Denver and Milford — he'd always thought all Sklorno looked alike, but Denver had more red in her eyestalks, and Milford's oily head of hair seemed to be thicker and longer than any of the others. If it weren't for jersey names and numbers, however, he wouldn't have been able to tell the difference between Scarborough, Hawick, Richfield, Mezquitic and the other Kraken receivers.

Pine grabbed a ball from the rack and squatted, just as he'd done in the VR practice field. The first Sklorno bent down into their strange starting stance — legs folded up like a grasshopper, tail sticking straight back to balance the forward-leaning body. The back of her jersey read "Hawick."

"Hut-hut!"

Pine took a three-step drop, planted and fired — *far* too high. In the millisecond after the ball left Pine's hand, Quentin figured it would sail forty yards downfield. But Hawick was already fifteen yards down field and turning. She didn't just stop and turn, like a Human receiver would do on a hook route, she stopped, turned and *jumped*. Quentin's jaw dropped as Hawick sprang ten feet into the air, like a 280-pound flea — the ball hit her square in the numbers. She landed and turned in the same motion, sprinting all the way to the end zone before stopping.

Quentin stared, barely able to believe what he'd seen. Such speed. Pine and Yitzhak hadn't been screwing with him in the VR room, Sklorno really were that fast. And that *leap*. It was one thing to see it on the 'net, quite another to see it in person.

Yitzhak took the next ball. The next Sklorno's jersey read "Mezquitic."

"Hut-hut!" Yitzhak dropped back three steps and fired — again seemingly far too high. Mezquitic sprang high, caught the ball, landed and streaked down the field. Quentin was still staring at the streaking Sklorno receiver when Pine poked him in the rib pads.

"You're up, boy."

Quentin grabbed the next ball from the rack and squatted down just behind the fifty. He looked to his right — "Scarborough" looked back at him, awaiting his signal.

"Hut-hut!" Quentin drove backward three steps and planted.

He started to throw but hesitated a half second because Scarborough was still a good eight yards from hooking up the route. In less time than it took to blink, Scarborough was there, turning, leaping and looking for the ball. Quentin threw as quickly as he could, but it was too late. Scarborough had hit the ground by the time the throw reached her — it sailed far over her head.

"Barnes!" Hokor barked. "What the *hell* was that?"

Quentin blushed.

"Get used to the timing, Barnes. With Sklorno receivers, passing is a three-dimensional game. You're not in the bush leagues anymore."

Practice continued for another hour. Quentin struggled with the Sklornos' blinding speed and leaping ability but made significant progress pass after pass. He had some trouble with Mezquitic, who dropped two of his passes, but he clicked well with the other receivers, particularly Denver. Only in the final five minutes did Hokor open it up for long patterns. Pine opened up by dropping back seven steps and firing a 55-yard strike to Hawick. The Sklorno receivers let out a series of rapid clicking noises.

"What is that sound they're making?" Quentin asked Yitzhak.

"Sklorno equivalent to *ooh* and *ahh*," Yitzhak said. "The ladies love the long ball."

Yitzhak threw next, hitting a 45-yard streak to Mezquitic. The receivers let out clicks, but they weren't as loud as they had been for Pine's pass.

Quentin smiled as he grabbed the ball and squatted down for his rep. Neither of these guys could match his arm strength, not even the once-great Donald Pine. Scarborough lined up to his right. Quentin barked out a "hut-hut." He dropped back the prescribed seven steps and kept going, finally setting up a good fifteen yards from where he'd "snapped" the ball. He watched Scarborough the whole way, his mind now somewhat accustomed to the receiver's 3.2 speed. Quentin unleashed the ball — the Sklorno's clicks started immediately as the ball arced through the air like a laser-guided bomb. Scarborough angled under it and caught it in stride at the back edge of the end zone.

The Sklornos not only clicked and chirped louder than ever,

they started jumping up and down and hugging each other. Raspers lolled, and spit flew everywhere.

"Damn," Pine said, shaking his head.

"That was seventy-five yards in the air," Yitzhak said. "And right on the money."

Quentin smiled, his hands patting out a quick *ba da-bap* on his stomach as he waited for accolades from his new coach.

"Silence!" Hokor shouted at the Sklorno. The anger in his voice seemed to terrify them. They huddled together, shaking and twitching in a mass of fear.

Hokor turned to Quentin. "What was that?"

"A touchdown," Quentin said.

"I know that, what was that drop?"

Quentin shrugged. "I just wanted to show you what I can do."

"And what you can do is drop back fifteen yards? What are you, a punter?"

Quentin felt his face flushing red once again. "Well, no, Coach ... I just wanted to show you how deep I could throw it."

"Well, if you like to show off so much, how about showing me how far you can run? Take ten laps around the field, we'll finish up reps without you."

Quentin blinked, his mind suddenly registering the coach's words. "Finish up ... *without* me?"

"I said take ten laps!" Hokor said. "Now move!"

Pine grabbed a ball and squatted down for the next rep while Denver crouched in readiness for her turn. Pine dropped back, Denver sprinted, and everyone seemed to ignore Quentin.

Coach Graber had never singled him out like that. Quentin's face felt hot. Anger swirled in his chest as he trotted to the edge of the field and started his first lap.

QUENTIN'S ROOM WAS EMPTY save for a bed, a table with two round stools, a large vertical equipment locker and a wide couch that sat in front of the holotank. He sat on the couch, staring at the life-sized image projected by the holotank.

The current image was a Human football player, his jersey a series of horizontal light blue and gray stripes. The computer droned away with stats.

[KITIARA LOMAX. THIRD-YEAR LINEBACKER FOR THE BIGG DIGGERS, NAMED ALL-PRO LAST YEAR. SIX-FOOT-TEN, FOUR-HUNDRED TWENTY-THREE POUNDS. LAST YEAR ACCUMULATED FIFTY-TWO TACKLES AND TWELVE SACKS, LAST CLOCKED TIME IN THE FORTY-YARD DASH, 4.1]

Quentin clicked his remote, and the image shifted to a Sklorno player, also dressed in a light blue-and-gray striped jersey.

[ARKHAM. FIFTH-YEAR CORNERBACK FOR THE BIGG DIGGERS ...]

The computer continued to rattle off statistics, but Quentin looked away from the image and stared at his blank wall. His legs gave off a subdued but ever-present burning feeling, the result of one hundred laps ran for a variety of transgressions, each one as unexpected as the last. His face also burned, but that wasn't from physical exertion. It was a new feeling, and he found it quite unacceptable.

A buzzer sounded, signaling a visitor at his door. The computer stopped the statistical litany.

[DONALD PINE AT YOUR DOOR]

"Enter," Quentin said in a toneless voice. He heard the swish of the door but didn't bother to get up. He hit the button on the remote. Arkham disappeared, replaced by a huge Ki lineman named Pret-Ah-Karat.

"Better watch out for him," Pine said quietly. "Last year he hit me so hard, he knocked me out of the game."

Quentin said nothing.

Pine crossed in front of Quentin and sat down on the couch. "We missed you at team dinner, kid. What's up?"

"Gotta study," Quentin said sullenly. "Hokor wants me to know all these damn players."

Pine nodded. "Yeah, you've got to know this stuff. But, hey, you've got to eat, right?"

"Not hungry now, I'll have something later." The truth was he was famished, but he had no intention of hitting the mess hall when the rest of the team was present — they'd all watched him run the endless laps, heard Hokor scream at him for various mistakes.

"It's no big deal, Hokor rips on all the rookies," Pine said, as if he read Quentin's thoughts. "He's got to shake out the weak ones. He's going to spend most of his time busting on you because you're a quarterback. It'll get worse before it gets better. Tomorrow we do route passing, but this time against the defensive backs. And the next day's practice is full-contact. So watch out for the Ki defensive linemen."

Quentin shrugged. "I'm not worried about some damn salamander, I just have to get these stupid players memorized."

Pine's eyebrows rose up in surprise. "*Salamander*, eh? Don't let them hear you say that, they'll tear your head off. Not worried about them? Our nose tackle, Mai-An-Ihkole, weighs 650 pounds and can bench-press 1,200 pounds, for crying out loud, and you're not worried? I've been on this team for two years, they're under strict orders not to hit me, and *I'm* worried."

Quentin turned and looked at Pine. He'd seen Pine run; the man had good reason to be worried. Quentin was faster, more agile, stronger and just plain tougher than Donald Pine.

"Thanks for the advice. Now if you don't mind, I've got studying to do."

Pine shrugged. "Suit yourself. If you need any help, let me know. Hey, maybe I can talk to Scarborough, get you some after-practice reps to get used to the speed of the game."

"I don't need help from a cricket."

Pine stared, then shook his head. "Yeah, you seem so normal on the outside, I forget where you come from. Just remember, kid, those *salamanders* and *crickets* are your teammates — you may have won games single-handedly back in the PNFL, but it doesn't work that way here."

"Thanks, pops, I'll remember that," Quentin said as he clicked the remote control to bring up the next player.

Pine stood, shook his head one more time and walked to the door. He stopped just as the door swished open and looked back at Quentin.

"Listen, kid, I'm not much for giving advice where it's not asked, but I feel you deserve to hear something. To play this game, you've got to know your history. Until the Creterakians took over, all the races were more likely to slaughter each other than talk, let alone work together. There's hatred here that goes way beyond anything related to sports. I'm not the greatest quarterback to ever play the game, but I figured out something a long time ago — for these warring races to play together as a team, someone has to step up and *lead*. Leading in the GFL means you forget your bigotry and get along with everyone. And it's a hard job. Damn near impossible. I expect everyone to get along and play as a unit. Warburg is one thing, but you're a quarterback, and as such, people tend to follow your lead. Your racism will cause problems, and I won't tolerate that. When you play for *my* team, you *will* respect your teammates."

Quentin felt his anger rising. *Who the hell did this guy think he was?*

"Your team?" Quentin said coldly. "Keep on living in that fantasy world, Pine, and you'll be a happy man in the retirement home. It's not going to be your team much longer."

Pine stared back hard, then sneered. "Whatever you say, rookie. It will be your team, all right. It will be your team when I decide to hang it up. Until then, you haven't got what it takes to be a starter, and you certainly don't have what it takes to beat *me*."

He walked out, the door swishing shut behind him.

Quentin turned off the holotank and stared at the blank wall. He hated salamanders, he hated crickets, and he hated blue-boy Donald Pine. But they would all learn. The Krakens were Quentin Barnes's team now, and sooner or later everyone would play by his rules.

THE SECOND DAY of practice saw Quentin, Pine and Yitzhak once again descend the lift into the orange end zone. The Sklorno receivers were there, this time in full pads, but so were Humans and Quyth Warriors — the linebackers — and eight new Sklorno — the defensive backs. All the defensive players wore black jerseys, while the offense wore orange.

"Do they worship Pine, too?" Quentin asked Yitzhak while pointing to the Sklorno defensive backs.

"They do, but in a different way, He leads the team, unifies us, and that makes him greater than a normal being. The receivers view catching a pass as a blessing, almost a gift from God. The defenders see a pass as a challenge given to them by God, a test of their will and physical abilities. To continuously fail to stop the passing game means they are unworthy, or something like that."

The three quarterbacks reached the end zone and started to warm up. Three orange-jerseyed Humans jogged from the center of the field to greet them. Warburg and the other two tight ends he had not yet met. Warburg gave Quentin a warm handshake.

Warburg introduced the other two men. "This is Yotaro Kobayasho and Pancho Saulsgiver." Quentin shook their hands. Yotaro was the biggest at 7-foot-1 and 380 pounds. He had a shaved head and three short, parallel scars on each cheek. Saulsgiver had pure white skin, like Yitzhak, with ice-blue eyes and white hair. At 6-foot-10 and about 355, he was the smallest of the three.

Hokor's hovercart floated down, and everyone pulled on their helmets.

"Let's get started," Hokor shouted before his hovercart even reached ground level. "Starting 'O' get on the goal line, we'll work the tight package."

Quentin started to move toward the goal line when he heard the words *Starting O*, then remembered he was not the starter.

Pine lined up on the goal line, back facing the end zone. Kobayasho lined up as the left tight end, and Warburg as the right. Scarborough lined up wide right, with Hawick two steps inside of Warburg and two steps behind him. The defensive backs showed bump-and-run coverage, playing directly in front of Scarborough and Hawick. Three linebackers spread out in their normal positions for a 3-4 defense. The outside linebackers were Quyth, one of whom wore number 58 — he was the guard that had stunsticked Mum-O-Killowe into submission on the landing dock at the *Combine*. The middle linebacker, number 50, was Human. He radiated lethality in a way Quentin had never seen or felt.

Pine barked out the signals, dropped back five steps, planted and bounced a half-step forward. The receivers sprinted out on their patterns: Scarborough on an in-route, Hawick on a post, Kobayasho on a ten-yard in-hook, Warburg in the flat.

The defense dropped into coverage. Sklorno defensive backs drifted into a zone, and the Human middle linebacker backpedaled straight back five yards. But it was the movement of the Quyth outside linebackers that shocked Quentin. They didn't run, they *rolled* to their positions, tucking up into a ball and rolling out — literally — to cover the flats before they popped up like some jumping spider, arms and pedipalps out and waiting.

Kobayasho was open on the hook, but Pine didn't throw. He checked through his reads, one-two-three-four, then turned and gunned the ball to Warburg, who had hooked up at four yards and drifted into the flat. Warburg caught the pass and turned upfield before Hokor blew the whistle. The players lined up again.

"Why didn't he hit Kobayasho?" Quentin asked Yitzhak.

"See number fifty there? That's John Tweedy, starting middle linebacker. All-Tier-Two last year. He's got phenomenal quickness. Kobayasho looked open, but even on a ten-yard bullet, Tweedy can get to the ball. He also pretends to be slower than he is. He'll do it for most of the game if he has to, to lull the quarterback into a pattern. When the ball is finally thrown to Tweedy's zone, it's because the QB thinks he can't get to it. He had six interceptions last year."

Quentin looked at the bulky linebacker. Something seemed to be on his face ... scrolling letters, hard to see but still legible under the facemask.

"What's up with his face? Does that say 'You rookies smell like nasty diarrhea'?"

Yitzhak laughed. "Yeah, probably. Tweedy has a full body tattoo."

"A tattoo? But it's moving."

"Sure, it's a image implant. Lots of guys in the league have tats. You've never seen one before?"

Quentin shook his head. "Not like that."

"They imbed little light emitters in the skin. They can make changing patterns, words, whatever. Tweedy went for the full package, complete skin coverage with a cyberlink. He can think of words and they play on his face, his forehead, chest, wherever."

Tweedy stood and pointed at Pine. "How's that arthritis, old man?" he said in a gravelly bellow.

Pine rose up from center. "A little rough, Johnny. You going to give me another rub-down like you did last night?"

The entire team laughed, including Tweedy, who flipped Pine off with both hands.

"Stop this Human bonding nonsense," Hokor called out. "Run the play."

Pine settled in under center and got back to business. Quentin watched carefully as the offense he'd studied on holos and on his messageboard came to life. Each play had several patterns for each receiver, depending on how the defense lined up. Were they in woman-to-woman? Were they in a prevent defense? Were they in a zone underneath with two-deep coverage over the top? At the snap of the ball, the receiver had to read the coverage and make route adjustments. These adjustments were just as planned as the original play itself — if the linebacker blitzed, the tight end changed his route from an out to a short hook; if the linebacker faded to a middle zone, the tight end kept his short hook; if the linebacker bit the run fake and came forward, then dropped back, the tight end changed from the short hook to a 15-yard streak.

The quarterback had to know the patterns for every receiver, for every play and the variations on every pattern based on the defensive alignment. On top of that, the quarterback had to know every pattern adjustment, for every route, based on the reaction of the defensive players after the snap of the ball. Each receiver had at least three pattern options. For a four-receiver play, that meant four patterns, multiplied by around six defensive sets, multiplied by three pattern options, resulting in seventy-two possible routes for every play. The quarterback had to read the defensive coverage while dropping back, know where his receivers were supposed to be, and usually make the decision to throw within four seconds of the snap. That was just the beginning — defenses did everything they could to disguise coverages, so the quarterback would think he saw one thing when in fact the defense was setting a trap. The quarterback had to be able to see through this ruse within his four seconds. The most complicated aspect of the whole thing was that the quarterback often had to read the defense and throw the ball before the receiver made his cut, so the ball would be there as soon as the receiver turned. For this to work, both the quarterback and the receiver had to make the same read at the same time, or the ball might sail long as the receiver turned up short for a hook pattern.

And then there was the obvious factor that most football fans forgot — the quarterback had to do all of this while 600-pound Ki linemen and 300-pound blitzing Human and Quyth Warrior linebackers and the occasional fast-as-lightning blitzing Sklorno safety were trying to get to him and forcibly remove his head from his shoulders.

And yet the stereotype of the "stupid jock" had persisted for centuries. It never ceased to amaze Quentin when people thought football players were just muscle-bound morons. He'd like to see a physics professor do algorithmic calculations while being chased around by a 600-pound monster that was known for eating its enemies alive.

Pine ran through all the plays, effortlessly reading every defensive adjustment. His skill clearly frustrated the defense, but at the same time Pine usually completed passes for only a five- or ten-yard gain. He ran through thirty plays with no interceptions, completing twenty-two passes — but only three for fifteen yards or more.

"Yitzhak," Hokor called out on his loudspeaker. "Take over."

Quentin bit his lip in anger. This second-rate benchwarmer was taking reps before he was. Quentin calmed himself — this early in the season, each quarterback would get the same amount of reps. Once the first game was out of the way, practice time would become so precious that very little of it could be used for the second- and third-string quarterbacks. But for now, he had to bite his tongue and wait.

If Pine made the offense look easy, Yitzhak illustrated how difficult it really was. He seemed to read the defense fairly well, but he did not possess Pine's pinpoint accuracy. Yitzhak finished his thirty plays with two interceptions, eighteen completions and only two passes that went for more than fifteen yards.

"Barnes!" Hokor barked. "Let's see what you can do. And remember, this isn't punting practice."

The defense laughed at Hokor's insult, and Quentin's face turned red. Obviously the entire team knew of his embarrassing incident the day before. Well, they wouldn't be laughing for long.

Quentin swaggered to the line. He'd watched the other two quarterbacks, and he'd watched the defenders — he knew how to run things. He lined up, feeling a surge of adrenaline pump through his veins. As Quentin bent down to start the play, the defensive players started calling out to him.

"Hey, rookie!" John Tweedy yelled. "Throw it my way, boy, make me look good for the Coach."

"Come on, Human," called Choto the Bright, the Quyth Warrior that played right outside linebacker. "You Nationalist racist scum, come make us sub-species look bad."

"You won't last, Human," said the left outside linebacker, number 58, Virak the Mean. "You're going back to your Third World planet in a body bag. I should have killed you on the landing dock at the *Combine* and just got it over with."

Quentin smiled. He hadn't been taunted since halfway through his first season of football back home. It had taken his opponents that long to learn what he was all about, that no matter what they said, he was going to tear their defense apart.

The defense closed in for bump-and-run. The cornerbacks Berea and Davenport lined up directly over Scarborough and Hawick, respectively. Quentin scanned through the rest of the defense, but he'd already seen what he needed to see.

"Hut-hut, *hut*!"

He took his strong five-step drop. Berea shoved Scarborough at the line of scrimmage, but Scarborough fought through the hit and streaked down the sideline. Quentin saw Stockbridge, the strong safety, moving over to help Berea, but it was already too late. Quentin waited, waited, then fired. The ball tore through the air on a shallow arc, hitting Scarborough in stride thirty yards downfield. Stockbridge pushed Scarborough out-of-bounds — a 35-yard gain.

The Sklorno receivers on the sidelines hooted and clicked and jumped with excitement.

"You took too long, Barnes," Hokor called. "You'd have never got that pass off. You've got to go through your reads quicker."

Quentin put his hands on his hips and stared up at Hokor, who hovered fifteen yards above the field in his little cart. Quentin stared for a few seconds more, then walked back to the line, shaking his head.

He called out the next set, which featured one tight end and three receivers. Scarborough lined up wide to the left, Hawick and Denver to the right, Kobayasho lined up at tight end. The defensive backs quickly shifted, taking out Choto the Bright, a linebacker, and bringing in another Sklorno defensive back. Quentin surveyed the field, running through the routes in his mind, matching them against the defensive set. Hawick was covered woman-to-woman by Davenport — Hawick's pattern in that coverage called for a post, and Quentin didn't think Davenport could handle Hawick's speed. Quentin tapped his stomach in a quick *ba-da-bap*, then barked out signals and snapped the ball.

He dropped back five steps, looked left to throw off the defense, then turned and launched the ball deep. As soon as he let it go, he saw his mistake: Davenport had broken off woman-to-woman and dropped into zone coverage, where she was responsible for defending a particular area of the field. Stockbridge, the strong safety, had the deep outside zone, where Quentin had thrown. Correctly reading the deep coverage of Stockbridge, Hawick broke off her post route and hooked up at fifteen yards — the ball sailed over her head, and Stockbridge swept in for an easy interception.

Tweedy let out a grating, evil, mocking laugh that sounded like a stuttering buzz saw. "Thanks, rookie!" he called out through cupped hands. "You just answered Hawick's prayers!" The Human defenders laughed. Quivering pedipalps showed the Quyth Warriors' amusement.

Quentin's face felt hot under his helmet. Davenport had easily disguised her coverage by running stride-for-stride with Hawick, until the defender reached her assigned zone coverage. It all happened so *fast* — seemingly twice as fast as anything happened back in the PNFL. Quentin had thrown too early.

The team fell silent as Hokor's cart lowered to the field. "Barnes, how many reads did you make that time?"

Quentin looked down. "One."

Hokor's pedipalps quivered, and clearly not from humor. "One. You just turned the ball over, again."

"Relax, Coach, I've got it now."

Hokor just stared at him with his one big eye. "Run it again," he said, then his cart rose noiselessly to fifteen feet and hovered behind the end zone.

Quentin lined up for another stab, but his confidence had suddenly abandoned him. Things were moving too fast. He ran the same play, saw the defensive coverage and opted for a short dump to the tight end. Even that was almost an interception: Virak the Mean tightened up into a ball and rolled sideways, not as fast as a Sklorno but pretty damn fast, a rolling blur that popped open at the last second when the ball drew near.

The next play, Quentin checked off his primary and secondary routes, which were covered, and fired a short crossing pass to the tight end — as soon as he let go, he knew he'd messed up again. Tweedy had seemed to be yards away from the play, but he stepped in front of Warburg and picked off the ball.

This time Hokor didn't come down, but it didn't matter — Tweedy's buzz-saw laughter roared across the field.

"You're my kind of quarterback," Tweedy called. "I just wish you were playing for Wallcrawlers instead of us. It would make my job easier."

Laughter and quivering pedipalps were all Quentin heard and saw. His face burned with embarrassment.

"You're not utilizing your arm strength."

Quentin turned to see Pine next to him.

"Tweedy is giving you the same cushion he gives me," Pine said quietly, practically whispering. "But you throw much harder than I do. If you want to shut them up, go after Tweedy again, but this time *hard*. These tight ends are much better than the guys you played with in the PNFL. As soon as you burn Tweedy a couple of times, he'll close the cushion, then call crossing routes over his head."

Now, Pine was giving him advice as if he were some schoolboy playing pickup ball. It was the final insult. Go after Tweedy, who'd just picked off a pass? Did Pine think Quentin was *stupid*? Pine obviously wanted to make him look bad.

"Get out of my huddle, Pine," Quentin growled. "I don't need any help from a blue-boy."

Pine leaned back as if he'd been slapped. He stared, shook his head sadly, then turned and jogged back to Yitzhak.

"Is Daddy helping Little Quentin play the game?" Tweedy called out loudly.

Quentin's patience hit a dead end. He pointed his finger at the linebacker. "Shuck *him*, and shuck *you*, Tweedy."

Tweedy's mocking smile turned into a gleeful snarl. "Well, show me what you got. So far you ain't got nothin'."

I'LL POKE OUT YOUR EYES AND CRAP ON YOUR BRAIN played across Tweedy's face tattoo. Quentin watched it for a second, then shook his head, trying to concentrate.

He ran through ten more plays, his frustration growing with each pass. He threw two more interceptions, his third and fourth of the day, one on a deep passes to Scarborough and one where Virak the Mean rolled *forward* in addition to *sideways* and sprang open right in front of a hooking Kobayasho.

"You've got two plays left, Barnes," Hokor called from his loudspeaker. "Let's see if you can continue your ineptitude."

The defense continued to taunt him. He was so mad he could

barely see, barely think. This hadn't been what he'd expected at all. He lined up for his second-to-last play, a three-receiver set with Warburg on the right. Quentin dropped back, trying to read the coverage. Within two seconds, he saw that all of the receivers were well-covered. He checked through the routes, but no one was open. Frustration exploded in his head as he read his last option — Warburg on a crossing route — only to see Tweedy lurking close by. Rage billowing over, Quentin reared back and vented all of his anger on a laser-blast pass. The ball was a blur as it shot forward. Tweedy sprang at it, but too late, and fell flat on his face. The ball slammed into Warburg's chest, hitting him so hard that it knocked him backward. Warburg stumbled, bobbled the ball, but hauled it in before he dropped to his butt.

For the first time that afternoon, the defense fell silent. Tweedy got up slowly, staring hatefully at Quentin.

Quentin blinked, his rage clearing away, and one thought echoing through his head. *If you want to shut them up, go after Tweedy again, but this time hard.*

The receivers returned to the mini-huddle. Quentin called his last play, a two tight end set, and made sure to include a deep crossing route behind Tweedy. At the snap he dropped back three steps and reared back to throw a hook to Warburg. Tweedy jumped forward, much sooner than he'd done all day. Quentin pump-faked, then tossed an easy pass over Tweedy's head to the crossing Kobayasho.

Quentin turned and looked back at Pine, who simply smiled and shrugged.

AFTER QUENTIN'S last pass, the team started jogging back to the tunnel, headed for the locker room. Quentin stopped when Hokor called out to him. As his teammates disappeared into the tunnel, Quentin waited while Hokor's cart floated down to the field.

"You have to make your reads faster," Hokor said.

Quentin felt embarrassed but couldn't argue. He felt like he was moving in slow-motion. He'd finished up ten-of-thirty with four interceptions — *four* — and only his first pass went for more than fifteen yards.

"Who's the second starting cornerback for the Wallcrawlers?" Hokor asked.

"Jacobina," Quentin said instantly. "Great vertical leap, but not very strong and easily blocked. Two-year vet."

"What's her weakness?"

"Trouble reaching maximum vertical leap during a full sprint."

"How do you beat her?"

"Throw deep and high, make the receiver have to really sprint and jump to make the catch. Jacobina usually can't match the jump if the ball is thrown correctly."

"Good," Hokor said. "And their second-string nose guard?"

Quentin opened his mouth to speak, then shut it. "Come on Coach, he's just a lineman. All I have to do is avoid him, I don't need to know anything about him."

Hokor's pedipalps twitched, just once. He pointed to the sidelines. "Start running."

Quentin groaned. "For how long?"

"Ten laps."

"Come on, Coach, that's crap!"

The pedipalps twitched, and this time kept twitching. "You're right, that is crap. Twenty laps."

"What? You just said ten!"

"Did I? I thought I said it thirty. Yes, I said thirty."

Quentin clenched his jaw tight. He felt helpless, out of his element. Hokor held all the cards and would until Quentin took over the starting spot. Quentin's mouth closed into a tight-lipped snarl. Hokor stared at him another five seconds, until Quentin jogged to the sidelines and started doing laps around the field.

Post patterns? Crossing routes? Woman-to-woman coverage? If you want to learn more about the passing game, hear the author explain the basics at http://www.scottsigler.com/passing101.

HOKOR THE HOOKCHEST sat in the control room mounted a hundred feet up from the practice field end zone. A dozen small holotanks lined the big window that looked out onto the field. The holotanks let him watch any of his players at any time, wherever they were in the ship.

The Ki slept together, as was their custom. They looked like a pile of legs and long bodies. The Ki section of the ship consisted of four large rooms — the communal room, the feeding room and sleeping rooms for offense and defense, respectively. He visited their communal room at least four or five times a season. It was decorated with multi-colored mosses and various slimes he was told were plants. He'd entered the defensive room once, and *only* once, because the place stank like a combination of rancid meat and animal offal. Ki family units slept together. It wasn't sexual — he'd heard stories about the Ki mating season and had no intention of ever witnessing such a brutal display.

He made the offense and defense sleep separately — they had to face off against each other in practice every day, and when they all slept as one big family unit, they were far too civil to each other. He needed violence and aggression on the practice field. It was the only way to prepare the team for the weekly war against the other GFL squads.

The Sklorno were deep into their morning worship. There were fourteen of the beings on the team, six receivers and eight defensive backs. Even after ten seasons of coaching, the Sklorno still seemed so bizarre to him. They worshipped strange things, like trees, the clouds on certain planets, works of literature and — strangest of all — quarterbacks and coaches. Three of the veteran receivers were high-ranking members of the Donald Pine church. Another two, both defensive backs, worshipped Frank Zimmer of the To Pirates. He didn't know what the rest worshipped, and didn't care, as long as it didn't complicate football.

He rarely checked up on the Quyth Warriors. He saved his spying for the sub-races. Warriors deserved the right to come and go as they pleased.

Eleven of his thirteen Humans were in bed, sleeping away. Ibrahim Khomeni, the 525-pounder from Vosor-3 was, of course, eating again. Hokor wondered how those HeavyG Human worlds maintained any economy at all, considering how much their subjects ate. Between Khomeni and Aleksandar Michnik, also from Vosor-3, they daily consumed enough food for ten normal-G Humans.

But while Hokor kept tabs on all of his players, he was really only concerned with one — Quentin Barnes. The Human rookie was in the virtual practice room, working away on the timing that had given him so much trouble in the first three days of practice.

The door to his control room hissed open. Hokor's antennae went up, briefly, long enough to sense the presence of Gredok. He stood, turned and brushed back his antennae.

"Don't bother, old friend," Gredok said. "Sit down, continue what you were doing."

Hokor sat and again turned his attention to Quentin. The Human surveyed his holographic players and the holographic team, then dropped back as the line erupted into holographic chaos. He took a strong five-step drop, set up and rifled the ball downfield. It fell short of the holographic Scarborough — a defender dove to intercept the ball.

"He's up early for a Human, isn't he?" Gredok asked.

"Just him and Ibrahim."

Gredok looked at the monitor that showed Ibrahim, sitting alone at a table with four heaping trays of food spread out before him.

"Females be saved," Gredok said with disgust. "Do these HeavyG Humans *ever* stop eating? I swear his salary is nothing compared to his food bill."

"If you could locate a 525-pound Quyth Warrior who can bench-press a thousand pounds, I'd be happy to trade for him."

Gredok watched Quentin run the same play. This time, he threw ahead of Scarborough for an incompletion.

"Does Barnes do this a lot?"

"He doesn't socialize with the other players," Hokor said. "He spends most of his time in the VR room, repeatedly running plays."

Gredok said nothing. Quentin lined up again, dropped back and ran the same play. This time the ball sailed over the leaping defender and hit the holographic Scarborough in full stride.

"Nice pass," Gredok said. "How long has he been at it?"

"Two hours."

"How's he doing?"

"Horrible," Hokor said. "But he's improving fast."

"Horrible? I watched him in practice yesterday. He threw 75-yard strikes like they were nothing."

Hokor turned to look at his *shamakath*. "He has only been playing the game for four years, and in a very low-quality league. He's never thrown to Sklorno receivers before, and he's not used to passing being a three-dimensional game instead of a two-dimensional game. Throwing routes is one thing, but he's not ready for the speed of real defensive backs."

"He'd better *get* ready for it. I went through a lot of trouble to get him."

"We had to get him now," Hokor said. "One more season, and every team in the GFL would have been after him. I just don't know how long he will take to develop."

"Need I remind you that this is your third season?" Gredok said coldly. "I don't care about development time, I care about *winning*. I want this team in Tier One next season. All the good trade routes require Tier One immunity. You know that."

Hokor did know that. *Trade routes* was a nice way of saying *smuggling routes*. Hokor didn't care for that part of the business at all, but that was the way the league worked.

"I'm sure that in two seasons, maybe three, Quentin will be the best player in the league."

"You don't have two seasons," Gredok said. "You wanted Donald Pine, I got you Donald Pine. You wanted Choto the Bright, I got him for you. You found out one of my lieutenants had Tier Three experience, so Virak the Mean is playing football instead of acting as my bodyguard and enforcer. I spent a *fortune* on Mum-O-Killowe, I gave up my drug distribution in Egypt City for him because you said we *had* to have him. I upgraded this ship because you said it would help us win games … do you think that was cheap?"

"No, *Shamakath*." Hokor knew the ship's retrofit had been horribly expensive, but he was a firm believer that if you wanted to play like a Tier One team, you had to practice like a Tier One team.

"I want Tier One and am willing to spend the money to get it," Gredok said. "But the time for investing in over, the time for profit is near. You will win the Quyth Irradiated Conference, get us into the Tier Two tournament and qualify us for Tier One next season or someone else will be around to watch Quentin Barnes turn into the best player in the league."

Gredok stood and walked out of the control room. Hokor slowly turned back to the holotank, just in time to see Quentin throw another interception. His pedipalps quivered in frustration.

6

ARRIVAL ON IONATH

HE WAS GLAD it was late because he could be alone in his room and no one would see his sweat, look at his wide eyes or hear his ragged breathing. The *Touchback* was about to punch-out.

Just relax just relax everything is fine …

Quentin had often heard that if things were to go wrong with punch drive travel, it would happen either on the punch-in or the punch-out of the space/time hole. Punching out always made him think of that ages-old Purist folk-saying: "It's not the fall that kills you, it's the landing."

Don't panic, breath, breath, it's almost here …

He felt the shimmer come, *felt*, not *saw*, because he couldn't bear to have his eyes open and see the reality wave lightly caress the ship and everything in it. And once again, nothing happened.

His held breath slipped out of his tense body, the tinge of horror clinging to his soul. He'd come to accept the fact that if he wanted his dream of glory and a GFL championship, he'd just have to ignore his fear of flying.

He felt the slight tug of the *Touchback*'s main engines kicking in, maneuvering the ship into orbit. Quentin moved to his view port and looked out onto the glowing red sphere that was Ionath, planet of Ionath City, the home of the Ionath Krakens.

He'd learned all about Ionath in school. In 2558, during the Third Galactic War, the Sklorno navy saturation-bombed the planet, rendering it a radioactive wasteland completely devoid of all life. That bombing was *proof*, the Holy Men liked to say, of the Sklorno's Satanic nature. It also *proved* that the Prawatt race, who had inhabited the planet, were also Satanic and suffered the wrath of the High One for their evil ways. Quentin had been only 9 when he noticed a pattern — just about everything bad that happened to other races or cultures was *proof* of Satanic tendencies. The only people who didn't suffer Satanic-related incidents were, coincidentally, the people of the Purist Nation.

But despite the bombing (or perhaps despite Satan), Ionath had not remained devoid of life. In 2573, the Quyth shocked the galaxy by establishing a permanent colony on the planet. In the 110 Earth-years that followed, the colony grew to a population of 500 million Quyth. In addition, the Quyth introduced flora and fauna that not only ignored radiation, but often used it in place of sunlight to capture energy. In just over a century, the Quyth transformed Ionath from a lifeless orb into a flourishing, growing, vibrant planet. The Holy Men cited this as *proof* of the Quyth's Satanic nature, for only a being from Hell could live on Hell itself.

While the Quyth flourished on Ionath, the radiation hadn't just gone away, and other sentient races could not survive on the planet's surface. The Quyth wanted commerce with other species, so Ionath — like the other irradiated planets of Whitok and Chik-chik — had several domed cities free of radiation. The domed areas acted as a downtown, a central hub of the non-protected areas. Ionath City boasted the largest rad-free dome on the planet. About 110,000 sentients lived inside the four-mile-diameter dome, while another 4.1 million Quyth lived outside. The football stadium, of course, sat inside the dome.

Ionath Stadium was also known as "The Big Eye." Quentin had dreamed of playing in such a place. Seating capacity: 185,000. An open-air stadium, but since it existed under the city dome the weather never changed — it was always 85 degrees Fahrenheit, the galaxy-accepted standard for multi-race environments. Eighty-five seemed hot to most Humans, a bit cool for Ki, borderline cold for Sklorno and Creterakians and ideal for Quyth. In the past, when the Krakens were a running team, rumor had it that for critical games, the temperature system for all of the Ionath City dome would often "malfunction," dropping the temp to 75 degrees or below, a temperature more suited to Human running backs.

His game was improving, but he'd been less than impressive during his four days with the team. He'd never even considered that he'd have such a hard time adjusting. They had two more days of practice, then the season opener against the Woo Wall-crawlers. And the second of those two days was a non-contact practice, a pre-game run-through.

That meant he really only had one more day to convince Hokor that he was ready to play Tier Two ball. But *was* he ready? Pine made everything look so easy, so smooth, and that only magnified Quentin's constant struggles. But if Pine could do it, Quentin could do it.

Mind games from Hokor. That's what all this crap was. Learn every opposing player, their stats, their history, run laps ... a bunch of busy work designed to show Quentin who was boss. Well, Quentin had broken Coach Graber, and Hokor would be no different. Yet, in the back of his mind, Quentin wondered if Hokor was different from Coach Graber. Hokor acted like he'd be perfectly willing to put Quentin on the next shuttle back to the Purist Nation. Was that just an act?

Quentin wasn't sure, and that gave him an uneasy feeling he'd never experienced before. He slid out of bed and started stretching. Today's practice would be very important, and he wanted to be ready.

THE ENTIRE TEAM assembled in the landing bay in a big half-circle around Gredok and Hokor. As usual, players mostly grouped with their own species. Quentin stood with Warburg and Yassoud.

Pine, as Quentin had come to expect, stood with one of the alien races, this time the Ki linemen.

"We will now be taking shuttles down to our facility on Ionath City," Gredok said. "Most of you know the drill. The shuttle will make four runs, veterans go down in the first two runs, then free agents new to the team, and finally rookies."

"After practice, my workers will show you to your apartments, which have already been assigned. All apartments are close to the stadium. The dome is a reasonably safe area, and as Krakens players, you will usually be awarded respect. However, Ionath City is not a vacation resort, so be careful. You are responsible for your body, and care for any injuries sustained while not on the practice or playing field will be docked from your pay. *Especially* you, Yassoud."

Yassoud looked as if his best friend had insulted his mother. "Me? Why would you say that?"

Gredok's pedipalps twitched once. "I've read your record, Yassoud. More tavern fight arrests than some of my low-level enforcers. If you insist on causing problems, you should pray that the police put you in jail instead of bringing you back to me. Understand?"

For once, Yassoud said nothing. Simply nodded instead.

"And as for you, Mum-O-Killowe," Gredok said, "I will be more than happy to send you home in a body bag if you act as you have when you played in the Sklorno leagues."

Shizzle appeared as if from nowhere, swooped over to Mum-O-Killowe and provided a quick translation. Mum-O-Killowe started saying something in his loud, harsh way, but before he managed a couple of syllables, another Ki lineman reached out with a long arm and flicked him in the vocal tubes. Quentin recognized the flicker as Mai-An-Ihkole, the veteran defensive tackle. Mum-O-Killowe looked offended, as near as Quentin could read Ki emotion. The rookie lineman fell silent.

"That is all," Gredok said. "The veterans will now board for the first run to Ionath City."

Veterans, including Pine, entered the shuttle as the rest of the team dispersed.

"What was that all about?" Quentin asked Yassoud. "You a trouble maker or something?"

Yassoud shrugged. "I've no idea. I've never caused a problem in my life."

"Where there's smoke, there's fire," Warburg said, looking down at the smaller Yassoud. "Just don't hang out with him in the city, Quentin. We don't need his influence to lead us astray."

Yassoud put a hand to his chest. "You offend me, sir. I would never think to corrupt a pious member of the church." He walked off, shaking his head in disbelief as if he'd been greatly misjudged.

Two Sklorno — Denver and Milford — approached. Warburg's demeanor instantly changed from doubt to intimidation, if not outright hostility. Denver's raspers dragged along the floor, actually leaving a thin trail of saliva on the flight deck. Her transparent carapace was so disconcerting — Quentin could actually see blood coursing through her veins, X-ray gray blurred by the clear chitin's X-ray white. Quentin felt a small shiver of disgust ripple down his spine.

Warburg stared. "What do *you* want?"

"Perhaps we are worthy to catch passes while running at full speed?" Denver said in her chirping voice.

Quentin and Warburg looked at each other in confusion, then back at Denver.

"What are you talking about, you stupid cricket?" Warburg said. His racial slur stopped all conversation — the players remaining on the flight deck turned to watch.

"Holy Pine said perhaps we could assist in Holy Quentin's passing. We run full speed, he blesses us with direct passes."

Quentin's face turned red, while Warburg started laughing.

Pine, Quentin thought. *How could he embarrass me like this?*

"Can we help?" Denver asked again.

"I don't need help!" Quentin spat. "Especially not from the likes of you!"

Denver's raspers rolled back up behind the chin plate. She leaned back a bit, her posture changing, but Quentin didn't know what that meant, and he was too furious to care.

"Oh, Pine really knows how to rub it in," Warburg said.

"Holy Quentin is angry?" Denver said. "But we are here to help."

It was too much to bear. Quentin turned and stormed away, heading out of the landing bay and back to his room. Help? From a damned unholy *Sklorno*? As if Quentin were some bush league quarterback who needed to work on his route passing? *Pine*. He'd show that jerk, one way or another, he'd *show* him!

QUENTIN HADN'T calmed down much by the time the shuttle, loaded up with the rookies, eased out of the landing bay and into space. It didn't help that Denver and Milford, the perpetrators of Pine's little practical joke, sat only a few feet away. At least this time they kept their distance.

The wasted red landscape of Ionath filled the front view screens. Plants colored orange, red and yellow seemed to flourish, but there was no plant large enough to hide the planet's war scars. Just over an Earth century had passed since Sklorno's 25,000-megaton bombs exterminated all life on the planet. The ten-mile-wide bomb craters remained clearly visible. Ionath City, in fact, was built inside one of those craters.

The clear dome gave off brilliant reflections from Ionath's sun. The sprawling city looked like a reddish egg, sunny-side up, with the dome being the yolk. As the shuttle approached the city, Quentin could see how Ionath Stadium got its nickname — the round stadium sat right under the dome's center and from this far up looked like an iris to the dome's cornea. *The Big Eye*. His new home, at least for this season.

Circular streets surrounded the dome in ever-widening bands, like flash-frozen ripples from a pebble dropped in a pond. Straight streets also radiated outward from the dome. Or more accurately, Quentin noticed, all streets led into the city center — straight to the stadium.

"I hear they really know how to party in Ionath City," Yassoud said, a wide smile on his face. "I can't wait to get out on the town."

"Isn't it a bit radioactive out there?"

Yassoud rolled his eyes. "Come on, hick — I'm not going into the outer city, I'm talking about nightlife under the dome. There's hundreds of bars and restaurants. And women. Lots of women."

Yassoud cast a glance back at the staring Sklorno receivers. "Human women," he said, giving Quentin a friendly elbow. "Unless you're committed to your harem over there."

Quentin's face turned red again, a feeling to which he was unfortunately becoming accustomed.

Red was also the predominant color of Ionath City. From outside the dome, buildings looked rugged and somewhat organic, more like they'd been grown than built. The tallest ones topped out at around forty stories.

The shuttle dove straight for the dome. The clear surface seemed to open like a living thing, and the shuttle passed through without slowing. Once inside the dome, the buildings looked more like what he'd seen in the Purist Nation's largest cities: towering, hexagonal structures with sides of smooth crystametal. The tallest buildings seemed to surround Ionath Stadium as if they wanted to peer down and watch the games. Only buildings at the dome center could hit such heights — the buildings farther out grew progressively smaller as the dome sloped down to meet the ground.

Quentin saw a huge holo ad running down the side of the city's tallest building — a quarterback dropping back for a pass, some words in Quyth. At first he thought it was Pine, but the player wore number fourteen — Yitzhak's number.

"Is that who I think it is?"

Yassoud nodded. "Yes indeed."

"What is that ad for?"

Yassoud stared for a moment, his lips moving slightly as he sounded out the Quyth writing. "Oh, yep, now I remember, it's an ad for Junkie Gin."

"Junkie Gin? But it's the biggest ad in the city, and it's Yitzhak. Why not Pine?"

"Because Yitzhak was born here, my friend. The Quyth Workers just love him, and they're the biggest market in any Quyth culture because there's so many of them. He doesn't see much playing time, but he makes more endorsement money than anyone else on the team. Pine included."

The shuttle dove toward the roof of a hexagonal, ten-story building attached to the stadium. Closer into the city, Quentin saw holo ads everywhere — on buildings, on sidewalks, floating above the streets. The innumerable ads gave the city a garish, carnival feel. At least half of those ads featured Krakens' players.

Even before the shuttle fully touched down, a pack of Quyth Workers swarmed out, ready to unload the players' baggage. Quentin and the other rookies stepped off the shuttle into the heat and high humidity of Ionath City.

Hokor was waiting for them, already sitting in his stupid flying cart. Next to the cart stood a Quyth worker wearing a neat blue jacket. Quentin thought the Worker looked rather like a bellboy or a doorman at some of the fancier Purist Nation hotels.

"This is Messal the Efficient," Hokor said to the rookies. "He will lead you to the locker room. Suit up and get your worthless asses to the field. Our scrimmage starts in thirty minutes. Remember, in two days at noon, we kick off against the Woo Wallcrawlers. We *must* win this game. Tomorrow's practice will be a no-contact walk-through, so today is your last chance to show me what you've got."

With that, Hokor's cart lifted up from the roof and flew off the edge, gently descending to the field. Quentin saw the veterans and the other players, just specks from this far, already on the field. He knew Pine would be down there, probably planning his next humiliating joke.

We'll see, Quentin thought. *We'll just see.*

QUENTIN SUITED UP quickly and ran out of the arching gate in the orange end zone. The seats, all 185,000 of them, sat empty. The quiet, massive structure reminded him of the Deliverance Temple in Landing City, built where Mason Stewart's scout craft had first touched down on new, holy soil. That historic moment marked the end of the Exodus from Earth, where Stewart and his four million surviving followers founded the Purist Church colony that would grow into to the four-planet Purist Nation. Quentin didn't have to be a convert to appreciate the powerful feeling of awe inspired by Deliverance Temple, just as he suspected someone didn't need to be a football fan to admire Ionath Stadium.

He knelt and rubbed his hands over the field's blue surface. At first he thought it was painted, but up close he saw that the playing surface was made up of densely packed, circular blue leaves, each smaller than his pinky nail. He pushed his hand down, feeling the blue plant give, then lifted his hand and watched it spring back.

Yassoud knelt next to him. "Getting in a quick prayer, Q?"

Quentin smiled. "No, just checking out the field. Never seen this stuff before."

"Nice, isn't it? I heard it's actually a plant that's native to Ionath. Called Iomatt. When they took over the planet, they got some from a plant museum, or something like that."

Quentin stood and ran a few steps, taking an experimental cut.

"Good resistance. Not quite as firm as the Carsengi Grass I'm used to, but not bad."

The other rookies filed past them, drawing their attention back to the task at hand. Hokor sat on the 50-yard line, in his cart, of course, surrounded by Krakens players. Humans, Quyth Warriors, Sklorno and — for the first time since he'd arrived — the huge and nightmarish Ki. The Ki were packed into two tight balls, each a mass of legs, tubular bodies and black eyes, like pictures of multi-headed demons Quentin had seen back on Micovi. One of the piles of Ki players wore black jerseys, for the defense, while the other pile wore orange, for the offense. Pine, Yitzhak and Quentin wore bright red jerseys — the standard football color for designating a "do not hit" player.

"In two days, we face off against the Woo Wallcrawlers," Hokor said. "It's a good start for us, as we know they have trouble with our offensive speed. They also went 2-7 last year, but don't let that fool you into thinking this is an easy game. It's the opening game of the season, and we have to win it if we're going to reach Tier One this year."

The players gave signs of agreement — nods from the Humans, Quyth Warriors rubbing their pedipalps together, unintelligible chirps and lolling tongues from the Sklorno and the Ki clacking their arms against their chest. Quentin didn't know how to read the other races, but he could see the commitment in the eyes of the Human players. They wanted to win, they wanted to reach Tier One.

"First offense," Hokor called out over his cart's loudspeaker. "Opening series."

Quentin jogged to the sidelines. Pine, the arrogant idiot, ran to the huddle with a confident stride. That was *Quentin's* huddle. He'd get it back, that was for sure. The ancient quarterback would have to make room for new blood.

Quentin stopped when he reached the sidelines and looked at the medical bays behind the bench. Five full bays, like a military field hospital. Re-juv tanks, cabinets that held bandages, surgical equipment and other things to help Doc and his staff repair damaged players and get them back on the field. Quentin could see just by looking that the med-bays were more advanced than anything he'd seen in the Purist Nation, even in a hospital. The bays were a reminder of the speed and strength and violence of the GFL — that and the money involved, because a hurt player was a wasted investment. Patch 'em up and put 'em back in.

Pine broke the huddle and the orange-jersey offense started on its own 20-yard line. The black-jersey defense lined up in a 4-3 set, showing woman-to-woman coverage. Quentin had never seen real GFL football in person, and it was an awesome sight to behold: the Ki linemen were thick, wide, six-foot-tall obstacles, like little buildings with legs, their spider-like, chitinous arms clacking against their chests as they talked to each other in their rhythmic combat language. The Quyth Warrior linebackers bounced in place, one-eyed creatures clad in thick Riddell padding. Sklorno receivers and defensive backs, with thin pads to allow for pure speed, gracefully flowed from one place to the next, almost as if they had no bones at all.

The first play was an off-tackle run by Mitchell Fayed, who even at three-quarter speed hit the hole harder than any PNFL running back Quentin had ever seen. Fayed came through the line, only to be met head-on by Choto the Bright, the right outside linebacker. With a loud "clack" of pads, the two players hit hard — Fayed managed two more short steps before Choto dragged him to the ground.

A shiver ran through Quentin's body. Drills were one thing, an important thing, but football is about *hitting*, and with that first clash of starting offense against starting defense, the season was actually *on*. The veterans had been practicing for months, but for the rookies, this was their first Upper Tier contact experience.

Pine guided the offense through the first series, mostly running plays. When he did drop back, he threw short, accurate passes. In his first twenty plays, he threw downfield only twice for one completion. Twice the defense got to Pine, but both times they slowed up before hitting him and just put a hand (or the applicable appendage) on his shoulder.

Yitzhak came in next and, by his mistakes, highlighted Pine's effectiveness. Hokor started subbing people on both sides of the ball. Yassoud Murphy came in for his first full-contact reps. When he carried the ball, he ran like a tank. His ever-present smile vanished, replaced by an expression that might have been more at home in a hand-to-hand ground war. The Sklorno rookie receivers, Denver and Milford, rotated in for several plays. Quentin waited and watched, trying to analyze the defensive weaknesses and trying — unsuccessfully — to be patient.

"Barnes!" Hokor finally called after an agonizing hour. Quentin practically sprinted out to the huddle — this is where he'd show Hokor, and the whole team for that matter, why he deserved to start. The offense was now a hodge-podge of first-stringers, second-stringers and rookies. Denver and Mezquitic stared at him reverently. Yassoud smiled. Warburg nodded.

"Okay, boys, let's take it to them. Pro-40 right flash, on two, on two, *break*."

The players moved quickly from the huddle to the line, and Quentin felt in control for the first time since leaving Micovi. The VR sim was an amazing tool, but this was *real*, this was his chance to show everyone. He lined up behind Bud-O-Shwek, the center — and suddenly realized he had no idea how to take a snap from a Ki.

Quentin stared at the long tubular body. This close up, Bud's body looked like a snake-skinned caterpillar with thick, multi-jointed spider legs. Pine and Yitzhak had made the snap look so natural Quentin hadn't even thought about it. Where the hell was he supposed to put his hands?

"Barnes!" Hokor shouted. "What is your difficulty?"

Quentin looked up at the coach in his little hovercart. "Well, I ... I'm not sure ..."

"Oh, rub me raw!" John Tweedy shouted. "The hick doesn't know how to take snap from a Ki!"

Laughter erupted on the field. Quentin flushed red. Everyone was laughing, laughing at *him*. Even Warburg was laughing, dammit.

Pine calmly stepped forward.

"Just like this, kid," Pine said, not a trace of laughter in his voice. Pine squatted down and slid his hands under Bud-O-Shwek's posterior. Quentin now saw that Pine squatted down deeper and reached in farther than he would with a Human center and had to stagger his feet a little bit in order to keep his balance.

"See?" Pine said. "It's not so different. Just keep your left foot back a step or so, so you can reach in without falling over. Hut-HUT!"

Bud-O-Shwek snapped the ball and shot forward, his body expanding quickly and violently. Pine tossed Bud the ball, then turned to Quentin.

"Got it, kid?"

Quentin nodded. Pine smiled, slapped him once on the shoulder pad, then jogged back behind the line.

"Let's go," Hokor called. "Run the play."

The offensive line formed up again. Quentin staggered his feet as Pine had done and reached far under Bud-O-Shwek. The Ki's rear felt cold and hard. He felt the pebbly skin against the back of his hands. A wave of revulsion tinged with a hint of fear swept through him. He was touching one of them. Bud-O-Shwek seemed indifferent: his front right leg curled around the ball, waiting for the snap-count.

Quentin looked over his center and surveyed the defense.

It was like looking straight out into a nightmare.

Mai-An-Ihkole and Per-Ah-Yet, the starting Ki defensive tackles, eyed him with obvious hunger, their black eyes glistening. Ki helmets consisted of a clear, circular visor that ran all the way around the head, accommodating their 360-degree vision. Above the visor, the black helmet pointed back like a dog's claw, protecting the delicate vocal tubes.

The two Ki tackles were flanked by defensive ends Aleksandar Michnik and Ibrahim Khomeni, both amongst the biggest Humans Quentin had ever seen. They both hailed from Vosor-3, a world with gravity three times that of Earth.

Once, in school, he'd seen pictures of an extinct creature called a "gorilla." The class had been on creation, how all creatures were created as-is by the High One. In the Planetary Union and the League of Planets, apparently, they believe that Humans had evolved from these gorillas. Quentin had agreed that the idea was absurd, that it was ridiculous to think gorillas had given birth to Human babies. But now, looking at the 525-pound Michnik, with arms bigger than Quentin's thighs and legs bigger than Quentin's chest, he suddenly had to wonder what a gorilla looked like if you shaved off all its fur and dressed it in football pads.

From the middle linebacker's spot, John Tweedy's evil laugh rang through the air. "Well, looks like we've got it easy now. The rookie is here to answer Sklorno prayers again."

EAT CRAP LOSER scrolled across Tweedy's face.

At left and right outside linebacker, respectively, Virak the Mean and Choto the Bright bounced in place: fast, vicious, powerful, one-eyed Quyth Warriors. Sometimes they moved on legs and arms, low to the ground and leaning forward, waiting to attack, and sometimes just on their legs, standing tall and surveying the field. If they blitzed, Quentin knew he'd have to react instantly to avoid them.

The Sklorno defensive backs added yet another horrific element to the defense, their translucent bodies and black skeletons showing clearly where the black jerseys and pads did not cover. Their armored eyestalks quivered with excitement.

He felt a flutter in his stomach, a queasy feeling he'd never experienced before on a football field. He knew the feeling, but vaguely, a distant echo of something he didn't have time to think about.

"Blue twenty-one," Quentin called. "Blue ... twenty-one."

Tweedy moved forward, his huge frame standing right at the line of scrimmage, in between Mai-An-Ihkole and Per-Ah-Yet.

"Here it comes, rookie!" Tweedy screamed, his face a contorted mask of psychotic rage. The strange feeling in Quentin's stomach grew in intensity. Was Tweedy just showing blitz, or was he coming for real?

"Flash, flash!" Quentin called out, audibling to a short-pattern pass. If Tweedy blitzed, Warburg would likely be open on a crossing route. "Hut-hut!"

The line erupted like nothing Quentin had ever seen or heard — so loud! The clatter of chitin and Ki battle screeches and Human grunts and smashing body armor filled the air like some medieval battle holo. Quentin pushed away from the line and reached the ball back for Yassoud to carry, then pulled it away at the last instant as a play-action fake. Quentin moved back four steps then turned and stood tall, looking for an open receiver.

Per-Ah-Yet ripped through the line and moved forward like a 560-pound, four-armed assassin. Quentin stepped up in the pocket and scrambled to the left to easily avoid the rush — or so he thought. A Human defensive tackle would have slipped by, momentum carrying him past as Quentin bounced forward toward the line. But Per-Ah-Yet wasn't Human. The Ki stopped on a dime and turned as his body contracted like an accordion. He expanded suddenly and violently, driving toward Quentin, long body trailing behind like a snake. Per's arms reached out much faster — and longer — than Quentin could have expected in his split-second decision to scramble. The long, thick, spider-like arms flashed out and hauled him in, lifting him off the ground, then driving him to the turf under all of Per-Ah-Yet's weight and momentum. Quentin hit the ground hard. His body armor protected him from cuts and joint injuries but couldn't do much to guard him from the concussive force of a 560-pound defensive lineman slamming him to the ground.

He suffered a second or two of confused blackness. He didn't know where he was. His brain couldn't process the situation — he'd scrambled like that hundreds of times in his short career, moving past defensive tackles as if they were statues, leaving them in awe of his speed and athleticism. No one caught him from behind. *No one.* He'd been almost ten yards from this Ki, a huge cushion, and the lineman knocked the living tar out of him.

Suddenly, Quentin recognized that feeling in his stomach — fear. The same feeling that ran through his mind and body for every punch-in and punch-out. The same fear he'd felt as a small boy, when the Holy Women that ran the orphanage had told stories about the nightmarish Ki, how they ate Humans, how they came in the night to snatch away bad little boys. He hadn't recognized it because he'd never before felt that emotion on a football field. Now the twelve-foot-long, multi-armed boogey-creature from his childhood nightmares wasn't just real, it was *on* him, *smothering* him.

"Get off me!" Quentin shouted as he tried to scramble out from under Per-Ah-Yet. The Ki's four-jointed arms grabbed Quentin's helmet and held it tight as he moved his face close enough to push against Quentin's facemask. Two of the five black eyespots stared into Quentin's eyes. Per-Ah-Yet's hexagonal mouth opened to expose the triangular black teeth.

"Grissach hadillit ai ai," it hissed, the sound from his worm-like vocal tubes muffled by the curving black helmet.

Quentin didn't understand the alien's words. Per-Ah-Yet pushed off him, heavily, and moved back to the defensive huddle.

Yassoud reached down to help Quentin up.

"He doesn't like you very much," Yassoud said.

"What did he say?"

"He said something to the effect that you'd look good roasting on a spit at his family picnic."

Quentin stood, his body emitting a dull throb of complaint. Defensive players weren't supposed to hit quarterbacks, not in practice. He'd just been leveled, and nobody seemed to care. Hokor, for one, wasn't saying anything. Quentin nodded. Now, he understood. Oh, yeah, he finally *got it*. This wasn't just a mind-game, he really wasn't going to start. No coach let the defense hit a starting QB.

He was just a rookie, and that meant he was fair game.

It was going to be a long day.

AT THE END of practice, Hokor gathered the team in the orange end zone. They circled around their little coach in his little cart, fifty tired and bruised players that looked like they'd just been through a battle.

"Good practice today," Hokor said. "We have only one more practice before we open the season. I know that is hard on you rookies, but most of you won't see much playing time. That is the nature of the league's schedule, and there is nothing we can do about it. Tomorrow's practice is a non-contact run-through."

Quentin thought the term "run-through" was a funny concept because he'd been hit so many times he could hardly walk, let alone run. The first-string defense had had a field day with him, blitzing every down, throwing stunts and overloads and everything else they could think of. The second-string defenders hadn't been any easier, especially Mum-O-Killowe, who attacked every play like he was seeking vengeance on someone who'd killed his family. The rookie Ki lineman had also delivered the biggest hit of the day — a cheap shot, a full two seconds after Quentin had thrown the ball.

He wasn't going to be the starter, his battered body told him that as clearly as if Hokor had spelled it out on paper. He'd played poorly — again — throwing three interceptions on thirty plays. He'd also thrown two touchdowns and gone 5-of-13 overall. But *three* interceptions! It was the freakin' speed of the game, he just couldn't get used to it. The defense came at him so much faster than he'd ever seen, and when he threw the ball, the Sklorno defensive backs broke on it like they'd been reading his mind.

He was third string. And right now, that's where he belonged.

"Prepare well for tomorrow's practice," Hokor said. "You are dismissed."

As the players walked off the field, Hokor's cart descended and landed in front of Quentin.

"Barnes, you are throwing behind your receivers. You've got to adjust your throws, and you've got to start getting the ball higher in the air when throwing to wide receivers. Do you forget that Sklorno can jump to catch the ball?"

"No, Coach … well, yeah, I do forget that sometimes."

"Well stop forgetting. If Pine goes down against the Wallcrawlers you're not ready to come in."

"Coach, I'm *ready*." The words were out of his mouth before he could think about it, but they rang hollow even to his own ears. "All I need is more reps, I'm getting the hang of things."

"Are you? Fine, then tell me who is the primary cornerback for the Wallcrawlers."

"Bangkok," Quentin said. He was exhausted and didn't want to play this ridiculous trivia game, but he would answer the questions asked of him. "Three-year veteran, Wallcrawlers MVP last year, started for the last two years, eleven interceptions last year."

"So with eleven interceptions, do we throw to her side of the field?"

"Not if we can help it," Quentin said.

"So if we don't throw at her, who is the strong safety?"

"Marlette. Five-year starter. Has lost an estimated five inches on her vertical leap since leg surgery at the end of last season. Throw high and deep on post patterns."

Hokor's pedipalps quivered lightly. "Good. Say it's third-and-seventeen. The nickel back comes in — who are you facing?"

Quentin started to answer, then had to stop and think. Nickel back for the Wallcrawlers ... who did they bring in for passing situations?

"Oshkosh!" Quentin said quickly when the name jumped into his head.

"And what's her weakness?"

"She ... she ..." Quentin tried to remember the one obscure fact about Oshkosh that could impact a game, but his tired mind came up with nothing.

"She has fused chitin plates near her hips," Hokor said. "They're too near her nervous center for anyone to operate safely. The fused plates greatly limit her ability to turn in mid-air, so if you throw to her area, you throw *behind* her, where she can't turn to get the ball. Your receivers know this already, and so should you. Now, think about that while you start running."

Quentin's head dropped. He was *exhausted*. And he had to run again?

"Hold on, Barnes," Hokor said. The diminutive alien turned and called through the cart's loudspeakers.

"Mum-O-Killowe!" Hokor shouted a few more syllables, all of which were pure gibberish to Quentin. The giant rookie lineman turned and scuttled over. He stopped three feet from Quentin. The Ki's black eyes burned into him in an expression of pure hatred (at least Quentin *wanted* to think it was hatred and not the emotion he suspected it might actually be, which was *hunger*). Hokor barked a few more syllables. Mum-O-Killowe suddenly roared and reared up on his last set of legs, briefly making him a ten-foot-tall, arm-waving monster.

Hokor, obviously unimpressed, simply pointed to the ground. Mum-O-Killowe dropped back down to six legs and fell quiet.

"I have told Mum-O-Killowe he is to be punished for his late hit. Such undisciplined play could have injured you, and someday you could be a valuable component of this team. Therefore, he will run with you until I am tired of thinking about it."

Quentin stared, dumbfounded, at his tiny coach. This thing wanted to kill him, and Hokor wanted the two of them to run laps like workout buddies?

"You've got to be kidding me, Coach," Quentin said. "This guy will come after me as soon as we're alone. He's already tried twice."

"Then you'd better learn to communicate with him, and fast. He is, after all, your teammate."

Hokor waddled to his cart, hopped in and flew off, leaving Quentin and Mum-O-Killowe staring at each other. Quentin shook his head and started to run but was careful to keep an eye on the young Ki. Mum-O-Killowe followed suit and ran alongside, staring at Quentin with his unblinking black spider eyes.

FIFTY-THREE LAPS later, Hokor apparently got tired of thinking about it. He called over the practice field's sound system, sending the two rookies to their respective locker rooms. They'd managed to run laps without an incident, to Quentin's surprise.

He pulled off his drenched uniform, each motion an exercise in ache. He was so soaked he wondered if even the plastic parts of his pads were sweat-logged. Quentin walked to a mirror and stared at himself — he already had discoloring bruises covering most of his right shoulder and chest, as well as darkening spots on both legs. *Bruises.* He hadn't had any bruises since his rookie season in the PNFL. That was the last time anyone laid a solid hit on him.

The locker room, of course, was empty except for Messal the Efficient, who busily gathered up Quentin's clothes and pads.

"Which way is the shower?" Quentin asked. Messal scrambled to open the first of a row of doors built into the wall.

Quentin sighed heavily — another nannite shower. It just wasn't what he needed.

"Don't you guys have a water shower here?"

Messal nodded immediately. "Yes, sir, we do."

Quentin felt a wave of relief wash over him. "Well, show me where it is."

Messal nodded again and started walking, Quentin followed as quickly as his exhausted and battered body would allow.

"If you'll follow me to the Ki locker room, sir," Messal said. "I will be happy to take you there."

Quentin stopped dead in his tracks. "The Ki locker room? Are you kidding me?"

Messal nodded. "Oh, no, sir. The Ki prefer running water to nannite cleansing."

"Well, so do some Humans!"

Messal nodded again. "No, sir, Humans prefer nannite cleansing."

"Not *this* Human, pal."

The nod, Quentin realized, was a gesture of subservience, not agreement. "Yes, sir, of course. I will take you to the water shower."

"Isn't there one in this locker room?"

Nod. "No, sir. It is in the Ki locker room. I will happily take you there so that you are satisfied with my service."

Quentin hung his head. He was bruised, beaten and exhausted, but he wasn't *that* tired. He waved Messal away and dragged himself to the nannite shower.

HE SAT IN HIS ROOM, marveling at how much a body could hurt after just one practice. It wasn't enough to stop him from playing. Nothing hurt that much. But it sure wasn't a walk in the park, either. Quentin's fingers deftly worked game controls as he guided his players around the holotank. Games were a good way to get his mind off of practice — he didn't know who "Madden" was, but "Madden 2683" was the best football sim he'd ever played. His To Pirates were up 22-16 over the Jupiter Jacks in a re-match of Galaxy Bowl XXIV.

His door-buzzer rang.

[MITCHELL FAYED IS AT YOUR DOOR]

Quentin hit pause and limped to the door. Fayed stood there, all 6-foot-9-inch, 350 granite-block pounds of him.

"Good evening, Quentin."

Quentin just nodded.

"Why are you not at second meal?"

Quentin shrugged. "Just wanted to relax after practice."

"You do not make friends easily with the rest of the team."

Quentin didn't know what to say. It was a statement, not a question.

"It does not matter," Fayed said. "I came to say something to you."

Fayed paused, as if waiting for permission.

"Well, go ahead," Quentin said.

"I have been in Tier Two for seven years now. Three with the Citadel Aquanauts and four with the Krakens. I have worked all my life to reach Tier One. That is all I want."

Quentin nodded.

"I came here to tell you that," Fayed said. "I hope reaching Tier One is as important to you as it is to me. If you should take over the quarterback position, I will support you. I think you have talent. I want you to be strong in these first few weeks. I suspect you have not been hit like this before?"

Quentin shrugged. "There were some big hits in the PNFL."

"And none of them reached you," Fayed said. "I have watched holos of your games. You are new to this level of hitting. And it will get worse during the games. Far worse."

Quentin tried to imagine how he could be hit any harder. Maybe if he crashed a hoversled into a brick wall at 180 miles per hour. Maybe.

"You get used to it," Fayed said. "You have a big, strong body, like me. I have watched you. You can take the hits. You may not know it yet, but you can take the hits. Be strong. Keep working hard, and good things will come."

Fayed then nodded once, turned and walked away.

Quentin stared out the door for a few seconds, then returned to his game. Did Fayed want something from him? Why was he being so nice? He didn't know what to make of the guy. Hell, he didn't know what to make of any of his teammates. But ... did Mitchell "The Machine" Fayed believe in him? Quentin shook his head. This had to be something else. Fayed had to have some kind of motive for this. Couldn't trust him. Couldn't trust anyone on this team. A voice in the back of his head reminded him he hadn't trusted anyone on the Raiders, either. Hadn't trusted anyone in a long, long time.

He picked up the controller, trying to ignore the pangs of loneliness as he focused on making his To Pirates will Galaxy Bowl XXIV.

BOOK THREE:
THE REGULAR SEASON

GAME ONE: Woo Wallcrawlers (0-0) at the Ionath Krakens (0-0)

An hour before the game, the Humans started dressing. The stadium was already mostly full. Even three stories below the stands, inside the locker room's thick walls, they heard the crowd's roar.

Music pumped from Yassoud's locker. He loved scrag music: loud, boisterous, boasting rhymes produced from the downtrodden culture of Rodina. Several people had asked Yassoud to turn it down, but John Tweedy liked the music, so nobody pressed the point.

Quentin sat on the bench, already dressed, his thoughts focused on the game ahead. His first Upper Tier game. He barely noticed his teammates or the music. He didn't come out of it until he felt someone near, staring at him. Quentin looked up and saw Don Pine only a few feet away. Quentin's eyes narrowed to hateful slits.

"What do you want, Pine?"

Pine shrugged. "Nothing."

"So go stare at someone else's booty."

"Kid, you need to relax."

"I really didn't appreciate your joke back on the landing platform."

"What joke? What are you talking about?"

"Denver. You had Denver come up to me — in front of everyone — and ask if I needed help with my passing."

Pine blinked a few times. "You thought that was a joke?"

"Not a very funny one," Quentin said. "You'll get yours."

Pine shook his head in amazement, then sighed. "Well, if you get in today, kid, good luck."

He turned and walked away. Quentin didn't return the sentiment.

THE KRAKENS PLAYERS GATHERED in the tunnel that led to the field.

The announcer said something in Quyth, then repeated it in Human: "Here is the visiting team, the WooooooOOOO Wallcrawlers!"

A scraping sound filled the stadium, like a million carpenters sanding a million rough boards. Quentin pressed his hands to the ear-holes of his helmet. He turned to Yitzhak. "What the *hell* is that?"

"Fur-scraping," Yitzhak said, leaning into Quentin and shouting so he could be heard over the horrible noise. "Workers scrape the bristly fur on their forearms together — it's kind of like a Human booing."

The Krakens packed tightly into the small space. Clean orange-and-black jerseys covered the bodies and armor of Human, HeavyG, Sklorno, Ki and Quyth Warrior. No one pushed, no one shoved, no one threatened. The very walls vibrated with the growing roar of the capacity 185,000-being crowd. Intangible electricity filled the air, making the skin on the back of Quentin's neck tingle with excitement.

Racial hatred disappeared. That wasn't quite true — it didn't disappear as much as it transformed, mutated, moving from alien teammates to the unified body of the enemy: the Woo Wallcrawlers. The Krakens players were no longer individual species, no longer individual beings with petty biases and hatreds and arguments.

They were warriors.

Headed to battle.

The announcer said something in Quyth, and the crowd erupted with the roar of the High One himself. The unified army of orange-and-black surged forward. The announcer repeated the call, this time in Human.

"Beings of all races, let's hear it for, *your*, Ionath, KRAAAAAA-KENNNNNNNS!"

Quentin found himself carried along in a wave of teammates. This was nothing like it had been on Micovi, where the starters were introduced one at a time, and the largest crowd he'd ever played before amounted to 24,500.

The team sprinted out through the tunnel mouth into the perfect daylight of Ionath Stadium. Quentin had never seen such a concentration of life. The crowd's roar hit like a physical, concussive force. At the sidelines, the Krakens gathered in a tight circle. Quentin found himself packed in: shoulder to shoulder against Milford on his right, pressed next to Mum-O-Killowe on his left and Killik the Unworthy behind him. In front of them all, at the center of the circle: Donald Pine.

"This is it," Pine said. He wasn't yelling, yet his words carried loudly despite the crowd's massive volume. "This is what we've worked for. The road to Tier One starts right here, right now."

His voice rang with authority and command. All around him, Quentin felt Krakens players leaning in toward Pine. The veteran quarterback radiated calm and utter confidence. Creterakian civilians dressed in tiny orange-and-black uniforms flittered about, translating Pine's words into Ki.

"We've got to go out there and establish ourselves *right now*," Pine said. "No waiting. They won the toss. Defense, I want the ball back. Offense, I want to score on our first drive. Then I want to score on our second drive. Then I want to score on our third drive. No letting up."

He raised his fist and the circle tightened in a convulsive surge. Hands, pedipalps, chitinous arms and raspers reached out to Pine, who stood in the center of it all like a battlefield hero. Quentin found, to his surprise, that he instinctively reached out his own hand as well — but he stopped himself only a few inches from the veteran quarterback, pretending that he couldn't quite reach.

Every player let out a single, deep, guttural grunt that transcended language, then the circle broke apart, the players gathering in groups: kickoff team, defense, offense and second-stringers. Across the field, the Woo Wallcrawlers broke from their own huddle. They wore pinkish leg armor and white jerseys with letters and numbers in light-blue rimmed by purple. Each jersey had the word "'Crawlers" stretched across the chest above their number. A stylized purple creature on the right shoulder of each jersey spread forth long tentacles: two down the chest, two down the back and two down the right arm (or arms, in the case of the Ki).

Five graceful, boneless Harrah floated onto the field. Their soft wings undulated in wave-like patterns, carrying them smoothly forward. They wore black-and-white striped jerseys custom fitted to their flat bodies. Quentin suddenly understood why the Harrah made great refs — they could fly up to monitor the twenty-foot-high, mid-air battles between Sklorno receivers and defensive backs. A grounded ref could never accurately judge interference.

Pine walked up next to Quentin. He saw the younger QB looking at the refs.

"Never seen flying refs before?"

Quentin shook his head. "No, but it's a great idea."

"Stupid zebes, they hate the Krakens. We always get crap calls."

"What's a *zebe*?"

"That's what they call refs."

"But what is it?"

"I think it's short for *zebra*."

"What's a zebra?"

Pine shrugged as he put on his helmet. "Beats me. Some animal with black and white stripes, I guess. From Satirli 6, I think."

The Krakens lined up for the kickoff. The crowd of 185,000

started beating their feet in place. Quentin looked at the stands behind him: the crowd was mostly Quyth, with Workers filling the higher rows and upper decks. Plenty of Humans, Quyth Warriors and Quyth Leaders filled the lower seats. He spotted the distinctive shape of many Sklorno females in the stands, most of whom wore replica Krakens jerseys with number 80, Hawick's number.

Special sections of the stands were packed with the bouncing, one-foot-diameter fuzzy balls that he now knew were Sklorno males. These sections were enclosed in clear crystametal. The males bounced up and down inside — there had to be a thousand of them in each enclosure, moving so fast he could barely make out individuals. Quentin wondered why, when looking at a stadium packed with a half-dozen races, the Sklorno males were segregated.

Quentin nudged Yitzhak. "Why are the Sklorno males in that cage?"

"The bedbugs? Because they get so turned on watching the females that they will rush the field and try to mate with them."

Quentin grimaced. "What? Really?"

"Oh, sure. They're horny little buggers. Watch out if you're around any of our receivers or DBs in public. The little scumbags lose it and will just start humping them. That's why the females wear full-body clothing in public; otherwise, the bedbugs might impregnate them."

The crowd's foot-pounding picked up in intensity and was joined by a low "oohhhhh" that quickly increased in pitch and volume. Quentin turned in time to see the kicker's foot slam into the ball exactly at the moment the crowd's "ohhh" turned into a sustained "ahhh!" of excitement. The ball sailed through the air as the Krakens' kickoff team pounded down the field.

Quentin saw Yassoud rushing downfield, that murderous look on his face. Denver and Milford were out there as well, sprinting like living missiles, pulling ahead of their teammates. A line of Human and Quyth Warrior Wallcrawlers formed a wedge and drove upfield, followed by a Sklorno carrying the brown ball. Denver and Milford launched themselves high into the air, arching over

the Wallcrawler wedge. Two pink-and-white clad Sklorno players shot through the air to meet them: one picked off Denver in
mid-air, and they fell in a heap. Milford twisted, and her defender sailed past. She landed on her feet as Yassoud and the other
Krakens smashed into the Wallcrawler wedge. Milford sprang forward — the Wallcrawler ball carrier tried to dodge, but Milford
brought her down at the 'Crawlers' fifteen-yard line.

The crowd roared so loudly that Quentin put his hands to his
helmet's ear-holes. He heard some kind of high-pitched screeching
from the stands and looked back — the Sklorno males bounced
maddeningly in their enclosures, hitting the crystametal walls so
hard they had to be injuring themselves.

John Tweedy led the defense onto the field. I AM THE BRINGER
OF DEATH scrolled across his face. The 'Crawlers offense came out
and huddled up, led by quarterback Kelley Moussay-Ed. Warburg
walked up and stood next to Quentin.

"Kelley's in for a long day," Warburg said. "This run-and-
shoot garbage doesn't work against Michnik and Khomeni."

Moussay-Ed snapped the ball and handed off to running back
Copu Soggang, who found nothing at the line. He cut right, but
Khomeni reached out his thick arms and dragged the runner to the
ground for no gain.

The 'Crawlers next ran a short out pass, good for three yards
before Berea leveled the receiver. On third-and-seven, Kelley
dropped back as four receivers snaked into the defensive backfield.
Michnik drove into the 'Crawlers' right tackle, then spun to the
inside and broke free. Moussay-Ed felt the pressure and threw the
ball away. The crowd roared in approval.

The defense ran off the field to congratulations and approv-
ing slaps from the offense and the second-stringers. The 'Crawlers
punted. Richfield called for a fair catch, and the Krakens' offense
took to the field for the first time. Pine led the offense onto the
field. Warburg waited a few seconds before leisurely trotting to
join the huddle.

Quentin moved to stand next to Yassoud. "What's it like out
there?"

"It's unbelievable," Yassoud said, his grin once again firmly in place. "The crowd is unreal, there's so much *energy*. You'll see soon enough."

Quentin shrugged. "Hopefully, the old fart won't last long."

"You never know," Yassoud said, neither agreeing nor disagreeing with Quentin's hopes.

First-and-ten on the Krakens' 45. Pine wasted no time exploiting the 'Crawlers' slow secondary. He hit Hawick for a twelve-yard slant, then Kobayasho for a six-yard out, then a deep crossing pattern to Warburg. Warburg caught the ball in full stride and turned upfield, all 365 pounds of him moving at top speed. 'Crawler defensive backs Seoul and Onoway closed in on him. Warburg turned to slam into Seoul head-to-head, knocking the 280-pound Sklorno defensive player backward. Warburg stumbled from the contact, and Onoway brought him down for a 22-yard gain that gave the Krakens first-and-ten on the Wallcrawler fifteen. Warburg and Onoway got up, Seoul didn't.

The game paused as a Harrah doctor flew onto the field, trailed by a floating cart. The Harrah looked exactly like Doc, except this one's backpack was pink and light-blue instead of orange-and-black. The doctor looked at Seoul for a long minute, then pushed the cart over the Sklorno's prone form. A hundred tiny wires shot out of the cart's underside, wrapping around Seoul in a hundred different places. The cart rose about a foot, and Seoul's body rose with it, still in the exact same position she'd been in on the ground. The doctor flew off the field, toward the tunnel to the locker room, the cart zipping along behind.

With the wounded player removed, the teams lined up once again.

The 'Crawlers blitzed on the next play, and Pine calmly delivered a seven-yard slant to Scarborough. He dropped back once more, standing tall and taking his time. His offensive line gave great protection, and after five full seconds, Pine fired a tight spiral to Hawick for a touchdown.

The stadium shuddered from the crowd's roar. Fireworks exploded overhead. The entire sky seemed to turn a deep orange.

Quentin ducked involuntarily, as if from the shadow of some giant bird flying close overhead.

"Relax, that's just the dome," Yassoud said. "They turn the whole thing orange when we score a touchdown."

The color blinked away, and the sky was once again clear and bright. Pine and the receivers ran off the field as the kicking team came on for the extra point.

"Oh, yep," Yassoud said. "He *is* an old fart. Five-for-five and a TD on the first drive. Man, we should get him a wheelchair and some oxygen before he collapses."

"Screw you," Quentin said. Yassoud just laughed.

The defense continued to pound the Wallcrawlers throughout the first half, shutting down Moussay-Ed. Michnik sacked him twice, and Tweedy got to him once with a devastating hit on a linebacker blitz.

Pine made good on his pregame plans, guiding the Krakens to scores on their next two drives. At the half, the Krakens were up 24-7. Pine added one more touchdown for good measure in the third quarter, a 32-yard strike to Scarborough. With each completion, Quentin grew angrier. He'd settled into his new-found role as a sideline spectator when, late in the fourth quarter, he heard Hokor's distinctive bark.

"Barnes!" the coach called. "Next series, you're in!"

Quentin stared at his coach, then back at the field. He was going in *before* Yitzhak. Was he second-string, then? Quentin's pulse beat double-time as he watched the Krakens' defense working against the 'Crawlers. Moussay-Ed hadn't made it past the third quarter before the 'Crawlers' coach pulled him. His replacement, second-year player Aniruddha Smith, didn't fare much better. Smith completed a short hook for a first down at the Krakens' 32.

"Come on, defense," Quentin said through gritted teeth. He looked up at the clock — 1:12 left to play.

He should have been able to predict what happened next — Tweedy showed blitz but slid into coverage as Smith dropped back. Mum-O-Killowe, who'd already notched one sack, furiously drove his opposing lineman back as he reached for

Smith. Smith dodged to the right, feeling the pressure. He threw a quick crossing pattern to a seemingly open tight end. Tweedy was playing his lame-duck act — he broke on the ball with a speed he hadn't shown the entire game and picked off the pass. The crowd roared in approval. As Tweedy & Co. came off the field, Quentin sprinted on, so excited he could barely think.

He stood in front of the huddle, a mix of first-string linemen and second-string skill players. Yassoud looked back at him, grinning. Denver and Milford were there, their armored eyestalks twitching in anticipation.

Quentin's head-up display activated automatically. Hokor's yellow and black, one-eyed face appeared, lifelike and right in front of Quentin's facemask.

"Base-block dive right, Barnes," Hokor said. "Keep it simple and hang onto the ball."

Quentin relayed the play to the Krakens. He broke the huddle and walked to the line. That feeling was back in his stomach again, the queasy feeling, the one he'd never known before that first full-contact practice two days earlier. His five Ki linemen looked like a giant wall of muscle. Yet if they were a wall, a fortress, beyond them were three Ki battering rams in white jerseys, waiting to blast through the offensive line and tear into him. Outside of them, two gigantic Human defensive ends, obviously HeavyG natives, so big they dwarfed the PNFL's biggest players. The first play, at least, he wouldn't have to worry about the front five.

Quentin squatted, left foot forward, right foot back, as he reached his hands under Bud-O-Shwek. He pressed his left hand up, but Bud felt wet. Quentin pulled his hands back out — black wetness smeared the back of his left hand. Bud was bleeding. Should he call a time-out? He quickly looked at his linemen — black blood smeared the orange numbers on their black jerseys, most of which were ripped in one place or another. Some of their arms were up and ready to block, while a few arms hung limp and lifeless, broken. Yet none of the Ki had come out of the game.

"Quentin, let's go!" Yassoud shouted from behind him. Quentin flashed a glance at the play clock — 1:05 and counting. He quickly wiped his hands on his jersey, then squatted and thrust his hands under Bud-O-Shwek.

"Blue, thirty-two!" Quentin called. "Blue, thirty-two, HUT-HUT!"

Bud-O-Shwek snapped the ball. Quentin felt it slap into his hands. He pulled it to his stomach and turned as he stepped back. Yassoud surged forward, back of his right hand on his chest, elbow high, his left hand across his stomach. Quentin reached the ball out and Yassoud slammed his arms together, taking the handoff and driving forward. He found no opening at the line, so he cut right. Vu-Ko-Will, the Krakens' right tackle, drove his defender backward. With nowhere else to go, Yassoud put his head down and followed Vu-Ko-Will. Defenders swarmed on him for a gain of only three.

The Krakens huddled. The clocked ticked past 1:00 and kept rolling.

"Screen pass," Hokor said. "X-Left."

Quentin looked to the sidelines and tapped the "transmit" button on his right wrist. "Come on, Coach. Their secondary is soft, let me go deep."

Quentin saw the little holographic of Hokor's yellow fur suddenly stand on end.

"Barnes, run the plays I call! Screen pass! X-Left."

Quentin nodded, turned to the huddle and called the play. He lined up again, noticing suddenly that the butterflies were worse than before. His stomach seemed to shrink, reducing itself to half-size, then quarter-size. And now he had to pee. Quite badly.

"Red ... sixteen! Red, *sixteen*! Hut-hut, HUT!"

The line clashed together once again. Quentin dropped back, holding the ball up by his ear, ready to pass. Suddenly the line parted, and the white-jersied battering rams surged forward, multi-jointed legs pumping and multi-jointed arms quivering. The monsters roared with unbridled fury as they charged toward him. He backpedaled as if he was avoiding the rush — just before the Ki defenders reached him, he turned and threw the ball to Yassoud in the flat. Kill-O-Yowet and Sho-Do-Thikit, the left tackle and left

guard, respectively, had released their blocks and moved to the flat
to block for Yassoud.

Yassoud caught the pass, but Quentin didn't see the results of
the play — three huge bodies bore down on him, driving him to
the ground. Almost a ton of defensive linemen smashed into him
as he hit the turf. His armor resisted most of the impact, but not
all. His lungs felt compressed, like he couldn't draw a full breath,
and he couldn't move a muscle.

Quentin heard a whistle, but the weight remained. He felt
the Ki's hot breath on his face and looked up into the hexagonal
mouth and sharp teeth. The mouth flexed as the Ki spoke in its
guttural tongue.

"Grissach hadillit eo."

"Heard it all before, loser," Quentin grunted out.

The huge creature shifted its weight, and suddenly Quentin felt
the tip of a chitinous arm reaching into his helmet. The arm moved
quickly, and he felt a searing pain across his cheek. More whistles
sounded, and the lineman pushed off him.

Quentin stood as he felt a hot wetness spread across his cheek.
He touched it, and his fingers came away streaked in his own
blood.

The butterflies in his stomach dried up and crumbled to dust.

Blossoming rage took their place.

The Krakens started to huddle up, but Quentin walked past
them, shouldering roughly past his own Ki linemen.

"You want to play with *me*?" Quentin shouted, pointed his
finger at the back of the Ki lineman who'd cut him. The name on
the back of the jersey read "Yag-Ah-Latis." The unblinking black
eyespots on the back of its head saw Quentin, of course. Yag-Ah-
Latis turned to face him.

"You want to play with me, you *salamander*?"

Yag-Ah-Latis simply put his bloody hand to his hexagonal
mouth. A blackish tongue slithered out and licked the red blood
clean.

Out of the corner of his eye, he saw yellow flags fly. Harrah
officials in their black-and-white striped jerseys flew between

Quentin and the Ki lineman. Quentin was about to shove them away and go after Yag-Ah-Latis when strong arms wrapped around his chest.

"Easy, kid," Yassoud said as he tried to hold Quentin back. "Come on now."

Quentin kept pointing and kept shouting. "You want to do that bush-league garbage with me?"

Another flag flew. Three black-and-white jerseys fluttered in front of him, helping to holding him back. A distant part of Quentin's rage-stoked brain found it interesting that a flying creature could display such considerable strength. A ref pushed him, and he almost fell backward. Quentin shoulder-tossed Yassoud, sending the rookie running-back sprawling on the ground, then reared back to hit the ref that pushed him. Hokor's voice in his ear screamed loud enough to make him wince.

"Barnes, no! You hit a ref, you're suspended for the season!"

The coach's words snapped Quentin out of his one-track intentions. A season-long suspension? Hell, nothing was worth that. He helped Yassoud up and walked back to the huddle, casting glances over his shoulder at Yag-Ah-Latis as he did.

"Barnes, that little act cost us fifteen yards," Hokor growled in his earpiece. "Now, take a knee and run out the clock."

Without looking at the sideline, Quentin reached down to his belt and calmly turned off his receiver. He looked up at the scoreboard and assessed the situation: 32 seconds to play, first-and-25 on the Krakens' 45.

As Quentin reached the huddle, he glared at his Ki linemen. Their eyespots stared back at him seemingly impassive. They didn't seem bothered in the least that their quarterback had just been cut by an opposing lineman.

"Hey," Yassoud said. "Call a time-out, chief, you're bleeding pretty bad."

"Shut up," Quentin growled. "No talking in my huddle. X-flash left, double deep. Denver and Milford, get deep fast and get open."

The two Sklorno started to quiver with excitement.

"Knock it off!" Quentin barked. "You want the whole stadium to know what we're doing?" The two receivers instantly fell stock-still.

"Shouldn't we just take a knee?" Yassoud asked.

Quentin reached out and grabbed Yassoud's facemask, twisting it and pulling his head forward. "*My* huddle. You talk one more time and you're out, got it?"

Yassoud, surprised and wide-eyed, nodded once.

Quentin let him go

"Line up like we're showing a QB kneel. As soon as we get to the line, Denver and Milford sprint to X-flash. Go on first sound, ready?"

"Break!" the players called in unison.

Quentin and the others jogged to the line. Denver and Milford lined up outside the left and right tight ends, respectively, then just as the defense settled in for the predictable situation, the Sklorno receivers sprinted out along the line of scrimmage.

Quentin saw Hokor's fur ruffle once more. The coach said something into his mouthpiece, but Quentin didn't hear it. Just as Hokor started to signal for a time-out, Quentin shouted "hut!" and the ball hit his hands. He dropped back five steps and planted, looking downfield. The crowd roared as Denver sprinted down the sideline, then angled toward the center of the field. Jacobina, the 'Crawlers' cornerback, matched Denver step-for-step with blanket coverage.

He suddenly realized that Mitchell Fayed had been right: this was nothing like practice. The Ki defensive tackles drove hard against the offensive linemen, roaring and punching and tearing. The offensive linemen gave as good as they got, backing up as they did, throwing punches and tearing at half-shredded jerseys. Huge bodies smashed against one another, flesh shuddering in concussive waves with each impact. Droplets of black blood flew in all directions as the pocket formed around Quentin — he stood at the eye of a storm of predatorial violence, where he was the prey.

Yag-Ah-Latis, his white jersey streaked with black, tried a spin move — it was amazing to see something so big move so fast, show such agility. Kill-O-Yowet managed to counter the spin move and stayed in front of the attacking lineman. The left defensive end had dropped into pass coverage, but the right end came with all his HeavyG force. The 535-pound monstrous Human drove forward, powered by thighs that looked like beer kegs, his thick arms pushing and pulling at Vu-Ko-Will, the Krakens' right tackle. As big as Vu-Ko-Will was, it was all he could do to stay in front of the attacking beast in a football uniform.

They didn't just want to tackle him, they wanted to *kill* him. For the first time since his rookie season in the PNFL, Quentin Barnes felt small.

Quentin waited, feeling the defensive pressure coming for him. His mind operated like a multi-processing machine, simultaneously measuring a hundred different inputs.

He let the ball fly, and it arced through the air. At first he thought he'd thrown a bit too far, and a bit too high, but Denver and Jacobina turned on the jets and burned downfield. Fifty yards downfield, Denver and her defender sprang high into the air — but Denver jumped higher. Fifteen feet up, Denver reached out and snagged the perfectly thrown ball. Her momentum carried her into the end zone — she landed for a touchdown.

The crowd volume reached deafening levels. Quentin knelt and picked up a few blades of Iomatt, torn up by the constant churning cleats. He held the circular blades to his nose and sniffed — smelled like cinnamon. He stood, then pointed straight at Yag-Ah-Latis.

"That touchdown was for *you*, baby!" Quentin shouted. "Now go translate this!" He grabbed his crotch and shook it three times. Yag-Ah-Latis' black eyespots shrunk to tiny pinholes, and he started to charge forward. This time the Harrah officials were ready. Flags flew again as four of them blocked Yag-Ah-Latis from coming after Quentin. The massive lineman could have effortlessly knocked the Harrah aside, but Yag-Ah-Latis wanted to sit out the season no more than Quentin did.

The offense ran off the field as the kicking team came on. Hokor's fur stood on end. "What was *that*? I told you to take a knee!"

Quentin shrugged. "Transmitter was broken, so I called a play."

Hokor's one eye stared hard at Quentin. "After the game I'll see you in my office, Barnes. Now, go get that cut fixed."

Quentin nodded, then smiled and walked to the bench.

Teammates thumped him on the helmet and shoulder pads. Pine approached and extended a hand. Quentin shook it before he realized what he was doing.

"Great pass," Pine said. Amazingly, he sounded genuinely happy, but Quentin knew the veteran was mocking him. Pine still had that grin on his face. "Perfectly timed for Denver's leaping ability."

"Thanks," Quentin said.

"How'd you know to throw it high and deep against Jacobina?"

"Well, I ... she can't do her maximum vertical when she's running full ..." Quentin's voice trailed off, a recent practice memory jumping into his head.

"Who's the starting cornerback for the Wallcrawlers?" Hokor had asked him.

"Jacobina. Great vertical leap, but not very strong and easily blocked. Two-year vet."

"What's her weakness?"

"Trouble reaching maximum vertical leap during a full sprint."

"How do you beat her?"

"Throw deep and high, make the receiver have to really sprint and jump to make the catch. Jacobina usually can't match the jump if the ball is thrown correctly."

Pine's grin widened, just a bit more, as recognition washed across Quentin's face.

"Maybe Hokor's instructions aren't 'busy work' after all, eh, rookie?"

Quentin looked away. Pine was right, and he didn't want to deal with the veteran's smugness.

A smiling Yitzhak came up and pounded Quentin on the shoulder pad. "Great throw! That's showing them!"

Doc floated over, his vocal processor kicking out more volume than usual to compensate for the crowd's incessant noise.

"That's a nasty cut, Quentin," Doc said. "Let's get to work on it."

Doc grabbed Quentin's arm and pulled him into one of the

med-bays behind the bench. Quentin's cleats *clacked* as he moved
from the soft field to the bay's metal-grate floor. Doc reached into
a drawer and pulled out a spray can and something wrapped in a
sealed plastic wrap. "First let's clean that up. Ki claws can produce
a nasty infection in Humans. Now, hold your breath. This will
sting just a bit."

Quentin took in a deep breath and held it as Doc sprayed the
can's contents on his cheek. The mist felt cool on his cheek.

"That didn't sting at all, Doc."

"I wasn't talking about the antiseptic," Doc said, and with one
smooth motion ripped open the plastic pouch and put a blue, wet,
rectangular cloth on Quentin's cheek. Pain leapt up immediately,
as if someone had placed a branding iron on his cheek. He stood
up with a start and pushed Doc away.

"High One, what the hell is *that*?" Quentin reached up to pull
the cloth away, but Doc's ribbon-like tentacle slapped his hand.

"Don't be a baby," Doc said. "That's nano-knit. It burns because nanocytes are ripping open a few cells to read your DNA."

The burning intensified. Quentin felt tears welling up in his
eyes. "Couldn't you just *stitch* the damn thing?"

Doc shuddered, a ripple that coursed through his boneless
body. "Don't insult me, Quentin. You're not in the barbarian lands
anymore."

Quentin danced in place, fighting to keep his hands off the
cloth, but already the burning feeling was subsiding.

"Has the burning ceased?"

Quentin nodded. A tingling sensation replaced the burning.

"The nanocytes have read your DNA to see exactly how your
skin is supposed to be. They are rebuilding the cut right now."

"How many of them are in there?"

"The patch contains roughly five hundred thousand."

"A half-million?"

"A trivial amount, I assure you. You would need ten times that
amount for muscle or ligament damage."

Quentin had never heard of such medical technology. And he
was receiving it on the sidelines of a football game. He could only

wonder just how advanced things were in an actual hospital. The Holy Men preached about the Nation's technical advancements, but most people knew the truth — that the Nation was decades behind rival systems like the Planetary Union and the League of Planets. Of course, he was in the GFL now, in the land of the big money, where no expense would be spared to keep oft-damaged players on the field. Still, he thought of the boy back on Micovi, the one he'd given his jersey to after the PNFL championship. Would this kind of treatment have helped that boy? Would it have saved his leg?

Doc reached out and removed the cloth. It was bloody and limp. He tossed it toward the bench, where it lay with other sideline debris like grass-stained tape, broken straps and broken buckles, torn jerseys and magni-cup rings.

"So what happens to the nanocytes now?"

"They'll run around, looking for more damaged skin, until they run out of energy."

"And then?"

"And then what? They stop working."

"But when do you take them out?"

"We don't do anything with them, Quentin. Your body will process them out like any other waste. Kidneys will filter them."

"So I'll pee them out?"

"That is correct. Now, if you'll excuse me, I must see what other injuries require my attention."

The game finished with the Krakens' defense on the field. Surprisingly, the crowd counted down the last ten seconds in English, and that grand football tradition sounded little different than it had back in the PNFL. Orange-and-black banners flew, colored streamers sailed, and fireworks blasted over the open stadium.

The Krakens, victorious, drifted in small groups off the field and into the tunnel. He saw Warburg and Seth Hanisek, the Wallcrawlers' stocky fullback and another Nationalite, praying at the 50-yard line. Quentin ignored them — he had always felt the High One had more important things to do than concern himself with football, and probably didn't listen to victory thanks.

He left the field, basking in the glow of his first GFL game. He hadn't played much, but he'd made the most of it: 2-of-2 for 80 yards and a TD. Hokor really had no choice now but to give him more playing time. Pine was great, but Quentin was the future, and now everybody knew it — the Krakens, their fans and *especially* Coach Hokor.

WALLCRAWLERS BOX SCORE

FINAL	1	2	3	4	T
Ionath	14	10	7	7	38
Woo	0	7	0	0	7

SCORING SUMMARY

1st QUARTER		ION	WOO
Ionath TD	Hawick 8-yard pass from Donald Pine (Arioch Morningstar kick)	7	0
Ionath TD	Hawick 22-yard pass from Donald Pine (Arioch Morningstar kick)	14	0

2nd QUARTER		ION	WOO
Ionath FG	Arioch Morningstar 32-yard kick	17	0
Woo TD	Copu Soggang 7-yard pass from Kelley Moussay-Ed (Frankie Darkness kick)	17	7
Ionath TD	Mitchell Fayed 12-yard run (Arioch Morningstar kick)	24	7

3rd QUARTER		ION	WOO
Ionath TD	Scarborough 32-yard pass from Donald Pine (Arioch Morningstar kick)	31	7

4th QUARTER		ION	WOO
Ionath TD	Denver 55-yard pass from Quentin Barnes (Arioch Morningstar kick)	38	7

TEAM STATISTICS	ION	WOO
First Downs	18	9
Third Down Efficiency	7-13	5-16
TOTAL NET YARDS	**442**	**193**
Total Plays	69	57
Average Gain Per Play	6.4	3.4
NET YARDS RUSHING	**136**	**72**
Rushes	31	25
Average Per Rush	4.4	2.9
NET YARDS PASSING	**306**	**116**
Pass Completion	28-38	16-32
Yards Per Pass	8.1	4.4
Times Sacked	0	5
Yards Lost To Sacks	0	26
Had Intercepted	0	3
PUNTS	**5**	**9**
Average Punt	39.6	36.0
PENALTIES	**4**	**7**
Penalty Yards	28	59
FUMBLES	**1**	**2**
Fumbles Lost	0	0
Time Of Possession	**36:01**	**23:59**

PASSING

KRAKENS	CMP	ATT	YDS	PCT	YPA	SACK	SYDS	TD	INT
Donald Pine	26	36	226	72.2	6.3	0	0	3	0
Quentin Barnes	2	2	80	100.0	40.0	0	0	1	0

WALLCRAWLERS	CMP	ATT	YDS	PCT	YPA	SACK	SYDS	TD	INT
Kelley Moussay-Ed	13	24	120	54.2	5.0	4	22	1	2
Aniruddia Smith	3	8	20	37.5	2.5	1	4	0	1

RUSHING

KRAKENS	ATT	YDS	AVG	LONG	TD	FUM
Mitchell Fayed	24	101	4.2	22	1	1
Paul Pierson	3	10	3.3	5	0	0
Yassoud Murphy	2	7	3.5	6	0	0
Tom Pareless	2	3	1.5	2	0	0

WALLCRAWLERS	ATT	YDS	AVG	LONG	TD	FUM
Copu Soggang	22	70	3.2	15	0	1
Braka the Beast	3	2	1.5	4	0	0

RECEIVING

KRAKENS	REC	YDS	AVG	LONG	TD	FUM
Hawick	8	92	11.5	22	2	0
Scarborough	6	47	7.8	32	1	0
Yotaro Kobayasho	5	26	5.2	18	0	0
Mezquitic	4	30	7.5	20	0	0
Rick Warburg	3	28	9.3	22	0	0
Denver	1	55	55.0	55	1	0
Yassoud Murphy	1	25	25.0	25	0	0
Mitchell Fayed	1	3	3.0	3	0	0

WALLCRAWLERS	REC	YDS	AVG	LONG	TD	FUM
Chatsworth	5	90	18.0	72	0	0
Eastwick	5	22	4.4	12	0	0
Copu Soggang	4	18	4.5	10	1	0
San Fernando	2	10	5.0	8	0	0

HE LOOKED AT his face in the mirror a dozen times in a dozen different ways, but he couldn't find any sign of that nasty cut. There was redness, like mild sunburn on the area where the bandage had been, but nothing else. Quentin tilted his head this way and that, pulled at his skin, amazed at what he didn't see.

John Tweedy walked by, dressed only in a towel. "Cut all gone, farm boy?"

Quentin looked at the bigger man and just nodded. YOU'RE A DUMB BACKWOODS CRACKER scrolled across Tweedy's forehead.

"You won't find the cut, you stupid hick, it's fixed," Tweedy said. He then put on a sarcastic, wide-eyed expression of wonder. "Oh, this here's some big magic, Quentin! Here in the big city, we fix people right up, like by magic! *Big magic* here!"

Quentin stared for a moment before he spoke. "What's your home planet, Tweedy?"

Tweedy pounded his chest three times. "Glory be to Thomas 3."

"Well, at least the Nation has something in common with Thomas 3."

"Oh? And what's that, rookie?"

"Based on your intelligence level, I gather Thomas 3 also has a major inbreeding problem."

Tweedy's sarcastic expression evaporated, replaced by a toothbared sneer. "You better watch your tongue, boy, or your butt is mine."

"Sorry, afraid I like women. I'm not your type."

Tweedy's right fist reared back, his taut muscles rippling under his skin. Quentin watched the hand and simultaneously watched Tweedy's eyes. The big man stepped forward and threw his hamsized fist, but Quentin moved so fast the punch might as well have been in slow motion. He stepped to the side, and the fist hit only empty air. Tweedy's momentum carried him forward a few awkward steps. In one smooth motion, Quentin reached out and snatched the towel from Tweedy's waist, holding one end in each hand: he pulled it tight then snapped his left hand forward. The towel shot out like a striking snake and snapped Tweedy's rear end — all of this before the big linebacker could even recover from his missed punch.

Tweedy stood straight up as he turned, his hands reaching back to cover his butt. His eyes grew wide with fury, and his lips curled back in a primitive snarl. Fists clenched, he took a step forward but stopped when Quentin held the towel tight once again, poised for another snap.

Tweedy pointed his finger at Quentin. "Put down that towel, you Purist piece of garbage, and we'll settle this right now."

"Sure thing, Johnny-boy," Quentin said. "Maybe this time I can snap Little Johnny right off your body." He twitched his shoulders as if to snap again, and the naked Tweedy took a hurried step back. Someone in the locker room started laughing.

"Barnes! Put that towel down!"

Quentin turned to see Hokor standing there, fur fluffed, his pedipalps trembling.

"Put it *down*."

Without looking, Quentin tossed the towel behind him. Tweedy caught it and wrapped it once again around his waist.

"In my office, now." Hokor stomped away, and Quentin followed.

Here we go, Quentin thought. *He saw how I play in a real game, and now, I'll get the talk about how he thinks I'm ready for more.*

Hokor's office was just off the central meeting room. Holo-frames lined the wall, showing Hokor with Krakens players as well as action shots of him on the sidelines of the D'Kow War Dogs, the Jupiter Jacks and the Chillich Spider-Bears. There were several pictures, the old-fashioned flat kind, showing Humans that Quentin didn't recognize. One had a brimmed, houndstooth-patterned hat pulled down almost over his eyes. He wore an antique suit and had Human players around him in crimson helmets with a white stripe and crimson jerseys with block white letters and numbers. Another showed a squat, smiling man in a long coat with thick black glasses and a buzz-cut. He was riding on the shoulders of two dirty, happy men in green uniforms with yellow helmets.

A football holo played in the center of the room: the Glory Warpigs playing host to the Krakens' next foe, the Grontak Hydras.

"How are the Hydras looking, Coach?" Quentin asked.

"They are my nightmare," Hokor said as he sat behind his desk. The desk was curved like half a circle, made of some hard plant material Quentin had never seen before. Yet, despite the alien wood in the alien city with the alien coach, Quentin couldn't help but think of Coach Graber, sitting behind his desk back on Micovi.

"They have great speed at receiver," Hokor said. "Their outside linebackers, Lokos the Bruised and Bilis the Destroyer, were All-GFL last year, and Wichita is without a doubt the best cornerback in Tier Two. She'll probably be able to shut Hawick down completely."

As the camera changed angles, a score flashed: Warpigs 22, Hydras 12.

"If they're so good, how come they're losing?"

Hokor stared for a moment before answering. "Barnes, the Hydras' score against the Warpigs doesn't matter. Nor does their record. Nor does it matter if the Hydras lose all their games. The only thing that matters is how they match up against *us*, and they match up very well indeed. Not that it matters to you."

"Of course, it matters to me, Coach. Why wouldn't it?"

"Because you're benched next week."

"*Benched*? Are you kidding me? For snapping John Tweedy on the butt?"

"I do not care about the silly bonding games you Human males play," Hokor said, his big eye flooding clear black. "You're benched for that pass you threw."

Quentin's jaw dropped. "What the hell are you talking about? I threw a 55-yard *touchdown*, for High One's sake!"

"A pass that I did not tell you to throw," Hokor said as he slapped the desktop with his pedipalps. "I told you to take a knee. And don't think I'm fooled by your trick of turning off your helmet receiver."

"Is this some kind of a rookie joke?"

"I do not joke."

"So how long am I out?"

"One game," Hokor said. "You will dress to lessen your shame, but you will not see any playing time. It is important that the team sees you as a competent backup to Pine, so we will keep this to ourselves. You are *going* to learn who is in charge here, Barnes."

Quentin stared at the diminutive coach. He wanted to come across the desk and punch out that one big eye. It didn't matter how he played, *nothing* was right in Hokor's eyes.

"This is all to protect Pine, isn't it," Quentin said. "You know damn well I should be starting."

"Right now you're not fit to start a grav-cab, let alone start for a Tier Two team," Hokor said. "The sooner you see that, the sooner we can start working to make you good enough to play in this league."

"I looked pretty flippin' good today."

"You were playing garbage time against the worst team in the division," Hokor said. "Hardly an impressive outing. Now leave, I must prepare for next week's game."

Quentin stood and stormed out of the office, making sure to accidentally bump his shoulder against one of the holoframes as he left. He heard the heavy thing crash into the floor, and heard Hokor's angry yell, but ignored both and walked back to the Human dressing room.

Pine was there, dressed in a sharp blue suit that complemented his blue skin. "Hell of a game today," he said with a wide smile. "And hell of a shot you put on Tweedy. The guy's left cheek is already black-and-blue. Where did you learn to do that?"

"In the mines," Quentin said as he sulked to his locker. "Roundbugs down there. Every kid carries a weighted rope. You learn early on how to snap the rope to kill any roundbugs you see — you don't learn how to do it right, you die."

Pine's face wrinkled in disbelief. "What, are you kidding me? How old were you when they taught you that?"

"Five," Quentin said. "That's when you start working in the mines."

"At *five*? Five years old? Working in a mine with poisonous ...

bugs, or whatever? Good God, Quentin, what kind of a place did you grow up in?"

"A chosen place," called the deep voice of Rick Warburg. "Where only the blessed can live."

Pine laughed. "Doesn't sound that blessed to me, champ."

"High One protects the faithful," Warburg said as he walked over.

"I see," Pine said, drawing out the last word. "The faithful. And so, therefore, if a little child is killed by one of these bugs, then that's because the child was not faithful. So the child dies, and it's the *child's* fault."

Warburg nodded.

Pine shook his head. "Nice place you guys come from. Say, Quentin, Yitzhak and I are heading out on the town. There's a great Chinese place just past the stadium."

Pine's audacity amazed Quentin. The guy was pulling every string in the book to keep his starting job and was two-faced enough to try and be friends.

"I've got a place Quentin would be more happy," Warburg said. "With his own people."

Pine looked at Warburg, then looked at Quentin, then shrugged and walked away.

"Finish getting dressed," Warburg said. "I've got a surprise for you."

"YOU'LL LOVE the neighborhood," Warburg said. "There's thousands of ex-patriot Nationalites on Ionath. Most of them came during the cleansing."

Their grav-cab floated along the magnetic track that led through the Human Cultural Area. Grav-cabs abounded in the domed city — you just hopped on, told it where you wanted to go, then enjoyed the ride. On Micovi, only the rich could afford any kind of car, let alone one with a driver. Here in Ionath City, cars were not only available to anyone at any time, they were also free.

The four-mile-diameter dome created twelve square miles of

ground, most of that space taken up by the main towering buildings of downtown Ionath City. The remaining space was home to the "Cultural Areas" of several species: Sklorno, Ki and Human; a fifty-story, high-pressure gas cylinder for the Harrah; aquatic centers for Leekee, Dolphins and Whitok. The Human Cultural Area consisted of only six city blocks, which didn't leave a lot of room for individual neighborhoods that reflected the thousands of various Human cultures. The Human District, as the residents called it, was a hodge-podge of cultural influences crammed together in a claustrophobically confined space.

"Wait 'til we eat," Warburg said. "An old couple owns the place, used to run a restaurant back on Allah, Down-home Nation cooking. They've got a habanero falafel biscuit that will put your mouth in punch-space."

Quentin marveled at the area's diversity. A hotel catering to League of Planets residents right next to a café that advertised food from the Tower Republic, next to a vodka-only liquor store that specialized in brands from across the galaxy. He saw dance clubs, restaurants, grocery stores, shops, all of which had signs written in Standard and hundreds of other languages. Shops and stores and restaurants packed one on top of the other and side by side. There were also dozens of places that — despite assorted cultural trappings — were easily identified by brightly lit signs showing stylized logos of liquor and beer, combined with some image of football. Bars, it seemed, looked the same all over in the galaxy.

People of every type walked the streets. Back home, he was used to the skin tones of his countrymen: black, brown, yellowish and pinkish. But here, those tones mingled with others that never set foot on Nation soil: blue, bleach-white, reddish and even the occasional deep purple skin of an amphibious Human from the Whitok Kingdom. The "mongrel" races, as they'd been called back home. And it wasn't just Humans. Gaudily dressed Ki businessmen freely walked the streets, as did Quyth Leaders, Quyth Warriors, tiny Sklorno males and floating Harrah.

Amidst the diversity, he suddenly realized that one species was notedly absent. "Where are the Creterakian soldiers?"

"There aren't any."

Quentin looked at Warburg. "There aren't any? But, how is that possible? They rule the universe."

Warburg shrugged. "They don't rule here. The Quyth are independent. The bats never conquered them."

The concept seemed impossible. All his life, he and his people had been ruled by Creterakians. Quentin had never known a time when the omnipresent bats hadn't controlled everything.

"So, in the war, the Quyth *won*?" The Quyth won while the Purist Nation was conquered were the words that went unsaid.

"They can thank Satan for that," Warburg said. "The Quyth are in league with the Low One. Temporary freedom for an eternity of fire, Quentin. It's hardly a good deal."

Music of many differing styles filtered out of windows and open bar doors. Smells of enticing foods combined with the stench of garbage and the ever-present onion scent of Quyth Workers. Quentin had never before experienced such a concentration of sights, sounds and smells.

"Look at this place," Warburg said, gesturing to the brightly lit signs of three different churches lined up side by side. "Look at all the blasphemy that goes on in the galaxy, Quentin. It's as if a new religion pops up every other day."

Churches of every type filled tiny buildings, offices and upper-story lofts. He'd never imagined there were so many different religions. On Micovi, you either followed the Purist way or you followed no way at all — practicing other religions in Nation space got you thrown in jail, if you were lucky, or dragged before a tribunal, which usually resulted in jail, public beatings or being stoned to death.

"Someday, Purist Nation troops will walk down this street," Warburg said. "Someday, all of these sinners will burn."

Quentin said nothing. He didn't feel anger or disgust, he felt excitement. Excitement at something new and different. He suddenly realized that, for the first time in his life, he was free of not only the Creterakian Empire's watchful eye, but also the Purist Church's constant restrictions.

"Here we are," Warburg said excitedly as he hit the stop button on the automated grav-cab. Quentin got out in front of a building with a flickering holosign of the infinity symbol. Below the flickering sign were the words "The Blessed Lamb" and below that a nondescript brown door. Some graffiti covered the plain black walls. Quentin couldn't make out most of the writing, but one message in Standard read *haters go home*.

Warburg walked in, and Quentin followed. There was a brief pause as the men entered and heads turned, followed by a chorus of cheers and calls of "Praise High One." Over half the crowd of fifty-plus patrons wore the blue. Most of the men bore the infinity tattoo on their foreheads.

"Welcome, Brother Warburg," said a fat man in priest's robes. "We enjoyed your performance today."

"Thank you, Father Harry." Warburg warmly shook the man's hand. "Three catches is a good day's work."

"Three catches for twenty-eight yards," said a man on their right. He wore Purist blue and held a coffee mug in his hand. "And let's not forget the highlight of the day, when you put that cricket in the hospital."

"Thanks, Elder Greyson. Any word on his condition?"

Father Harry smiled. "ESPN reports the beast is out for two to three games. Said her leg was nearly severed at the knee!"

A snarl-smile covered Warburg's face, and he pumped his fist. "I tried to make the thing come right off."

The words shocked Quentin. He stared at Warburg, wondering if the man was joking. Had he really *tried* to maim the Wallcrawler defensive back?

Warburg stood tall and raised his voice. "Hey, listen everybody. I want to introduce you to the latest Purist Nation export, Quentin Barnes."

A round of cheers and applause filled the small bar. Hands reached out to pat Quentin's shoulder or shake his hand. He couldn't help but smile at the outpouring of affection. These were Nationalites, church members, and they seemed to instantly accept him. Quentin didn't know what to make of it.

"A blessed game you played today, my son," Father Harry said. "Two-for-two, for eighty yards and a touchdown! Now that's showing the galaxy what a Nationalite can do."

"Maybe you'll be starting soon," Greyson said. "Get some more passes to Rick, here. High One knows he'd have more catches if that damn blue-boy quarterback would stop throwing to that scum Kobayasho. He doesn't even have half of Rick's skills!"

Warburg shrugged and held up his hands as if to say *what can I do?*

Quentin's thoughts came back to football, and he felt his face turn red with embarrassment. He wouldn't be starting, he wouldn't even be *playing* in the next game. Benched. *Benched*.

Quentin and Warburg were the center of attention as the bar owners, a husband-and-wife team named Brother Guido and Monica Basset, brought plate after plate of classic Nation dishes. The conversation revolved around the hated Planetary Union, the hated League of Planets, the hated Tower Republic, the demonic Ki, the demonic Sklorno, the demonic Quyth, et cetera, et cetera. It was the same conversation Quentin had heard every day of his life, yet somehow, in this alien city, with his alien teammates probably only a few blocks away at their own cultural centers, the conversation seemed out of place. It even seemed *wrong*. He suddenly wanted to be somewhere else.

And, he wanted a beer. Several beers. Back on Micovi, he didn't care who he offended with his preference of beverage, but these people were so nice, and Warburg really had tried hard to make him feel at home. For the first time in his life, he didn't *want* to offend the people around him.

Quentin finished his fourth helping of habanero falafel biscuits, his mouth a dichotomy of tasty pleasure and fiery, burning pain. He stood and smiled. "Thank you all for your hospitality."

"You're leaving?" Warburg said amidst the groans from the other patrons.

"This is my first time in the city," Quentin said apologetically. "I want to walk around a bit."

"You want me to come with you?"

Quentin shook his head. "No, thanks. You stay. I just want to take in the sights by myself."

Warburg stood and shook Quentin's hand, starting a cavalcade of hand-shaking and back-patting from smiling, happy expatriot Nationalites.

Father Harry stood. That took some effort thanks to his ample girth. He handed Quentin a plastic call chit. "Quentin, my son, if there's anything you need, anything at all, you have but to call. We have a network of Nationalite business owners and travelers who can help you no matter what the problem."

Quentin took the chit. The offer didn't surprise him — he'd received preferential treatment ever since he'd started his first game two years ago. But this was different. Before, he'd been treated with deference just because he was a quarterback, but here he had the feeling it had nothing to do with football. Well, *almost* nothing. It was mostly because he was a Nationalite.

"There is one thing."

"What is it, my son?"

"I ... I'm looking for my parents."

"Are they on Ionath?"

"I, um, I don't know. I haven't seen them since I was maybe three. I think they left Micovi, but I don't know."

Father Harry nodded knowingly, a sad nod, a supporting nod. "I see. Don't be embarrassed, Quentin. Your story is quite common. Many of us, even in this room, had to leave the Nation suddenly, either leave or die. Families are scattered throughout the universe."

"So how do I find them?"

"What are their names?"

"I don't know," Quentin said, staring at the ground. "I don't remember. I know their last name is Barnes, but that's all."

"Do you have any other family?"

Quentin held his breath. *Here it comes*, he thought. *Now they find out I have no family, and they treat me like garbage, just like they treated me back on Micovi.*

"Quentin, do you have any other family? Brothers? Aunts or uncles?"

"No," Quentin said in a whisper.

Father Harry clapped Quentin on the shoulder. "Then we'll have to start from scratch, my son. We'll put the word out. Last name Barnes, left Micovi about sixteen years ago?"

Quentin looked up, into Father Harry's eyes. The man was still smiling, still supportive. "Yeah, fifteen or sixteen years ago."

"If they can be found, we will find them. Now, go enjoy your sightseeing. You are welcome here anytime."

Quentin mumbled thanks, then walked outside. He didn't know what to make of it. These people were a support network, a small tribe in a hostile land. He felt the sense of community, of brotherhood. They offered to help him not because he was a football player, but because they automatically considered him to be one of them. He had to travel hundreds of light-years from his home to be accepted by his own people. It was so confusing it made his head hurt.

He started walking. He'd never been treated like that before. Those people were so nice to him, so gracious and friendly and loving — just because he was a Nationalite. And yet, those same people hated everything that was different from them. Not just *hated*, but wanted to *destroy*.

He had walked only a few short minutes when the environment changed. The buildings looked the same, but the glowing signs showed alien words. Strange music flowing from open doors. If you could call it music — some horrible screeching sound with rhythm. Quentin looked around him, realizing he'd walked right through the Human District and into the Sklorno Cultural Area. Tall Sklorno females wrapped in heavy clothing walked about. Sklorno males abounded, but here the tiny creatures moved in an orderly, calm fashion, nothing like the bouncing madness he'd seen at the game.

He also realized he'd drawn a crowd. Looking about, he saw he was surrounded by Sklorno females. They kept their distance, a good fifteen feet, but ringed him nonetheless.

"Well, well, well, look who's out on the town!"

Quentin cringed when he heard the deep Human voice — John

Tweedy. He turned to see Tweedy and Yassoud standing there. Perhaps leaning was a better description. Both men held magnicans of beer, and both looked like they'd been drinking for hours. They were both stylishly dressed, although the clothes looked a bit worse for the wear, as if they'd both fallen down several times during the night. Tweedy also wore a bandoleer filled with magnicans. TAKE ONE DOWN PASS IT AROUND scrolled across Tweedy's forehead.

"Hey, Q," Yassoud said.

"Hey," Quentin said, staring at Tweedy, bracing himself for some kind of conflict.

"So what's a racist waste of skin like you doin' in the Sklorno District?" Tweedy said, his words slurring slightly.

Quentin started to answer, but Yassoud cut him off. "Aw, leave him alone, Johnny. He's here, ain't he?"

Tweedy seemed to seriously consider this for almost five seconds, as if it were an advanced trigonometry problem. "Uh ... yeah," he finally said with a definitive nod of the head.

Yassoud laughed. "I'm finding our world-class linebacker ain't too sharp after you get a few in him."

Tweedy reached into his bandolier and pulled out a magnican. "Hey, Q, you want a beer?"

It was the last thing he'd expected to hear from John Tweedy. "Sure," Quentin said and took the offered can. He twisted the top, feeling the can grow instantly cold in his hand. He took a long drink — the amazing taste exploded in his mouth. He looked at the can: Miller Lager.

"Where the hell did you get this?"

Tweedy's face furrowed in confusion. "From a beer store."

"Yeah, but, I mean, how much did this *cost*?"

Yassoud laughed. "Five credits for a ten-pack."

"Five credits? You're joking."

Yassoud and Tweedy looked at each other, then at Quentin, and both laughed.

"Okay, fine, so it's cheap beer," Yassoud said. "Go to the store and get what you want."

"No, no, it's great!" Quentin took another long pull, draining the can. "I don't know how you got it for that price. Is there any left at that store?"

Yassoud laughed and shook his head. "Are you kidding me? There's a whole wall of it."

They had to be joking, of course. Miller Lager was ten credits a can back home.

Tweedy and Yassoud started to walk toward a door. Quentin didn't know what the building was until he saw the glowing holo sign: some logo he didn't recognize, with words he couldn't read, but in the middle of it was the familiar outline of a football — a sports bar. Tweedy and Yassoud made it as far as the wall before they fell down in a heap. Yassoud attempted to rise, while Tweedy didn't move.

Quentin sighed. All of the sudden he was the sober one and knew he had to get his teammates home. He signaled a grav-cab and helped Yassoud stumble in. Then he struggled to lift Tweedy's 310-plus pounds, breaking a sweat before he rolled the big, muscular man onto the cab's floor. The vehicle was built to carry all types of sentients, including Ki, which meant there was still plenty of room.

"The Krakens' Building," Quentin said. The grav-cab slid noiselessly down the track.

WEEK ONE LEAGUE ROUNDUP
(Courtesy of Galaxy Sports network)

Opening week of the Quyth Irradiated schedule held few surprises. The **Glory Warpigs** (1-0) topped the **Grontak Hydras** (0-1) thanks to a pair of interceptions by the Warpigs' All-Pro cornerback Toyonaka.

Last year's rookie sensation Condor Adrienne showed why he's the hope of the **Whitok Pioneers** (1-0), throwing for 334 yards and three touchdowns in a 42-10 blowout win over the **Quyth Survivors** (0-1).

Donald Pine, quarterback of the **Ionath Krakens** (1-0), showed no signs of his age, throwing three TD passes in a 31-7 win over the **Woo Wallcrawlers** (0-1).

The **Sheb Stalkers** (0-1) couldn't manage any answer to "The Mad" Ju Tweedy, who ran for 212 yards to lead the **Orbiting Death** (1-0) to a 32-7 win. Ju notched three rushing touchdowns and knocked two Stalkers defenders out for the season.

The **Bigg Diggers** (1-0) edged out a 21-16 win over the **Sky Demolition** (0-1).

DEATHS:

Princeton, a kick returner for the Bigg Diggers, was killed on a tackle by Yalla the Biter. League officials ruled that it was a clean hit.

WEEK ONE PLAYERS OF THE WEEK:

Offense: Condor Adrienne, quarterback, Whitok Pioneers. 31-of-42, 334 yards, three TDs, no INTs.

Defense: Arkham, cornerback, Bigg Diggers. Six tackles, one sack, two interceptions, five passes defended.

GAME TWO: Grontak Hydras (0-1) at the Ionath Krakens (1-0)

QUYTH IRRADIATED CONFERENCE STANDINGS

Bigg Diggers	1-0
Glory Warpigs	1-0
Ionath Krakens	1-0
Orbiting Death	1-0
Whitok Pioneers	1-0
Grontak Hydras	0-1
Quyth Survivors	0-1
Sheb Stalkers	0-1
Sky Demolition	0-1
Woo Wallcrawlers	0-1

THE HYDRAS WERE 0-1, but drastically better than the Woo Wallcrawlers. The Hydras wore white jerseys with bright red numbers and yellow trim. The jerseys looked normal, but their leg armor was painted a bizarre red-and-yellow checkerboard pattern. Red facemasks adorned pure red helmets free of any logo.

Quentin watched from the sidelines, his black jersey and orange leg armor pristine and unblemished with dirt or sweat or blood or the blue streaks from the plants that made up the playing field.

Pine's uniform, on the other hand, was far from clean. A cut on his left forearm had spilled blood all over his shoes and his orange leg armor. He'd been sacked three times. Iomatt-blue stains and dirt marks spotted his uniform. His black jersey had come half-untucked, and he'd never bothered to fix it.

Pine had taken a beating. In addition to the three sacks, he'd been knocked down four times and hurried ten. His classic pocket-passing style ran into problems against the Hydras' defense. The Hydras' secondary played a lot of woman-to-woman, bump-and-run style, taking away Pine's accurate short-passing game. That gave the defensive line more time to get to him, which had resulted in the pounding he'd taken thus far. Hokor countered with running plays to keep the defense on its toes. The woman-to-woman coverage also meant receivers were eventually going to get free — Pine had torched the secondary with two long TD passes, putting the Krakens up 23-17. Both TDs went to the right side of the field, to Scarborough. The Hydras' star cornerback, Wichita, had shut down Hawick on the left side all day long.

Quentin watched with mixed emotions. He knew he could have used his speed and mobility to avoid the defense. Each time Pine went down, he felt a smug satisfaction that Hokor was sleeping in the bed he had made for himself. Yet at the same time, Quentin wanted to win — when Pine threw a completion, he found himself hissing "yes!" between clenched teeth. Pine kept getting knocked down, knocked down *hard*, and he kept getting back up. Slower each time, it seemed, but he refused to stay down.

The game was a real nail-biter, but Hokor seemed to have things under control. Up 23-17 with 1:41 to play, ball on the Krakens' 32, Hokor relied on running plays to Mitchell "The Machine" Fayed.

From the sidelines, Quentin saw where he got his nickname. The punishing Hydra defense brought it all against Fayed, delivering big-time hit after big-time hit. Yet after each bone-crushing impact, some so devastating they made other players wince just from watching, Fayed simply popped up and ran back to the huddle. He smashed into the line again and again, dishing out as many hits as he took.

Paul Pierson, Fayed's backup, had also seen several carries. Quentin hadn't been that impressed and wondered if Yassoud could do better.

On second-and-six, Pine dropped back and stood tall in the pocket. Wichita, the defensive back, lined up over Hawick, took two steps back as if in pass coverage, then came full speed on a blindside blitz.

As Pine checked through his receivers, Wichita closed the fifteen-yard distance in only two seconds, a white-red-yellow blur of speed. Pine saw the blitz at the last second and fired a pass to Fayed in the flat, just before Wichita dove at Pine's legs. Even from the sidelines, despite the roar of another 185,000-plus capacity crowd, Quentin heard the snap.

Wichita hit Pine at the thigh, seemingly bending him in half and driving him to the side. His orange-colored leg armor split into two pieces and spun away like large chunks of shrapnel. The two players hit the ground, Wichita on top, Pine already howling in pain. As Wichita rolled off, Pine's hands flew to his thigh. His leg suddenly seemed to have an extra joint — the thigh flopped sickeningly halfway between the hip and the knee, more like a Ki's leg than a Human's. At this new, unnatural joint, his cool-suit stuck out at a weird angle. A growing circle of bright blood stained the microtubule fabric.

Whistles blew as Harrah refs swarmed to the downed quarterback. Doc flew out onto the field, the med-sled stretcher automatically following slowly behind. A hush fell over the crowd as Pine rolled to one side, then the next, clutching his leg, his face a scrunched-up vision of agony.

As Doc reached Pine, Quentin noticed the Sklorno players

trembling on the field. Not the excited trembling he'd seen before, but something else, something disturbing. They huddled together, Kraken and Hydra both, raspers linked like a pile of entangled snakes. All but Wichita, who stood a few yards away from Pine. Her arms were spread out to her sides, and her eyes looked up to the sky. Quentin didn't know what to make of the strange behavior.

Doc put a small device to Pine's neck, and one second later Pine stopped moving. Thin wires snaked out from the grav-sled, sliding under Pine and lifting him up off the ground. With Pine dangling motionless underneath, the med-sled glided noiselessly off the field towards the end-zone tunnel, Doc flying gracefully by its side.

"Barnes," Hokor called loudly.

Quentin blinked a few times, not sure if he'd heard right. He was benched. Yitzhak would be going in, not him.

"Barnes!"

Quentin pulled on his helmet as he ran to the coach. Without being told, he knelt on one knee so he could look Hokor in the eye. Hokor put a pedipalp on Quentin's shoulder and drew him close.

"Barnes, we're in a bad spot. We need to play for field position and let our defense win this thing, you understand?"

Quentin nodded vigorously.

"You run the plays that I call, and we'll win this game."

Quentin nodded again.

"If we have to pass, they're going to come hard. That's why I need you now, Yitzhak can't scramble the way you can. R-set, dive right, tell Fayed to get that first down."

Quentin stood and ran onto the field. The crowd roared approval, but he didn't hear them. A glance at the scoreboard told him Fayed had picked up five yards on the last play, making it third-and-one. He felt like he was floating instead of running. He reached the huddle. It was different this time — all first-string players — dirty, bloody, intense and mean. This wasn't garbage time. Every one of the ten sentients in the huddle wanted to win. They looked at him, some with suspicion, some with hope. Warburg smiled at him and gave him a quick thumbs-up.

"R-set," Quentin said, surprised to hear his voice crack like a pubescent teenager. He cleared his throat. "R-set, dive right. We need a first down here! On two, on two, ready?"

"Break," the huddle called in unison.

Quentin walked to the line, adrenaline racing through his body, making him feel like a vibrating holosign. The Human and Quyth linebackers looked at him like he was a mortal enemy, the Ki defensive linemen looked at him like he was a meal.

The Krakens lined up with two tight ends, Tom Pareless at fullback and Fayed at tailback. Hawick lined up wide left, Wichita only two yards off in bump-and-run coverage.

"Blue, fifteen!" Quentin's eyes swept the defense. "Blue, fifteen!" The Hydras lined up in a 5-2 with the defensive backs up close — a run-stopping formation. The right cornerback played in tight, and the free safety was cheating up to the line. Like everyone in the stadium, they knew it was a run, that Fayed would get the ball. That was the safe thing to do, the smart thing to do. Quentin's mind flashed a light-year a minute, calculating the positions and intended directions of each defensive player.

"Hut-hut!"

BLINK

The world around him slowed to half-speed. The ball slapped into his hands, and the line exploded into a melee. Quentin pivoted for the handoff, and as he did he saw the free safety drive forward and the right cornerback come in for a run-blitz. The Hydras hoped to jam the off-tackle hole, and the cornerback would keep Fayed from bouncing to the outside. Fayed would have nowhere to run.

Quentin reached the ball back for Fayed — then at the last second, he pulled it just out of Fayed's reach.

Fayed tried to turn, looking to the ground as if there was a fumble, but his forward momentum carried him into the line. The free safety slipped through the hole and hit Fayed at the waist. The blitzing cornerback came in fast and saw too late that Quentin still had the ball.

Quentin tucked the ball and drove to his right. The cornerback planted her feet, but he was by her before she could change direction. As soon as he moved past her, he cut up-field at an angle. The corner chased him — he'd never seen a player change direction that fast. The strong safety came at him from the defensive backfield, eliminating any cutback. The Quyth Warrior outside linebacker, number 52, Bilis the Destroyer, went into a side-roll, quickly moving back at an angle that put him in front of Quentin. Bilis popped out of his roll, suddenly on all fours, strong pedipalps sticking out and ready.

Quentin threw a head-and-shoulders juke to his left, to the inside. Bilis bought it, and Quentin instantly drove to his right, to the outside, in a cut that would leave the linebacker grasping air.

Bilis the Destroyer instantly matched the move.

No way, Quentin had time to think before Bilis leveled him, catching him under the chin and knocking his head back. Quentin's feet flew out from under him as his body spun backward until the back of his head smashed into the ground. He bounced once and rolled to an ungraceful stop.

BLINK

The world rushed back to normal, some unseen force seeming to tap off the "mute" button in his brain — the sound of 185,000-plus hit him like a hammer.

He stood up, energy pumping through every molecule in his body while pain radiated through his brain. He'd thrown that same move at least a thousand times in his PNFL career. It always left the defenders in the dust. But the Quyth Warrior linebacker ... he'd never seen such amazing lateral movement. Bilis the Destroyer had matched his in-cut and his out-cut as if he were Quentin's mirror-image. On all-fours, their low center of gravity let them move side to side far faster than any Human.

The Hydras called a time-out, stopping the clock at 1:36. The ref signaled first down, and the chains moved forward. Quentin jogged back to the huddle. He'd picked up eleven yards on the play.

Hokor's faced popped to life in the holographic heads-up display.

"Barnes, what the hell was that?"

"A first down, Coach."

"I called a dive right."

"That's what I ran, Coach," Quentin said as he reached the huddle. "Only I missed the handoff, so I improvised."

"Well, stop improvising!" Hokor screamed so loud Quentin wondered if Quyth Leaders had vocal cords that could rupture.

"Okay, Coach, no problem."

"Good. Same play. And this time, *hand it off.*"

First-and-10 on the Krakens' 43. Quentin turned to the huddle. The Humans were smiling at him, the Sklorno stared at him with newfound reverence, and the Ki just looked at him in their unemotional way.

"Okay, let's do it again, X-set, dive right, on one."

"You gonna hand it off this time?" Fayed asked without a hint of irritation.

"Yeah. Get me some yards."

Fayed nodded once.

The Krakens lined up. He handed off to Fayed: this time the free safety stayed off the line, and the right corner waited, making sure Quentin didn't have the ball. Bilis the Destroyer came free and swung his arm in a vicious hook that caught Fayed in the throat, lifting the Human off the ground and snapping him back after a three-yard gain. Quentin watched in horror, fully expecting Fayed to lay on the ground with a broken neck. But the whistles blew, Fayed popped up good as new and ran back to the huddle smiling.

Hydras used their second time-out: 1:29 to go.

Hokor's voice came over the transmitter. "Off-tackle left, tell Fayed to keep that ball covered up."

Quentin nodded and called the play in the huddle. The crowd roared like a hundred take-off rockets, so loud their combined voices shook the very ground. The ball snapped into his hands. As he turned he watched the defenders — once again they were selling out, coming to stop the run and *only* the run. Quentin handed off to Fayed, who avoided a would-be tackler that broke through the line. Fayed spun to his left, back inside, but there was nowhere to run. He plowed into the line for no gain.

The Hydras used their last time-out.

Third down and seven on the 46, 1:22 to play.

Quentin reached to his belt and tapped the transmit button. "Coach, they're bringing everyone to stop the run. I can do a quick slant for the first down."

Hokor's face appeared in the heads-up display. "Dive left," he said.

"Coach, we won't get a first down! They'll get the ball back."

"We chew up another thirty seconds, punt, and make them work the length of the field."

"But, Coach –"

"Hand off the damn ball!" Hokor's voice was loud enough to make Quentin flinch. The coach's fur puffed out, and his eye flooded a deep black.

Quentin walked to the huddle. "Okay, okay, we've got this in the bag. X-set dive left, on two, on two. Break!"

The Krakens jogged to the line. The Hydras players looked like characters from some war movie, dug-in deep and ready for a heroic last stand against the enemy. The ballgame hinged on this one play. If the Hydras stopped the Krakens here, they'd get the ball back with just under a minute to play. No time-outs, but they'd have a chance to win. If the Krakens got the first down, Quentin would just take a knee on the next two plays, and the game was over. If they got the first down, they controlled the win instead of giving the Hydras a chance to snatch the victory.

Quentin stood behind the center and surveyed the defense.

"Red, nineteeeeen! Red, *nineteen*!"

All the defenders moved up to the line. The free safety and the safety stood only a few yards back from the linebackers, who had lined up just two yards off the line of scrimmage. With the defense packed in like that, there was nowhere for Fayed to run.

As Quentin bent to take the snap, he stole a glance at Wichita, the Hydras' cornerback: she was only one yard off the blindingly fast Hawick. Too close. Hawick could run a seven-yard slant in less than a second. All Quentin had to do was take the snap, stand and throw as fast as he could, and Hawick would be seven yards downfield.

"Flash! Flash!" Quentin called. Krakens' heads turned to look at him in amazement. "Blue thirty-two, blue-thirty two!" With the audible, the Krakens players had their new instructions. Heads turned back to face front. He'd win this game and win it right now.

"Hut, *hut*!"

The ball snapped into his hands. Quentin stood, turned and fired. Hawick was a blur, Wichita a half-step behind. The ball ripped through the air like a laser — but a misguided laser, just a bit behind the target. Wichita closed so fast Quentin's mind couldn't even process the movement. Hawick reached back, but Wichita cut in front of her, snatched the ball out of the air and, in the same motion, cut back to the outside and angled for the Krakens' end zone.

Quentin turned reactively to pursue, but it was already too late — in the time it took him to change direction and head downfield, Wichita already had a ten-yard lead. Hawick, the only player with a hope of catching her, gave chase but didn't have enough time to catch up. Wichita ran the fifty yards to the end zone in less than four seconds.

Hydras 23, Krakens 23.

The Hydras' kicker, Kash Wallace, and the kicking team ran onto the field. The sandpapery sound filled the stadium, along with other derisive noises from the smattering of other species present. It was the loudest "boo" Quentin had ever heard. He stood there, dumbfounded.

Hokor's face appeared once again in the heads-up display. His fur was puffed out all the way, but there was nothing cute about it this time. His eye was blacker than even a Ki's unblinking spot. "Barnes! Get your stupid, inbred face off my field."

Quentin turned and ran to the sidelines, feeling like a condemned man walking his last mile. Teammates stood on the sidelines, glaring at him, some shaking their heads in disbelief, some pounding the ground in rage.

He said a quick prayer to the High One, but the High One wasn't listening — Wallace's extra point sailed through the uprights.

Hydras 24, Krakens 23, 1:13 to play.

Special teams ran onto the field for the kickoff.

Quentin ran to Hokor and kneeled down. Hokor's eye swirled with colors: blacks and reds, the colors of anger and hate. "What did I tell you to call?"

"Dive left."

"And what did you run?"

"Slant pass left."

Hokor nodded and glared. Something about the look said *I told you so*. Quentin felt his face turn red, and he dropped his head in shame. He'd just cost his team the game.

"You want to prove yourself? " Hokor said. "Well, here's your chance. We've got a minute left to win this game. We've only got one time-out left. Your arm is going to do it for us."

Quentin looked up. Hokor was putting him back in, back in to win the game. Quentin felt a new rush of adrenaline. This is what he was born to do.

"I won't screw up again, Coach."

Hokor nodded. "If you do, Gredok will probably have you killed."

The crowd roared as the kickoff sailed through the air. Richfield caught the ball at the five. She ran up-field, then cut right. The Hydras closed in, weaving through blockers or just running them over. Quentin recognized the Hydra with the number 23 — Wichita — dodge around blockers as if they weren't even there.

Richfield cut back inside and jumped high to avoid the tackle, but Wichita read the cut and launched herself through the air. She hit Richfield dead-center and at top speed — Richfield's torso snapped backward, her legs still moving forward.

First-and-ten on the Krakens' fifteen.

Quentin led the offense onto the field. Arioch Morningstar, the Krakens' kicker, could hit from 45 yards out, sometimes from 50. That meant the Krakens had to get at least to the Hydras' 35-yard line to get into Morningstar's range, and they had 1:08 in which to do it.

"X-set," said Hokor's voice in Quentin's ear. "Pulse-34, work the sidelines."

Quentin nodded and looked over his huddle. They all looked at him, expecting him to lead them.

"X-set, pulse-34," Quentin said. "Make sure you get out of bounds."

He broke the huddle and came up the line.

The Hydras dug in, knowing it was now their game to lose. Bilis the Destroyer crowded the line, showing blitz. The crowd's roar grew so loud Quentin could barely hear himself call the signals. Hawick and Scarborough lined up wide to the left, Denver and Mezquitic wide to the right. Wichita again lined up over Scarborough, in bump-and-run coverage. Quentin looked to his right, to Denver. If Bilis the Destroyer came on the blitz, Denver would angle in and run a hook in Bilis's abandoned coverage area.

"Blue, sixteeeen!" Quentin shouted, trying to be heard over the crowd's roar. Bilis took another step forward, edging in between his Ki defensive tackle and his Human defensive end.

"Hut-hut!"

BLINK

The ball slapped into his hands as the clock started ticking. Quentin dropped back, ball held high, looking for Denver's route. Bilis didn't blitz — instead, he backpedaled on all fours, scurrying back to cover the short zone, right where Quentin had hoped Denver would run. Denver saw the coverage and angled for the sidelines, but she was covered. Quentin looked left: Scarborough hooked up at the sidelines, but she was also covered. Hawick ran a post — she was wide-open, no defender. Quentin planted, after only three steps of his five-step drop, and started to throw even before he saw the blur of motion coming from his left.

Nothing can move that fast flashed through his head just before Wichita, on a corner blitz, caught him dead in the chest. Two hundred eighty pounds of power moving at blinding speed knocked Quentin back like a rag doll. His helmet popped off, seemed to hang in mid-air as he was driven backward. A pain stabbed through his mouth, but all he could think about was the fact that the ball was no longer in his hands. He turned as he fell, his naked face sliding across the grass.

He saw the brown ball bouncing on the blue Iomatt, wobbling towards the sidelines. Quentin scrambled to get up, but Wichita was much faster. She popped to her feet.

Quentin's breath froze in his chest. All players converged on the loose ball.

But Wichita got to it first.

BLINK

The world returned to normal speed as the whistle blew. The ref flew in and repeatedly thrust a tentacle toward the Krakens' end zone — Hydras' ball. Quentin's heart sank right down out of his chest, through his legs and into the ground. It was all over but the crying. He felt a hard something in his mouth. He spit; a bloody white tooth landed on the blue field.

The game was over. A corner blitz. He'd successfully handled that same defensive tactic more times than he could count, but Wichita had come so fast, arriving perhaps two full seconds sooner than any Human corner could have ever managed. Quentin picked up his helmet and walked off the field, head hung low, the taste of his own blood salty in his mouth.

The Hydras' quarterback took a knee on first down. The Krakens used up their last time-out. Two more knees, and the clock ticked down to zero.

Hydras 24, Krakens 23.

The sandpaper-bristle sound rose to even new heights, loud enough to make the High One himself cover his ears.

Game over. Quentin didn't get a chance to be the hero, he was only the goat.

MANY THINGS HAD CHANGED in the course of eight centuries of football. Equipment changed, rules changed, strategy changed, even species changed. But at least two things remained constant — the feeling of the winners and the feeling of the losers.

A noise-killing shadow seemed to hang over the Human locker room. There was almost no conversation, only the clicks and clacks of armor being removed and tossed into lockers. The shadow seemed deepest and most oppressive in front of the locker belonging to one Quentin Barnes, who sat on the bench, head hung, his gear still on.

He'd had his chance and he'd blown it. Instead of doing what he was told, instead of giving the defense the chance to win the game, he'd stupidly gone for the kill and wound up losing.

Yassoud came out of the nano-shower dressed only in a towel. His right shoulder was one solid bruise, angry blue and painful purple beneath his light brown skin. He saw Quentin, head hung low, and walked over.

"How you doin', champ?"

Quentin looked up without lifting his head, then returned his gaze to the floor. His tongue played with the painful spot where his right front tooth had once been. "Leave me alone."

"Hey, you threw a pick, it happens."

"It shouldn't have happened. Hokor called a run play, I audibled."

"So?"

"*So*? What do you mean *so*? I cost us the game."

Yassoud shrugged his shoulders. "Maybe. A lot of factors went into that loss. The defense gave up ten points in the third quarter. You threw an interception. It was a team loss, Q."

Quentin shook his head. "It was my game to win, and I blew it."

Yassoud patted him on the shoulder. "That's nothing a night on the town won't cure, my friend. Let's go out and drink away our sorrows!"

Quentin stood and started unbuckling his armor. "No, thanks. I've got to get back to my room and study some holo."

"Hey, man, you've got to take a break sometime."

"I'll take a break after we win."

Yassoud gave a little smile that seemed to say suit yourself, then returned to his locker.

He was the only one that spoke to Quentin that night. The others simply ignored him.

HYDRAS BOX SCORE

Final	1	2	3	4	T
Ionath	7	10	3	3	23
Grontak	0	7	10	7	24

SCORING SUMMARY

1st QUARTER		ION	GRO
Ionath TD	Scarborough 37-yard pass from Donald Pine (Arioch Morningstar kick)	7	0

2nd QUARTER		ION	GRO
Grontak TD	Trace Bannister 21-yard run (Kash Wallace kick)	7	7
Ionath TD	Scarborough 41-yard pass from Donald Pine (Arioch Morningstar kick)	14	7
Ionath FG	Arioch Morningstar 26-yard field goal	17	7

3rd QUARTER		ION	GRO
Grontak TD	Trace Bannister 12-yard run (Kash Wallace kick)	17	14
Grontak FG	Kash Wallace 22-yard field goal	17	17
Ionath FG	Arioch Morningstar 21-yard field goal	20	17

4th QUARTER		ION	GRO
Ionath TD	Arioch Morningstar 29-yard field goal	23	17
Grontak TD	Wichita 48-yard interception return off of Quentin Barnes pass (Kash Wallace kick)	23	24

TEAM STATISTICS	ION	GRO
First Downs	12	13
Third Down Efficiency	6-14	7-16
TOTAL NET YARDS	**315**	**283**
Total Plays	55	61
Average Gain Per Play	5.7	4.6
NET YARDS RUSHING	**133**	**130**
Rushes	38	32
Average Per Rush	3.5	4.1
NET YARDS PASSING	**182**	**153**
Pass Completion	13-17	15-29
Yards Per Pass	10.7	5.3
Times Sacked	4	2
Yards Lost To Sacks	17	7
Had Intercepted	1	0
PUNTS	**8**	**9**
Average Punt	39.2	42.0
PENALTIES	**5**	**3**
Penalty Yards	45	30
FUMBLES	**2**	**0**
Fumbles Lost	1	0
Time Of Possession	**29:23**	**31:37**

PASSING

KRAKENS	CMP	ATT	YDS	PCT	YPA	SACK	SYDS	TD	INT
Donald Pine	13	16	199	81.3	12.4	3	12	2	0
Quentin Barnes	0	1	0	0.0	0.0	1	5	0	1

HYDRAS	CMP	ATT	YDS	PCT	YPA	SACK	SYDS	TD	INT
Sir Douglas Yee	15	29	160	51.7	5.5	2	7	0	0

RUSHING

KRAKENS	ATT	YDS	AVG	LONG	TD	FUM
Mitchell Fayed	31	99	3.2	31	0	0
Paul Pierson	5	17	3.4	7	0	0
Quentin Barnes	1	11	11	11	0	0
Yassoud Murphy	1	6	6.0	6	0	0

HYDRAS	ATT	YDS	AVG	LONG	TD	FUM
Trace Bannister	20	83	4.2	21	2	0
Christian Sorrenson	12	47	3.9	11	0	0

RECEIVING

KRAKENS	REC	YDS	AVG	LONG	TD	FUM
Scarborough	5	109	21.8	41	2	0
Hawick	2	19	9.5	10	0	0
Yotaro Kobayasho	2	10	5.0	6	0	0
Denver	1	28	28.0	28	0	0
Paul Pierson	1	18	18.0	18	0	0
Yassoud Murphy	1	10	10	10	0	0
Mitchell Fayed	1	5	5	5	0	0

HYDRAS	REC	YDS	AVG	LONG	TD	FUM
Galveston	8	101	12.6	34	0	0
Pleasanton	3	30	10.0	12	0	0
Sedro Wolley	3	15	5.0	11	0	0
Ariel Goldman	1	14	14.0	14.0	0	0

WEEK TWO LEAGUE ROUNDUP
(Courtesy of Galaxy Sports network)

Condor Adrienne continued his hot streak, throwing for 342 yards and four touchdowns as the **Whitok Pioneers** (2-0) notched a 26-12 win over the **Bigg Diggers** (1-1).

The **Sheb Stalkers** (1-1) put one in the win column with a 18-16 thriller over the **Sky Demolition** (0-2). Kicker Bernard Alexander rocked home a 51-yard field goal as time expired to give the Stalkers the victory.

An injury to star quarterback Donald Pine let the **Grontak Hydras** (1-1) pull out an upset win over the **Ionath Krakens** (1-1). Defensive back Wichita picked off a fourth-quarter pass from Krakens' rookie Quentin Barnes and returned it for a touchdown, giving the Hydras a 24-23 win.

Orbiting Death (2-0) continues to look strong, notching a convincing 35-21 win over the **Woo Wallcrawlers** (0-2). Ju Tweedy rushed for 121 yards and two TDs in the win but also fumbled three times, resulting in two turnovers.

The **Glory Warpigs** (2-0) remained tied for first thanks to a narrow 17-14 win over the **Quyth Survivors** (0-2). Keluang, Wellington and Alamo each grabbed an interception as the Warpigs held the Survivors to 102 yards passing and 182 yards total offense.

DEATHS:
No deaths to report this week.

WEEK TWO PLAYERS OF THE WEEK:
Offense: Ju Tweedy, running back, Orbiting Death. 121 yards on 23 carries, two TDs.
Defense: Wichita, cornerback, Grontak Hydras. Nine tackles, two sacks, one forced fumble, one fumble recovery, one INT, returned for a TD.

GAME THREE: Ionath Krakens (1-1) at Whitok Pioneers (2-0)

QUYTH IRRADIATED CONFERENCE STANDINGS

Glory Warpigs	2-0
Orbiting Death	2-0
Whitok Pioneers	2-0
Bigg Diggers	1-1
Grontak Hydras	1-1
Ionath Krakens	1-1
Sheb Stalkers	1-1
Quyth Survivors	0-2
Sky Demolition	0-2
Woo Wallcrawlers	0-2

HALF-DRESSED FOR PRACTICE and head hung low, Quentin trudged into the center dressing room. Hokor had summoned him to his office. Quentin had never felt like such a failure. He'd had his chance and he'd blown it. Pissed it away because he still didn't understand how fast things moved in the GFL. *Logically*, he understood, sure, but subliminally, at that primitive level where thought ceased and instinct took over, where split-second decisions were made, he just didn't get it.

Quentin's tongue played against the back of the thin plastic that lined his front teeth. Doc said it would take the rest of the day to finish growing the tooth. The working nanocytes tingled in his gums.

Was Hokor just benching him again, or was he giving him a one-way ticket back to the Purist Nation? Quentin went to buzz the door, but it was already open, waiting for him like an execution chamber. He hesitated a moment then stepped inside.

"You wanted to see me, Coach?"

Hokor's pedipalp waved him in. The coach stood in the middle of the floor, staring into a holo of the Whitok Pioneers' 32-14 win over the Bigg Diggers. The holo was set to one-third size, making a six-foot-tall player project at two feet high, just a bit shorter than Hokor.

"Have a seat, Quentin."

Quentin did as he was told. A pallor seemed to hang over his soul. He hadn't felt this way since the orphanage nuns had caught him eating food, eating more than his share by far. He'd tried to lie his way out of it, only making the nuns' wrath all the more severe. That had been his first public whipping, tied up in the city square, with hundreds watching as Sister Akira gave him fifteen lashes. It was the longest day of a 7-year-old's life.

Hokor said nothing. On the field, the Diggers lined up in a three wide receiver set with a tight end and a single running back. The defense closed in, showing tight woman-to-woman. Hokor paused the game. He worked the controls so that the field spun until Quentin was behind the offensive line.

"What do you see?"

"They're showing woman-to-woman, but I think they're set up for a cover-two."

"Why do you say that?"

"The right corner's eyes are in the offensive backfield. If it was pure woman-to-woman, she'd be more concerned with the receiver in front of her."

Hokor nodded once. "Very good. And if that was you, and I'd called a post-cross, what would you audible?"

Quentin stared at the field. His heart sank in his chest. He started to answer, then stopped, his mind suddenly blank.

"I wouldn't audible anything. I've had enough audibling for awhile."

Hokor again nodded just once. "If I put you in the game again, will you run the plays I call?"

"Yeah."

"Good. You're starting this week."

Quentin stared, dumbfounded.

"Surely your backwater ears understand what I'm telling you. You're starting this week."

"But ... but I lost the game."

"Yes, you did. And you lost it because you didn't do what I told you to do. But this week, you *will* do what I tell you to do."

Quentin nodded.

"Pine is out this week and next," Hokor said. "The broken bone ruptured an artery. I don't think you're ready, but you give us the best chance of winning. The Pioneers have a good secondary but only a moderate pass rush — your mobility should be enough to keep you from getting sacked. We're 1-and-1, Quentin, we've got to win this game! The Pioneers are 2-and-0 and very tough. I need you to run a tight, ball-control offense so we can get a lead and chew up the clock."

"Yes, sir," Quentin said, wondering if a man could die from excitement.

"I need a strong week of practice from you. You're going to lead this team to a win."

"Yes, sir!"

"Good. We practice here today, then it's a two-day flight to Whitok. That gives us two days of practice on the ship and two days at Whitok Stadium. There's a big time change, we'll be playing late at night our time, so we need to be extra sharp. Let's have a good practice."

Quentin stood and practically sprinted out of the room. *Starting!* His first GFL start! He'd thought himself out of a job, but Hokor was giving him the reins. He'd learned his lesson — this time he'd play it Hokor's way.

As he headed toward the main tunnel, Denver came out of the Sklorno locker room.

"I speak please," she said.

Quentin started to ignore the Sklorno receiver and keep walking, but something made him stop. "What do you want?"

"I shame myself when we speak last. I only offer help."

"I didn't appreciate Pine's sense of humor."

"Not understand," Denver said. "I serve, run routes and catch passes so your greatness increase. Please forgive, I mean no sacrilege, only praise. Praise for Quentin Barnes. I help make you greater?"

She was asking him again, this disgusting cricket was asking him again if he needed her help. Quentin felt the flush of embarrassed rage start to spill over him once again — then something odd happened. His mind flashed back to the Hydras game, to the last play. The sheer speed of Wichita — if he'd just thrown to Hawick the second he saw her open, would he have completed the pass? He'd waited a half-second, and that had been too long. There was no getting around the fact that he'd lost because he still wasn't used to Sklorno speed.

His anger faded away. Denver wasn't being rude, Denver was being honest. Quentin's game wasn't as sharp as it needed to be. But still, he'd figure it out, and *without* help from a cricket.

"Thanks for the offer, but no thanks," Quentin said, surprised to hear his voice come out normal, not snotty and hateful.

Denver backed away, slinking back into the Sklorno locker room. Quentin didn't know much about alien behavior, but Denver seemed like she'd just been severely rebuked for some untoward behavior.

Quentin turned and ran out the tunnel. He didn't have time to worry about it. He had a game to win.

FROM SPACE, Whitok's upper atmosphere looked a lime green. As the shuttle sliced into the soupy air, Quentin saw the all-encompassing cloud cover was actually a sulphurous yellow. The blazing light of the blue star at the center of the Whitok system reflected off the yellow outer atmosphere, the two colors combining for a peaceful green. That peaceful sensation faded away as the shuttle dove toward the planet: the closer they came to the surface, the darker it became. Miles-long bursts of lightning rippled through the dark sky, illuminating the ubiquitous clouds in milky-yellow explosions of light. Within minutes of the descent, all sunlight faded away, the shuttle coursing through Whitok's perpetual twilight.

"Is it always this dark?" Quentin asked Shizzle, who fluttered about the small cabin.

"Is, and has been for the last 145 years," Shizzle said. The little creature fluttered to a stop on Quentin's shoulder.

"Find your own seat, pal," Quentin said as he gently brushed

Shizzle away. The Creterakian fluttered twice, then landed on the seat's armrest.

"The Sklorno navy used relativity bombs on Whitok in 2524. They fired about fifty dense projectiles at near-light speeds. At that speed, the projectiles literally punched right through the core and out the other side. The entry and exit points alone were the sources of devastation like nothing the galaxy had ever seen, the shock-waves destroyed surface life for thousands of miles in all directions. But the projectiles also mixed up Whitok's inner molten nickel core and the outer layer of molten iron. That caused huge shifts in the tectonic plates. Whitok suffered decades of massive quakes and volcanoes. Gasses from the core filled the atmosphere, killing any life that survived the initial impacts.

"Whitok's climate was forever changed. It was seventy-five years before the tectonic plates settled into relative stability. The key word is *relative*, mind you, because the surface is still plagued with volcanoes that reach as high as five miles into the air. Some estimate it will be another five hundred to a thousand years before the crust settles completely and the volcanoes become dormant."

"How come Ionath isn't like that? The Sklorno also sat-bombed Ionath, right?"

"They did, but they didn't use relativity bombs, which caused so much damage to Whitok that they've never been used again. The results even scared the Sklorno, who wondered if such destructive weapons might someday be utilized against their home-world. For future wars, they instead developed the massive nuclear bombs that were used on Ionath and Gritchlik."

"Wow," Quentin said. "That was awfully nice of them."

"They are a one-minded species," Shizzle said. "They're part of the reason we Creterakians took over. We feared that if left to yourselves, the warlike races of Human, Ki, Harrah and especially Sklorno might completely exterminate one another."

Quentin looked out the window at the blank darkness. "Save me the lecture, Shizzle. I've heard it all before."

"The amazing thing is that despite the almost complete destruction of Whitok, and the fact that the planet is among the

most hostile places in the galaxy, the Quyth managed to successfully develop permanent cities. Ah, we're coming out of the clouds
now — behold, the Port of Whitok."

Quentin pressed against the view port, eager to see his second
alien city. As the lightless clouds thinned to nothing, however, he
briefly wondered if he'd been tricked — it looked like a smaller
version of his new home. The domed downtown looked the same,
and the roads radiated out in the familiar spoke-like pattern.

"It looks like Ionath City," Quentin said.

"The Port of Whitok was built well after the success of Ionath
and Gritchlik," Shizzle said. "The Quyth's first pioneers landed
fifty-one years after the relativity bombing, but the planet's surface
was still so violent they could barely survive. It was another fifty
years before they built an actual port that allowed large-craft landings, so the city is really only about sixty years old."

The shuttle swooped down toward the huge dome. Just like
Ionath City, the dome's surface seemed to open just for the speeding shuttle. Inside the dome, right at the city center, sat a perfectly
round stadium.

"It looks bigger than ours," Quentin said.

"EA&M Stadium," Shizzle said. "Seats 181,500, every game is
a sellout. There's no sunlight on the planet's surface, which hinders
outdoor activities. There's not much to do, so beings on Whitok
take football very seriously."

"More seriously than Ionath?"

"Last week there were five murders involving tickets for the
game against the Bigg Diggers."

The shuttle banked a landing pad atop a building attached
to the stadium. Even the buildings looked very similar to Ionath
City's. As the vehicle lowered for the landing, Quentin stared out
the window at the field. Here the surface wasn't blue, but a pale
yellow with black lines and numbers. He had read up on the stadium in his effort to prepare as completely as possible — the plant
that made up the field was reportedly a bit oily, making for poor
traction and quickly stained uniforms.

How would he run the offense in such poor footing? How

would that affect the patterns of his receivers? Shizzle's history lesson faded away. Quentin's mind switched into full-out strategy mode, even before the shuttle touched down.

QUENTIN WALKED OUT of the Holy Light bar and onto the streets of Port Whitok. The Holy Light was similar to the Blessed Lamb back on Ionath, a Purist-only place where you could get heaping helpings of good food, religion and reasons to hate every being except those that hailed from Purist Nation space. He ate politely, made friends. At the end, he asked if they could help him track down his parents. The people in the Holy Light acted exactly the way Father Harry had, offering to help him unconditionally. Quentin still had trouble believing that Nationalites liked him and wanted to help him, even though he was an orphan. Being an orphan, it seemed, had little meaning to people who had fled the home planets in fear of their lives, leaving behind family, belongings and culture.

Warburg had taken him to the Holy Light. Quentin excused himself shortly after dinner. Warburg meant well enough, but Quentin grew tired of the man's constant verbal attacks on anyone and anything that was not Nationalite. Quentin hated the subraces too, sure, but he didn't need to talk about it every second of every day.

The street outside the Holy Light might as well have been in Ionath City's Human District, save for the fact that Port Whitok was perpetually under the blanket of night thanks to the huge volcanoes that spilled fumes into the upper atmosphere. Earthquakes, too, were a daily occurrence. But here, he'd learned, every building — even the huge stadium — rested on a mag-grav suspension system. So did the streets and any utilities like pipes, power transmitters or atmosphere processors. Quakes hit four or five times a day: things shook, everyone waited, things stopped shaking, everyone went on about their business. Port Ionath sat in the center of a tectonic plate, so significant ground cracks seldom posed a problem.

The fact that 8.0 quakes shuddered the ground on a regular basis and that poisonous gas filled the air outside the dome didn't bother the Quyth, 1.2 million of whom lived outside the curved downtown dome. It seemed these beings could live just about anywhere, and therein lay their advantage. For all his countrymen's talk about being the High One's "chosen people," Humans couldn't survive for ten minutes on the surface of Whitok.

Quentin walked alone down the street, weaving through the crowds of Quyth, Ki, Human and Sklorno. He had a lot on his mind. Practice was going well, although he still had problems adjusting to the speed of his receivers and the defensive backs. His pass release had been slow when he arrived, and he hadn't even known it. Now he got rid of the ball twice as fast as he had when with the Raiders. That helped, but it didn't solve the main problem, which was adjusting his eyes to take in the whole field. Back home, he could see a twenty-yard radius and know, instantly, who could move how far within that space. Thanks to the amazing speed of the Sklorno race, now he needed to see a radius of forty to fifty yards, even more if he wanted to throw downfield. He had to drop back, instantly account for every Sklorno defensive back, know how far they could go, how high they could jump and at what angle, then make the decision whether or not to throw and deliver the ball on target.

What was worse, the Krakens seemed to simply tolerate him as opposed to accepting him as their leader. They were Pine's players. But why did they follow that has-been? Quentin was a better quarterback, albeit less experienced, and everyone on the team knew it. They followed Pine's commands without question — when Quentin commanded, he often got glares or bored looks before anyone complied. The Ki didn't block as well for him as they did for Pine. The Human players were no better. Aside from Warburg, the Humans starters showed little respect — except for Mitchell Fayed, who ran every play as if his life depended in it.

They were obviously all jealous of his talent. They wanted to keep their little status quo with their buddy Don Pine, and they resented new blood coming in to take over. Well, that was their problem, and they'd have to learn to deal with it. It was Quentin's team now, and they'd all learn that come game time.

He was so lost in his thoughts he didn't hear the flutter of Creterakian wings right beside him. He didn't even know the little creature was there until it spoke.

"Quentin Barnes?" asked a small voice.

Quentin turned to look at the bat. It had light yellow skin with mottled brown spots and wore a plain brown outfit. It hovered near his head, reminding Quentin of a big, noisy hummingbird — a disgusting one with six eyes.

"Yes, that's me."

"My name is Maygon, and I'd like a word with you. Or, more precisely, my employer would like a word with you."

"And who is your employer?"

Maygon handed him a business disc. Quentin thumbed the button at the center, and a small hologram appeared above it: Maygon, talent scout, To Pirates.

Quentin felt his heart beat faster. "You're really from the Pirates?"

"Yes, but it's better if we don't talk here. Your teammates might see. Follow me." Maygon flew down a side street. Quentin followed him into the street, then into a small door. He had to duck to get through. Once inside he was able to stand, but just barely, his hair touching the ceiling. The place was full of Quyth workers in various states of intoxication. Some danced to strange music, some leaned against numerous three-foot-high poles that filled the room, and some laid on the floor. The smell of juniper filled the air.

"What is this place?"

"A gin joint," Maygon said as he fluttered down atop one of the poles. He was the only Creterakian in the room. For that matter, Quentin was the only Human.

"I forgot that you don't know much about the galaxy. Gin, the same thing you Humans distill and consume, has a powerful narcotic effect on the Quyth. Most alcohol doesn't affect them, but there's something in gin that really knocks them out."

Quentin thought back to the time he'd seen an opium den back on Micovi. Human or Quyth Worker, stoners all looked the same.

"It's pathetic," Quentin said.

"If you think these Workers are bad now, you should see the ones that are hooked on raw juniper berries. At least the gin is distilled to take out some of the poisons."

Quentin took another quick look around, then turned to Maygon. "Okay, so what's this about? What do the Pirates want?"

"They want you."

The words hit like an injection of pure excitement. His body coursed with eagerness and hope.

"What, they want me now?"

"Not now, idiot," Maygon said. "At the end of the season. Kirani-Ah-Kollok will give you a three-year contract."

A *three-year* contract, with the *To Pirates*, the greatest franchise in GFL history — his childhood dream come true!

"That sounds great," Quentin said. "Tell Mr. Kollok I'm very interested."

"Of course you're interested, backwater. It's the To Pirates. Everybody is interested. But there's one catch."

"Which is?"

"You have to make sure the Krakens don't make the playoffs."

Quentin's face furrowed. "But why not? What difference does that make?"

Maygon fluttered his wings, a clear sign of irritation. "Because, backwater, if the Krakens make the playoffs and make it into Tier One, all players are protected for two years. That means that the Pirates, or any other team for that matter, can't touch you unless the Krakens cut you."

"Oh, yeah," Quentin said, some of his excitement fading away. "Yeah, I forgot about that."

"But it doesn't look like it's going to be a problem," Maygon said. "You guys are already one-and-one, and there's no way you're going to beat the Pioneers, so you'll be two games out of first place. Just make sure the Krakens lose any games you start, and you'll be wearing the blood red before you know it. Mr. Kollok thinks there's big things in your future. If I need to talk to you again, I'll contact you, but we can't be seen together. If the league finds out we're talking, the Pirates will be fined and you'll be suspended."

"*Suspended*?" Quentin quickly looked around the bar but still saw only drunken Quyth Workers. "Why didn't you say that before we started talking?"

"Not my fault if you don't know GFL regulations. Now if you'll excuse me, I want to go. I can't stand the stink of Humans."

With that, Maygon fluttered up and flew out the door. Quentin stared after him. The To Pirates. The *To Pirates*! Winners of five GFL championships, more than any other team. The Pirates, with their legendary blood-red jerseys, they wanted him.

Just make sure you lose the games you start.

Those words pushed to the forefront of his brain, dissipating his excitement. Tank a game or two? Sure, they had one loss, but with a win against the Pioneers, the Krakens were right back in the race.

Quentin shook his head and walked out of the gin joint. He'd never thrown a game in his life, but odds were he wouldn't have to. The Pioneers were the best team in the Quyth Irradiated Conference. They'd probably walk all over the Krakens' defense. It wouldn't come down to Quentin tanking the game.

At least he *hoped* it wouldn't.

HE STOOD AT THE FRONT of the pack. The Krakens players crammed into the tunnel. It seemed wider than the one at Ionath Stadium. Wider and newer. In fact, everything about the stadium reeked of newness, from the full wall of multi-race vending machines in the team lobby, to the smart-paint lockers that changed color to suit each player's preference. The communications equipment was state of the art, but what else would you expect from a stadium sponsored by a telecom company like Earth Ansible & Messenger?

The stadium's quality, however, faded to insignificance as the game-fever started to overtake Quentin. The Krakens players grunted, and clacked, and chirped, and bounced, and twitched with the anticipation of battle. Pheromones filled the air: the thick scent of Ki aggression combining with the tang of Human sweat. An electrical charge ripped through the unified mass of players, cycling from one end to the other and back again.

"Time to draw the battle line," Yassoud said from somewhere in the back, his voice muffled by the tight press of bodies packed into the tunnel. Human grunts acknowledged his words.

"We will accept Condor's gifts," a Sklorno called out, referring to Condor Adrienne, the Pioneer's star quarterback. The other Sklornos chirped excitedly, all of them bouncing up and down, unable to contain the energy that filled their bodies.

The sensation built up quickly, thickly, so intense that Quentin couldn't even think, he could only *feel*, like an animal waiting to pounce. It was like the last two games, but it was different — this time they were *his* to command, *his* to lead. This was the moment he'd waited for all of his life.

The announcer introduced the Ionath Krakens.

"Kree-goll-ramoud!" Mum-O-Killowe roared in his deep, warlike voice, and the team surged out of the tunnel to the deafening sound of boos. Small, hard items plinked off their armor. Bits of wet matter, both cold and hot, spilled down on them as they ran onto the field. Quentin covered his head as he looked up into the stands and saw an endless sea of midnight-blue and neon-green, the colors of the Whitok Pioneers.

He reached the sidelines. The Krakens surged around him like a python, everywhere at once, pressing in, their eyes on him, their breath in his face and on his neck. They bounced and surged and punched and clawed like a tiger in a cage.

Quentin started to speak, but John Tweedy beat him to it.

"This is it," Tweedy shouted. "This is it! We need this win, we want it more than they do! We must destroy this house!"

The Krakens roared and clicked and jumped and pushed. Quentin felt a rush of anger — he was the quarterback, the team should be looking to him, not Tweedy.

"Pine is out, so we've got to pull together," Tweedy shouted.

"This is *war*. *We* take the battle to *them*. Now let's go kick their asses!"

The team surged even tighter one last time, bouncing Quentin about like a cork in a typhoon. Then the huddle broke and the players wandered away, preparing for the game.

Quentin fumed on the sidelines. They still didn't give him enough respect. Well, they would all be jealous when he suited up in the blood red for Tier One season, and they were all at home, watching the holos.

The Pioneers won the toss, received the kick and started with the ball on their own 28. Condor Adrienne wasted no time, dropping back on the first play. His offensive line, a huge wall of Ki averaging 630 pounds, gave him all the time in the world. Adrienne launched a deep pass to a streaking receiver, who sprang high in the air. Davenport, the Krakens' right cornerback, went up high as well, but she was just a step behind. The ball floated down just an inch away from her outstretched tentacles to drop perfectly into the hands of Bangor, the Pioneers' receiver. The two players came down as one, but Davenport stumbled on impact. Bangor sprinted the remaining fifteen yards into the end zone.

"Ain't that a pain," Yassoud said. The crowd roared like a thousand-pound bomb. Giant pompons and flags, all midnight blue lined with neon green, waved in the air, making the 181,500-plus crowd seem a single, massive anemone.

The kick was good. The first play of the game found the Whitok Pioneers up 7-0.

"Looks like we've got our work cut out for us, men," Mitchell Fayed shouted as the offense gathered to take the field. "Let's get that one back."

Richfield returned the kick to the Krakens' 30. The offense ran onto the field to the concentrated boos of 181,500 fans. The pompons and banners vanished, like that same anemone pulling in its flowery tentacles at the first hint of danger.

As the players huddled up, Quentin took one quick look around the stadium. "Boy, they love us here, don't they?"

"We won here two seasons ago," said Yotaro Kobayasho, the

tight end. "The crowd rioted. Twenty-seven beings died before they got it under control."

"They take this stuff seriously," said Tom Pareless, the fullback. "You've got to love it."

"Okay, boys, let's take care of business," Quentin said. He tapped his right ear-hole to activate the heads-up display inside his visor. Hokor had already specified the first twenty offensive plays. Quentin knew them by heart, having re-read the list at least a hundred times to make sure he knew every step of every player for each and every play (fifteen running plays and five short passing plays — not a bomb in the bunch). But he checked again, just to be sure. The first play: Y-set, belly right. He tapped the button and the list of plays disappeared from the visor.

"Y-set, belly right. On one, on one, ready ..."

"Break!"

The Krakens moved to the line. The booing intensified. Pure hate distilled from 181,500-plus.

He surveyed the defense. The Pioneers' "D" had given up 21 points a game — they won games with Adrienne's arm. The middle linebacker, Kagan the Crazy, was a thickly built Quyth Warrior and the most dangerous player on the team. He loved to blitz, especially delayed blitzes, and already had three sacks in the first two games. The defensive line was nothing special, allowing an average of 168 yards on the ground — hence Hokor's emphasis on running. Hokor wanted to control the ball and keep Adrienne off the field as much as possible. Quentin scanned the defensive backfield and recognized his opponents for the afternoon: Palatine, the right corner, Tumwater, the safety, Westland, the free safety, and Belgrade, the left corner.

The stats and tendencies of all four defensive backs suddenly popped into his thoughts. Information seemed to flood into his brain as if from an outside pipeline. Belgrade had poor speed, she often gave up long passes over the top. Tumwater was playing with a hurt right tentacle, and in the last game she had avoided big hits. Palatine was a good right corner but lacked the height and jumping ability to match premier receivers. Westland, a five-year vet, built much thicker than most Sklorno, was known for her devastating hits.

"Greeeeen, nineteen!" Quentin shouted, barely able to hear himself over the crowd. "Green, nineteen!"

Quentin turned to the right and handed off to Fayed. The Pioneers' linebackers came quickly on a run-blitz, knocking Fayed backward, stuffing the play at the line.

Quentin looked to the sidelines, but Hokor said nothing over the ear-speaker. Quentin tapped his heads-up display to double-check the next play: another run. He sighed and formed up the huddle.

AS THE FIRST QUARTER wore on, it became obvious that the Pioneers weren't going to let Mitchell "The Machine" Fayed run wild. They run-blitzed, they stacked linebackers in the gaps. They didn't use pass-coverage formations like the nickel package, even on third downs. The Krakens' first two possessions were three-and-out. Quentin didn't even throw his first pass until the end of the first quarter, a completion to Kobayasho for seven yards. The Pioneers clearly didn't fear this rookie quarterback in his first start — they practically dared Hokor to beat them with the pass.

Adrienne struck again in the second quarter, hitting Westchester for a 52-yard strike. Quentin burned with jealousy at the Pioneer quarterback's long TD passes. He knew he could match the performance, especially against the run-oriented Pioneers defense, but he wasn't going to question Hokor anymore. He'd run the plays that were called.

He felt his pulse quicken when he took the field late in the second quarter and Hokor finally outlined a passing attack.

"Y-set, double-post," Hokor said. "Test them downfield. If it's not open, don't throw, you got it?"

Quentin nodded as he moved to the huddle and called the play. The team seemed a bit listless in the huddle, as if they had already conceded defeat. The only way to get them going, Quentin knew, was with a sustained drive or a big play. He broke the huddle and lined up. The Pioneers still showed a run defense, leaving Hawick and Scarborough covered with only woman-to-woman. Quentin calmed himself, knowing he had to be cool to take advantage of this opportunity.

"Blue, fifteeeeeen! Blue, fifteen … hut-*hut*!"

He dropped straight back, eyes following Hawick, over to Scarborough, then back to Hawick again. She already had a step on her defender. Quentin stepped up to throw, but the pocket collapsed almost immediately. A huge Ki lineman bore down on him from the left. Quentin dodged to his right, still looking downfield, but he sensed pressure on that side as well. He stepped up into the pocket, where Kagan met him head-on with a hit that knocked Quentin flat on his back. It was like being smacked with a wrecking ball. His eyes scrunched in pain. Quentin heard the continuing "ooohhh" of the crowd as the holomonitors in each end zone replayed the hit.

With second-and-long, Hokor called another pass. Kagan blitzed again. Quentin didn't have time to throw downfield and had to settle for a quick five-yard strike to Warburg. The Krakens tried a draw on the next play and got nowhere. Defeated once again, the offense ran off the field as the punt team came on.

Quentin took off his helmet and threw it at the bench in disgust. He couldn't make things happen if he didn't have time to throw. He'd studied the Pioneers games over and over again — their defensive line wasn't anything special. He had to get his O-line motivated. He stood and started walking down the bench to where the Ki linemen were huddled in their big ball but stopped — Donald Pine was already in front of them.

Pine leaned heavily on his crutches, their tops digging into his armpits, leaving his hands free to flail about. He wildly gestured first to the linemen, then to the field, then up in the air, then back again. Pine looked furious, madder than Quentin had ever seen him. Pine was screaming them up one side and down the other, and Quentin didn't have to wonder what for.

Why is he doing that? Quentin thought. *That's my job.*

Why was he doing it? Because the linemen *listened* to Pine.

Once again, Pine seemed to be helping Quentin, not sabotaging him. Had he done the same thing in making Denver offer help for passing practice?

AT HALFTIME, the game seemed to have slipped away. The Krakens were down 21-3, their only score coming on a nice 52-yard field goal by Arioch Morningstar. Quentin saw possibilities on almost every play, or *thought* he saw them, but he wasn't about to alter Hokor's calls. Maybe it was like before, like in the Hydras game, and Hokor knew something that he didn't. He'd made the most out of the few opportunities that came his way, hitting five of his eleven passes for 82 yards. The completions were nice, but he spent most of the first half flat on his back either knocked down after the pass or dragged down for one of the three first-half sacks. That was more sacks than he'd suffered his entire *season* with the Raiders. No touchdowns and one interception when a Ki tentacle deflected his pass at the line of scrimmage. He had also scrambled for 22 rushing yards — far more out of necessity than choice. On the Krakens' home field, he could have run for much more, but the Pioneer field's slippery footing made it hard for him to make sharp cuts.

The visitors' central locker room was filled with beings dressed in orange leg armor with black trim and orange jerseys stained with streaks of oily yellow. Hokor stood in the middle of the circular room, his fur extended to its full length. He ranted and raved about the offensive line's poor showing, but much like Pine's lecture on the sidelines, nobody seemed to care.

THE PIONEERS WALKED away with the game, winning by an embarrassing score of 35-10. Fayed had managed one big play, breaking three tackles for a 24-yard run and the Krakens' only contribution to the weekly ESPN highlight reel.

Quentin undressed at his locker, feeling neither happy nor sad about the outcome. He'd played as well as could be expected under the circumstances, the circumstances being that the offensive line didn't really give a crap about protecting him. He'd finished the day 15-of-35 for 186 yards, with 37 yards rushing. His body felt like he'd gone ten rounds in the octagon with Korak the Cutter. He'd thought he'd taken some blows in practice, but now he knew that his own defenders had been holding back, if only just a bit.

The Krakens changed in almost total quiet. They had one win, two losses, and were already two games out of first. Their chances of moving up to Tier One seemed near nil. Nobody spoke, except for Yassoud, who went from player to player, asking who was up for a night in Port Whitok's gambling district.

As Quentin pulled off his chest armor, Donald Pine hobbled over, the crutches making him awkward as he slowly sat.

"You played well out there, Q."

Quentin shrugged. "Not that any of my so-called teammates would notice. Or care, for that matter."

Pine nodded. "Oh, they noticed. But you're right, they didn't *care*. I told you before, there's more to being a quarterback than skill and talent."

"Listen, gramps, I don't need a lecture. Now take off."

Pine didn't move. "You *do* need a lecture, Quentin. So did the offensive line, but I already gave them one. Several, as a matter of fact."

Quentin started to speak, then stopped. He remembered Pine on the sidelines, arms waving like a madman, yelling his head off at 3,000-plus pounds of offensive line. No one else had done that. Not Warburg, not Hokor, not Quentin himself. Just Pine.

"Okay," Quentin said quietly. "Say what you've got to say."

"Q, you've got all the talent in the world. It pours off you like stink from a skunk. Your brain works overtime — I see you come up with play adjustments that are *almost* as good as those of another Krakens quarterback I know." Pine smiled with the joke. Quentin felt some of his stress fade away — Pine's smile had a way of making people feel comfortable.

"Yeah," Quentin said, "that Yitzhak is pretty damn creative."

Pine laughed. "Right, right. So you've got all the tools, but as you saw today, the greatest general in the world can't win if the troops won't go to war. The Ki linemen are not some random beings from their culture, they are *soldiers*. I've seen normal Ki citizens, have you?"

Quentin shrugged. "Just a few on the streets in Ionath."

"And did they look violent? Did they look strong?"

Quentin thought back, then shook his head. They didn't look violent at all. In fact, they were Human-sized, weighing probably 250 pounds or so, half the weight of a Kraken lineman. He hadn't realized that fact until this moment.

"The difference between citizen and warrior isn't as dramatic as it is in the Quyth culture, where there's a completely separate sub-species built for fighting, but it's there. Ki soldiers are selected from a very young age, like the equivalent of three years old in Humans. They're trained from that time in how to fight, how to kill, how to endure pain and hardship that Humans couldn't come close to handling. Most of our linemen have taken sentient life, Quentin, some with their bare hands. So to speak. All of them participated in ground combat at one point or another."

"And that's supposed to excuse them for piss-poor blocking?"

Pine shook his head. "No, you don't get it. They *love* blocking, they *love* tackling. Physical combat is a huge part of their culture. But they aren't in control of this game. They're not calling the plays, they're just doing what they're told to do. Someone has to *lead* them. And if they don't respect that someone, they simply don't try as hard."

Quentin thought about Pine's words. "So what you're telling me is that the big, mean, deadly Ki are kind of ... sensitive?"

Pine smiled and nodded. "If you don't respect them, they're sure not going to respect you. And if they don't respect you, they're not *following* you, they're just going through the motions."

Quentin looked off in the distance. Yassoud flitted about Tom Pareless like a big mosquito. Pareless kept pushing him away, but Yassoud just buzzed back again — he obviously had run out of people to go gambling with, and Pareless was his last hope.

"Okay," Quentin said, looking back at Pine. "So what do I do about it?"

"You really want to know? You're not going to like it."

Quentin waved his left hand in an inner circular motion, as if to say *come on, come on.*

"The Ki are a very tight species," Pine said. "They send nerve impulses through their skin and antenna. That's why they cluster up like that all the time, on the sidelines and at night. When they're touching, they can kind of talk without speaking. That also makes for closeness among them, gives them a sense of tribe, or of family."

"So they're not just *sensitive*," Quentin said in a deadpan. "They're also *touchy-feely*?"

Pine shrugged his shoulders. "I didn't cause their evolution, I just study it. You act like they're revolting."

"They are."

"So what?" Pine said angrily. "So *what*? So they're revolting. Do you want to win games or not?"

Quentin nodded.

"Fine. You have to stop acting like they have the plague. Touch them. Hug them the way you would any Human player who did something good."

"I, uh, don't really do hugs."

"You know what I mean, jerk. Get it in your head that you have to stop thinking of different races, and start seeing all of them, Ki, Quyth and Sklorno, as your *teammates*."

Quentin's face wrinkled up in guarded suspicion. "I don't know, man. This seems a little too, well, like Creterakian propaganda, that we all have to get along as one giant race of sentients. I mean, come on, does this stuff really *work*?"

Pine smiled and held up his right hand, fingers outstretched. Glittering championship rings adorned his middle and ring fingers.

The point finally clicked home. Quentin nodded. Pine wasn't his enemy. The man was trying to help him, probably had been all along. Quentin had trouble getting his thoughts around the concept — no one had ever helped him before, not without wanting something in return. And Pine not only wanted nothing, he had everything to lose by helping Quentin. The more Pine helped, the more likely he was to lose his starting job. It just didn't make any sense.

And Pine was an expert on the subject, proof positive being his two Galaxy Bowl wins. Quentin realized he'd been a damn fool — he had one of the greatest players in the game trying to help him, and he'd treated that help like some kind of underhanded trick.

"Pine, why are you doing this?"

"Doing what?"

"Helping me."

Pine looked confused. "Because you need it, why else?"

"Yeah, but, if you help me, and I get better ..." Quentin's voice trailed off.

Pine nodded. "Oh, now, I understand. I'm helping you because you're *on my team*. You get that yet? I need a backup that can win games. Besides, my career only has a few years left, I know that. It would be nice to, well, have someone to teach. Someone to ... to ... I don't know."

"Carry on the Don Pine tradition?"

Pine smiled. "Sure, that works. Someone to carry on the Don Pine tradition."

"Thank you," Quentin said. He extended his right hand, which Pine shook. "I've got a good idea on how to take your advice."

Pine nodded and hobbled away on his crutches. Quentin stood and finished removing his armor. He pulled on a robe, then hit the service button in his locker. Messal appeared as if out of thin air.

"You rang, sir?"

"Messal, I've had it with these nannite showers."

"Is there a problem, sir?"

"No problem some steaming hot water won't fix. Get Shizzle here immediately, then take me to the Ki locker room."

"YOU SURE you want to do this?" Shizzle asked as he flew small circles around Quentin's head. "They have been known to *eat* Humans, you know."

"Just be quiet until I need you to translate."

Messal led them into the Ki locker room. "Ki eyes take in a larger spectrum of light than Human eyes. Consequently, only a few purple lights provide any illumination. So watch your step."

The Ki locker room was dark. And hot. And humid enough to compete with the geothermal steam baths back on Stewart. Goodwill or no goodwill, there was no denying that the place stank. He'd thought pregame Ki odors were bad, but his nose let him know those were nothing compared to the post-game scents. Smelled like rotten fish mixed in with decomposed chicken guts. Quentin ignored the smell and followed Messal to the back.

Quentin heard the hiss of water jets, and his skin tingled in anticipation. He suddenly realized it had been *weeks* since he'd had a real shower.

Messal opened a door and bowed as Quentin passed. Steam billowed out of the open door and up onto the ceiling, making hazy purple clouds where it crossed in front of the dim lights. Quentin stood at the open door for one second, swallowed and stepped through.

One step inside the door, he stopped cold. If he had somehow accidentally stumbled upon a scene like this, he probably would have turned and ran. This was far worse than any Holy Man propaganda horror holo he'd seen back home.

A deep pool of water sat in the middle of the circular room. The low lights made the water look black. Dozens of showerheads ringed the ceiling, angling water down to the mass of creatures bundled up in the pool's center.

They sat there, a giant, entwined ball of worm-like bodies, multi-jointed legs, pinkish mouths lined with black teeth, muscular multi-jointed arms, orangish skin without end and thousands of reddish-brown spots of enamel, each wet and glistening like a black ruby. They looked like a coiled, multi-headed dragon straight out of the Holy Book.

As a kid, Quentin had seen educational movies of snakes. There was a strange mating practice for some snakes, where hundreds of them twisted into a giant, writhing pile of skin and scales and mucus. That's what the Ki cluster reminded him of, only these snakes were twelve feet long and could bench-press 1,300 pounds.

They didn't turn their heads to look when he came in — they didn't have to, their unblinking black eyes let them see everything at once. The ball of bodies seemed to move, to *slide* just a bit, and one figure slithered out of the pack. The long, thick body splashed water out of the pool and onto the tile floor as it moved slowly toward Quentin.

Oddly enough, he instantly recognized the oncoming Ki. Maybe they didn't all look alike after all.

Great, he thought. *Mum-O-Killowe as the Welcome Wagon*. The temperamental rookie walked up until he was only a few inches from Quentin, then barked out words in his guttural language.

Messal translated. "He wants to know what you think you're doing here."

Quentin swallowed. There was a whole room of them, and he was dressed in only a robe. He wanted to leave ... but he wanted to win more. Two losses were enough.

"This is the only room with water showers," Quentin said. Shizzle started translating before the second word was even out of his mouth, and he finished only a fraction of a second after Quentin stopped.

Mum-O-Killowe barked again.

"He says that you should go."

Quentin stepped to Mum-O-Killowe's right, gently shouldering past the huge Ki as he did. The boldness of the move seemed to surprise Mum-O, for it was a full second before Quentin sensed the lineman reaching out for him. Quentin avoided the multi-jointed arms by quickly diving into the water.

The water was almost scalding. It felt miraculous against his skin. He arched and swam upward, his face breaking the surface only a few feet from the giant ball of alien linemen. Mum-O-Killowe roared something and started to splash toward Quentin, but Kill-O-Yowet, the left tackle, barked one short, definitive syllable.

Mum-O-Killowe stopped short of Quentin, stared at him for a second, then slithered back into the ball.

"Kill-O-Yowet says you can stay," Shizzle said. Quentin kicked back to the pool's edge. He draped his arms on the tile and his body sank in up to his chest. Water sprayed down on his closed eyes and smiling face. The wet heat felt wonderful on his bruised body. Maybe his effort to bond with the Ki linemen would work, maybe it wouldn't, but at least he'd get a decent shower out of the thing.

PIONEERS BOX SCORE

Final	1	2	3	4	T
Ionath	0	3	0	7	10
Whitok	7	14	7	7	35

SCORING SUMMARY

1st QUARTER		ION	WHI
Whitok TD	Bangor 72-yard pass from Condor Adrienne (Pos Mercur kick)	0	7
Whitok TD	Westchester 52-yard pass from Condor Adrienne (Pos Mercur kick)	0	14

2nd QUARTER		ION	WHI
Ionath FG	Arioch Morningstar 52-yard field goal	3	14
Whitok TD	Andrew Collins 4-yard run (Pos Mercur kick)	3	21

3rd QUARTER		ION	WHI
Whitok TD	Bangor 23-yard pass from Condor Adrienne (Pos Mercur kick)	3	28

4th QUARTER		ION	WHI
Ionath TD	Mitchell Fayed 24-yard run (Arioch Morningstar kick)	10	28
Whitok TD	Apollo Weinhardt 4-yard run (Pos Mercur kick)	10	35

TEAM STATISTICS	ION	WHI
First Downs	9	16
Third Down Efficiency	5-13	10-15
TOTAL NET YARDS	**258**	**408**
Total Plays	66	68
Average Gain Per Play	3.9	6.0
NET YARDS RUSHING	**109**	**72**
Rushes	31	36
Average Per Rush	3.5	2.0
NET YARDS PASSING	**149**	**336**
Pass Completion	15-35	22-32
Yards Per Pass	4.3	10.5
Times Sacked	5	1
Yards Lost To Sacks	37	4
Had Intercepted	2	0
PUNTS	**8**	**5**
Average Punt	41.2	36.3
PENALTIES	**6**	**4**
Penalty Yards	50	25
FUMBLES	**1**	**1**
Fumbles Lost	0	1
Time Of Possession	**25:38**	**34:12**

PASSING

KRAKENS	CMP	ATT	YDS	PCT	YPA	SACK	SYDS	TD	INT
Quentin Barnes	15	35	186	42.9	5.3	5	37	0	2

PIONEERS	CMP	ATT	YDS	PCT	YPA	SACK	SYDS	TD	INT
Condor Adrienne	22	32	340	68.8	10.6	1	4	3	0

RUSHING

KRAKENS	ATT	YDS	AVG	LONG	TD	FUM
Mitchell Fayed	15	60	4.0	24	1	1
Quentin Barnes	9	37	4.1	22	0	0
Yassoud Murphy	5	10	2.0	4	0	0
Tom Pareless	2	2	1.0	1	0	0

PIONEERS	ATT	YDS	AVG	LONG	TD	FUM
Andrew Collins	24	50	2.1	12	1	1
Apollo Weinhardt	12	22	1.8	5	1	0

RECEIVING

KRAKENS	REC	YDS	AVG	LONG	TD	FUM
Hawick	4	74	18.5	37	0	0
Yotaro Kobayasho	3	38	12.7	14	0	0
Scarborough	3	35	11.7	19	0	0
Rick Warburg	2	17	8.5	12	0	0
Mezquitic	1	8	8.0	8	0	0
Denver	1	8	8.0	8	0	0
Yassoud Murphy	1	6	6.0	6	0	0

PIONEERS	REC	YDS	AVG	LONG	TD	FUM
Bangor	12	175	14.6	72	2	0
Westchester	5	112	22.4	52	1	0
Borris McGraw	3	32	10.7	21	0	0
Leningrad	1	11	11.0	11	0	0
Akbar Blue	1	10	10.0	10	0	0

THREE HOURS AFTER the game, the Ionath Krakens began shuttling back up to the *Touchback*. Yassoud had managed, somehow, to cram in two hours worth of partying. He and Tom Pareless showed up in time for the last shuttle, drunk enough that they could barely walk, but not so drunk that they couldn't sing "My Girl from Satirli 6" at the top of their lungs.

Quentin felt sore all over, and he knew it was only a harbinger of things to come the next morning, yet the hot soak in the Ki pool had lifted his spirits.

It's a game, he thought to himself. *What goes on off the field is as much of a game as what happens on the field.* He'd been thinking about it all wrong. He hadn't needed to bond with his teammates back in the PNFL because he'd been good enough to win games almost single-handedly. But in the GFL, even at Tier Two, *everyone* was good. These players were the best a galaxy had to offer. The game, his *new* game, would be making them play as a team.

He stood on the launch platform, gazing up at the twilight sky of Port Whitok. He sensed someone approaching. Quentin turned to find himself facing the squat, powerful form of a Quyth Warrior. Shayat the Thick, the backup right outside linebacker. He played behind John Tweedy, which meant that he didn't play much at all. Tweedy rarely came out of the game, thanks to his skills at defending both the run and the pass.

"You played well," Shayat said. It was, Quentin realized, the first time Shayat had ever spoken to him.

"Thanks," Quentin said. "It wasn't enough."

Shayat's carapace was a deep, silvery black. A painted unit insignia adorned his left shoulder. Under the insignia were horizontal lines, each of which, Quentin had learned, represented a combat mission. Shayat's lines ran from his insignia almost to his wrist. Enameled graphics covered his carapace — the most prominent of which was a Krakens logo emblazoned across his midriff. On his back was an Earth crab wearing a crown and holding a football — the logo of the Yucatan Sea-Kings, a Tier Three team. A ring of white surrounded Shayat's single eye, making him look even more bug-eyed than Hokor or any of the other Quyth. But they didn't call him Shayat the Thick for nothing: layers and layers of powerful muscles graced his frame. His pedipalps were so heavy they looked like John Tweedy's arms, and Shayat's arms were so thick they might have been Tweedy's huge legs. Shayat wore a backpack that looked to be completely stuffed.

"We need to win next week," Shayat said.

Quentin nodded. "That we do."

After a moment of silence, Shayat spoke. "Do you like money?"

It seemed a strange question, but straightforward enough. "I like money just fine."

"Do you want to make more?"

Quentin said nothing, but he suddenly knew what was coming next. The dark underbelly of the GFL had avoided him — until now, it seemed.

"This is all juniper berries," Shayat said, his left pedipalp reaching behind him to pat the backpack. "Worth a fortune on Ionath. Human races control gin production. They drive up the price. But Workers will pay big money for raw juniper berries. They crush them and mix them with fermented digestive acids from collowacks, a kind of insect back on Quyth."

"I thought juniper berries were illegal," Quentin said.

"They are. Very illegal. But the System Police can't search us, remember? If they do, the Creterakians might pull Port Whitok's GFL franchise rights. You know what would happen to the local government if that happened?"

Quentin shrugged.

"There would be riots. Beings love football. Basically, whatever we can carry on our backs is ignored."

Quentin nodded, wondering what a bulging backpack of processed opium might be worth back on Stewart.

"I've got the berries, mesh, weed, heroin, sleepy, conot-root, you name it. Everything that's selling back home."

"So why are you telling me this?"

"I've got a nice pipeline going," Shayat said. "Every away

game, I bring out a load of money. My contacts bring me a load of juniper berries, which I buy and bring with me when we return to Ionath. On Ionath, berries go for five to ten times what I paid for them, depending on supply."

Quentin whistled. "At least a five hundred-percent markup, eh? Not bad."

"I want to make more. If you carry a shipment next time, you'll get half the profit."

"Why only half?"

"My contacts, my network."

Quentin nodded. "I guess that's fair enough."

"So you're in?"

Quentin shook his head. "I'm not in. I don't want any part of your smuggling ring, you got that? And if you ask me again, you and I are going to go a few rounds."

Shayat's pedipalps twitched in laughter. "You think you could go even *one* round with me, Human?"

Quentin nodded. "Maybe, maybe not, but if you don't get out of my face, we're sure going to find out." He stared with cold-hearted disdain at the larger alien. Shayat turned and walked away.

BACK ONBOARD THE *Touchback*, Quentin walked through the Sklorno section of the ship. While the Human section was fairly spartan and decorated in subdued tones (when the decor wasn't Krakens orange-and-black), the Sklorno section paraded a mind-boggling maze of electric colors. Blues, purples, reds, yellows, greens, oranges ... all ranging from near-black to near-neon intensity. Patterns, colors and pictures covered the floor, the walls and the ceiling. It was intensely beautiful and disgustingly ugly all at the same time. He found it ironic that the species with no color on their bodies decorated with more colors than anyone else.

He checked his messageboard, which displayed a map of the ship guiding him to Denver's room. Without the map, he'd have quickly become lost in the Technicolor intensity. Like all doors in this section, Denver's door was oblong, tall and narrow, like the outline of an egg stretched lengthwise. It was different, but a door was a door — it struck Quentin that this was something (minor, but something) that the different races had in common: a need for privacy, or perhaps just a need to put up walls. Except the Ki, that was ... he wasn't sure if the Ki even understood the concept of privacy.

Quentin pushed the door buzzer. There was a brief pause. The door slid open. Denver stood there for a moment, then started to tremble. Her raspers unrolled, hitting the ground.

"Quentin Barnes," she said.

Quentin nodded. "Um, listen ... I know I've been a bit rude to you."

Denver simply stared. Stared and trembled. From inside the room, Milford walked up behind her. Milford also began to tremble. They both looked at him like he was some kind of ... well ... alien. To them, he was an alien, probably as weird and disgusting as they were to him.

"So I was hoping that your offer was still good."

"We participate in making you even greater?"

"Yes, I would appreciate that."

Denver began to bounce lightly in place. Milford did the same. Quentin could see into the room and noticed that the ceilings were at least twenty feet high.

"When-when-when-when!" Denver said.

Quentin shrugged. "Well, I'm going to be sore as hell tomorrow, so how about we get few reps in right now? I know the VR field is open, and we —"

The two receivers raced out of the room, cutting his words short as they inadvertently shoved him against the far wall. They sprinted down the hall with all their flat-out Sklorno speed, headed for the ship's center section and the VR field.

Like little kids the morning of Giving Day, he thought, and laughed to himself as he followed them down the hall.

• • •

WITH ALL THE ROOM'S lights turned off, the only illumination came from the row of holotanks. The moving, flashing images cast an uneven and unsteady light onto Hokor's face. Some of his players were taking the loss very hard, and others didn't seem to care at all.

Michnik and Khomeni were in the cafeteria, drowning their sorrows in food. The Ki were also about to start their meal. Hokor heard the pitiful bleat of their prey animal. He punched a button on his remote control, turning off that monitor before the Ki started eating. Some players were in the infirmary, Doc tending to their wounds. In a way, Hokor wished more of his players were in the infirmary, as dozens of injuries might be a way to console himself at the humiliating loss.

The Krakens were 1-2, their chances of qualifying for the Tier Two tournament almost completely destroyed. The Glory Warpigs and the Whitok Pioneers both sat at 3-0. The way Condor Adrienne was playing, he didn't see the Pioneers losing more than two games at most. The Krakens had to win their next six to even have a chance at the playoffs.

The Krakens' next game against the 0-3 Sky Demolition was the only chance to get back in the race — at least mathematically. A loss ... well, another loss meant the end of the playoff hopes and the end of Hokor's tenure with Ionath.

This would be his last season as Krakens coach, he knew that. Gredok wouldn't stand for it. If only Pine hadn't gone down! That was why he went after Quentin, but the talented young Nationalite needed more time. Time Hokor didn't have.

"Computer, where is Quentin Barnes?"

[QUENTIN BARNES IS UTILIZING THE KRIEGS-BALLOK VIRTUAL PRACTICE SYSTEM]

Nothing new there. Hokor punched a button to call up a holo of the VR practice room. Barnes was there, as he always was. The Human had taken quite a beating thanks to an offensive line that simply did not want to block for him. Yet he had kept getting up and kept playing as hard as he could. And now, only hours after the game, he was practicing yet again. Barnes dropped back, stepped up, and threw a hard crossing pattern. The throw was a bit behind the receiver. Hokor expected to see the ball pass through the out-stretched holographic arms and go bouncing down the field, but it hit the arms and stuck.

Hokor leaned forward. The VR players faded away, leaving not only Quentin, but Denver and Milford as well. Hokor could scarcely believe his eyes. The two Sklorno receivers ran back to Quentin and lined up for another play.

WEEK THREE LEAGUE ROUNDUP
(Courtesy of Galaxy Sports network)

Can any team stop Condor Adrienne? Maybe, but that team certainly isn't the **Ionath Krakens** (1-2), who let Adrienne throw for 340 yards and three touchdowns on 22-of-32 passing. Adri-enne's **Whitok Pioneers** (3-0) torched the **Ionath Krakens** (1-2) for a 35-10 win.

So will Adrienne be stopped? If so, it might be this week when the Pioneers travel to the **Glory Warpigs** (3-0). The 'Pigs remained tied for first thanks to a narrow 14-12 win over **Orbiting Death** (2-1). The Death couldn't manage a touchdown against the Warpigs' defense, which ranks first in all of Tier Two.

Finally a win on the home planet as the **Quyth Survivors** (1-2) defeated the **Bigg Diggers** (1-2), 29-24.

Sheb Stalkers (2-1) got back into the playoff hunt with a 19-14 win over the **Grontak Hydras** (1-2), and the **Woo Wallcrawlers** (1-2) notched their first victory of the season with a 42-6 drubbing of the winless **Sky Demolition** (0-3).

DEATHS:
This week we mourn the passing of two players, Demolition de-fensive lineman **Kok-O-Thalla** and Bigg Diggers' receiver **Martins-ville**. Martinsville died on a clean hit by Survivors' defensive back Topinabee, and Kok-O-Thalla died during a fumble pileup. The league has not ruled it a clean death and is still investigating, al-though no Wallcrawlers player has yet been fined.

WEEK THREE PLAYERS OF THE WEEK:

Offense: Condor Adrienne, quarterback, Whitok Pioneers. 22-of-32, 340 yards, three TDs, no INTs.

Defense: Yalla the Biter, linebacker, Sky Demolition. Eleven tackles, two sacks and a fumble recovery.

GAME FOUR: Ionath Krakens (1-2) at Sky Demolition (0-3)

QUYTH IRRADIATED CONFERENCE STANDINGS

Glory Warpigs	3-0
Whitok Pioneers	3-0
Sheb Stalkers	2-1
Orbiting Death	2-1
Bigg Diggers	1-2
Grontak Hydras	1-2
Ionath Krakens	1-2
Quyth Survivors	1-2
Woo Wallcrawlers	1-2
Sky Demolition	0-3

WITH THE TOUCHBACK hovering in orbit, the shuttle flew Quentin and the other rookies down to Ionath City. This time, however, when they got out, there were Quyth Workers and Quyth Leaders dressed in white uniforms. A red line glowed on the roof of the Krakens' Building.

"Players, line up on the red line," said a blue-furred Quyth Leader.

Quentin lightly elbowed Yassoud. "What's this all about?"

"It's a customs check," Yassoud said. "Quyth System Police. Don't worry about it, league rules apply in the Concordia just like they do everywhere else in the galaxy. The customs guys can't touch you, so whatever you're carrying, they can't do a thing."

Quentin looked down the line and saw Shayat the Thick with his bulging backpack. He then looked at other players and saw that several of them carried a bag of some sort. Yassoud held a small satchel — Quentin didn't want to know what was inside.

They stood on the red line with the other rookies. The blue-furred Quyth Leader walked down the line, looking at each one of them in turn. Two white-uniformed workers slid a grav-cart into the shuttle.

"I am Kotop the Observer," the leader said. "My team will be checking you each time you come back from out-system. I'm sure nobody here is smuggling anything, right?"

Yassoud started laughing, his curly beard jiggling in time.

"Yes, it is all so very funny," Kotop said. Quentin stared at the little Leader — did he detect sarcasm in the alien's voice?

Kotop said nothing else, just stared, his one eye a deep shade of black. The workers came out of the shuttle.

"No explosives, no weapons," one of them said to Kotop.

"You may all go," Kotop said. He sounded disgusted.

"WE'RE IN TROUBLE," Hokor said quietly. Despite the fact that every Krakens player was crammed into the central meeting area, Hokor didn't need volume to be heard. Nobody made a sound. There had been some joking and laughing and boasting as the players filtered out of their respective locker rooms and into the central area, but all of that faded when Hokor used his holopen to decorate the far wall with three large, glowing orange marks.

The marks were the number one, a dash and the number two. 1-2.

"We're a losing team," Hokor said. "A *losing* team. How does that sound to you?"

No one answered.

"Tweedy, how does that sound to you?"

"Sounds like I'd rather eat a poop sandwich, Coach."

"Right," Hokor said. "So why did we allow the Pioneers to throw for 340 yards on us, when we only sacked Adrienne once?"

Tweedy said nothing.

"Berea," Hokor said to the right corner back, who immediately began to tremble. "What number do you like more, one-and-two, or 340 yards passing?"

Berea said nothing. Instead, she fell on the floor and lay flat, trembling like a damaged moth.

"And you, Barnes? How does it feel to be on your first losing team?"

"Humiliating, Coach," Quentin said quietly.

"And you, Kill-O-Yowet?" Hokor's voice rose in intensity. "I've got some numbers for you, too. Which do you like better, one-and-two, or five sacks? *Five* sacks."

Kill-O-Yowet said nothing.

"Do you realize that in one game, we went from allowing the fewest sacks in the conference to allowing the second most? Do you realize that you and your brethren on the offensive line are now the *second worst* unit in the Quyth Irradiated Conference?"

Kill-O-Yowet let out a low growl, but that was all.

Hokor hit a button, and the "1-2" vanished. He wrote three new symbols.

0-3.

"This is the record of Sky Demolition. They are the worst team in the conference. If they beat us, then, by default we're the worst team in the conference. If you think you feel bad now, imagine how you will feel if we lose to them."

Hokor paused dramatically. A deathly silence filled the locker room.

He cleared the numbers again. Three names flashed up on the screen: Brady Entenabe, San Mateo and Yalla the Biter. The holo-tank flashed two pictures: a tall, blonde-haired Human frozen in mid-throw and a sprinting Sklorno. Both were dressed in the uniforms of the Sky Demolition: light purple leg armor, deep purple jersey with light purple numbers trimmed in white and deep purple helmets with three white stripes down the center.

"Brady Entenabe is a second-year quarterback having a surprisingly good year, despite the Demolition's record. In three games, he has seven touchdown passes and has run for two more. Four of those touchdown passes have gone to San Mateo. Entenabe has also given up five interceptions. He's thrown for 812 yards, 260 of which have gone to San Mateo. We are going to stop that combination. There is no alternative."

Hokor hit a button. The pictures faded away, replaced by a moderate-sized Quyth Warrior.

"Yalla the Biter is fast, perhaps the fastest linebacker in the conference. He is faster than John Tweedy. He is faster than Virak the Mean. He has four sacks on the season, along with two interceptions and seventeen tackles. He is the Demolition's biggest defensive threat. He also has six unnecessary roughness penalties, three for late hits on the quarterback. Last week he was thrown out of the game for fighting. In Week One he killed Princeton, kick returner for Bigg Diggers, on a clean hit. Last week he severed the leg of the Wallcrawlers' tight end, ending the Human's career. If the offensive line plays as poorly this week as they did against the Pioneers, I suspect our quarterbacks will be sledded off the field."

Hokor cleared the pictures. The room remained quiet. "The Sky Demolition is not a deep team — if we stop those three, we win. I don't care about the Tier Two tournament anymore. All I care about is the Sky Demolition. This game is all that matters to us. Let's practice like we want to win back our honor."

Quentin felt the change in the locker room. There was no yelling, no pushing, no testosterone-oriented boasting, but the air had changed nonetheless. Hokor's quiet speech had affected them all, himself included. Quentin had four days to change the team. Four days to get them playing as a unit.

But was that enough time?

THE TOUCHBACK was in punch drive, en route to Orbital Station Two, home of the Sky Demolition. Quentin shut down the holotank in his room. He'd looked at the Demolition defensive players over and over again — now it was time to put that study into practical use. He headed for the VR practice field. Last night's practice had gone well. The repetitive throws to the receivers had started to give him a better perspective on the speed involved. Practicing with holograms was effective, but a hologram couldn't catch the ball and, therefore, couldn't give him a truly realistic idea of where to put a ball so that a talented receiver could haul it in.

Quentin walked into the VR field, expecting to see Denver and Milford — it shocked him to see not only the two rookies, but Hawick and Scarborough as well. In addition, two reserve defensive backs — Saugatuck and Rehoboth — stood ready to play.

"If Quentin Barnes approves," Denver said with the Quyth equivalent of a submissive bow, "these humble players would like to partake in the receiving of your gifts."

Quentin felt slightly embarrassed to see Hawick and Scarborough, two starting receivers. Yet as soon as that feeling crossed his brain, he chased it away — he was the starting quarterback and should have asked those two to practice with him from the beginning. The fact that they had come on their own, well, that was both emotionally flattering and strategically encouraging. Now he'd have an even more realistic version of a game situation.

"I approve," Quentin said. "And thank you."

All the Sklorno bowed as one. Quentin smiled as he walked to the rack of footballs, realizing that these teammates, at least, had accepted him as an equal.

FOR QUENTIN, the days blurred past, a run-on sentence crammed with practice and study with little of the punctuation that sleep would provide. He woke four hours before first meal, studied Sky Demolition defensive players, formations and plays, then went to eat with the team. He then sat in position meetings with Pine, Yitzhak and Hokor. Then team practice. Doc had said Pine could dress for the game, but he was not to practice, which meant Quentin took eighty-five percent of all reps. After practice came second meal, which Quentin now took with the rest of the team. He tried talking to as many teammates as he could. He got the impression his teammates knew he was trying, and it seemed to be making a difference.

After second meal, he studied some more. When most of the team went to sleep, Quentin set up shop in the VR field. By the third day, every Sklorno on the team was showing up for the late-night sessions: Quentin practiced with three or four receivers, depending on the set, and a full complement of defensive backs. The extra reps proved invaluable, and his timing started to improve, but it was the defenders that really got him over the hump. He could run whatever play he wanted, as many times as he wanted, gradually building up an instinctive knowledge of how fast the defenders could break on the ball and how far away they had to be to constitute an "open" receiver.

And he made sure they came at him with plenty of safety and corner blitzes.

It would be a long time before Sklorno-level speed became second-nature to him, the way Human-level speed had been back on Micovi. But as he ran rep after rep, threw pass after pass, he regained the belief that he could handle the offense and throw with total confidence.

QUENTIN HAD ASSUMED that no construct could be larger than Emperor One.

He was wrong.

Orbital Station Two, or "The Deuce" as it was known across most of the Human worlds, reminded Quentin of an animal he'd seen in his science classes: the sea urchin. The Deuce was spherical, like a moon or a planet, with hundreds of massive, orderly hollow spires jutting up and away from the surface.

He looked around the *Touchback*'s viewing bay. All of the rookies were there, of course, as they were to see any new planet. All of the Quyth Warriors were present, as was Hokor and at least two dozen Quyth Workers. Quentin hadn't even known that many Quyth Workers were on the ship. All of them — Warriors, Leaders and Workers alike — stared at the viewscreen with a suffused reverence.

He looked for someone to talk to. Every minute of every day, he tried to find any opportunity to communicate with his teammates, to forge the bonds that Pine said were so critical to winning. He realized he'd spent absolutely no time with Quyth Warriors. He walked across the viewing deck to stand next to Virak the Mean.

"Just how big are those things," Quentin asked, gesturing to the urchin-spikes that jutted from the space station.

Virak turned and looked at him. A Quyth Leader's eye is a huge, glassy sphere that looks about as resilient as a Giving Day tree ornament. A Quyth Warrior's eye, on the other hand, looks out from beneath thick, bony ridges. Even though a Warrior is more than twice the size of a Leader, a Warrior's eye is about two-thirds the size of a Leader's. A heavy eyelid, thick as Mason leather and coated with overlapping scales of tough chitin, hooded Virak's eye from the top. Quentin's childhood combat training taught him that the eye was the best place to attack a Quyth Warrior, but combat sims with realistic robots were a long way away from facing one in being-to-being combat. Now that he'd seen Quyth Warriors move in person, and on the field, the idea of poking out a Quyth Warrior's baseball-sized eye seemed much easier said than done.

Virak looked at him with a combination of amusement and disdain. Of all the races, the Quyth seemed to share the most Human-like emotions. When Virak spoke, it was with an air of boredom. "They are about two miles long."

"Two miles? That's amazing, they look so thick to be that tall."

"The spikes are about an eighth of a mile thick. They are beautiful."

Quentin stared at them and nodded. The symmetrical placement of the spikes did give the space station an ironically delicate appearance.

"The spikes are a life form," Virak said. "A silica-based organism that grows in a dense crystalline matrix. They are like bacteria. They grow, feed and reproduce in numbers beyond comprehension. Only the outside of the spike is alive — the inside is nothing but dead skeletons, but it is incredibly dense and hard. The crystalline structure gives it the strength to reach such massive heights."

"What are they for?"

"They serve two purposes. They reach down to the core. We can vent energy through them to propel the station in any direction. They are also the main supports of The Deuce's framework. Crossbeams connect to the spikes. You can see one below the equator, there."

Virak pointed. Quentin saw another long, green structure, although this one was horizontal rather than vertical. It ran between two spikes.

"Why is there only that one crossbeam?"

"There are thousands of them, but they are buried," Virak said. "The Deuce is built in stages, and each stage takes several cycles. With that crossbeam in place, workers will add to the station's mass."

As Quentin watched, a small, speckle-coated asteroid drifted down below the spike points and toward the surface. It took his brain a second to register the scale involved — the speckles were actually ships, and the asteroid had to be at least ten miles across and five miles thick. As he watched, the speckle-ships (which were each probably larger than the *Touchback*) drove the asteroid down. About a half-mile from the surface, the speckle-ships broke off, flying away from the asteroid like a slow-moving cloud of gnats. The massive rock continued its descent until it smashed into the surface with a huge, billowing cloud of dust and debris. The cloud seemed to hang in the air, floating lightly, pulled back down ever so slowly by The Deuce's weak gravity.

"That is how it gets bigger," Virak said. "Every day ships go out and find asteroids. They bring them back to add to the surface. As the mass continues to grow, so does the gravity, and so does the density of The Deuce's core. Additional matter on the surface compresses the core. The original living levels have long since been smashed flat by gravity. Workers constantly dig new levels, creating an exponentially increasing living area to accommodate a high birth rate. Immigration to the Orbital Stations fell to a near standstill after Whitok and Ionath were colonized. Now those seeking to escape the overpopulation of Quyth head to those planets instead of the Orbital Stations."

Quentin stared at the asteroid, a small pebble in a slightly larger crater. Crater and asteroid both barely a pimple on the surface.

"How long does it take to bring the asteroids in?"

Virak thought for a moment. "It depends on the materials needed. Some trips take only a few months. Others seek out asteroids comprised of rare or vital minerals, such as platinum or iridium. Those missions can take hundreds of years. It is common for a crew to leave The Deuce knowing that they will be long dead of old age before the ship returns, and their children or grandchildren will pilot the vessel home."

"How many ships are there?"

"Somewhere around a hundred thousand."

"A hundred ... just how long does it take to build that thing out there?"

"The Deuce has been growing for almost three hundred years, and The Ace is just over three hundred and fifty years old."

Quentin shook his head in amazement. All his life he'd been told the Quyth were only semi-intelligent beasts. Yet here was an engineering project that rivaled the terraforming of Solomon, a race so unified in purpose that they sacrificed themselves to build a home for future generations.

"It's not *that* big," Quentin said. "I mean, for an artificial construct, it's massive. But from a strategic perspective, I can't see how the Creterakians could take over entire planets that were twenty times as large, but not be able to take The Deuce."

"They took over other planets by swarming across the surface and overwhelming the enemy by sheer numbers," Virak said. "Here, the surface doesn't support life. They had to fight their way into the shaft to get at the living levels. They tried the same technique they used against the big ships — launching thousands of landing vessels, trying to overwhelm our shaft defenses. We slaughtered their people by the millions."

Quentin raised an eyebrow. "You sound like you actually fought here or something."

"I did," Virak said. "I was born here. When my time came, I fought not for new breeding grounds, but for defense of my birth-home."

Virak absently brushed a pedipalp hand across a long list of short, alien words etched into the chitin of his right arm."

"What are those?" Quentin asked, gesturing to the writing.

"Names of Warriors in my fighting pack. Warriors I had lived with most of my life. They died in the battles. I lost everyone in my fighting pack, but the Creterakians paid a terrible price for their assault."

"How many died?"

"Over two million Quyth," Virak said. "Including all my family. We estimate around 22 million Creterakians died trying to capture The Deuce. We kept rough count up to 10 million, but they just kept coming, and counting the dead was last on our list of needs."

Quentin tried to imagine fighting an enemy without number that came in wave after wave after wave. "That many, and they never broke through?"

"They eventually created a beachhead on Shaft Two and Shaft Four. We let them bring in troops and resources, then we used nuclear weapons to destroy those shafts before they could penetrate further. Eventually, technologists from Satirli 6 were brought in to engineer a way through the two miles that separated the surface from the living levels."

"Did they get in?"

"Yes, several times. But we distributed tactical nuclear weapons throughout The Deuce. Citizens were under strict orders — at the first sign of a breakthrough, seal off their section and detonate."

Quentin's jaw dropped. "At first sign? But how long did it take to evacuate the sections before you nuked them?"

Virak looked back into space. "There was no evacuation. Citizens sealed their section, then detonated."

"How many Quyth would that kill?"

Virak thought for a moment. "Depending on the section, anywhere from 150,000 to 250,000. It did not matter — as long as the Creterakians did not establish a beachhead on the living levels, from which they could re-supply and swarm through the entire station, any sacrifice was worth it."

"But to kill a quarter-million of your own people ..."

"It was necessary," Virak said. "The Creterakians do not control us. Freedom isn't free."

Quentin tried to imagine even the most hard-core Holy Man pulling the trigger on a nuke that would take out not only him, but 250,000 of his people.

"We maintained maneuverability," Virak said. "As big as it is, the whole station can enter punch-space. We moved toward the home planet, to help defend it. The three Orbital Stations are more than just ships, they are self-contained ecosystems with planetary-level manufacturing infrastructures and resources that are inexhaustible in the short term. That meant we were moving three full war-factories to defend the homeworld. We left the Creterakians with one choice — completely destroy the orbital stations, exterminating all life or fight the ships the stations produced for decades to come."

"So why didn't they blow up The Deuce and the others?"

"We don't know," Virak said. "Maybe they didn't have the technology. Relativity bombs, like the Sklorno used on Whitok, would have completely destroyed The Deuce, but the Creterakians either do not have them or did not use them. It doesn't matter anymore. We beat them back once, we'll beat them back again. The Quyth protect their homelands."

There was more than a hint of condescension in that comment. The Quyth, who despite their military presence were considered the galaxy's poor cousin of intelligence, had resisted the swarming Creterakians when all the "superior" governments had surrendered. The fact that most of the Quyth planets were irradiated wastelands seemed irrelevant, at least to them.

The conversation faded away as the *Touchback* maneuvered toward a massive shaft, perhaps two miles wide. Rows of lights ran down the sides, disappearing into the depths, reminiscent of the mine shafts back home. Ships, large and small, flew in and out of the huge opening. As the *Touchback* approached, traffic faded to nothing — exit traffic ceased, and entry traffic hovered in place.

"Why is all the shipping stopped?"

"Because they clear everything out when a bus comes in," Virak said. "They need to prevent possible terrorist attacks. If a ship even gets within a half mile of a team bus, it is destroyed."

The *Touchback* descended the shaft, sinking like a pebble into a miles-deep, dark-water chasm. Large ships docked against greenish projections that jutted out from the walls up and down the length of the shaft. He saw thousands of small ships, but many larger ones as well: cargo tugs hauling long lines of hexagonal boxes, space liners sporting sleek lines, bulky freighters loading or unloading payload to haul to other systems and something that Quentin had never seen — warships.

There were dozens of warships, big and small, bristling with bulky shield generators and the long, thin, unmistakable shapes of weapons. Quentin felt a shiver, thinking of the days when weapon-loaded ships like these had permeated the universe, fighting and killing more often than not.

The *Touchback* slowed, almost imperceptibly. A light jarring motion indicated they had docked.

[BEINGS ON FIRST SHUTTLE FLIGHT, MOVE TO THE LANDING BAY. FIRST SHUTTLE FLIGHT LEAVES IN FIFTEEN MINUTES.]

"You come with me," Virak said.

"But I'm on the third flight."

"I have more to show you," Virak said. "You come with me."

Quentin followed the muscular Quyth warrior from the viewing deck down to the landing bay. He boarded — a few of the veteran starters gave him a quick look, but most shrugged (or gave the respective alien equivalent of a shrug) and went back to whatever they had been doing. The shuttle slid out of the landing bay and descended the shaft.

The shuttle finally slipped past the bottom of the shaft and into a cavernous, dome-shaped space. Endless rails of the green crystal ran in curved arms along the dome shell up toward the two-mile-wide shaft mouth, which was also ringed by a thick band of green. Ships, probably personal cars judging from their tiny dimensions, flew in every direction like a thick swarm of gnats.

The air looked crowded with vehicles, but not around the

shuttle. Off the port side, he noticed a squat yellow and black ship, lethal-looking and bristling with weapons. It struck him as an artistic interpretation of a bumblebee crossed with an automated factory robot. He didn't know the reason for its rather un-aerodynamic shape, but there was no mistaking the ship was a fighter.

He watched the fighter out the window. It matched speed and altitude with the shuttle. Then he noticed another fighter, and another, also matching speed. He looked out windows on the other side, and saw many more. Dozens of mechanical bees formed a sort of protective sphere-web with the shuttle at its center.

The Deuce reminded Quentin of Ionath City and Port Whitok — a huge, dome-shaped city. Although this time the dome was twice as large, at least eight miles in diameter and over two miles high. There was no sprawling city playing away from the downtown — here bare rock marked the city's edge. A winding river, at this height no more than a blue-green ribbon, ran through the center of the city, emanating from one domewall and disappearing into another on the far side.

This place did not have the fine radial symmetry of Ionath City. Rather, it spread outward from the center the way a bacteria colony might grow on a petri dish: orderly but in a biological fashion, as if it had grown naturally without the guiding hand of a city engineer. Lights glowed from almost every building, adding to the city's biological feel, as if it were a bioluminescent colonial organism in some deep ocean. Roads wound through the city with little more order than the meandering river.

"How did they put a river in there?"

"Comet harvesters," Virak said. "Same as the asteroid harvesters. Water is very important for life. Females breed in water. On Ionath and Whitok, we have special water-filled facilities for breeding, but here we can do it naturally, right out in the open like it is done on Quyth."

The buildings had looked squat from the shaft mouth, but as the shuttle descended, Quentin saw that was just an illusion. The towering, organic-looking hexagonal structures reached to heights of two hundred stories and more. The shuttle banked to the left and followed the line of the river. Buildings seemed to link together, their green crystalline structure branching out like neurons to connect to all their neighbors, several times at several heights. The number of buildings, their densely packed proximity, their height — Quentin's head spun with one obvious question.

"How many beings live on The Deuce?"

"The last census put us somewhere around 742 million. It's not as open as Ionath City, but it's not nearly as crowded as the homeworld."

All in a space less than half the size of the Earth's moon. The Quyth homeworld was only slightly larger than Earth — and populated with 72 billion Quyth. The race seemed to have mastered dense-population living.

The shuttle dropped to a hundred feet above the water as the river banked sharply to the right. Around that bend lay Demolition Stadium. A smaller affair than its counterparts on Ionath and Whitok, it had purple seats 500 rows high running parallel to each sideline. Demolition Stadium looked kind of like a freeze-frame sculpture of a thick book being closed. Both end zones were open, free of the towering bleachers that rose at such a steep angle, Quentin wondered how anyone could climb the steps. The field surface was a pale, milky white, with yard markers written in a deep blue.

"The surface is Tiralik," Virak said. "Very springy and giving. Soft surface cuts down on injuries but stains jerseys badly."

A multi-shaded purple building dominated one end zone, while a platform of some kind dominated the other. The shuttle set down on the purple building.

Virak turned to Quentin and grabbed one arm with a pedipalp. Quentin managed to not wince at the painful grab — he knew the full strength of a Quyth Warrior, and this grab was not meant to hurt.

"You watch yourself," Virak said. "Orbital Stations are a lot older than Ionath City. Races have mingled here for centuries. This is one of the few places in the galaxy that there are no Creterakians, so a lot of criminal elements come and go, or just come and stay."

"So why don't your people do something about it?"

"For a long time it was difficult to trade with other systems. No one wanted to bother with the Quyth. Smugglers brought in many goods, and they needed a place to hide out. And when the war came, they fought and died right along with us. For that, we leave them be as long as they don't make too much trouble."

Quentin noted the phrase *too much trouble*, as opposed to *as long as they don't make any trouble*. As he disembarked onto the roof of the purple building, he wondered what kind of activities might fall under the threshold of *too much trouble*.

"Just be careful," Virak said as the races moved to their separate locker rooms. "And you'd do best to keep to yourself."

THE DEUCE HAD no haven for Purist Nation ex-patriots, so Rick Warburg decided to stay in the Demolition Building. Quentin had no intention of staying in. He opted for dinner with Yassoud and John Tweedy. The city's bizarre architecture drew him out into the streets. Ionath City was orderly and new, a highly regimented place built with careful planning and meticulous attention to detail. The Deuce, on the other hand, felt far more organic. Not just streets but entire levels had sprung up over the centuries, many without any official sanction or knowledge. Caverns and tunnels, both rough and smoothly engineered, ran through the artificial planetoid like a giant termite colony.

Like Ionath City and Port Whitok, the football stadium lay in a bustling downtown area packed with many species, noise, grav-cars and multiple forms of entertainment. It surprised him to see so many representatives of the different races. Some of the Human families, he'd been told, had lived on The Deuce for eight or more generations, two centuries of life, and considered themselves citizens of the Quyth Concordia with no association whatsoever to the Human systems.

Quentin thought of his own lineage — his ancestors had come over on the first flotilla, some 240 years ago. A great-great-great-great grandfather, supposedly, had come from someplace on Earth called "Dallas." Quentin only remembered that tidbit because one of the original football teams had played there. He, and his parents, and his parents' parents before him, thought of themselves as citizens of the Purist Nation, as separate from Earth as the Human citizens of The Deuce were to any Human government. Still, it was hard to think of Humans proudly boasting their citizenship to a nation of radioactivity-proof aliens.

Buildings towered above, some reaching a mile into the air. The green crystalline mass that made up the buildings' framework looked bubbly, almost alive, with the soft ripples and curves of a large icicle. Massive arcs of that same green crystal reached from building to building, across narrow spans, across streets, some across entire blocks. Some arcs reached from a building to another arc, and a few even ran from one arc to another, forming a stringy, organic latticework.

"Bet you never saw anything like this back on the farm, eh, Quentin?" Yassoud said as the trio headed to the first building with a holographic football/beer bottle sign.

"You can say that again," Quentin said. "Virak told me to watch my back in this place. I hear it's dangerous."

"Relax, backwater," Tweedy said with a grin. "We're football players. Nobody is gonna mess with us. We can beat the tar out of them and no one can send us to jail. GFL immunity is great, I tell ya. Let's just enjoy the place and tie one on tonight."

"Oh, yep," Yassoud said. "Let us delve into the seedy underbelly of this strange and alien city."

As if pulled by some unseen magnetism, Yassoud and Tweedy suddenly turned as one and walked toward a door marked with a familiar glowing sign of a football on top of a Miller logo. Quentin paused before entering. The bar was so packed part of the crowd stood on the street, mag-glasses in hand. Where Ionath City and Port Whitok had "species-specific" areas, this bar seemed to have everything: Humans, Creterakian civilians, female Sklorno, more than a few Ki, Harrah and, of course, dozens of Quyth Workers, Warriors and Leaders.

The crowd parted for the three men as they walked into the

bar, mostly because the ever-scowling Tweedy led the way, head tilted down, eyes peering out from his thick eyebrows. KRAKENS RULE THE UNIVERSE scrolled across his forehead. The bar's counter was a black, onyx-like surface set at just two feet off the ground, the perfect height for Quyth Workers to sit and relax. Quentin, Tweedy and Yassoud sat at three seats, which seemed to magically open before them as three normal-sized Humans got up and left upon their approach.

"Bartender!" Yassoud screamed as he sat. A wide, white-toothed smile nearly split his face in two. "*Bartender!* Three Millers!"

A Quyth Worker waddled over. A shriveled stub on his left cheek remained of what had once matched the yellow-and-orange furred pedipalp on his right. He reached under the bar and quickly served up three mag-cans of Miller. Yassoud, still smiling, ceremoniously opened all three cans, passing one to Quentin and one to John Tweedy.

"Tonight we drink to turning things around," Yassoud said, his can held high. "Here's to kicking in the Demolition's face! Oh, yep!"

All three men drank as the crowd, obviously Demolition fans, let out low-volume jeers. Quentin noticed how many beings wore Demolition clothing of one type or another: purple hats and jackets and shirts marked with three white stripes.

Quentin took a couple of swallows. When he set his can down, Yassoud and Tweedy were still drinking. Both men drained their mag-cans, hit the decompress button on the top and set the now de-charged and empty metal ring on the bar top.

"*Bartender!*" Yassoud screamed. "Another round please."

John Tweedy poked a finger at Quentin's can, still three-quarters full. "What's the matter, rookie? Not thirsty?"

"Um, we have a game in two days."

"So?" Yassoud and Tweedy said in unison.

"I'm not going to get drunk. We've got to be at our best for the game."

Tweedy waved a hand in front of his face as if Quentin had

farted. "Dang, backwater, I thought you were fun, like Yassoud here."

Yassoud, smiling, just shrugged.

"I'm fun," Quentin said. "I just don't wanna mess anything up this week."

"Yeah, you're tons of fun," Yassoud said. "The way you spend all your time in the VR room, man, you're a regular ball of laughs. I wanna party with you, kid."

Tweedy laughed. Quentin felt his face turn a bit red.

"Hey, I'm out tonight, right?" Quentin said, "Give me at least that much."

Yassoud nodded vigorously. "Oh, yep, you're right, you're here so I'll quit bagging on you."

The second round hit the bar top. Within seconds, John and Yassoud had knocked that one back as well.

"*Bartender!*" Yassoud screamed. Quentin slowly shook his head. It was going to be a long night.

RIGHT ABOUT THE TIME John Tweedy, now eight beers heavier, started challenging anyone and everyone in the bar to a fight, Quentin (only two beers heavier) walked outside. He had a good feeling he'd need a grav-cab to get Tweedy and Yassoud back to their rooms. How they could hope to practice the next day was beyond Quentin's understanding.

The streets remained packed with grav-cars. Pedestrians filled the sidewalks and moved in and out of bars and buildings. The green tinged buildings soared above, their endless network of arms reaching out to each other like tentacled lovers caught in a freeze-frame.

A pair of Human hand-holding women walked by, one with blue skin, the other with white, both wearing matching see-through body suits that left nothing to the imagination. A month ago, he would have sneered at the two shameless women, both for their sinful dress and for the color of their skin. Now however, something did rise as they walked by, but it wasn't his lip.

You're changing so fast you can barely keep score, Quentin

thought to himself. Maybe it was being immersed in alien cultures that made even blue- and white-skinned women look alluring. They didn't seem so *different* anymore, not like they had back on Micovi, where you only saw colored skin in the holos. The white-skinned girl turned and looked at him as she walked by, her blue-painted lips flashing a seductive smile.

He watched her walk down the sidewalk, his eyes following first her shapely booty, then her legs, then her friend's booty, then her friend's legs, then Maygon.

Maygon?

Quentin blinked twice, but there was nothing wrong with his vision. Maygon, the Creterakian representative of the To Pirates, was two buildings down the street, dressed in a fuchsia suit with yellow stripes, and waving at him with one wing. No, not waving, *beckoning*.

Quentin felt his face flush red. He looked around quickly but saw no one he recognized and no one staring at him. Well, no *unusual* stares — a seven-foot-tall being drew plenty of stares in a city where the average citizen stood just over four feet.

Maygon waved again, this time faster, more demanding.

Quentin swallowed, looked in the bar to make sure Yassoud and Tweedy weren't watching, then walked to Maygon.

"What do you want?' Quentin said. "We can't be seen together."

"A chance you'll have to take. Kirani-Ah-Kollok has a message for you."

"Well, then make it quick."

"I'll only be a second, relax. I just wanted to let you know you did a good job last week. Your effort looked *very* convincing, yet you still lost by twenty-five points."

Quentin suddenly realized that once he'd taken that first snap, he hadn't even *thought* about throwing the game. He felt doubly humiliated — first because he'd considered tanking and second because he'd played his tail off, lost, and this *bat* thought he'd lost on *purpose*. Quentin felt an anger brewing in him like he'd never felt before.

"Just keep it up, backwater," Maygon said. "One more loss

and you'll be wearing the blood red before Tier One season starts. Just letting you know that I'm here, and I'm watching. Now piss off, I want to chase some tail."

Quentin stood for a moment, then turned, the rage so thick in his head it was hard to think. *One more loss* ... the phrase echoed in his mind. The To Pirates, his childhood dream, and all he needed was one more loss. He walked toward the bar. It was time to get those two drunks out of there and go back to the rooms.

He was so mad he didn't notice the things around him, like the crowd parting before him the way it had for John Tweedy or the two huge Ki that blocked the sidewalk and weren't about to part for anybody. Quentin almost walked right into them.

"Excuse me," he said, but the Ki didn't move. Quentin looked at them for a moment, their expressionless black eyes staring back, then he tried to walk around them.

They moved to block his path.

"You guys have a problem?"

The Ki said nothing. A Creterakian, this one dressed in lemon yellow with long flowing streamers of dark yellow, flew up and perched on one of the Ki's shoulders.

"Quentin Barnes," the Creterakian said. "My boss would like a word with you."

Did the To Pirates think he was a moron? "I already heard the sermon. Now leave me alone."

"You haven't heard anything," the Creterakian said, "until you've heard it from the boss. And the boss wants to speak with you."

"I'm heading back to my room. Now get these beasts out of my way."

"The boss wants to talk with you *now*," the Creterakian said. The Ki moved quickly, multi-jointed arms reaching out. Quentin immediately started dodging to the left, but they were too close and he'd been caught off guard. Eight strong Ki arms grabbed him and held him concrete-tight. Quentin in tow, they scuttled into a building. It all happened so fast Quentin barely knew what was happening before the Ki tossed him unceremoniously onto the floor. The noise of the street faded away behind a closed door. He stood up with an athlete's quickness, but the Ki were already off him, backed up against the door to prevent his escape. The yellow-suited Creterakian was also in the room, only now he was perched on the shoulder of a black-and-tan furred Quyth Leader.

This is bad, Quentin thought instantly. *This is very bad.* He wanted out and he wanted out quickly. He leaned forward and started lunging for the Ki.

They both pulled knives, and he stopped short, almost stumbling into the glittering points.

Knives wasn't the right word. He'd used knives in his military training. *Knives* were a foot long at most. The blades were three feet long, serrated on one side, gleaming sharpness on the other.

"Stop being a pansy," the Quyth Leader said in a gravelly voice. "You're here until I tell you to leave, so stop being a pansy."

Quentin backed away from the sword-wielding Ki. The room had another door, but it was behind the Quyth Leader. Quentin suspected if he rushed for that way out, the Ki might cut him down before he could get the thing open.

"I am Mopuk the Sneaky," the Quyth Leader said. He then gestured to the Creterakian. "This is Sobox. If you see Sobox again, know that he is carrying my voice."

"I don't care if he's carrying your nuts in a paper baggie, you want to tell me what this is about?"

"This is about Donald Pine."

Quentin hadn't expected that. "What about him?"

"He works for me," Mopuk said. "You might say he's a seasonal employee. Donald Pine owes me a lot of money. He pays off his debt by playing the way I tell him to play."

Quentin felt stunned. "You're trying to tell me that Pine throws games for you?"

Mopuk's pedipalps quivered once.

"Well, you're out of luck then, moron, because Pine's hurt and I'm playing this week."

"That's why you're here," Mopuk said. "I want the Demolition to win. You will make sure that happens."

Quentin was getting tired of people telling him to lose. *Damn tired.*

"There's cash in it for you," Mopuk said. He held out one pedipalp, into which Sobox dropped a credit chit. Mopuk tossed it to Quentin. "That's a chit for a half million. I believe your entire salary for the season is only one million?"

Quentin looked at the small black chit. Indeed, the readout said c500,000.00. The *payable* button, however, did not glow the blue of an active transaction.

"One million, what a joke," Sobox said. "You need an agent, backwater."

"Just take care of business, and that light glows blue," Mopuk said. "Make sure the Demolition wins by at least a touchdown. That's all you have to do."

Quentin stared at the chit. Five hundred thousand — that was half of what he made for the whole season. More than half, if he counted in the tithe he had to pay to the Purist Nation. And hell, they'd probably lose anyway …

He shook his head, trying to clear away such thoughts. He wasn't throwing the game. And besides, if he did, Gredok might find out, and that would be very, very bad.

"Do you know who owns the Krakens?" Quentin asked. "Any idea at all, moron?"

"I know who owns the Krakens," Mopuk said. "And if you go run and tell him, he won't be happy. But right now he doesn't know anything. And if he *does* find out, I'll be sure to implicate you in every way possible. I'm protected, *gatholi*, but you're not. Who do you think is going to come out of this with their head still attached to their body? You just throw the game and everyone is happy."

Quentin shook his head. "I've got a better idea. Why don't you let me use those pedipalps to clean my toilet? I had some Tower food that didn't agree with me, and it's a mess. Your furry little things would clean it up good."

Sobox flapped once, and the Ki were on him. There was no space to maneuver in the small room. Quentin managed one good punch at the first Ki but didn't know if his blow did any damage before he went down under a thousand pounds of heavy alien. He felt sudden blows to his ribs and one to his jaw. The world spun awkwardly around him as the weight suddenly lifted. Quentin slowly stood up, rubbing his jaw, his ribs feeling like someone had jabbed a baseball bat into him handle-first. He felt something in his mouth. He spit — his front right tooth shot out and landed in a loogie of his blood.

Dammit. I just finished growing that thing back.

"Now, shut up and listen," Mopuk said. "I'm done negotiating. The money is off the table, no more deal there, you blew it. The Demolition wins. You do it for free. End of story. And they win by a touchdown. Got that? *Seven points*, at least. If this doesn't happen, you're going back to the Purist Nation in a coffin."

Quentin looked at the two Ki. He was stuck in this room, and if they wanted, they could easily kill him.

"Yeah," he said, the word coming out stilted from his already swelling jaw. "I got it."

One of the Ki opened the door and stood aside. Quentin walked out onto the busy street. The door shut behind him.

RED "NO TOUCH" JERSEY flapping in a light breeze, Quentin dropped back and planted. His feet slid slightly on the white Tiralik. The footing felt like grass — if you covered grass with a light coating of kitchen grease, that is. He was quickly adjusting to the slickness. He looked downfield to his primary receiver and gunned the pass to Hawick. The ball covered fifteen yards in a half-second and hit Hawick dead-on.

"Good job, Barnes," Hokor called in his headset.

"Thanks, Coach." It was strange to hear a compliment, and this had been Hokor's fourth of the practice. Everything seemed to be flowing now, the players — both offense and defense — part of a huge dance. More and more he knew where each receiver would move and where their defensive "dance partner" would move in response. Things were starting to feel natural, the way they did back on Micovi. Still, this was against a defense he practiced with not only daily, but nightly as well. He'd started to subconsciously absorb the aggressive tendencies of Berea and Stockbridge, the one-step-too-late break of Perth and the too-cautious defense of Davenport. Against the Demolition's top-rated pass defense, however, it would be a different story.

"You're looking good, backwater."

Quentin turned to look at Donald Pine, who was dressed in civy clothes. The crutches were gone, replaced by just a cane. The cane made him look like the old man that he was. How long had he been throwing games? Quentin could barely look at Pine without feeling sick and angry. One of the best QBs of all time, and he threw games like some punk.

"Bend your left knee more when you drop back," Pine said. "You're handling the slickness okay now, but in the second half, the field will be really beat up and way more slippery. You need that extra springiness a bent knee will give you to keep your balance."

Quentin nodded but didn't say anything. Once again, he couldn't trust what Pine had to say. Had Mopuk & Co. told Pine to make sure Quentin tanked? Was Pine going to play subversive mind games to ensure a loss?

A long whistle blew as Hokor's cart descended to the 50-yard line. The team gathered from all over the field — practice was over, and Hokor had to cover any last important notes before the players headed to the locker rooms. Tomorrow this same field would be filled with 110,000 screaming fans, as well as 44 players wearing the multi-shaded purple of the Sky Demolition.

Quentin turned away from Pine and jogged to the mid-field gathering. Tomorrow was game day. Do-or-die day. One more loss and the season was shot.

Not under my watch.

The thought popped into Quentin's head. The team probably wouldn't make the Tier Two tournament. But if that happened, it would be because Don Pine threw a game, not Quentin Barnes.

Forget Pine.

Forget Mopuk.

Hell, for that matter, forget the To Pirates.

Quentin wasn't taking a dive for anyone. He would not let his teammates down.

Live feed from UBS GameDay holocast coverage

"Hello, football fans, welcome back to this UBS holocast of GFL football. This is Masara the Observant, here with Chick Mc-Gee, the galaxy's favorite color commentator. Well, Chick, despite the score, we've seen some good football in the first half. The Demolition is up 14-3, but the Krakens' defense has played well."

"You've got that right, Masara. Let's take a look at the Bombay Gin Halftime StatBoard. Nothing eases a Worker's day like the tasty taste of Gin from Bombay. Hmmm, that's *tasty*."

"Chick, you shouldn't be drinking that in the booth."

"Hey, how can I endorse it without sampling the product? Brady Entenabe is showing why he's one of the top-rated passers in the Quyth Irradiated. He's 12-of-17 for 203 and a pair of touchdowns, both to San Mateo. The Krakens' secondary has done a good job of containing the Demolition pass attack but gave up two big plays, a 68-yard TD strike from Entenabe to San Mateo and another 27-yard TD that came on a crucial third-and-12 right at the end of the half. If they'd held them there, the Krakens would only be back by a touchdown."

"Chick, what does the Krakens *offense* have to do to put some points on the board?"

"Well, Masara, they've got to do three things. First, rookie QB Quentin Barnes has to work on his footing. He's not used to playing on this kind of surface — he's already fallen twice on his drop-backs, slipping when he plants to step up and throw. Second, the Krakens have to start blocking. The Demo has sacked Barnes three times so far, knocked him down three more and hurried him another four. Barnes has thrown two interceptions, both caused by heavy pass-rush pressure. If it wasn't for his running ability, the Krakens would be worse off than they already are. Barnes has twenty-six yards on the ground on five rushing attempts, all of them scrambles. I tell ya, that Human has been chewed up like a Sklorno larvae during a famine."

"Um, Chick, I hardly think our Sklorno viewers would appreciate that ..."

"Yes, you're right there, Masara. Sorry, folks — sometimes this old game of football gets me so fired up I slip back into cute colloquialisms. No offense intended."

"So, let's move on. We've got hotter footing, then blocking, what's the third thing?"

"Masara, the third thing is play calling. Hokor the Hookchest is being very predictable. The Krakens are running first, throwing second, and the Demolition knows it. The only time the Krakens throw is when they *have* to throw, and then the Demolition brings Yalla the Biter on a blitz almost every time."

"So, why isn't Barnes changing the plays at the line?"

"You've got me, Masara. The kid seems like he knows the offense very well, but either he's afraid to change the play or Hokor isn't letting him audible."

"Next up we'll take a look at the first-half highlights, brought to you by Ju-Ku-Killok Shipping. Remember, if you've got to ship it across the galaxy, don't you want to ship it with a Ki? Any way you look at it, Chick, it seems something's got to change if the Krakens are going to get back into this game."

"You got that right, Masara. Otherwise the Krakens have about as much chance as a naked nun at a Purist Nation rapist convention."

"Chick! Now come on—"

"Sorry, Masara. Sorry, beings at home ..."

QUENTIN HISSED ONCE as Doc wrapped the cool blue patch around the right side of his neck. He'd been tackled by the neck on the last sack, a Ki arm tearing away a good six square inches of skin. He thought he'd been in the clear but still hadn't accounted for how far the Ki could jump out of a gather. The right side of Quentin's jersey was deeply stained with his own blood, and he couldn't swallow without an explosion of throbbing pain. The patch's sting set in immediately — it only added to his anger. Pine sat on his left, cane in hand, and Yitzhak sat on his right.

"We've got to execute better on first down," Hokor told the assembled players. "We're not getting off to a good start."

That's because all you want to do is hand the ball off to Fayed, Quentin thought.

"And we've got to start blocking on the offensive line," Hokor said. "I don't care what cultural crap you Ki are dealing with, but block."

Block, that's right, Hokor, now you're really leading, *aren't you, you pint-sized idiot.*

"Defensively, we've got to get our coverages in sync."

Block, crap crap crap crap, this hurts.

"Entenabe is taking advantage of every blown rotation."

Tired of getting sacked, you scumbags ...

"So, let's get back to our game plan. We don't —"

"Game plan?" Quentin stood so suddenly his chair shot out from behind him. "The game plan is *not* for me to spend four quarters getting pummeled like a half-frozen roundbug!"

"Barnes!" Hokor said. "Sit down and —"

"I'm *sick* of it!" Quentin strode toward the Ki linemen. They sat on one side of the locker room, a huge mass of dangerous strength dressed in orange jerseys and multi-legged, orange leg armor stained white from the oily field.

"You call that blocking? You garbage-eating cowardly scumbags! *Scumbags!*"

"Barnes!"

"Shut *up*, half-pint!" Quentin flashed a wide-eyed stare at Hokor before turning back to the Ki linemen.

Pine leaned over to Yitzhak. "He's lost it."

Yitzhak leaned back. "Yeah. Should we help him?"

Pine shrugged. "Naw, this is kind of fun. They'll either block for him or eat him, I'm not sure which."

"You worthless *losers*! You're not fit to clean the toilets in this place, you weak-willed pansies! After this game we're gonna settle up, salamanders. Settle up with the lot of you!"

The Ki didn't move a muscle.

Quentin turned and stormed out of the locker room, stopping along the way to kick over a water bucket and smash a chair into the wall. There was a brief silence, broken by an angry bark from Sho-Do-Thikit.

"Don't talk threats," Pine said. He spoke quietly, but his voice carried to every ear. When he talked, the entire team turned to look at him. "Yes, he insulted you. And you deserved it. All five of you. And you all know it."

THE THIRD QUARTER was pure torture. Quentin saw play after play where he could have audibled a pass that would have burned the defense, but he stuck to the plays that Hokor called. Entenabe, however, didn't seem to have such restrictions. He struck for a 24-yard TD pass at the end of the third, putting the Demolition up 21-3 going into the fourth.

The blocking, however, seemed somewhat improved. Quentin had time to set up and survey the field. He went 6-of-10 for 34 yards in the third quarter but couldn't string together enough passes to constitute a drive. With the extra time to set up, however, he started marking defensive nuances. Slowly but steadily, his mind began to place the Demolition defenders like a chess master marking out his opponent's likely moves.

With 10:02 to play in the fourth, the Krakens' "D" forced a punt, which Richfield returned to the Demolition 45. Quentin couldn't stand it any longer. They had to score, and they had to score now. He ran to Hokor.

"Coach," Quentin said as he kneeled down. "Coach, how about letting me audible out there?"

"Just run the plays I call, Barnes."

"But Coach, we're losing!"

"I know that, Barnes. Now shut up or I'm going to turn you

loose this time. Just do what I say, and *run the plays that I call,* got it?"

Quentin felt frustration welling up inside of him, but he nodded.

"We've run on seven of the last eight first downs," Hokor said. "Go deep this time. Z-set, play-action, 42-fly."

Quentin felt his pulse quicken. He ran onto the field. Z-set put two tight ends in the game, along with Fayed and Pareless, the fullback. The only receiver would be Hawick on the left flank. Bud-O-Shwek snapped it, and Quentin turned to the left, stabbing the ball toward the onrushing Fayed. He pulled it away at the last second, putting the ball on his left hip and letting his right hand brush Fayed's belly. Fayed put both arms together, just as he would if he'd been handed the ball, and smashed into the line. The Krakens hadn't used play action all day, and the fake drew in the run-oriented defense. Quentin tucked down to hide the ball even as he dropped back. After five steps, he turned and stood ...

... and saw Yalla the Biter, already through the line and coming right for him.

BLINK

Quentin juked left, which Yalla instantly matched. Quentin started to juke right, his patented double-move that always got him out of trouble in the PNFL, but in a millisecond's time he knew Yalla could effortlessly mirror that move with the amazing lateral movement and reaction time of a Quyth Warrior.

Quentin's instincts took over. He suddenly saw Yalla's direction as if there were an arrow pointing forward, like a video game, and sensed the linebacker's force and momentum like a growing pressure in his thoughts. *Timing, it's all in the timing ...*

Yalla leaned far forward to deliver the hit, suddenly coming off all-fours, pedipalps and arms reaching out. At just that instant Quentin spun violently to the right. The quarterback pushed off with his right hand as he spun, the ball in his left hand, his body between Yalla and the ball. He spun so fast he almost fell over from the momentum, but the move worked. Juke moves took too much time against Quyth Warriors, but a spin move, just as Yalla came off all-fours to deliver the hit, didn't give the linebacker enough time to react: one millisecond Quentin was there, the next he was two feet right of where he had been.

Yalla's momentum carried him past the spinning quarterback, but his powerful pedipalps grabbed a double-handful of jersey on the way past. Quentin felt himself sliding backward on the slick white surface. He instinctively tucked the ball and started pumping his legs with short, quick, jabbing steps. The Quyth linebacker fell to the ground ... Quentin planted his legs and pushed against the weight dragging him down ... a ripping sound, and suddenly Quentin lurched forward, free to move once again.

He instantly stood tall and looked downfield — Hawick streaked down the sidelines, a full two steps ahead of her defender.

Quentin fired the ball downfield high and long — as usual, he had no problem hitting an open receiver, and Hawick sailed fifteen feet into the air, caught the ball and landed in full stride. The left cornerback was behind her and didn't stand a chance ... the safety came over to help, but she'd also lost a step with the play-action fake. Hawick strode into the end zone untouched.

BLINK

The crowd booed, but without much intensity. Quentin flipped them off en masse as he ran off the field, his torn jersey flapping around him. Morningstar knocked in the extra point, cutting the lead to 21-10.

Quentin sat on the bench, his heart racing, a feeling of pure ecstasy coursing through his brain. Teammates came up to shake his hand, slap his shoulder pads or just grunt some unintelligible alien words of encouragement.

Pine slid onto the bench next to him. "You've got to watch Yalla's feet," he said. "He's showing blitz when he's on his toes. When he's flat-footed, he's in run coverage."

Quentin nodded. He didn't know if he could trust Pine, but that bit of advice sounded reliable.

Pine smiled and thumped Quentin on the shoulder pad. "Nice pass, kid, you just need a couple more."

Pine hobbled away. Messal approached with a box in his

arms. He set the box down and removed a gleaming metal device that looked like a combination of a small pistol and a pair of pliers.

"What the hell is that?" Quentin asked.

"For your uniform," Messal said. His strong pedipalps lined up the torn edges of Quentin's jersey. Messal pinched the bottom edges together and slid them into the opening of the gun-pliers. The machine made a small whirring noise, and Messal expertly slid it up the length of the ripped Kevlar fabric, knitting the shreds into a ugly but neat line.

"Hey, not bad," Quentin said as he pulled at the new seam. It held tight.

Messal simply bowed and scuttled off to attend to some other managerial duty.

THEY WERE STILL DOWN two scores, but the Krakens seemed suddenly energized. Entenabe had faced little pressure on the day. Hokor suddenly changed strategy, sending a blitz after the Demolition quarterback on nearly every play. Entenabe managed one completion before Mai-An-Ihkole sacked him on a second down, and Virak the Mean got him on third for a 10-yard loss. The Demolition's drive chewed up only three minutes. Richfield signaled fair catch on the punt — Krakens' ball on their own 41, 6:52 to play in the game.

Quentin ran out onto the field, Hokor's one-eyed face in the heads-up display.

"Now they're watching out for you," Hokor said. "This time go X-set, 42-base draw play ... we'll see if Fayed can finally make something happen."

Quentin called the play and walked to the line. The defensive backs had moved to five-yard cushions instead of their one-yard bump-and-run. The linebackers had moved back as well. At the snap, Quentin held the ball to his ear, showing pass as he dropped back five steps. The defensive backs and the linebackers immediately backpedaled into pass coverage. At the end of his drop,

Quentin suddenly handed the ball off to Fayed, who dashed into the line. He cut left into a big hole created by Kill-O-Yowet and Sho-Do-Thikit. Warburg moved to block Yalla the Biter. Yalla tucked his head and drove his right arm into Warburg, crushing the big tight end to the ground. Warburg barely slowed Yalla at all, but it was enough for Fayed to slip by, and suddenly the running back was in the defensive backfield. The d-backs converged on him and brought him down, but not before he'd picked up 23 yards and moved the ball to the Demolition 36.

6:28 and counting …

Paul Pierson came in for Fayed at tailback. The Krakens had dled up, electricity and momentum filling the small space.

The Krakens players looked tired, but their eyes blazed sharply and their intensity felt ubiquitous.

His earpiece crackled. "We need to score and score quick," Hokor said. "Y-set, 42-post, look for Pierson on the delayed route over the middle, we may catch Yalla sleeping."

Quentin called the play and surveyed the defense as the Krakens lined up. The Demolition showed a normal 3-4, which left them with four defensive backs. Quentin's instincts told him to watch for the blitz, but Yalla's feet looked flat.

At the snap Quentin dropped back. Hawick and Scarborough streaked downfield then cut inside on an angle, drawing the free safety and safety with them. Pierson ran to the line acting like he would block, then released and sprinted down the field. Yalla tried to cover him, but Pierson's superior speed carried him past. Quentin feathered a light toss that sailed just beyond Yalla and hit Pierson in stride. Yalla dove, covering ten yards in the leap, and brought Pierson down from behind after a 22-yard gain.

First-and-10, ball on the Demolition 14, 6:02 to play.

Whistles blew as Harrah officials flew to Pierson, who rolled on the ground in obvious pain. The officials waved their tentacles madly to the Krakens' sidelines. Before Doc arrived with his cart, Quentin saw Pierson roll to his back, his bloody hands clutching at his foot — which dangled sickly from only a scrap of skin and a few strands of bloody muscle. Yalla's tackle had ripped the man's leg in half. Blood shot out of his ravaged leg, splashing on the white field, on Doc, and staining the zebes' black-and-white uniforms.

Fayed came back in as Doc's med-sled rushed Pierson off the field.

"High One," said a wide-eyed Quentin. "Did you see that? His whole leg almost came off!"

"Give me the ball," Fayed said. Intensity narrowed his eyes to angry slits. "I'll show that cheap-shotting motherless tool."

Fortunately, Hokor called a dive right — exactly what Fayed wanted. The team lined up. Quentin took the snap and pivoted. Fayed nearly ripped the ball out of his hands and drove forward like a tank. Yalla the Biter came at him, and the two hit head-on like a pair of rams. Yalla fell backward, and Fayed stumbled over him, falling for a five-yard gain. Fayed stood and tossed the ball to the ground in front of Yalla, who was slow getting up.

"I'm here all day!" Fayed shouted, thumping his fist against his chest. "Just see if you can tear *my* leg off."

Fayed walked back to the huddle. Quentin felt a wave of awe wash over him — Yalla the Biter had just crippled Paul Pierson, and on the very next play, Fayed not only carried the ball, but went headhunting for Yalla. The play energized the entire team. If Fayed could show that kind of courage, so could everyone else.

Another running play put the Krakens on the Demolition 5-yard line.

"S-set, double-cross," Hokor barked. Quentin relayed the play to the Krakens' huddle. He felt the pure vibe of control now, the rhythm of the game coursing through him, *answering* to him, obeying his every whim. The huddle broke and he strode to the line, his predator's eyes sweeping over the defense. S-set was a single-back set: Fayed in the backfield, five offensive linemen, Hawick and Mezquitic split out left, Warburg in the right slot and Scarborough wide right. It was the first time that day the Krakens used such a setup, and the Demolition scrambled to adjust. They quickly fell into woman-to-woman coverage with a linebacker wide on either side. That left four down linemen and a single middle linebacker — Yalla — in the middle.

Quentin knew what he wanted to do even before he snapped the ball.

"Red, ninety-one, red, ninety-one, hut-*hut*!"

The receivers drove off the line and cut inside at six yards. Quentin dropped back as Fayed rolled to the right flat. Yalla moved with him, and Quentin made his decision — after just a three step drop, he planted and bounced forward, his 360 pounds hitting top speed almost instantly. The sudden change caught the onrushing defense off-guard, and he slipped past them without so much as a single cut. Yalla was already moving to the right to cover Fayed — the linebacker drove back to the left but was far too late to match Quentin's quickness.

Quentin strode into the end zone untouched.

Demolition 21, Krakens 16.

Quentin started to run off the field when he saw Hokor signaling to him to stay.

"We're going for two," Hokor called calmly over the earpiece. "I-set, show left dive, naked boot right. Kobayasho blocks inside and releases to the right. Hit him for the conversion."

Quentin nodded, but his mind raced with possibilities. A two-point conversion would pull them to within three points, one field goal away from tying. With the game on the line, Hokor was calling a naked boot, which meant Quentin rolled to the right with no blockers. It was both an insult and a compliment: an insult, because the Demolition still wouldn't think Hokor would put the game on a rookie's shoulders, and a complement because Hokor *was* putting the game on his shoulders.

He felt palpable excitement in the huddle. All eyes looked to him, awaiting his words. There was victory in the air, every being felt it. All they had to do was reach out and *take* it. Warburg and Kobayasho, the tight ends, were in the huddle, as was Pareless the fullback. Scarborough and Mezquitic were back on the sidelines — it was a two-tight end set with a fullback, clearly a running formation.

"I-set, show left dive, and Fayed, make it *count*. Naked boot right. Kobayasho, block in and release *deep*. If I have to run, I don't want the guy covering you able to stop me from scoring, got it?"

Kobayasho nodded, as did the other players.

"Break!"

The Krakens lined up. The Demolition dug in. Quentin surveyed the defense and saw Yalla drifting to the offense's right. Quentin's instincts screamed at him to call an audible, change the play to a dive left to take advantage of the cheating middle linebacker.

Run the plays I call, Quentin heard in his mind.

"Hut hut!"

The ball slapped into his hands, and he pivoted to the left. He put the ball in Fayed's stomach and turned with the running back, guiding him to the line. Just before Fayed crashed into the mass of bodies, Quentin pulled the ball out and pivoted hard to his right. He sprinted to the sidelines. The defense had bought the fake, all were converging on Fayed … all but Yalla the Biter. The monstrous, pitch-black-eyed Quyth Warrior linebacker went into a side-roll, staying flat to the goal line as he matched Quentin's horizontal movement. Kobayasho bounced to the outside, but he was covered by the Demolition cornerback.

Quentin thought about the pass for one more second then tucked the ball and sprinted for the corner of the end zone. Kobayasho instantly reacted to the situation, turning and blocking his defender, taking her out of the play.

That left only Quentin and Yalla the Biter.

Yalla popped out of his roll and sprang forward, hitting Quentin at the two-yard line.

You wanna mess with me? Quentin thought as he switched the ball to his right hand and threw his left forward in a vicious, snarling upper-cut. His fist slammed into Yalla's chest, bounced up and nailed the Quyth Warrior right between the pedipalps. Yalla reached out and grabbed at Quentin's jersey as sharp teeth slashed Quentin's left hand. Yalla's full weight slammed into him — Quentin stumbled, but recovered, and drove forward. His momentum pushed Yalla backward, just a touch, but it was enough. They both started to fall … Quentin managed two more powerful strides on the way down and landed after the ball just crossed the goal line.

Demolition 21, Krakens 18.

Flags flew. Unnecessary roughness on Yalla the Biter, to be assessed on the kickoff. The Krakens offense ran off the field to the boos of the Demolition faithful. Yalla's bite had torn open the skin on the back of Quentin's left hand, a bloody gash running from the knuckle on his index finger to the middle of his forearm. Blood poured from the wound, leaving an intermittent trail on the white playing field. Pine met him halfway, his cane doing a double-time that barely kept up the pace.

"Quentin, you idiot, why didn't you audible out of that? I could see from here that Yalla knew the play, and I *know* you saw it!"

"I call the plays that are given to me," Quentin said as he ran back to the bench, leaving the crippled Pine behind him.

"Doc!" Quentin shouted, oblivious to the shoulder pad and helmet slaps his appreciative teammates threw his way. "Doc, get over here!"

The Harrah doctor glided over, his tentacles immediately grabbing Quentin's wrist in a surprisingly strong grip.

"Sit still," Doc said firmly. "This is a deep cut, we've got to get you to the locker room for the healing tank."

"Forget that!" Quentin yanked his hand away. Blood flew in all directions. Teammates stopped what they were doing and stared at him, but he saw nothing except Doc, who was now no more than another obstacle trying to stop him from winning.

"You fix this up right now!" Quentin's face twisted into a mask of challenge and fury. "I've got to put another three on the board."

"You're out of the game!" Doc yelled back.

Quentin's eyes widened to giant white balls spotted with flecks of pure black. He suddenly rushed Doc, grabbing his floating body, finding it surprisingly light. He started to shake Doc when Yitzhak and Yassoud grabbed him, pulling him away.

"Jesus Christ, Quentin, stop it!" Yitzhak shouted as he stepped between Quentin and Doc.

Quentin ignored him, looking over Yitzhak's shoulder and shaking his blood-dripping finger at Doc. "If you don't fix up my hand, I'll bounce you off the ground like a damn *toy*, you got that?

I don't care if you have to cauterize it with a damned branding iron, *stop the bleeding*."

Doc hung there for a second, then reached into his bag and pulled out the now-familiar blue strip. He wrapped it around Quentin's shredded skin. Yitzhak and Yassoud let Quentin go, cautiously, as if he might snap again at any second. Quentin hissed as the acid-like sting spread through his hand. Blood pooled up around the edges of the blue strip and dripped to the trampled white plants below. He looked down, seeing that his blood had stained his orange jersey with stripes and splotches of bright red.

Doc held Quentin's hand tight as he removed the blood-soaked strip, now a deep purple, and applied another.

Yitzhak, leaned in to examine the extent of injury. "Hey, won't that put too many nanocytes in his body? Can't that cause liver damage?"

"Shut up," Quentin growled at Yitzhak. "And don't bother getting warmed up, I'm going back in."

The second strip also turned purple with blood. Quentin felt as if his hand was being cooked from the inside out.

"It's not working," Doc said. "The lacerations are too large, and you've got an arterial tear. The nanocytes can't bind it up. We need to put your hand in the healing tank, Quentin. The gel in the tank is programmed to hold your skin together long enough for the nanocytes to do their work."

"I don't have time for the damned tank!" A string of spittle flew from Quentin's mouth to dangle from the bottom bar of his facemask. He looked up at the scoreboard: 3:12 to play, the Demolition with the ball, second and three on their own 32. As soon as the defense stopped them, the Krakens' "O" would have a chance to win the game. *He* wanted to be on that field, and *he* wanted to win. He quickly looked around the sidelines, searching for an answer.

Then he saw Messal.

"Messal! Get your box and get over here, *now*!"

The manager turned at the sound of Quentin's bellowing voice, quivering as if a Quyth Leader had done the yelling. He scrambled to grab his box off the bench, then ran to Quentin.

"Get that thing you used to fix my jersey," Quentin said.

Messal pulled out the gun-pliers. Doc took one look at the device, then looked at the ugly stitch running up the front of Quentin's jersey.

"Absolutely not!" Doc said. "We will not use *stitches* on Human flesh!"

"Do it, Messal," Quentin said.

"Use that on him and I'll have Gredok fire you," Doc said. "I mean it, Messal."

Messal started to put the gun-pliers away. Quentin reached down with his right hand and grabbed the short Quyth Worker by his left pedipalp.

"You use that thing on *this*," Quentin said, holding up his bloody left hand, "or I will *kill* you, *cook* you and *eat* you."

Messal quivered like a tuning fork. He reached out and gently pinched together the skin on both sides of the cut. Yassoud moved in and wrapped his arms around Quentin's left arm, holding it still. Quentin felt Ki arms snake around his chest, their strength holding him immobile. He looked over his shoulder — Kill-O-Yowet's black eyes stared at him, only inches from his own.

Messal looked up, the obvious question burning in his one eye.

"Do it," Quentin said through clenched teeth.

Messal pulled the trigger. Quentin's eyes grew wider still as a new level of pain seared through his arm. He tried to pull back, but Yassoud and Kill-O-Yowet held him still. Messal slid the gun-pliers up the cut in a smooth stroke, and it was over. Quentin stared at his arm — the edges of the skin pursed out a quarter inch from his arm, smeared with blood and roughly stitched together with Kevlar thread, like the seam of his jersey. Echoes of the needle-and-thread pain ripped through his arm, but through that he still felt the burning of the nanocytes. That burning intensified on the stitch itself — the tiny machines were trying to do their job.

"That's going to leave a horrible scar," Doc said angrily. "And it's not going to heal the arterial tear. You've got ten minutes, tops, before you pass out."

Quentin heard boos from the crowd. He looked up at the scoreboard, his heart leaping when he saw the magic words "4th down, 6 to go, ball on the Demolition's 44." The clock counted down ... 1:12 ... 1:11 ... 1:10 ...

"Barnes, get your lazy butt up here," Hokor's voice said in his helmet. Quentin ran to his coach and knelt. Hokor stared at him, and Quentin saw his own reflection in Hokor's big eye: jersey torn and stitched up the chest, making the left side of his number 10 slightly higher than the right; the orange fabric stained bright red with blood; his arm a bloody mess with an ugly, black-threaded stitch running from his hand to his elbow.

"You sure you can make it?" Hokor asked.

Quentin nodded and smiled. "Just give me the ball, Coach."

Hokor's pedipalps reached out, each one lightly touching Quentin's shoulder pads. "We've pulled a lot of new strategies on them this quarter, so they'll be ready for anything, but at the same time, they won't focus on any one area. We're going to spread it out, so you'll have room to move — if you're in doubt, tuck it and run, but no more *head-to-head* battles, I can't have you getting hurt. When you run, you take a slide before they tackle you, you got it?"

Quentin nodded quickly. Hokor called the first play.

The Demolition punt sailed through the air. Richfield signaled a fair catch at the Krakens' 17-yard line. Quentin looked at the clock, then nodded again, to himself, this time — he had his work cut out for him: he needed to go 83 yards in 56 seconds.

The Krakens' offense ran onto the field. In the huddle, the players seemed different, staring at him with near reverence. Quentin noticed that blood streaked all of the Ki linemen jerseys. Red blood. But Ki blood was black ... it took him a second to realize that Kill-O-Yowet had rubbed blood, *Quentin's blood*, on each jersey. The pain in his arm faded away as a new dose of adrenaline pumped through his veins.

"We're going to get back in the hunt for Tier One *right now*,"

Quentin said. "We've got 56 seconds to put these motherless losers away. A field goal ties it, but I want a *win*. X-set, 21-base. All routes break off at twenty yards." Quentin reached up and grabbed Hawick's facemask, but when he spoke, it was to another receiver.

"Scarborough," Quentin said, his eyes still locked on Hawick. "Their nickel back will be on you. She can't handle your speed." Scarborough quivered once, then stopped and stood stock-still. "You sprint downfield on a post, and when I throw you the ball, you damn well catch it. Let's step on their throats right now and put this one away. Ready?"

"*Break!*"

The crowd roared as Quentin's team stepped to the line. He moved up with a step left, a half-bounce left, a step right, a half-bounce right. He stood behind Bud-O-Shwek, his hands tapping out a quick left-right-left *ba-da-bap* on the Ki's carapace. As he suspected, the defense moved to key on Hawick.

The ball snapped into his hands, and he dropped back five long steps. He planted, left knee bent deep, and slid two yards across the oily white surface before his cleats caught and he bounced forward a half-step. Standing tall at the 6-yard line, he locked his eyes on Hawick. She drove downfield and suddenly broke off at the 37, cutting back on a hook route. The motion was enough to freeze the safety, only for a moment, but in that moment Scarborough turned on the afterburners.

Wait for it … Quentin thought as the pocket started to collapse around him.

She sprinted past the 40 … the 50 …

Wait for it …

She sprinted past the 40 … the 30 …

Kill-O-Yowet lost his grip on his defender and fell to the ground. The defender's body gathered for a vicious blow even as he ran forward, multi-jointed limbs reaching out like a hungry, long-armed spider.

Quentin reared back and launched the ball just before the defensive lineman extended and smashed into him at full force.

Quentin was knocked ten yards to his right, the wind *whuffing* out of his lungs. He hit and rolled. The ball was in the air so long he actually stumbled to his feet before it finished its long parabola.

Scarborough leapt into the air, the safety a good three feet behind her. At the 12-yard line, 81 yards from where he'd released it, the ball landed in Scarborough's tentacles. Her feet touched down at the 7-yard line, and she strolled into the end zone standing up.

Krakens 25, Demolition 21.

Quentin stumbled off the field, his mind still fuzzy from the devastating hit he'd taken just after releasing the ball. Morningstar added the extra point to put the Krakens up by five. The hit had also opened up the cut on the back of Quentin's hand, although most of the gash remained sutured shut. From there on, things were a bit of a blur. Someone guided him to a med-sled and sat him on the back edge. The med-sled moved down the sidelines and into the tunnel. The crowed seemed a massive blur of colors and shapes and sounds. The med-sled cruised into the visitor's locker room — Quentin had an impression of someone (or something) helping him off the sled before his legs gave out and everything went black.

DEMOLITION BOX SCORE

Final	1	2	3	4	T
Ionath	0	3	0	22	25
Orbital Station 2	7	7	7	0	21

SCORING SUMMARY

1st QUARTER		OS2	ION
OS2 TD	San Mateo 68-yard pass from Brady Entenabe (Duke Dichenzo kick)	7	0

2nd QUARTER		OS2	ION
Ionath FG	Arioch Morningstar 32-yard field goal	7	3
OS2 TD	San Mateo 27-yard pass from Brady Entenabe (Duke Dichenzo kick)	14	3

3rd QUARTER		OS2	ION
OS2 TD	Madrid 24-yard pass from Brady Entenabe (Duke Dichenzo kick)	21	3

4th QUARTER		OS2	ION
Ionath TD	Hawick 45-yard pass from Quentin Barnes (Arioch Morningstar kick)	21	10
Ionath TD	Quentin Barnes 14-yard run. (Quentin Barnes run for 2-point conversion is good.)	21	18
Ionath TD	Scarborough 83-yard pass from Quentin Barnes (Arioch Morningstar kick)	21	25

TEAM STATISTICS	OS2	ION
First Downs	12	13
Third Down Efficiency	8-14	9-15
TOTAL NET YARDS	**368**	**383**
Total Plays	59	67
Average Gain Per Play	6.2	5.7
NET YARDS RUSHING	**92**	**136**
Rushes	33	32
Average Per Rush	2.8	4.4
NET YARDS PASSING	**276**	**247**
Pass Completion	20-36	17-40
Yards Per Pass	7.9	6.6
Times Sacked	2	3
Yards Lost To Sacks	9	14
Had Intercepted	0	2
PUNTS	**6**	**6**
Average Punt	40.1	38.4
PENALTIES	**7**	**5**
Penalty Yards	55	30
FUMBLES	**2**	**0**
Fumbles Lost	1	0
Time Of Possession	**25:38**	**34:12**

PASSING

KRAKENS	CMP	ATT	YDS	PCT	YPA	SACK	SYDS	TD	INT
Quentin Barnes	17	35	261	48.5	7.5	3	14	2	2

DEMOLITION	CMP	ATT	YDS	PCT	YPA	SACK	SYDS	TD	INT
Brady Entenabe	20	36	285	55.5	7.9	2	9	3	0

RUSHING

KRAKENS	ATT	YDS	AVG	LONG	TD	FUM
Mitchell Fayed	21	82	3.9	23	0	0
Yassoud Murphy	4	12	3.0	5	0	0
Quentin Barnes	7	42	6.0	14	1	0

DEMOLITION	ATT	YDS	AVG	LONG	TD	FUM
H. Gladstone	12	50	4.2	15	0	0
Yuri Schwartz	11	42	3.8	6	0	2

RECEIVING

KRAKENS	REC	YDS	AVG	LONG	TD	FUM
Hawick	6	92	15.3	45	1	0
Yotaro Kobayasho	4	33	8.3	8	0	0
Scarborough	3	100	33.3	83	1	0
Paul Pierson	1	22	22.0	22	0	0
Rick Warburg	1	6	6.0	6	0	0
Mezquitic	1	8	8.0	8	0	0

DEMOLITION	REC	YDS	AVG	LONG	TD	FUM
San Mateo	9	132	14.7	68	2	0
Madrid	5	92	18.4	24	1	0
Gloucester	3	51	17.0	35	0	0
Yuri Schwartz	3	10	3.3	5	0	0

WEEK FOUR LEAGUE ROUNDUP
(Courtesy of Galaxy Sports network)

With a thrilling 28-24 win over the **Glory Warpigs** (3-1), the **Whitok Pioneers** (4-0) took sole possession of first place in the Quyth Irradiated Conference.

Rookie QB Quentin Barnes kept the **Ionath Krakens** (2-2) in the playoff hunt with an 83-yard TD pass to Scarborough, giving the Krakens a 25-21 win over the winless **Sky Demolition** (0-4).

The **Grontak Hydras** (2-2) edged out a 35-31 win over the **Bigg Diggers** (1-3).

Orbiting Death (3-1) is only one game out of first thanks to a 28-7 drubbing of the **Quyth Survivors** (1-3).

The **Sheb Stalkers** (3-1) shut out the **Woo Wallcrawlers** (1-3) 17-0.

DEATHS:
No deaths to report this week.

WEEK FOUR PLAYERS OF THE WEEK:
Offense: **Condor Adrienne**, quarterback, Whitok Pioneers. 31-of-42, 334 yards, three TDs, no INTs.

Defense: **Arkham**, cornerback, Bigg Diggers. Six tackles, one sack, three interceptions, including one returned for a TD, her second of the year.

GAME FIVE: Sheb Stalkers (3-1) at Ionath Krakens (2-2)
QUYTH IRRADIATED CONFERENCE STANDINGS

Whitok Pioneers	4-0
Glory Warpigs	3-1
Orbiting Death	3-1
Sheb Stalkers	3-1
Grontak Hydras	2-2
Ionath Krakens	2-2
Bigg Diggers	1-3
Quyth Survivors	1-3
Woo Wallcrawlers	1-3
Sky Demolition	0-4

QUENTIN WALKED SLOWLY from his locker to the central meeting room and to Hokor's office. Two days of rest hadn't completely removed the pulsing, dull-nova ache that lived inside his skull. Concussion-proof helmets. Right.

He'd notched his first GFL win as a starter, but he'd paid a price. The concussion had him puking his guts out the rest of the night, and well into the next day, even though there was nothing left to puke. And with each stomach-clenching burst, his breath locked up and his muscles tightened — when he finally breathed and the muscles relaxed, the sudden rush of blood to his brain elevated his omnipresent headache to new levels.

While his teammates celebrated the win, Quentin spent the rest of that night in bed, which was where he spent the next day, and most of the day after that. He tried to get up and run through VR practice, but Hokor himself came to his room and told him to stay put, on Doc's orders.

Now, two days later, he didn't feel one ounce better. But pain or no pain, he wasn't going to miss one single rep of actual practice. He wasn't going to let his teammates down, not when this week's game put them up against the 3-1 Sheb Stalkers.

Quentin walked through the door to Hokor's office.

"You wanted to see —" he ended his sentence when he saw Pine in the room, fully dressed for practice.

"Come in, Barnes," Hokor said. "Shut the door."

Quentin did as he was told, a double-sick feeling growing in the pit of his stomach. *Double*-sick: once because he couldn't stand to look at Pine the Tanker and once because he instantly knew the reason for this closed-door meeting.

"Barnes, you did an amazing job last week," Hokor said. "You put us back on the board. If we can beat the Sheb Stalkers this week, we're 3-2 and back in the running."

Quentin nodded slightly.

"You've generated a lot of respect," Hokor continued. "The team is now confident in your abilities. There's a new feeling in the locker room that we have a guy who can come off the bench and play big time ball.

"Come off the *bench*," Quentin said quietly.

"The bench," Hokor echoed. "Pine is our starter, and he's healthy."

Quentin breathed deeply through his nose. That *tanker* was starting again.

"I just wanted to let you know in person," Hokor said. "I know your goal is to start, and I wouldn't want it any other way. You're the future of this franchise, but right now, it's Pine's team. You understand?"

Just run the plays that are called. The throbbing in his head suddenly kicked up a few notches.

"Yeah, sure," he said. "I understand. Can I go now?"

Hokor nodded. Quentin turned. He meant to just tap the door-open button, but his fist hit it so hard the red plastic plate cracked. The door hissed open, and Quentin walked out into the meeting room.

Forget this team. They can all go straight to hell.

Quentin stormed out of the locker room and through the tunnel. He had just about reached the field when a hand grabbed his shoulder and gently stopped him. Quentin turned violently, eyes wide, nostrils flaring, and looked into the surprised eyes of Donald Pine.

"Hey, kid, take it easy," Pine said with a smile. "Try to relax a little."

"Screw *you*," Quentin said, pushing Pine's chest to emphasize the last word.

Pine stumbled back a step. His tone changed, and his smile faded away. "Why don't you just simmer down? I know you're pissed. I would be, too, but you've got to play your role on this team."

"And what's my role? Just what, exactly, is *my role*? Sit on the bench?"

"If you have to, yes!" Pine's expression had faded from smile to blankness, now it twisted into a mask of frustrated anger. "Sit on the damn bench, Quentin, and pay your dues. I know you think you're hot stuff, but I've about had it with your attitude that you're better than me. I've tried to help you, you stubborn moron, but you better pull your head out."

"Oh, is that right?"

"*Yeah*, that's right!" Pine's voice dropped to a whispered shout. "You're going to be great, but right now you're *not* as good as *me*! Just relax and learn the system 'til your time comes."

"And when will that come? The next time you throw a game for Mopuk?"

Pine blinked rapidly and his breath stopped short, as if a knife had slid noiselessly into his heart. He took a small step back, then looked to his right and left, seeing if anyone had heard. The two quarterbacks were alone on the field.

"I don't know what you're talking about," Pine said.

"Your party friends paid me a visit the day before the Demolition game," Quentin said. "Mopuk said you were his property, Pine. That you throw games whenever he wants."

Pine looked down, and in that instant, Quentin knew it was true. He felt a part of his childhood die, right there on the spot — a man he'd idolized was a *tanker*.

"Why?" Quentin asked. "Why the hell do you do it?"

"Because he'll kill me if I don't," Pine said quietly. "I ... I gamble, a bit. I've gotten in over my head."

Quentin spat on the ground then looked into Pine's shame-filled eyes. "How much do you owe?"

Pine looked away and shrugged. Quentin grabbed him by the

shoulder pads, shook once and pulled Pine close until their eyes were only inches apart.

"How *much*?"

Pine paused, then answered. "Four million."

"Four *million*?" The number seemed staggering, but then he remembered a Tier Two QB of Pine's caliber made three or four million a year. On top of that, he had the endorsement deals that put his picture on almost as many ads as Yitzhak.

"So, why don't you pay it?" Quentin asked. "You've got that much, don't you?"

Pine slowly shook his head. "Already went through everything I got. Savings, my salary ... I'm still four mil in the hole."

"How long has this been going on?"

Pine looked away again. Quentin gave him a quick, single shake. Pine looked at his feet. "Since '79."

Quentin's eyes widened as he did the math. "Since '79? You've been tanking for *four years*?"

"I bet a lot of money on the '77 semi-final game with the To Pirates," Pine said. "That put me in the hole. I've been working my way out ever since, and I'm *almost* out."

"Four mil in the hole and you think you're almost out?"

"I just need to win a couple of bets, that's all, and I'll be out!"

Quentin pushed him away. The two men stood in silence.

"You going to tell Hokor?" Pine asked.

Quentin thought for a moment, then shook his head.

"Why not?" Pine asked. "That would give you the starting position."

He met this comment with a shrug. Pine was right, but Quentin didn't *want* to win it that way. He wanted to *earn* it. The first players started to filter out of the tunnel for practice.

"Don't do it again," Quentin said quietly. "You do and I'll take you down."

Pine looked at him with the eyes of a haunted man, a man hunted from all directions for far too long. "You'll take me down if I don't do what you want? Hey, welcome to the club."

Pine walked to the sidelines. Quentin stormed to a ball rack on the 30-yard line, anger and emotions whipping through his head. Without saying a word to them, Denver, Milford and Richfield lined up, waiting for Quentin to call out patterns.

"Deep," he said, the word coming out as a bark. Denver shot down the field. Quentin dropped back to the 20, then threw the ball with a grunt. He'd put all of his strength into the throw. It sailed so far past Denver she didn't even bother jumping — the ball arced through the air, sailing past the end zone, past the grass at the back of the end zone and bounced off the glass dome six floors up at the far end of the field.

"Dang," Quentin said quietly. He grabbed the next ball, oblivious to the fact he'd just thrown the ball over a hundred yards in the air.

From the Ionath City Gazette

Pine leads Krakens to second-straight win
By Kigin the Witty

IONATH CITY (Associated Press) — You can't keep a good veteran down.

At least that's what Ionath fans are thinking following a 21-7 Krakens win over the Sheb Stalkers, a win that might as well be named "The Donald Pine Show."

Pine missed two games with a broken femur but showed that the time off didn't affect him in the least. He went 21-for-34 on the day, throwing for 312 yards with two TDs and no interceptions. The Stalkers (3-2) came into the game with only one loss and were favored by nine points, but couldn't find an answer for Pine's accurate short-passing game.

"We did everything we could," said Stalkers middle linebacker Brian Badrocke. "If we blitzed, he hit us short. If we didn't blitz, he hit us long. It was a really long, frustrating day."

The Krakens' offensive line, which has given up eight sacks in the last two games, offered Pine laser-proof protection the entire game. It was the first time the Krakens didn't give up a sack since Week One.

"Anyone could have thrown well with that much time," Pine said after the game. "All the credit goes to the offensive line. They're true warriors."

Following Ionath's come-from-behind win over Sky Demolition in Week Four, many Krakens fans saw a potential quarterback controversy between Pine and rookie Quentin Barnes. Pine, however, put those thoughts to rest with his flawless performance against the Stalkers.

The Krakens' defense was a key factor in the win, holding the Stalkers to just 68 yards rushing while snagging four turnovers. Aleksandar Michnik notched three sacks, and Berea grabbed two interceptions.

STALKERS BOX SCORE

Final	1	2	3	4	T
Ionath	7	0	7	7	21
Sheb	0	0	0	7	7

SCORING SUMMARY

1st QUARTER		ION	SHE
Ionath TD	Rick Warburg 12-yard pass from Don Pine (Arioch Morningstar kick)	7	0

3rd QUARTER		ION	SHE
Ionath TD	Mitchell Fayed 24-yard run (Arioch Morningstar kick)	14	0

4th QUARTER		ION	SHE
Sheb TD	Lo Familia 2-yard run (Bernard Alexander kick)	14	7
Ionath TD	Hawick 46-yard pass from Don Pine (Arioch Morningstar)	21	7

TEAM STATISTICS	SHE	ION
First Downs	11	16
Third Down Efficiency	4-10	9-15
TOTAL NET YARDS	**281**	**424**
Total Plays	49	76
Average Gain Per Play	5.7	5.6
NET YARDS RUSHING	**68**	**112**
Rushes	18	42
Average Per Rush	3.8	2.7
NET YARDS PASSING	**213**	**312**
Pass Completion	20-31	21-34
Yards Per Pass	6.9	9.2
Times Sacked	4	0
Yards Lost To Sacks	20	0
Had Intercepted	3	0
PUNTS	**6**	**6**
Average Punt	37.2	38.4
PENALTIES	**11**	**5**
Penalty Yards	115	34
FUMBLES	**1**	**0**
Fumbles Lost	1	0
Time Of Possession	**21:12**	**38:48**

PASSING

KRAKENS	CMP	ATT	YDS	PCT	YPA	SACK	SYDS	TD	INT
Donald Pine	21	34	312	61.7	9.2	0	0	2	0

STALKERS	CMP	ATT	YDS	PCT	YPA	SACK	SYDS	TD	INT
Roblnar Kupanji	20	31	233	64.5	7.5	3	20	0	3

RUSHING

KRAKENS	ATT	YDS	AVG	LONG	TD	FUM
Mitchell Fayed	35	104	2.7	24	1	0
Tom Pareless	7	8	1.1	3	0	0

STALKERS	ATT	YDS	AVG	LONG	TD	FUM
Lo Familia	14	56	4.0	22	1	1
Jiang Bakuti	4	12	3.0	6	0	0

RECEIVING

KRAKENS	REC	YDS	AVG	LONG	TD	FUM
Hawick	6	113	18.9	46	1	0
Scarborough	4	56	14.0	32	0	0
Rick Warburg	4	50	12.5	17	1	0
Denver	2	34	17.0	20	0	0
Mezquitic	1	14	14.0	14	0	0
Milford	1	22	22.0	22	0	0
Yotaro Kobayasho	1	10	10.0	10	0	0
Tom Pareless	1	9	9.0	9	0	0
Mitchell Fayed	1	4	4.0	4	0	0

DEMOLITION	REC	YDS	AVG	LONG	TD	FUM
L.A.	6	72	12.0	34	0	0
Shreveport	4	60	15.0	42	0	0
Falujia	4	52	13.0	22	0	0
Jiang Bakuti	3	39	13.0	14	0	0
Thomas Jewell	3	10	3.3	6	0	0

WEEK FIVE LEAGUE ROUNDUP
(Courtesy of Galaxy Sports network)

The big story this week is the **Whitok Pioneers'** (4-1) 24-21 loss at the hands of **Orbiting Death** (4-1). The Death's win puts them in a three-way tie for first with the Pioneers and the **Glory Warpigs** (4-1), who put another mark in the win column with an easy 42-17 drubbing of Sky Demolition (0-5). The Pioneers' loss is even more devastating considering the injury to league-leading quarterback **Condor Adrienne,** who suffered severe damage to his right elbow. Adrienne is out for three to four weeks.

The **Bigg Diggers** (2-3) defeated the **Woo Wallcrawlers** (1-4) 22-6. The **Quyth Survivors** (2-3) edged out the **Grontak Hydras** (2-3) in a 23-20 overtime thriller.

DEATHS:
Chicago, wide receiver for the Sky Demolition, was killed by a gang-tackle involving Glory Warpigs defensive backs Keluang and Wellington. League officials ruled it was a clean hit.

WEEK FIVE PLAYERS OF THE WEEK:
Offense: Donald Pine, quarterback, Ionath Krakens. 21-of-34, 312 yards, two TDs, no INTs.
Defense: Sven Draupnir, linebacker, Quyth Survivors. Sixteen tackles, one interception, one forced fumble.

GAME SIX: Ionath Krakens (3-2) at Orbiting Death (4-1)

QUYTH IRRADIATED CONFERENCE STANDINGS

Orbiting Death	4-1
Whitok Pioneers	4-1
Glory Warpigs	4-1
Sheb Stalkers	3-2
Ionath Krakens	3-2
Grontak Hydras	2-3
Bigg Diggers	2-3
Quyth Survivors	2-3
Woo Wallcrawlers	1-4
Sky Demolition	0-5

QUENTIN WALKED into the central locker room to find the place already half-full of players and buzzing with excitement. The players crowded around the holotank in the center of the room.

"What's going on?" Quentin asked.

"Oh, yep," Yassoud said, making room for Quentin. "Check out our first break of the season."

The holotank showed two Human broadcasters, Christoff Berman and Dr. Mary Warwick, reviewing a holographic replay projected on the desk between them. The ESPN GameDay logo circled above them.

"The Orbiting Death's upset win over the Whitok Pioneers puts the Death in a three-way tie for first," Berman said. "But the bigger story is this injury to the Pioneers' money-man, Condor Big-Playdrianne. Just how long is Adrienne out for, Mary?"

The replay froze, and she poked the tip of a plastic pointer into the holographic display. In the display, Condor Adrienne had his right hand on the ground, obviously trying to keep himself from going down. A defensive lineman for the Orbiting Death, dressed in a white jersey with black trim and metalflake-red helmet, was also frozen in mid-fall, leaning against Adrienne's arm. Quentin suddenly realized that Adrienne's arm was bent the wrong way.

"As you can see here, the elbow is badly hyper-extended," Dr.

Warwick said. The replay moved forward another second, then froze. Adrienne's arm bent further, and a bone poked out of his skin accompanied by a freeze-frame flash of blood. A groan of disgust rippled through the Krakens players.

The holo started to move forward, then backward in rewind, then forward again, over and over to show the injury.

"Like a chicken wing!" Yassoud shouted joyfully.

Dr. Warwick continued. "Here we see severe bone and ligament damage to Adrienne's arm. This will require major reconstructive surgery. He could be out three to four weeks while they rebuild the joint."

Quentin felt bad for the man but also felt a surge of excitement. With him gone, the Pioneers were no longer the unbeatable machine they had been for the first four weeks. The Pioneers' win over the Krakens meant that even if the Krakens won out, and the Pioneers only lost one more, both teams would finish at 7-2 and the Pioneers would win the conference on the head-to-head tiebreaker. But if the Pioneers lost *two* games, the Krakens had a chance to win the conference outright. The Orbiting Death was also 4-1, but they only had to lose one more game — that week's game, against the Krakens.

If the Krakens prevailed against the Orbiting Death, both teams would hold 4-2 records. However, that same head-to-head tiebreaker would this time favor the Krakens. Even though the Krakens' shot at a conference title meant they had to win their last four games, the injury to Adrienne and the upcoming match with the Death made all things seem quite possible.

To Quentin, it felt like a shroud had lifted. In a two-game span, the team had gone from falling to 1-2 and losing its starting QB to crawling back to 3-2 with an outside shot at a title.

Two days of practice on the *Touchback*, then two days at Orbital Station One, home of Orbiting Death. Orbital Station One, The Ace, was even larger than The Deuce. Even the fact that Quentin was about to see yet another new world was not enough to offset his rage.

He was still on the bench, backing up a tanker.

• • •

IT WAS ONLY A FEW minutes after breaking out of punch space
that Quentin found himself in the observatory, looking out at another massive, mobile, artificial world. The Ace was an order of
magnitude larger than The Deuce. Where The Deuce had seemed
like a spherical sea urchin, complete with long, tapering spines,
The Ace looked more like a medieval mace. Short, blue, stubby
points dotted its spherical shape — the remnants of framework
spikes, like on The Deuce, but with the area between filled in by
harvested space debris.

Quentin walked up to Virak the Mean. "Just how big is that?"

"Largest artificial construct in the galaxy's history," Virak
said. "Much larger than Emperor One."

Quentin let out a long whistle. "I bet the Creterakians don't
like that."

"They hate it."

"How many beings live on that thing?"

"One-point-one billion."

Quentin shook his head. That was more beings than all the
Purist Nation's outlying colonies *combined*. Hell, it was more than
two entire planets, Allah and Stewart. The Ace wasn't a station, it
was a whole *world*. Still, while Allah and Stewart, especially Stewart, looked alive and vibrant, The Ace looked like a rock studded
with blue metallic points.

"Not much to see from space," Quentin said.

"Inside it is amazing," Virak said. "Even better than Orbital
Station Two."

Quentin didn't have to wait long to see the inside. The *Touchback* locked into orbit near an entrance shaft. Quentin rode down
on the first shuttle. He wasn't starting, yet he was listed on the
starters' shuttle. He didn't know what that meant — what he did
know was he didn't want to talk to Donald Pine on the way down.

Pine couldn't even meet Quentin's eyes. The older quarterback
spent most of the trip staring out the window, ignoring the hateful
glances Quentin couldn't help but shoot his way.

If Pine tanked a game, the Krakens were out of the playoff hunt, plain and simple. But if Quentin told anyone, it would destroy not only Pine's career, but the man's reputation and legacy as well. Maybe Pine was a moron for getting himself into trouble, but he was also a two-time Tier One champion. Did Quentin have the right to ruin that?

Pine wasn't the only one acting odd. John Tweedy sat in a chair, left fist methodically punching into right hand. *Whap.* Pause. *Whap.* Pause. *Whap* …

MOM ALWAYS DID LOVE YOU BEST scrolled across his forehead.

Quentin nudged the massive Khomeni, then gestured at Tweedy.

"What's his deal?"

"This is the biggest game of the year for him," Khomeni said in a voice that sounded like a deep well full of gravel. "The Death's running back is Ju Tweedy, John's brother."

Quentin had read about "The Mad" Ju Tweedy, Tier Two's leading rusher, in the weekly reports and seen him run on the highlight reels, but he had never connected the last name.

"John looks like he's about to kill someone," Quentin said. "He and Ju get along?"

Khomeni laughed as he pulled a large sandwich out of his duffel bag. "Yeah, they get along." He took a big bite, then spoke around a mouthful of ham on rye. "They get along about as well as the Purist Nation gets along with the League of Planets."

Quentin left Khomeni to his sandwich as the shuttle slid into the entrance shaft. At The Deuce, the crystalline growths had been mostly straight, like green quartz crystals. Here, they curved in all directions, like crystals of blue gypsum, sometimes spiraling outward like a ram's horn. Curls grew off of curls that grew off of curls, until the walls of the shaft were like a tangled jungle overgrowth of translucent blue. There were also smooth facets, their polished surface matching the contour of the shaft's outer diameter.

"Why isn't it as orderly as The Deuce? This looks like crap."

Virak seemed to wince at the comment, and before Quentin

could ask why, Choto the Bright slid out of his seat and stormed over. Choto's eye flooded a deep green. His strong pedipalps reached for Quentin. Quentin felt a blast of adrenaline rip through him in response to the oncoming 400-pound linebacker. Without even thinking, his fists balled up and he started to look for an opening.

Before either he or Choto could take a swing, however, Virak stepped between them.

"Back off, Choto!" Virak said, catching the bigger Quyth Warrior in mid-step. Choto's one eye peeked around Virak's shoulder. It was a scene identical to one Quentin had witnessed Humans perform more times than he could remember — one being holding another one back to prevent a fight.

"Human rookie said my world looks like feces!" Choto said. He tried to swing a pedipalp over the top, the Quyth Warrior equivalent of the Human "swim technique" used to get past an offensive lineman, but Virak effortlessly matched the move.

"He did not mean it," Virak said. "Quentin, tell him you did not mean it."

Choto pushed again, and Virak had to take a step back to keep his balance. Suddenly two Ki linemen, Kill-O-Yowet and Sho-Do-Thikit, grabbed Choto and held him tight. Choto's pedipalps quivered violently, and his eye flooded a deep black.

"I'm sorry," Quentin said quickly, stepping around Virak to place a hand on Choto's chest. "I did not mean to offend."

The words and the touch seemed to stop Choto cold.

"You called my world *feces*."

"A figure of speech on my world," Quentin said quickly. "I was not actually calling your world *feces*. I apologize if I offended you."

Choto's eye quickly faded from deep green to crystal-clear. His body relaxed, and the Ki linemen cautiously released their holds.

"Apology accepted," Choto said.

"So why does this shaft look so different from The Deuce," Quentin asked.

"Orbital Station One is older than The Deuce," Choto said.

"About fifty Human years older. The crystal growth technology was not as developed."

"It looks like it grows great."

"Yes, but too fast," Choto said. "That was fine when The Ace was small, a population of about two hundred million beings. But the larger the crystalline matrix grew, the more silicate organisms there were, and growth rates increased exponentially. Engineers cut it away when it grows into populated areas, but it grows unchecked through the nonliving areas. It is a problem we've been trying to fix for over a century."

The shuttle dropped through the entrance shaft and into a brightly lit underground city.

"High One," Quentin murmured. He now understood why larger ships weren't allowed through the shaft.

If the entrance shaft had resembled overgrown underbrush, the city was a full-out wilderness. Sprawling blue-tinted crystals reached out from every part of the domed ceiling, curving up and over so that the city seemed to exist within a living-but-artificial jungle canopy.

"We have over a million beings employed just to remove overgrowth," Choto said. "It is our biggest tax burden."

The shuttle slowed considerably and angled for a large gap in the arching crystalline canopy. As it slid past, the crystal growths seemed so close that Quentin unconsciously gripped a bulkhead to steady himself.

The ship slipped past the upper canopy and into an open space between the canopy and the city buildings. A ship off to the left had dozens of long legs and clung to a crystalline growth like an insect clinging to a plant stem. At the base of the ship, a long, multi-jointed arm held a concentrated beam of white-hot energy. The beam moved back and forth across the blue crystalline growth, until suddenly the growth snapped free, trailing thick globs of molten crystal. Growth and ship together plunged downward, but only for a second before the ship's engine caught and it hovered, newly cut prize still clutched in insectile legs. The ship flew up, carefully threading its way through the crystalline canopy.

"They will send that off into deep space," Choto said. "There is no use for it."

"Why don't the city engineers just replace this growth with the more successful variety from The Deuce?"

"It has been attempted. The original growth is much more aggressive than the new. New growth has been introduced several times — it is either choked out, overgrown or actually converted into original growth."

"Couldn't you just come up with a virus or something?"

"The planet is now some sixty percent original growth," Choto said. "Any virus might spread to the core and destroy the structural integrity. We would be killing our own planet."

"So you can't kill it, you can't replace it, and you can't stop it," Quentin said.

Choto's pedipalps quivered. He seemed oddly proud of the growth. "Much like the Quyth themselves."

The shuttle banked to the right. Here Quentin could discern no "downtown" because all of the huge buildings reached up into the crystalline canopy. Three centuries had given the buildings plenty of time to grow to towering heights. Like The Deuce, thick tendrils connected the city's buildings. Unlike The Deuce, however, wherever the shuttle flew, Quentin could see hundreds of the insect-like ships cutting away at unwanted growths. Thousands of small curls spiraled out from every possible place — the start of new growths that also would eventually need thinning.

"How many beings live here, in this city?"

"This is the city of Madderch, with fifty million residents in the city proper, which you see before you, and another hundred million in the underlying tunnels. It is the biggest city on The Ace because it is the only one that supports life for non-Quyth. All other cities were completely irradiated when the Creterakians attacked."

Quentin shook his head in amazement. Such numbers. Fifty million in what he saw before him, in a space only a few miles across. The same amount of space in New Mecca housed only ten million, and he had thought that impossibly overpopulated.

Another bank to the right ended the conversation as Beefeater Gin Stadium, home of the Orbiting Death, came into view. It was a round stadium, set deep in the ground. The first two decks were actually below the city's surface level. The next two decks towered high above, both sets connected by steeply sloped seats. Long, thick, curved buttresses arced out from four equidistant spots around the curved stadium, reaching up to support the upper decks. The playing field looked impossibly tiny and distant, a testament to the stadium's size. He'd seen several colors of playing surface, but this was the most unusual yet — jet-black. So black the white lines and numbers popped out in contrast, so sharp he could read them from the shuttle. The fact that the translucent blue stadium sat deep in the ground had caused some witty Human of years gone by to dub the stadium the "Ace Hole." The name had stuck.

Where all other parts of the city seemed to be fighting a losing battle against the slow-but-wild growth of crystal, the stadium seemed to be a perfect, shimmering, symmetrical jewel. Quentin saw several dozen insectile ships working away on the stadium, carving away even the smallest budding protuberance.

The shuttle banked over the stadium, then actually flew *inside* a hole in one of the huge buttresses. Once the ship set down, Quentin stepped out into a massive crystal room as elegant as an imperial palace. A short hallway, decorated with holoframes and memorabilia of the Orbiting Death, led the team to the visitor's central locker room.

As the races filed into their respective dressing rooms, Quentin stopped to look at the back wall, painted metalflake-red with a ten-foot-high flat-black circle.

"What the hell does that mean, anyway," Quentin asked Choto.

"That is the Quyth symbol for death," Choto said. "The circle. No beginning, no ending — a fighting death for one Quyth means life for many others."

Quentin nodded to himself as Choto walked to the Quyth Warrior locker room. The Orbiting Death wanted to die fighting? No problem, because Quentin Barnes aimed to please.

• • •

QUENTIN JUST WANTED to be alone. He didn't want to see his teammates. He didn't want to think about riding the bench. But that was all he *could* think about.

He sat in a mixed-race bar, hiding in a shadowy back-corner booth, a Sports Illustrated messageboard in one hand and a mag-can of Miller in the other. His eyes merely glazed over the words and pictures. His mind couldn't get around the fact that he was backup to a tanker.

"Hello, Quentin."

Quentin looked up to see Mitchell Fayed and Virak the Mean.

"Are we disturbing you?" Fayed asked.

Quentin shrugged. "Just wanted some time to myself, you know?"

Fayed nodded. "We saw you and wanted to invite you to join us for dinner. We're going to discuss ways to keep our winning streak alive. But if you want to be left alone, we understand."

"Thanks."

Fayed put his hand on Quentin's shoulder. It made Quentin uncomfortable, but he didn't knock it away. "Stay strong," Fayed said. "Keep working hard and good things will come."

With that, Fayed walked away and Virak followed. Quentin stared after them, hating Fayed for his positive attitude. He finished his Miller. Then another. Then another. He lost count — it wasn't until he stood to leave some four hours later that he felt the effects. The room spun around him, and he had to put a hand on the table to keep his balance.

A Creterakian civilian flew up and perched on his table. Quentin stared for a second, then recognized him — Sobox, the voice of Mopuk the Sneaky.

"You messed up, Human," Sobox said.

"What are you talkin' 'bout," Quentin said. His words sounded slurred — his balance wasn't the only thing failing him.

"Mopuk told you what to do, and you didn't do it. Now you've got to pay."

Quentin saw two large shadows move toward him. Not shadows — Ki, so big they blocked out the bars' lights. He saw a blur before something smashed into his face and the room twisted wildly. He fell back into his booth. Hot blood coursed out of his nose and onto his upper lip.

"You're never going to play again," Sobox said. "My boys will see to that."

A blow to his stomach. Air shot out of him — he tried to breathe in, but couldn't. His mouth gasped open like a fish out of water. Strong arms lifted him up out of the booth and held him up.

"You're going to pay," Sobox said quietly.

"Put him down ... *now*." The voice was quiet but carried deadly authority.

Quentin finally drew a gasping breath. The two Ki enforcers held him by his armpits. Sobox was still on the table. All three faced Virak the Mean and Mitchell Fayed.

"I said, put him down," Virak said.

Sobox glared at the Quyth Warrior. "Mind your own business, you grunt. You don't want to mess with Mopuk the Sneaky."

Virak turned from the Ki and stared directly at Sobox. "You insignificant worm. Gredok is my *shamakath*. He is also the *shamakath* of Mopuk the Sneaky. Quentin Barnes is Gredok's property. Now you put him down, or this will get ugly."

Sobox stared hatefully for a moment, then gestured to his enforcers. "Put him down. Let's go. You haven't heard the last of this, Virak."

"Yes, I have," Virak said. He turned to the two Ki enforcers. "You two face me again, in any capacity, and I'll kill you."

The Ki grunted some kind of return threat, then scuttled away, Sobox hovering over their heads as they left the bar.

"Quentin, are you okay?" Fayed said as he grabbed a napkin and held it to the bleeding nose.

"Ya, fine," Quentin mumbled.

"What was that about?" Virak said. "What are you doing associating with Mopuk the Sneaky? What did he want with you?"

"Beats me," Quentin said. "Maybe he didn't like my hair."

"Stop lying," Virak said, his voice a dark growl. "I have to tell Gredok about this."

"No!" Quentin said, feeling his buzz suddenly fade away. "You can't do that."

"I have to," Virak said. "He is my *shamakath*, and I must tell him."

"Virak, don't," Quentin said, a pleading tone tingeing his voice.

"Why not?" A shade of light purple colored Virak's eye.

"You … you just can't, okay?"

"That is not okay. It is my duty. Mopuk is in Gredok's organization."

Quentin groaned inside. "Mopuk works *for* Gredok? Oh, this sucks."

"If Mopuk is making a move, Gredok has to know about it."

"He's not making a move, it's … something else."

"I must tell Gredok, and you must tell him also, everything about this."

Quentin stood and looked Virak in the eye. "You have to trust me. If you tell Gredok, it will destroy our season."

"Why?" Fayed asked. "Why would it destroy our season?"

"It just will," Quentin said. "Virak, please, you have to trust me on this. Do it for your team."

"For … my team?"

Quentin nodded. "I'm telling you, we have to keep this quiet. I can't tell you why. Just trust me."

Virak stared for a long moment. "It is a sign of disrespect to not tell Gredok, and he does not take disrespect lightly."

Quentin stayed quiet. He'd said his piece.

"Virak, we can't let anything ruin our season," Fayed said. "Don't tell Gredok."

Virak looked at Fayed, then back to Quentin.

"I will not say anything," Virak said. "I will … trust you, Quentin. But do not betray that trust."

Quentin nodded, a grateful smile crossing his face.

"Thank you, Virak. And thanks, guys, for helpin' me out. I would have got my face kicked in."

"We will return to the rooms," Fayed said. "Will you join us this time?"

Quentin nodded. The three teammates left the bar together.

THE BUG-SHIPS WERE nowhere to be seen. There wouldn't have been any room for them anyway — the Ace Hole had been transformed into a living sea of flat-black clothing, flat-black banners and flat-back flags, surrounded by the shimmering beauty of ice-like blue crystal with a playing field of pitch-black grass.

The residents of Orbital Station Two didn't call the stadium the Ace Hole — they called it the Black Hole. Four decks of seating provided a capacity of 132,000. Attendance for this game stood at 133,412.

The crowd roared and surged and whistled and chirped as the Krakens gathered in the tunnel. Battle scent rolled through the orange and white and black clad warriors. Another week, another war. This war they would win; this war they *had* to win.

"This is our chance to make up for lost time," Pine said in his ringing tone of command. "This is our chance to get back in the *hunt*."

The team let out primitive barks of agreement, yet the veteran's words held little sway over Quentin. Was the fix in for this game?

The loudspeaker called out a welcome to the visiting Ionath Krakens, and the team swarmed onto the field. Yet as soon as they did, a sound hit Quentin's ears like a thunderbolt.

Or rather, a *lack* of sound.

The Black Hole instantly lived up to its name as most of the 133,412 fans fell stone silent. There were a few thin cheers from Krakens' faithful, but even those sounds quickly ended, as if the fans felt suddenly self-conscious about making noise in the midst of funeral-like quiet. The transition from cacophony to total silence made Quentin stop in his tracks — the players behind him nearly ran him over. Regaining his wits, he jogged to the sidelines with his teammates.

Quentin looked across the silent fans, head whipping from one

side, then to the next. His brain could barely process the phenomenon. He walked to Yitzhak. "What the hell is this all about?"

"The silent treatment? That's what the Death fans do for every
home game. Kind of cool, isn't it?"

Quentin nodded absently. "Yeah, kind of cool."

"Well, it doesn't last long, so get ready —"

Yitzhak's words were cut off by an instant and all-encompassing roar from over 133,000 fans, a roar so abrupt and total it felt
like a physical blow. The Orbiting Death players took the field,
resplendent in their flat-black uniforms with metalflake-red numbers and blue trim. Stadium lights gleamed off their metalflake-red
helmets, each decorated with a flat-black circle.

"Wow," Quentin said. "That's pretty impressive."

Yitzhak nodded. "They really put on a show. It's all a head
game, and they've got over a hundred-thousand fans playing along
perfectly with the script."

"Yeah," Quentin said. "Just a head game." He hoped Yitzhak
didn't see that the "head game" had registered an impact. The
roar-to-silence-to-roar definitely unnerved him. For a second, he
was happy that Pine would be taking the first snap and not him.

But it was a brief second.

THE ORBITING DEATH wasted no time showing why they were
4-1 — that reason being running back Ju Tweedy. At 6-foot-9,
385 pounds and with a 40-yard dash time of 3.6, John Tweedy's
younger brother was a Human wrecking ball. Add to those stats
a few more: he had a vertical leap of 64 inches, could squat 1,500
pounds and could knock out 47 reps on the standard 300-pound
bench press test.

Virak the Mean, Choto the Bright and, of course, John Tweedy
had been waiting weeks for this moment, waiting to show the
league their mettle, but Quentin wondered if they now wished
they'd just stayed home. The three linebackers brought the house
on every tackle, but through the first quarter, he had yet to see Ju
knocked backward, even once. "The Mad Ju," as he was called

in the papers, rumbled into the hole, lowered his thick head like a medieval battering ram and plowed forward with great pain and suffering to all those that stood in his way.

Death quarterback Ganesha Fritz wasn't the greatest signal-caller in the galaxy, but he provided exactly what the Death needed — short, accurate passes to keep the linebackers from constantly keying on Ju. The Death utilized a simple strategy: hold onto the ball, pass when the linebackers cheat up and keep giving the rock to Ju.

By the end of the first quarter, The Mad Ju had racked up 52 yards on seven carries, with one phenomenal 12-yard TD run in which he broke tackle attempts by Mai-An-Ihkole at the line of scrimmage, John Tweedy at the 9, Choto at the 6 and Berea at the 1. Well, Quentin couldn't exactly call that last one a "broken tackle" because all Berea really did was get in front of Ju and then get run over. That last hit drew roars of approval from the crowd and broke Berea's left leg. Tiburon filled the cornerback spot while Doc tended to the wounded Sklorno defender.

"They'll keep pounding on him," Yitzhak said, referring to the linebackers' never-ending suicide assaults on Ju. "He's got one weakness — he can't hold onto the pellet."

Quentin nodded at this wisdom but wondered that if a fumble ever did occur, would there be anything left of Choto, Virak or John Tweedy to jump on it?

Ju's performance seemed to inspire Mitchell Fayed, who ran like a man possessed. Fans of the running game were not disappointed by the Krakens vs. the Orbiting Death. And it was a good thing that Fayed ran so well because Donald Pine was simply not his usual self. By the end of the first quarter, the two-time champ, the King of the Short Game, was 5-for-12 for 27 yards.

Quentin watched him. Watched him carefully.

Is he tanking or just playing bad? Quentin found himself trying to give Pine the benefit of the doubt, but his eyes told him a different story. The Death's defensive secondary just didn't seem that impressive. Hawick and Scarborough looked open several times, but Pine's passes either fell short or were never thrown at all.

With each possession, Quentin's anger grew.

Possession #1: A run, one incomplete pass, a sack — three-and-out.

Possession #2: Sacked on third-and-long.

Possession #3: Two completions, three incompletions, punt.

Possession #4: Three straight completions, then an interception.

Possession #5: Two strong runs, then a sack and a fumble — Death's ball.

"Jesus," Yitzhak said quietly. "Three sacks already. Pine never gets sacked. And he *never* fumbles. We're in some deep doo-doo, my friend."

Quentin kept watching. If it was a tank, as soon as the Death got up by two or three scores, Pine would strike to make it close.

As the second quarter dragged on, The Mad Ju ripped off a 28-yard TD run, putting the Death up 17-0. Richfield returned the following kick to the Krakens' 12, but Quentin had eyes only for Pine.

If he's tanking, he'll come back strong to make it look good.

Pine dropped back on the first snap. He planted — no busy feet this time, he stood tall in the pocket, like a heroic statue.

"She's open!" Yitzhak's excited voice called to Quentin's right, but Quentin just watched Pine. A defensive lineman, the same one who already had two sacks, closed in, gathering up for a perfect blindside blast on Pine's back.

"Take them deep!" Yitzhak screamed.

Pine cocked back and let the ball fly — he didn't have Quentin's strength, but there was nothing weak about the throw. The ball shot downfield …

But Quentin watched Pine. The lineman closed in, only a half-second behind the throw, expanding violently for a blindside shot.

Pine took one small step forward. The lineman shot past to fall in a clumsy, sliding heap on the ground.

Pine, you tanking jerk.

That same lineman, making that same blindside approach, had earlier racked up two sacks. Yet, this time, Pine had slipped by as if he had eyes in the back of his head.

Not eyes in the back of his head, Quentin thought. *He just knows where every player is at all times.* After watching Pine up close and personal for six weeks, he *knew* the veteran was letting those sacks happen. Pine was so good, so unbelievably in control of his game, that he could choreograph a tanking without anyone suspecting. After all, what quarterback can dodge a blindside sack, right?

Donald Pine. That's who.

The crowd booed deeply as Hawick crossed the goal line for an 88-yard touchdown. Yitzhak ran onto the field for the extra point, as Pine ran off. Quentin's anger rose another ten degrees, then *popped*, almost audibly.

Quentin met Pine on the sidelines.

"Nice pass, you piece of garbage," Quentin said.

Pine just nodded and kept walking toward the bench.

"Hey, *loser*, I'm talking to you!" Quentin grabbed Pine's shoulder pad and whipped him around. Pine's eyes went wide with surprise, then narrowed with anger.

"Leave me alone," Pine said.

"You throw two more TDs and I'll leave you alone, you *coward*." Quentin pointed his finger straight at Pine's nose. Other players turned to watch the confrontation.

"Shut up, kid," Pine said. "I've got a game to play."

"A game? Is *that* what you call it?"

Pine stepped forward, going chest-to-chest and nose-to-nose with Quentin.

"You wanna make a move, rookie, then make it now!"

Quentin cocked his left fist and started to swing but was jerked away by strong Human hands. Quentin's anger soared to a new level. He twisted and threw a hard left cross at this new foe. His fist smashed into Mitchell Fayed's jaw. Fayed's head snapped back and to his left. He slowly turned his head back to look into Quentin's eyes, working his jaw from side to side.

"Are you finished?" Fayed asked. "Or do I have to hit you back?"

Quentin felt his anger seep away. His face felt scaldingly hot.

"Aw, Mitch, I'm sorry."

"I said, are you finished?"

Quentin nodded.

"Good. This is not the place for this behavior, Quentin. Now calm down. You're disturbing the team."

Quentin nodded again. He'd never felt so embarrassed. Once again, his temper had got the best of him. Maybe he could make it up to Fayed later. Then again, maybe not — he'd just hit the man in front of 133,000 fans and probably another three billion watching at home. He walked down the sidelines, away from Pine. Anger returned, but this time it was a cold, calculating anger.

Not now. Not now, Pine, old kid, not when we can climb back into the hunt.

Quentin had to think. He looked around the sidelines, searching for an answer. He couldn't tell Hokor, not now, the coach wouldn't believe him. Even if he did, Pine's career was over (not to mention, when Gredok found out, probably his life).

Quentin didn't know what he was looking for until he saw it.

Shayat the Thick.

The drug dealer.

"Holy crap," Quentin said to himself. "We might win this game after all."

"YOU WANT DRUGS *now*," Shayat said in a whispered hiss. "It's the middle of a game. What do you want sleepy for?"

"Just *give* it to me," Quentin said. "I know you've got it in your locker. I know you wouldn't let your shipment out of your sight. Now, you either give me enough to knock a Human out *cold* or you and I are going to hook right now."

Shayat's eye went from clear to light translucent green.

"I would kill you, Human."

"Maybe so," Quentin said. "But if you and I go, I'll make sure I hurt you enough to keep you out of the game. And you don't want that today, do you?" Quentin gestured to Virak the Mean and Choto the Bright — both Quyth Warriors were on training tables, Doc and Quyth Leader trainers tending to their wounds. Choto's right pedipalp quivered sickeningly, even as he lay perfectly still on the table. The pedipalp looked broken, a very painful injury, from what Quentin had heard. John Tweedy might have been hurt, but no one knew because he stood in front of his locker, bashing his forehead into the metal grate. His tattoo scrolled nothing but gibberish, his lips were frozen in a permanent snarl, and tears of rage trickled down his cheeks.

"But I get to start the second half," Shayat said. "You wouldn't do that to me, I haven't had a chance to play first-string all year."

"Sure," Quentin said. "You'll start, *if* you give me what I want."

Shayat looked back at Quentin, and the eye slipped back to clear.

"I will give you the drug."

Quentin smiled a malicious smile. He was halfway home.

HOKOR WORKED the holoboard, outlining a new defensive strategy designed to shut down Ju. The defensive players, except for Virak and Choto, crowded around the board, pointing excitedly and offering suggestions. The Krakens were down 17-7, yet the defense showed no sign of letting up. They couldn't wait to get back on the field and take another crack at Ju. Especially John Tweedy. The Human linebacker's eyes were as wide as wide could be, his nostrils flared in and out, and every word was a guttural scream. HATEYOUHATEYOUHATEYOU scrolled across his sweaty forehead tattoo — he couldn't concentrate on it long enough to make a message. John looked like a man infused with the living, hunting energy of an entire special forces platoon.

Hokor had already finished with the offense. There wasn't much to talk about, really — everyone knew that to get back in the game, Donald Pine had to stop getting sacked, start completing passes and hold onto the ball. Everyone knew this, yet there wasn't one evil eye cast his way. The team knew that if it could be done, Pine would do it. If Pine couldn't do it, well, then neither could anyone else. Pine was the kind of quarterback who could throw five interceptions in a game, yet never be pulled, because his next three passes might hit for touchdowns.

That was, of course, when he was *trying*.

Pine sat in front of his locker, a portable holotank in front of him, reviewing defensive sets. Holding a water bottle, Quentin walked up and sat down. Pine glared at him with a look that combined hate and shame.

"Come to yell at me some more, kid?"

Quentin shook his head. "I came to apologize."

Pine raised a suspicious eyebrow. "Apologize? You?"

Quentin shrugged again. "Look, you've got some stuff to deal with, I shouldn't have lit into you on the field. We can talk about it later." He handed Pine the water bottle. Pine took it, his eyes never leaving Quentin's face.

"This isn't my choice," Pine said quietly. "I just want you to know that."

"I know," Quentin said and walked away.

Pine took a long drink from the water bottle, then turned back to the holotank.

THE ORBITING DEATH received the second-half kickoff. Choto the Bright lasted only three plays, until he tried to "arm-tackle" The Mad Ju. Trying to take down Ju with a broken pedipalp was a bad idea at best. Ju ripped through Choto's valiant effort, leaving the Quyth Warrior writhing on the ground.

Shayat the Thick ran onto the field to take Choto's place. Samuel Darkeye was Choto's normal backup at outside linebacker, but Hokor needed Shayat's size to try and stop The Mad Ju. The Krakens' "D" kept hammering at Ju, and Ju kept hammering back, yet the fumble-fruit of his so-called slippery hands never seemed to materialize. At the end of the drive, to quite literally add insult to injury, Ju crossed the goal line with John Tweedy on his back.

Extra point: good.

Orbiting Death 24, Krakens 7.

Richfield returned the ensuing kick. The Krakens' "O" took the field, starting from their own 34. Quentin watched carefully. He'd given Pine enough sleepy to knock out a Ki lineman. If he gave too much, the overdose could easily cause brain hemorrhaging. Quentin hoped that wouldn't happen, but he had a game to win.

The huddle broke and Pine walked up to the line. He seemed to walk slower than normal. He looked around a few times, then shook his head violently and lined up under center. A handoff to Fayed picked up four yards. The team returned to the huddle, but Pine stayed where he was, staring down at the grass as if it were the most interesting thing in the known universe. A blast of anticipation adrenaline shot through Quentin's body — it was working.

Fayed walked up to Pine, who continued to stare at the ground. A Harrah ref floated up to both Humans. Pine stared at the zebe as if he'd never seen such a thing before. A steady murmur burbled through the capacity crowd: like most of the players, they wondered what was going on. Pine turned to Fayed and said something. Fayed instantly signaled for a time-out.

"Barnes!" Hokor called. "Let's go!"

Quentin followed Hokor onto the field. They ran up to Fayed and Pine.

"What in the name of the Mother of All is going on here?" Hokor barked, his fur fluffed up with anger.

"Um ..." Fayed said. "I, uh, think Pine was hit in the head or something."

"Heyyyyy," Pine said with a smile, never looking away from Fayed. "I can see right into Fayed's brain. *Right inside!*"

"Pine!" Hokor barked. "Pine, snap out of it!"

"Fayed is thinking about a ham sandwich."

"No, I'm not," Fayed said.

"Pine, you okay?" Hokor asked.

"Ham sandwich with Texas mustard," Pine said. "Don't deny it, you liar. I can *see* your thoughts!"

"Pine!" Hokor said. "You're going to have to sit out a few." Hokor signaled to Doc for the med-sled.

"But I'm not lying," Fayed said. "I don't like mustard."

Hokor turned to Quentin. "Okay, Barnes, it's up to you now. We need some points on the board. Just run —"

"The plays that are called, yeah, I know, Coach."

"Ham and you are a beautiful thing!" Pine screamed. "Don't fight your urges, Fayed!"

Doc flew up to Pine, the med-sled right behind him. Pine pointed a finger in Fayed's face. "You know how many pigs die every year? Their lives are on your conscience! *Swine-eater!*"

"I kind of *hate* mustard," Fayed said.

Quentin sat Pine down on the med-sled. "Doc, get him out of here, now." Doc led the sled off the field — Pine carefully watched the grass go by.

Quentin and Fayed walked back to the huddle. The team looked at him with a new expression.

Like I'm the savior, Quentin thought. *They think I can pull this one out.* The thing was, *he* thought he could pull it out. They'd spent a half-game of futility and had only seven points to show for it. Quentin knew he needed to get these guys some momentum, and he needed to do it quick.

"Okay, they've been blitzing all day. Let them come. We're going quarterback draw on two, on two. Just give them a good fit and let them come on by." The huddle seemed revived with electricity.

"Dive right to Fayed," Hokor called in his earpiece. Quentin nodded then broke the huddle. Hokor's plays would have to wait — he knew what his team needed, they needed a burst of excitement, not a methodical ground game.

Quentin surveyed the defense as he lined up behind center. He'd guessed right — they showed blitz all the way. Orbiting Death ran a 5-2, and both Quyth linebackers leaned forward on all-fours, weight on their arms.

"Red, twenty-one! Red, twenty-one!" The linebackers leaned farther forward. Quentin waited a second to give the Ki linemen a chance to pick their targets.

"Hut!" The Death linemen and linebackers surged forward with a metal-plastic crash against their backpedaling offensive enemy. Quentin dropped back three steps, planted and sprang forward. The blitzing defense didn't even have a chance to slow down before Quentin was past them, moving like a tall, strong wind. His first five steps took him ten yards downfield, leaving seven defenders behind him. The defensive backs reacted instantly, but the three-step drop had given Hawick and Scarborough a chance to move into blocking position. The two receivers danced with the safety and free safety that tried to avoid them — they weren't good blocks by any means, but with Quentin's speed, they were more than enough for him to shoot past.

BLINK

Everything moved in slow motion, and Quentin suddenly saw every last detail the field had to offer. The left cornerback came from his right side — she dove for his legs. Quentin planted and spun outside, a whirling blur, the cornerback grasping only empty air as he straightened and moved downfield. The right cornerback closed on him and he bounced outside. He saw *everything*, her raspers hanging out just a bit from her chin-plate, her flat-black uniform flapping slightly with each powerful thrust of her long legs. She moved in, reached out.

Quentin felt a blast of something primitive. His lip curled up of its own accord. He felt the strength of a supernova in his limbs. He switched the ball to his right hand and reached out with his left, grabbing the cornerback by the neck just as she tried to wrap around his waist. He squeezed and lifted — she was so *light*. Like a tribesman carrying a spear, he ran another five yards with her neck in his hand, her feet dangling uselessly, her eyestalks showing sudden pain and fear. He casually tossed her away as one might discard an apple core. She flew through the air, landing heavily on her head, tumbling in a rolling heap.

He felt something grab at his back and try to pull him down. The extra weight slowed him, but only for a second, his legs pumped with the power of an entire universe. The weight fell away, and he was once again free. He distantly heard the roaring *booo* of the crowd, a faraway noise that was none of his concern.

He crossed the goal line, and the world *blinked* back to real-time with a rush of deafening sound. He tossed the ball to the floating Harrah ref, then knelt and plucked a few blades of black grass. He sniffed deeply — smelled like a sappy pine tree. Hawick and Scarborough arrived suddenly and leapt on him hard enough to knock him over.

"*Touchdown, Krakens, 62-yard run by Quentin Barnes,*" the loudspeaker blared amidst the crowd's boo and the hiss of Quyth Workers scraping in derision. Quentin laughed and pushed aside Hawick and Scarborough. He stood, only to be knocked down again, this time by Fayed and Kobayasho.

"What an excellent *run*!" Fayed screamed at him, his facemask smashed against Quentin's. "A much better use of energy than punching me in the face!"

Quentin managed to stand amidst friendly-but-hard slaps to his head and shoulder pads. He ran to the sidelines and was engulfed by teammates. They seemed energized as if they were up by four touchdowns instead of down 24-14.

"Barnes!" Hokor screamed in his headset. "What was that? I called a dive!"

"Sorry Coach," Quentin said. "I thought you said QB draw."

"You dirty, lying Human! Run the plays that I call!"

"Yes, Coach. Got ya."

The long touchdown run was like the harbinger of doom for Orbiting Death. Two plays later, John Tweedy came free on a linebacker stunt and put the first really solid hit on his brother Ju. The ball popped free, wobbled on the ground, where Shayat the Thick smothered it. The Death had the lead, but something intangible had changed hands. After a pair of passes to Kobayasho, Fayed scored on a 15-yard run to cut the lead to 24-21.

In the fourth quarter, Quentin dissected the Death secondary as he knew Pine should have done, hitting Scarborough for two TD passes. Ju fumbled one more time, setting up the second TD strike to Scarborough, but the wrecking-ball running back couldn't be completely stopped. He scored on a long 44-yard run that left John Tweedy on his rear and put Shayat on the sidelines for the rest of the game.

When the final gun sounded, Quentin had led the Krakens to a 35-31 win — 28 of those points coming in the second half.

THERE WAS A NOTICEABLE difference between a 1-2 locker room and a 4-2 locker room. Players laughed and joked and shouted. The Pioneers had lost again, were now 4-2 and still had two games to go without their star quarterback. The Glory Warpigs had soundly whipped the Woo Wallcrawlers 35-3 to move to 5-1. The Krakens were now only one game out of first and had to go head-to-head with the 'Pigs in Week 8.

A conference title was no longer a fantasy — they were three wins (their own) and one loss (by the Pioneers) away from winning the championship.

Every Human took a turn coming up to Quentin and giving their respects.

"You're a stone-bred *monster*!" John Tweedy shouted, hugging Quentin with his powerful arms.

"*Huge* comeback, kid!" Yitzhak said with a massive grin, tousling Quentin's hair as if he were a little boy. Quentin pushed Yitzhak's hand away but laughed along with him.

Everyone wanted to congratulate him. Everyone, it seemed, except Donald Pine. Pine's ham-sandwich fixated buzz had worn off just as the fourth quarter ended. He sat alone in front of his locker, still dressed in his soiled uniform, his head hanging in his hands. Quentin felt a pang of pity for the man, but he chased that thought away — Pine made his own bed, and if sleeping in it sucked, then that was the breaks. Quentin had kept his secret, and even that was more than Pine deserved. It didn't matter, the Krakens were 4-2 and almost — *almost* — in control of their own destiny.

WEEK SIX LEAGUE ROUNDUP
(Courtesy of Galaxy Sports network)

The Quyth Irradiated Conference standings saw a major shakeup this week. The **Ionath Krakens** (4-2) crawled another thin notch higher in the standings with a 35-31 upset win over **Orbiting Death** (4-2). The Krakens continue to show no continuity at quarterback, as this week veteran Donald Pine was ineffective while rookie backup Quentin Barnes led the team to a come-from-behind win.

The **Whitok Pioneers** (4-2) seemed to be walking away with the conference title, but without star quarterback Condor Adrienne they lost their second straight game, this time 24-8 to the **Grontak Hydras** (3-3).

First place now belongs solely to the **Glory Warpigs** (5-1), who thrashed the **Woo Wallcrawlers** (1-5) by a score of 24-6.

The **Sheb Stalkers** (4-2) remained in contention with a key 17-14 win over the **Bigg Diggers** (2-4). Arkham, All-Pro cornerback for the Diggers, notched her tenth and eleventh interceptions of the season. She leads the Quyth Irradiated in interceptions for the season, well ahead of the Warpigs' Toyonaka, who has eight picks so far this year.

Sky Demolition (0-6) still can't find a win, this time losing 32-10 to the **Quyth Survivors** (3-3).

DEATHS:
Shak-Ah-Tallo, offensive guard for Quyth Survivors, was killed on an illegal hit by Yalla the Biter. Yalla has been suspended for two games.

WEEK SIX PLAYERS OF THE WEEK:
Offense: St. Petersburg, wide receiver, Glory Warpigs. Hauled in 12 catches for 162 receiving yards and three TDs.
Defense: Kitiara Lomax, linebacker, Bigg Diggers. nine tackles, one interception.

ORBITING DEATH BOX SCORE

Final	1	2	3	4	T
Ionath	0	7	14	14	35
OS1	7	10	7	7	31

SCORING SUMMARY

1st QUARTER		ION	OS1
OS1 TD	Ju Tweedy, 12-yard run (Shi-Ki-Kill kick)	0	7

2nd QUARTER		ION	OS1
OS1 FG	34-yard FG by Shi-Ki-Kill is good.	0	10
OS1 TD	Ju Tweedy, 28-yard run (Shi-Ki-Kill kick)	0	17
Ionath TD	Hawick 88-yard pass from Don Pine (Arioch Morningstar kick)	7	17

3rd QUARTER		ION	OS1
OS1 TD	Ju Tweedy, 4-yard run (kick by Shi-Ki-Kill)	7	24
Ionath TD	Quentin Barnes 62-yard run (Arioch Morningstar kick)	14	24
Ionath TD	Mitchell Fayed 15-yard run (Arioch Morningstar kick)	21	24

4th QUARTER		ION	OS1
Ionath TD	Scarborough 22-yard pass from Quentin Barnes (Arioch Morningstar kick)	28	24
Ionath TD	Scarborough 17-yard pass from Quentin Barnes (Arioch Morningstar kick)	35	24
OS1 TD	Ju Tweedy 44-yard run (Shi-Ki-Kill kick)	35	31

TEAM STATISTICS	OS1	ION
First Downs	16	15
Third Down Efficiency	8-13	9-14
TOTAL NET YARDS	**308**	**460**
Total Plays	63	73
Average Gain Per Play	4.9	6.3
NET YARDS RUSHING	**185**	**180**
Rushes	40	31
Average Per Rush	4.6	5.8
NET YARDS PASSING	**123**	**280**
Pass Completion	12-23	22-42
Yards Per Pass	5.3	6.7
Times Sacked	2	3
Yards Lost To Sacks	7	20
Had Intercepted	0	1
PUNTS	**5**	**5**
Average Punt	32.8	39.1
PENALTIES	**3**	**6**
Penalty Yards	15	40
FUMBLES	**2**	**1**
Fumbles Lost	2	1
Time Of Possession	**34:22**	**25:38**

PASSING

KRAKENS	CMP	ATT	YDS	PCT	YPA	SACK	SYDS	TD	INT
Donald Pine	10	24	135	41.7	5.6	3	20	1	1
Quentin Barnes	12	18	165	66.7	9.2	0	0	2	0

ORBITING DEATH	CMP	ATT	YDS	PCT	YPA	SACK	SYDS	TD	INT
Ganesha Fritz	12	23	130	52.2	5.7	2	7	0	0

RUSHING

KRAKENS	ATT	YDS	AVG	LONG	TD	FUM
Mitchell Fayed	25	96	3.8	18	1	0
Tom Pareless	4	20	5.0	10	0	0
Quentin Barnes	2	64	32.0	62	1	0

ORBITING DEATH	ATT	YDS	AVG	LONG	TD	FUM
Ju Tweedy	36	179	5.0	44	4	2
Bimidji Billings	4	6	1.5	3	0	0

RECEIVING

KRAKENS	REC	YDS	AVG	LONG	TD	FUM
Hawick	5	120	24.0	88	1	0
Scarborough	5	68	13.6	22	2	0
Yotaro Kobayasho	4	34	8.5	12	0	0
Milford	2	26	13.0	14	0	0
Rick Warburg	2	17	8.5	16	0	0
Tom Pareless	2	12	6.0	10	0	0
Denver	1	12	12.0	12	0	0
Mezquitic	1	11	11.0	11	0	0

DEMOLITION	REC	YDS	AVG	LONG	TD	FUM
Brian Johnson	5	52	10.4	16	0	0
Brazilia	4	50	12.5	24	0	0
Parker Schmoz	1	18	18.0	18	0	0
Ju Tweedy	1	6	6.0	6	0	0
Bimidji Billings	1	4	4.0	4	0	0

YASSOUD, OF COURSE, wanted to drag *everyone*, non-Humans included, out to the nightclub district. Quentin put a stop to it, saying the team had to stay sharp in a dangerous place like The Ace — and after beating the Orbiting Death, many of the city's residents would have been most happy to mess with an Ionath Kraken. Instead, most of the team headed to The Dead Fly, a laid-back bar owned by Choto the Bright's family. Choto's family shut the bar down for the impromptu private party. Quentin wanted the team to stay together — most came along, although I'me wanted to be alone, and Quentin wasn't going to argue with him.

Liquor flowed, which Quentin didn't mind as long as everyone stayed inside. The quarantine angered Yassoud and Tweedy, but Choto backed up Quentin's desire to keep the team off the streets. Quentin started feeding Yassoud and Tweedy beers, and after six or seven, the two stopped complaining and started enjoying the night.

While drink was in plentiful supply, food was another story.

"But you are hungry," Virak said to Quentin. "There is nothing wrong with this food."

Quentin worked hard to keep a straight face as he stared down onto a tray covered with fried critters that looked a lot like foot-long centipedes, only not quite as appetizing.

"I don't think so, those look like ..."

His voice trailed off as Choto the Bright walked up, a gin-and-tonic in hand, his eye a hazy shade of orange. Choto's family had made the food, and Quentin could only imagine Choto's reaction if he called it "crap."

"It's fine to eat," Yitzhak said. He reached out and picked up one of the fried critters by a long front leg. He dangled it over his mouth, biting off a two-inch chunk. "Just bio-mass, perfectly digestible. Quyth and Human digestive physiology are quite compatible, you know."

Virak and Choto stared at Quentin, obviously waiting for him to eat. He gingerly reached out and picked up a critter by its leg, as Yitzhak had done. He held it in front of his eyes, his stomach simultaneously growling with hunger and churning at the thought of that *thing* in his belly.

"Eat!" Choto said. "Is good!"

Quentin lifted the thing to dangle over his lips. He opened his mouth and started to lower it, when Virak's phone buzzed loudly. Quentin set the critter down, pretending to be polite, as Virak answered the call. The Quyth Warrior's eye changed from orange, the color of happiness, to pitch black almost instantly.

"What's the matter," Quentin said as Virak put the phone away.

"Donald Pine is in the hospital. He has been attacked."

QUENTIN WALKED into the room not knowing what he'd see. He didn't want to feel guilty — he hadn't been the one to gamble up a huge debt and start throwing games, after all — but when he saw Pine in the hospital bed, he couldn't stop waves of the nasty stuff from washing over his soul.

Pine was resting at a 45-degree angle, his bandaged head up high, both legs immersed in the pink liquid of a rejuvenation tank. A large, enamel-white, tube-like machine hid most of his left arm. Light-blue bandages covered his forehead and his right cheek.

The hospital room would have seemed large were there fewer beings in it. With three Ki linemen, John Tweedy and Mitchell Fayed present, Quentin could barely see the walls.

"Hey, kid," Pine said. "Great game."

"Thanks," Quentin said automatically.

"I watched it on tape. Seems I wasn't in much of a condition to watch it live."

"Yeah," Quentin said. He didn't know what else to say.

Tweedy's brow seemed larger than ever. SOMEBODY'S GOTTA PAY scrolled across his forehead in black letters. "We're gonna find the sentients that did this," he said in a low growl. "Nobody messes with our quarterback and lives."

The Ki linemen — Sho-Do-Thikit, Kill-O-Yowet and Bud-O-Shwek — grunted in monosyllabic agreement. Quentin had a brief image of wandering into a dark alley and facing Tweedy and the linemen. He shivered at the thought then pushed it away.

"Virak, Kopor the Climber and Shayat are out looking for the culprits," Fayed said. "They think it was someone from the Bigg Diggers, trying to soften us up for next week. Virak thought it could be the Glory Warpigs, seeing as it might be us or them for the championship, but the doctors say your injuries may be healed by that time."

"Too bad for them," Tweedy said. "Our number two can win games just like our number one, eh, boys?"

Fayed nodded, the Ki made their one grunt, they all looked at Quentin with pride.

"I need to talk to Quentin," Pine said. "Alone. You guys give us a minute?"

The five Krakens players filtered out of the room, leaving Pine to stare at Quentin.

"I haven't had a hit of sleepy since my Tier Three days," Pine said. "I'd forgotten what a great trip it is. You ever hit that stuff?"

Quentin shook his head.

"I didn't think so," Pine said. "Wonderboy would never touch a drug like that, eh? Well, at least he'd never *take* a drug like that. But I'll bet that if he wanted to, he could get his hands on an extra-large dose."

"It's not my fault you're in here, so don't try and guilt me out," Quentin said, although he was about as guilted-out as one could get. He should have known better than to leave Pine alone when Mopuk's goons would be looking for revenge.

Pine nodded. "I know it's not your fault, kid."

There was an uncomfortable pause. "They messed you up pretty bad," Quentin said finally.

Pine shrugged. "Not so bad, really. They didn't want to mess up their investment. Notice they didn't touch the right arm, and they didn't touch the eyes. Hell, if rehab goes well, I'm back in the lineup in two weeks."

Quentin looked up and down Pine's body. The man had been in surgery and then in a hospital room for three hours. With the speed of modern medicine, the fact that he still looked so rough was a testament to the beating he'd taken. Mopuk's men had probably cut on him for quite a while.

"Don't think this guilt trip is going to go over on me," Quentin said, mustering far more conviction than he felt. "I'm keeping the starting spot this time."

Pine nodded slowly. "Maybe. Maybe, kid." He looked away. "I guess I've messed things up pretty bad. If I don't start ... well ... I guess I'm not much use to them anymore."

Pine wasn't begging for his starting spot, just talking out loud. Yet the sentence hit home to Quentin, even more than the injuries, even more than his own run-ins with Mopuk. Pine owed money. As long as he could throw games, he was an asset to Mopuk. If he wasn't starting, if his career was on the way out, well, Mopuk would have to do something about the debt. Quentin had seen Stedmar Osborne deal with enough fixers and loan sharks back on Micovi to know what would happen. If Pine wasn't playing ball, he was a good as dead.

"I'll take care this," Quentin said.

Pine looked hard at him for a few seconds. "Stay out of it. This ain't your business. You did the right thing, taking me out of the game. We're still in the playoff hunt, thanks to you. I brought this on myself. You get involved, you're just going to get messed up."

"I can't let you go alone on this, Pine."

The veteran laughed. "You can't? Why not? You hate my guts. You've wanted me out of the picture since your first day with the team. Well, now you've got what you want, so just let it be. I don't want to destroy two careers with my stupidity."

"Can we go to Gredok?"

Pine looked away. "He'll kill me faster than Mopuk would. Gredok finds out I threw his games, I'm dead. Hell, I guess it doesn't matter, I'm dead one way or another."

Quentin nodded once, then walked out of the room. Outside, Tweedy, Fayed and the linemen were waiting. They started to talk, but Quentin held up a hand, silencing them.

"Call a team meeting, immediately. Get everyone, especially Shayat. Tell Choto to clear out The Dead Fly, we'll meet there. No coaches. Hokor and Gredok can't find out about it."

"What's this about?" Fayed asked.

326   SCOTT SIGLER

"Just trust me," Quentin said.

"What about Virak?" Tweedy asked. "He's one of Gredok's bodyguards, totally loyal to him."

"Get him, too. And tell him not to say a word to Gredok, that I'll explain later. Tell him our playoff hopes hinge on his silence."

QUENTIN WALKED into The Dead Fly bar. He saw a sea of familiar faces (or what passed for faces) looking back at him. There were no other patrons in the place, only Krakens.

"This better be good," Virak said. "Gredok does not like secrecy."

"He's not going to find out," Quentin said. "No one is going to tell him. No one is going to say a word about this ... this *stuff*, to anyone. That's the way it's going to be. Got it?"

Quentin looked around the room. There was no sign of dissent. He'd called all these players together, and they'd come. They looked back at him, waiting to hear what he had to say. Quentin realized that his on-field performance had elevated his status amongst his teammates. At this moment, he was their *leader*.

"Shayat," Quentin said. "How much merchandise can you get your hands on?"

"I've already got my load," Shayat said. "All I can carry."

"I didn't ask that. What if you had more carriers? Say, forty-three other carriers, how much could you get then?"

Shayat looked at Quentin, then around the room, his eye shifting to a translucent red of surprise. "A lot. Enough for everyone."

"What is this?" Virak said. "You want us to smuggle drugs?"

Quentin nodded. "That's right. All of you. As much as you can carry."

A cacophony of shouting questions filled the room. Virak and Choto's eyes turned deep blackish-green.

"Shut *up!*" Quentin's voice exploded in the small room, creating instant, stunned silence.

"Pine owes money," Quentin said. "That's why he was beat up, because he can't pay. We're his teammates. We're going to pay off his debt. Everyone does it, no exceptions, and no one talks."

The statement left a sea of stunned faces.

"This is serious," Virak said. "Gredok ignores individual efforts. It's one of the benefits of being a player. The amount is insignificant compared to what he ships on the team bus. But the whole team smuggling? That's not something you ignore, Quentin. That's not being enterprising, that's being *competition*. Gredok doesn't like competition."

"We don't do it, Pine's a dead man," Quentin said.

"That's no reason to lie to Gredok," Virak said. "He is our *shamakath*."

"He's *your shamakath*," Quentin said. "Donald Pine is the *shamakath* for the rest of us. He's the team leader. So you've got to make a choice."

Virak's eye swirled from blackish-green to purple, a visible mark of his confusion.

"Virak," Quentin said, "do you want to be a bodyguard or a Tier One football player?"

Virak said nothing. Quentin continued. "Without Pine, our chances of making the playoffs are pretty dim. Even if we don't make it, it doesn't matter, he's our *teammate* and we're going to help him. We either do this, *all* of us, together, or Donald Pine is dead. We can't go to Gredok, you all just have to trust me on this. Now, does anyone want to back out?" He asked the question, but his eyes and demeanor clearly said that no one would be *allowed* to back out.

And no one did. Except Rick Warburg.

"Forget this," Warburg said. "I'm not putting my career on the line for Pine."

Quentin glared at him. "Yes, you are, Warburg. You're in."

"No way. I'm not going through this for a *blue-boy*, and neither should you. It's a sin to help Satan's children."

"He's not a *blue-boy*, you idiot. He's your teammate."

"I collect a paycheck. I don't have *teammates*, not from other races. I thought *you* were my teammate, but I guess I was wrong."

"Yeah," Quentin said. "I guess you were."

Warburg stared at him for a few seconds, then walked out of the bar, head held high.

"Anyone else?"

None of the other players said a word. Maybe it was their love for Pine. Maybe it was Quentin's will. Maybe it was both.

"Good," Quentin said. "We've got three hours before the *Touchback* leaves. Shayat, make it happen."

GAME SEVEN: Bigg Diggers (2-4) at Ionath Krakens (4-2)

QUYTH IRRADIATED CONFERENCE STANDINGS

Glory Warpigs	5-1
Ionath Krakens	4-2
Orbiting Death	4-2
Whitok Pioneers	4-2
Sheb Stalkers	4-2
Grontak Hydras	3-3
Quyth Survivors	3-3
Bigg Diggers	2-4
Woo Wallcrawlers	1-5
Sky Demolition	0-6

THE SHUTTLE BANKED DOWN to the customs platform and into the express lane reserved for diplomats and foreign dignitaries. The team filed out and stood single-file on the yellow waiting line. Three Quyth Workers dressed in the white uniforms of the Quyth System Police slid hoversleds into the shuttle. The hoversleds were loaded with the typical weapon- and explosive-scanning suites.

Kotop the Observer walked down the line of Krakens players. It was a performance they went through each time the shuttle returned from out-system.

"The food must be very good on Orbital Station One," Kotop said with disgust. "You've all gained weight."

Quentin, like the other Human players, wore a baggy sweatsuit — with a bulging, rounded belly. All the players had some new bulky area on their body: the Ki linemen had bulging backs, Sklorno tails were fatter and longer, and even the Quyth Warriors thighs seemed far thicker than normal.

Kotop stood in front of Virak.

"This must be a very proud day for a warrior like yourself," Kotop said. "I wonder who will be hurt by your newfound wealth."

Virak said nothing. He simply stared straight ahead so he didn't have to look at Kotop. His eye showed no color. Moments later, the technicians exited the ship.

"No weapons, no explosives," one of them said to Kotop. The Quyth Leader clapped his pedipalps together once, then gestured to the ship.

"You football players think you're so special," Kotop said. "You flaunt the law right in front of us, and there's nothing we can do. Someday … someday things will change."

"YOU SURE THIS IS the right way to do this?" Quentin sat in the back of a cramped hovercab. Virak the Mean sat on one side, Choto the Bright sat on the other.

"Do you want Pine's debt cleared?" Virak asked.

Quentin nodded.

"Then we have to show strength. A Leader like Mopuk will not let go of a choice debtor like Pine. Not easily. You need to convince Mopuk it's in his best interest."

Quentin nodded again. He'd started this, and he'd finish it, but he hadn't expected anything like what was about to go down. Virak, Choto, Shayat and John Tweedy were well versed in violence. Real violence, the kind where beings died. Quentin could hold his own in any fight, but this was something different.

He looked out the side of the open cab. They were in Ionath City's club district, a seemingly endless row of bars and dance halls, the street lit with brightly colored holosigns. Beings of all shapes and sizes crowded the streets. At least two fights were already in progress, one down the street to the left, one just off to their right. Quyth Warrior constables casually worked their way through the crowd to break up the altercations.

"We move now." Virak slipped over the cab's edge and onto the street. Choto hopped out the other side. Quentin followed suit, walking behind the two Quyth Warriors toward a club called the Bootleg Arms. A holosign above the bar showed a Quyth Worker using his pedipalps to repeatedly pour a gin & tonic. A line of beings, mostly Quyth Workers, although all kinds were represented, extended out the door and down the street.

A Quyth Worker and three Ki — large, but not as large as GFL linemen — stood near the door. The Quyth Worker instantly recognized the three Krakens players and gestured for them to walk past the line. Virak and Choto entered first, moving in front of Quentin like the blades of a snowplow. They ignored the Quyth Worker and the Ki.

"Elder Barnes," the Quyth Worker said, perfectly pronouncing the respectable Purist Nation title. "Welcome to the Bootleg Arms. If there is anything you need, I am Tikad the Groveling, and I assure you I will tend to your needs."

"We want to see Mopuk," Quentin said.

Tikad bowed. "Mr. Mopuk may be busy, Elder Barnes."

"Go get him," Quentin said. "Right now."

Tikad bowed lower, said something to the Ki guards, then walked through the door. Virak and Choto followed Tikad, Quentin only a step behind them. They walked through the door and onto a lighted floor that swayed with dancers of all species. He wondered how any being could dance to that crappy Tower Republic music, but it was all the rage in the clubs.

Floating flashbugs gracefully avoided the swirling dancers. The bugs emitted bright colors in time to the music's beat. The floor shook with the song's low bass tones, frequencies that seemed to vibrate every atom in Quentin's body. Smells filled his nostrils — like most clubs, designer pheromones permeated the air, guaranteed to put an erotic edge on every patron regardless of their species. He kept his eyes on Virak and Choto, doing his best to ignore the sensory assault.

The crowd parted before the two Quyth Warriors. Quentin couldn't help but feel important. The two of them moved like walking statues that radiated confidence mixed with lethality. They followed Tikad to a back wall that seemed to vibrate slightly, in time to the bass beat — a hologram. Two Quyth Warriors stood by the wall, not-so-gently pushing back any dancers that moved too close. Tikad walked between them and right through the holographic wall.

As soon as they were through, the music dropped off to a distant thud of bass and nothing more. Soft lighting seemed a direct contrast to the dance floor's garish flashbugs. Thick couches, some for all species but mainly tailored for the small bodies of Quyth Leaders, lined the walls of the small room. A large oval table sat in the middle, a clear glass top revealing a tank of swarming insect-like creatures.

On a chair behind the table sat Mopuk. His Ki bodyguards flanked him, one on each side. Quentin recognized them — they'd beaten the crap out of him back on The Deuces and had tried to rough him up on The Ace. That was when Virak the Mean told the bodyguards that if he faced them again, he'd kill them. Quentin wondered if the two guards remembered the threat.

Tikad stood nervously, his pedipalps repeatedly cleaning his eye, which glowed a deep yellow. Mopuk's eyes, of course, remained perfectly clear. Sobox, Mopuk's Creterakian lieutenant, perched comfortably on Mopuk's small shoulder.

Virak and Choto each took a small step to the side. Quentin walked between them and sat down on a Human chair, directly across the table from Mopuk.

"Quentin Barnes," Mopuk said quietly. "You saved me the time of coming to find you again. You've cost me a lot of money this season, money you will have to repay."

"I owe you nothing," Quentin said. "But I am here about money. He pulled out a contract box and slid it across the table. As the box crossed the glass, the insect-like creatures swarmed toward it, pressing hungrily against the glass top's underside.

Mopuk picked up the contract box. "What's this?"

"Four-point-one million. Every penny that Donald Pine owes you."

Mopuk's eye instantly changed to translucent black. He slid the contract box back across the glass. The bugs vainly tried again to eat it.

"That's not enough," Sobox said. "Mopuk the Sneaky does not accept your offer."

"He'd better," Quentin said. "Pine's debt to you is paid. Now you stay away from him, and everyone else on the Krakens."

Mopuk's eye shifted to an even deeper shade of black.

"You come in *here* and tell *me* what to do? I say that's not enough money." Mopuk gestured to the glass table. "Get out of here before I feed you to my pets."

"You will accept this," Quentin said, leaning forward. "You don't have a choice."

Mopuk leaned back, seemingly speechless, then looked to his left and gestured a pedipalp at one of the Ki. The two big creatures started to move forward but hadn't even managed two steps before Virak and Choto launched into action.

Virak moved forward at blinding linebacker speed. He touched his pedipalps together once — when he pulled them apart, a thin glowing silvery line ran from one to the other. He looped this line around the first surprised Ki and then yanked it tight — black blood exploded like a water balloon as the Ki's upper torso fell away from the lower body.

Choto moved almost as fast, producing a fat blade from a hiding spot inside the carapace of his right arm. He jammed the blade into the second Ki's hexagonal mouth, bent it downward and thrust it right down the Ki's throat.

Sobox flew up in alarm and reached into his tiny vest. Quentin didn't know if they made entropic accelerators that small, but he wasn't waiting to find out. He threw the contract box like a missile. It smashed into Sobox, knocking the Creterakian backward. Sobox hit the wall and fell to the floor, limp.

Just before Choto's opponent hit the floor, Tikad pressed a button on his belt. The holographic wall vanished and an alarm screeched through the bar. The music kept playing, joined by noises of fear and surprise from the patrons. Flashbugs started filtering in, pre-programmed to diffuse evenly through any open space.

The two Ki bodyguards were not Mopuk's only protection. Two Quyth Warriors sprinted toward the back room, each pulling a small pistol as they ran. Before the guns cleared their concealed holsters, flashes of black cloth hit them like phantasms. Both guards went down under the weight of a pair of Sklorno females: Hawick and Scarborough on one, Mezquitic and Denver on the other. As soon as the Quyth Warriors hit the ground, John Tweedy slid out of a booth, head down, hateful eyes up, moving like a silent tiger. DON'T MESS WITH DON PINE scrolled across his forehead. With a growling snarl, he put his fist clear through the first Quyth Warrior's eye and deep into the brain. Clear liquid splashed up and out, covering Tweedy's psychotic face.

The second Quyth Warrior kicked out, knocking Denver on her back. The Warrior's pedipalps whipped like snakes, wrapping around Mezquitic's slender neck. Tweedy flew through the air, dropping all his weight on the prone Warrior.

As John Tweedy and the Warrior grappled, deafening roars erupted, far louder than the bass-driven music. Five sets of waving tentacles drew all eyes as the Krakens' offensive line, who had been quietly dancing only moments earlier, stood tall on their rear legs, twelve-feet high and more imposing than a rabid Mullah Hills bull-cat. Bar patrons needed no further urging — they ran for the door, a stampede of every species moving as one panicked mass.

Tweedy rolled on top of the Quyth Warrior, grabbed his thick head in both hands and jerked to the right. A loud *crack* marked the end of the conflict as the Quyth Warrior quivered once, then fell still, motionless save for a quivering pedipalp.

"Touch *my* quarterbacks, you loser," Tweedy said in a growl. "Losers don't get to make that mistake twice."

Black blood spread across the floor like a giant amoeba. Quentin had never imagined Ki had so much blood in their tubular body. He felt his lunch rising up in his stomach, but he steeled himself against the sickness. The game was on, and he'd stick with it.

Tikad cowered on the floor, his body already covered in black gore as he rolled about, quietly begging not to be killed. Mopuk was still in his chair, his eye now the pure blue of total fear. Streaks of black blood covered him, even on his eye — he was too stunned to clean it off. Virak and Choto stood rock still on either side of him, awaiting Quentin's orders.

Quentin picked the contract box up off the ground. He walked back to his chair and sat, then slid the contract box across the table once again. The insects seemed angrier than ever, but the glass still held them at bay. The contract box slid off the glass and onto Mopuk's lap.

"Last chance," Quentin said. "You get your money, Pine is free and clear. Do you accept?"

Mopuk picked up the contract box in his trembling pedi-palps. He slid the tip of one pedipalp into the contract box. The box's light switched from red to green, signifying a completed transaction.

"That's that," Quentin said. "Now that you're paid, I don't have to worry about you coming after us. I don't want to see you again. And don't think of letting it slip to Gredok as a way of getting back at Pine. You know what will happen to Pine if Gredok finds out, but you also know what will happen to *you* if Gredok finds out you were messing with his team and his players, right?"

"Yes," Mopuk said. "I agree. We will keep this to ourselves."

"And what about them?" Quentin asked, gesturing to the two dead Ki that took up half the floor and the two dead Quyth Warriors.

"An accident," Mopuk said. "You will not be involved."

Quentin nodded again. The music continued to blare, but over the horrible noise he heard the high-pitched rhythmic chirp of constables approaching.

"Tikad," Quentin said. The Quyth Worker didn't seem to hear. Quentin reached out with a toe and kicked him.

"Yes Elder Barnes!" said Tikad the Groveling. "Please is there anything I can do for you?"

"You got a back door in this place?"

"Yes, Elder Barnes! Right this way!" Tikad scrambled to his feet, his body trailing dripping black strands of thick Ki blood. He ran deeper into the club. Quentin followed, Virak and Choto in front of him once again the rest of his teammates behind. As the first constables ran into the Bootleg Arms, Quentin and the rest of the Krakens were nowhere to be seen.

IN LESS THAN twenty-four hours, the bandages were gone, the rejuv bath had been removed, and Don Pine's healed arms crossed over his chest as he lay back in his hospital bed, staring incredulously at Quentin.

"So you *paid* it?" Pine said. "Are you kidding me?" While his eyes showed doubt, they also showed just a flicker of hope.

"Yes," Quentin said. "The debt is paid."

They were alone in the room. Teammates sat outside. Not a moment had gone by when there weren't at least two Krakens players guarding their veteran quarterback.

"But they're not going to just let me go," Pine said, shaking his head. "They make more on one game than my debt is worth, easy."

Quentin shrugged. "It's taken care of."

Pine looked away. "Those Ki scumbags that broke my legs, cut me up ... they'll be after me again, I know it."

"They won't be after anyone, ever," Quentin said. "Virak and Choto saw to that."

Pine's expression relaxed into wide-eyed amazement. "But why, Quentin? Why would you do this?"

"I didn't do it, the team did it."

Pine nodded. "Yeah, I'm sure of that, but off the field most of these guys can't even stand to look at each other. Someone had to make them work together, and I know it wasn't Virak and Choto. It was you. So why did you do it? All you had to do was stay out of it, and the team was yours."

Quentin looked at the floor. "I don't know. You needed help, and I helped. That's it."

Pine extended his blue-skinned hand. Quentin had shaken the

man's hand before, but this was different. Quentin stared at it for a second. Ten weeks ago, to think a blue-boy would be a true friend, well, that was simply unthinkable.

Quentin shook Donald Pine's hand.

"I won't forget this," Pine said. "Not ever."

QUENTIN ROLLED to the left as the rest of the team moved right. Hokor had held the naked boot in reserve all day but played that card late in the fourth quarter. The Krakens held on to a slim 20-19 lead, and they needed to put the Bigg Diggers away.

Surveying his options, Quentin kept the ball on his left hip as he started turning upfield at the Diggers' 28. Kitiara Lomax, the Diggers' all-pro linebacker, saw the naked boot and gave chase, but he was the only one. Quentin looked downfield — Rick Warburg had blocked down then bounced left on a 10-yard out, and Denver was angling for the end zone's back left corner, covered closely by Arkham.

Run or pass. With the speed of a supercomputer, the options flashed through Quentin's brain. He had three or four steps on Lomax. Arkham already had three interceptions on the day and had kept her team in the game by preying on Quentin's passes like a piranha on raw meat. Rick Warburg was open — but he was also a racist jerk.

BLINK

Quentin tucked the ball under his left arm and angled for the sidelines. He sensed everything: the home Krakens crowd jumping and roaring, the missing patches of Iomatt where cleats had torn up the turf, the smell of dirt and sweat and blood, Lomax's desperate efforts to cut him off, Warburg's look of fury when he realized that Quentin wasn't going to throw.

He leaned into the run, his legs chewing up the yards. Lomax was faster than he'd calculated and dove for Quentin just as the young QB reached the sidelines and turned upfield. But Warburg was there, coming free and fast, and blindsided Lomax with a devastating, head-snapping hit.

Quentin's long, graceful strides belied his speed. The yards slid by like water on glass. Denver tried to block Arkham, but the cornerback effortlessly pushed the receiver aside and came up the sidelines at Quentin. It would be a head-to-head battle.

Intercept me? Payback time, lady.

Arkam's legs blurred as she kamikazied her way forward. At the eleven, Quentin screamed and lowered his head, smashing into Arkham, more a linebacker delivering a concussive blow than a quarterback scrambling for yards. Arkham was bigger than most Sklorno, and faster, and she carried a devastating amount of force.

Quentin ran her right over.

He stumbled after the hit, legs pumping high to avoid a trip. Arkham crashed to the ground, defeated, crushed. Her raspers reached out at the last second, scraping long strips of skin from the backs of Quentin's hands.

BLINK

The world slammed back to reality as Quentin crossed the goal line trailing a stream of his own blood. He chucked the ball into the stands, then stood with both arms outstretched, redness dripping to stain the grass, his tilted head looking at the roaring, adoring crowd.

That's right, he thought as he turned, surveying his fans. *You do* not *mess with Quentin Barnes.*

From the Ionath City Gazette

Backup leads Krakens to fourth straight win
By Toyat the Inquisitive

It seems that the Purist Nation finally has an export that interests citizens of the Quyth Concordia.

That export is Quentin Barnes.

The rookie quarterback once again came to the Krakens' rescue, filling in for oft-damaged starter Donald Pine, who was out with unspecified injuries. Barnes led the Krakens (5-2) to a 27-19 win over the Bigg Diggers (2-5) and put on a showcase that combined unstoppable talent, rookie inexperience and more speed than any Human has a right to possess. Barnes threw for 305 yards and two touchdowns, as well as running for 82 yards and adding another touchdown on the ground. This all-pro caliber performance was marred by inconsistent passing — Barnes was 19-for-35, including three interceptions.

"They (the Diggers) threw some coverages at me I hadn't prepared for," said Barnes. "Arkham robbed me blind all day long."

Arkham, the Diggers' crafty veteran cornerback, repeatedly disguised her coverage and capitalized on Barnes's inexperience. Arkham notched all three interceptions but was knocked out of the game late in the fourth quarter with a crushed right thorax and torn upper right tentacle. She will be out for the rest of the season.

BIGG DIGGERS BOX SCORE

Final	1	2	3	4	T
Ionath	7	10	3	7	27
Bigg	0	10	6	3	19

SCORING SUMMARY

1st QUARTER		ION	BIG
Ionath TD	Hawick 38-yard pass from Quentin Barnes (Arioch Morningstar kick)	7	0

2nd QUARTER		ION	BIG
Bigg TD	Clearwater 12-yard pass from Dre Azerbaijan (Vladimir Popa kick)	7	7
Bigg FG	34-yard FG by Vladimir Popa is good.	7	10
Ionath TD	Yotaro Kobayasho 3-yard pass from Quentin Barnes (Arioch Morningstar kick)	14	10
Ionath FG	44-yard FG by Arioch Morningstar is good.	17	10

3rd QUARTER		ION	BIG
Bigg FG	24-yard FG by Vladimir Popa is good.	17	13
Ionath FG	27-yard FG by Arioch Morningstar is good.	20	13
Bigg FG	17-yard FG by Vladimir Popa is good.	20	16

4th QUARTER		ION	BIG
Bigg FG	32-yard FG by Vladimir Popa is good.	20	19
Ionath TD	Quentin Barnes 28-yard run (Arioch Morningstar kick)	27	19

TEAM STATISTICS	BIG	ION
First Downs	13	17
Third Down Efficiency	6-17	10-16
TOTAL NET YARDS	**283**	**422**
Total Plays	61	81
Average Gain Per Play	4.6	5.2
NET YARDS RUSHING	**89**	**117**
Rushes	22	46
Average Per Rush	4.0	2.5
NET YARDS PASSING	**194**	**305**
Pass Completion	20-39	19-35
Yards Per Pass	5.0	8.7
Times Sacked	2	0
Yards Lost To Sacks	15	0
Had Intercepted	2	3
PUNTS	**11**	**6**
Average Punt	46.8	40.1
PENALTIES	**9**	**8**
Penalty Yards	85	56
FUMBLES	**2**	**0**
Fumbles Lost	1	0
Time Of Possession	**23.48**	**36.12**

PASSING

KRAKENS	CMP	ATT	YDS	PCT	YPA	SACK	SYDS	TD	INT
Quentin Barnes	19	35	305	54.3	8.7	0	0	2	3

DIGGERS	CMP	ATT	YDS	PCT	YPA	SACK	SYDS	TD	INT
Dre Azerbaijan	20	39	209	51.3	5.4	2	15	1	2

RUSHING

KRAKENS	ATT	YDS	AVG	LONG	TD	FUM
Quentin Barnes	12	82	6.8	28	1	0
Mitchell Fayed	30	45	1.5	7	0	0
Yassoud Murphy	4	-10	-2.5	2	0	0

DIGGERS	ATT	YDS	AVG	LONG	TD	FUM
Kraga the Big-Handed	22	89	4.0	12	0	2

RECEIVING

KRAKENS	REC	YDS	AVG	LONG	TD	FUM
Hawick	3	89	29.7	42	1	0
Denver	5	88	17.6	20	0	0
Milford	4	42	10.5	14	0	0
Yotaro Kobayasho	3	34	11.3	21	1	0
Scarborough	3	27	9.0	13	0	0
Mezquitic	1	25	25.0	25	0	0

DIGGERS	REC	YDS	AVG	LONG	TD	FUM
Cosmopolis	6	92	15.3	66	0	0
Clearwater	5	56	11.2	31	1	0
Alcanar	4	37	9.3	14	0	0
Islington	3	14	4.7	8	0	0
Billopillya	2	10	5.0	6	0	0

WEEK SEVEN LEAGUE ROUNDUP
(Courtesy of Galaxy Sports network)

Woes and misery continue on Whitok, where the **Whitok Pioneers** (4-3) dropped their third straight game, this time to the previously winless **Sky Demolition** (1-6) on a last-second field goal that gave the Demo a 21-19 win. Even though starting QB Condor Adrienne returns to the lineup this week as the Pioneers travel to the **Woo Wallcrawlers** (2-5), Whitok is basically out of the running for the division title.

The Wallcrawlers notched their second win of the year by topping the **Quyth Survivors** (3-4) 28-24.

The **Ionath Krakens** (5-2) made it four-in-a-row, topping the **Bigg Diggers** (2-5) 27-19. Ionath rookie Quentin Barnes showed that the Krakens may be the team to beat in the future, but are they good enough to prevail in this week's showdown against the **Glory Warpigs**? It's winner-take-all at Warpigs Stadium — the 'Pigs (6-1) are in sole possession of first place thanks to this week's 32-10 drubbing of the **Sheb Stalkers** (4-3).

Orbiting Death (5-2) remain in the running for the title but need the Warpigs to lose their last two games and the Krakens to lose as well. Death hung a 17-7 defeat on the **Grontak Hydras** (3-4).

DEATHS:
Percy Gaines, tight end for the Woo Wallcrawlers, died on a clean hit by Topinabee, the head-hunting defensive back for the Quyth Survivors.

WEEK SEVEN PLAYERS OF THE WEEK:
Offense: Quentin Barnes, quarterback, Ionath Krakens. 19-of-35 for 305 yards, two TDs, three INTs. Also ran for 82 yards on 12 carries, one rushing TD.
Defense: Arkham, cornerback, Bigg Diggers. Eight tackles, three INTs.

GAME EIGHT: Ionath Krakens (5-2) at Glory Warpigs (6-1)
QUYTH IRRADIATED CONFERENCE STANDINGS

Glory Warpigs	6-1
Ionath Krakens	5-2
Orbiting Death	5-2
Whitok Pioneers	4-3
Sheb Stalkers	4-3
Grontak Hydras	3-4
Quyth Survivors	3-4
Bigg Diggers	2-5
Woo Wallcrawlers	2-5
Sky Demolition	1-6

"BARNES, YOU'RE PLAYING much better, but you've got to improve your passing."

"Come on, Coach, I was the offensive player of the week! Can't you lighten up a bit?"

"There is no lightheartedness in interceptions."

Quentin nodded. "Yeah, that throwing for 305 yards and two TDs, that's pathetic."

Hokor's fur fluffed, then settled. "Sure, those stats are great, but you threw *three* interceptions!"

"Come *on*, Coach! We *won* the damn game."

Hokor's fur ruffled again, and this time stayed ruffled. "The season hangs in the balance this week, Barnes. We win, we take over first place. The Warpigs have the best secondary in the league — they're only allowing 150 passing yards a game!"

Quentin waved a hand dismissively. "Big deal," he said. "They haven't faced us yet, we'll light 'em up."

"Pine's well enough to dress this week."

Quentin suddenly sat forward, eyes narrow. "*I* got us to this position, and you know it."

Hokor's eye turned translucent black.

"You're not in charge here, Barnes, I am. You're starting, you've earned it for this game. But I'm letting you know that if you keep throwing interceptions, I'm going to have to sit you down. I would have pulled you last week, but Yitzhak couldn't have done any better. Pine can."

Quentin felt his temper boiling up to the top, but he concentrated, holding it in check. "I've studied like mad for this game, I've worked the holosim over and over again. I know those defenders. I just won't throw interceptions, how's that?"

"Ball control," Hokor said. "That's what we need. We turn it over against them, we lose. You're doing a great job, Quentin, but you're still a little rough around the edges. Don't take it personally."

"Oh I don't," Quentin lied. "Not at all."

He stood and walked out of the office.

Transcript from the "Galaxy's Greatest Sports Show with Dan & Akbar & Tarat the Smasher"

CALLER: I'm glad Barnes gets the start. Pine is washed up.

AKBAR: You moron! How can you say he's washed up?

CALLER: He's always hurt.

AKBAR: He got mugged, for crying out loud. *Mugged*. This wasn't some on-field injury.

DAN: Well, there was the injury earlier this year.

AKBAR: Hey, you don't recover from a broken femur that quick if you're fragile, you know.

CALLER: But he can't win the big games!

AKBAR: What, two Galaxy Bowls aren't big enough for you?

TARAT: That was years ago, Akbar.

CALLER: Ancient history.

AKBAR: Well, I can't believe you people. Aside from Condor Adrienne, Pine is still the best quarterback in Tier Two.

DAN: But that's Tier Two! The fans are sick of Tier Two, I'm sick of Tier Two, and so are you. Barnes is the key to Tier One, like I've been saying all along.

AKBAR: He's too young.

DAN: Too young? Who cares! Look what he's done so far. His come-from-behind win over the Orbiting Death kept the Krakens in the playoff hunt, and he dusted the Bigg Diggers.

AKBAR: Dusted? What game were you watching?

DAN: The one where he threw two TDs and ran for another, racked up 387 all-purpose yards.

AKBAR: Oh, *that* game. Is that the same one where he threw three interceptions? Why, yes, I think it is. Three interceptions against a mediocre defensive secondary that gives up an average, *an average*, of 280 yards a game? Are you kidding me?

TARAT: Well when I played the game, all we cared about was the win. Barnes got the win.

DAN: That's right, he wins games.

AKBAR: Well, he's not going to win against the Warpigs, I'll tell you that for free. They've got the best secondary in all of football, not just Tier Two.

TARAT: One could easily argue that the Bartell Water Bugs or the Hullwalkers have the best secondary.

AKBAR: Am I in a house of morons, here? Am I? Those are *Tier One* teams contending for the championship this year. The best of the best. And the Warpigs' secondary is right up there. Look at the stats: left corner Keluang, four interceptions; safety Wellington, three interceptions and a pair of sacks; free safety Alamo, two interceptions; and let's not forget right corner Toyonaka, all-pro two years running, *eight interceptions* on the season, averaging more than one a game.

DAN: Look, Quentin Barnes is the future of this team. I said it before, I'll say it again, I've said it all along, Barnes needs to start.

AKBAR: You're crazy and stupid. Pine needs to start this game.

DAN: Well, we'll see what happens at game-time. Caller, thanks for the call. Next we've got Amos from Jones 2. Hello, Amos, you're on the space …

QUENTIN RUBBED SWEAT from his eyes. He'd never faced a secondary like this one.

Arkham had robbed him blind last week, but the rest of the

secondary had been mortal. The only reason Arkham had inter-
cepted him three times was he wanted to go after her, he wanted
to complete passes to her side of the field. Hokor had told him to
avoid her, but Quentin hid from no one. You just don't give up a
whole side of the field. If he'd have stayed away from Arkham,
gone to the easy side of the field, he probably would have come out
with no interceptions at all.

But the Warpigs were different — there *was* no easy side of
the field. The Warpigs didn't have anyone as good as Arkham,
but they had *four* players who were almost in her ballpark. *Four.*
Every time Quentin dropped back, every receiver seemed covered.
And if they looked open, they probably weren't. He'd learned that
lesson the hard way, throwing two interceptions in the first quarter, including one that Keluang, the Warpigs' corner, took to the
house for a 33-yard touchdown. The secondary switched from
woman-to-woman to zone in the same play, zone to woman-to-
woman the next, two-deep with zone under the next. The 'Pigs
linebackers were also damn good, covering passes over the middle
and in the flat, trying to take away dump-passes to the tight ends
and running backs.

His arm hadn't done anything for the Krakens. What had
worked, however, were two pairs of Human feet — his and Mitchell Fayed's. Late in the second quarter, Fayed already had 80 yards
on the ground and a TD. Quentin had added a rushing TD and another 40 rushing yards, mostly from scrambling because there was
no one to pass to. Those two touchdowns put 14 on the board, to
match the Warpigs' two TDs.

Second-and-4 on the Krakens' 22. Quentin looked to the sidelines as the Krakens huddled up.

"Keep it on the ground," Hokor said into his earpiece. "Forty-
six sweep right."

Quentin breathed a sigh of relief, then felt a wave of anger
swarm across his thoughts. What kind of a pansy was he turning
into? He'd felt *happy* because Hokor called a run play? Quentin
called the play in the huddle, then walked to the line, marveling at
how this defense had taken him right out of his game.

"Red, twenty-one … red, twenty-one, hut-hut!"

The ball slapped into his hands. Quentin stepped to his left, planted his left foot and pivoted backward all the way around in a smooth motion. Holding the ball in front of him with both hands, he gently flipped it to Fayed, who moved left, five yards back and parallel to the line of scrimmage. Right guard Wen-E-Daret pulled to lead the block, taking a few steps back and then scuttling right, horizontal to the line. The big Ki lineman got in front of Fayed, leading the running back to the outside as they both looked to cut upfield. The Warpigs' outside linebacker picked up the play and drove straight at Wen-E. The two collided, and Fayed slipped past the block, trying to find open space. Keluang, the Warpigs' left cornerback, came up fast, a streaking blur of black jersey with teal numbers and a teal helmet. Fayed tried to cut outside, but Keluang dove and tripped up the running back, taking him down for a four-yard loss.

Third and 8.

Quentin's stomach churned with butterflies. He had to pee. Tie game, passing down.

"Spread right, twenty-two post," Hokor said. "Look for Kobayasho's out-cut. Don't go deep, Quentin, we need to hold onto the ball and play for field position."

Quentin watched his team gather in the huddle. He looked back at the Warpigs, who were gathering in their own huddle.

Was Keluang *limping*? Was she hurt?

Quentin's mind raced. If she was hurt, he had to go after her. He called the play and the Krakens lined up for the snap. Twenty-two post held a couple of options — Hawick on a deep post down the left side, Kobayasho on an out-cut and Scarborough on a flag right, which would put her head-to-head against Keluang, deep down the field.

"Bluuuueeee, sixteen, hut-hut!"

Quentin dropped back, ball held high, eyes watching the entire field at once.

BLINK

The receivers sprinted downfield in that weird real-time slow-motion dance. He saw Kobayasho cut out to the right, where he already had a step on the linebackers. Hawick was covered like stink on a skunk. Quentin planted and stepped up — at fifteen yards, Scarborough broke right on her flag cut, a half-step ahead of Keluang.

Quentin fired the ball on a rope. The brown missile streaked through the air at eighty miles an hour, so fast that Keluang never had a chance at it. Scarborough turned back, the ball hit her in the chest so hard it knocked her over. She slid out of bounds twenty yards downfield.

First-and-10 on the Krakens' 42. Three minutes to play in the half.

Keluang turned and ran back to her huddle. She *was* limping, just a bit. Her stats flashed through his head: four-year veteran, played two seasons of Tier Three ball with the New Orleans Saints of the Earth League. She'd clocked a 3.1 forty in full pads, while Scarborough's best was 3.2. She could also jump twenty-two feet into the air. And she'd missed two games last season with a fissured left lower leg.

The same leg she seemed to be favoring now.

"Nice pass," Hokor said in his earpiece. "Now back to the ground-attack. Basic package, sweep left."

Quentin looked to the sidelines. Hokor stood there, clipboard in hand. Pine stood next to him, helmet under his arm like a picture off of a Wheaties box. "But Coach, Keluang looks hurt, let's go after her."

"Keluang looks hurt?" Hokor said. He turned to Pine, who viciously shook his head *no*.

"Stick to the ground," Hokor said, turning back to look onto the field. "Pine says Keluang is faking it."

"*Faking* it?"

"Just run the plays I call, Barnes!"

Quentin jogged back to the huddle, his eye on the play clock. He had to get this play off in fifteen seconds or suffer a delay-of-game penalty.

Faking? What defensive back would *fake* an injury and allow a twenty-yard pass? She wasn't *faking*, she was hurt.

"Okay, kiddies," Quentin said to his huddle. "Let's get this play off quick. Y-set, roll out left, double post. Scarborough, does Keluang seem slow to you?"

"Yes," Scarborough said. "Not as fast as before."

"Then you bust your little rear end downfield, got it? We're going to take the wind out of their sails right now."

Quentin broke the huddle and sauntered up behind center. A quick *ba-da-bap* on the center's carapace.

"Red, twelve, red, twelve, hut-hut!"

The trenches clashed as Quentin, a lefty, dropped back and rolled out to his left, eyes constantly scanning downfield. Hawick looked open for a second, but the free safety came over to help out the right cornerback, taking away that option. Fayed ran a five-yard out pattern, staying in front of Quentin, while Tom Pareless shuffled to his left, looking to block the first defender that broke through the offensive line. The right defensive end slipped past Kill-O-Yowet's block, then Pareless undercut the multi-legged Ki with a nasty head-first dive. The Ki crumbled clumsily to the ground, leaving Quentin completely free of pressure.

Scarborough was already forty yards downfield.

And Keluang was a full-step behind.

Quentin launched the ball, a deep, arcing, perfect spiral.

"Come on, baby," he whispered as the ball started its descent.

Suddenly, Keluang's small limp vanished. Her legs moved perfectly as she strode downfield, her eyes turned back to the ball.

"No," Quentin whispered as the ball continued downward.

Keluang and Scarborough simultaneously leapt upward, but Keluang leapt higher.

She picked the ball out of the air. The two Sklorno fell to the ground, just as Quentin dropped to his knees.

"Crap-crap-crap-*crap!*" He screamed, leaning forward until his helmet touched the ground. "Crap-crap-*crapcrap!*"

"Barnes!" Hokor screamed in his earpiece. "Get your worthless face off my field *now!*"

Quentin stood, ignoring the crowd's boos as he ran off the

field. He didn't bother stopping to talk to Hokor, he just ran to the bench and sat.

He wasn't going anywhere else for the rest of the game, and he knew it.

Pine jogged over and sat next to him. "Q, you've got to stop going for the homerun on every play!"

"Go somewhere else and die," Quentin hissed as he pulled off his helmet. He wanted to *blame* Pine, blame anyone, for that matter. Wounded duck ploy, and he'd fell for it hook, line and sinker.

"I warned you," Pine said. "But as usual, you don't listen."

"Scarborough couldn't catch a ball if I shoved it right down her throat."

"No, you *don't*," Pine said. "Don't go blaming her. You threw to a covered receiver, against a defender that has four interceptions this season."

"Six," Quentin said morosely. "That was her second of the day."

"Right, *six*. I told you all week you can't play home-run ball against the Warpigs, so don't you dare blame your teammate for your mistake."

"Didn't I tell you to go somewhere else?" Quentin said, turning and snarling at his friend.

"No," Pine said with a smile. "You told me to go somewhere else *and die*. Big difference."

Quentin wanted to knock those smiling teeth into a little pile on the ground. Pine started laughing, and Quentin wanted to tear his head right from his shoulders.

"Take it easy, Q," Pine said. "You've bailed me out enough this season, let me bail *you* out this time."

"Oh sure," Quentin said. "Like you can just go in there and tear up their secondary!"

Pine nodded. "Just watch me. You're playing their game. Now I'm going to make them play mine."

• • •

THE WARPIGS MANAGED to add insult to injury by marching downfield for a touchdown before the half, making the score 21-14. That made Quentin's stats perfect — three interceptions, all three resulting in touchdowns. *Crap-crap-crap.*

His mind hunted for someone to blame, but this time the blame fell on only one being.

Himself.

It was his second start in a row, his fourth start of the season. He'd had starter's reps in practice for two full weeks. He couldn't blame lack of practice time. He couldn't blame poor coaching — for crying out loud, he'd been *warned* right before the play that took him out of the game.

No one to blame but himself. It was a new feeling, and one he didn't like at all. Not one bit. It occurred to him, suddenly and savagely, that for most of his problems, he'd really had no one to blame but himself all along.

IN THE SECOND HALF, Pine wasted no time. He opened up with an entire series of X-set, which put four wide receivers on the field. The Warpigs started out in woman-to-woman, which left the slower free safety covering either Mezquitic or the blindingly fast rookie Denver. Pine showed his repaired legs were as good as new, rolling out to escape inside blitzes and giving Denver more time to make long crossing routes where her superior speed gained her a couple of steps.

His first three plays were three completions, for seven, sixteen and nine yards. He scrambled on the fourth play, a very *un*-Pine thing to do, picking up a first down before sliding to the ground to avoid a hit. The home crowd ate it up. After a half of interceptions and incompletions, they screamed their heads off for anything positive.

Quentin watched as Hawick drove deep downfield against Toyonaka, the two speedsters a combined flash of orange and black, white and black and teal. The ball was in the air before Hawick even stopped, and when she turned, it hit her dead in the chest. Toyonaka was faster, but at such speeds her reaction time wasn't enough to match deadly pin-point passing on a timed route.

Fifteen yards.

Pine ran the same play again for twelve yards.

He was merciless — he ran the same play a third time, but pump-faked when Toyonaka anticipated the throw. Hawick shot downfield as Pine launched a soft fade pass. Toyonaka tried to catch up, but Hawick brought the ball in as delicately as a mother holding her new baby.

The crowd roared so loud Quentin wondered if the anti-radiation dome might collapse on their heads. Morningstar knocked in the extra point.

Krakens 21, Warpigs 21.

Quentin shook his head in amazement. Toyonaka was an all-pro, and Pine had gone right after her, victimizing her in just three plays.

Jealousy burned in his chest as Pine put the Krakens on the board two of the next three possessions, one a 21-yard field goal by Morningstar and the other a lucky break when Keluang fell while trying to tackle Denver. The stumble turned a short out pattern into a 67-yard TD: you only got one chance to tackle Denver.

The Warpigs came back, but the Krakens' defense showed new energy in the second half. Two fumbles killed critical Warpig drives. The momentum steadily dripped over to the Krakens' side of the field. Fayed broke a long 52-yard run, his longest of the season, to put the final nail in the coffin.

The clock ticked down to 0:00.

Krakens 38, Warpigs 28.

The team ran off the field and into the locker room, the feeling of elation running rampant through their hearts and minds — they were now in sole possession of first place, one game away from the Tier Two Tournament and a possible Tier One berth.

WARPIGS BOX SCORE

Final	1	2	3	4	T
Ionath	7	7	17	7	38
Glory	7	14	7	0	28

SCORING SUMMARY

1st QUARTER		ION	GLO
Ionath TD	Quentin Barnes 12-yard run (Arioch Morningstar kick)	7	0
Glory TD	Keluang 33-yard interception off Quentin Barnes (Pra-Ka-Hiti kick)	7	7

2nd QUARTER		ION	GLO
Ionath TD	Mitchell Fayed 4-yard run (Arioch Morningstar kick)	14	7
Glory TD	Mayville 78-yard pass from Hiawatha Harrison (Pra-Ka-Hiti kick)	14	14
Glory TD	Mayville 18-yard pass from Hiawatha Harrison (Pra-Ka-Hiti kick)	14	21

3rd QUARTER		ION	GLO
Ionath TD	Hawick 44-yard pass from Don Pine (Arioch Morningstar kick)	21	21
Ionath FG	22-yard FG by Arioch Morningstar is good.	24	21
Ionath TD	Denver 67-yard pass from Don Pine (Arioch Morningstar kick)	31	21
Glory TD	Mayville 69-yard pass from Hiawatha Harrison (Pra-Ka-Hiti kick)	31	28

4th QUARTER		ION	GLO
ION TD	Mitchell Fayed 52-yard run (Arioch Morningstar kick)	38	28

TEAM STATISTICS	GLO	ION
First Downs	14	21
Third Down Efficiency	8-11	11-18
TOTAL NET YARDS	**385**	**475**
Total Plays	69	75
Average Gain Per Play	5.6	6.3
NET YARDS RUSHING	**104**	**205**
Rushes	33	36
Average Per Rush	3.1	5.7
NET YARDS PASSING	**281**	**270**
Pass Completion	28-36	24-39
Yards Per Pass	7.8	6.9
Times Sacked	4	2
Yards Lost To Sacks	21	12
Had Intercepted	2	3
PUNTS	3	7
Average Punt	36.1	41.8
PENALTIES	**8**	**3**
Penalty Yards	62	40
FUMBLES	**2**	**1**
Fumbles Lost	1	0
Time Of Possession	**23:04**	**34:56**

PASSING

KRAKENS	CMP	ATT	YDS	PCT	YPA	SACK	SYDS	TD	INT
Quentin Barnes	8	18	72	44.4	4.0	2	12	0	3
Don Pine	16	21	210	76.2	10.0	0	0	2	0

WARPIGS	CMP	ATT	YDS	PCT	YPA	SACK	SYDS	TD	INT
Hiawatha Harrison	28	36	302	77.8	8.4	4	21	3	2

RUSHING

KRAKENS	ATT	YDS	AVG	LONG	TD	FUM
Mitchell Fayed	26	150	5.8	52	2	0
Quentin Barnes	6	40	6.7	16	1	0
Yassoud Murphy	3	4	1.3	2	0	0
Don Pine	1	11	11.0	11	0	0

WARPIGS	ATT	YDS	AVG	LONG	TD	FUM
Parker Catrell	16	43	2.7	15	0	1
Lomenzo Carelli	8	25	3.1	13	0	1
Pino Koryat	6	20	3.3	8	0	0
Hiawatha Harrison	3	16	5.3	10	0	0

RECEIVING

KRAKENS	REC	YDS	AVG	LONG	TD	FUM
Hawick	6	102	17.0	44	1	0
Denver	2	85	42.5	67	1	0
Mezquitic	5	35	7.0	16	0	0
Scarborough	6	25	4.2	20	0	0
Tom Pareless	3	21	7.0	13	0	0
Milford	1	9	9.0	9	0	0
Yotaro Kobayasho	1	5	5.0	5	0	0

WARPIGS	REC	YDS	AVG	LONG	TD	FUM
Mayville	12	191	15.9	78	3	1
Kinji Kataro	6	49	8.2	31	0	0
Znojmo	5	46	9.2	19	0	0
Salado Creek	5	16	3.2	8	0	0

WEEK EIGHT LEAGUE ROUNDUP
(Courtesy of Galaxy Sports network)

The impossible comeback looks possible, but which quarterback will lead the **Ionath Krakens** (6-2) into their final game against the **Quyth Survivors** (3-5). The Krakens' musical-chairs quarterbacking continued this week in a 38-28 win over the **Glory Warpigs** (6-2). Rookie QB Quentin Barnes started the game but couldn't handle the pressure of the Warpigs' top-rated defensive secondary. Veteran Donald Pine led the Krakens to the win. After a 1-2 start, the Krakens have won five straight and now need to beat the Survivors to win the Quyth Irradiated Conference title.

Orbiting Death (5-3) pounded the **Bigg Diggers** (3-5) 31-17, the **Grontak Hydras** (4-4) topped the **Sky Demolition** (1-7) 21-12, the **Sheb Stalkers** (5-3) defeated the **Quyth Survivors** (3-5) by a score of 17-10 and the **Whitok Pioneers** (5-3) trounced the **Woo Wallcrawlers** (2-6) 52-3.

DEATHS:
No deaths to report this week.

WEEK EIGHT PLAYERS OF THE WEEK:
Offense: Mayville, receiver, Glory Warpigs. Twelve catches for 191 yards, three TDs.
Defense: Sven Draupnir, outside linebacker, Quyth Survivors. Twelve tackles, two sacks.

GAME NINE: Ionath Krakens (6-2) at Quyth Survivors (3-5)

QUYTH IRRADIATED CONFERENCE STANDINGS

Ionath Krakens	6-2
Glory Warpigs	6-2
Orbiting Death	5-3
Whitok Pioneers	5-3
Sheb Stalkers	5-3
Grontak Hydras	4-4
Quyth Survivors	3-5
Bigg Diggers	3-5
Woo Wallcrawlers	2-6
Sky Demolition	1-7

THEY MIGHT AS WELL have been preparing for a gladiatorial fight to the death or perhaps a pitched battle to save their own families. That's how intense it felt as the Krakens practiced for the final regular-season game against the Quyth Survivors. There had been smiles and jokes and hard work and intensity as the Krakens crawled from 1-2 and fought their way to first place. The smiles and jokes were gone.

The Krakens had fought too long and too hard to grab sole possession of first place and weren't about to take a team lightly simply because of a 3-5 record.

Hokor gave the starting job to Pine. Quentin was mad as could be, jealous, enraged and dejected, but after his performance against the Warpigs, he couldn't blame Hokor. The difference this time, however, was that Quentin and Pine evenly split all practice reps.

After the second practice, with two more to go before game time, Quentin was glad he was not a Quyth Survivor. Later that night they'd take the shuttle up to the *Touchback* and depart for the planet Quyth, seat of the Quyth Concordia and home of the Survivors.

As he peeled off his armor after practice, Messal waddled over to him. The Quyth Worker stood there, waiting to be addressed.

"What is it?" Quentin asked. He hated how the Workers were so subservient they wouldn't speak unless spoken to.

"Gredok wishes to see you," Messal said.

Quentin's blood ran ice-cold. Gredok hadn't talked to him since that first shuttle trip from the *Combine* to the *Touchback*. "What does he want?"

"As I said, Gredok wishes to see you."

Quentin nodded. "Tell him I'll be right up as soon as I finish dressing."

"He is not here," Messal said. "He is in town. I am to take you to him immediately."

Quentin took a deep breath. *In town.* Gredok wasn't even on the *Touchback*. Had he found out about the team-wide smuggling effort? Or, far worse, about Pine?

"Come on, Messal, give me a hint. What's this about?"

"It is not my place to say," Messal said with a little bow.

"Okay, let me shower up first."

"If I may be so bold, I suggest you skip the shower and come with me immediately. Gredok seemed … *agitated.*"

"Agitated," Quentin echoed. That couldn't be good. He'd never seen Gredok angry, let alone agitated. He quickly finished removing his armor, then threw on pants and a Krakens sweatshirt.

THE HOVERCAB STOPPED in front of the Bootleg Arms.

"Uh-oh," Quentin said.

Virak the Mean was waiting by the front door. They walked forward as soon as the cab stopped. Virak's eye showed a thin coloring of translucent pink.

"Gredok is inside," Virak said. "Come with me."

Quentin thought of running for it, but where would he go? He was in an alien city. He knew only his teammates and a handful of die-hard Purist Nation citizens. He could easily outrun Virak. But where after that? This was Gredok's city. Virak was also apparently in trouble — pink was the color of fear.

"Okay," Quentin said. "Let's go."

They walked inside. Quentin couldn't help but think of the parallels to the last time he'd been here. Messal led the way this time, instead of Tikad the Groveling. Virak was with him once again, but this time they were side-by-side.

The bar was empty. Somehow Quentin knew it would be. They walked past the dance floor and into the back room.

Gredok sat comfortably in Mopuk's chair. Two Quyth Warriors Quentin didn't recognize stood on either side of him, each holding a gun.

"Hello, Quentin," Gredok said. "I think you remember Mopuk." Gredok gestured to the table. The strange, insect-like creatures filled one-half of the table, separated from the other end by a glowing force field. The bugs kept running at the force field and were constantly thrown backward by some small shock. After every blast, they ran forward again, only to be shocked again. Inside the other end lay Mopuk, bound tight. His eye glowed the bright, neon pink of pure terror.

"Of course, I remember him," Quentin said.

"I'm not happy with you, Quentin," Gredok said. "You or your teammates."

Quentin just looked at Gredok. He wasn't about to volunteer any information.

"You used my team to smuggle a large shipment of goods," Gredok said. "I don't want that to happen again."

Quentin nodded.

"I've learned that Donald Pine was throwing games. *My* games."

"I doubt it," Quentin said. "He's a great quarterback."

"Don't lie to me. Your body heat and pulse tell me when you're lying."

Gredok's fur raised slightly. Quentin had seen Hokor angry, all puffed up like a fur ball, but Gredok's fur had always lain flat and smooth.

"The problem has been solved," Quentin said calmly. "We took care of it as a team."

"You solved *nothing*." Gredok pointed to Mopuk. "This, this *yakochat* caused my team to *lose*."

"I'm sorry, *Shamakath*!" Mopuk screamed. "Please, give me a chance to make it up to you!"

"Be quiet."

"But *Shamakath*, I swear, it was a mistake — "

Gredok's pedipalp reached for a small button built into the tabletop, and Mopuk instantly fell silent.

"This weak one has already told me everything," Gredok said. "So do not lie to me again, Quentin. Was Pine throwing games?"

Quentin thought for a moment, then nodded.

"Was this one responsible for that?" Gredok asked, his other pedipalp tapping on the glass, right next to the button.

Quentin nodded again.

Gredok pressed the button.

The force field dissipated, and the ever-attacking bug-like creatures swarmed over Mopuk, covering his legs and stomach in the blink of an eye. He started to scream as the living carpet swept up his chest and onto his face — but the scream choked as dozens crawled into his mouth. His jaws clamped shut, sending quirts of yellow bug blood against the inner glass. His mouth stayed shut only a second — he opened it to scream again, and more poured into the opening. He jerked and thrashed against his bindings, his body lurching against the strong glass, smashing more of the creatures against the smooth surface, streaking it with blobs of dripping yellow and bits of crushed body parts. The table shook with his jerking pain but did not break.

He's shrinking, Quentin thought for a second, then realized the bugs were draining Mopuk of fluid, like a swarm of demonic mosquitoes.

His kicks and lurches slowed.

He had one more panicked burst of twitches, then he slowed again.

And finally stopped.

The bugs kept swarming over him, a shimmering bodysuit of living death.

"That is what happens to those who betray me," Gredok said. He looked quite satisfied with himself. "If you keep information from me again, I will be angry. But for now, I am pleased with your resourcefulness. I think you handled the situation much as I would have. You will be the starter this week against the Survivors. I am not happy with my bodyguard, who abandoned his main duties in favor of his place on the team. Virak will perform *ghiris* as an example to others in my organization."

"Ghiris?"

The pinkness deepened in Virak's eye.

"It is a ritualistic suicide," he said. "I will kill myself while the others watch to prove my loyalty to my *shamakath*."

"Kill yourself? Are you nuts? Come on, Gredok, he didn't know you'd be this mad, he was just trying to help the team!"

Gredok said nothing.

"I knew exactly what would happen if we were discovered," Virak said quietly. "I knew the consequences, and I am prepared to pay the price."

Quentin stared, first at Virak, then at Gredok, then back. Virak had known helping Pine might bring about his own death, yet he helped anyway.

The temper starting to burn at the back of his brain, Quentin turned to Gredok. "And what about Pine?"

"Pine will suffer a fate similar to Mopuk."

"No," Quentin said.

Gredok looked at him. "Are you refusing my orders?"

"Yes," Quentin said. "I am a football player. Donald Pine is a football player. Virak is a football player."

"Those two *betrayed* me."

"I don't give a crap what they did. They are my teammates."

"Did you not hear me?" Gredok said. "I said you're the *starter*. These two don't concern you."

"Virak stays on the team," Quentin said. "Pine stays on the team. No one dies."

Gredok leaned forward. "Who do you think you're talking to? I'm your *shamakath*, you insolent Human."

"You are the team owner," Quentin said. "You are not my *shamakath*."

Gredok's fur ruffled out to full length. He looked like a little black puffball.

"Don't bother getting all pissy," Quentin said. "You do anything to Pine, or Virak dies, and I walk. Do you understand what that means?"

"You walk? You *quit*? Do you think I can't get another quarterback?"

"Not like me you can't, baby," Quentin said, slowly shaking his head side-to-side. "There isn't anyone like me and you know it. Never was. Never will be. And I walk *now*, Greedy, right this second. That means your starter against the Quyth Survivors is Yitzhak. You think Yitzhak can win that game?"

"Yes, he can," Gredok said. "The Survivors are 3-5, we can beat them without *you*."

Quentin nodded. "Maybe. But can he win in the playoffs? Can he beat the Texas Earthlings? Can he beat the undefeated Chillich Spider-Bears?"

Gredok's eye turned a deep, iridescent black.

"You remember the playoffs," Quentin said. "That thing we need to win to reach Tier One? Don't you *want* to win Tier One?"

Gredok's pedipalps trembled. "You smelly Human. You don't even really understand who you're talking to."

"Sure I do," Quentin said. "I'm talking to the team owner. I'm not in your mob, Gredok. I'm a football player. I'm not disrespecting you in any way, I promise you that. I'm telling you the way it's going to be with my team, or I catch the first liner back to Purist Nation space."

"And what if I put you inside this table right now?"

Quentin shrugged. "I would die a miserable death, but you know what? You still *lose*. You don't reach Tier One. It's that simple. So here's the deal. Pine plays. Virak plays. In fact, Virak is so good, why don't you get some of the other monkey-boys to do your muscle work? He needs to concentrate on the Survivors and on the tournament. It's your call, Greedy. What's it going to be?"

Gredok's eye swirled black-hole black then slowly faded to clear. He stared for another full minute then finally spoke.

"Hakat, Jokot," he said to the guards on either side. "See these *football players* out. But know this, Quentin — your deal lasts only as long as you keep winning. If you *don't* make Tier One, you and I will settle up."

Quentin winked. "We're going to the top, boss. You can bank on it."

If only he felt as confident as he sounded.

ALONE, GREDOK SAT in the Bootleg Arms for several minutes. He contemplated the scenario, unlike any he'd been through in a long, long time. Gredok had controlled countless sentients over the years, everything from Ki to Sklorno to Leekee, even a Dolphin or two. And hundreds of Quyth Leaders, the most intelligent, controlling beings in the known universe. And, of course, Humans. *Many* Humans.

Humans were often the easiest to control because they were so poorly trained at hiding their emotions. Quyth Leaders had the obvious "tell," their ever-shifting eye color. But Quyth Leaders aspiring for power quickly learned how to repress those color changes or even consciously manipulate them. Those who didn't, well, they didn't last long. Human "tells," however, were much more difficult to control — body heat, heart rate, pupil dilation, alpha waves, respiration. A trained Quyth Leader could read all of these tells.

Knowing your opponent's true intentions, *that* was the game. Knowing what was important to them, knowing what they could and couldn't live without. Knowing when they were lying.

Quentin Barnes had not been lying.

The young Human had been willing to walk away from the Krakens, from the GFL. To protect a Quyth Warrior he barely knew. To protect a man that had thrown games, a man that had betrayed the team, the entire *sport*. And *nothing* was more important to Quentin than the sport of football. That fact was obvious in every tell. With Pine out of the way, Quentin became the permanent starting quarterback, the thing he claimed he'd wanted all his life. But he'd put all that on the line until he got his way. What could compel a Human to do something that was so contrary to his own best interests?

The answer seemed obvious loyalty. Quentin Barnes was loyal to a fault, loyal to the point he'd throw his own future away to protect a friend. In Gredok's world, loyalty often went to the highest bidder, or at least to the *shamakath* that provided the most opportunities for advancement and wealth and power.

Gredok looked at the shriveled shape of Mopuk, drained of fluid. His fur lay in ugly clumps at the bottom of the glass table. Fat *shushuliks*, newly bloated with Mopuk's blood, moved lazily through the piles of fur. Mopuk had claimed to be loyal. That brand of loyalty, the brand with which Gredok was most familiar, lasted only until the next potential payday. Quentin's loyalty, well, that was another story.

That kind of loyalty Gredok could put to good use. If the Krakens could win two more games, if they could reach the elite ranks of Tier One, Gredok would find a way to use that loyalty indeed.

THE *TOUCHBACK* SHUDDERED out of punch-space. Quentin let out his long-held breath in a slow, steady exhale. He'd made it yet again. The anxiety was the same, but this time he wasn't hiding in his room. He stood on the viewing deck, next to Virak the Mean.

"Flying scares you?" Virak asked calmly.

"It's not the flight," Quentin said. "It's the punch-out."

He looked at the view screens, amazed at the sight of the Quyth homeworld. They'd arrived on the nighttime side, yet there wasn't one dark patch to be seen. Every last square mile seemed covered with the soft glow of civilization.

"High One," Quentin said. "Is the whole thing covered?"

"There is no more open land," Virak said. "Nor much open water."

"Seventy-two billion," Quentin said in amazement. The population of Quyth seemed so staggering he had to say it out loud to appreciate it.

"Now you understand why we expand. We either find new worlds or stop breeding, and that is not an option."

They said nothing more, simply stared at the overpopulated planet. The Purist Nation planets were relatively unpopulated. Earth, however, was at 18 billion and counting. He wondered how long it would be until the Earth, like the Quyth homeworld, was just one big city without boundaries or borders.

PINE DRESSED for the game, but had about as much a chance of seeing field time as the Purist Nation had of winning the Intergalactic Sentient Peace award for good deeds done to other species. The team still didn't know, save for Virak and Quentin.

But Hokor knew.

Gredok had obviously informed his workaholic coach that Donald Pine, two-time Galaxy Bowl Champion, one-time League MVP and erstwhile savior of the Ionath Krakens franchise had been taking Hokor's detailed game plans and basically using them to wipe his butt. Pine had gone from starter to the doghouse faster than a ship moving in punch drive.

At least thus far, Hokor hadn't told anyone else. Too many beings now knew. It was only a matter of time before the rest of the team discovered Pine's horrible secret. And when it came out, Pine's presence would be most unwelcome in the Krakens' locker room.

But Quentin didn't have time to worry about that right now. It wasn't his problem anymore. He had a whole new set of problems. Forty-four of them, to be precise, each one wearing the metallic silver uniforms of the Quyth Survivors.

A losing team, my rear end, Quentin thought. *The only thing that matters is how they match up against us, and they match up very well indeed*. The Survivors weren't a losing team, they were an enemy, an obstacle standing between him and his dream. No, far more importantly, they were standing between *his team* and *his team's dream*. There wouldn't be any interceptions today, just completions, just a calm, methodical march down the field and a strangulating game of ball control and field position. He wasn't going to give the Survivors any chances to get into this game and get a very erroneous thought in their brains that they had any right to be on the same field with the Ionath Krakens.

Ball control, Quentin thought. *Ball control, patience, field position*.

THE PLANTS LOOKED just like Carsengi Grass, but the blades blazed a fluorescent orange. Black lines and numbers popped off the field in stark contrast.

First offensive play of the game. Krakens' ball, first-and-10 from their own 33.

Is that what I think it is? Are those idiots in woman-to-woman when I've got three burners on the field?

Ba-da-bap went his hands on the center's carapace.

Forget ball control, let's go downtown.

"Flash, flash!" Quentin shouted.

Heads and eyestalks turned to look at him, waiting for the audible. He was changing the play at the line.

"Blue twenty-two!" He shouted down the left side of the line. Hawick had been lined up three feet to the left of Rick Warburg. Hawick jogged another ten yards to the left, almost to the sideline, her defender following. She stopped, stood and waited for the snap.

"Bluuuee, twenty two!" He shouted down the right side of the line. Scarborough and Mezquitic stood at five and seven yards, respectively, away from the right tackle Vu-Ko-Will, Mezquitic on the line of scrimmage, Scarborough one step back from it. With the audible, Mezquitic took one step forward, while Scarborough took a step back, then went in motion to the sidelines, a slow jog that took her fifteen yards out.

"Blue, twenty-two!" Quentin shouted behind him. Tom Pareless and Mitchell Fayed had been in an I-formation, Tom in a three-point stance, Fayed two yards behind him, hands on his knees, head up high. They quickly adjusted so that they stood side-by-side in a pro-set.

Quentin turned back to the line. "Hut-hut!"

The line erupted with crashes and clacks and grunts for the game's first trench battle. Pareless and Fayed each took a step up and a step outside, where they crouched, waiting for the first opportunity to block. Quentin dropped straight back, slipping between the two running backs like they were centurions guarding some ancient gate. Hawick and Mezquitic shot downfield on streak patterns, while Scarborough ran forward for fifteen yards, then angled to the middle of the field on a post pattern.

Those patterns drew single coverage from the two cornerbacks and the safety. Quentin watched the free safety, the key to the play. Hawick and Scarborough were both running even with their defenders, but Quentin could tell they still had an extra step in their gas tanks. The safety ran to the outside to pick up the Krakens' most deadly threat — Hawick.

That was all Quentin needed to see.

He cocked his arm and threw just as Tom Pareless undercut the first Ki defender that broke through the line. The ball arced downfield, not a perfect spiral this time, but marred by a tiny bit of wobble. It didn't look pretty, but it was on target. Scarborough remained step-for-step with her defender for another two seconds, then put on a sudden burst of speed that took her just a few feet past. She timed the ball perfectly, leaping high into the air to catch the ball without a single mid-air twist or turn or alteration. The defender reached for her, but Scarborough kicked out with her right leg, hitting the defender in the chest. The blow knocked the defender back, just a bit, and when the two hit the ground she had a good three steps of clearance, more than any Sklorno needed just fifteen yards from the goal line.

Scarborough ran into the end zone.

First play from scrimmage, a 67-yard touchdown strike.

• • •

THE REST OF THE GAME brought more of the same. Quentin had never felt so in sync before, not even in his Purist Nation days. He knew exactly where his receivers were at all times. The receivers seemed to read his thoughts, breaking off patterns to find the ball already in the air, moving to open spots in perfect time with any of Quentin's scrambling efforts. He saw every defender, every disguised coverage, every blitz. He saw the sideways-rolling Quyth Warrior linebackers and knew when they would pop up into a pass-coverage stance. When he ran, he knew when they would lean in for the tackle, when their balance was all forward, and that told him just when to spin: juke moves didn't work on them, but half the time spin moves left them falling flat on their face. He saw Ki defensive linemen raging past his offensive line, he saw them gather and knew when to step forward just as they released, springing violently forward to grasp only empty air. He saw the speed and timing of the Sklorno defensive backs and knew just where to throw to avoid them. He even saw a safety blitz and two corner blitzes — but each time he threw in a fraction of a second, hitting the open receiver before the streaking d-back could close on him.

Nothing could touch him.

The Krakens' defense played its best game of the season. Aside from one long run by Chooch Motumbo, the Survivors tailback, the defense shut down everything. By the end of the third quarter, the Krakens were up 28-7 and in clear control of the game.

That was when disaster struck.

THIRD-AND-3 on the Survivors' 35.

Quentin surveyed the defense. He could have audibled to a slant pass, because the linebacker was cheating inside, but opted to go with the called play, a sweep to the right. He didn't want to put the ball in the air now, nothing that might give the Survivors a chance to get back in the game. Dressed in metallic silver jerseys, leg armor and helmets, the Survivors' defense looked like a bunch of old-time science-fiction robots, ones that had been through a losing battle, and were now covered in orange grass stains, dirt and blood. Lots of blood. Still, they weren't giving up, and even though they were having their asses handed to them, the Survivors' defense fought as hard as they could on every play.

"Hut-HUUUT!"

The ball slapped into Quentin's hands. He pivoted backward off his right foot, coming all the way around before softly pitching the ball to Fayed. Already moving right, Fayed caught the ball and ran parallel to the line of scrimmage, Kopor the Climber out in front to block. Sho-Do-Thikit, the left guard, stepped back and pulled to the right, giving Fayed two blockers on the quick pitch. The play's design was simple — get outside as fast as possible and try to cut up and out. A good block on the outside linebacker could leave Fayed one-on-one with the slender Sklorno defensive backs, a punishing equation that would almost always end with Fayed driving the defender back for positive yards, if not breaking the tackle outright for a big gain.

Quentin watched the three Krakens sweep right, orange jerseys with black numbers and orange trim, orange leg armor with black piping, orange and black helmets. The outside linebacker, a powerful HeavyG giant from Rodina named Sven Draupnir, drove upfield as the middle linebacker, Kylee Cannell, used his impressive speed to dash toward the sidelines, trying to stay just inside of Fayed's left shoulder, preventing an inside cutback that could go for big yards. Draupnir crashed forward like a tank. Wen-E-Deret tried to reach him, but Draupnir stepped to the right tackle's outside shoulder and drove past, batting away strong Ki arms like some mere annoyance. Wen-E-Deret gathered and leapt, but was too late. Kopor stepped up and met Draupnir head-on — the resulting collision sent a *clack* so loud it was heard in the upper deck, even over the roar of the crowd. Kopor was knocked back as if he were a child, rolling feet-over-head right into Fayed.

Fayed reached one arm down as his feet came off the ground. His extended hand met Kopor's shoulder pad. Fayed pushed off quickly, an amazingly athletic move, his arm absorbing the shock.

Instead of being knocked over, he was simply knocked back — his lithe feet landed on the ground, he stumbled once, then recovered and headed for the sidelines.

Fayed's athleticism was a wonder to behold, but Cannell was no slouch and used Fayed's momentary stumble to close the gap. Cannell dove, his big fingers grabbing handfuls of Fayed's jersey. Fayed's strong legs pumped away, dragging the prone, 420-pound Cannell along the ground.

Topinabee raced up field at top speed, a silver streak headed for the encumbered Fayed. Fayed started to lower his shoulder, but like a water-skier bouncing up from some trick, Cannell slid to his feet, his fingers still deeply wrapped in Fayed's jersey. With a primal grunt, Cannell planted his feet and *swung*. The motion first stopped Fayed cold, then ripped him in a blurring, backward horizontal arc. At the end of the arc, almost 360 degrees from where he started, the orange-jerseyed blur met the oncoming silver-jerseyed blur of Topinabee, with a *crack* that made the Draupnir/Kopor collision sound quiet by comparison. Quentin winced as the two came together. The crowd "ooohheed" in satisfaction, most of them probably wincing themselves.

Cannell pounded his chest, playing to the crowd.

Topinabee slowly rose to her feet, stumbled, then fell.

Fayed didn't get up.

His foot twitched, and the fingers of his left hand opened and closed spasmodically, but he didn't get up. He was laying face-down — actually, he *should* have been face-down, because his stomach and chest were on the ground, but his face was actually looking up.

"Oh, High One," Quentin said, then ran to his teammate.

Fayed's eyes were wide with terror. He tried to breathe but couldn't seem to draw air. His head was turned so far around, he could almost have looked down and seen his own spine.

"Fayed!" Quentin said. He reached for his teammate, then kept his hands away, remembering someone telling him once not to touch a head or neck injury.

"The banana … meteors …" Fayed said. His foot kept twitching, but his hand suddenly stopped the spasmodic opening and closing. The fingers froze in mid-move, curled rigid like a talon.

Quentin was distantly aware of a med-sled racing out, of Doc fluttering down next to Fayed. Quentin felt a hand, or a tentacle, he didn't know, grab his shoulder pad and gently pull him back.

Doc pulled a laser scalpel from his bag and deftly sliced off Fayed's back armor. Doc then removed a small, rectangular device. He punched a few buttons on the device, then pressed it against Fayed's back. There was a sickening squelching sound as tendrils reached out of both sides of the device and penetrated Fayed's skin, curling in toward his spine. A soft orange light started flashing on the device — *blink, blink, blink, blink ...*

Doc zipped to the med-sled and maneuvered it over the top of Fayed's body. The metallic tendrils reached down. The med-sled lifted, and Fayed rose off the ground without his body moving an iota, like some magician's trick of levitation. Doc flew off the field, the med-sled moving behind him, slowly, so as not to jostle Fayed.

As the cart and patient slid noiselessly toward the tunnel, Quentin's sharp eyes remained fixated on the orange light.

Blink, blink ... blink .... blink ....

Then nothing.

Before Fayed slid into the tunnel, Quentin knew the orange light had stopped flashing.

HE FINISHED THE GAME. He didn't know how he did it, but he did it nonetheless. He even scored another touchdown, this one a twelve-yard run. He had to do the running himself — Yassoud's face went pale each time Hokor called his number, and he ran with all the intensity of a galley cook. When the game was on, Quentin didn't have to think about it, he either ran the offense on the field, every last scrap of his intellect devoted to analyzing the defense, or he sat on the sidelines, intently studying a holotable of the last series, in case he found a weakness to use on the next possession.

But when the final seconds ticked off the clock, and the scoreboard read Krakens 38, Survivors 13, he didn't have anything else to distract him. The team gathered in the central meeting room. Hokor stood in front of the holoboard, as usual.

Except this time, his eye wasn't black or orange or even pink.

It was deep purple. Opaque purple.

Quentin had never seen that color before, but somehow he knew exactly what it meant.

"First of all, I want to sing all of your praises for a hard-fought game," Hokor said. "We played, and won, as a team. I have very little to say of negative things. The Ionath Krakens are now the champions of the Quyth Irradiated Conference."

A half-hour ago, that same phrase would have drawn a deafening roar from the assembled players. Now, it was met with silence, a silence broken only by some Human trying to clear phlegm from his throat.

"We have lost one of our warriors," Hokor said. He looked down at a palmtop. "Mitchell Fayed suffered a severed spinal cord and a collapsed lung. Doc tried to used a Galthier Spinal Cord Controller to regulate Fayed's breathing and heart rate, but there was too much damage, too soon. Attempts to repair the damage and reanimate him failed."

There was a loud sob. Quentin looked over to the source of the sound. John Tweedy, big, dangerous, deadly John Tweedy, sat on a bench, his elbow on his knee, his forehead propped on his hand, his eyes squeezed shut, his solid shoulders shaking in time with his sobs.

The noise seemed to open a dam of emotion. Other Humans started sobbing, or sniffling, or coughing to hide their self-perceived weakness.

One of the Ki linemen produced a long, serrated knife. They passed it from one to the next, taking turns cutting a long gash into their own upper left arm. With each cut, black blood spilled down in a noisy, splattering rivulet, spreading out across the tile floor.

They're letting out their own blood, Quentin thought. *So it can join Fayed's blood on the field of battle.*

Messal the Efficient silently slipped out of the Quyth Warrior locker room. He walked over to Virak the Mean who sat limply on the floor. Messal opened the box and removed a metallic, pen-like instrument. The instrument hummed lightly as Messal started moving it across the chitin on Virak's left forearm. Choto the Bright stood behind Virak, Killik the Unworthy behind him, a line of Quyth Warriors slowly forming. Quentin didn't recognize the new writing on Virak's shell, but he knew it was a Quyth rendition of Fayed's name. It stunned Quentin to see a Human name being written on a Quyth Warrior's shell.

But that's what Fayed's constant, punishing work ethic had meant to everyone.

Quentin felt cold. Fayed had been on the field with him, battling away, not even an *hour* ago. And now he was gone. Horrible injuries were part of the game. Big bodies, *strong* bodies, and speed. Force equals mass times acceleration. Beings got hurt, but then beings got fixed. All the plaques he'd seen in all the stadiums, commemorating those who died on the field — it had seemed somehow *distant*, something from the game's past, from *before* the reality that embraced him once he joined the ranks of the elite.

Fayed was dead.

Quentin wasn't about to let that death be for nothing.

He looked at Donald Pine. Instinctively, he expected Pine to stand and say something, anything, talk of how the team would win for Fayed. But Pine said nothing, he just sat there, head bowed. He was a disgraced man, and even though the team didn't know it, *he* knew it. Pine was broken, his mantle of leadership ... gone.

With sudden clarity, Quentin realized that he now held that mantle.

Something had to be said. And *he* was only one who could say it.

The team started to head to their separate dressing rooms when Quentin stood and spoke.

"I need to say a few words."

The players stopped where they were. They looked back at him. They looked at him in the same way he'd just looked at Pine.

They wanted someone to lead them.

"Fayed ... " he started to talk, but his voice cracked. He felt his throat thicken and tears try to fight their way out of his eyes. He held his eyes shut tight and took a deep breath.

"The Machine, he was a great running back," Quentin said. "All he wanted to do was play Tier One ball. It was his dream."

Quentin looked around the room, in turn looking each player in the eye. His voice suddenly changed, from on-the-verge-of-tears to a cold, steel baritone that rang through the soul of every being in the room.

"He's with us, he's still on this team," Quentin said. "And if we make it to Tier One, *he* makes it to Tier One. No one in this room will let him down. Coach, who do we play?"

Hokor tapped a button on his palmtop. "We have the second-best record in the tournament, based on a points-scored tiebreaker with the Texas Earthlings. That means we have a bye the first round. We play the winner of the Texas Earthlings and the Aril Archers."

Quentin nodded slowly, turning so that he could look every player right in the eyes. None of them said a word.

"A bye. That means we're automatically in the semi-finals. We win that game, that *one* game, and we're in Tier One. We win that game, and Fayed gets his dream."

Tweedy's sobbing slowed, becoming just a sniffle.

"I don't care who steps on that field," Quentin said. "Earthlings, Archers, it doesn't make any difference. Either way, they're going *down*."

Quentin nodded once then walked to the Human locker room.

SURVIVORS BOX SCORE

Final	1	2	3	4	T
Ionath	14	14	3	7	38
Quyth	0	7	6	0	13

SCORING SUMMARY

1st QUARTER		ION	QUY
Ionath TD	Scarborough 67-yard pass from Quentin Barnes (Arioch Morningstar kick)	7	0
Ionath TD	Denver 8-yard pass from Quentin Barnes (Arioch Morningstar kick)	14	0

2nd QUARTER		ION	QUY
Ionath TD	Hawick 8-yard pass from Quentin Barnes (Arioch Morningstar kick)	21	0
Quyth TD	Chooch Motumbo 52-yard run (Karen Eubanks kick)	21	7
Ionath TD	Scarborough 17-yard pass from Quentin Barnes (Arioch Morningstar kick)	28	0

3rd QUARTER		ION	QUY
Ionath FG	31-yard FG by Arioch Morningstar is good.	31	7
Quyth FG	34-yard FG by Karen Eubanks is good.	31	10
Quyth FG	29-yard FG by Karen Eubanks is good.	31	13

4th QUARTER		ION	QUY
Ionath TD	Quentin Barnes 12-yard run (Arioch Morningstar kick)	38	13

TEAM STATISTICS	QUY	ION
First Downs	10	19
Third Down Efficiency	5-15	15-20
TOTAL NET YARDS	**297**	**417**
Total Plays	65	69
Average Gain Per Play	4.6	6.0
NET YARDS RUSHING	**120**	**145**
Rushes	29	33
Average Per Rush	4.1	4.4
NET YARDS PASSING	**177**	**272**
Pass Completion	14-36	22-36
Yards Per Pass	4.9	7.6
Times Sacked	2	0
Yards Lost To Sacks	7	0
Had Intercepted	0	0
PUNTS	**10**	**5**
Average Punt	45.7	38.4
PENALTIES	**7**	**4**
Penalty Yards	59	25
FUMBLES	**3**	**1**
Fumbles Lost	2	1
Time Of Possession	**28:55**	**31:05**

PASSING

KRAKENS	CMP	ATT	YDS	PCT	YPA	SACK	SYDS	TD	INT
Quentin Barnes	22	36	272	61.1	7.6	0	0	4	0

SURVIVORS	CMP	ATT	YDS	PCT	YPA	SACK	SYDS	TD	INT
Smiley Bates	14	36	184	38.9	5.1	2	7	0	0

RUSHING

KRAKENS	ATT	YDS	AVG	LONG	TD	FUM
Mitchell Fayed	22	101	4.6	17	0	1
Quentin Barnes	4	32	8.0	19	1	0
Yassoud Murphy	7	12	1.7	4	0	0

SURVIVORS	ATT	YDS	AVG	LONG	TD	FUM
Chooch Motumbo	24	106	4.4	52	1	1
Pikor the Killer	5	14	2.8	7	0	0

RECEIVING

KRAKENS	REC	YDS	AVG	LONG	TD	FUM
Scarborough	7	115	16.4	67	2	0
Denver	3	45	15.0	21	1	0
Hawick	3	40	13.3	18	1	0
Mezquitic	3	31	10.3	14	0	0
Milford	2	20	10.0	12	0	0
Tom Pareless	2	12	6.0	8	0	0
Yotaro Kobayasho	2	9	4.5	7	0	0

SURVIVORS	REC	YDS	AVG	LONG	TD	FUM
Milan	4	56	14.0	24	0	1
Vladivostok	5	48	9.6	30	0	0
Juno	4	44	11.0	26	0	0
Craig Marlahan	1	36	36.0	36	0	1

WEEK NINE LEAGUE ROUNDUP
(Courtesy of Galaxy Sports network)

The **Ionath Krakens** (7-2) completed their improbable comeback, winning their sixth-straight game 38-13 over the **Quyth Survivors** (3-6). With the win the Krakens locked up the Quyth Irradiated Conference title and earned a trip to the Tier Two playoffs.

The **Glory Warpigs** (7-2) finished up an excellent season with a 25-13 win over the **Bigg Diggers** (3-6).

The **Whitok Pioneers** (6-3) look ready for next year, as quarterback Condor Adrienne threw for five TDs in a 52-27 thrashing of the **Sheb Stalkers** (4-5).

Also in action last week, the **Woo Wallcrawlers** (4-5) upset the **Grontak Hydras** (4-5) by a score of 17-14, and **Orbiting Death** (6-3) pounded on the **Sky Demolition** (1-8), 37-10.

DEATHS:
Mitchell "The Machine" Fayed, killed on a clean hit by Tobinabee, free safety for the Quyth Survivors.

WEEK NINE PLAYERS OF THE WEEK:
Offense: Ju Tweedy, running back, Orbiting Death. 205 yards on 32 carries, three TDs.
Defense: Bray-O-Haka, tackle, Woo Wallcrawlers. Four sacks, seven tackles.

PLAYOFFS ROUND #1
SEEDING FOR THE TIER TWO TOURNAMENT

#1	Chillich Spider-Bears	9-0
#2	Ionath Krakens	7-2
#3	Texas Earthlings	7-2
#4	Shorah Chieftains	6-3
#5	Citadel Aquanauts	6-3
#6	Aril Archers	6-3

From the Ionath City Gazette

Earthlings face Krakens in Tier Two semifinals
By Kigin the Witty

EARTH (Associated Press) — In a game that really wasn't as close as the score indicates, the Texas Earthlings defeated the Aril Archers 21-17 to advance to the Tier Two semi-finals. The Earthlings face the Ionath Krakens, champions of the Quyth Irradiated Conference.

The Earthlings' defense led the way, allowing only 10 points. The Archers managed one defensive score to keep it close, a 22-yard interception return for a touchdown by Minneapolis.

Earthlings' linebacker Alonzo Castro was named the game's MVP. Castro, a rookie from the Sigurd Norsemen of the PNFL, had eight solo tackles along with an interception and a critical quarterback sack, his fifth of the season.

"Castro's speed has taken our defense to a new level," said Earthlings coach Pata the Calculating. "Teams have to watch out for him, and that helps keep double-teams off of Chok-Oh-Thilit."

Chok-Oh-Thilit, the Earthlings' All-Pro defensive tackle, finished the day with two sacks and five tackles.

"He (Chok-Oh-Thilit) was basically unblockable," said Archers' coach David Djadin. "We couldn't do anything with him. He injured three linemen — I'm glad the season is over because we couldn't even field an offensive line right now. He's the hardest hitter in the game."

Offensively, the Earthlings moved the ball with efficiency and didn't give up a single turnover. Quarterback Case Johanson went 21-of-34 for 225 yards and a 12-yard touchdown pass to running back Peter Lowachee. The Earthlings utilized a ball-control offense, chewing up the clock by relying on running back Pookie Chang. Chang racked up 122 yards on 27 carries, including touchdown runs of 3 and 7 yards.

• • •

QUENTIN HAD never been to Earth.

In fact, most citizens of the Purist Nation had never been there. Earth, after all, was the capital of the Planetary Union, the historical enemy of the Purist Nation. Earth was also the cradle of Satan, the birth place of evil, the home of the Human betrayers and the Brother-Killers. Centuries ago, the powerful people of Earth had cast out the Faithful, sending Stewart and his followers on a perilous journey across the Void. Only the hand of the High One himself had saved the chosen people, delivered them to a green place from which the Purist Nation flourished.

At least that was the story.

Quentin couldn't help but believe some of it. That story, after all, had been drummed into his head since before he could speak. Yet, that didn't dull his excitement as the *Touchback* prepared to drop out of the punch-space near Earth orbit. *Earth*. The beginning of Humanity. Regardless of the Purist Nation's current politics, Earth was where it had all begun.

Not for just the species, like Quentin could give a crap about that.

Earth was the birthplace of *football*.

Quentin could barely contain his excitement. What would he see first? The legendary Kraft Cheese Stadium? The 200-year-old Ford Orbital Stadium, site of *five* Galaxy Bowls, site of all the Earth Football League Championships from 2482 until the end of the league in 2566? The Professional Football Hall Of Fame, in some place called Canton? Perhaps one of the many universities where they still played collegiate football, a historic if quaint anachronism. Some had even called college football "Tier Four" football, a place for people to play when they weren't good enough to cut it on a Tier Three team. Rumor was the entire Krakens squad would be guests at one of the most historical games in the sport, eight hundred years of tradition marked by a game with a team called "Michigan" versus a team called "Ohio State."

His excitement ran at such a high level he almost forgot to be afraid of punch-out. Almost. The *Touchback* shuddered as he slipped back into reality. View screens changed from pitch-black to a stunning view of a cloud-speckled blue world.

Earth.

A dozen orbital stations, the biggest only a twentieth the size of The Ace or Emperor Two, floated in Earth's near-space. Two of those stations had long, thin tubes running down toward the surface of Earth, stretching out so far that the silvery tendrils faded away into nothing. Quentin wondered if they were some kind of communications assembly.

It was the most highly populated Human planet at eighteen billion beings, although a good five billion of those were of the Whitok and Dolphin species that lived in the planet's vast oceans. The Whitokians living there, of course, were the original catalyst that resulted in Mason Stewart and his followers leaving Earth on their long pilgrimage to the Promised Land. That anti-alien bias had permeated every aspect of Purist life. Quentin now knew this and knew that he could never go back to living in such a place, not when he fought on the field with his alien teammates day-in and day-out. He had no place to call home. Maybe someday, after he retired, he'd come and live on Earth.

The *Touchback* veered toward one of the orbital stations with the long tendril. As it drew close, Quentin saw that the tendril was far from thin — it was a massively thick tube that stretched down and down and down. Like other orbital stations, this one had many long piers that jutted out from a central radius. Each pier reached out for miles, dotted with ships of all makes and colors. The *Touchback* gently approached a pier and shuddered lightly as mechanical arms reached out to lash the bus to an anchoring port.

[TEAM DISEMBARK] the computer voice said. [ALL PLAYERS DIS-EMBARK]

"Aren't we taking the shuttle down?" Quentin asked Yitzhak as the team walked out.

"Shuttle? Not on Earth, buddy. No shuttle traffic allowed. Everyone takes the tube to get to and from the surface."

A recorded voice droned over hidden loudspeakers.

[WELCOME TO HUDSON BAY STATION. PLEASE WATCH YOUR

STEP ON THE MOVING SIDEWALK. NO WEAPONS OF ANY KIND ARE ALLOWED ON HUDSON BAY STATION. WELCOME TO HUDSON BAY STATION ...]

Just outside the hatch, a long, two-band moving sidewalk ran off into the distance, toward the station's central spine. The band on the outside moved at a decent clip, while the central band seemed to move twice as fast. Just past the moving sidewalk was a large, clear tube. Inside the tube were two more tubes, side-by-side, each filled with water. Bubbles and bits of flotsam showed the nearest tube flowed toward the station's core, while the one on the other side flowed out to the end of the pier. Inside the tube, Quentin saw Whitokians, Dolphins and Leekee swimming along like fish in a packed aquarium.

The team filtered onto the walkway, which briskly moved them along the pier. Quentin watched Yitzhak casually step onto the first band. As he moved away, he carefully stepped on to the central band. He shot down the pier moving at least twenty miles an hour. Quentin followed suit. He stepped on the first band and almost lost his balance at the sudden shift in momentum. He steadied himself, then stepped onto the second band to experience another surge of acceleration. He jogged down the central strip until he caught up with Yitzhak.

"Why don't they use shuttles?"

Yitzhak laughed. "Because they don't want to get blown up, that's why. Anything that gets below the 80,000-feet boundary is instantly attacked and destroyed by a flight of Creterakian fighters."

"Destroyed? But why?"

Yitzhak looked at Quentin for a moment, a quizzical look on his face. "Are you serious?"

Quentin felt a little stupid, but he nodded.

"Because of the suicide attacks," Yitzhak said. "Purist Nation terrorists. They attack any chance they get, blow themselves up as long as they can inflict heavy casualties."

Quentin felt defensive anger swarm to the front of his thoughts. "What makes you think they're from the Purist Nation?"

Yitzhak put a hand on Quentin's shoulder. "Don't get mad at me, Q. There's a dozen terrorist groups on Earth, and after an attack, they contact the media and actually claim responsibility. Their goal is supposedly to drive all aliens off the planet. The Purist Repatriation Assembly is the worst. Two years ago the PRA managed to nuke a Whitok city in the Atlantic, killed three million Whitok, Dolphins and Humans. That was just the initial blast. That area of the Atlantic has been utterly devastated. They're still working on the radiological cleanup. Some people wanted to bring in a big team of Quyth engineers, who are the experts on cleaning up radiation, but there's too much suspicion that the Quyth will squat on that spot the way they did on Ionath and Whitok."

Virak overheard the conversation and walked over. "Those fears are stupid. Why would we want to start a colony on a planet that does not live in freedom?"

Yitzhak shrugged. "That's Earth citizens for you. You know how suspicious they are. But hey, if you'd lived through 280 years of terrorism, your people would be suspicious, too."

The walkway zipped along the pier, passing a regular progression of dock-locks. Most locks were closed, but some were open, and Quentin saw just about every species represented. The fast-moving sidewalks seemed to control congestion on the pier, but it was still a very busy place indeed.

"I hope there's no construction this time," Yitzhak said. "I'd really like to get down to the surface sometime in the near future."

"There's *always* construction," Virak said.

The walkway entered a large, noisy, domed open space. Ornate lights lined the ceiling, and voices in all languages repeatedly echoed through the cavernous space.

[THE RED ZONE IS FOR LOADING AND UNLOADING OF PASSENGERS ONLY, PLEASE DO NOT LOITER IN THE RED ZONE.]

[NO WEAPONS ARE ALLOWED ON HUDSON BAY STATION. IF YOU ARE CARRYING A WEAPON OF ANY KIND, PLEASE REPORT TO THE NEAREST CONSTABLE AND TURN IT IN. CARRYING A WEAPON ON HUDSON BAY STATION IS A CAPITOL OFFENSE.]

The team moved toward a huge line of beings. Waist-high silver stands dotted the length of the line, a red velvety rope hanging between each of the stands.

Off in the distance, the line emptied into a cavernous, hexagonal central area. A massive circle, at least two hundred feet in diameter, dotted each of the hexagon's sides. Three of the circles were nothing but a large blank space surrounded by a wide ring of deck. A huge platform sat in the center of the fourth circle. Concentric rings of seats filled the platform. Different colors denoted different sections, like slices of pizza, and each color had a different type of seat to accommodate either Ki, Sklorno, Quyth, Leekee or Human. Beings steadily exited the line and moved onto the platform, taking their respective seats. Once the seats filled (some species sat in seats that didn't quite fit them right, but they didn't seem to mind much), the platform simply dropped out of sight.

The last two platforms were blocked off by rings of orange and white barrels with small, flashing orange lights on top. Tools and equipment littered the area, although Quentin saw no workers. A sign read, "Your tax dollars at work! Upgrades to the Armstrong Elevator — faster drop-engines, to be complete in September 2684."

"Construction," Yitzhak said. "I swear, they're *never* finished with this place."

"*Two* platforms are down?" Virak moaned. "We're going to be here forever."

Quentin waited patiently. While the line did move slowly, it didn't bother him as much as is seemed to bother some of his teammates. Apparently, they'd never spent four or five hours standing in line while the Starvation Trucks dispensed food to an entire city of hungry people.

Finally the Krakens players reached the end of the line. Platform #3 rose up like some giant Leviathan, noiselessly filling the giant, empty circle that matched its circumference. They wandered onto the platform along with other passengers. Quentin found a seat next to Yitzhak, sat down and waited.

"You ever been on the chute before?" Yitzhak asked.

Quentin shook his head.

"Hope you don't get motion sick," Yitzhak said. "And if you do, don't puke on me."

[PLEASE FASTEN YOUR SEAT RESTRAINTS. THE PLATFORM WILL DESCEND IN TEN SECONDS.]

Quentin watched Yitzhak fasten a seatbelt around his waist and followed suit. He silently counted to ten, and then the bottom dropped out of his world.

The huge platform simply *fell*. His hands flew to the armrests, fingers digging into the worn plastic. Falling. *Falling*. All around the platform, metal walls slid by at a sickening speed. Then suddenly the walls were gone, and he was looking at nothing but blue sky and clouds. His stomach roiled, and he felt dizzy. Yitzhak's warning echoed in his thoughts, and he wondered if, indeed, he might puke. He closed his eyes and gritted his teeth against an onset of nausea.

After five minutes, just when he thought he couldn't handle it anymore, the seat seemed to push against his butt, and the floor seemed to press against his feet. They were decelerating. Quentin tried to calm his breathing for the next two minutes, as the platform steadily pushed against him. Finally, it slowed to an almost imperceptible speed and stopped with a slight, shaking jar.

[WELCOME TO HUDSON BAY SURFACE STATION,] the computer voice echoed. [WE HOPE YOU ENJOY YOUR STAY.]

Quentin followed along as the passengers disembarked. The ground station looked like an exact copy of the orbital station, with the exception that the walls were clear and offered a breathtaking view of Hudson Bay and the surrounding complex. Waves crashed into clear walls, sending up clouds of droplets that sparkled in the sunlight before misting back down. He'd never seen so much water before, yet the footing was as rock-solid as dry land.

To the east sprawled the Hudson Bay Airport, a flat rectangle two miles across and three miles long. The airport, elevated about a hundred feet above the water level, rested on two dozen thick black pylons that ran below the surface. Each pylon, he was told, connected to a sub-surface pontoon some three hundred feet below the surface. Dynamic positioning systems controlled the depth and position of each pontoon, ensuring fixed positioning even in the worst storms. He watched a triangular passenger plane land, escorted in by a flight of boxy-looking Creterakian fighters.

To the north sat Quentin's destiny: Hudson Bay Stadium. Unlike the airport, the bottom levels of the stadium dome actually rested below the water, with the playing field sitting some 150 feet beneath the surface. A compartmentalized triple-walled hull kept the Hudson Bay waters in check, and rumor had it the stadium housed over a thousand water pumps to control leaks ranging from a tiny pin-hole to the kind of gaping wound caused by a terrorist attack.

The massive lower bowl also rested below the surface, the top seats just peeking out above the water line. The second and third decks rested within a gleaming, crystal-clear dome that rose hundreds of feet into the air.

To the south sat the floating wonder of Hudson Bay City. Centuries ago, the city was built to house Human and Whitok workers harvesting untold amounts of oil and natural gas from deep below the surface. The high-tech boom town saw many decades of prosperous growth, until the natural resources started to run out about the same time demand for those resources dropped due to new technologies. City officials then used the platform's isolation as a trump card to win a contract for the Earth's second orbital elevator, the first having been built over the English Channel.

With the orbital elevator in place, Hudson Bay City blossomed. As one of two main hubs for interstellar commerce, Hudson Bay's economy transformed from drilling to shipping. City officials also lured tourist dollars by building the largest football stadium on Earth. The city's former isolation turned out to be its strongest asset — set in the middle of Hudson Bay, the stadium was easily defended from the airborne terrorist attacks that plagued many other Earth facilities.

Messal the Efficient scurried about, his helpers gathering the Krakens players.

"We are taking the tram to the stadium," Messal said, loud enough to be heard by forty-four Krakens and other team staff. "Please follow me."

The mass of players moved toward the underwater tram that would take them to the stadium, the area around them clear of other beings. Quentin noticed black-uniformed Human police all around the platform, each one armed, each one staring at the crowds of travelers with a look that promised severe trouble if anyone approached the football players. Fleeting shadows slashed across the floor — Creterakian soldiers flying through the complex, scouting for trouble.

Quentin smiled. Hudson Bay City had trouble, alright — trouble in the form of the Ionath Krakens. Trouble for the Texas Earthlings.

ONE LAST PRACTICE. One last practice before the biggest game of the year.

Quentin flowed through the plays as if he'd been created just for this one game, as if he'd been meticulously engineered to be a perfect quarterbacking machine. Lines of energy seemed to radiate from all his receivers. He saw them all in perfect clarity, delivering the ball in tight, rope-like spirals that arrived dead-center in passing windows no larger than ten inches across.

He had to be perfect. Yassoud had the potential to be a great running back, but he was at least two seasons away from that level. Even then, it was doubtful he'd match Mitchell Fayed's powerful, punishing style. The defense wasn't going to consider Yassoud a major threat — most of the defensive pressure would come via blitzing and extra defensive backs, probably both at the same time. The Earthlings would make the Krakens win the game on the ground.

Well, forget that. Quentin was going to beat them through the air, drive that ball so far down their throats they'd crap leather for a month. Everything had finally come together — he knew the moves, the speed, the tendencies of Hawick, Scarborough, Mezquitic, Denver, Milford and even Richfield. It wasn't just the wide receivers. He had Warburg and Kobayasho down cold, and fullback Tom Pareless was a hidden receiving weapon coming out of the backfield.

"Huuut-hut, hut!"

The ball slapped his hands and he dropped back, watching the Krakens defensive backs try in vain to cover the Krakens receivers. Quentin checked through, his mind racing at bio-computer speed: Hawick, covered; Scarborough, open in another ten yards; Warburg, open on a short hook — back to Scarborough, open, as he knew she would be. He fired the pass in a straight line, drilling Scarborough right on the money twenty-five yards downfield. Scarborough cut upfield, adding another six yards before Perth gave her a little tap — full contact was out, they didn't want any last-second injuries gumming up the works.

Next play: he dropped back and fired a long TD strike to Hawick, who was playing so well she now had to be considered one of the top five receivers in all of Tier Two.

Next play: short hook to Kobayasho, who cut upfield and went down easy on a light hit from John Tweedy.

Next play: Quentin dropped back, checked off his three receivers — all covered. He turned and threw the safety-valve pass to Yassoud, who hauled in the tight pass and cut upfield.

The snap was so loud it stopped everyone in their tracks.

Yassoud planted his right foot, and when he cut upfield, the snap rang out like a gunshot. He let out a yell, then fell, both hands holding his right knee before his body hit the ground.

The ball rolled free, wobbling to a slow stop.

Forty-three spirits collectively sank.

Doc floated onto the field. Yassoud writhed, his face a twisted mask of agony, his hands still clutched on his knee in white-knuckle desperation. A freak injury, from nothing more than making a sharp upfield cut.

"Pareless!" Hokor barked from his floating cart. "Move to tailback. Kopor, you're in at fullback."

Four days from the biggest game of the year, the last obstacle to Tier One ball, and the Ionath Krakens had just run out of tailbacks.

QUENTIN WALKED into Hokor's office and sat down. Hokor stared at the wall, his eye a translucent mauve. Quentin waited for the coach to acknowledge his presence, but the little Quyth Leader just sat there.

"Coach?" Quentin said lightly.

Hokor turned suddenly, his eye instantly going clear.

"Barnes," Hokor said. "I didn't see you there."

"It's okay, Coach. You strategizing?"

Hokor's fur ruffled once, then lay flat. "Strategizing, yes. Trying to find an answer for our lack of tailbacks."

"And?"

"There is no answer. You'll have to carry the game, Quentin — Pareless can run, but the Earthlings won't consider him a threat, nor should they. He's a great blocking back and good for short yardage but basically worthless as an open-field runner. They're going to blitz on every play."

Quentin sat for a second, considering his words. Hokor started staring at the wall again.

"There is one answer," Quentin said.

Hokor turned to look at him once again.

"Which is?"

"I'll play tailback."

Hokor kept staring.

"I've got the size and the speed," Quentin said. "I know the offense inside and out."

Hokor nodded. "Except for the small detail of who will play quarterback. You think Yitzhak can handle the Earthlings' defensive backs?"

"I'm not talking about Yitzhak," Quentin said.

Hokor looked blank for another second, then his eye flooded a deep black.

"Absolutely not! I will not have that *betrayer* run my team ever again."

Quentin leaned forward. "It's our only chance, Coach! You've got to let him back in."

"No! I'd rather lose than see him on the field again."

"Would you?" Quentin said. "Would you really rather *lose* than have him at quarterback? Because I'd rather do *anything* than lose! It doesn't matter what he did, Coach, all that matters is that we give ourselves the best possible chance to win tomorrow."

Hokor sat silent for a moment. "We won't even get a chance to practice."

"Who cares? It's Donald Pine! You remember him? The guy who won two Galaxy Bowls? It's not like he dropped off into re-tard-land in the one week he's been gone. Get him in here."

Hokor stared, his eye slowly fading from deep black to clear. "You would do this? You would give up the quarterback spot in the biggest game of the year? That's not like you, Barnes."

Quentin shrugged. "It's like me now, Coach. I want to win. I want to play Tier One ball."

"Do you *know* what you're doing? Do you understand the level of punishment a tailback takes in a game?"

"I'll do whatever it takes to reach Tier One."

Hokor said nothing. They stared at each other for a long min-ute, the seconds ticking away on some unseen, slow-motion clock. Finally, Hokor pressed a button on his desk. Messal the Efficient ap-peared as if he'd been standing just outside the door the entire time.

"How may I help you, *Shamakath*?"

"Find Donald Pine. Get him in here, immediately."

Transcript from the "Galaxy's Greatest Sports Show with Dan & Akbar & Tarat the Smasher"

DAN: Thanks, caller, great point about the reliability of Morn-ingstar. You know, Akbar, in all the commotion over Fayed's death, we've kind of overlooked the quality performances from some of the Krakens players. That and with the quarter-back controversy.

AKBAR: Well, luckily the quarterback controversy is over.

DAN: It is?

AKBAR: Of *course*, it is.

DAN: Okay, then who won it?

AKBAR: Barnes, for crying out loud.

TARAT: Barnes is starting against the Earthlings.

DAN: And that means the controversy is over?

TARAT: You saw him last week. Barnes was sensational.

DAN: Sure, against the Quyth Survivors. My mother-in-law could pass on the Quyth Survivors.

AKBAR: Come on, Dan, just admit it — Barnes is the man.

DAN: Are you insane? Are you completely brain-damaged? The kid couldn't cut it against the Warpigs, Pine had to come in and bail him out.

AKBAR: So he had one bad game …

DAN: He throws interceptions! He's the friggin' King of Interception-Land! And now you think he's the *man*?

AKBAR: But Pine's not even practicing with the team.

DAN: That's just a rumor.

TARAT: My sources say it's true, he's not practicing at all.

DAN: Then it's a head-game, don't you morons see that? Hokor is up to his old tricks again.

AKBAR: So what are you saying, Pine should start?

DAN: Damn right!

AKBAR: So he can choke again, like he has the last two years?

TARAT: He does seem to blow big games.

DAN: It's the playoffs! You know, where teams play other teams that are pretty damn good?

AKBAR: Oh, come on, Dan! Pine couldn't finish a hot dog without choking on it.

DAN: He won two Galaxy Bowls!

TARAT: Oh, not that again …

DAN: Screw you, Tarat! And screw you, Akbar! Next caller, dammit, next caller!

Playoffs Round Two:
Ionath Krakens (7-2) at Texas Earthlings (8-2)

The Krakens gathered in the dimly lit tunnel of Hudson Field. The 250,000 fans crowded into the stadium stamped their feet in unison, *boom-boom … boom-boom … boom-boom …* The walls and floor vibrated from the blood-thirsty beast's stomping.

Quentin felt nearly mad with the hunger of battle. He was stepping into it this time, taking the hand-to-hand combat into the field instead of sitting behind his wall of Ki linemen. The Earthlings would be coming after him relentlessly, literally trying to knock him out of the game. Cheap shots would abound. He knew damn well he was in for the beating of his life. But he was going to give as good as he got.

[INTRODUCING THE CHAMPIONS OF THE HUMAN CONFERENCE, PLEASE WELCOME THE TEXAAAAAAASSSSSS EARTHLINNNNNGS!]

The crowd's choreographed stomping evaporated, replaced by the nova-like roar of mostly Human fans. It was a hostile environment — broadcasters had estimated 200,000 of the fans were Texas Earthlings supporters, another 20,000 were Krakens faithful, and the remaining 30,000 were mostly fans from other teams in the Human Conference. All that added up to a nice home game for the Earthlings.

The Krakens swayed back and forth, one organism, one collective brain set on grabbing the prey and tearing it to shreds, tearing it apart with tooth and claw and tentacle and rasper and bare hands. Society slipped away to some abstract concept — for now there was only the battle, there was only the intense, primitive *pleasure* of destroying another sentient being.

High One help those who stood in the Krakens' way.

[AND NOW, THE CHAMPIONS OF THE QUYTH IRRADIATED CONFERENCE, THE IONAAAAAAAATH KRAAAAAAAAAAAAAAKEEEEEEEEEEENS!]

Quentin waited for Pine to call out to the team, to rally them into one cohesive, violent machine ready to crush and to punish and, if need be, to kill.

But instead of his trademark leader's voice, Pine said only one soft sentence.

"Quentin, it's your team now, lead us out."

Forty-three sets of eyes turned to look at Quentin, who wore a warm-up jacket over his uniform. Pine's words filled Quentin with raw emotion. It was *his* team now, now and forever. Pine had passed the torch in full view of his teammates.

He wasn't a rookie anymore. He was the battle-hardened leader of this team, the general who led his soldiers into war. He'd fought and bled with these beings, won and lost with these beings, felt ultimate joy and faced the ultimate sadness. Somewhere during the season, and he didn't know where, Quentin Barnes had become a man.

The team waited for Quentin to speak. He quickly looked from player to player, taking the time to measure up each Krakens' emotions. They were all ready to go.

Instead of talking, he slipped off his warm-up jacket to show his orange jersey. Underneath, instead of his number 10, the black numbers with orange trim read 47.

Fayed's jersey.

"Screw the Earthlings," Quentin said.

A brief pause, then a barbaric roar so raw and loud it made the 250,000-being crowd sound weak by comparison. The Krakens shot out of the tunnel like the fiery breath of some legendary dragon. They raced onto the surface, which was made up of a thick, emerald-green plant marked with bright white stripes and numbers. It was finer and softer than Micovi's Carsengi Grass.

Quentin's mind raced, not with thoughts, but a *lack* of thoughts, a mental blankness created by a primitive violence that suffused his every last atom. He walked out onto the center of the field for the coin toss, Hawick on his left, John Tweedy on his right. A zebe waited at the 50-yard line, right in the middle of the multi-colored GFL logo painted on the lush green grass. On the other side of the zebe waited their enemy: Case "Hot Pepper" Johanson, the Earthlings quarterback, and Chok-Oh-Thilit, their All-Pro defensive tackle. The Earthlings wore bright-red jerseys with blue letters and silver trim, blue leg armor with silver piping and silver helmets decorated with a blue-trimmed white star.

Johanson stared at Quentin. "What's with the number change, boy?"

Quentin just stared back. Johanson had played three seasons of Tier One ball with the Earthlings before their fall from grace last season down into Tier Two.

"Don't you know it's bad luck to wear a dead man's number?" Johanson asked, his face twisted into a half-smile/half-sneer.

"Keep talking, douche bag," Tweedy growled. "*You're* wearing a dead man's number, you just don't know it yet."

JOHANSON THROWS LIKE A GIRL scrolled across Tweedy's forehead.

Johanson's sneer faded, briefly, but it faded nonetheless. The hotshot quarterback's attentions turned from Quentin to John Tweedy, who just stared and grinned his I'm-not-quite-sane grin. Johanson didn't say anything else.

"Krakens are the visiting team," the zebe said, his voice amplified by the stadium loudspeakers so that it cracked like the sound of the High One himself. "Who will call the toss for the Krakens?"

"She will," Quentin said, pointing at Hawick. She had been given that duty, and she shook with an intense fervor. Quentin didn't understand how the coin toss factored into the Sklorno's strange religion, but apparently it was an honor that surpassed even the cathartic thrill of catching a long touchdown pass.

"This is heads," the zebe said, showing a metal coin with a picture of a Creterakian head. "This is tails." He flipped the coin to show stylized planet — Creterak.

"Call it in the air," the zebe said, and he tossed the coin.

"Heads!" Hawick screamed, more rapture than excitement. The coin bounced on the grass, flipped three times, then landed flat.

Heads.

Hawick collapsed and lay on the ground, quivering.

"Krakens win the toss," said the zebe, echoed by the loudspeakers. "Do you wish to receive or defer?"

"We want the ball," Quentin said.

"A stay of execution," Tweedy said, staring straight at Johanson, who no longer looked as cocky.

Quentin and Tweedy picked up Hawick and carried her to the sidelines. Quentin let out a slow, controlled breath. He wouldn't have long to wait — one quick kickoff, and he'd be on the field, squaring off against Chok-Oh-Thilit and the other Earthlings defenders.

"*Ohhhhhhhhhhh,*" the crowd started the low, tribal, pre-kick-off chant. Adrenaline poured through Quentin's veins, so thick it might have spilled out of his pores and dripped onto the green grass at his feet. He tried to breathe slow but found it difficult — his breath came in shallow, ragged gasps. He blinked rapidly, gritting his teeth, waiting for the coming battle.

"OHHHHHHHHH …"

A hand on his shoulder. Donald Pine.

"Relax, kid," Pine said, his smile easy and genuine. "We're going to do this together. Once you get that first hit, you'll be fine."

Quentin nodded, then turned back to the field.

"AHHHHHHH-*AH!*"

The ball sailed through the air. Richfield jogged back past the goal line, her eyes fixed on the tiny brown dot in the sky.

"Just take a knee," Pine said, more to himself than anyone else.

The ball descended as the Krakens' special teamers formed up into the wall.

Thunk, the ball dropped down in Richfield's arms at the very back edge of the end zone. She looked up, hesitated for half a second, then ripped forward at a dead sprint.

"No!" Pine said.

Quentin just watched.

Earthlings "wall-breakers" smashed into the Krakens' wedge at the 10-yard line. Bodies flew in all directions. Richfield ran up into the wall and disappeared among the carnage.

"Well, there goes field posi —"

Pine's sentence died on his lips as Richfield popped out the other side, untouched and moving at top speed. In the blink of an eye, she passed the 30, then the 40 and moved across mid-field.

"Well slap my face and call me Sally," Pine said.

Sklorno Earthlings took deep angles of pursuit. Serj Tanakian, the Earthlings' kicker, ran upfield, trying to cut down Richfield's running angles. She ran right at him, cut once to the left, then to the right, then to the left again. Tanakian matched the first move, stumbled on the second and fell face-first on the third.

Richfield shot by him. She sprang ten feet into the air as a Sklorno defender leapt for her feet and became the second player in a row to hit the grass empty handed. One last red-and-blue clad Sklorno angled between Richfield and the end zone. She didn't cut this time, she reached out a hard tentacle as the two players met at the ten, "stiffarming" her foe. They ran side-by-side for another five yards, then the defender — knocked off balance by the stiffarm — fell to the ground.

Richfield went into the end zone standing up.

Quentin looked back downfield, but there were no flags.

[TOUCHDOWN, KRAKENS! RICHFIELD SCORES ON A 102-YARD KICKOFF RETURN, A NEW PLAYOFF RECORD!]

The extra-point team ran onto the field. The Krakens had just taken a huge jump, but Quentin found it hard to be excited — he had to wait for the first hit, and he had to pee.

Morningstar knocked in the extra point. First play of the game, Krakens 7, Earthlings 0.

Quentin tried to draw a full breath while the kickoff team took the field. Morningstar nailed a low squib kick — Hokor didn't want a long return that might give the Earthlings momentum.

Utgard, the Earthlings' kick returner, handled the line-drive kick and brought the ball back to the 28 before being brought down.

John Tweedy & Company took the field. As he looked at the defense — Tweedy, Virak the Mean, Choto the Bright, Michnik and Khomeni, Mai-An-Ihkole and Per-Ah-Yet — Quentin felt a pang of sorrow for Johanson. Those seven players had thought of nothing for the last week other than the total destruction of the Earthlings' quarterback. Quentin figured the Earthlings defense had probably done the same thing, preparing for him — how would they react when he lined up at tailback, and Donald Pine took the snaps?

The Earthlings started out running, a sweep to Pookie Chang. Virak the Mean drove through two blockers and brought Chang down for a one-yard loss. Johanson tried a simple out pass on the next snap, but Berea broke up the play.

On third and long, Tweedy crowded the line, showing blitz all the way. Johanson dropped back — Tweedy's blitz drew the fullback's block, and Khomeni broke through almost immediately. Johanson felt the pressure and calmly threw the ball away.

Three and out.

Quentin had to pee so bad he could barely stand up straight.

"Here we go, kid," Pine said as he pulled on his helmet. "It's show time."

Richfield vibrated with anticipation as the punt sailed through the air, but it had excellent hang-time and she was forced to call a fair catch at the Krakens' 35.

Quentin and the offense ran onto the field for the first time.

"JUST WHAT IN the *heck* is going on here, Masara?"

"I don't know, Chick, but it looks to me like Donald Pine is calling the play in the huddle."

"But I thought Pine wasn't even *practicing* with the team."

"That's what everyone was told, Chick. But Krakens Coach Hokor the Hookchest and Earthlings' Coach Pata the Calculating are two of the trickiest strategists in the game. Word has it that Pata the Calculating has something up his many sleeves — he wouldn't allow any media in his practices for the last two weeks. And as for Pine not practicing with the team, maybe Hokor was just being disingenuous."

"Hey, now, easy on the big words, Masara!"

"It's not a *big* word, it's a very common —"

"Hold on there, Vocabulistic Vinnie! The Krakens are lining up for the play, and — what the *heck*, that's Mitchell Fayed's number in the backfield."

"Someone get us a close-up of that guy!"

"Well, grease me up like a well-used sock monkey, Masara, that's *Quentin Barnes* at tailback!"

"Is he crazy, Chick? The defense will tear him apart!"

"Well, this makes about as much sense as a Sklorno receiver walking unclothed into a bedbug convention, but it's definitely a new wrinkle that I don't think the Earthlings are ready for."

"The defense looks a bit anxious, Chick."

"That they do, Masara, like the mother of three hot triplets who just realized her jailbait daughters are well into puberty and drawing the attention of the void-bike gang next door."

"Chick, take it easy …"

"Sorry, Masara, sorry, folks at home, here go the Krakens in I-formation …"

QUENTIN LIGHTLY RESTED his hands on his slightly bent knees. He stood directly behind Tom Pareless, who crouched in a three-point stance. Donald Pine looked down the left side of the line, then the right, barking out signals.

"Blue, sixteen! Bluueeee, sixteen!"

The play was an off-tackle left — away from Chok-Oh-Thilit, a strategy the Krakens would try to follow for most of the day. No point in wasting time, Quentin had to get it over with if he was going to be effective.

"Hut-HUT!"

Pine turned as Pareless drove to the left. Quentin followed him, his eyes fixed on the ball held in Pine's outstretched hands.

Don't fumble don't fumble don't fumble —

Quentin raised his right elbow high, the back of his hand on his chest. His left hand rested against his lower stomach, thumb forward — the way he'd been taught to take a handoff. Pine stabbed the ball toward his stomach, holding it so that the ball's points were parallel to Quentin's body. Quentin's left hand cupped the bottom of the ball as his right elbow *snapped* down, trapping the ball between his thick forearms. Only after he felt the ball was snugly in place did he look up to run.

Pareless pushed through the hole and notched a solid fit on the linebacker. Quentin ran straight into the hole. Like some evil magical portal, the hole instantly vanished. Defenders appeared in front, on his right and left — Quentin put his head down and drove forward.

WhamWHAM!

Two hits in rapid succession, one from the left, the next from the right, as the defensive tackle and then the middle linebacker smashed into him. Quentin's right arm went instantly numb, but he held onto the ball as the two big bodies dragged him down. He wound up on his back, looking straight up into the face of his countryman Alonzo Castro.

"What in the void could you be thinking, boy?" Alonzo asked, a look of concern on his face. "You need to get your tail back behind that big offensive line of yours, or you're going to get hurt."

Quentin's right arm felt all tingly and hot — not in any shape to push Alonzo away — so he laid still and tried to play it cool.

"Good to see you again," Quentin said. "But if anybody's going to get hurt, it's going to be you when I run you over."

Alonzo laughed, not an evil laugh, but as if an old friend had told him a good joke. He stood and reached out a hand.

"We'll see about that," Alonzo said as he helped Quentin off the ground.

Quentin ran back to the huddle. He could barely move his arm, but the tingling feeling was already fading away. If that was the best hit Alonzo had to offer, Quentin thought he might make it through the game after all. He ran to the back of the huddle to stand in the tailback's spot, thinking how strange it was to watch someone else call the play.

"Quentin!" Pine barked. "Take it easy when I hand you the freakin' ball, you almost took my hand off."

"Oh ... sorry."

"Don't sweat it. You feel better now?"

The question confused Quentin for just a second, then he realized the butterflies were gone and he no longer had to pee.

"Yeah," he said with a grin. "I guess I do."

Pine nodded, just once, then his eager eyes swept the offensive players. "Okay, they're already confused by Quentin, and they'll be looking for him, so we go play-action right, toward Chok-Oh-Thilit, hot-pass to Warburg."

"At least *someone* will throw me the ball," Warburg said.

"Shut up, racist," Pine said. "Keep your mouth shut in my huddle, got it?"

Warburg glared but nodded.

"Okay, on two, on two, ready ..."

Quentin lined up in the I-formation once again. Pine barked out the signals. The linemen smashed together. Quentin drove to the right, left hand on his chest, left elbow high. Pine stabbed the ball toward his stomach again, and Quentin brought his forearms together, except this time there was no ball at his stomach. He put his head down and leaned forward, charging into the line. He ran just outside Wen-Eh-Deret's right side: the hit came from his right, enough to spin him around, then a freight train smashed into his chest. The world spun in a wild circle, and something hit him hard in the left shoulder — it took him a full second before he realized that last hit had been the ground.

Quentin gazed up into the black eyes of Chok-Oh-Thilit, who looked down at him the way a spider looks at a bug caught in its web.

Alonzo's grinning head appeared next to Chok-Oh-Thilit's. "Don't he just hit like a *tank*?"

"My ... gramma ... hits harder," Quentin said, although his voice cracked just a bit when he said it. Alonzo helped him up once again.

In the huddle the Krakens were excited and eager for the next play. Quentin realized he had no idea if the play had been successful — he looked at the scoreboard: first-and-10 on the Earthlings' 44.

Warburg stood and looked back at Quentin. "So *that's* what it's like to catch a pass."

Pine reached out and slapped Warburg hard in the head. "Dammit, Warburg, shut your pie-hole!" Warburg turned and bent, leaning over in standard huddle position so the players behind him could see Pine.

"Okay, now we go for the throat," Pine said. "B-set, twenty-two post. Hawick, I'm putting the ball in the air whether you're covered or not. You go get it or I'll *never* throw you another pass as long as you live."

A silence filled the huddle. Quentin just stared, amazed at Pine's ruthlessness — it would have been like telling a Holy Man that if he didn't catch the ball, he'd been damned to hell by St. Stewart himself. Hawick started to shake.

"Shake all you want, sissy girl, every defensive back on the field is going to know it's coming to you when I drop back, and it doesn't matter — you don't catch the ball, and you're excommunicated from the Church of Donald Pine, do you understand?"

Hawick's raspers rolled and unrolled involuntarily, over and over again.

"Do you understand?"

"Yes," Hawick chirped.

Pine nodded once. "On three, on three, ready ..."

The Krakens lined up in a pro-set, Quentin five yards behind Pine and two yards to his left, Tom Pareless five yards behind Pine and two yards to his right. Warburg lined up at left tight end and Scarborough split left. Wide right, all alone, stood Hawick, still shaking. The defensive backs keyed on Hawick's shake — Toronto called a defensive audible. The backs shifted: Toronto moved up one yard off Hawick for woman-to-woman coverage, while Volgograd lined up ten yards behind her — Hawick was facing double coverage.

"Red, twelve!" Pine shouted. "Red, *twelve.*"

Alonzo jumped forward after the call, lining up over the left guard and showing blitz. If he came, he was Quentin's responsibility. Alonzo stood quickly and pointed at Quentin.

"Here it comes, pretty-boy! Here comes the hurt!" Alonzo

squatted, fists shaking with adrenaline rage, eyes wide as a nocturnal predator.

"Hut-huuuut … *hut!*"

Pine took the snap and dropped back smooth as silk. Quentin stepped forward, with one step to the left, legs bent and hands up in front of him. The left defensive tackle drove toward the center as Alonzo took a small step back and moved quickly to his right, away from center.

A linebacker stunt, Quentin thought.

The slashing defensive tackle drew blocks from both Sho-Do Thikit, the left guard, and Bud-O-Shwek, the center. Warburg blocked the defensive end. Alonzo stepped up through the sudden opening, coming free and unobstructed like a rabid bearcat.

Block him or Pine goes down, Quentin thought quickly as he stepped up and leaned forward. Alonzo bent forward at the exact same moment, bringing his right arm forward in a vicious undercut. Quentin recognized the rip-move at the last second — Alonzo would power by his right side and have a free shot at Pine. Quentin lunged to his right, desperately trying to correct his mistake. Alonzo hit him with all of his considerable strength, driving his rip move from his feet through his thick thighs to his powerful arm, all with a strong twist of the hips to make the move as concussive as a heavyweight's knockout uppercut. Quentin was off-balance from his desperate dive, and without his feet planted, he had no strength to counter the move — Alonzo's forearm hit him under the chin, lifting him off his feet and knocking him backward. Quentin saw nothing but bright lights and felt a quick tug on his chin before his helmet spun through the air like a decapitated head. He landed on his butt and rolled backward, feet-over-head. The world whirled around him, a blur of green grass and red leg armor. He felt a foot kick him in the ribs, then the weight of another player landing on top of him. Quentin rolled backward one more time, then lay flat — there was a ringing in his ears.

But there was also a roar.

A roar of the crowd.

Suddenly a hand grabbed his, yanking him to his feet.

"Great block, kid!" Pine said, shaking Quentin's shoulders as he screamed in his face. "We got 'em!"

"Wha …" Quentin stammered.

"Touchdown, kid, *touchdown!*"

Quentin felt something in his mouth. He spit — his front right tooth landed in a clot of blood, red-and-white on green.

That thing is never going to heal right, Quentin thought as he limped off the field.

"THAT'S GOT TO BE the greatest catch I've ever seen, Masara!"

"Amazing! Amazing! Let's see the replay on this."

"Hawick is double-covered from the get-go, Masara. Watch the move she puts on Toronto to get clear, but then she's still got Volgograd in woman-to-woman. She's totally covered."

"But if she's double-covered, why would Pine throw that ball, Chick? He just put it up for grabs!"

"He knows his players, Masara. He's always known his players. Watch Hawick go up in the air. Check the live analysis, Masara — the computer says she jumped *twenty-three feet* in the air."

"She jumped like her life depended on it."

"Something like that, Masara. But Volgograd is known for her leaping ability, and she actually got a hand on the ball. But watch Hawick rip it away from her! She went after that ball like a hooker diving after a tight-wad trick!"

"Chick! For crying out loud—"

"Sorry, Masara, and sorry, folks at home, but watch her come down with it — she hit the ground upside down and *still* held onto the ball."

"And there you have it, the High Priestess of the Church of Donald Pine puts the Krakens up by two touchdowns, and we're still in the first quarter."

QUENTIN WOKE with a start, the smell of something acidic and horrible filling his nostrils. He twisted his face to avoid the stench, which seemed to follow his nose. He blinked a few times and saw that Doc was waving something in his face.

"Knock it off!" Quentin said, pushing Doc's tentacle away. He looked around. He was on the sidelines. "What happened?"

"You don't remember?"

Quentin started to shake his head and realized too late just how much that hurt. "No, I don't."

"You ran a sweep right and tried to cut back — Chok-Oh-Thilit beat his block and laid you out."

"A sweep right?"

"Yes," Doc said.

"When?"

"First drive of the second quarter."

"Second ... the first quarter is over?"

Doc floated up to look Quentin in the eye. "You don't remember the first quarter?"

Quentin shrugged. "Some of it."

"What's the last thing you remember?"

"Hawick's touchdown."

"Quentin, you carried the ball five times for sixteen yards after that. You don't remember?"

Quentin thought for a second, then shrugged. "Nope, not a thing." His head throbbed as if a miniature Ki were in his brain, whipping jointed limbs to and fro in a dance of destructed gray matter. It felt like someone was jabbing a screwdriver into the right side of his jaw. He gingerly touched there — no screwdriver, at least, but he couldn't be certain about the miniature Ki. The tip of his tongue played with the space where his missing right front tooth should have been.

"I don't feel so good."

"How many tentacle tips am I holding up?"

Quentin squinted. At first he saw four tentacle tips, then his vision cleared and the tentacle tips blended together into a solid shape.

"Two."

"Good," Doc said, patting Quentin on the shoulder pad. "You're ready to go back in." Doc floated away.

"That's what you think," Quentin muttered, looking at the ground. He definitely did not feel ready to go back in. He noticed the right side of his orange jersey was stained with blood. Only then did he notice a tingling along his ribs. Left hand told the story: right-side rib armor ripped half away, temporarily patched with bulkhead tape. He slid his fingers under the shoddy repair job and felt the familiar texture of a nanocyte bandage.

He saw a tiny pair of yellow-furred feet and looked up into the eye of Hokor the Hookchest.

"Great job out there, Barnes," Hokor said. "You ready for more?"

Quentin nodded. Just once, because nodding *yes* hurt as much as shaking no. "Just give me the ball, Coach."

"Good, good! Well, you're going to get the ball now. We're up 14-0 so we want to keep the ball on the ground as much as possible and chew up clock. You ready to take some hits?"

Quentin raised an eyebrow. "I haven't taken some already?"

"Whatever you do, *hold onto the ball*." Hokor walked back to the edge of the field. The Krakens defense was on the field, but Quentin didn't have the energy to get up and watch. Quentin took a deep breath and let out a heavy sigh — he had at least one more half of this to go.

KRAKENS FANS were scattered around the stadium, with most sitting in the north end zone. The south end zone, however, was the sole domain of die-hard Texas Earthlings fans, dressed in a sea of red, blue and white. As the Krakens lined up at their own 3-yard line, the fans roared as if a thousand mouths were pressed right up against Quentin's ear.

Pine's shoulders shook as he called out the signals, but Quentin couldn't hear him. The Earthlings fans wanted a break, something *good* to happen for their team, which was down 14-0.

Quentin watched carefully — Pine's head bobbed down when he said "Hut!" and the snap was on three. He had to time it right. There was no room for mistakes this close to your own goal line.

One bob.

Alonzo cheated up the line, his eyes locked on Quentin.

Bob-*bob*.

Even as Quentin ran right to take the handoff, he saw Chok-Oh-Thilit driving inward, a Ki tank chewing up flesh. Wen-E-Deret tried to stop him but suddenly bent backward at a funny angle, multi-jointed limbs spamming in a symphony of pain. Chok-Oh-Thilit roared through the line, already a yard past the goal line. Quentin concentrated on taking the handoff. Once he felt the ball firmly in his arms, he put his head down and drove forward. It was like running into a swinging 600-pound wrecking ball. Every atom in his body jarred backward. He couldn't see. He felt arms wrapping around him. Quentin spun to the right, his free hand viciously punching away — it hit some armor and glanced off. Arms tried to drag him down, but he kept pumping his legs, running with a pure animal fury — like *hell* he'd be tackled for a safety. He felt the Ki arms slip away, and he cut upfield — only to feel a shoulder pad drive deep into his stomach, and short-but-powerful Human arms wrapping around his waist. Air shot out of his stomach and his body jarred backward, every atom shaking from the impact. His feet came off the ground, and he landed on his back, head *snapping* into the turf. Whistles blew. The crowd roared.

He gasped for air, but nothing came in or out. He opened his eyes and looked at the ground. It was painted in Earthlings' red.

Safety.

Krakens 14, Earthlings 2.

Alonzo pushed off him, looked to the sky and screamed a primitive roar of triumph. He looked down at Quentin and smiled.

"Good thing I'm a *little small* for a linebacker, or that hit might have actually hurt you."

Quentin sill couldn't breathe. He weakly lifted his right hand and flipped Alonzo the bird. Alonzo laughed just before his defensive teammates swarmed over him, shouting excitedly in at least four different languages.

• • •

DESPITE DOC'S URGING, Quentin refused to lie down. He knew that if he did, he wouldn't get up. Not ever again. He'd just sleep for a long, long time. But Doc wouldn't put IVs in him if he stood, so he compromised and sat through Hokor's halftime adjustments.

"This is the game we wanted to play," Hokor said.

Quentin held out his right arm, allowing Doc to inject an IV needle. He watched the pointed needle slide into his skin but didn't feel a thing.

"Fluids," Doc said quietly. "You're dehydrated."

"The defense has shut them down," Hokor said. "No points, can we keep it up?"

"Yes!" shouted Tweedy. "Johanson talking garbage! I say the only way that loser gets off the field at the end of the game is on a stretcher!"

The Ki linemen let out a roar of approval, banging their forearms against their chest armor.

Another needle, this time in his right arm.

"Blood," Doc said. "You lost a lot from those cuts on your ribs. We need to get your blood count back to normal."

"Offensively, we're doing okay," Hokor said. "Aka-Na-Tak, I know you're facing Chok-Oh-Thilit, but you've got to *step up*. You've got to play above your level. You can't let him come through."

Wen-E-Deret had been hurt on the play that gave the Earthlings a safety. After preliminary treatment on the sidelines, Doc had carted him to the locker room, and from there a grav-ambulance had rushed him off to Hudson Bay Hospital. Someone had mumbled something about a severed nervous cord, a very serious Ki injury, but the team didn't talk about it. After the game, there would be plenty of time to either visit him in the hospital or the funeral home.

"I know you can stop him, Aka-Na-Tak," Pine said. The veteran quarterback looked like he'd been mugged all over again. After Wen-E-Deret's injury, Chok-Oh-Thilit had sacked Pine three times, each one more devastating than the last. Aka-Na-Tak, a backup tackle, just couldn't handle the all-pro's savage defensive strength. "You've *got* to stop him. The honor of your family is riding on this."

Aka-Na-Tak suddenly sat up straighter.

"You know what he told me after the last sack?" Pine said. "He put his face right against mine and said *dijo malach we yokot*."

All the Ki in the room shuddered with instant anger. All eyes turned to Aka-Na-Tak, who stood stock-still.

"What's that mean?" Quentin whispered to Doc.

"It means 'your lineman is my girlfriend,' roughly."

Quentin nodded slowly, appreciating the severity of the comment.

"Can you believe he said that?" Pine said. "Although, if you look at the beating I took on *your* missed blocks, it's hard to argue with him."

Suddenly all eyes turned away from Aka-Na-Tak, as if everyone in the room felt embarrassed for him.

Hokor commanded everyone's attention. "Yes, well, anyway, let's get on with the halftime adjustments."

Doc slid away to tend to other players, leaving the needles sticking out of Quentin's arms. Messal the Efficient ran up, a new set of rib-armor in his hands. The Quyth Worker pulled away the blue bandages covering Quentin's wounds. They weren't quite healed yet, but they didn't have time to wait.

Hokor walked through offensive adjustments, and Quentin tried to pay attention. But all he could hear, really, were the words *we're going to run the ball more*, repeated over and over again.

THE KRAKENS WEREN'T the only ones making halftime adjustments.

The Earthlings received the second-half kickoff and ran it back to their own 37. They lined up in something that Quentin had never seen before — two tight ends, with three running backs lined up side-by-side, about five yards behind Johanson.

"Well, ain't that something," Yitzhak murmured. "The Wing-T."

Krakens defenders shouted to each other, already nervous

about the new formation. The Earthlings hadn't run this formation, not once, all season long.

The ball snapped. Quentin watched Johanson hand off to the Pookie Chang. Chang's big arms folded over the ball. He plowed into the line and disappeared into a pile of bodies.

But there was no whistle.

Johanson still had the ball. He'd faked the handoff to Chang — he put it into the hands of tailback Peter Lowachee, who folded his arms around the ball the same way Chang had. Johanson "rode" the handoff, seemingly holding onto the ball as Lowachee cut into the off-tackle hole. Johanson then ran to the sidelines, pretending to carry the ball.

Every play is a triple-threat, Quentin thought. *Fullback, tailback or quarterback. And the way they fold over the ball, you can't see if they have it or not.*

Most of the Krakens' defense had bought the fullback's dive, leaving plenty of room for Lowachee, who broke through the line and cut upfield. After a half of watching running back Pookie Chang's big body rumble along, the fleet-footed Lowachee was like poetry in motion. At only 210 pounds he was a featherweight, but man could he *move*.

Lowachee chewed up fifteen yards before Perth brought him down at the Krakens' 48.

The Earthlings lined up in the Wing-T again, and this time Pookie Chang took the handoff. He popped through a tiny hole next to the center, moving forward at top speed. Tweedy had been watching Lowachee and hadn't come forward — Chang hit like a big-shouldered boulder, knocking Tweedy flat on his back. Chang stumbled on the fallen linebacker, giving Virak the Mean time to drag him down after an eight-yard gain.

The next play saw the same thing. The linemen and linebackers stepped up to stop Chang, but he didn't have it. Defensive backs converged on Lowachee as Johanson rode him through the line. Lowachee went down under Perth and Berea — but *he* didn't have the ball either. Suddenly Johanson was cutting up the sidelines, all alone. Stockbridge came from the far side of the field, her speed easily surpassing Johanson's. Instead of taking the hit, Johanson casually stepped out of bounds after a 37-yard gain.

"Uh-oh," Yitzhak said. "I bet it's been two centuries since anyone ran this offense. This could be trouble."

The Earthlings lined up at the Krakens' 3-yard line, once again in the two tight-end Wing-T. The Krakens' goal line defense packed around the line, shifting here and there, still not sure how to set up to stop the new offensive attack. The ball snapped, and Johanson went through the cycle: put ball in Chang's arms, put ball in Lowachee's arms and ride him in, then run to the sidelines. Quentin tried to find the ball. Chang went down. Lowachee's fake was bad — Johanson still had the ball, running for the corner of the end zone. Perth closed on him like a black-and-orange-and-white blur — but Johanson pulled up and threw a light pass to Lowachee, who had released into the flat, behind the streaking Perth.

Wide open.

Touchdown, Earthlings.

Extra point good, Krakens 14, Earthlings 9.

ON THIRD AND 11 at the Krakens' 22, Aka-Na-Tak went down again, Chok-Oh-Thilit came through again, and Pine was sacked again. He came up bleeding from the right cheek, madder than Quentin had ever seen him. Pine reared back and threw the ball with all his strength — at Chok-Oh-Thilit, who was only five yards away. The ball smashed into Chok-Oh-Thilit's helmet, then bounced high into the air.

Chok-Oh-Thilit turned and roared and ran at Pine, who snarled and drove forward, fists swinging. Whistles blew. The crowd roared. Quentin jumped on Chok-Oh-Thilit's back. Zebes swarmed in as players attacked each other. The game was suddenly a sea of legs and tentacles and raspers and red-blue-silver-orange-black-white.

Whistles shrieked, players swore in four different languages. Something hit Quentin in the back, right at the kidneys. He rolled off Chok-Oh-Thilit and lay on the ground. Pine had his helmet off and was swinging it like a war hammer, blood coursing down his face, his white eyes wide against his red-stained blue skin.

More black and white. Zebes poured out of the woodwork, at least fifteen of them, flying in with stun-sticks. Quentin heard the *zap* of the sticks, smelled burnt ozone and saw players dropping. Chok-Oh-Thilit fell from a dozen blasts, Pine only needed two.

When it was over, the Krakens' punt team came onto the field. Fifteen yards back, of course, for Pine's personal foul.

THE DAMN WING-T was like watching a living puzzle box. It was a magician's offense, sleight-of-hand and loathsome chicanery. Who had the ball? Pookie Chang? Peter Lowachee? Case Johanson? Was it a run? Was it a pass?

The Earthlings marched downfield again, chewing up five and six yards a pop. The Krakens started to adjust, but the vanishing-ball trick had them tackling the wrong player more often than not. Chang for six. Lowachee for ten. Pass for fifteen. Chang for another four.

Twelve plays and seven minutes after the Krakens' post-fight punt, Pookie Chang carried it in from four yards out to give the Earthlings the lead. Without missing a beat, they again lined up in the Wing-T for the two-point conversion. The Krakens' defense still didn't know how to stop that offense — Pookie Chang slipped through a trap-block and walked into the end zone standing up.

Earthlings 17, Krakens 14.

QUENTIN FOLLOWED Tom Pareless into the hole. Pareless nailed a stumbling Alonzo, putting the linebacker into the ground. Quentin hurdled them both and tried to cut outside. Kipir the Assassin, the outside linebacker, dove for him and grabbed his jersey, standing Quentin almost straight up as he tried to move forward. Jurong, the free safety, came in untouched like an armor-piercing bullet. She smashed into Quentin's ribs. He heard a *crack* from his pads and another *snap* from inside his body.

He'd never been stabbed in the ribs, but he knew it had to feel just like this.

Quentin lay on the ground, big hands clutched tightly around the football. They could kill him, but they couldn't make him fumble. His eyes scrunched tight with the agony in his side, and he waited for the med-sled to cart him off the field.

Someone kicked his leg.

Quentin opened his eyes, squinting through the pain, to look up at Donald Pine.

"Get up, loser."

Pine still had a blue bandage on his cheek. The cut had been deep, and despite constant application of nanocytes, it had opened up two more times. The front of his orange jersey was a sheet of red.

"I said get up, you pansy."

Quentin tried to blink away the pain. He had broken ribs. *Broken ribs*.

"I've got broken ribs," Quentin said.

"And I care," Pine said. "Now get up, rookie, and back in the huddle or I will kick you in those same ribs until you do."

Quentin stared at Pine. He hated Pine. He had thought Pine was his friend, but he'd been crazy to think that. He'd always hated Don Pine. Don Pine was a loser.

Quentin slowly hauled himself back to a standing position and followed Pine to the Krakens' huddle.

THE FOURTH QUARTER started just as the Earthlings took over. They kept moving the ball, seemingly at will. Chang for five. Lowachee for seven. Chang for another four.

Then it happened.

Johanson put the ball in Chang's belly as the thick running back slammed into the line. He then put it in Lowachee's arms, and rode the fleet-footed running back through the hole. Quentin had adjusted to the offense and now saw the pulling guard running past the off-tackle hole, toward the outside — that mean Johanson had the ball.

And Quentin wasn't the only one to see it.

Virak the Mean saw it, too.

The Earthlings' pulling guard moved forward to block Virak, but the Quyth Warrior dropped to all-fours and stutter-stepped left, then right, then left again, using his low center of gravity to create the impossible lateral motion of a truly talented Quyth Warrior. The guard matched the first two moves, but stumbled off-balance and Virak shot past. He came free with a good five yards to pick up speed. Johanson tried to cut inside to avoid the reaching arms of Mum-O-Killowe — he didn't see Virak until it was too late.

Virak threw himself forward like a flying switchblade, his helmet *smashing* into Johanson's stomach. The quarterback went down hard. The ball popped free, but Pookie Chang hopped on it.

Whistles blew. Johanson got up ... slowly. He limped back to the huddle, barely able to walk on his right leg.

THE EARTHLINGS TRIED running the Wing-T a few more times, but everyone knew the limping Johanson wasn't going to carry the ball. With him removed as a threat, the Krakens' defense concentrated on Chang and Lowachee. As the clock ticked past 8:00, the Earthlings punted the ball away and wouldn't run the Wing-T again for the rest of the game.

PINE GOT UP slowly after his fifth sack. He was bleeding again, this time from a cut on his arm. At least he got up — Aka-Na-Tak still lay on the ground, a limp tubular body with limp multi-jointed arms. A thin, recurring squirt of black blood jetted up from his back, like a little on-off geyser of oil. Chok-Oh-Thilit had destroyed his second right tackle of the game.

After starting on their own 15, the Krakens had put together a 30-yard drive, but on third-and-long Chok-Oh-Thilit smashed through Aka-Na-Tak and dragged Pine down. The Krakens offense ran off the field to be replaced by the punt team as Doc's med-sled floated Aka-Na-Tak off the field. There were only five minutes left to play. The defense had to come up with one more stop.

THE DEFENSE HELD. The Krakens got the ball back with 2:12 to play in the game, ball on their own 35.

Quentin sat at the bottom of the pile, face-down, the football pressing into his diaphragm, so much weight on top of him that he couldn't draw in a full breath. Not that that was necessarily a bad thing — when he took a full breath, his ribs screamed and his chest ached with the effort. Another assassination attempt by Chok-Oh-Thilit had torn away Quentin's second set of rib armor, along with more of his skin and blood — Doc said not to worry, though ... he'd be fine after an hour in the rejuv tank. The injury wouldn't stop Quentin from finishing the game. Gosh. Thanks, Doc.

Cay-Oh-Kiware was the third Krakens guard to face Chok-Oh-Thilit, and he wasn't doing much better than had Wen-E-Deret or Aka-Na-Tak.

The weight lifted from Quentin's back one chunk at a time, until the last player rolled off. Quentin pushed his way up. He didn't want to get up, he wanted to lay there, maybe take a nice nap. But he'd be damned before he'd show those Earthlings one more ounce of weakness or pain.

"How you holding up, champ?" Alonzo asked. "It's not going to stop, you know. Maybe you should just stay down."

"Then you better quit fooling around and dig out your A-game," Quentin said as he stood tall and walked back to the huddle, ignoring the invisible knife buried deep in his ribs. "'Cause what you got ain't bothering me all that much."

He was the last one back to the huddle. Pine stood there, hands on his hips, glaring at him as he walked around to the back of the huddle and took his place.

"Finished catching up on old times?" Pine asked him.

"Hey, he started talking crap, I just —"

"Just nothing," Pine snapped. "Shut your mouth and get back to the huddle, got it?"

"Hey! I'm not going to take this, he — "

"Quentin! Shut up! Jesus, you Purist Nation guys don't ever stop running at the mouth. Next play you get your butt back to the huddle and don't say a word, you *got* it?"

Quentin started to protest one more time then closed his mouth. He was furious that Pine was talking to him this way, but it was Pine's huddle. Pine looked at the sidelines then shook his head.

"No," he said. "Let's keep it on the ground."

An unheard voice said something to Pine. He nodded toward the sidelines and turned back to the huddle.

"Okay, we've pounded it up the middle enough for now, let's mix it up. Y-set, screen pass right. Quentin, maybe this time you could actually *run* with the ball instead of pussyfooting it to the line so they can smack you around like a little girl?"

Quentin's eyes widened with rage. "What are you talking about?"

"We'd have this game wrapped up if we had Fayed, or even Yassoud, but all we've got is *you*, you lazy backwater rookie."

Without thinking, he pushed his way forward to slide between Kill-O-Yowet and Sho-Do-Thikit, who were in front of him, bent down so the players behind them could see Pine. Quentin raised his right fist to swing at Pine, but two sets of hands and one set of tentacles grabbed him from all sides and held him back.

"Hey," Pine said, holding his hands out, palms up, that arrogant grin on his bloody face. "You want a piece of me, you little spoiled racist *brat*?"

The word seemed to slip into Quentin's brain like a branding iron. He jerked against the hands holding him back as the huddle shifted and broke apart.

"You wanna mess with *me*, Pine?" Quentin screamed. He tried to break loose. From behind, a strong arm wrapped around his neck and squeezed, lightly, just enough for Quentin to feel pressure on his windpipe — just enough to know he'd pass out if the arm tightened further.

"Stop this right now," Tom Pareless said quietly. "I let you go, you run the play, deal?"

Quentin nodded, or at least he moved his head — he couldn't nod with Pareless' thick arm wedged around his neck and under his chin.

"WHAT'S GOING ON there, Chick? The Krakens are fighting in the huddle."

"Well, Masara, it looks like tempers might be flaring. Can we get a close-up of Barnes' face? Now, run it in slow-mo."

"You want to see if you can tell what this argument is about, Chick?"

"You got it, Masara. Look at that guy, he's as wide-eyed-mad as a Brahma bull getting a three-pound suppository. Hold on, let me see what he's saying … *well*, it seems that Quentin Barnes had a few choice words. He said — "

"I think the viewers have a good idea what he said, Chick."

"Yeah, but he called Donald Pine a — "

"And we're back to the action on the field! The Krakens are lining up in an I-formation with Hawick wide left, Scarborough wide right and Kobayasho at right tight end."

QUENTIN LINED UP in the I-formation, right behind Tom Pareless. He was so mad he could barely see, barely hear the snap count. So now he knew what kind of a man Pine really was — screw all the favors Quentin had given him, screw the fact that Quentin had saved the man's reputation and career: when the going got tough, Donald Pine passed the buck.

"Green, twenty-eight!" Pine shouted.

Quentin couldn't even stand the sound of that blue-boy's voice. How could he have been so stupid to give up the quarterback spot for the biggest game of the year? He *asked* Hokor for this!

"*Greeeeeeen*, twenty-eight!"

Well, he and Pine would settle up once the game was over. That old man was going to get his, that was for certain.

"Hut-hut!"

Quentin drove forward and to the right as Pareless stood, hands out, to pass-block. On the screen pass, Quentin's job was to block down on the defensive tackle, then bounce outside and wait for the pass. Cay-Oh-Kiware and Vu-Ko-Will, the right guard and tackle, respectively, would make half-hearted blocks, enough so that the defense could go right by, then bounce to the right and block for Quentin. The defensive line would chase after Pine, who would back up, drawing them in — when Pine threw the little dump-pass to Quentin, those same defenders would be too far away from the play to do anything about it.

Quentin ran up as Chok-Oh-Thilit spun around Vu-Ko-Will's pseudo-block.

I'll show you, Pine.

Quentin launched himself forward just as Chok-Oh-Thilit finished his spin. Quentin's elbow smashed into the Ki lineman's helmet, snapping his head back. Chok-Oh-Thilit stumbled, then fell to the ground.

BLINK

The world decelerated: Quentin bounced to the right and looked back. Three defensive linemen closed in on Pine, who back pedaled and looked confused. The linemen gathered and shot forward toward the scrambling quarterback — who at the last possible second deftly tossed a floating pass. Quentin watched the ball in total fascination. It moved so slow he could read the small letters burned into the ball (Riddell GFL-licensed) and count the pebbles in the leather grain. The ball slowly spun toward him, until his hands seemed to reach out and pull it in like an old friend.

He turned upfield. Vu-Ko-Will and Cay-Oh-Kiware were already in front of him, two biological bulldozers moving forward on multi-jointed legs. Kipir the Assassin tried to cut past Vu-Ko, but the Ki lineman managed to get a partial block. Kipir spun and stumbled by, off-balance but reaching for Quentin. Quentin switched the ball to his right arm, reared back with his left and delivered a crushing forearm to the linebacker. Kipir's feet came out from under him, and he went down hard.

Quentin stayed behind Cay-Oh, who ran as fast as his little Ki legs would carry him. Jurong tried to reach Quentin, but she was fighting off a running block from Scarborough. Montrouge, the cornerback, came free, but had a bad angle — she tried to make a cut around Cay-Oh-Kiware, but the Ki lineman gathered at the last second and launched forward. Even in Quentin's Zen-state, he heard the crowd's "OHHH" when Cay-Oh Kiware smashed Montrouge into a limp Sklorno puddle.

Quentin cut outside, zipping past Jurong who couldn't separate from Scarborough's block. Suddenly, there, was no one left. Quentin sprinted forward, big legs chewing up the yardage. The goal line loomed before him like the gate to heaven. He looked to his left — Volgograd closing in. Quentin watched in seeming slow-mo as she gathered for a touchdown-saving leap. Quentin's brain effortlessly timed the Sklorno's dive — when she went horizontal, diving at his feet, he launched himself lengthwise into the air. Volgograd passed by where his feet had just been, her tentacles flailing as she tried to grab a foot, a leg, a shoelace, *anything*, but came up with only air.

Quentin's facemask hit the ground first — he slid forward, realizing, suddenly, that the grass he looked down upon wasn't green.

It was red, the color painted in the end zones.

BLINK

The world rushed back in a hammer-blow of noise and color and intensity.

[TOUCHDOWN, KRAKENS! A 45-YARD PASS FROM PINE TO QUENTIN BARNES!]

Quentin looked for flags but saw none. The Harrah zebe signaled a touchdown. He glanced up at the scoreboard.

Krakens 20, Earthlings 17.

1:31 left to play.

His teammates swarmed around him as he ran off the field. The Krakens faithful in the stands were a blur of jumping, screaming excitement — two sections of anarchy set amidst a stadium of disappointment.

Now it was all up to the defense.

• • •

QUENTIN STOOD on the sidelines, as far away from Don Pine as he could get. Case Johanson limped onto the field, and Quentin felt a bond of brotherhood. Even from thirty yards away, Quentin could see the look in Johanson's eyes — he was ready to sacrifice anything to get the win.

Morningstar had knocked in the extra point, giving the Krakens a 21-17 lead. His following kickoff had sailed into the end zone. The Earthlings started their last drive at their own 20.

Pookie Chang lined up as a single back. The Earthlings lined up in a "big" set — single back, two tight ends, two wide receivers. John Tweedy moved up onto the line, immediately showing blitz. His right leg twitched with anticipation, each hand tightened into a flesh-and-bone mace.

Johanson dropped back five steps, limping slightly, then stood tall. Tweedy slipped between the linemen, but Chang picked him up and knocked him down with a perfect block. Johanson looked right, then turned left and delivered a tight crossing pass to Norfolk, who caught the ball and ran out of bounds just before Virak the Mean could tear off her head.

Twelve-yard gain. First and 10 at the Earthlings' 32, 1:17 to play.

Mai-An-Ihkole and Choto the Bright ran off the field, Mum-O-Killowe and Tiburon ran on as Hokor switched to a nickel package.

The Earthlings again lined up in a big set. Johanson hobbled back in a five-step drop. Quentin looked downfield, his mind on offense, instinctively looking for the open routes. Mum-O-Killowe drove forward with his characteristic un-Ki-like agility, spinning and thrashing, trying to blast past the double-team that held him in check. Johanson felt the pressure, cocked his arm and delivered another short pass, this time to Bates McGee, the tight end. Complete for six yards, Virak the Mean on the tackle.

Second and 4.

Johanson signaled a time-out.

Clock at 1:09.

The Earthlings huddled up during the time-out and then hit the line in a three wide receiver shotgun. The defense settled in like an invading army awaiting the signal to attack. Mum-O-Killowe roared and came forward like a nightmare, two linemen punishing him all the way, yet he still drove toward Johanson.

Quentin looked downfield — Norfolk ran a post, and was pulling away from Berea.

"Oh crap," Quentin whispered.

Johanson side-stepped Mum-O-Killowe's madman rush, looked downfield and saw the same thing Quentin had seen. The undauntable quarterback stepped up, cocked his arm —

— and then there was Michnik. The massive HeavyG defensive end came from the blindside. He connected just before the Johanson's arm started to come forward. Michnik hit him in the small of the back, 525 pounds moving at full speed — Johanson looked like a rag doll bent in half at the spine. The ball flopped away on a wobbly backward arc. Johanson's body just started to move back to normal alignment when Michnik drove him into the ground. They hit so hard, Quentin wondered if there would be an impact crater.

The ball descended, hit the ground and squirted in a spinning dance to the right. It took almost a full second for the offensive and defensive linemen to see the ball on the ground. An offensive tackle lunged for it, but his jointed legs seemed to misjudge the ball's speed — he managed only to hit it, sending it farther into the backfield. The ball bounced back past the 25-yard line like a wildly spinning brown windmill. Time ceased to exist — 250,000 sets of eyes watched its unpredictable motion, 250,000 beings held their breath.

Three players dove for the ball simultaneously, and it squirted up into the air.

Where Mum-O-Killowe snatched it.

The rookie defensive tackle scuttled for the corner as the crowd's roar erupted into a combination of excitement and anticipated doom. Pookie Chang ran after Mum-O-Killowe. The big Ki lineman scuttled across the 15 and headed for the end zone. Pookie's speed closed the distance in less than five yards, and he latched onto Mum-O-Killowe's torso. The Ki lineman sagged to the right under the extra 310 pounds, but he kept plodding forward. Pookie ripped at the ball, ripped at Mum-O-Killowe's eyes, his mouth, at anything, desperate to save the touchdown that meant the end of the Earthlings' chances.

The moving war passed the 10 yard line.

Mum-O-Killowe reached out his two right arms and lifted Pookie Chang right off the ground.

Stunned at such a display of power, Quentin watched Mum-O-Killowe cross the goal line, the ball tucked under his left arms, Pookie Chang tucked under his right.

The Krakens' sidelines erupted into a shouting, screaming, clicking, clacking, jumping melee of exploding joy.

Krakens 27, Earthlings 17.

Fifty-two seconds to play.

Quentin found himself jumping up and down and hugging teammates just like everyone else. The joy seemed to gush out of him like a volcano, limitless and unstoppable. Tier One! *Tier One!*

The extra-point team ran onto the field. One more kick, and the Krakens were up by two scores with less than a minute to play.

The extra-point team stopped as whistles blew. Johanson hadn't got up. The Earthlings' docs flew onto the field, their med-sled floating behind them. They took a quick look at Johanson, then put the med-sled over him. The tiny cables shot out, simultaneously immobilizing and lifting Johanson's prone body. The med-sled and the docs headed for the tunnel. Normally, all the players would have silently watched the procession, but not this time — this time they could barely stop themselves from screaming at the docs to get Johanson's weak butt off the field.

The extra-point team lined up.

Quentin found himself standing next to Donald Pine.

"Nice touchdown run, Q," Pine said, grinning. "Ever notice how you play better when you're mad?"

Quentin stared at Pine for a second, then it sank in. His face turned red with embarrassment. Even in the biggest game of the year, Pine, the master manipulator, had goaded him into a rage. It hadn't been personal, it had been calculated. Quentin realized that when the rage hit, he'd forgotten all about his battered body and just *played*.

Quentin smiled as Pine tousled his hair. Together, they turned to watch the extra point.

Morningstar knocked it through.

Krakens 28, Earthlings 17.

"WELL, CHICK, I think you can say this one is pretty much over. The Earthlings' backup quarterback, Dan Erlewine, just isn't the same caliber as Case Johanson."

"I think the Earthlings are about as done as a three-day-old dog turd, Masara."

"Chick … we've only got a few minutes left, can't you just *try* to knock it off?"

"Masara, you're as uptight as an anal-retentive accountant."

"You know what? I give up."

"Hey, Masara, you can't *leave* the booth, the game is still on! … well, um, folks, Chick McGee here, now on play-by-play. Dan Erlewine is in the shotgun, and he looks nervous. He's got to come up with two touchdowns in less than forty seconds. He drops back, looking, looking, he's going deep to Norfolk! The pass looks short, and Berea's got it! Interception! That's the ballgame, folks. The Earthlings are headed to the showers, and the Ionath Krakens are headed to Tier One!"

AN HOUR AFTER the game, every player remained crammed into the communal center room. Mitchell Fayed's jersey had been taped up to the holoboard. Grass stains darkened the orange jersey, as did Quentin's red blood and several streaks of Ki black. It hung there, a memorial to their fallen comrade, as if Fayed watched over them, participating in their celebration.

Pine walked up to Quentin, and they hugged like long-lost brothers. He didn't feel any pain this time — with the game over, Doc had injected several brands of rather efficient painkillers.

"You did it, old man!"

"No, you did it, Q!" Pine said, his blazing genuine smile as different from his arrogant grin as night was from day. "You're a *quarterback*, and you rushed for 64 yards and caught for another 82. You're the hero of the game."

"An MVP performance, eh?"

Pine laughed and shook his head. "Sorry, the MVP goes to Mum-O-Killowe — three sacks and the fumble-recovery for a TD."

Quentin shrugged and laughed. He'd get his playoff MVP someday. Mum-O-Killowe had savaged the Earthlings offensive line and sealed the game with the fumble return for a TD. He deserved it as much as anyone else.

"Well, he earned it," Quentin said.

"Brother, we *all* earned it."

"Looks like we're in another QB controversy. Tier One season is only a month away!" Quentin said it jokingly, but Pine's smile faded.

"Hey," Quentin said. "Did I say something wrong?"

Pine shook his head. "No. And there isn't a QB controversy, anymore. *You're* the guy."

Quentin stared at the veteran. "Don, you just put the team back into Tier One. I'm not going to go down without a fight, but you finally did it."

Pine shook his head again. "No. I had my chances. I had five seasons of chances, and I pissed them away. I wouldn't even *be* here if it weren't for you. This team won because of *you*, Quentin, because of your leadership. I used to have that ability, but not anymore, not like you have it. Look around you — any one of these beings would follow you straight into hell. And believe me, Q, that's what Tier One is — hell on a football field. They'll follow you. *I'll* follow you."

The words stunned Quentin. Donald Pine, two-time Galaxy Bowl champ, one-time League MVP, was going to be his backup.

Permanently. Quentin Barnes, dirt-faced orphan from a backwater planet in a backwater system, would lead the Ionath Krakens into Tier One.

"Don't stand there with your jaw open," Pine said. "I swear, you Purist Nation guys never shut your mouth. Now, go congratulate your teammates."

Quentin moved from player to player, thanking them, congratulating them, celebrating with them. It struck him as he danced with Sklorno, hugged Humans, clacked his armor off the chest of Ki and butted heads with Quyth Warriors (the most annoying of all the various races' celebratory habits), he no longer thought of them as aliens. They were *Krakens*, pure and simple. They were his teammates, his fellow warriors. He'd been through hell and back with them, fought together on the field and off, killed and been killed, all in the name of winning.

Winning together.

Winning as a team.

He could never go back to the Purist Nation.

He reveled in the joy of accomplishing his second-highest goal. His ultimate goal? Winning a Tier One championship.

He was on a collision course with that now, on a collision course with a Tier One championship. The only variable was time ...

EARTHLINGS BOX SCORE

Final	1	2	3	4	T
Ionath	7	7	0	14	28
Texas	0	2	15	0	17

SCORING SUMMARY

1st QUARTER		ION	TEX
Ionath TD	Richfield 102-yard kickoff return (Arioch Morningstar kick)	7	0

2nd QUARTER		ION	TEX
Ionath TD	Hawick 44-yard pass from Don Pine (Arioch Morningstar kick)	14	0
Texas SF	Alonzo Castro safety	14	2

3rd QUARTER		ION	TEX
Texas TD	Peter Lowachee 3-yard pass from Case Johanson (Napoleon Utube kick)	14	9
Texas TD	Pookie Chang 4-yard run (Pookie Chang run for conversion)	14	17

4th QUARTER		ION	TEX
Ionath TD	Quentin Barnes 45-yard pass from Don Pine (Arioch Morningstar kick)	21	17
Ionath TD	Mum-O-Killowe 31-yard fumble return (Arioch Morningstar kick)	28	17

TEAM STATISTICS	TEX	ION
First Downs	17	16
Third Down Efficiency	7-14	9-20
TOTAL NET YARDS	**185**	**277**
Total Plays	56	67
Average Gain Per Play	3.3	4.1
NET YARDS RUSHING	**121**	**78**
Rushes	38	42
Average Per Rush	3.2	2.2
NET YARDS PASSING	**34**	**199**
Pass Completion	10-18	15-25
Yards Per Pass	5.2	8.8
Times Sacked	5	5
Yards Lost To Sacks	29	22
Had Intercepted	1	0
PUNTS	**7**	**11**
Average Punt	43.6	42.1
PENALTIES	**9**	**10**
Penalty Yards	73	72
FUMBLES	**2**	**0**
Fumbles Lost	1	0
Time Of Possession	**32:44**	**27:12**

PASSING

KRAKENS	CMP	ATT	YDS	PCT	YPA	SACK	SYDS	TD	INT
Don Pine	15	25	221	60.0	8.8	5	22	2	0

EARTHLINGS	CMP	ATT	YDS	PCT	YPA	SACK	SYDS	TD	INT
Case Johanson	10	17	93	58.8	5.5	5	29	1	0
Dan Erlewine	0	1	0	0.0	0	0	0	0	1

RUSHING

KRAKENS	ATT	YDS	AVG	LONG	TD	FUM
Quentin Barnes	28	64	2.3	11	0	0
Tom Pareless	14	29	2.1	6	0	0

EARTHLINGS	ATT	YDS	AVG	LONG	TD	FUM
Pookie Chang	18	68	3.8	21	1	1
Peter Lowachee	10	26	2.6	15	0	0
Case Johanson	6	16	2.7	14	0	0
Jules Ardetto	4	11	2.8	5	0	0

RECEIVING

KRAKENS	REC	YDS	AVG	LONG	TD	FUM
Hawick	4	88	22.0	44	1	0
Quentin Barnes	4	82	20.5	45	1	0
Scarborough	2	21	10.5	16	0	0
Mezquitic	2	10	5.0	8	0	0
Denver	1	10	10.0	10	0	0
Rick Warburg	1	5	5.0	5	0	0
Milford	1	5	5.0	5	0	0

EARTHLINGS	REC	YDS	AVG	LONG	TD	FUM
Norfolk	4	48	12.0	23	0	0
Bates McGee	3	18	6.0	11	0	0
Peter Lowachee	2	18	9.0	15	1	0
Jules Ardetto	1	9	9.0	9	0	0

EPILOGUE

PLAYOFFS ROUND THREE:
KRAKENS VS. CHILLICH SPIDER-BEARS

From the Ionath City Gazette

Hometown Hero Leads Krakens to Championship
By Toyat the Inquisitive

EARTH — Last night the Planetary Union shook in fear under the weight of the Quyth Concordia's newest and best home-grown secret weapon: Yitzhak Goldman.

Goldman, a Human native of Ionath City, led the Krakens to a 24-19 win in the Tier Two Championship game, played at Hudson Bay Stadium on Earth. Goldman, who was named the game's MVP, threw for two touchdown passes on the day, one to Milford and the second to Richfield. Goldman, who has been third on the depth chart for most of the season, was tapped to lead the team in this critical championship match-up.

"We had two injured quarterbacks, and Goldman stepped up," said Krakens head coach Hokor the Hookchest. "Our semifinal game left us with a lot of beat-up players. With the Tier One season only a few weeks away, we needed to rest some beings."

Another key performer was Krakens running back Yassoud Murphy, who posted the first 100-yard game of his young Upper Tier career. Murphy picked up most of the yardage on a stunning 44-yard touchdown run late in the third quarter, a play that gave the Krakens a commanding 24-12 lead.

"The offensive line opened up a huge hole, and I ran through it," Murphy said. "I'm buying those guys a beer. In fact, I'm buying them a lot of beers. Hey, you want a beer? I'm buying."

Murphy's jubilance was echoed in the Krakens' locker room, where quarterbacks Donald Pine and Quentin Barnes drenched Goldman in the football tradition of a "champagne shower."

The Krakens move into Tier One for the first time in ten seasons. They don't have much time to rest, however, as the Tier One season begins in only four weeks with a visit to the Isis Ice Storm of the Tower Republic.

THE END

EXCERPTS

From "Religion of an Empire: Mason Stewart's Purist Church"

It has been argued for centuries whether Mason Stewart was, indeed, a true prophet or just the right man in the right place at the right time.

Earth's ancient history is fraught with war and hatred between the dominant religions. Three religions, in particular — Christianity, Judaism and Islam — have been at each other's throats for millennia. Historians can only estimate the number of deaths caused by altercations among these sects, and yet the most ironic part is that all three, essentially, worship the very same god.

It was this "one true god" that Mason Stewart called upon when he founded the Purist Nation just three months after Humanity's first interstellar contact: the historic "Message from Space" sent out by the Whitok race in 2395. Humanity's reaction to the discovery of life on other planets was mixed at best, ranging from boundless optimism to prophecies of doom and destruction. Elements of all three major religions railed against the concept of intelligent life on other planets. Stewart's fire-and-brimstone speeches catered to these elements. His single most brilliant tactic was that he didn't embrace an existing religion, but rather started his own. His was not an offshoot of Christianity or Islam or Judaism, but an entirely new church that incorporated elements of all three.

Many historians feel that Stewart's incorporation of religious elements is proof positive that he was a calculating opportunist, that he skillfully created a philosophy "familiar enough" to be comfortable for members of all three religions. Members of the Purist Nation, however, say Stewart was a direct conduit for God, whom Stewart called the "High One." Stewart painted a picture that the three religions were not "wrong," just that man's interpretation hadn't been quite "right."

The presence of alien life caused a great schism in the three religions. The leaders of Christianity, Judaism and Islam supported Humanity's involvement with other races, yet millions of rank-and-file members did not. Fundamentalist movements sprang up all over the world, growing in numbers and strength when Whitokians established a permanent colony on Earth in 2406. Severe violence marked the various schisms as fundamentalists sought to kill Whitokians, drive them from Earth and take control away from "blasphemous" church leaders. As Stewart's church gained strength, his message called out to these fundamentalists. He gave them exactly what they wanted: an organized, religiously justified platform from which to hate alien races.

The Purist Nation boldly claimed responsibility for terrorist actions that cost the lives of thousands of Whitokian immigrants. The crackdown of 2431, however, put a permanent end to those terrorist acts. Governments and religions around the world cooperated to capture or kill Purist Nation terrorists. With his best shock troops eliminated, Stewart faced a turning point in his power base. Instead of trying to play politics, he called upon the immense wealth of his church to outfit a fleet of starships. Over five million followers of the Purist Nation fled Earth at the end of 2431.

The journey was difficult, to say the least. Poor technology, overcrowding and accidents caused the loss of some thirty ships and over one million lives before the Purist Nation fleet colonized their first planet, named "Stewart" after their bold leader. Many elements of this "exodus" have been incorporated into the Purist Nation's holy texts. The new planet gave the Purist Nation a home free of cultural influence from Earth.

From "Rise to Power: The Quyth Concordia 2752 to present," written by Viler the Meek

It is often mentioned in galactic history texts that the Quyth Concordia's rise to power is merely a fluke of biology. The Quyth, after all, are the only sentient species that can completely ignore latent radiation, even when that radiation reaches levels high enough to kill Humans, Ki, Sklorno, Harrah, Whitok, Leekee and Creterakians.

This innate ability allowed the Quyth to expand from one planet to a five-planet empire rich in mineral wealth. In the seminal year of 2573, the Quyth shocked the galaxy by establishing a permanent, flourishing colony on the planet Gritchlik, which the Sklorno irradiated during the Quyth-Sklorno war. By the end of 2573, the Quyth had also colonized three other irradiated worlds—Whitok, Ionath and Chikchik. This marked the fastest expansion in the galaxy's history and instantly catapulted the Quyth from a galactic second-stringer to a major player on the political landscape.

Yet despite the Concordia's continued success, and despite the fact that the Concordia is one of only six systems to remain independent from the Creterakian Empire, sociologists from other species continue to say that the Quyth's success relies solely on resistance to radiation. These so-called "experts" like to point out that the Quyth's expansion was largely unchallenged because no government could justify fighting a war over a "dead" planet. An interesting stance, but how logical is it?

Humans, for example, target planets rich in oxygen with Earth-like gravity. The Tower Republic and Leekee Collective have cooperatively shared planets in the same system, with the Republic taking the land and the Collective claiming domain over the oceans. Is that not a perfect example of a "biological fluke" resulting in expansion of territory? The Republic and the Collective do not war over planets because they each occupy noncompetitive ecological niches.

The Harrah, as another example, are the only species in the galaxy that can live on gas-giant planets. And yet how many "experts" point out the "biological fluke" that has led the Harrah to become a five-planet empire of immense military and political power? And how many of these mostly-Human "experts" point out the obvious, that while all Human governments bend to the will of the Creterakian Empire, the Quyth Concordia remains independent?

From "Species Biology & Football," written by Cho-Ah-Huity

It is well known that the Ki are the best linemen in football. While many call me biased, as I am a proud subject of the Ki Empire, I support this claim with facts.

First of all, there is the size factor. A Ki lineman stands on average six feet high vertically, with another six feet reaching back from the vertical body. It is the six-foot-long "ground-body" that provides amazing stability. Six legs support the ground-body, giving the Ki lineman the lowest center of gravity of any species. Because of this, it is very difficult to knock a Ki lineman to the ground.

Then there is the strength factor. In the "bench press," a Human test of strength that is uniquely suited to measuring football prowess, the average Human lineman benches 720 pounds while the average Ki lineman benches 1,130 pounds. Quyth Warriors, the only other species capable of playing on the line, bench around 600 pounds. Humans from HeavyG worlds are becoming more of a factor in the game, yet they average around 900 pounds in the bench press. Clearly, the Ki is the strongest species in the game.

It has been noted, repeatedly, that both Quyth Warriors and HeavyG Humans are faster than Ki, have better lateral movement and faster reaction time due to their smaller size — mostly because they have less mass to move. These factors make both species excellent linebackers and defensive ends. However, those factors are usually not enough to offset the Ki's advantage in size and strength. Depending on the offensive scheme, Quyth and HeavyG Humans can make good run-blockers, but if you want to throw the ball, you need the pass-blocking prowess of the Ki species.

As for defense, the middle of the line might as well be sovereign territory of the Ki Empire. With massive strength and the low center of gravity, Ki nose guards and defensive tackles are specialists at shutting down the run. The Ki are also able to lay devastating hits due to their "gather" ability, where they can briefly compact their tubular body from twelve feet to eight feet, then suddenly expand with violent force. The "gather" lets them deliver crushing hits anywhere in a ten-foot radius. It is a common technique in tackling as well as in block-destruct.

**From "Species Biology & Football,"
written by Cho-Ah-Huity**

Sklorno were once considered the bane of the galaxy. An aggressive, fast-growing species, Sklorno females reach reproductive maturity in seven years. They also can breed up to twice a year, with potential broods of ten to twelve children. This would create severe overpopulation, save for the fact that in Sklorno society cannibalism is not only socially acceptable, it is considered a normal part of life. When the population exceeds the food supply, the government simply selects the individuals that are to become food themselves.

This behavior is indicative of what makes the Sklorno so "alien" to the other sentient species. The Sklorno have little or no concern for individual life. What matters in their culture is the success of the entire species, the "macro-environmental" scale if you will. Because of this attitude, the Sklorno were a vicious warring race and tried several times to exterminate other species and expand their territory via war. The Sklorno, in fact, started the First Intergalactic War when they conquered the planet Withrit and exterminated all intelligent life (amounting to about 2.1 billion Whitokians). The Sklorno were also the first species to destroy a planet's ability to sustain life when they saturation-bombed Ionath, which then belonged to the Prawatt Jihad.

So what does this history lesson have to do with Species Biology & Football? You must understand the culture of the Sklorno if you are to understand their strengths and weaknesses as football players. Individual life holds little meaning for the Sklorno, while the success of the overall species is all-important. This attitude translates literally to the gridiron. Sklorno do whatever it takes to put the team ahead.

On top of that, they're the fastest and most agile species in the galaxy. With 40-yard dash speeds up to a blistering 3.0, and vertical leaps of up to fifteen feet, they seem almost genetically engineered to play wide receiver and defensive back. A Sklorno receiver fully extended and at top jumping height can pull down a ball that's thrown twenty feet over her head. Despite their speed, the Sklorno are the least strong of the playing races. Improvements in inertia-based protective equipment have greatly reduced Sklorno deaths, although during a given Upper Tier season, one can still expect five to eight deaths.

Creterakian officials introduced football in Sklorno space just 23 years ago. It has become a massive cultural phenomenon. Football is the number-one spectator sport, surpassing the traditional sports of spot-racing and even soccer, which the Sklorno have dominated since Humans introduced it 62 years ago. With military expansion halted by Creterakian rule, young Sklorno females have few outlets for their aggressive tribal tendencies. Football has filled that gap.

A societal quirk has developed due to the GFL, where Sklorno players (and some fans) put their team on a slightly higher level than their species. For many Sklorno, football isn't like a religion, it is a religion. Sociologists say that the team-based nature of the GFL is a perfect, microcosmic replica of the warring culture, and it appeals to the Sklorno at a very instinctive level. With the success of the species always at the forefront of their thoughts, Sklorno tend to idolize those that define a team's success — coaches and quarterbacks. There are actual churches spread throughout Sklorno space that are dedicated to coaches, like To Pirates coach Yuri Rockmananoff, and quarterbacks, like Hittoni Hull-walkers legend Sam London and two-time Tier One Championship MVP Donald Pine.

From "Creterak: The Unforeseen Dynasty," written by Hammond Gomez

It is almost inconceivable to anyone under the age of 40 that once, not so long ago, no one had even heard of a "Creterakian." Considering that race's almost total control over the galaxy, it is just as inconceivable to those people that the Creterakians were once looked at as an asset to be claimed, not a military power to be feared.

Creterak is a medium-sized planet, disadvantageously located in a political "hot zone" near the galactic core. The planet borders the Harrah Tribal Accord, The Quyth Concordia and the Rewall Association. It is also uncomfortably close to the last known position of the Prawatt Jihad fleet. This proximity proved to be a spark for military conflict.

The Creterakians were centuries behind other races in most technologies but surprisingly advanced in some areas. Signal detection, for example, is an area in which that race completely outclasses all others. The Creterakians managed to "hide" their planet from detection for over 250 years and were completely unknown until they achieved FTL capability in 2639.

The existence of a sentient race hidden within in a well-explored area stunned every scientist in the galaxy. Military officials of three separate systems saw a potential asset near the border of potential enemies. Within hours of the announcement, the Tribal Accord, the Association and the Concordia sent "diplomatic" fleets to Creterak. All three systems immediately claimed the rights to the new planet.

Even as the Galactic Council met to discuss claims to Creterak, skirmishes erupted between the Harrah and Quyth fleets just three days after the planet's discovery. Within a week, the skirmishes evolved into minor naval battles claiming well over 50,000 lives. What had begun as an amazing discovery quickly grew into the potential for a Fifth Galactic War. Each government sent reinforcements, resulting in three armada-class fleets circling the planet.

In a claimed effort to stem the violence, the Creterakians sent delegates to every ship in all three fleets. Again, it is inconceivable to young people today that the fleets fell for such a simple ruse. But look at it from the historical standpoint: the Creterakians were small, seemingly harmless creatures, they had no inter-species battle experience, and they had no military craft. Humans have even described Creterakians as "cute." Nothing was known of them other than the fact that they had FTL capability and could speak every known language, which they had absorbed from centuries of signal monitoring.

One small delegate vessel traveled to each ship in all three fleets, but no one suspected just how many Creterakians could pack into such a confined space. In primitive shuttles that would seat four humans in relative comfort, the Creterakians packed over 300 shock troops. In addition, no one had ever faced soldiers that moved as fast as the Creterakians, who can fly up to 45 miles per hour. The results were almost instant — the Creterakians seized control of three entire fleets as their soldiers tore through the ships with unheard of speed, killing most of the crew even before alarms could be sounded.

With their borders secure, the Creterakians launched the largest invasion force the galaxy has ever seen. Like a cell bursting with a deadly virus, over 50,000 transport vessels departed from Creterak and spread throughout the galaxy. Each vessel contained at least one million Creterakian soldiers — a force 50 billion strong. Subsequent research shows the Creterakians had been planning their attack for 125 years, all the while going undetected by every race in the galaxy.

The Creterakians also shocked established navies with a new tactic — attack by attrition. The landing ships ignored navies and headed straight for the surface of every inhabited planet in the galaxy. Defending navies destroyed tens of thousands of ships, but it's estimated at least five landing vessels touched down on each planet — giving the invading Creterakians a ground force of at least five million soldiers that could fly at 45 miles per hour and were armed with high-power entropic accelerator rifles. As astonishing as the figure sounds, the Creterakians conquered every planet within one week of landing.

By 2642, the Creterakians had the complete surrender of the Planetary Union, League of Planets, Ki Empire, Ki Rebel Alliance, Purist Nation, Tower Republic, Leekee Collective, Harrah Tribal Accord and the Sklorno Dynasty. The Quyth Concordia and the Rewall Association managed to fight off the invading forces and remain independent to this day.

TIMELINE

Partial galactic history of major events leading up
to the founding and operation of the GFL

PRE-HISTORY

TERTIARY EPOCH:

Other than the sprawling deep-space construct known as "The Reef,"
very little evidence remains of the Tertiary Epoch. It is known, however, that the period was a clear example of the "batching" phenomenon.
Batching is defined as several species on separate planets achieving sentience and FTL technology in a relatively limited time span. Considering
the number of variables involved with a species achieving sentience, it
is theorized that with certain types of planets, evolution of sentience is
inevitable and will happen in a certain time frame based upon a planet
cooling enough to support self-replicating chemical compounds. As large
areas of mass condensed to form stars and planets, these areas possibly provided similar "starting points" at which this inevitable path to
sentience began. This theory is highly controversial, countered by most
mathematicians, astronomers and, of course, those that theorize batching
is caused by galactic panspermia efforts.

QUATERNARY EPOCH:

Little is known about this period that occurred some two million years
ago. The batching phenomena occurred in this time, with several species

attaining sentience and achieving faster-than-light and/or gate technology. The Quaternary Epoch lasted approximately 500,000 years. Most academicians agree that ancestors of the Givers and Collectors cultures began in this period.

Galactic Timeline:
all times in Earth Time (ErT)

MODERN EPOCH:

1967   Collector gate built on Ki homeworld. Ki race subjugated (date estimated).

1988   Collector orbital arrives at Earth.

2008   Collectors fail in multiple attempts to invade Earth.

2009   Ki uprising against Collector homeworld. All contact lost with Collector race. Ki destroy all technology, dark age begins.

2015   Prawatt race created and exterminated on Earth (date estimated).

2345   Rewalls complete first successful test of the Punch Drive, achieve FTL status.

2387   Humans independently develop the Punch Drive.

2392   Rewalls establish colony on Loshal.

2401   Humans become first peaceful interstellar ambassadors, landing on Whitok.

2406   Humans (with help of Terran Dolphins) sign treaty with Whitok.
- Whitok inhabit Earth's waters, humans inhabit Whitok lands.
- Purist movement forms on Earth. Some humans believe Whitok are tools of the devil and that they should be destroyed.

2407   Humans colonize Capizzi 7, located in the Whitok system.

2409   Rewall colonize Yewalla.

2410   Prawatt race seeded on new homeworld.

2412   Terrorist attack on Whitok city by Purists, 120 Whitok killed.

2414   Purist movement gains power. They want "Satanic" Whitok removed form Earth.

2420   Whitok become third interstellar race, achieving FTL with help of human scientists.

2430   Estimated time the Givers arrive in galaxy.

2431   Terrorist attacks on Whitok increase. Earth authorities heavily punish Purists in order to pacify enraged Whitok. Purists flee persecution and leave Earth in small fleet of ships. They predict destruction of Earth as they escape "Satanic" Whitok.

2431   Earthlings colonize Satirli 6.

2432   Givers land on Harrah homeworld.

2433   Capizzi 7 achieves self-sufficiency.

2434   Prawatt achieve FTL capability.

2438   Prawatts attack peaceful Rewall research vessel. First interstellar combat. Both ships break off fighting and return to home systems.

2439   Kuluko establish radio contact with Whitok, Rewalls and Earth. Purists land on Jason 2, renaming it Allah. Begin massive re-tooling of fleet to create fighting navy.

2440   Prawatt, with a navy of only 20 ships, attack Yewalla in first interstellar war. Prawatt forces defeat token Rewall defenders and land on Yewalla but are driven off by Rewall land forces.

2445   Purists colonize Stewart.

2448   Harrah achieve FTL capability. Givers depart.

2450   Satirli 6 achieves self-sufficiency.
       • Earth, Capizzi 7 and Satirli 6 form Planetary Union.

2453   Purists declare war on Planetary Union in First Holy War. The Purists only have 12 ships — the war is clumsy and short-lived.

2454   Purists, fearing a retaliatory attack, sue for peace. Union accepts.

2455   Givers land on Kurgurk homeworld.

2456   Prawatt conquer Kuluko, exterminating the intelligent race. Ambassadors from Union, Whitok and Rewall Accord are executed. None of the three systems are able to respond in time to help Kuluko.

2460   Rewalls colonize Lotharis.

2461   Whitok colonize New Whitok.

2468   Planetary Union colonizes Thomas 3, which is in the same system
        as New Whitok.

2470   Leekee achieve FTL capability.

2478   • Prawatt colonize Lewarth and Basadah.

        • Kurgurk achieve FTL capability. Givers depart.

2486   Prawatt fleet (estimated at 72 ships) attack Yewalla again. Rewall
        ships, now prepared for combat, destroy Prawatt fleet (an esti-
        mated 25 ships returned to Prawatt).

2489   • Satirli 6 secedes from Planetary Union.

        • Civil war erupts between Union and Satirli 6.

2490   Whitok colonize Withrit.

2491   Satirli 6 successfully defends itself. Planetary Union officially rec-
        ognizes it as an independent government.

2502   Sklorno achieve FTL capability.

2503   Thomas 3 admitted to Planetary Union.

2504   Grasslop achieve FTL capability.

2506   Grasslop ship meets Leekee ship in neutral space. Leekee attack
        and destroy Grasslop ship.

2510   Leekee declare war on Grasslop.

2511   Leekee conquer Grasslop.

2512   • Rewalls colonize Yashan.

        • Purists colonize Mason.

2514   • Satirli 6 colonizes Wilson 4 and Wilson 6 and immediately de-
          clares them both independent protectorates, to be completely
          free as soon as they are self-sufficient.

        • Satirli 6 opens trade with Planetary Union and Whitok Kingdom.

2515   Satirli 6 opens its doors to Union immigrants and they come by
        the millions. Satirli 6 rapidly becoming economic giant.

2517   Purists, seeing Satirli 6's massive growth and assuming they hate
        the Union, invite Satirli 6 to join the Purist Nation. Satirli 6 re-
        fuses and Purists declare war on the infidels.

2518   Givers land on Ki homeworld.

2519   • Purists can't keep up long-distance offensive war against Satirli 6.

        • Purists offer peace, Satirli 6 accepts.

        • Satirli 6, Wilson 4 and Wilson 6 form League of Planets to defend themselves against future Purist aggression.

First Galactic War, 2520-2524

2520   • Sklorno launch massive (150 ship) attack against Withrit, destroying all intelligent life on planet.

        • Whitok kingdom immediately declares war on Sklorno.

        • Planetary Union joins its ally and declares war on Sklorno.

2521   Purists see the Union at war and declare Second Holy War on the infidels.

2522   Whitok send delegation to Rewalls. Rewalls understand message and declare war on Sklorno.

2523   • League of Planets declares defensive war on Purist Nation.

        • Prawatt, who have waited until Rewall navy is committed against Sklorno, attack Yewalla.

        • Sklorno are days away from conquering Whitok.

        • Purists get first look at Sklorno. They immediately break off their war with the Union.

        • League of Planets stops attacks on Purist ships, allowing them to return back to their system.

        • Rewall forced to break off attacks on Sklorno to deal with Prawatt.

        • In a last-ditch effort, the Whitok navy suicide-attacks the Sklorno forces off of the Whitok homeworld. The attack stops the movement on Whitok homeworld, but costs the Kingdom 50 percent of an already crippled fleet.

2524   Planetary Union brings full force to bear on Sklorno navy, which has regrouped and is heading for Whitok homeworld. The largest battle of the war ensues. Union forces drive off Sklorno, but not before the Sklorno saturation-bomb Whitok homeworld. Most life on Whitok destroyed and planet is uninhabitable.

2525   • Ki achieve FTL capability. Eat givers for dinner.

      • Rewall and Prawatt stalemate ends when Rewall leave a ravaged Yewalla for the Prawatt Jihad.

2526   Whitok offer Reiger 2 to Planetary Union in thanks after refusing to join Union. Addition of Reiger 2 leaves New Whitok, the Kingdom's only remaining planet, well inside Union borders.

2527-
2549   The Age Of Colonization.

      • Planetary Union adds Jones, New Earth, Rodina (all three in same system) and Home to its ranks.

      • Sklorno destroy avian race on Yall and add Chikchik.

      • Whitok spend trillions on colonization, adding Whipath and Whirod (same system), Whopol, Whirot and all-water giant Wheresh

      • Prawatt add Ionath.

      • Rewall add Loshall.

      • Leekee add Grinkas and Replas.

      • League of Planets adds Vosor 3 and distant Tower 1.

      • Purists add Solomon.

      • Kurgurk add Rfgh and Drghp.

      • Ki add Ol 3 and Re 4.

2530   Portath achieve FTL capability. Within 4 years (estimated), Portath colonize Thew and Faskah.

2531   • League of Planets forces sent from Tower on peaceful mission are lost when they enter the Portath Cloud.

      • Portath send a message to the galaxy not to enter the cloud.

      • League sends large navy to protect Tower from potential threat.

2533   Sklorno, despite warnings from Planetary Union, attack New Whitok. Whitok Kingdom's new navy has been waiting for revenge for nine years and defeat Sklorno in pitched battle.

2535   Planetary Union signs treaty of friendship with Purist Nation. League of Planets and Whitok Kingdom voice their objections to treaty.

Second Galactic War, 2536-2540

2536   Leekee attack Whiropt in an effort to gain new territory. Whitok barely repel attack. Whitok, seeing a double threat to a navy that hasn't even recovered fully from the last war, begin to spend all money on defense.

2537   Leekee, trying to surprise Whitok forces at Whiropt, travel into Portath Cloud. Forty-seven ships are never heard from again as entire force disappears. (Editor's Note: this was the Leekee's biggest blunder, as it gave Whitok time to rebuild its navy. Had Leekee attacked directly, it could have claimed half of the Whitok Kingdom's territory.)

2538   • Purist Nation launches major fleet in effort to add Tower 1.
       • League of Planets promises war if Purists touch Tower.
       • Purists claim the Union cannot allow hostile League ships through its space as it would be a violation of the friendship treaty of 2535. Caught in the diplomatic trap and wanting to avoid war with Purists, the Union claims neutrality and refuses to allow League ships through.
       • Purist force, unaware of large Tower navy, are defeated in first battle for Tower.

2539   • League tries to send ships though Union space. Union blockades the movement. Minor firefight ensues with League returning to system.
       • League forces are stonewalled by Purist defenses outside Jones system. League helpless to protect Tower.
       • August 4: Tower's Captain Markos surprises Purist forces at Stewart. Purists suffer heavy losses but still maintain vast numerical superiority. Tower's hopes for peace are dashed as Purists send 80-ship armada to conquer Tower once and for all.
       • November 21: Markos, pursued by 78 Purist vessels, leads Tower's final 14 ships into the Portath Cloud. Markos baits Purists into cloud and scatters his fleet. Seven Tower ships returned home, and all 78 Purist ships were lost. Captain Markos was never heard from again.

2540   • Portath send message to Purists: "Attack again, and we will destroy you."
       • Purist government, unsure of how Tower destroyed most of its fleet, offers Tower peace. Tower accepts.

- Tower secedes from League of Planets. League blames Union for loss of planet, hostile feelings remain today.
- Union, angered at being used in the Tower conflict, breaks off treaty with Purist Nation. Purists warn of consequences.

2551
- Ki navy makes its first appearance, attacking Leekee forces at Replas. Ki navy wins battle, then returns home.
- Ki navy attacks Harrah forces. Harrah win soundly and declare war on Ki for unprovoked aggression.

2552
- Planetary Union, trying to prevent a war so close to its borders, calls Galactic Peace Conference, attended by all except Prawatt.
- Quyth achieve FTL capability.

Third Galactic War, 2553-2557

2553
- Ki sign peace treaty with Harrah (at Galactic Peace Conference). Ki people outraged.
- Ol and Re secede from Ki Empire.
- Ships stationed at Ol and Re attack Ki, trying to oust cowardly government.
- Leekee see potential for war if Rebels win and decide to support Ki government, attacking the rebels near Ol.
- Rebels hold off Leekee and press closer to Ki. Some landings take place, resulting in numerous ground wars.

2554
- Rewalls, who have had excellent relations with the Ki government, threaten war unless rebels retreat. Rebels continue attacks and Rewall engage rebel forces at Re.
- Whitok, spurred on by the memory of unprovoked attacks by Leekee, send "advisors" to help rebels on Leekee border.
- Tower, wary of rebuilt Purist navy and hungry for allies, sends ships to help Leekee.
- Purists, seeing another chance to snatch Tower, side with Rebels for "religious purposes."
- Planetary Union warns Purists to stay away from Tower.

2556
- A minor altercation on the Prawatt/Sklorno border erupts into a full-scale war.

- Harrah join in fight against the Rebels, supporting the government that made the peace treaty.
- April 27: First battle for Ki. Synchronized attack by the Purists, Whitok and Rebels overwhelm Rewall and Leekee forces. Rebels take Ki but not before royal family can be evacuated.
- Purists attack Tower forces at Tower. Union immediately moves to attack Purists.

2557
- Battle for Asteroid X7. Union forces meet Purist forces at Asteroid X7. Union wins by small margin. Purists fall back to regroup. (Editor's Note: the fall back is considered the biggest tactical mistake of the war. The Union could not mount another offensive for at least three months, and the Purists could have brought up reserves and regrouped right on the front lines.)
- June 12: Tower, Rewall and Leekee forces seize opportunity and attack Rebels in second battle for Ki. Whitok navy late in arriving and is turned back by organized Rewall defenses.
- July 23: Leekee, Tower and Loyal Ki forces re-take planet. Rebels on planet-side are ousted and Rebel forces return to Re and Ol.

2558
- Tower turns down offer to join Union. Instead, they join new Tri-Alliance (Ki Empire, Leekee Collective and Tower Republic).
- Prawatt/Sklorno war is a stalemate.
- Sklorno saturate Ionath, killing all sentient life.
- Prawatt saturate Chikchik, killing all sentient life.

2559 Rewall, hot off their victory over the Ki Rebels, launch a surprise attack against Prawatt-controlled Yewalla. They quickly defeat the Prawatts, who are still weak from war with Sklorno. Rewalls execute all Prawatts in retaliation for actions of 2525.

2561 Ki declare themselves trading capital of the galaxy and sign non-aggression pacts with every system, excluding Prawatt.

2562 Tower and Leekee conduct The Great Planet Trade. Leekee added one of Tower's moons (New Leekee). Tower adds two planets in Leekee system (Fortress and Citadel).

2563 Ki colonize To.

2568 Harrah claim Satah, which is deep in Whitok space. Whitok are unable to use planet but still threaten war. Union enters as intermediary; Harrah buy the planet from Whiok for c50 trillion.

2569   Harrah claim Lorah, which Planetary Union has rights to but cannot live on. Caught in same argument they used against Whitok, Union reluctantly sells planet to Harrah for c57 trillion.

2572   • February 12: 23-year galactic peace shattered when Quyth send 400 ships against Reiger, crushing defenses and enslaving population.

• February 17: Quyth strike again, sending another fleet of 300 ships against Sklorno-held Gritchlik. They take planet and send Sklorno citizens back to Sklorno.

• March 4: Quyth expansion halted by Rewall when they defeat 500-ship force at Loshall.

• March 27: Union forces attack Quyth at Reiger. Union loses 26 ships, Quyth lose 112. Quyth win with incredible numerical superiority (estimated at 4 to 1).

• April 10: Sklorno re-take Gritchlik in costly battle.

• May 22: Quyth re-take Gritchlik with navy returning from Loshall. Sklorno saturate planet before pulling out.

2573   • Quyth shock the galaxy when it is discovered they have a permanent colony on radioactive Gritchlik.

• June 4: Quyth colonize and claim Whitok.

• July 6: Quyth colonize and claim Ionath.

• July 17: Quyth colonize and claim Chikchik.

• July 21: Whitok declare war on Quyth for landing on Whitok (even though it will be another three million years before any Whitokian can even set foot on the planet).

• Through three battles, Whitok lose half of their 300-ship navy while destroying 1,012 Quyth ships.

2574   Quyth retaliate to "unprovoked" attacks and send 600 ships to attack New Whitok. Combined Union and Whitok force meet Quyth fleet. Quyth lost 450 ships before retreating, Whitok lost 78 and Union lost 45 (Editor's Note: largest single battle in Galaxy's history). Whitok and Quyth agree to a cease-fire.

2581   Sklorno attack Drghp. Kurgurk unleash asteroid battleships and destroy Sklorno invaders.

2582 Whitok, fearing an attack from Leekee (their navy was still very weak from Quyth war), trade rights to Whopol to Ki for weapons, ships and credit.

2584 Ki develop deep mineral sights on Whopol that the Whitok were unaware of. Resulting wealth thrusts Ki Empire past League of Planets into top economic power in the galaxy.

2587 Pirate attacks begin in earnest on Ki shipping lanes.

2588 • Harrah boldly claim Yarah, a planet on the Quyth/Rewall border. Both systems are so surprised and slow to react that Harrah set up heavy defenses before either system could respond. Harrah allowed to keep planet without war.

• Whitok spend defense money hand over fist and begin to borrow from gracious Ki Empire.

2589 Ki Imperial Navy capturing more pirates, finding most to be Human with some Ki.

Fourth Galactic War, 2591-2600

2591 Purists use seven captured Unions ships (captured in the last war) to attack convoy just off of To. Ki cripple one ship, which the Purists have filled with captured Union soldiers (also from the last war). Ki troops find only dead Union soldiers.

2592 • September 5: Despite claims of innocence from the Union, Ki government decides war would be good for economy and declares war on Union for sponsoring pirates.

• Ki force Whitok, who are deeply in debt to the Empire, to stay out of war.

• Ki manipulate treaty agreement of 2558 as well as threaten to cut off trade to bring Tower and Leekee into the war.

2593 • No battles have yet taken place. Purist Nation gladly joins the fight against the warmongering, satanic Union.

• League of Planets, realizing that they will be next on Ki and Purist target list if the two defeat the most powerful navy in the galaxy, join the Union in the war.

• January 17: Ki and Union forces meet off of Harrah homeworld. Union forces are defeated and retreat to stronghold at Thomas 3.

- July 2: Ki Rebel Establishment takes advantage of Empire's troubles and pounces on Ak, an Imperial protectorate, adding it to the Establishment.

2594
- Ki, who don't think war is progressing fast enough, negotiate a deal with the Sklorno to attack the Union.
- Whitok, ashamed of their stance in the war and not helping its Union ally, attack the hated Sklorno with vigor.
- Battles rage across galaxy. Ki side is winning due to greater numbers and more money.
- Empire manages to keep solid trade lines going with all her allies except the Sklorno.

2595
- January 12: Ki and Tower forces defeat main Union force and conquer Thomas 3.
- February 14: Purists conquer Jones 2.

2596 Planetary Union very close to surrender. Fleet operating at 34 percent of original numbers. Death toll reaching 70 million.

2597
- January 12: Rewall enters war suddenly by conquering Demos. Ki must defend against Rewall's constant harassment sorties and lose numerical superiority over Union.
- May 19: The Great Sneak Attack. League of Planets forces invoke new stealth technology to travel to Allah, defeating Purist forces and conquering Purist capital.
- Purists immediately pull every ship out of war and head for Allah, abandoning weakening Ki forces. When Purist ships arrive in Allah system, League leaves without a fight.
- Harrah offer aid to Union for far-flung Whitok outpost. Union and Whitok, who can no longer hold back Sklorno, agree to terms.

2598
- Union forces, led by Harrah frigates, conquer Ki forces and re-take Thomas 3.
- Ki Rebels declare all debts owed to Ki Empire invalid and sneak attack Ki homeworld.
- Ki immediately retreat to deal with new threat.
- Tower/Leekee forces attack Rebels at Re. They are defeated and the Tri-Alliance members withdraw from war, leaving Ki Empire with no allies.

2600 • Ki Empire surrenders to combined delegation of League, Union, Rebel and Rewall forces.

• Harrah claim Whitok outpost, christening it Mathara.

• Harrah give Sklorno cease-fire ultimatum. Sklorno return to their system.

• September 6: Galactic Accord signed. Ki navy limited to 100 active ships and 100 dismantled and in reserve for defensive purposes. Union Watchdogs installed on all Ki ships to ensure compliance with treaty. Ki allowed to hold all of its possessions. Rebels demand Ki homeworld for their part in the war. Other systems just want peace and officially end war with promises of retaliating any hostile Rebel actions.

The Great Peace

2601 Planetary Union buys back Jones 2. Purists sell because they do not want to go to war in their weakened state.

2610 The Great Mapping Conference. System borders are hammered out to everyone's satisfaction. The new map clearly marks territory and makes it obvious to identify the aggressor. This brings about a relative peace.

2634 Quyth claim that map is incorrect, that Sklorno border is too close to Gritchlik and Chikchik.

2636 Second Galactic Peace Conference held. Quyth and Sklorno are not liked by anyone, and little attention is paid to their border dispute.

2637 • Tiring of constant border raids by Quyth, Sklorno send major force to border.

• Quyth respond by sending a major force.

• Ki achieve pre-war economic status.

2638 Tensions on Quyth/Sklorno border continue to rise, war seems imminent.

• Prawatts announce their intention of backing the Quyth if war should break (Editor's Note: a major turning point in the history of galaxy, as it was the Jihad's first political move).

• Purists, who now have their navy functioning again, claim rights to Jones 2, saying that they were coerced into selling the planet, for a fraction of its worth. Purists say that Union would have destroyed Allah had the Nation not sold Jones 2.

- Rodina threatens secession from the Union.

The Creterakian Age, 2639-

2639   Creterakians achieve FTL capability. Quyth, Rewalls and Harrah claim Creterak. Creterakians claim allegiance to no one and friendship to all. (Editor's Note: the Creterakians had been quietly monitoring the galactic events of the past 200 years without being discovered. They knew exactly what was going on when they announced their presence. They are far ahead of where any other race was at the FTL discovery phase of their histories).

2640   • Quyth, Rewall and Harrah fleets converge on Creterak, tensions soaring — none of the three governments is willing to give up rights to the world, while the rest of the galaxy tries to decide how to handle this unprecedented situation.

- Skirmishes erupt among the three fleets.

- Creterakians claim self-sufficiency, send delegations to the three fleets to negotiate a settlement.

- The three fleets welcome the tiny, seemingly harmless Creterakian delegations. The Creterakians are far from harmless. Swarming by the thousands, the small, flying creatures erupt from landing bays and within hours have captured all ships from the three fleets.

- The Creterakians launch 50,000 landing ships that have been concealed on the planet. This reveals a level of technology not only unsuspected by the rest of the galaxy but unknown to anyone (Editor's Note: the Creterakians planned their galactic attack for over 125 years).

- Each ship contains at least one million Creterakians. Fifty billion Creterakians spread through the galaxy within days. Thousands of ships are destroyed, but at least four ships land on every colonized planet in the galaxy. The Creterakians completely bypass navies, choosing to land on planets instead.

- Once on a planet, the Creterakian flocks unleash a devastating ground attack. Their speed, natural flight and high-powered weaponry make them an unstoppable force. Within one week, all ground armies are overwhelmed.

- Whitokian governments, based underwater, remain intact, but all land is overtaken.

- Prawatt Jihad has more time to react, being at the edge of the galaxy. They irradiate outlying worlds and colonies and fall back to their system. They manage to destroy all of the Creterakian ships targeted for their core system.

- Quyth government retreats to irradiated worlds, where the Creterakians choose not to attack.

- Planetary Union forces, led by Admiral Joshua Baugh, attempt a desperate attack on the Creterakian homeworld. The Creterakians use their captured warships to hold off the attack.

- League of Planets Blue Fleet, numbering over 1,000 vessels, joins the assault, but the Creterakians are waiting — they have discovered a design flaw in League ships, and manage to use small boarding vessels to swarm the League ships capturing all ships in one devastating tactical stroke.

- Ki Empire and Ki Rebellion navies join forces in an attack on the Creterakian homeworld but are soundly defeated by the technologically advanced captured League ships.

- Almost 900 Creterakian warships and landing vessels enter the Portath Cloud and are never heard from again.

2641
- Creterakians demand the surrender of all navies. Initially all systems refuse, but the Cretarakians begin to execute thousands of hostages every day.

- The Planetary Union surrenders first, on the orders of Admiral Joshua Baugh.

- The Ki Empire surrenders.

- The Ki Rebellion manages to evacuate government officials to a warship and declare themselves a space-faring race, abandoning their planets.

- Purist Nation surrenders.

- Tower Republic surrenders.

- Leekee Collective surrenders.

- League of Planets surrenders.

2642
- Creterakians abandon efforts to pacify Rewall Association and Kurgurk. Scientists aren't even sure if the Kurgurk knew the

Creterakians were on their planets — the Creterakian armies were completely ignored.

- Harrah Tribal Accord surrenders.
- Sklorno Dynasty surrenders.
- Creterakians abandon efforts to pacify irradiated Quyth Concordia planets.
- Creterakians abandon efforts to pacify Whitok Kingdom — Whitokian underwater combat technology too great to overcome.

2643   • Creterakians in clear control of the Galaxy. Most species suspect existing governments are working with the Creterakians, creating an overpowering, Cold War atmosphere of distrust.

- Murder rates skyrocket, as do isolationist cults and cross-species violence.

2644   In an effort to control cross-species violence and racism, the Creterakians take over all shipping between worlds.

2645   Creterakian shipping proves to be clumsy and poorly communicated. Goods and services are delivered late, often not at all, and industry begins to suffer heavily.

2646   • The Galaxy dives headlong into economic depression. Despite strict Creterakian discipline, murder and violence rates continue to climb. In cities and planets that formerly encouraged diversification, violence becomes a daily occurrence.

- The Creterakians begin to realize they don't understand the behavior of other species. Creterakian scientists assumed that once they had control of all military forces, a great peace would ensue.

2647   • The Dark Time — the depression hits the worst levels ever, with galactic unemployment at 25 percent.

- Cross-species relations reach an all-time low.
- Organized crime swells to new heights, providing unobtainable goods and services for exorbitant prices.

2648   The Cretarakians give up on their role as the galaxy's shippers, turning the duties over to the Ki Empire.

2649   The Ki Empire provides an overall organizational structure, coordinating the shipping fleets of all subjugated governments.

Almost overnight, the demand for imported goods and services skyrockets as items once again become available on most worlds.

2650   The Planetary Union introduces a galactic supply-and-demand computing system, tying all shipping vessels into one gigantic, coordinated fleet. Economic recovery continues to boom.

2651   • Despite increased trade, cross-species violence is still a major problem, so severe it interferes with shipping as vessels are illegally searched and crews harassed or detained based on race.

    • Ki Rebellion piracy becoming a major problem.

    • Organized crime grows stronger by preying on shipping.

    • Creterakians refuse to give any government warships to deal with the piracy problem.

2652   Cross-species violence becomes an epidemic as terrorists do the unthinkable, simultaneously nuking three cities (one each on the Planetary Union's Earth, Leekee Collective's Grinkas and Ki Empire's Ki). Purist Nation is suspected, but there is no proof.

2653   • Creterakians ask for help in controlling cross-species violence and piracy. Planetary Union officials introduce a plan for "System Police" departments — para-military forces made up of indigenous species that protect their various governments.

    • SP ships are armed but are significantly weaker than Creterakian warships.

    • SP ships are given limited search-and-seizure powers.

2654   • Creterakians finally admit they need help in improving species relations. League of Planets steps up, introducing noncontact galactic sporting events.

    • Sports have historically brought races together, not only for humans, but for all sentient species.

    • League scientists believe group dynamics that have held true for intra-species race relations will also hold true for inter-species relations.

2657   • The sporting events prove to be a boon to the entertainment and travel industries but are not producing the predicted cross-species cooperation.

    • Physiology results in single species dominating various sports.

    • Harrah dominate all racing events.

- Ki dominate all strength, hand-to-hand combat and throwing events.

- Sklorno dominate noncontact field sports like soccer.

- Humans dominate all hand-eye coordination sports like hockey, archery, etc.

The Galactic Football League Era

2650 • League scientist Demarkus Johnson unveils a plan for the Galactic Football League.

- Football is the only sport where various positions cater to the different physiologies.

- The Creterakians readily accept, funding a test league of 12 teams.

2659-
2661 The GFL is an immediate success, as it forces species to work together. In addition, it is the first occurrence in decades where fans of one species root for players of another.

2662 The GFL expands to 14 teams.

2663 • Purist Nation citizens rise up against Creterakian control. System-wide riots occur as citizens attack Creterakian garrisons. Creterakians bring in military reinforcements to quell uprising.

- Human death count uncertain, at least 12,000.

- Creterakian death count: 7,213.

- Reverend Abdul Smith uses situation to mount bloody coup, takes over church leadership.

- Smith works with Creterakians to investigate uprising, uses investigation to remove potential enemies.

- Millions flee Purist Nation as Smith's Creterakian death squads spread through system.

2664 • Demand for teams is so great that the GFL expands to 18 teams.

- Station 1 Givers, Buddah City Elite, Hittoni Hullwalkers and Srabian Salient added.

2665 • "The Disaster." Purist Nation police under Abdul Smith's orders impounds the New Rodina Astronauts' team bus. The

Purist Nation police accuse the Astronauts of spying — all non-Human players are executed.

- Governments are outraged — anti-Human violence soars.
- The GFL season is canceled.
- Purist Nation church coup results in Smith's death. Mullah Abigail Chase new leader.

2666 • Creterakian officials decide to eliminate the GFL.
- Club football teams flourish.
- A Ki businessman starts a new 12-team league to fill the gap, the Inter-Galactic Football League (IGFL). The IGFL is open to any team.

2667 • Despite low caliber of players, limited traveling ability and a lack of security, the IGFL swells to 26 teams and is an instant hit with football fans.
- The Fangs, a Ki-based team, are killed when a terrorist bomb destroys their team bus.
- Tower Football Club members are killed in a freak cosmic-ray accident.

2668 • The IGFL swells to 32 teams. It is a great year for attendance and a bad year for teams: four teams are lost in shipping accidents or terrorist acts.
- Illegal search-and-seizure by SP forces continues to plague the league, resulting in harassment, beatings and several injuries that impact game outcomes.

2669 • Faced with mounting deaths from unregulated IGFL teams, the Creterakians again start up the GFL.
- GFL "team busses" are given diplomatic immunity — they cannot be stopped or searched by any SP forces.
- The 18 former GFL teams are reinstated, and four IGFL teams are added to the ranks.
- The Creterakians disband the IGFL, breaking it down into six smaller leagues that play all games within the borders of a single government. Acts of SP harassment drop considerably.

2670 The 22-team GFL enjoys a successful season without any violence.

2671 League officials are flooded with requests by teams wanting to join the GFL.

2672   The GFL reorganizes, absorbing the former IGFL teams as "Second Tier" teams.

2682   The present.

League Structure: Tier One

- There are 22 Tier One teams, broken into two 11-team divisions (the Solar Division and the Planet Division).
- Teams play a 12-game season, with 10 games against their Division teams and two cross-divisional games.
- The top four teams in each division end the season with a single-elimination playoff.
- The two division champs face off in the GFL Championship.
- The team in each division with the worst record drops into the Second Tier.
- The top two Second Tier teams move into the First Tier.
- Players on Second Tier teams that move up are protected for two seasons, to give new First Tier teams a chance to win without their talent being raided.

League Structure: Tier Two

- Human League (Planetary Union, League of Planets, Purist Nation)
- Tower League (Tower, Leekee)
- Ki League (Ki, former Ki Rebel Alliance planets)
- Harrah League
- Quyth Irradiated League
- Sklorno League

Modern-Day Political Alignment

Creterakian Controlled

Human	Planetary Union
Human	League of Planets
Ki	Ki Empire
Ki	Ki Rebel Alliance
Human	Purist Nation
Human, Leekee	Tri-Alliance
Leekee	Leekee
Quyth	Quyth Concordia (non-irradiated planets)
Harrah	Harrah Tribal Accord

Not Creterakian Controlled

Quyth	Quyth Concordia
Whitok	Whitok Kingdom
Rewall	Rewall Association
Portath	Portath Cloud
Kurgurk	Kurgurk
Prawatt	Prawatt Jihad

GLOSSARY

The Ace: Quyth Orbital Station I, called "The Ace" by Humans. A massive artificial structure, The Ace was created as a solution to overcrowding on the Quyth homeworld. The Ace is over 350 Earth years old and has a population of 1.1 billion. Also known as "The City of Ice" for the crystaline blue material that makes up buildings and support structures.

The Big Eye: Slang term for Ionath City Stadium.

Bedbug: Slang for Sklorno males because all they want to do is get the females into bed.

Bureau of Species Interaction: Also known as the BSI, the Bureau is the agency responsible for helping the different races get along. The Creterakians hate war and violence and will go to great lengths to end the deadly rivalries between the major races.

The *Combine*: A station orbiting Creterak that functions as the Galactic Football League's headquarters. All rookies are brought to the *Combine* for extensive testing before being allowed to play.

Cricket: Racial, derogatory term for Sklorno.

Cross-crescent-star: The symbol of the Purist church, combining the Christian Cross, the Islamic Crescent and the Star of David.

The Deuce: Quyth Orbital Station II, called "The Deuce" by Humans. A massive artificial structure, The Deuce was created as a solution to overcrowding on the Quyth homeworld. The Deuce is almost 300 Earth years old and has a population of 740 million.

Five Star Circle: The symbol of the Quyth Concordia, with one star representing each of the Concordia's five planets.

Flashbugs: Robots that emit patterns of colored lights. Used in nightclubs.

Fly (flies): Racial, derogatory term for Creterakians.

Fur scraping: Derisive sound made by Quyth Workers, caused by rubbing their forearms. Hard bristles of fur make the noise — equivalent to a "boo" from a Human fan.

Gatholi: Quyth equivalent of "craphead."

Giving Day: The Purist Nation's version of Christmas.

HeavyG Human: A Human born and raised on a planet with 1.5 to 2 times the gravity of Earth. HeavyG Humans tend to be far stronger than normal Humans and have thicker builds. Where an average Human male stands 6 feet tall and weighs 190 pounds, an average HeavyG Human stands 6-foot-1 and weighs 260 pounds.

High One: The Purist Nation's name for God.

Hiropt's Disease: Neurological disorder caused by bacteria carried in the saliva of roundbugs, an indigenous species of Mining Colony Six. Symptoms include constant shaking, uncontrollable muscle spasms and overall weakness.

Holy Man: A religious leader of the Purist religion.

Mae gong ka olll: Quyth battle cry. Literal English translation: "Now we take the war to you."

Med-sled: Hovercart used by team medical staffers to move injured players off the field.

Messageboard: A flat screen about the size of an 8.5x11 piece of paper. Holds 50 terabytes of data.

Mesh: A cybernetic drug comprised of semi-intelligent bacteria. "Mesh bugs" measure and amplify neurotransmitters, as well as flock to active areas of the brain. Mesh acts as an "intensifier," greatly increasing sensory response and causing highly realistic hallucinations.

Mission marks: Horizontal stripes enameled onto the arms of Quyth Warriors, signifying combat missions, battles or tours of duty.

Punch motor: Faster-than-light technology developed independently by Humans, The Givers and other races. A zero-mass envelope field surrounds a microscopic singularity. This singularity is used to "punch" a hole in space/time.

Pyuli: Hallucinogenic drug that affects Humans, distilled from the Pyuli plant that grows on Ki and Ki-terraformed worlds. Causes intense hallucinations.

Referee's Guild: The GFL's official licensing body for officials. All officials must attend the annual Guild conference, held at Skygod Orbital Station off planet Shorah.

The Red Moon: A glowing red moon is the symbol of the Sklorno Dynasty. In 2391 ErT, the Sklorno traveled to their moon. Their moon had a flourishing ecosystem, complete with a primitive sentient species. The Sklorno exterminated that species and took the Red Moon as the symbol for the Dynasty.

Roundbug: A native predator of Mining Colony Six. Roundbugs bite their prey, infecting them with a deadly bacteria, and wait several days for the prey to die. The bacteria are not fatal to Humans, but can cause permanent neurological damage to Human children (known as Hiropt's Disease).

Salamander: Racial, derogatory term for a Ki.

Shamakath: Quyth word for "leader," most commonly used in military terms or attributed to the main boss of a syndicate.

The Takeover: The three-year span during which the Creterak conquered the galaxy.

The Tri: Quyth Orbital Station III, called "The Tri" by Humans. A massive artificial structure, The Tri was created as a solution to overcrowding on the Quyth homeworld. It was built shortly before the Quyth Concordia achieved FTL technology and was the last such massive engineering project before the government expansion strategy switched to colonizing "dead" worlds. The Tri is about 150 Earth years old and has a population of 112 million.

Wartimes: Creterakian-approved phrase for all history prior to The Takeover.

Xerchit: Quyth word for lieutenant, most commonly attributed to the leader of a syndicate cell.

Yakochat: Quyth word for one who betrays so much he would murder his own mother.

Zebe: A football official, a "zebra."

Zoroastrian Guild: Subversive organization dedicated to ending Creterakian rule.

About the Author

New York Times best-selling novelist Scott Sigler is the author of **NOCTURNAL, ANCESTOR, INFECTED** and **CONTAGIOUS**, hardcover thrillers from Crown Publishing, and the co-founder of Dark Øverlord Media, which produces his Galactic Football League series: **THE ROOKIE, THE STARTER, THE ALL-PRO,** and **THE MVP**.

Before he was published, Scott built a large online following by giving away his self-recorded audiobooks as free, serialized podcasts. His loyal fans, who named themselves "Junkies," have downloaded over fifteen million individual episodes of his stories and interact daily with Scott and each other in the social media space.

Photograph by Amy Davis Roth of Surlyramics.com

GREAT
BRITAIN

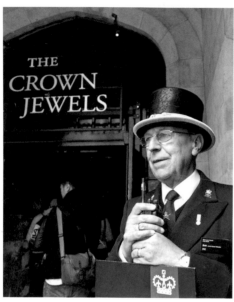

THE
CROWN
JEWELS

CONTENTS

Welcome to Rick Steves' Europe

Travel is intensified living—maximum thrills per minute and one of the last great sources of legal adventure. Travel is freedom. It's recess, and we need it.

I discovered a passion for European travel as a teen and have been sharing it ever since—through my tours, public television and radio shows, and travel guidebooks. Over the years, I've taught thousands of travelers how to best enjoy Europe's blockbuster sights—and experience "Back Door" discoveries that most tourists miss.

This book offers you a balanced mix of Great Britain's biggies (such as Big Ben and Stonehenge) and more intimate locales (ancient Roman lookouts and misty Scottish isles). And it's selective: There are dozens of hikes in the Lake District; I recommend only the best ones. My self-guided museum tours and city walks give insight into the country's vibrant history and today's living, breathing culture.

I advocate traveling simply and smartly. Take advantage of my money- and time-saving tips on sightseeing, transportation, and more. Try local, characteristic alternatives to expensive hotels and restaurants. In many ways, spending more money only builds a thicker wall between you and what you traveled so far to see.

We visit Great Britain to experience it—to become temporary locals. Thoughtful travel engages us with the world, as we learn to appreciate other cultures and new ways to measure quality of life.

Judging from the positive feedback I receive from readers, this book will help you enjoy a fun, affordable, and rewarding vacation—whether it's your first trip or your tenth.

Have a brilliant holiday! Happy travels!

Rick Steves

GREAT BRITAIN

What's so great about Britain? Plenty. You can watch a world-class Shakespeare play, do the Beatles blitz in Liverpool, and walk along a windswept hill in the footsteps of Wordsworth. Climb cobblestone streets as you wander Edinburgh's Royal Mile, or take a ferry to a remote isle. Ponder a moody glen, lonesome stone circle, or ruined abbey. Try getting your tongue around a few Welsh words, relax in a bath in Bath, and enjoy evensong at Westminster Abbey. Stroll through a cute-as-can-be Cotswold town, try to spot an underwater monster in Loch Ness, and sail along the Thames past Big Ben. Great Britain has it all.

Regardless of the revolution we had 230-some years ago, many American travelers feel that they "go home" to Great Britain. This popular tourist destination retains a strange influence and power over us.

The Isle of Britain is small (about the size of Idaho)— 600 miles long and 300 miles at its widest point. Its highest mountain (Scotland's Ben Nevis) is 4,406 feet, a foothill by our standards. The population is a fifth that of the US. At its peak in the mid-1800s, Great Britain owned one-fifth of the world and accounted for over half of the planet's industrial output. Today, though its landholdings have greatly diminished, its impact remains huge.

Great Britain is a major global player, with a rich heritage, lively present, and momentous future. Whether its

In Britain, the people are down-to-earth and the scenery is charming and iconic.

impending departure from the European Union ("Brexit") speeds up or slows down its progress, the result is sure to be interesting.

It's easy to think that "Britain" and "England" are one and the same. But actually, three unique countries make up Great Britain: England, Wales, and Scotland. (Add Northern Ireland and it's called the United Kingdom—but you'll need a different guidebook.) Let's take a quick tour through Great Britain's three nations.

ENGLAND

England is a cultural, linguistic touchstone for the almost one billion humans who speak English. It's the core of the United Kingdom: home to four out of five UK citizens, the seat of government, the economic powerhouse, and the center of higher learning.

South England, which includes London, has always had more people and more money than the north. Blessed with rolling hills, wide plains, and the Thames River, this region for centuries was rich with farms and its rivers flowed with trade. Then and now, high culture flourished in London, today a thriving metropolis of eight million people.

Britain's Pub Hub

In Britain, a pub is a home-away-from-home. Spend some time in one and you'll have your finger on the pulse of the community. These cozy hangouts are extended living rooms, where locals and travelers alike can eat, drink, get out of the rain, watch a sporting event, and meet other people.

Britain's pubs are also national treasures, with great cultural value and rich history, not to mention good beer and grub. Crawling between classic pubs is more than a tipsy night out—it's bona fide sight-seeing. Each offers a glimpse—and a taste—of traditional British culture.

Pubs' odd names can go back hundreds of years. Because many medieval pub-goers were illiterate, pubs were simply named for the picture hung outside (e.g., The Crooked Stick, The Queen's Arms—meaning her coat of arms).

The Golden Age for pub-building was in the late Victorian era (c. 1880–1905). In this class-conscious time, pubs were divided by screens (now mostly gone), allowing the wealthy to drink in a more refined setting. Pubs were really "public houses," featuring nooks (snugs) for groups and clubs to meet, friends and lovers to rendezvous, and families to get out of the house at night.

Pubs are neighborhood hang-outs with a personality, a quaint name, and a cozy or even elegant setting.

Fancy, late-Victorian pubs often come with heavy embossed wall-paper ceilings, decorative tile work, fine-etched glass, ornate carved stillions (the big central hutch for storing bottles and glass), and even urinals equipped with a place to set your glass. The "former-bank pubs" represent a more modern trend in pub-building. As banks increasingly go electronic, they're moving out of lavish, high-rent old buildings. ▶▶▶

▶▶▶ Many of these former banks are being refitted as pubs with elegant bars and freestanding stillions, which provide a fine centerpiece.

Pubs often serve traditional dishes, such as "bangers and mash" (sausages and mashed potatoes) and roast beef with Yorkshire pudding, but you're just as likely to find pasta, curried dishes, and quiche.

And, of course, there's the number-one reason people have always flocked to pubs: beer. The British take great pride in their brews. Many Brits think that drinking beer cold and carbonated, as Americans do, ruins the taste. Most pubs will have lagers (cold, refreshing, American-style beer), ales (amber-colored, cellar-temperature beer), bitters (hop-flavored ale, perhaps the most typical British beer), and stouts (dark and somewhat bitter, like Guinness). At pubs, long-handled pulls are used to pull the traditional, rich-flavored "real ales" up from the cellar. These are the connoisseur's favorites: fermented naturally, varying from sweet to bitter, often with a hoppy or nutty flavor. Short-handled pulls mean colder, fizzier, mass-produced, and less interesting keg beers. Mild beers are sweeter, with a creamy malt flavoring. Irish cream ale is a smooth, sweet experience. Try the draft cider (sweet or dry)... carefully.

Pubs offer hearty food (such as bangers and mash), various ales and beer, and friendly service.

Like in days past, people go to a pub to be social. If that's your aim, stick by the bar (rather than a table) and people will assume you're in the mood to talk. Go pubbing in the evening for a lively time, or drop by during the quiet late morning (from 11:00) for some lunchtime grub.

No matter what time of day, a visit to a historic pub is an enriching experience. Slow down, try a local beer, and make yourself at home. You'll likely gain a broader perspective, some interesting stories, and maybe even a new friend or two. ∎

North England tends to be hilly with poor soil, so the traditional economy was based on livestock (grazing cows and sheep). Known today for England's most beautiful landscapes, in the 19th century it was dotted with belching smokestacks as its major cities and its heartland became centers of coal and iron mining and manufacturing. Now its working-class cities and ports (such as Liverpool) are experiencing a comeback, buoyed by tourism, vibrant arts scenes, and higher employment.

England's economy can stand alongside many much larger nations. It boasts high-tech industries (software, chemicals, aviation), international banking, and textile manufacturing, and is a major exporter of beef. England is an urban, industrial, and post-industrial colossus, yet its farms, villages, and people are down-to-earth.

For the tourist, England offers a little of everything we associate with Britain: castles, cathedrals, and ruined abbeys; chatty locals nursing beers in village pubs; mysterious prehistoric stone circles and Roman ruins; tea, scones, and clotted cream; hikes across unspoiled, sheep-speckled hillsides; and drivers who cheerfully wave from the "wrong" side of the road. And then there's London, a world in itself, with famous cathedrals (St. Paul's), museums (the British Museum), and royalty (Buckingham Palace). London rivals New York as the

Bustling London offers nonstop entertainment while England's countryside provides a tranquil retreat.

best scene for live theater, and England entertains millions of people with its movies and music.

For a thousand years, England has been the cultural heart of Britain. Parliamentary democracy, science (Isaac Newton), technology (Michael Faraday), and education (Cambridge and Oxford) were nurtured here. In literature, England has few peers in any language, producing great legends (King Arthur, *Beowulf*, and *The Lord of the Rings*), poetry (by Chaucer, Wordsworth, and Byron), novels (by Dickens, Austen, and J. K. Rowling), and plays (by Shakespeare).

You can trace the evolution of England's long, illustrious history as you travel. Prehistoric peoples built the mysterious stone circles of Stonehenge and Avebury. Then came the Romans, who built Hadrian's Wall and the baths at Bath. Viking invaders left their mark in York, and the Normans built the Tower of London. As England Christianized, the grand cathedrals of Salisbury, Wells, and Durham arose. Next came the castles and palaces of the English monarchs (Windsor) and the Shakespeare sights from the era of Elizabeth I (Stratford-upon-Avon). Then tiny England became a maritime empire (the *Cutty Sark* at Greenwich) and the world's first industrial power (Ironbridge Gorge). England's Romantic poets were inspired by the unspoiled nature and villages of the Lake District and the Cotswolds. In the 20th century, gritty Liverpool gave the world the Beatles. Today London is on the cutting edge of 21st-century trends.

WALES

Humble, charming Wales is traditional and beautiful—it seems trapped in a time warp. At first, you'll feel you're still in England, but soon you'll awaken to the crusty yet poetic vitality of this small country. Don't ask for an "English breakfast" at your B&B—they'll politely remind you that it's a "Welsh breakfast," made with Welsh ingredients.

For the tourist, Wales is a land of stout castles (Conwy, Caernarfon, and more), salty harbors, chummy community choirs, slate-roofed villages, and a landscape of mountains, moors, and lush green fields dotted with sheep. Snowdonia National Park is a hiker's paradise, with steep but manageable mountain trails, cute-as-a-hobbit villages (Beddgelert

Wales builds its towns with native stone (Beddgelert, left) and boasts Europe's longest town name, with 58 letters, nicknamed Llanfair PG.

and Betws-y-Coed), and scenery more striking than most anything in England. Fascinating slate-mine museums (such as at Blaenau Ffestiniog), handy home-base towns (Conwy and Caernarfon), and enticing offbeat attractions round out Wales' appeal.

Culturally, Wales is "a land of poets and singers"—or so says the national anthem. From the myths of Merlin and King Arthur to the 20th-century poetry of Dylan Thomas, Wales has a long literary tradition. In music, the country nourishes its traditional Celtic folk music (especially the harp).

You'll enjoy hearing the locals speak Welsh with one another (before effortlessly switching to English for you). Their tongue-twisting, fun-to-listen-to language, with its mix of harsh and melodic tones, transports listeners to another time and place.

SCOTLAND

Rugged, feisty, and spirited Scotland is the home of kilts, bagpipes, golf, shortbread, haggis, and whisky—to wash down the haggis.

Scotland consists of two parts: the Lowlands (flatter, southern, and urban) and the Highlands (rugged, northern, and remote). The Lowlands star the Scottish capital of Edinburgh, with its bustling Royal Mile and stirring hilltop

castle. The underrated city of Glasgow has a friendly, down-to-earth appeal and youthful vibe, while St. Andrews has world-famous golf courses and sandy beaches.

To commune with the traditional Scottish soul, head for the Highlands' hills, lochs (lakes), castles, and whisky distilleries (where sampling is encouraged). The Highlands are bisected by the engineering marvel of the Caledonian Canal, which includes the famous Loch Ness (wave hi to Nessie). Hardy souls set sail from Oban for nearby islands.

While the Scots are known for their telltale burr and some unique words (aye, just listen for a wee blether), they're also trying to keep alive their own Celtic tongue: Gaelic (pronounced "gallic"). Few Scots speak Gaelic in everyday life, but legislation protects it, and it's beginning to be used on road signs. That's just one small sign of the famously independent Scottish spirit. Since the days of William "Braveheart" Wallace, the Scots have chafed under English rule. Thanks to the recent trend of "devolution," Scotland has become increasingly autonomous and has its own parliament.

Whether you're going to Scotland, Wales, England, or (my choice) all three, you'll have a grand adventure—and a great experience—in Great Britain. Cheerio!

Great Britain's Top Destinations

There's so much to see in Great Britain and so little time. This overview breaks Britain's top destinations into must-see sights (to help first-time travelers plan their trip) and worth-it sights (for those with extra time or special interests). I've also suggested a minimum number of days to allow per destination.

PLACES COVERED IN THIS BOOK

▲▲▲ Must See
▲▲ Try Hard to See
▲ Worthwhile

INVERNESS & LOCH NESS

GLENCOE & FORT WILLIAM

OBAN & THE INNER HEBRIDES

STIRLING & NEARBY

ST. ANDREWS

GLASGOW

EDINBURGH

SCOTLAND

50 Kilometers
50 Miles

DURHAM & N.E. ENGLAND

LAKE DISTRICT

Irish Sea

YORK

North Sea

LIVERPOOL

NORTH WALES

IRONBRIDGE GORGE

ENGLAND

STRATFORD-UPON-AVON

WALES

THE COTSWOLDS

SOUTH WALES

WINDSOR & CAMBRIDGE

Atlantic Ocean

BATH

LONDON

GLASTONBURY & WELLS

AVEBURY, STONEHENGE & SALISBURY

English Channel

MUST-SEE DESTINATIONS

These top cities give you an excellent, diverse sampler of the best of Great Britain.

▲▲▲ London (allow 3-4 days)
London has world-class museums, bustling markets, and cutting-edge architecture sharing the turf with the Tower of London and St. Paul's Cathedral. Enjoy London's cuisine scene, parks, grand squares, and palaces. Live theater takes center stage at night.

▲▲▲ Bath (2 days)
Bath is a genteel Georgian showcase city, built around an ancient Roman bath. Its glorious abbey, harmonious architecture, engaging walking tours, and small-town feel make it a good candidate for your first stop in Britain. Fun day trips include Glastonbury, Wells, Stonehenge, and more.

▲▲▲ York (1-2 days)
The walled medieval town has a grand Gothic cathedral (with a divine evensong) and fine museums (Viking, Victorian, and railway). Classy restaurants hide out in the atmospheric old center, with its "snickelway" passages and colorful Shambles shopping lane.

▲▲▲ Edinburgh (2 days)
The proud, endlessly entertaining Scottish capital has an imposing castle, attractions-studded Royal Mile, and excellent museums. You'll see all the clichés (ghost tours, whisky tastings, haggis, bagpipes, and kilts) and enjoy exuberant nightlife, especially during the city's famous festivals in August, featuring theater, music, and dance.

London's Millennium Bridge leading to St. Paul's, Bath's ancient Roman Baths museum and riverside setting, and a street festival in Edinburgh in August

WORTH-IT DESTINATIONS

You can weave any of these destinations—rated ▲ or ▲▲—into your itinerary. They're listed in the order they appear in the book. It's easy to add some destinations based on proximity (if you're going to the Cotswolds, Stratford-upon-Avon is next door), but some out-of-the-way places (such as Hadrian's Wall or Inverness) can also merit the journey, depending on your time and interests.

▲▲ Windsor and Cambridge (1-2 days)
Good day trips from London include Windsor, starring the Queen's impressive home-sweet-castle. Cambridge, one of England's best university towns, features the stunning King's College Chapel and Wren Library.

▲▲ Glastonbury and Wells (1 day)
Little Glastonbury has a mystical, New Age vibe, with its Holy Grail and King Arthur lore. The enjoyable town of Wells has an ingeniously fortified cathedral. Both towns are easy to visit from Bath.

▲▲ Avebury, Stonehenge, and Salisbury (1 day)
For spine-tingling stone circles, see famed Stonehenge (worth ▲▲▲ on its own) and the smaller, less touristy Avebury. Nearby is Salisbury and its striking cathedral.

▲▲ The Cotswolds (1-2 days)
These quaint villages—the cozy market town of Chipping Campden, popular Stow-on-the-Wold, and the handy transit hub of Moreton-in-Marsh—are scattered over a hilly countryside, which can be fun to explore on foot, by bike, or by car.

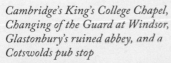

Cambridge's King's College Chapel, Changing of the Guard at Windsor, Glastonbury's ruined abbey, and a Cotswolds pub stop

▲ **Stratford-upon-Avon** (half-day to 1 day)
Shakespeare's pretty hometown, featuring residences that belonged to the bard and his loved ones, is the top venue for performances of his plays.

▲ **Ironbridge Gorge** (half-day to 1 day)
Boasting the planet's first iron bridge, this unassuming village was the birthplace of the Industrial Revolution, with sights and museums that tell the world-changing story.

▲ **Liverpool** (half-day to 1 day)
The rejuvenated port city is the Beatles' hometown, with a host of related sights (including the homes of John and Paul), museums, and pub-and-club nightlife.

▲▲ **The Lake District** (2 days)
This peaceful region, dotted with lakes, hills, and sheep, is known for its enjoyable hikes, joyrides, time-passed valleys, and William Wordsworth and Beatrix Potter sights.

▲ **Durham and Northeast England** (1-2 days)
The youthful workaday town has a magnificent cathedral, plus (nearby) an open-air museum, the Roman remains of Hadrian's Wall, Holy Island, and Bamburgh Castle.

▲▲ **North Wales** (1-2 days)
The scenically rugged land features castle towns (Conwy, Caernarfon, and Beaumaris), the natural beauty of Snowdonia National Park, tourable slate mines (Blaenau Ffestiniog),

colorful Welsh villages (Beddgelert and Llangollen), and charming locals who speak a tongue-twisting old language.

▲▲ South Wales (1-2 days)

The revitalized Welsh capital of Cardiff, poetic Tintern Abbey, castle towns (Caerphilly and Chepstow), and an open-air museum of Welsh culture offer an easy, rewarding look at Wales from Bath or the Cotswolds.

▲▲ Glasgow (1-2 days)

The best sight of Scotland's underrated, cultural "second city" may be its chatty, welcoming locals, with its nightlife a close second. The city is a hotbed of 20th-century architecture, thanks to native son Charles Rennie Mackintosh.

▲ Stirling and Nearby (half-day to 1 day)

Stirling, one of Scotland's top castles (home of the Stuart kings), overlooks a historic plain, with great sights nearby—from sculptures of giant horse heads to a Ferris wheel for boats to the time-warp village of Culross.

▲▲ St. Andrews (1 day)

Famous for golf, this is the only town in Britain where tee time is more prized than tea time. St. Andrews also boasts Scotland's top university and has a long sandy beach, both of which contribute to the town's youthful vibe.

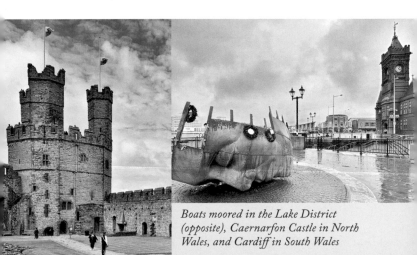

Boats moored in the Lake District (opposite), Caernarfon Castle in North Wales, and Cardiff in South Wales

▲▲ Oban and the Inner Hebrides (1-2 days)

The port town of Oban, with an easy-to-visit distillery, is a handy anchor for boat trips to the isles of the Inner Hebrides: rugged Mull, spiritual Iona, and remote Staffa's puffin colony and striking basalt columns.

▲ Glencoe and Fort William (half-day to 1 day)

The village of Glencoe is near the stirring "Weeping Glen," where government Redcoats killed the clansmen who sheltered them. Today the region offers lush Highland scenery and fine hikes, plus the transit-hub town of Fort William.

▲▲ Inverness and Loch Ness (half-day to 1 day)

The pleasant, regional capital is a launchpad for day trips to Highland sights, including Culloden Battlefield (Scotland's Alamo) and monster-spotting at the famous Loch Ness.

Touring Glasgow's museums, golfing at St. Andrews, and visiting the idyllic isle of Iona

Planning Your Trip

To plan your trip, you'll need to design your itinerary—choosing where and when to go, how you'll travel, and how many days to spend at each destination. For my best advice on sightseeing, accommodations, restaurants, and transportation, see the Practicalities chapter.

DESIGNING AN ITINERARY

As you read this book and learn your options...

Choose your top destinations.
My recommended itinerary (on the next page) gives you an idea of how much you can reasonably see in three weeks, but you can adapt it to fit your own interests and time frame.

If you enjoy big cities, you could easily spend a week in London (top-notch museums, food, street life, and entertainment); Edinburgh and Glasgow are also engaging and lively. For a slower pace of life, settle in any of Britain's many appealing towns, such as York or Bath. If villages beckon, linger in the Cotswolds, where time has all but stopped.

Nature lovers get wonderfully lost in the Lake District, Wales, and the Scottish Highlands. Sailors depart from Oban for islands beyond.

Literary fans make a pilgrimage to Stratford-upon-Avon (Shakespeare), Bath (Austen), and the Lake District (Wordsworth and Potter). Beatles fans from here, there, and everywhere head to Liverpool.

Britain's Best Three-Week Trip by Car

While this three-week itinerary is designed to be done by car, it can also be done by public transportation with modifications (see the itinerary later in this chapter).

Day	Plan	Sleep in
1	Arrive in London, connect to Bath (by train or bus)	Bath
2	Sightsee Bath	Bath
3	Pick up car, visit Avebury, Wells, Glastonbury	Bath
4	South Wales, Cardiff, Tintern	Chipping Campden
5	Explore the Cotswolds, Blenheim	Chipping Campden
6	Stratford	Ironbridge Gorge
7	Ironbridge Gorge to North Wales	Conwy
8	Highlights of North Wales	Conwy
9	Liverpool	Liverpool
10	South Lake District	Keswick area
11	North Lake District	Keswick area
12	Drive up west coast of Scotland	Oban
13	Explore the Highlands, Loch Ness	Edinburgh
14	Edinburgh	Edinburgh
15	Edinburgh	Edinburgh
16	Hadrian's Wall, Beamish Museum, Durham's cathedral and evensong	Durham
17	Drive to York, turn in car	York
18	York	York
19	Early train to London	London
20	London	London
21	London	London
22	Whew!	

History buffs choose their era: prehistoric (Stonehenge), ancient Roman (Bath and Hadrian's Wall), medieval (York), Industrial Revolution (Ironbridge Gorge), royal (Tower of London, Windsor Castle, Edinburgh Castle), and many more. If you've ever wanted to storm a castle before afternoon tea, you're in the right place.

Decide when to go.

July and August are peak season—with long days, the best weather, and a busy schedule of tourist fun. May and June

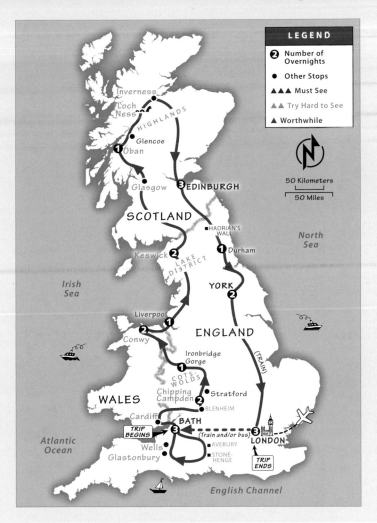

can be lovely anywhere. Spring and fall offer decent weather and smaller crowds.

Winter travelers encounter few crowds and soft room prices (except in London), but sightseeing hours are shorter and the weather is reliably bad. In the countryside, some attractions open only on weekends or close entirely (Nov-Feb). While rural charm falls with the leaves, city sightseeing is fine in winter.

For weather specifics, see the climate chart in the appendix.

23

Expect a mix of sun and clouds, whether at Scotland's gigantic Kelpies or England's top-of-the-world Lake District.

Connect the dots.

Link your destinations into a logical route. Determine which cities you'll fly into and out of. Begin your search for transatlantic flights at Kayak.com.

Decide if you'll travel by car or public transportation, or both. A car is helpful for exploring places where public transportation can be sparse or time-consuming (such as the Cotswolds, Ironbridge Gorge, the Lake District, and the Scottish Highlands), but is useless in big cities (park it). Some travelers rent a car on site for a day or two, and use public transportation for the rest.

Trains are faster and more expensive than buses (which rarely run on Sundays). Minibus tours can cover regional sights efficiently for travelers without wheels.

For approximate transportation times between destinations, study the driving chart (see the Practicalities chapter) or train schedules (www.nationalrail.co.uk or ww.bahn.com).

If traveling beyond Britain, consider taking the Eurostar train (London to Paris) or a budget flight; check Skyscanner.com for flights within Europe.

Write out a day-by-day itinerary.

Figure out how many destinations you can comfortably fit in. Don't overdo it—few travelers wish they'd hurried more. Allow enough days per stop (see estimates in "Great Britain's Top Destinations," earlier). Minimize one-night stands, especially consecutive ones. It can be worth a late-afternoon drive or train ride to get settled in a town for two nights.

Britain's Best Three-Week Trip by Public Transportation

For three weeks without a car, cut back on the sights with the most frustrating public transportation (parts of Wales, Ironbridge Gorge, and the Scottish Highlands). Lacing together the cities by train is slick (though some journeys in this itinerary involve transfers—usually just one). Buses, slower and cheaper, can get you where the trains don't go (but service is scarce on Sundays).

Day	Plan	Sleep in
1	Arrive in London, connect to Bath (by train or bus)	Bath
2	Sightsee Bath	Bath
3	Stonehenge and Avebury by minibus day tour	Bath
4	To Cotswolds by train to Moreton-in-Marsh (2.5 hours), then bus to Chipping Campden (0.5 hour)	Chipping Campden (or Moreton-in-Marsh)
5	Cotswolds, or day-trip to Stratford (1.5 hours by bus), or Blenheim (1 hour by train-plus-bus)	Chipping Campden (or Moreton-in-Marsh)
6	To North Wales by train (5-6 scenic hours)	Conwy
7	See highlights of North Wales on a leisurely train and bus loop	Conwy
8	To Liverpool by train (2 hours)	Liverpool
9	To Lake District by train to Penrith, then bus to Keswick (about 3 hours)	Keswick
10	Explore Lake District on foot and/or by bus or boat	Keswick
11	To Oban, Scotland, by train (5-6 scenic hours)	Oban
12	Boat tour of islands of Mull, Iona, and possibly Staffa	Oban
13	To Glasgow by train or bus (3 hours)	Glasgow
14	More Glasgow, then to Edinburgh by train (1 hour)	Edinburgh
15	Edinburgh	Edinburgh
16	Edinburgh	Edinburgh
17	To York by train (2.5 hours)	York
18	York	York
19	Early train to London (2 hours)	London
20	London	London
21	London	London
22	Whew!	

Include sufficient time for transportation; whether you travel by car or public transit, it'll take you a half-day to get between most destinations.

Staying in a home base (like London or Bath) and making day trips can be more time-efficient than changing locations and hotels.

Take sight closures into account. Avoid visiting a town on the one day a week its must-see sights are closed. Check if any holidays or festivals fall during your trip—these attract crowds and can close sights (for the latest, visit Britain's tourist website, www.visitbritain.com).

Give yourself some slack. Every trip, and every traveler, needs downtime for doing laundry, picnic shopping, people-watching, and so on. Pace yourself. Assume you will return.

Cosmopolitan London celebrates cultural festivals. Make time for people-watching.

Trip Costs Per Person

Run a reality check on your dream trip. You'll have major transportation costs in addition to daily expenses.

Flight: A round-trip flight from the US to London costs about $1,000-2,000, depending on where you fly from and when.

Public Transportation: For a three-week trip, allow $725 for second-class trains and bus travel ($1,050 for first class plus buses), and $30 for the London Tube. A BritRail pass is a good value; buy it before you go.

Car Rental: Allow roughly $250 per week, not including tolls, gas, parking, and insurance. If you need the car for three weeks or more, leasing can be cheaper.

AVERAGE DAILY EXPENSES PER PERSON

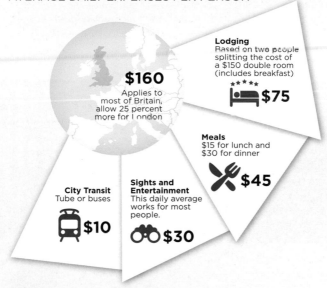

$160
Applies to most of Britain, allow 25 percent more for London

Lodging
Based on two people splitting the cost of a $150 double room (includes breakfast)
$75

Meals
$15 for lunch and $30 for dinner
$45

City Transit
Tube or buses
$10

Sights and Entertainment
This daily average works for most people.
$30

Budget Tips

You can cut your daily expenses by taking advantage of the deals you'll find throughout Britain and mentioned in this book.

City transit passes (for multiple rides or all-day usage) decrease your cost per ride. For example, it's smart to get an Oyster card in London, valid on the Tube and buses.

Avid sightseers buy combo-tickets or passes that cover multiple museums. If a town doesn't offer deals, visit only the sights you most want to see, and seek out free sights and experiences (offered even in London).

Some businesses—especially hotels and walking-tour companies—offer discounts ▶▶▶

▶▶▶ to my readers (look for the RS% symbol in the hotel listings in this book).

Book your rooms directly with the hotel via email or phone for the best rates. Some hotels offer a discount if you pay in cash and/or stay three or more nights (check online or ask). Rooms cost less outside of peak season (July and Aug). And even seniors can sleep cheap in hostels (some have double rooms) for as little as $30 per person. Or check Airbnb-type sites for deals.

It's no hardship to eat cheap in Britain. You can get tasty, inexpensive meals at pubs, cafeterias, chain restaurants, ethnic eateries, and fish-and-chips joints. Some upscale restaurants offer early-bird dinner specials. Most grocery stores sell ready-made sandwiches; cultivate the art of picnicking in atmospheric settings.

When you splurge, choose an experience you'll always remember, such as an elegant afternoon tea or a splashy London musical. Minimize souvenir shopping—how will you get it all home? Focus instead on collecting wonderful memories. ▮

Indian food is "going local" in Britain. Save money when you can, but splurge on experiences, like a play in London.

BEFORE YOU GO

You'll have a smoother trip if you tackle a few things ahead of time. For more information on these topics, see the Practicalities chapter (and www.ricksteves.com, which has helpful travel tips and talks).

Make sure your passport is valid. If it's due to expire within six months of your ticketed date of return, you need to renew it. Allow up to six weeks to renew or get a passport (www.travel.state.gov).

Arrange your transportation. Book your international flights early. Figure out your main form of transportation within Britain: You can rent a car, get a rail pass, or buy train tickets as you go. (You can wing it in Europe, but it may cost more.)

Book rooms well in advance, especially if your trip falls during peak season or any major holidays or festivals (such as Edinburgh's busy festival month, August).

Reserve or buy tickets ahead for must-see plays, special tours, or sights. If there's a show you're set on seeing, you can buy tickets before you go. At Stonehenge, most visitors are happy to view the stones from a distance, but to go inside the circle, you'll need reservations. To tour the interior of the Lennon and McCartney homes in Liverpool, reserve ahead.

Edinburgh is crowded in August during festival time. Book ahead for any events you must see (theater, dance, and the Military Tattoo). You can also book online for Edinburgh Castle. To golf at St. Andrews' famous Old Course, you'll need to reserve the previous fall, or put your name in for the "ballot" two days before. When you're in London, you can buy Fast Track tickets for some popular sights in advance, saving you time in line. Specifics on making reservations are in the chapters

Consider travel insurance. Compare the cost of the insurance to the cost of your potential loss. Check whether your existing insurance (health, homeowners, or renters) covers you and your possessions overseas.

Call your bank. Alert your bank that you'll be using your debit and credit cards in Europe. Ask about transaction fees, and get the PIN number for your credit card. You don't need to bring pounds for your trip; you can withdraw currency from cash machines in Europe.

Use your smartphone smartly. Sign up for an international service plan to reduce your costs, or rely on Wi-Fi in Europe instead. Download any apps you'll want on the road, such as maps, transit schedules, and Rick Steves Audio Europe (see sidebar).

Rip up this book! Turn chapters into mini guidebooks: Break the book's spine and use a utility knife to slice apart chapters, keeping gummy edges intact. Reinforce the chapter spines with clear wide tape; use a heavy-duty stapler; or make or buy a cheap cover (see www.ricksteves.com), swapping out chapters as you travel.

Pack light. You'll walk with your luggage more than you think. Bring a single carry-on bag and a daypack. Use the packing checklist in the appendix as a guide.

∩ Stick This Guidebook in Your Ear!

My free Rick Steves Audio Europe app makes it easy for you to download my audio tours of many of Europe's top attractions and listen to them offline during your travels. For Great Britain, these include major museums and neighborhoods in London and my Royal Mile Walk in Edinburgh. Sights covered by audio tours are marked in this book with this symbol: ∩. The app also offers insightful travel interviews from my public radio show with experts from Great Britain and around the globe. It's all free! You can download the app via Apple's App Store, Google Play, or Amazon's Appstore. For more info, see www.ricksteves.com/audioeurope.

Travel Smart

If you have a positive attitude, equip yourself with good information (this book) and expect to travel smart, you will.

Read—and reread—this book. To have an "A" trip, be an "A" student. As you study up on sights, note opening hours of sights, closed days, and crowd-beating tips. Check the latest at www.ricksteves.com/update.

Be your own tour guide. As you travel, get up-to-date info on sights, reserve tickets and tours, reconfirm hotels and travel arrangements, and check transit connections. Visit local tourist information offices. Upon arrival in a new town, lay the groundwork for a smooth departure; confirm the train, bus, or road you'll take when you leave.

Outsmart thieves. Pickpockets abound in crowded places where tourists congregate. Treat commotions as smokescreens for theft. Keep your cash, credit cards, and passport secure in a money belt tucked under your clothes; carry only a day's spending money in your front pocket. Don't set valuable items down on counters or café tabletops, where they can be quickly stolen or easily forgotten.

Minimize potential loss. Keep expensive gear to a minimum. Bring photocopies or take photos of important documents (passport and cards) to aid in replacement if they're lost or stolen.

Guard your time and energy. Taking a taxi can be a good value if you're too tired to tackle the Tube or wait for a bus. To avoid long lines, follow my crowd-beating tips, such as making advance reservations, or sightseeing early or late.

Be flexible. Even if you have a well-planned itinerary,

expect changes, strikes, closures, sore feet, bad weather, and so on. Your Plan B could turn out to be even better.

Connect with the culture. Interacting with locals carbonates your experience. Enjoy the friendliness of the British people. Ask questions; most locals are happy to point you in their idea of the right direction. Set up your own quest for the friendliest pub, favorite castle, best London show, or silliest name for a sweet treat. When an opportunity pops up, make it a habit to say "yes."

Great Britain...here you come!

ENGLAND

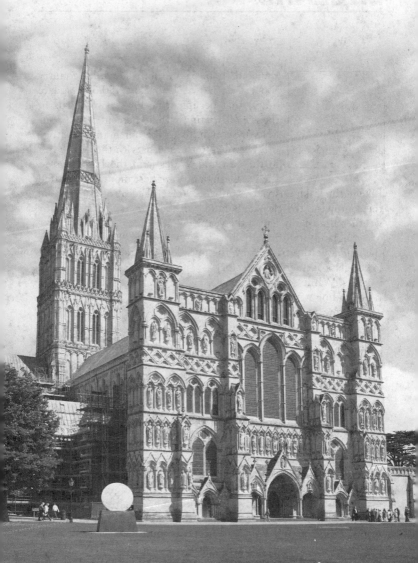

ENGLAND

England (pop. 55 million) is a hilly country about the size of Louisiana (50,346 square miles) that occupies the lower two-thirds of the isle of Britain (with 80 percent of its population). Scotland is to the north and the English Channel to the south, with the North Sea to the east and Wales (and the Irish Sea) to the west. England's highest mountain (Scafell Pike in the Lake District) is only 3,206 feet. Fed by ocean air from the southwest, the climate is mild, with a chance of cloudy, rainy weather almost any day of the year.

England traditionally has been very class-conscious, with the land-wealthy aristocracy, the middle-class tradesmen, and the lower-class farmers and factory workers. While social stratification is fading with the new global economy, regional differences remain strong. Locals can often identify where someone is from by their dialect or local accent—Geordie, Cockney, or Queen's English.

One thing that sets England apart from its fellow UK countries (Scotland, Wales, and Northern Ireland) is its ethnic makeup. Traditionally, those countries had Celtic roots, while the English mixed in Saxon and Norman blood. In the 20th century, England welcomed many Scots, Welsh, and Irish as low-wage workers. More recently, it's become home to immigrants from former colonies of its worldwide empire—particularly from India/Pakistan/Bangladesh, the Caribbean, and Africa—and to many workers from poorer Eastern European countries. These days it's not a given that every "English" person speaks English. Nearly one in three citizens does not profess the Christian faith. As the world becomes interconnected by communications technology, it's possible for many immigrants to physically inhabit the country while

England

SCOTLAND

Berwick-upon-Tweed
Holy Island

HADRIAN'S WALL

Hexham • Newcastle

North Sea

Carlisle

Keswick •

LAKE DISTRICT

• Durham

Windermere •

NORTH YORK MOORS

• Whitby

Lancaster •

• York

Blackpool •

• Leeds

Kingston-upon-Hull

Irish Sea

Liverpool •

Conwy •

• Manchester

Chester •

MIDLANDS

• Lincoln

ENGLAND

IRONBRIDGE GORGE ■

• Birmingham

• Coventry

King's Lynn

NORFOLK

Norwich •

• Warwick

WALES

COTSWOLDS

• Stratford upon-Avon

Chipping Campden •

■ BLENHEIM PALACE

• Oxford

Cambridge

ESSEX

Harwich •

Cardiff •

• Bath

▲ AVEBURY

London

Wells •

WILTSHIRE

Windsor •

⊛

Canter-bury

Glastonbury •

STONE-HENGE ■

• Salisbury

Greenwich •

Dartmoor Nat'l Park →■

SOMERSET

• Exeter

DORSET

SUSSEX

KENT

Dover •

DEVON

Weymouth •

Bourne-mouth

• Brighton

CORNWALL

Portsmouth

• Penzance

English Channel

50 Kilometers
50 Miles

remaining closely linked to their home culture—rather than truly assimilating into England.

This is the current English paradox. England—the birthplace and center of the extended worldwide family of English speakers—is losing its traditional Englishness. Where Scotland, Wales, and Northern Ireland have cultural movements to preserve their local languages and customs, England does not. Politically, there is no "English" party in the UK Parliament. While Scotland, Wales, and Northern Ireland have their own

parliaments to decide local issues, England must depend on the decisions of the UK government at large. Except for the occasional display of an English flag (the red St. George's cross on a white background) at a football (soccer) match, many English people don't really think of themselves as "English"—more as "Brits," a part of the wider UK.

Today, England tries to preserve its rich past as it races forward as a leading global player. There are still hints of its legacy of farms, villages, Victorian lamplighters, and upper-crust dandies. But it's also a jostling world of unemployed factory workers, investment bankers, football matches, rowdy "stag parties," and faux-Tudor suburbs. Modern England is a culturally diverse land in transition. Catch it while you can.

LONDON

London is more than 600 square miles of urban jungle—a world in itself and a barrage on all the senses. On my first visit, I felt extremely small.

London is more than its museums and landmarks. It's the L.A., D.C., and N.Y.C. of Britain—a living, breathing, thriving organism...a coral reef of humanity. The city has changed dramatically in recent years, and many visitors are surprised to find how "un-English" it is. ESL (English as a second language) seems like the city's first language, as white people are now a minority in major parts of the city that once symbolized white imperialism. London is a city of eight million separate dreams, inhabiting a place that tolerates and encourages them. Arabs have nearly bought out the area north of Hyde Park. Chinese takeouts outnumber fish-and-chips shops. Eastern Europeans pull pints in British pubs, and Italians express your espresso. Many hotels are run by people with foreign accents (who hire English chambermaids), while outlying suburbs are home to huge communities of Indians and Pakistanis.

But with Britain's recent vote to exit the EU, the British people have decided to pull up the drawbridge. From a practical standpoint, travelers heading to London soon likely won't see much of a post-"Brexit" difference...other than a cheaper pound sterling and plenty to talk about with your new British friends.

The city, which has long attracted tourists, seems perpetually at your service, with an impressive slate of sights, entertainment, and eateries, all linked by a great transit system. With just a few days here, you'll get no more than a quick splash in this teeming human tidal pool. But with a good orientation, you'll find London manageable and fun. You'll get a sampling of the city's top sights, history, and cultural entertainment, and a good look at its ever-changing human face.

Blow through the city on the open deck of a double-decker orientation tour bus, and take a pinch-me-I'm-in-London walk through the West End. Ogle the crown jewels at the Tower of London, gaze up at mighty Big Ben, and see the Houses of Parliament in action. Cruise the River Thames, and take a spin on the London Eye. Hobnob with poets' tombstones in Westminster Abbey, and visit with Leonardo, Botticelli, and Rembrandt in the National Gallery. Enjoy Shakespeare in a replica of the Globe theater and marvel at a glitzy, fun musical at a modern-day theater. Whisper across the dome of St. Paul's Cathedral, then rummage through our civilization's attic at the British Museum. And sip your tea with pinky raised and clotted cream dribbling down your scone.

PLANNING YOUR TIME

The sights of London alone could easily fill a trip to England. It's a great one-week getaway. But on a three-week tour of England, I'd give London three busy days. You won't be able to see everything, so don't try. You'll keep coming back to London. After dozens of visits myself, I still enjoy a healthy list of excuses to return. If you're flying in to one of London's airports, consider starting your trip in Bath and making London your English finale. Especially if you hope to enjoy a play or concert, a night or two of jet lag is bad news.

Here's a suggested three-day schedule:

Day 1

Use my Westminster Walk to link the following sights:

9:00	Be in line at Westminster Abbey (opens at 9:30, closed Sun), to tour the place with fewer crowds.
11:00	Visit the Churchill War Rooms.
13:00	Eat lunch at the Churchill War Rooms café or nearby, or grab a later lunch near Trafalgar Square.
15:00	Visit the National Gallery and any nearby sights that interest you (National Portrait Gallery or St. Martin-in-the-Fields Church).
Evening	Dinner and a play in the West End.

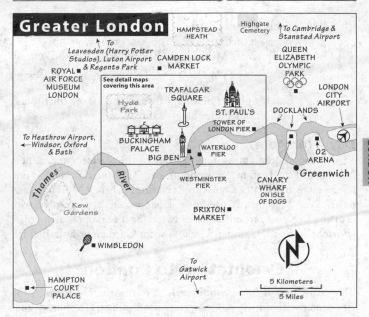

Day 2

8:30	Take a double-decker hop-on, hop-off London sightseeing bus tour (from Victoria Station or Green Park).
10:00	Hop off at Trafalgar Square and walk briskly to Buckingham Palace to secure a spot to watch the Changing of the Guard.
11:00	Buckingham Palace (guards change most days May-July at 11:00, alternate days Aug-April—confirm online).
14:00	After lunch, tour the British Museum.
16:00	Tour the British Library.
Evening	Choose from a play, concert, or walking tour, or do some shopping at one of London's elegant department stores (Harrod's, Liberty, and Fortnum & Mason are open until 20:00 or 21:00 except on Sun).

Day 3

9:00	Tower of London (crown jewels first, then Beefeater tour and White Tower; note that the Tower opens at 10:00 Sun-Mon).
12:00	Grab a picnic, catch a boat at Tower Pier, and have lunch on the Thames while cruising to Blackfriars Pier.

13:00	Tour St. Paul's Cathedral and climb its dome for views (cathedral closed Sun except for worship).
15:00	Walk across Millennium Bridge to the South Bank to visit the Tate Modern, Shakespeare's Globe, or other sights.
Evening	Catch a play at Shakespeare's Globe, or see the other suggestions under Days 1 and 2.

Day 4 (or More)

Visit London's remaining top-tier sights: the Victoria and Albert Museum, Tate Britain, or London Eye. Or you can choose one of the city's many other museums (Natural History Museum, Imperial War Museum, Museum of London, etc.); take a day trip, cruising to Kew Gardens or Greenwich; or hit an open-air market (Portobello Road, Camden Lock, Covent Garden, or Spitalfields).

Orientation to London

To grasp London more comfortably, see it as the old town in the city center without the modern, congested sprawl. (Even from that perspective, it's still huge.)

The River Thames (pronounced "tems") runs roughly west to east through the city, with most of the visitor's sights on the North Bank. Mentally, maybe even physically, trim down your map to include only the area between the Tower of London (to the east), Hyde Park (west), Regent's Park (north), and the South Bank (south). This is roughly the area bordered by the Tube's Circle Line. This four-mile stretch between the Tower and Hyde Park (about a 1.5-hour walk) looks like a milk bottle on its side (see map), and holds 80 percent of the sights mentioned in this chapter.

The sprawling city becomes much more manageable if you think of it as a collection of neighborhoods.

Central London: This area contains Westminster and what Londoners call the West End. The Westminster district includes Big Ben, Parliament, Westminster Abbey, and Buckingham Palace—the grand government buildings from which Britain is ruled. Trafalgar Square, London's gathering place, has many major museums. The West End is the center of London's cultural life, with bustling squares: Piccadilly Circus and Leicester Square host cinemas, tourist traps, and nighttime glitz. Soho and Covent Garden are thriving people zones with theaters, restaurants, pubs, and boutiques. And Regent and Oxford streets are the city's main shopping zones.

North London: Neighborhoods in this part of town—including Bloomsbury, Fitzrovia, and Marylebone—contain such major sights as the British Museum and the overhyped Madame Tus-

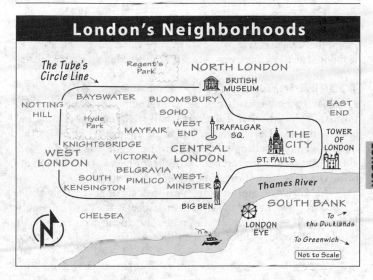

London's Neighborhoods

The Tube's Circle Line

Regent's Park

NORTH LONDON

BRITISH MUSEUM

BAYSWATER

BLOOMSBURY

NOTTING HILL

Hyde Park

SOHO

EAST END

WEST END

MAYFAIR

TRAFALGAR SQ.

THE CITY

TOWER OF LONDON

KNIGHTSBRIDGE

CENTRAL LONDON

WEST LONDON

VICTORIA

ST. PAUL'S

BELGRAVIA

SOUTH KENSINGTON

PIMLICO

WEST-MINSTER

Thames River

CHELSEA

BIG BEN

LONDON EYE

SOUTH BANK

To the Docklands

To Greenwich

Not to Scale

LONDON

sauds Waxworks. Nearby, along busy Euston Road, is the British Library, plus a trio of train stations (one of them, St. Pancras International, is linked to Paris by the Eurostar "Chunnel" train).

The City: Today's modern financial district, called simply "The City," was a walled town in Roman times. Gleaming skyscrapers are interspersed with historical landmarks such as St. Paul's Cathedral, legal sights (Old Bailey), and the Museum of London. The Tower of London and Tower Bridge lie at The City's eastern border.

East London: Just east of The City is the East End—the former stomping ground of Cockney ragamuffins and Jack the Ripper, and now an increasingly gentrified neighborhood of hipsters, "pop-up" shops, and an emerging food scene.

The South Bank: The South Bank of the River Thames offers major sights (Tate Modern, Shakespeare's Globe, London Eye) linked by a riverside walkway. Within this area, Southwark (SUTH-uck) stretches from the Tate Modern to London Bridge. Pedestrian bridges connect the South Bank with The City and Trafalgar Square.

West London: This huge area contains neighborhoods such as Mayfair, Belgravia, Pimlico, Chelsea, South Kensington, and Notting Hill. It's home to London's wealthy and has many trendy shops and enticing restaurants. Here you'll find a range of museums (Victoria and Albert Museum, Tate Britain, and more), my top hotel recommendations, lively Victoria Station, and the vast green expanses of Hyde Park and Kensington Gardens.

Outside the Center: The Docklands, London's version of Manhattan, is farther east than the East End. Historic Greenwich is southeast of London and across the Thames. Kew Gardens and Hampton Court Palace are southwest of London. To the north of London is the Warner Bros. Studio Tour (for Harry Potter fans).

TOURIST INFORMATION

It's amazing how hard it can be to find unbiased sightseeing information and advice in London. You'll see "Tourist Information" offices advertised everywhere, but most are private agencies that make a big profit selling tours and advance sightseeing and/or theater tickets; others are run by Transport for London (TFL) and are primarily focused on providing public-transit advice.

The **City of London Information Centre** next to St. Paul's Cathedral (just outside the church entrance) is the city's only publicly funded—and impartial—"real" TI (Mon-Sat 9:30-17:30, Sun 10:00-16:00; Tube: St. Paul's, tel. 020/7332-1456, www.visitthecity.co.uk).

While officially a service of The City (London's financial district), this office also provides information about the rest of London. It sells Oyster cards, London Passes, advance "Fast Track" sightseeing tickets (all described later), and some National Express bus tickets. It also stocks various free publications: *London Planner* (a free monthly that lists all the sights, events, and hours), some walking-tour brochures, the *Official London Theatre Guide*, a free Tube and bus map, the *Guide to River Thames Boat Services*, and brochures describing self-guided walks in The City (various themes, including Dickens, modern architecture, Shakespeare, and film locations).

The TI gives out a free map of The City and sells several city-wide maps; ask if they have yet another, free map with various coupons for discounts on sights. Skip their room-booking service (charges a commission) and theater box office (may charge a commission).

Visit London, which serves the greater London area, doesn't have an office you can visit in person—but does have an info-packed website (www.visitlondon.com).

Fast Track Tickets: To skip the ticket-buying queues at certain London sights, you can buy Fast Track tickets (sometimes called "priority pass" tickets) in advance—and they can be cheaper than tickets sold right at the sight. They're particularly smart for the Tower of London (a voucher you exchange for a ticket at the Tower's group ticket window), the London Eye, The Shard, and Madame Tussauds Waxworks, all of which get very busy in high season. They're available through various sales outlets (including the City of London TI, souvenir stands, and faux-TIs scattered throughout touristy areas).

London Pass: This pass, which covers many big sights and lets you skip some lines, is expensive but potentially worth the investment for extremely busy sightseers. Among the many sights it includes are the Tower of London, Westminster Abbey, Churchill War Rooms, and Windsor Castle, as well as many temporary exhibits and audioguides at otherwise "free" biggies. Think through your sightseeing plans, study their website to see what's covered, and do the math before you buy (£62/1 day, £85/2 days, £101/3 days, £139/6 days; days are calendar days rather than 24-hour periods; comes with 160-page guidebook, also sold at major train stations and airports, tel. 020/7293-0972, www.londonpass.com).

ARRIVAL IN LONDON

For more information on getting to or from London, see "London Connections" at the end of this chapter.

By Train: London has nine major train stations, all connected by the Tube (subway). All have ATMs, and many of the larger stations also have shops, fast food, exchange offices, and luggage storage. From any station, you can ride the Tube or taxi to your hotel.

By Bus: The main intercity bus station is Victoria Coach Station, one block southwest of Victoria train/Tube station.

By Plane: London has six airports. Most tourists arrive at Heathrow or Gatwick airport, although flights from elsewhere in Europe may land at Stansted, Luton, Southend, or London City airport. For hotels near Heathrow and Gatwick, see page 182.

HELPFUL HINTS

Theft Alert: Wear your money belt. The Artful Dodger is alive and well in London. Be on guard, particularly on public transportation and in places crowded with tourists, who, considered naive and rich, are targeted. The Changing of the Guard scene is a favorite for thieves. And more than 7,500 purses are stolen annually at Covent Garden alone.

Pedestrian Safety: Cars drive on the left side of the road—which can be as confusing for foreign pedestrians as for foreign drivers. Before crossing a street, I always look right, look left, then look right again just to be sure. Most crosswalks are even painted with instructions, reminding foreign guests to "Look right" or "Look left." While locals are champion jaywalkers, you shouldn't try it; jaywalking is treacherous when you're disoriented about which direction traffic is coming from.

Medical Problems: Local hospitals have good-quality 24-hour-a-day emergency care centers, where any tourist who needs help can drop in and, after a wait, be seen by a doctor. Your hotel has details. St. Thomas' Hospital, immediately across the river from Big Ben, has a fine reputation.

Sightseeing Tips: Many of London's museums are free, which also means they're crowded; visit early or late (many have evening hours). The Tower of London and British Museum are especially crowded on weekends, when street markets are lively and most worth visiting. On Sunday, most theaters take the day off, and Westminster Abbey and St. Paul's are open during the day for worship but closed to sightseers. Visit Westminster Abbey on a weekday afternoon, then stay for the 17:00 evensong.

Busy sightseers should consider the London Pass: It's expensive but lets you to skip the lines at some major sights. Fast Track tickets are also available for a few key sights, like the Tower of London and Westminster Abbey (see page 42 for details).

Getting Your Bearings: London is well-signed for visitors. Through an initiative called Legible London, the city has erected thoughtfully designed, pedestrian-focused maps around town—especially handy when exiting Tube stations. In this sprawling city—where predictable grid-planned streets are relatively rare—it's also smart to buy and use a good map. For suggestions, see page 1021.

Festivals: For one week in February and another in September, fashionistas descend on the city for **London Fashion Week** (www.londonfashionweek.co.uk). The famous **Chelsea Flower Show** blossoms in late May (book ahead for this popular event at www.rhs.org.uk/chelsea). During the annual **Trooping the Colour** in June, there are military bands and pageantry, and the Queen's birthday parade (https://qbp.army.mod.uk). Tennis fans pack the stands at the **Wimbledon Tennis Championship** in late June to early July (www.wimbledon.org), and partygoers head for the **Notting Hill Carnival** in late August.

Traveling in Winter: London dazzles year-round, so consider visiting in winter, when airfares and hotel rates are generally cheaper and there are fewer tourists. For ideas on what to do, see the "Winter Activities in London" article at www.ricksteves.com/winteracts.

Wi-Fi: In addition to the Wi-Fi that's likely available at your hotel, many major museums, sights, and even entire boroughs offer free access. For example, **O2 Wifi** hotspots let you connect for free in Trafalgar Square, Leicester Square, and Piccadilly (www.o2wifi.co.uk). Consider a free account with **The Cloud,** a Wi-Fi service found in most London train stations and many museums, coffee shops, cafés, and shopping centers (though the connection can be slow). When you sign up at www.skywifi.cloud, you'll be asked to enter a street address and postal code; it doesn't matter which one (use your hotel's,

or the Queen's: Buckingham Palace, SW1A 1AA). Then use
the **Sky WiFi app** to locate hotspots.

Most **Tube stations** and trains have Wi-Fi, but it's free
only to those with a British Virgin Media account. However,
the Tube's Wi-Fi always lets you access Transport for London's "Plan a Journey" feature (www.tfl.gov.uk), making it
easy to look up transit options—and get real-time updates on
delays—once you're in a station. To use the Tube's pay Wi-Fi,
you'll pay £2 for a one-day pass, or £5 for a one-week pass
(http://my.virginmedia.com/wifi).

Useful Apps: Mapway's free **Tube Map London Underground**
and **Bus Times London** (www.mapway.com) apps show the
easiest way to connect Tube stations and provide bus stops
and route information. When you're online, the apps provide
live updates about delays, closures, and time estimates for
your journey. The handy **Citymapper** app for London covers
every mode of public transit in the city. **City Maps 2Go** lets
you download searchable offline maps; their London version
is quite good. And **Time Out London**'s free app has reviews
and listings for theater, museums, and movies (download the
"Make Your City Amazing" version—it's updated weekly—
not the boilerplate "Travel Guide" version).

Travel Bookstores: Located between Covent Garden and Leicester Square, the very good **Stanfords Travel Bookstore** stocks
a huge selection of guidebooks (including current editions
of my titles), travel-related novels, maps, and gear (Mon-Sat
9:00-20:00, Sun 11:30-18:00, 12 Long Acre, second entrance
on Floral Street, Tube: Leicester Square, tel. 020/7836-1321,
www.stanfords.co.uk).

Two impressive **Waterstones** bookstores have the biggest
collection of travel guides in town: on Piccadilly (Mon-Sat
9:00-22:00, Sun 12:00-18:30, café, great views from top-floor
bar—see sidebar on page 117, 203 Piccadilly, tel. 0843-290-
8549) and on Trafalgar Square (Mon-Sat 9:00-21:00, Sun
12:00-18:00, Costa Café on second floor, tel. 020/7839-4411).

Daunts Books, housed in a church-like Edwardian
building full of oak accents and stained-glass windows, is a
North London staple known for arranging books by geography, regardless of subject or author (Mon-Sat 9:00-19:30, Sun
11:00-18:00, 83 Marylebone High Street, Tube: Baker Street,
tel. 020/7724-2295, www.dauntbooks.co.uk).

Baggage Storage: Train stations have replaced lockers with more
secure left-luggage counters. Each bag must go through a
scanner (just like at the airport). Expect long waits in the
morning to check in (up to 45 minutes) and in the afternoon to
pick up (each item-£12.50/24 hours, most stations daily 7:00-

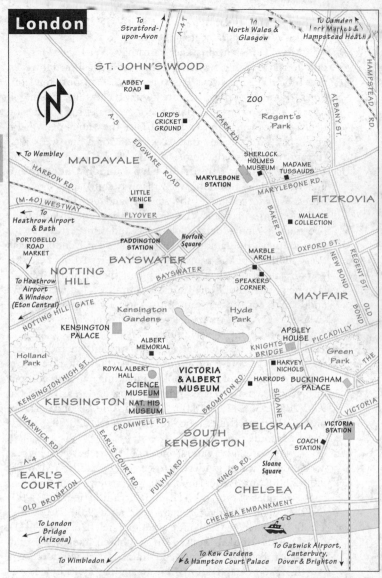

London

LONDON

23:00). You can also store bags at the airports (similar rates and hours, www.left-baggage.co.uk).

"Voluntary Donations": Some London sights automatically add a "voluntary donation" of about 10 percent to their admission fees. The prices posted and quoted in this chapter include the donation, though it's perfectly fine to pay the base price without the donation. Some of London's free museums also ask for donations as you enter, but again, it's completely optional.

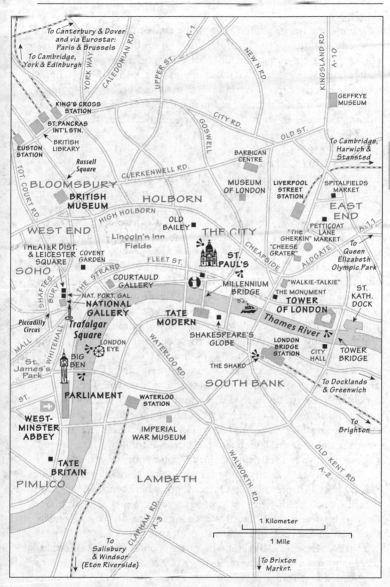

LONDON

GETTING AROUND LONDON

To travel smart in a city this size, you must get comfortable with public transportation. London's excellent taxis, buses, and subway (Tube) system can take you anywhere you need to go—a blessing for travelers' precious vacation time, not to mention their feet. And, as the streets become ever more congested, the key is to master the Tube.

For more information about public transit (bus and Tube), the best single source is the helpful *Hello London* brochure, which includes both a Tube map and a handy schematic map of the best bus routes (available free at TIs, museums, hotels, and at www.tfl.gov. uk). For specific directions on how to get from point A to point B on London's transit, detailed bus maps, updated prices, and general information, check www.tfl.gov.uk or call the automated info line at 0843-222-1234.

Tickets and Cards

London's is the most expensive public transit in the world. While the transit system has six zones, almost all tourist sights are within Zones 1 and 2, so those are the prices I've listed. For more information, visit www.tfl.gov.uk/tickets. A few odd special passes are available, but for nearly every tourist, the answer is simple: Get the Oyster card and use it.

Individual Tickets: Individual paper tickets for the Tube are ridiculously expensive (£5 per Tube ride). Tickets are sold at any Tube station, either at (often-crowded) ticket windows or at easy-to-use self-service machines (hit "Adult Single" and enter your destination). Tickets are valid only on the day of purchase. But unless you're literally taking only one Tube ride your entire visit, you'll save money (and time) with an Oyster card.

Oyster Card: A pay-as-you-go Oyster card (a plastic card embedded with a microchip) allows you to ride the Tube, buses, Docklands Light Railway (DLR), and Overground (mostly suburban trains) for about half the rate of individual tickets. To use it, simply touch the card against the yellow card reader at the turnstile or entrance. It flashes green and the fare is automatically deducted. (You must also tap your card again to "touch out" as you exit.)

Buy the card at any Tube station ticket window, or look for nearby shops displaying the Oyster logo, where you can purchase a card or add credit without the wait. You'll pay a £5 refundable deposit up front, then load it with as much credit as you'll need. One ride in Zones 1 and 2 during peak time costs £2.90; off peak is a little cheaper (£2.40/ride). The system comes with an automatic price cap that guarantees you'll never pay more than £6.60 in one day for rides within Zones 1 and 2. If you think you'll take more than two rides in a day, £6.60 of credit will cover you, but it's smart to add a little more if you expect to travel outside the city center. If you're staying five or more days, consider adding a 7-Day Travel-card to your Oyster card (details later).

Note that Oyster cards are not shareable among companions taking the same ride; each traveler will need his or her own. If your balance gets low, simply add credit—or "top up"—at a ticket window, machine, or shop. You can always see how much credit remains on your card (along with a list of where you've traveled) by touching it to the pad at any ticket machine.

You'll see advertisements for "contactless payment" using a credit card or mobile device, but that service is intended for residents, not travelers (who would rack up international transaction fees for every ride).

Remember to turn in your Oyster card after your last ride (you'll get back the £5 deposit and unused balance up to £10) at a ticket window or by selecting "Pay as you go refund" on any ticket machine that gives change. This will deactivate your card. For balances of more than £10, you must go to a ticket window for your refund. If you don't deactivate your card, the credit never expires—you can use it again on your next trip.

LONDON

Passes and Discounts

7-Day Travelcard: Various Tube passes and deals are available. Of these, the only option of note is the 7-Day Travelcard. This is the best choice if you're staying five or more days and plan to use public transit a lot (£33 for Zones 1-2; £60.20 for Zones 1-6). For most travelers, the Zone 1-2 pass works best. Heathrow Airport is in Zone 6, but there's no need to buy the Zones 1-6 version if that's the only ride outside the city center you plan to take—instead you can pay a small supplement to cover the difference. You can add the 7-Day Travelcard to your Oyster card or purchase the paper version at any National Rail train station.

Families: A paying adult can take up to four kids (10 and under) for free on the Tube, Docklands Light Railway (DLR), Overground, and buses. Kids 11-15 get a discount. Explore other child and student discounts at www.tfl.gov.uk/tickets or ask a clerk at a Tube ticket window which deal is best.

River Cruises: A Travelcard gives you a 33 percent discount on most Thames cruises (see page 62). The Oyster card gives you roughly a 10 percent discount on Thames Clippers (including the Tate Boat museum ferry).

The Bottom Line

On a short visit (three days or fewer), I'd get an Oyster card and add £20-25 of credit (£6.60 daily cap times three days, plus a little extra for any rides outside Zones 1-2). If you'll be taking fewer rides, £15 will be enough (£2.90 per ride during peak time gets you 5 rides); if not, you can always top up. For a visit of five days or more, the 7-Day Travelcard—either the paper version or on an Oyster card—will likely pay for itself.

By Tube

London's subway system is called the Tube or Underground (but never "subway," which, in Britain, refers to a pedestrian underpass). The Tube is one of this planet's great people-movers and usually the fastest long-distance transport in town (runs Mon-Sat about 5:00-24:00, Sun about 7:00-23:00; Central, Jubilee, Northern, Piccadilly, and Victoria lines also run Fri-Sat 24 hours). Two other commuter rail lines are tied into the network

and use the same tickets: the Docklands Light Railway (called DLR) and the Overground. The new Crossrail system will eventually cut through central London connecting Heathrow with Paddington, Bond, and Liverpool Street Tube stations on the Elizabeth line before continuing to the city's outlying eastern neighborhoods.

Get your bearings by studying a map of the system, free at any station (or download a transit app—described earlier).

Each line has a name (such as Circle, Northern, or Bakerloo) and two directions (indicated by the end-of-the-line stops). Find the line that will take you to your destination, and figure out roughly which direction (north, south, east, or west) you'll need to go to get there.

At the Tube station, there are two ways to pass through the turnstile. With an Oyster card, touch it flat against the turnstile's yellow card reader, both when you enter and exit the station. With a paper ticket or paper Travelcard, feed it into the turnstile, reclaim it, and hang on to it—you'll need it later.

Find your train by following signs to your line and the (general) direction it's headed (such as Central Line: east). Since some tracks are shared by several lines, double-check before boarding: Make sure your destination is one of the stops listed on the sign at the platform. Also, check the electronic signboards that announce which train is next, and make sure the destination (the end-of-the-line stop) is the direction you want. Some trains, particularly on the Circle and

District lines, split off for other directions, but each train has its final destination marked above its windshield.

Trains run about every 3-10 minutes. (The Victoria line brags that it's the most frequent anywhere, with trains coming every 100 seconds at peak time.) A general rule of thumb is that it takes 30 minutes to travel six Tube stops (including walking time within stations), or roughly five minutes per stop.

When you leave the system, "touch out" with your Oyster card at the electronic reader on the turnstile, or feed your paper ticket into the turnstile (it will eat your now-expired ticket). With a paper Travelcard, it will spit out your still-valid card. Check maps and signs for the most convenient exit.

The system can be fraught with construction delays and breakdowns. Pay attention to signs and announcements explaining necessary detours. Rush hours (8:00-10:00 and 16:00-19:00) can be packed and sweaty. If one train is stuffed—and another is coming in three minutes—it may be worth a wait to avoid the sardine routine. If you get confused, ask for advice from a local, a blue-vested staffer, or at the information window located before the turnstile entry. Online, get help from the "Plan a Journey" feature at www.tfl.gov.uk, which is accessible (via free Wi-Fi) on any mobile device within most Tube stations before you go underground.

Tube Etiquette and Tips
- When your train arrives, stand off to the side and let riders exit before you board.
- When the car is jampacked, avoid using the hinged seats near the doors of some trains—they take up valuable standing space.
- If you're blocking the door when the train stops, step out of the car and off to the side, let others off, then get back on.
- Talk softly in the cars. Listen to how quietly Londoners communicate and follow their lead.
- On escalators, stand on the right and pass on the left. But note that in some passageways or stairways, you might be directed to walk on the left (the direction Brits go when behind the wheel).
- Discreet eating and drinking are fine (nothing smelly); drinking alcohol and smoking are banned.
- Be zipped up to thwart thieves.
- Carefully check exit options before surfacing to street level. Signs point clearly to nearby sights—you'll save lots of walking by choosing the right exit.

By Bus

If you figure out the bus system, you'll swing like Tarzan through the urban jungle of London (see sidebar for a list of handy routes). Get in the habit of hopping buses for quick little straight shots, even just to get to a Tube stop. However, during bump-and-grind rush hours (8:00-10:00 and 16:00-19:00), you'll usually go faster by Tube.

You can't buy single-trip tickets for buses, and you can't use cash to pay when boarding. Instead, you must have an Oyster card, a paper Travelcard, or a one-day Bus & Tram Pass (£5, can buy on day of travel only—not beforehand, from ticket machine in any Tube station). If you're using your Oyster card, any bus ride in downtown London costs £1.50 (capped at £4.50/day).

The first step in mastering London's bus system is learning how to decipher the bus-stop signs. The accompanying photo shows a typical sign listing the buses (the N91, N68, etc.) that come by here and their destinations (Oakwood, Old Coulsdon, etc.). In the first column, find your destination on the list—e.g., to Paddington (Tube and rail station). In the next column, find a bus that goes there—the #23 (routes marked "N" are night-only). In the final column, a letter within a circle (e.g., "H") tells you exactly which nearby bus stop to use. Find your stop on the accompanying bus-stop map, then make your way to that stop—

Nunhead Inverton Road	N343	⊘
O		
Oakwood ⇐	N91	⊘ ⊘
Old Coulsdon	N68	Aldwych
Old Ford	N8	Oxford Circus
Old Kent Road Canal Bridge	53, N381	⊘ ⊘ ⊘
	453	⊘
	N21	⊘
Old Street ⇐	243	Aldwych
Orpington	N47	⊘
Oxford Circus ⇐	Any bus	⊘
	N18	⊘
P		
Paddington ⇐ ⊜	23, N15	⊘ ⊘ ⊘
Palmers Green	N29	⊘
Park Langley	N3	⊘ ⊘
Peckham	12	⊘
	N89, N343	⊘ ⊘
	N136	⊘ ⊘
	N381	⊘
Penge Pawleyne Arms	176	⊘
	N5	⊘ ⊘
Petts Wood	N47	⊘
Pimlico Grosvenor Road	24	⊘
Plaistow Greengate	N15	⊘ ⊘
Plumstead	53	⊘
Plumstead Common	53	⊘
Ponders End	N279	⊘
Poplar All Saints ⊡	N15, N551	⊘ ⊘

you'll know it's yours because it will have the same letter on its pole.

When your bus approaches, it's wise to hold your arm out to let the driver know you want on. Hop on and confirm your destination with the driver (often friendly and helpful).

As you board, touch your Oyster card to the card reader, or show your paper Travelcard or Bus & Tram Pass to the driver. Unlike on the Tube, there's no need to show or tap your card when you hop off. On the older heritage "Routemaster" buses without card-readers (used on the #15 route), you simply take a seat, and the conductor comes around to check cards and passes.

To alert the driver that you want to get off, press one of the red buttons (on the poles between the seats) before your stop.

With a mobile phone, you can find out the arrival time of the next bus by texting your bus stop's five-digit code (posted at the stop, above the timetable) to 87287 (if you're using your US phone, text the code to 011-44-7797-800-287). Or try the helpful London Bus Checker app, with route maps and real-time bus info.

By Taxi

London is the best taxi town in Europe. Big, black, carefully regulated cabs are everywhere—there are about 25,000 of them. (While historically known as "black cabs," London's official taxis are sometimes covered with wildly colored ads.)

I've never met a crabby cabbie in London. They love to talk,

and they know every nook and cranny in town. I ride in a taxi each day just to get my London questions answered. Drivers must pass a rigorous test on "The Knowledge" of London geography to earn their license.

If a cab's top light is on, just wave it down. Drivers flash lights when they see you wave. They have a tight turning radius, so you can hail cabs going in either direction. If waving doesn't work, ask someone where you can find a taxi stand. Telephoning a cab will get you one in a few minutes, but costs a little more (tel. 0871-871-8710).

Rides start at £2.60. The regular tariff #1 covers most of the day (Mon-Fri 5:00-20:00), tariff #2 is during "unsociable hours" (Mon-Fri 20:00-22:00 and Sat-Sun 5:00-22:00), and tariff #3 is for nighttime (22:00-5:00) and holidays. Rates go up about 40 percent with each higher tariff. Extra charges are explained in writing on the cab wall. All cabs accept credit and debit cards, including American cards. Tip a cabbie by rounding up (maximum 10 percent).

Connecting downtown sights is quick and easy, and will cost you about £8-10 (for example, St. Paul's to the Tower of London, or between the two Tate museums). For a short ride, three adults in a cab generally travel at close to Tube prices—and groups of four or five adults should taxi everywhere. All cabs can carry five passengers, and some take six, for the same cost as a single traveler.

Don't worry about meter cheating. Licensed British cab meters come with a sealed computer chip and clock that ensures you'll get the correct tariff. The only way a cabbie can cheat you is by taking a needlessly long route. One serious pitfall, however, is taking a cab when traffic is bad to a destination efficiently served by the Tube. On one trip to London, I hopped in a taxi at South Kensington for Waterloo Station and hit bad traffic. Rather than spending 20 minutes and £2 on the Tube, I spent 40 minutes and £16 in a taxi.

If you overdrink and ride in a taxi, be warned: Taxis charge £40 for "soiling" (a.k.a., pub puke). If you forget this book in a taxi, call the Lost Property office and hope for the best (tel. 0845-330-9882).

By Uber

Uber faces legal challenges in London and may not be operating when you visit. If Uber is running, it can be much cheaper than a taxi and is a handy alternative if there's a long line for a taxi or if

Handy Bus Routes

The best views are upstairs on a double-decker. Check the bus stop closest to your hotel—it may be convenient to your sightseeing plans. Here are some of the most useful routes:

Route #9: High Street Kensington to Knightsbridge (Harrods) to Hyde Park Corner to Trafalgar Square to Somerset House.

Route #11: Victoria Station to Westminster Abbey to Trafalgar Square to St. Paul's and Liverpool Street Station and the East End.

Route #15: Trafalgar Square to St. Paul's to Tower of London (sometimes with heritage "Routemaster" old-style double-decker buses).

Routes #23 and #159: Paddington Station (#159 begins at Marble Arch) to Oxford Circus to Piccadilly Circus to Trafalgar Square; from there, #23 heads east to St. Paul's and Liverpool Street Station, while #159 heads to Westminster and the Imperial War Museum. In addition, several buses (including #6, #12, and #139) also make the corridor run between Marble Arch, Oxford Circus, Piccadilly Circus, and Trafalgar Square.

Route #24: Pimlico to Victoria Station to Westminster Abbey to

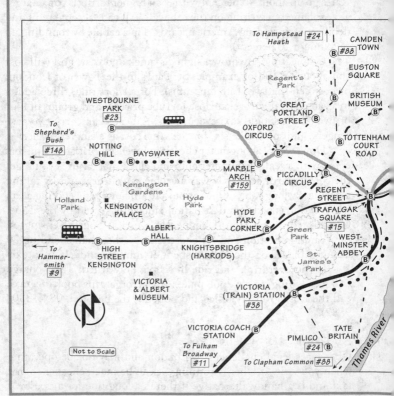

Trafalgar Square to Euston Square, then all the way north to Camden Town (Camden Lock Market).

Route #38: Victoria Station to Hyde Park Corner to Piccadilly Circus to British Museum.

Route #88: Tate Britain to Westminster Abbey to Trafalgar Square to Piccadilly Circus to Oxford Circus to Great Portland Street Station (Regent's Park), then north to Camden Town.

Route #148: Westminster Abbey to Victoria Station to Notting Hill and Bayswater (by way of the east end of Hyde Park and Marble Arch).

Route #RV1 (a scenic South Bank joyride): Tower of London to Tower Bridge to Southwark Street (five-minute walk behind Tate Modern/Shakespeare's Globe) to London Eye/Waterloo Station, then over Waterloo Bridge to Somerset House and Covent Garden.

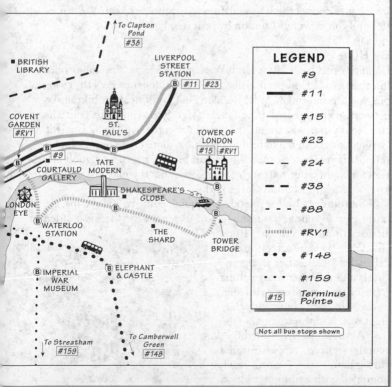

no cabs are available. Uber drivers generally don't know the city as well as regular cabbies, and they don't have the access to some fast lanes that taxis do. Still, if you like using Uber, it can work great here.

By Car

If you have a car, stow it—you don't want to drive in London. An £11.50 **congestion charge** is levied on any private car entering the city center during peak hours (Mon-Fri 7:00-18:00, no charge Sat-Sun and holidays). You can pay the fee either online or by phone (www.cclondon.com, from within the UK call 0343/222-2222, from outside the UK call 011-44-20/7649-9122, phones answered Mon-Fri 8:00-22:00, Sat 9:00-15:00, be ready to give the vehicle registration number and country of registration). There are painfully stiff penalties for late payments. The system has cut down traffic jams, bolstered London's public transit, and made buses cheaper and more user-friendly. Today, the vast majority of vehicles in the city center are buses, taxis, and service trucks.

By Boat

It's easy to connect downtown London sights between Westminster and the Tower of London by boat (see later).

By Bike

London operates a citywide bike-rental program similar to ones in other major European cities, and new bike lanes are still cropping up around town. Still, London isn't (yet) ideal for biking. Its network of designated bike lanes is far from complete, and the city's many one-way streets (not to mention the need to bike on the "wrong" side) can make biking here a bit more challenging than it sounds. If you're accustomed to urban biking, it can be a good option for connecting your sightseeing stops, but if you're just up for a joyride, stick to London's large parks.

Santander Cycles, intended for quick point-to-point trips, are fairly easy to rent and a giddy joy to use, even for the most jaded London tourist. These "Boris Bikes" (as they are affectionately called by locals, after cycle enthusiast and former mayor Boris Johnson) are cruisers with big, cushy seats, a bag rack with elastic straps, and three gears.

Approximately 700 bike-rental stations are scattered throughout the city, each equipped with a computer kiosk.

To rent a bike, you'll pay an access fee (£2/day). The first 30 minutes are free; if you keep the bike for longer, you'll be charged £2 for every additional 30-minute period.

When you're ready to ride, press "Hire a Cycle" and insert your credit card when prompted. You'll then get a ticket with a five-digit code. Take the ticket to any bike that doesn't have a red light (those are "taken") and punch in the number. After the yellow light blinks, a green light will appear: Now you can (firmly) pull the bike out of the slot.

When your ride is over, find a station with an empty slot, then push your bike in until it locks and the green light flashes.

You can hire bikes as often as you like (which will start your free 30-minute period over again), as long as you wait five minutes between each use. There can be problems, of course—stations at popular locations (such as entrances to parks) can temporarily run out of bikes, and you may have trouble finding a place to return a bike—but for the most part, this system works great. To make things easier, get a map of the docking stations—pick one up at any major Tube station. The same map is also available online at www.tfl.gov.uk (click on "Santander Cycles") and as a free app (http://cyclehireapp.com).

Helmets are not provided, so ride carefully. Stay to the far-left side of the road and watch closely at intersections for *left*-turning cars. Be aware that in most parks (including Hyde Park/Kensington Gardens) only certain paths are designated for bike use—you can't ride just anywhere. Maps posted at park entrances identify bike paths, and non-bike paths are generally clearly marked.

Some bike tour companies also rent bikes—for details, see page 62.

Tours in London

🎧 To sightsee on your own, download my free Rick Steves Audio Europe app with **audio tours** that illuminate some of London's top sights and neighborhoods, including my Westminster Walk, Historic London: The City Walk, and tours of the British Museum, British Library, and St. Paul's Cathedral (see sidebar on page 30 for details).

▲▲▲BY HOP-ON, HOP-OFF DOUBLE-DECKER BUS

London is full of hop-on, hop-off bus companies competing for your tourist pound. I've focused on the two companies I like the most: **Original** and **Big Bus.** Both offer essentially the same two tours of the city's sightseeing highlights. Big Bus tours are a little

Combining a London Bus Tour and the Changing of the Guard

For a grand and efficient intro to London, consider catching an 8:30 departure of a hop-on, hop-off overview bus tour, riding most of the loop (which takes just over 1.5 hours, depending on traffic). Hop off just before 10:00 at Trafalgar Square (Cockspur Street, stop "S") and walk briskly to Buckingham Palace to find a spot to watch the Changing of the Guard ceremony at 11:00.

more expensive (£35, cheaper in advance online), while Original tours are cheaper (£26 with this book).

These once-over-lightly bus tours drive by all the famous sights, providing a stress-free way to get your bearings and see the biggies: Piccadilly Circus, Trafalgar Square, Big Ben, St. Paul's, the Tower of London, Marble Arch, Victoria Station, and elsewhere. With a good guide, decent traffic, and nice weather, I'd sit back and enjoy the entire tour. (If traffic is bad or you don't like your guide, you can hop off and try your luck with the next departure.)

Each company offers at least one route with live (English-only) guides, and a second (sometimes slightly different route) with recorded, dial-a-language narration. In addition to the overview tours, both Original and Big Bus include the River Thames boat trip by City Cruises (between Westminster and the Tower of London) and several walking tours. Employees for both companies will try hard to sell you tickets and Fast Track admissions to various sights in London. Review your sightseeing plan carefully in advance so you can take advantage of offers that will save you time or money, but skip the rest.

Pick up a map from any flier rack or from one of the countless salespeople, and study the color-coded system. Sunday morning—when traffic is light and many museums are closed—is a fine time for a tour. Traffic is at its peak around lunch and during the evening rush hour (around 17:00).

Buses run daily about every 10-15 minutes in summer and every 10-20 minutes in winter, starting at about 8:30. The last full loop usually leaves Victoria Station at about 20:00 in summer, and at about 17:00 in winter.

You can buy tickets online in advance, or from drivers or from staff at street kiosks (credit cards accepted at kiosks at major stops such as Victoria Station, ticket valid 24 hours in summer, 48 hours in winter).

Original London Sightseeing Bus Tour

They offer two versions of their basic highlights loop, both marked with a yellow triangle (confirm version with the driver before boarding): **The Original Tour** (live guide) and the **City Sightseeing Tour** (same route but with recorded narration, a kids' soundtrack option, and a stop at Madame Tussauds). Other routes include the orange-triangle **British Museum Tour** (connecting the museum and King's Cross neighborhoods with central London), and the blue-triangle **Royal Borough Tour** (high-end shopping and regal hang-outs). The black- and purple-triangle routes act more like shuttles, linking major train stations and Madame Tussauds to the central route. All routes are covered by the same ticket (£32, £6 less with this book, limit four discounts per book, they'll rip off the corner of this page—raise bloody hell if the staff or driver won't honor this discount; also online deals, info center at 17 Cockspur Street sells discounted tickets to Tower of London, St. Paul's Cathedral, and London Eye; Mon-Sat 8:00-18:00, Sun until 17:30; tel. 020/7389-5040, www.theoriginaltour.com).

Big Bus London Tours

For £35 (up to 30 percent discount online—print tickets or have them delivered to your phone), you get the same basic overview tours: Red buses come with a live guide, while the blue route has a recorded narration and a one-hour longer path that goes around Hyde Park. These pricier Big Bus tours tend to have more departures—meaning shorter waits for those hopping on and off (tel. 020/7808-6753, www.bigbustours.com).

BY BUS OR CAR

London by Night Sightseeing Tour

Various companies offer a 1- to 2-hour circuit, but after hours, with no extras (e.g., walks, river cruises), at a lower price. While the narration can be lame, the views at twilight are grand—although note that it stays light until late on summer nights, and London just doesn't do floodlighting as well as, say, Paris. **Golden Tours** buses depart at 19:00 and 20:00 from their offices on Buckingham Palace Road (tel. 020/7630-2028; www.goldentours.com). **See London By Night** buses offer live English guides and daily departures from Green Park (next to the Ritz Hotel) at 19:30, 20:00, 20:30, 21:15, 21:45, and 22:15; October-March at 19:30 and 21:20 only (tel. 020/7183-4744, www.seelondonbynight.com). For a memorable and economical evening, munch a scenic picnic dinner on the top deck. (There are plenty of takeaway options near the various stops.)

Driver-Guides

These guides have cars or a minibus (particularly helpful for travelers with limited mobility), and also do walking-only tours:

Janine Barton (£390/half-day, £560/day, tel. 020/7402-4600, http://seeitinstyle.synthasite.com, jbsiis@aol.com); covering **Hugh Dickson** and **Mike Dickson** (£345/half-day, £535/day, overnights also possible, both registered Blue Badge guides; Hugh's mobile 07771/602-069, hughdickson@hotmail.com; Mike's mobile 07769/905-811, michael.dickson5@btinternet.com); and **David Stubbs** (£225/half-day, £330/day, about £50 more for groups of 4-6 people, also does tours to the Cotswolds, Stonehenge, and Stratford, mobile 07775-888-534, www.londoncountrytours.co.uk, info@londoncountrytours.co.uk).

▲▲ON FOOT

Top-notch local guides lead (sometimes big) groups on walking tours through specific slices of London's past. Look for brochures at TIs or ask at hotels. *Time Out,* the weekly entertainment guide, lists some, but not all, scheduled walks. Check with the various tour companies by phone or online to get their full picture.

To take a walking tour, simply show up at the announced location and pay the guide. Then enjoy two chatty hours of Dickens, Harry Potter, the Plague, Shakespeare, street art, the Beatles, Jack the Ripper, or whatever is on the agenda.

London Walks

This leading company lists its extensive and creative daily schedule online, as well as in a beefy *London Walks* brochure (available at hotels and in racks all over town). Just perusing their fascinating lineup opens me up to dimensions of the city I never considered and inspires me to stay longer in London. Their two-hour walks, led by top-quality professional guides (ranging from archaeologists to actors), cost £10 (cash only, walks offered year-round, private tours for groups-£140, tel. 020/7624-3978 for a live person, tel. 020/7624-9255 for a recording of today's or tomorrow's walks and the Tube station they depart from, www.walks.com).

London Walks also offers day trips into the countryside, a good option for those with limited time (£18 plus £36-64 for transportation and admission costs, cash only: Stonehenge/Salisbury, Oxford/Cotswolds, Cambridge, Bath, and so on). These are economical in part because everyone gets group discounts for transportation and admissions.

Sandemans New London "Free Royal London Tour"

This company offers free tours covering the basic London sights in a youthful, light, and irreverent way that can be both entertaining and fun, but it's misleading to call them "free," as tips are expected. Given that London Walks offers daily tours at a reasonable price, taking this "free" tour makes no sense to me (daily at 10:00,

11:00, and 13:00; meet at Covent Garden Piazza by the Apple Store, Tube: Covent Garden). Sandemans also offers guided tours for a charge, including a Pub Crawl (£15, nightly at 19:30, meet at Brewmaster, 37 Cranbourn Street, Tube: Leicester Square, www.newlondon-tours.com).

Beatles Walks
Fans of the still-Fab Four can take one of three Beatles walks (London Walks has two that run 5 days/week; for more on Beatles sights, see page 109).

Jack the Ripper Walks
Each walking tour company seems to make most of its money with "haunted" and Jack the Ripper tours. Many guides are historians and would rather not lead these lightweight tours—but, in tourism as in journalism, "if it bleeds, it leads" (which is why the juvenile London Dungeon is one of the city's busiest sights).

Two reliably good two-hour tours start every night at the Tower Hill Tube station exit. **London Walks** leaves nightly at 19:30 (£10, pay at the start, tel. 020/7624-3978, recorded info tel. 020/7624-9255, www.jacktheripperwalk.com). **Ripping Yarns,** which leaves earlier, is guided by off-duty Yeoman Warders—the Tower of London "Beefeaters" (£8, pay at end, nightly at 18:30, mobile 07813-559-301, www.jack-the-ripper-tours.com). After taking both, I found the London Walks tour more entertaining, informative, and with a better route (along quieter, once hooker-friendly lanes, with less traffic), starting at Tower Hill and ending at Liverpool Street Station. Groups can be huge for both, and one group can be nearly on top of another, but there's always room—just show up.

Private Walks with Local Guides
Standard rates for London's registered Blue Badge guides are about £160-200 for four hours and £260 or more for nine hours (tel. 020/7611-2545, www.guidelondon.org.uk or www.britainsbestguides.org). I know and like five fine local guides: **Sean Kelleher,** an engaging storyteller who knows his history (tel. 020/8673-1624, mobile 07764-612-770, sean@seanlondonguide.com); **Britt Lonsdale** (£250/half-day, £350/day, great with families, tel. 020/7386-9907, mobile 07813-278-077, brittl@btinternet.com); **Joel Reid,** an imaginative guide who specializes in off-the-beaten-track London (mobile 07887-955-720, joelyreid@gmail.com); and two others who work in London when they're not on the road leading my Britain tours: **Tom Hooper** (mobile 07986-048-047, tomh@ricksteves.net), and **Gillian Chadwick** (mobile 07889-976-598, gillychad@hotmail.co.uk). If you have a particular

interest, London Walks (see earlier) can book a guide for your exact focus (£180/half-day).

BY BIKE

Many of London's best sights can be laced together with a pleasant pedal through its parks. Confirm schedules in advance.

London Bicycle Tour Company

Three tours covering London are offered daily from their base at Gabriel's Wharf on the South Bank of the Thames. Sunday is the best, as there is less car traffic (**Classic Tour**—£25, daily at 10:30 and 11:00, 6 miles, 3 hours, includes Westminster, Buckingham Palace, Covent Garden, and St. Paul's; **Love London Tour**—£25, April-Oct daily at 14:30, Nov-March daily at 12:00 if at least 4 people show up, 7 miles, 3 hours, includes Westminster, Buckingham Palace, Hyde Park, Soho, and Covent Garden; **Old Town Tour**—£28.50, April-Oct Sat-Sun at 14:00, Nov-March Sat-Sun at 12:00, 9 miles, 3.5 hours, includes south side of the river to Tower Bridge, then The City to the East End; book ahead for off-season tours). They also rent bikes (£3.50/hour, £20/day; office open daily April-Oct 9:30-18:00, shorter hours Nov-March, west of Blackfriars Bridge on the South Bank, 1 Gabriel's Wharf, tel. 020/7928-6838, www.londonbicycle.com).

Fat Tire Bike Tours

Nearly daily bike tours cover the highlights of downtown London, on two different itineraries (£2 discount with this book): **Royal London** (£22, April-Oct daily at 11:00, mid-May-mid-Sept also at 15:30, Nov-March Thu-Mon at 11:00, 7 miles, 4 hours, meet at Queensway Tube station; includes Parliament, Buckingham Palace, Hyde Park, and Trafalgar Square) and **River Thames** (£30, nearly daily in summer at 10:30, March-Nov Thu-Sat at 10:30, 4.5 hours, reservations required, meet just outside Southwark Tube Station; includes London Eye, St. Paul's, Tower of London, and London Bridge). Their guiding style wears its learning lightly, mixing history with humor. Reservations are easy online, and required for River Thames tours and kids' bikes (off-season tours also available, mobile 078-8233-8779, www.fattirebiketourslondon.com). They also offer a range of walking tours that include a fish-and-chips dinner, a beer-tasting pub tour, and theater packages.

▲▲BY CRUISE BOAT

London offers many made-for-tourist cruises, most on slow-moving, open-top boats accompanied by entertaining commentary about passing sights. Several companies offer essentially the same trip. Generally speaking, you can either do a **short city center cruise** by riding a boat 30 minutes from Westminster Pier to Tower

Thames Boat Piers

Thames boats stop at these piers in the town center and beyond. While Westminster Pier is the most popular, it's not the only dock in town. Consider all the options (listed from west to east, as the Thames flows—see the color maps in the back of this book).

Millbank Pier (North Bank): At the Tate Britain Museum, used primarily by the Tate Boat ferry service (express connection to Tate Modern at Bankside Pier).

Westminster Pier (North Bank): Near the base of Big Ben, offers round-trip sightseeing cruises and lots of departures in both directions (though the Thames Clippers boats don't stop here). Nearby sights include Parliament and Westminster Abbey.

London Eye Pier (a.k.a. **Waterloo Pier,** South Bank): At the base of the London Eye; good, less-crowded alternative to Westminster, with many of the same cruise options (Waterloo Station is nearby).

Embankment Pier (North Bank): Near Covent Garden, Trafalgar Square, and Cleopatra's Needle (the obelisk on the Thames). This pier is used mostly for special boat trips, such as some RIB (rigid inflatable boats) and lunch and dinner cruises.

Festival Pier (South Bank): Next to the Royal Festival Hall, just downstream from the London Eye.

Blackfriars Pier (North Bank): In The City, not far from St. Paul's.

Bankside Pier (South Bank): Directly in front of the Tate Modern and Shakespeare's Globe.

London Bridge Pier (a.k.a. **London Bridge City Pier,** South Bank): Near the HMS *Belfast*.

Tower Pier (North Bank): At the Tower of London, at the east edge of The City and near the East End.

St. Katharine's Pier (North Bank): Just downstream from the Tower of London.

Canary Wharf Pier (North Bank): At the Docklands, London's new "downtown."

Greenwich, Kew Gardens, and **Hampton Court Piers:** These outer London piers may also come in handy.

Pier (particularly handy if you're interested in visiting the Tower of London anyway), or take a **longer cruise** that includes a peek at the East End, riding from Westminster all the way to Greenwich (save time by taking the Tube back).

Each company runs cruises daily, about twice hourly, from morning until dark; many reduce frequency off-season. Boats come go from various docks in the city center (see sidebar). The most popular places to embark are Westminster Pier (at the base of Westminster Bridge across the street from Big Ben) and London Eye Pier (also known as Waterloo Pier, across the river).

A one-way trip within the city center costs about £10; going all the way to Greenwich costs about £2.50 more. Most companies charge around £4 more for a round-trip ticket. Others sell hop-on, hop-off day tickets (around £19). But I'd rather savor a one-way cruise, and then zip home by Tube.

You can buy tickets at kiosks on the docks. A Travelcard can snare you a 33 percent discount on most cruises (just show the card when you pay for the cruise); the pay-as-you-go Oyster card nets you a discount only on Thames Clippers. Because companies vary in the discounts they offer, always ask. Children and seniors generally get discounts. You can purchase drinks and scant, over-priced snacks on board. Clever budget travelers pack a picnic and munch while they cruise.

The three dominant companies are **City Cruises** (handy 45-minute cruise from Westminster Pier to Tower Pier; www.citycruises.com), **Thames River Services** (fewer stops, classic boats, friendlier and more old-fashioned feel; www.thamesriverservices.co.uk), and **Circular Cruise** (full cruise takes about an hour, operated by Crown River Services, www.circularcruise.london). I'd skip the **London Eye**'s River Cruise from London Eye Pier—it's about the same price as Circular Cruise, but 20 minutes shorter. The speedy **Thames Clippers** (described later) are designed more for no-nonsense transport than lazy sightseeing.

To compare all of your options in one spot, head to Westminster Pier, which has a row of kiosks for all of the big outfits.

Cruising Downstream, to Greenwich: Both **City Cruises** and **Thames River Services** head from Westminster Pier to Greenwich. The cruises are usually narrated by the captain, with most commentary given on the way to Greenwich. The companies' prices are the same, though their itineraries are slightly different (Thames River Services makes only one stop en route and takes just an hour, while City Cruises makes two stops and adds about 15 minutes). The **Thames Clippers** boats, described later, are cheaper and faster (about 20-45 minutes to Greenwich), but have no commentary and no up-top seating. To maximize both efficiency and sightseeing, I'd take a narrated cruise to Greenwich one way, and go the other way on the DLR (Docklands Light Railway), with stop in the Docklands (Canary Wharf station).

Cruising Upstream, to Kew Gardens and Hampton Court Palace: Thames River Boats leave for Kew Gardens from Westminster Pier (£13 one-way, £20 round-trip, cash only, discounts with Travelcard, 2-4/day depending on season, 1.5 hours, boats sail April-Oct, about half the trip is narrated, www.wpsa.co.uk). Most boats continue on to Hampton Court Palace for an additional £4 (and another 1.5 hours). Because of the river current, you can save 30 minutes cruising from Hampton Court back into town (depends on the tide—ask before you commit). Romantic as these rides sound, it can be a long trip...especially upstream.

Commuting by Clipper

The sleek, 220-seat catamarans used by **Thames Clippers** are designed for commuters rather than sightseers. Think of the boats as express buses on the river—they zip through London every 20-30 minutes, stopping at most of the major docks en route, including Canary Wharf (Docklands) and Greenwich. They're fast: roughly 20 minutes from Embankment to Tower, 10 more minutes to Docklands, and 15 more minutes to Greenwich. The boats are less pleasant for joyriding than the cruises described earlier, with no commentary and no open deck up top (the only outside access is on a crowded deck at the exhaust-choked back of the boat, where you're jostling for space to take photos). Any one-way ride in Central London (roughly London Eye to Tower Pier) costs £8; a one-way ride to East London (Canary Wharf and Greenwich) is £8.70, and a River Roamer all-day ticket costs £18.50 (discounts with Travelcard and Oyster card, www.thamesclippers.com).

Thames Clippers also offers two express trips. The **Tate Boat** ferry service, which directly connects the Tate Britain (Millbank Pier) and the Tate Modern (Bankside Pier), is made for art lovers (£8 one-way, covered by River Roamer day ticket; buy ticket at kiosks or self-service machines before boarding or use Oyster Card; for frequency and times, see www.tate.org.uk/visit/tate-boat). The **O2 Express** runs only on nights when there are events at the O2 arena (departs from London Eye Pier).

WEEKEND TOUR PACKAGES FOR STUDENTS

Andy Steves (Rick's son) runs **Weekend Student Adventures** (WSA Europe), offering 3-day and 10-day budget travel packages across Europe including accommodations, skip-the-line sightseeing, and unique local experiences. Locally guided and DIY unguided options are available for student and budget travelers in 13 of Europe's most popular cities, including London (guided trips from €199, see www.wsaeurope.com for details). Check out Andy's tips, resources, and podcast at www.andysteves.com.

London at a Glance

▲▲▲**Westminster Abbey** Britain's finest church and the site of royal coronations and burials since 1066. **Hours:** Mon-Fri 9:30-16:30, Wed until 19:00, Sat until 14:30, closed Sun to sightseers except for worship. See page 70.

▲▲▲**Churchill War Rooms** Underground WWII headquarters of Churchill's war effort. **Hours:** Daily 9:30-18:00. See page 81.

▲▲▲**National Gallery** Remarkable collection of European paintings (1250-1900), including Leonardo, Botticelli, Velázquez, Rembrandt, Turner, Van Gogh, and the Impressionists. **Hours:** Daily 10:00-18:00, Fri until 21:00. See page 84.

▲▲▲**British Museum** The world's greatest collection of artifacts of Western civilization, including the Rosetta Stone and the Parthenon's Elgin Marbles. **Hours:** Daily 10:00-17:30, Fri until 20:30 (selected galleries only). See page 98.

▲▲▲**British Library** Fascinating collection of important literary treasures of the Western world. **Hours:** Mon-Fri 9:30-18:00, Tue-Thu until 20:00, Sat until 17:00, Sun 11:00-17:00. See page 104.

▲▲▲**St. Paul's Cathedral** The main cathedral of the Anglican Church, designed by Christopher Wren, with a climbable dome and daily evensong services. **Hours:** Mon-Sat 8:30-16:30, closed Sun except for worship. See page 111.

▲▲▲**Tower of London** Historic castle, palace, and prison housing the crown jewels and a witty band of Beefeaters. **Hours:** Tue-Sat 9:00-17:30, Sun-Mon from 10:00; Nov-Feb closes one hour earlier. See page 118.

▲▲▲**Victoria and Albert Museum** The best collection of decorative arts anywhere. **Hours:** Daily 10:00-17:45, Fri until 22:00 (selected galleries only). See page 141.

▲▲**Houses of Parliament** London landmark famous for Big Ben and occupied by the Houses of Lords and Commons. **Hours:** When Parliament is in session, generally open Oct-late July Mon-Thu, closed Fri-Sun and during recess late July-Sept. Guided tours offered year-round on Sat and most weekdays during recess. See page 75.

▲▲**Trafalgar Square** The heart of London, where Westminster, The City, and the West End meet. See page 83.

▲▲**National Portrait Gallery** A *Who's Who* of British history, featuring portraits of this nation's most important historical figures. **Hours:** Daily 10:00-18:00, Fri until 21:00, first and second floors open Mon at 11:00. See page 89.

LONDON

▲▲**Covent Garden** Vibrant people-watching zone with shops, cafés, street musicians, and an iron-and-glass arcade that once hosted a produce market. See page 91.

▲▲**Changing of the Guard at Buckingham Palace** Hour-long spectacle at Britain's royal residence. **Hours:** May-July daily at 11:00, Aug-April every other day. See page 95.

▲▲**London Eye** Enormous observation wheel, dominating—and offering commanding views over—London's skyline. **Hours:** Daily June-Aug 10:00-20:30 or later, Sept-May 11:00-18:00. See page 126.

▲▲**Imperial War Museum** Exhibits examining military conflicts from the early 20th century to today. **Hours:** Daily 10:00-18:00. See page 127.

▲▲**Tate Modern** Works by Monet, Matisse, Dalí, Picasso, and Warhol displayed in a converted powerhouse complex. **Hours:** Daily 10:00-18:00, Fri-Sat until 22:00. See page 130.

▲▲**Shakespeare's Globe** Timbered, thatched-roof reconstruction of the Bard's original "wooden O." **Hours:** Theater complex, museum, and actor-led tours generally daily 9:00-17:30; April-Oct generally morning theater tours only. Plays are also staged here. See page 132.

▲▲**Tate Britain** Collection of British painting from the 16th century through modern times, including works by William Blake, the Pre-Raphaelites, and J. M. W. Turner. **Hours:** Daily 10:00-18:00. See page 135.

▲▲**Natural History Museum** A Darwinian delight, packed with stuffed creatures, engaging exhibits, and enthralled kids. **Hours:** Daily 10:00-18:00. See page 144.

▲▲**Greenwich** Seafaring borough just east of the city center, with *Cutty Sark* tea clipper, Royal Observatory, other maritime sights, and a pleasant market. **Hours:** Most sights open daily, typically 10:00-17:00. See page 145.

▲**Wallace Collection** One of the finest private family art collections anywhere—free and open to the public—with paintings by such masters as Rembrandt, Rubens, and Velázquez. **Hours:** Daily 10:00-17:00. See page 107.

▲**East End** Explore the haunt of Jack the Ripper, but also happier locales such as the colorful Spitalfields, Petticoat Lane, and Truman markets, and the curry-scented streets of "Banglatown." See page 125.

Westminster Walk

Just about every visitor to London strolls along historic Whitehall from Big Ben to Trafalgar Square. This self-guided walk gives meaning to that touristy ramble (most of the sights you'll see are described in more detail later). Under London's modern traffic and big-city bustle lie 2,000 fascinating years of history. You'll get a whirlwind tour as well as a practical orientation to London. ∩ You can download a free, extended audio version of this walk; see page 30.

Start halfway across ❶ **Westminster Bridge** for that "Wow, I'm really in London!" feeling. Get a close-up view of the **Houses of Parliament** and **Big Ben** (floodlit at night). Downstream you'll see the **London Eye,** the city's giant Ferris wheel. Down the stairs to Westminster Pier are boats to the Tower of London and Greenwich (downstream) or Kew Gardens (upstream).

En route to Parliament Square, you'll pass a ❷ **statue of Boadicea,** the Celtic queen who unsuccessfully resisted Roman invaders in A.D. 60. Julius Caesar was the first Roman general to cross the Channel, but even he was weirded out by the island's strange inhabitants, who worshiped trees, sacrificed virgins, and went to war painted blue. Later, Romans subdued and civilized them, building roads and making this spot on the Thames—"Londinium"—a major urban center.

You'll find four red phone booths lining the north side of ❸ **Parliament Square** along Great George Street—great for a phone-box-and-Big-Ben photo op.

Wave hello to Winston Churchill and Nelson Mandela in Parliament Square. To Churchill's right is the historic **Westminster Abbey,** with its two stubby, elegant towers. The white building (flying the Union Jack) at the far end of the square houses Britain's **Supreme Court.**

Head north up Parliament Street, which turns into ❹ **Whitehall,** and walk toward Trafalgar Square. You'll see the thought-provoking ❺ **Cenotaph** in the middle of the boulevard, reminding passersby of the many Brits who died in the last century's world wars. To visit the **Churchill War Rooms,** take a left before the Cenotaph, on King Charles Street.

Continuing on Whitehall, stop at the barricaded and guarded ❻ **#10 Downing Street** to see the British "White House," the traditional home of the prime minister since the position was created in the early 18th century. Break the bobby's boredom and ask him a question. The huge building across Whitehall from Downing Street is the **Ministry of Defence** (MOD), the "British Pentagon."

Nearing Trafalgar Square, look for the 17th-century ❼ **Banqueting House** across the street, which is just about all that re-

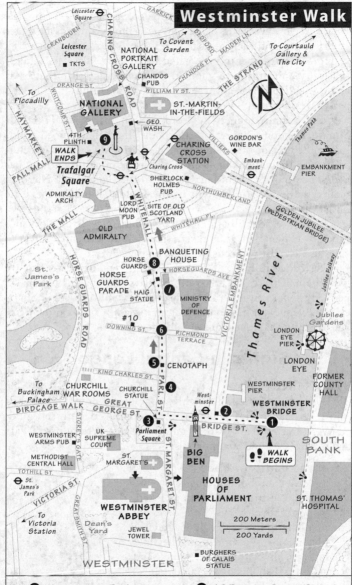

Westminster Walk

Leicester Square

GARRICK

To Covent Garden

BEDFORD

MAIDEN LN.

To Courtauld Gallery & The City

CRANBOURN

CHARING CROSS ROAD

Leicester Square

■ TKTS

NATIONAL PORTRAIT GALLERY

CHANDOS PL.

THE STRAND

ORANGE ST.

CHANDOS PUB

To Piccadilly

WILLIAM IV ST.

HAYMARKET

WHITCOMB ST.

NATIONAL GALLERY

ST.-MARTIN-IN-THE-FIELDS

GEO. WASH.

N

Thames Path

4TH PLINTH

❾

CHARING CROSS STATION

GORDON'S WINE BAR

VILLIERS

WALK ENDS

Charing Cross

Embankment

EMBANKMENT PIER

PALL MALL

Trafalgar Square

SHERLOCK HOLMES PUB

NORTHUMBERLAND

ADMIRALTY ARCH

LORD MOON PUB

SITE OF OLD SCOTLAND YARD

WHITEHALL PL.

GOLDEN JUBILEE (PEDESTRIAN BRIDGE)

THE MALL

HORSE GUARDS ROAD

OLD ADMIRALTY

WHITEHALL

VICTORIA EMBANKMENT

Thames River

Jubilee Walkway

St. James's Park

HORSE GUARDS PARADE

HORSE GUARDS

❽

BANQUETING HOUSE

HORSEGUARDS AVE.

❼

HAIG STATUE

MINISTRY OF DEFENCE

#10

DOWNING ST.

❻

RICHMOND TERRACE

Jubilee Gardens

LONDON EYE PIER

LONDON EYE

To Buckingham Palace

❺

CENOTAPH

KING CHARLES ST.

❹

PARL ST.

WESTMINSTER PIER

FORMER COUNTY HALL

BIRDCAGE WALK

CHURCHILL WAR ROOMS

CHURCHILL STATUE

GREAT GEORGE ST.

West-minster

WESTMINSTER BRIDGE

WESTMINSTER ARMS PUB

STOREY'S GATE

UK SUPREME COURT

❸

Parliament Square

❷

BRIDGE ST.

SOUTH BANK

METHODIST CENTRAL HALL

ST. MARGARET'S

ST. MARGARET ST.

BIG BEN

❶

👣 WALK BEGINS

TOTHILL ST.

St. James's Park

VICTORIA ST.

GREAT SMITH ST.

WESTMINSTER ABBEY

HOUSES OF PARLIAMENT

ST. THOMAS' HOSPITAL

To Victoria Station

Dean's Yard

JEWEL TOWER

200 Meters

200 Yards

WESTMINSTER

BURGHERS OF CALAIS STATUE

❶ Westminster Bridge
❷ Statue of Boadicea
❸ Parliament Square
❹ Walking Along Whitehall
❺ Cenotaph

❻ 10 Downing Street & Ministry of Defence
❼ Banqueting House
❽ Horse Guards
❾ Trafalgar Square

mains of what was once the biggest palace in Europe—Whitehall Palace. If you visit, you can enjoy its ceiling paintings by Peter Paul Rubens, and the exquisite hall itself. Also take a look at the ❽ **Horse Guards** behind the gated fence. For 200 years, soldiers in cavalry uniforms have guarded this arched entrance that leads to Buckingham Palace. These elite troops constitute the Queen's personal bodyguard.

The column topped by Lord Nelson marks ❾ **Trafalgar Square,** London's central meeting point. The stately domed building on the far side of the square is the **National Gallery,** which is filled with the national collection of European paintings, and has a classy café in the Sainsbury wing. To the right of the National Gallery is the 1722 **St. Martin-in-the-Fields Church** and its Café in the Crypt.

To get to Piccadilly from Trafalgar Square, walk up Cockspur Street to Haymarket, then take a short left on Coventry Street to colorful **Piccadilly Circus** (see map on page 90).

Near Piccadilly, you'll find several theaters. **Leicester Square** (with its half-price TKTS booth for plays—see page 159) thrives just a few blocks away. Walk through trendy **Soho** (north of Shaftesbury Avenue) for its fun pubs. From Piccadilly or Oxford Circus, you can take a taxi, bus, or the Tube home.

Sights in Central London

WESTMINSTER

These sights are listed in roughly geographical order from Westminster Abbey to Trafalgar Square, and are linked in my self-guided Westminster Walk (earlier) and the 🎧 free Westminster Walk audio tour (see page 30 for details).

▲▲▲Westminster Abbey

The greatest church in the English-speaking world, Westminster Abbey is where the nation's royalty has been wedded, crowned, and buried since 1066. Indeed, the histories of Westminster Abbey and England are almost the same. A thousand years of English history—3,000 tombs, the remains of 29 kings and queens, and hundreds of memorials to poets, politicians, scientists, and warriors—lie within its stained-glass splendor and under its stone slabs.

Cost and Hours: £22, £44 family ticket (covers 2 adults and 1 child), includes cloister and audioguide; Mon-Fri 9:30-16:30, Wed until 19:00 (main church only), Sat until 14:30, last entry one hour before closing, closed Sun to sightseers but open for services, guided tours available; cloister—daily 8:00-18:00; Tube: Westminster or St. James's Park, tel. 020/7222-5152, www.westminster-abbey.org.

When to Go: The place is most crowded every day at mid-morning and all day Saturdays and Mondays. Visit early, during lunch, or late to avoid tourist hordes. Weekdays after 14:30—especially Wed—are less congested; come late and stay for the 17:00 evensong (note that the Wed 17:00 evensong is generally spoken, not sung). The main entrance, on the Parliament Square side, often has a sizable line. You can skip it by booking tickets in advance via the Abbey's website. Show your ticket to the marshal at the entrance; only tickets bought directly through the Abbey's website qualify.

Church Services and Music: Mon-Fri at 7:30 (prayer), 8:00 (communion), 12:30 (communion), 17:00 evensong (except on Wed, when the evening service is generally spoken—not sung); **Sat** at 8:00 (communion), 9:00 (prayer), 15:00 (evensong; May-Aug it's at 17:00); **Sun** services generally come with more music: at 8:00 (communion), 10:00 (sung Matins), 11:15 (sung Eucharist), 15:00 (evensong), 18:30 (evening service). Services are free to anyone, though visitors who haven't paid church admission aren't allowed to linger afterward. Free **organ recitals** are usually held Sun at 17:45 (30 minutes). For a schedule of services or recitals on a particular day, look for posted signs with schedules or check the Abbey's website.

Tours: The included **audioguide** is excellent, taking some of the sting out of the steep admission fee. The Westminster Abbey Official Tour **app** includes an audio tour narrated by Jeremy Irons. To add to the experience, you can take an entertaining **guided tour** from a verger—the church equivalent of a museum docent (£5, schedule posted both outside and inside entry, up to 6/day in summer, 2-4/day in winter, 1.5 hours).

➲ Self-Guided Tour: You'll have no choice but to follow the steady flow of tourists through the church, along the route laid out for the audioguide. My tour covers the Abbey's top stops.
• *Walk straight through the north transept. Follow the crowd flow to the right and enter the spacious...*

❶ Nave: Look down the long and narrow center aisle of the church. Lined with the raying hands of the Gothic arches, glowing with light from the stained glass, this is more than a museum. With saints in stained glass, heroes in carved stone, and the bodies of England's greatest citizens under the floor stones, Westminster Abbey is the religious heart of England.

The king who built the Abbey was Edward the Confessor.

Westminster Abbey Tour

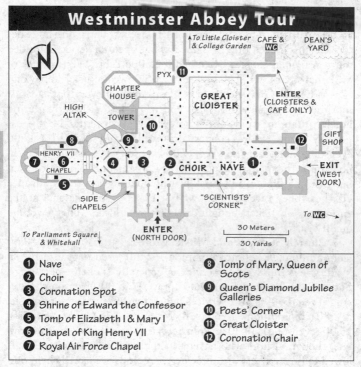

To Little Cloister & College Garden

CAFÉ & WC

DEAN'S YARD

PYX

11

CHAPTER HOUSE

GREAT CLOISTER

ENTER (CLOISTERS & CAFÉ ONLY)

HIGH ALTAR

TOWER

10

8

9

GIFT SHOP

12

HENRY VII

7 **6** **5** CHAPEL

4 **3**

2 CHOIR NAVE **1**

EXIT (WEST DOOR)

SIDE CHAPELS

"SCIENTISTS' CORNER"

To WC →

ENTER (NORTH DOOR)

To Parliament Square & Whitehall

30 Meters

30 Yards

1 Nave
2 Choir
3 Coronation Spot
4 Shrine of Edward the Confessor
5 Tomb of Elizabeth I & Mary I
6 Chapel of King Henry VII
7 Royal Air Force Chapel

8 Tomb of Mary, Queen of Scots
9 Queen's Diamond Jubilee Galleries
10 Poets' Corner
11 Great Cloister
12 Coronation Chair

Find him in the stained-glass windows on the left side of the nave (as you face the altar). He's in the third bay from the end (marked *S: Edwardus rex...*), with his crown, scepter, and ring. The Abbey's 10-story nave is the tallest in England. The chandeliers, 10 feet tall, look small in comparison (16 were given to the Abbey by the Guinness family).

On the floor near the west entrance of the Abbey is the flower-lined Grave of the Unknown Warrior, one ordinary WWI soldier buried in soil from France with lettering made from melted-down weapons from that war. Take time to contemplate the million-man army from the British Empire, and all those who gave their lives. Their memory is so revered that, when Kate Middleton walked up the aisle on her wedding day, by tradition she had to step around the tomb (and her wedding bouquet was later placed atop this tomb, also in accordance with tradition).

• *Walk up the nave toward the altar. This is the same route every future monarch walks on the way to being crowned. Midway up the nave, you pass through the colorful screen of an enclosure known as the...*

2 **Choir:** These elaborately carved wood and gilded seats are where monks once chanted their services in the "quire"—as it's known in British churchspeak. Today, it's where the Abbey boys' choir sings the evensong. You're approaching the center of a cross-shaped church. The "high" (main) altar (which usually has a cross and candlesticks atop it) sits on the platform up the five stairs in front of you.

• *It's on this platform that the monarch is crowned.*

❸ **Coronation Spot:** The area immediately before the high altar is where every English coronation since 1066 has taken place. Royalty are also given funerals here. Princess Diana's coffin was carried to this spot for her funeral service in 1997. The "Queen Mum" (mother of Elizabeth II) had her funeral here in 2002. This is also where most of the last century's royal weddings have taken place, including the unions of Queen Elizabeth II and Prince Philip (1947), Prince Andrew and Sarah Ferguson (1986), and Prince William and Kate Middleton (2011).

• *Veer left and follow the crowd. Pause at the wooden staircase on your right.*

❹ **Shrine of Edward the Confessor:** Step back and peek over the dark coffin of Edward I to see the tippy-top of the green-and-gold wedding-cake tomb of King Edward the Confessor—the man who built Westminster Abbey.

God had told pious Edward to visit St. Peter's Basilica in Rome. But with the Normans thinking conquest, it was too dangerous for him to leave England. Instead, he built this grand church and dedicated it to St. Peter. It was finished just in time to bury Edward and to crown his foreign successor, William the Conqueror, in 1066. After Edward's death, people prayed at his tomb, and, after getting good results, Pope Alexander III canonized him. This elevated, central tomb—which lost some of its luster when Henry VIII melted down the gold coffin-case—is surrounded by the tombs of eight kings and queens.

• *At the top of the stone staircase, veer left into the private burial chapel of Queen Elizabeth I.*

❺ **Tomb of Queens Elizabeth I and Mary I:** Although

only one effigy is on the tomb (Elizabeth's), there are actually two queens buried beneath it, both daughters of Henry VIII (by different mothers). Bloody Mary—meek, pious, sickly, and Catholic—enforced Catholicism during her short reign (1553-1558) by burning "heretics" at the stake.

Elizabeth—strong, clever, and Protestant—steered England on an Anglican course. She holds a royal orb symbolizing that she's queen of the whole globe. When

26-year-old Elizabeth was crowned in the Abbey, her right to rule was questioned (especially by her Catholic subjects) but none questioned considered the bastard seed of Henry VIII's unsanctioned marriage to Anne Boleyn. But Elizabeth's long reign (1559-1603) was one of the greatest in English history, a time when England ruled the seas and Shakespeare explored human emotions. When she died, thousands turned out for her funeral in the Abbey. Elizabeth's face on the tomb, modeled after her death mask, is considered a very accurate take on this hook-nosed, imperious "Virgin Queen" (she never married).

• *Continue into the ornate, flag-draped room up a few more stairs, directly behind the main altar.*

❻ Chapel of King Henry VII (The Lady Chapel): The light from the stained-glass windows; the colorful banners overhead; and the elaborate tracery in stone, wood, and glass give this room the festive air of a medieval tournament. The prestigious Knights of the Bath meet here, under the magnificent ceiling studded with gold pendants. The ceiling—of carved stone, not plaster (1519)—is the finest English Perpendicular Gothic and fan vaulting you'll see (unless you're going to King's College Chapel in Cambridge). The ceiling was sculpted on the floor in pieces, then jigsaw-puzzled into place. It capped the Gothic period and signaled the vitality of the coming Renaissance.

• *Go to the far end of the chapel and stand at the banister in front of the modern set of stained-glass windows.*

❼ Royal Air Force Chapel: Saints in robes and halos mingle with pilots in parachutes and bomber jackets. This tribute to WWII flyers is for those who earned their angel wings in the Battle of Britain (July-Oct 1940). A bit of bomb damage has been preserved—look for the little glassed-over hole in the wall below the windows in the lower left-hand corner.

• *Exit the Chapel of Henry VII. Turn left into a side chapel with the tomb (the central one of three in the chapel).*

❽ Tomb of Mary, Queen of Scots: The beautiful, French-educated queen (1542-1587) was held under house arrest for 19 years by Queen Elizabeth I, who considered her a threat to her sovereignty. Elizabeth got wind of an assassination plot, suspected Mary was behind it, and had her first cousin (once removed) beheaded. When Elizabeth died childless, Mary's son—James VI, King of Scots—also became King James I of England and Ireland. James buried his mum here (with her head sewn back on) in the Abbey's most sumptuous tomb.

• *Exit Mary's chapel. Continue on, until you emerge in the south transept. Look for the doorway that leads to a stairway and elevator to the...*

❾ Queen's Diamond Jubilee Galleries: In the summer of 2018, the Abbey will open a space that has been closed off for 700 years—an internal gallery 70 feet above the main floor known as the triforium. This balcony will house the new Queen's Diamond Jubilee Galleries, a small museum where you'll see exhibits covering royal coronations, funerals, and much more from the Abbey's 1,000-year history. There will also be stunning views of the nave straight down to the Great West Door. Because of limited access to the galleries, it's likely visitors will need a timed-entry ticket (see the Abbey website for details).

• *After touring the Queen's Galleries, return to the main floor. You're in...*

🔟 **Poets' Corner:** England's greatest artistic contributions are in the written word. Here the masters of arguably the world's

most complex and expressive language are remembered: Geoffrey Chaucer *(Canterbury Tales)*, Lord Byron, Dylan Thomas, W. H. Auden, Lewis Carroll *(Alice's Adventures in Wonderland)*, T. S. Eliot *(The Waste Land)*, Alfred Tennyson, Robert Browning, and Charles Dickens. Many writers are honored with plaques and monuments; relatively few are actually buried here. Shakespeare is commemorated by a fine statue that stands near the end of the transept, overlooking the others.

• *Exit the church (temporarily) at the south door, which leads to the...*

⓫ **Great Cloister:** The buildings that adjoin the church housed the monks. Cloistered courtyards gave them a place to meditate on God's creations.

• *Go back into the church for the last stop.*

⓬ **Coronation Chair:** A gold-painted oak chair waits here under a regal canopy for the next coronation. For every English coronation since 1308 (except two), it's been moved to its spot before the high altar to receive the royal buttocks. The chair's legs rest on lions, England's symbol.

▲▲Houses of Parliament (Palace of Westminster)

This Neo-Gothic icon of London, the site of the royal residence ~~fro~~m 1042 to 1547, is now the meeting place of the legislative ~~bran~~ch of government. Like the US Capitol in Washington, DC, the complex is open to visitors. You can view parliamentary sessions in either the bickering House of Commons or the sleepy House of Lords. Or you can simply wander on your own (through a few closely monitored rooms) to appreciate the historic building itself.

The Palace of Westminster has been the center of political power in England for nearly a thousand years. In 1834, a horrendous fire gutted the Palace. It was rebuilt in a retro, Neo-Gothic style that recalled England's medieval Christian roots—pointed arches, stained-glass windows, spires, and saint-like statues. At the same time, Britain was also retooling its government. Democracy was on the rise, the queen became a constitutional monarch,  and Parliament emerged as the nation's ruling body. The Palace of Westminster became a symbol—a kind of cathedral—of democracy. A visit here offers a chance to tour a piece of living history and see the British government in action.

Cost and Hours: Free when Parliament is in session, otherwise must visit with a paid tour (see later); hours for nonticketed entry to House of Commons—Oct-late July Mon 14:30-22:30, Tue-Wed 11:30-19:30, Thu 9:30-17:30; for House of Lords—Oct-late July Mon-Tue 14:30-22:00, Wed 15:00-22:00, Thu 11:00-19:30; last entry depends on debates; exact schedule at www.parliament.uk.

Tours: Audioguide-£18.50, guided tour-£25.50, Sat year-round 9:00-16:30 and most weekdays during recess (late July-Sept), 1.5 hours. Confirm the tour schedule and book ahead at www.parliament.uk or by calling 020/7219-4114. The ticket office also sells tour tickets, but there's no guarantee same-day spaces will be available (ticket office open Mon-Fri 10:00-16:00, Sat 9:00-16:30, closed Sun, located in Portcullis House next to Westminster Tube station, entrance on Victoria Embankment).

Choosing a House: The House of Lords is less important politically, but they meet in a more ornate room, and the wait time is shorter (likely less than 30 minutes). The House of Commons is where major policy is made, but the room is sparse, and wait times are longer (30-60 minutes or more).

Crowd-Beating Tips: For the public galleries, lines tend to be longest at the start of each session, particularly on Wednesdays; for the shortest wait, try to show up later in the afternoon (but don't push it, as things sometimes close down early).

⊙ Self-Guided Tour: Enter midway along the west side the building (across the street from Westminster Abbey),

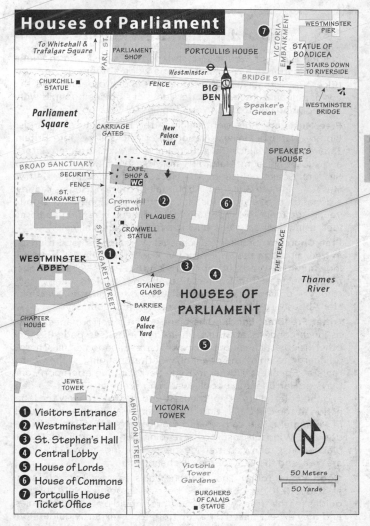

Houses of Parliament

To Whitehall & Trafalgar Square

PARL. ST.

PARLIAMENT SHOP

PORTCULLIS HOUSE

VICTORIA EMBANKMENT

WESTMINSTER PIER

STATUE OF BOADICEA

STAIRS DOWN TO RIVERSIDE

CHURCHILL STATUE

Westminster

BRIDGE ST.

FENCE

BIG BEN

Parliament Square

CARRIAGE GATES

New Palace Yard

Speaker's Green

WESTMINSTER BRIDGE

BROAD SANCTUARY

SECURITY FENCE

ST. MARGARET'S

CAFÉ, SHOP & WC

Cromwell Green

❷

PLAQUES

❻

SPEAKER'S HOUSE

CROMWELL STATUE

WESTMINSTER ABBEY

❶

ST. MARGARET STREET

STAINED GLASS

BARRIER

Old Palace Yard

❸

❹

HOUSES OF PARLIAMENT

THE TERRACE

Thames River

CHAPTER HOUSE

❺

JEWEL TOWER

ABINGDON STREET

VICTORIA TOWER

Victoria Tower Gardens

BURGHERS OF CALAIS STATUE

50 Meters

50 Yards

LONDON

❶ Visitors Entrance
❷ Westminster Hall
❸ St. Stephen's Hall
❹ Central Lobby
❺ House of Lords
❻ House of Commons
❼ Portcullis House Ticket Office

a tourist ramp leads to the ❶ **visitors entrance.** Line up for the airport-style security check. You'll be given a visitor badge. If you

have questions, the attendants are extremely helpful.

• *First, take in the cavernous...*

❷ **Westminster Hall:** This vast hall—covering 16,000 square feet—survived the 1834 fire, and is one of the oldest and most important buildings in England. England's vaunted legal system

Affording London's Sights

London is one of Europe's most expensive cities, with the dubious distinction of having some of the world's steepest admission prices. But with its many free museums and affordable plays, this cosmopolitan, cultured city offers days of sightseeing thrills without requiring you to pinch your pennies (or your pounds).

Free Museums: Free sights include the British Museum, British Library, National Gallery, National Portrait Gallery, Tate Britain, Tate Modern, Wallace Collection, Imperial War Museum, Victoria and Albert Museum, Natural History Museum, Science Museum, Sir John Soane's Museum, the Museum of London, the Geffrye Museum, and the Guildhall. About half of these museums request a donation of a few pounds, but whether you contribute is up to you. If you feel like supporting these museums, renting audioguides, using their café, and buying a few souvenirs all help.

Free Churches: Smaller churches let worshippers (and tourists) in free, although they may ask for a donation. The big sightseeing churches—Westminster Abbey and St. Paul's—charge higher admission fees, but offer free evensong services nearly daily (though you can't stick around afterward to sightsee). Westminster Abbey also offers free organ recitals most Sundays.

Other Freebies: London has plenty of free performances, such as lunch concerts at St. Martin-in-the-Fields (see page 89). For other freebies, check out www.whatsfreeinlondon.co.uk. There's no charge to enjoy the pageantry of the Changing of the Guard, rants at Speakers' Corner in Hyde Park (on Sun afternoon), displays at Harrods, the people-watching scene at Covent Garden, and the colorful streets of the East End. It's free to view the legal action at the Old Bailey and the legislature at work in the Houses of Parliament. You can get into the chapels at the Tower of London and Windsor Castle by attending Sunday services at each place. And, Greenwich is an inexpensive outing. Many of its sights are free, and the DLR journey is cheap.

Good-Value Tours: The London Walks tours with professional guides (£10) are one of the best deals going. (Note that the guides for the "free" walking tours are unpaid by their companies, and they expect tips—I'd pay up front for an expertly guided tour instead.) Hop-on, hop-off big-bus tours, while expensive (around

was invented in this hall, as this was the major court of the land for 700 years. King Charles I was tried and sentenced to death here. Guy Fawkes was condemned for plotting to blow up the Halls of Parliament in 1605.

• *Continue up the stairs, and enter...*

   ❸ **St. Stephen's Hall:** This long, beautifully lit room was the original House of Commons. Members of Parliament (MPs) sat in

£30), provide a great overview and include free boat tours as well as city walks. (Or, for the price of a transit ticket, you could get similar views from the top of a double-decker public bus.) A one-hour Thames ride to Greenwich costs about £12 one-way, but most boats come with entertaining commentary. A three-hour bicycle tour is about £25.

Pricey...but Worth It? Big-ticket sights worth their hefty admission fees (£15-30) are the Tower of London, Kew Gardens, Shakespeare's Globe, and the Churchill War Rooms. The London Eye has become a London must-see—but you may feel differently when you see the prices (£25). St. Paul's Cathedral (£18) becomes more worthwhile if you climb the dome for the stunning view. While Hampton Court Palace is expensive (£23), it is well-presented and a reasonable value if you have an interest in royal history. The Queen charges royally for a peek inside Buckingham Palace (£23, open Aug-Sept only) and her fine art gallery and carriage museum (adjacent to the palace, £10 each). Madame Tussauds Waxworks is pricey but still hard for many to resist (£35, see page 108 for info on discounts). Harry Potter fans gladly pay the Hagrid-sized £39 fee to see the sets and props at the Warner Bros. Studio Tour (but those who wouldn't know a wizard from a Muggle needn't bother).

Totally Pants (Brit-speak for Not Worth It): The London Dungeon, at £28, is gimmicky, overpriced, and a terrible value...despite the long line. The cost of the wallet-bleeding ride to the top of The Shard—£31—is even more breathtaking than the view from Western Europe's tallest skyscraper.

Theater: Compared with Broadway's prices, London's theater can be a bargain. Seek out the freestanding TKTS booth at Leicester Square to get discounts from 25 to 50 percent on good seats (and full-price tickets to the hottest shows with no service charges; see page 158). Buying direct at the theater box office can score you a great deal on same-day tickets, and even the most popular shows generally have some seats under £20 (possibly with obstructed views)—ask. A £5 "groundling" ticket for a play at Shakespeare's Globe is the best theater deal in town (see page 161). Tickets to the Open Air Theatre at north London's Regent's Park start at £25 (see page 162).

church pews on either side of the hall—the ruling faction on one side, the opposition on the other

• *Next you reach the...*

❹ **Central Lobby:** This ornate, octagonal, high-vaulted room is often called the "heart of British government," because it sits midway between the House of Commons (to the left) and the House of Lords (right). Video monitors list the schedule of meetings and events in this 1,100-room governmental hive. This is the best place to admire the Palace's carved wood, chandeliers, statues, and floor tiles.

• This lobby marks the end of the public space where you can wander freely. To see the House of Lords or House of Commons, you must wait in line and check your belongings.

❺ House of Lords: When you're called, you'll walk to the Lords Chamber by way of the long Peers' Corridor—referring to the House's 800 unelected members, called "Peers." Paintings on the corridor walls depict the antiauthoritarian spirit brewing under the reign of Charles I.

When you reach the House of Lords Chamber, you'll watch the proceedings from the upper-level visitors gallery. Debate may occur among the few Lords who show up at any given time, but these days, the Peers' role is largely advisory—they have no real power to pass laws on their own.

The Lords Chamber is church-like and impressive, with stained glass and intricately carved walls. At the far end is the Queen's gilded throne, where she sits once a year to give a speech to open Parliament. In front of the throne sits the woolsack—a cushion stuffed with wool. Here the Lord Speaker presides, with a ceremonial mace behind the backrest. To the Lord Speaker's right are the members of the ruling party (a.k.a. "government") and to his left are the members of the opposition (the Labour Party). Unaffiliated Crossbenchers sit in between

❻ House of Commons: The Commons Chamber may be much less grandiose than the Lords', but this is where the sausage gets made. The House of Commons is as powerful as the Lords, prime minister, and Queen combined.

Of today's 650-plus MPs, only 450 can sit—the rest have to stand at the ends. As in the House of Lords, the ruling party sits on the right of the Speaker—in his canopied Speaker's Chair—and opposition sits on the left. Keep an eye out for two red lines on the floor, which must not be crossed when debating the other side. (They're supposedly two sword-lengths apart, to prevent a literal clashing of swords.) The clerks sit at a central table that holds the ceremonial mace, a symbol of the power given Parliament by the monarch, who is not allowed in the Commons Chamber.

When the prime minister visits, her ministers (or cabinet) join her on the front bench, while lesser MPs (the "backbenchers") sit behind. It's often a fiery spectacle, as the prime minister defends her policies, while the opposition grumbles and harrumphs in displeasure. It's not unheard-of for MPs to get out of line and be escorted out by the Serjeant at Arms.

Nearby: Across the street from the Parliament building's S⁻ Stephen's Gate, the **Jewel Tower** is a rare remnant of the old Pala of Westminster, used by kings until Henry VIII. The crude stone tower (1365-1366) was a guard tower in the palace wall, overlooking a moat. It contains a fine exhibit on the medieval Westminster Palace and the tower (£5.20, daily 10:00-18:00, Oct until 17:00; Nov-March Sat-Sun until 16:00, closed Mon-Fri; tel. 020/7222-2219). Next to the tower (and free) is a quiet courtyard with picnic-friendly benches.

Big Ben, the 315-foot-high clock tower at the north end of the Palace of Westminster, is named for its 13-ton bell, Ben. The light above the clock is lit when Parliament is in session. The face of the clock is huge—you can actually see the minute hand moving. For a good view of it, walk halfway over Westminster Bridge.

▲▲▲Churchill War Rooms

This excellent sight offers a fascinating walk through the underground headquarters of the British government's WWII fight against the Nazis in the darkest days of the Battle of Britain. It has two parts: the war rooms themselves, and a top-notch museum dedicated to the man who steered the war from here, Winston Churchill. For details on all the blood, sweat, toil, and tears, pick up the excellent, essential, and included audioguide at the entry, and dive in. Though you can buy your ticket in advance online, you may still find yourself waiting up to 30 minutes (on busy days) in the security line before entering. Allow 1-2 hours for your visit.

Cost and Hours: £19, includes audioguide, daily 9:30-18:00, last entry one hour before closing; on King Charles Street, 200 yards off Whitehall—follow signs, Tube: Westminster; tel. 020/7930-6961, www.iwm.org.uk/churchill. The museum's gift shop is great for anyone nostalgic for the 1940s.

Cabinet War Rooms: The 27-room, heavily fortified nerve center of the British war effort was used from 1939 to 1945. Churchill's

room, the map room, and other rooms are just as they were in 1945. As you follow the one-way route, take advantage of the audioguide, which explains each room and offers first-person accounts of wartime happenings here. Be patient—it's well worth it. While the rooms are spartan, you'll see how British gentility survived even as the city was bombarded—posted signs informed those working underground what the weather was like outside, and a cheery notice reminded them to turn off the light switch to conserve electricity.

LONDON

Churchill Museum: Don't bypass this museum, which occupies a large hall amid the war rooms. It dissects every aspect of the man behind the famous cigar, bowler hat, and V-for-victory sign. It's extremely well-presented and engaging, using artifacts, quotes, political cartoons, clear explanations, and interactive exhibits to bring the colorful statesman to life. You'll get a taste of Winston's wit, irascibility, work ethic, passion for painting, American ties, writing talents, and drinking habits. The exhibit shows Winston's warts as well: It questions whether his party-switching was just political opportunism, examines the basis for his opposition to Indian self-rule, and reveals him to be an intense taskmaster who worked 18-hour days and was brutal to his staffers (who deeply respected him nevertheless).

A long touch-the-screen timeline lets you zero in on events in his life from birth (November 30, 1874) to his first appointment as prime minister in 1940. Many of the items on display—such as a European map divvied up in permanent marker, which Churchill brought to England from the postwar Potsdam Conference—drive home the remarkable span of history this man influenced. Imagine: Churchill began his military career riding horses in the cavalry and ended it speaking out against nuclear proliferation. It's all the more amazing considering that, in the 1930s, the man who would become my vote for greatest statesman of the 20th century was considered a washed-up loony ranting about the growing threat of fascist Germany. When World War II broke out, Prime Minister Chamberlain's appeasement policies were discredited, and—on the day that Germany invaded the Netherlands—the king appointed Churchill prime minister. Churchill guided the nation through its darkest hour. His greatest contribution may have been his stirring radio speeches that galvanized the will of the British people.

Eating: Rations are available at the **$$ museum café** or, better, get a pub lunch at the nearby **$$ Westminster Arms** (food served downstairs, on Storey's Gate, a couple of blocks south of the museum).

Horse Guards

The Horse Guards change daily at 10:30 (9:30 on Sun), and a colorful dismounting ceremony takes place daily at 16:00. The rest of the day, they just stand there—making for boring video (at Horse Guards Parade on Whitehall, directly across from the Banqueting House, between Trafalgar Square and 10 Downing Street, Tube: Westminster, www.householddivision.org.uk—search "Changing the Guard").

Buckingham Palace pageantry is canceled when it rains, but the Horse Guards change regardless of the weather.

▲**Banqueting House**

England's first Renaissance building (1619-1622) is still standing. Designed by Inigo Jones, built by King James I, and decorated by his son Charles I, the Banqueting House came to symbolize the Stuart kings' "divine right" management style—the belief that God himself had anointed them to rule. The house is one of the few London landmarks spared by the 1698 fire and the only surviving part of the original Palace of Whitehall. Today it opens its doors to visitors, who enjoy a restful 10-minute audiovisual history, a 45-minute audioguide, and a look at the exquisite banqueting hall itself. As a tourist attraction, it's basically one big room, with sumptuous ceiling paintings by Peter Paul Rubens. At Charles I's request, these paintings drove home the doctrine of the legitimacy of the divine right of kings. Ironically, in 1649—divine right ignored—King Charles I was famously executed right here.

Cost and Hours: £8, includes audioguide, Fri-Wed 10:00-17:00, closed Thu, may close for government functions—although it stays open at least until 13:00 (call ahead for recorded info), immediately across Whitehall from the Horse Guards, Tube: Westminster, tel. 020/3166-6155, www.hrp.org.uk.

ON TRAFALGAR SQUARE

Trafalgar Square, London's central square worth ▲▲, is at the intersection of Westminster, The City, and the West End. It's the

climax of most marches and demonstrations, and is a thrilling place to simply hang out. A remodeling of the square has rerouted car traffic, helping reclaim the area for London's citizens. At the top of Trafalgar Square (north) sits the domed National Gallery with its grand staircase, and to the right, the steeple of St. Martin-in-the-Fields, built in 1722, inspiring the steeple-over-the-entrance style of many town churches in New England. In the center of the square, Lord Nelson stands atop his 185-foot-tall fluted granite column, gazing out toward Trafalgar, where he lost his life but defeated the French fleet. Part of this 1842 memorial is made from is victims' melted-down cannons. He's surrounded by spraying ntains, giant lions, hordes of people, and—until recently—even e pigeons. A former London mayor decided that London's "fly-

LONDON

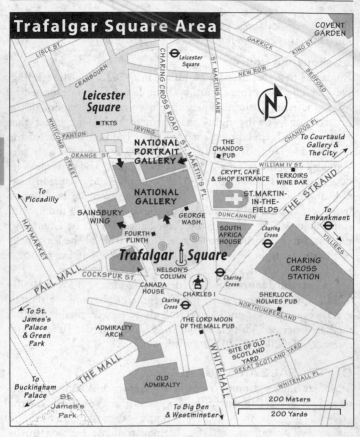

Trafalgar Square Area

ing rats" were a public nuisance and evicted Trafalgar Square's venerable seed salesmen (Tube: Charing Cross).

▲▲▲National Gallery

Displaying an unsurpassed collection of European paintings from 1250 to 1900—including works by Leonardo, Botticelli, Velázquez, Rembrandt, Turner, Van Gogh, and the Impressionists—this is one of Europe's great galleries. You'll peruse 700 years of art—from gold-backed Madonnas to Cubist bathers.

Cost and Hours: Free, £5 suggested donation, special exhibits extra, daily 10:00-18:00, Fri until 21:00, last entry to special exhibits 45 minutes before closing, on Trafalgar Square, Tube: Charing Cross or Leicester Square.

Information: Helpful £1 floor plan available from information desk; free one-hour overview tours leave from Sainsbury Wing info desk daily at 11:30 and 14:30, plus Fri at 19:00; excellent £4 audioguides—choose from one-hour highlights tour, several theme tours, or an option that lets you dial up info on any painting in the museum; tel. 020/7747-2885, www.nationalgallery.org.uk.

Eating: Consider splitting afternoon tea at the excellent **$$$ National Dining Rooms,** on the first floor of the Sainsbury Wing (see page 204). The **$$$ National Café,** located near the Getty Entrance, has a table-service restaurant and a **$ café.** Seek out the **$ Espresso Bar,** near the Portico and Getty entrances, for sandwiches, pastries, and soft couches.

◐ Self-Guided Tour: Enter through the Sainsbury Entrance (in the smaller building to the left of the main entrance), and approach the collection chronologically.

Medieval and Early Renaissance: In the first rooms, you see shiny paintings of saints, angels, Madonnas, and crucifixions floating in an ethereal gold never-never land. Art in the Middle Ages was religious, dominated by the Church. The illiterate faithful could meditate on an altarpiece and visualize heaven. It's as though they couldn't imagine saints and angels inhabiting the dreary world of rocks, trees, and sky they lived in.

After leaving this gold-leaf peace, you'll stumble into Uccello's *Battle of San Romano* and Van Eyck's *The Arnolfini Portrait*,

called by some "The Shotgun Wedding." This painting—a masterpiece of down-to-earth details—was once thought to depict a wedding ceremony forced by the lady's swelling belly. Today it's understood as a portrait of a solemn, well-dressed, well-heeled couple, the Arnolfinis of Bruges, Belgium (she likely was not pregnant—the fashion of the day was to gather up the folds of one's extremely full-skirted dress).

Italian Renaissance: In painting, the Renaissance meant realism. Artists rediscovered the beauty of nature and the human body, expressing the optimism and confidence of this new age. Look for Botticelli's *Venus and Mars*, Michelangelo's *The Entombment*, and Raphael's *Pope Julius II*.

In Leonardo's *The Virgin of the Rocks*, Mary plays with her son Jesus and little Johnny the Baptist (with cross, at left) while an androgynous angel looks on. Leonardo brings this holy scene right down to earth by setting it among rocks, stalactites, water, nd flowering plants. But looking closer, we see that Leonardo has

LONDON

MEDIEVAL & EARLY RENAISSANCE
1 ANONYMOUS – The Wilton Diptych
2 UCCELLO – Battle of San Romano
3 VAN EYCK – The Arnolfini Portrait

ITALIAN RENAISSANCE
4 LEONARDO – The Virgin of the Rocks
5 BOTTICELLI – Venus and Mars
6 CRIVELLI – The Annunciation, with Saint Emidius

HIGH RENAISSANCE & MANNERISM
7 LEONARDO – Virgin and Child with St. Anne and St. John the Baptist
8 MICHELANGELO – The Entombment
9 RAPHAEL – Pope Julius II
10 BRONZINO – An Allegory with Venus and Cupid
11 TINTORETTO – The Origin of the Milky Way

NORTHERN PROTESTANT ART
12 VERMEER – A Young Woman Standing at a Virginal
13 VAN HOOGSTRATEN – A Peepshow with Views of the Interior of a Dutch House
14 REMBRANDT – Belshazzar's Feast
15 REMBRANDT – Self-Portrait at the Age of 63

BAROQUE & FRENCH ROCOCO
16 RUBENS – The Judgment of Paris
17 VELÁZQUEZ – The Rokeby Venus
18 VAN DYCK – Equestrian Portrait of Charles I
19 CARAVAGGIO – The Supper at Emmaus
20 BOUCHER – Pan and Syrinx

BRITISH ROMANTIC ART
21 CONSTABLE – The Hay Wain
22 TURNER – The Fighting Téméraire

To Leicester Square ⊖
(5 min. walk)

SAINSBURY WING
ENTRANCE ON LEVEL 0

SELF-GUIDED TOUR
STARTS ON LEVEL 2

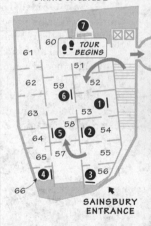

deliberately posed his people into a pyramid shape, with Mary's head at the peak, creating an oasis of maternal stability and serenity amid the hard rock of the earth.

In *The Origin of the Milky Way* by Venetian Renaissance painter Tintoretto, the god Jupiter places his illegitimate son, baby Hercules, at his wife's breast. Juno says, "Wait a minute. That's not my baby!" Her milk spurts upward, becoming the Milky Way.

Northern Protestant: While Italy had wealthy aristocrats and the powerful Catholic Church to purchase art, the North's patron

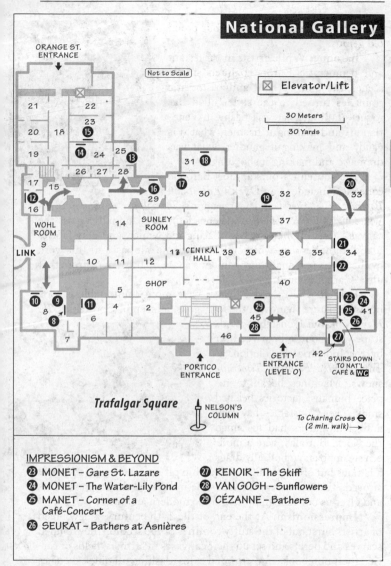

National Gallery

ORANGE ST.
ENTRANCE

Not to Scale

⊠ Elevator/Lift

30 Meters
30 Yards

LONDON

WOHL ROOM
LINK
SUNLEY ROOM
CENTRAL HALL
SHOP

PORTICO ENTRANCE

GETTY ENTRANCE (LEVEL 0)

STAIRS DOWN TO NAT'L CAFÉ & **WC**

Trafalgar Square

NELSON'S COLUMN

To Charing Cross ⊖
(2 min. walk) →

IMPRESSIONISM & BEYOND

23 MONET – *Gare St. Lazare*
24 MONET – *The Water-Lily Pond*
25 MANET – *Corner of a Café-Concert*
26 SEURAT – *Bathers at Asnières*

27 RENOIR – *The Skiff*
28 VAN GOGH – *Sunflowers*
29 CÉZANNE – *Bathers*

were middle-class, hardworking, Protestant merchants. They wanted simple, cheap, no-nonsense pictures to decorate their homes and offices. Greek gods and Virgin Marys are out, and hometown folks and hometown places are in.

Highlights include Vermeer's *A Young Woman Standing at a Virginal* and Rembrandt's *Belshazzar's Feast*. Rembrandt painted his *Self-Portrait at the Age of 63* in the year he would die. He throws the light of truth on...himself. He was bankrupt, his mistress had just passed away, and he had also buried several of his children. We see a disillusioned, well-worn, but proud old genius.

Baroque: While artists in Protestant and democratic Europe painted simple scenes, those in Catholic and aristocratic countries turned to the style called Baroque—taking what was flashy in Venetian art and making it flashier, what was gaudy and making it gaudier, what was dramatic and making it shocking.

The museum's outstanding Baroque collection includes Van Dyck's *Equestrian Portrait of Charles I* and Caravaggio's *The Supper at Emmaus.* In Velázquez's *The Rokeby Venus,* Venus lounges diagonally across the canvas, admiring herself, with flaring red, white, and gray fabrics to highlight her rosy-white skin and inflame our passion. This work by the king's personal court painter is a rare Spanish nude from that ultra-Catholic country.

British: The reserved British were more comfortable cavorting with nature than with the lofty gods, as seen in Constable's *The Hay Wain.* But Constable's land-

scape was about to be paved over by the Industrial Revolution, as Turner's *The Fighting Téméraire* shows. Machines began to replace humans, factories belched smoke over Constable's hay cart, and cloud-gazers had to punch the clock. But alas, here a modern steamboat symbolically drags a famous but obsolete sailing battleship off into the sunset to be destroyed. Turner's messy, colorful style influenced the Impressionists and gives us our first glimpse into the modern art world.

Impressionism: At the end of the 19th century, a new breed of artists burst out of the stuffy confines of the studio. They donned scarves and berets and set up their canvases in farmers' fields or carried their notebooks into crowded cafés, dashing off quick sketches in order to catch a momentary...impression. Check out Impressionist and Post-Impressionist masterpieces such as Monet's *Gare St. Lazare* and *The Water-Lily Pond,* Renoir's *The Skiff,* Seurat's *Bathers at Asnières,* and Van Gogh's *Sunflowers.*

Van Gogh was the point man of his culture. He added emotion to Impressionism, infusing life even into inanimate objects. His sunflowers, painted with characteristic swirling brushstrokes, shimmer and writhe in either agony or ecstasy—depending on your own mood. Van Gogh painted these during his stay in southern

France, a time of frenzied creativity, when he hovered between despair and delight, bliss and madness. A year later, he shot himself.

Cézanne's *Bathers* are arranged in strict triangles. Cézanne uses the Impressionist technique of building a figure with dabs of paint (though his "dabs" are often larger-sized "cube" shapes) to make solid, 3-D geometrical figures in the style of the Renaissance. In the process, his cube shapes helped inspire a radical new style—Cubism—bringing art into the 20th century.

▲▲National Portrait Gallery

LONDON

Put off by halls of 19th-century characters who meant nothing to me, I used to call this museum "as interesting as someone else's yearbook." But a selective walk through this 500-year-long *Who's Who* of British history is quick and free, and puts faces on the story of England. The collection is well-described, not huge, and in historical sequence, from the 16th century on the second floor to today's royal family, usually housed on the ground floor. Highlights include Henry VIII and wives; portraits of the "Virgin Queen" Elizabeth I, Sir Francis Drake, and Sir Walter Raleigh; the only real-life portrait of William Shakespeare; Oliver Cromwell and Charles I with his head on; portraits by Gainsborough and Reynolds; the Romantics (William Blake, Lord Byron, William Wordsworth, and company); Queen Victoria and her era; and the present royal family, including the late Princess Diana and the current Duchess of Cambridge—Kate.

Cost and Hours: Free, £5 suggested donation, special exhibits extra; daily 10:00-18:00, Fri until 21:00, first and second floors open Mon at 11:00, last entry to special exhibits one hour before closing; excellent audioguide-£3, floor plan-£1; entry 100 yards off Trafalgar Square (around the corner from National Gallery, opposite Church of St. Martin-in-the-Fields), Tube: Charing Cross or Leicester Square, tel. 020/7306-0055, recorded info tel. 020/7312-2463, www.npg.org.uk.

▲St. Martin-in-the-Fields

The church, built in the 1720s with a Gothic spire atop a Greek-type temple, is an oasis of peace on wild and noisy Trafalgar Square. St. Martin cared for the poor. "In the fields" was where the first church stood on this spot (in the 13th century), between Westminster and The City. Stepping inside, you still feel a compassion for the needs of the people in this neighborhood—the church serves the homeless and houses a Chinese community center. The modern east window—with grillwork bent into the shape of a warped cross—was installed in 2008 to replace one damaged in World War II.

A freestanding glass pavilion to the left of the church serves as the entrance to the church's underground areas. There you'll find the concert ticket office, a gift shop, brass-rubbing center, and the recommended support-the-church Café in the Crypt.

Cost and Hours: Free, donations welcome; hours vary but generally Mon-Fri 8:30-13:00 & 14:00-18:00, Sat 9:30-18:00, Sun 15:30-17:00; services listed at entrance; Tube: Charing Cross, tel. 020/7766-1100, www.stmartin-in-the-fields.org.

Music: The church is famous for its concerts. Consider a free lunchtime concert (£3.50 suggested donation; Mon, Tue, and Fri at 13:00), an evening concert (£9-28, several nights a week at 19:30), or Wednesday night jazz at the Café in the Crypt (£8-15 at 20:00). See the church's website for the concert schedule.

THE WEST END AND NEARBY

To explore this area during dinnertime, see my recommended restaurants on page 183.

▲Piccadilly Circus

Although this square is slathered with neon billboards and tacky attractions (think of it as the Times Square of London), the surrounding streets are packed with great shopping opportunities and swimming with youth on the rampage.

Nearby Shaftesbury Avenue and Leicester Square teem with fun-seekers, theaters, Chinese restaurants, and street singers. To the northeast is London's Chinatown and, beyond that, the funky Soho neighborhood (described next). And curling to the northwest from Piccadilly Circus is genteel Regent Street, lined with exclusive shops.

▲Soho

North of Piccadilly, once-seedy Soho has become trendy—with many recommended restaurants—and is well worth a gawk. It's the epicenter of London's thriving, colorful youth scene, a fun and funky *Sesame Street* of urban diversity.

Soho is also London's red light district (especially near Brewer and Berwick Streets), where "friendly models" wait in tiny rooms up dreary stairways, voluptuous con artists sell strip shows, and eager male tourists are frequently ripped off. But it's easy to avoid trouble if you're not looking for it. In fact, the sleazy joints shathe block with respectable pubs and restaurants, and elderly couples stroll past neon signs that flash *Licensed Sex Shop in Basement*.

▲▲Covent Garden

This large square teems with people and street performers—jugglers, sword swallowers, and guitar players. London's buskers (in-

cluding those in the Tube) are auditioned, licensed, and assigned times and places where they are allowed to perform.

The square's centerpiece is a covered marketplace. A market has been here since medieval times, when it was the "convent" garden owned by Westminster Abbey. In the 1600s, it became a housing development with this courtyard as its center, done in the Palladian style by Inigo Jones. Today's fine iron-and-glass structure was built in 1830 (when such buildings were all the Industrial Age rage) to house the stalls of what became London's chief produce market. Covent Garden remained a produce market until 1973, when its venerable arcades were converted to boutiques, cafés, and antique shops. A tourist market thrives here today (for details, see page 157).

The "Actors' Church" of St. Paul, the Royal Opera House, and the London Transport Museum (described next) all border the square, and theaters are nearby. The area is a people-watcher's delight, with cigarette eaters, Punch-and-Judy acts, food that's good for you (but not your wallet), trendy crafts, and row after row of boutique shops and market stalls. For better Covent Garden lunch deals, walk a block or two away from the eye of this touristic hurricane (check out the places north of the Tube station, along Endell and Neal Streets).

▲London Transport Museum

This modern, well-presented museum, located right at Covent Garden, is fun for kids and thought-provoking for adults (if a bit overpriced). Whether you're cursing or marveling at the buses and Tube, the growth of Europe's third-biggest city (after Istanbul and Moscow) has been made possible by its public transit system.

After you enter, take the elevator up to the top floor...and the year 1800, when horse-drawn vehicles ruled the road. Next, you descend to the first floor and the world's first underground Metro system, which used steam-powered locomotives (the Circle Line, c. 1865). On the ground floor, horses and trains are replaced by motorized vehicles (cars, taxis, double-decker buses, streetcars), re-

LONDON

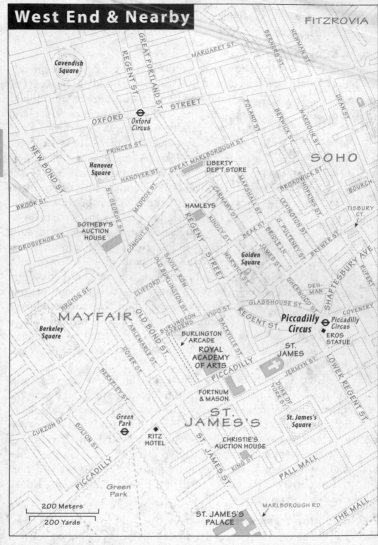

West End & Nearby

FITZROVIA

Cavendish Square

SOHO

OXFORD STREET

Oxford Circus

Hanover Square

LIBERTY DEP'T STORE

HAMLEYS

SOTHEBY'S AUCTION HOUSE

Golden Square

MAYFAIR

Berkeley Square

BURLINGTON ARCADE

ROYAL ACADEMY OF ARTS

Piccadilly Circus

EROS STATUE

ST. JAMES

PICCADILLY

FORTNUM & MASON

Green Park

ST. JAMES'S

St. James's Square

RITZ HOTEL

CHRISTIE'S AUCTION HOUSE

PALL MALL

PICCADILLY

Green Park

THE MALL

200 Meters

200 Yards

MARLBOROUGH RD.

ST. JAMES'S PALACE

sulting in 20th-century congestion. How to deal with it? In 2003, car drivers in London were slapped with a congestion charge, and today, a half-billion people ride the Tube every year.

Cost and Hours: £17.50, ticket good for one year, free for kids under 18, Sat-Thu 10:00-18:00, Fri from 11:00, last entry 45 minutes before closing; pleasant upstairs café with Covent Garden view; in southeast corner of Covent Garden courtyard, Tube: Covent Garden, switchboard tel. 020/7379-6344, recorded info tel. 020/7565-7299, www.ltmuseum.co.uk.

LONDON

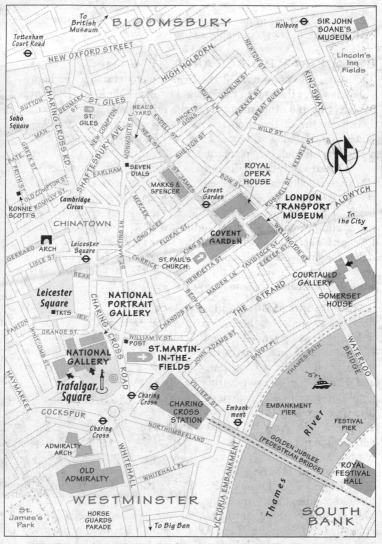

▲Courtauld Gallery

This gallery, part of the Courtauld Institute of Art, is set to close in mid-2018 for a multiyear renovation. If it's open when you visit, you'll see medieval European paintings and works by Rubens, the Impressionists (Manet, Monet, and Degas), Post-Impressionists (Cézanne and an intense Van Gogh self-portrait), and more. The gallery is located within the grand Somerset House; enjoy the riverside eateries and the courtyard featuring a playful fountain.

Cost and Hours: £7, price can change with exhibit; daily 10:00-18:00, occasionally Thu until 21:00; in Somerset House on the Strand, Tube: Temple or Covent Garden, recorded info tel. 020/7848-2526, www.courtauld.ac.uk.

BUCKINGHAM PALACE AREA

The working headquarters of the British monarchy, Buckingham Palace is where the Queen carries out her official duties as the head of state. She and other members of the royal family also maintain apartments here. The property hasn't always been this grand—James I (1603-1625) first brought the site under royal protection as a place for his mulberry plantation, for rearing silkworms.

Ticketing Options: Three palace sights require admission—the State Rooms (open Aug-Sept only), the Queen's Gallery, and the Royal Mews. You can pay for each separately (prices listed later), or buy a combo-ticket: A £39.50 "Royal Day Out" combo-ticket admits you to all three sights; a £17.70 version covers the Queen's Gallery and Royal Mews. For more information or to book online, see www.royalcollection.org.uk. Many tourists are more interested in the Changing of the Guard, which costs nothing at all to view. For locations, see map on page 96.

▲State Rooms at Buckingham Palace

This lavish home has been Britain's royal residence since 1837, when the newly ascended Queen Victoria moved in. When today's Queen is at home, the royal standard flies (a red, yellow, and blue flag); otherwise, the Union Jack flaps in the wind. The Queen opens her palace to the public—but only in August and September, when she's out of town.

Cost and Hours: £23 for State Rooms and throne room, includes audioguide; Aug-Sept only, daily 9:30-18:30, until 19:00 in Aug, last admission 17:15 in Aug, 16:15 in Sept; limited to 8,000 visitors a day by timed entry; come early to the palace's Visitor Entrance (opens at 9:00), or book ahead in person, by phone, or online; Tube: Victoria, tel. 0303/123-7300—but Her Majesty rarely answers.

Queen's Gallery at Buckingham Palace

A small sampling of Queen Elizabeth's personal collection of art is on display in five rooms in a wing adjoining the palace. Her 7,000 paintings, one of the largest private art collections in the world, are actually a series of collections built upon by each successive monarch since the 16th century. The Queen rotates the paintings, enjoying some privately in her many palatial residences while sharing others with her subjects in public galleries in Edinburgh and London. The exhibits change two or three times a year and are lovingly described by the included audioguide.

Because the gallery is small and security is tight (involving lines), I'd suggest visiting this gallery only if you're a patient art lover interested in the current exhibit.

Cost and Hours: £10.30 but can change depending on exhibit, daily 10:00-17:30, from 9:30 Aug-Sept, last entry one hour before closing, Tube: Victoria, tel. 0303/123-7301. Men shouldn't miss the mahogany-trimmed urinals.

Royal Mews

A visit to the Queen's working stables is likely to be disappointing unless you follow the included audioguide or the hourly guided tour (April-Oct only, 45 minutes), in which case it's fairly entertaining—especially if you're interested in horses and/or royalty. You'll see only a few of the Queen's 30 horses (most active between 10:00 and 12:00), a fancy car, and a bunch of old carriages, finishing with the Gold State Coach (c. 1760, 4 tons, 4 mph). Queen Victoria said absolutely no cars. When she died, in 1901, the mews got its first Daimler. Today, along with the hay-eating transport, the stable is home to five Bentleys and Rolls-Royce Phantoms, with at least one on display.

Cost and Hours: £10, April-Oct daily 10:00-17:00, Nov-March Mon-Sat 10:00-16:00, closed Sun; last entry 45 minutes before closing, generally busiest immediately after changing of the guard, guided tours on the hour in summer; Buckingham Palace Road, Tube: Victoria, tel. 0303/123-7302.

▲▲Changing of the Guard at Buckingham Palace

This is the spectacle every visitor to London has to see at least once: stone-faced, red-coated (or in winter, gray-coated), bearskin-hatted

guards changing posts with much fanfare, in an hour-long ceremony accompanied by a brass band.

The most famous part takes place right in front of Buckingham Palace at 11:00. But there actually are several different guard-changing ceremonies and parades going on simultaneously, at different locations within a few hundred yards of the palace. All of these spectacles converge around Buckingham Palace in a perfect storm of red-coated pageantry.

To plan your sightseeing strategy (and understand what's going on), see the blow-by-blow account in the "Changing of the Guard Timeline."

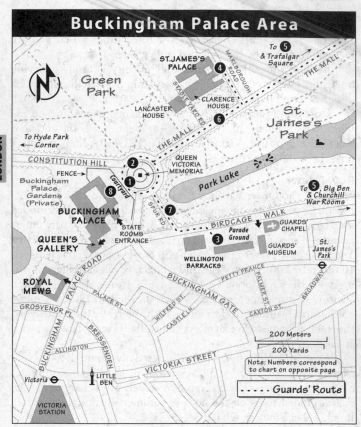

Buckingham Palace Area

Green Park

To Hyde Park Corner →

CONSTITUTION HILL

← FENCE

Buckingham Palace Gardens (Private)

BUCKINGHAM PALACE

Courtyard

STATE ROOMS ENTRANCE

QUEEN'S GALLERY

ROYAL MEWS

GROSVENOR PL.

PALACE ROAD

PALACE ST.

WILFRED ST.

CASTLE LN.

BRESSENDEN

ALLINGTON

Victoria ⊖

VICTORIA STATION

Little Ben

VICTORIA STREET

ST. JAMES'S PALACE

MARLBOROUGH RD.

STABLE YARD RD.

THE MALL

To ⑤ & Trafalgar Square →

THE MALL

CLARENCE HOUSE

LANCASTER HOUSE

St. James's Park

④

⑥

②
①

⑧

⑦

QUEEN VICTORIA MEMORIAL

Park Lake

SPUR RD.

BIRDCAGE WALK

Parade Ground

WELLINGTON BARRACKS

③

GUARDS' MUSEUM

GUARDS' CHAPEL

St. James's Park

To ⑤ Big Ben & Churchill War Rooms →

BUCKINGHAM GATE

PETTY FRANCE

PALMER ST.

CAXTON ST.

BROADWAY

200 Meters

200 Yards

Note: Numbers correspond to chart on opposite page

- - - - Guards' Route

Cost and Hours: Free, May-July daily at 11:00, every other day Aug-April, no ceremony in very wet weather; exact schedule subject to change—call 020/7766-7300 for the day's plan, or check www.householddivision.org.uk (search "Changing the Guard"); Buckingham Palace, Tube: Victoria, St. James's Park, or Green Park. Or hop into a big black taxi and say, "Buck House, please."

Sightseeing Strategies: Most tourists just show up and get lost in the crowds, but those who anticipate the action and know where to perch will enjoy the event more. The action takes place in stages over the course of an hour, at multiple locations; see the map. There are several ways to experience the pageantry. Get out your map (or download the official app at www.royalcollection.org.uk) and strategize. Here are a few options to consider:

Watch near the Palace: The main event is in the forecourt right in front of Buckingham Palace (between the palace and the fence) from 11:00 to 11:30. You'll need to get here as close to 10:00 as possible to get a place front and center, next to the fence. The key to good viewing is to get either right up front along the road

Changing of the Guard Timeline

When	What
10:00	Tourists begin to gather. Arrive now for a spot front and center by the **1** fence outside Buckingham Palace in anticipation of the most famous event—when the "Queen's Guard" does its shift change at 11:00.
10:30	**2** By now, the Victoria Memorial in front of the palace—the best all-purpose viewing spot—is crowded.
10:30-10:45	Meanwhile, at the nearby **3** Wellington Barracks, the "New Guard" gathers for inspection and the "Old Guard" gathers for inspection at **4** St. James's Palace.
10:30 (9:30 Sun)	Farther away, along Whitehall, the Horse Guard also changes guard, and begins parading down **5** the Mall.
10:43	Relieved of duty, the tired St. James's Palace guards march down **6** the Mall, heading for Buckingham Palace.
10:57	Fresh replacement troops (led by a marching band) head in a grand parade from Wellington Barracks down **7** Spur Road to Buckingham Palace.
11:00	All guards gradually converge around the Victoria Memorial in front of the palace. The ceremony approaches its climax.
11:00-11:30	Now, the famous Changing of the Guard ceremony takes place **8** inside the fenced courtyard of Buckingham Palace. Everyone parades around, the guard changes, and they pass the regimental flag (or "colour")—all with much shouting. The band plays a happy little concert and then they march out.
11:40	The tired "Old Guard" (led by a band) heads up Spur Road for Wellington Barracks. The fresh "New Guard" heads up the Mall for St. James's Palace.
11:45	As the fresh "New Guard" takes over at St. James's Palace, there's a smaller changing of the guard ceremony. And with that—"Tourists...d-i-i-s-missed!"

fence, or find some raised surface to stand or sit on—a balustrade or a curb—so you can see over people's heads.

Watch near the Victoria Memorial: The high ground on the circular Victoria Memorial provides the best overall view (come before 10:30 to get a place). From a high spot on the memorial, you have good (if more distant) views of the palace as well as the arriving and departing parades along The Mall and Spur Road. The actual Changing of the Guard in front of the palace is a nonevent.

It is interesting, however, to see nearly every tourist in London gathered in one place at the same time.

Watch near St. James's Palace: If you don't feel like jostling for a view, stroll down to St. James's Palace and wait near the corner for a great photo-op. At about 11:45, the parade marches up The Mall to the palace and performs a smaller changing ceremony—with almost no crowds. Afterward, stroll through nearby St. James's Park.

Follow the Procession: You won't get the closest views, but you'll get something even better—the thrill of participating in the action. Start with the "Old Guard" mobilizing in the courtyard of St. James's Palace (10:30). Arrive early, and grab a spot just across the road (otherwise you'll be asked to move when the inspection begins). Just before they prepare to leave (at 10:43), march ahead of them down Marlborough Street to The Mall. Pause here to watch them parade past, band and all, on their way to the Buckingham Palace, then cut through the park and head to the Wellington Barracks—where the "New Guard" is getting ready to leave for Buckingham (10:57). March along with full military band and fresh guards from the barracks to the palace. At 11:00 the two guard groups meet in the courtyard, the band plays a few songs, and soldiers parade and finally exchange compliments before returning to Wellington Barracks and St. James's Palace (11:40). Use this time to snap a few photos of the guards—and the crowds—before making your way across the Mall to Clarence House (on Stable Yard Road), where you'll see the "New Guard" pass one last time on their way to St. James's Palace. On their way, the final piece of ceremony takes place—one member of the "Old Guard" and one member of the first-relief "New Guard" change places here.

Join a Tour: Local tour companies such as **Fun London Tours** more or less follow the self-guided route above but add in history and facts about the guards, bands, and royal family to their already entertaining march. These walks add color and good value to what can otherwise seem like a stressful mess of tourists (£17, Changing of the Guard tour starts at Piccadilly Circus at 9:40, must book online in advance, www.funlondontours.com).

Sights in North London

▲▲▲British Museum

Simply put, this is the greatest chronicle of civilization...anywhere. A visit here is like taking a long hike through *Encyclopedia Britannica* National Park. The vast British Museum wraps around its Great Court (the huge entrance hall), with the most popular sections filling the ground floor: Egyptian, Assyrian, and ancient Greek, with the famous frieze sculptures from the Parthenon in

Athens. The museum's stately Reading Room—famous as the place where Karl Marx hung out while formulating his ideas on communism and writing *Das Kapital*—sometimes hosts special exhibits.

Cost and Hours: Free, £5 donation requested, special exhibits usually extra (and with timed ticket); daily 10:00-17:30, Fri until 20:30 (selected galleries only), least crowded late on weekday afternoons, especially Fri; Great Russell Street, Tube: Tottenham Court Road, ticket desk tel. 020/7323-8181, www.britishmuseum.org.

Visitor Information and Tours: Info desks offer a basic map (£2 donation), but it's not essential; the *Visitor's Guide* (£5) offers 15 different tours and skimpy text. Free 30- to 40-minute **EyeOpener tours** are led by volunteers, who focus on select rooms (daily 11:00-15:45, generally every 15 minutes). Free 45-minute **gallery talks** on specific subjects are offered Tue-Sat at 13:15; a free 20-minute **spotlight** tour runs on Friday evenings. The £6 **multimedia guide** offers dial-up audio commentary and video on 200 objects, as well as several theme tours (must leave photo ID). There's also a fun family multimedia guide (£5). Or ⌂ download my free audio tour.

❷ Self-Guided Tour: From the Great Court, doorways lead to all wings. To the left are the exhibits on Egypt, Assyria, and Greece—the highlights of your visit.

Enjoy the Great Court, Europe's largest covered square, which is bigger than a football field. This people-friendly court—delightfully spared from the London rain—was for 150 years one of London's great lost spaces...closed off and gathering dust. Since the year 2000, it's been the 140-foot-wide hub of a two-acre cultural complex.

Egypt: Start with the Egyptian section. Egypt was one of the world's first "civilizations"—a group of people with a government, religion, art, free time, and a written language. The Egypt we think of—pyramids, mummies, pharaohs, and guys who walk funny—lasted from 3000 to 1000 B.C. with hardly any change in the government, religion, or arts. Imagine two millennia of Nixon.

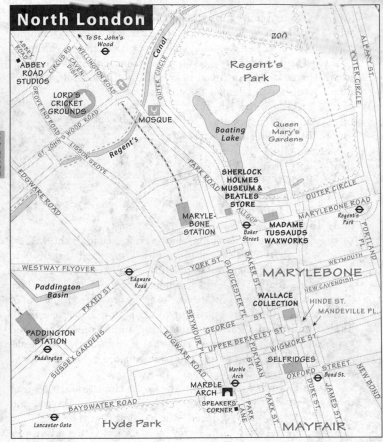

North London

To St. John's Wood

ABBEY ROAD STUDIOS

LORD'S CRICKET GROUNDS

MOSQUE

Regent's

Canal

OUTER CIRCLE

ZOO

Regent's Park

Boating Lake

Queen Mary's Gardens

ALPART ST.

OUTER CIRCLE

SHERLOCK HOLMES MUSEUM & BEATLES STORE

MARYLEBONE STATION

Baker Street

MADAME TUSSAUDS WAXWORKS

OUTER CIRCLE

MARYLEBONE ROAD

Regent's Park

PORTLAND PL.

WESTWAY FLYOVER

Paddington Basin

Edgware Road

YORK ST.

MARYLEBONE

WEYMOUTH

NEW CAVENDISH

PADDINGTON STATION

Paddington

PRAED ST.

SUSSEX GARDENS

EDGWARE ROAD

SEYMOUR PL.

GEORGE ST.

UPPER BERKELEY ST.

PORTMAN ST.

WALLACE COLLECTION

HINDE ST.

MANDEVILLE PL.

WIGMORE ST.

SELFRIDGES

OXFORD STREET

Bond St.

NEW BOND ST.

DUKE ST.

JAMES ST.

BAYSWATER ROAD

Lancaster Gate

Hyde Park

Marble Arch

MARBLE ARCH

SPEAKERS' CORNER

PARK LANE

PARK ST.

MAYFAIR

The first thing you'll see in the Egypt section is the **Rosetta Stone**. When this rock was unearthed in the Egyptian desert in 1799, it was a sensation in Europe. This black slab, dating from 196 B.C., caused a quantum leap in the study of ancient history. Finally, Egyptian writing could be decoded.

The hieroglyphic writing in the upper part of the stone was indecipherable for a thousand years. Did a picture of a bird mean "bird"? Or was it a sound, forming part of a larger word, like "burden"? As it turned out, hieroglyphics are a complex combination of the two, surprisingly more phonetic than symbolic. (For example, the hieroglyph that looks like a mouth or an eye is the letter "R.")

The Rosetta Stone (see photo, next page) allowed linguists to break the code. It contains a single inscription repeated in three languages. The bottom third is plain old Greek, while the middle is medieval Egyptian. By comparing the two known languages with the one they didn't know, translators figured out the hieroglyphics.

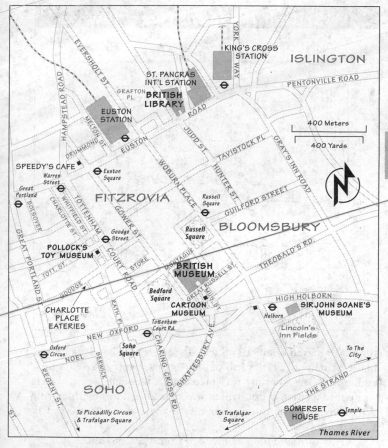

Next, wander past the many **statues,** including a seven-ton Ramesses, with the traditional features of a pharaoh (goatee, cloth headdress, and cobra diadem on his forehead). When Moses told the king of Egypt, "Let my people go!" this was the stony-faced look he got. You'll also see the Egyptian gods as animals—these include Amun, king of the gods, as a ram, and Horus, the god of the living, as a falcon.

At the end of the hall, climb the stairs or take the elevator to **mummy** land. To mummify a body is much like following a recipe. First, disembowel it (but leave the heart inside), then pack the cavities with pitch, and dry it with natron, a natural form of sodium carbonate (and, I believe,

LONDON

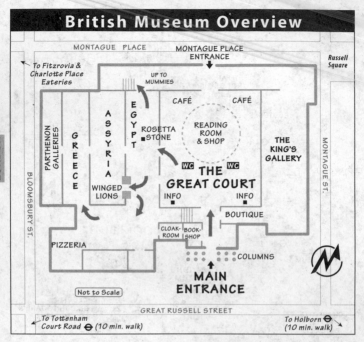

British Museum Overview

MONTAGUE PLACE

MONTAGUE PLACE ENTRANCE

Russell Square

To Fitzrovia & Charlotte Place Eateries

UP TO MUMMIES

EGYPT

ASSYRIA

CAFÉ   CAFÉ

GREECE

PARTHENON GALLERIES

ROSETTA STONE

READING ROOM & SHOP

THE KING'S GALLERY

MONTAGUE ST.

WC   WC

THE GREAT COURT

WINGED LIONS

INFO   INFO

BLOOMSBURY ST.

BOUTIQUE

CLOAK-ROOM   BOOK-SHOP

PIZZERIA

COLUMNS

Not to Scale

MAIN ENTRANCE

GREAT RUSSELL STREET

To Tottenham Court Road ⊖ (10 min. walk)

To Holborn ⊖ (10 min. walk)

the active ingredient in Twinkies). Then carefully bandage it head to toe with hundreds of yards of linen strips. Let it sit 2,000 years, and...*voilà!* The mummy was placed in a wooden coffin, which was put in a stone coffin, which was placed in a tomb. The result is that we now have Egyptian bodies that are as well preserved as Larry King.

Many of the mummies here are from the time of the Roman occupation, when fine memorial portraits painted in wax became popular. X-ray photos in the display cases tell us more about these people. Don't miss the animal mummies. Cats were popular pets. They were also considered incarnations of the cat-headed goddess Bastet. Worshipped in life as the sun god's allies, preserved in death, and memorialized with statues, cats were given the adulation they've come to expect ever since.

Assyria: Long before Saddam Hussein, Iraq was home to other palace-building, iron-fisted rulers—the Assyrians, who conquered their southern neighbors and dominated the Middle East for 300 years (c. 900-600 B.C.).

Their strength came from a superb army (chariots, mounted cavalry, and siege engines), a policy of terrorism against enemies ("I tied their heads to tree trunks all around the city," reads a royal inscription), ethnic cleansing and mass deportations of the vanquished, and efficient administration (roads and express postal service). They have been called the "Romans of the East."

The British Museum's valuable collection of Assyrian artifacts has become even more priceless since the recent destruction of ancient sites in the Middle East by ISIS terrorists.

Standing guard over the Assyrian exhibit halls are two human-headed **winged lions**. These stone lions guarded an Assyrian palace (11th-8th century B.C.). With the strength of a lion, the wings of an eagle, the brain of a man, and the beard of ZZ Top, they protected the king from evil spirits and scared the heck out of foreign ambassadors and left-wing newspaper reporters. (What has five legs and flies? Take a close look. These winged quintupeds, which appear complete from both the front and the side, could guard both directions at once.)

Carved into the stone between the bearded lions' loins, you can see one of civilization's most impressive achievements—writing. This wedge-shaped **(cuneiform)** script is the world's first written language, invented 5,000 years ago by the Sumerians (of southern Iraq) and passed down to their less-civilized descendants, the Assyrians.

The **Nimrud Gallery** is a mini version of the throne room and royal apartments of King Ashurnasirpal II's Northwest Palace at Nimrud (9th century B.C.). It's filled with royal propaganda reliefs, 30-ton marble bulls, and panels depicting wounded lions (lion-hunting was Assyria's sport of kings).

Greece: The history of ancient Greece (600 B.C.-A.D. 1) could be subtitled "making order out of chaos." While Assyria was dominating the Middle East, "Greece"—a gaggle of warring tribes roaming the Greek peninsula—was floundering in darkness. But by about 700 B.C., these tribes began settling down, experimenting with democracy, forming self-governing city-states, and making ties with other city-states. During their civilization's Golden Age (500-430 B.C.), the ancient Greeks set the tone for all of Western civilization to follow. Democracy, theater, literature, mathematics, philosophy, science, gyros, art, and architecture as we know them, were virtually all invented by a single generation of Greeks in a small town of maybe 80,000 citizens.

Your walk through Greek art history starts with pottery, usually painted red and black, and a popular export product for the sea-trading Greeks. The earliest featured geometric patterns (eighth century B.C.), then a painted black silhouette on the natural orange clay, then a red figure on a black background. Later, painted vases show a culture really into partying.

The highlight is the **Parthenon Sculptures**—taken from the temple dedicated to Athena—the crowning glory of an enormous urban-renewal plan during Greece's Golden Age. While the build-

LONDON

ing itself remains in Athens, many of the Parthenon's best sculptures are right here in the British Museum. The sculptures are also called the Elgin Marbles, named for the shrewd British ambassador who had his men hammer, chisel, and saw them off the Parthenon in the early 1800s. Al-

though the Greek government complains about losing its marbles, the Brits feel they rescued and preserved the sculptures.

These much-wrangled-over bits of the Parthenon (from about 450 B.C.) are indeed impressive. The marble panels you see lining the walls of this large hall are part of the frieze that originally ran around the exterior of the Parthenon, under the eaves. The statues at either end of the hall once filled the Parthenon's triangular-shaped pediments and showed the birth of Athena. The relief panels known as metopes tell the story of the struggle between the forces of human civilization and animal-like barbarism.

The Rest of the Museum: Be sure to venture upstairs to see artifacts from **Roman Britain** that surpass anything you'll see at Hadrian's Wall or elsewhere in the country. Also look for the Sutton Hoo Ship Burial artifacts from a seventh-century royal burial on the east coast of England (Room 41). A rare Michelangelo cartoon (preliminary sketch) is in Room 90 (level 4).

▲▲▲British Library

Here, in just two rooms, are the literary treasures of Western civilization, from early Bibles to Shakespeare's *Hamlet* to Lewis Carroll's *Alice's Adventures in Wonderland* to the *Magna Carta*. You'll see the Lindisfarne Gospels transcribed on an illuminated manuscript, Beatles lyrics scrawled on the back of a greeting card, and Leonardo da Vinci's genius sketched into his notebooks. The British Empire built its greatest monuments out of paper; it's through literature that England made her most lasting and significant contribution to civilization and the arts.

Cost and Hours: Free, £5 suggested donation, admission charged for special exhibits; Mon-Fri 9:30-18:00, Tue-Thu until 20:00, Sat until 17:00, Sun 11:00-17:00; 96 Euston Road, Tube: King's Cross St. Pancras or Euston, tel. 019/3754-6060 or 020/7412-7676, www.bl.uk.

Tours: There are no guided tours or audioguides for the permanent collection, but you can ∩ download my free British Library audio tour. There are guided tours of the building itself—the archives and reading rooms. Touch-screen computers in the permanent collection let you page virtually through some of the rare books.

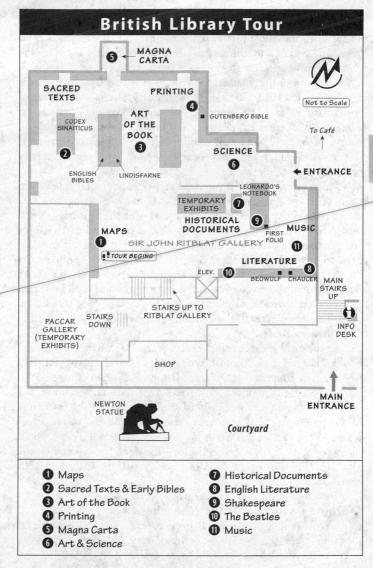

British Library Tour

LONDON

1. Maps
2. Sacred Texts & Early Bibles
3. Art of the Book
4. Printing
5. Magna Carta
6. Art & Science
7. Historical Documents
8. English Literature
9. Shakespeare
10. The Beatles
11. Music

◆ Self-Guided Tour: Entering the library courtyard, you'll see a big statue of a naked Isaac Newton bending forward with a compass to measure the universe. The statue symbolizes the library's purpose: to gather all knowledge and promote humanity's endless search for truth.

Stepping inside, a 50-foot-tall wall of 65,000 books teasingly exposes its shelves in the middle of the building. In 1823 King George IV gifted the collection to the people under the condition the books remain on display for all to see. The high-tech book-shelf—with moveable lifts to reach the highest titles—sits behind glass, inaccessible to commoners but ever-visible. Likewise, the reading rooms upstairs are not open to the public.

Everything that matters for your visit is in a tiny but exciting area variously called "The Sir John Ritblat Gallery," "Treasures of the British Library," or just "The Treasures." We'll concentrate on a handful of documents—literary and historical—that changed the course of history. Note that exhibits change often, and many of the museum's old, fragile manuscripts need to "rest" periodically in order to stay well-preserved.

Upon entering the Ritblat Gallery, start at the far side of the room with the display case of historic ❶ maps showing how humans' perspective of the world expanded over the centuries. Next, move into the area dedicated to ❷ sacred texts and early Bibles from several cultures, including the Codex Sinaiticus. This early bound book from around A.D. 350 is one of the oldest complete Bibles in existence—one of the first attempts to collect various books by different authors into one authoritative anthology. Nearby, you may find another early Bible: the Codex Alexandrinus (from A.D. 425). These two early Bibles contain some writings not included in most modern Bibles.

In the display cases called ❸ Art of the Book, you'll find beautifully illustrated, or "illuminated," Bibles from the early medieval period, including the Lindisfarne Gospels (A.D. 698). The text is in Latin, the language of scholars ever since the Roman Empire, but you can read an electronic copy of these manuscripts by using one of the touch-screen computers scattered around the room. Elsewhere in the Art of the Book (or possibly in Sacred Texts), you'll likely see some Early English Bibles—the King James Version, the Wycliffe Bible, or others—dating from the 15th, 16th, and 17th centuries.

In the glass cases featuring early ❹ printing, you'll see the Gutenberg Bible, the first book printed in Europe using movable type (c. 1455)—a revolutionary document. Suddenly, the Bible was available for anyone to read, fueling the Protestant Reformation.

Through a nearby doorway is a small room that holds versions of the ❺ Magna Carta, assuming they're not "resting" when you visit (though historians talk about *the* Magna Carta, several different versions of the document exist). The basis for England's constitutional system of Government, this

"Great Charter" listing rules about mundane administrative issues was radical because of the simple fact that the king had agreed to abide by them as law. Until then, kings had ruled by God-given authority, above the laws of men. Now, for the first time, there were limits—in writing—on how a king could treat his subjects.

Return to the main room to find display cases featuring trail-blazing ❻ **art and science** documents by early scientists such as Galileo, Isaac Newton, and many more. Pages from Leonardo da Vinci's notebook show his powerful curiosity, his genius for invention, and his famous backward and inside-out handwriting. Nearby are many more ❼ **historical documents.** The displays change frequently, but you may see letters by Henry VIII, Queen Elizabeth I, Darwin, Freud, Gandhi, and others.

Next, trace the evolution of ❽ **English literature.** Check out the A.D. 1000 manuscript of *Beowulf,* the first English literary masterpiece, and the *The Canterbury Tales* (c. 1410), Geoffrey Chaucer's bawdy collection of stories. The Literature wall is often a greatest-hits sampling of literature in English, from Brontë to Kipling to Woolf to Joyce to Dickens. The original *Alice's Adventures in Wonderland* by Lewis Carroll created a fantasy world, where grown-up rules and logic were turned upside down. The most famous of England's writers—❾ **Shakespeare**—generally gets his own display case. Look for the First Folio—one of the 750 copies of the first complete collection of his plays, published in 1623. If the First Folio is not out for viewing, the library should have other Shakespeare items on display.

Now fast-forward a few centuries to ❿ **The Beatles.** Look for photos of John Lennon, Paul McCartney, George Harrison,

and Ringo Starr before and after their fame, as well as manuscripts of song lyrics written by Lennon and McCartney. In the ⓫ **music** section, there are manuscripts by Mozart, Beethoven, Schubert, and others (kind of an anticlimax after the Fab Four, I know). George Frideric Handel's famous oratorio, the *Messiah* (1741), is often on display and marks the end of our tour. Hallelujah.

▲Wallace Collection

Sir Richard Wallace's fine collection of 17th-century Dutch Masters, 18th-century French Rococo, medieval armor, and assorted aristocratic fancies fills the sumptuously furnished Hertford House on Manchester Square. From the rough and intimate Dutch lifescapes of Jan Steen to the pink-cheeked Rococo fantasies of François Boucher, a wander through this little-visited mansion makes you nostalgic for the days of the empire. This collection would be a big deal in a midsized city, but here in London it gets pleasantly lost. Because this is a "closed collection" (nothing new is acquired and nothing permanent goes on loan), it feels more like visiting a classic English manor estate than a museum. It's thoroughly enjoyable.

Cost and Hours: Free, £5 suggested donation, daily 10:00-17:00, audioguide-£4; free guided tours or lectures almost daily at 11:30, 13:00, and 14:30—call or check online to confirm times; just north of Oxford Street on Manchester Square, Tube: Bond Street, tel. 020/7563-9500, www.wallacecollection.org.

▲Madame Tussauds Waxworks

This waxtravaganza is gimmicky, crass, and crazily expensive, but dang fun...a hit with the kind of tourists who skip the British Museum. The original Madame Tussaud did wax casts of heads lopped off during the French Revolution (such as Marie-Antoinette's). She took her show on the road and ended up in London in 1835. Now it's all about singing with Lady Gaga, partying with Benedict Cumberbatch, and hanging with the Beatles. In addition to posing with all the eerily realistic wax dummies—from the Queen and Will and Kate to the Beckhams—you'll have the chance to learn how they created this waxy army; hop on a people-mover and cruise through a kid-pleasing "Spirit of London" time trip; and visit with Spider-Man, the Hulk, and other Marvel superheroes. A nine-minute "4-D" show features a 3-D movie heightened by wind, "back ticklers," and other special effects.

Cost: £35, kids-£30 (free for kids under 5), up to 25 percent discount and shorter lines if you buy tickets in advance on their website; combo-deal with the London Eye.

Hours: Roughly July-Aug and school holidays daily 8:30-18:00, Sept-June Mon-Fri 10:00-16:00, Sat-Sun 9:00-17:00, these are last entry times—it stays open roughly two hours later; check website for the latest times as hours vary widely depending on season, Marylebone Road, Tube: Baker Street, tel. 0871-894-3000, www.madametussauds.com.

Crowd-Beating Tips: This popular attraction can be swamped. The ticket-buying line can be an hour or more (believe the posted signs about the wait). Once inside, there can be more waits for some popular exhibits. To avoid the ticket line, buy a Priority Entrance ticket and reserve a time slot at least a day in advance. Or, purchase a Fast Track ticket in advance (available from souvenir stands and shops or at the TI), which gives you access to a dedicated entrance with shorter lines. The place is less crowded (for both buying tickets at the door and for simply enjoying the place) if you arrive after 15:00.

▲Sir John Soane's Museum

Architects love this quirky place, as do fans of interior decor, eclectic knickknacks, and Back Door sights. Tour this furnished home on a bird-chirping square and see 19th-century chairs, lamps, wood-paneled nooks and crannies, sculptures, and stained-glass skylights just as they were when the owner lived here. As professor of architecture at the Royal Academy, Soane created his home to be a place of learning, cramming it floor to ceiling with ancient relics, curios, and famous paintings, including several excellent Canalettos and Hogarth's series on *The Rake's Progress* (which is hidden behind a panel in the Picture Room and opened randomly at the museum's discretion, usually twice an hour). In 1833, just before his death, Soane established his house as a museum, stipulating that it be kept as nearly as possible in the state he left it. If he visited today, he'd be entirely satisfied by the diligence with which the staff safeguards his treasures. You'll leave wishing you'd known the man.

Cost and Hours: Free, but donations much appreciated; Tue-Sat 10:00-17:00, open and candlelit the first Tue of the month 18:00-21:00 (limited to 250 people), closed Sun-Mon; often long entry lines (especially Sat), knowledgeable volunteers in most rooms, guidebook-£5; £10 guided tour must be booked ahead online and runs Tue and Thu-Sat at 12:00; 13 Lincoln's Inn Fields, quarter-mile southeast of British Museum, Tube: Holborn, tel. 020/7405-2107, www.soane.org.

Beatles Sights

London's city center is surprisingly devoid of sights associated with the famous '60s rock band. To see much of anything, consider taking a guided walk (see page 60).

For a photo op, go to **Abbey Road** and walk the famous cross-

LONDON

walk pictured on the *Abbey Road* album cover (Tube: St. John's Wood, get information and buy Beatles memorabilia at the small kiosk in the station). From the Tube station, it's a five-minute walk west down Grove End Road to the intersection with Abbey Road. The Abbey Road recording studio is the low-key white building to the right of

Abbey House (it's still a working studio, so you can't go inside). Ponder the graffiti on the low wall outside, and...imagine. To re-create the famous cover photo, shoot the crosswalk from the round-about as you face north up Abbey Road. Shoes are optional.

Nearby is **Paul McCartney's current home** (7 Cavendish Avenue): Continue down Grove End Road, turn left on Circus Road, and then right on Cavendish. Please be discreet.

The **Beatles Store** is at 231 Baker Street (Tube: Baker Street). It's small—some Beatles-logo T-shirts, mugs, pins, and old vinyl like you might have in your closet—and has nothing of historic value (open eight days a week, 10:00-18:30, tel. 020/7935-4464, www.beatlesstorelondon.co.uk; another rock memorabilia store is across the street).

Sherlock Holmes Museum

A few doors down from the Beatles Store, this meticulous recre-ation of the (fictional) apartment of the (fictional) detective sits at the (real) address of 221b Baker Street. The first-floor replica (so to speak) of Sherlock's study delights fans with the opportunity to play Holmes and Watson while sitting in authentic 18th-century chairs. The second and third floors offer fine exhibits on daily Victorian life, show-ing off furniture, clothes, pipes, paintings, and chamber pots; in other rooms, models are posed to enact key scenes from Sir Ar-thur Conan Doyle's famous books.

Cost and Hours: £15, daily 9:30-18:00, expect to wait 15 minutes or more—up to 2 hours in peak season; buy tickets inside the gift shop first, then get in line outside the mu-seum (if you're traveling with a partner, send one person in to buy tickets while the other waits in the entrance line); large gift shop for Holmes connoisseurs, including souvenirs from the BBC-TV series; Tube: Baker Street, tel. 020/7935-8866, www.sherlock-holmes.co.uk.

Nearby: Fans of BBC-TV's "Sherlock" series—which this museum doesn't cover—may want to grab a bite or snap a photo at Speedy's Café, the filming location for the show's 221b exterior (at 187 North Gower Street, an easy Tube ride to Euston Square).

Sights in The City

When Londoners say "The City," they mean the one-square-mile business center in East London that 2,000 years ago was Roman Londinium. The outline of the Roman city walls can still be seen in the arc of roads from Blackfriars Bridge to Tower Bridge. Within The City are 23 churches designed by Sir Christopher Wren, mostly just ornamentation around St. Paul's Cathedral. Today, while home to only 10,000 residents, The City thrives with around 400,000 office workers coming and going daily. It's a fascinating district to wander on weekdays, but since almost nobody actually lives there, it's dull in the evening and on Saturday and Sunday.

You can 🎧 download my free audio tour of The City, which peels back the many layers of history in this oldest part of London.

▲▲▲St. Paul's Cathedral

Sir Christopher Wren's most famous church is the great St. Paul's, its elaborate interior capped by a 365-foot dome. There's been a

church on this spot since 604. After the Great Fire of 1666 destroyed the old cathedral, Wren created this Baroque masterpiece. And since World War II, St. Paul's has been Britain's symbol of resilience. Despite 57 nights of bombing, the Nazis failed to destroy the cathedral, thanks to St. Paul's volunteer fire watchmen, who stayed on the dome.

Cost and Hours: £18, £16 in advance online, includes church entry, dome climb, crypt, tour, and audio/videoguide; Mon-Sat 8:30-16:30 (dome opens at 9:30), closed Sun except for worship; book ahead online to skip the line, 15-30-minute wait at busy times; Tube: St. Paul's; recorded info tel. 020/7246-8348, reception tel. 020/7246-8350, www.stpauls.co.uk.

Music and Church Services: Worship times are available on the church's website. Communion is generally Mon-Sat at 8:00 and 12:30. On Sunday, services are held at 8:00, 10:15 (Matins),

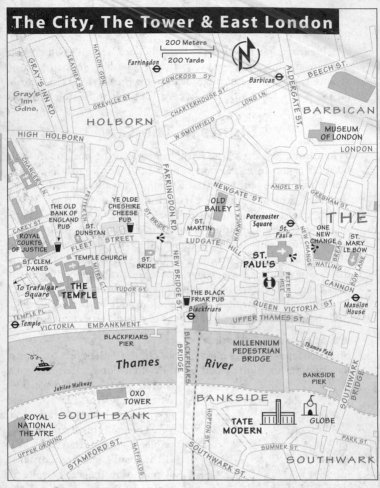

The City, The Tower & East London

11:30 (sung Eucharist), 15:15 (evensong), and 18:00. The rest of the week, evensong is at 17:00 (Mon is spoken—not sung). For more on evensong, see page 163. If you come 20 minutes early for evensong worship (under the dome), you may be able to grab a big wooden stall in the choir, next to the singers. On some Sundays, there's a free organ recital at 16:45.

Tours: Admission includes an **audioguide** (with video clips), as well as a 1.5-hour guided **tour** (Mon-Sat at 10:00, 11:00, 13:00, and 14:00; call 020/7246-8357 to confirm or ask at church). Free 20-minute **introductory talks** are offered throughout the day. You can also 🎧 download my free St. Paul's Cathedral **audio tour.**

○ **Self-Guided Tour:** Even now, as skyscrapers encroach, the 365-foot-high dome of St. Paul's rises majestically above the roof-tops of the neighborhood. The tall dome is set on classical colum

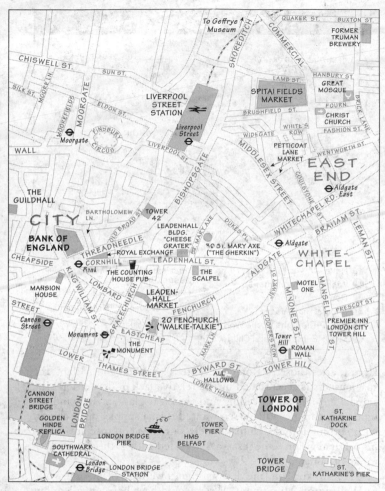

capped with a lantern, topped by a six-foot ball, and iced with a cross. As the first Anglican cathedral built in London after the Reformation, it is Baroque: St. Peter's in Rome filtered through clear-eyed English reason. Though often the site of historic funerals (Queen Victoria and Winston Churchill), St. Paul's most famous ceremony was a wedding—when Prince Charles married Lady Diana Spencer in 1981.

Enter, buy your ticket, pick up the free visitor's map, and stand at the far back of the ❶ **nave,** behind the font. This big church feels big. At 515 feet long and 250 feet wide, it's Europe's fourth

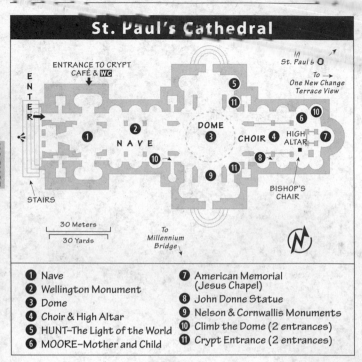

St. Paul's Cathedral

ENTRANCE TO CRYPT
CAFÉ & WC

ENTER

STAIRS

DOME ❸

NAVE

CHOIR ❹

HIGH ALTAR

BISHOP'S CHAIR

In St. Paul's 🅞

To → One New Change Terrace View

❶ ❷ ❺ ❻ ❼ ❽ ❾ ❿ ⓫

30 Meters
30 Yards

To Millennium Bridge

❶ Nave
❷ Wellington Monument
❸ Dome
❹ Choir & High Altar
❺ HUNT–The Light of the World
❻ MOORE–Mother and Child
❼ American Memorial (Jesus Chapel)
❽ John Donne Statue
❾ Nelson & Cornwallis Monuments
❿ Climb the Dome (2 entrances)
⓫ Crypt Entrance (2 entrances)

LONDON

largest, after those in Rome (St. Peter's), Sevilla, and Milan. The spaciousness is accentuated by the relative lack of decoration. The simple, cream-colored ceiling and the clear glass in the windows light everything evenly. Wren wanted this: a simple, open church with nothing to hide. Unfortunately, only this entrance area keeps his original vision—the rest was encrusted with 19th-century Victorian ornamentation.

Ahead and on the left is the towering, black-and-white ❷ **Wellington Monument.** Wren would have been appalled, but his church has become so central to England's soul that many national heroes are buried here (in the basement crypt). General Wellington, Napoleon's conqueror at Waterloo (1815) and the embodiment of British stiff-upper-lippedness, was honored here in a funeral packed with 13,000 fans.

The ❸ **dome** you see from here, painted with scenes from the life of St. Paul, is only the innermost of three. From the painted interior of the first dome, look up through the opening to see the light-filled lantern of the second dome. Finally, the whole thing is covered on the outside by the third and final dome, the shell of lead-covered wood that you see from the street. Wren's ingenious three-in-one design was psychological as well as functional—he wanted a low, shallow inner dome so worshippers wouldn't feel diminished. The ❹ **choir** area blocks your way, but you can see the **high altar** at the far end under a golden canopy.

Do a quick clockwise spin around the church. In the north transept (to your left as you face the altar), find the big painting ❺ *The Light of the World* (1904), by the Pre-Raphaelite William Holman Hunt. Inspired by Hunt's own experience of finding Christ during a moment of spiritual crisis, the crowd-pleasing work was criticized by art highbrows for being "syrupy" and "simple"—even as it became the most famous painting in Victorian England.

Along the left side of the choir is the modern statue ❻ *Mother and Child*, by the great modern sculptor Henry Moore. Typical of Moore's work, this Mary and Baby Jesus—inspired by the sight of British moms nursing babies in WWII bomb shelters—renders a traditional subject in an abstract, minimalist way.

The area behind the altar, with three bright and modern stained-glass windows, is the ❼ **American Memorial Chapel**—honoring the Americans who sacrificed their lives to save Britain in World War II. In colored panes that arch around the big windows, spot the American eagle (center window, to the left of Christ), George Washington (right window, upper-right corner), and symbols of all 50 states (find your state seal). In the carved wood beneath the windows, you'll see birds and foliage native to the US. The Roll of Honor (a 500-page book under glass immediately behind the altar) lists the names of 28,000 US servicemen and women based in Britain who gave their lives during the war.

Around the other side of the choir is a shrouded statue honoring ❽ **John Donne** (1621–1631), a passionate preacher in old St. Paul's, as well as a great poet ("never wonder for whom the bell tolls—it tolls for thee"). In the south transept are monuments to military greats ❾ **Horatio Nelson,** who fought Napoleon, and **Charles Cornwallis,** who was finished off by George Washington at Yorktown.

❿ **Climbing the Dome:** You can climb 528 steps to reach the dome and great city views. Along the way, have some fun in the **Whispering Gallery** (257 steps up). Whisper sweet nothings into the wall, and your partner (and anyone else) standing far away can hear you. For best effects, try whispering (not talking) with your mouth close to the wall, while your partner stands a few dozen yards away with his or her ear to the wall.

A long, tight metal staircase takes you to the very top of the cupola, the **Golden Gallery.** Once at the top, you emerge to stunning, unobstructed views of the city. Looking west, you'll see the London Eye and Big Ben. To the south, across the Thames, is the rectangular smokestack of the Tate Modern, with Shakespeare's Globe nestled nearby. To the east sprouts a glassy garden of skyscrapers, including the 600-foot-tall, black-topped Tower 42, the

London's Best Views

Though London is a height-challenged city, you can get lofty perspectives on it from several high-flying places. For some viewpoints, you need to pay admission, and at the bars or restaurants, you'll need to buy a drink; the only truly free spots are Primrose Hill, the rooftop terrace of One New Change shopping mall (behind St. Paul's Cathedral), the Sky Garden at 20 Fenchurch, and the viewpoint in front of Greenwich's Royal Observatory.

London Eye: Ride the giant Ferris wheel for stunning London views. See page 126.

St. Paul's Dome: You'll earn a striking, unobstructed view by climbing hundreds of steps to the cramped balcony of the church's cupola. See page 115.

One New Change Rooftop Terrace: Get fine, free views of St. Paul's Cathedral and surroundings—nearly as good as those from St. Paul's Dome—from the rooftop terrace of the One New Change shopping mall just behind and east of the church.

Tate Modern: Take in a classic vista across the Thames from the restaurant/bar on the museum's sixth level and from the new Blavatnik Building (a.k.a. the Switch House). See page 130.

20 Fenchurch (a.k.a. "The Walkie-Talkie"): Get 360-degree views of London from the mostly enclosed Sky Garden, complete with a thoughtfully planned urban garden, bar, restaurants, and lots of locals. It's free to access but you'll need to make reservations in advance and bring photo ID (Mon-Fri 10:00-18:00, Sat-Sun 11:00-21:00, 20 Fenchurch Street, Tube: Monument, www.skygarden. london). If you can't get a reservation, try arriving before 10:00 (or 11:00 on weekends) and ask to go up. Once in, you can stay as long as you like.

National Portrait Gallery: A mod top-floor restaurant peers over

bullet-shaped 30 St. Mary Axe building (nicknamed "The Gherkin"), and two more buildings easily ID'd by their nicknames—"The Cheese Grater" and "The Walkie-Talkie." Demographers speculate that the rapidly growing East End and Docklands may eventually replace the West End and The City as the center of London. So as you look to the east, you're gazing into London's future.

⑪ Visiting the Crypt: The crypt is a world of historic bones and interesting cathedral models. Many legends are buried here—Horatio Nelson, who wore down Napoleon; the Duke of Wellington, who finished Napoleon off; and even Wren himself. Wren's actual tomb is marked by a simple black slab with no statue, although he considered this church to be his legacy. Back up in the nave, on the floor directly under the dome, is Christopher Wren's name and epitaph (written in Latin): "Reader, if you seek his monument, look around you."

Trafalgar Square and the Westminster neighborhood.

Waterstones Bookstore: Its hip, low-key, top-floor café/bar has reasonable prices and sweeping views of the London Eye, Big Ben, and the Houses of Parliament (see page 45, on Sun bar closes one hour before bookstore, www.5thview.co.uk).

OXO Tower: Perched high over the River Thames, the building's upscale restaurant/bar boasts views over London and St. Paul's, with al fresco dining in good weather (Barge House Street, Tube: Blackfriars or Southwark, tel. 020/7803-3888, www.harveynichols.com/restaurant).

London Hilton, Park Lane: You'll spot Buckingham Palace, Hyde Park, and the London Eye from Galvin at Windows, a 28th-floor restaurant/bar in an otherwise nondescript hotel (22 Park Lane, Tube: Hyde Park Corner, tel. 020/7208-4021, www.galvinatwindows.com).

The Shard: The observation decks that cap this 1,020-foot-tall skyscraper offer London's most commanding views, but at an outrageously high price. See page 134.

Primrose Hill: For dramatic 360-degree city views, head to the huge grassy expanse at the summit of Primrose Hill, just north of Regent's Park (off Prince Albert Road, Tube: Chalk Farm or Camden Town, www.royalparks.org.uk/parks/the-regents-park).

The River Thames: Various companies run boat trips on the Thames, offering a unique vantage point and unobstructed, ever-changing views of great landmarks (see page 62).

Royal Observatory Greenwich: Enjoy sweeping views of Greenwich's grand buildings in the foreground, the Docklands' skyscrapers in the middle ground, and The City and central London in the distance. See page 149.

LONDON

▲Old Bailey

To view the British legal system in action—lawyers in little blond wigs speaking legalese with an upper-crust accent—spend a few minutes in the visitors' gallery at the Old Bailey courthouse, called the "Central Criminal Court." Don't enter under the dome; continue up the block about halfway to the modern part of the building—the entry is at Warwick Passage.

Cost and Hours: Free, generally Mon-Fri 10:00-13:00 & 14:00-17:00 depending on caseload, last entry at 12:40 and 15:40 but often closes an hour or so earlier, closed Sat-Sun, fewer cases in Aug; no kids under 14; 2 blocks northwest of St. Paul's on Old Bailey Street (down a tunnel called Warwick Passage, follow signs to public entrance), Tube: St. Paul's, tel. 020/7248-3277 www.cityoflondon.gov.uk.

Bag Check: Old Bailey has a strictly enforced policy of no bags, mobile phones, cameras, computers, or food. Small purses are OK (but no phones or cameras inside). You can check bags at many nearby businesses, including the Capable Travel agency just down the street at 4 Old Bailey (£5/bag and £1/phone or camera).

The Guildhall

Hiding out in The City six blocks northeast of St. Paul's on Gresham Street, the Guildhall offers visitors a grand medieval hall and a delightful painting gallery for free (Mon-Sat 10:00-17:00, Sun 12:00-16:00). This gathering place served as the meeting spot for guilds in medieval times and still hosts about 100 professional associations. The Guildhall Art Gallery gives insight into old London society with mostly Victorian paintings

▲Museum of London

This museum tells the fascinating story of London, taking you on a walk from its pre-Roman beginnings to the present. It features London's distinguished citizens through history—from Neanderthals, to Romans, to Elizabethans, to Victorians, to Mods, to today. The displays are chronological, spacious, and informative without being overwhelming. Scale models and costumes help you visualize everyday life in the city at different periods. There are enough whiz-bang multimedia displays (including the Plague and the Great Fire) to spice up otherwise humdrum artifacts. This regular stop for the local school kids gives the best overview of London history in town.

Cost and Hours: Free, daily 10:00-18:00, last entry one hour before closing, see the day's events board for special talks and tours, café, baggage lockers, 150 London Wall at Aldersgate Street, Tube: Barbican or St. Paul's plus a 5-minute walk, tel. 020/7001-9844, www.museumoflondon.org.uk.

The Monument

Wren's recently restored 202-foot-tall tribute to London's 1666 Great Fire is at the junction of Monument Street and Fish Street Hill. Climb the 311 steps inside the column for a monumental view of The City (£4.50, £11 combo-ticket with Tower Bridge, cash only, daily 9:30-18:00, until 17:30 Oct-March, Tube: Monument).

▲▲▲Tower of London

The Tower has served as a castle in wartime, a king's residence in peacetime, and, most notoriously, as the prison and execution site of rebels. You can see the crown jewels, take a witty Beefeater tour, and ponder the executioner's block that dispensed with Anne Boleyn, Sir Thomas More, and troublesome heirs to the throne. You'll find more bloody history per square inch in this original tower of power than anywhere else in Britain.

Cost and Hours: £28, family-£70, entry fee includes Beef-

eater tour (described later),
Tue-Sat 9:00-17:30, Sun-
Mon from 10:00, Nov-Feb
until 16:30, skippable au-
dioguide-£4; Tube: Tower
Hill, tel. 0844-482-7788,
www.hrp.org.uk.

Advance Tickets:
To avoid the long ticket-
buying lines, and save a
few pounds off the gate price, buy a **voucher** in advance. You can
purchase vouchers at the Trader's Gate gift shop, located down the
steps from the Tower Hill Tube stop (pick it up on your way to
the Tower; vouchers here can be used any day), or on the Tower
website (£24, family-£59, vouchers purchased online are valid any
day up to 7 days after the date you select). All vouchers, regardless
of where purchased, must be exchanged for tickets at the Tower's
group ticket office (see map).

You can also try buying tickets, with credit card only, at the
Tower Welcome Centre to the left of the normal ticket lines—
though on busy days they may turn you away. Tickets are also sold
by phone (tel. 0844-482-7788 within UK or tel. 011-44-20-3166-
6000 from the US; £2 fee, pick up your tickets at the Tower's group
ticket office).

More Crowd-Beating Tips: It's most crowded in summer, on
weekends (especially Sundays), and during school holidays. Any
time of year, the line for the crown jewels—the best on earth—can
be just as long as the line for tickets. For fewer crowds, arrive before
10:00 and go straight for the jewels. Alternatively, arrive in the afternoon, tour the rest of the Tower first, and see the jewels an hour
before closing time, when crowds die down.

Yeoman Warder (Beefeater) Tours: Today, while the Tower's
military purpose is history, it's still home to the Beefeaters—the
35 Yeoman Warders and their families. (The original duty of the
Yeoman Warders was to guard the Tower, its prisoners, and the
jewels.) Free, worthwhile, one-hour Beefeater tours leave every 30
minutes from just inside the entrance gate (first tour Tue-Sat at
10:00, Sun-Mon at 10:30, last one at 15:30—or 14:30 in Nov-Feb).
The boisterous Beefeaters are great entertainers, whose historical
talks include lots of bloody anecdotes and corny jokes.

Sunday Worship: For a refreshingly different Tower experience, come on Sunday morning, when visitors are welcome on the
grounds for free to worship in the Chapel Royal of St. Peter ad
Vincula. You get in without the lines, but you can only see the chapel—no sightseeing (9:15 Communion or 11:00 service with fine

Tower of London Tour

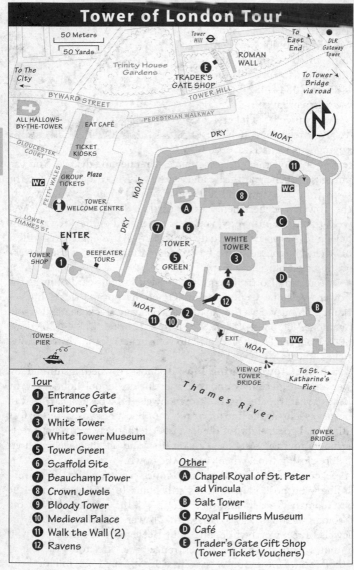

50 Meters
50 Yards

To East End

DLR Gateway Tower

Tower Hill

ROMAN WALL

Trinity House Gardens

To The City

TRADER'S GATE SHOP   E

BYWARD STREET

TOWER HILL

To Tower Bridge via road

ALL HALLOWS-BY-THE-TOWER

EAT CAFÉ

PEDESTRIAN WALKWAY

GLOUCESTER COURT

TICKET KIOSKS

DRY MOAT

N

WC   GROUP TICKETS   Plaza

PETTY WALES

TOWER WELCOME CENTRE

LOWER THAMES ST.

DRY MOAT

A

11

WC

ENTER

7   6

C

TOWER SHOP   1   BEEFEATER TOURS

TOWER GREEN   5

8

WHITE TOWER

3

B

4

D

9

12

MOAT

11   10   2

EXIT   MOAT

WC

TOWER PIER

VIEW OF TOWER BRIDGE

To St. Katharine's Pier

Thames River

TOWER BRIDGE

Tour
1. Entrance Gate
2. Traitors' Gate
3. White Tower
4. White Tower Museum
5. Tower Green
6. Scaffold Site
7. Beauchamp Tower
8. Crown Jewels
9. Bloody Tower
10. Medieval Palace
11. Walk the Wall (2)
12. Ravens

Other
A. Chapel Royal of St. Peter ad Vincula
B. Salt Tower
C. Royal Fusiliers Museum
D. Café
E. Trader's Gate Gift Shop (Tower Ticket Vouchers)

choral music, meet at west gate 30 minutes early, dress for church, may be closed for ceremonies—call ahead).

→ **Self-Guided Tour:** Even an army the size of the ticket line couldn't storm this castle. The **①** **entrance gate** where you'll show your ticket was just part of two concentric rings of complete defenses. As you go in, consult the daily event schedule, and consider catching the Beefeater tour.

When you're all set, go 50 yards straight ahead to the ❷ traitor's gate. This was the boat entrance to the Tower from the Thames. Many English leaders who fell from grace entered through here—only a lucky few walked back out.

Turn left to pass under the archway into the inner courtyard. The big William I, still getting used to his new title of "the Conqueror," built the stone ❸ "White Tower" (1077-1097) in the middle to keep the Londoners in line. Standing high above the rest of old London, the White Tower provided a gleaming reminder of the monarch's absolute power over subjects. If you made the wrong move here, you could be feasting on roast boar in the banqueting hall one night and chained to the walls of the prison the next. The Tower also served as an effective lookout for seeing invaders coming up the Thames.

This square, 90-foot-tall tower was the original structure that gave this castle complex of 20 towers its name. William's successors enlarged the complex to its present 18-acre size. Because of the security it provided, the Tower of London served over the centuries as a royal residence, the Royal Mint, the Royal Jewel House, and, most famously, as the prison and execution site of those who dared oppose the Crown.

Inside the White Tower is a ❹ museum with exhibits re-creating medieval life and chronicling the torture and executions that took place here. In the Royal Armory, you'll see some suits of armor of Henry VIII—slender in his youth (c. 1515), heavyset by 1540—with his bigger-is-better codpiece. On the top floor, see the Tower's actual execution ax and chopping block.

Back outside, the courtyard to the left of the White Tower is the ❺ Tower Green. In medieval times, this spacious courtyard within the walls was the "town square" for those who lived in the castle. The ❻ scaffold site, in the middle of Tower Green, looks pleasant enough today. A modern sculpture encourages visitors to ponder those who died here. It was here that enemies of the crown would kneel before the king for the final time. With their hands tied behind

their backs, they would say a final prayer, then lay their heads on a block, and—*shlit*—the blade would slice through their necks, their heads tumbling to the ground. Tower Green was the most prestigious execution site at the Tower. Henry VIII axed a couple of his ex-wives here (divorced readers can insert their own joke), including Anne Boleyn and his fifth wife, teenage Catherine Howard (for more on Henry, see the sidebar).

LONDON

Henry VIII (1491-1547)

The notorious king who single-handedly transformed England was a true Renaissance Man—six feet tall, handsome, charismatic, well-educated, and brilliant. He spoke English, Latin, French, and Spanish. A legendary athlete, he hunted, played tennis, and jousted with knights and kings. He played the lute and wrote folk songs; his "Pastime with Good Company" is still being performed. When 17-year-old Henry, the second monarch of the House of Tudor, was crowned king in Westminster Abbey, all of England rejoiced.

Henry left affairs of state in the hands of others, and filled his days with sports, war, dice, women, and the arts. But in 1529, Henry's personal life became a political atom bomb, and it changed the course of history. Henry wanted a divorce, partly because his wife had become too old to bear him a son, and partly because he'd fallen in love with Anne Boleyn, a younger woman who stubbornly refused to be just the king's mistress. Henry begged the pope for an annulment, but—for political reasons, not moral ones—the pope refused. Henry went ahead and divorced his wife anyway, and he was excommunicated.

The event sparked the English Reformation. With his defiance, Henry rejected papal authority in England. He forced monasteries to close, sold off some church land, and confiscated everything else for himself and the Crown. Within a decade, monastic institutions that had operated for centuries were left empty and gutted (many ruined sites can be visited today, including the abbeys of Glastonbury, St. Mary's at York, Rievaulx, and Lindisfarne). Meanwhile, the Catholic Church was reorganized into the (Anglican) Church of England, with Henry as its head. Though Henry himself basically adhered to Catholic doctrine, he discouraged the veneration of saints and relics, and commissioned an English translation of the Bible. Hard-core Catholics had to assume a low profile. Many English welcomed this break from Italian religious influence, but others rebelled. For the next few generations, England would suffer through bitter Catholic-Protestant differences.

Henry famously had six wives. The issue was not his love life (which could have been satisfied by his numerous mistresses), but the politics of royal succession. To guarantee the Tudor family's dominance, he needed a male heir born by a recognized queen.

Henry's first marriage, to Catherine of Aragon, had been arranged to cement an alliance with her parents, Ferdinand and Isabel of Spain. Catherine bore Henry a daughter, but no sons. Next came Anne Boleyn, who also gave birth to a daughter. After a turbulent few years with Anne and several miscarriages, a frustrated Henry had her beheaded at the Tower of London. His next wife, Jane Seymour, finally had a son (but Jane died soon after giving birth). A blind-marriage with Anne of Cleves ended quickly when she proved to be both politically useless and ugly—the "Flanders Mare." Next, teen bride Catherine Howard ended up cheating on Henry, so she was executed. Henry finally found comfort—but no children—in his later years with his final wife, Catherine Parr.

In 1536 Henry suffered a serious accident while jousting. His health would never be the same. Increasingly, he suffered from festering boils and violent mood swings, and he became morbidly obese, tipping the scales at 400 pounds with a 54-inch waist.

Henry's last years were marked by paranoia, sudden rages, and despotism. He gave his perceived enemies the pink slip in his signature way—charged with treason and beheaded. (Ironically, Henry's own heraldic motto was "Coeur Loyal"—true heart.) Once-wealthy England was becoming depleted, thanks to Henry's expensive habits, which included making war on France, building and acquiring palaces (he had 50), and collecting fine tapestries and archery bows.

Henry forged a large legacy. He expanded the power of the monarchy, making himself the focus of a rising, modern nation-state. Simultaneously, he strengthened Parliament—largely because it agreed with his policies. He annexed Wales, and imposed English rule on Ireland (provoking centuries of resentment). He expanded the navy, paving the way for Britannia to soon rule the waves. And—thanks to Henry's marital woes—England would forever be a Protestant nation.

When Henry died at age 55, he was succeeded by his nine-year-old son by Jane Seymour, Edward VI. Weak and sickly, Edward died six years later. Next to rule was Mary, Henry's daughter from his first marriage. A staunch Catholic, she tried to brutally reverse England's Protestant Reformation, earning the nickname "Bloody Mary." Finally came Henry's daughter with Anne Boleyn—Queen Elizabeth I, who ruled a prosperous, expanding England, seeing her father's seeds blossom into the English Renaissance.

London abounds with "Henry" sights. He was born in Greenwich (at today's Old Royal Naval College) and was crowned in Westminster Abbey. He built a palace along Whitehall and enjoyed another at Hampton Court. At the National Portrait Gallery, you can see portraits of some of Henry's wives, and at the Tower you can see where he executed them. Henry is buried alongside his third wife, Jane Seymour, at Windsor Castle.

The north side of the Green is bordered by the stone **Chapel Royal of St. Peter ad Vincula** ("in Chains"), where Anne Boleyn and Catherine Howard are buried. Overlooking the scaffold sight is the ❼ **Beauchamp Tower,** one of several places in the complex that housed Very Important Prisoners. You can climb upstairs to a room where the walls are covered by graffiti carved into the stone by despondent inmates.

Across from the White Tower is the entrance to the ❽ **crown jewels.** Here you'll pass through a series of rooms with videos and exhibits showing the actual coronation items in the order they're used whenever a new king or queen is crowned. The Sovereign's Scepter is encrusted with the world's largest cut diamond—the 530-carat Star of Africa, beefy as a quarter-pounder. The Crown of the Queen Mother (Elizabeth II's famous mum, who died in 2002) has the 106-carat Koh-I-Noor diamond glittering on the front (considered unlucky for male rulers, it only adorns the crown of the king's wife). The Imperial State Crown is what the Queen wears for official functions such as the State Opening of Parliament. Among its 3,733 jewels are Queen Elizabeth I's former earrings (the hanging pearls, top center), a stunning 13th-century ruby look-alike in the center, and Edward the Confessor's ring (the blue sapphire on top, in the center of the Maltese cross of diamonds).

At the far end of the Tower Green is the ❾ **Bloody Tower** (where 13-year-old King Edward V and his kid brother are thought to have died) and beyond that, the ❿ **Medieval Palace,** built in 1240 by Henry III. From the medieval palace's throne room you can continue up the stairs to ⓫ **walk the walls.** The Tower was defended by state-of-the-art walls and fortifications in the 13th century. Walking along them offers a good look at the walls, along with a fine view of the famous Tower Bridge, with its twin towers and blue spans.

Between the White Tower and the Thames are cages housing ⓬ **ravens:** According to tradition, the Tower and the British throne are only safe as long as ravens are present here. Other sights at the Tower include the Salt Tower and the Royal Fusiliers Regimental Museum. After your visit, consider taking the boat to Greenwich from here (see "Tours in London: By Cruise Boat" earlier).

Tower Bridge

The iconic Tower Bridge (often mistakenly called London Bridge) was built in 1894 to accommodate the growing East End. While fully modern and hydraulically powered, the drawbridge was designed with a retro Neo-Gothic look.

The bridge is most interesting when the drawbridge lifts to let ships pass, as it does a thousand times a year (best viewed from the Tower side of the Thames). For the bridge-lifting schedule, check the website (see below) or call.

You can tour the bridge at the **Tower Bridge Exhibition,** with a history display and a peek at the Victorian-era engine room that lifts the span. Included in your entrance is the chance to cross the bridge—138 feet above the road along a partially see-through glass walkway. As an exhibit, it's overpriced, though the adrenaline rush and spectacular city views from the walkway may help justify the cost.

Cost and Hours: £9, £11 combo-ticket with The Monument, daily 10:00-18:00 in summer, 9:30-17:30 in winter, enter at northwest tower, Tube: Tower Hill, tel. 020/7403-3761, www.towerbridge.org.uk.

Nearby: The best remaining bit of London's **Roman Wall** is just north of the Tower (at the Tower Hill Tube station). The chic **St. Katharine Dock,** just east of Tower Bridge, has private yachts and mod shops. Across the bridge, on the South Bank, is the upscale Butlers Wharf area, as well as City Hall, museums, the Jubilee Walkway, and, towering overhead, the Shard. Or you can head north to Liverpool Street Station and stroll London's East End (described next).

Sights in East London

▲East End

The East End has a long history as London's poorer side of town— even in medieval times. These days, it still lacks the posh refinement of the West End—but the area just beyond Liverpool Street Station is now one of London's hippest, most fun spots. It boasts a colorful mix of bustling markets, late-night dance clubs, the Bangladeshi neighborhood (called "Banglatown"), and tenements of Jack the Ripper's London, all in the

shadow of glittering new skyscrapers. Head up Brick Lane for a meal in "the curry capital of Europe," or check out the former Truman Brewery, which now houses a Sunday market, cool shops, and Café 1001 (good coffee). This neighborhood is best on Sunday afternoons, when the Spitalfields, Petticoat Lane, and Backyard markets thrive (for more on these markets, see page 155).

▲Geffrye Museum

This low-key but well-organized museum—housed in an 18th-century almshouse—is located north of Liverpool Street Station (closed for renovation until 2020). It's a strip of 11 rooms, each furnished as a living room from a different age and each very well-described. It's an intimate peek at the middle class as its comforts evolved from 1600 to 2000. In summer, explore the fragrant herb garden.

Cost and Hours: Free, £3 suggested donation, Tue-Sun 10:00-17:00, closed Mon, garden open April-Oct, 136 Kingsland Road, tel. 020/7739-9893, www.geffrye-museum.org.uk.

Getting There: Take the Tube to Liverpool Street, then ride the bus 10 minutes north (bus #149 or #242—leave station through Bishopsgate exit and head left a few steps to find stop; hop off at the Pearson Street stop, just after passing the brick museum on the right). Or take the East London line on the Overground to the Hoxton stop, which is right next to the museum (Tube tickets and Oyster cards also valid on Overground).

Sights on the South Bank

The South Bank of the Thames is a thriving arts and cultural center, tied together by the riverfront Jubilee Walkway. For fun lunch options in this area, consider one of the nearby street food markets (see page 157).

▲Jubilee Walkway

This riverside path is a popular pub-crawling pedestrian promenade that stretches all along the South Bank, offering grand views of the Houses of Parliament and St. Paul's. On a sunny day, this is the place to see Londoners out strolling. The Walkway hugs the river except just east of London Bridge, where it cuts inland for a couple of blocks. It has been expanded into a 60-mile "Greenway" circling the city, including the 2012 Olympics site.

▲▲London Eye

This giant Ferris wheel, towering above London opposite Big Ben, is one of the world's highest observational wheels and London's answer to the Eiffel Tower. Riding it is a memorable experience, even though London doesn't have much of a skyline, and the price is borderline outrageous. Whether you ride or not, the wheel is a sight to behold.

The experience starts with an engaging, four-minute show combining a 4-D movie with wind and water effects. Then it's time to spin around the Eye. Designed like a giant bicycle wheel, it's a pan-European undertaking: British steel and Dutch engineering, with Czech, German, French, and Italian mechanical parts. It's also very "green," running extremely efficiently and virtually silently. Twenty-eight people ride in each of its 32 air-conditioned capsules (representing the boroughs of London) for the 30-minute rotation (you go around only once). From the top of this 443-foot-high wheel—the second-highest public viewpoint in the city—even Big Ben looks small.

Cost: £24.95, about 10 percent cheaper if bought online. Combo-tickets save money if you plan on visiting Madame Tussauds. Buy tickets in advance at www.londoneye.com or try in person at the box office (in the corner of the County Hall building nearest the Eye), though day-of tickets are often sold out.

Hours: Daily June-Aug 10:00-20:30 or later, Sept-May generally 11:00-18:00, check website for latest schedule, these are last-ascent times, closed Dec 25 and a few days in Jan for maintenance, Tube: Waterloo or Westminster. Thames boats come and go from London Eye Pier at the foot of the wheel.

Crowd-Beating Tips: The London Eye is busiest between 11:00 and 17:00, especially on weekends year-round and every day in July and August. You may wait up to 30 minutes to buy your ticket, then another 30-45 minutes to board your capsule—it's best to prebook your ticket during these times. Print your advance ticket at home, retrieve it from an onsite ticket machine (bring your payment card and confirmation code), or stand in the "Ticket Collection" line. Even if you buy in advance, you may wait a bit to board the wheel. You can pay an extra £8 for a Fast Track ticket, but since you still may wait up to 30 minutes, it's probably not worth the expense.

▲▲Imperial War Museum

This impressive museum covers the wars and conflicts of the 20th and 21st centuries—from World War I biplanes, to the rise of fascism, the Cold War, the Cuban Missile Crisis, the Troubles in

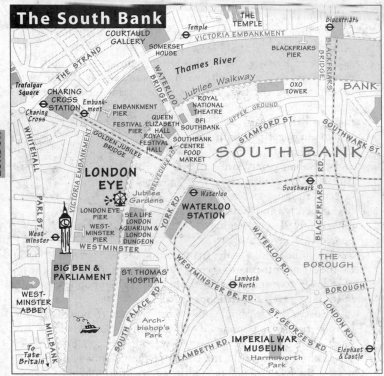

The South Bank

COURTAULD GALLERY
Temple
THE TEMPLE
Blackfriars
SOMERSET HOUSE
VICTORIA EMBANKMENT
THE STRAND
BLACKFRIARS PIER
BLACKFRIARS BRIDGE
Thames River
Jubilee Walkway
Trafalgar Square
CHARING CROSS STATION
Embankment
OXO TOWER
BANK
Charing Cross
EMBANKMENT PIER
ROYAL NATIONAL THEATRE
WATERLOO BRIDGE
UPPER GROUND
FESTIVAL PIER
QUEEN ELIZABETH HALL
BFI SOUTHBANK
STAMFORD ST.
SOUTHWARK ST.
WHITEHALL
GOLDEN JUBILEE BRIDGE
ROYAL FESTIVAL HALL
SOUTHBANK CENTRE FOOD MARKET
SOUTH BANK
LONDON EYE
Jubilee Gardens
BELVEDERE RD.
Waterloo
Southwark
BLACKFRIARS RD.
PARL ST.
VICTORIA EMBANKMENT
LONDON EYE PIER
WEST-MINSTER PIER
SEA LIFE LONDON AQUARIUM & LONDON DUNGEON
YORK RD.
WATERLOO STATION
Westminster
WESTMINSTER
WATERLOO RD.
THE BOROUGH
BIG BEN & PARLIAMENT
ST. THOMAS' HOSPITAL
WESTMINSTER BR. RD.
Lambeth North
BOROUGH
WEST-MINSTER ABBEY
SOUTH PALACE RD.
ST. GEORGE'S RD.
LONDON RD.
MILLBANK
Arch-bishop's Park
LAMBETH RD.
IMPERIAL WAR MUSEUM
Elephant & Castle
To Tate Britain
Harmsworth Park

Northern Ireland, the wars in Iraq and Afghanistan, and terrorism. Rather than glorify war, the museum encourages an understand-

ing of the history of modern warfare and the wartime experience, including the effect it has on the everyday lives of people back home. The museum's coverage never neglects the human side of one of civilization's more uncivilized, persistent traits.

Allow plenty of time, as this powerful museum—with lots of artifacts and video clips—can be engrossing. War wonks love the place, as do general history buffs who enjoy patiently reading displays. For the rest, there are enough interactive experiences and multimedia exhibits and submarines for the kids to climb in to keep it interesting.

Cost and Hours: Free, £5 suggested donation, special exhibits extra, daily 10:00-18:00, last entry one hour before closing, Tube:

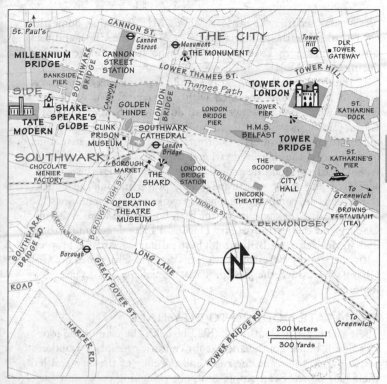

To St. Paul's · CANNON ST. · THE CITY · Tower Hill · DLR TOWER GATEWAY
MILLENNIUM BRIDGE · Cannon Street · Monument · THE MONUMENT · CANNON STREET STATION · LOWER THAMES ST. · TOWER HILL
BANKSIDE PIER · SOUTHWARK BRIDGE · CANNON · Thames Path · TOWER OF LONDON
SIDE · LONDON BRIDGE · TOWER PIER · ST. KATHARINE DOCK
SHAKE-SPEARE'S GLOBE · GOLDEN HINDE · LONDON BRIDGE PIER · H.M.S. BELFAST · TOWER BRIDGE
TATE MODERN · CLINK PRISON MUSEUM · SOUTHWARK CATHEDRAL · London Bridge · ST. KATHARINE'S PIER
SOUTHWARK · CHOCOLATE MENIER FACTORY · BOROUGH MARKET · THE SHARD · LONDON BRIDGE STATION · TOOLEY · THE SCOOP · CITY HALL · To Greenwich
BOROUGH HIGH ST. · OLD OPERATING THEATRE MUSEUM · ST. THOMAS ST. · UNICORN THEATRE · BERMONDSEY · BROWNS RESTAURANT (TEA)
SOUTHWARK BRIDGE RD. · MARSHALSEA · Borough · LONG LANE · GREAT DOVER ST.
ROAD · HARPER RD. · TOWER BRIDGE RD. · To Greenwich
300 Meters · 300 Yards

Lambeth North or Elephant and Castle; buses #3, #12, and #159 from Westminster area; tel. 020/7416-5000, www.iwm.org.uk.

Visiting the Museum: Start with the atrium to grasp the massive scale of warfare as you wander among and under notable battle machines, then head directly for the museum's latest pride and joy: the WWI galleries, recently renovated to commemorate the 100-year anniversary of that conflict. Here firsthand accounts connect the blunt reality of a brutal war with the contributions, heartache, and efforts of a nation. Exhibits cover the various theaters and war at sea, as well as life on the home front.

Pause to ponder the irony of how different this museum would be if the war to end all wars had lived up to its name. Instead, the museum, much like history, builds on itself. Ascending to the first floor, you'll find the permanent **Turning Points** galleries progressing up to and through World War II and including sections explaining the Blitzkrieg and its effects (see an actual Nazi parachute bomb like the ones that devastated London). For a deeper understanding of life during these decades, visit the **Family in Wartime** exhibit to see London through the eyes of an ordinary family.

The second floor houses the **Secret War** exhibit, which peeks into the intrigues of espionage in World Wars I and II through present-day security. You'll learn about MI5 (Britain's domestic spy corps), MI6 (their international spies—like the CIA), and the Special Operations Executive (SOE), who led espionage efforts during World War II.

The third floor houses various (and often rotating) temporary art and film exhibits speckled with military-themed works including (when not on its own tour of duty) **John Singer Sargent**'s *Gassed* (1919), showing besieged troops in World War I, and other giant canvases. The fourth-floor section on the **Holocaust,** one of the best on the subject anywhere, tells the story with powerful videos, artifacts, and fine explanations. While it's not the same as actually being at one of Europe's many powerful Holocaust sites, the exhibits are compelling enough to evoke the same emotions.

Crowning the museum on the fifth floor is the Lord Ashcroft Gallery and the **Extraordinary Heroes** display. Here, more than 250 stories celebrate Britain's highest military award for bravery with the world's largest collection of Victoria Cross medals. Civilians who earned the George Cross medal for bravery are also honored.

FROM TATE MODERN TO CITY HALL

These sights are in Southwark (SUTH-uck), the core of the tourist's South Bank. Southwark was for centuries the place Londoners would go to escape the rules and decency of the city and let their hair down. Bearbaiting, brothels, rollicking pubs, and theater—you name the dream, and it could be fulfilled just across the Thames. A run-down warehouse district through the 20th century, it's been gentrified with classy restaurants, office parks, pedestrian promenades, major sights (such as the Tate Modern and Shakespeare's Globe), and a colorful collection of lesser sights. The area is easy on foot and a scenic—though circuitous—way to connect the Tower of London with St. Paul's.

▲▲Tate Modern

Dedicated in the spring of 2000, the striking museum fills a derelict old power station across the river from St. Paul's—it opened the new century with art from the previous one. Its powerhouse collection includes Dalí, Picasso, Warhol, and much more.

Cost and Hours: Free, £4 donation appreciated, fee for special exhibits; open daily 10:00-18:00, Fri-Sat until 22:00, last entry to special exhibits 45 minutes before closing, especially crowded on weekend days (crowds thin out Fri and Sat evenings); view restaurant on top floor; tel. 020/7887-8888, www. tate.org.uk.

Tours: Multimedia guide-£4.75, free 45-minute guided tours at 11:00, 12:00, 14:00, and 15:00.

Getting There: Cross the Millennium Bridge from St. Paul's; take the Tube to Southwark, London Bridge, St. Paul's, Mansion House, or Blackfriars and walk 10-15 minutes; or catch Thames Clippers' Tate Boat ferry from the Tate Britain (Millbank Pier) for a 15-minute crossing (£8 one-way, every 40 minutes Mon-Fri 10:00-16:00, Sat-Sun 9:15-18:40, www.tate.org.uk/visit/tate-boat).

Visiting the Museum: The permanent collection is generally on levels 2 through 4 of the Boiler House. Paintings are arranged according to theme—such as "Poetry and Dream"—not chronologically or by artist. Paintings by Picasso, for example, are scattered all over the building.

Since 1960, London has rivaled New York as a center for the visual arts. You'll find British artists displayed here—look for work by David Hockney, Henry Moore, and Barbara Hepworth. American art is also prominently represented—keep an eye out for abstract expressionist works by Mark Rothko and Jackson Pollock, and the pop art of Andy Warhol and Roy Lichtenstein. Don't just come to see the Old Masters of modernism. Push your mental envelope with more recent works by Miró, Bacon, Picabia, Beuys, Twombly, and others.

Of equal interest are the many temporary exhibits featuring cutting-edge art. Each year, the main hall features a different monumental installation by a prominent artist—always one of the highlights of the art world. The Tate recently opened a new wing to the south: This new Blavatnik Building (Switch House) gave the Tate an extra quarter-million square feet of display space. Besides showing off more of the Tate's impressive collection, the space hosts changing themed exhibitions, performance art, experimental film, and interactive sculpture incorporating light and sound.

▲Millennium Bridge

The pedestrian bridge links St. Paul's Cathedral and the Tate Modern across the Thames. This is London's first new bridge in a century. When it opened, the $25 million bridge wiggled when people walked on it, so it promptly closed for repairs; 20 months and $8 million later, it reopened. Nicknamed the "blade of light" for its sleek minimalist design (370 yards long, four yards wide, stainless steel with teak planks), its clever aerodynamic handrails deflect wind over the heads of pedestrians.

▲▲Shakespeare's Globe

This replica of the original Globe Theatre was built, half-timbered and thatched, as it was in Shakespeare's time. (This is the first thatched roof constructed in London since they were outlawed after the Great Fire of 1666.) The Globe originally accommodated 2,200 seated and another 1,000 standing. Today, slightly smaller and leaving space for reasonable aisles, the theater holds 800 seated and 600 groundlings.

Its promoters brag that the theater melds "the three A's"—actors, audience, and architecture—with each contributing to the play. The working theater hosts authentic performances of Shakespeare's plays with actors in period costumes, modern interpretations of his works, and some works by other playwrights. For details on attending a play, see page 161.

The Globe complex has four parts: the Globe theater itself, the box office, a museum (called the Exhibition), and the Sam Wanamaker Playhouse (an indoor Jacobean theater around back). The Playhouse, which hosts performances through the winter, is horseshoe-shaped, intimate (seating fewer than 350), and sometimes uses authentic candle-lighting for period performances. The repertoire focuses less on Shakespeare and more on the work of his contemporaries (Jonson, Marlow, Fletcher), as well as concerts.

Cost: £16 for adults, £9 for kids 5-15, free for kids 5 and under, family ticket available; ticket includes Exhibition, audioguide, and 40-minute tour of the Globe; when theater is in use, you can tour the Exhibition only for £6.

Hours: The complex is open daily 9:00-17:30. Tours start every 30 minutes; during Globe theater season (late April-mid-Oct), last tour Mon at 17:00, Tue-Sat at 12:30, Sun at 11:30—it's best to arrive for a tour before noon; located on the South Bank over the Millennium Bridge from St. Paul's, Tube: Mansion House or London Bridge plus a 10-minute walk; tel. 020/7902-1400, box office tel. 020/7401-9919, www.shakespearesglobe.com.

Visiting the Globe: You browse on your own in the **Exhibition** (with the included audioguide) through displays of Elizabethan-era costumes and makeup, music, script-printing, and special effects (the displays change). There are early folios and objects that were dug up on site. Videos and scale models help put Shakespearean theater within the context of the times. (The Globe opened in 1599, eleven years after England mastered the seas by defeating the Spanish Armada. The debut play was Shakespeare's *Julius Caesar*.)

You'll also learn how they built the replica in modern times, using Elizabethan materials and techniques. Take advantage of the touch screens to delve into specific topics.

You must **tour the theater** at the time stamped on your ticket, but you can come back to the Exhibition museum afterward. A guide (usually an actor) leads you into the theater to see the stage and the various seating areas for the different classes of people. You take a seat and learn how the new Globe is similar to the old Globe (open-air performances, standing-room by the stage, no curtain) and how  it's different (female actors today, lights for night performances, concrete floor). It's not a backstage tour—you don't see dressing rooms or costume shops or sit in on rehearsals—but the guides are energetic, theatrical, and knowledgeable, bringing the Elizabethan period to life.

Eating: The **$$$$ Swan at the Globe** café offers a sit-down restaurant (for lunch and dinner, reservations recommended, tel. 020/7928-9444), a drinks-and-plates bar, and a sandwich-and-coffee cart (Mon-Fri 8:00-closing, depends on performance times, Sat-Sun from 10:00).

The Clink Prison Museum

Proudly the "original clink," this was, until 1780, where law-abiding citizens threw Southwark troublemakers. Today, it's a low-tech torture museum filling grotty old rooms with papier-mâché gore. There are storyboards about those unfortunate enough to be thrown in the Clink, but little that seriously deals with the fascinating problem of law and order in Southwark, where 18th-century Londoners went for a good time.

Cost and Hours: Overpriced at £7.50 for adults, £5.50 for kids 15 and under, family ticket available; July-Sept daily 10:00-21:00; Oct-June Mon-Fri 10:00-18:00, Sat-Sun until 19:30; 1 Clink Street, Tube: London Bridge, tel. 020/7403-0900, www.clink.co.uk.

▲Southwark Cathedral

While made a cathedral only in 1905, this has been the neighborhood church since the 13th century, and comes with some interesting history. The enthusiastic docents give impromptu tours if you ask.

Cost and Hours: Free, £1 map serves as photo permit, Mon-

Fri 8:00-18:00, Sat-Sun 8:30-18:00, guidebook-£4.50, Tube: London Bridge, tel. 020/7367-6700, www.cathedral.southwark. anglican.org.

Music: The cathedral hosts evensong Sun at 15:00, Tue-Fri at 17:30, and some Sat at 16:00; organ recitals are Mon at 13:15 and music recitals Tue at 15:15 (call or check website to confirm times).

▲Old Operating Theatre Museum and Herb Garret

Climb a tight and creaky wooden spiral staircase to a church attic where you'll find a garret used to dry medicinal herbs, a fascinating exhibit on Victorian surgery, cases of well-described 19th-century medical paraphernalia, and a special look at "anesthesia, the defeat of pain." Then you stumble upon Britain's oldest operating theater, where limbs were sawed off way back in 1821.

Cost and Hours: £6.50, borrowable laminated descriptions, daily 10:30-17:00, closed Dec 15-Jan 5, at 9a St. Thomas Street, Tube: London Bridge, tel. 020/7188-2679, http://oldoperatingtheatre.com.

The Shard

Rocketing dramatically 1,020 feet above the south end of the London Bridge, this addition to London's skyline is by far the tallest building in Western Europe. Designed by Renzo Piano (best known as the co-architect of Paris' Pompidou Center), the glass-clad pyramid shimmers in the sun and its prickly top glows like the city's nightlight after dark. Its uppermost floors are set aside as public viewing galleries, but the ticket price is as outrageously high as the building itself. The Aqua Shard bar on the 31st floor offers views from half the height for the price of a fancy drink (www.aquashard.co.uk). For cheaper view opportunities in London, see the sidebar on page 116.

Cost and Hours: £31 (cheaper if booked online at least a day in advance); book as soon as you have reasonable chance of assuring decent weather, least crowded on weekday mornings, but perhaps better photo opportunities in the early evening (less haze); daily 10:00-22:00, shorter hours Oct-March; Tube: London Bridge—use London Bridge exit and follow signs, tel. 0844-499-7111, www.theviewfromtheshard.com.

HMS *Belfast*

This former Royal Navy warship, a veteran of World War II that took part in the D-Day invasion, clogs the Thames just upstream from the Tower Bridge. The huge vessel—now manned with wax sailors—thrills kids who always dreamed of sitting in a turret shooting off their imaginary guns. If you're into WWII warships, this is the ultimate. Otherwise, it's just lots of exercise with a nice view of the Tower Bridge.

Cost and Hours: Adult-£16, £8 for kids 5-15, family ticket for 2 adults and up to 3 kids-£41, free for kids under 5, includes audioguide, daily March-Oct 10:00-18:00, Nov-Feb until 17:00, last entry one hour before closing, Tube: London Bridge, tel. 020/7940-6300, www.iwm.org.uk/visits/hms-belfast.

City Hall

The glassy, egg-shaped building near the south end of Tower Bridge is London's City Hall, designed by Sir Norman Foster, the architect who worked on London's Millennium Bridge and Berlin's Reichstag. Nicknamed "the Armadillo," City Hall houses the office of London's mayor—it's here that the mayor consults with the Assembly representatives of the city's 25 districts. An interior spiral ramp allows visitors to watch and hear the action below in the Assembly Chamber ride the lift to floor 2 (the highest visitors can go) and spiral down. On the lower ground floor is a large aerial photograph of London and a handy cafeteria. Next to City Hall is the outdoor amphitheater called The Scoop (see page 164).

Cost and Hours: Free, open to visitors Mon-Thu 8:30-18:00, Fri until 17:30, closed Sat-Sun; Tube: London Bridge station plus 10-minute walk, or Tower Hill station plus 15-minute walk; tel. 020/7983-4000, www.london.gov.uk.

Sights in West London

▲▲Tate Britain

One of Europe's great art houses, the Tate Britain specializes in British painting from the 16th century through modern times. This is people's art, with realistic paintings rooted in the individuals, landscape, and stories of the British Isles. The Tate shows off Hogarth's stage sets, Gainsborough's ladies, Blake's angels, Constable's clouds, Turner's tempests, the naturalistic realism of the Pre-Raphaelites, and the camera-eye portraits of Hockney and Freud.

Cost and Hours: Free, £4 donation suggested, admission fee for special exhibits; daily 10:00-18:00, last entry 45 minutes before closing, map-£1 suggested donation; free tours generally daily at 11:00, 12:00, 14:00, and 15:00, or download the Tate's handy app for a room-by-room guide; café and restaurant, tel. 020/7887-8888, www.tate.org.uk.

Getting There: It's on the River Thames, south of Big Ben

LONDON

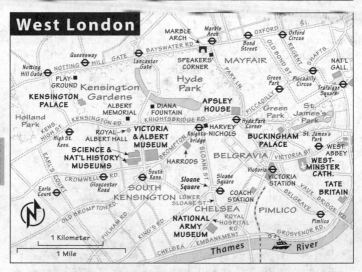

and north of Vauxhall Bridge. Tube to Pimlico, then walk seven minutes. Or hop on the Tate Boat museum ferry from Tate Modern (for details, see page 65).

Visiting the Museum: Works from the early centuries are located in the west half of the building, 20th-century art is in the east half, the works of J. M. W. Turner and John Constable are in an adjacent wing (the Clore Gallery), and William Blake's work is upstairs. The Tate's great strength is championing contemporary British art in special exhibitions. There are generally two exhibition spaces: one in the east half of the main floor (often free), and another downstairs (usually requiring separate admission). The Tate rotates its vast collection of paintings, so it's difficult to predict exactly which works will be on display. Pick up the latest map as you enter or download the museum's helpful app.

1700s—Art Blossoms: With peace at home (under three King Georges), a strong overseas economy, and a growing urban center in London, England's artistic life began to bloom. As the English grew more sophisticated, so did their portraits. Painters branched out into other subjects, capturing slices of everyday life (find William Hogarth, with his unflinchingly honest portraits, and Thomas Gainsborough's elegant, educated women).

1800-1850—The Industrial Revolution: Newfangled inventions were everywhere. Many artists rebelled against "progress" and the modern world. They escaped the dirty cities to commune with nature (Constable and the Romantics). Or they found a new spirituality in intense human emotions (dramatic scenes from history or literature). Or they left the modern world altogether. William Blake, whose work hangs in a darkened room upstairs to protect his watercolors from deterioration, painted angels, not the dull material world. He turned his gaze inward, illustrating the glorious visions of the soul. His pen and watercolor sketches glow with an unearthly aura. In visions of the Christian heaven or Dante's hell, his figures have superhero musculature. The colors are almost translucent.

1837-1901—The Victorian Era: In the world's wealthiest nation, the prosperous middle class dictated taste in art. They admired paintings that were realistic (showcasing the artist's talent and work ethic), depicting Norman Rockwell-style slices of everyday life. Some paintings tug at the heartstrings, with scenes of parting couples, the grief of death, or the joy of families reuniting.

Overdosed with the gushy sentimentality of their day, a band of 20-year-old artists—including Sir John Everett Millais, Dante Gabriel Rossetti, and William Holman Hunt—said "Enough!" and dedicated themselves to creating less saccharine art (the Pre-Raphaelites). Like the Impressionists who followed them, they donned their scarves, barged out of the stuffy studio, and set up out-

doors, painting trees, streams, and people, like scientists on a field trip. Still, they often captured nature with such a close-up clarity that it's downright unnatural.

British Impressionism: Realistic British art stood apart from the modernist trends in France, but some influences drifted across the Channel (Rooms 1890 and 1900). John Singer Sargent (American-born) studied with Parisian Impressionists, learning the thick, messy brushwork and play of light at twilight. James Tissot used Degas' snapshot technique to capture a crowded scene from an odd angle. And James McNeill Whistler (born in America, trained in Paris, lived in London) composed his paintings like music—see some of his paintings' titles.

1900-1950—World Wars: As two world wars whittled down the powerful British Empire, it still remained a major cultural force. British art mirrored many of the trends and "-isms" pioneered in Paris (room marked *1930*). You'll see Cubism like Picasso's, abstract art like Mondrian's, and so on. But British artists also continued the British tradition of realistic paintings of people and landscapes. Henry Moore's statues—mostly female, mostly reclining—catch the primitive power of carved stone. He captured the human body in a few simple curves, with minimal changes to the rock itself.

With a stiff upper lip, Britain survived the Blitz, World War II, and the loss of hundreds of thousands of men—but at war's end, the bottled-up horror came rushing out. Francis Bacon's deformed half-humans/half-animals express the existential human predicament of being caught in a world not of your making, isolated and helpless to change it.

1950-2000—Modern World: No longer a world power, Britain in the Swinging '60s became a major exporter of pop culture. British art's traditional strengths—realism, portraits, landscapes, and slice-of-life scenes—were redone in the modern style. Look for works by David Hockney, Lucian Freud, Bridget Riley, and Gilbert and George.

The Turner Collection: Walking through J. M. W. Turner's life's work, you can trace his progression from a painter of realistic historical scenes, through his wandering years, to Impressionist paintings of color-and-light patterns. You'll also see how Turner dabbled in different subjects: landscapes, seascapes, Roman ruins, snapshots of Venice, and so on. The corner room of the Clore Gallery is dedicated to Turner's great rival and contemporary,

porary, John Constable, who brought painting back into the real world. He painted the English landscape as it was—realistically, without idealizing it.

▲National Army Museum

This museum tells the story of the British army from 1415 through the Bosnian conflict and Iraq, and how it influences today's society. The five well-signed galleries are neatly arranged by theme— "Army," "Battle," "Soldier," "Society," and "Insight"—with plenty of interactive exhibits for kids. History buffs appreciate the carefully displayed artifacts that bring school lessons to life, from 17th-century uniforms to Wellington's battle cloak. Other highlights of the collection include the skeleton of Napoleon's horse, Lawrence of Arabia's silk robe, and Burberry's signature Trench coat (originally designed for WWI soldiers).

Cost and Hours: Free, £5 suggested donation, daily 10:00-17:30, Wed until 20:00, free tours daily at 11:00 and 14:00, Royal Hospital Road, Chelsea, Tube: 10 minute walk from Sloane Square, exit the station and head south on Lower Sloan Street, turn right on Royal Hospital Road, the museum is two long blocks ahead on the left, tel. 020/7730-0717, www.nam.ac.uk.

HYDE PARK AND NEARBY

A number of worthwhile sights border this grand park, from Apsley House on the east to Kensington Palace on the west.

▲Apsley House (Wellington Museum)

Having beaten Napoleon at Waterloo, Arthur Wellesley, the First Duke of Wellington, was once the most famous man in Europe.

He was given a huge fortune, with which he purchased London's ultimate address, Number One London. His refurbished mansion offers a nice interior, a handful of world-class paintings, and a glimpse at the life of the great soldier and two-time prime minister. The highlight is the large ballroom, the Waterloo Gallery, decorated with Anthony van Dyck's *Charles I on Horseback* (over the main fireplace), Diego Velázquez's earthy *Water-Seller of Seville* (to the left of Van Dyck), and Jan Steen's playful *Dissolute Household* (to the right). Just outside the door, in the Portico Room, is a large portrait of the Duke of Wellington by Francisco Goya. The place is well-described by the included audioguide, which has sound bites from the current Duke of Wellington (who still lives at Apsley).

Cost and Hours: £10.30, Wed-Sun 11:00-17:00, closed Mon-Tue, 20 yards from Hyde Park Corner Tube station, tel. 020/7499-5676, www.english-heritage.org.uk.

Nearby: Hyde Park's pleasant rose garden is picnic-friendly. **Wellington Arch,** which stands just across the street, is open to the public but not worth the £5.50 charge (or £12.50 combo-ticket with Apsley House; elevator up, lousy views and boring exhibits).

▲Hyde Park and Speakers' Corner

London's "Central Park," originally Henry VIII's hunting grounds, has more than 600 acres of lush greenery, Santander Cycles rental stations, the huge man-made Serpentine Lake (with rental boats and a lakeside swimming pool), the royal Kensington Palace (described next), and the ornate Neo-Gothic Albert Memorial across from the Royal Albert Hall (for more about the park, see www.royalparks.org.uk/parks/hyde-park). The western half of the park is known as Kensington Gardens. The park is huge—study a Tube map to choose the stop nearest to your destination.

On Sundays, from just after noon until early evening, **Speakers' Corner** offers soapbox oratory at its best (northeast corner of the park, Tube: Marble Arch). Characters climb their stepladders, wave their flags, pound emphatically on their sandwich boards,

and share what they are convinced is their wisdom. Regulars have resident hecklers who know their lines and are always ready with a verbal jab or barb. "The grass roots of democracy" is actually a holdover from when the gallows stood here and the criminal was allowed to say just about anything he wanted to before he swung. I dare you to raise your voice and gather a crowd—it's easy to do.

The **Princess Diana Memorial Fountain** honors the "People's Princess," who once lived in nearby Kensington Palace. The low-key circular stream, great for cooling off your feet on a hot day, is in the south-central part of the park, near the Albert Memorial and Serpentine Gallery (Tube: Knightsbridge). A similarly named but different sight, the **Diana, Princess of Wales Memorial Playground,** in the park's northwest corner, is loads of fun for kids (Tube: Queensway).

Kensington Palace

For nearly 150 years (1689-1837), Kensington was the royal residence, before Buckingham Palace became the official home of the monarch. Sitting primly on its pleasant parkside grounds, the palace gives a barren yet regal glimpse into royal life—particularly that of Queen Victoria, who was born and raised here.

After Queen Victoria moved the monarchy to Buckingham Palace, lesser royals bedded down at Kensington. Princess Diana lived here both during and after her marriage to Prince Charles (1981-1997). More recently, Will and Kate moved in. However—as many disappointed visitors discover—none of these more recent apartments are open to the public. The palace hosts a revolving series of temporary exhibits, some great, others not so. To see what's on during your visit, check online.

Cost and Hours: £19, daily 10:00-18:00, Nov-Feb until 16:00; a long 10-minute stroll through Kensington Gardens from either High Street Kensington or Queensway Tube stations, tel. 0844-482-7788, www.hrp.org.uk.

Nearby: Garden enthusiasts enjoy popping into the secluded Sunken Garden, 50 yards from the exit. Consider afternoon tea at the nearby Orangery (see page 202), built as a greenhouse for Queen Anne in 1704.

▲▲▲Victoria and Albert Museum

The world's top collection of decorative arts—also one of the most eclectic collections—encompasses 2,000 years of art and design (ceramics, stained glass, fine furniture, clothing, jewelry, carpets, and more). Known as "the V&A," this museum presents a surprisingly interesting and diverse assortment of crafts from the West, as well as Asian and Islamic cultures. There's much to see, including Raphael's tapestry cartoons, a cast of Trajan's Column that depicts the emperor's conquests, one of Leonardo da Vinci's notebooks, ladies' underwear through the ages, a life-size *David* with detachable fig leaf, and Mick Jagger's sequined jumpsuit. From the worlds of Islam and India, there are stunning carpets, the ring of the man who built the Taj Mahal, and a mechanical tiger that eats Brits. Best of all, the objects are all quite beautiful. You could spend days in the place.

Cost and Hours: Free, £5 donation requested, extra for some special exhibits, daily 10:00-17:45, some galleries open Fri until 22:00, £1 suggested donation for much-needed museum map, free tours daily, on Cromwell Road in South Kensington, Tube: South Kensington, from the Tube station a long tunnel leads directly to museum, tel. 020/7942-2000, www.vam.ac.uk.

◆ Self-Guided Tour: In the Grand Entrance lobby, look up to see the colorful **chandelier/sculpture** by American glass artist Dale Chihuly. This elaborate piece epitomizes the spirit of the V&A's collection—beautiful manufactured objects that demonstrate technical skill and innovation, wedding the old with the new, and blurring the line between arts and crafts.

Keep looking up to the balcony to see the **Hereford Screen,** a 35-by-35-foot, eight-ton rood screen (built for the Hereford Cathedral's sacred altar area) that looks medieval, but was created with the most modern materials the Industrial Revolution could produce. George Gilbert Scott (1811-1878), who built the screen, redesigned much of London in the Neo-Gothic style, restoring old churches such as Westminster Abbey, renovating the Houses of Parliament, and building new structures like St. Pancras Station and the Albert Memorial—some 700 buildings in all.

The V&A has (arguably) the best collection of **Italian Renaissance sculpture** outside Italy. One prime example is *Samson Slaying a*

LONDON

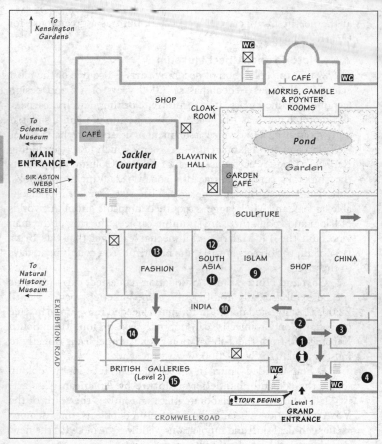

Philistine, by Giambologna (c. 1562), carved from a single block of marble, which shows the testy Israelite warrior preparing to decapitate a man who'd insulted him. The statue's spiral-shaped pose is reminiscent of works by Michelangelo.

A long set of rooms shows off the museum's eclectic nature, including the **Becket Casket** in Room 8, a blue-and-gold box that contains the mortal remains (or relics) of St. Thomas Becket, who was brutally murdered. Pieces of his DNA were conserved in this enamel-and-metal work box, a specialty of Limoges, France. In Room 10a, you'll run right into the **Boar and Bear Hunt Tapestry**. Though most medieval art depicted the Madonna and saints, this colorful wool tapestry—woven in Belgium—provides a secular slice of life.

Two floors up, you'll see how the foundation of civilization laid in medieval times would launch the Renaissance. In Room 64b, you'll find the tiny, pocket-size **notebook by Leonardo da Vinci** which dates from the years when he was living in Milan,

Victoria & Albert Museum Tour

1 Dale Chihuly Chandelier
2 Hereford Screen (above lobby)
3 GIAMBOLOGNA – Samson Slaying a Philistine
4 Medieval & Renaissance Galleries
5 Becket Casket
6 Boar & Bear Hunt Tapestry
7 Stairs to Leonardo Notebook
8 Michelangelo Casts
9 Islamic Art
10 Shiva Nataraja Statue
11 Possessions of Emperor Shah Jahan
12 Tipu's Tiger
13 Fashion Galleries
14 RAPHAEL – Tapestry Cartoons
15 British Galleries
16 Stairs up to Jewelry, Theater & British Silver

TEMPORARY EXHIBITS

To 16

JAPAN

CAST COURT

ROOM 46

CAST COURT

WC

STAIRS TO CAST COURTS VIEW

KOREA

BROMPTON ROAD

⊠ ELEVATOR/LIFT

Not to Scale

To Harrods & Hyde Park Corner →

LONDON

shortly before undertaking his famous *Last Supper* fresco. The book's contents are all over the map: meticulous sketches of the human head, diagrams illustrating nature's geometrical perfection, a horse's leg for a huge equestrian statue, and even drawings of the latest ballroom fashions.

The museum's **Islamic art** reflects both religious influences and sophisticated secular culture. Many Islamic artists expressed themselves with beautiful but functional objects, like the 630-square-foot Ardabil Carpet (1539-1540), which likely took a dozen workers years to make. Also in the room are more ceramics (mostly blue-and-white or red-and-white) and glazed tile—all covered top to bottom in complex patterns. The intricate interweaving, repetition, and unending lines suggest the complex, infinite nature of God (Allah). Notice floral patterns (twining vines, flowers, arabesques) and geometric designs (stars, diamonds). But the most common pattern is calligraphy—elaborate lettering of an inscription in Arabic, the language of the Quran.

A few rooms down, switch gears with a trip through centuries of **English fashion**, corseted into 40 display cases along a runway. You'll see the evolution of fashion from ladies' underwear, hoop skirts, and rain gear to high-society evening wear, men's suits, and more. The mantua dress, on the far right, is an example of court couture from the mid-18th century. Circle the room and reminisce about old trends—and how some are becoming new again.

Head back upstairs to the **British Galleries,** which sweep chronologically through 400 years of British high-class living (1500-1900). Look for rare miniature portraits—a popular item of Queen Elizabeth I's day—including Hilliard's oft-reproduced *Young Man Among Roses* miniature, capturing the romance of a Shakespeare sonnet. A room dedicated to Henry VIII has a portrait of him, his writing box (with quill pens, ink, and sealing wax), and a whole roomful of the fancy furniture, tapestries, jewelry, and dinnerware that may have decorated his palaces.

Back in the Grand Entrance lobby, find the staircase to level 3 for the understandably popular **jewelry collection.** In one long, glittering gallery, you can trace the evolution of jewelry from ancient Egyptian, Greek, and Roman to the 20th century. The Art Nouveau style of Parisian jeweler Rene Lalique is hard not to love. Also on this floor, the **theater and performance rooms** have artifacts from Hamlet skulls to rock-and-roll tour posters. Kids will enjoy the costumes from *The Lion King* and

the dress-up costume box. Nearby, aging boomers will see Mick Jagger's jumpsuit...and marvel that he used to fit into it.

▲▲Natural History Museum

Across the street from the Victoria and Albert, this mammoth museum is housed in a giant and wonderful Victorian, Neo-Romanesque building. It was built in the 1870s specifically for the huge collection (50 million specimens). Exhibits are wonderfully explained, with lots of creative, interactive displays. It covers everything from life ("creepy crawlies," human biol-

ogy, our place in evolution, and awe-inspiring dinosaurs) to earth science (meteors, volcanoes, and earthquakes).

Cost and Hours: Free, £5 donation requested, fees for (optional) special exhibits, daily 10:00-18:00, open later last Fri of the month, helpful £1 map, long tunnel leads directly from South Kensington Tube station to museum (follow signs), tel. 020/7942-5000, exhibit info and reservations tel. 020/7942-5011, www.nhm. ac.uk. Free visitor app available via the "Visit" section of the website.

▲Science Museum

Next door to the Natural History Museum, this sprawling wonderland for curious minds is kid-perfect, with themes such as measuring time, exploring space, climate change, the evolution of modern medicine, and the Information Age. It offers hands-on fun, with trendy technology exhibits, a state-of-the-art IMAX theater (shows-£11, £9 for kids, £27/£30 for families of 3 or 4), the Garden—a cool play area for children up to age seven, plus several other pay-to-enter attractions, including a virtual-reality spacecraft descent to Earth (£7) and Wonderlab kids area (£8 for adults, £6 for kids). Look for the family "What's On" brochure and ask about tours and demonstrations at the info desk.

Cost and Hours: Free, £5 donation requested, daily 10:00-18:00, until 19:00 during school holidays, last entry 45 minutes before closing, Exhibition Road, Tube: South Kensington, tel. 0333-241-4000, www.sciencemuseum.org.uk.

Sights in Greater London

EAST OF LONDON
▲▲Greenwich

This borough of London—an easy boat trip or DLR (light rail) journey from downtown—combines majestic, picnic-perfect parks; the stately trappings of Britain's proud nautical heritage; and the Royal Observatory Greenwich, with a fine museum on the evolution of seafaring and a chance to straddle the eastern and western hemispheres at the prime meridian. An affordable jaunt from central London, and boasting several top-notch museums (including some free ones), Greenwich is worth considering and easy to combine with a look at the Docklands (described next).

Getting There: Ride a boat to Greenwich for the scenery and commentary, and take the Docklands Light Rail (DLR) back—especially if you want to stop at the Docklands on the way home. Various **tour boats** with commentary and open-deck seating (2/hour, 30-75 minutes), as well as faster Thames Clippers (departs every 20-30 minutes from several piers in central London, 20-45 minutes) leave from several piers in central London. Thames Clip-

LONDON

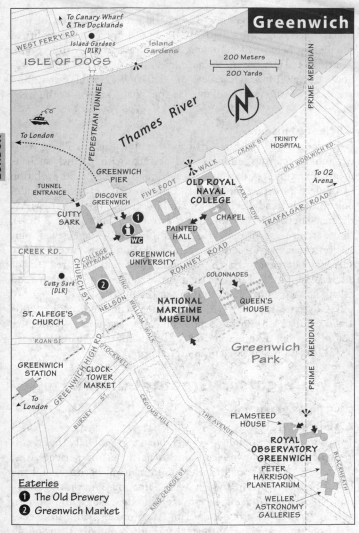

Greenwich

To Canary Wharf & The Docklands

WEST FERRY RD.

Island Gardens (DLR)

Island Gardens

ISLE OF DOGS

200 Meters
200 Yards

PRIME MERIDIAN

Thames River

To London

PEDESTRIAN TUNNEL

GREENWICH PIER

FIVE FOOT WALK

PARK ROW

CRANE ST.

TRINITY HOSPITAL

OLD WOOLWICH RD.

To O2 Arena

TUNNEL ENTRANCE

DISCOVER GREENWICH

OLD ROYAL NAVAL COLLEGE

CHAPEL

TRAFALGAR ROAD

CUTTY SARK

WC

PAINTED HALL

CREEK RD.

COLLEGE APPROACH

GREENWICH UNIVERSITY

ROMNEY ROAD

COLONNADES

CHURCH ST.

Cutty Sark (DLR)

KING WILLIAM WALK

NELSON RD.

NATIONAL MARITIME MUSEUM

QUEEN'S HOUSE

ST. ALFEGE'S CHURCH

ROAN ST.

Greenwich Park

PRIME MERIDIAN

GREENWICH STATION

STOCKWELL ST.

GREENWICH HIGH RD.

CLOCK-TOWER MARKET

To London

BURNEY ST.

CROOMS HILL

THE AVENUE

FLAMSTEED HOUSE

ROYAL OBSERVATORY GREENWICH

BLACKHEATH

KING GEORGE ST.

PETER HARRISON PLANETARIUM

WELLER ASTRONOMY GALLERIES

Eateries
1 The Old Brewery
2 Greenwich Market

pers also connects Greenwich to the Docklands' Canary Wharf Pier (2-3/hour, 10 minutes).

By DLR, ride from Bank-Monument Station in central London to Cutty Sark Station in central Greenwich; it's one stop before the main—but less central—Greenwich Station (departs at least every 10 minutes, 20 minutes, all in Zone 2). Alternately, catch bus #188 from Russell Square near the British Museum (about 45 minutes to Greenwich).

Combining Greenwich with the Docklands: It's easy to connect Greenwich with the Docklands by DLR or by boat. You could sightsee Greenwich in the morning and early afternoon, then make a brief stop at the Docklands on your way back to central London. Or, to reach Greenwich from the Docklands, hop a DLR train bound for Greenwich or Lewisham, then get off at Cutty Sark station.

Eating in Greenwich: Greenwich's parks are picnic-friendly, especially around the National Maritime Museum and Royal Observatory. Greenwich has almost 100 pubs, with some boasting that they're mere milliseconds from the prime meridian. **$$$ The Old Brewery,** in the Discover Greenwich center, is a gastropub decorated with all things beer. From Yorkshire pudding to paella to Thai cuisine, food stalls at the Greenwich Market (described next) offer an international variety of tasty options.

Markets: Thanks to its markets, Greenwich throbs with browsing Londoners on weekends. The **Greenwich Market** is an entertaining mini Covent Garden, located in the middle of the block between the Cutty Sark DLR station and the Old Royal Naval College (farmers market, arts and crafts, and food stands; daily 10:00-17:30; antiques Mon, Tue, Thu, and Fri, www. greenwichmarketlondon.com).

▲▲Cutty Sark

When first launched in 1869, the Scottish-built *Cutty Sark* was the last of the great China tea clippers and the queen of the seas. She

was among the fastest clippers ever built, the culmination of centuries of ship design. With 32,000 square feet of sail—and favorable winds—she could travel 300 miles in a day. But as a new century dawned, steamers began to outmatch sailing ships for speed, and by the mid-1920s the *Cutty Sark* was the world's last operating clipper ship.

In 2012, the ship was restored and reopened with a spectacular new glass-walled display space (though one critic groused that the ship now "looks like it has run aground in a giant greenhouse"). Displays explore the *Cutty Sark*'s 140-year history and the cargo she carried—everything from tea to wool to gunpowder—as she raced between London and ports all around the world.

Cost and Hours: £13.50, £7 for kids 5-15, free for kids under age 5, family tickets available, combo-ticket with Royal Observatory-£18.50—saves money if you plan to visit both sights, kids combo-ticket-£8.50; daily 10:00-17:00; reserve ahead online or by phone on school holidays and on weekends, or just try showing up around 13:00; unnecessary £5 guidebook, reservation tel. 020/8312-6608, www.rmg.co.uk.

▲Old Royal Naval College: The Painted Hall and the Chapel

Despite the name, these grand structures were built (1692) as a veterans' hospital to house disabled and retired sailors who'd served their country. King William III and Queen Mary II spared no expense. They donated land from the former royal palace and hired the great Christopher Wren to design the complex (though other architects completed it). Wren created a virtual temple to seamen. It was perfectly symmetrical, with classical double-columned arcades topped by soaring domes. The honored pensioners ate in the Painted Hall and prayed in the Chapel of Sts. Peter and Paul.

In 1873, the hospital was transformed into one of the world's most prestigious universities for training naval officers. Here they studied math, physics, and engineering for use at sea. During World War II, the college was a hive of activity, as Britain churned out officers to face the Nazis. Today, the buildings host university students, music students, business conventions, concerts, and film crews drawn to the awe-inspiring space.

Cost and Hours: Both the Painted Hall and Chapel are free (£3 suggested donation), daily 10:00-17:00, sometimes closed for private events, service Sun at 11:00 in chapel—all are welcome, www.ornc.org. The Painted Hall interior may be covered with scaffolding when you visit. During these renovations, you can see the painted ceiling up close on a £10 guided tour (book online in advance).

▲National Maritime Museum

Great for anyone interested in the sea, this museum holds everything from a giant working paddlewheel to the uniform Admiral Horatio Nelson wore when he was killed at Trafalgar (look for the bullet hole, in the left shoulder). A big glass roof tops three levels of slick, modern, kid-friendly exhibits about all things seafaring, including the All Hands gallery, where they can send secret messages by Morse code. Along with displays of lighthouse technology, you'll see model ships and weapons, and various salty odds and ends.

Cost and Hours: Free, daily 10:00-17:00, tel. 020/8858-4422, www.rmg.co.uk. The museum hosts frequent family-oriented events—singing, treasure hunts, and storytelling—particularly on weekends; ask at the desk. Inside, listen for announcements alerting visitors to free tours on various topics.

▲▲Royal Observatory Greenwich

Located on the prime meridian (0° longitude), this observatory is famous as the point from which all time and distances on earth are measured. It was here that astronomers studied the heavens in order to help seafarers navigate. In the process, they used the constancy of the stars to establish standards of measurement for time and distance used by the whole world.

A visit here gives you a taste of the sciences of astronomy, timekeeping, and seafaring—and how they all meld together—along with great views over Greenwich and the distant London skyline. Outside, you can snap a selfie straddling the famous prime meridian line in the pavement. Within, there's the original 1600s-era **observatory** and several early telescopes. You'll see the famous clocks from the 1700s that first set the standard of global time, as well as ingenious more-recent timekeeping devices. The **Weller Astronomy Galleries** has interactive, kid-pleasing displays allowing you to guide a space mission and touch a 4.5-billion-year-old meteorite. And the state-of-the-art, 120-seat **Peter Harrison Planetarium** offers entertaining and informative shows several times a day where they project a view of the heavens onto the interior of the dome.

Cost and Hours: Observatory—£9.50, includes audioguide, combo-ticket with *Cutty Sark*-£18.50, combo-ticket with planetarium-£12.50, daily 10:00-17:00, until later in summer; astronomy galleries—free, daily 10:00-17:00; planetarium—£7.50; 30-minute shows generally run every hour (Mon-Fri 13:00-16:00, Sat-Sun 11:00-16:00, fewer in winter, confirm times in advance and consider calling ahead to order tickets; tel. 020/8858-4422, reservations tel. 020/8312-6608, www.rmg.co.uk.

▲▲The Docklands

Once the primary harbor for the Port of London, the Docklands has been transformed into a vibrant business center, with  ultra-tall skyscrapers, subterranean supermalls, trendy pubs, and peaceful parks with pedestrian bridges looping over canals. It also boasts the very good Museum of London Docklands. While not full of the touristy sights that many are seeking in London, the Docklands offers a refreshing look at the British version of a 21st-century city. It's best at the end of the workday, when it's lively with office workers. It's ideal to see on your way back from Greenwich, since both line up on the same train tracks.

Getting There: Coming from central London, take the Tube to a DLR stop (the Bank/Monument stops are the most central), then take the Lewisham line to South Quay. If you're coming from Greenwich, take any northbound DLR line to South Quay.

▲Museum of London Docklands

This modern and interesting museum, which fills an old sugar warehouse, gives the Docklands historic context. In telling the story of the world's leading 19th-century port, it also conveys the story of London. This 2,000-year walk through the story of commerce on the Thames includes a re-creation of the fuel pipeline that was laid under the English Channel to supply the Allies on the Continent during WWII, and a walk through gritty "Sailortown," where you'll listen to the salty voices of those who lived and worked in quarters like these.

Cost and Hours: Free, £2.50 suggested donation, daily 10:00-18:00, last entry one hour before closing, tel. 020/7001-9844, www.museumoflondon.org.uk/docklands.

WEST OF LONDON

Kew Gardens/Hampton Court Blitz: Because these two sights are in the same general direction (about £20 for a taxi between the two), you can visit both in one day. Here's a game plan: Start your morning at Hampton Court, tour the palace and garden, and have a Tudor-style lunch in the atmospheric dining hall. After lunch, take bus #R68 from Hampton Court Station to Richmond (40 minutes), then transfer to bus #65, which will drop you off at the Kew Gardens gate (5 minutes). After touring the gardens, have tea in the Orangery, then Tube or boat back to London.

▲▲Kew Gardens

For a fine riverside park and a palatial greenhouse jungle to swing through, take the Tube or the boat to every botanist's favorite escape, Kew Gardens. While to most visitors the Royal Botanic Gardens of Kew are simply a delightful opportunity to wander among 33,000 different types of plants, to the hardworking organization that runs them, the gardens are a way to promote the understanding and preservation of the botanical diversity of our planet.

Garden lovers could spend days exploring Kew's 300 acres. For a quick visit, spend a fragrant hour wandering through three buildings: the Palm House, a humid Victorian world of iron, glass, and tropical plants that was built in 1844; a Waterlily House that Monet would swim for; and the Princess of Wales Conservatory, a meandering modern greenhouse with many different climate zones growing countless cacti, bug-munching carnivorous plants, and more. Check out the Xstrata Treetop Walkway, a 200-yard-long scenic steel walkway that puts you high in the canopy 60 feet above the ground. Young kids will love the Climbers and Creepers

Indoor/outdoor playground and little zip line, and a slow and easy ride on the hop-on, hop-off Kew Explorer tram.

Cost and Hours: £16.50, June-Aug £11 after 16:00, £3.50 for kids 4-16, free for kids under 4; April-Aug Mon-Thu 10:00-18:30, Fri-Sun 10:00-19:30, closes earlier Sept-March—check schedule online, glasshouses close at 17:30 in high season—earlier off-season, free one-hour walking tours daily at 11:00 and 13:30, tel. 020/8332-5000, recorded info tel. 020/8332-5655, www.kew.org.

Getting There: If taking the Tube, ride to Kew Gardens; from the Tube station, cross the footbridge over the tracks, which drops you in a little community of plant-and-herb shops, a two-block walk from Victoria Gate (the main garden entrance). Another option is to take a boat, which runs April-Oct between Kew Gardens and Westminster Pier (see page 64).

Eating: For a sun-dappled lunch or snack, walk 10 minutes from the Palm House to the **$$ Orangery Cafeteria** (Mon-Thu 10:00-17:30, Fri-Sun until 18:30, daily until 15:15 in winter, closes early for events).

▲Hampton Court Palace

Fifteen miles up the Thames from downtown, the 500-year-old palace of Henry VIII is worth ▲▲ for palace aficionados. Actu-

ally, it was originally the palace of his minister, Cardinal Wolsey. When Wolsey, a clever man, realized Henry VIII was experiencing a little palace envy, he gave the mansion to his king. The Tudor palace was also home to Elizabeth I and Charles I. Sections were updated by Christopher Wren for William and Mary. The stately palace stands overlooking the Thames and includes some fine Tudor rooms, including a Great Hall with a magnificent hammer-beam ceiling. The industrial-strength Tudor kitchen was capable of keeping 600 schmoozing courtiers thoroughly—if not well—fed. The sculpted garden features a rare Tudor tennis court and a popular maze.

The palace tries hard to please, but it doesn't quite sparkle. From the information center in the main courtyard, you can pick up audioguides for self-guided tours of various wings of the palace (free but slow, aimed mostly at school-age children). For more in-depth information, strike up a conversation with the costumed characters or docents posted in each room. The Tudor portions of the castle, including the rooms dedicated to the young Henry, are most interesting; the Georgian rooms are pretty dull. The maze in the nearby garden is a curiosity some find fun (maze free with palace ticket, otherwise £4.70).

Cost and Hours: £23, family-£57; online discounts, daily April-Oct 10:00-18:00, Nov-March until 16:30, last entry one hour before closing, café, tel. 0844-482-7777 or 020/3166-6000, www.hrp.org.uk.

Getting There: From London's Waterloo Station, take a South West train. The train will drop you on the far side of the river from the palace—just walk across the bridge (2/hour, 35 minutes, Oyster cards OK). Consider arriving at or departing from the palace by boat (connections with London's Westminster Pier, see page 64); it's a relaxing and scenic three- to four-hour cruise past two locks and a fun new/old riverside mix.

NORTH OF LONDON
The Making of Harry Potter:
Warner Bros. Studio Tour London

While you can visit several real-life locations where the Harry Potter movies were filmed, there's only one way to see imaginary places like Hogwarts' Great Hall, Diagon Alley, Dumbledore's office, and #4 Privet Drive: Visit the Warner Bros. Studio in Leavesden, 20 miles northwest of London. You'll see the actual sets, costumes, and props used in the movies, video interviews with the actors and filmmakers, and exhibits about how the films' special effects were created. The visit culminates with a stroll down Diagon Alley and a room-sized 1:24-scale model of Hogwarts.

It's essential to reserve your visit online far in advance (entry possible only with reserved time slot). Allowing about three hours at the studio, plus nearly three hours to get there and back, this experience will eat up the better part of a day.

Cost and Hours: £39, kids 5-15-£31, family ticket for 2 adults and 2 kids-£126; opening hours flex with season—first tour at 9:00 or 10:00, last tour as early as 14:30 or as late as 18:30; audio/videoguide-£5, café, tel. 0845-084-0900, www.wbstudiotour.co.uk.

Getting There: Take the frequent train from London Euston to Watford Junction (about 5/hour, 20 minutes), then catch the brightly painted Mullany's Coaches shuttle bus to the studio (2-4/hour, 15 minutes, £2.50 round-trip, buy ticket from driver). Alternately, book a Golden Tours **bus** trip (multiple trips daily, price includes round-trip bus and studio entrance: adults-£60-70, kids-£55-65; reserve ahead at www.goldentours.com).

Shopping in London

Most stores are open Monday through Saturday from roughly 9:00 or 10:00 until 17:00 or 18:00, with a late night on Wednesday or Thursday (usually until 19:00 or 20:00). Many close on Sundays. Large department stores stay open later during the week (until about 21:00 Mon-Sat) with shorter hours on Sundays. If you're looking for bargains, visit one of the city's many street markets.

SHOPPING STREETS

London is famous for its shopping. The best and most convenient shopping streets are in the West End and West London (roughly between Soho and Hyde Park). You'll find mid-range shops along **Oxford Street** (running east from Tube: Marble Arch), and fancier shops along **Regent Street** (stretching south from Tube: Oxford Circus to Piccadilly Circus) and

Knightsbridge (where you'll find Harrods and Harvey Nichols; Tube: Knightsbridge). Other streets are more specialized, such as **Jermyn Street** for old-fashioned men's clothing (just south of Piccadilly Street) and **Charing Cross Road** for books. **Floral Street,** connecting Leicester Square to Covent Garden, is lined with fashion boutiques.

FANCY DEPARTMENT STORES

Harrods

Harrods is London's most famous and touristy department store. With more than four acres of retail space covering seven floors, it's a place where some shoppers could spend all day. (To me, it's still just a department store.) Big yet classy, Harrods has everything from elephants to toothbrushes (Mon-Sat 10:00-21:00, Sun 11:30-18:00; baggage check outside on Basil Street—follow *left luggage* signs at back of the store, a hefty £25/bag; Brompton Road, Tube: Knightsbridge, tel. 020/7730-1234, www.harrods.com).

Harvey Nichols

Once Princess Diana's favorite and later Duchess Kate's, "Harvey Nick's" remains the department store *du jour* (Mon-Sat 10:00-20:00, Sun 11:30-18:00, near Harrods, 109 Knightsbridge, Tube: Knightsbridge, tel. 020/7235-5000, www.harveynichols.com).

Want to pick up a £20 scarf? You won't do it here, where they're more like £200. The store's fifth floor is a veritable food fest, with a gourmet grocery store, a fancy restaurant, a Yo! Sushi bar, and a lively café. Consider a takeaway tray of sushi to eat on a bench in the Hyde Park rose garden two blocks away.

Fortnum & Mason

The official department store of the Queen, Fortnum & Mason embodies old-fashioned, British upper-class taste. While some feel it is too stuffy, you won't find another store with the same storybook atmosphere. With rich displays and deep red carpet, Fortnum's feels classier and more relaxed than Harrods (Mon-Sat 10:00-21:00, Sun 11:30-18:00, elegant tea served in their Diamond Jubilee Tea Salon—see page 203, 181 Piccadilly, Tube: Green Park, tel. 020/7734-8040, www.fortnumandmason.com).

Liberty

Designed to make well-heeled shoppers feel at home, this half-timbered, mock-Tudor emporium is a 19th-century institution that thrives today. Known for its gorgeous "Liberty Print" floral fabrics, well-stocked crafts department, and castle-like interior, this iconic shop was a favorite of writer Oscar Wilde, who called it "the chosen resort of the artistic shopper" (Mon-Sat 10:00-20:00, Sun 12:00-18:00, Great Marlborough Street, Tube: Oxford Circus, tel. 020/7734-1234, www.liberty.co.uk).

STREET MARKETS

Antique buffs, foodies, people-watchers, and folks who brake for garage sales love London's street markets. There's good early-morning market activity somewhere any day of the week. The best markets—which combine lively stalls and a colorful neighborhood with cute and characteristic shops of their own—are Portobello Road and Camden Lock Market. Hagglers will enjoy the no-holds-barred bargaining encouraged in London's street markets. **Greenwich** (a quick DLR ride from central London) also has its share of great markets, especially lively on weekends.

Warning: Markets attract two kinds of people—tourists and pickpockets.

Portobello Road Market (Notting Hill)

Arguably London's best street market, Portobello Road stretches for several blocks through the delightful, colorful, funky-yet-quaint Notting Hill neighborhood. Already-charming streets lined with pastel-painted houses and offbeat antique shops are enlivened on Fridays and Saturdays with 2,000 additional stalls (9:00-19:00), plus food, live music, and more. (The best strategy is to come on Friday; most stalls are open, with half the crowds of Saturday.)

If you start at Notting Hill Gate and work your way north, you'll find these general sections: antiques, new goods, produce, vintage clothing, more new goods, a flea market, and more food. While Portobello Road is best on Fridays and Saturdays, it's enjoyable to stroll this street on most other days as well, since the quirky shops are fun to explore (Tube: Notting Hill Gate, near recommended accommodations, tel. 020/7727-7684, www.portobelloroad.co.uk).

Camden Lock Market (Camden Town)

This huge, trendy arts-and-crafts festival is divided into three areas, each with its own vibe. The main market, set alongside the pictur-

esque canal, features a mix of shops and stalls selling boutique crafts and artisanal foods. The market on the opposite side of Chalk Farm Road is edgier, with cheap ethnic food stalls, lots of canalside seating, and punk crafts. The Stables, a sprawling, incense-scented complex, is dec-orated with fun statues of horses and squeezed into tunnels under the old rail bridge just behind the main market. It's a little lowbrow and wildly creative, with cheap clothes, junk jewelry, and loud music (daily 10:00-19:00, busiest on weekends, tel. 020/3763-9999, www.camdenmarket.com).

Leadenhall Market (The City)

One of London's oldest, Leadenhall Market stands on the original Roman center of town. Today, cheese and flower shops nestle be-tween pubs, restaurants, and fashion boutiques, all beneath a beau-tiful Victorian arcade (Harry Potter fans may recognize it as Di-agon Alley). This is not a "street market" in the true sense, but more a hidden gem in the midst of London's financial grind (Mon-Fri 10:00-18:00, tel. 020/7332-1523, Tube: Monument or Liverpool; off Gracechurch Street near Leadenhall Street and Fenchurch).

East End Markets

Most of these East End markets are busiest and most interesting on Sundays; the Broadway Market is best on Saturdays.

Spitalfields Market: This huge, mod-feeling market hall combines a shopping mall with old brick buildings and sleek mod-ern ones, all covered by a giant glass roof. The shops, stalls, and a rainbow of restaurant options are open every day, tempting you with ethnic eateries, crafts, trendy clothes, bags, and an antiques-and-junk market (Mon-Fri 10:00-17:00, Sat from 11:00, Sun from 9:00, Tube: Liverpool Street; from the Tube stop, take Bishopsgate

East exit, turn left, walk to Brushfield Street, and turn right; www. spitalfields.co.uk).

Petticoat Lane Market: Just a block from Spitalfields Market, this line of stalls sits on the otherwise dull, glass-skyscraper-filled Middlesex Street; adjoining Wentworth Street is grungier and more characteristic. Expect budget clothing, leather, shoes, watches, jewelry, and crowds (Sun 9:00-14:00, sometimes later; smaller market Mon-Fri on Wentworth Street only; Middlesex Street and Wentworth Street, Tube: Liverpool Street).

Truman Markets: Housed in the former Truman Brewery on Brick Lane, this cluster of markets is in the heart of the "Banglatown" Bangladeshi community. Of the East End market areas, these are the grittiest and most avant-garde, selling handmade clothes and home decor as well as ethnic street food. The markets are in full swing on Sundays (roughly 10:00-17:00), though you'll see some action on Saturdays (11:00-18:00). The Boiler House Food Hall and the Backyard Market (hipster arts and crafts) go all weekend—and the Vintage Market (clothes) even operates on Thursdays and Fridays (11:00-16:00). Surrounding shops and eateries, including a fun courtyard of food trucks tucked off Brick Lane, are open all week (Tube: Liverpool Street or Aldgate East, tel. 020/7770-6028, www.bricklanemarket.com).

Columbia Road Flower Market: From the Truman Brewery complex, Brick Lane is lined with Sunday market stalls all the way up to Bethnal Green Road, about a 10-minute walk. Continuing straight (north) about five more minutes takes you to Columbia Road, where you can turn right (east) to find a colorful shopping street made even more so by the Sunday-morning commotion of shouting flower vendors (Sun 8:00-15:00, http://columbiaroad. info). Halfway up Columbia Road, be sure to loop left up little Ezra Street, with characteristic eateries, boutiques, and antique vendors.

Broadway Market: Saturdays are best for the festive market sprawling through this aptly named neighborhood—ground zero for London's hipsters. A bit farther out, this market can be tricky to reach; it's easiest to take the Overground from Liverpool Street Station three stops to London Fields, then walk through that park to the market. Several blocks are filled with foodie delights, along with a few arts and crafts. The Broadway Schoolyard section is home to popular food trucks—many of them satellites of brick-and-mortar restaurants spread across London—selling trendy, affordable bites (Sat 9:00-17:00, www.broadwaymarket.co.uk). On sunny days, the London Fields park just north of the market is filled with thousands of picnicking and sunbathing locals.

West End Markets

Covent Garden Market: Originally the convent garden for West-minster Abbey, the iron-and-glass market hall hosted a produce market until the 1970s (earning it the name "Apple Market"). Now it's a mix of fun shops, eateries, markets, and a more modern-day Apple store on the corner. Mondays are for antiques, while arts and crafts dominate the rest of the week. Yesteryear's produce stalls are open daily 10:30-18:00, and on Thursdays, a food market brightens up the square (Tube: Covent Garden, tel. 020/7395-1350, www.coventgardenlondonuk.com).

Jubilee Hall Market: This market features antiques on Mondays (5:00-17:00); a general market Tuesday through Friday (10:30-19:00); and arts and crafts on Saturdays and Sundays (10:00-18:00). It's located on the south side of Covent Garden (tel. 020/7379-4242, www.jubileemarket.co.uk).

South London Markets

Borough Market: London's oldest fruit-and-vegetable market has been serving the Southwark community for over 800 years. These days there are as many people taking photos as buying fruit, cheese, and beautiful breads, but it's still a fun carnival atmosphere with fantastic stall food. For maximum market and minimum crowds, join the locals on Thursdays (full market open Wed-Sat 10:00-17:00, Fri until 18:00, surrounding food stalls open daily; south of London Bridge, where Southwark Street meets Borough High Street; Tube: London Bridge, tel. 020/7407-1002, www.boroughmarket.org.uk).

Southbank Centre Food Market: You'll find some of the city's most popular vendors in this paradise of street food near the London Eye (Fri-Sat 12:00-20:00, Sun-Mon until 18:00, closed midweek; between the Royal Festival Hall and BFI Southbank at Hayward Gallery, Tube: Waterloo, or Embankment and cross the Jubilee Bridge; tel. 020/3879-9555, www.southbankcentre.co.uk).

Ropewalk (Maltby Street Market): This short-but-sweet, completely untouristy food bazaar bustles on weekends under a nondescript rail bridge in the shadow of the Shard. Two dozen vendors fill the narrow passage with a festival of hipster/artisan food carts, offering everything from gourmet burgers to waffles to scotch eggs to ice-cream sandwiches (Sat 9:00-16:00, Sun from 11:00, www.maltby.st).

Brixton Market: This multicultural neighborhood south of the Thames features yet another thriving market. Here the food, clothing, and music reflect a burgeoning hipster scene (shops and stalls open Mon-Sat 8:00-18:00, Wed until 15:00, farmers market Sun 10:00-14:00 but otherwise dead on Sun; Tube: Brixton, www.brixtonmarket.net).

Entertainment in London

For the best list of what's happening and a look at the latest London scene, check www.timeout.com/london. The free monthly *London Planner* covers sights, events, and plays, though generally not as well as the *Time Out* website.

THEATER (A.K.A. "THEATRE")

London's theater scene rivals Broadway's in quality and sometimes beats it in price. Choose from 200 offerings—Shakespeare, musicals, comedies, thrillers, sex farces, cutting-edge fringe, revivals starring movie celebs, and more. London does it all well.

Seating Terminology: Just like at home, London's theaters sell seats in a range of levels—but the Brits use different terms: stalls (ground floor), dress circle (first balcony), upper circle (second balcony), balcony (sky-high third balcony), and slips (cheap seats on the fringes). Discounted tickets are called "concessions" (abbreviated as "conc" or "s"). For floor plans of the various theaters, see www.theatremonkey.com.

Big West End Shows

Nearly all big-name shows are hosted in the theaters of the West End, clustering around Soho (especially along Shaftesbury Avenue) between Piccadilly and Covent Garden. With a centuries-old tradition of pleasing the masses, they present London theater at its grandest.

I prefer big, glitzy—even bombastic—musicals over serious chamber dramas, simply because London can deliver the lights, booming voices, dancers, and multimedia spectacle I rarely get back home. If that's not to your taste—or you already have access to similar spectacles at home—you might prefer some of London's more low-key offerings.

Well-known musicals may draw the biggest crowds, but the West End offers plenty of other crowd-pleasers, from revivals of classics to cutting-edge works by the hottest young playwrights. These productions tend to have shorter runs than famous musicals. Many productions star huge-name celebrities—London is a magnet for movie stars who want to stretch their acting chops.

You'll see the latest offerings advertised all over the Tube and elsewhere. The free *Official London Theatre Guide*, updated weekly, is a handy tool (find it at hotels, box offices, the City of London TI, and online at www.officiallondontheatre.co.uk). You can check reviews at www.timeout.com/london.

Most performances are nightly except Sunday, usually with two or three matinees a week. The few shows that run on Sundays are mostly family fare (such as *The Lion King*). Tickets range from about £25 to £120 for the best seats at big shows. Matinees are generally cheaper and rarely sell out.

Buying Tickets for West End Shows

For most visitors, it makes sense to simply buy tickets in London. Most shows have tickets available on short notice—likely at a discount. But if your time in London is limited—and you have your heart set on a particular show that's likely to sell out (usually the newest shows, and especially on weekends)—you can buy peace of mind by booking your tickets from home.

Advance Tickets: It's generally cheapest to buy your tickets directly from the theater, either through its website or by calling the theater box office. Often, a theater will reroute you to a third-party ticket vendor such as Ticketmaster. You'll pay with a credit card, and generally be charged a per-ticket booking fee (around £3). You can have your tickets emailed to you or pick them up before show time at the theater's Will Call window. Note that many third-party websites sell London theater tickets, but these generally charge higher prices and fees. It's best to try the theater's website or box office first.

Discount Tickets from the TKTS Booth: This famous outlet at Leicester Square sells discounted tickets (25-50 percent off)

for many shows (£3/ticket service charge included, open Mon-Sat 10:00-19:00, Sun 11:00-16:30). TKTS offers a wide variety of shows on any given day, though they may not have the hottest shows in town. You must buy in person at the kiosk, and the best deals are same-day only.

The list of shows and prices is posted outside the booth and updated throughout the day. The same info is available on their constantly refreshed website (www.tkts.co.uk), which is worth checking before you head to Leicester Square. For the best choice and prices, come early in the day—the line starts forming even before the booth opens (it moves quickly). Have a second-choice show in mind, in case your first choice is sold out by the time you reach the ticket window. If you're less picky, come later in the day, when lines (and choices) diminish.

TKTS also sells advance tickets for some shows (but not as cheaply) and some regular-price tickets to extremely popular shows—convenient, but no savings. If TKTS runs out of its ticket allotment for a certain show, it doesn't necessarily mean the show is sold out—you can still try the theater's box office.

Take note: The real TKTS booth (with its prominent sign) is a freestanding kiosk at the south edge of Leicester Square. Several dishonest outfits nearby advertise "official half-price tickets"— avoid these, where you'll rarely pay anything close to half-price.

Tickets at the Theater Box Office: Even sif a show is "sold out," there's usually a way to get a seat. Many theaters offer various discounts or "concessions": same-day tickets, cheap returned tickets, standing-room, matinee, senior or student standby deals, and more. Start by checking the show's website, call the box office, or simply drop by (many theaters are right in the tourist zone).

Same-day tickets (called "day seats") are generally available only in person at the box office starting at 10:00 (people start lining up well before then). These tickets (£20 or less) tend to be either in the nosebleed rows or have a restricted view (behind a pillar or extremely far to one side).

Another strategy is to show up at the box office shortly before show time (best on weekdays) and—before paying full price—ask about any cheaper options. Last-minute return tickets are often sold at great prices as curtain time approaches.

For a helpful guide to "day seats," consult www.theatremonkey.com/dayseatfinder.htm; for tips on getting cheap and last-minute tickets, visit www.londontheatretickets.org and www.timeout.com/london/theatre.

Booking Through Other Agencies: Although booking through a middleman such as your hotel or a ticket agency is quick and easy (and may be your last resort for a sold-out show), prices are greatly inflated. Ticket agencies and third-party websites are often just scalpers with an address. If you do buy from an agency, choose one who is a member of the Society of Ticket Agents and Retailers (look for the STAR logo—short for "secure tickets from authorized retailers"). These legitimate resellers normally add a maximum 25 percent booking fee to tickets.

Scalpers (or "Touts"): As at any event, you'll find scalpers hawking tickets outside theaters. And, just like at home, those people may either be honest folk whose date just happened to cancel at the last minute...or they may be unscrupulous thieves selling forgeries. London has many of the latter.

Theater Beyond the West End

Tickets for lesser-known shows tend to be cheaper (figure £15-30), in part because most of the smaller theaters are government-subsidized. Remember that plays don't need a familiar title or famous actor to be a worthwhile experience—read up on the latest offerings online; *Time Out*'s website is a great place to start.

Major Noncommercial Theaters

One particularly good venue is the **National Theatre,** which has a range of impressive options, often starring recognizable names. While the building is ugly on the outside, the acts that play out upon its stage are beautiful—as are the deeply discounted tickets it commonly offers (looming on the South Bank by Waterloo Bridge, Tube: Waterloo, www.nationaltheatre.org.uk).

The **Barbican Centre** puts on high-quality, often experimental work (right by the Museum of London, just north of The City, Tube: Barbican, www.barbican.org.uk), as does the **Royal Court Theatre,** which has £12 tickets for its Monday shows (west of the West End in Sloane Square, Tube: Sloane Square, www.royalcourttheatre.com).

Menier Chocolate Factory is a small theater in Southwark popular for its impressive productions and intimate setting. Check their website to see what's on—they tend to have a mix of plays, musicals, and even an occasional comedian (behind the Tate Modern at 53 Southwark Street, Tube: Southwark, www.menierchocolatefactory.com).

Royal Shakespeare Company: If you'll ever enjoy Shakespeare, it'll be in Britain. The RSC performs at various theaters around London and in Stratford-upon-Avon year-round (for details, see page 417 in the Stratford-upon-Avon chapter). To get a schedule, contact the RSC (Royal Shakespeare Theatre, Stratford-upon-Avon, tel. 0844-800-1110, box office tel. 01789/403-493, www.rsc.org.uk).

Shakespeare's Globe

To see Shakespeare in a replica of the theater for which he wrote his plays, attend a play at the Globe. In this round, thatch-roof, open-air theater, the plays are performed much as Shakespeare intended—under the sky, with no amplification.

The play's the thing from late April through early October (usually Tue-Sat 14:00 and 19:30, Sun either 13:00 and/or 18:30, tickets can be sold out months in advance). You'll pay £5 to stand and £20-45 to sit, usually on a backless bench. Because only a few rows and the pricier Gentlemen's Rooms have seats with backs, £1 cushions and £3 add-on backrests are considered a good investment by many. Dress for the weather.

The £5 "groundling" tickets—which are open to rain—are most fun. Scurry in early to stake out a spot on the stage's edge, where the most interaction with the actors occurs. You're a crude peasant. You can lean your elbows on the stage, munch a picnic dinner (yes, you can bring in food), or walk around. I've never enjoyed Shakespeare as much as here, performed as it was meant to be in the "wooden O." If you can't get a ticket, consider waiting around. Plays can be long, and many groundlings leave before the end. Hang around outside and beg or buy a ticket from someone leaving early (groundlings are allowed to come and go). A few non-Shakespeare plays are also presented each year. If you can't attend a show, you can take a guided tour of the theater and museum by day (see page 132).

The indoor Sam Wanamaker Playhouse allows Shakespearean-era plays and early-music concerts to be performed through the winter. Many of the productions in this intimate venue are one-offs and can be quite pricey.

To reserve tickets for plays at the Globe or Sam Wanamaker, call or drop by the box office (Mon-Sat 10:00-18:00, Sun until 17:00, open one hour later on performance days, New Globe Walk entrance, no extra charge to book by phone, tel. 020/7401-9919). You can also reserve online (www.shakespearesglobe.com, £2.50 booking fee). If the tickets are sold out, don't despair; a few often free up at the last minute. Try calling around noon the day of the performance to see if the box office expects any returned tickets. If so, they'll advise you to show up a little more than an hour before the show, when these tickets are sold (first-come, first-served).

The theater is on the South Bank, directly across the Thames over the Millennium Bridge from St. Paul's Cathedral (Tube: Mansion House or London Bridge). The Globe is inconvenient for public transport, but during theater season, a regular supply of black cabs wait nearby.

Outdoor and Fringe Theater

In summer, enjoy Shakespearean drama and other plays under the stars at the **Open Air Theatre,** in leafy Regent's Park in north London. You can bring your own picnic, order à la carte from the theater menu, or preorder a picnic supper from the theater at least 24 hours in advance (tickets from £25, available beginning in mid-Jan, season runs late May-mid-Sept; book at www.openairtheatre. org or—for an extra booking fee—by calling 0844-826-4242; grounds open 1.5 hours before evening performances, one hour before matinees; 10-minute walk north of Baker Street Tube, near Queen Mary's Gardens within Regent's Park; detailed directions and more info at www.openairtheatre.org).

London's rougher evening-entertainment scene is thriving. Choose from a wide range of **fringe theater** and comedy acts (find posters in many Tube stations, or search for "fringe theater" on www.timeout.com; tickets can start as cheap as £14).

CONCERTS AT CHURCHES

For easy, cheap, or free concerts in historic churches, attend a **lunch concert,** especially:

Evensong

One of my favorite experiences in Britain is to attend evensong at a great church. Evensong is an evening worship service that is typically sung rather than said (though some parts—including scripture readings, a few prayers, and a homily—are spoken). It follows the traditional Anglican service in the Book of Common Prayer, including prayers, scripture readings, canticles (sung responses), and hymns that are appropriate for the early evening—traditionally the end of the working day and before the evening meal. In major churches with resident choirs, this service is filled with quality, professional musical elements. A singing or chanting priest leads the service, and a choir—usually made up of both men's and boys' voices (to sing the lower and higher parts, respectively)—sings the responses. The choir usually sings a cappella, or is accompanied by an organ. While regular attendees follow the service from memory, visitors—who are welcome—are given an order of service or a prayer book to help them follow along. (If you're not familiar with the order of service, watch the congregation to know when to stand, sit, and kneel.)

The most impressive places for evensong include London (Westminster Abbey, St. Paul's, Southwark Cathedral, or St. Bride's Church), Cambridge (King's College Chapel), York Minster, and Durham Cathedral. While this list includes many of the grandest churches in England, be aware that evensong typically takes place in the small choir area—which is far more intimate than the main nave. (To see the full church in action, a concert is a better choice.) Evensong generally occurs daily between 17:00 and 18:00 (often two hours earlier on Sundays)—check with individual churches for specifics. At smaller churches, evensong is sometimes spoken, not sung.

Note that evensong is not a performance—it's a somewhat somber worship service. If you enjoy worshipping in different churches, attending evensong can be a trip-capping highlight. But if regimented church services aren't your thing, consider getting a different music fix. Most major churches also offer organ or choral concerts—look for posted schedules or ask at the information desk or gift shop.

- St. Bride's Church, with free half-hour lunch concerts twice a week at 13:15 (usually Tue and Fri—confirm in advance, church tel. 020/7427-0133, www.stbrides.com).
- St. James's at Piccadilly, with 50-minute concerts on Mon, Wed, and Fri at 13:10 (suggested £3.50 donation, info tel. 020/7734-4511, www.sjp.org.uk).
- St. Martin-in-the-Fields, offering concerts on Mon, Tue, and Fri at 13:00 (suggested £3.50 donation, church tel. 020/7766-1100, www.stmartin-in-the-fields.org).

St. Martin-in-the-Fields also hosts fine **evening concerts** by candlelight (£9-28, several nights a week at 19:30) and live jazz in its underground Café in the Crypt (£8-15, Wed at 20:00).

Evensong services are held at several churches, including St. Paul's Cathedral, Westminster Abbey, Southwark Cathedral, and St. Bride's Church (Sun at 17:30).

Free **organ recitals** are usually held on Sunday at 17:45 in Westminster Abbey (30 minutes, tel. 020/7222-5152). Many other churches have free concerts; ask for the *London Organ Concerts Guide* at the TI.

SUMMER EVENINGS ALONG THE SOUTH BANK

If you're visiting London in summer, consider hitting the South Bank neighborhood after hours.

Take a trip around the **London Eye** while the sun sets over the city (the wheel spins until late—last ascent at 20:30 or later in summer). Then cap your night with an evening walk along the pedestrian-only **Jubilee Walkway,** which runs east-west along the river. It's where Londoners go to escape the heat. This pleasant stretch of the walkway—lined with pubs and casual eateries—goes from the London Eye past Shakespeare's Globe to Tower Bridge (you can walk in either direction).

If you're in the mood for a movie, take in a flick at the **BFI Southbank,** located just across the river, alongside Waterloo Bridge. Run by the British Film Institute, the state-of-the-art theater shows mostly classic films, as well as art cinema (Tube: Waterloo or Embankment, check www.bfi.org.uk for schedules and prices).

Farther east along the South Bank is **The Scoop**—an outdoor amphitheater next to City Hall. It's a good spot for movies, concerts, dance, and theater productions throughout the summer—with Tower Bridge as a scenic backdrop. These events are free, nearly nightly, and family-friendly. For the latest event schedule, see www.morelondon.com and click on "Events" (next to City Hall, Riverside, The Queen's Walkway, Tube: London Bridge).

SPORTING EVENTS

Tennis, cricket, rugby, football (soccer), and horse races all take place within an hour of the city. In summer Wimbledon draws a half-million spectators (www.wimbledon.com), while big-name English Premier League soccer clubs—including Chelsea, Arsenal, Tottenham Hotspur, and West Ham United—take the pitch in London to sell-out crowds (www.premierleague.com). The two biggest horse races of the year take place in June: the Royal Ascot Races (www.ascot.co.uk) near Windsor and the Epsom Derby (www.epsomderby.co.uk) in Surrey are both once-in-a-lifetime experiences.

Securing tickets to anything sporting-related in London can be difficult—and expensive. Check the official team or event website several months in advance; tickets can sell out within minutes of going on sale to the general public. Third-party booking companies such as SportsEvents 365 (www.sportsevents365.com) and Ticketmaster (www.ticketmaster.co.uk) often have tickets to popular events at a premium price—a godsend for die-hard fans. Many teams also offer affordable, well-run stadium tours—check your favorite side's official website for details. Even if you can't attend a sports event in person, consider cheering on the action in a London pub.

Sleeping in London

London is an expensive city for lodging. Cheaper rooms are relatively dumpy. Don't expect £160 cheeriness in an £80 room. For £80, you'll get a double with breakfast in a safe, cramped, and dreary place with minimal service and the bathroom down the hall. For £100, you'll get a basic, reasonably cheery double with worn carpet and a private bath in a usually cramped, somewhat outdated, cracked-plaster building, or a soulless but comfortable room without breakfast in a huge Motel 6-type place. My London splurges, at £160-300, are spacious, thoughtfully appointed places good for entertaining or romancing.

I rank accommodations from $ budget to $$$$ splurge. To get the best deal, contact my family-run hotels directly by phone or email. If you go direct, the owner avoids a roughly 20 percent commission and may be able to offer you a discount. Book your accommodations well in advance if you'll be traveling during peak season or if your trip coincides with a major holiday or festival (see page 1074). For information and tips on hotel rates and deals, making reservations, finding a short-term rental, and more, see page 1030.

Looking for Hotel Deals Online: Given London's high hotel prices, it's worth searching for a deal. For some travelers, short-term, Airbnb-type rentals can be a good alternative; search for places in my recommended hotel neighborhoods. Various websites list rooms in London in high-rise, three- and four-star business hotels. You'll give up the charm and warmth of a family-run establishment, and breakfast probably won't be included, but you might find that the price is right.

Start by browsing the websites of several chains to get a sense of typical rates and online deals (see "Big, Good-Value, Modern Hotels," later). Pricier London hotel chains include Millennium/Copthorne, Grange, Firmdale, Thistle, InterContinental/Holiday Inn, Radisson, Hilton, and Red Carnation. Auction-type sites

London's Hotel Neighborhoods

(such as Priceline and Hotwire) match flexible travelers with empty hotel rooms, often at prices well below the hotel's normal rates. You can also browse these accommodation discount sites: www.londontown.com (an informative site with a discount booking service), athomeinlondon.co.uk and www.londonbb.com (both list central B&Bs), www.lastminute.com, www.visitlondon.com, and www.eurocheapo.com.

VICTORIA STATION NEIGHBORHOOD

The streets behind Victoria Station teem with little, moderately-priced-for-London B&Bs. It's a safe, surprisingly tidy, and decent area without a hint of the trashy, touristy glitz of the streets in front of the station. I've divided these accommodations into two broad categories: Belgravia, west of the station, feels particularly posh, while Pimlico, to the east, is still upscale and dotted with colorful eateries. While I wouldn't go out of my way just to dine here, each area has plenty of good restaurants (see "Eating in London," later). All of my recommended hotels are within a five-minute walk of the Victoria Tube, bus, and train stations. On hot summer nights, request a quiet back room; most of these B&Bs lack air-conditioning and may front busy streets.

Laundry: The nearest laundry option is **Pimlico Launderette,** on the east—Pimlico—side about five blocks southwest of Warwick Square. Low prices and friendly George brighten your chore (self-service and same-day full service, daily 8:00-19:00, last wash at 17:30; 3 Westmoreland Terrace—go down Clarendon Street, turn right on Sutherland, and look for the launderette on the left at the end of the street; tel. 020/7821-8692).

Parking: The 400-space Semley Place **NCP parking garage** is near the hotels on the west/Belgravia side (£42/day, possible discounts with hotel voucher, just west of Victoria Coach Station at Buckingham Palace Road and Semley Place, tel. 0845-050-7080, www.ncp.co.uk). **Victoria Station car park** is cheaper but a quarter of the size; check here first, but don't hold your breath (£30/day on weekdays, £15/day on weekends, entrance on Eccleston Bridge between Buckingham Palace Road and Bridge Place, tel. 0345-222-4224, www.apcoa.co.uk).

West of Victoria Station (Belgravia)

In Belgravia, the prices are a bit higher and your neighbors include some of the world's wealthiest people. These two places sit on tranquil Ebury Street, two blocks over from Victoria Station (or a slightly shorter walk from the Sloane Square Tube stop). You can cut the walk from Victoria Station to nearly nothing by taking a short ride on frequent bus #C1 (leaves from Buckingham Palace Road side of Victoria Station and drops you off on corner of Ebury and Elizabeth streets).

$$$$ Lime Tree Hotel, enthusiastically run by Charlotte and Matt, is a gem, with 28 spacious, stylish, comfortable, thoughtfully decorated rooms, a helpful staff, and a fun-loving breakfast room (small lounge opens onto quiet garden, 135 Ebury Street, tel. 020/7730-8191, www.limetreehotel.co.uk, info@limetreehotel.co.uk, Laura manages the office).

$$$ B&B Belgravia comes with bright rooms, high ceilings, and spring-loaded slamming doors. It's a little worn around the edges and feels less than homey, but still offers good value for the location. Most of its 26 rooms come with closets and larger-than-average space. If you're a light sleeper, ask for a room in the back (family rooms, 64 Ebury Street, tel. 020/7259-8570, www.bb-belgravia.com, info@bb-belgravia.com).

East of Victoria Station (Pimlico)

This area feels a bit less genteel than Belgravia, but it's still plenty inviting, with eateries and grocery stores. Most of these hotels are on or near Warwick Way, the main drag through this area. Generally the best Tube stop for this neighborhood is Victoria (though the Pimlico stop works equally well for the Luna Simone). Bus #24 runs right through the middle of Pimlico, connecting the Tate Britain to the south with Victoria Station, the Houses of Parliament, Trafalgar Square, the British Museum, and much more to the north.

$$$ Luna Simone Hotel rents 36 fresh, spacious, remodeled rooms with modern bathrooms. It's a smartly managed place, run for more than 40 years by twins Peter and Bernard—and Ber-

LONDON

Victoria Station Neighborhood

Hotels
1. Lime Tree Hotel
2. B&B Belgravia
3. Luna Simone Hotel
4. Bakers Hotel
5. New England Hotel
6. Best Western Victoria Palace
7. Jubilee Hotel
8. Cherry Court Hotel
9. EasyHotel Victoria

Eateries
10. La Bottega Deli
11. The Thomas Cubitt
12. To The Duke of Wellington
13. The Orange
14. Daylesford Deli
15. La Poule au Pot
16. Grumbles
17. Pimlico Fresh
18. Seafresh Fish Restaurant
19. The Jugged Hare
20. St. George's Tavern
21. Boisdale Restaurant

Services
22. Grocery Stores (3)
23. To Launderette
24. Hop-On Bus Tours (3)
25. Tube, Taxis, City Buses
26. Green Line Coach Terminal
27. Buses to Luton & Stansted Airports

nard's son Mark—and they still seem to enjoy their work (RS%, family rooms, 47 Belgrave Road near the corner of Charlwood Street, handy bus #24 stops out front, tel. 020/7834-5897, www. lunasimonehotel.com, stay@lunasimonehotel.com).

$$ Bakers Hotel shoehorns 12 brightly painted rooms into a seedy building, but it's conveniently located and offers modest prices and a small breakfast (RS%, cheaper rooms with shared bath, family rooms, 126 Warwick Way, tel. 020/7834-0729, www. bakershotel.co.uk, reservations@bakershotel.co.uk, Amin Jamani).

$$ New England Hotel, run by Jay and the Patel family, has very worn public spaces but well-priced rooms in a tight, old corner

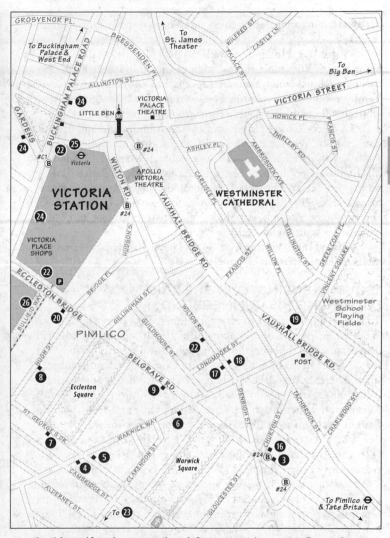

building (family rooms, breakfast is very basic, 20 Saint George's Drive, tel. 020/7834-8351, www.newenglandhotel.com, mystay@ newenglandhotel.com).

$$ Best Western Victoria Palace offers modern business-class comfort compared with some of the other creaky old hotels listed here. Choose from the 43 rooms in the main building (elevator, at 60 Warwick Way), or pay about 20 percent less by booking a nearly identical room in one of the annexes, each a half-block away—an excellent value for this neighborhood if you skip breakfast (breakfast extra, air-con, no elevator, 17 Belgrave Road and 1 Warwick Way, reception at main building, tel. 020/7821-7113, www.

bestwesternvictoriapalace.co.uk, info@bestwesternvictoriapalace.co.uk).

$$ Jubilee Hotel is a well-run but slightly shabby slumbermill with 26 simple rooms, high ceilings, and neat beds. The cheapest rooms, which share bathrooms, are just below street level (family rooms, 31 Eccleston Square, tel. 020/7834-0845, www.jubileehotel.co.uk, stay@jubileehotel.co.uk, Bob Patel).

$ Cherry Court Hotel, run by the friendly and industrious Patel family, rents 12 very small but bright and well-designed rooms with firm mattresses in a central location. Considering London's sky-high prices, this is a fine budget choice (family rooms, fruit-basket breakfast in room, air-con, laundry, 23 Hugh Street, tel. 020/7828-2840, www.cherrycourthotel.co.uk, info@cherrycourthotel.co.uk, daughter Neha answers emails and offers informed restaurant advice).

$ EasyHotel Victoria, at 34 Belgrave Road, is part of the budget chain described on page 181.

"SOUTH KENSINGTON," SHE SAID, LOOSENING HIS CUMMERBUND

To stay on a quiet street so classy it doesn't allow hotel signs, make "South Ken" your London home. The area has plenty of colorful restaurants, and shoppers like being a short walk from Harrods and the designer shops of King's Road and Chelsea. When I splurge, I splurge here. Sumner Place (where my first two listings are located) is just off Old Brompton Road, 200 yards from the handy South Kensington Tube station (on Circle Line, two stops from Victoria Station; and on Piccadilly Line, direct from Heathrow).

$$$$ Aster House, in a lovely Victorian town house, is run with care by friendly Simon and Leonie Tan, who've been welcoming my readers for years (I call it "my home in London"). It's a great value, with 13 comfy and quiet rooms, a cheerful lobby, and lounge. Enjoy breakfast or just kicking back in the whisper-elegant Orangery, a glassy greenhouse (RS%, air-con, TV, 3 Sumner Place, tel. 020/7581-5888, www.asterhouse.com, asterhouse@gmail.com).

$$$$ Number Sixteen, for well-heeled travelers, packs over-the-top class into its 41 artfully imagined rooms, plush designer-chic lounges, and tranquil garden. It's in a labyrinthine building, with boldly modern decor—perfect for an urban honeymoon (breakfast extra, elevator, 16 Sumner Place, tel. 020/7589-5232, US tel. 1-888-559-5508, www.numbersixteenhotel.co.uk, sixteen@firmdale.com).

$$$$ The Pelham Hotel, a 52-room business-class hotel with crisp service and a pricey mix of pretense and style, is genteel, with low lighting and a pleasant drawing room among the many

South Kensington Neighborhood

Accommodations
1. Aster House
2. Number Sixteen Hotel
3. The Pelham Hotel

Eateries & Other
4. Exhibition Road Food Circus

5. Moti Mahal Indian Rest.
6. Bosphorus Kebabs & Beirut Express
7. Franco Manca
8. The Anglesea Arms Pub
9. Rocca
10. Groceries (2)

perks (breakfast extra, air-con, elevator, fitness room, 15 Cromwell Place, tel. 020/7589-8288, US tel. 1-888-757-5587, www.pelhamhotel.co.uk, reservations.thepelham@starhotels.com).

NORTH OF KENSINGTON GARDENS

From the core of the tourist's London, the vast Hyde Park spreads west, eventually becoming Kensington Gardens. Three good accommodations neighborhoods line up side by side along the northern edge of the park: Bayswater (with the highest concentration of good hotels) anchors the area; it's bordered by Notting Hill to the west and Paddington to the east. This area has quick bus and Tube access to downtown and, for London, is very "homely" (Brit-speak for cozy).

Bayswater

Most of my Bayswater accommodations flank a tranquil, tidy park called Kensington Gardens Square (not to be confused with the much bigger Kensington Gardens adjacent to Hyde Park), a block west of bustling Queensway, north of Bayswater Tube station. These hotels are quiet for central London, but the area feels a bit sterile, and the hotels here tend to be impersonal. Popular with young international travelers, the Bayswater street called Queensway is a multicultural festival of commerce and eateries (see page 197).

$$$ **Vancouver Studios** offers one of the best values in this neighborhood. Its 45 modern, tastefully furnished rooms come with fully equipped kitchenettes (utensils, stove, microwave, and fridge) rather than breakfast. It's nestled between Kensington Gardens Square and Prince's Square and has its own tranquil garden patio out back (30 Prince's Square, tel. 020/7243-1270, www.vancouverstudios.co.uk, info@vancouverstudios.co.uk).

$$$ **Garden Court Hotel** is understated, with 40 simple, homey-but-tasteful rooms (family rooms, includes continental breakfast, elevator, 30 Kensington Gardens Square, tel. 020/7229-2553, www.gardencourthotel.co.uk, info@gardencourthotel.co.uk).

$$$ **Phoenix Hotel** offers spacious public spaces and 125 modern-feeling rooms. Its prices—which range from fine-value to rip-off—are determined by a greedy computer program (elevator, 1 Kensington Gardens Square, tel. 020/7229-2494, www.phoenixhotel.co.uk, reservations@phoenixhotel.co.uk).

$$$ **Princes Square Guest Accommodation** is a crisp (if impersonal) place renting 50 businesslike rooms with pleasant, modern decor. It's well located, practical, and a very good value, especially if you can score a good rate (elevator, 23 Prince's

Square, tel. 020/7229-9876, www.princessquarehotel.co.uk, info@princessquarehotel.co.uk).

$$ London House Hotel has 103 spiffy, modern, cookie-cutter rooms on Kensington Gardens Square. Its rates are great considering the quality and fine location (family rooms, breakfast extra, elevator, 81 Kensington Gardens Square, tel. 020/7243-1810, www.londonhousehotels.com, reservations@londonhousehotels.com).

$$ Kensington Gardens Hotel, with the same owners as the Phoenix Hotel, laces 17 rooms together in a tall, skinny building (breakfast extra—served at Phoenix Hotel, 9 Kensington Gardens Square, tel. 020/7243-7600, www.kensingtongardenshotel.co.uk, info@kensingtongardenshotel.co.uk).

$$ Bayswater Inn Hotel's 140 tidy, perfectly adequate rooms come with dated style, an impersonal feel, and outrageously high official rack rates. But rooms commonly go for much lower prices, making this a decent—sometimes great—budget option (family rooms, elevator, 8 Prince's Square, tel. 020/7727-8621, www.bayswaterinnhotel.com, reservations@bayswaterinnhotel.com).

Notting Hill and Nearby

The Notting Hill neighborhood, just west of Bayswater (spreading out from the northwest tip of Kensington Gardens) is famous for two things: It's the site of the colorful Portobello Road Market (see "Shopping in London," earlier) and the setting of the 1999 Hugh Grant/Julia Roberts film of the same name. While the neighborhood is now a bit more upscale and less funky than the one shown in that film, it's still a pleasant place to stay.

$$$$ Portobello Hotel is on a quiet residential street in the heart of Notting Hill. Its 21 rooms are funky yet elegant—both the style and location give it an urban-fresh feeling (elevator, 22 Stanley Gardens, tel. 020/7727-2777, www.portobellohotel.com, stay@portobellohotel.com).

Near Holland Park: English is definitely a second language at ¢ **Norwegian YWCA (Norsk K.F.U.K.)**—which is open to any Norwegian woman and to non-Norwegian women under 30. (Men must be under 30 with a Norwegian passport.) Located on a quiet, stately street, it offers a study, TV room, piano lounge, and an open-face Norwegian ambience (goat cheese on Sundays!). They have mostly quads, so those willing to share with strangers are most likely to get a bed (private rooms available, 52 Holland Park, Tube: Holland Park, tel. 020/7727-9346, www.kfukhjemmet.org.uk, kontor@kfukhjemmet.org.uk). With each visit, I wonder which is easier to get—a sex change or a Norwegian passport?

LONDON

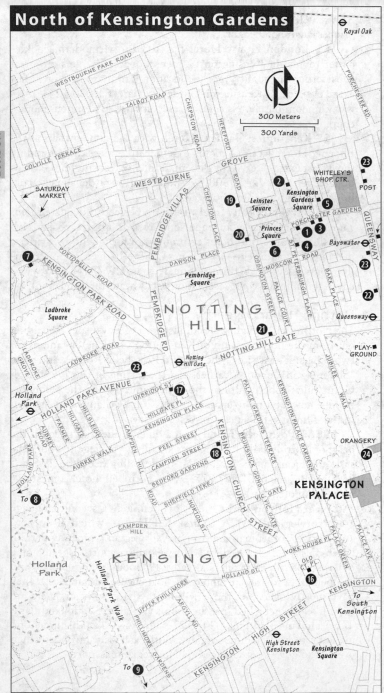

North of Kensington Gardens

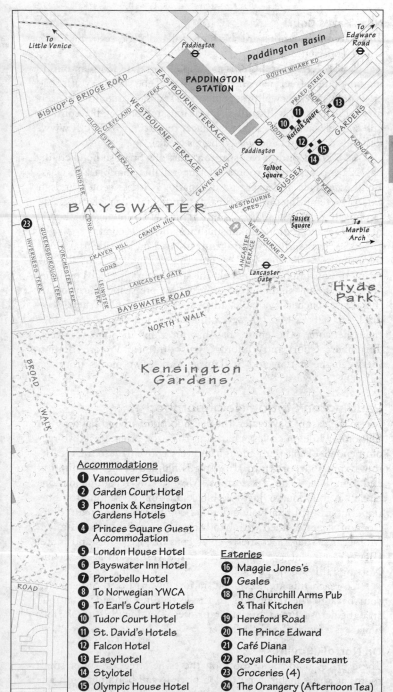

Accommodations

1. Vancouver Studios
2. Garden Court Hotel
3. Phoenix & Kensington Gardens Hotels
4. Princes Square Guest Accommodation
5. London House Hotel
6. Bayswater Inn Hotel
7. Portobello Hotel
8. To Norwegian YWCA
9. To Earl's Court Hotels
10. Tudor Court Hotel
11. St. David's Hotels
12. Falcon Hotel
13. EasyHotel
14. Stylotel
15. Olympic House Hotel

Eateries

16. Maggie Jones's
17. Geales
18. The Churchill Arms Pub & Thai Kitchen
19. Hereford Road
20. The Prince Edward
21. Café Diana
22. Royal China Restaurant
23. Groceries (4)
24. The Orangery (Afternoon Tea)

Near Earl's Court

These accommodations are south of Holland Park, near the Earl's Court Tube station.

$$$$ K+K Hotel George occupies a grand Georgian building on a quiet street near the Earl's Court Tube station. With spacious public areas, a wellness center, and standard amenities in each of its 154 rooms, it has all the makings for predictable comfort (air-con, elevator, 1 Templeton Place, tel. 020/7598-8700, www.kkhotels.com, hotel.george@kkhotels.co.uk).

$$$ NH London Kensington, part of a Spanish hotel chain, has 121 business-style rooms offering reliable comfort and class. Bonuses include a pleasant garden patio, a fitness center, and an extensive, tempting optional breakfast buffet (air-con, elevator, 202 Cromwell Road, tel. 020/7244-1441, www.nh-hotels.com/hotel/nh-london-kensington, nhkensington@nh-hotels.com).

$$$ The **Nadler Kensington,** situated on a residential block five minutes' walk from Earl's Court tube station, offers 65 self-catering rooms. High ceilings help the smallish rooms feel a bit larger, and in-room kitchenettes are great for preparing cheap meals (breakfast vouchers available, air-con, elevator, 25 Courtfield Gardens, tel. 020/7244-2255, www.thenadler.com, kensington.info@thenadler.com). The chain also has locations in Soho (between Tottenham Court and Oxford Circus) and near Victoria Station (between the station and St. James's Park—two blocks from the palace).

Paddington Station Neighborhood

Just to the east of Bayswater, the neighborhood around Paddington Station—while much less charming than the other areas I've recommended—is pleasant enough and very convenient to the Heathrow Express airport train. The area is flanked by the Paddington and Lancaster Gate Tube stops. Most of my recommendations circle Norfolk Square, just two blocks in front of Paddington Station, but are still relatively quiet and comfortable. The main drag, London Street, is lined with handy eateries—pubs, Indian, Italian, Moroccan, Greek, Lebanese—plus convenience stores and more. (Better restaurants are a short stroll to the west, near Bayswater and Notting Hill—see page 197.)

To reach this area, exit the station toward Praed Street (with your back to the tracks, it's to the left). Once outside, continue straight across Praed Street and down London Street; Norfolk Square is a block ahead on the left.

On Norfolk Square

These places (and many more on the same street) all offer small rooms at a reasonable-for-London price in tall buildings with lots of stairs and no elevator. I've chosen the ones that offer the most reasonable prices and the warmest welcome.

$$$ Tudor Court Hotel has 38 tired, tight rooms with prefab plastic bathrooms and creaky plumbing. It's run by Connan and the Gupta family (family rooms, 10 Norfolk Square, tel. 020/7723-5157, www.tudorcourtpaddington.co.uk, reservations@tudorcourtpaddington.co.uk).

$$ St. David's Hotels, run by the Neokleous family, has 60 basic but comfortable rooms in several interconnected buildings. The friendly staff members treat you like a member of the family and are happy to share their native London knowledge. Their rooms with shared bath are a workable budget option (Wi-Fi in lobby, 14 Norfolk Square, tel. 020/7723-3856, www.stdavidshotels.com, info@stdavidshotels.com).

$$ Falcon Hotel, a lesser value, has less personality and 19 simple, old-school, slightly dingy rooms (family rooms, 11 Norfolk Square, tel. 020/7723-8603, www.falcon-hotel.com, info@falcon-hotel.com).

$ EasyHotel, a budget chain described later under "Big, Good-Value, Modern Hotels," has a branch at 10 Norfolk Place.

On Sussex Gardens

To reach these hotels, follow the directions to Norfolk Square (earlier), but continue away from the station past the square to the big intersection with Sussex Gardens; you'll find them immediately to the left.

$$ Stylotel feels like the stylish, super-modern, aluminum-clad big sister of the EasyHotel chain. Their tidy 39 rooms come with hard surfaces—hardwood floors, prefab plastic bathrooms, and metallic walls. While rooms can be cramped, the beds have space for luggage underneath. You may feel like an astronaut in a retro science-fiction film, but if you don't need ye olde doilies, this place offers a good value (family rooms, elevator, 160 Sussex Gardens, tel. 020/7723-1026, www.stylotel.com, info@stylotel.com, well-run by Andreas). They have eight fancier, pricier, air-conditioned suites across the street with kitchenettes and no breakfast.

$$ Olympic House Hotel has clean public spaces and a no-nonsense welcome, but its 38 business-class rooms offer predictable comfort and fewer old-timey quirks than many hotels in this price range (air-con extra, elevator, pay Wi-Fi, 138 Sussex Gardens, tel. 020/7723-5935, www.olympichousehotel.co.uk, olympichousehotel@btinternet.com).

NORTH LONDON

$$$$ The Sumner Hotel rents 19 rooms in a 19th-century Georgian townhouse sporting large contemporary rooms and a lounge

LONDON

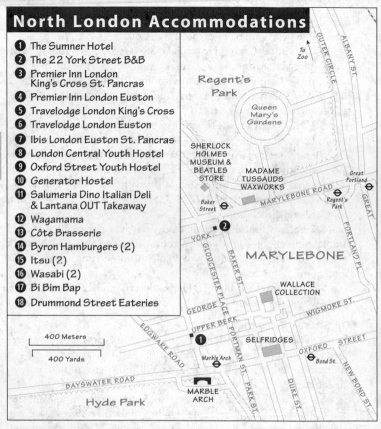

North London Accommodations

1 The Sumner Hotel
2 The 22 York Street B&B
3 Premier Inn London King's Cross St. Pancras
4 Premier Inn London Euston
5 Travelodge London King's Cross
6 Travelodge London Euston
7 Ibis London Euston St. Pancras
8 London Central Youth Hostel
9 Oxford Street Youth Hostel
10 Generator Hostel
11 Salumeria Dino Italian Deli & Lantana OUT Takeaway
12 Wagamama
13 Côte Brasserie
14 Byron Hamburgers (2)
15 Itsu (2)
16 Wasabi (2)
17 Bi Bim Bap
18 Drummond Street Eateries

400 Meters

400 Yards

with fancy modern Italian furniture. This swanky place packs in all the amenities and is conveniently located north of Hyde Park and near Oxford Street, a busy shopping destination—close to Selfridges and a Marks & Spencer (RS%, air-con, elevator, 54 Upper Berkeley Street, a block and a half off Edgware Road, Tube: Marble Arch, tel. 020/7723-2244, www.thesumner.com, reservations@thesumner.com).

$$$$ Charlotte Street Hotel has 52 rooms with a bright countryside English garden motif, and inviting public spaces in the up-and-coming Fitzrovia neighborhood close to the British Museum. Their rooms start at twice the cost of my favorite London B&Bs—but are worth considering if you want to splurge (connecting family rooms, air-con, elevator, 15 Charlotte Street, Tube: Tottenham Court Road, tel. 020/7806-2000, www.charlottestreethotel.com, reservations@charlottestreethotel.com).

$$$$ The Mandeville Hotel, at the center of the action just one block from Bond Street Tube station, has a genteel British vibe, with high ceilings, tasteful art, and just-vibrant-enough col-

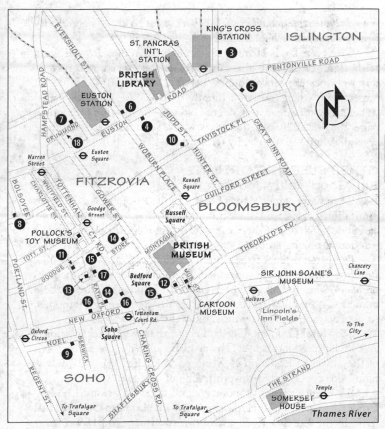

ors. It's a worthy splurge for its amenities and location, especially if you score a good deal (breakfast extra, air-con, elevator, Mandeville Place, tel. 020/7935-5599, www.mandeville.co.uk, info@mandeville.co.uk).

$$$$ The Fielding Hotel is a simple and slightly more affordable place lodged in the center of all the action—just steps from Covent Garden—on a quiet lane. They rent 25 basic rooms, serve no breakfast, and have almost no public spaces. Grace, the manager, sticks with straight pricing (family rooms, air-con, 4 Broad Court off Bow Street, Tube: Covent Garden—for location see map on page 186, tel. 020/7836-8305, www.thefieldinghotel.co.uk, reservations@thefieldinghotel.co.uk).

$$$ The 22 York Street B&B offers a casual alternative in the city center, with an inviting lounge and 10 traditional, hardwood, comfortable rooms, each named for a notable London landmark (near Marylebone/Baker Street: From Baker Street Tube station, walk 2 blocks down Baker Street and take a right to 22 York Street—no sign, just look for #22; tel. 020/7224-2990, www.22yorkstreet.co.uk,   mc@22yorkstreet.co.uk,   energetically run by Liz and Michael Callis).

$$ Seven Dials Hotel's 18 no-nonsense rooms are plain and fairly tight, but they're also clean, reasonably priced, and incredibly well located. Since doubles here all cost the same, request a larger room when you book (family rooms, 7 Monmouth Street, Tube: Leicester Square or Covent Garden—for location see map on page 186, tel. 020/240-0823, www.sevendialshotel.co.uk, info@sevendialshotel.co.uk, run by friendly and hardworking Hanna).

OTHER SLEEPING OPTIONS
Big, Good-Value, Modern Hotels

If you can score a double for £90-100 (or less—often possible with promotional rates) and don't mind a modern, impersonal, American-style hotel, one of these can be a decent value in pricey London (for details on chain hotels, see page 1029).

I've listed a few of the dominant chains, along with a quick rundown on their more convenient London locations (see the map on page 178 to find chain hotels in North London). Some of these branches sit on busy streets in dreary train-station neighborhoods, so use common sense after dark and wear a money belt.

$$ Motel One, the German chain that specializes in affordable style, has a branch at **Tower Hill,** a 10-minute walk north of the Tower of London (24 Minories, tel. 020/7481-6427, www.motel-one.com, london-towerhill@motel-one.com).

$$ Premier Inn has more than 70 hotels in greater London. Convenient locations include a branch inside **London County Hall** (next to the London Eye), at **Southwark/Borough Market** (near Shakespeare's Globe, 34 Park Street), **Southwark/Tate Modern** (Great Suffolk Street), **Kensington/Earl's Court** (11 Knaresborough Place), **Victoria** (82 Eccleston Square), and **Leicester Square** (1 Leicester Place). In North London, the following branches cluster between King's Cross St. Pancras and the British Museum: **King's Cross St. Pancras, St. Pancras, Euston,** and **Brook House.** Avoid the **Tower Bridge** location, south of the bridge and a long walk from the Tube—but **London City Tower Hill,** north of the bridge on Prescot Street, works fine (www.premierinn.com, tel. 0871-527-9222; from North America, dial 011-44-1582-567-890).

$$ Travelodge has close to 70 locations in London, including at **King's Cross** (200 yards in front of King's Cross Station, Gray's Inn Road) and **Euston** (1 Grafton Place). Other handy locations include **King's Cross Royal Scot, Marylebone, Covent Garden, Liverpool Street, Southwark,** and **Farringdon;** www.travelodge.co.uk.

$$ Ibis, the budget branch of the AccorHotels group, has a few dozen options across the city, with a handful of locations convenient to London's center, including **Euston St. Pancras** (on a quiet street a block west of Euston Station, 3 Cardington Street), **London City Shoreditch** (5 Commercial Street), and the more design-focused **Ibis Styles** branches at **Kensington** (15 Hogarth Road) and **Southwark,** with a theater theme (43 Southwark Bridge Road); www.ibishotel.com.

$ EasyHotel, with several branches in good neighborhoods, has a unique business model inspired by its parent company, the EasyJet budget airline. The generally tiny, super-efficient, no-frills rooms feel popped out of a plastic mold, down to the prefab ship's head-type "bathroom pod." Rates can be surprisingly low (with doubles as cheap as £30 if you book early enough)—but you'll pay à la carte for expensive add-ons, such as TV use, Wi-Fi, luggage storage, fresh towels, and daily cleaning (breakfast, if available, comes from a vending machine). If you go with the base rate, it's like hosteling with privacy—a hard-to-beat value. But you get what you pay for (thin walls, flimsy construction, noisy fellow guests, and so on). They're only a good deal if you book far enough ahead to get a good price and skip the many extras. Locations include **Victoria** (34 Belgrave Road—see map on page 168), **South Kensington** (14 Lexham Gardens), **Earl's Court** (44 West Cromwell Road), and **Paddington** (10 Norfolk Place); www.easyhotel.com.

Hostels

Hostels can slash accommodation costs while meeting your basic needs. The following places are open 24 hours, have private rooms as well as dorms, and come with Wi-Fi.

¢ London Central Youth Hostel is the flagship of London's hostels, with all the latest in security and comfortable efficiency. Families and travelers of any age will feel welcome in this wonderful facility. You'll pay the same price for any bed—so try to grab one with a bathroom (families welcome to book an entire room, book long in advance, between Oxford Circus and Great Portland Street Tube stations at 104 Bolsover Street—see map on page 178, tel. 0845-371-9154, www.yha.org.uk, londoncentral@yha.org.uk).

¢ Oxford Street Youth Hostel is right in the shopping and clubbing zone in Soho (14 Noel Street—see map on page 178, Tube: Oxford Street, tel. 0845-371-9133, www.yha.org.uk, oxfordst@yha.org.uk).

¢ St. Paul's Youth Hostel, near St. Paul's Cathedral, is modern, friendly, well-run, and a bit scruffy (36 Carter Lane, Tube: St. Paul's, tel. 020/7236-4965 or 0845-371-9012, www.yha.org.uk, stpauls@yha.org.uk).

¢ Generator Hostel is a brightly colored, hip hostel with a café and a DJ spinning the hits. It's in a renovated building tucked behind a busy street halfway between King's Cross and the British

Museum (37 Tavistock Place—see map on page 178, Tube: Russell Square, tel. 020/7388-7666, www.generatorhostels.com, london@generatorhostels.com).

¢ A cluster of three **St. Christopher's Inn** hostels, south of the Thames near London Bridge, have cheap dorm beds; one branch (the Oasis) is for women only. All have loud and friendly bars attached (must be over 18 years old, 161 Borough High Street, Tube: Borough or London Bridge, reservations tel. 020/8600-7500, www.st-christophers.co.uk, bookings@st-christophers.co.uk).

Apartment Rentals

Consider this option if you're traveling as a family, in a group, or staying five days or longer. Websites such as Airbnb and VRBO let you correspond directly with European property owners or managers, or consider one of the sites listed below. Some specialize in London, while others also cover areas outside of London. For more information on short-term rentals, see page 1034 in the Practicalities chapter.

LondonConnection.com is a Utah-based company that owns and rents several properties around London. The owner, Thomas, prides himself on providing personal service.

OneFineStay.com focuses on finding stylish, contemporary flats (most of them part-time residences) in desirable London neighborhoods. While pricey, it can be a good choice if you're seeking a hip, nicely decorated home away from home.

SuperCityUk.com gives travelers a taste of what local London life is like, renting chic, comfortable aparthotels and serviced apartments in three buildings.

Other options include **Cross-Pollinate.com, Coach House Rentals** (www.chsrentals.com), **APlaceLikeHome. co.uk,** HomeFromHome.co.uk, London-House.com, and GoWithIt.co.uk.

Staying near the Airports

It's so easy to get to Heathrow and Gatwick from central London, I see no reason to sleep at either one. But if you do, here are some options.

Heathrow: A **Yotel** is inside the airport (Terminal 4), while **EasyHotel** and **Hotel Ibis London Heathrow** are a short bus or taxi ride away.

Gatwick: The South Terminal has a **Yotel,** while **Gatwick Airport Central Premier Inn** rents cheap rooms 350 yards away, and **Gatwick Airport Travelodge** has budget rooms about two miles from the airport.

Eating in London

Whether it's dining well with the upper crust, sharing hearty pub fare with the blokes, or joining young professionals at the sushi bar, eating out has become an essential part of the London experience. You could try a different cuisine for each meal and never eat "local" English food, even on a lengthy stay in London. The sheer variety of foods—from every corner of Britain's former empire and beyond—is astonishing.

But the thought of a £50 meal in Britain generally ruins my appetite, so my London dining is limited mostly to easygoing, fun, moderately priced alternatives. I've listed places by neighborhood—handy to your sightseeing or hotel. Considering how expensive London can be, if there's any good place to cut corners to stretch your budget, it's by eating cheaply here. Pub grub (at one of London's 7,000 pubs) and ethnic restaurants (especially Indian and Chinese) are good low-cost options. Of course, picnicking is the fastest and cheapest way to go. Good grocery stores and sandwich shops, fine park benches, and polite pigeons abound in Britain's most expensive city.

I rank restaurants from $ budget to $$$$ splurge. For even more advice on eating in London, including information on pubs, beer, and ethnic eats, plus details on restaurant pricing, tipping, eating on a budget, English breakfasts, and afternoon tea, see page 1037.

CENTRAL LONDON

I've arranged these options by neighborhood, but they're all within about a 15-minute walk of each other. Survey your options before settling on a place. A large number of trendy chain restaurants permeate Central London. There's no need to clutter up my listings and maps with these—like Starbucks or McDonald's, you can count on seeing them wherever you go without worrying about an address. They're generally fast, good, and reasonably priced, and they range from glorified fast food to impressively classy dining experiences. The main sense you get wandering these streets: Trendy people fill trendy places and millennials with money rule the world. Weekends and later in the evenings, bars overflow as the sidewalks and even the streets become congested with people out clubbing.

If you're looking for peace and quiet and a calm meal, avoid Friday and Saturday evenings here and come early on other nights.

Soho and Nearby

London has a trendy scene that many Beefeater seekers miss. Foodies who want to eat well dine in Soho. Make it a point to experience Soho at least once to feel the pulse of London's eclectic urban melting pot of international flavors. These restaurants are scattered throughout a chic, creative, and once-seedy zone that teems with hipsters, theatergoers, and London's gay community. Even if you plan to have dinner elsewhere, it's a treat just to wander around Soho in the evening, when it's seething with young Londoners out and about.

On and near Wardour Street

$$ Princi is a vast, bright, efficient, wildly popular Italian deli/bakery with Milanese flair. Along one wall is a long counter with display cases offering a tempting array of *pizza rustica, panini* sandwiches, focaccia, pasta dishes, and desserts. Order your food at the counter, then find a space to share at a long table; or get it to go. They also have a classy restaurant section with reasonable prices if you'd rather have table service (daily 8:00-24:00, 135 Wardour Street, tel. 020/7478-8888).

$$$ The Gay Hussar, dressy and tight, squeezes several elegant tables into what the owners say is the only Hungarian restaurant in England. It's traditional Hungarian fare: cabbage, sauerkraut, sausage, paprika, and pork, as well as duck and chicken and, of course, Hungarian wine (Mon-Sat 12:15-14:30 & 17:30-22:45, closed Sun, 2 Greek Street, tel. 020/7437-0973).

$$$ Bocca di Lupo, a stylish and popular option, serves half and full portions of classic regional Italian food. Dressy but with a fun energy, it's a place where you're glad you made a reservation. The counter seating, on cushy stools with a view into the lively open kitchen, is particularly memorable, or you can take a table in the snug, casual back end (daily 12:30-15:00 & 17:15-23:00, 12 Archer Street, tel. 020/7734-2223, www.boccadilupo.com).

$$ Yalla Yalla is a bohemian-chic hole-in-the-wall serving up high-quality Beirut street food—hummus, baba ghanoush, tabbouleh, and *shawarmas*. It's tucked down a seedy alley across from a sex shop. Eat in the cramped and cozy interior or at one of the few outdoor tables (£4 sandwiches and *meze*, £8 *mezes* platter available until 17:00, daily 10:00-24:00, 1 Green's Court—just north of Brewer Street, tel. 020/7287-7663).

Gelato: Across the street from Bocca di Lupo (see earlier) is its sister *gelateria,* **Gelupo,** with a wide array of ever-changing but always creative and delicious dessert favorites. Take away or enjoy their homey interior (daily 11:00-23:00, 7 Archer Street, tel. 020/7287-5555).

Cheap Eats near Carnaby Street

The area south of Oxford Circus between Regent Street and Soho Gardens entices hungry shoppers with attention-grabbing, gimmicky restaurants that fill the niche between chains and upscale eateries. Stroll along Ganton, Carnaby, or Great Marlborough streets for something that fits your budget and appetite, or try one of these restaurants, all within a five-minute walk of each other.

$$ Mother Mash is a bangers-and-mash version of a fish-and-chips shop. For £10, choose your mash, meat, and gravy and enjoy this simple, satisfying, and thoroughly British meal (daily 10:00-22:00, 26 Ganton Street, tel. 020/7494-9644).

$ Potato Project features imaginative fillings that turn baked "jacket" potatoes into gourmet creations (Mon-Fri 10:00-18:00, closed Sat-Sun, 27 Noel Street, tel. 020/3620-1585).

Next door, **$ Melt Room** crafts anything-but-Kraft grilled cheese masterpieces—including a bacon-cheese doughnut (Mon-Fri 8:00-20:00, Sat-Sun 11:00-18:00, 26 Noel Street, tel. 020/7096-2002).

Lexington Street, in the Heart of Soho

$$$ Andrew Edmunds Restaurant is a tiny candlelit space where you'll want to hide your camera and guidebook and not act like a tourist. This little place—with a jealous and loyal clientele—is the closest I've found to Parisian quality in a cozy restaurant in London. The extensive wine list, modern European cooking, and creative seasonal menu are worth the splurge (daily 12:30-15:30 & 17:30-22:45, these are last-order times, come early or call ahead, request ground floor rather than basement, 46 Lexington Street, tel. 020/7437-5708, www.andrewedmunds.com).

$$ Mildred's Vegetarian Restaurant, across from Andrew Edmunds, has a creative, fun menu and a tight, high-energy interior filled with happy herbivores (Mon-Sat 12:00-23:00, closed Sun, vegan options, 45 Lexington Street, tel. 020/7494-1634).

$$$ Bao is a tight, minimalist eatery selling top-quality Taiwanese cuisine, specializing in delicate and delectable steamed-bun sandwiches. This is a foodie fave with a steady line across the street (they take no reservations, so try to arrive early or late). While it's pricey (portions are small), it's a great experience and worth the splurge (Mon-Sat 12:00-15:00 & 17:30-22:00, closed Sun, 53 Lexington Street).

$$ Fernandez & Wells is a cozy, convivial, delightfully simple little wine, cheese, and ham bar. Grab a stool as you belly up to the big wooden bar. Share a plate of tapas, top-quality cheeses, and/or Spanish, Italian, or French hams with fine bread and oil, all while sipping a nice glass of wine (Mon-Sat 11:00-23:00, Sun

LONDON

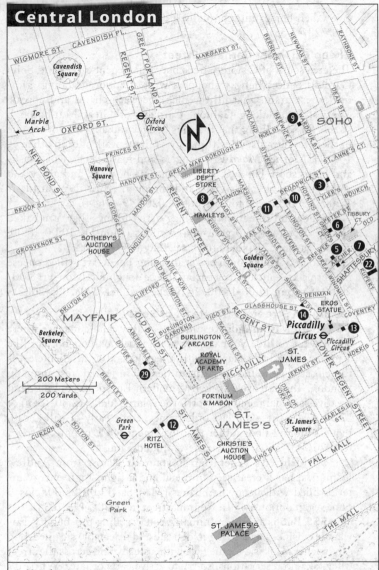

Central London

Hotels

❶ The Fielding Hotel
❷ Seven Dials Hotel

Eateries

❸ Princi Italian Deli
❹ The Gay Hussar
❺ Bocca di Lupo
❻ Yalla Yalla

❼ Gelupo Gelato
❽ Mother Mash
❾ Potato Project & Melt Room
❿ Andrew Edmunds Restaurant
⓫ Mildred's Vegetarian Rest.;
   Bao; Fernandez & Wells
⓬ The Wolseley
⓭ The Savini at the Criterion
⓮ Brasserie Zédel

LONDON

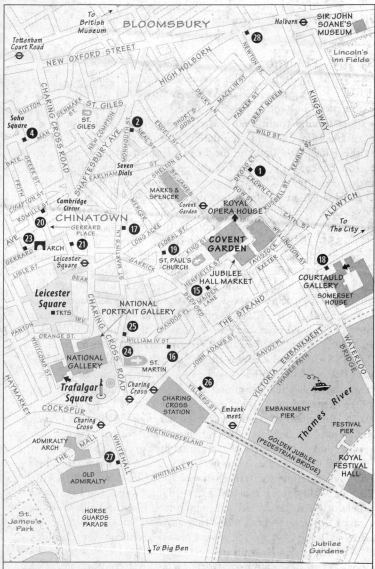

⑮ Rules Restaurant	㉓ Dumplings' Legend
⑯ Terroirs Wine Bar	㉔ St. Martin-in-the-Fields Café in the Crypt
⑰ Dishoom	㉕ The Chandos Pub
⑱ Shapur Indian Restaurant	㉖ Gordon's Wine Bar
⑲ Lamb & Flag Pub	㉗ The Lord Moon of the Mall
⑳ Y Ming Chinese Restaurant	㉘ The Princess Louise
㉑ Jen Café	㉙ Brown's Hotel Tea Room
㉒ Wong Kei	

until 18:00, quality sandwiches at lunch, 43 Lexington Street, tel. 020/7734-1546).

Swanky Splurges

$$$$ **The Wolseley** is the grand 1920s showroom of a long-defunct British car. The last Wolseley drove out with the Great Depression, but today this old-time bistro bustles with formal waiters serving traditional Austrian and French dishes in an elegant black-marble-and-chandeliers setting fit for its location next to the Ritz. Although the food can be unexceptional, prices are reasonable considering the grand presentation and setting. Reservations are a must (cheaper soup, salad, and sandwich "café menu" available in all areas of restaurant, daily 7:00-24:00, 160 Piccadilly, tel. 020/7499-6996, www.thewolseley.com). They're popular for their fancy cream tea or afternoon tea (for details, see page 202).

$$$$ **The Savini at the Criterion** is a palatial dining hall offering an Italian menu in a dreamy neo-Byzantine setting from the 1870s. It's right on Piccadilly Circus but a world away from the punk junk, with fairly normal food served in an unforgettable Great Gatsby space. It's a deal for the visual experience during lunch or early (before 19:00) or late (after 22:00)—and if you order the £29-36 fixed-price meal or £16 cream tea (daily 12:00-23:30, 224 Piccadilly, tel. 020/7930-1459, www.saviniatcriterion.co.uk).

$$$ **Brasserie Zédel** is the former dining hall of the old Regent Palace Hotel, which was the biggest hotel in the world when it was built in 1915. Climbing down the stairs from street level, you're surprised by a gilded grand hall that feels like a circa-1920 cruise ship, filled with a boisterous crowd enjoying big, rich French food—old-fashioned brasserie dishes. With vested waiters, fast service, and paper tablecloths, it's great for a group of friends. After 21:30 the lights dim, the candles are lit, and it gets more romantic with live jazz (nightly inexpensive *plats du jour*, daily 11:30-23:00, 20 Sherwood Street, tel. 020/7734-4888). Across the hall is the hotel's original Bar Américain (which feels like the 1930s) and the Crazy Coqs venue—busy with "Live at Zédel" music, theater, comedy, and literary events (see www.brasseriezedel.com for schedule).

$$$$ **Rules Restaurant,** established in 1798, is as traditional as can be—extremely British, classy yet comfortable. It's a big, borderline-stuffy place, where you'll eat in a plush Edwardian atmosphere with formal service and plenty of game on the menu. (A warning reads, "Game birds may contain lead shot.") This is the place to dress up and splurge for classic English dishes (daily 12:00-23:00, between the Strand and Covent Garden at 34 Maiden Lane, tel. 020/7836-5314, www.rules.co.uk).

Near Covent Garden

Covent Garden bustles with people and touristy eateries. The area feels overrun, but if you must eat around here, you have some good choices.

$$$ Terroirs Wine Bar is an enticing place with a casual but classy ambience that exudes happiness. It's a few steps below street level, with a long zinc bar that has a kitchen view and two levels of tables. The fun menu is mostly Mediterranean and designed to share. The meat and cheese plates complement the fine wines available by the glass (Mon-Sat 12:00-15:00 & 17:30-23:00, closed Sun, reservations smart, just two blocks from Trafalgar Square but tucked away from the tourist crowds at 5 William IV Street, tel. 020/7036-0660, www.terroirswinebar.com).

$$$ Dishoom is London's hotspot for upscale Indian cuisine, with top-quality ingredients and carefully executed recipes. The dishes seem familiar, but the flavors are a revelation. People line up early (starting around 17:30) for a seat, either on the bright, rollicking, brasserie-like ground floor or in the less appealing basement. Reservations are possible only until 17:45 (daily 8:00-23:00, 12 Upper St. Martin's Lane, tel. 020/7420-9320). They also have locations near King's Cross Station, Carnaby Street, and in Shoreditch.

$$$ Shapur Indian Restaurant is a well-respected place serving classic Indian dishes from many regions, fine fish, and a tasty £19 vegetarian *thali* (combo platter). It's small, low energy, and dressy with good service (Mon-Fri 12:00-14:30 & 17:30-23:30, Sat 15:00-23:30, closed Sun, next to Somerset House at 149 Strand, tel. 020/7836-3730, Syed Khan).

$$ Lamb and Flag Pub is a survivor—a spit-and-sawdust pub serving traditional grub (like meat pies) two blocks off Covent Garden, yet seemingly a world away. Here since 1772, this pub was a favorite of Charles Dickens and is now a hit with local workers. At lunch, it's all food. In the evening, the ground floor is for drinking and the food service is upstairs (long hours daily, 33 Rose Street, across from Stanfords bookstore entrance on Floral Street, tel. 020/7497-9504).

Chinatown and Good Chinese Nearby

The main drag of Chinatown (Gerrard Street, with the ornamental archways) is lined with touristy, interchangeable Chinese joints—but these places seem to have an edge.

$$ Y Ming Chinese Restaurant—across Shaftesbury Avenue from the ornate gates, clatter, and dim sum of Chinatown—has dressy, porcelain-blue European decor, serious but helpful service, and authentic Northern Chinese cooking. London's food critics consider this well worth the short walk from the heart of Chinatown for food that's a notch above (good £15 meal deal offer

12:00-18:00, open Mon-Sat 12:00-23:30, closed Sun, 35 Greek Street, tel. 020/7734-2721, run for 22 years by William).

$ **Jen Café,** across the little square called Newport Place, is a humble Chinese corner eatery much loved for its homemade dumplings. It's just stools and simple seating, with fast service, a fun and inexpensive menu, and a devoted following (Mon-Wed 11:00-20:30, Thu-Sun until 21:30, cash only, 4 Newport Place, tel. 020/7287-9708).

$$ **Wong Kei** Chinese restaurant, at the Wardour Street (west) end of the Chinatown drag, offers a bewildering variety of dishes served by notoriously brusque waiters in a setting that feels like a hospital cafeteria. Londoners put up with the abuse and lack of ambience to enjoy one of the satisfying BBQ rice dishes or hot pots. Individuals and couples are usually seated at communal tables, while larger parties are briskly shuffled up or down stairs (£10-15 chef special combos, daily 11:30-23:30, cash only, 41 Wardour Street, tel. 020/7437-8408).

$$$ **Dumplings' Legend** is a cut above Wong Kei if you'd like to spend a bit more. They serve a standard Chinese menu with full dim sum only until 18:00 (open daily for lunch and dinner, no reservations, on pedestrian main drag, 15 Gerrard Street, tel. 020/7494-1200).

Pubs and Crypts near Trafalgar Square

These places, all of which provide a more "jolly olde" experience than high cuisine, are within about 100 yards of Trafalgar Square.

$$ **St. Martin-in-the-Fields Café in the Crypt** is just right for a tasty meal on a monk's budget—maybe even on a monk's tomb. You'll dine sitting on somebody's gravestone in an ancient crypt. Their enticing buffet line is kept stocked all day, serving breakfast, lunch, and dinner (hearty traditional desserts, free jugs of water). They also serve a restful £10 afternoon tea (daily 12:00-18:00). You'll find the café directly under St. Martin-in-the-Fields, facing Trafalgar Square—enter through the glass pavilion next to the church (generally about 8:00-20:00 daily, profits go to the church, Tube: Charing Cross, tel. 020/7766-1158). On Wednesday evenings you can dine to the music of a live jazz band at 20:00 (£8-15 tickets). While here, check out the concert schedule for the busy church upstairs (or visit www.stmartin-in-the-fields.org).

$$ **The Chandos Pub's Opera Room** floats amazingly apart from the tacky crush of tourism around Trafalgar Square. Look for it opposite the National Portrait Gallery (corner of William IV Street and St. Martin's Lane) and climb the stairs—to the left or right of the pub entrance—to the Opera Room. This is a fine Trafalgar rendezvous point and wonderfully local pub. They serve sandwiches and a better-than-average range of traditional pub

meals for £10—meat pies and ~~~~~~~~~~d-chips are their specialty.
The ground-floor pub is stuffed ~~~~~lars and offers snugs (private booths) and more serious be~~~~~ing. To eat on that level,
you have to order upstairs and car~~~~~wn (kitchen open daily
11:30-21:00, Fri until 18:00, order a~~~~~at the bar, 29 St. Martin's Lane, Tube: Leicester Square, te~~~7836-1401).

$$ Gordon's Wine Bar is a candl~~~~~h-century wine cellar
filled with dusty old bottles, faded Briti~~~~~norabilia, and nine-
to-fivers. At the "English rustic" buffet, c~~~~~a hot meal or cold
meat dish with a salad (figure around £1~~~~); the £12 cheese
plate comes with two big hunks of cheese (fr~~~~our choice of 20),
bread, and a pickle. Then step up to the wine~~~~nd consider the
many varieties of wine and port available by t~~~~loss (this place
is passionate about port—even the house port~~~~xcellent). The
low carbon-crusted vaulting deeper in the back se~~~~; to intensify
the Hogarth-painting atmosphere. Although it's c~~~~ded—often
downright packed—you can normally corral two ch~~~s and grab
the corner of a shared table. When sunny, the crowd sp~~~s out onto
the tight parkside patio, where a chef often cooks at a BBQ grill for
a long line of happy customers (daily 11:00-23:00, 2 blocks from
Trafalgar Square, bottom of Villiers Street at #47—the door is
locked but it's just around the corner to the right, Tube Embank-
ment, tel. 020/7930-1408, manager Gerard Menan).

$ The Lord Moon of the Mall Pub is a sloppy old eating
pub, actually filling a former bank, right at the top of Whitehall.
While nothing extraordinary, it's a very handy location and cranks
out cheap, simple pub grub and fish-and-chips all day (long hours
daily, 16 Whitehall, Tube: Charing Cross, tel. 020/7839-7701).

Near the British Museum

To avoid the touristy crush right around the museum, head a few
blocks west to the Fitzrovia area. Here, tiny Charlotte Place is lined
with small eateries (including the first two listed next); nearby, th~
much bigger Charlotte Street has several more good options. T~
higher street signs you'll notice on Charlotte Street are a hold~
from a time when they needed to be visible to carriage drivers~
area is a short walk from the Goodge Street Tube station—
nient to the British Museum. See the map on page 178 ~
tions.

$ Salumeria Dino serves up hearty £5 sandwiches~
Italian coffee. Dino, a native of Naples, has run his l~
more than 30 years and has managed to create a class~
ian deli (cheap takeaway cappuccinos, Mon-Fri 9:0~
Sat-Sun, 15 Charlotte Place, tel. 020/7580-3938)~

$ Lantana OUT, next door to Salumeria ~
lian coffee shop that sells modern soups, sand~

LONDON

...ppreciation

...e people's Britain, where all manner of
The pub is the hea...ns, found their respite from work and a
folks have, for ge... While pubs have been around for cen-
home away from...eally came alive in the late Victorian era
turies, the pub s... g this period, pubs were independently
(c. 1880-1905)....es were high enough to make it worthwhile
owned and lan...hem up. The politics were pro-pub as well:
to invest in fi...cked by Big Beer, were in, and temperance-
Conservative...vere out. For more on Britain's pub hub culture,
minded Libe...
see page 7....ing historic pubs are worth seeking out during
The f...London:
your trave...place to see the very oldest-style tavern in the
The ...tradition" is at
"domest...

$$ Ye ...e Cheshire Cheese,
which ...as rebuilt in 1667
(after ...e Great Fire) from
a 16t...century tavern (pub
grub,...pricier meals in the res-
taurant, open daily, 145 Fleet
Street, Tube: Blackfriars, tel.
020/735-6170). Imagine this
mazelike place, with three sep-
arate bars, in the pre-Victorian
era: With no bar, drinkers gath-

ered around the fireplaces, while tap boys shuttled tankards up
from the cellar. (This was long before barroom taps were con-
nected to casks in the cellar. Oh, and don't say "keg"—that's a
gassy modern thing.)

Late-Victorian pubs are more common, such as the lovingly
restored **$$ Princess Louise,** dating from 1897 (daily midday until
23:00, lunch and dinner served Mon-Sat 12:00-21:00 in less atmo-

spheric upstairs lounge, no food Sun,
208 High Holborn, see map on page
187, Tube: Holborn, tel. 020/7405-
8816). These places are fancy, often
with heavily embossed wallpaper
ceilings, decorative tile work, fine-
etched glass, ornate carved stillions
(the big central hutch for storing
bottles and glass), and even urinals
equipped with a place to set your
glass.

London's best Art Nouveau pub
is **$$ The Black Friar** (c. 1900-1915),
with fine carved capitals, lamp hold-
ers, and quirky phrases worked into
the decor (daily until 23:00, food

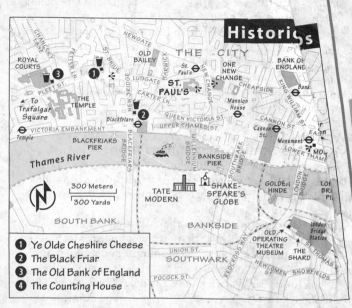

Historic ...s

THE CITY

ROYAL COURTS

NEWGATE

OLD BAILEY

FETTER ST.

ST BRIDE

St. Paul's

ONE NEW CHANGE

BANK OF ENGLAND

LUDGATE

WARWICK

NEW BRIDGE ST.

CARTER LN.

ST. PAUL'S

CHEAPSIDE

Bank

KING WILLIAM ST.

FLEET ST.

To Trafalgar Square

THE TEMPLE

Mansion House

CANNON ST.

Cannon St.

VICTORIA EMBANKMENT

Blackfriars

QUEEN VICTORIA ST.

UPPER THAMES ST.

Monument

LOWER THAMES

EA...

MO...

Temple

BLACKFRIARS PIER

BLACKFRIARS BRIDGE

Thames River

MILLENNIUM BRIDGE

BANKSIDE PIER

SOUTHWARK BRIDGE

GOLDEN HINDE

LONDON BRIDGE

LO... BR... PI...

300 Meters

300 Yards

TATE MODERN

SHAKE-SPEARE'S GLOBE

SOUTH BANK

BANKSIDE

London Bridge Station

UNION ST.

SOUTHWARK

REDCROSS WAY

OLD OPERATING THEATRE MUSEUM

THE SHARD

ST. THOMAS ST.

POCOCK ST.

NEWCOMEN ST.

SNOWFIELDS

❶ Ye Olde Cheshire Cheese
❷ The Black Friar
❸ The Old Bank of England
❹ The Counting House

served until 22:00, outdoor seating, 174 Queen Victoria Street, Tube: Blackfriars, tel. 020/7236-5474).

These days, former banks are being repurposed as trendy, lavish pubs. Three such places are **$$$ The Old Bank of England** (Mon-Fri 11:00-23:00, food served until 21:00, Sat 12:00-18:00, closed Sun, 194 Fleet Street, Tube: Temple, tel. 020/7430-2255),

$$ The Jugged Hare (open daily, 172 Vauxhall Bridge Road—see map on page 168, Tube: Victoria, tel. 020/7614-0134, also see listing on page 195), and **$$ The Counting House,** with great sandwiches, homemade meat pies, fish, and fresh vegetables (ope... Mon-Fri 11:00-23:00, foo... served until 22:00, clo... Sat-Sun; gets really busy ... the buttoned-down crowd after 12:15, especially Thu-Fri; 50 Cornhill, Tube: B... 020/7283-7123).

At night, pubs are convivial watering-holes. To ... the calmer side of pub tradition, drop by in late mo... 11:00), when the pub is empty and filled with mem... tails on beer and pub food, see the Practicalities ch...

their takeaw... ow (£8 daily hot dish). **Lantana IN** is an adjacent sit-dov... hat serves pricier meals (both open long hours daily, 13 C... Place, tel. 020/7637-3347).

$$ In...od near the British Library: Drummond Street (running i... t of Euston Station) is famous for cheap and good Indian ve... n food. For a good, moderately priced *thali* (combo platter) c... **Chutneys** (124 Drummond, tel. 020/7388-0604) and **Rav...nkar** (135 Drummond, tel. 020/7388-6458, both open lor... rs daily).

WEST...NDON
Near...toria Station Accommodations

These ...aurants are within a few blocks of Victoria Station—and all are...ces where I've enjoyed eating. As with the accommodations... his area, I've grouped them by location: east or west of the statio...see the map on page 168).

...heap Eats: For groceries, try the following places (all open long... ours daily). Inside Victoria Station you'll find an **M&S Simply Fo**d (near the front, by the bus terminus) and a **Sainsbury's Local**(at rear entrance, on Eccleston Street). A larger Sainsbury's is on Wilton Road near Warwick Way, a couple of blocks southeast of the station (closes early on Sun). A string of good ethnic restaurants lines Wilton Road. For affordable if forgettable meals, try the row of cheap little eateries on Elizabeth Street.

West of Victoria Station (Belgravia)

$ La Bottega is an Italian delicatessen that fits its upscale Belgravia neighborhood. It offers tasty, freshly cooked pastas, lasagnas, and salads, great sandwiches, and a good coffee bar with Italian pastries. It's fast (order at the counter). Grab your meal to go, or enjoy the Belgravia good life with locals, either sitting inside or at a sidewalk table (Mon-Fri 8:00-19:00, Sat-Sun 9:00-18:00, on corner of Ebury and Eccleston Streets, tel. 020/7730-2730).

$$$ The Thomas Cubitt, named for the urban planner who ...signed much of Belgravia, is a trendy neighborhood gastropub ...ked with young professionals. It's pricey, a pinch pretentious, ...popular for its modern English cooking. With a bright but ... cramped interior and fine sidewalk seating, it's great for a ... meal. Upstairs is a more refined and expensive restaurant ...ame kitchen (food served daily 12:00-22:00, reservations ...ded, 44 Elizabeth Street, tel. 020/7730-6060, www. ...bitt.co.uk).

...Duke of Wellington pub is a classic neighborhood ...ttable grub, sidewalk seating, and an inviting in-...e lowbrow than my other Belgravia listings, this ...shot at meeting a local (food served Mon-Sat

12:00-15:00 & 18:00-21:00, Sun lunch only, 63 Eaton Terrace, tel. 020/7730-1782).

South End of Ebury Street: A five-minute walk down Ebury Street, where it intersects with Pimlico Road, you'll find a pretty square with a few more eateries to consider—including **$$$ The Orange,** a high-priced gastropub with the same owners and a similar menu to The Thomas Cubitt (described earlier); **$ Daylesford,** the deli and café of an organic farm (light meals to go—a good picnic option); and **$$$$ La Poule au Pot,** serving classic French dishes (daily 12:00-23:00, reservations smart, 231 Ebury Street, tel. 020/7730-7763, www.pouleaupot.co.uk).

East of Victoria Station (Pimlico)

$$$ Grumbles brags it's been serving "good food and wine at non-scary prices since 1964." Offering a delicious mix of "modern eclectic French and traditional English," this unpretentious little place with cozy booths inside (on two levels) and a few nice sidewalk tables is the best spot to eat well in this otherwise workaday neighborhood. Their traditional dishes are their forte (early-bird specials, open daily 12:00-14:30 & 18:00-23:00, reservations wise, half a block north of Belgrave Road at 35 Churton Street, tel. 020/7834-0149, www.grumblesrestaurant.co.uk).

$$ Pimlico Fresh's breakfasts and lunches feature fresh, organic ingredients, served up with good coffee and/or fresh-squeezed juices. Choose from the dishes listed on the wall-sized chalkboard that lines the small eating area, then order at the counter. This place is heaven if you need a break from your hotel's bacon-eggs-beans routine (takeout lunches, plenty of vegetarian options; Mon-Fri 7:30-18:30, breakfast served until 15:00; Sat-Sun 9:00-18:00; 86 Wilton Road, tel. 020/7932-0030).

$$ Seafresh Fish Restaurant is the neighborhood place for plaice—and classic and creative fish-and-chips cuisine. You can either take out on the cheap or eat in, enjoying a white-fish ambience. Though Mario's father started this place in 1965, it feels like the chippy of the 21st century (Mon-Sat 12:00-15:00 & 17:00-22:30, closed Sun, 80 Wilton Road, tel. 020/7828-0747).

$$ The Jugged Hare, a 10-minute walk from Victoria Station, fills a lavish old bank building, with vaults replaced by kegs of beer and a kitchen. They have a traditional menu and a plush, vivid pub scene good for a meal or just a drink (food served Mon-F 11:00-21:00, Sat-Sun until 20:00, 172 Vauxhall Bridge Road, 020/7828-1543).

$$ St. George's Tavern is the neighborhood's best pub full meal. They serve dinner from the same menu in three on the sidewalk to catch the sun and enjoy some people-wa in the ground-floor pub, and in a classier downstairs dini with full table service. The scene is inviting for just a beer, too (food served daily 12:00-22:00, corner of Hugh Street and Belgrave Road, tel. 020/7630-1116).

South Kensington

These places are close to several recommended hotels and just a couple of blocks from the Victoria and Albert Museum and Natural History Museum (Tube: South Kensington; for locations see map on page 171).

$$ Exhibition Road Food Circus, a one-block-long road (on the Victoria and Albert Museum side of the South Kensington Tube station), is a traffic-free pedestrian zone lined with enticing little eateries, including **Fernandez and Wells** (if you want wine, fine meats, and cheese), **Thai Square** (for good Thai), **Comptoir Libanais** (a Lebanese canteen), **Casa Brindisa** (for tapas and shared Mediterranean-style dishes), **Le Pain Quotidien** (hearty soups and sandwiches on homemade rustic bread), **Daquise** (a venerable Polish restaurant much loved by the local Polish community—and the only non-chain mentioned here; at 20 Thurloe Street), and much more.

$$$ Moti Mahal Indian Restaurant, with minimalist-yet-upscale ambience and attentive service, serves delicious, mostly Bangladeshi cuisine. Consider chicken *jalfrezi* if you like spicy food, and buttery chicken if you don't (daily 12:00-14:30 & 17:30-23:30, 3 Glendower Place, tel. 020/7584-8428).

$ Bosphorus Kebabs is the student favorite for a quick, fast, and hearty Turkish dinner served with a friendly smile. While mostly for takeaway, they have a few tight tables indoors and on the sidewalk (daily 10:30-24:00, 59 Old Brompton Road, tel. 020/7584-4048).

$ Beirut Express has fresh, well-prepared Lebanese cuisine. In the front, you'll find takeaway service as well as barstools for a quick bite. In the back is a pricier sit-down restaurant (daily 12:00-24:00, 65 Old Brompton Road, tel. 020/7591-0123).

$ Franco Manca, a taverna-inspired pizzeria, is part of a chain serving Neapolitan-style pies using organic ingredients and boasting typical Italian charm. If you skip the pricey drinks you can feast very cheaply here (daily 11:30-23:00, 91 Old Brompton Road, tel. 020/7584-9713).

$$$ The Anglesea Arms, with a great terrace buried in a busy South Kensington residential area, is a destination pub that feels like the classic neighborhood favorite. It's a thriving and happy place with a woody ambience. While the food is the main draw, it's also a fine place to just have a beer. Don't let the crowds here scare you off. Behind all the drinkers, in back, is an elegant, mellow sit-down dining room a world away from any tourism (meals served daily 12:00-15:00 & 18:00-22:00; heading west from Old Brompton Road, turn left at Onslow Gardens and go down a few blocks to 15 Selwood Terrace; tel. 020/7373-7960).

$$ Rocca is a bright and dressy Italian place with a heated terrace (daily 11:30-23:30, 73 Old Brompton Road, tel. 020/7225-3413).

Supermarkets: Tesco Express (50 Old Brompton Road) and **Little Waitrose** (99 Old Brompton Road) are both open long hours daily.

Near Bayswater and Notting Hill Accommodations

For locations, see the map on page 174.

$$$$ Maggie Jones's has been feeding locals for more than 50 years. Its countryside antique decor and candlelight make a visit a step back in time. It's a longer walk than most of my recommendations, but you'll get solid English cuisine. The portions are huge (especially the meat-and-fish pies, their specialty), and prices are a bargain at lunch. You're welcome to split your main course. The candlelit upstairs is the most romantic, while the basement is kept lively with the kitchen, tight seating, and lots of action. The staff is young and slightly aloof (daily 12:00-14:00 & 18:00-22:30, reservations recommended, 6 Old Court Place, east of Kensington Church Street, near High Street Kensington Tube stop, tel. 020/7937-6462, www.maggie-jones.co.uk).

$$$ Geales, which opened its doors in 1939 as a fish-and-chips shop, has been serving Notting Hill ever since. Today, while the menu is more varied, the emphasis is still on fish. The interior is casual, but the food is upscale. The crispy battered cod that put them on the map is still the best around (£10 two-course express lunch menu; Tue-Sun 12:00-15:00 & 18:00-22:00, closed Mon, reservations smart, 2 Farmer Street, just south of Notting Hill Gate Tube stop, tel. 020/7727-7528, www.geales.com).

$$ The Churchill Arms Pub and Thai Kitchen is a comb establishment that's a hit in the neighborhood. It offers good b and a thriving old-English ambience in front and hearty £9 plates in an enclosed patio in the back. You can eat the Th in the tropical hideaway (table service) or in the atmosph section (order at the counter). The place is festooned with memorabilia and chamber pots (including one with Hi it—hanging from the ceiling farthest from Thai Kit cure the constipation of any Brit during World W 18:00 or after 21:00 to avoid a line (food served 119 Kensington Church Street, tel. 020/772 or 020/7792-1246 for restaurant, www.chur co.uk).

$$$ Hereford Road is a cozy, mod eatery tucked away on Leinster Square. It's stylish but not pretentious, serving heavy, meaty English cuisine made with modern panache. Cozy two-person booths face the open kitchen up top; the main dining room is down below. There are also a few sidewalk tables (daily 12:00-15:00 & 18:00-22:00, reservations smart, 3 Hereford Road, tel. 020/7727-1144, www.herefordroad.org).

$$ The Prince Edward serves good grub in a comfy, family-friendly, upscale-pub setting and at its sidewalk tables (daily 10:30-22:30, 2 blocks north of Bayswater Road at the corner of Dawson Place and Hereford Road, 73 Prince's Square, tel. 020/7727-2221).

$ Café Diana is a healthy little eatery serving sandwiches, salads, and Middle Eastern food. It's decorated—almost shrine-like—with photos of Princess Diana, who used to drop by for pita sandwiches. You can dine in the simple interior, or order to-go (daily 8:00-23:00, cash only, 5 Wellington Terrace, on Bayswater Road, opposite Kensington Palace Garden gates, where Di once lived, tel. 020/7792-9606, Abdul).

On Queensway: The road called Queensway is a multiethnic food circus, lined with lively and inexpensive eateries—browse the options along here and choose your favorite. For a cut above, head for **$$$ Royal China Restaurant**—filled with London's Chinese, who consider this one of the city's best eateries. It's dressed up in black, white, and gold, with candles and brisk waiters. While it's pricier than most neighborhood Chinese restaurants, the food is noticeably better (£9-10 dim sum menu served until 17:00, £25-40 special dishes, daily 12:00-23:00, 13 Queensway, tel. 020/7221-2535).

Supermarkets: Tesco is a half-block from the Notting Hill Gate Tube stop (near intersection with Pembridge Road at 114 Notting Hill Gate). Queensway is home to several supermarkets, including **Sainsbury's Local** and **Tesco Express** (both next to Bayswater Tube stop; a larger **Tesco** is near the post office farther along Queensway), and **Marks & Spencer** (inside Whiteleys Shopping Centre). All open early and close late (except on Sun).

LONDON

heritage of welcoming immigrants, it's no surprise that East End is its up-and-coming foodie mecca. Lively restaurants, trucks, and "pop-ups" come here to get a toehold in culinary scene. When in-the-know young locals for East London—especially trendy Shoreditch. area is what Soho was 40 years ago (before ation): a bit raw, unapologetically edgy, and sights, sounds, and flavors. I've focused on

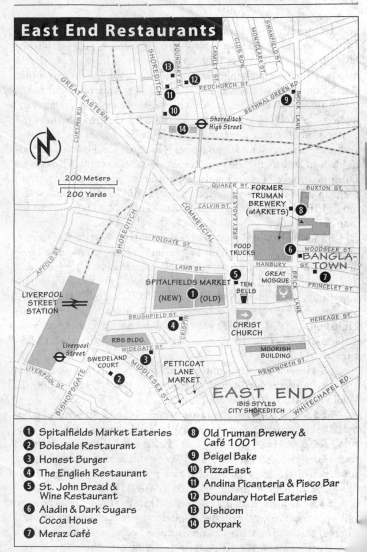

East End Restaurants

1 Spitalfields Market Eateries
2 Boisdale Restaurant
3 Honest Burger
4 The English Restaurant
5 St. John Bread & Wine Restaurant
6 Aladin & Dark Sugars Cocoa House
7 Meraz Café
8 Old Truman Brewery & Café 1001
9 Beigel Bake
10 PizzaEast
11 Andina Picanteria & Pisco Bar
12 Boundary Hotel Eateries
13 Dishoom
14 Boxpark

three areas: around Liverpool Street Station and Spitalfields Market; along Brick Lane; and near the Shoreditch High Street station. For tips on street markets in this area, see page 155

Near Liverpool Street Station and Spitalfields Market

Outside the station and around the market, you'll find able chains. For something more interesting, check Market and the surrounding streets.

In Spitalfields Market: This cavernous market hall is a festival of tempting eateries—some chains, others well-established favorites, and still others that sign a "pop-up" lease of just a few months. The lineup changes constantly, but look for these options: At the north end of the old market are **$$ Androuet** (takeaway toasted cheese baguettes, sit-down cheese pastas and raclette; attached shop sells even more cheese) and **$$$ Wright Brothers** (£1 oysters and other sea-to-plate specialties). Also inside the market—and just outside, along Lamb Street—look for food trucks, including **$ Sud Italia**'s mobile oven (piping-hot pizzas) and **Crosstown Donuts** (gourmet sourdough doughnuts). Nearby is a wall of **$** cheap eats: **Poppies** (fish-and-chips), **Indi Go Go** (Indian street food), **Pilpel** (falafel), and other Italian, Turkish, Mexican, and Indian counters.

$$$$ Boisdale Restaurant, down narrow Swedeland Court, is part of a small local chain of brasserie/piano bars specializing in Scottish fare. It offers tartan touches, a meat-heavy menu, and live jazz, blues, and soul music nearly nightly (steaks and seafood; downstairs restaurant Mon-Fri 12:00-15:00 & 18:00-late, closed Sat-Sun; reservations recommended, live music Tue-Fri 19:30-21:30, tel. 020/7283-1763, www.boisdale.co.uk). Other locations include Belgravia (see map on page 168), Canary Wharf, and Mayfair.

$$ Honest Burger, another small local chain, is a good place to try Britain's version of an American staple (daily 11:30-22:00, 12 Widegate Street, tel. 020/3693-3423).

$$$$ The English Restaurant, across from the south end of Spitalfields Market, started out as a Jewish bakery in the 17th century. Today it serves up traditional British cuisine with a Belgian flair—like updated bread-and-butter pudding—in a snug dining room or a bistro-style bar area (Mon-Fri 8:00-23:00, Sat-Sun 9:30-18:00, 52 Brushfield Street, tel. 020/7247-4110).

$$$ St. John Bread and Wine Restaurant, with a "nose to tail" philosophy, is especially popular at breakfast—served until ⌐oon and featuring their award-winning bacon sandwich on thick ⌐ead with homemade ketchup (see if you can guess the special ⌐oning). They also have good lunches and dinners (daily 8:00-⌐, 94 Commercial Street, tel. 020/7251-0848).

Brick Lane

⌐ladeshi and Indian Food: Brick Lane—nicknamed ⌐n"—boasts a row of popular curry houses popular both ⌐ and with London's Bangladeshi community. Curb-⌐pitch each eatery's "award-winning" pedigree (eager ⌐rcent discount), but little actually distinguishes the ⌐re. Compare menus and deals, and take your pick.

Aladin, at #132, has a good reputation—the same chef has been spicing up an extensive menu of delicious *madras* and *balti* curries, *tikka masala,* and other specialty items for 30 years (daily 12:00-23:00, tel. 020/7247-8210). **Meraz Café,** just off Brick Lane, offers a small, simple menu of Indian, Pakistani, and Bangladeshi dishes and homemade chutney with a focus on quality over variety (daily 11:00-23:00, 56 Hanbury Street, tel. 020/7247-6999). And many places have very cheap and filling lunch specials.

Other Options on Brick Lane: Brick Lane is more than just curry houses—particularly once you get north of the **Old Truman Brewery,** which hosts a fun courtyard of **$ food trucks** surrounded by prominent street art (check out the Shepard Fairey mural). Inside the brewery, **Café 1001** is a good place for coffee and cheap cafeteria fare. A bit farther north, at **Dark Sugars Cocoa House,** the sweet aroma of rich chocolate wafts through the open doors. Pop in for a taste—ask about their signature cardamom orange truffle or one of the fun pipettes (daily 10:00-22:00, 124 Brick Lane, mobile 07429-472-606). **$ Beigel Bake,** unpretentious and old-school, is justifiably popular, but well worth the short wait in line for fresh-baked bagels—served plain, smothered with cream cheese, or topped with salted beef, smoked salmon, salami, or chopped herring (open daily 24 hours, no seating—stand at the counter or take away, 159 Brick Lane, tel. 0171/729-0616).

Near Shoreditch High Street Tube Station

For upmarket, trendy, sit-down restaurants, head for the epicenter of East London's foodie scene: Shoreditch High Street. These choices are within a short walk of the area's Tube stop. Just north of here, Kingsland Road is nicknamed "Pho Mile" for its many Vietnamese eateries.

$$$ PizzaEast delivers modern Italian pizzas and main dishes (crispy pork belly), all baked in their wood oven. Happy crowds perch on stools at communal tables under concrete rafters in this subway-tiled industrial space. For dessert, their salted caramel tart is a favorite. It can get noisy at dinnertime and on Sundays with the market crowd; for a quieter ambience, come at lunch (daily 12:00-24:00, 56 Shoreditch High Street, tel. 020/7729-1888).

$$ Andina Picanteria & Pisco Bar is a colorful, contemporary Peruvian place known for its ceviche (Mon-Fri 12:00-2..., Sat-Sun from 16:00, 1 Redchurch Street at the corner of Sho... High Street, tel. 020/7920-6499).

$$$$ Boundary Restaurant is a trendy splurge wh... foodies go for special occasions. In the cellars of Bound... you'll dine on sophisticated French haute cuisine ur... ceilings and soft lighting (Mon-Sat 18:30-22:30, clo... ervations smart, 2 Boundary Street, tel. 020/772...

theboundary.co.uk). The hotel also houses the **$$$ Albion shop and café** (British favorites and homemade bread/pastries, daily 8:00-23:00) and a **$$$ rooftop bar and restaurant** with good views and pricey cocktails (daily 10:00-23:00).

$$$ Dishoom's original Shoreditch location offers a similar upmarket Indian menu (and the same wild popularity) as its Covent Garden outpost (listed earlier), with seating in the British Imperialist dining room or outdoor enclosed veranda. Try their creative cocktails while you wait for a table (long hours daily, 7 Boundary Street, entrance tucked around the corner from busy Shoreditch High Street, tel. 020/7420-9324).

Boxpark Food Court: Just outside the Shoreditch High Street Tube station, you'll find this elevated food court housed in repurposed train boxcars. Entrepreneurs rent time-limited "pop-up" space—an approach that allows them more stability than traveling to food markets, without the financial risk of opening a full restaurant. Wander through and see what's available—usually a sampling of ethnic food with a modern twist (like Korean BBQ burritos). Their website lists the current lineup and each vendor's story (Mon-Sat 8:00-23:00, Sun 12:00-22:00, 2 Bethnal Green, tel. 020/7033-2899, www.boxpark.co.uk).

TAKING TEA IN LONDON

While visiting London, consider partaking in this most British of traditions. While some tearooms—such as the wallet-draining £50-a-head tea service at Claridges and the finicky Fortnum & Mason—still require a jacket and tie, most others happily welcome tourists in jeans and sneakers. Most tearooms are usually open for lunch and close about 17:00. At all the places listed below, it's perfectly acceptable for two people to order one afternoon tea and one cream tea and share the afternoon tea's goodies. For details on afternoon tea, see page 1044.

Traditional Tea Experiences

$$$ The Wolseley serves a good afternoon tea between their meal service. Split one with your companion and enjoy two light meals a great price in classic elegance (£13 cream tea, £30 afternoon £40 champagne tea, generally served 15:00-18:30 daily, see full on page 188).

$$$ The Orangery at Kensington Palace serves a £28 "Orea" and a £35 champagne tea in its bright white hall near and Kate's residence. You can also order treats à la carte. s aren't huge, but who can argue with eating at a royal on the terrace? (Tea served 12:00-18:00; a 10-min-ugh Kensington Gardens from either Queensway or ensington Tube stations to the orange brick building, about 100 yards from Kensington Palace—see map on page 174; tel. 020/3166-6113, www.hrp.org.uk.)

$$$$ The Capital Hotel, a luxury hotel a half-block from Harrods, caters to weary shoppers with its intimate five-table, linen-tablecloth tearoom. It's where the ladies-who-lunch meet to decide whether to buy that Versace gown they've had their eye on. Even so, casual clothes, kids, and sharing plates are all OK (£30 afternoon tea, daily 14:00-17:30, call to book ahead—especially on weekends, 22 Basil Street—see West London color map in the back of this book, Tube: Knightsbridge, tel. 020/7591-1202, www.capitalhotel.co.uk).

$$$$ Fortnum & Mason department store offers tea at several different restaurants within its walls. You can "Take Tea in the Parlour" for £22 (including ice cream and scones; Mon-Sat 10:00-19:30, Sun 11:30-17:00). The pièce de resistance is their Diamond Jubilee Tea Salon, named in honor of the Queen's 60th year on the throne (and, no doubt, to remind visitors of Her Majesty's visit for tea here in 2012 with Camilla and Kate). At these royal prices, consider it dinner (£48, Mon-Sat 12:00-19:00, Sun until 18:00, dress up a bit—no shorts, "children must be behaved," 181 Piccadilly, smart to reserve at least a week in advance, tel. 020/7734-8040, www.fortnumandmason.com).

$$$$ Brown's Hotel in Mayfair serves a fancy £55 afternoon tea (you're welcome to ask for second helpings of your favorite scones and sandwiches) in its English tearoom. Said to be the inspiration for Agatha Christie's *At Bertram's Hotel,* the wood-paneled walls and inviting fire set a scene that's more contemporary-cozy than pinky-raising classy (daily 12:00-18:00, reservations smart, no casual clothing, 33 Albemarle Street—see map on page 186, Tube: Green Park, tel. 020/7518-4155, www.roccofortehotels.com).

Other Places to Sip Tea

Taking tea is not just for tourists and the wealthy—it's a true English tradition. If you want the teatime experience but are put off by the price, consider these options.

$$$ Browns Restaurant at Butler's Wharf serves a £14 afternoon tea with brioche sandwiches, traditional scones, and sophisticated desserts (daily 14:30-17:00, 26 Shad Thames facing Tower Bridge, tel. 020/7378-1700).

$$ The Café at Sotheby's, on the ground floor of the auction giant's headquarters, gives shoppers a break from fashionable New Bond Street (£9-26, tea served Mon-Fri 15:00-16:45, reservations smart, 34 New Bond Street—see map on page 186, Tube: Bond Street or Oxford Circus, tel. 020/7293-5077, www.sothebys.com cafe).

At **$ Waterstones'** bookstore you can put together a spread for less than £10 in their fifth-floor view café (203 Piccadilly).

Museum Cafés: Many museum restaurants offer a fine inexpensive tea service. The **$$$ National Dining Rooms,** within the Sainsbury Wing of the National Gallery on Trafalgar Square, serves a £7 cream tea and £18 afternoon tea with a great view from 14:30 to 16:30 (tea also served in National Café at the museum's Getty entrance, from 14:30 to 17:30; Tube: Charing Cross or Leicester Square, tel. 020/7747-2525). The **$$ Victoria and Albert Museum** café serves a classic cream tea in an elegant setting that won't break your budget and the **$$$ Wallace Collection** serves reasonably priced afternoon tea in its atrium.

Shop Cafés: You'll find good-value teas at various cafés in shops and bookstores across London. Most department stores on Oxford Street (including those between Oxford Circus and Bond Street Tube stations) offer an afternoon tea.

London Connections

BY PLANE

London has six airports; I've focused my coverage on the two most widely used—Heathrow and Gatwick—with a few tips for using the others (Stansted, Luton, London City, and Southend).

For accommodations at or near the major airports, see page 182. For more on flights within Europe, see page 1069.

Heathrow Airport

Heathrow Airport is one of the world's busiest airports. Think about it: 75 million passengers a year on 500,000 flights from 185 destinations traveling on 80 air-
lines, like some kind of global maypole dance. For Heathrow's airport, flight, and transfer information, call the switchboard at 0844-335-1801, or visit the helpful website www.heathrow. com (airport code: LHR).

Heathrow's terminals are numbered T-1 through T-5. Though T-1 is now closed for arrivals and departures, it still supports other terminals with baggage, and the newly renovated T-2 ("Queen's Terminal") will likely expand into the old T-1 digs eventually. Each terminal is served by different airlines and alliances; for example, T-5 is exclusively for British Air and Iberia Air flights, while T-2 serves mostly Star Alliance flights, such as United and Lufthansa. Screens posted throughout the airport identify which

LONDON

London's Airports

Luton

✈ Luton

✈ Stansted

N
Not to Scale

#757 & A1

ST. PANCRAS

PADDINGTON

LIVERPOOL STREET

Southend

Reading

Windsor
#71 & 77

✈ Southend

VICTORIA

Tube

D.L.R.

Rail Air Link

To Bath

Heathrow

VICTORIA COACH STN.

London City

✈

London

Thames

Guildford

EUROSTAR

✈ *Gatwick*

Ashford

Rail
Eurostar Rail
Tube & D.L.R.
Bus

ALL BUSES ARE NATIONAL EXPRESS
UNLESS NOTED

↓To Brighton

To Paris →

English Channel

terminal each airline uses; this information should also be printed on your ticket or boarding pass.

You can walk between T-2 and T-3. From this central hub (called "Heathrow Central"), T-4 and T-5 split off in opposite directions (and are not walkable). The easiest way to travel between the T-2/T-3 cluster and either T-4 or T-5 is by Heathrow Express train (free to transfer between terminals, departs every 15-20 minutes). You can also take a shuttle bus (free, serves all terminals), or the Tube (requires a ticket, serves all terminals).

If you're flying out of Heathrow, it's critical to confirm wh~~i~~ terminal your flight will use (look at your ticket/boarding check online, or call your airline in advance)—if it's T-4 ~~o~~ allow extra time. Taxi drivers generally know which termir~~a~~ need based on the airline, but bus drivers may not.

Services: Each terminal has an airport informatio~~n~~ long hours daily), car-rental agencies, exchange bure~~a~~ pharmacy, a VAT refund desk (tel. 0845-872-7627~~,~~ ent the VAT claim form from the retailer here to g~~et~~ on purchased items—see page 1020 for details) age (£6/item up to 2 hours, £11/item for 2-2~~4~~ daily, www.left-baggage.co.uk). Heathrow ~~a~~ and pay Internet access points (in each ter~~r~~

cations). You'll find a post office on the first floor of T-3 (departures area). Each terminal also has cheap eateries.

Heathrow's small **"TI"** (tourist info shop), even though it's a for-profit business, is worth a visit if you're nearby and want to pick up free information, including the *London Planner* visitors guide (long hours daily, 5-minute walk from T-3 in Tube station, follow signs to Underground; bypass queue for transit info to reach window for London questions).

Getting Between Heathrow and Downtown London

You have several options for traveling the 14 miles between Heathrow Airport and downtown London: Tube (about £6/person), bus (£8-10/person), express train with connecting Tube or taxi (about £10/person for slower train, £22-25/person for faster train, price does not include connecting Tube fare), car service (from £32/car), or taxi (about £75/group). The one that works best for you will depend on your arrival terminal, your destination in central London, and your budget.

By Tube (Subway): The Tube takes you from any Heathrow terminal to downtown London in 50-60 minutes on the Piccadilly Line (6/hour, buy ticket at Tube station ticket window or self-service machine). Depending on your destination in London, you may need to transfer (for example, if headed to the Victoria Station neighborhood, transfer at Hammersmith to the District line and ride six more stops). If you plan to use the Tube for transport in London, it makes  sense to buy a pay-as-you-go Oyster card (possibly adding a 7-Day Travelcard) at the airport's Tube station ticket window. (For details these passes, see page 48.) If you add a Travelcard that covers Zones 1-2, you'll need to pay a small supplement for the initial m Heathrow (Zone 6) to downtown.

u're taking the Tube from downtown London *to* the air- that Piccadilly Line trains don't stop at every terminal. r stop at T-4, then T-2/T-3 (also called Heathrow Cen- order; or T-2/T-3, then T-5. When leaving central Tube, allow extra time if going to T-4 or T-5, and board in the station to make sure that the train rminal before you board.

buses depart from the outdoor common area Station, a five-minute walk from the T-2/T-

3 complex. To connect between T-4 or T-5 and the Central Bus Station, ride the free Heathrow Express train or the shuttle buses.

National Express has regular service from Heathrow's Central Bus Station to Victoria Coach Station in downtown London, near several of my recommended hotels. While slow, the bus is affordable and convenient for those staying near Victoria Station (£8-10, 1-2/hour, less frequent from Victoria Station to Heathrow, 45-75 minutes depending on time of day, tel. 0871-781-8181, www.nationalexpress.com). A less-frequent National Express bus goes from T-5 directly to Victoria Coach Station.

By Train: Two different trains run between Heathrow Airport and London's Paddington Station. At Paddington Station, you're in the thick of the Tube system, with easy access to any of my recommended neighborhoods—my Paddington hotels are just outside the front door, and Notting Hill Gate is just two Tube stops away. The **Heathrow Connect** train is the slightly slower, much cheaper option, serving T-2/T-3 at a single station called Heathrow Central; use free transfers to get from either T-4 or T-5 to Heathrow Central (£10.30 one-way, £20.70 round-trip, 2/hour Mon-Sat, 1-2/hour Sun, 40 minutes, tel. 0345-604-1515, www.heathrowconnect.com). By the time you visit, the new **Crossrail Elizabeth line** may be operational, connecting Heathrow Central and T-4 to Paddington (and most likely replacing the Heathrow Connect train service).

The **Heathrow Express** train is fast and runs more frequently, but it's pricey (£22-25 one-way, price depends on time of day, £37 round-trip, £5 more if you buy your ticket on board, covered by BritRail pass; 4/hour, daily 5:00-24:00, 15 minutes to downtown from Heathrow Central Station serving T-2/T-3, 21 minutes from T-5; for T-4 take free transfer to Heathrow Central, tel. 0345-600-1515, www.heathrowexpress.co.uk). At the airport, you can use the Heathrow Express as a free transfer between terminals.

By Car Service: Just Airports offers a private car service between five London airports and the city center (see website for price quote, tel. 020/8900-1666, www.justairports.com).

By Taxi: Taxis from the airport cost £45-75 to west and central London (one hour). For four people traveling together, this can be a reasonable option. Hotels can often line up a cab back to the airport for about £50. If running, Uber also offers London airport pickup and drop-off.

Gatwick Airport

More and more flights land at Gatwick Airport, which way between London and the south coast (airport co tel. 0844-892-0322, www.gatwickairport.com). Gatw terminals, North and South, which are easily conne monorail (two-minute trip, runs 24 hours daily). Note that board-ing passes say "Gatwick N" or "Gatwick S" to indicate your termi-nal. British Airways flights generally use Gatwick South. The Gat-wick Express trains (described next) stop only at Gatwick South. Schedules in each terminal show only arrivals and departures from that terminal.

Getting Between Gatwick and Downtown London: The best way into London from this airport, **Gatwick Express trains** shuttle conveniently between Gatwick South and London's **Victo-ria Station,** with many of my recommended hotels close by (£20 one-way, £35 round-trip, at least 10 percent cheaper if purchased online, Oyster cards accepted but no discount offered, 4/hour, 30 minutes, runs 5:00-24:00 daily, a few trains as early as 3:30, tel. 0845-850-1530, www.gatwickexpress.com). If you buy your tick-ets at the station before boarding, ask about possible group deals. (If you see others in the ticket line, suggest buying your tickets together.) When going *to* the airport, at Victoria Station note that Gatwick Express has its own ticket windows right by the platform (tracks 13 and 14). You'll also find easy-to-use ticket machines nearby.

A train also runs between Gatwick South and **St. Pancras International Station** (£10.40, 3-5/hour, 45-60 minutes, www.thetrainline.com)—useful for travelers taking the Eurostar train (to Paris or Brussels) or staying in the St. Pancras/King's Cross neighborhood.

While even slower, the **bus** is a cheap and handy option to the Victoria Station neighborhood. National Express runs a bus from Gatwick direct to Victoria Station (£9, at least hourly, 1.5 hours, tel. 0871-781-8181, www.nationalexpress.com); easyBus has one going to near the Earls Court Tube stop (£2-10 depending on how far ahead you book, 2-3/hour, www.easybus.co.uk).

London's Other Airports

Stansted Airport: From Stansted (airport code: STN, tel. 0844-335-1803, www.stanstedairport.com), you have several options r getting into or out of London. Two different **buses** connect airport and London's Victoria Station neighborhood: National ress (£9-12, every 15 minutes, 2 hours, runs 24 hours a day, up and stops throughout London, ends at Victoria Coach or Liverpool Street Station, tel. 0871-781-8181, www.express.com) and Terravision (£4-10, 2/hour, 1.5-2 hours, reen Line Coach Station just south of Victoria Station). n take the faster, pricier Stansted Express **train** (£19, booked online, connects to London's Tube system at ale or Liverpool Street, 4/hour, 45 minutes, 4:30-

23:00, www.stanstedexpress.com). Stansted is expensive by cab; figure £100-120 one-way from central London.

Luton Airport: For Luton (airport code: LTN, airport tel. 01582/405-100, www.london-luton.co.uk), the fastest way to go into London is by **train** to St. Pancras International Station (£10-14 one-way, 1-5/hour, 35-45 minutes—check schedule to avoid slower trains, tel. 0345-712-5678, www.eastmidlandstrains.co.uk); catch the 10-minute shuttle bus (every 10 minutes) from outside the terminal to the Luton Airport Parkway Station. You can purchase a shuttle bus and train combo-ticket from kiosks or ticket machines inside the airport. When buying your train ticket *to* Luton, make sure you select "Luton Airport" as your destination rather than "Parkway Station" to ensure the shuttle fare is included.

The **National Express bus** A1 runs from Luton to Victoria Coach Station (£7-11 one-way, 2/hour, 1-1.5 hours, runs 24 hours, tel. 0871-781-8181, www.nationalexpress.com). The **Green Line express bus** #757 runs to Buckingham Palace Road, just south of Victoria Station, and stops en route near the Baker Street Tube station—best if you're staying near Paddington Station or in North London (£10 one-way, 2-4/hour, 1-1.5 hours, runs 24 hours, tel. 0344-800-4411, www.greenline.co.uk). If you're sleeping at Luton, consider EasyHotel.

London City and Southend Airports: To get into the city center from London City Airport (airport code: LCY, tel. 020/7646-0088, www.londoncityairport.com), take the Docklands Light Railway (DLR) to the Bank Tube station, which is one stop east of St. Paul's on the Central Line (less than £6 one-way, covered by Travelcard, a bit cheaper with an Oyster card, 20 minutes, www.tfl.gov.uk/dlr). Some EasyJet flights land farther out, at Southend Airport (airport code: SEN, tel. 01702/538-500, www.southendairport.com). Trains connect this airport to London's Liverpool Street Station (£16.20 one-way, 3-8/hour, 55 minutes, www.abelliogreateranglia.co.uk).

Connecting London's Airports by Bus

A handy **National Express bus** runs between Heathrow, Stansted, and Luton airports—easier than having to the center of London—although traffic can be bad an travel times (tel. 0871-781-8181, www.nationalexp

From Heathrow Airport to: Gatwick Ai hour, about 1.5 hours—but allow at least t flights), **Stansted Airport** (£27, 1-2/hour dir **Airport** (£27, roughly hourly, 1 hour).

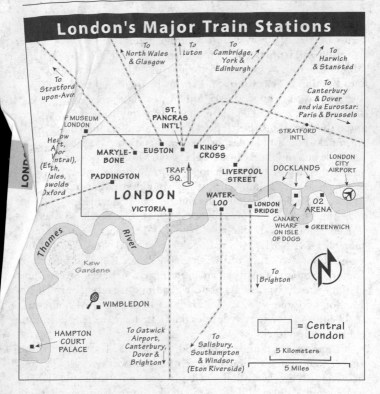

London's Major Train Stations

BY TRAIN

London, the country's major transportation hub, has a different train station for each region. There are nine main stations (see the map):

Euston: Serves northwest England, North Wales, and Scotland.

St. Pancras International: Serves north and south England, the Eurostar to Paris or Brussels (see "Crossing the Channel,"

King's Cross: Serves northeast England and Scotland, including Edinburgh.

Liverpool Street: Serves east England, including Essex and

London Bridge: Serves south England, including Brighton. **Waterloo** Serves south England, including Salisbury and

Victoria Gatwick Airport, Canterbury, Dover, and

Paddington south and southwest England, including

Public Transportation near London

Heathrow Airport, Windsor, Bath, Oxford, South Wales, and the Cotswolds.

Marylebone: Serves southwest and central England, including Stratford-upon-Avon.

In addition, London has several smaller train stations that you're less likely to use, such as **Charing Cross** (serves southeast England, including Dover) and **Blackfriars** (serves Brighton).

Any train station has schedule information, can make reservations, and can sell tickets for any destination. Most stations of a baggage-storage service (£12.50/bag for 24 hours, look fo *luggage* signs); because of long security lines, it can take a w check or pick up your bag (www.left-baggage.co.uk). For tails on the services available at each station, see www.n co.uk/stations. UK train and bus info is available at w org.uk. For information on tickets and rail passes, s the Practicalities chapter.

Train Connections from London
To Points West
From Paddington Station to: Windsor tral Station, 2/hour, 35 minutes, easy c hour, 1.5 hours), **Moreton-in-Mars** (2/hour, 2 hours).

From Waterloo Station to: Windsor (to Windsor & Eton Riverside Station, 2/hour, 1 hour), **Salisbury** (2/hour, 1.5 hours).

To Points North
From King's Cross Station: Trains run at least hourly, stopping in **York** (2 hours), **Durham** (3 hours), and **Edinburgh** (4.5 hours). Trains to **Cambridge** also leave from here (4/hour, 1 hour).

From Euston Station to: Conwy (nearly hourly, 3.5 hours, transfer in Chester), **Liverpool** (at least hourly, 3 hours, more with transfer), **Keswick** (hourly, 4 hours, transfer to bus at Penrith), **Glasgow** (1-2/hour, 4.5 hours).

From Marylebone Station: Trains leave for **Stratford-upon-Avon** from this station, located near the southwest corner of Regent's Park (2/day direct, 2.5 hours hours; also 1-2/hour, 2 hours, transfer in Leamington Spa, Dorridge, or Birmingham Moor).

BY BUS
Buses are slower but considerably cheaper than trains for reaching destinations around Britain and beyond. Most depart from **Victoria Coach Station,** which is one long block south of Victoria Station (near many recommended accommodations, Tube: Victoria). Inside the station, you'll find basic eateries, kiosks, and a helpful information desk stocked with schedules and staff ready to point you to your bus or answer any questions. Watch your bags carefully—luggage thieves thrive at the station.

Ideally you'll buy your tickets online (for tips on buying tickets and taking buses, see page 1058 of the Practicalities chapter). But if you must buy one at the station, try to arrive an hour before the bus departs, or drop by the day before. Ticketing machines are scattered around the station (separate machines for National Express/Eurolines and Megabus; you can buy either for today or for tomorrow); there's also a ticket counter near gate 21. For UK train and info, check www.traveline.org.uk.

National Express buses go to: **Bath** (nearly hourly, 3 hours; consider a guided Evan Evans tour by bus—see page 321), (every 60-90 minutes, 2 hours), **Cardiff** (hourly, 3.5 tford-upon-Avon** (3/day, 3.5 hours), **Liverpool** (8/day rs, overnight available), **York** (4/day direct, 5 hours), direct, 7 hours, train is better), **Glasgow** (2-4/day in is much better), **Edinburgh** (2/day direct, 10 stead).

nd:** This bus/boat journey, operated by Eu-s (£40, 1/day, departs Victoria Coach Sta-h passport one hour before). Consider a nstead.

ally in summer, buses run to destinations all over Europe, including Paris, Amsterdam, Brussels, and Germany (sometimes crossing the Channel by ferry, other times through the Chunnel). For any international connection, you need to check in with your passport one hour before departure. For details, call 0871-781-8181 or visit www.eurolines.co.uk.

CROSSING THE CHANNEL
By Eurostar Train

The Eurostar zips you (and up to 800 others in 18 sleek cars) from downtown London to downtown **Paris** or **Brussels** at 190 mph in 2.5 hours (1-2/hour). The tunnel crossing is a 20-minute, silent, 100 mph nonevent. Your ears won't even pop.

Eurostar recently expanded its reach with direct service from London to **Amsterdam** (2/day, 4 hours; also stops at Rotterdam). Initially trains will only run direct from London to Amsterdam—those traveling from Amsterdam will need to change trains in Brussels and go through passport control. Direct service from Amsterdam may be running by late 2019. Eurostar also runs direct service to **Lyon, Avignon,** and **Marseille** (5/week in summer, less frequent off-season). Germany's national railroad is also looking to run bullet trains between Frankfurt, Amsterdam, and London.

Eurostar Routes

ENGLAND
Amsterdam
North Sea
NETH.
London
Ebbsfleet
Rotterdam
Ashford
Calais-
Fréthun
Lille-
Europe
Brussels
BELG.
English
Channel
FRANCE
Paris

Not to Scale

Eurostar
Channel Tunnel

Eurostar Tickets and Fares: A one-way ticket between London and Paris, Brussels, or Amsterdam can vary widely in price; for instance, $45-200 (Standard class), $160-310 (Standard Premier), and $400 (Business Premier). Fares depend on how far ahead you reserve and whether you're eligible for any discounts—available for children (under age 12), youths (under 26), and adults booking months ahead or purchasing roundtrip. You can book tickets 4 months in advance. Tickets can be exchanged before the scheduled departure for a fee (about $45 plus the cost of any price increase but only Business Premier class allows any refund.

You can buy tickets online using the print-at-home eticket option (see www.ricksteves.com/eurostar or www.eurostar.co can also order by phone through Rail Europe (US tel. 8 6782) for home delivery before you go, or through Eur 0843-218-6186, priced in euros) to pick up at the station. tickets are issued only at the Eurostar office in St. Panc tional Station. In continental Europe, you can buy Eu at any major train station in any country or at any travel agency that handles train tickets (expect a booking fee). Seat reservations for travelers with a Eurail Pass covering France, Belgium, or the Netherlands are available at Eurostar departure stations, through US agents, or by phone with Eurostar, but they may be harder to get at other train stations and travel agencies ($34 in Standard, $44 in Standard Premier, can sell out, no benefit with BritRail Pass).

Taking the Eurostar: Eurostar trains depart from and arrive at London's St. Pancras International Station. Check in at least 30 minutes in advance (remember that times listed on tickets are local times; Britain's time zone is one hour earlier than France, the Netherlands, or Belgium's). Pass through airport-like security, show your passport to customs officials, and locate your departure gate (shown on a TV monitor). The waiting area has shops, newsstands, horrible snack bars, and cafés (bring food for the trip from elsewhere), free Wi-Fi, and a currency-exchange booth.

Crossing the Channel Without Eurostar

For speed and affordability, look into cheap flights (see page 1069). Or consider the following old-fashioned ways of crossing the Channel (cheaper but more complicated and time-consuming than the Eurostar).

By Train and Boat: To reach **Paris,** take a train from London's St. Pancras International Station, Charing Cross Station, or Victoria Station to Dover's Priory Station (hourly, 1-2 hours), then catch a P&O ferry to Calais, France (hourly, 1.5 hours, www. poferries.com). From Calais, take the TGV train to Paris.

For **Amsterdam,** consider Stena Line's Dutchflyer service, which combines train and ferry tickets. Trains go from London's Liverpool Street Station to the port of Harwich (hourly, 1.5 hours, most transfer in Manningtree). From Harwich, Stena Line ferries sail to Hoek van Holland (8 hours), where you can catch a train to Amsterdam (book ahead for best price, 13 hours total, www. stenaline.co.uk, Dutch train info at www.ns.nl). For additional European ferry info, visit www.aferry.to.

By Bus and Boat: The bus from London's Victoria Coach Station goes direct to **Paris** (£40-45, 4-5/day, 8-10 hours), **Brussels** (£?-40, 4/day, 9 hours), or **Amsterdam** (4/day, 12 hours) via ferry or tunnel (day or overnight; £36-70 one-way, cheaper in advance, 70-514-3219, www.eurolines.co.uk).

CRUISE SHIP

...ises begin, end, or call at one of several English ports ...sy access to London. Cruise lines favor two ports: ...n, 80 miles southwest of London; and Dover, 80 miles ...London. If you don't want to bother with public transportation, most cruise lines offer transit-only excursion packages into London. For more details, see my *Rick Steves Scandinavian & Northern European Cruise Ports* guidebook.

Southampton Cruise Port

Within Southampton's sprawling port (www.cruisesouthampton. com), cruises use two separate dock areas, each with two terminals.

To reach London, it's about a 1.5-hour train ride. To get to Southampton Central Station from the cruise port, you can take a taxi or walk 10-15 minutes to the public ferry dock (Town Quay), where you can ride the QuayConnect bus to the train station. From there, trains depart at least every 30 minutes for London's Waterloo Station.

If you have time to kill in port, consider taking the train to Portsmouth (50-60 minutes), best known for its Historic Dockyard and many nautical sights, or stick around Southampton and visit the excellent SeaCity Museum, with a beautifully presented exhibit about the *Titanic*, which set sail from here on April 10, 1912.

Dover Cruise Port

Little Dover has a huge port. Cruises put in at the Western Docks, with two terminals. Trains go hourly from Dover Priory Station to London. From either cruise terminal, the best way into town (or to the train station) is by taxi or shuttle bus (take it to Market Square, then walk 15 minutes to the train station). From Dover's station, a fast train leaves for London's St. Pancras International Station (2/hour, 1 hour); direct trains go to Victoria Station and Charing Cross Station (hourly, 2 hours, more with transfers).

If you have extra time in port, Dover Castle, perched upon chalk cliffs, is well worth a visit for its WWII-era Secret Wartime Tunnels. Or take the train to Canterbury (2/hour, less than 30 minutes), notable for its important cathedral and fine historic core.

GARTER

rarely open). T...
residence, and...
hangs her cro...
workaday gri...
Her Majesty...
above the ro...
blue flag) in...

While...
some enjoy...
charm, w...
sider over...
are easy,...
poundin...

W

GETT...
By Tr...
tral ar...
conn...
easy...
day...
wit'...
er—...
ret...

HELPFUL HINTS

Supermarkets: Pick up picnic supplies at **Marks & Spencer** (Mon-Sat 8:00-19:00, Sun 11:00-17:00, 130 Peascod Street, tel. 01753/852-266) or at **Waitrose** (Mon-Fri 8:00-21:00, Sat until 20:00, Sun 11:00-17:00, King Edward Court Shopping Centre, just south of Windsor & Eton Central Station, tel. 01753/860-565). Just outside the castle, you'll find long benches near the statue of Queen Victoria—great for people-watching while you munch.

Bike Rental: Extreme Motion, near the river in Alexandra Gardens, rents 21-speed mountain bikes (£12.50/4 hours, £18/day, includes helmet, £150 credit-card deposit required, bring passport as ID, summer daily 10:00-18:00, Sat-Sun only off-season, tel. 01753/830-220).

Sights in Windsor

▲▲WINDSOR CASTLE

Windsor Castle, the official home of England's royal family for 900 years, claims to be the largest and oldest occupied castle in the world. Thankfully, touring it is simple. You'll see sprawling grounds, lavish staterooms, a crowd-pleasing dollhouse, a gallery of Michelangelo and Leonardo da Vinci drawings, and an exquisite Perpendicular Gothic chapel.

Cost: £20.50, includes entry to castle grounds and all exhibits inside. Tickets are valid for one year of reentry (get it stamped at the exit).

Hours: Grounds and most interiors open daily 9:30-17:15, Nov-Feb 9:45-16:15, except St. George's Chapel, which is closed Sun to tourists (but open to worshippers; wait at the exit gate to be escorted in). Last entry to grounds and St. George's Chapel is 75 minutes before closing. Last entry to State Apartments and Queen Mary's Dolls' House is 45 minutes before closing.

Information: Tel. 020/7766-7324, www.royalcollection.org.uk.

Crowd Control: Ticket lines can be long in summer. You can expect the worst crowds between 11:00-13:00 any time of year. Avoid the wait by purchasing tickets in advance online at www.royalcollection.org.uk (collect them at the prepaid ticket window), in person at the Buckingham Palace ticket office in London), or anywhere in Windsor to buy advance tickets.

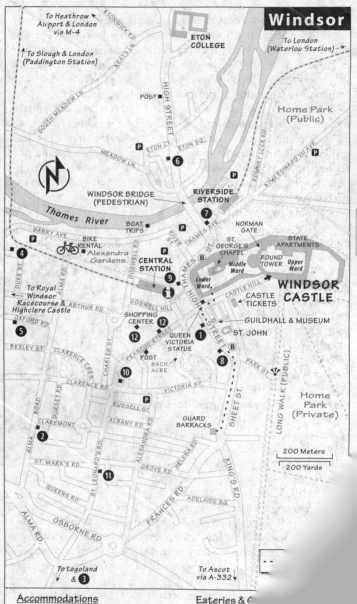

WINDSOR & CAMBRIDGE

Map labels:

To Heathrow Airport & London via M-4

ETONWICK RD.

KEATS LN.

ETON COLLEGE

To London (Waterloo Station)

To Slough & London (Paddington Station)

SOUTH MEADOW LN.

POST

HIGH STREET

Home Park (Public)

MEADOW LN.

ETON CT.

ETON SQ.

P

❻

ROMNEY LOCK RD.

KING EDWARD VII AVE.

WINDSOR BRIDGE (PEDESTRIAN)

RIVERSIDE STATION

❼

NORMAN GATE

ST. GEORGE'S CHAPEL

STATE APARTMENTS

Thames River

BOAT TRIPS

RIVER ST.

THAMES AVE.

Middle Ward

ROUND TOWER

Upper Ward

N

BARRY AVE.

BIKE RENTAL

Alexandra Gardens

CENTRAL STATION

P

❾

HIGH ST.

THAMES ST.

B

Lower Ward

CASTLE HILL

WINDSOR CASTLE

DUKE ST.

❹

ALMA RD.

GOSWELL RD.

To Royal Windsor Racecourse & Highclere Castle

ARTHUR RD.

GOSWELL HILL

CASTLE TICKETS

GUILDHALL & MUSEUM

OXFORD RD.

SHOPPING CENTER

❶❷

ST. JOHN

❺

BEXLEY ST.

CLARENCE CRES.

CHARLES ST.

PEASCOD STREET

QUEEN VICTORIA STATUE

❶

HIGH STREET

B

❽

PARK ST.

LONG WALK (PUBLIC)

POST

BACH. ACRE

❿

CLARENCE RD.

VICTORIA ST.

ROAD

DORSET RD.

RUSSELL ST.

P

Home Park (Private)

ALMA

CLAREMONT

❷

ALBANY RD.

ALEXANDRA RD.

GUARD BARRACKS

SHEET ST.

ST. MARK'S RD.

⓫

GROVE RD.

HELENA RD.

KING'S RD.

200 Meters

200 Yards

QUEENS RD.

ST. LEONARD'S RD.

FRANCES RD.

ADELAIDE SQ.

ALMA RD.

OSBORNE RD.

To Legoland & ❸

To Ascot via A-332

Accommodations

❶ MGallery Castle Hotel Windsor

❷ Langton House B&B

❸ To Park Farm B&B

❹ 76 Duke Street B&B

❺ Dee & Steve's B&B

❻ Crown & Cushion Rooms

Eateries & O

❼ Bel & T

❽ Corn

❾ Th

❿ M

⓫

Possible Closures: On rare occasions when the Queen is entertaining guests, the State Apartments close (and tickets are reduced to £11.30). Sometimes the entire castle closes. It's smart to call ahead or check the website (especially in mid-June) to make sure everything is open when you want to go. While you're at it, confirm the Changing of the Guard schedule.

Tours: An included **audioguide** (dry, reverent, informative) covers both the grounds and interiors. For a good overview—and an opportunity to ask questions—consider the free 30-minute **guided walk** around the grounds (usually 2/hour, schedule posted next to audioguide desk). The official £5 guidebook is full of gorgeous images and makes a fine souvenir, but the information within is covered by the audioguide and tour.

Changing of the Guard: The Changing of the Guard takes place Monday through Saturday at 11:00 (April-July) and on alter-

nating days the rest of the year (confirm schedule on website; get there by 10:30 or earlier if you expect a line for tickets). There is no Changing of the Guard on Sundays or in very wet weather. The fresh guards, led by a marching band, leave their barracks on Sheet Street and march up High Street, hanging a right at Victoria, then a left into the castle's Lower Ward, arriving at about 11:00. After about a half-hour, the tired guards march back the way the new ones came. To watch the actual ceremony inside the castle, you'll need to have already bought your ticket, entered the grounds, and ̄aked out a spot. Alternatively, you could ̄t for them to march by on High Street or on the lower half of ̄e Hill.

̄ensong: An evensong takes place in the chapel nightly at ̄e for worshippers, line up at exit gate to be admitted).

̄iew: While you can get great views of the castle from ̄, the classic views are from the wooded avenue called ̄, which stretches south of the palace and is open to

are no real eateries inside (other than shops sell- ̄colates and bottled water), so consider bring-

̄d going through the security check-

The Order of the Garter

In addition to being the royal residence, Windsor is the home of the Most Noble Order of the Garter—Britain's most prestigious chivalrous order. The castle's history is inexorably tied to this order.

Founded in 1348 by King Edward III and his son (the "Black Prince"), the Order of the Garter was designed to honor returning Crusaders. This was a time when the legends of King Arthur and the Knights of the Round Table were sweeping England, and Edward III fantasized that Windsor could be a real-life Camelot. (He even built the Round Tower as an homage to the Round Table.)

The order's seal illustrates the story of the order's founding and unusual name: a cross of St. George encircled with a belt and a French motto loosely translated as "Shame be upon he who thinks evil of it." Supposedly while the king was dancing with a fair maiden, her garter slipped off onto the floor; in an act of great chivalry, he rescued her from embarrassment by picking it up and uttering those words.

The Order of the Garter continues to the present day as the single most prestigious honor in the United Kingdom. There can be only 24 knights at one time (perfect numbers for splitting into two 12-man jousting teams), plus the sitting monarch and the Prince of Wales. Aside from royals and the nobility, past Knights of the Garter have included Winston Churchill, Bernard "Monty" Montgomery, and Ethiopian Emperor Haile Selassie. In 2008, Prince William became only the 1,000th knight in the order's 669-year history. Other current members include various ex-military officers, former British Prime Minister John Major, and a member of the Colman's Mustard family.

The patron of the order is St. George—the namesake of the State Apartments' most sumptuous hall and of the castle's own chapel. Both of these spaces—the grandest in all of Windsor--are designed to celebrate and to honor the Order of the Garter.

point, pick up your audioguide and start strolling along the p... through...

The Grounds: Head up the hill, enjoying the first of fine castle views you'll see today. The tower-topped conical your left represents the historical core of the castle. Wi¹ Conqueror built this motte (artificial mound) and baile stockade around it) in 1080—his first castle in Engl the later monarchs who spiffed up Windsor were Edv with French war booty, he made it a palace fit for king), Charles II (determined to restore the mon the 1660s), and George IV (Britain's "Bling Ki... many such vanity projects in the 1820s). On you...

bandstand platform has a seal of the Order of the Garter, which has important ties to Windsor (see sidebar).

Passing through the small gate, you approach the stately St. George's Gate. Peek through here to the Upper Ward's **Quadrangle,** which is surrounded by the State Apartments (across the field) and the Queen's private apartments (to the right).

Turn left and follow the wall. On your right-hand side, you enjoy great views of the **Round Tower** atop that original motte; running around the base of this artificial hill is the delightful, peaceful garden of the castle governor. The unusual design of this castle has not one "bailey" (castle yard), but three, which today make up Windsor's Upper Ward (where the Queen lives, which you just saw), Middle Ward (the ecclesiastical heart of the complex, with St. George's Chapel, which you'll soon pass on the left), and Lower Ward (residences for castle workers).

Continue all the way around this mini moat to the **Norman Gate,** which once held a prison. Walking under the gate, look up to see the bottom of the portcullis that could be dropped to seal off the inner courtyard. Three big holes are strategically situated for dumping boiling goo or worse on whoever was outside the gate. Past the gate are even finer views of the Quadrangle.

Do a 180 and head back toward the Norman Gate, but before you reach it, go down the staircase on the right. You'll emerge onto a fine **terrace** overlooking the flat lands all around. It's easy to understand why this was a strategic place to build a castle. That's Eton College across the Thames. Imagine how handy it's been for royals ⬤ be able to ship off their teenagers to an elite prep school so close at they could easily keep an eye on them...literally. The power-⬤t cooling towers in the distance mark the workaday burg of ⬤h (rhymes with "plow," immortalized as the setting for Brit-⬤iginal version of the television series *The Office*).

ight and wander along the terrace. You'll likely see two lines. The
⬤ads to Queen Mary's Dolls' House, then to the State Apart-
⬤hort line skips the dollhouse and heads directly to the apart-
the following descriptions and decide if the dollhouse is
for (or try again later in the day, when the line sometimes
⬤ see the Drawings Gallery and the China Museum

⬤'s Dolls' House: This palace in miniature (1:12 "the most famous dollhouse in the world." It was a gift for the adult Queen Mary (the wife of King George V, and the current Queen's grandmother), who greatly enjoyed miniatures. It's basically one big, dimly lit room with the large dollhouse in the middle, executed with an astonishing level of detail. Each fork, knife, and spoon on the expertly set banquet table is perfect and made of real silver—and the tiny pipes of its plumbing system actually have running water. But you're kept a few feet away by a glass wall, and are constantly jostled by fellow sightseers in this crowded space, making it difficult to fully appreciate. Unless you're a dollhouse devotee, it's probably not worth waiting half an hour for a five-minute peek at this, but if the line is short it's definitely worth a look.

Drawings Gallery and China Museum: Positioned at the exit of Queen Mary's Dolls' House, this gallery displays a changing array of pieces from the Queen's collection—usually including some big names, such as Michelangelo and Leonardo. The China Museum features items from the Queen's many exquisite settings for royal shindigs.

State Apartments: Dripping with chandeliers, finely furnished, and strewn with history and the art of a long line of kings

and queens, they're the best I've seen in Britain. This is where Henry VIII and Charles I once lived, and where the current Queen wows visiting dignitaries. Take advantage of the talkative docents in each room, who are happy to answer your questions.

You'll climb the Grand Staircase up to the **Grand Vestibule,** decorated with exotic items seized by British troops during their missions to colonize various corners of the world. Ask a docent to help you find which one of the many glass cases contains the bullet that killed Lord Nelson at Trafalgar. In the next room, the magnificent wood-ceilinged **Waterloo Chamber** is wallpapered with portraits of figures from the pan-European alliance that defeated Napoleon. Find the Duke of Wellington (high on the far wall, in red) who outmaneuvered him at Waterloo, and Pope Pius VII (right wall, in red and white) whom Napoleon befriended...then imprisoned. Next, you'll pass through a **series of living rooms**—bedchambers, dressing rooms, and drawing rooms of the king and queen (who traditionally maintained separate quarters). Many rooms are decorated with canvases by Rubens, Van Dyck, and Holbein. Finally, you'll emerge into **St. George's Hall,** decorated with emblems representing the knights of the prestigious Order of the Garter (see sidebar). This is the s of some of the most elaborate royal banquets—imagine one long table stretching from one end of the hall to the other and seating 160 VIPs. From here, you'll proceed into the rooms that were restored after a fire in 1992, including the "Semi-State Apartments." The **Garter Throne Room** is where new members of the Order of the Garter are invested (ceremonially granted their titles).

• *Exiting the State Apartments, you have one more major sight to see. Get out your castle-issued map or follow signs to find...*

St. George's Chapel: This church is known for housing numerous royal tombs (and as the site of the 2018 wedding of Prince Harry and Meghan Markle), and is an exquisite example of the Perpendicular Gothic style (dating from about 1500). Pick up a free map and circle the interior clockwise, finding these highlights:

Stand at the back and look down the **nave,** with its classic fan-vaulting spreading out from each slender pillar and nearly every joint capped with an elaborate and colorful roof boss. Most of these emblems are associated with the Knights of the Garter, who consider St. George's their "mother church." Under the upper stained-glass windows, notice the continuous frieze of 250 angels, lovingly carved with great detail, ringing the church.

In the corner (#4 on your church-issued map), take in the melodramatic monument to **Princess Charlotte of Wales,** the only child of King George IV. Heir to the throne, her death in 1817 (at 21, in childbirth) devastated the nation. Head up the left side of the nave and find the simple chapel (#6) containing the tombs of the current Queen's parents, **King George VI and "Queen Mum" Elizabeth;** the ashes of her younger sister, Princess Margaret, are also kept here (see the marble slab against the wall). It's speculated that the current Queen may choose this chapel for her final resting place. Farther up the aisle is the tomb of **Edward IV** (#8), who expanded St. George's Chapel.

Stepping into the **choir area** (#12), you're immediately aware that you are in the inner sanctum of the Order of the Garter. The banners lining the nave represent the knights, as do the fancy helmets and half-drawn swords at the top of each wood-carved seat. These symbols honor only living knights; on the seats are some 800 golden panels memorializing departed knights. Under your feet lies the **Royal Vault** (#13), burial spot of Mad King George III (nemesis of American revolutionaries). Strolling farther up the aisle, notice the marker in the floor: You're walking over the burial site of **King Henry VIII** (#14) and Jane Seymour, Henry's favorite wife (perhaps because she was the only one who died before he could behead her). The body of King Charles I, who was beheaded by Oliver Cromwell's forces at the Banqueting House (see page 83), was also discovered here...with its head sewn back on.

On your way out, you can pause at the door of the sumptuous 13th-century **Albert Memorial Chapel** (#28), redecorated in 1861 after the death of Queen Victoria's husband, Prince Albert, and dedicated to his memory.

• *On exiting the chapel, you come into the castle's...*

Lower Ward: This area is a living town where some 160 people who work for the Queen reside; they include clergy, military, and castle administrators. Just below the chapel, you may be able to enter a tranquil little horseshoe-shaped courtyard ringed with residential doorways—all of them with a spectacular view of the chapel's grand entrance.

Back out in the yard, look for the guard posted at his pillbox. Like those at Buckingham Palace, he's been trained to be a ruthless killing machine...just so he can wind up as somebody's photo op. Click!

MORE SIGHTS IN WINDSOR
Legoland Windsor

Paradise for Legomaniacs under age 12, this huge, kid-pleasing park has dozens of tame but fun rides (often with very long lines) scattered throughout its 150 acres. The impressive Miniland has 40 million Lego pieces glued together to create 800 tiny buildings and a mini tour of Europe. Several of the more exciting rides involve getting wet, so dress accordingly or buy a cheap disposable poncho in the gift shop. While you may be tempted to hop on the Hill Train at the entrance, it's faster and more convenient to walk down in the park. Food is available in the park, but you can save money bringing a picnic.

Cost: £60 but varies by day, significant savings when b? online at least 7 days in advance, 10 percent discount at W TI, free for ages 3 and under, optional Q-Bot ride-reservati? get allows you to bypass lines (£20-80 depending on whe? and how much time you want to save).

Hours: Generally late July-Aug daily 10:00-18

March-late July and Sept-Oct Mon-Fri until 17:00, Sat-Sun until 18:00, often closed Tue-Wed; closed Nov-mid-March. Check website for exact schedule, tel. 0871-222-2001, www.legoland.co.uk.

Getting There: A £5 round-trip shuttle bus runs from opposite Windsor's Theatre Royal on Thames Street, and from the Parish Church stop on High Street (2/hour). If day-tripping from London, ask about rail/shuttle/park admission deals from Paddington or Waterloo train stations. For drivers, the park is on B-3022 Windsor/Ascot road, two miles southwest of Windsor and 25 miles west of London. Legoland is clearly signposted from the M-3, M-4, and M-25 motorways. Parking is easy (£6).

Eton College

Across the bridge from Windsor Castle is the most famous "public" (the equivalent of our "private") high school in Britain. Eton was founded in 1440 by King Henry VI; today it educates about 1,300 boys (ages 13-18), who live on campus. Eton has molded the characters of 19 prime ministers as well as members of the royal family—most recently princes William and Harry. Sparse on actual sights, the college is closed to visitors except via guided tour, where you may get a glimpse of the schoolyard, chapel, cloisters, and the Museum of Eton Life. For more information visit www.etoncollege.com or call 01753/370-100.

Eton High Street

Even if you're not touring the college, it's worth the few minutes it takes to cross the pedestrian bridge and wander straight up Eton's High Street. A bit more cutesy and authentic-feeling than Windsor (which is given over to shopping malls and chain stores), Eton has a charm that's fun to sample.

Windsor and Royal Borough Museum

Tucked into a small space beneath the Guildhall (where Prince Charles remarried), this little museum does its best to give some insight into the history of Windsor and the surrounding area. They also have lots of special activities for kids. Ask at the desk whether tours are running to the Guildhall itself (visits only possible with a guide); if not, it's probably not worth the admission.

Cost and Hours: £2, includes audioguide, Tue-Sat 10:00-
:00, Sun from 12:00, closed Mon, located in the Guildhall on
h Street, tel. 01628/685-686, www.rbwm.gov.uk.

Trips

up and down the Thames River for classic views of the
he village of Eton, Eton College, and the Royal Windsor
rse. Choose from a 40-minute or two-hour tour, then relax
nd nibble a picnic. Boats leave from the riverside prom-
cent to Barry Avenue.

Visiting Highclere Castle

If you're a fan of *Downton Abbey*, consider a day trip from London to Highclere Castle, the stately house where much of the show was filmed. Though the hugely popular TV series was set in Yorkshire, the actual house is located in Hampshire, about an hour's train ride west of London. Highclere has been home to the Earls of Carnarvon since 1679, but the present Jacobean-style house was rebuilt in the 1840s by Sir Charles Barry, who also designed London's Houses of Parliament. Noted landscape architect Capability Brown laid out the traditional gardens in the mid-18th century. The castle's Egyptian exhibit features artifacts collected by Highclere's fifth Earl, George Herbert, a keen amateur archaeologist. When Howard Carter discovered King Tut's tomb in 1922, he waited three weeks for his friend and patron Herbert to join him before looking inside. The Earl died unexpectedly a few months later, giving birth to the legend of a "mummy's curse."

Cost: £22 for castle, garden, and Egyptian exhibit; £15 for castle and garden only, or Egyptian exhibit and garden only; £7 for garden only.

Hours: Admission by timed entry only, mid-July–mid-Sept Sun-Thu castle open 10:30-17:00, grounds open 9:00-17:00, last entry one hour before closing, closed Fri-Sat; generally closed mid-Sept–mid-July except for special events; reserve well in advance online—tickets available several months ahead; 24-hour info tel. 01635/253-204, www.highclerecastle.co.uk.

Getting There: Highclere is six miles south of Newbury, about 70 miles west of London, off A-34.

By Train and Taxi: Great Western trains run from London's Paddington Station to Newbury (1-2/hour, 50-70 minutes, £25-56 same-day return, tel. 0345-700-125, www.gwr.com). From Newbury train station, you can take a taxi (£15-25 one-way, higher price is for Sun, taxis wait outside station) or reserve a car and driver (must arrange in advance, £12.50/person round-trip; £25 minimum, Webair, tel. 07818/430-095, mapeng@msn.com).

By Tour: Brit Movie Tours offers an all-day bus tour of *Downton Abbey* filming locations, including Highclere Castle and the fictional village of Downton (sells out early, £80, includes transport and castle/garden entry, £5 extra for Egyptian exhibit, 9 hours, depart London from outside Glouceste_ Road Tube Station, reservations required, tel. 0844-247-10C from the US or Canada call 011-44-20-7118-1007, ww_ britmovietours.com).

WINDSOR & CAMBRIDGE

Cost and Hours: 40-minute tour-£8.50, family pass-about £23, mid-Feb-Oct 1-2/hour daily 10:00-17:00, fewer and Sat-Sun only in Nov; 2-hour tour—£14.50, family pass-about £40, late March-Oct only, 1-2/day; closed Dec-mid-Feb; online discounts, tel. 01753/851-900, www.frenchbrothers.co.uk.

Horse Racing

The horses race near Windsor every Monday at the Royal Windsor Racecourse (£25 entry, online discounts, under age 18 free with an adult, April-Aug and Oct, no races in Sept, sporadic in Aug, off A-308 between Windsor and Maidenhead, tel. 01753/498-400, www.windsor-racecourse.co.uk). The romantic way to get there from Windsor is by a 10-minute shuttle boat (£7 round-trip, www.frenchbrothers.co.uk). The famous Ascot Racecourse (described next) is also nearby.

NEAR WINDSOR
Ascot Racecourse

Located seven miles southwest of Windsor and just north of the town of Ascot, this royally owned track is one of the most famous horse-racing venues in the world. The horses first ran here in 1711, and the course is best known for June's five-day Royal Ascot race meeting, attended by the Queen and 299,999 of her loyal subjects. For many, the outlandish hats worn on Ladies Day (Thu) are more interesting than the horses. Royal Ascot is usually the third week in June. The pricey tickets go on sale the preceding November; while the Friday and Saturday races tend to sell out far ahead, tickets for the other days are often available close to the date (check website). In addition to Royal Ascot, the racecourse runs the ponies year-round—funny hats strictly optional.

Cost: Regular tickets generally start from £18 and go as high as £80—may be available at a discount at TI, kids ages 17 and under sometimes free; parking from free to £20, depending on event; dress code enforced in some areas and on certain days, tel. 0844-346-3000, www.ascot.co.uk.

Sleeping in Windsor

t visitors stay in London and do Windsor as a day trip. But here few suggestions for those staying the night.

$$$ **MGallery Castle Hotel Windsor,** part of the bou- vision of Accor Hotels, offers 108 rooms and elegant public a central location just down the street from Her Maj- kend retreat (breakfast extra, air-con, parking-£20/day, reet, tel. 01753/851-577, www.castlehotelwindsor.com, .com).

$$ Langton House B&B is a stately Victorian home with five spacious, well-appointed rooms lovingly maintained by Paul and Sonja Fogg (continental breakfast included but full English breakfast extra, family rooms, guest kitchen, 46 Alma Road, tel. 01753/858-299, www.langtonhouse.co.uk, bookings@langtonhouse.co.uk).

$$ Park Farm B&B, bright and cheery, is most convenient for drivers. But even if you're not driving, this beautiful place is such a good value, and the welcome is so warm, that you're unlikely to mind the bus ride into town (cash only—credit card solely for reservations, family room with bunk beds, shared fridge and microwave, free off-street parking, 1 mile from Legoland on St. Leonards Road near Imperial Road, 5-minute bus ride or 1-mile walk to castle, £5 taxi ride from station, tel. 01753/866-823, www.parkfarm.com, stay@parkfarm.com, Caroline and Drew Youds).

$$ 76 Duke Street has two nice rooms, but only hosts one set of guests at a time. While the bathroom is (just) outside your bedroom, you have it to yourself (15-minute walk from station at—you guessed it—76 Duke Street, tel. 01753/620-636 or 07884/222-225, www.76dukestreet.co.uk, bandb@76dukestreet.co.uk, Julia).

$ Dee and Steve's B&B is a friendly four-room place above a window shop on a quiet residential street about a 10-minute walk from the castle and station. The rooms are cozy, Dee and Steve are pleasant hosts, and breakfast is served in the contemporary kitchen/lounge (169 Oxford Road, tel. 01753/854-489, www.deeandsteve.com, dee@deeandsteve.com).

$ Crown and Cushion is a good option on Eton's High Street, just across the pedestrian bridge from Windsor's waterfront (a short uphill walk to the castle). While the pub it's situated over is worn and drab, you're right in the heart of charming Eton, and the eight creaky rooms—with uneven floors and old-beam ceilings—are nicely furnished (free parking, 84 High Street in Eton, tel. 01753/861-531, www.thecrownandcushioneton.co.uk, info@thecrownandcushioneton.com).

Eating in Windsor

Elegant Spots with River Views: Several places flank Windsor Bridge, offering romantic dining after dark. The riverside promenade, with cheap takeaway stands scattered about, is a delightful place for a picnic lunch or dinner with the swans. If you don't see anything that appeals, continue up Eton's High Street, which is also lined with characteristic eateries.

In the Tourist Zone Around the Palace: Strolling the streets and lanes around the palace entrance—especially in the shopping zone near Windsor & Eton Station—you'll find countless trendy and inviting eateries. The central area also has a sampling of dependable British chains (including a Wagamama, Gourmet Burger Kitchen, and Thai Square). Residents enjoy a wide selection of unpretentious little eateries (including a fire station turned pub-and-cultural center) just past the end of pedestrian Peascod Street.

$$$ Bel & The Dragon is the place to splurge on high-quality classic British food in a charming half-timbered building with an upscale-rustic dining space (food served daily 12:00-15:00 & 18:00-22:00, afternoon tea served between lunch and dinner, bar open longer hours, on Thames Street near the bridge to Eton, tel. 01753/866-056).

$$$ Cornucopia a la Russe, with a cozy, woody atmosphere, serves tasty international dishes (two- and three-course lunch deals, open Mon-Sat 12:00-14:30 & 18:00-21:30, Fri-Sat until 22:00, closed Sun, 6 High Street, tel. 01753/833-009).

$$ The Duchess of Cambridge's friendly staff serves up the normal grub in a pub that's right across from the castle walls, and with an open fireplace to boot (daily 11:00-23:00 or later, 3 Thames Street, tel. 01753/864-405). While the pub predates Kate, it was named in her honor following a recent remodel, and has the photos to prove her endorsement.

$$ Meimo offers "Mediterranean/Moroccan" cuisine in a nicely subdued dining room at the quieter end of the pedestrian zone (several fixed-price meal options, daily 10:00-22:00, 69 Peascod Street, tel. 01753/862-222).

$$ Saffron restaurant, while a fairly long walk from the castle, is the local choice for South Indian cuisine, with a modern interior and attentive waiters who struggle with English but are fluent at bringing out tasty dishes. Their vegetarian *thali* is a treat (daily 12:00-14:30 & 17:30-23:30, 99 St. Leonards Road, tel. 01753/855-467).

Cambridge

Cambridge, 60 miles north of London, is world-famous for its prestigious university. Wordsworth, Isaac Newton, Tennyson, Darwin, and Prince Charles are a few of its illustrious alumni. The university dominates—and owns—most of Cambridge, a historic town of about 125,000 people. Cambridge is the epitome of a university town, with busy bikers, stately residence halls, plenty of bookshops, and proud locals who can point out where DNA was originally modeled, the atom first split, and electrons discovered.

In medieval Europe, higher education was the domain of the Church and was limited to ecclesiastical schools. Scholars lived in

"halls" on campus. This academic community of residential halls, chapels, and lecture halls connected by peaceful garden courtyards survives today in the colleges that make up the universities of Cambridge and Oxford. By 1350, Cambridge had eight colleges, each with a monastic-type courtyard, chapel, library, and lodgings. Today, Cambridge has 31 colleges, each with its own facilities, and about 12,000 undergrads. In the town center, these grand old halls date back centuries, with ornately decorated facades that try to one-up each other. While students' lives revolve around their independent colleges, the university organizes lectures, presents degrees, and promotes research.

The university schedule has three terms: Lent term from mid-January to mid-March, Easter term from mid-April to mid-June, and Michaelmas term from early October to early December. During exams (roughly the month of May), the colleges are closed to visitors, which can impede access to some of the town's picturesque little corners. But the main sights—King's College Chapel and the Wren Library at Trinity College—stay open, and Cambridge is never sleepy.

PLANNING YOUR TIME

Cambridge can easily be seen as a day trip from London. A good five-hour plan is to follow my self-guided walk, spend an hour on a punt ride, tour the Fitzwilliam Museum (closed Mon), and see the Wren Library at Trinity College (open Mon-Sat for only two hours a day, so plan ahead). For a little extra color, consider joining a walk through town with a local guide from the TI (2 hours, repeats much of my self-guided walk but splices in local flavor). The TI's town walk includes King's College Chapel, so don't do that on your own.

If you're in town for the evening, the evensong service at King's College Chapel (Mon-Sat at 17:30, Sun at 15:30) is a must. If you like plays and music, events are always happening in this thriving cultural hub.

GETTING TO CAMBRIDGE

By Train: It's an easy trip from London and less than an hour a Catch the train from London's King's Cross Station (2/hour, t leave King's Cross at :15 and :44 past the hour, 45 minutes, £ one-way standard class, £24.60 same-day return after 9:3

0845-748-4950, www.nationalrail.co.uk). Cheaper direct trains also run from London's Liverpool Street Station, but take longer (2/hour, 1.5 hours).

By Bus: National Express X90 coaches run from London's Victoria Coach Station to the Parkside stop in Cambridge (every 60-90 minutes, 2 hours, £12-22, discounted fares may be available in advance online, tel. 0871-781-8181, www.nationalexpress.co.uk).

Orientation to Cambridge

Cambridge is small. Everything is within a pleasant walk. The town has two main streets, separated from the River Cam by the most interesting colleges. The town center, brimming with tearooms, has a TI and a colorful open-air market square. The train station is about a mile to the southeast.

TOURIST INFORMATION

Cambridge's TI is well run and well signposted, just off Market Hill Square in the town center. They offer walking tours (see "Tours in Cambridge," later) and sell bus tickets and a £2.50 map/guide (Mon-Sat 10:00-17:00, Easter-Sept also Sun 11:00-15:00—otherwise closed Sun, phones answered from 9:00, Peas Hill, tel. 01223/791-500, www.visitcambridge.org). In the same building as the TI, you can duck into a former courtroom to catch a free video overview of the town and its history.

ARRIVAL IN CAMBRIDGE

By Train: Cambridge's train station doesn't have baggage storage or a TI. You can pick up a free map at the small info desk on the platform and other brochures on an interior wall to the left of the turnstiles.

To get from the station to downtown Cambridge, you can **walk** for about 25 minutes (exit straight ahead on Station Road, bear right at the war memorial onto Hills Road, and follow it into town); take public **bus** #1, #3, or #7 (referred to as "Citi 1," "Citi 3," and so on in schedules, but buses are marked only with the number; £1.70, pay driver, runs every 5-10 minutes, turn left when exiting station, cross the street, and walk half a block to find bus stands, get off when you see the Lion Yard shopping mall on the left); pay about £6 for a **taxi;** or take a City Sightseeing **bus tour** (described er).

By Car: To park in the middle of town, follow signs from the 1 motorway to any of the central (but expensive) short-stay g lots—including one at the Lion Yard shopping mall. Or

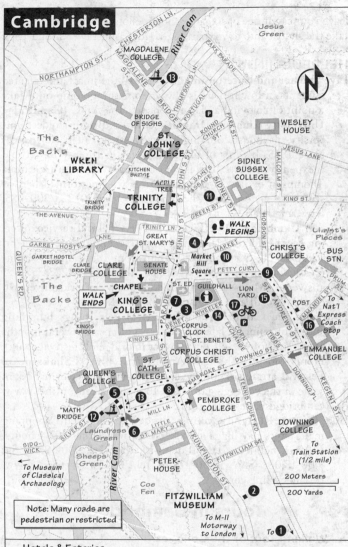

Cambridge

WINDSOR & CAMBRIDGE

Hotels & Eateries
1 To Lensfield Hotel
2 Hotel du Vin
3 The Eagle Pub; Bread & Meat
4 Michaelhouse Café
5 The Anchor Pub
6 The Mill Pub
7 Agora at The Copper Kettle &
King's College Visitors Center
8 Fitzbillies
9 Healthy Fast Food Chains
10 Marks & Spencer
11 Sainsbury's

Other
12 Cambridge Chauffeur Punts
13 Scudamore's Punts (2)
14 Cambridge Live Tickets
15 Bus from Train Station
16 Bus to Train Station
17 Bike Rental

Note: Many roads are pedestrian or restricted

leave your car at one of six park-and-ride lots outside the city, then take the shuttle into town (parking-£1/day; shuttle-£3 round-trip).

HELPFUL HINTS

Live Theater and Entertainment: With all the smart and talented students in town, there is always something going on. Make a point of enjoying a play or concert. The ADC (**Cambridge University Amateur Dramatic Club**) is Britain's oldest university playhouse, offering a steady stream of performances since 1855. It's lots of fun and casual, with easy-to-get and inexpensive tickets. This is your chance to see a future Emma Thompson or Ian McKellen—alums who performed here as students—before they become stars (tel. 01223/300-085, www.adctheatre.com).

　　Cambridge Live Tickets is a very helpful service, offering event info and ticket sales in person and online (Mon-Fri 12:00-18:00, Sat from 10:00, Sun from 18:00 until 30 minutes before showtime, 2 Wheeler Street, tel. 01223/357-851 answered Mon-Sat 10:00-18:00, www.cambridgelivetrust.co.uk). The TI also has lists of what's on.

Festivals: The **Cambridge Folk Festival** gets things humming and strumming in late July (tickets go on sale several months ahead and often sell out; www.cambridgefolkfestival.co.uk). From mid-July through August, the town's **Shakespeare Festival** attracts 25,000 visitors for outdoor performances in some of the college's gardens (£16, book tickets online, www.cambridgeshakespeare.com).

Bike Rental: Rutland Cycling, inside the Lion Yard shopping mall, offers pay luggage lockers and rents bikes (£7/4 hours, £10/day, helmets-£1, £60 deposit); Mon-Fri 8:00-18:00, Sat 9:00-18:00, Sun 10:00-17:00; tel. 01223/307-655, www.rutlandcycling.com.

Tours in Cambridge

▲▲Walking Tour of the Colleges

A walking tour is the best way to understand Cambridge's mix of "town and gown." The walks can be more educational (read: dry) than entertaining, but they do provide a good rundown of the historic and scenic highlights of the university, some fun local gossip, and plenty of university trivia.

　　The TI offers **daily walking tours** that include the King's College Chapel, as well as another college—usually Queen's College 0, 2 hours, includes entry fees; July-Aug daily at 11:00, 12:00, 0, and 14:00, no 11:00 tour on Sun; generally fewer tours rest e year—check website for schedule; tel. 01223/791-500, www.

visitcambridge.org). Groups are limited to 20, so it's smart to call ahead or drop in at the TI in advance to reserve a spot. Note that the 12:00 tour overlaps with the limited opening times of the Wren Library, so you'll miss out on the library if you take the noon tour.

Private guides are available through the TI and affordable if you can assemble a group to share the cost (2-hour tour-£97.50; does not include individual college entrance fees, tel. 01223/791-500, tours@visitcambridge.org).

Walking Ghost Tour

If you're in Cambridge on the weekend, consider a £6.50 "ghost walk" to where spooky sightings have been reported (Fri-Sat at 18:00, organized by the TI, tel. 01223/791-500).

Bus Tours

City Sightseeing hop-on, hop-off bus tours are informative and cover the outskirts, including the American WWII Cemetery. But keep in mind that buses can't go where walking tours can—right into the center (£15.50, 80 minutes for full 19-stop circuit, buy ticket with credit card at the bus-stop kiosk or pay cash to driver when you board, departs every 20 minutes in summer, every 40 minutes in winter, first bus leaves train station around 10:00, last bus around 17:30, recorded commentary, tel. 01223/433-250, www.city-sightseeing.com). If arriving by train, you can buy your ticket from the kiosk directly in front of the station, then ride the bus into town.

Cambridge Town Walk

Cambridge is built along its dreamy little river and around its 31 colleges (the first, Peterhouse, was founded in the 1280s). It's easy to sort out. There's a small and youthful commercial center—quiet and traffic free (except for lots of bikes), one important museum (the Fitzwilliam), and lots of minor museums (all generally free). The River Cam has boat tours, three public bridges, and a strip of six colleges whose gardens basically own the river through the center of town and make it feel like an exclusive park. The university includes two dominant colleges (Trinity with its famous Wren Library, and King's College with its famous chapel), but also plenty of minor ones, each with a grand front gate. The city is filled with students year-round—scholars throughout the regular terms and visiting students enjoying summer programs.

In the following self-guided walk, I cover the essential town sights (including two less-visited colleges), finishing at King's College Chapel. Trinity College and the Fitzwilliam Museum are covered in "Sights in Cambridge," later. To trace the route, see the Cambridge map, earlier.

Cambridge Colleges 101

Colleges are central to life at Cambridge, and are where students spend most of their time. Cambridge has 31 colleges, which house, feed, and parent the students, while the overall university offers formal teaching and lectures. Each college also has a "home professor" who coaches students as they navigate the higher education system.

Some colleges are free to visit and welcoming to the public, some are closed off and very private, and others are famous and make money by charging for visits. Most are open only in the afternoons, and all have a similar design and etiquette. At their historic front gates, you'll find a porter's lodge where the porter keeps an eye on things. He delivers mail, monitors who comes and goes, and keeps people off the grass. The exclusive putting-green quality of the courtyard lawns is a huge deal here: Only fellows (senior professors) can walk on the courts, which are the centerpiece of each college campus. Whether a college is open to visitors or private, you can usually at least pop in through the gate, chat with the porter, and enjoy the view of the grassy court.

The court is ringed by venerable buildings, always including a library, dormitories, a dining hall, and a chapel. The dining halls are easy to identify because they have big bay windows that mark the location of a "high table" where VIPs eat. A portrait of the college's founder usually hangs above the high table, and paintings of rectors and important alumni also decorate the walls. Students still eat in these halls, which is why they are rarely open to the public (but you can look in from the main door). A college's chapel is the building that most often allows visitors (including at evensong services, usually at 17:30 or 18:00). In the chapel, seating is usually arranged in several rows of pews that face each other to allow for antiphonal singing and chanting—where one side starts and the other responds. The chapels often contain memorials to students who died in World Wars I and II. Libraries are treasured and generally not open to the public. There's also a Senior Common Room (like a teachers' lounge but much fancier), where fellows share ideas in an exclusive social hall, creating a fertile intellectual garden. Students live on campus not along halls but in "staircases" (never open to the public). Their address includes their college, their staircase, and their room number.

• Start this self-guided walk on Market Hill Square (the TI is just half a block away). To find the square from the lively street called King's Parade—which feels like the center of town and is where this walk ends—go behind Great St. Mary's Church (with the tall tower).

Market Hill Square

This square has been a center of commerce for more than a thousand years. Think of the history this place has seen: Romans first built a bridge over the Cam in A.D. 43, Anglo-Saxons and Danes established a market here in the Dark Ages, and Normans built a castle here (now gone) in the 11th century.

But the big year was 1209, when scholars and students first arrived. After scuffles in Oxford between its townsfolk and university (which is roughly 100 years older than Cambridge), Oxford's students and professors fled here and settled. (The Oxford-Cambridge rivalry just seems natural.) Where's the university? Everywhere, mixed into the town, with the 31 individual colleges, university halls, and student dorms scattered about. Even on this square you can see dorms (the more modern, tasteless buildings around you). Cambridge suffered no bomb damage in World War II, so the older buildings you see are originals. As you walk, notice how peaceful the town is. Almost no cars, but bikes everywhere—be careful! They are silent and pack a punch.

The Guildhall facing this square (the seat of the city council today) overlooks market stalls. The big market is on Sunday (9:30-16:30) and features produce, arts, and crafts. On other days, you'll find mostly clothes and food (Mon-Sat generally 9:30-16:00).

• *Facing the Guildhall, exit the square to your left down Petty Cury Lane, a modern pedestrian shopping street. At its end (with three fast-food places: Eat, Pret, and Wasabi) you hit St. Andrews Street. On the left side of the street is the fine 16th-century gatehouse of Christ's College. Step inside to enjoy the classic court, next to a bust of Charles Darwin (a notable alum). The college is open to the public daily 9:00-16:00 if you want to poke around. Otherwise continue down St. Andrews Street a long block to Emmanuel College.*

Emmanuel College

This college welcomes the public and offers a classic peek at a typical Cambridge college (free, open 9:00-18:00). Emmanuel was founded in 1584 as a Protestant college on land that had once been a Dominican friary. (Like many monasteries and convents in the 16th century, the friary had been dissolved by the English king in an epic power struggle that left England with its own version of Christianity and the government with lots of land once owned by the Catholic Church.)

Facing the court, with the big clock, is one of two chapels in town designed by the famed architect Christopher Wren. Above the church is the Senior Common Room, a social hall for colle fellows. On the left is the dining hall—marked by its big bay w' dow.

At this point you could visit the church (find the por of John Harvard—the Emmanuel College student who we America and founded another prestigious school—in the s glass on the left), look through the doorway into the dining hall, enjoy the garden behind the chapel (typical of these colleges; the fish pond goes back to monastic days when the fish were part of the diet), or chat with the porter.

• *Leaving Emmanuel College, walk straight ahead along Downing Street. You'll pass several museums that are owned by the university to support various fields of study (generally free to enter). Downing Street ends at King's Parade, with Pembroke College on the left and the recommended Fitzbillies café on the right (famous for its local cinnamon roll, the Chelsea Bun).*

Pembroke College

Founded in 1347, Pembroke is the third-oldest college in Cambridge. Step into the court, past the porter's lodge—it's polite to say hello and ask whether you can wander around. Survey the court. Two chapels face it. The original chapel (on the left) was replaced by the bigger one on the right. Ahead of you is the medieval dining hall. The fancy building with the pointed clock tower is the library (the statue in front is alumnus William Pitt the Younger—a great 18th-century prime minister), with a charming garden beyond.

The highlight here is the chapel on the right, which dates from about 1660 and is the first building Christopher Wren completed. Before stepping inside to enjoy the interior, pause for a moment at the somber WWI and WWII memorial.

• *From Pembroke College, cross King's Parade and follow Mill Lane directly down to the River Cam and its mill pond.*

River Cam, the Mill Pond, and Punting

From this perch you see the "harbor action" of Cambridge. The city was a sort of harbor in medieval times: Trading vessels from the North Sea could navigate to here. Today a weir divides the River Cam from the River Granta (on the left), which leads through idyllic countryside to the town of Grantchester. Filling the mill pond is a commotion of the iconic Cambridge boats called punts (note that punts cannot cross the weir). Students hustle to take visitors on a 45-minute trip along the park known as "the Backs," with views of the backs of colleges that line the river from here to the far side of town (about £20, see page 247). You can share a boat with others and enjoy a colorful narration as you're poled past fine college architecture. Skilled residents rent boats for themselves, as do not-so-skilled tourists—much to the amusement of locals who their beer while watching clumsy visitors fumble with the boats ich are tougher to maneuver than they look).

Walk along the harbor past the recommended Anchor Pub waterfront tables and fancier seating upstairs) to the Silver Bridge. From here you can watch more punt action and check out the famous "Mathematical Bridge," which links the old and new buildings of Queens' College. This wooden bridge, although curved, is made of straight boards. (It was not designed by Isaac Newton, as a popular fable would have it—Newton died before the bridge was constructed.)

Gazing upstream past the wooden bridge, you see the start of "the Backs" stretch of six colleges, most with bridges connecting campus grounds or buildings on both sides of the river.

• *Walk up Silver Street, back to King's Parade, and turn left toward this walk's finale—King's College. On the first corner, find the fancy gilded clock.*

The Corpus Clock, Benet Street, and Eagle Pub

Designed and commissioned by Corpus Christi College alum John Taylor, this clock was unveiled by Cambridge physicist Stephen Hawking in a 2008 ceremony. Perched on top is the Chrono phage—the "time eater"—a grotesque giant grasshopper that keeps the clock moving and periodically winks at passersby. The message? Time is passing, so live every moment to the fullest.

The Eagle Pub, a venerable joint, is just down Benet Street on the left. This is Cambridge's oldest pub and a sight in itself. Poke into the courtyard and atmospheric rooms even if you don't eat or drink here.

From the courtyard outside, look up at the balcony of second-floor guest rooms that date back to when this was a coachmen's inn as well as a pub. (It's said that in Shakespeare's time, plays were performed from this perch to entertain guests below.) The faded *Bath* sign indicates that this was a posh place—you could even wash. Notice that the window on the right end is open; any local will love to tell you why.

Step past the "glancing stones" that protected the corner from careening coaches. During World War II, US Army Air Corps pilots famously hung out here before missions over Germany. The fun interior is plastered with stickers of air crews and WWII memorabilia. Next to the fireplace a photo and plaque remember two esteemed regulars—Francis Crick and James Watson—the scientists who first described the structure of DNA. They announced their finding here in 1953, and if you'd like to drink to that, there's a beer on tap for you—a bitter called DNA.

St. Benet's Church, across the street from the pub, is the oldest surviving building in Cambridgeshire. The Saxons who built the church in the 11th century included circular holes in its bell tower to encourage owls to roost there and keep the mouse population under control.

• *Return to the creepy grasshopper clock and turn right, continuing do*

King's Parade past the regal front facade of King's College Chapel (we'll return here shortly) to the...

Senate House

This stately classical building with triangular pediments is the ceremonial and administrative heart of the University of Cambridge and the meeting place of the university's governing body. In June, you may notice green boxes lining the front of this house. Traditionally, at the end of the term, students came to these boxes to see whether they earned their degree; those not listed knew they had flunked. Amazingly, until 2010 this was the only notification students received about their status. (Now they first get an email.)

Looming across the street from the Senate House is **Great St. Mary's Church** (a.k.a. the University Church), with a climbable bell tower (£4, Mon-Sat 9:30-

16:30, Sun 12:30-16:00, 123 stairs). On the corner nearby is **Ryder and Amies** (22 King's Parade), which has been the official university outfitter for 150 years. It's a great shop for college gear: sweaters, ties, and so on. Upstairs, if you ask, you can try on an undergraduate gown and mortar board.

• *Just after the Senate House, take the first left possible (on Senate House passage); at the end, bear left on Trinity Lane to reach the gate where you pay to enter...*

▲▲King's College Chapel

Built from 1446 to 1515 by Henrys VI through VIII, England's best example of Perpendicular Gothic architecture is the single most impressive building in Cambridge.

Cost and Hours: £9, erratic hours depending on school events; during academic term usually Mon-Fri 9:30-15:30, Sat until 15:15, Sun 13:15-14:30; during breaks (see page 233) usually daily 9:30-16:30; recorded info tel. 01223/331-1212. Buy tickets at the King's College visitors center at 13 Kings Parade, across the street from the main entrance gate.

Evensong: When school's in session, you're welcome to enjoy an evensong service in this glorious space, with a famous choir made up of men and boys (free, Mon-Sat at 17:30, Sun at 15:30; for more on evensong, see page 163). Line up at the front entrance (on King's Parade) by 17:00 if you want prime seats in the choir.

Visiting the Chapel: Stand inside, look up, and marvel, as Christopher Wren did, at what was then the largest single span of **vaulted roof** anywhere. Built between 1512 and 1515, its 2,000 tons of incredible fan vaulting—held in place by the force of gravity—are a careful balancing act resting delicately on the buttresses visible outside the building.

While Henry VI—who began work on the chapel—wanted it to be austere, his successors on the throne decided it should glorify the House of Tudor (of which Henry VI's half-nephew Henry VII, was the first king). Lining the walls are giant **Tudor coats-of-arms.** The shield is supported by symbolism for each branch of the family: the fleur-de-lis is there because an earlier

ancestor, Edward III, woke up one day and somewhat arbitrarily declared himself king of France; a rose and the dragon of Wales represent the family of Henry VII's father, Edmund Tudor; and the greyhound holding the shield and the portcullis (the iron grate) symbolize the family of Henry VII's mother, Lady Margaret Beaufort.

The 26 **stained-glass windows** date from the 16th century. It's the most Renaissance stained glass anywhere in one spot. (Most

of the stained glass in English churches dates from Victorian times, but this glass is three centuries older.) The lower panes show scenes from the New Testament, while the upper panes feature corresponding stories from the Old Testament. Considering England's turbulent history, it's miraculous that these windows have survived for nearly half a millennium in such a pristine state. After Henry VIII separated from the Catholic Church in 1534, many such windows and other Catholic features around England were destroyed. (Think of all those ruined abbeys dotting the English countryside.) However, since Henry had just paid for these windows, he couldn't bear to destroy them. A century later, in the days of Oliver Cromwell, another wave of iconoclasm destroyed more windows around England. Though these windows were slated for removal, they stayed put. (Historians speculate that Cromwell's troops, who were garrisoned in this building, didn't want the windows removed in the chilly wintertime.) Finally, during World War II, the windows were taken out and hidden away for safekeeping, then painstakingly replaced after the war ended. The only nonmedieval windows are on the west wall (opposite the altar). These are in the Romantic style from the 1880s; when Nazi bombs threatened the church, all agreed they should be left in place.

The **choir screen** that bisects the church was commissioned by King Henry VIII to commemorate his marriage to Anne Boleyn. By the time it was finished, so was she (beheaded). But it was too late to remove her initials, which were carved into the screen (look on the far left and right for *R.A.*, for *Regina Anna*—"Queen Anne"). Behind the screen is the **choir** area, where the King's College Choir performs a daily evensong (during school terms). On Christmas Eve, a special service is held here and broadcast around the world on the BBC—a tradition near and dear to British hearts.

Walk to the altar and admire Rubens' masterful *Adoration of the Magi* (1634). It's actually a family portrait: The admirer in the front (wearing red) is a self-portrait of Rubens, Mary looks an awful lot like his much-younger wife, and the Baby Jesus resembles their own newborn at the time. The chapel to the right of the altar is a moving memorial to those who died in the two world wars.

Finally, check out the long and fascinating series of rooms that run the length of the nave on the left. Dedicated to the history and art of the church, these are a great little King's College Chapel museum (including a model showing how the fan vaults were constructed).

• *Exit the church opposite where you entered, into the college court. From here you can stroll the rich grounds all the way to the River Cam and then back, passing through the grand entry gate and onto King's Parade.*

Sights in Cambridge

My self-guided walk takes you to most of the main sights in Cambridge, but not all. Visiting the following places in and near town is also worthwhile.

▲▲Trinity College and Wren Library

More than a third of Cambridge's 83 Nobel Prize winners have come from this richest and biggest of the town's colleges, founded in 1546 by Henry VIII. The college has three sights to see: the entrance gate, the grounds, and the magnificent Wren Library.

Cost and Hours: Grounds—£3, daily 10:00-17:00; library—free, Mon-Fri 12:00-14:00, during full term also Sat 10:30-12:30, closed Sun year-round; only 20 people allowed in at a time, tel. 01223/338-400, www.trin.cam.ac.uk.

Visiting the College: To see the Wren Library without paying for the grounds, access it from the riverside entrance (a long walk around the college via the Garret Hostel Bridge).

Trinity Gate: You'll notice gates like these adorning facades of colleges around town. Above the door is a statue of **King Henry**

VIII, who founded Trinity because he feared that Cambridge's existing colleges were too cozy with the Church. Notice Henry's right hand holding a chair leg instead of the traditional scepter with the crown jewels. This is courtesy of Cambridge's Night Climbers, who first replaced the scepter a century ago, and continue to periodically switch it out for other items. According to campus legend, decades ago some of the world's most talented mountaineers enrolled at Cambridge... in one of the flattest parts of England. (Cambridge was actually a seaport until Dutch engineers drained the surrounding swamps.) Lacking opportunities to practice their skill, they began scaling the frilly facades of Cambridge's college buildings under cover of darkness (if caught, they'd have been expelled). In the 1960s, climbers actually managed to haul an entire automobile onto the roof of the Senate House. The university had to bring in the army to cut it into pieces and remove it. Only 50 years later, at a class reunion, did the guilty parties finally fess up.

In the little park to the right, notice the lone **apple tree.** Supposedly, this tree is a descendant of the very one that once stood in the garden of Sir Isaac Newton (who spent 30 years at Trinity). According to legend, Newton was inspired to investigate gravity when

an apple fell from the tree onto his head. This tree stopped bearing fruit long ago; if you do see apples, they've been tied on by mischievous students.

Beyond the gate are the Trinity grounds. Note that there's often a fine and free view of Trinity College courtyard—if the gate is open—from Trinity Lane (leading, under a uniform row of old chimneys, around the school to the Wren Library).

Trinity Grounds: The grounds are enjoyable to explore. Inside the **Great Court,** the clock (on the tower on the right) double-rings at the top of each hour. It's a college tradition to take off running from the clock when the high noon bells begin (it takes 43 seconds to clang 24 times), race around the courtyard, touching each of the four corners without setting foot on the cobbles, and try to return to the same spot before the ringing

ends. Supposedly only one student (a young lord) ever managed the feat—a scene featured in *Chariots of Fire* (but filmed elsewhere).

The **chapel** (entrance to the right of the clock tower)—which pales in comparison to the stunning King's College Chapel—feels like a shrine to thinking, with statues honoring great Trinity minds both familiar (Isaac Newton, Alfred, Lord Tennyson, Francis Bacon) and unfamiliar. Who's missing? The poet Lord Byron, who was such a hell-raiser during his time at Trinity that a statue of him was deemed unfit for Church property; his statue stands in the library instead.

Wren Library: Don't miss the 1695 Christopher Wren-designed library, with its wonderful carving and fascinating original manuscripts. Just outside the library entrance, Sir Isaac Newton clapped his hands and timed the echo to measure the speed of sound as it raced down the side of the cloister and back. In the library's 12 display cases (covered with cloth that you flip back), you'll see handwritten works by Sir Isaac Newton and John Milton, alongside A. A. Milne's original *Winnie the Pooh* (the real Christopher Robin attended Trinity College). Unlike the other libraries at Cambridge, Wren designed his to be used from the first floor up—instead of the damp, dark ground floor. As a result, Wren's library is flooded with light, rather than water (and it's also brimming with students during exam times).

▲▲Fitzwilliam Museum

Britain's best museum of antiquities and art outside London is the Fitzwilliam. Housed in a grand Neoclassical building, a 10-minute walk south of Market Square, it's a palatial celebration of beauty and humankind's ability to create it.

Cost and Hours: Free but £5 donation suggested, Tue-Sat 10:00-17:00, Sun 12:00-17:00, closed Mon, lockers, Trumpington Street, tel. 01223/332-900, www.fitzmuseum.cam.ac.uk.

Visiting the Museum: The Fitzwilliam's broad collection is like a mini-British Museum/National Gallery rolled into one; you're bound to find something you like. Helpful docents—many with degrees or doctorates in art history—are more than willing to answer questions about the collection. The ground floor features an extensive range of antiquities and applied arts—everything from Greek vases, Mesopotamian artifacts, and Egyptian sarcophagi to Roman statues, fine porcelain, and suits of armor.

Upstairs is the painting gallery, with works that span art history: Italian Venetian masters (such as Titian and Canaletto), a worthy English section (featuring Gainsborough, Reynolds, Hogarth, and others), and a notable array of French Impressionist art (including Monet, Renoir, Picsarro, Degas, and Sisley). Rounding out the collection are old manuscripts, including some musical compositions from Handel.

Museum of Classical Archaeology

Although this museum contains no originals, it offers a unique chance to study accurate copies (19th-century casts) of virtually every famous ancient Greek and Roman statue. More than 450 statues are on display. If you've seen the real things in Greece, Istanbul, Rome, and elsewhere, touring this collection is like a high school reunion..."Hey, I know you!" But since it takes some time to get here, this museum is best left to devotees of classical sculpture.

Cost and Hours: Free, Mon-Fri 10:00-17:00, Sat 10:00-13:00 during term, closed Sun year-round, Sidgwick Avenue, tel. 01223/330-402, www.classics.cam.ac.uk/museum.

Getting There: The museum is a five-minute walk west of Silver Street Bridge; after crossing the bridge, continue straight until you reach a sign reading *Sidgwick Site*.

▲Punting on the Cam

For a little levity and probably more exercise than you really want, try renting one of the traditional flat-bottom punts at the river and pole yourself up and down (or around and around, more likely) the lazy Cam. This is one of the best memories the town has to offer, and once you get the hang of it, it's a fine way to enjoy the scenic side of Cambridge. It's less crowded in late afternoon (and less embarrassing).

Several companies rent

punts and also offer punting tours with entertaining narration. Hawkers try to snare passengers in the thriving people zone in front of King's College. Prices are soft in slow times—try talking them down a bit before committing.

Scudamore's has two locations: on Mill Lane, just south of the central Silver Street Bridge, and at the less convenient Quayside at Magdalene Bridge, at the north end of town (£27.50/hour, credit-card deposit required; 45-minute tours-£19/person, ask for discount; open daily 9:00-dusk, tel. 01223/359-750, www.scudamores.com).

Cambridge Chauffeur Punts, just under the Silver Street Bridge, also rents punts. Take yourself and up to five friends for a spin, or they will chauffeur (£24/hour; passport, credit card, or £60 cash deposit required; 45-minute shared tours-£16/person; open daily March-Nov 9:00-dusk, tel. 01223/354-164, www.punting-in-cambridge.co.uk).

NEAR CAMBRIDGE
Imperial War Museum Duxford

This former airfield, nine miles south of Cambridge, is popular with aviation fans and WWII history buffs. Wander through seven exhibition halls housing 200 vintage aircraft (including Spitfires, B-17 Flying Fortresses, a Concorde, and a Blackbird, some of which you can enter) as well as military land vehicles and special displays on Normandy and the Battle of Britain. The American Air wing thoughtfully portrays the achievements and controversies of British/US wartime collaboration, including the stories of American airmen based at Duxford. On many weekends, the museum holds special events, such as air shows (extra fee)—check the website for details.

Cost and Hours: £18, show local bus ticket for discount, daily 10:00-18:00, off-season until 16:00, last entry one hour before closing; tel. 01223/835-000, www.iwm.org.uk/visits/iwm-duxford.

Getting There: The museum is located off the A-505 in Duxford. On Sundays, direct Myalls bus #132 runs to the museum from the train station (4/day, 45 minutes, www.travelineeastanglia.org.uk). The rest of the week, it's best to take a taxi from Cambridge: Catch one at the taxi stand on St. Andrews Street next to the Lion Yard shopping mall (about £25 one-way).

Sleeping in Cambridge

While Cambridge is an easy side-trip from London (and you can enjoy an evening here before catching a late train back), its subtle charms may convince you to spend a night or two. Cambridge has few accommodations in the city center, and none in the tight maze of colleges and shops where you'll spend most of your time. These recommendations (each just past the Fitzwilliam Museum) are about a 10-minute walk south of the town center, toward the train station. (Though weak in hotel offerings, Cambridge does have plenty of B&Bs, which you can research and book online.)

$$$ Lensfield Hotel, popular with visiting professors, has 40 comfortable rooms—some old-fashioned, some refurbished (spa and fitness room, 53 Lensfield Road, tel. 01223/355-017, www. lensfieldhotel.co.uk, enquiries@lensfieldhotel.co.uk).

$$$ Hotel du Vin is a pretentious place that rents 41 decent rooms at a high price. It has duck-your-head character and a good location (breakfast extra, Trumpington Street 15, tel. 01223/928 991, www.hotelduvin.com, reception.cambridge@hotelduvin. com).

Eating in Cambridge

$$$ The Eagle Pub, near the TI and described earlier in my town walk, is the oldest pub in town. While the food is mediocre, the pub is a Cambridge institution with a history so rich that a visit here practically qualifies as sightseeing (food served daily 11:00-22:00, 8 Benet Street, tel. 01223/505-020).

$ Michaelhouse Café is a heavenly respite from the crowds, tucked into the repurposed St. Michael's Church, just north of Great St. Mary's Church. At lunch, choose from salads and sandwiches, as well as a few hot dishes and a variety of tasty baked goods (Mon-Sat 8:00-17:00, breakfast served until 11:30, lunch served 11:30-15:50, closed Sun, Trinity Street, tel. 01223/309-147). Between 15:00 and 17:00 whatever they have left from lunch is half-price.

$$$ The Anchor Pub's claim to fame is as the setting of Pink Floyd's first gig. Today it's known for the best people-watching—and some locals say best food—in Cambridge. Choose from its outdoor riverside terrace, inside bar, or more romantic upstairs restaurant (all seating areas serve the same menu, but the upstairs menu has a few added specials; daily 12:00-21:30, on the riverfront at Silver Street, tel. 01224/353-554).

$$ The Mill Pub is a livelier, less formal alternative to The Anchor, but enjoys a similar location right on the river. The clientele is a mixture of students and tourists; the tipples are craft brews, local ales, and ciders; and the food is an eclectic mix ranging from updated pub standards to Indian and Asian options (daily 11:00-23:00, 14 Mill Lane, tel. 01223/311-829).

$ Bread & Meat serves simple soups and hearty sandwiches. Grab a signature *porchetta* sandwich to take away or snag a rustic table in the small dining room (Sun-Thu 11:00-19:30, Fri-Sat 10:00-21:00, 4 Benet Street, tel. 0791/808-3057).

$$ Agora at The Copper Kettle is a popular place for Greek and Turkish *meze,* beautifully situated facing King's College on King's Parade (also fish-and-chips at lunch, daily 8:00-20:30, later in summer, 4 King's Parade, tel. 01223/308-448).

$$ Fitzbillies, long a favorite for cakes (Chelsea Buns) and coffee, offers inviting lunch and afternoon tea menus (daily, 51 Trumpington Street, tel. 01223/352-500).

$ Fast Food: For healthy fast-food chains, the corner of Petty Cury Lane and Sidney Street (a long block off Market Hill Square) has several good options.

Supermarkets: There's a **Marks & Spencer Simply Food** at the train station (daily until 23:00) and a larger Marks & Spencer department store on Market Hill Square (Mon-Tue 8:00-18:00, later Wed-Sat, Sun 11:00-17:00). **Sainsbury's** supermarket has longer hours (Mon-Sat 7:30-23:30, Sun 11:00-17:00, 44 Sidney Street, at the corner of Green Street).

A good picnic spot is Laundress Green, a grassy park on the river, at the end of Mill Lane near the Silver Street Bridge punts. There are no benches, so bring something to sit on. Remember, the college lawns are private property, so walking or picnicking on the grass is generally not allowed. When in doubt, ask at the college's entrance.

Cambridge Connections

From Cambridge by Train to: York (hourly, 2.5 hours, transfer in Peterborough), **London** (King's Cross Station: 2/hour, 45 minutes; Liverpool Street Station: 2/hour, 1.5 hours). Train info: Tel. 0345-748-4950, www.nationalrail.co.uk.

By Bus to: London (every 60-90 minutes, 2 hours), **Heathrow Airport** (1-2/hour, 2-3 hours). Bus info: Tel. 0871-781-8181, www.nationalexpress.com.

BATH

The best city to visit within easy striking distance of London is Bath—just a 1.5-hour train ride away. Two hundred years ago, this city of 90,000 was the trendsetting Tinseltown of Britain. If ever a city enjoyed looking in the mirror, Bath's the one. It has more "government-listed" or protected historic buildings per capita than any other town in England. Built of the creamy warm-tone limestone called "Bath stone," it beams in its cover-girl complexion. An architectural chorus line, it's a triumph of the Neoclassical style of the Georgian era—named for the four Georges who sat as England's kings from 1714 to 1830. Proud locals remind visitors that the town is routinely banned from the "Britain in Bloom" contest to give other towns a chance to win. Bath's narcissism is justified. Even with its mobs of tourists (2 million per year) and greedy prices, Bath is a joy to visit.

Bath's fame began with the allure of its (supposedly) healing hot springs. Long before the Romans arrived in the first century, Bath was known for its curative waters. Romans named the popular spa town Aquae Sulis, after a local Celtic goddess. The town's importance carried through Saxon times, when it had a huge church on the site of the present-day abbey and was considered the religious capital of Britain. Its influence peaked in 973 with King Edgar's sumptuous coronation in the abbey. Later, Bath prospered as a wool town.

Bath then declined until the mid-1600s, wasting away to just a huddle of huts around the abbey, with hot, smelly mud and 3,000 residents, oblivious to the Roman ruins 18 feet below their dirt floors. In fact, with its own walls built upon ancient ones, Bath was no bigger than that Roman town. Then, in 1687, Queen Mary, fighting infertility, bathed here. Within 10 months, she gave birth to a son...and a new age of popularity for Bath.

The revitalized town boomed as a spa resort. Most of the buildings you'll see today are from the 18th century. The classical revivalism of Italian architect Andrea Palladio inspired a local father-and-son team—both named John Wood (the Elder and the Younger)—to build a "new Rome." The town bloomed in the Neoclassical style, and streets were lined not with scrawny sidewalks but with wide "parades," upon which women in their stylishly wide dresses could spread their fashionable tails.

Beau Nash (1673-1762) was Bath's "master of ceremonies." He organized the daily social regimen of aristocratic visitors, and he made the city more appealing by lighting the streets, improving security, banning swords, and opening the Pump Room. Under his fashionable baton, Bath became a city of balls, gaming, and concerts—the place to see and be seen in England. This most civilized place became even more so with the great Neoclassical building spree that followed.

These days, modern tourism has stoked the local economy, as has the fast morning train to London. (A growing number of Bath-based professionals catch the 7:13 train to Paddington Station every weekday morning.) And, with renewed access to Bath's soothing hot springs at the Thermae Bath Spa, the venerable waters are in the spotlight again, attracting a new generation of visitors in need of a cure or a soak.

PLANNING YOUR TIME

Bath deserves two nights even on a quick trip. On a three-week England getaway, spend three nights in Bath, with one day for the city and one day for side-trips (see next chapter). Ideally, use Bath as your jet-lag recovery pillow (easy access from Heathrow Airport), and do London at the end of your trip.

Consider starting your English vacation this way:

Day 1: Land at Heathrow. Connect to Bath either by train via London Paddington, direct bus, or bus/train combination via Reading (for details, see page 289). You can also consider flying into Bristol, which has easy bus connections with Bath. While you don't need or want a car in Bath, those who land early and pick up their cars at the airport can visit Windsor Castle (near Heathrow) on their way to Bath. If you have the evening free in Bath, take a walking tour.

Day 2: 9:00—Tour the Roman Baths; 10:30—Catch the free city walking tour; 12:30—Picnic on the open deck of a tour bus; 14:00—Visit the abbey, then free time in the shopping center of old Bath; 15:30—Tour the No. 1 Royal Crescent Georgian house and Fashion Museum or Museum of Bath at Work. At night, consider seeing a play, take the evening walking tour (unless you did last night), enjoy the Bizarre Bath comedy walk, or go for an evening soak in the Thermae Bath Spa.

Day 3 (and Possibly 4): By car or bus, explore nearby sights such as Glastonbury and Wells (see the next chapter). Without a car or to go farther afield, consider a one-day Avebury/Stonehenge/cute towns minibus tour from Bath (Mad Max tours are best; see "Tours in Bath," later).

Continuing from Bath: Consider linking Bath to the Cotswolds via South Wales (see the South Wales chapter).

Orientation to Bath

Bath's town square, three blocks in front of the bus and train station, is a cluster of tourist landmarks, including the abbey, Roman Baths, and the Pump Room. Bath is hilly. In general, you'll gain elevation as you head north from the town center.

TOURIST INFORMATION

The TI is in the abbey churchyard (Mon-Sat 9:30-17:30, Sun 10:00-16:00, tel. 0844-847-5256, www.visitbath.co.uk). It sells tickets for the Roman Baths, allowing you to skip the (often long) line.

ARRIVAL IN BATH

The Bath Spa **train station** has a staffed ticket desk and ticket machines. Directly in front of the train station is the SouthGate Bath shopping center. To get from the train station to the TI, exit straight ahead and continue up Manvers Street for about five minutes, then turn left at the triangular "square" overlooking the riverfront park, following the small TI arrow on a signpost. The **bus station** is immediately west of the train station, along Dorchester Street. There is a handy luggage-check service a half block away (see "Helpful Hints," next).

HELPFUL HINTS

Getting to Bath and Stonehenge by Tour: Several companies offer guided bus tours from London to Stonehenge, Salisbury, and Bath; you can abandon the tour in Bath, essentially using the tour as one-way transport; see page 320.

Festivals: In late May, the 10-day **Bath Festival** celebrates

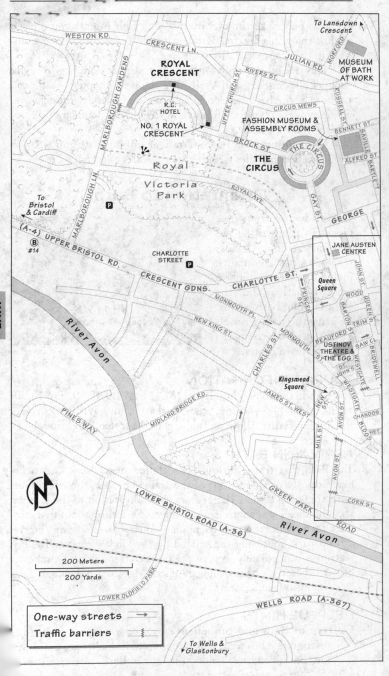

WESTON RD.

CRESCENT LN.

To Lansdown
Crescent

JULIAN RD.

MORFORD

ROYAL
CRESCENT

MUSEUM
OF BATH
AT WORK

RIVERS ST.

CIRCUS MEWS

R.C.
HOTEL

UPPER CHURCH ST.

RUSSELL ST.

BENNETT ST.

SAVILLE ST.

NO. 1 ROYAL
CRESCENT

FASHION MUSEUM &
ASSEMBLY ROOMS

BROCK ST.

THE CIRCUS

ALFRED ST.

BAKTLE

MARLBOROUGH GARDENS

THE
CIRCUS

Royal

Victoria
Park

ROYAL AVE.

GAY ST.

To
Bristol
& Cardiff

MARLBOROUGH LN.

P

GEORGE

(A-4) UPPER BRISTOL RD.

B
#14

CHARLOTTE
STREET

P

JANE AUSTEN
CENTRE

CRESCENT GDNS.

CHARLOTTE ST.

Queen
Square

JOHN ST.

PRINCES ST.

WOOD

MONMOUTH PL.

QUEEN

River Avon

NEW KING ST.

CHARLES ST.

MONMOUTH

BARTON ST.

TRIM ST.

BEAUFORD SQ.

BRIDEWELL

SAW CL.

USTINOV
THEATRE &
THE EGG

JOHN'S ST.

WESTGATE ST.

Kingsmead
Square

NEW ST.

WESTGATE
BLDGS.

PINES WAY

MIDLAND BRIDGE RD.

JAMES ST. WEST

CHANDOS

MILK ST.

AVON ST.

HET

GREEN PARK

N

LOWER BRISTOL ROAD (A-36)

River Avon

CORN ST.

ROAD

200 Meters

200 Yards

LOWER OLDFIELD PARK

WELLS ROAD (A-367)

One-way streets →

Traffic barriers

To Wells &
Glastonbury

BATH

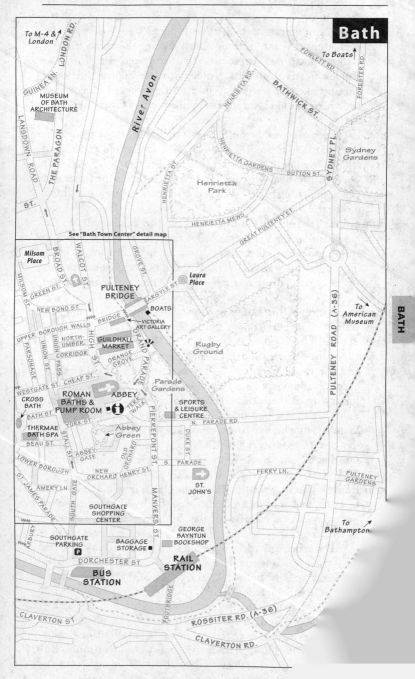

music, and literature (bathfestivals.org.uk/the-bath-festival/), overlapped by the eclectic **Bath Fringe Festival** (theater, walks, talks, bus trips; www.bathfringe.co.uk). The **Jane Austen Festival** unfolds genteelly in late September (www.janeausten.co.uk/festival). And for three weeks in December, the squares around the abbey are filled with a **Christmas market.**

Bath's festival **box office** sells tickets for most events (but not for those at the Theatre Royal), and can tell you exactly what's on tonight (housed inside the TI, tel. 01225/463-362, www.bathfestivals.org.uk). The city's weekly paper, the *Bath Chronicle*, publishes a "What's On" events listing each Thursday (www.thisisbath.com).

Bookstore: Topping & Company, an inviting bookshop, has frequent author readings, free coffee and tea, a good selection of maps, and tables filled with tidy stacks, including lots of books on the Bath region (daily 9:00-20:00, near the bottom of the street called "The Paragon"—where it meets George Street, tel. 01225/428-111, www.toppingbooks.co.uk).

Baggage Storage: The Luggage Store, a half block in front of the train station, checks bags for £2.50 each per day (daily 8:00-22:00, 13 Manvers Street, tel. 01225/312-685).

Laundry: The **Spruce Goose Launderette** is between the Circus and the Royal Crescent, on the pedestrian lane called Margaret's Buildings. Bring £1 coins for washing and £0.20 coins for drying, as there are no change machines (self-service, daily 8:00-20:00, last load at 19:00). **Speedy Wash** can pick up your laundry anywhere in town on weekdays before 9:30 for same-day service (Mon-Fri 8:00-17:30, Sat until 13:00 but no pickup, closed Sun, no self-service, most hotels work with them, 4 Mile End, London Road, tel. 01225/427-616).

Car Rental: Ideally, take the train or bus from downtown London to Bath, and rent a car as you leave Bath. Most offices close Saturday afternoon and all day Sunday, which complicates weekend pickups.

Enterprise provides a pickup service for customers to and ~~fr~~om their hotels (extra fee for one-way rentals, at Lower Bris~~tol~~ Road outside Bath, tel. 01225/443-311, www.enterprise.~~com~~). Others include **Thrifty** (pickup service and one-way ~~rentals~~ available, in the Burnett Business Park in Keynsham— ~~between~~ Bath and Bristol, tel. 01179/867-997, www.thrifty.~~com~~), **Hertz** (one-way rentals possible, at Windsor Bridge, ~~tel. 01225/7~~09-3004, www.hertz.co.uk), and **National/Eu**~~ropcar~~ ~~(one-~~way rentals available, about £7 by taxi from the ~~station, a~~t Brassmill Lane—go west on Upper Bristol ~~Road, tel. 01225/3~~84-9985, www.europcar.co.uk). Skip **Avis**—

it's a mile from the Bristol train station; you'd need to rent a car to get there.

Parking: As Bath becomes increasingly pedestrian-friendly, city-center street parking is disappearing. **Park & Ride** service is a stress-free, no-hassle option to save time and money. Shuttles from Newbridge, Lansdown, and Odd Down (all just outside of Bath) offer free parking and 10-minute shuttle buses into town (daily every 15 minutes, £3.30 round-trip).

If you drive into town, be aware that short-term lots fill up fast (£1.60/hour, 2-4-hour maximum). You'll find more spots in long-stay lots for about the same cost. The SouthGate Bath shopping center lot on the corner of Southgate and Dorchester streets is a five-minute walk from the abbey (£5/up to 3 hours, £14/24 hours, cash or credit card, open 24/7); the Charlotte Street car park is the most convenient. For more info on parking (including Park & Ride service), see the "Travel and Maps" section of http://visitbath.co.uk.

Tours in and near Bath

BATH

IN THE CITY
▲▲▲Free City Walking Tours

Free two-hour tours are led by **The Mayor's Corps of Honorary Guides,** volunteers who want to share their love of Bath with its many visitors (as the city's mayor first did when he took a group on a guided walk back in the 1930s). These chatty, historical, and gossip-filled walks are essential for your understanding of this town's amazing Georgian social scene. How else would you learn that the old "chair ho" call for your sedan chair evolved into today's "cheerio" farewell? Tours leave from outside the Pump Room in the abbey churchyard (free, no tips, year-round Sun-Fri at 10:30 and 14:00, Sat at 10:30 only; additional evening walks May-Sept Tue and Thu at 19:00; www.bathguides.org.uk). Tip for theatergoers: When your guide stops to talk outside the Theatre Royal, skip out for a moment, pop into the box office, and see about snaring a great deal on a play for tonight.

The Honorary Guides also lead free two-hour Pulteney Estate walks, including Pulteney Street and Sydney Gardens (May-Sept, Tue and Thu at 11:00).

Private Tours

For a private tour, call the local guides' bureau, **Bath Parade Guides** (£90/2 hours, tel. 01225/337-111, www.bathparadeguides.co.uk, bathparadeguides@yahoo.com). For **Ghost Walks** and **Bizarre Bath** tours, see "Nightlife in Bath," later.

Bath at a Glance

▲▲▲**Free City Walking Tours** Top-notch tours helping you make the most of your visit, led by The Mayor's Corps of Honorary Guides. **Hours:** Sun-Fri at 10:30 and 14:00, Sat at 10:30 only; additional evening walks offered May-Sept Tue and Thu at 19:00. See page 257.

▲▲▲**Roman Baths** Ancient baths that gave the city its name, tourable with good audioguide. **Hours:** Daily 9:00-18:00, July-Aug until 22:00, Nov-Feb 9:30-17:00. See page 261.

▲▲**Bath Abbey** 500-year-old Perpendicular Gothic church, graced with beautiful fan vaulting and stained glass. **Hours:** Mon-Sat 9:00-17:30, Sun 13:00-14:30 & 16:30-17:30. See page 265.

▲▲**Circus and Royal Crescent** Stately Georgian (Neoclassical) buildings from Bath's 18th-century glory days. See page 267.

▲▲**No. 1 Royal Crescent** Your best look at the interior of one of Bath's high-rent Georgian beauties. **Hours:** Mon 12:00-17:30, Tue-Sun 10:30-17:30. See page 268.

▲**Pump Room** Swanky Georgian hall, ideal for a spot of tea or a taste of unforgettably "healthy" spa water. **Hours:** Daily 9:30-17:00 for breakfast, lunch, and afternoon tea (open 18:00-21:00 for dinner July-Aug and Christmas holidays only). See page 264.

BATH

▲▲City Bus Tours

City Sightseeing's hop-on, hop-off bus tours zip through Bath. Jump on a bus anytime at one of 17 signposted pickup points, pay the driver, climb upstairs, and hear recorded commentary about Bath. City Sightseeing has two 45-minute routes: a city tour and a "Skyline" route outside town. Try to get one with a live guide (June-Sept city tour usually at :24 and :48 past the hour, Skyline route on the hour—confirm with driver); otherwise, bring your own earbuds if you've got 'em (the audio recording on the other buses can be barely intelligible with the headsets provided). On a sunny day, this is a multitasking tourist's dream come true: You can munch a sandwich, work on a tan, snap great photos, and learn a lot—all at once. Save money by doing the bus tour first—your ticket get you minor discounts at many sights (£15, ticket valid for hours and both tour routes, generally 4/hour daily in summer 0-17:30, in winter 10:00-15:30, tel. 01225/330-444, www.city-seeing.com).

▲**Pulteney Bridge and Parade Gardens** Shop-strewn bridge and relaxing riverside gardens. **Hours:** Bridge—always open; gardens—daily 10:00-18:00, shorter hours Oct-Easter. See page 266.

▲**Victoria Art Gallery** Paintings from the late 17th century to today. **Hours:** Daily 10:30-17:00. See page 267.

▲**Fashion Museum** 400 years of clothing under one roof, plus the opulent Assembly Rooms. **Hours:** Daily 10:30-18:00, Nov-Feb until 17:00. See page 269.

▲**Museum of Bath at Work** Gadget-ridden circa-1900 engineer's shop, foundry, factory, and office. **Hours:** Daily 10:30-17:00, Nov and Jan-March weekends only, closed in Dec. See page 270

▲**American Museum** Insightful look primarily at colonial/early-American lifestyles, with 18 furnished rooms and eager-to-talk guides. **Hours:** Tue-Sun 12:00-17:00, late Nov-mid-Dec until 16:30, closed Mon except in Aug, closed early Nov and late Dec-mid-March. See page 272.

▲**Thermae Bath Spa** Relaxation center that put the bath back in Bath. **Hours:** Daily 9:00-21:30. See page 273.

BATH

Taxi Tours

Local taxis, driven by good talkers, go where big buses can't. A group of up to four can rent a cab for an hour (about £40; try to negotiate) and enjoy a fine, informative, and—with the right cabbie—entertaining private joyride. It's probably cheaper to let the meter run than to pay for an hourly rate, but ask the cabbie for advice.

NEARBY SIGHTS

Bath is a good launchpad for visiting nearby Glastonbury, We Avebury, Stonehenge, and more.

Mad Max Minibus Tours

Operating daily from Bath, Maddy offers thoughtfully org informative tours run with entertaining guides and limi people per group. Check their website for the latest off book ahead—as far ahead as possible in summer. The S Avebury, and Villages full-day tour, by far their m covers 110 miles and visits Stonehenge; the Avebury photogenic Lacock (LAY-cock); and Castle Combe, the southern-most Cotswold village (£42 plus Stonehenge entry fee, tours depart daily at 8:30 and return at 17:30). Three additional all-day itineraries do a good job covering other areas surrounding Bath: **Avebury & Cotswold Villages** (includes Avebury Stone Circles, Lacock, and Castle Combe; £35, April-Oct Tue and Sat at 11:00); **Heart of the Cotswolds** (visits a handful of villages; £40, March-Oct Mon, Wed, and Fri at 9:00); **Wells and Glastonbury** (includes scenic Cheddar Gorge, £42, April-Sept Tue, Thu, and Sun at 9:00).

All tours depart from outside the Abbey Hotel on Terrace Walk in Bath, a one-minute walk from the abbey. Arrive 15 minutes before your departure time and bring cash (or book online with a credit card at least 48 hours in advance, Rick Steves readers get £10 rebate with online purchase of two separate tour itineraries, request by email at time of booking; mobile 07990-505-970, phone answered daily 8:00-18:00, www.madmaxtours.co.uk, maddy@madmaxtours.co.uk).

Lion Tours

This well-run outfit gets you to Stonehenge on their half-day **Stonehenge and Lacock** tour (£39 including Stonehenge entry fee; leaves daily at 12:15 and returns at 17:30, in summer this tour also leaves at 8:30 and returns at 12:00). They also run full-day tours of **Cotswold Villages** and **King Arthur's Realm.** If you ask in advance, you can bring your luggage along and use this tour to get to Stow. Or, for £10 extra per person or group, you can hop off in Moreton-in-Marsh for easy train connections to Oxford and bus connections to Chipping Campden. Lion's tours depart from the same stop as Mad Max Tours—see earlier (mobile 07769-668-668, book online at www.liontours.co.uk).

Other Tour Options

Scarper Tours runs four-hour narrated minibus tours to Stonehenge—giving you two hours at the site (£20 transportation only, £35 including Stonehenge entry fee, departs from behind the abbey on Terrace Walk; daily mid-March-mid-Oct at 9:30 and 14:00; mid-Oct-mid-March at 13:00; sally@scarpertours.com, www. rpertours.com).

Celtic Horizons offers tours from Bath to destinations such onehenge, Avebury, and Wells. They can provide a convenient r service (to or from London, Heathrow, Bristol Airport, swolds, and so on), with or without a tour itinerary en llow about £35/hour for a group (comfortable minivans or 8 people) and £140 for Heathrow-Bath transfers (1-4 lake arrangements and get pricing by email at info@ s.com (tel. 01373/800-500, US tel. 855-895-0165, rizons.com).

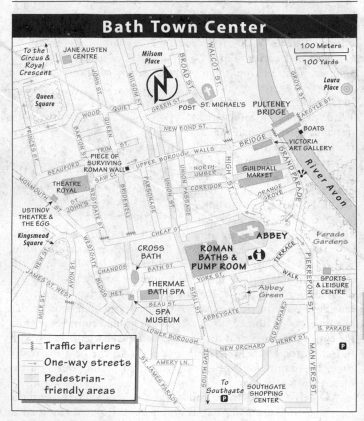

Bath Town Center

Sights in Bath

IN THE TOWN CENTER
▲▲▲Roman Baths

In ancient Roman times, high society enjoyed the mineral sprin
at Bath. From Londinium, Romans traveled so often to Ac
Sulis, as the city was called, to "take a bath" that finally it be
known simply as Bath. Today, a fine museum surrounds
cient bath. With the help of a great audioguide, you'll wa
well-documented displays, Roman artifacts, a temple
with an evocative bearded face, a bronze head of the g
Minerva, excavated ancient foundations, and the ac
the health-giving spring. At the end, you'll have a
around the big pool itself, where Romans once l
splashed, and thanked the gods for the gift of the

Cost and Hours: £15.50, includes audiog
ticket includes Fashion Museum and Victori
rary exhibits, family ticket available, dail

until 22:00, Nov-Feb 9:30-17:00, last entry one hour before closing, tel. 01225/477-784, www.romanbaths.co.uk.

Crowd-Beating Tips: Long ticket lines are typical in the summer. You can avoid them by purchasing a combo-ticket at the Fashion Museum or by buying a ticket at the nearby TI. With voucher or combo-ticket in hand, enter through the "fast track" lane, to the left of the general admission line. On any day, try to visit early or late; peak time is between 13:00 and 15:00. If you're here in July or August, the best time is after

19:00, when the baths are romantic, gas-lit, and all yours.

Tours: Take advantage of the included essential **audioguide,** which makes your visit easy and informative. In addition to the basic commentary, look for posted numbers to key into your audioguide for specialty topics—including a kid-friendly tour and musings from American expat writer Bill Bryson. For those with a big appetite for Roman history, in-depth **guided tours** leave from the end of the museum at the edge of the actual bath (included with ticket, on the hour, a poolside clock is set for the next departure time, 20-40 minutes depending on the guide). You can revisit the museum after the tour.

➲ Self-Guided Tour: Follow the one-way route through the bath and museum complex. This self-guided tour offers a basic overview; for more in-depth commentary, make ample use of the audioguide.

Begin by walking around the upper **terrace,** overlooking the Great Bath. This terrace—lined with sculptures of VIRs (Very Important Romans)—evokes ancient times but was built in the 1890s. The ruins of the bath complex sat undisturbed for centuries before finally being excavated and turned into a museum in the late 19th century.

At the end of the terrace, before going downstairs, peer down into the **spring,** where water bubbles remind you that 240,000 gallons of water emerge daily. If magically, it must have seemed to pilgrims—at a constant 115°F. Geologists now know, heated more than a mile below the earth's surface, first fell

to earth as rain onto nearby hills about 10,000 years ago...making the Romans seem relatively recent.

Now you'll head down to the museum, where exhibits explain the dual purpose of the buildings that stood here in Roman times: a bath complex, for relaxation and for healing; and a temple dedicated to the goddess Sulis Minerva, who was believed to be responsible for the mysterious and much-appreciated thermal springs. Cut-away diagrams and models resurrect both parts of this complex and help establish your bearings among the remaining fragments and foundations—including the original entrance (just off the main suspended walkway, on your right, as you pass through the temple courtyard and Minerva section).

The fragments of the **temple pediment**—carved by indigenous Celtic craftsmen but with Roman themes—represent a remarkable

cultural synthesis. Sit and watch for a while as a slide projection fills in historians' best guesses as to what once occupied the missing bits. The identity of the circular face in the middle puzzles researchers. (God? Santa Claus?) It could be the head of the Gorgon monster after it was slain by Perseus—are those snakes peeking through its hair and beard? And yet, the Gorgon was traditionally depicted as female. Perhaps instead it's Neptune, the god of the sea—appropriate for this aquatic site.

The next exhibits examine living, dying, and worshipping in Aquae Sulis (the settlement here) in antiquity. Much like the pilgrimage sites of the Middle Ages, this spot exerted a powerful pull on people from all over the realm, who were eager to partake in its healing waters and to worship at the religious site. A display of the **Beau Street Hoard**—more than 17,500 Roman coins dating from 32 B.C. to A.D. 274 that were found near the Baths—emphasizes just how well-visited this area was.

You'll also see some of the small but extremely heavy carved-stone tables that pilgrims hauled here as an offering to the gods. Take time to read some of the requests (inscribed on sheets of pewter or iron) that visitors made of the goddess—many are comically spiteful and petty, offering a warts-and-all glimpse into day-to-day Roman culture.

As you walk through the temple's original foundations, keep an eye out for the sacrificial altar. The gilded-bronze head of the goddess **Sulis Minerva** (in the display case) once overlooked a flaming cauldron inside the temple, where only priest were allowed to enter. Similar to the Greek goddess Athena, Sul

Minerva was considered to be a life-giving mother goddess.

Engineers enjoy a close-up look at the spring overflow and the original **drain system**—built two millennia ago—that still carries excess water to the River Avon. Marvel at the cleverness and durability of Roman engineering, created in (what we usually imagine to be) a "primitive" time. A nearby exhibit on pulleys and fasteners lets you play with these inventions.

Head outside to the **Great Bath** itself (where you can join one of the included guided tours for a much more extensive visit—look for the clock with the next start time). Take a slow lap (by foot) around the perimeter, imagining the frolicking Romans who once immersed themselves up to their necks in this five-foot-deep pool. The water is greenish because of algae—don't drink it. The best views are from the west end, looking back toward the abbey. Nearby is a giant chunk of roof span, from a time when this was a cavernous covered swimming hall. At the corner, you'll step over a small canal where hot water still trickles into the main pool. Nearby, find a length of original lead pipe, remarkably well preserved since antiquity.

Symmetrical bath complexes branch off at opposite ends of the Great Bath (perhaps dating from a conservative period when the Romans maintained separate facilities for men and women). The **East Baths** show off changing rooms and various bathing rooms, each one designed for a special therapy or recreational purpose (immersion therapy tub, sauna-like heated floor, and so on), as described in detail by the audioguide.

When you're ready to leave, head for the **West Baths** (including a sweat bath and a *frigidarium*, or "cold plunge" pool) and take another look at the spring and more foundations. After returning your audioguide, pop over to the fountain for a free taste of the spa water. Then pass through the gift shop, past the convenient public WCs (which use plain old tap water), and exit through the **Pump Room**—or stay for a spot of tea.

▲Pump Room

For centuries, Bath was forgotten as a spa. Then, in 1687, the previously barren Queen Mary bathed here, became pregnant, and bore a male heir to the throne. A few years later, Queen Anne found the water eased her painful gout. Word of its miraculously curative waters spread, and Bath earned its way back on the aristocratic map. High society soon turned the place into one big pleasure

palace. The Pump Room, an elegant Georgian hall just above the Roman Baths, offers visitors their best chance to raise a pinky in Neoclassical grandeur. Above the clock, a statue of Beau Nash himself sniffles down at you. Come for a light meal, or to try a famous (but forgettable) "Bath bun" with your spa water (the same water that's in the fountain at the end of the baths tour; also free in the Pump Room if you present your ticket). The spa water is served by an appropriately attired waiter, who will tell you the water is pumped up from nearly 100 yards deep and marinated in 43 wonderful minerals. Or for just the price of a coffee, drop in anytime—except during lunch—to enjoy live music (string trio or piano; times vary) and the atmosphere. Even if you don't eat here, you're welcome to enter the foyer for a view of the baths and dining room.

The **$$$ Pump Room** is open daily 9:30-17:00 for breakfast, lunch, and afternoon tea (tea service starts at 14:30; last orders at 16:00), tea/coffee and pastries also available in the afternoons; open 18:00-21:00 for dinner July-Aug and Christmas holidays only; tel. 01225/444-477.

▲▲Bath Abbey

The town of Bath wasn't much in the Middle Ages, but an important church has stood on this spot since Anglo-Saxon times. King Edgar I was crowned here in 973, when the church was much bigger (before the bishop packed up and moved to Wells). Dominating the town center, today's abbey—the last great church built in medieval England—is 500 years old and a fine example of

the Late Perpendicular Gothic style, with breezy fan va~
enough stained glass to earn it the nickname "Lantern c~

Cost and Hours: £4 suggested donation, Mon-S~
Sun 13:00-14:30 & 16:30-17:30, handy flier narra~
tour, ask about schedule of events—including c~
and evensong—also posted on the door and onli~
462, www.bathabbey.org.

Evensong: Though the evensong servic~

on Monday through Saturday, it's still a beautiful 20 minutes of worship (nightly at 17:30, choral evensong 15:30 on Sun only).

Visiting the Abbey: Take a moment to appreciate the abbey's architecture from the square. The facade (c. 1500, but mostly restored) is interesting for some of its carvings. Look for the angels going down the ladder. The statue of Peter (to the left of the door) lost its head to mean-spirited iconoclasts; it was recarved out of Peter's once supersized beard.

Going inside is worth the small suggested contribution. The glass, red-iron lamps and the heating grates on the floor are all remnants of the 19th century. (In a sustainable, 21st-century touch, the heat now comes from the baths' hot runoff water.) The window behind the altar shows 52 scenes from the life of Christ. A window to the left of the altar shows Edgar's coronation. Note that a WWII bomb blast destroyed the medieval glass; what you see today is from the 1950s.

Climbing the Tower: You can reach the top of the tower only with a worthwhile 50-minute guided tour. You'll hike up 212 steps for views across the rooftops of Bath and a peek down into the Roman Baths. In the rafters, you walk right up behind the clock face on the north transept, and get an inside-out look at the fan vaulting. Along the way, you'll hear a brief town history as you learn all about the tower's bells. If you've always wanted to clang a huge church bell for all the town to hear, this is your chance—it's oddly satisfying (£6, sporadic schedule but generally at the top of each hour when abbey is open, more often during busy times; Mon-Sat 10:00-17:00, Nov-March 11:00-15:00, these are last tour-departure times; today's tour times usually posted outside abbey entrance, no tours Sun, buy tickets in abbey gift shop).

▲Pulteney Bridge and Parade Gardens

Bath is inclined to compare its shop-lined Pulteney Bridge with Florence's Ponte Vecchio. That's pushing it. But to best enjoy a

ny day, pack a picnic lunch
ay £1.50 to enter the Parade
s below the bridge (daily
3:00, shorter hours Oct-
ludes deck chairs, ask
rts held some Sun
mmer, entrance a
bridge). Relax-
t the riverside
ul break (and
bridge at Pulteney Weir, tour boat companies
ivities in Bath," later.
he free city walking tours covers Pulteney

Bridge, Pulteney Street, and Sydney Gardens (see "Tours in Bath," earlier)

Guildhall Market

The little old-school shopping mall located across from Pulteney Bridge is a frumpy time warp in this affluent town. It's fun for browsing and picnic shopping, and its recommended Market Café is a cheap place for a bite.

▲Victoria Art Gallery

This small gallery, next to Pulteney Bridge, has two parts: The ground floor houses temporary exhibits, while the upstairs is filled with paintings from the late 17th century to the present, along with a small collection of decorative arts.

Cost and Hours: Free, temporary exhibits-£4 or covered by £21.50 combo-ticket with Roman Baths and Fashion Museum, daily 10:30-17:00, tel. 01225/477-233, www.victoriagal.org.uk.

Visiting the Gallery: The permanent painting collection presents an intimate world of portraiture and Bath-scapes. On the back wall, find Thomas Gainsborough's portrait of *Thomas Rumbold and Son*. During the 18th century, members of high society flocked to Bath and employed Gainsborough to paint their portraits as a souvenir. Thanks to this fad, Gainsborough found steady employment in this city.

Scan the wall on the left to find *Bath from the East*—just below eye level—for a look at preindustrial Bath. Riffle through the white chests of drawers on either side of the room to find even more scenes of Bath throughout the years. As you exit the museum, a clever donation box on the staircase invites you to watch an artist at work; it's worth a small coin to see him in action.

NORTHWEST OF THE TOWN CENTER

Several worthwhile public spaces and museums can be found slightly uphill 10-minute walk away.

▲▲The Circus and the Royal Crescent

If Bath is an architectural cancan, these are its knicker first Georgian "condos"—built in the mid-18th centu father-and-son John Woods (the Circus by the Elde Crescent by the Younger)—are well explained by th tours. "Georgian" is British for "Neoclassical." The complexes, conveniently located a block apart fro quintessential Georgian and quintessential Bat

Circus: True to its name, this is a circu Picture it as a coliseum turned inside out. It rinthian capital decorations pay homage gin, and are a reminder that Bath (with

BATH

"the Rome of England." The frieze above the first row of columns has hundreds of different panels representing the arts, sciences, and crafts. The ground-floor entrances were made large enough that aristocrats could be carried right through the door in their sedan chairs, and women could enter without disturbing their sky-high hairdos. The tiny round windows on the top floors were the servants' quarters. While the building fronts are uniform, the backs are higgledy-piggledy, infamous for their "hanging loos" (bathrooms added years later). Stand in the middle of the Circus among the grand plane trees, on the capped old well. Imagine the days when there was no indoor plumbing, and the servant girls gathered here to fetch water—this was gossip central. If you stand on the well, your clap echoes three times around the circle (try it).

Royal Crescent: A long, graceful arc of buildings—impossible to see in one glance unless you step way back to the edge of the big park in front—evokes the wealth and gentility of Bath's glory days. As you cruise the Crescent, strut like an aristocrat.

Now imagine you're poor: Notice the "ha ha fence," a drop-off in the front yard that acted as a barrier, invisible from the windows, for keeping out sheep and peasants. The refined and stylish **Royal Crescent Hotel** sits virtually unmarked in the center of the Crescent (with the giant rhododendron growing over the door). You're welcome to (politely) drop in to explore its fine ground-floor public spaces and back garden, where a gracious and traditional tea is served (£16.50 cream tea, £35 afternoon tea, daily 13:30-16:30, sharing is OK, reserve a ⸻ay ahead—a week ahead for Sat-Sun, tel. 01225/823-333, www. ⸻alcrescent.co.uk).

⸻. 1 Royal Crescent

⸻seum (corner of Brock Street and Royal Crescent) takes ⸻hind one of those classy Georgian facades, offering your ⸻to a period house—and how the wealthy lived in 18th- ⸻Docents in each room hand out placards, but take ⸻with them to learn many more fascinating details ⸻such as how high-class women shaved their eye- ⸻ carefully trimmed strips of mouse fur in their

⸻10, £12.50 combo-ticket with Museum of ⸻12:00-17:30, Tue-Sun 10:30-17:30, last ⸻?8-126, http://no1royalcrescent.org.uk/.

Visiting the Museum: Start with the **parlor,** the main room of the house used for breakfast in the mornings, business affairs in the afternoon, and various other everyday activities throughout the evening. The bookcase was a status symbol of knowledge and literacy. In the **gentleman's retreat,** find a machine with a hand crank. This "modern" device was thought to cure ailments by shocking them out of you—give it a spin and feel for yourself. Shops in town charged for these electrifying cures; only the wealthiest had in-home shock machines. Upstairs in the **lady's bedroom** are trinkets befitting a Georgian socialite; look for a framed love letter, wig scratcher, and hidden doorway (next to the bed) providing direct access to the servants' staircase. The **gentleman's bedroom** upstairs is the masculine equivalent of the lady's room—rich colors, scenes of Bath, and manly decor. The back staircase leads directly to the **servants' hall.** Look up to find Fido, who spent his days on the treadmill powering the rotisserie.

Finally, you'll end in the **kitchen.** Notice the wooden rack hanging from the ceiling—it kept the bread, herbs, and ham away from the mice. The scattered tools here helped servants create the upper-crust lifestyle overhead.

▲Fashion Museum

Housed underneath Bath's Assembly Rooms, this museum displays four centuries of fashion on one floor. It's small, but the fact-filled

included audioguide can stretch a visit to an informative and enjoyable hour. Like fashion itself, the exhibits change all the time. A major feature is the "Dress of the Year" display, for which a fashion expert anoints a new frock each year. Ongoing since 1963, it's a chance to view more than a half-century of fashion trends in one sweep of the head. (The menswear version—awarded sporadically—shows a bit less variation, but has flashes of creativity.) Many of the exhibits are organized by theme (bags, shoes, underwear, wedding dresses). You'll see how fashion evolved—just like architecture and other arts—from one historical period to the next: Georgian, Regency, Victorian, the Swinging '60s, and so on. If you're intrigued by all those historic garments, go ahead and lace up your own trainer corset (which looks more like a life jacket) and try on a hoop underdress.

Cost and Hours: £9, includes audioguide; £21.50 combo-ticket includes Roman Baths and Victoria Art Gallery tempo rary exhibits, family ticket available; daily 10:30-18:00, Nov-Fe until 17:00, last entry one hour before closing; free 30-minute guided tour in summer at 12:00 and 16:00, in winter at 12:00 and 13:00; self-service café, Bennett Street, tel. 01225/477-789, www.fashionmuseum.co.uk.

Assembly Rooms

Above the Fashion Museum, these grand, empty rooms—where card games, concerts, tea, and dances were held in the 18th century (before the advent of fancy hotels with grand public spaces made them obsolete)—evoke images of dashing young gentlemen mingling with elegant ladies in a *Who's Who* of high society. Note the extreme symmetry (pleasing to the aristocratic eye) and the high windows (assuring privacy). After the Allies bombed the historic and well-preserved German city of Lübeck, the Germans picked up a Baedeker guide and chose a similarly lovely city to bomb: Bath. The Assembly Rooms—gutted in this wartime tit-for-tat by WWII bombs—have since been restored to their original splendor. (Only the chandeliers are original.)

Cost and Hours: Free, same hours and contact information as Fashion Museum.

Nearby: Below the Assembly Rooms and Fashion Museum (to the left as you exit, 20 yards away at the door marked *14* and *Alfred House*) is one of the few surviving sets of **iron house hardware.** "Link boys" carried torches through the dark streets, lighting the way for big shots in their sedan chairs as they traveled from one affair to the next. The link boys extinguished their torches in the black conical "snuffers." The lamp above was once gas-lit. The crank on the left was used to hoist bulky things to various windows (see the hooks). Few of these sets survived the dark days of the WWII Blitz, when most were collected and melted down, purportedly to make weapons to feed the British war machine. (Not long ago, these well-meaning Brits finally found out that all of their patriotic extra commitment to the national struggle had been for naught, since the metal ended up in junk heaps.)

Shoppers head down **Bartlett Street,** just below the Fashion Museum, to browse the boutique shops.

▲Museum of Bath at Work

This modest but informative museum explains the industrial history of Bath. If you want to learn about the unglamorous workaday side to the spa town, this is the place.

Cost and Hours: £6, includes audioguide, daily 10:30-17:00, Nov and Jan-March weekends only, closed Dec, last entry one hour before closing, Julian Road, 2 steep blocks up Russell Street from Assembly Rooms, tel. 01225/318-348, www.bath-at-work.org.uk.

Visiting the Museum: The core of the museum is the well-preserved, circa-1900 fizzy-drink business of one Mr. Bowler. It includes a Dickensian office, engineer's shop, brass foundry, essence room lined with bottled scents (see photo), and factory floor. It's just a pile of meaningless old gadgets—until the included audioguide resurrects Mr. Bowler's creative genius. Each item has its own story to tell.

Upstairs are display cases featuring other Bath creations through the years, including a 1914 Horstmann car, wheeled sedan chairs (this *is* Bath, after all), and versatile plasticine (colorful proto-Play-Doh—still the preferred medium of Aardman Studios, creators of the stop-motion animated Wallace & Gromit movies). At the snack bar, ask about buying your own historic fizzy drink (a descendant of the ones once made here). On your way out, don't miss the intriguing collection of small exhibits on the ground floor, featuring cabinetmaking, the traditional methods for cutting the local "Bath stone," a locally produced six-stroke engine, and more.

Sightseeing Tip: Notice the proximity of this museum to the Fashion Museum (described earlier). Museum attendants told me that, while some folks appreciate both places, they see more men visiting the Museum of Bath at Work while their female traveling companions tour the Fashion Museum. Maybe it's time to divide and conquer?

Jane Austen Centre

This exhibition focuses on Jane Austen's tumultuous, sometimes-troubled five years in Bath (circa 1800, during which time her father died) and the influence the city had on her writing. There's little of historic substance here. You'll walk through a Georgian townhouse that she didn't live in (one of her real addresses in Bath was a few houses up the road, at 25 Gay Street), and you'll see mostly enlarged reproductions of things associated with her writing as well as her overhyped waxwork likeness, but none of that seems to bother the steady stream of happy Austen fans touring the house.

The exhibit does describe various places from two novels set in Bath (*Persuasion* and *Northanger Abbey*). Costumed guides give an intro talk (on the first floor, 15 minutes, 3/hour, on the hour and at :20 and :40 past the hour) about the romantic but down-to-earth Austen, who skewered the silly, shallow, and arrogant aristocrats' world, where "the doing of nothing all day prevents one from doin anything." They also show a 15-minute video; after that, you're free to wander through the rest of the exhibit. The well-stocked gift shop—with "I love Mr. Darcy" tote bags and Colin Firth's visage emblazoned on teacups, postcards, and more—is a shopping spree in the making for Austen fans.

Cost and Hours: £11; April-Oct daily 9:45-17:30, July-Aug until 18:00; Nov-March Sun-Fri 11:00-16:30, Sat from 10:00; last entry one hour before closing, between Queen's Square and the Circus at 40 Gay Street, tel. 01225/443-000, www.janeausten.co.uk.

Tea: Upstairs, the award-winning $ **Regency Tea Rooms** (free entrance) hits the spot for Austen-ites with costumed wait-staff and themed teas (£8-10), including the all-out "Tea with Mr. Darcy" for £18 (also serves sandwiches, opens at 11:00, closes same time as the center, last order taken one hour before closing).

Museum of Bath Architecture

This unique collection offers an intriguing behind-the-scenes look at how the Georgian city was actually built, covering everything from the innovative town planning to the plasterwork. Near the entrance, an aerial map outlines Bath's expansion from its 17th-century origins to today's neighborhoods. In the back of the museum, an interactive model highlights town sights. Compare the 1694 Gilmore map—one of Bath's first tourist maps—with the one you're using today.

Cost and Hours: £6, £12.50 combo-ticket with No. 1 Royal Crescent, Tue-Fri 14:00-17:00, Sat-Sun 10:30-17:00, closed Mon and Dec-mid-Feb, 10-minute intro film runs on a loop, a short walk north of the city center on a street called "The Paragon," tel. 01225/333-895, www.museumofbatharchitecture.org.uk.

George Bayntun Bindery and Bookshop

This high-end bookshop and working bindery is worth a peek. While the workshop is not open to the public, their bookshop—with a reverent, Oxford-library feel—welcomes visitors to browse through an impressive back-room collection of rare editions and old prints for sale (Mon-Fri 9:00-13:00 & 14:00-17:30, closed Sat-Sun, on Manvers Street near the train station, tel. 01225/466-000).

OUTER BATH
▲American Museum

I know, you need this in Bath like you need a Big Mac. The UK's sole museum dedicated to American history, this may be the only place that combines Geronimo and Groucho Marx. It has thought-ful exhibits on the history of Native Americans and the Civil War, but the museum's heart is with the decorative arts and cultural artifacts that reveal how Americans lived from colonial times to the mid-19th century. The 18 completely furnished rooms (from a plain 1600s Massachusetts dining/living room to a Rococo Revival explosion in a New Orleans bedroom) are hosted by eager guides waiting to fill you in on the everyday items that make domestic Yankee history surprisingly interesting. (In the Lee Room, look for the original mouse holes, strategically backlit in the floorboards.) One room is a quilter's nirvana. It's interesting to see your own country through British eyes—but on a nice day, the surrounding gardens and view of the hills might be the best reasons to visit. You could easily spend an afternoon here, enjoying the gardens, arboretum, and trails.

Cost and Hours: £12, Tue-Sun 12:00-17:00, late Nov-mid-Dec until 16:30, closed Mon except in Aug, closed early Nov and late Dec-mid-March, at Claverton Manor, tel. 01225/460-503, www.americanmuseum.org.

Getting There: The museum is outside of town, but a free hourly shuttle from Terrace Walk just behind the abbey gets you there in 15 minutes (5/day, call or check their website for times; keep your eye out for a white van with the museum's name on it—or hop a taxi for about £10).

BATH

Activities in Bath

▲Thermae Bath Spa

After simmering unused for a quarter-century, Bath's natural thermal springs once again offer R&R for the masses. The state-of-the-

art spa is housed in a complex of three buildings that combine historic structures with new glass-and-steel architecture.

Is the Thermae Bath Spa worth the time and money? The experience is pretty pricey and humble compared to similar German and Hungarian spas. The tall, modern building in the city center lacks a certain old-time elegance. Jets in the pools are very limited, and the only water toys are big foam noodles. There's no cold plunge—the only way to cool off between steam rooms is to step onto a small, unglamorous balcony. The Royal Bath's two pools are essentially the same, and the water isn't particularly hot in either—in fact, the main attraction is the rooftop view from the top one (best with a partner or as a social experience).

All that said, this is the only natural thermal spa in the UK and your one chance to actually bathe in Bath. Bring your swimsuit and come for a couple of hours (Fri night and all day Sat-Sun are most crowded). Consider an evening visit, when—on a chilly day—Bath's twilight glows through the steam from the rooftop pool.

Cost: The cheapest spa pass is £35 for two hours (£38 on weekends), which includes towel, robe, and slippers and gains you access to the Royal Bath's large, ground-floor "Minerva Bath"; four steam rooms and a waterfall shower; and the view-filled, open-air, rooftop thermal pool. Longer stays are £10 for each additional hour. If you arrived in Bath by train, your used rail ticket will score you a four-hour session for the price of two hours (Mon-Fri only). The much-hyped £47 Twilight Package includes three hours and a meal (one plate, drink, robe, towel, and slippers). The appeal of this package is not the mediocre meal, but being on top of the building at a magical hour (which you can do for less money at the regular rate).

Thermae has all the "pamper thyself" extras: massages, mud wraps, and various healing-type treatments, including "watsu"—water shiatsu (£45-98 extra). Book treatments in advance by phone.

Hours: Daily 9:00-21:30, last entry at 19:00, pools close at 21:00. No kids under 16.

Information: It's 100 yards from the Roman Baths, on Beau Street (tel. 01225/331-234, www.thermaebathspa.com). There's a salad-and-smoothies café for guests.

The Cross Bath: Operated by Thermae Bath Spa, this renovated circular Georgian structure across the street from the main spa provides a simpler and less-expensive bathing option. It has a hot-water fountain that taps directly into the spring, making its water hotter than the spa's (£18-20/1.5 hours, daily 10:00-19:30, last entry at 18:00, check in at Thermae Bath Spa's main entrance across the street and you'll be escorted to the Cross Bath, changing rooms, no access to Royal Bath, no kids under 12).

Spa Visitor Center: Also across the street, in the Hetling Pump Room, this free one-room exhibit explains the story of the spa (Mon-Sat 10:00-17:00, Sun 11:00-16:00, audioguide-£2).

Walking

The Bath Skyline Walk is a six-mile wander around the hills surrounding Bath (leaflet at TI, or see www.nationaltrust.org.uk/bath-skyline). Another option—with scenic access to the Kennet and Avon Canal—is a walk through the park behind the Holburne Museum—any local can point the way on a city map. Plenty of other scenic paths are described in the TI's literature. For additional options, get *Country Walks around Bath*, by Tim Mowl (£4.50 at TI or bookstores).

Hiking the Canal to Bathampton

An idyllic towpath leads three miles from the Bath Spa train station, along the Kennet and Avon Canal, to the sleepy village of
Bathampton. Immediately behind the station in Bath, cross the
footbridge, turn left, and find where the canal hits the River Avon.
Head northeast along the small canal, noticing the series of Industrial Age locks and giving thanks that you're not a horse pulling
a barge. After the path crisscrosses the canal a few times, you'll
mostly walk with the water on your right. You'll be in Bathampton
in about an hour, where the George Inn, a classic pub, awaits with
a nice meal and beer (reservations smart, tel. 01225/425-079, www.
chefandbrewer.com), or try The Bathampton Mill pub, with garden
tables overlooking the waterway (tel. 01225/469-758).

Slow Cruise to Bathampton

The *Pulteney Princess* cruises to the neighboring village of Batham̄p
ton about hourly from Pulteney Weir. It's a sleepy float with sporadic commentary, but it's certainly relaxing, and boats come with
picnic-friendly sundecks. The good news: The fine Bathampton
Mill pub awaits at the dock in Bathampton (see previous listing).
Consider combining the cruise with a walk along the riverside trail
back into town, as described earlier (£5 one-way, up to 12/day in
good weather, one hour to Bathampton and back, WCs on board,
mobile 07791-910-650, £10 taxi back to Bath if dining late).

Boating

The Bath Boating Station, in an old Victorian boathouse, rents
rowboats, canoes, and punts (£7/person for first hour, then £4/
hour; all day for £18; Wed-Sun 10:00-18:00, closed Mon-Tue and
Oct-Easter, intersection of Forester and Rockcliffe roads, one mile
northeast of center, tel. 01225/312-900, www.bathboating.co.uk).

Swimming and Kids' Activities

The Bath Sports and Leisure Centre has a fine pool for laps as well
as lots of waterslides. Kids will also enjoy the "Zany Zone" indoor
playground (swimming-£4/adult, £3/kid, family discounts, Mon-
Fri 6:30-22:00, Sat 10:30-19:00, Sun 8:00-20:00, kids' hours limited, call for open-swim times, just across the bridge on North Parade Road, tel. 01225/486-905, www.better.org.uk—enter "Bath"
under "By postcode/location").

Shopping

There's great browsing between the abbey and the Assembly
Rooms. Shops close at about 17:30, and many are open on Sunday
(11:00-16:00). Explore the antique shops around Bartlett Street
below the Fashion Museum.

Nightlife in Bath

For an up-to-date list of events, pick up the local weekly newspaper, the *Bath Chronicle*, which includes a "What's On" schedule (www.thisisbath.com).

▲▲Bizarre Bath Street Theater

For an entertaining walking-tour comedy act "with absolutely no history or culture," follow Toby or Noel on their creative and lively Bizarre Bath walk. This 1.5-hour "tour," which combines stand-up comedy with cleverly executed magic tricks, plays off unsuspecting passersby as well as tour members. It's a belly laugh a minute.

Cost and Hours: £10, £8 if you show this book, April-Oct nightly at 20:00, smaller groups Mon-Thu, promises to insult all nationalities and sensitivities, just racy enough but still good family fun, leaves from The Huntsman Inn near the abbey (confirm at TI or see www.bizarrebath.co.uk).

▲Theatre Royal Performance

The restored 18th-century, 800-seat Theatre Royal, one of England's loveliest, offers a busy schedule of London West End-type plays, including many "pre-London" dress-rehearsal runs. The Theatre Royal also oversees performances at two other theaters around the corner from the main box office: Ustinov Studio (edgier, more obscure titles, many of which are premier runs in the UK) and "the egg" (for children, young people, and families).

Cost and Hours: £20-40 plus small booking fee; shows generally start at 19:30 or 20:00, matinees at 14:30, box office open Mon-Sat 10:00-20:00, Sun from 12:00 if there's a show; book in person, online, or by phone; on Saw Close, tel. 01225/448-844, www.theatreroyal.org.uk.

Ticket Deals: Forty nosebleed spots on a bench (misnamed "standbys") go on sale at noon Monday through Saturday for that day's evening performance in the main theater (£7.50, 2 tickets maximum). If the show is sold out, same-day "standing places" go on sale at 18:00 (12:00 for matinees) for £4 (cash only). Also at the box office, you can snatch up any "last minute" seats for £15-20 a half-hour before "curtain up" (cash only). Shows in the Ustinov Theatre go for around £20, with no cheap-seat deals.

Sightseeing Tip: During the free Bath walking tour, your guide stops here. Pop into the box office, ask what's playing, and see if there are many seats left for that night. If plenty of seats remain unsold, you're fairly safe to come back 30 minutes before curtain time to buy a ticket at the cheaper price. Oh...and if you smell jasmine, it's the ghost of Lady Grey, a mistress of Beau Nash.

Evening Walks

Take your choice: comedy (Bizarre Bath, described earlier), history, or ghost tour. Free city walking tours (a daily standard, described on page 257) are offered on some summer evenings (2 hours, May-Sept Tue and Thu at 19:00, leave from Pump Room). Ghost Walks are a popular way to pass the after-dark hours (£8, cash only, 1.5 hours, year-round Thu-Sat at 20:00, leave from The Garrick's Head pub—to the left and behind Theatre Royal as you face it, tel. 01225/350-512, www.ghostwalksofbath.co.uk). The cities of York and Edinburgh—which have houses thought to be actually haunted—are better for ghost walks.

Pubs

Most pubs in the center are very noisy, catering to a rowdy twentysomething crowd. But on the top end of town, you can still find some classic old places with inviting ambience and live music. See the map on page 285 for locations.

The Old Green Tree, conveniently right in the town center, is a rare traditional pub offering a warm welcome (locally brewed real ales, no TVs, 12 Green Street, tel. 01225/448-259).

The Star Inn is much appreciated by local beerlovers for its fine ale and "no machines or music to distract from the chat." It's a throwback to the manly pubs of yesteryear, and its long bench, nicknamed "death row," still comes with a complimentary pinch of snuff from tins on the ledge. Try the Bellringer Ale, made just up the road (daily 12:00-14:30 & 17:30-late, no food served, 23 The Vineyards, top of The Paragon/A-4 Roman Road, tel. 01225/425-072, generous and friendly welcome from Paul, who runs the place).

The Bell has a jazzy, pierced-and-tattooed, bohemian feel, but with a mellow older crowd. After learning the much-beloved bar would be sold to an outsider, 536 locals—plus a few well-known celebrities—banded together to save it. Thanks to their efforts, some kind of activity continues to brew nearly nightly, usually involving live music (daily 11:30-23:00, 103 Walcot Street, tel. 01225/460-426, www.thebellinnbath.co.uk).

Summer Nights at the Baths

In July and August, you can stretch your sightseeing day at the Roman Baths, open nightly until 22:00 (last entry 21:00), when the gas lamps flame and the baths are far less crowded and more atmospheric. To take a dip yourself, consider popping over to the Thermae Bath Spa (last entry at 19:00).

BATH

Sleeping in Bath

Bath is a busy tourist town. Reserve in advance, and keep in mind B&Bs favor those lingering longer. Accommodations are expensive, and low-cost alternatives are rare. By far the best budget option is the YMCA—it's central, safe, simple, very well-run, and has plenty of twin rooms available. At B&Bs, it's worth asking for a weekday, three-nights-in-a-row, or off-season deal. Friday and Saturday nights are tightest (with many rates going up by about 25 percent)—especially if you're staying only one night. If you're driving to Bath, stowing your car near the center will cost you (though some less-central B&Bs have parking)—see "Parking," earlier under "Helpful Hints," or ask your hotelier.

NEAR THE ROYAL CRESCENT

These listings are all a 5- to 10-minute walk from the town center, and an easy 15-minute walk from the train station. With bags in tow you may want to either catch a taxi (£5-7) or (except for Brocks Guest House) hop on bus #4 (direction: Weston, catch bus inside bus station, pay driver £2.20, get off at the Comfortable Place stop—just after the park starts on the right, cross the street and backtrack 100 yards).

Marlborough, Brooks, and Cornerways all face a busy arterial street (Upper Bristol Road, also known as Crescent Gardens); while the noise is minimal by urban standards and these B&Bs have well-insulated windows, light sleepers should request a rear- or side-facing room.

$$$ **Marlborough House,** exuberantly run by hands-on owner Peter, mixes modern style with antique furnishings and features a welcoming breakfast room with an open kitchen. Each of the six rooms comes with a sip of sherry (RS%, air-con, minifridges, free parking, 1 Marlborough Lane, tel. 01225/318-175, www.marlborough-house.net, mars@manque.dircon.co.uk).

$$$ **Brocks Guest House** rents six rooms in a Georgian townhouse built by John Wood in 1765. Located between the prestigious Royal Crescent and the courtly Circus, it's been redone in a way that would make the great architect proud. Each room has its own Bath-related theme (little top-floor library, 32 Brock Street, tel. 01225/338-374, www.brocksguesthouse.co.uk, brocks@brocksguesthouse.co.uk, Marta and Rafal).

$$ **Brooks Guesthouse** is the biggest and most polished of the bunch, albeit the least personal, with 22 modern rooms and classy public spaces, including an exceptionally pleasant breakfast room (limited pay parking, 1 Crescent Gardens, Upper Bristol Road, tel. 01225/425-543, www.brooksguesthouse.com, info@brooksguesthouse.com).

$$ Parkside Guest House rents five large, thoughtfully appointed Edwardian rooms. It's tidy, clean, homey, and well-priced—and has a spacious back garden (RS%, limited free parking, 11 Marlborough Lane, tel. 01225/429-444, www.parksidebandb. co.uk, post@parksidebandb.co.uk, kind Inge Lynall).

$$ Cornerways B&B is centrally located, simple, and pleasant, with three rooms and old-fashioned homey touches (RS%, DVD library, free parking, 47 Crescent Gardens, tel. 01225/422-382, www.cornerwaysbath.co.uk, info@cornerwaysbath.co.uk, Sue Black).

EAST OF THE RIVER

These listings are a 5- to 10-minute walk from the city center. From the train station, it's best to take a taxi, as there are no good bus connections.

$$$$ The Roseate Villa rents 21 stately yet modern rooms in a freestanding Victorian townhouse, with a park on one side and an extensive lawn on the other. In a city that's so insistently Georgian, it's fun to stay in a mansion that's Victorian (family rooms, free parking for those booking direct, in quiet residential area on Henrietta Street, tel. 01225/466-329, http://roseatehotels.com/bath/ theroseatevilla, reception.trvb@roseatehotels.com)

$$$ The Kennard is a short walk from the Pulteney Bridge. Each of the 12 rooms is colorfully and elaborately decorated (free street parking permits, peaceful little Georgian garden out back, 11 Henrietta Street, tel. 01225/310-472, www.kennard.co.uk, reception@kennard.co.uk, Priya and Ajay).

$$$ Henrietta House, with large rooms, hardwood floors, and daily homemade biscuits and jam, is cloak-and-cravat cozy. Even the name reflects English aristocracy, honoring the daughter of the mansion's former owner, Lord Pulteney. Now it's smartly run by Peter and another Henrietta (family-size suites, pay parking available, 33 Henrietta Street, tel. 01225/632-632, www. henriettahouse.co.uk, reception@henriettahouse.co.uk).

$$$ The Ayrlington, next door to a lawn-bowling green, rents 19 spacious rooms, each thoughtfully decorated in classic old-English style. Though this well-maintained hotel fronts a busy street, it's reasonably quiet and tranquil, hinting of a more genteel time. Rooms in the back have pleasant views of sports greens and Bath beyond. For the best value, request a standard top-floor double with a view of Bath (fine garden, free and easy parking, 24 Pulteney Road, tel. 01225/425-495, www.ayrlington.com, theayrlington@gmail.com).

$$ At Apple Tree Guesthouse, near a shady canal, hostess Ling rents five comfortable rooms sprinkled with Asian decor (family rooms, 2-night minimum Fri-Sat nights, free parking,

BATH

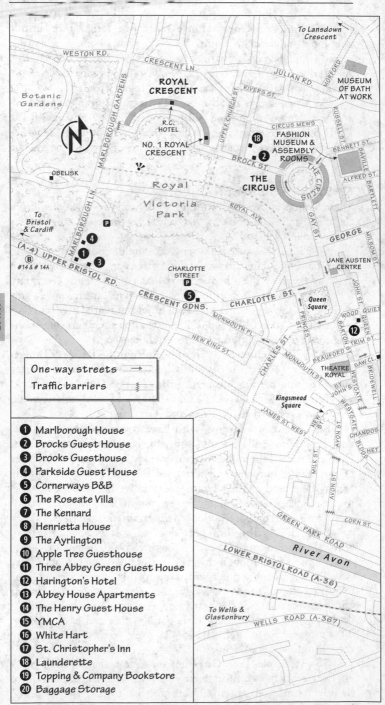

TO Lansdown Crescent

WESTON RD.

CRESCENT LN.

JULIAN RD.

MORFORD

MUSEUM OF BATH AT WORK

Botanic Gardens

ROYAL CRESCENT

RIVERS ST.

RUSSELL ST.

R.C. HOTEL

UPPER CHURCH ST.

CIRCUS MEWS

FASHION MUSEUM & ASSEMBLY ROOMS

BENNETT ST.

NO. 1 ROYAL CRESCENT

BROCK ST.

SAVILLE ROW

BARTLETT ST.

ALFRED ST.

THE CIRCUS

OBELISK

MARLBOROUGH GARDENS

Royal

Victoria Park

ROYAL AVE.

THE CIRCUS

GAY ST.

GEORGE

To Bristol & Cardiff

MARLBOROUGH LN.

MILSOM ST.

JANE AUSTEN CENTRE

(A-4) UPPER BRISTOL RD.

CHARLOTTE STREET

QUEEN ST.

JOHN ST.

Quiet

(B) #14 & #14A

CRESCENT GDNS.

CHARLOTTE ST.

Queen Square

WOOD ST.

MONMOUTH PL.

PRINCES ST.

BARTON ST.

TRIM ST.

NEW KING ST.

CHARLES ST.

MONMOUTH ST.

BEAUFORD SQ.

SAW CL.

BRIDEWELL

WESTGATE

THEATRE ROYAL

One-way streets →

Traffic barriers

JOHN'S CT.

ST.

Kingsmead Square

JAMES ST. WEST

NEW ST.

CHANDOS BLDGS.

① Marlborough House
② Brocks Guest House
③ Brooks Guesthouse
④ Parkside Guest House
⑤ Cornerways B&B
⑥ The Roseate Villa
⑦ The Kennard
⑧ Henrietta House
⑨ The Ayrlington
⑩ Apple Tree Guesthouse
⑪ Three Abbey Green Guest House
⑫ Harington's Hotel
⑬ Abbey House Apartments
⑭ The Henry Guest House
⑮ YMCA
⑯ White Hart
⑰ St. Christopher's Inn
⑱ Launderette
⑲ Topping & Company Bookstore
⑳ Baggage Storage

AVON ST.

WALK ST.

MILK ST.

AVON ST.

CORN ST.

GREEN PARK ROAD

River Avon

LOWER BRISTOL ROAD (A-36)

To Wells & Glastonbury

WELLS ROAD (A-367)

BATH

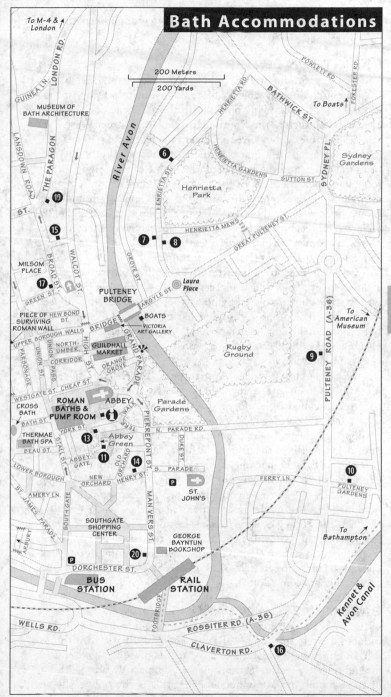

Bath Accommodations

To M-4 & London

200 Meters
200 Yards

MUSEUM OF BATH ARCHITECTURE

River Avon

THE PARAGON

LONDON RD.

GUINEA LN.

LANSDOWN ROAD

POWLETT RD.

FORESTER RD.

BATHWICK ST.

To Boats

HENRIETTA RD.

Sydney Gardens

SYDNEY PL.

19

6

HENRIETTA ST.

HENRIETTA GARDENS

SUTTON ST.

Henrietta Park

15

BROAD ST.

WALCOT ST.

7 **8**

HENRIETTA MEWS

GREAT PULTENEY ST.

MILSOM PLACE

GREEN ST.

17

GROVE ST.

Laura Place

PULTENEY BRIDGE

ARGYLE ST.

To American Museum

PULTENEY ROAD (A-36)

PIECE OF SURVIVING ROMAN WALL

NEW BOND ST.

BRIDGE ST.

BOATS

VICTORIA ART GALLERY

UPPER BOROUGH WALLS

UNION ST.

NORTH-UMBER-LAND PASS.

CORRIDOR

HIGH ST.

GRAND PARADE

GUILDHALL MARKET

ORANGE GROVE

Rugby Ground

9

PARSONAGE

WESTGATE ST.

CHEAP ST.

CROSS BATH

ROMAN BATHS & PUMP ROOM

ABBEY

ABBEY CHURCH YARD

Parade Gardens

PIERREPONT ST.

THERMAE BATH SPA

PATH ST.

YORK ST.

i

Abbey Green

N. PARADE RD.

13

STALL ST.

BEAU ST.

11

ABBEY GATE

OLD ORCHARD

14

DUKE ST.

S. PARADE

LOWER BOROUGH

NEW ORCHARD

HENRY ST.

P

FERRY LN.

10

PULTENEY GARDENS

ST. JAMES LN.

AMERY LN.

ST. JOHN'S

ARBURY

SOUTH GATE

MAN VERS ST.

To Bathampton

ST. JAMES PARADE

SOUTHGATE SHOPPING CENTER

GEORGE BAYNTUN BOOKSHOP

P

20

DORCHESTER ST.

BUS STATION

RAIL STATION

Kennet & Avon Canal

WELLS RD.

FOOTBRIDGE

ROSSITER RD. (A-36)

CLAVERTON RD.

16

BATH

7 Pulteney Gardens, tel. 01225/337-642, www.appletreebath.com, enquiries@appletreebath.com).

IN THE TOWN CENTER

You'll pay a premium to sleep right in the center. And, since Bath is so pleasant and manageable by foot, a downtown location isn't essential. Still, the following options are all well-located; or consider a chain hotel, such as the **Premier Inn** on James Street West.

$$$ **Three Abbey Green Guest House,** renting 10 spacious rooms, is located in a quiet, traffic-free courtyard only 50 yards from the abbey and the Roman Baths. Some of the bright, cheery rooms overlook the trees in the courtyard (family rooms, 2-night minimum on weekends, limited free parking, 2 ground-floor rooms work well for those with limited mobility, tel. 01225/428-558, www.threeabbeygreen.com, stay@threeabbeygreen.com, Sue, Derek, daughter Nicola, and son-in-law Alan). They also rent a self-catering apartment (2-night minimum).

$$$ **Harington's Hotel** rents 13 fresh, modern rooms on a quiet street. This stylish place feels like a boutique hotel, but with a friendlier, laid-back vibe (RS%, pay parking, 8 Queen Street, tel. 01225/461-728, www.haringtonshotel.co.uk, post@haringtonshotel.co.uk, manager Eve). Owners Melissa and Peter also rent several self-catering apartments down the street (2-night minimum on weekdays).

$$$ At **Abbey House Apartments,** Laura rents five flats on Abbey Green and many others scattered around town. The apartments called Abbey Green (with a washer and dryer), Abbey View, and Abbey Flat have views of the abbey from their nicely equipped kitchens. Laura provides a simple breakfast, but it's fun and cheap to stock the fridge. When Laura meets you to give you the keys, you become a local (2-night minimum, rooms can sleep four with Murphy and sofa beds, Abbey Green, tel. 01225/464-238, www.laurastownhouseapartments.co.uk, bookings@laurastownhouseapartments.co.uk).

$$ **The Henry Guest House** is a simple, vertical place, renting seven clean rooms. It's friendly, well-run, and just two blocks from the train station (family rooms, 2-night minimum on weekends, 6 Henry Street, tel. 01225/424-052, www.thehenry.com, stay@thehenry.com, Colin).

BARGAIN ACCOMMODATIONS

¢ The **YMCA,** centrally located on a leafy square, has 210 beds in industrial-strength rooms—all with sinks and basic furnishings. Although it smells a little like a gym, this place is a godsend for budget travelers—safe, secure, quiet, and efficiently run. With lots of twin rooms and a few double beds, this is the only easily accessible budget option in downtown Bath (family rooms, includes continental breakfast, free linens, rental towels, lockers, laundry facilities, down a tiny alley off Broad Street on Broad Street Place, tel. 01225/325-900, www.bathymca.co.uk, stay@bathymca.co.uk).

¢ **White Hart** is a friendly and colorful place in need of a little updating, but offering good, cheap stays in four private rooms or a dorm (fine garden out back, 5-minute walk behind the train station at Widcombe—where Widcombe Hill hits Claverton Street, tel. 01225/313-985; if no one answers, ring the bar at tel. 01225/338-053, www.whitehartbath.co.uk). The White Hart also has a pub with a reputation for good food.

¢ **St. Christopher's Inn,** in a prime central location, is part of a chain of low-priced, high-energy hubs for backpackers looking for beds and brews. Rooms are basic, clean, and cheap because they know you'll spend money on their beer. The inn sits above the lively, youthful Belushi's pub, which is where you'll find the reception (cheaper to book online, no guests under 18, laundry facilities, lounge, 9 Green Street, tel. 01225/481-444, www.st-christophers.co.uk).

Eating in Bath

Bath is bursting with eateries. There's something for every appetite and budget—just stroll around the center of town. A picnic dinner of deli food or take-out fish-and-chips in the Royal Crescent Park or down by the river is ideal for aristocratic hoboes. The restaurants I recommend are mostly small and popular—reserve a table for dinner—especially on Friday and Saturday. Most pricey little bistros offer big savings with their two- and three-course lunches and "pre-theatre" specials. Look for early-bird specials: As long as you order within the time window, you're in for a less-expensive meal.

UPSCALE ENGLISH

$$$$ Clayton's Kitchen is fine for a modern English splurge in a woody, romantic, candlelit atmosphere, where Michelin-star chef Rob Clayton aims to offer affordable British cuisine without pretense. The food is artfully prepared and presented—and they love their scallops (daily from noon and from 18:00, a few outside tables, live jazz on Sundays, 15 George Street, tel. 01225/585-100, www.claytonskitchen.com).

$$$$ The Circus Restaurant is a relaxing little eatery serving well-executed English cuisine with European flair. Choose between the modern interior—with seating on the main floor or in the less-charming cellar—and the four tables on the peaceful street connecting the Circus and the Royal Crescent (Mon-Sat

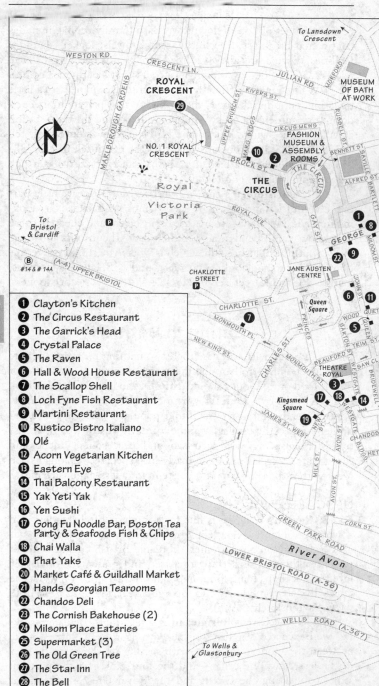

BATH

1 Clayton's Kitchen
2 The Circus Restaurant
3 The Garrick's Head
4 Crystal Palace
5 The Raven
6 Hall & Wood House Restaurant
7 The Scallop Shell
8 Loch Fyne Fish Restaurant
9 Martini Restaurant
10 Rustico Bistro Italiano
11 Olé
12 Acorn Vegetarian Kitchen
13 Eastern Eye
14 Thai Balcony Restaurant
15 Yak Yeti Yak
16 Yen Sushi
17 Gong Fu Noodle Bar, Boston Tea Party & Seafoods Fish & Chips
18 Chai Walla
19 Phat Yaks
20 Market Café & Guildhall Market
21 Hands Georgian Tearooms
22 Chandos Deli
23 The Cornish Bakehouse (2)
24 Milsom Place Eateries
25 Supermarket (3)
26 The Old Green Tree
27 The Star Inn
28 The Bell
29 Royal Crescent Hotel (Tea)

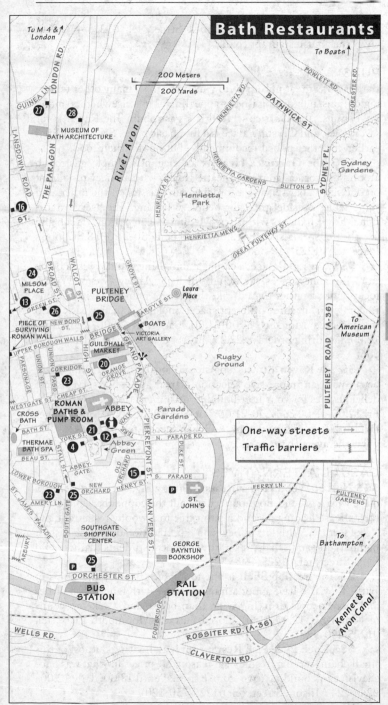

Bath Restaurants

To M 4 &
London

To Boats↑

POWLETT RD.

FORESTER RD.

GUINEA LN.

LONDON RD.

BATHWICK ST.

SYDNEY PL.

27

28

MUSEUM OF
BATH ARCHITECTURE

THE PARAGON

LANSDOWN ROAD

River Avon

HENRIETTA RD.

HENRIETTA GARDENS

SUTTON ST.

Sydney
Gardens

HENRIETTA ST.

Henrietta
Park

16

ST.

GREAT PULTENEY ST.

HENRIETTA MEWS

200 Meters
200 Yards

24

MILSOM
PLACE

BROAD ST.

WALCOT ST.

GROVE ST.

PULTENEY
BRIDGE

Laura
Place

PULTENEY ROAD (A-36)

To
American
Museum

13

GREEN ST.

26

25

NEW BOND
ST.

SARGYLE ST.

BRIDGE

GRAND PARADE

PIECE OF
SURVIVING
ROMAN WALL

BOATS

VICTORIA
ART GALLERY

GUILDHALL
MARKET

HIGH ST.

UPPER BOROUGH WALLS

PARSONAGE

UNION ST.

NORTHUMBERLAND

A-4

CORRIDOR

23

20

ORANGE
GROVE

Rugby
Ground

CHEAP ST.

WESTGATE ST.

CROSS
BATH

ROMAN
BATHS &
PUMP ROOM

ABBEY

Parade
Gardens

One-way streets

Traffic barriers

BATH ST.

21

12

N. PARADE RD.

YORK ST.

TERR.

THERMAE
BATH SPA

4

Abbey
Green

PIERREPONT ST.

DUKE ST.

BEAU ST.

STALL ST.

ABBEY-
GATE

OLD
ORCHARD

S. PARADE

LOWER BOROUGH

ST. JAMES PARADE

23

AMERY LN.

25

NEW
ORCHARD

15

HENRY ST.

MANVERS ST.

P

ST.
JOHN'S

FERRY LN.

PULTENEY
GARDENS

To
Bathampton

SOUTHGATE

SOUTHGATE
SHOPPING
CENTER

GEORGE
BAYNTUN
BOOKSHOP

ARBURY

25

P

DORCHESTER ST.

BUS
STATION

RAIL
STATION

WELLS RD.

FOOTBRIDGE

ROSSITER RD. (A-36)

CLAVERTON RD.

Kennet &
Avon Canal

10:00-24:00, closed Sun, 34 Brock Street, tel. 01225/466-020, www.thecircusrestaurant.co.uk).

PUBS

Bath is not a great pub-grub town, and with so many other tempting options, pub dining isn't as appealing as it is elsewhere. Among my listings, The Garrick's Head is a gastropub, The Raven is for savory pies, and Crystal Palace is a fun, basic place. See "Nightlife," earlier, for other pubs I recommend—but not for their food.

$$$ **The Garrick's Head** is an elegantly simple gastropub around the corner from the Theatre Royal, with a pricey restaurant on one side, a bar serving affordable pub classics on the other, and some tables outside great for people-watching. They serve traditional English dishes with a few Mediterranean options (lunch and pre-theater specials, daily 12:00-14:30 & 17:30-21:00, 8 St. John's Place, tel. 01225/318-368).

$$$ **Crystal Palace,** a casual and inviting standby just a block from the abbey, faces the delightful little Abbey Green. With a focus on food rather than drink, they serve "pub grub with a Continental flair" in three different spaces, including an airy back patio (food served Mon-Fri 11:00-21:00, Sat until 20:00, Sun from 12:00, last drink orders at 22:45, 10 Abbey Green, tel. 01225/482-666).

$$ **The Raven** attracts a boisterous local crowd. It emphasizes beer—with an impressive selection of real ales—but serves some delicious pies for your non-liquid nourishment (food served Mon-Fri 12:00-15:00 & 17:00-21:00, Sat-Sun 12:30-20:30, open longer for drinks; no kids under 14, 6 Queen Street, tel. 01225/425-045, www.theravenofbath.co.uk).

CASUAL ALTERNATIVES

$$$ **Hall & Wood House Restaurant** is a big, slick, high-energy place with a ground-floor pub (check out the copper bar) and a spiral staircase leading around a palm tree to a woody restaurant and a roof terrace. With lots of beers on tap, traditional English dishes, hamburgers, and salads, it's a hit with local students (daily, 1 Old King Street, tel. 01225/469-259).

$$ **The Scallop Shell** is the top choice for fish-and-chips in Bath. They also have a modern restaurant—with fancier fish dishes and more people drinking wine than beer—and a takeout counter (Mon-Sat 12:00-21:30, closed Sun, 27 Monmouth Place, tel. 01225/420-928).

$$$ **Loch Fyne Fish Restaurant** is an inviting outpost of this small chain, serving fresh fish at reasonable prices in what was once a lavish bank building (two-course special until 18:00, daily 12:00-22:00, 24 Milsom Street, tel. 01225/750-120).

ITALIAN AND SPANISH

$$$$ Martini Restaurant, a hopping, purely Italian place with jovial waiters, has class (open daily 12:00-14:30 & 18:00-22:30, veggie options, daily fish specials, extensive wine list, 9 George Street, tel. 01225/460-818; Nunzio, Franco, and chef Luigi).

$$$$ Rustico Bistro Italiano, nestled between the Circus and the Royal Crescent, is precisely what its name implies. Franco and his staff are kept busy by a local crowd (no pizza, check chalkboard for specials, Tue-Sun 12:00-14:30 & 18:00-22:00, closed Mon, just off Brock Street at 2 Margaret's Buildings, tel. 01225/310-064).

$$ Olé bounces to a flamenco beat, turning out tasty tapas from their minuscule kitchen. If you're hungry for a trip to Spain, arrive early or make a reservation, as there are only a handful of tables (Sun-Thu 12:00-22:00, Fri-Sat until 23:00, up the stairs at 1 John Street, tel. 01225/466-440).

VEGETARIAN AND ASIAN

$$$$ Acorn Vegetarian Kitchen is pricey but highly rated and ideal for the well-heeled vegetarian. Its tight interior has an understated vibe (daily 12:00-15:00 & 17:30-21:30, 2 North Parade Passage, tel. 01225/446-059).

$$$ Eastern Eye entices with large portions of Indian and Bangladeshi dishes served in an impressive, triple-domed Georgian hall. Service is uneven but the food doesn't disappoint (Mon-Fri 12:00-14:30 & 18:00-23:30, Sat-Sun 12:00-23:30, 8A Quiet Street, tel. 01225/422-323).

$$ Thai Balcony Restaurant's open, spacious interior is so plush, it'll have you wondering, "Where's the Thai wedding?" While residents debate which of Bath's handful of Thai restaurants serves the best food or offers the lowest prices, there's no doubt that Thai Balcony's fun and elegant atmosphere makes for a memorable and enjoyable dinner (daily 12:00-14:30 & 18:00-22:00, Saw Close, tel. 01225/444-450).

$$ Yak Yeti Yak is a fun Nepalese restaurant with both Western and sit-on-the-floor seating. Sera and his wife, Sarah, along with their cheerful, hardworking Nepali team, cook up great traditional food (including plenty of vegetarian plates) at prices that would delight a sherpa (daily 12:00-14:00 & 18:00-22:00, downstairs at 12 Pierrepont Street, tel. 01225/442-299).

$$ Yen Sushi is your basic little Japanese sushi bar—plain and sterile, with stools facing a conveyor belt that constantly tempts you with a variety of freshly made delights on color-coded plates (daily 12:00-15:00 & 17:30-22:30, 11 Bartlett Street, tel. 01225/333-313).

Ethnic Fast Food: Kingsmead Square is surrounded by several **$** cheap and cheerful joints where you can grab a bite and sit on the leafy square—best for lunch or early dinner. **Gong Fu Noodle Bar** is a favorite with Chinese students studying in Bath (daily 11:00-23:00). **Chai Walla** serves up satisfying, simple Indian street food (12:00-17:00, closed Sun). **Phat Yaks** is a phunky little cafe with Himalayan flair, plus teas and cakes (Mon-Sat 8:00-18:00, Sun 11:00-16:00).

SIMPLE LUNCH OPTIONS
$ Market Café, in the Guildhall Market across from Pulteney Bridge, is where you can munch really cheaply on a homemade meat pie or sip tea while surrounded by stacks of used books and honest-to-goodness old-time locals (traditional English meals including fried breakfasts all day, Mon-Sat 8:00-17:00, closed Sun, tel. 01225/461-593 a block north of the abbey, on High Street).

$ Hands Georgian Tearooms is an understated, family-run place a stone's throw from the Abbey and the Baths. It's a good option for breakfast, lunch, or afternoon tea right in the center of the tourist bustle (daily 10:00-17:00, 1 Abbey Street, tel. 01225/463-928).

$ Boston Tea Party is what Starbucks aspires to be—the neighborhood coffeehouse and hangout. Its extensive breakfasts, light lunches, and salads are fresh and healthy. The outdoor seating overlooks a busy square. Their walls are decorated with works by local artists (Mon-Sat 7:00-19:30, Sun 9:00-19:00, 19 Kingsmead Square, tel. 01225/314-826).

$ Chandos Deli has good coffee, breakfast pastries, and tasty £3-5 sandwiches made on artisan breads—plus meats, cheese, baguettes, and wine for assembling a gourmet picnic. Upscale yet casual, this place satisfies dedicated foodies who don't want to pay too much (Mon-Fri 8:00-17:30, Sat from 9:00, Sun 10:00-17:00, 12 George Street, tel. 01225/314-418).

$ Seafoods Fish & Chips is respected by lovers of greasy fried fish. There's diner-style and outdoor seating, or you can get your food to go (Mon-Wed 11:30-21:00, Thu-Sat until 22:00, Sun 12:00-19:00, 38 Kingsmead Street, tel. 01225/465-190).

$ The Cornish Bakehouse has freshly baked £3 takeaway pasties (Mon-Sat 8:30-17:30, Sun 10:00-17:00, kitty-corner from Marks & Spencer at 1 Lower Borough Walls, second location off High Street at 11A The Corridor, tel. 01225/426-635).

Chain Eateries at Milsom Place: A pleasant hidden courtyard holds several dependable chain eateries.

Supermarkets: With a good salad bar, **Waitrose** is great for picnics (Mon-Sat 7:30-21:00, Sun 11:00-17:00, just west of Pulteney Bridge and across from post office on High Street). **Marks & Spencer,** near the bottom end of town, has a grocery at the back of its department store and two eateries: **M&S Kitchen** on the ground floor and the pleasant, inexpensive **Café Revive** on the top floor (Mon-Sat 8:00-19:00, Sun 11:00-17:00, 16 Stall Street). **Sainsbury's Local,** across the street from the bus station, has the longest hours (daily 7:00-23:00, 2 Dorchester Street).

Bath Connections

Bath's train station is called Bath Spa (tel. 0345-748-4959). The National Express bus station is just west of the train station (bus info tel. 0871-781-8181, www.nationalexpress.com). For all public bus services in southwestern England, see www.travelinesw.com.

From Bath to London: You can catch a **train** to London's Paddington Station (2/hour, 1.5 hours, best deals for travel after 9:30 and when purchased in advance, www.gwr.com), or save money—but not time—by taking the National Express **bus** to Victoria Coach Station (direct buses nearly hourly, 3.5 hours, avoid those with layover in Bristol, one-way-£5-12, round-trip-£10-18, cheapest to purchase online several days in advance).

Connecting Bath with London's Airports: To get to or from **Heathrow,** it's fastest and most pleasant to take the **train via London;** with a Britrail pass, it's also the cheapest option, as the whole trip is covered. Without a rail pass, it's the most expensive way to go (£60 total for off-peak travel without rail pass, £10-20 cheaper bought in advance, up to £60 more for full-fare peak-time ticket; 2/hour, 2.25 hours depending on airport terminal, easy change between First Great Western train and Heathrow Express at London's Paddington Station).

The **National Express bus** is direct and often much cheaper for those without a rail pass, but it's relatively infrequent and can take nearly twice as long as the train (nearly hourly, 3-3.5 hours, £24-40 one-way depending on time of day, tel. 0871-781-8181, www.nationalexpress.com). Doing a **train-and-bus combination** via the town of Reading can make sense for travelers without a rail pass, as it's more frequent, can take less time than the direct bus—allow 2.5 hours total—and can be much cheaper than the train via London (RailAir Link shuttle bus to Reading: 2-3/hour, 45 minutes; train from Reading to Bath: 2/hour, 1 hour; £31-41 for off-peak, nonrefundable travel booked in advance—but up to double for peak-time trains; tel. 0118-957-9425, buy bus ticket from www.railair.com, train ticket from www.gwr.com). Another option is the **minibus** operated by recommended tour company Celtic Horizons (see page 260).

You can get to **Gatwick** by train with a transfer in Reading (hourly, 3 hours, £55-75 one-way depending on time of day, cheaper in advance; avoid transfer in London, where you'll have to change stations; www.gwr.com or by bus with a transfer at Heathrow (6/day, 4 hours, about £30 one-way, transfer at Heathrow Airport, www.nationalexpress.com).

Connecting Bath and Bristol Airport: Located about 20 miles west of Bath, this airport is closer than Heathrow and has good connections by bus. From Bristol Airport, your most convenient option is the Bristol Air Decker bus #A4 (£14, 2/hour, 1.25 hours, www.airdecker.com). Otherwise, you can take a taxi (£40) or call Celtic Horizons (see page 260).

From Bath by Train to: Salisbury (hourly direct, 1 hour), **Moreton-in-Marsh** (hourly, 2.5 hours, 1 transfer, more with additional transfers), **York** (hourly with transfer in Bristol, 4.5 hours, more with additional transfers), **Cardiff** (hourly, 1.5 hours), and **points north** (via Birmingham, a major transportation hub, trains depart for Scotland and North Wales; use a train/bus combination to reach Ironbridge Gorge and the Lake District).

From Bath by Bus to: Salisbury (hourly, 3 hours; or National Express #300 at 17:05, 1.5 hours), **Avebury** (hourly, 2-2.5 hours, transfer in Devizes), **Stratford-upon-Avon** (1/day, 4 hours, transfer in Bristol. For bus connections to **Glastonbury** and **Wells,** see the next chapter.

GLASTONBURY & WELLS

The countryside surrounding Bath holds two particularly fine cathedral towns. Glastonbury (perhaps a.k.a. Avalon) is the ancient resting place of King Arthur, and home (maybe) to the Holy Grail. It can be covered well in two to three hours: See the abbey, climb the tor, and ponder your hippie past (and where you are now).

Nearby, medieval Wells gathers around its grand cathedral. Wells is simply a cute small town, much smaller and more medieval than Bath, with a uniquely beautiful cathedral that's best experienced at the 17:15 evensong service (Sun at 15:00)—though the service isn't usually held in July and August.

GETTING AROUND THE REGION

By Car: Glastonbury and Wells are each about 20-25 miles from Bath and 140 miles from London. Drivers can do a 51-mile loop from Bath to Glaston-

bury (25 miles) to Wells (6 miles) and back to Bath (20 miles). Extend the trip to a 131-mile loop that includes two places covered in the next chapter: Drive from Bath to Avebury (25 miles) to Stonehenge (30 miles) to Glastonbury (50 miles) to Wells (6 miles) and back to Bath (20 miles).

By Bus and Train: The nearest train station is in Bath, served by regular trains from London's Paddington Station (2/hour, 1.5

Glastonbury & Wells Area

GLASTONBURY & WELLS

hours). Wells and Glastonbury are both easily accessible by bus from Bath. Bus #173 goes direct from Bath to **Wells** (nearly hourly, less frequent on Sun, 1.5 hours), where you can continue on to **Glastonbury** by catching bus #376 (2/hour, 25 minutes, drops off directly in front of abbey entrance on Magdalene Street). Note that there are no direct buses between Bath and Glastonbury. First Bus Company's £7.50 day pass is a good deal if you plan on connecting Glastonbury and Wells from your Bath home base. Wells and Glastonbury are also connected to each other by a 10-mile foot and bike path (unfortunately neither town offers bike rental).

Glastonbury

Marked by its hill, or "tor," and located on England's most powerful line of prehistoric sites, the town of Glastonbury gurgles with history and mystery.

In A.D. 37, Joseph of Arimathea—Jesus' wealthy uncle—reputedly brought vessels containing the blood of Jesus to Glastonbury, and with him, Christianity came to England. (Joseph's visit is plausible—long before Christ, locals traded lead and tin to merchants from the Levant.)

While this story is "proven" by fourth-century writings and accepted by the Church, the King-Arthur-and-the-Holy-Grail legends it inspired are not. Those medieval tales came when England needed a morale-boosting folk hero for inspiration during a war with France. They pointed to the ancient Celtic sanctuary at Glastonbury as proof enough of the greatness of the fifth-century warlord Arthur. In 1191, after a huge fire, Arthur's supposed remains (along with those of Queen Guinevere) were dug up from the abbey garden. Reburied in the abbey choir, Arthur and Guinevere's gravesite is a shrine today. Many think the Grail trail ends at the bottom of the Chalice Well, a natural spring at the base of the Glastonbury Tor.

By the 10th century, Glastonbury Abbey was England's most powerful and wealthy, and was part of a nationwide network of monasteries that by 1500 owned one-quarter of all English land and had four times the income of the Crown. Then Henry VIII dissolved the abbeys in 1536. He was particularly harsh on Glastonbury—he not only destroyed the abbey but also hung and quartered the abbot, sending the parts of his body on four different national tours...at the same time. This was meant as a warning to other religious clerics, and it worked.

But Glastonbury rebounded. In an 18th-century publicity campaign, thousands signed affidavits stating that they'd been healed by water from the Chalice Well, and once again Glastonbury was on the tourist map. Today, Glastonbury and its tor are a cen-

ter for "searchers"—too creepy
for the mainstream Church but
just right for those looking for a
place to recharge their crystals.
Glastonbury is also synonymous
with its summer music-and-arts
festival, a long-hair-and-mud
Woodstock re-creation that's a
rite of passage for young music
lovers in Britain.

Part of the fun of a visit to Glastonbury is just being in a town
where every other shop and eatery is a New Age place. Locals who
are not into this complain that on High Street, you can buy any
kind of magic crystal or incense—but not a roll of TP. But, as this
counterculture is their town's bread and butter, they do their best to
sit in their pubs and go "Ommmmm."

Orientation to Glastonbury

TOURIST INFORMATION

The TI is on High Street—as are many of the dreadlocked folks
who walk it. It occupies a fine 15th-century townhouse called
The Tribunal (Mon-Sat 10:00-15:00, closed Sun, 9 High Street,
tel. 01458/832-954, www.glastonburytic.co.uk). The TI sells several booklets about cycling and walking in the area, including the
Glastonbury and Street Guide, with local listings and a map (£1.50);
and the *Glastonbury Millennium Trail* pamphlet, which sends visitors on a historical scavenger hunt, following 20 numbered marble
plaques embedded in the pavement throughout the town (£1).

Above the TI is the marginally interesting **Lake Village Museum,** with two humble rooms featuring tools made of stones,
bones, and antlers. Preserved in and excavated from the local peat
bogs, these tools offer a look at the lives of marshland people. In
pre-Roman times, these ancients chose to live in the shadow of a
mystical hill crossed by two equally mystical "ley lines"—supposed
energy paths that circle the globe (£3.50, extensive descriptions,
same hours as TI, tel. 01458/832-954).

HELPFUL HINTS

Market Day: Tuesday is market day for crafts, knickknacks, and
local produce on the main street. There's also a country market
Tuesday mornings in the Town Hall.

Glastonbury Festival: Nearly every summer (around the June
solstice), the gigantic Glastonbury Festival—billing itself as
the "largest music and performing arts festival in the world"—
brings all manner of postmodern flower children to its no-

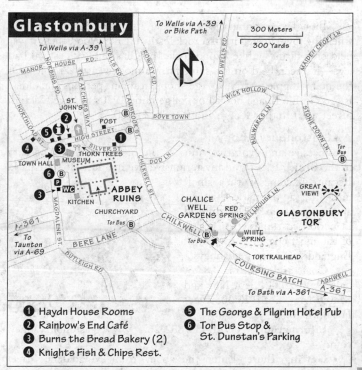

Glastonbury

To Wells via A-39
or Bike Path

300 Meters
300 Yards

To Wells via A-39

MANOR RD.
NORBINS HOUSE RD.
THE ARCHER'S WAY
WELLS RD.
ROWLEY RD.
LAMBROOK ST.
OLD WELLS RD.
MAIDEN CROFT LN.
WICK HOLLOW
BOVE TOWN
BULWARKS LN.
STONE DOWN LN.

ST. JOHN'S
POST
HIGH STREET
SILVER ST.
THORN TREES
MUSEUM
TOWN HALL
KITCHEN
WC
P
ABBEY RUINS
CHURCHYARD
NORTHLOAD ST.
MAGDALENE ST.
DOD LN.
CHILKWELL ST.
CHALICE WELL GARDENS
RED SPRING
WHITE SPRING
WELLHOUSE LN.
GREAT VIEW!
GLASTONBURY TOR
Tor Bus
Tor Bus
Tor Bus
CHILKWELL
TOR TRAILHEAD
COURSING BATCH
ASHWELL
A-361

A-361
To Taunton via A-69
BERE LANE
BUTLEIGH RD.
To Bath via A-361

❶ Haydn House Rooms
❷ Rainbow's End Café
❸ Burns the Bread Bakery (2)
❹ Knights Fish & Chips Rest.
❺ The George & Pilgrim Hotel Pub
❻ Tor Bus Stop &
    St. Dunstan's Parking

toriously muddy "Healing Fields." Music fans and London's beautiful people make the trek to see the hottest British and American bands. If you're near Glastonbury during the festival, anticipate increased traffic and crowds (especially on public transit; more than 165,000 tickets generally sell out), even though the actual music venue—practically a temporary city of its own—is six miles east of town (www.glastonburyfestivals. co.uk).

Sights in Glastonbury

I've listed these sights in the order you'll reach them, moving from the town center to the tor.

Glastonbury Town

The tiny town itself is worth a pleasant stroll. The abbey came first, and Glastonbury grew up to serve it. For example, the George and Pilgrim Hotel was originally a freestanding structure built in the 15th century to house pilgrims. And St. John's Church, which dates from the same century, was constructed to give townsfolk a place to worship, as they weren't allowed in the abbey. The Market Cross at the base of High Street dates from around 1800.

Though Glastonbury is much older, its character dates to 1970, when the town hosted its first rock festival. Like Woodstock, it was held on a farm. Unlike Woodstock, the Glastonbury Festival had legs—it's been held on the same farm almost every year since. Of the many hippie and New Age shops in town, perhaps the oldest is the Gothic Image bookshop, of genuine 1970s vintage (7 High Street, next to the George and Pilgrim Hotel).

▲▲Glastonbury Abbey

The massive and evocative ruins of the first Christian sanctuary in the British Isles stand mysteriously alive in a lush 36-acre park.

Because it comes with a small museum, a dramatic history, and enthusiastic guides dressed in period costumes, this is one of the most engaging to visit of England's many ruined abbeys.

Cost and Hours: £8.25, daily 9:00-20:00, Sept-Nov and March-May until 18:00, Dec-Feb until 16:00.

Information: Tel. 01458/832-267, www.glastonburyabbey.com.

Getting There: Enter the abbey from Magdalene Street (around the corner from High Street, near the St. Dunstan's parking lot). Pay parking is nearby.

Tours and Demonstrations: Costumed guides offer 30-minute tours (generally daily March-Oct on the hour from 10:00). As you enter, confirm these times, and ask about other tour and show times.

Eating: Picnicking is encouraged—bring something from one of the shops in town (see "Eating in Glastonbury," later), or buy food at the small café on site (open May-Sept).

Background: The space that these ruins occupy has been sacred ground for centuries. The druids used it as a pagan holy site, and during Joseph of Arimathea's supposed visit here, he built a simple place of worship. In the 12th century—because of that legendary connection—Glastonbury was the leading Christian pilgrimage site in all of Britain. The popular abbey grew powerful and very wealthy, employing a thousand people to serve the needs of the pilgrims.

In 1184, there was a devastating fire in the monastery, and in 1191, the abbot here "discovered"—with the help of a divine dream—the tomb and bodies of King Arthur and Queen Guinevere. Of course, this discovery boosted the pilgrim trade in Glastonbury, and the new revenues helped to rebuild the abbey.

Then, in 1539, King Henry VIII ordered the abbey's destruction. When Glastonbury Abbot Richard Whiting questioned the king's decision, he was branded a traitor, hung at the top of Glastonbury Tor (after carrying up the plank that would support his noose), and his body cut into four pieces. His head was stuck over the gateway to the former abbey precinct. After this harsh example, the other abbots accepted the king's dissolution of England's abbeys, with many returning to monastic centers in France. Glastonbury Abbey was destroyed. With the roof removed, it fell into ruin and was used as a quarry.

Today, the abbey attracts both the curious and pious. Tie-dyed, starry-eyed pilgrims seem to float through the grounds, naturally high. Others lie on the grave of King Arthur, whose burial site is marked off in the center of the abbey ruins.

◑ Self-Guided Tour: After buying your ticket, pick up a map and tour the informative **museum** at the entrance building. A model shows the abbey in its pre-Henry VIII splendor, and exhibits tell the story of a place "grandly constructed to entice the dullest minds to prayer." Knowledgeable costumed guides are eager to share the site's story and might even offer an impromptu tour.

Next, head out to explore the green park, dotted with bits of the **ruined abbey.** You come face-to-face with the abbey's Lady Chapel, the site of first wattle-and-daub church, possibly dating to the first century. Today, the crypt is dug out and exposed; posted information helps you imagine its 12th-century splendor.

The Lady Chapel became the abbey's west entry when the church expanded. The abbey was long and skinny, but vast. Measuring 580 feet, it was the longest in Britain (larger than York Minster is today) and Europe's largest building north of the Alps.

Before poking around the ruins, circle to the left behind the entrance building to find the two **thorn trees.** According to legend, when Joseph of Arimathea came here, he climbed nearby Wearyall Hill and stuck his staff into the soil. A thorn tree sprouted, and its descendant still stands there today; the trees here in the abbey are its offspring. In 2010, vandals hacked off the branches of the original tree on Wearyall Hill, but miraculously, the stump put out small green shoots the following spring. The trees inside the abbey grounds bloom twice a year, at Easter and at Christmas. If the story seems far-fetched to you, don't tell the Queen—a blossom from the abbey's trees sits proudly on her breakfast table every Christmas morning.

Ahead and to the left of the trees, inside what was the north wall, look for two trap doors in the ground. Lift up the doors to see surviving fragments of the abbey's original tiled floor.

Now hike through the remains of the ruined complex to the far end of the abbey. You can stand and, from what was the altar, look down at what was the gangly nave. Envision the longest church nave in England. In this area, you'll find the tombstone (formerly in the floor of the church's choir) marking the spot where the supposed relics of **Arthur and Guinevere** were interred.

Continue around the far side of the abbey ruins, feeling free to poke around the park. Imagine all of this green space—just a tiny part of the lands the abbey owned—bustling with the daily business of a powerful monastic community.

All those monks needed to eat. Take a look at the abbot's conical **kitchen,** the only surviving intact building on the grounds. Its size, and its simple exhibit about life in the abbey, give you an idea of how big the community once was.

NEAR GLASTONBURY TOR

These sights are about a 15-minute walk from the town center, toward the tor (see "Getting There," on page 299).

Chalice Well Gardens

According to tradition, Joseph of Arimathea brought the chalice from the Last Supper to Glastonbury in A.D. 37. Supposedly it ended up in the bottom of a well, which is now the centerpiece of a peaceful and inviting garden. Even if the chalice is not at the bottom of the well (another legend says it made the trip to Wales), and the water is red from iron ore and not Jesus' blood, the tranquil setting attracts pilgrims still. If you're a fan of gardens—or want to say

you've completed your grail quest—this place is worth a visit. To find the well itself, follow the well-marked path uphill alongside the gurgling stream, passing several places where you can drink from or wade in the healing water, as well as areas designated for silent reflection. The stones of the well shaft date from the 12th century and are believed to have come from the church in Glastonbury Abbey (which was destroyed by fire). In the 18th century, pilgrims flocked to Glastonbury for the well's healing powers. Have a drink or take some of the precious water home—they sell empty bottles to fill.

Cost and Hours: £4.30, daily 10:00-18:00, Nov-March until 16:30, on Chilkwell Street/A-361, tel. 01458/831-154, www.chalicewell.org.uk.

Red and White Spring Waters

If you'd just like to sample the fabled water, two waterspouts are just around the corner from the Chalice Well Gardens entrance (just beyond the trailhead to the tor, where the bus drops off). The spout on the Chalice Well side comes from the Red Spring; the other spout's source is the White Spring. Try both and see which you prefer.

▲Glastonbury Tor

Seen by many as a Mother Goddess symbol, the Glastonbury Tor—a natural plug of sandstone on clay—has an undeniable geological charisma. Climbing the tor is the essential activity on a visit to Glastonbury. A fine Somerset view rewards those who hike to its 520-foot summit.

Getting There: The tor is a steep hill at the southeastern edge of the town (it's visible from just about everywhere). The base of the tor is a 20-minute **walk** from the TI and town center. From the base, a trail leads up to the top (figure another 15-20 uphill minutes, if you keep a brisk pace). While you can hike up the tor from either end, the less-steep approach (which most people take) starts next to the Chalice Well.

If you're without a car and don't want to walk to the tor trailhead, you have two options: The **Tor Bus** shuttles visitors from the town center to the base of the tor, stopping at the Chalice Well en route (£3 round-trip, 2/hour, departs from St. Dunstan's parking lot next to the abbey on the half-hour, April-Sept daily 10:00-12:30 & 14:00-17:00, doesn't run Oct-March). If you have a **car**, you won't find any parking nearby so expect a bit of a hike. A **taxi** to the tor trailhead costs about £5 one-way—an easier and more economical choice for couples or groups. Remember, these take you only to the bottom of the tor; to reach the top, you have to hike.

A good plan is to ride the shuttle bus to the tor, climb to the top, hike down, drop by Chalice Well Gardens, and stroll back into town from there.

Climbing the Tor: Hiking up to the top of the tor, you can survey the surrounding land—a former swamp, inhabited for 12,000 years, which is still below sea level at high tide. Up until the 11th century you could actually sail to the tower. The ribbon-like man-made drainage canals that glisten as they slice through the farmland are the work of Dutch engineers—Huguenot refugees imported centuries ago to turn the marshy wasteland into something arable.

Looking out, find Glastonbury (at the base of the hill) and

Wells (marked by its cathedral) to the right. Above Wells, a TV tower marks the 996-foot high point of the Mendip Hills. It was lead from these hills that attracted the ancient Romans (and, perhaps, Jesus' uncle Joe) so long ago. Stretching to the left, the Mendip Hills define what was the coastline before those Dutch engineers arrived.

The tor-top tower is the remnant of a chapel dedicated to St. Michael. Early Christians often employed St. Michael, the warrior angel, to combat pagan gods. When a church was built upon a pagan holy ground like this, it was frequently dedicated to Michael. But apparently those pagan gods fought back: St. Michael's Church was destroyed by an earthquake in 1275.

Sleeping and Eating in Glastonbury

Sleeping: $ Haydn House rents three rooms in a centrally located 19th-century red-brick house (13a Silver Street, tel. 01458/834-771, www.haydnhouseglastonbury.com, haydnhouseglastonbury@gmail.com, Sharon and Jon).

Eating: These restaurants are on or near High Street.

$ Rainbow's End is one of several fine, healthy, vegetarian lunch cafés for hot meals (different every day), salads, herbal teas, soups, yummy homemade sweets, and New Age people-watching. If you're looking for a midwife or a male-bonding tribal meeting, check their notice board (vegan and gluten-free options, counter service, daily 10:00-16:00, a few doors up from the TI, 17 High Street, tel. 01458/833-896).

$ Burns the Bread has two locations in town, making hearty pasties (savory meat pies) as well as fresh pies, sandwiches, delicious cookies, and pastries. Ask for a sample of the Torsy Moorsy Cake (a type of fruitcake made with cheddar), or try a gingerbread man made with real ginger. Grab a pasty and picnic with the ghosts of Arthur and Guinevere in the abbey ruins (Mon-Sat 6:00-17:00, Sun 11:00-17:00, main location at 14 High Street; smaller shop in St. Dunstan's parking lot next to the abbey, tel. 01458/831-532).

$ Knights Fish and Chips Restaurant has been in the same family since 1909 and is the town's top chippy. It's another fine option for a picnic at the abbey (more for table service, Mon-Sat 12:00-21:30, Sun 12:00-19:30, closed Sun off-season, 5 Northload Street, tel. 01458/831-882, Kevin and Charlotte).

$$ The George & Pilgrim Hotel's wonderfully Old World pub might be exactly what the doctor ordered for visitors suffering a New Age overdose. The local owners serve up a traditional pub-grub menu (food served daily 12:00-14:45 & 18:00-20:45, 1 High Street, tel. 01458/831-146). They also rent **$$** rooms.

Glastonbury Connections

The nearest train station is in Bath. Local buses are run by First Bus Company (tel. 0845-602-0156, www.firstgroup.com).

From Glastonbury by Bus to: Wells (2/hour, 25 minutes, bus #376 headed to Bristol), **Bath** (nearly hourly, allow 2 hours, take bus to Wells, transfer to bus #173 to Bath, 1.5 hours between Wells and Bath). Buses are sparse on Sundays (generally one bus every other hour). If you're heading to points west, you'll likely connect through **Taunton** (which is a transfer point for westbound buses from Bristol).

Wells

Because this well-preserved little town has a cathedral, it can be called a city. It's England's smallest cathedral city (pop. just under 12,000), with one of its most interesting cathedrals and a wonderful evensong service (generally not offered July-Aug). Wells has more medieval buildings still doing what they were originally built to do than any town you'll visit, and you can still spot a number of the wells, water, and springs that helped give the town its name. Market day fills the town square on Wednesday (farmers' market) and Saturday (general goods).

Orientation to Wells

TOURIST INFORMATION

The TI is in the lobby of the Wells Museum, across the green from the cathedral. Consider purchasing their town map for £0.50, or the £1 *Wells City Trail* booklet (Mon-Sat 10:00-17:00, Nov-March until 16:00, closed Sun year-round, 8 Cathedral Green, tel. 01749/673-477, www.wellssomerset.com). Ask TI staff about one-hour walking tours of town for £6 on Wednesdays at 11:00 (www.wellswalkingtours.co.uk). The TI's attached museum houses displays on the archaeology and geology of nearby Mendip Hills and Wookey Caves, along with an exhibit on World War I (£3, same hours as TI).

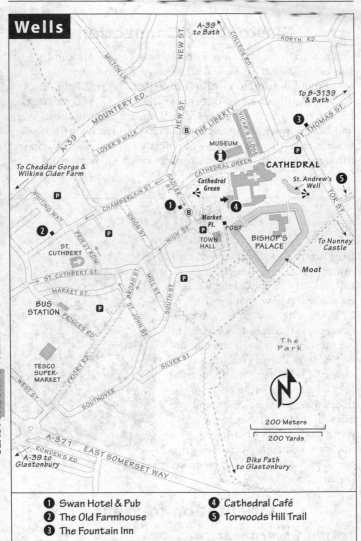

Wells

A-39
to Bath

NORTH RD.

NEW ST.

COLLEGE RD.

MOUNTERY RD.

MILTON LN.

A-39

LOVER'S WALK

NEW ST.

THE LIBERTY

VICAR'S CLOSE

ST. THOMAS ST.

To B-3139
& Bath

❸

MUSEUM ℹ

CATHEDRAL GREEN

CATHEDRAL

To Cheddar Gorge &
Wilkins Cider Farm

WHITING WAY

P

CHAMBERLAIN ST.

SADLER ST.

Cathedral
Green

ⓑ

Market
Pl.

POST

St. Andrew's
Well

❺

TOR ST.

❶

ⓑ

❹

P

UNION ST.

PRIEST ROW

❷

ST.
CUTHBERT

P

HIGH ST.

TOWN
HALL

BISHOP'S
PALACE

To Nunney
Castle

ST. CUTHBERT ST.

Moat

MARKET ST.

BROAD ST.

MILL ST.

SOUTH ST.

P

BUS
STATION

PRINCES RD.

ST. JOHN ST.

The
Park

TESCO
SUPER-
MARKET

PRIORY RD.

SILVER ST.

SOUTHOVER

N

WEST ST.

200 Meters

200 Yards

A-371

EAST SOMERSET WAY

ROWDEN'S RD.

A-39 to
Glastonbury

Bike Path
to Glastonbury

GLASTONBURY & WELLS

❶ Swan Hotel & Pub
❷ The Old Farmhouse
❸ The Fountain Inn
❹ Cathedral Café
❺ Torwoods Hill Trail

ARRIVAL IN WELLS

If you're coming by **bus,** you can get off in the city center at the Sadler Street stop, around the corner from the cathedral (tell the driver that's your stop). Or you can disembark at the big, well-organized bus station/parking lot (staffed Mon-Fri 9:30-13:30, closed Sat-Sun), about a five-minute walk from the town center at the south end of town. Find the Wells map at the head of the stalls to get oriented (the big church tower you see is *not* the cathedral); the signpost at the main pedestrian exit directs you downtown.

Drivers will find pay parking right on the main square, but because of confusing one-way streets, it's hard to reach; instead, it's simpler to park at the Princes Road lot next to the bus station (enter on Priory Road) and walk five minutes to the cathedral.

HELPFUL HINTS

Wells Carnival: Every November Wells hosts what it claims is the world's biggest illuminated carnival, featuring spectacular floats, street performers, and a market fair (carnival also travels to nearby towns; see www.wellssomerset.com for details).

Best Views: It's hard to beat the grand views of the cathedral from the green in front of it...but the reflecting pool tucked inside the Bishop's Palace grounds tries hard. For a fine cathedral-and-town view from your own leafy hilltop bench, hike 10 minutes up Torwoods Hill. The trail starts on Tor Street behind the Bishop's Palace.

Sights in Wells

▲▲WELLS CATHEDRAL

The city's highlight is England's first completely Gothic cathedral (dating from about 1200). Locals claim this church has the largest collection of medieval statuary north of the Alps. It certainly has one of the widest and most elaborate facades I've seen, and unique figure-eight "scissor arches" that are unforgettable.

Cost and Hours: Free but £6 donation requested, daily 7:00-19:00, Oct-Easter until 18:00, daily evensong service (except July-Aug)—described later. Tel. 01749/674-483, www.wellscathedral.org.uk.

Tours: Free one-hour tours run Mon-Sat at 10:00, 11:00, 13:00, 14:00, and 15:00; Nov-March usually at 12:00 and 14:00—unless other events are going on in the cathedral.

Eating: A handy café is right by the entrance (described in "Eating in Wells," later).

❍ Self-Guided Tour

Begin on the large, inviting **green** in front of the cathedral. In the Middle Ages, the cathedral was enclosed within "The Liberty," an area free from civil jurisdiction until the 1800s. The Liberty included the green on the west side of the cathedral, which, from the 13th to the 17th century, was a burial place for common folk, including 17th-century plague victims. The green became a cricket pitch, then a field for grazing animals and picnicking people. Today, it's the perfect spot to marvel at an impressive cathedral.

Peer up at the magnificent **facade.** The west front displays almost 300 original 13th-century carvings of kings and the Last

Judgment. The bottom row of niches is empty, too easily reached by Cromwell's men, who were hell-bent on destroying "graven images." Stand back and imagine it as a grand Palm Sunday welcome with a cast of hundreds—all gaily painted back then, choristers singing boldly from holes above the doors and trumpets tooting through the holes up by the 12 apostles.

Now head **inside.** Visitors enter by going to the right, through the door under the small spire, into the lobby and welcome center.

At the **welcome center,** you'll be warmly greeted and reminded how expensive it is to maintain the cathedral. Pay the donation and pick up a map of the cathedral's highlights. Then head through the cloister and into the cathedral.

At your first glance down the nave, you're immediately struck by the general sense of light and the unique "scissors" or hourglass-shaped **double arch** (added in 1338 to transfer weight from the south—where the foundations were sinking under the tower's weight—to the east, where they were firm). Until Henry VIII and the Reformation, the interior was opulently painted in golds, reds, and greens. Later it was whitewashed. Then, in the 1840s, the church experienced the Victorian "great scrape," as locals peeled moldy whitewash off and revealed the bare stone we see today. The floral ceiling painting is based on the original medieval design: A single pattern was discovered under the 17th-century whitewash and repeated throughout.

Small, ornate, 15th-century pavilion-like chapels flank the altar, carved in lacy Gothic for church VIPs. On the right, the **pulpit** features a post-Reformation, circa-1540 English script—rather than the standard Latin (see where the stonemason ran out of space when carving the inscription—we've all been there). Since this was not a monastery church, the Reformation didn't destroy it as it did the Glastonbury Abbey church.

We'll do a quick clockwise spin around the cathedral's interior. First walk down the left aisle until you reach the north transept. The medieval **clock** does a silly but much-loved joust on the quarter-hour. If you get to watch the show, notice how—like clockwork—the same rider gets clobbered, as he has for hundreds of years. The clock's face, which depicts the earth at the center of the universe, dates from 1390. The outer ring shows hours, the middle ring shows minutes, and the inner ring shows the dates of the month and phases of the moon. Above and to the right of the clock is Jack Blandiver, a chap carved out of wood in the 14th century. Beneath the clock, the fine **crucifix** (1947) was carved out of a yew tree. Also in the north transept is a door with well-worn steps leading up to the **Chapter House,** a grand space for huddles among church officials. Its sublime "tierceron" vaulting—a forerunner of the fan vaults you

can see in later English Gothic style—make this one of the most impressive medieval ceilings in the country.

Now continue down the left aisle. On the right is the entrance to the **choir** (or "quire," the central zone where the daily services are sung). Go in and take a close look at the embroidery work on the cushions, which celebrate the hometowns of important local church leaders. Up above the east end of the choir is "Jesse's Window," depicting Jesus' family tree. It's also called the "Golden Window," because it's bathed in sunlight each morning.

Head back out to the aisle the way you came in, and continue to the end of the church. On the outside wall, on the left, is the entry to the undercroft, now a cathedral history exhibit worth a look. In the apse you'll find the **Lady Chapel.** Examine the medieval stained-glass windows. Do they look jumbled? In the 17th century, Puritan troops trashed the precious original glass. Much was repaired, but many of the broken panes were like a puzzle that was never figured out. That's why today many of the windows are simply kaleidoscopes of colored glass.

Next to the chapel is the oldest known piece of wooden furniture in England: a **"cope chest,"** which is still used to store the clergy's garments. It is so large it can't be moved out through any of the cathedral's doors. Historians theorize the chest is older than the existing building, and was originally installed around A.D. 800, in the Saxon church that predated the cathedral.

Now circle around and head up the other aisle. As you walk, notice that many of the black **tombstones** set in the floor have decorative recesses that aren't filled with brass (as they once were).

After the Reformation in the 1530s, the church was short on cash, so they sold the brass lettering to raise money for roof repairs.

Once you reach the south transept, you'll find several items of interest. The **old Saxon font** survives from the previous church (A.D. 705) and has been the site of Wells baptisms for more than a thousand years. (Its carved arches were added by Normans in the 12th century, and the cover is from the 17th century.) In the far end of this transept (in the shade of the fancy chapels), a little of the original green and red wall painting, which wasn't whitewashed, survives.

Nearby, notice the **carvings** in the capitals of the freestanding pillars, with whimsical depictions of medieval life. On the first pillar, notice the man with a toothache and another man with a thorn in his foot. The second pillar tells a story of medieval justice: On the left, we see thieves stealing grapes; on the right, the woodcutter (with an axe) is warning the farmer (with the pitchfork) what's happening. Circle around to the back of the pillar for the rest of the story: On the left, the farmer chases one of the thieves, grabbing him by the ear. On the right, he clobbers the thief over the head with his pitchfork—so hard the farmer's hat falls off.

Also in the south transept, you'll find the entrance to the cathedral **Reading Room** (free, April-Oct Mon-Sat 11:00-13:00 & 14:30-16:30 only; it's often possible to step in for a quick look on weekday mornings and afternoons). Housing a few old manuscripts, it offers a peek into a real 15th-century library. At the back of the Reading Room, peer through the doors and notice the irons chaining the books to the shelves—a reflection perhaps of the trust in the clergy at that time.

Head out into the cloister, then cross the courtyard back to the welcome center, shop, café, and exit. Go in peace.

MORE CATHEDRAL SIGHTS
▲▲Cathedral Evensong Service

The cathedral choir takes full advantage of heavenly acoustics with a nightly 45-minute evensong service. You'll sit right in the old "quire" as you listen to a great pipe organ and the world-famous Wells Cathedral choir.

Cost and Hours: Free, Mon-Sat at 17:15, Sun at 15:00, generally no service when school is out July-Aug unless a visiting choir performs, to check call 01749/674-483 or visit www.wellscathedral.org.uk. At 17:05 (Sun at 14:50), the verger ushers visitors to their seats. There's usually plenty of room.

Returning to Bath After the Evensong: Confirm the departure time for the last direct bus to Bath in advance—it's usually around 18:30. If you need to catch the 17:50 bus instead, request a seat on the north side of the presbytery, so you can slip out the side door without disturbing the service (10-minute walk from cathedral to station, bus may also depart from The Liberty stop—a 4-minute walk away; your other option is a bus and train connection via Bristol—explained later, under "Wells Connections").

Other Cathedral Concerts: The cathedral also hosts several evening concerts each month (most about £20, generally Thu-Sat at 19:00 or 19:30, buy tickets by phone or at box office in cathedral gift shop; Mon-Sat 10:00-16:30, Sun 11:00-16:30; tel. 01749/672-773). Concert tickets are also sometimes available at the TI, along with pamphlets listing what's on.

Vicars' Close

Lined with perfectly pickled 14th-century houses, this is the oldest continuously occupied complete street in Europe (since 1348; just a block north of the ca-thedral—go under the big arch and look left). It was built to house the vicar's choir, and it still houses church officials and choristers. These dwellings were bachelor pads until the Reformation allowed clerics to marry; they were then redesigned to accommodate families. Notice how the close gets narrower at the top, creating the illusion that it is a longer lane than it is. Notice also the elevated passageway connecting these choristers' quarters with the church.

▲Bishop's Palace

Next to the cathedral stands the moated Bishop's Palace, built in the 13th century and still in use today as the residence of the bishop

of Bath and Wells. While the interior of the palace itself is dull, the grounds and gardens surrounding it are the most tranquil and scenic spot in Wells, with wonderful views of the cathedral. It's just the place for a relaxing walk in the park. Watch the swans ring the bell—hanging over the water just left of the entry gate—when they have an attack of the munchies.

Cost and Hours: £8; daily 10:00-18:00, Nov-March until 16:00, often closed on Sat for special events—call to confirm; multimedia guide available for small fee; tel. 01749/988-111, www.bishopspalace.org.uk.

Visiting the Palace and Gardens: The palace's spring-fed moat was built in the 14th century to protect the bishop during squabbles with the borough. Bishops would generously release this potable water into the town during local festivals. Now the moat serves primarily as a pool for mute swans. The bridge was last drawn in 1831. Crossing that bridge, you'll buy your ticket and enter the grounds (past the old-timers playing a proper game of croquet—several times a week after 13:30). On your right, pass through the evocative ruins of the Great Hall (which was deserted and left to gradually deteriorate), and stroll through the chirpy south lawn. If you're feeling energetic, hike up to the top of the ramparts that encircle the property.

Circling around the far side of the mansion, walk through a door in the rampart wall, cross the wooden bridge, and follow a path to a smaller bridge and the wells (springs) that gave the city its name. Surrounding a reflecting pool with the cathedral towering overhead, these flower-bedecked pathways are idyllic.

Nearby are an arboretum, picnic area, and sweet little pea-patch gardens.

After touring the gardens, the mansion's interior is a letdown—despite the borrowable descriptions that struggle to make the dusty old place meaningful. Have a spot of tea in the café (with outdoor garden seating—free access), or climb the creaky wooden staircase to wander long halls lined with portraits of bishops past.

SIGHTS NEAR WELLS

The following stops are best for drivers.

Cheddar Cheese

If you're in the mood for a picnic, drop by any local aromatic cheese shop for a great selection of tasty Somerset cheeses. Real farmhouse cheddar puts Velveeta to shame. The **Cheddar Gorge Cheese Company,** eight miles west of Wells, gives guests a chance to see the cheese-making process and enjoy a sample (£2, daily 10:00-15:30; take the A-39, then the A-371 to Cheddar Gorge; tel 01934/742-810, www.cheddargorgecheeseco.co.uk).

Scrumpy Farms

Scrumpy is the wonderfully dangerous hard cider brewed in this part of England. You don't find it served in many pubs because of the unruly crowd it attracts. Scrumpy, at around 7 percent alcohol, will rot your socks—this is potent stuff. "Scrumpy Jack," carbonated mass-produced cider, is not real scrumpy. The real stuff is "rough farmhouse cider." It's said some farmers throw a side of beef into the vat, and when fermentation is done only the teeth remain. (Some use a pair of old boots, for the tannin from the leather.)

TIs list cider farms open to the public, such as **Wilkins Cider Farm** (also known as Land's End Farm)—a great Back Door travel experience (free, Mon-Sat 10:00-20:00, Sun until 13:00; west of Wells in Mudgley, take the B-3139 from Wells to Wedmore, then the B-3151 south for 2 miles, farm is a quarter-mile off the B-3151—tough to find, get close and ask locals; tel. 01934/712-385, www.wilkinscider.com).

Apples are pressed from August through December. Hard cider, while not quite scrumpy, is also typical of the West Country, but more fashionable, "decent," and accessible. You can get a pint of hard cider at nearly any pub, drawn straight from the barrel—dry, medium, or sweet.

Nunney Castle

The centerpiece of the charming and quintessentially English village of Nunney (between Bath and Glastonbury, off the A-361) is a striking 14th-century castle surrounded by a fairy-tale moat. Its rare, French-style design brings to mind the Paris Bastille. The year 1644 was a tumultuous one for Nunney. Its noble family was royalist (and likely closet Catholics). They defied Parliament, so Parliament ordered their castle "slighted" (deliberately destroyed) to ensure that it would threaten the order of the land no more. Looking at this castle, so daunting in the age of bows and arrows, you can see how it was no match for the modern cannon. The pretty Mendip village of Nunney, with its little brook, is also worth a wander.

Cost and Hours: Free, visitable at "any reasonable time," tel. 0370/333-1181, www.english-heritage.org.uk.

Sleeping and Eating in Wells

Sleeping: Wells is a pleasant overnight stop, with a few accommodation options.

$$$ Swan Hotel, a Best Western Plus facing the cathedral, is a big, comfortable, 50-room hotel. Prices for their Tudor-style rooms vary based on whether you want extras like a four-poster bed or a cathedral view. They also rent five apartments in the village (Sadler Street, tel. 01749/836-300, www.swanhotelwells.co.uk, info@swanhotelwells.co.uk).

$$ The Old Farmhouse, a five-minute walk from the town center, welcomes you with a secluded front garden and two tastefully decorated rooms (2-night minimum, secure parking, next to the gas station at 62 Chamberlain Street, tel. 01749/675-058, theoldfarmhousewells@hotmail.com, charming owners Felicity and Christopher Wilkes).

Eating: Downtown Wells is tiny. A fine variety of eating options are within a block or two of its market square, including classic pubs and little delis, bakeries, and takeaway places serving light meals.

$$ The Fountain Inn, on a quiet street 50 yards behind the cathedral, serves good pub grub (daily 12:00-14:00 & 18:00-21:00, no lunch on Mon, pub open until later, St. Thomas Street, tel. 01749/672-317).

$ The café in the cathedral welcome center offers a handy if not heavenly lunch (Mon-Sat 10:00-17:00, Sun 11:00-16:30, may close earlier in winter, tel. 01749/676-543).

$$ The Swan Hotel pub serves lunches in their garden across the street with a view over the green and cathedral (Sadler Street, tel. 01749/836-300).

Wells Connections

The nearest train station is in Bath. The bus station in Wells is at a well-organized bus parking lot at the intersection of Priory and Princes roads. Local buses are run by First Bus Company (for Wells, tel. 0845-602-0156, www.firstgroup.com), while buses to and from London are run by National Express (tel. 0871-781-8181, www.nationalexpress.com).

From Wells by Bus to: Bath (nearly hourly, less frequent on

Sun, 1.5 hours; if you miss the last direct bus to Bath, catch the bus to Bristol—runs hourly and takes one hour, then a 15-minute train ride to Bath), **Glastonbury** (3-4/hour, 25 minutes, take bus #376 toward the town of Street), **London**'s Victoria Coach Station (£21-30, 1/day direct, 4 hours; otherwise hourly with a change in Bristol).

into an easy-to-use website covering southwest England (www. travelinesw.com, tel. 0871-200-2233).

By Tour: From Bath, if you don't have a car, the most convenient and quickest way to see Avebury and Stonehenge is with a minibus tour. Mad Max is the liveliest of the tours leaving from Bath (see "Tours in and near Bath" on page 257).

Avebury

Avebury is an open-air museum of prehistory, with a complex of fascinating Neolithic sites all gathered around the great stone henge (circle). Among England's many stone circles (see sidebar), Avebury is unique for its vast size—a village is tucked into its center, and roads rumble between its stones. Because the surrounding area sports only a thin skin of topsoil over chalk,

it is naturally treeless (similar to the area around Stonehenge). Perhaps this unique landscape—where the land connects with the big sky—made it the choice of prehistoric societies for their religious monuments. Whatever the case, Avebury dates to 2800 B.C.—six centuries older than Stonehenge. This complex, the St. Peter's Basilica of Neolithic civilization, makes for a fascinating visit. Some visitors enjoy it even more than Stonehenge.

Orientation to Avebury

Avebury is the name of a huge stone circle, as well as the tiny village that sits surrounded by its stones. It's easy to reach by car, but more difficult by public transportation (see "Getting Around the Region," page 291).

Tourist Information: There's no TI, but the National Trust hands out maps and answers questions from a trailer in the parking lot (daily April-Oct 10:30-16:30). For more information on the Avebury sights, see www.english-heritage.org.uk or www. nationaltrust.org.uk.

Tours: The National Trust offers daily one-hour guided tours of the stone circle (£3, check schedule at trailer in the parking lot or at the Alexander Keiller Museum's Barn Gallery).

Parking: There's no public parking in the village center. Visitors park in a flat-fee National Trust lot along the A-4361—a five-

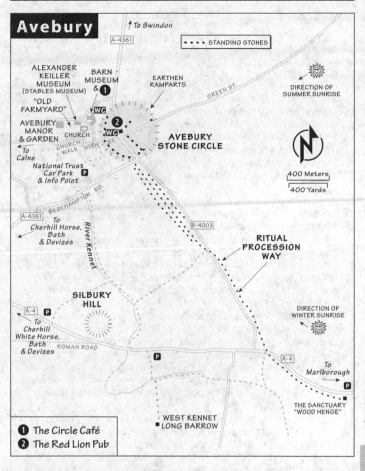

Avebury

↑ *To Swindon*

A-4361

• • • • STANDING STONES

ALEXANDER
KEILLER
MUSEUM
(STABLES MUSEUM)

BARN
MUSEUM
& ❶

EARTHEN
RAMPARTS

GREEN ST.

DIRECTION OF
SUMMER SUNRISE

"OLD
FARMYARD"

WC

AVEBURY
MANOR
& GARDEN

CHURCH

❷

WC

HIGH ST.

CHURCH WALK

*To
Calne*

AVEBURY
STONE CIRCLE

N

400 Meters

400 Yards

National Trust
Car Park
& Info Point P

BECKHAMPTON RD.

A-4361

*To
Cherhill Horse,
Bath
& Devizes*

River Kennet

B-4003

RITUAL
PROCESSION
WAY

SILBURY
HILL

A-4

P

*To
Cherhill
White Horse,
Bath
& Devizes*

ROMAN ROAD

DIRECTION OF
WINTER SUNRISE

P

A-4

*To
Marlborough*

P

THE SANCTUARY
"WOOD HENGE"

P

WEST KENNET
■ LONG BARROW

❶ The Circle Café
❷ The Red Lion Pub

minute walk from the village (£7, £4 after 15:00 and in winter, pay with coins at the machine or with cash at the trailer, open summer 9:30-18:30, off-season until 16:30).

Sights in Avebury

All of Avebury's prehistoric sights—which spread over a wide area—are free to visit and always open. The underwhelming museum and mansion charge admission and have limited hours. I've linked the sights with directions for drivers who want to make a targeted visit to all that Avebury has to offer.

• *From the official National Trust parking lot, follow the path five minutes through fields to the village center. On your right, you'll see the first access point to the big stone circle. (To pass through the gate, slide the*

Stone Circles: The Riddle of the Rocks

Britain is home to roughly 800 stone circles, most of them rudimentary, jaggedly sparse boulder rings that lack the iconic upright-and-lintel form of Stonehenge. But their misty, mossy settings provide curious travelers with an intimate and accessible glimpse of the mysterious people who lived in prehistoric Britain.

Bronze Age Britain (2000-600 B.C.) was populated by farming folk who had mastered the craft of smelting heated tin and copper together to produce bronze, which was used to make durable tools and weapons. Late in the Bronze Age, many of these clannish communities also put considerable effort into gathering huge rocks and arranging them into circles, perhaps for use in rituals with long-forgotten meanings. Some scholars believe the circles may have been used as solar observatories—used to calculate solstices and equinoxes to help plan life-sustaining seasonal crop-planting cycles. A few human remains have been discovered in the centers of some circles, but their primary use seems to have been ceremonial, not as burial sites. The superstitious people of the Middle Ages believed Stonehenge was arranged by giants (makes sense to me); nearby circles were thought to be petrified partiers who had dared to dance on the Sabbath.

Britain's stone circles generally lie in Scotland, Wales, and at the fringes of England, clustering mostly in the southwest (particularly on the Cornwall peninsula), north of Manchester, and in eastern Scotland (near Aberdeen). You'll find them marked in the Ordnance Survey atlas and signposted along rural roads. Ask a local farmer for directions—and savor the experience (wear shoes impervious to grass dew and sheep doo).

I've highlighted my favorites in this book, and described each one in case you're being selective.

Stonehenge is by far the most famous, the only one with horizontal "lintels" connecting the monoliths, and comes with the most insightful visitors center.

Avebury is by far the biggest—so large that a small village was built inside it. Less crowded and easier to visit than Stonehenge, it's easy and fun to explore on your own.

Castlerigg is a pretty standard-issue stone circle, but it's handy for those going to the Lake District (just off the main road into Keswick; see page 490).

Clava Cairns (in Scotland just outside Inverness—see page 980) is quite different, with a collection of stone enclosures in a forest clearing (the inspiration for the stone circle in *Outlander*).

*handle sideways rather than lifting it.) Take some time exploring the
remarkable...*

▲▲Avebury Stone Circle

The Neolithic stone circle at Avebury is 1,400 feet wide—that's 16
times as big as Stonehenge. It's so vast that it dwarfs the village
that grew up in its midst. You're free to wander among 100 stones,
ditches, mounds, and curious patterns from the past.

In the 14th century, in a frenzy of ignorance and religious
paranoia, Avebury villagers buried many of these mysterious
pagan stones. Their 18th-century descendants hosted social events
in which they broke up the remaining pagan stones (topple, heat
up, douse with cold water, and scavenge broken stones as building blocks). In modern times, the buried stones were dug up and
re-erected. Concrete markers show where the missing broken-up
stones once stood.

Explore. Touch a chunk of prehistory. While even just a short
walk to a few stones is rewarding, you can stroll the entire half-
mile around the circle, much of it along an impressive earthwork
henge—a 30-foot-high outer bank surrounding a ditch 30 feet
deep, making a 60-foot-high rampart. This earthen rampart once
had stones standing around the perimeter, placed about every 30
feet, and four grand causeway entries. Originally, two smaller circles made of about 200 stones stood within the henge.

• *Directly across from the parking-lot trail, follow signs into the "Old
Farmyard"—a little courtyard of rustic buildings near Avebury Manor.
Today these house museums, WCs, a shop, a recommended café, and the
two sights described next. (Note: These sights pale in comparison to the
prehistoric sights.)*

Alexander Keiller Museum

This museum, named for the archaeologist who led excavations at
Avebury in the late 1930s, is housed in two buildings (covered by
the same ticket). The 17th-century **Barn Gallery** illustrates 6,000
years of Avebury history, with kid-friendly interactive exhibits
about the landscape and the people who've lived here—from the
Stone Age to Victorian times. Across the farmyard, the small, old-
school **Stables Gallery** displays artifacts and skeletons from past
digs and a re-creation of what Neolithic people might have looked
like.

Cost and Hours: £5, daily 10:00-18:00, Nov-March until
16:00, tel. 01672/539-250.

• *Behind the Stables Gallery is the...*

Avebury Manor and Garden

Archaeologist Alexander Keiller's former home, a 500-year-old
estate, was restored by a team of historians and craftspeople in col-

laboration with the BBC (for their 2001 documentary *The Manor Reborn*). Nine rooms were decorated in five different period styles showing the progression of design, from a Tudor wedding chapel to a Queen Anne-era bedroom to an early-20th-century billiards room. The grounds were also spruced up with a topiary and a Victorian kitchen garden. While it's fun to tour—and the docents enjoy explaining how each room was painstakingly researched and re-created by the BBC—it's pricey and far from authentic...and it has nothing to do with Avebury's impressive circle.

Cost and Hours: £10, limited number of timed tickets sold per day; April-Oct daily 11:00-17:00, shorter hours off-season, closed Jan-mid-Feb and Mon-Wed in Nov-Dec; last entry one hour before closing, buy tickets at Alexander Keiller Museum's Barn Gallery, tel. 01672/539-250, www.nationaltrust.org.uk.

• *The following sights are a long walk or a short drive from the center of Avebury.*

First, from the Avebury village center, the road southeast toward West Kennet and Malborough (B-4003, a.k.a. West Kennet Avenue) is evocatively lined with an "avenue" of stones. This is known as the...

▲Ritual Procession Way

This double line of stones provided a ritual procession way leading from Avebury to a long-gone wooden circle dubbed "The Sanctuary." This "wood henge," thought to have been 1,000 years older than everything else in the area, is considered to have been the genesis of Avebury and its big stone circle. (You can see the site of the former Sanctuary—turn left onto A-4, look for the marked pullout on the left, and walk across the road—but all you'll see is an empty field with concrete blocks marking where the circle once stood.) Most of the stones standing along the procession way today were reconstructed in modern times.

• *From the end of the Ritual Procession Way, you can turn right (west) on the A-4. After just a mile or so, watch on the right for the dome-shaped green hill. Just beyond it is a handy parking lot. (Walkers can reach this by heading to the National Trust parking lot, crossing the road, and hiking up and over the hill.)*

▲Silbury Hill

This pyramid-shaped hill (reminiscent of Glastonbury Tor) is a 130-foot-high, yet-to-be-explained mound of chalk just outside of Avebury. More than 4,000 years old, this mound is considered the largest man-made object in prehistoric Europe (with the surface area of London's Trafalgar Square and the height of the Nelson Column). It's a reminder that we've only just scratched the surface of England's mysterious and ancient religious landscape.

Inspired by a legend that the hill hid a gold statue in its center, locals tunneled through Silbury Hill in 1830, undermining the

structure. Work is currently underway to restore the hill, which remains closed to the public. Archaeologists (who date things like this by carbon-dating snails and other little critters killed in its construction) figure Silbury Hill took only 60 years to build, in about 2200 B.C. This makes Silbury Hill the last element built at Avebury and contemporaneous with Stonehenge. Some think it may have been an observation point for all the other bits of the Avebury site. You can still see evidence of a spiral path leading up the hill and a moat at its base.

The Roman road detoured around Silbury Hill. (Roman engineers often used features of the landscape as visual reference points when building roads. Their roads would commonly kink at the crest of hills or other landmarks, where they realigned with a new visual point.) Later, the hill sported a wooden Saxon fort, which likely acted as a lookout for marauding Vikings. And in World War II, the Royal Observer Corps stationed men up here to count and report Nazi bombers on raids.

Nearby: Across the road from Silbury Hill (a 15-minute walk through the fields) is **West Kennet Long Barrow.** This burial chamber, the best-preserved Stone Age chamber tomb in the UK, stands intact on a ridge. It lines up with the rising sun on the summer solstice. You can walk inside the barrow, or sit on its roof and survey the Neolithic landscape around you.

• *The final sight is about four miles west of Avebury, along the A-4 toward Calne (and Bath), just before the village of Cherhill. Pull over at the Avebury end of the village and look for the hill-capping obelisk; below it, carved into the hillside, is the...*

Cherhill Horse

Throughout England, you'll see horses (and other objects) like this one carved into the downs, or chalk hills. There is one genuinely prehistoric white horse in England (the Uffington White Horse); the Cherhill Horse, like all the others, is an 18th-century creation. Prehistoric discoveries were all the rage in the 1700s, and it was a fad to make your own fake ones. Throughout southern England, you can cut into the thin layer of topsoil and find chalk. Now, so they don't have to weed, horses like this are cemented and painted white. Above the horse are the remains of an Iron Age hill fort known as Oldbury Castle—described on an information board at the pullout.

AVEBURY, STONEHENGE & SALISBURY

Eating in Avebury

$ The Circle Café is practical and pleasant, serving healthy lunches, including vegan and gluten-free dishes, and cream teas on most days (daily 10:00-17:30, Nov-March until 16:00, no hot food after 14:30, in the Barn Gallery on the Old Farmyard, tel. 01672/539-250).

$$ The Red Lion—a classic thatched-roof pub right in the heart of Avebury village—has updated but unpretentious pub grub; a creaky, well-worn, dart-throwing ambience; a medieval well in its dining room; and ample outdoor seating (Mon-Sat 12:00-21:00, Sun until 20:00, High Street, tel. 01672/539-266).

Stonehenge

As old as the pyramids, and far older than the Acropolis and the Colosseum, this iconic stone circle amazed medieval Europeans, who figured it was built by a race of giants. And it still impresses visitors today. As one of Europe's most famous sights, Stonehenge, worth ▲▲▲, does a valiant job of retaining an air of mystery and majesty (partly because cordons, which keep hordes of tourists from trampling all over it, foster the illusion that it stands alone in a field). Although  cynics manage to be underwhelmed by Stonehenge, most of its almost one million annual visitors agree that it's well worth the trip. At few sights in Europe will you overhear so many awe-filled comments.

GETTING TO STONEHENGE

Stonehenge is about 90 miles southwest of central London. To reach it from London, you can take a bus tour; go on a guided tour that uses public transportation; or do it on your own using public transit, connecting via Salisbury. It's not worth the hassle or expense to rent a car just for a Stonehenge day trip.

By Bus Tour from London: Several companies offer big-bus day trips to Stonehenge from London, often with stops in Bath, Windsor, Salisbury, and/or Avebury. These generally cost about £45-85 (including Stonehenge admission), last 8-12 hours, and pack a 45-seat bus. Some include hotel pickup, admission fees, and meals; understand what's included before you book. The more destinations listed for a tour, the less time you'll have at any one stop. Well-known companies are **Evan Evans** (their bare-bones Stonehenge Express gets you there and back for £48, tel. 020/7950-1777 or US tel. 866-382-6868, www.evanevanstours.co.uk) and **Golden Tours** (£48, tel. 020/7630-2028 or US toll-free tel. 800-509-2507, www.goldentours.com). **International Friends** runs pricier but smaller 16-person tours that include Windsor and Bath (£139, tel. 01223/244-555, www.internationalfriends.co.uk).

By Bus Tour from Bath: For tours of Stonehenge from Bath (Mad Max is best), see page 259.

By Guided Tour on Public Transport from London: London Walks offers a guided "Stonehenge and Salisbury Tour" from London by train and bus on Tuesdays from May through October (£78, includes all transportation, Salisbury walking tour, entry fees, and guided tours of Stonehenge and Salisbury Cathedral; pay guide, cash only, Tue at 8:45, meet at Waterloo Station's main ticket office, opposite Platform 16, verify price and schedule online, advance booking not required, tel. 020/7624-3978, recorded info tel. 020/7624-9255, www.walks.com).

On Your Own on Public Transport via Salisbury: From London or Bath, you can catch a train to Salisbury, then go by bus or taxi to Stonehenge. **Trains** to Salisbury run from London's Waterloo Station (around £38 for same-day return leaving weekdays after 9:30, 2/hour, 1.5 hours, tel. 0871-200-4950 or 0345-748-4950, www.southwesttrains.co.uk or www.nationalrail.co.uk). For details on trains to Salisbury from Bath, see "Getting Around the Region" at the beginning of this chapter.

From Salisbury, take **The Stonehenge Tour bus** to the site. These distinctive double-decker buses leave from the Salisbury train station, stop in Salisbury's center, then make a circuit to Stonehenge and Old Sarum, with lovely scenery and a decent light commentary along the way (£15, £29 includes Stonehenge as well as Old Sarum—whether you want it or not; tickets good all day, pay driver; daily June-Aug 10:00-18:00, 2/hour; may not run June 21 because of solstice crowds, shorter hours and hourly departures off-season; 30 minutes from station to Stonehenge, tel. 01202/338-420, timetable at www.thestonehengetour.info).

A **taxi** from Salisbury to Stonehenge can make sense for groups (about £40-50). Try City Cabs (inexpensive, tel. 01722/505-055) or Value Cars Taxis (tel. 01722/505-050, www.salisbury-valuecars.co.uk), or a local cabbie named Brian (tel. 01722/339-781, briantwort@ntlworld.com).

By Car: Stonehenge is well-signed just off the A-303, about 15 minutes north of Salisbury, an hour southeast of Bath, an hour east of Glastonbury, and an hour south of Avebury.

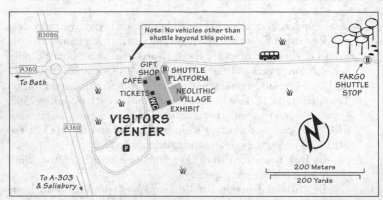

Stonehenge is about 70 miles and 1.5 hours west of **London Heathrow** (barring traffic). From the M-25 ring road, connect with the M-3 toward Southampton. Past Basingstoke, exit to the A-303. Continue west past Andover to Amesbury. In 3.5 miles, turn onto northbound A-360 at the roundabout, and follow "From Salisbury" directions from that point (see next).

From **Salisbury,** head north on A-360 (at the St. Paul's roundabout, take the second exit, direction: Devizes). Continue for eight miles, crossing the A-303 roundabout. In one more mile you'll encounter another roundabout; follow it around to the exit for the well-marked visitors center.

ORIENTATION TO STONEHENGE

The visitors center, located 1.25 miles west of the circle, is a minimalist steel structure with a subtly curved roofline, evoking the landscape of Salisbury Plain.

Cost: £17.50, includes shuttle-bus ride to stone circle, best to buy in advance online, covered by English Heritage Pass (see page 1024). In peak times, you'll pay £5 to park, but that will be refunded when you buy your ticket.

Hours: Daily June-Aug 9:00-20:00, April-May and Sept-mid-Oct 9:30-19:00, mid-Oct-March 9:30-17:00. Ticket sales stop two hours before closing. Expect shorter hours and possible closures June 20-22 due to huge, raucous solstice crowds.

Advance Tickets and Crowd-Beating Tips: Up to 9,000 visitors are allowed to enter each day. While Stonehenge rarely sells out completely, you can avoid the long ticket-buying line by prebooking at least 24 hours in advance at www.english-heritage.org.uk/stonehenge. Either print out an e-ticket or bring the booking number from your confirmation email to the designated window at the entrance.

When prebooking, you'll be asked to select a 30-minute

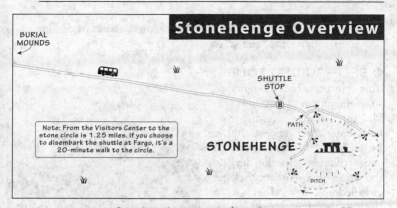

Stonehenge Overview

BURIAL MOUNDS

SHUTTLE STOP

B

PATH

Note: From the Visitors Center to the stone circle is 1.25 miles. If you choose to disembark the shuttle at Fargo, it's a 20-minute walk to the circle.

STONEHENGE

DITCH

entry window, but don't stress about being on time: You can typically enter anytime on the day of your ticket.

Even if you prebook, you may have to wait in line for the shuttle bus to and from the stones. For a less crowded, more mystical experience, come early or late. Things are pretty quiet before about 10:30 (head out to the stones first, then circle back to the exhibits); at the end of the day, aim to arrive just before the "last ticket" time (two hours before closing). Stonehenge is most crowded when school's out: summer weekends (especially holiday weekends) and anytime in August.

Information: Tel. 0870-333-1181, www.english-heritage.org.uk/stonehenge.

Tours: Worthwhile audioguides are available behind the ticket counter (included with Heritage Pass, otherwise £3). Or you can use the visitors center's free Wi-Fi to download the free "Stonehenge Audio Tour" app; be sure it's working before boarding the shuttle bus.

Visiting the Inner Stones: For the true Stonehenge fan, special one-hour access to the stones' inner circle is available early in the morning (times vary depending on sunrise; the earliest visit is at 5:00 in June and July) or after closing to the general public. Touching the stones is not allowed. Only 30 people are allowed at a time, so reserve well in advance (£35, allows you to revisit the site the same day at no extra charge, tel. 0370-333-0605). For details see the English Heritage website (select "Prices and Opening Times," then "Stone Circle Access").

Length of This Tour: Allow at least two hours to see everything.

Services: The visitors center has WCs, a large gift shop, and free Wi-Fi. Services at the circle itself are limited to emergency WCs. Even in summer, carry a jacket, as there are no trees to act as a wind-break and there's a reason Salisbury Plain is so green.

Eating: A large **$ café** within the visitors center serves hot drinks, soup, sandwiches, and salads.

❍ SELF-GUIDED TOUR

This commentary is designed to supplement the sight's audioguide. Start by touring the visitors center, then take a shuttle (or walk) to the stone circle. If you arrive early in the day, do the stones first—before they get crowded—then circle back to the visitors center.

• *As you enter the complex, on the right is the...*

Permanent Exhibit

This excellent, state-of-the-art exhibit uses an artful combination of multimedia displays and actual artifacts to provide context for the stones.

You'll begin by standing in the center of a virtual Stonehenge, watching its evolution through 5,000 years—including simulated solstice sunrises and sunsets.

Then, you'll head into the exhibits, where prehistoric bones, tools, and pottery shards tell the story of the people who built Stonehenge, how they lived, and why they might have built the stone circle. Find the forensic reconstruction of a Neolithic man, based on a skeleton unearthed in 1863. Small models illustrate how Stonehenge developed from a simple circle of short, stubby stones to the stout ring we know today. And a large screen shows the entire archaeological area surrounding Stonehenge (which is just one of many mysterious prehistoric landmarks near here). In 2010, within sight of Stonehenge, archaeologists discovered another 5,000-year-old henge, which they believe once encircled a wooden "twin" of the famous circle. Recent excavations revealed that people had been living on the site since around 3,000 B.C.—about five centuries earlier than anyone had realized.

In the small side room, an exhibit examines the iconic status of Stonehenge, including its frequent appearances in popular culture (strangely, no Spinal Tap) and its history as a tourist destination. See the vintage Guinness ad showing smiling people having a picnic on the rocks.

Then step outside and explore a village of reconstructed **Neolithic huts** modeled after the traces of a village discovered just northeast of Stonehenge. Step into the thatched-roof huts to see primitive "wicker" furniture and straw blankets. Docents demon-

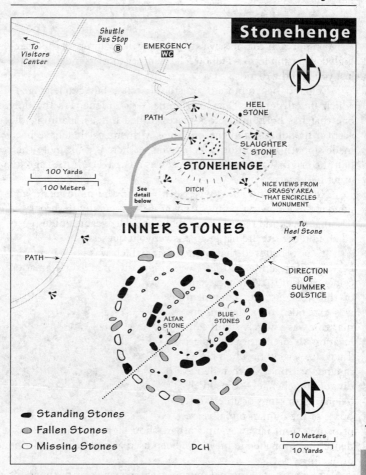

Stonehenge

To Visitors Center

Shuttle Bus Stop B

EMERGENCY WC

PATH

HEEL STONE

SLAUGHTER STONE

STONEHENGE

DITCH

NICE VIEWS FROM GRASSY AREA THAT ENCIRCLES MONUMENT

100 Yards
100 Meters

See detail below

INNER STONES

To Heel Stone

PATH

DIRECTION OF SUMMER SOLSTICE

ALTAR STONE

BLUE-STONES

● Standing Stones
◓ Fallen Stones
○ Missing Stones

DCH

10 Meters
10 Yards

strate Neolithic tools—made of wood, flint, and antler. You'll also see a huge, life-size replica of the rolling wooden sledge thought to have been used to slo-o-owly roll the stones across Salisbury Plain. While you can't touch the stones at the site itself, you can touch the one loaded onto this sledge.

• Shuttle buses to the stone circle depart every 5–10 minutes from the platform behind the gift shop (there may be a wait). The trip takes six minutes. If you'd prefer, you can walk 1.25 miles through the fields to the site (use the map you receive with your ticket, or ask a staff member for directions).

Along the way, you have the option of stopping at **Fargo Plantation,** where you can see several burial mounds (tell the shuttle attendant if you want to disembark here). After wandering through the burial mounds, you'll need to walk the rest of the way to the stone circle (about 20 minutes).

Stone Circle

As you approach the massive structure, walk right up to the knee-high cordon and let your fellow 21st-century tourists melt away. It's just you and the druids...

England has hundreds of stone circles, but Stonehenge—which literally means "hanging stones"—is unique. It's the only one that has horizontal cross-pieces (called lintels) spanning the vertical monoliths, and the only one with stones that have been made smooth and uniform. What you see here is a bit more than half the original structure—the rest was quarried centuries ago for other buildings.

Now do a slow **clockwise spin** around the monument, and ponder the following points. As you walk, mentally flesh out the missing pieces and re-erect the rubble. Knowledgeable guides posted around the site are happy to answer your questions.

It's now believed that Stonehenge, which was built in phases between 3000 and 1500 B.C., was originally used as a cremation cemetery. But that's not the end of the story, as the monument was expanded over the millennia. This was a hugely significant location to prehistoric peoples. There are several hundred burial mounds within a three-mile radius of Stonehenge—some likely belonging to kings or chieftains. Some of the human remains are

of people from far away, and others show signs of injuries—evidence that Stonehenge may have been used as a place of medicine or healing.

Whatever its original purpose, Stonehenge still functions as a celestial calendar. As the sun rises on the summer solstice (June 21), the **"heel stone"**—the one set apart from the rest, near the road—lines up with the sun and the altar at the center of the stone circle. A study of more than 300 similar circles in Britain found that each was designed to calculate the movement of the sun, moon, and stars, and to predict eclipses in order to help early societies know when to plant, harvest, and party. Even in modern times, as the summer solstice sun sets in just the right slot at Stonehenge, pagans boogie.

Some believe that Stonehenge is built at the precise point where six **"ley lines"** intersect. Ley lines are theoretical lines of magnetic or spiritual power that crisscross the globe. Belief in the power of these lines has gone in and out of fashion over time. They are believed to have been very important to prehistoric peoples, but then were largely ignored until the early 20th century, when the

English writer Alfred Watkins popularized them (to the scorn of serious scientists). More recently, the concept has been embraced by the New Age movement. Without realizing it, you follow these ley lines all the time: Many of England's modern highways follow prehistoric paths, and most churches are built over prehistoric monuments—placed where ley lines intersect. If you're a skeptic, ask one of the guides at Stonehenge to explain the mystique of this paranormal tradition that continued for centuries; it's creepy...and convincing.

Notice that two of the stones (facing the shuttle bus stop) are blemished. At the base of one monolith, it looks like someone has pulled back the stone to reveal a concrete skeleton. This is a clumsy **repair job** to fix damage done long ago by souvenir seekers, who actually rented hammers and chisels to take home a piece of Stonehenge. Look to the right of the repaired stone: The back of another stone is missing the same thin layer of protective lichen that covers the others. The lichen—and some of the stone itself—was sandblasted off to remove graffiti. (No wonder they've got Stonehenge roped off now.) The repairs were intentionally done in a different color, so as not to appear like the original stone.

Stonehenge's builders used two different types of stone. The tall, stout monoliths and lintels are sandstone blocks called **sarsen stones.**

Most of the monoliths weigh about 25 tons (the largest is 45 tons), and the lintels are about 7 tons apiece. These sarsen stones were brought from "only" 20 miles away. Scientists have chemically matched the shorter stones in the middle—called **bluestones**—to outcrops on the south coast of Wales...240 miles away (close if you're taking a train, but far if you're packing a megalith). Imagine the logistical puzzle of floating six-ton stones across Wales' Severn Estuary and up the River Avon, then rolling them on logs about 20 miles to this position...an impressive feat, even in our era of skyscrapers.

Why didn't the builders of Stonehenge use what seem like perfectly adequate stones nearby? This, like many other questions about Stonehenge, remains shrouded in mystery. Think again about the ley lines. Ponder the fact that many experts accept none of the explanations of how these giant stones were transported. Then imagine congregations gathering here 5,000 years ago, raising thought levels, creating a powerful life force transmitted along the ley lines. Maybe a particular kind of stone was essential for maximum energy transmission. Maybe the stones were levitated here. Maybe psychics really do create powerful vibes. Maybe not. It's as unbelievable as electricity used to be.

Salisbury

Salisbury, an attractive small city set in the middle of the expansive Salisbury Plain, is the natural launch pad for visiting nearby Stonehenge. But it's also a fine destination in its own right, with a walkable core, a famously soaring cathedral (with England's tallest spire and largest green), and a thriving twice-weekly market (Tue and Sat). While well-cared-for, practical Salisbury isn't particularly cute or quaint. But that's part of its charm.

As the city most associated with Stonehenge, it's no surprise that Salisbury also has a very long history: It was originally settled during the Bronze Age—possibly as early as 600 B.C.—and later became a Roman town called Sarum (located on a hill above today's city). When the old settlement outgrew its boundaries, the townspeople relocated to the river valley below.

Today, sightseers flow through Salisbury on their way to Stonehenge. But if you have time to spare, spend some of it exploring this fine town.

Orientation to Salisbury

Salisbury (pop. 45,000) stretches along the River Avon in the shadow of its huge landmark cathedral. The heart of the city clusters around the vast Market Place. A few short blocks to the south is the walled complex of the Cathedral Close.

TOURIST INFORMATION

The TI is just off Market Place. If you're headed to Stonehenge, you can buy tickets here (Mon-Fri 9:00-17:00, Sat 10:00-16:00, Sun 10:00-14:00, free Wi-Fi, corner of Fish Row and Queen Street, tel. 01722/342-860, www.visitwiltshire.co.uk).

Ask the TI about the 1.5-hour **town walking tours** (£6, daily at 11:00, Nov-March Sat-Sun only) or the Friday-evening **Ghost Walk** (£6, May-Sept Fri at 20:00); both depart from TI.

For walking-tour information call 07873/212-941 or visit www.salisburycityguides.co.uk.

ARRIVAL IN SALISBURY

By Train: From the train station, it's a 10-minute walk into the town center: Exit to the left, then bear right on Fisherton Street, and follow it into town.

By Bus: Buses stop at several points along Market Place (on Blue Boar Road) and around the corner on Endless Street. A handy bus information and ticket office is between Market Place and the cathedral (Mon-Fri 8:30-17:00, Sat 9:00-15:00, closed Sun, New Canal 6).

By Car: Drivers will find several pay parking lots. Follow the blue *P* signs (specific parking options, and available spaces, are noted on signs as you approach). To get as close as possible to the cathedral, look for a space at the corner of High Street and North Walk, just inside the cathedral's High Street Gate (£7/day). The Old George Mall parking garage, between Market Place and the cathedral, is handy, but closes Mon-Sat at 20:00 and Sun at 17:00. The "Central" lot, behind the giant red-brick Sainsbury's store, is farther out but still walkable, and has plenty of spaces—even when others are full (enter from Churchill Way West or Castle Street, open 24/7). Overnight, your best bet is the Culver Street garage, located a few blocks east of Market Place (free after 15:00 and all day Sun).

HELPFUL HINTS

Market Days: Don't miss Salisbury's market days (big markets Tue and Sat, smaller markets some Fri and Wed). For details, see "Market Days" under "Sights in Salisbury," later.

Festivals: The **Salisbury International Arts Festival** normally runs for just over two weeks at the end of May and beginning of June (www.salisburyfestival.co.uk). It's on hiatus in 2018, but is likely to return in 2019.

Laundry: Washing Well has two-hour full-service (Mon-Sat 8:30-17:00) as well as self-service (Mon-Sat 15:30-21:00, Sun from 7:00, last self-service wash one hour before closing; 28 Chipper Lane, tel. 01722/421-874).

Getting to the Stone Circles: You can get to Stonehenge from Salisbury on **The Stonehenge Tour** double-decker bus in summer or (more expensively) by **taxi** (see page 321). For buses to Avebury's stone circle, see "Salisbury Connections," later.

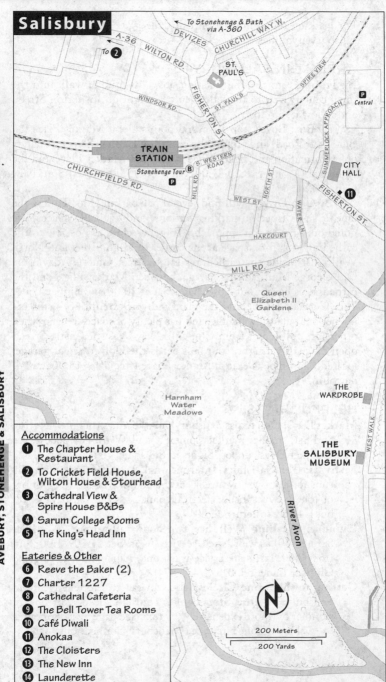

Salisbury

To Stonehenge & Bath via A-360

DEVIZES

CHURCHILL WAY W.

A-36 WILTON RD.

To ②

ST. PAUL'S

WINDSOR RD.

FISHERTON ST.

ST. PAUL'S

SPIRE VIEW

SUMMERLOCK APPROACH

P Central

TRAIN STATION

Stonehenge Tour B

S. WESTERN ROAD

CHURCHFIELDS RD.

P

MILL RD.

WEST ST.

NORTH ST.

WATER LN.

CITY HALL

FISHERTON ST.

◆ ⑪

HARCOURT

MILL RD.

Queen Elizabeth II Gardens

Harnham Water Meadows

THE WARDROBE

WEST WALK

THE SALISBURY MUSEUM

River Avon

N

200 Meters
200 Yards

Accommodations

1. The Chapter House & Restaurant
2. To Cricket Field House, Wilton House & Stourhead
3. Cathedral View & Spire House B&Bs
4. Sarum College Rooms
5. The King's Head Inn

Eateries & Other

6. Reeve the Baker (2)
7. Charter 1227
8. Cathedral Cafeteria
9. The Bell Tower Tea Rooms
10. Café Diwali
11. Anokaa
12. The Cloisters
13. The New Inn
14. Launderette
15. Bus Ticket Office

AVEBURY, STONEHENGE & SALISBURY

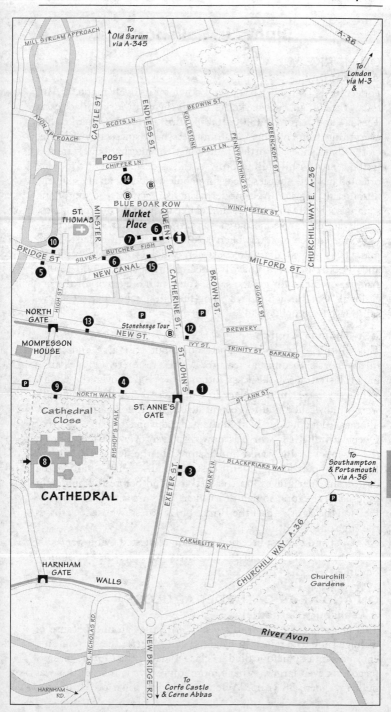

Sights in Salisbury

ON MARKET PLACE
▲Market Day

For centuries, Salisbury has been known for its lively markets. And today, the big "charter market" still fills the vast Market Place each Tuesday and Saturday (8:00-16:00). This all-purpose market has everything from butchers, fishmongers, and spices to hardware, clothes, and shoes. A little "food court" of international stands is in the center. While fun to browse, this is decidedly not a tourist-oriented market—but it's great for people-watching an age-old tradition still going on in a modern English city. At the top of the square is a handy row of bars and coffee shops with outdoor tables.

Every other Wednesday is the farmers' market. And increasingly, the city council has been hosting a variety of other themed markets: Fridays alternate between vintage, French products, and "Foodie Friday" (typically once monthly each, 10:00-16:00). And if you brake for garage sales, you'll pull a U-turn for the occasional "Car Boot Sundays." For the latest schedule, see www.salisburycitycouncil.gov.uk.

▲St. Thomas' Church

This Gothic space—short and squat, but still airy and light-filled—boasts an unusual feature: A fully restored "Doom Painting" (illustration of the Last Judgment, c. 1475, over the choir). While these are commonplace in Continental churches, England's were whitewashed and forgotten during the Reformation. But St. Thomas'—long hidden behind the painted wooden coat-of-arms of Queen Elizabeth I, which is now displayed over the red door on the right—was uncovered and restored in the late 19th century. Examine the exquisite, Flemish-style details: Angels pulling the dead from their graves (on the left) to stand before the judgment of Jesus (at the top); some unfortunate souls are sent to the jaws of Hell (on the right)—past the Prince of Darkness, whose toe crosses the edge of the Gothic arch.

Cost and Hours: Free but donation requested, Mon-Sat 9:00-17:00, Sun from 12:00, just west of Market Place on St. Thomas' Square.

ON AND NEAR CATHEDERAL CLOSE
▲▲Salisbury Cathedral

This magnificent cathedral is visible for miles around because of its huge spire (the tallest in England at 404 feet). The surrounding enormous grassy field (called a "close") makes the Gothic master-piece look even larger. What's more impressive is that all this was built in a mere 38 years. When the old hill town of Sarum was

moved down to the valley, its cathedral had to be replaced in a hurry. So, in 1220, the townspeople began building, and in 1258 their sparkling-new cathedral was ready for ribbon-cutting. Since the structure was built in just a few decades, its style is uniform, rather than the centuries-long patchwork common in cathedrals of the time. The cathedral also displays a remarkably well-preserved original copy of the Magna Carta (in the Chapter House).

Cost and Hours: £7.50 suggested donation, Mon-Sat 9:00-17:00, Sun 12:00-16:00, can be closed for special events. This working cathedral opens early for services: Be respectful if you arrive when one is in session. Tel. 01722/555-156, www.salisburycathedral.org.uk.

Tower Tours: Imagine building a cathedral on this scale before the invention of cranes, bulldozers, or modern scaffolding. An excellent tower tour (1.5-2 hours) helps visitors understand how it was done. You'll climb in between the stone arches and the roof to inspect the vaulting and trussing; see a medieval winch that was used in the construction; and finish with the 332-step climb up the narrow tower for a sweeping view of the Wiltshire countryside. Because only 12 people are allowed on each tour, it's smart to reserve by phone or online a few days ahead—or even longer on summer weekends (£12.50; early Mon-Sat at 11:15, 12:15, 13:15, 14:15, and 15:15, Sun at 13:15 and 14:15; fewer Oct-March but usually one at 13:15; tel. 01722/555-156, www.salisburycathedral.org.uk/visit/tower-tours).

Evensong: Salisbury's daily choral evensong (Mon-Sat at 17:30, Sun at 16:30, about 45 minutes) is just as beautiful as the one in Wells Cathedral (see page 303). Arrive up to 15 minutes early and enter through the north door. Spectators can sit in the nave, but you can also ask to be seated in the beautiful wood-carved seats of the choir.

Eating: The cathedral has two fine eating options: a glassed-in cafeteria and an outdoor café with prime views (see "Eating in Salisbury," later).

❷ Self-Guided Tour: You'll enter through the cloister, around the right side of the building. Entering the church, you'll instantly feel the architectural harmony. Volunteer guides posted strategically throughout the church stand ready to answer your questions. (Free guided tours of the cathedral nave are offered every hour or so, when enough people assemble.)

Step into the center of the **nave,** noticing how the stone col-

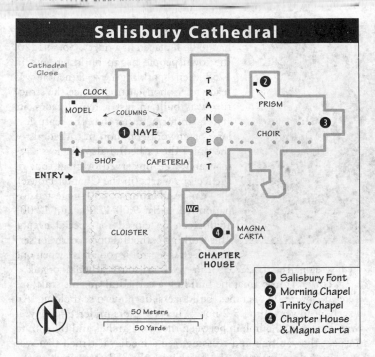

Salisbury Cathedral

Cathedral Close

CLOCK

MODEL

COLUMNS

1 NAVE

SHOP

CAFETERIA

ENTRY →

TRANSEPT

PRISM

2

CHOIR

3

CLOISTER

WC

4 MAGNA CARTA

CHAPTER HOUSE

50 Meters

50 Yards

1 Salisbury Font
2 Morning Chapel
3 Trinity Chapel
4 Chapter House & Magna Carta

umns march identically down the aisle—like a thick gray forest of tree trunks. The arches overhead soar to grand heights, helping churchgoers appreciate the vast and amazing heavens. Now imagine the interior surfaces painted in red, blue, green, and gold, as they would have been prior to the whitewashing of the English Reformation.

Head to the far wall (the back-left corner), where an interesting **model** shows how this cathedral was built so quickly in the 13th century. A few steps toward the front of the church is the "oldest working clock in existence," dating from the 14th century (the hourly bell has been removed, so as not to interrupt worship services). On the wall by the clock is a bell from the decommissioned ship HMS *Salisbury*. Look closely inside the bell to see the engraved names of crew members' children who were baptized on the ship.

Wander down the aisle past monuments and knights' tombs, as well as tombstones set into the floor. About halfway down the nave, you'll see (and hear) the gurgling **Salisbury Font**—a modern, oxidized-bronze baptismal font dedicated in 2008 to honor the cathedral's 750th birthday. While it looks like a modern sculpture, it's also used for baptisms—one of many ways in which it's clear that this church is full of life.

When you reach the transept, gape up at the **columns.** These posts were supposed to support a more modest bell tower, but when a heavy tower was added 100 years later, the columns bent under the enormous weight, causing the tower to lean sideways. Although the posts were later reinforced, the tower still tilts about two and a half feet.

Step into the **choir**, with its finely carved seats. This area hosts an evensong late each afternoon (well worth attending—see details earlier).

Head down the left side of the choir and dip into the **Morning Chapel** (on the left). At the back of this chapel, find the glass prism engraved with images of Salisbury—donated to the church in memory of a soldier who died at the D-Day landing at Normandy.

The oldest part of the church is at the apse (far end), where construction began in 1220: the **Trinity Chapel**. The giant, modern stained-glass window ponders the theme "prisoners of conscience."

Retrace your steps and exit back into the cloister. Turn left and follow signs around to the medieval **Chapter House**—so called because it's where the daily Bible verse, or chapter, was read. These spaces often served as gathering places for conducting church or town business. Enter the little freestanding tent for a look at the best preserved of the four original copies of the **Magna Carta.** This "Great Charter" is as important to the English as the Constitution is to Americans. Dating from 1215, the Magna Carta settled a dispute between England's King John and some powerful barons by guaranteeing that the monarch was not above the law. To this day, lawyers and political scientists admire this very early example of "checks and balances"—a major victory in the centuries-long tug-of-war between monarchs and nobles. Notice the smudge marks on the glass case, where historians have bumped their noses squinting at the miniscule script.

▲Cathedral Close

The enormous green surrounding the cathedral is the largest in England, and one of the loveliest. It's cradled in the elbow of the River Avon and ringed by row houses, cottages, and grand man-

sions. The church owns the houses on the green and rents them to lucky people with holy connections. A former prime minister, Edward Heath, lived on the green, not because of his political influence, but because he was once the church organist.

The benches scattered around the green are an excellent place for having a romantic moonlit picnic or for gazing thoughtfully at the leaning spire. Although you may be tempted to linger until it's late, don't—this is still private church property...and the heavy medieval gates of the close shut at about 22:00.

A few houses are open to the public, such as the overpriced Mompesson House and the medieval Wardrobe. The most interesting is...

▲The Salisbury Museum

Occupying the building just opposite the cathedral entry, this eclectic and sprawling collection was heralded by American expat travel writer Bill Bryson as one of England's best. While that's a stretch, the museum does offer a little something for everyone.

Cost and Hours: £7.50, Mon-Sat 10:00-17:00, Sun from 12:00 except closed Sun Oct-May, check with desk about occasional tours, 65 The Close, tel. 01722/332-151, www.salisburymuseum.org.uk.

Visiting the Museum: The highlight is the Wessex Gallery (to the left as you enter), with informative, interactive exhibits covering this area's rich prehistory—from Neanderthal axe heads to Iron Age cremation urns. Check out the ancient Roman mosaic floor and sarcophagus, and the sculpture fragments from the original Old Sarum cathedral. One exhibit details the excavation of Stonehenge, which began as early as 1620—back when it was believed to be Roman rather than druid.

The museum continues to the right of the entry, with a musty, dimly lit, but endearing collection of Salisbury's historic bric-a-brac—including the true-to-its-name "Salisbury Giant" puppet once used by the tailors' guild during parades, and some J. M. W. Turner paintings of the cathedral interior. Upstairs is a historical clothing exhibit and a collection of exquisite Wedgwood china and other ceramics.

JUST OUTSIDE SALISBURY

These two rewarding sights are practically on Salisbury's doorstep—within a 10-minute drive of Market Place. While neither is worth planning your day around, either can easily be combined with a trip to or from Stonehenge.

Old Sarum

Today, little remains of the original town of "Old Sarum," but a little imagination can transport you back to *very* Olde England. The city was originally founded on a slope overlooking the plain below. Uniquely, it combined both a castle and a cathedral within an Iron Age fortification. Old Sarum was eventually abandoned, leaving only a few stone foundations. The grand views of Salisbury from here have in-"spired" painters for ages and provided countless picnickers with a scenic backdrop (bring lunch or snacks).

Cost and Hours: £5, daily 10:00-18:00, Oct until 17:00, Nov-March until 16:00, tel. 01722/335-398, www.english-heritage.org.uk.

Getting There: It's on the edge of Salisbury, two miles north of the city center off the A-345. The Stonehenge Tour bus stops here, or you can take Salisbury Reds bus #X5 or Activ bus #8.

Background: Human settlement in this area stretches back to the Bronze Age, and the Romans, Saxons, and Normans all called this hilltop home. From about 500 B.C. through A.D. 1220, Old Sarum flourished, giving rise to a motte-and-bailey castle, a cathedral, and scores of wooden homes along the town's outer ring. The town grew so quickly that by the Middle Ages, it had outgrown its spot on the hill. In 1220, the local bishop successfully petitioned to move the entire city to the valley below, where space and water was plentiful. So, stone by stone, Old Sarum was packed up and shipped to New Sarum, where builders used nearly all the rubble from the old city to create a brand-new town with a magnificent cathedral.

Visiting the Site: From the parking lot or bus stop, you'll cross over the former moat to reach the core of Old Sarum. Inside you'll find a few scant walls and foundations. Colorful information plaques help resurrect the rubble. Additional ruins line the road between the site and the main road.

▲Wilton House and Garden

This sprawling estate, with a grand mansion and tidy gardens, has been owned by the Earls of Pembroke since King Henry VIII's time. The Pembrokes are a classy clan, and—unlike the many borderline-scruffy aristocratic homes in Britain—their home and garden are in exquisite repair and oozing with pride. The grounds are compact and well-organized, allowing for as short or long a visit as you'd like. Jane Austen fans particularly enjoy this stately home, where parts of 2005's Oscar-nominated *Pride and Prejudice* were filmed. But, alas, Mr. Darcy has checked out. Note the unusual weekend closure—the Pembrokes like to have the place to themselves on Fridays and Saturdays.

Cost and Hours: House and gardens-£15, gardens only-£6.25; house open Easter weekend and May-Aug Sun-Thu 11:30-17:00, closed Fri-Sat except holiday weekends, closed Sept-April; gardens open May-mid-Sept Sun-Thu 11:00-17:30, closed Fri-Sat, closed mid-Sept-April; tel. 01722/746-728, www.wiltonhouse.com.

Getting There: It's five miles west of Salisbury via the A-36, to Wilton's Minster Street. You can also reach it on Salisbury Reds bus #R3, park-and-ride bus #PR3, or—on Sundays—Salisbury Reds bus #3.

Visiting the Estate: The first stop is the **Old Riding School,** which houses a faintly interesting (but skippable) 15-minute film about the family and their house, and a fine collection of luxury cars old and new.

Inside the **mansion,** you'll tour several gorgeous rooms decorated with classical sculpture and paintings by Rubens, Rembrandt, Van Dyck, and Brueghel. You'll also see plenty of family portraits and some quirky odds and ends, such as a series of paintings of the Spanish Riding School, and a lock of Queen Elizabeth I's hair. The perfectly proportioned Double Cube Room has served as everything from a 17th-century state dining room to a secret D-Day planning room during World War II...if only the portraits could talk. Fortunately, the docents posted in each room do—since there's no posted information, be sure to ask plenty of questions.

You'll exit to the garden—flat and perfectly tended, with pebbly paths and a golf course-quality lawn, stretching along the gurgling River Nadder and decorated with a few Neoclassical ornaments.

Nearby: The village of Wilton itself is a proud, workaday burg that's fun to explore. It boasts the Wilton House at one end of town, a cozy green at its center, and at the far end of town, the Italianate **Church of Sts. Mary and Nicholas**—dating from the Romantic period of the mid-19th century, when world travelers brought some of their favorite styles back home. The can't-miss-it church, along West Street, looks like it'd be more at home in the Veneto than on Salisbury Plain.

Sleeping in Salisbury

Salisbury's town center has very few accommodations. Noisy roads rumble past most of these places: Light sleepers can try asking for a quieter room in back (or pack earplugs). Drivers should ask about parking when reserving. The town gets particularly crowded during the arts festival (late May through early June). If you're in a pinch, there's a **Premier Inn** two miles outside of town.

$$$ The Chapter House is a boutique hotel with 17 stylish, modern rooms in a creaky old shell. The rooms are above their trendy restaurant, immediately across from the side entrance to the Cathedral Close (9 St. John's Street, tel. 01722/341-277, www. thechapterhouseuk.com).

$$$ Cricket Field House, a cozy little compound just outside of town on the A-36 toward Wilton, overlooks a cricket pitch and golf course. It has 10 large, comfortable rooms, its own gorgeous garden, and plenty of parking (Wilton Road, tel. 01722/322-595,

www.cricketfieldhouse.co.uk, cricketfieldcottage@btinternet.com;
Brian and Margaret James). While this place works best for drivers,
it's a 20-minute walk from the train station or a five-minute bus
ride from the city center.

$$ Cathedral View B&B is a classic, traditional B&B rent-
ing four rooms just off the Cathedral Close. Wenda and Steve are
generous with travel tips, and Steve is an armchair town historian
with lots of insights (cash only, 2-night minimum on weekends,
no kids under age 10, 83 Exeter Street, tel. 01722/502-254, www.
cathedral-viewbandb.co.uk, info@cathedral-viewbandb.co.uk).

$$ Spire House B&B, with splashy decor, feels younger and
fresher (rather than a big English breakfast, they bring croissants
to your room). Owners Lois and John rent three rooms, but when
they're traveling—which is often—they rent out the entire place
on Airbnb (84 Exeter Street, tel. 01722/339-213, www.salisbury-
bedandbreakfast.com, spire.enquiries@btinternet.com).

$$ Sarum College is a theological college that rents 40 rooms
in its building right on the peaceful Cathedral Close. Much of
the year, it houses visitors to the college, but it usually has rooms
for tourists as well. The well-worn, slightly institutional but clean
rooms share hallways with libraries, bookstores, and offices; the
five attic rooms come with dramatic cathedral views from their
dormer windows (meals available, elevator, limited free parking,
19 The Close, tel. 01722/424-800, www.sarum.ac.uk, hospitality@
sarum.ac.uk).

$$ The King's Head Inn rents 33 modern rooms above a chain
Wetherspoon pub. While impersonal, it's a decent value and con-
veniently located—in a handsome old sandstone building between
Market Place and the train station—and likely to have room when
others are full (breakfast extra, deeply discounted Sun nights, air-
con, elevator to some rooms, 1 Bridge Street, tel. 01722/438-400,
www.jdwetherspoon.com, kingsheadinn@jdwetherspoon.co.uk).

Eating in Salisbury

There are plenty of atmospheric pubs all over town. For the best
variety of restaurants, head to the Market Place area. Some places
offer "early bird" specials before 19:00.

$ Reeve the Baker crafts an array of high-calorie delights and
handy pick-me-ups for a fast and affordable lunch. Peruse the long
cases of pastries and savory treats, and notice the locals waiting
patiently at the fresh bread counter in back (Mon-Sat 7:30-17:30,
Sun 10:00-16:00, tel. 01722/320-367). The main branch, on Market Place (at 2 Butcher Row), has seating both upstairs and out on
the square—either with a nice view of the busy market. A much

smaller second branch is at the corner of Market and Bridge streets at 61 Silver Street.

$$$ The Chapter House is a lively and popular restaurant with an enticing menu of British, South African, and international fare in a trendy setting (Mon-Sat 12:00-15:00 & 18:00-22:00, Sun until 20:00, 9 St. John's Street, tel. 01722/341-277).

$$$$ Charter 1227 is a high-end splurge (by Salisbury standards) filling a contemporary dining room upstairs, overlooking Market Place. The short, selective menu is much more affordable at lunch for their mid-week "early bird" specials (open Tue-Sat 12:00-14:30 & 18:00-21:30, closed Sun-Mon, lunch specials Tue-Thu, reservations smart, 6 Ox Row, enter from Market Place, tel. 01722/333-118, www.charter1227.co.uk).

At the Cathedral: For lunch near the cathedral, you have two great choices. The **$ cafeteria** has a full menu and fills a winter garden squeezed between the buttresses and the cloister, with additional seating in the cloister itself (open same hours as cathedral). But on a sunny day, it's hard to imagine a nicer setting than **$ The Bell Tower Tea Rooms,** with outdoor tables on England's biggest close, peering up at its tallest cathedral tower (drinks, deli sandwiches, and affordable teas—£5 cream tea, afternoon tea is £24/2 people; choose a table, then order at the counter; daily 10:00-17:00).

Indian: If you're going to try Indian food, do it in Salisbury. These two excellent options both serve creative variations on the typical "curry house" fare: **$$$ Café Diwali** takes an "Indian street food" approach, with delicious, well-executed, and creative dishes served thali-style, on big silver platters (daily 12:00-14:00 & 18:00-22:30, 90 Crane Street, tel. 01722/329-700). And **$$$ Anokaa** serves up updated Indian cuisine in a dressy, contemporary setting (daily 12:00-14:00 & 17:30-23:00, 60 Fisherton Street, tel. 01722/414-142, www.anokaa.com).

Pubs: $$ The Cloisters is the best all-around choice, with reliable pub fare and atmosphere, and leather couches under heavy beams (daily 11:00-23:00, 83 Catherine Street, tel. 01722/338-102). **$$ The New Inn,** the local rugby pub, fills a creaky, atmospheric, 15th-century house rumored to have a tunnel leading directly into the cathedral—perhaps dug while the building housed a brothel? On a sunny day, their back garden is altogether pleasant (daily 11:00-24:00, 41 New Street, tel. 01722/326-662).

Salisbury Connections

From Salisbury by Train to: London's Waterloo Station (2/hour, 1.5 hours), **Bath** (hourly direct, 1 hour). Train info: tel. 0345-748-4950, www.nationalrail.co.uk.

By Bus to: Bath (hourly, 3 hours, www.travelinesw.com; or National Express #300 at 10:35, 1.5 hours, tel. 0871-781-8181, www.nationalexpress.com), **Avebury** (hourly, 2-2.5 hours, transfer in Devizes, www.travelinesw.com). Many of Salisbury's long-distance buses are run by Salisbury Reds (tel. 01722/336-855 or 01202/338-420, www.salisburyreds.co.uk).

Near Salisbury

The most appealing sights in the Salisbury area are Stonehenge and Avebury. But if you have extra time here (or en route to your next stop), these possibilities are worth considering. While best for drivers, and not worth going out of your way to see, they may appeal if you have a special interest in gardens, ruined castles, or cute villages.

Stourhead House and Gardens

Stourhead, designed by owner Henry Hoare II in the mid-18th century, is a sprawling 2,650-acre estate of rolling hills, meandering paths, placid lakes, and colorful trees, punctuated by classically inspired bridges and monuments. The creaky old mansion strains to make its obscure aristocratic owners interesting (with eager docents in each room), but the gardens are the real highlight: Take a two-mile loop hike down and around the lake. It's not rewarding enough for the time it demands, but those who enjoy strolling through gardens may find it worthwhile.

Cost and Hours: £16 includes house and garden, after 16:00 you can pay £9.60 for the garden alone; house open March-Oct daily 11:00-16:30, garden open year-round daily 9:00-18:00; tel. 01747/841-152, www.nationaltrust.org.uk. It's 28 miles (40 minutes) west of Salisbury in the village of Stourton.

Corfe Castle

Built by William the Conqueror in the 11th century, this was a favorite residence for medieval kings until it was destroyed by a massive gunpowder blast during a 17th-century siege. Today its jagged ruins cap a steep, conical hill, offering a fun excuse for a

AVEBURY, STONEHENGE & SALISBURY

hike and sweeping views over the Dorset countryside. Park at the Castle View Visitors Center, then follow the path that curls around the back of the castle to the village (about 10 minutes). There you can buy your ticket, cross the drawbridge, and hike up. The castle is mostly an empty husk, with little to bring its dramatic history to life, but it's fun to scramble along its rocky remnants.

Cost and Hours: £10, daily 10:00-18:00, closes earlier Oct-March, tel. 01929/481-294, www.nationaltrust.org.uk). It's 44 miles (about one hour) south of Salisbury.

▲Cerne Abbas

Dorset County's most adorable village is cuddly, one-street Cerne Abbas (surn AB-iss)—about 45 miles (one hour) southwest of Salisbury. It's lined with half-timbered buildings and draped with ivy and wisteria. Park your car and go for a walk. Head up Abbey Street, passing the lovely St. Mary's Church on ywour way up to the village's namesake abbey. Let yourself in the gate and explore the mysterious, beautiful grounds. If you need a break, the town has some appealing pubs and the fine Abbots Tea Room (7 Long Street, tel. 01300/341-349).

The village is best known for the large chalk figure that's scraped into a nearby hillside: the famous **Cerne Abbas Giant.**

(To find it, head up the street just past Abbots Tea Room—by car or by foot; you can also follow brown road signs to *Giant Viewpoint*.) Chalk figures such as this one can be found in many parts of the region. Because the soil is only a few inches deep, the overlying grass and dirt can easily be removed to expose the bright white chalk bedrock beneath, creating the outlines. While nobody is sure exactly how old this figure is, or what its original purpose was, the giant is faithfully maintained by the locals, who mow and clear the fields at least once a year. This particular figure, possibly a fertility god, looks friendly... maybe a little too friendly. Locals claim that if a woman who's having trouble getting pregnant sleeps on the giant for one night, she will soon be able to conceive a child. (A few years back, controversy surrounded this giant, as a 180-foot-tall, donut-hoisting Homer Simpson was painted onto the adjacent hillside. No kidding.)

The area around Cerne Abbas can be fun to explore—with names seemingly invented on a bet by pub patrons on tuppence-ale night. Piddle Lane leads out of town to villages with names like Piddletrenthide, Piddlehinton (both on the aptly named River Piddle), Plush, Mappowder, Ansty, Lower Ansty, and, of course, Higher Ansty. More entertainment rewards careful map-readers in the surrounding hills: King's Stag, Fifehead Neville, Maiden Newton, Hazelbury Bryan, Poopton-upon-Piddle, Stock Gaylard, Bishop's Caundle, Alton Pancras, Melbury Bubb, Beer Hackett, Sturminster Newton, Nether Cerne, and Margaret Marsh. Believe it or not, only one of these names is made up.

THE COTSWOLDS

*Chipping Campden • Stow-on-the-Wold •
Moreton-in-Marsh • Blenheim Palace*

The Cotswold Hills, a 25-by-90-mile chunk of Gloucestershire, are dotted with enchanting villages and graced with England's greatest countryside palace, Blenheim. As with many fairy-tale regions of Europe, the present-day beauty of the Cotswolds was the result of an economic disaster. Wool was a huge industry in medieval England, and Cotswold sheep grew the best wool. A 12th-century saying bragged, "In Europe the best wool is English. In England the best wool is Cotswold." The region prospered. Wool money built fine towns and houses. Local "wool" churches are called "cathedrals" for their scale and wealth. Stained-glass slogans say things like "I thank my God and ever shall, it is the sheep hath paid for all."

But with the rise of cotton and the Industrial Revolution, the woolen industry collapsed. Ba-a-a-ad news. The wealthy Cotswold towns fell into a depressed time warp; the homes of impoverished nobility became gracefully dilapidated. Today, visitors enjoy a harmonious blend of man and nature—the most pristine of English countrysides decorated with time-passed villages, rich wool churches, tell-me-a-story stone fences, and "kissing gates" you wouldn't want to experience alone. Appreciated by throngs of 21st-century Romantics, the Cotswolds are enjoying new prosperity.

The north Cotswolds are best. Two of the region's coziest towns, Chipping Campden and Stow-on-the-Wold, are eight and four miles, respectively, from Moreton-in-Marsh, which has the best public transportation connections. Any of these three towns makes a fine home base for your exploration of the thatch-happiest of Cotswold villages and walks.

PLANNING YOUR TIME

The Cotswolds are an absolute delight by car and, with a well-organized plan—and patience—are enjoyable even without one. Do your homework in advance; read this chapter carefully. Then decide if you want to rent a car, rely on public transportation (budgeting for an inevitable taxi ride), or reserve a day with a tour company or private driver. Whatever you choose, on a three-week countrywide trip, I'd spend at least two nights and a day in the Cotswolds. The Cotswolds' charm has a softening effect on many uptight itineraries. You could enjoy days of walking from a home base here.

Home Bases: Quaint without being overrun, **Chipping Campden** and **Stow-on-the-Wold** both have good accommodations. Stow has a bit more character for an overnight stay and offers the widest range of choices, but Chipping Campden is more peaceful. The plainer town of **Moreton-in-Marsh** is the only one of the three with a train station, and only worth visiting as a transit hub. While Moreton has the most convenient connections, it's possible for nondrivers to home-base in Chipping Campden or Stow—especially if you don't mind sorting through bus schedules or springing for the occasional taxi to connect towns. (This becomes even more challenging on Sundays, when there is essentially no bus service.) With a car, consider really getting away from it all by staying in one of the smaller villages.

Nearby Sights: England's top countryside palace, **Blenheim,** is located at the eastern edge of the Cotswolds, between Moreton and Oxford (see the end of this chapter). For drivers, Blenheim fits well on the way into or out of the region. If you want to take in some Shakespeare, note that Stow, Chipping Campden, and Moreton are only a 30-minute drive from **Stratford,** which offers a great evening of world-class entertainment (see next chapter).

One-Day Driver's Cotswold Blitz: Use a good map and re-shuffle this plan to fit your home base:

 9:00   Browse through Chipping Campden, following my self-guided walk.

10:30   Joyride through Snowshill, Stanway, and Stanton.

12:30   Have lunch in Stow-on-the-Wold, then follow my self-guided walk there.

15:00   Drive to the Slaughters, Bourton-on-the-Water, and Bibury; or, if you're up for a hike instead of a drive, walk from Stow to the Slaughters to Bourton, then catch the bus back to Stow.

18:00   Have dinner at a countryside gastropub (reserve in advance), then head home; or drive 30 minutes to Stratford-upon-Avon for a Shakespeare play.

Two-Day Plan by Public Transportation: This plan is best for any day except Sunday—when virtually no buses run—and assumes you're home-basing in Moreton-in-Marsh.

Day 1: Take the morning bus to Chipping Campden (likely departing around 9:30) to explore that town. Hike up Dover's Hill and back (about one-hour round-trip), or take the bus to Mickleton and walk (uphill, 45 minutes) to Hidcote Manor Garden for a visit there. Eat lunch in Chipping Campden, then squeeze in either Broad Campden or Broadway before returning directly from either town to Moreton by bus #1 or #2.

Day 2: Take a day trip to Blenheim Palace via Oxford (train to Oxford, bus to palace—explained on page 397). Or take a morning bus to Stow. After poking around the town, hike from Stow through the Slaughters to Bourton-on-the-Water (about 3 hours at a relaxed pace), then return by bus or taxi to Moreton for dinner.

TOURIST INFORMATION

Local TIs stock a wide array of helpful resources and can tell you about any local events during your stay. Ask for the *Cotswold Lion*, the biannual newspaper, which includes suggestions for walks and hikes (spring/summer); bus schedules for the routes you'll be using; and the *Attractions and Events Guide* (with updated prices and hours for Cotswold sights). Each village also has its own assortment of brochures, often for a small fee. While being asked to pay for these items seems chintzy, realize that Cotswold TIs have lost much of their government funding and are struggling to make ends meet (some are run by volunteers).

GETTING AROUND THE COTSWOLDS
By Car

Joyriding here truly is a joy. Winding country roads seem designed to spring bucolic village-and-countryside scenes on the driver at every turn. Distances are wonderfully short, and easily navigable with GPS. As a backup, you could invest in the Ordnance Survey map of the Cotswolds, sold locally at TIs and newsstands (the £9 Explorer OL #45 map is excellent but almost too detailed for drivers; a £5 tour map covers a wider area in less detail). Here are driving distances from Moreton: **Stow-on-the-Wold** (4 miles), **Chipping Campden** (8 miles), **Broadway** (10 miles), **Stratford-upon-Avon** (17 miles), **Warwick** (23 miles), **Blenheim Palace** (20 miles).

Car hiking is great. In this chapter, I cover the postcard-perfect (but discovered) villages. With a car and a good map (either

GPS or the local Ordnance Survey), you can easily ramble about and find your own gems. The problem with having a car is that you are less likely to walk. Consider taking a taxi or bus somewhere, so that you can walk back to your car and enjoy the scenery (see suggestions next).

Car Rental: The easiest option is to rent a car in Oxford then drive (30-45 minutes) into the Cotswolds. One place near Moreton-in-Marsh rents cars by the day, but you'll need to reserve in advance. **Robinson Goss Self Drive** is six miles north of town and won't bring the car to you in Moreton (£31-61/day plus extras like GPS and gas, Mon-Fri 8:30-17:00, Sat until 12:00, closed Sun, tel. 01608/663-322, www.robgos.co.uk).

By Bus

The Cotswolds are so well-preserved, in part, because public transportation to and within this area has long been miserable. For-

tunately, trains link the region to larger towns, and a few key buses connect the more interesting villages. Centrally located Moreton-in-Marsh is the region's transit hub—with the only train station and several bus lines.

To explore the towns, use the bus routes that hop through the Cotswolds about every 1.5 hours, lacing together main stops and ending at rail stations. In each case, the entire trip takes about an hour. Individual fares are around £4. If you plan on taking more than two rides in a day, consider the Cotswolds Discoverer pass, which offers unlimited travel on most buses including those listed next (£10/day, www.escapetothecotswolds.org.uk/discoverer).).

The TI hands out easy-to-read bus schedules for the key lines described here (or check www.traveline.org.uk, or call the Traveline info line, tel. 0871-200-2233). Put together a one-way or return trip by public transportation, making for a fine Cotswold day. If you're traveling one-way between two train stations, remember that the Cotswold villages—generally pretty clueless when it comes to the needs of travelers without a car—have no official baggage-check services. You'll need to improvise; ask sweetly at the nearest TI or business.

Note that no single bus connects the three major towns described in this chapter (Chipping Campden, Stow, and Moreton); to get between Chipping Campden and Stow, you'll have to change buses in Moreton. Since buses can be unreliable and connections

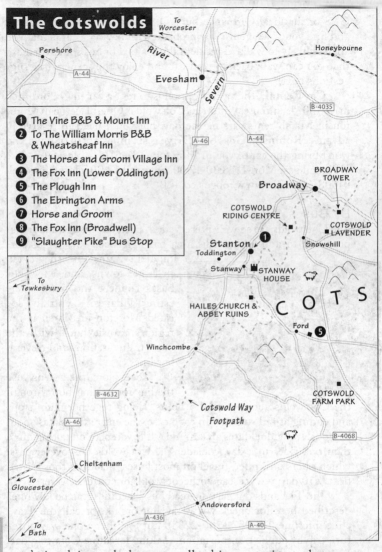

The Cotswolds

To Worcester

Pershore

River

Honeybourne

A-44

Evesham

Severn

B-4035

1 The Vine B&B & Mount Inn
2 To The William Morris B&B
  & Wheatsheaf Inn
3 The Horse and Groom Village Inn
4 The Fox Inn (Lower Oddington)
5 The Plough Inn
6 The Ebrington Arms
7 Horse and Groom
8 The Fox Inn (Broadwell)
9 "Slaughter Pike" Bus Stop

A-46   A-44

BROADWAY
TOWER

Broadway

COTSWOLD
RIDING CENTRE

COTSWOLD
LAVENDER

Stanton   1   Snowshill

Toddington

Stanway

STANWAY
HOUSE

To
Tekwesbury

C O T S

HAILES CHURCH &
ABBEY RUINS

Ford   5

Winchcombe

B-4632

COTSWOLD
FARM PARK

A-46   Cotswold Way
            Footpath

B-4068

Cheltenham

To
Gloucester

Andoversford

A-436   A-40

To
Bath

COTSWOLDS

aren't timed, it may be better to call a driver or taxi to go between Chipping Campden and Stow.

The following bus lines are operated by Johnsons Coaches (tel. 01564/797-070, www.johnsonscoaches.co.uk): Buses **#1** and **#2** run from Moreton-in-Marsh to Batsford to Bourton-on-the-Hill to Blockley, then either to Broadway or Broad Campden on their way to Chipping Campden, and pass through Mickleton before ending at Stratford-upon-Avon.

The following buses are operated by Pulham & Sons Coaches (tel. 01451/820-369, www.pulhamscoaches.com): Bus **#801**

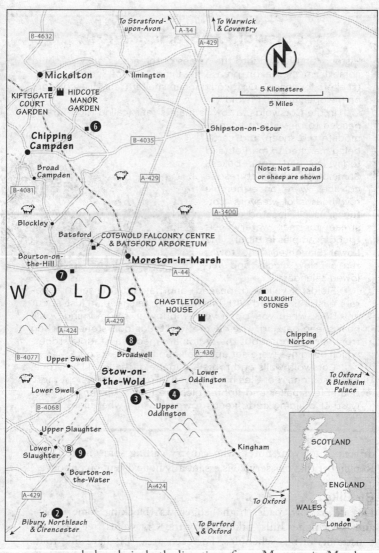

To Stratford-upon-Avon

A-34

To Warwick & Coventry

A-429

B-4632

• Mickelton

• Ilmington

N

5 Kilometers

5 Miles

KIFTSGATE COURT GARDEN

HIDCOTE MANOR GARDEN

6

• Shipston-on-Stour

Chipping Campden

B-4035

• Broad Campden

A-429

Note: Not all roads or sheep are shown

B-4081

A-3400

• Blockley

Batsford

COTSWOLD FALCONRY CENTRE & BATSFORD ARBORETUM

Bourton-on-the-Hill

Moreton-in-Marsh

W O L D S

7

A-44

CHASTLETON HOUSE

ROLLRIGHT STONES

A-429

A-424

Chipping Norton

B-4077

Upper Swell

8

Broadwell

A-436

To Oxford & Blenheim Palace

Lower Oddington

Lower Swell

Stow-on-the-Wold

3

4

B-4068

Upper Oddington

Upper Slaughter

Lower Slaughter

B

9

Kingham

Bourton-on-the-Water

A-424

A-429

To Oxford

2

To Bibury, Northleach & Cirencester

To Burford & Oxford

SCOTLAND

ENGLAND

WALES

London

goes nearly hourly in both directions from Moreton-in-Marsh to Stow-on-the-Wold to Bourton-on-the-Water; most continue on to Northleach and Cheltenham (limited service on Sun in summer). Bus #855 goes from Moreton-in-Marsh and Stow to Northleach to Bibury to Cirencester.

Warning: Unfortunately, the buses described here aren't particularly reliable—it's not uncommon for them to show up late, early, or not at all. Leave yourself a sizeable cushion if using buses to make another connection (such as a train to London), and always have a backup plan (such as the phone number for a few taxis/

Cotswold Appreciation 101

History can be read into the names of the area. *Cotswold* could come from the Saxon phrase meaning "hills of sheep's cotes" (shelters for sheep). Or it could mean shelter ("cot" like cottage) on the open upland ("wold").

In the Cotswolds, a town's main street (called High Street) needed to be wide to accom- modate the sheep and cattle being marched to market (and today, to park tour buses). Some of the most picturesque cottages were once humble row houses of weavers' cot- tages, usually located along a stream for their waterwheels (good examples in Bibury and Lower Slaughter). The towns run on slow clocks and yel- lowed calendars.

Fields of yellow (rapeseed) and pale blue (linseed) sepa- rate pastures dotted with black and white sheep. In just about any B&B, when you open your window in the morning you'll hear sheep baa-ing. The decorative "toadstool" stones dotting front yards throughout the region are medieval staddle stones, which buildings were set upon to keep the rodents out.

Cotswold walls and roofs are made of the local limestone. The limestone roof tiles hang by pegs. To make the weight more bearable, smaller and lighter tiles are higher up. An extreme- ly strict building code keeps towns looking what many locals

drivers or for your hotel, who can try calling someone for you). Remember that bus service is essentially nonexistent on Sundays.

By Bike

Despite narrow roads, high hedgerows (blocking some views), and even higher hills, bikers enjoy the Cotswolds free from the constraints of bus schedules. For each area, TIs have fine route planners that indicate which peaceful, paved lanes are particularly scenic for biking. In summer, it's smart to book your rental bike a couple of days ahead. Note that only Chipping Campden and Bourton-on-the-Water have shops that rent out bikes.

In **Chipping Campden** your only choice is **Cycle Cotswolds,** at the Volunteer Inn pub (£12/day, daily 7:00-dusk, Lower High Street, mobile 07549-620-597, www.cyclecotswolds.co.uk). If you make it to **Bourton-on-the-Water,** you can rent bicycles through **Hartwells** on High Street (£10/3 hours, £14/day, includes helmet,

COTSWOLDS

call "overly quaint."

While you'll still see lots of sheep, the commercial wool industry is essentially dead. It costs more to shear a sheep than the 50 pence the wool will fetch. In the old days, sheep lived long lives, producing lots of wool. When they were finally slaughtered, the meat was tough and eaten as "mutton." Today, you don't find mutton much because the sheep are raised primarily for their meat, and slaughtered younger. When it comes to Cotswold sheep these days, it's lamb (not mutton) for dinner (not sweaters).

Towns are small, and everyone seems to know everyone. The area is provincial yet ever-so-polite, and people commonly rescue themselves from a gossipy tangent by saying, "It's all very... mmm...yaaa."

In contrast to the village ambience are the giant manors and mansions whose private gated driveways you'll drive past. Many of these now belong to A-list celebrities, who have country homes here. If you live in the Cotswolds, you can call Madonna, Elizabeth Hurley, and Kate Moss your neighbors.

This is walking country. The English love their walks and vigorously defend their age-old right to free passage. Once a year the Ramblers, Britain's largest walking club, organizes a "Mass Trespass," when each of the country's 50,000 miles of public footpaths is walked. By assuring that each path is used at least once a year, they stop landlords from putting up fences. Any paths found blocked are unceremoniously unblocked.

Questions to ask locals: Do you think foxhunting should have been banned? Who are the Morris men? What's a kissing gate?

route map, and locks; Mon-Sat 9:00-18:00, Sun from 10:00; tel. 01451/820-405, www.hartwells.supanet.com).

If you're interested in a biking vacation, **Cotswold Country Cycles** offers self-led bike tours of the Cotswolds and surrounding areas (tours last 2-7 days and include accommodations and luggage transfer, see www.cotswoldcountrycycles.com).

By Foot

Walking guidebooks and leaflets abound, giving you a world of choices for each of my recommended stops (choose a book with clear maps). If you're doing any hiking whatsoever, get the excellent Ordnance Survey Explorer OL #45 map, which shows every road, trail, and ridgeline (£9 at local TIs). Nearly every hotel and B&B has a box or shelf of local walking guides and maps, including Ordnance Survey #45. Don't hesitate to ask for a loaner. For a quick **circular hike** from a particular village, peruse the books and brochures offered by that village's TI, or search online for maps and route descriptions; one good website is www.nationaltrail.co.uk—select "Cotswold Way," then "Be Inspired," then "Circular Walks." Villages are generally no more than three miles apart, and most have pubs that would love to feed and water you.

For a list of **guided walks,** ask at any TI for the free *Cotswold Lion* newspaper. The walks range from 2 to 12 miles, and often involve a stop at a pub or tearoom (*Lion* newspaper also online at www.cotswoldsaonb.org.uk—click on "News," then "Publications").

Another option is to leave the planning to a company such as **Cotswold Walking Holidays,** which can help you design a walking vacation, provide route instructions and maps, transfer your bags, and even arrange lodging. They also offer five- to six-night walking tours that come with a local guide. Walking through the towns allows you to slow down and enjoy the Cotswolds at their very best—experiencing open fields during the day and arriving into towns just as the day-trippers depart (www.cotswoldwalks.com).

There are many options for hikers, ranging from the "Cotswold Way" path that leads 100 miles from Chipping Campden all the way to Bath, to easy loop trips to the next village. Serious hikers enjoy doing a several-day loop, walking for several hours each day and sleeping in a different village each night. One popular route is the **"Cotswold Ring"**: Day 1—Moreton-in-Marsh to Stow-on-the-Wold to the Slaughters to Bourton-on-the-Water (12 miles); Day 2—Bourton-on-the-Water to Winchcombe (13 miles); Day 3—Winchcombe to Stanway to Stanton (7 miles), or all the way to Broadway (10.5 miles total); Day 4—On to Chipping Campden (just 5.5 miles, but steeply uphill); Day 5—Chipping Campden to Broad Campden, Blockley, Bourton-on-the-Hill, or Batsford, and back to Moreton (7 miles).

Realistically, on a short visit, you won't have time for that much hiking. But if you have a few hours to spare, consider venturing across the pretty hills and meadows of the Cotswolds. Each of the home-base villages I recommend has several options. Stow-on-the-Wold, immersed in pleasant but not-too-hilly terrain, is within easy walking distance of several interesting spots and is probably the best starting point. Chipping Campden sits along a ridge, which means that hikes from there are extremely scenic, but also more strenuous. Moreton—true to its name—sits on a marsh, offering flatter and less picturesque hikes.

Recommended Hikes

Here are a few hikes to consider, in order of difficulty (easiest first). I've selected these for their convenience to the home-base towns and because the start and/or end points are on bus lines, allowing you to hitch a ride back to where you started (or on to the next town) rather than backtracking by foot.

Stow, the Slaughters, and Bourton-on-the-Water: Walk from Stow to Upper and Lower Slaughter, then on to Bourton-on-the-Water (which has bus service back to Stow on #801). One big advantage of this walk is that it's mostly downhill (4 miles, about 2-3 hours one-way). For details, see page 378.

Chipping Campden, Broad Campden, Blockley, and Bourton-on-the-Hill: From Chipping Campden, it's an easy mile walk into charming Broad Campden, and from there, a more strenuous hike to Blockley and Bourton-on-the-Hill (which are both connected by buses #1 and #2 to Chipping Campden and Moreton). For more details, see page 357.

Winchcombe, Stanway, Stanton, and Broadway: You can reach the charming villages of Stanway and Stanton by foot, but it's tough going—lots of up and down. The start and end points (Winchcombe and Broadway) have decent bus connections, and in a pinch some buses do serve Stanton (but carefully check schedules before you set out).

Broadway to Chipping Campden: The hardiest hike of those I list here, this takes you along the Cotswold Ridge. Attempt it only if you're a serious hiker (5.5 miles).

Bibury and the Coln Valley are pretty, but limited bus access makes hiking there less appealing.

By Taxi or Private Driver

Two or three town-to-town taxi trips can make more sense than renting a car. While taking a cab cross-country seems extravagant, the distances are short (Stow to Moreton is 4 miles, Stow to Chipping Campden is 10), and one-way walks are lovely. If you call a cab, confirm that the meter will start only when you are actually picked up. Consider hiring a private driver at the hourly "touring rate" (generally around £35), rather than the meter rate. For a few more bucks than taking a taxi, you can have a joyride peppered with commentary. Whether you book a taxi or a private driver, expect to pay about £25 between Chipping Campden and Stow and about £20 between Chipping Campden and Moreton.

Note that the drivers listed here are not typical city taxi services (with many drivers on call), but are mostly individuals—it's smart to call ahead if you're arriving in high season, since they can be booked in advance on weekends.

To scare up a taxi in Moreton, try Stuart and Stephen at **ETC**, "Everything Taken Care of" (tel. 01608/650-343 or toll-free 0800-955-8584, www.cotswoldtravel.co.uk); see also the taxi phone numbers posted outside the Moreton train station office. In Stow, try **Tony Knight** (mobile 07887-714-047, anthonyknight205@

COTSWOLDS

The Cotswolds at a Glance

Chipping Campden and Nearby

▲▲**Chipping Campden** Picturesque market town with finest High Street in England, accented by a 17th-century Market Hall, wool-tycoon manors, and a characteristic Gothic church. See page 356.

▲▲**Stanway House** Grand, aristocratic home of the Earl of Wemyss, with the tallest fountain in Britain and a 14th-century tithe barn. **Hours:** June-Aug Tue and Thu only 14:00-17:00, closed Sept-May. See page 367.

▲**Stanton** Classic Cotswold village with flower-filled exteriors and 15th-century church. See page 369.

▲**Snowshill Manor** Eerie mansion packed to the rafters with eclectic curiosities collected over a lifetime. **Hours:** July-Aug Wed-Mon 11:30-16:30, closed Tue; April-June and Sept-Oct Wed-Sun 12:00-17:00, closed Mon-Tue; closed Nov-March. See page 370.

▲**Hidcote Manor Garden** Fragrant garden organized into color-themed "outdoor rooms" that set a trend in 20th-century garden design. **Hours:** March-Sept daily 10:00-18:00; Oct daily until 17:00; Nov-Dec Sat-Sun 11:00-16:00, closed Mon-Fri; closed Jan-Feb. See page 372.

▲**Broad Campden, Blockley, and Bourton-on-the-Hill** Trio of villages with sweeping views and quaint homes, far from the madding crowds. See page 373.

Stow-on-the-Wold and Nearby

▲▲**Stow-on-the-Wold** Convenient Cotswold home base with charming shops and pubs clustered around town square, plus popular day hikes. See page 373.

▲**Lower and Upper Slaughter** Inaptly named historic villages—home to a working waterwheel, peaceful churches, and a folksy museum. See page 385.

COTSWOLDS

btinternet.com). In Chipping Campden, call James at **Cotswold Private Hire** (mobile 07980-857-833), or **Les Proctor,** who offers village tours and station pick-ups (mobile 07580-993-492, Les also co-runs Cornerways B&B—see page 364). Tim Harrison at **Tour the Cotswolds** specializes in tours of the Cotswolds and its gardens, but will also do tours outside the area (mobile 07779-030-820, www.tourthecotswolds.co.uk).

▲**Bourton-on-the-Water** The "Venice of the Cotswolds," touristy yet undeniably striking, with petite canals and impressive Cotswold Motoring Museum. See page 386.

▲**Cotswold Farm Park** Kid-friendly park with endangered breeds of native British animals, farm demonstrations, and tractor rides. **Hours:** Daily 10:30-17:00, Nov-Dec until 16:00, closed Jan. See page 387.

▲**Mechanical Music Museum** Tiny museum brimming with self-playing musical instruments, demonstrations, and Victorian music boxes. **Hours:** Daily 10:00-17:00. See page 389.

▲**Bibury Village** of antique weavers' cottages, ideal for outdoor activities like fishing and picnicking. See page 390.

▲**Cirencester** Ancient 2,000-year-old city noteworthy for its crafts center and museum, showcasing artifacts from Roman and Saxon times. See page 390.

Moreton-in-Marsh and Nearby
▲**Moreton-in-Marsh** Relatively flat and functional home base with the best transportation links in the Cotswolds and a bustling Tuesday market. See page 392.

▲**Chastleton House** Lofty Jacobean-era home with a rich family history. **Hours:** Wed-Sun 13:00-17:00, closed Nov-mid-March and Mon-Tue year-round. See page 396.

▲▲▲**Blenheim Palace** Fascinating, sumptuous, still-occupied aristocratic abode—one of Britain's best. **Hours:** Mid-Feb-Oct daily 10:30-17:30, Nov-mid-Dec generally closed Mon-Tue, park open but palace closed mid-Dec-mid-Feb. See page 397.

COTSWOLDS

By Tour
Departing from Bath, **Lion Tours** offers a Cotswold Discovery full-day tour, and can drop you and your luggage off in Stow (£5/person) or in Moreton-in-Marsh (£7.50/person; minimum two people for either). If you want to get back to London in time for a show, ask to be dropped off at Kemble Station; it's best to arrange drop-offs in advance (see page 259 of the Bath chapter).

Cotswold Tour offers a smartly arranged day of sightseeing for people with limited time and transportation. Reserve your spot online, then meet Becky at Moreton-in-Marsh's train station at 10:00. The tour follows a set route that includes a buffet lunch and cream tea served in her cottage and returns to the station by 16:30—good timing for day-trippers to return to London for the evening (£95/person, must reserve ahead online, tel. 01608/674-700, www.cotswoldtourismtours.co.uk). No luggage is allowed—if you're traveling with bags you'll have to find somewhere in Moreton to store them for the day (Becky recommends leaving them at the launderette a few minutes' walk from the station).

Go Cotswolds comes recommended by readers. Tom will pick you up from Stratford-upon-Avon or Moreton-in-Marsh for a day tour of several highlights including Chipping Campden, Stow-on-the-Wold and Bourton-on-the-Water. The tours operate Wednesdays, Fridays, and Sundays (£40/person, tel. 07786-920-166, info@gocotswolds.co.uk, www.gocotswolds.co.uk).

While none of the Cotswold towns offers regularly scheduled walks, many have voluntary **warden groups** who love to meet visitors and give walks for a small donation (see specific contact information below for Chipping Campden).

Chipping Campden

Just touristy enough to be convenient, the north Cotswold town of Chipping Campden (CAM-den) is a ▲▲ sight. This market town, once the home of the richest Cotswold wool merchants, has some incredibly beautiful thatched roofs. Both the great British historian G. M. Trevelyan and I call Chipping Campden's High Street the finest in England.

Orientation to Chipping Campden

TOURIST INFORMATION

Chipping Campden's TI is tucked away in the old police station on High Street. Get the £1.50 town guide with map, or the local *Footpath Guide* for £2.50 (April-Oct daily 9:30-17:00; Nov-March Mon-Thu 9:30-13:00, Fri-Sun until 16:00; tel. 01386/841-206, www.chippingcampdenonline.org).

HELPFUL HINTS

Festivals: The **Cotswold Olimpicks** are a series of tongue-in-cheek countryside games (such as competitive shin-kicking) held atop Dover's Hill, just above town (generally in late spring; check www.olimpickgames.co.uk to see if the games are on). Chipping Campden also has a **music festival** in May and an **open gardens festival** the third weekend in June.

Bike Rental: Call **Cycle Cotswolds** (see page 350).

Taxi: Try **Cotswold Private Hire** or **Tour the Cotswolds** (see page 354).

Parking: Find a spot anywhere along High Street and park for free with no time limit. There's also a pay-and-display lot on High Street, across from the TI (2-hour maximum). If those are full, there is free parking on the street called Back Ends. On weekends, you can also park for free at the school (see map).

Tours: The local members of the **Cotswold Voluntary Wardens** are happy to show you around town for a small donation to the Cotswold Conservation Fund (suggested donation-£4/person, 1.5-hour walks run June-Sept Tue at 14:00 and Thu at 10:00, meet at Market Hall; tel. 0776/156-5661, Vin Kelly).

Walks and Hikes from Chipping Campden: Since this is a particularly hilly area, long-distance hikes are challenging. The easiest and most rewarding stroll is to the thatch-happy hobbit village of **Broad Campden** (about a mile, mostly level). From there, you can walk or take the bus (#2) back to Chipping Campden.

Or, if you have more energy, continue from Broad Campden up over the ridge and into picturesque **Blockley**—and, if your stamina holds out, all the way to **Bourton-on-the-Hill** (Blockley and Bourton-on-the-Hill are also connected by buses #1 and #2 to Chipping Campden and Moreton).

Alternatively, you can hike up to **Dover's Hill,** just north of the village. Ask locally about this easy, circular one-hour walk that takes you on the first mile of the 100-mile-long Cotswold Way (which goes from here to Bath).

For more about hiking, see "Getting Around the Cotswolds—By Foot," earlier.

Chipping Campden Walk

This self-guided stroll through "Campden" (as locals call their town) takes you from the Market Hall west to the old silk mill, and then back east the length of High Street to the church. It takes about an hour.

Market Hall: Begin at Campden's most famous monument—the Market Hall. It stands in front of the TI, marking the town center. The Market Hall was built in 1627 by the 17th-century Lord of the Manor, Sir Baptist Hicks. (Look for the Hicks family coat of arms on the east end of the building's facade.) Back then, it was an elegant—even over-the-top—shopping hall for the towns-

folk who'd come here to buy their produce. In the 1940s, it was almost sold to an American, but the townspeople heroically raised money to buy it first, then gave it to the National Trust for its preservation.

The timbers inside are true to the original. Study the classic Cotswold stone roof, still held together with wooden pegs nailed in from underneath. (Tiles were cut and sold with peg holes, and stacked like waterproof scales.) Buildings all over the region still use these stone shingles. Today, the hall, which is rarely used, stands as a testimony to the importance of trade to medieval Campden.

Adjacent to the Market Hall is the sober WWI monument—a reminder of the huge price paid by nearly every little town. Walk around it, noticing how 1918 brought the greatest losses.

Between the Market Hall and the WWI monument you'll find a limestone disc embedded in the ground marking the ceremonial start of the Cotswold Way (you'll find its partner in front of the abbey in Bath—100 miles away—marking the southern end).

The TI is just across the street, in the old police courthouse. If it's open, you're welcome to climb the stairs and peek into the **Magistrate's Court** (free, same hours as TI, ask at TI to go up). Under the open-beamed courtroom, you'll find a humble little exhibit on the town's history.

• *Walk west, passing the town hall and the parking lot that was originally the sheep market, until you reach the Red Lion Inn. Across High Street (and a bit to the right), look for the house with a sundial and sign over the door reading...*

"Green Dragons": The house's decorative black cast-iron fixtures (originally in the stables) once held hay and functioned much like salad bowls for horses. Fine-cut stones define the door, but "rubble stones" make up the rest of the wall. The pink stones are the same limestone

Chipping Campden

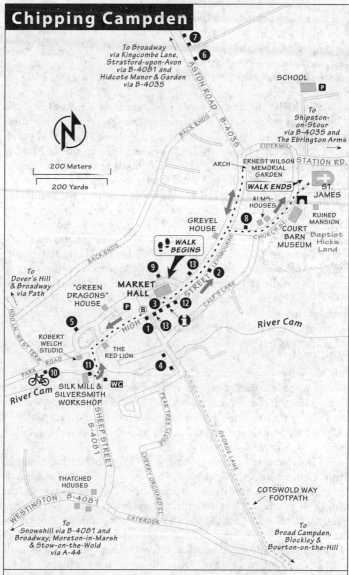

To Broadway
via Kingcombe Lane,
Stratford-upon-Avon
via B-4081 and
Hidcote Manor & Garden
via B-4035

ASTON ROAD
B-4035

SCHOOL
P

To
Shipston-
on-Stour
via B-4035 and
The Ebrington Arms

BACK ENDS

CIDERMIL

STATION RD.

N

200 Meters

200 Yards

ARCH

ERNEST WILSON
MEMORIAL
GARDEN

WALK ENDS

ALMS-
HOUSES

ST.
JAMES

RUINED
MANSION

GREVEL
HOUSE

COURT
BARN
MUSEUM

Baptist
Hicks
Land

CHURCH ST.

BACK ENDS

To
Dover's Hill
& Broadway
via Path

**WALK
BEGINS**

"GREEN
DRAGONS"
HOUSE

**MARKET
HALL**

9

13

2

LEYSBOURNE STREET

CALF'S LANE

River Cam

P

B

3

12

5

1

13

i

HIGH STREET

HOO LN. WEST TERR.

ROBERT
WELCH
STUDIO

THE
RED LION

PARK ROAD

11

10

4

River Cam

WC

SILK MILL &
SILVERSMITH
WORKSHOP

SHEEP STREET
B-4081

PEAR TREE CLOSE

CHERRY ORCHARD CL.

GEORGE LANE

COTSWOLD WAY
FOOTPATH

THATCHED
HOUSES

WESTINGTON   B-4081

CATBROOK

To
Snowshill via B-4081 and
Broadway, Moreton-in-Marsh
& Stow-on-the-Wold
via A-44

To
Broad Campden,
Blockley &
Bourton-on-the-Hill

COTSWOLDS

Accommodations
1 Noel Arms Hotel
2 The Lygon Arms Hotel & Pub
3 Badgers Hall B&B
4 Cornerways & Stonecroft B&Bs
5 The Old Bakehouse & Butty's
6 Cherry Trees B&B
7 The Chance B&B & Bramley House

Eateries & Other
8 Eight Bells Pub
9 Michael's
10 Maharaja Indian Restaurant
   & Cycle Cotswolds
11 Campden Coffee Company
12 Bantam Tea Rooms
13 Grocery (2)

but have been heated, and likely were scavenged from a house that burned down.

• *At the Red Lion, leave High Street and walk a block down Sheep Street. At the little creek just past the public WC, a 30-yard-long lane on the right leads to an old Industrial-Age silk mill (and the Hart silversmith shop).*

Silk Mill: The tiny River Cam powered a mill here since about 1790. Today it houses the handicraft workers guild and some interesting history. In 1902, Charles Robert Ashbee (1863-1942) revitalized this sleepy hamlet of 2,500 by bringing a troupe of London artisans and their families (160 people in all) to town. Ashbee was a leader in the romantic Arts and Crafts movement—craftspeople repulsed by the Industrial Revolution who idealized the handmade crafts and preindustrial ways. Ashbee's idealistic craftsmen's guild lasted only until 1908, when most of his men grew bored with their small-town, back-to-nature ideals. Today, the only shop surviving from the originals is that of **silversmith David Hart.** His grandfather came to town with Ashbee, and the workshop (upstairs in the mill building) is an amazing time warp—little has changed since 1902. Hart is a gracious man as well as a fine silversmith, and he, his son William, and nephew Julian welcome browsers six days a week (Mon-Fri 9:00-17:00, Sat until 12:00, closed Sun, tel. 01386/841-100). They're proud that everything they make is a "one-off."

• *While you could continue 200 yards farther to see some fine thatched houses, this walk instead returns to High Street. On the corner is the studio shop of* **Robert Welch***, a local industrial designer who worked in the spirit of the Arts and Crafts movement. His son and daughter carry on his legacy in the fine shop (with a little museum case in the back). Turn right, and walk through town.*

High Street: Chipping Campden's High Street has changed little architecturally since 1840. (The town's street plan and property lines survive from the 12th century.) As you now walk the length of England's finest historic High Street, study the skyline, see the dates on the buildings, and count the sundials. Notice the harmony of the long rows of buildings. While the street comprises different styles through the centuries, everything you see was made of the same Cotswold stone—the only stone allowed today.

To remain level, High Street arcs with the contour of the hillside. Because it's so wide, you know this was a market town. In past centuries, livestock and packhorses laden with piles of freshly shorn fleece would fill the streets. Campden was a sales and distribution center for the wool industry, and merchants from as far away as Italy would come here for the prized raw wool.

High Street has no house numbers: Locals know the houses by their names. In the distance, you'll see the town church (where this walk ends). Notice that the power lines are buried underground, making the scene delightfully uncluttered.

As you stroll High Street, you'll find the finest houses on the uphill side—which gets more sun. Decorative features (like the Ionic capitals near the TI) are added for nonstructural touches of class. Most High Street buildings are half-timbered, but with cosmetic stone facades. You may see some exposed half-timbered walls. Study the crudely beautiful framing, made of hand-hewn oak (you can see the adze marks) and held together by wooden pegs.

Peeking down alleys, you'll notice how the lots are narrow but very deep. Called "burgage plots," this platting goes back to 1170. In medieval times, rooms were lined up long and skinny like train cars: Each building had a small storefront, followed by a workshop, living quarters, staff quarters, stables, and a garden at the very back. Now the private alleys that still define many of these old lots lead to comfy gardens. While some of today's buildings are wider, virtually all the widths are exact multiples of that basic first unit (for example, a modern building may be three times wider than its medieval counterpart).

• *Hike the length of High Street toward the church, to just before the first intersection. In front of the door of the old schoolhouse on the left side of the street, notice the rude gargoyle carved by the town's former stonemason. There are more gargoyles hanging out above you a few houses down at the...*

Grevel House: In 1367, William Grevel built what's considered Campden's first stone house. Sheep tycoons had big homes. Imagine back then, when this fine building was surrounded by humble wattle-and-daub huts. It had newfangled chimneys, rather than a crude hole in the roof. (No more rain inside!) Originally a "hall house" with just one big, tall room, it got its upper floor in the 16th century. The finely carved central bay window is a good early example of the Perpendicular Gothic style. The gargoyles scared away bad spirits—and served as rain spouts. The boot scrapers outside each door were fixtures in that muddy age—especially in market towns, where the streets were filled with animal dung.

• *Continue up High Street for about 100 yards. Go past Church Street (which we'll walk up later). On the right, at a big tree behind a low stone wall, you'll find a small Gothic arch leading into a garden.*

Ernest Wilson Memorial Garden: Once the church's vegetable patch, this small and secluded garden is a botanist's delight today. Pop inside if it's open. The garden is filled with well-labeled plants that the Victorian botanist Ernest Wilson brought back to England from his extensive travels in Asia. There's a complete history of the garden on the board to the left of the entry.

• *Backtrack to Church Street. Turn left, walk past the recommended*

COTSWOLDS

Eight Bells pub, and hook left with the street. Along your right-hand side stretches...

Baptist Hicks Land: Sprawling adjacent to the town church, the area known as Baptist Hicks Land held Hicks' huge estate and manor house. This influential Lord of the Manor was from "a family of substance," who were merchants of silk and fine clothing as well as money-lenders. Beyond the ornate gate (which you'll see ahead, near the church), only a few outbuildings and the charred corner of his **mansion** survive. The mansion

was burned by royalists in 1645 during the Civil War—notice how Cotswold stone turns red when burned. Hicks housed the poor, making a show of his generosity, adding a long row of almshouses (with his family coat of arms) for neighbors to see as they walked to church. These almshouses (lining Church Street on the left) house pensioners today, as they have since the 17th century. Across the street is a ditch built as a "cart wash"—it was filled with water to soak old cart wheels so they'd swell up and stop rattling.

On the right, filling the old **Court Barn,** is a small, fussy museum about crafts and designs from the Arts and Crafts movement, with works by Ashbee and his craftsmen (£5, Tue-Sun 10:00-17:00, Oct-March until 16:00, closed Mon year-round, tel. 01386/841-951, www.courtbarn.org.uk).

• *Next to the Hicks gate, a scenic, tree-lined lane leads to the front door of the church. On the way, notice the 11 lime trees: Planted in about 1760, there used to be one for each of the apostles, until a tree died recently (sorry, no limes).*

St. James Church: One of the finest churches in the Cotswolds, St. James Church graces one of its leading towns. Both the town and the church were built by wool wealth. Go inside. The church is Perpendicular Gothic, with lots of light and strong verticality. Notice the fine vestments and altar hangings (intricate c. 1460 embroidery) behind protective blue curtains (near the back of the church). Tombstones pave the floor in the chancel (often under protective red carpeting)—memorializing great wool merchants through the ages.

At the altar is a brass relief of William Grevel, the first owner of the Grevel House (described earlier), and his wife. But it is Sir Baptist Hicks who dominates the church. His huge canopied tomb is the ornate final resting place for Hicks and his wife, Elizabeth. Study their faces, framed by fancy lace ruffs (trendy in the 1620s). Adjacent—as if in a closet—is a statue of their daughter,

COTSWOLDS

Lady Juliana, and her husband, Lutheran Yokels.
Juliana commissioned the
statue in 1642, when her
husband died, but had it
closed up until *she* died
in 1680. Then, the doors
were opened, revealing
these two people hold-
ing hands and living hap-
pily ever after—at least in

marble. The hinges were likely used only once.

Just outside as you leave the church, look immediately around
the corner to the right of the door. A small tombstone reads "Thank
you Lord for Simon, a dearly loved cat who greeted everyone who
entered this church. RIP 1980."

Sleeping in Chipping Campden

In Chipping Campden—as in any town in the Cotswolds—B&Bs
offer a better value than hotels. Try to book well in advance, as
rooms are snapped up early in the spring and summer by happy
hikers heading for the nearby Cotswold Way. Rooms are also generally tight on Saturdays (when many charge a bit more and are
reluctant to rent to one-nighters) and in September, another peak
month. Parking is never a problem. Always ask for a discount if
staying longer than one or two nights.

ON OR NEAR HIGH STREET

Located on the main street (or just off of it), these places couldn't
be more central.

$$$ **Noel Arms Hotel,** the characteristic old hotel on the
main square, has welcomed guests for 600 years. Its lobby was re-
modeled in a medieval-meets-modern style, and its 27 rooms are
well-furnished with antiques (some ground-floor doubles, attached
restaurant/bar and café, free parking, High Street, tel. 01386/840-
317, www.noelarmshotel.com, reception@noelarmshotel.com).

$$$ **The Lygon Arms Hotel** (pronounced "lig-un"), at-
tached to the popular pub of the same name, has small public
areas and 10 cheery, open-beamed rooms (free parking, High
Street, go through archway and look for hotel reception on
the left, tel. 01386/840-318, www.lygonarms.co.uk, sandra@
lygonarms.co.uk, Sandra Davenport).

$$ **Badgers Hall,** above a tearoom, rents four somewhat
overpriced rooms with antique furnishings beneath wooden
beams (2-night minimum, no kids under age 18, High Street, tel.

01386/840-839, www.badgershall.com, badgershall@talk21.com, Karen). Their delightful half-timbered tearoom (open to guests only except on Fri and Sat) offers a selection of savory dishes, homemade cakes, crumbles, and scones.

$$ Cornerways B&B is a fresh, bright, and comfy home (not "oldie worldie") a block off High Street. It's run by the delightful Carole Proctor, who can "look out the window and see the church where we were married." The two huge, light, airy loft rooms are great for families. If you're happy to exchange breakfast for more space, ask about the cottage across the street (2-night minimum, cash only, off-street parking, George Lane, just walk through the arch beside Noel Arms Hotel, tel. 01386/841-307, www.cornerways.info, carole@cornerways.info). For a fee, Les can pick you up from the train station, or take you on village tours.

$$ Stonecroft B&B, next to Cornerways, has three polished, well-maintained rooms (one with low, slanted ceilings—unfriendly to tall people). The lovely garden with a patio and small stream is a tranquil place for meals or an early-evening drink (family rooms but no kids under 12, George Lane, tel. 01386/840-486, www.stonecroft-chippingcampden.co.uk, info@stonecroft-chippingcampden.co.uk, Roger and Lesley Yates).

$$ The Old Bakehouse, run by energetic young mom Zoe, rents two small but pleasant rooms in a 600-year-old home with exposed beams and cottage charm (cash only, Lower High Street, near intersection with Sheep Street, tel. 01386/840-979, mobile 07717-330-838, www.theoldbakehouse.org.uk, zoegabb@yahoo.co.uk).

A SHORT WALK FROM TOWN ON ASTON ROAD

The B&Bs below are a 10-minute walk from Market Hall. They are listed in the order you would find them when strolling from town (if arriving by bus, ask to be dropped off at Aston Road).

$$ Cherry Trees B&B, set well off the road, is bubbly Angie's spacious, modern home, with three king rooms and one superior king room with balcony (free parking, Aston Road, tel. 01386/840-873, www.cherrytreescampden.com, sclrksn7@tiscali.co.uk).

$$ The Chance B&B—a modern home with Cotswold charm—has two tastefully decorated rooms with king beds (which can also be twins if requested) and a breakfast room that opens onto a patio. They also offer two self-catering cottages in town, next to the silk mill (cash only, free parking, 1 Aston Road, tel. 01386/849-079, www.the-chance.co.uk, enquiries@the-chance.co.uk, Sally and Paul).

$$ Bramley House, which backs up to a farm, has a spacious garden suite with a private outdoor patio and lounge area (bath-

COTSWOLDS

room downstairs from bedroom) and a superior king double. Crisp white linens and simple country decor give the place a light and airy feel (2-night minimum, homemade cake with tea or coffee on arrival, locally sourced/organic breakfast, 6 Aston Road, tel. 01386/840-066, www.bramleyhouse.co.uk, dppovey@btinternet.com, Jane and David Povey).

Eating in Chipping Campden

This town—filled with wealthy residents and tourists—comes with many choices. I've listed some local favorites below. If you have a car, consider driving to one of the excellent countryside pubs mentioned in the sidebar on page 382.

$$$ Eight Bells pub is a charming 14th-century inn on Leysbourne with a classy and woody restaurant and a more rustic pub. Neil and Julie keep their seasonal menu as locally sourced as possible. They serve a daily special and always have a good vegetarian dish. As this is the best deal going in town for top-end pub dining, reservations are smart (daily 12:00-14:00 & 18:30-21:00, tel. 01386/840-371, www.eightbellsinn.co.uk).

$$ The Lygon Arms pub is cozy and inviting, with a good, basic bar menu. You can order from the same menu in the colorful pub or the more elegant dining room across the passage (daily 11:30-14:30 & 18:00-22:00, tel. 01386/840-318).

$$$ Michael's, a fun Mediterranean restaurant on High Street, serves hearty portions and breaks plates at closing every Saturday night. Michael, who runs his place with a contagious love of life, is from Cyprus: The forte here is Greek, with plenty of *mezes*—small dishes (Tue-Sun 11:00-14:30 & 19:00-22:00, closed Mon, tel. 01386/840-826).

$$ Maharaja Indian Restaurant in the Volunteer Inn serves decent Indian standards (£10-15 meals, daily 18:00-22:30, grassy courtyard out back, Lower High Street, tel. 01386/849-281).

LIGHT MEALS

If you want a quick takeaway sandwich, consider these options. Munch your lunch on the benches on the little green near the Market Hall.

$ Butty's offers tasty sandwiches and wraps made to order (Mon-Sat 7:30-14:00, closed Sun, Lower High Street, tel. 01386/840-401).

$ Campden Coffee Company is a cozy little café with local goodies including salads, sandwiches, and homemade sweets (Sat-Mon 10:00-16:15, Tue-Fri from 9:00, on the ground floor of the Silk Mill, tel. 01386/849-251).

Picnic: The **Co-op** grocery is the town's small "supermarket" (Mon-Sat 7:00-22:00, Sun from 8:00, next to TI on High Street).

COTSWOLDS

Tokes, on the opposite end of High Street, has a tempting selection of cheeses, meats, and wine for a make-your-own ploughman's lunch (Mon-Fri 9:00-18:00, Sat 10:00-17:00, Sun 10:00-16:00, just past the Market Hall, tel. 01386/849-345.)

Afternoon Tea: To visit a cute tearoom, try the good-value **$ Bantam Tea Rooms,** near the Market Hall (daily 10:00-16:00, High Street, tel. 01386/840-386). On Fridays and Saturdays, the recommended **$$ Badgers Hall** opens their lunch and afternoon tea service to visitors not staying at their B&B.

Near Chipping Campden

Because the countryside around Chipping Campden is particularly hilly, it's also especially scenic. This is a very rewarding area to poke around and discover little thatched villages.

WEST OF CHIPPING CAMPDEN

Due west of Chipping Campden lies the famous and touristy town of Broadway. Just south of that, you'll find my nominations for the cutest Cotswold villages. Like marshmallows in hot chocolate, Stanway, Stanton, and Snowshill nestle side by side, awaiting your arrival. (Note the Stanway House's limited hours when planning your visit.)

Broadway

This postcard-pretty town, a couple of miles west of Chipping Campden, is filled with inviting shops and fancy teahouses. With a "broad way" indeed running through its middle, it's one of the bigger towns in the area. This means you'll likely pass through at some point if you're driving—but, since all the big bus tours seem to stop here, I usually give Broadway a miss. However, with a new road that allows traffic to skirt the town, Broadway has gotten cuter than ever. Broadway has good bus connections with Chipping Campden.

Just outside Broadway, on the road to Chipping Campden, you might spot signs for the **Broadway Tower,** which looks like a turreted castle fortification stranded in the countryside without a castle in sight. This 55-foot-tall observation tower is a "folly"—a uniquely English term for a quirky, outlandish novelty erected as a giant lawn ornament by some aristocrat with more money than taste. If you're also weighted down with too many pounds, you can relieve yourself of £5 to climb to its top for a view over the pastures. But the view from the tower's park-like perch is free, and almost as impressive (daily 10:00-17:00).

Stanway

More of a humble crossroads community than a true village, sleepy Stanway is worth a visit mostly for its manor house, which offers an intriguing insight into the English aristocracy today. If you're in the area when it's open, it's well worth visiting.

▲▲Stanway House

The Earl of Wemyss (pronounced "Weemz"), whose family tree charts relatives back to 1202, opens his melancholy home and

grounds to visitors just two days a week in the summer. Walking through his house offers a unique glimpse into the lifestyles of England's eccentric and fading nobility.

Cost and Hours: £9 ticket covers house and fountain, £3 to visit the watermill; ticket includes a wonderful and intimate audioguide, narrated by the lordship himself; June-Aug Tue and Thu only 14:00-17:00, closed Sept-May, tel. 01386/584-469, www.stanwayfountain.co.uk.

Getting There: By car, leave the B-4077 at a statue of (the Christian) George slaying the dragon (of pagan superstition); you'll round the corner and see the manor's fine 17th-century Jacobean gatehouse. Park in the lot across the street. There's no public transportation to Stanway.

Visiting the Manor: The bitchin' **Tithe Barn** (near where you enter the grounds) dates to the 14th century, and predates the manor. It was originally where monks—in the days before money—would accept one-tenth of whatever the peasants produced. Peek inside: This is a great hall for village hoedowns. While the Tithe Barn is no longer used to greet motley peasants and collect their feudal "rents," the lord still gets rent from his vast landholdings, and hosts community fêtes in his barn.

Stepping into the obviously very lived-in **manor,** you're free to wander around pretty much as you like, but keep in mind that a family does live here. His lordship is often roaming about as well. The place feels like a time warp. Ask a staff member to demonstrate the spinning rent-collection table. In the great hall, marvel at the one-piece oak shuffleboard table and the 1780 Chippendale exercise chair (half an hour of bouncing on this was considered good for the liver).

The manor dogs have their own cutely painted "family tree," but the Earl admits that his last dog, C. J., was "all character and no breeding." Poke into the office. You can psychoanalyze the lord by the books that fill his library, the DVDs stacked in front of his bed (with the mink bedspread), and whatever's next to his toilet.

The place has a story to tell. And so do the docents stationed in each room—modern-day peasants who, even without family trees, probably have relatives going back just as far in this village. Talk to these people. Probe. Learn what you can about this side of England.

Wandering through the expansive back yard you'll see the earl's pet project: restoring "the tallest **fountain** in Britain"—300 feet tall, gravity-powered, and running for 30 minutes twice a day (at 14:45 and 16:00).

Signs lead to a working **watermill**, which produces flour from wheat grown on the estate (about 100 yards from the house, requires separate ticket to enter).

Hailes Church and Abbey

A three-mile drive or pleasant two-and-a-half-mile walk from Stanway House along the Cotswold Way leads you to a fine Norman church and abbey ruins. Richard, Earl of Cornwall (and younger brother of King Henry III) founded the abbey after surviving a shipwreck, but it was his son Edmund who turned it into a pilgrimage site after buying a vial of holy blood and bringing the relic to Hailes around 1270. Thanks to Henry VIII's dissolution of monasteries in the 16th century, not much remains of the abbey today (£6.20, daily 10:00-17:00, closed Nov-March). However, the church—which predates the abbey by about a century—houses some of its original tiles and medieval stained glass. It's worth a look inside the humble church for its 800-year-old baptismal font and faded but evocative murals (including St. Christopher, patron saint of travelers, and a hunting scene attributed to a local knight). Check out the wooden screen added long after the original construction—look closely and you'll see how the arch had to be cut away in order for the screen to fit.

From Stanway to Stanton

These towns are separated by a row of oak trees and grazing land, with parallel waves echoing the furrows plowed by medieval farmers. Centuries ago, farmers were allotted long strips of land called "furlongs." The idea was to dole out good and bad land equitably. (One square furlong equals 10 acres.) Over centuries of plowing these, furrows were formed. Let someone else drive, so you can hang out the window under a canopy of oaks, passing stone walls and sheep. Leaving Stanway on the road to Stanton, the first building you'll see (on the left, just outside Stanway) is a thatched cricket pavilion overlooking the village cricket green. Originally built for *Peter Pan* author J. M. Barrie, it dates from 1930 and is raised up (as medieval buildings were) on rodent-resistant staddle stones. Stanton is just ahead; follow the signs.

▲Stanton

Pristine Cotswold charm cheers you as you head up the main street of the village of Stanton, served by a scant few buses. Go on a photo

safari for flower-bedecked doorways and windows.

Stanton's **Church of St. Michael** (with the pointy spire) betrays a pagan past. It's safe to assume any church dedicated to St. Michael (the archangel who fought the devil) sits upon a sacred pagan site. Stanton is actually at the intersection of two ley lines (a line connecting prehistoric or ancient sights). You'll see St. Michael's well-worn figure (and, above that, a sundial) over the door as you enter. Inside, above the capitals in the nave, find the pagan symbols for the sun and the moon (see photo). While the church probably dates back to the ninth century, today's building is mostly from the 15th century, with 13th-century transepts. On the north transept (far side from entry), medieval frescoes show faintly through the 17th-century whitewash. (Once upon a time, these frescoes were considered too "papist.") Imagine the

church interior colorfully decorated throughout. Original medieval glass is behind the altar. The list of rectors (at the very back of the church, under the organ loft) goes back to 1269. Finger the grooves in the back pews, worn away by sheepdog leashes. (A man's sheepdog accompanied him everywhere.)

Horse Riding: Jill Carenza's **Cotswolds Riding Centre,** set just outside Stanton village, is in the most scenic corner of the region. The facility's horses can take anyone from rank beginners to more experienced riders on a scenic "hack" through the village and into the high country (per-hour prices: £32/person on a group hack, £42/person semiprivate hack, £52 private one-person hack; lessons, longer/expert rides, and pub tours available; tel. 01386/584-250, www.cotswoldsriding.co.uk,

info@cotswoldsriding.co.uk). From Stanton, head toward Broadway and watch for the riding center on your right after about a third of a mile.

Sleeping in Stanton: $$ The Vine B&B has five rooms in a characteristic old Cotswold house near the center of town, next to the cricket pitch (ask if any matches are on if you're there on a Saturday in summer). It's owned by no-nonsense Jill, whose daughter, Sarah Jane, welcomes you to their large, lovingly worn family home. While it suffers from absentee management, the Vine is convenient if you want to ride all day (most rooms with four-poster beds, some stairs; for contact info, see listing for riding center, above).

Eating in Stanton: High on a hill at the far end of Stanton's main drag, nearest to Broadway, the aptly named **$$$ Mount Inn** serves up pricey, upscale meals on its big, inviting terrace with grand views of Stanton rooftops and the Cotswold hills (food served daily 12:00-14:00 & 18:00-21:00, may be closed Mon off-season, Old Snowshill Road, tel. 01386/584-316).

Snowshill

Another nearly edible little bundle of cuteness, the village of Snowshill (SNOWS-hill) has a photogenic triangular square with a characteristic pub at its base.

▲Snowshill Manor

Dark and mysterious, this old palace is filled with the lifetime collection of Charles Paget Wade. It's one big, musty celebration of craftsmanship, from finely carved spinning wheels to frightening samurai armor to tiny elaborate figurines carved by prisoners from the bones of meat served at dinner. Taking seriously his family motto, "Let Nothing Perish," Wade dedicated his life and fortune to preserving things finely crafted. The house (whose management made me promise not to promote it as an eccentric collector's pile of curiosities) really shows off Wade's ability to recognize and acquire fine examples of craftsmanship. It's all very...mmm...yaaa.

Cost and Hours: £12; manor house open July-Aug Wed-Mon 11:30-16:30, closed Tue; April-June and Sept-Oct Wed-Sun 12:00-17:00, closed Mon-Tue; closed Nov-March; gardens and ticket window open at 11:00, last entry one hour before closing, restaurant, tel. 01386/852-410, www.nationaltrust.org.uk/snowshillmanor.

Getting There: The manor overlooks the town square, but there's no direct access from the square; instead, the entrance and parking lot are about a half-mile up the road toward Broadway. Park there and follow the long walkway through the garden to get to the house. A golf-cart-type shuttle to the house is available for those who need assistance.

Getting In: This popular sight strictly limits the number of entering visitors by doling out entry times. No reservations are possible; to get a slot, you must report to the ticket desk. It can be up to an hour's wait—even more on busy days, especially weekends (when they can sell out for the day as early as 14:00). Tickets go on sale and the gardens open at 11:00. A good strategy is to arrive close to the opening time, and if there's a wait, enjoy the gardens (it's a 10-minute walk to the manor). If you have more time to kill, head into the village of Snowshill itself (a half-mile away) to wander and explore—or get a time slot for later in the day, and return in the afternoon.

Cotswold Lavender

In 2000, farmer Charlie Byrd realized that tourists love lavender. He planted his farm with 250,000 plants, and now visitors come to wander among his 53 acres, which burst with gorgeous lavender blossoms from mid-June through late August. His fragrant fantasy peaks late each July. Lavender—so famous in France's Provence—is not indigenous to this region, but it fits the climate and soil just fine. A free flier in  the shop explains the variations of blooming flowers. Farmer Byrd produces lavender oil (an herbal product valued since ancient times for its healing, calming, and fragrant qualities) and sells it in a delightful shop, along with many other lavender-themed items. In the café, enjoy a pot of lavender-flavored tea with a lavender scone.

Cost and Hours: Free to enter shop and café, £3.50 to walk through the fields and the distillery; generally open June-Aug daily 10:00-17:00, closed Sept-May, schedule changes annually depending on when the lavender blooms—call ahead or check their website; tel. 01386/854-821, www.cotswoldlavender.co.uk.

Getting There: It's a half-mile out of Snowshill on the road toward Chipping Campden (easy parking). Entering Snowshill from the road to the manor (described earlier), take the left fork, then turn left again at the end of the village.

EAST OF CHIPPING CAMPDEN

Hidcote Manor Garden is just northeast of Chipping Campden, while Broad Campden, Blockley, and Bourton-on-the-Hill lie roughly between Chipping Campden and Stow (or Moreton)—handy if you're connecting those towns.

▲Hidcote Manor Garden

This is less "on the way" between towns than the other sights in this section—but the grounds around this manor house are well worth a detour if you like gardens. Hid-

cote is where garden designers pioneered the notion of creating a series of outdoor "rooms," each with a unique theme (such as maple room, red room, and so on) and separated by a yew-tree hedge. The garden's design, inspired by the Arts and Crafts movement, is most formal near the house and becomes more pastoral as it approaches the country-side. Follow your nose through a clever series of small gardens that lead delightfully from one to the next. Among the best in England, Hidcote Gardens are at their fragrant peak from May through August. But don't expect much indoors—the manor house has only a few rooms open to the public.

Cost and Hours: £13; March-Sept daily 10:00-18:00, Oct until 17:00; Nov-Dec Sat-Sun 11:00-16:00, closed Mon-Fri; closed Jan-Feb; last entry one hour before closing, café, restaurant, tel. 01386/438-333, www.nationaltrust.org.uk/hidcote.

Getting There: If you're driving, it's four miles northeast of Chipping Campden—roughly toward Ilmington. The gardens are accessible by bus, then a 45-minute country walk uphill. Buses #1 and #2 take you to Mickleton (one stop past Chipping Campden), where a footpath begins next to the churchyard. Continuing more or less straight, the path leads through sheep pastures and ends at Hidcote's driveway.

Nearby: Gardening enthusiasts will also want to stop at **Kifts-gate Court Garden,** just across the road from Hidcote. While not as impressive, these private gardens are a fun contrast since they were designed at the same time and influenced by Hidcote (£8.50; May-July Sat-Wed 12:00-18:00, Aug from 14:00, closed Thu-Fri; April and Sept Sun-Mon and Wed only 14:00-18:00; closed Oct-March; tel. 01386/438-777, www.kiftsgate.co.uk).

▲Broad Campden, Blockley, and Bourton-on-the-Hill

This trio of pleasant villages lines up along an off-the-beaten-path road between Chipping Campden and Moreton or Stow. **Broad**

Campden, just on the outskirts of Chipping Campden, has some of the cutest thatched-roof houses I've seen. **Blockley,** nestled higher in the pictur-esque hills, is a popular setting for films. The same road contin-ues on to **Bourton-on-the-Hill** (pictured), with fine views look-ing down into a valley and an excellent gastropub (Horse and Groom, described on page 382). All three of these towns are connected to Chipping Campden by bus #1 and #2, or you can walk (easy to Broad Campden, more challenging to the other two—see page 351).

Stow-on-the-Wold

Located 10 miles south of Chipping Campden, Stow-on-the-Wold—with a name that means "meeting place on the uplands"—is the highest point of the Cots-wolds. Despite its crowds, it retains its charm, and it merits ▲▲. Most of the tourists are day-trippers, so nights—even in the peak of summer—are peaceful.

COTSWOLDS

Stow has no real sights other than the town itself, some good pubs, antiques stores, and cute shops draped seductively around a big town square. Visit the church, with its evocative old door guarded by an-cient yew trees and the tombs of wool tycoons. A visit to Stow is not complete until you've locked your partner in the stocks on the village green.

Orientation to Stow-on-the-Wold

TOURIST INFORMATION

A small visitor information center staffed by volunteers is run out of the library in St. Edwards Hall on the main square (hours erratic, generally Mon-Sat 10:00-14:00, sometimes as late as 17:00, closed Sun, tel. 08452-305-420). Aside from the meager rack of brochures, don't expect much information—get your serious questions answered in Moreton-in-Marsh instead (see page 392).

HELPFUL HINTS

Taxi: See "Getting Around the Cotswolds—By Taxi," earlier.

Parking: Park anywhere on Market Square free for two hours, and overnight between 18:00 and 9:00 (combining overnight plus daily 2-hour allowances means you can park free 16:00-11:00—they note your license, so you can't just move to another spot after your time is up; £50 tickets for offenders). You can also park for free on some streets farther from the center (such as Park Street and Well Lane) for an unlimited amount of time. A convenient pay-and-display lot is at the bottom of town (toward the Oddingtons), and there's a free lot at Tesco Supermarket—an easy five-minute walk north of town (follow the signs).

Stow-on-the-Wold Walk

This four-stop self-guided walk covers about 500 yards and takes about 45 minutes.

Start at the **Stocks on the Market Square.** Imagine this village during the era when people were publicly ridiculed here as a punishment. Stow was born in pre-Roman times; it's where three trade routes crossed at a high point in the region (altitude: 800 feet). This square was the site of an Iron Age fort, and then a Roman garrison town. Starting in 1107, Stow was the site of an international fair, and people came from as far away as Italy to shop for wool fleeces

on this vast, grassy expanse. Picture it in the Middle Ages (minus all the parked cars, and before the buildings in the center were

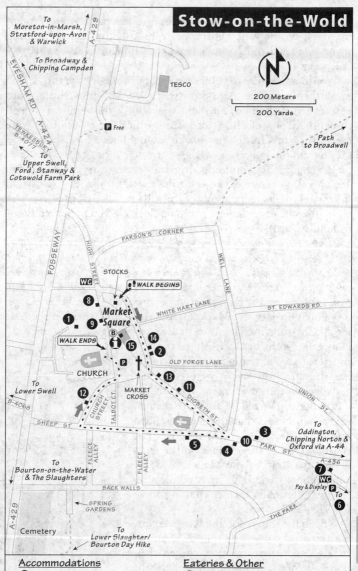

Stow-on-the-Wold

To Moreton-in-Marsh, Stratford-upon-Avon & Warwick

To Broadway & Chipping Campden

EVESHAM RD. A-424

TEWKESBURY B-4077

To Upper Swell, Ford, Stanway & Cotswold Farm Park

A-429

TESCO

P Free

200 Meters
200 Yards

Path to Broadwell

FOSSEWAY

HIGH STREET

PARSON'S CORNER

STOCKS

WC

WALK BEGINS

Market Square

WHITE HART LANE

WELL LANE

ST. EDWARDS RD.

WALK ENDS

B

CHURCH

To Lower Swell

B-4068

OLD FORGE LANE

UNION ST.

MARKET CROSS

CHURCH STREET

TALBOT CT.

DIGBETH ST.

SHEEP ST.

To Oddington, Chipping Norton & Oxford via A-44

PARK ST.

A-436

FLEECE ALLEY

FLEECE ALLEY

To Bourton-on-the-Water & The Slaughters

BACK WALLS

WC

Pay & Display P

To

A-429

SPRING GARDENS

THE PARK

Cemetery

To Lower Slaughter/ Bourton Day Hike

COTSWOLDS

Accommodations
1. Stow Lodge Hotel & Restaurant
2. The Kings Arms
3. Number Nine
4. Cross Keys Cottage
5. The Pound
6. To Little Broom B&B

Eateries & Other
7. The Bell at Stow
8. The Queen's Head
9. Huffkins Bakery & Tea Rooms
10. Park Street Eateries
11. The Old Bakery Tearoom
12. Speedwells Café
13. Cotswold Chocolate Company
14. Grocery
15. St. Edwards Hall & Library

added): a public commons and grazing ground, paths worn through the grass, and no well. Until the late 1800s, Stow had no running water; women fetched water from the "Roman Well" a quarter-mile away.

With as many as 20,000 sheep sold in a single day, this square was a thriving scene. And Stow was filled with inns and pubs to keep everyone housed, fed, and watered. A thin skin of topsoil covers the Cotswold limestone, from which these buildings were made. The **Stow Lodge** (next to the church) lies a little lower than the church; the lodge sits on the spot where locals quarried stones for the church. That building, originally the rectory, is now a hotel. The church (where we'll end this little walk) is made of Cotswold stone, and marks the summit of the hill upon which the town was built. The stocks are a great photo op (lock Dad up for a great family holiday card).

• *Walk past The White Hart Inn to the market, and cross to the other part of the square. Notice how locals stop to chat with each other to catch up on local news: This is a tight-knit little community. Enjoy the stone work and the crazy rooflines. Observe the cheap signage and think how shops have been coming and going for centuries in buildings that never change.*

For 500 years, the **Market Cross** stood in the market reminding all Christian merchants to "trade fairly under the sight of God."

Notice the stubs of the iron fence in the concrete base—a reminder of how countless wrought-iron fences were cut down and given to the government to be melted down during World War II. (Recently, it's been disclosed that all that iron ended up in junk heaps—frantic patriotism just wasted.) One of the plaques on the cross honors the Lord of the Manor, who donated money back to his tenants, allowing the town to finally finance running water in 1878.

Scan the square for **The Kings Arms,** with its great gables and spindly chimney. It was once where travelers parked their horses before spending the night. In the 1600s, this was considered the premium "posting house" between London and Birmingham. Today, The Kings Arms cooks up pub grub and rents rooms upstairs.

During the English Civil War, which pitted Parliamentarians against royalists, Stow-on-the-Wold remained staunchly loyal to the king. (Charles I is said to have eaten at The Kings Arms before a great battle.) Because of its allegiance, the town has an abundance of pubs with royal names (King's This and Queen's That).

The stately building in the center of the square with the wooden steeple is **St. Edwards Hall.** Back in the 1870s, a bank couldn't locate the owner of an account containing a small fortune, so it donated the funds to the town to build this civic center. It serves as a city hall, library, TI, and meeting place. When it's open, you can wander around upstairs to see the largest collection of Civil War portrait paintings in England.

• *Walk past The Kings Arms down Digbeth Street. At the bottom of Digbeth you'll pass the traditional Lambournes butcher and a fragrant cheesemonger across the street. Digbeth ends at a little triangular park in front of the former Methodist Church and across from the Porch House Hotel (dating from 947; it claims—along with about 20 others—to be the oldest in England).*

Just beyond the small grassy triangle with benches was the place where locals gathered for bloody cockfights and bearbaiting (watching packs of hungry dogs tear at bears). Today this is where—twice a year, in May and October—the Stow Horse Fair attracts nomadic Roma (sometimes called Gypsies) and Irish Travellers from far and wide. They congregate down the street on the Maugersbury Road. Locals paint a colorful picture of the Roma, Travellers, and horses inundating the town. The young women dress up because the fair also functions as a marriage market.

• *Hook right and hike up the wide street.*

As you head up **Sheep Street,** you'll pass a boutique-filled former brewery yard (on the left). Notice its fancy street-front office, with a striking flint facade. Sheep Street was originally not a street, but a staging place for medieval sheep markets. The sheep would be gathered here, then paraded into the Market Square down narrow alleys—just wide enough for a single file of sheep to walk down, making it easier to count them. You'll see several of these so-called "fleece alleys" as you walk up the street.

• *Walk a couple blocks until about 50 yards before the streetlight and the highway, then make a right onto Church Street, which leads to the church.*

Before entering the **church,** circle it. On the back side, a wooden door is flanked by two ancient yew trees. While many see the door and think of the Christian scripture, "Behold, I stand at the door and knock," J. R. R. Tolkien fans see something quite different. Tolkien hiked the Cotswolds, and had a passion for sketching evocative trees such as this. *Lord of the Rings* enthusiasts are convinced this must be the inspiration for the Doors of Durin, leading into Moria.

While the church (usually open 9:00-18:00, except during services) dates from Saxon times, today's structure is from the 15th century. Its history is played up in leaflets and plaques just inside the door. The floor is paved with the tombs of big shots who made their money from wool and are still boastful in death. (Find the tombs crowned with the bales of wool.) Most of the windows are traditional Victorian (19th century) designs, but the two sets high up in the clerestory are from the dreamier Pre-Raphaelite school.

On the right wall as you approach the altar, a monument remembers the many boys from this small town who were lost in World War I (50 out of a population of 2,000). There were far fewer in World War II. The biscuit-shaped plaque remembers an admiral from Stow who lost four sons defending the realm. It's sliced from an ancient fluted column (which locals believe is from Ephesus, Turkey).

During the English Civil War in the mid-1600s, the church was ransacked, and more than 1,000 soldiers were imprisoned here. The tombstone in front of the altar remembers the royalist Captain Francis Keyt. His long hair, lace, and sash indicate he was a "cavalier," and true-blue to the king (Cromwellians were called "round heads"—named for their short hair). Study the crude provincial art—childlike skulls and (in the upper corners) symbols of his service to the king (armor, weapons).

Finally, don't miss the kneelers tucked in the pews. These are made by a committed band of women known as "the Kneeler Group." They meet most Tuesday mornings (except sometimes in summer) at 10:30 in the Church Room to needlepoint, sip coffee, and enjoy a good chat. (The vicar assured me that any tourist wanting to join them would be more than welcome. The help would be appreciated and the company would be excellent.) If you'd rather sing, the choir practices on the first and third Fridays of the month at 18:00, and visitors are encouraged to join in. And with Reverend Martin Short for the pastor, the services could be pretty lively.

Hiking from Stow

Stow/Lower Slaughter/Bourton Day Hike

Stow is made to order for day hikes. The most popular is the downhill stroll to Lower Slaughter (3 miles), then on to Bourton-on-the-Water (about 1.5 miles more). It's a two-hour walk if you keep up a brisk pace and don't stop, but dawdlers should allow three to four hours. At the end, from Bourton-on-the-Water, a bus can bring you back to Stow. While those with keen eyes can follow this walk by spotting trail signs, it can't hurt to bring a map (ask to borrow one at your B&B). Note that these three towns are described in more detail starting on page 385.

To reach the trail, find the cemetery (from the main square, head down Church Street, turn left on Sheep Street, right into Fleece Alley, right onto Back Walls, and left onto Spring Gardens, which has no street sign). Walk past the community's big pea patch, then duck right through the cemetery to the far end. Here, go through the gate and walk down the footpath that

runs alongside the big A-429 road for about 200 yards, then cross the road and catch the well-marked trail (gravel road with green sign noting *Public Footpath/Gloucestershire Way*, next to Quarwood Cottage). Follow this trail for a delightful hour across farms, through romantic gates, across a fancy driveway, and past Gainsborough-painting vistas. You'll enjoy an intimate backyard look at local farm life. Although it seems like you could lose the trail, tiny easy-to-miss signs (yellow *Public Footpath* arrows—sometimes also marked *Gloucestershire Way* or *The Monarch's Way*—usually embedded in fence posts) keep you on target—watch for these very carefully to avoid getting lost. Finally, passing a cricket pitch, you reach **Lower Slaughter,** with its fine church and a mill creek leading up to its mill.

Hiking from Lower Slaughter up to **Upper Slaughter** is a worthwhile one-mile detour each way, if you have the time and energy.

From Lower Slaughter, it's a less-scenic 25-minute walk into the bigger town of **Bourton-on-the-Water.** Leave Lower Slaughter along its mill creek, then follow a bridle path back to A-429 and into Bourton. Walking through Bourton's burbs, you'll pass two different bus stops for the ride back to Stow; better yet, to enjoy some time in Bourton itself, continue all the way into town and—when ready—catch the bus from in front of the Edinburgh Woolen Mill (bus #801 departs roughly hourly, none on Sun except May-Aug when it runs about 2/day, 10-minute ride).

Sleeping in Stow

$$$ Stow Lodge Hotel fills the historic church rectory with lots of old English charm. Facing the town square, with its own sprawling and peaceful garden, this lavish old place offers 21 large, thoughtfully appointed rooms with soft beds, stately public spaces, and a cushy-chair lounge (closed Jan, free parking, The Square,

tel. 01451/830-485, www.stowlodge.co.uk, enquiries@stowlodge.
co.uk, helpful Hartley family).

$$ The Kings Arms, with 10 rooms above a pub, manages
to keep its historic Cotswold character while still feeling fresh
and modern in all the right ways (steep stairs, three "cottages"
out back, free parking, Market Square, tel. 01451/830-364, www.
kingsarmsstow.co.uk, info@kingsarmsstow.co.uk, Lucinda and
Felicity).

$$ Number Nine has three large, bright, refurbished, and
tastefully decorated rooms. This 200-year-old home comes with
watch-your-head beamed ceilings and beautiful old wooden doors
(9 Park Street, tel. 01451/870-333, mobile 07779-006-539, www.
number-nine.info, enquiries@number-nine.info, friendly James
and Carol Brown and their dog Snoop).

$$ Cross Keys Cottage offers four smallish but smartly up-
dated rooms—some bright and floral, others classy white—with
modern bathrooms. Kindly Margaret and Roger Welton take care
of their guests in this 17th-century beamed cottage (RS%, call
ahead to confirm arrival time, Park Street, tel. 01451/831-128,
www.crosskeyscottage.co.uk, rogxmag@hotmail.com).

$ The Pound is the quaint,
centuries-old, slanty, cozy,
and low-beamed home of Pa-
tricia Whitehead. She offers
two bright, inviting rooms and
a classic old fireplace lounge
(cash only, downtown on Sheep
Street next to the inn with the
Sheep sign, tel. 01451/830-229,
patwhitehead1@live.co.uk).

NEAR STOW

$ Little Broom B&B hides out in the neighboring hamlet of
Maugersbury, which enjoys the peace Stow once had. It rents
three cozy rooms that share a lush garden and pool (cash only, tel.
01451/830-510, www.cotswolds.info/webpage/little-broom.htm,
brendarussell1@hotmail.co.uk). Brenda has racehorses, and her
greenhouse keeps the pool warm throughout the summer (guests
welcome). It's an easy eight-minute walk from Stow: Head east on
Park Street and stay right toward Maugersbury. Turn right into
Chapel Street and take the first right uphill to the B&B.

COTSWOLDS

Eating in and near Stow

While Stow has several good dining options, consider venturing out of town for a meal. You can walk to the pub in nearby Broadwell, or—better yet—drive to one of several enticing gastropubs in the surrounding villages (see sidebar on page 382).

IN STOW

These places are all within a five-minute walk of each other, either on the main square or downhill on Queen and Park streets. For good sit-down fish-and-chips, go to either pub on the main square: The Queen's Head or The Kings Arms. For dessert, consider munching a locally made chocolate treat under the trees on the square's benches and watching the sky darken, the lamps come on, and visitors having their photo fun in the stocks.

Restaurants and Pubs

$$ Stow Lodge is *the* choice of the town's proper ladies. There are two parts: The formal but friendly bar serves fine pub grub (daily 12:00-14:00 & 19:00-20:30); the restaurant serves a popular £30 three-course dinner (nightly, veggie options, good wines, just off main square, tel. 01451/830-485, Val). On a sunny day, the pub serves lunch in the well-manicured garden, where you'll feel quite aristocratic.

$$ The Bell at Stow, at the end of Park Street (on the edge of town), has a great scene and fun pub energy for a drink or for a full meal. They serve up classic English dishes with a lighter, sometimes Asian twist. Produce and fish are locally sourced (daily 12:00-21:00, reservations recommended, tel. 01451/870-916, www.thebellatstow.com). Enjoy live music on Sunday evenings.

$$ The Queen's Head faces the Market Square, near Stow Lodge. With a classic pub vibe, it's a great place to bring your dog and watch the eccentrics while you eat pub grub and drink the local Cotswold brew, Donnington Ale. They have a meat pie of the day, good fish and chips, and live music on Saturdays (beer garden out back, daily 12:00-14:30 & 18:30-21:00, tel. 01451/830-563, Johnny).

$$ Huffkins Bakery and Tea Rooms is a cute, old-school institution overlooking the center of the market square with to-go lunches and a well-worn tearoom for bakery-fresh meals—soups, sandwiches, all-day breakfast, tea and scones, and gluten-free options (Mon-Sat 9:00-17:00, Sun 10:00-14:00, tel. 01451/832-870).

Cheaper Options and Ethnic Food

Head to the grassy triangle where Digbeth hits Sheep Street; there you'll find takeout fish-and-chips, Chinese, and Indian food. You

Great Country Gastropubs

These places—known for their high-quality meals and fine settings—are very popular. Arrive early or phone in a reservation. (If you show up at 20:00, it's unlikely that they'll be able to seat you for dinner if you haven't called first.) These pubs allow "well-behaved children," have overnight accommodations, and are practical only for those with a car. If you have wheels, make a point to dine at one (or more) of these—no matter where you're sleeping. In addition to these fine choices, other pubs serving worth-a-trip food are **$$$ Eight Bells** in Chipping Camden (described on page 365) and **$$$$ The Wheatsheaf Inn** in Northleach (see page 388).

Near Stow

The first two (in Oddington, about three miles from Stow) are more trendy and fresh, yet still in a traditional pub setting. The Plough (in Ford, a few miles farther away) is your jolly olde dark pub.

$$$$ The Fox Inn, a different Fox Inn than the one in Broadwell (see "Pub Dinner Hike from Stow"), has a long history but a fresh approach. It's a popular choice among local foodies for its delicately prepared, borderline-pretentious but still reasonably priced updated pub classics and more creative dishes. They've perfected their upmarket rustic-chic vibe, with a genteelly Old World interior that's fresh and candle-lit and a delightful back terrace and garden (extensive wine list, Mon-Fri 12:00-14:30 & 18:30-21:30, Sat-Sun 12:00-15:00, in Lower Oddington, tel. 01451/870-555, www.thefoxatoddington.com).

$$$$ The Horse and Groom Village Inn in Upper Oddington is a smart place in a 16th-century inn, serving modern English and Continental food with a good wine list (38 wines by the glass) and top honors as pub of the year for its serious attention to beer. It boasts a wonderful fireplace and lots of meat on the menu (food served daily 12:00-14:00 & 18:00-21:00, tel. 01451/830-584, www.horseandgroomoddington.com).

Between Stow and Chipping Campden

$$$ The Plough Inn, in the hamlet of Ford, fills a fascinating old building—once an old coaching inn, later a courthouse, and now a tribute to all things horse racing (it sits across from the Jackdaws

Castle racehorse training facility). Ask the bar staff for some fun history—like what "you're barred" means. Eat from the same traditional English menu in the restaurant, bar, or garden. They are serious about their beer, and serve up heaping portions of stick-to-your-ribs pub-grub classics—a bit more traditional and less refined than others listed here (food served daily 12:00-14:00 & 18:00-21:00, all day long Fri-Sun and June-Aug, 6 miles from Stow on the road to Tewkesbury, reservations smart, tel. 01386/584-215, http://theploughinnford.co.uk).

Near Chipping Campden
$$$$ The Ebrington Arms is a quintessential neighborhood pub with 21st-century amenities: modern British cuisine, home-brewed beer, an extensive wine list, and friendly service. Rub elbows with locals in the crowded bar—energetic any day of the week. The restaurant and rotating menu are classy without being pretentious, and owners Jim and Claire make you feel welcomed but not smothered (food served daily 12:00-14:30 & 18:00-21:00, Sun until 15:30 and 20:30, 3 miles from Chipping Campden, reservations smart, tel. 01386/593-223, www.theebringtonarms.co.uk).

Near Moreton-in-Marsh, in Bourton-on-the-Hill
The hill-capping Bourton—about a five-minute drive (or two-mile uphill walk) above Moreton—offers sweeping views over the Cotswold countryside. Perched at the top of this steep, picturesque burg is an enticing destination pub.

   $$$$ Horse and Groom melds a warm welcome with a tempting menu of delicious modern English fare. Of the pubs listed here, they seem to hit the best balance of old and new, combining unassumingly delicious food with a convivial spit-and-sawdust spirit. Choose between the lively, light, spacious interior or—in good weather—the terraced picnic-table garden out back (food served Mon-Sat 12:00-14:00 & 19:00-21:00, Sun 12:00-14:30 only, tel. 01386/700-413 (www.horseandgroom.info, enquiries@horseandgroom.info). Don't confuse this with The Horse and Groom Village Inn in Upper Oddington, near Stow (described earlier).

COTSWOLDS

can picnic at the triangle, or on the benches by the stocks on Market Street.

$ Greedy's Fish and Chips, on Park Street, is the go-to place for takeout. There's no seating, but they have benches out front (Mon-Sat 12:00-14:00 & 16:30-21:00, closed Sun, tel. 01451/870-821).

$ Jade Garden Chinese Take-Away is appreciated by locals who don't want to cook (Wed-Mon 17:00-23:00, closed Tue, 15 Park Street, tel. 01451/870-288).

$$ The Prince of India offers good Indian food to take out or eat in (nightly 18:00-23:30, 5 Park Street, tel. 01451/830-099).

$ The Old Bakery Tearoom is a local favorite hidden away in a tiny mall at the bottom of Digbeth Street with tradition cakes and light lunches (Mon-Wed & Fri-Sat 10:00-16:00, closed Thu and Sun, Digbeth Street, Alan and Jackie).

$$ Speedwells Cafe provides a nice break from the horses-and-hounds traditional cuisine found elsewhere. You can get your food to go, or eat here—there's pleasant garden seating out back (good coffee, daily 9:00-18:00, Church Street, tel. 01451/870-802).

The **Cotswold Chocolate Company** creates handmade chocolate bars, bon-bons, truffles, and more. Pop in to watch Tony working through a window in the back of the shop (his wife, Heidi, does the decorating after he's done). The friendly shopkeepers are happy to offer suggestions. If you're struggling to decide, try the fruit-and-chili bar, or the chocolate-covered...anything (daily 10:00-17:30, Digbeth Street, tel. 01451/798-082).

Groceries: Small grocery stores face the main square (the **Co-op** is open daily 7:00-22:00; next to The Kings Arms), and a big **Tesco** supermarket is 400 yards north of town.

PUB DINNER HIKE FROM STOW

From Stow, consider taking a half-hour countryside walk to the village of Broadwell, where you'll find a traditional old pub serving good basic grub in a convivial atmosphere. **$$ The Fox Inn** serves pub dinners and draws traditional ales—including the local Donnington ales (food served Mon-Sat 11:30-14:00 & 18:30-21:00, Sun 12:00-14:00 only, outdoor tables in garden out back, on the village green, reservations smart, tel. 01451/870-909, www.foxbroadwell.co.uk, Mike and Carol).

Getting There: If you walk briskly, it's just 20 minutes downhill from Stow. While the walk is not particularly scenic (it's one-third paved lane, and the rest on an arrow-straight bridle path), it is peaceful, and the exercise is a nice way to start and finish your meal. The trail is poorly marked, but it's hard to get lost: Leave Stow at Parson's Corner, continue downhill, pass the town well, follow the bridle path straight until you hit the next road, then turn

COTSWOLDS

right at the road and walk downhill into the village of Broadwell. You can often hitch a ride with someone from the pub back to Stow after you eat.

Near Stow-on-the-Wold

These sights are all south of Stow: Some are within walking distance (the Slaughters and Bourton-on-the-Water), and one is 20 miles away (Cirencester). The Slaughters and Bourton are tied together by the countryside walk described on page 378.

▲Lower and Upper Slaughter

"Slaughter" has nothing to do with lamb chops. It likely derives from an Old English word, perhaps meaning sloe tree (the one used to make sloe gin).

Lower Slaughter is a classic village, with ducks, a charming little church, a working water mill, and usually an artist busy at her easel somewhere. The Old Mill Museum is a folksy ensemble with a tiny museum, shop, and café complete with a delightful terrace overlooking the mill pond, enthusiastically run by Gerald and his daughter Laura, who just can't resist giving generous tastes of their homemade ice cream (£2.50 for museum, daily 10:00-18:00, Nov-Feb until dusk, tel. 01451/822-127, www.oldmill-lowerslaughter. com). Just behind the Old Mill, two kissing gates lead to the path that goes to nearby Upper Slaughter, a 15-minute walk or 2-minute drive away (leaving the Old Mill, take two lefts, then follow sign for *Wardens Way*). And if you follow the mill creek downstream, a bridle path leads to Bourton-on-the-Water (described next).

In **Upper Slaughter,** walk through the yew trees (sacred in pagan days) down a lane through the raised graveyard (a buildup of centuries of graves) to the peaceful church. In the back of the fine cemetery, the statue of a wistful woman looks over the tomb of an 18th-century rector (sculpted by his son). Notice the town is missing a war memorial—that's because every soldier  who left Upper Slaughter for World War I and World War II survived the wars. As a so-called "Doubly Thankful Village" (one of only 13 in England and Wales), the town instead honors those who served in war with a simple wood plaque in the town hall.

Getting There: Though the stop is not listed on schedules, you should be able to reach these towns on bus #801 (from Moreton

COTSWOLDS

or Stow) by requesting the "Slaughter Pike" stop (along the main road, near the villages). Confirm with the driver before getting on. If driving, the small roads from Upper Slaughter to Ford and Kineton (and the Cotswold Farm Park, described later) are some of England's most scenic. Roll your window down and joyride slowly.

▲Bourton-on-the-Water

I can't figure out whether they call this "the Venice of the Cotswolds" because of its quaint canals or its miserable crowds. Either way, this town—four miles south of Stow and a mile from Lower Slaughter—is very pretty. But it can be mobbed with tour groups during the day: Sidewalks become jammed with disoriented tourists wearing nametags. Perhaps the most touristy town in Britain, Bourton-on-the-Water charges 20 pence to pee and has a turnstile to be sure it gets the coin.

If you can avoid the crowds, it's worth a drive-through and maybe a short stop. It's pleasantly empty in the early evening and after dark.

Bourton's attractions are tacky tourist traps, but the three listed below might be worth considering. All are on High Street in the town center. In addition to these, consider Bourton's **leisure center** (big pool and sauna, a five-minute walk from town center off Station Road; Mon-Fri 6:30-22:00, Sat-Sun 8:00-20:00; shared with the school—which gets priority for use, tel. 01451/824-024).

Getting There: It's conveniently connected to Stow and Moreton by bus #801.

Parking: Finding a spot here can be tough. Even during the busy business day, rather than park in the pay-and-display parking lot a five-minute walk from the center, drive right into town and wait for a spot on High Street just past the village green (where the road swings left, turn right to go down High Street; there's a long row of free 1.5 hour spots starting in front of the Edinburgh Woolen Mills Shop, on the right).

Tourist Information: The TI is tucked across the stream a short block off the main drag, on Victoria Street, behind The Victoria Hall (Mon-Fri 9:30-17:00, Sat until 17:30, Sun 10:00-14:00 except closed Sun Oct-April, closes one hour earlier Nov-March, tel. 01451/820-211).

Bike Rental: Hartwells on High Street rents bikes by the hour or day and includes a helmet, map, and lock (£10/3 hours;

£14/day, Mon-Sat 9:00-18:00, Sun from 10:00, tel. 01451/820-405, www.hartwells.supanet.com).

▲Cotswold Motoring Museum

Lovingly presented, this good, jumbled museum shows off a lifetime's accumulation of vintage cars, old lacquered signs, thread-

bare toys, prewar memorabilia, and sundry British pop culture knick-knacks. If you appreciate old cars, this is nirvana. Wander the car-and-driver displays, which range from the automobile's early days to slick 1970s models, including period music to set the mood. Talk to an elderly Brit who's touring the place for some personal memories.

Cost and Hours: £5.75, daily 10:00-18:00, closed late Dec-mid-Feb, in the mill facing the town center, tel. 01451/821-255, www.cotswoldmotoringmuseum.co.uk.

Model Railway Exhibition

This exhibit of three model railway layouts is impressive only to train buffs (£3, June-Aug daily 11:00-17:00; closed Jan and Mon-Fri off-season; located in the back of a hobby shop, in the center of town).

Model Village

This light but fun display re-creates the town on a 1:9 scale in a tiny outdoor park, and has an attached room full of tiny models showing off various bits of British domestic life.

Cost and Hours: £3.60, daily 10:00-18:00, until 16:00 in winter, at the edge of town, behind The Old New Inn, a few minutes' walk from the center.

Walk to the Slaughters

From Bourton-on-the-Water, it's about a 30-minute walk (or a two-minute drive) to Upper and Lower Slaughter (described previously); taken together, they make for an easy two-hour round-trip walk from Bourton. (You could also walk from Stow through the Slaughters to Bourton—hike described on page 378.)

▲Cotswold Farm Park

Here's a delight for young and old alike. This park is the private venture of the Henson family, who are passionate about preserving rare and endangered breeds of native British animals. While it feels like a kids' zone (with all the family-friendly facilities you can imagine), it's actually a fascinating chance for anyone to get up close and (very) personal with piles of mostly cute animals, including the sheep that made this region famous—the big and woolly Cotswold Lion. The "listening posts" deliver audio information on each rare breed.

A busy schedule of demonstrations gives you a look at local farm life—check the events board as you enter for times for the milking, "farm safari," shearing, and well-done "sheep show." Join the included 20-minute tractor ride, with live narration. Buy a bag of seed upon arrival, or have your map eaten by munchy goats as I did. Tykes love the little tractor rides, maze, and zip line, but the "touch barn" is where it's at for little kids.

Cost and Hours: £12, kids-£10.50, family ticket for 2 adults and 2 kids-£40, daily 10:30-17:00, Nov-Dec until 16:00, closed Jan, good guidebook (£6), decent cafeteria, tel. 01451/850-307, www.cotswoldfarmpark.co.uk.

Getting There: It's well-signposted about halfway between Stow and Stanway (15 minutes from either), just off Tewkesbury Road (B-4077, toward Ford from Stow). A visit here makes sense if you're traveling from Stow to Chipping Campden.

Northleach

One of the "untouched and untouristed" Cotswold villages, Northleach is worth a short stop. The town's impressive main square and church attest to its position as a major wool center in the Middle Ages. Park in the square called The Green or the adjoining Market Place. The town has no TI, but you may find a free town map and visitor guide at the Mechanical Music Museum, at the post office on the Market Place, or at other nearby shops. Information: www.northleach.gov.uk.

Getting There: Northleach is nine miles south of Stow, down the A-429. Bus #801 connects it to Stow and Moreton.

Eating in Northleach: Tucked along unassuming Northleach's main drag is a foodies' favorite, **$$$$ The Wheatsheaf Inn.** With a pleasantly traditional dining room and a gorgeous sprawling garden, they offer an intriguing eclectic menu of modern English cuisine proudly served with a warm welcome, relaxed

COTSWOLDS

service, and a take-your-time approach to top-quality food. Reservations are smart (daily, on West End, tel. 01451/860-244, www. cotswoldswheatsheaf.com).

▲Mechanical Music Museum

This delightful little one-room place offers a unique opportunity to listen to 300 years of amazing self-playing musical instruments. It's run by people who are passionate about the restoration work they do on these musical marvels. The curators delight in demonstrating about 20 of the museum's machines with each hour-long tour. You'll hear Victorian music boxes and the earliest polyphones (record players) playing cylinders and then discs—all from an age when music was made mechanically, without the help of electricity. The admission fee includes an essential hour-long tour.

Cost and Hours: £8, daily 10:00-17:00, last entry at 16:00, tours go constantly—join one in progress, High Street, Northleach, tel. 01451/860-181, www.mechanicalmusic.co.uk.

Church of Saints Peter and Paul

This fine Perpendicular Gothic church has been called the "cathedral of the Cotswolds." It's one of the Cotswolds' two finest "wool" churches (along with Chipping Campden's), paid for by 15th-century wool tycoons. Find the oldest tombstone, and the baptismal font with carved devils being crushed at its base. The brass plaques on the floor memorialize big  shots, showing sheep and sacks of wool at their long-dead feet, and inscriptions mixing Latin and Old English (daily 9:00-17:00 or until dusk, tel. 01451/861-132).

Coln Valley

Drivers will enjoy exploring the scenic Coln Valley, linking Northleach to Bibury as you pass through the enigmatic villages of Coln St. Dennis, Coln Rogers, Coln Powell, and Winson.

Chedworth Roman Villa

Secluded in thick woods in the Coln Valley are the remains of one of the finest aristocratic villas of fourth-century Roman Britain. Though well off the beaten path now, in its heyday of the late fourth century this wealthy farmstead was not far from a major Roman thoroughfare. You'll find a small museum and visitors center, and extensive, well-preserved floor mosaics. Rounding out the site are the remains of a small bath complex and a mossy spring once surrounded by an ostentatious water shrine. For history buffs with their own transportation, this is worth seeking out.

Cost and Hours: £10.50, daily 10:00-17:00, until 16:00 off season, audioguide-£1, tel. 01242/890-256, www.nationaltrust. org.uk/chedworth.

Getting There: A half-mile beyond Northleach on the A-429, turn right and follow brown *Roman Villa* signs another 4 miles to the villa. Note: Don't follow *Chedworth* signs; these lead to Chedworth village.

▲Bibury

Six miles northeast of Cirencester, this village is a favorite with British picnickers fond of strolling and fishing. Bibury (BYE-bree) offers some relaxing sights, including a row of very old weavers' cottages, a trout farm, a stream teeming with fat fish and proud ducks, and a church surrounded by rosebushes, each tended by a volunteer of the parish. A protected wetlands area on the far side of the stream hosts newts and water voles.  Walk up the main street, then turn right along the old weavers' Arlington Row and back on the far side of the marsh, peeking into the rushes for wildlife.

For a closer look at the fish, cross the little bridge to the 15-acre **Trout Farm,** where you can feed them—or catch your own (£4.50 to walk the grounds, fish food-£0.60; daily 8:00-17:30, Oct and March until 17:00, Nov-Feb until 16:00; catch-your-own only on weekends March-Oct 10:00-17:00, no fishing in winter, call or email to confirm fishing schedule, tel. 01285/740-215, www. biburytroutfarm.co.uk).

Getting There: Take bus #801 from Moreton-in-Marsh or Stow, then change to #855 in Northleach or Bourton-on-the-Water (3/day, 1 hour total).

Sleeping in Bibury: To spend the night in tiny Bibury, consider **$$ The William Morris B&B,** named for the 19th-century designer and writer (2 rooms, tearoom, 200 yards from the bridge toward the church at 11 The Street, tel. 01285/740-555, www. thewilliammorris.com, ian@ianhowards.wanadoo.co.uk).

▲Cirencester

Almost 2,000 years ago, Cirencester (SIGH-ren-ses-ter) was the ancient Roman city of Corinium. Larger and less cute than other

Cotswold towns, but with a pleasant historic center, it's 20 miles from Stow down the A-429, which was called Fosse Way in Roman times. The **TI,** in the shop at the Corinium Museum, answers questions and sells a town map and a town walking-tour brochure (same hours as museum, tel. 01285/654-180).

Getting There: By bus, take #801 from Moreton-in-Marsh or Stow, then change to #855 in Northleach or Bourton-on-the-Water for Cirencester (3/day, 1.5 hours total). Drivers follow *Town Centre* signs and find parking right on the market square; if it's full, retreat to the Waterloo pay-and-display lot (a 5-minute walk away).

Visiting Cirencester: Stop by the impressive **Corinium Museum** to find out why they say, "If you scratch Gloucestershire, you'll find Rome." The museum chronologically displays well-explained artifacts from the town's rich history, with a focus on Roman times—when Corinium was the second-biggest city in the British Isles (after Londinium). You'll see column capitals and fine mosaics before moving on to the Anglo-Saxon and Middle Ages exhibits (£5.40, Mon-Sat 10:00-17:00, Sun from 14:00, Park Street, tel. 01285/655-611, www.coriniummuseum.org).

Cirencester's **church** is the largest of the Cotswold "wool" churches. The cutesy **New Brewery Arts** crafts center entertains visitors with traditional weaving and potting, workshops, an interesting gallery, and a good coffee shop (www.newbreweryarts.org.uk). Monday and Friday are general-**market** days, Friday features an antique market, and a crafts market is held every Saturday.

COTSWOLDS

Moreton-in-Marsh

This workaday town—worth ▲—is like Stow or Chipping Campden without the touristy sugar. Rather than gift and antique shops, you'll find streets lined with real shops: ironmongers selling cottage nameplates and carpet shops strewn with the remarkable patterns that decorate B&B floors. A traditional market of 100-plus stalls fills High Street each Tuesday, as it has for the last 400 years (8:00-15:30, handicrafts, farm produce, clothing, books, and people-watching; best if you go early). The Cotswolds has an economy aside from tourism, and you'll feel it here.

Orientation to Moreton-in-Marsh

Moreton has a tiny, sleepy train station two blocks from High Street, lots of bus connections, and the best **TI** in the region. Peruse the racks of fliers, confirm rail and bus schedules, and consider the £0.50 *Town Trail* self-guided walking tour leaflet. Ask about discounted tickets for Blenheim Palace, easily visited between here and Oxford; see page 397 (TI open Mon 8:45-16:00, Tue-Thu until 17:15, Fri until 16:45, Sat 10:00-13:00—until 12:30 in winter, closed Sun, good public WC, tel. 01608/650-881).

HELPFUL HINTS

Baggage Storage: While there's no formal baggage storage in town, the **Black Bear Inn** (next to the TI) might let you leave bags there—especially if you buy a drink.

Laundry: The handy launderette is a block in front of the train station on New Road (daily 7:00-19:00, last self-service wash at 18:00, drop-off service options available—call ahead to arrange, tel. 01608/650-888).

Bike Rental, Taxis, and Car Rental: See "Getting Around the Cotswolds," earlier.

Parking: It's easy—anywhere on High Street is fine any time, as long as you want, for free (though there is a 2-hour parking limit for the small lot in the middle of the street). On Tuesdays, when the market makes parking tricky, try the **Budgens** supermarket, where you can park for two hours.

Hikes and Walks from Moreton-in-Marsh: As its name implies, Moreton-in-Marsh sits on a flat, boggy landscape, making it a

COTSWOLDS

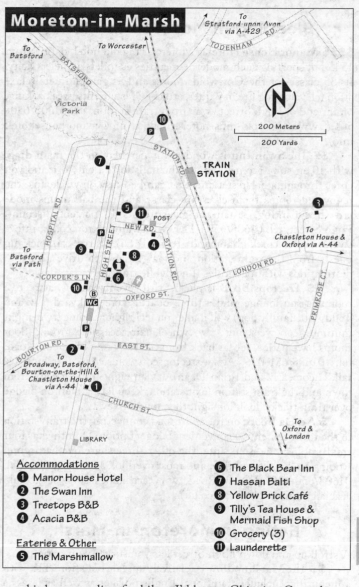

Moreton-in-Marsh

To Stratford-upon-Avon via A-429

To Worcester

To Batsford

TODENHAM RD.

Victoria Park

BATSFORD RD.

STATION RD.

TRAIN STATION

200 Meters

200 Yards

HOSPITAL RD.

NEW RD.

POST

HIGH STREET

STATION RD.

To Chastleton House & Oxford via A-44

To Batsford via Path

CORDER'S LN.

OXFORD ST.

LONDON RD.

PRIMROSE CT.

WC

BOURTON RD.

EAST ST.

To Broadway, Batsford, Bourton-on-the-Hill & Chastleton House via A-44

CHURCH ST.

To Oxford & London

LIBRARY

Accommodations
1. Manor House Hotel
2. The Swan Inn
3. Treetops B&B
4. Acacia B&B

Eateries & Other
5. The Marshmallow
6. The Black Bear Inn
7. Hassan Balti
8. Yellow Brick Café
9. Tilly's Tea House & Mermaid Fish Shop
10. Grocery (3)
11. Launderette

COTSWOLDS

bit less appealing for hikes; I'd bus to Chipping Campden or to Stow, both described earlier, for a better hike (this is easy, since Moreton is a transit hub). If you do have just a bit of time to kill in Moreton, consider taking a fun and easy walk a mile out to the arboretum and falconry center in **Batsford** (described later).

874 Rick Steves Great Britain

Sleeping in Moreton-in-Marsh

$$$$ Manor House Hotel is Moreton's big old hotel, dating from 1545 but sporting such modern amenities as toilets and electricity. Its 35 classy-for-the-Cotswolds rooms and its garden invite relaxation (elevator, log fire in winter, attached restaurants, free parking, on far end of High Street away from train station, tel. 01608/650-501, www.cotswold-inns-hotels.co.uk, info@manorhousehotel.info).

$$ The Swan Inn is wonderfully perched on the main drag, with 10 en-suite rooms. Though the halls look a bit worn and you enter through a bar/restaurant that can be noisy on weekends, the renovated rooms themselves are classy and the bathrooms modern (free parking, restaurant gives guests 10 percent discount, High Street, tel. 01608/650-711, www.swanmoreton.co.uk, info@swanmoreton.co.uk, Sara and Terry Todd). Terry can pick up guests from the train station and may be able to drive guests to destinations within 20 miles if no public transport is available.

$$ Treetops B&B is plush, with seven spacious, attractive rooms, a sun lounge, and a three-quarter-acre backyard. Liz and Teddy (the family dog) will make you feel right at home (two-night minimum on weekends, two wheelchair-accessible ground-floor rooms have patios, set far back from the busy road, London Road, tel. 01608/651-036, www.treetopscotswolds.co.uk, treetops1@talk21.com, Liz and Brian Dean). It's an eight-minute walk from town and the train station (exit station, keep left, go left on bridge over train tracks, look for sign, then long driveway).

$ Acacia B&B, on the short road connecting the train station to the town center, is a convenient budget option. Dorothy has four small rooms: one is en suite, the other three share one bathroom. Rooms are bright and tidy, and most overlook a lovely garden (tel. 01608/650-130, 2 New Road, www.acaciainthecotswolds.co.uk, acacia.guesthouse@tiscali.co.uk).

Eating in Moreton-in-Marsh

A stroll up and down High Street lets you survey your options.

$$ The Marshmallow is relatively upscale but affordable, with a menu that includes traditional English dishes as well as lasagna and salads (afternoon tea, Mon 10:00-16:00, Tue-Sat until 20:00, Sun 10:30-18:00, closed for dinner in Jan, reservations smart, shady back garden for dining, tel. 01608/651-536, www.marshmallow-tea-restaurant.co.uk).

$$$ The Black Bear Inn offers traditional English food. Choose between the dining room on the left or the pub on the right

COTSWOLDS

(restaurant daily 12:00-14:00 & 18:30-21:00, pub daily 10:30-23:30, tel. 01608/652-992).

$$ Hassan Balti, with tasty Bangladeshi food, is a fine value for sit-down or takeout (daily 12:00-14:00 & 17:30-23:30, tel. 01608/650-798).

$$ Yellow Brick Café, run by Tom and Nicola, has a delightful outdoor patio, cozy indoor seating, and a tempting display of homemade cakes. It's good for a late breakfast, midday lunch, or early dinner after a full day of Cotswolds exploring (daily 9:00-17:00, 3 Old Market Way, tel. 01608/651-881).

$ Tilly's Tea House serves fresh soups, salads, sandwiches, and pastries for lunch in a cheerful spot on High Street across from the TI (good cream tea, Mon-Sat 9:00-17:00, Sun 10:00-16:00, tel. 01608/650-000).

$ Mermaid fish shop is popular for its takeout fish and tasty selection of traditional savory pies (Mon-Sat 11:30-14:00 & 17:00-22:00, closed Sun, tel. 01608/651-391).

Picnic: There's a small **Co-op** grocery on High Street (Mon-Sat 7:00-20:00, Sun 8:00-20:00), and a **Tesco Express** two doors down (Mon-Fri 6:00-23:00, Sat-Sun from 7:00). The big **Budgens** supermarket is indeed super (Mon-Sat 8:00-22:00, Sun 10:00-16:00, far end of High Street). You can picnic across the street in pleasant Victoria Park (with a playground).

Nearby: The excellent **$$$$ Horse and Groom** gastropub in Bourton-on-the-Hill is a quick drive or two-mile uphill walk (see page 383).

Moreton-in-Marsh Connections

Moreton, the only Cotswold town with a train station, is also the best base for exploring the region by bus (see "Getting Around the Cotswolds" on page 346).

From Moreton by Train to: London's Paddington Station (every 1-2 hours, 2 hours), **Bath** (hourly, 3 hours, 1-2 transfers), **Oxford** (2/hour, 40 minutes), **Ironbridge Gorge** (hourly, 3 hours, 2 transfers; arrive Telford, then catch a bus or cab 7 miles to Ironbridge Gorge—see page 429), **Stratford-upon-Avon** (hourly, 3 hours, 2 transfers, slow and expensive, better by bus). Train info: Tel. 0345-748-4950, www.nationalrail.co.uk.

From Moreton by Bus to: Stratford-upon-Avon (#1 and #2 go via Chipping Campden: Mon-Sat 8/day, none on Sun, 1-1.5 hours, Johnsons Coaches, tel. 01564/797-070, www.johnsonscoaches. co.uk).

COTSWOLDS

Near Moreton-in-Marsh

▲Chastleton House

This stately home, located about five miles southeast of Moreton-in-Marsh, was lived in by the same family from 1607 until 1991.
It offers a rare peek into a Jaco-
bean gentry house. (Jacobean,
which comes from the Latin for
"James," indicates the style from
the time of King James I—the
early 1600s.) Built, like most
Cotswold palaces, with wool
money, it gradually declined
with the fortunes of its aristocratic family, who lost much of
their wealth in the war—not

World War II, but the English Civil War in the 1640s. They stuck
it out for centuries until, according to the last lady of the house,
the place was "held together by cobwebs." It came to the National
Trust on the condition that they would maintain its musty Jacobean ambience. It's so authentic that the BBC used it to film scenes
from its adaptation of *Wolf Hall* (a best-seller about Henry VIII's
chief minister, Thomas Cromwell, who masterminded Henry's divorce, marriage to Anne Boleyn, and break with Rome). Wander
on creaky floorboards, many of them original, chat with the knowledgeable volunteer guides, and understand this frozen-in-time relic
revealing the lives of nobles who were land rich but cash poor. The
docents are proud to play on one of the best croquet teams in the region (the rules of croquet were formalized in this house in 1868—
if you fancy a round, the ticket counter can lend you a set). Page
through the early 20th-century family photo albums in the room
just off the entry.

Cost and Hours: £10.50; Wed-Sun 13:00-17:00, closed Nov-
mid-March and Mon-Tue year-round; ticket office opens at 12:30,
last entry one hour before closing, recorded info tel. 01494/755-
560, www.nationaltrust.org.uk/chastleton.

Getting In: Tickets are first-come, first-served and reservations are not possible. On busy days, entries are timed, and you may
have to wait a bit. Fridays are the quietest days, with the shortest
wait times.

Getting There: Chastleton House is well-signposted (be sure
you follow signs to the house, not the town), about a 10-minute
drive southeast of Moreton-in-Marsh off the A-44. It's a five-minute hike to the house from the free parking lot.

COTSWOLDS

Batsford

This village has two side-by-side attractions that might appeal if you have a special interest or time to kill.

Getting There: Batsford is an easy 45-minute, 1.5-mile country walk west of Moreton-in-Marsh. It's also connected to Moreton by buses #1 and #2.

Cotswold Falconry Centre

Along with the Cotswolds' hunting heritage comes falconry—and this place, with dozens of specimens of eagles, falcons, owls, and other birds, gives a sample of what these deadly birds of prey can do. You can peruse the cages to see all the different birds, but the demonstration, with vultures or falcons swooping inches over your head, is what makes it fun.

Cost and Hours: £10, ticket good for 10 percent discount at Batsford Arboretum; daily mid-Feb-mid-Nov 10:30-17:30, closed rest of the year; flying displays at 11:30, 13:30, and 15:00, plus in summer at 16:30; Batsford Park, tel. 01386/701-043, www.cotswold-falconry.co.uk.

Batsford Arboretum

This sleepy grove, with 2,800 trees from around the world, pales in comparison to some of the Cotswolds' genteel manor gardens. But it's next door to the Falconry Centre, and handy to visit if you'd enjoy strolling through a diverse wood. The arboretum's café serves lunch and tea on a terrace with sweeping views of the Gloucestershire countryside.

Cost and Hours: £8, ticket good for 10 percent discount at Falconry Centre, daily 9:00-17:00, last entry 45 minutes before closing, tel. 01386/701-441, www.batsarb.co.uk.

Blenheim Palace

Conveniently located halfway between the Cotswolds and Oxford, Blenheim Palace is one of Britian's best—worth ▲▲▲. Too many palaces can send you into a furniture-wax coma, but as a sightseeing experience and in simple visual grandeur, this palace is among Europe's finest. The Duke of Marlborough's home— one of the largest in England—is still lived in, which is wonderfully obvious as you prowl through it. The 2,000-acre yard, well-designed by Lancelot "Capability" Brown, is as majestic to some as the palace itself. Note: Americans who pronounce the place "blen-HEIM" are the butt of jokes. It's "BLEN-em."

John Churchill, first duke of Marlborough, achieved Europe-wide renown with his stunning victory over Louis XIV of France's armies at the Battle of Blenheim in 1704. This was a major turning point in the War of the Spanish Succession—one of Louis's repeated attempts to gain hegemony over the continent. A thankful Queen Anne rewarded Churchill by building him this nice home, perhaps the finest Baroque building in England. Eleven dukes of Marlborough later, the palace is as impressive as ever. In 1874, a later John Churchill's American daughter-in-law, Jennie Jerome, gave birth at Blenheim to another historic baby in that line...and named him Winston.

GETTING TO BLENHEIM PALACE

Blenheim Palace sits at the edge of the cute cobbled town of Woodstock. The train station nearest the palace (Hanborough, 1.5 miles away) has no taxi or bus service.

If you're coming from the **Cotswolds,** your easiest train connection is from Moreton-in-Marsh to Oxford, where you can catch the bus to Blenheim (note that bus #S3 doesn't always stop at the Oxford train station—you may have to walk 5 minutes to the bus station).

From **Oxford,** take bus #S3 (3/hour, 40 minutes; bus tel. 01865/772-250, www.stagecoachbus.com). Catch it from the bus station at Gloucester Green (may also pick up in the center on George Street—ask). It stops twice near Blenheim Palace: the "Blenheim Palace Gates" stop is along the main road about a half-mile walk to the palace itself; the "Woodstock/Marlborough Arms" stop puts you right in the heart of the village of Woodstock (handy if you want to poke around town before heading to the palace; this adds just a few more minutes' walking). The Woodstock stop also offers the most spectacular view of the palace and lake.

Drivers head for Woodstock (from the Cotswolds, follow signs for *Oxford* on the A-44); the palace is well-signposted once in town, just off the main road. Buy your ticket at the gate, then drive up the long driveway to park near the palace.

ORIENTATION TO BLENHEIM PALACE

Cost and Hours: £24.90, park and gardens only-£14, discount palace tickets that save £3 are available at TIs in surrounding towns—including Oxford and Moreton-in-Marsh—or on the #S3 bus from Oxford; family ticket for two adults and two kids-£60, £5.50 guidebook; open mid-Feb-Oct daily 10:30-

17:30, Nov-mid-Dec generally closed Mon-Tue, park open but palace closed mid-Dec-mid-Feb. Doors to the palace close at 16:45, it's "everyone out" at 17:30, and the park closes at 18:00. Late in the afternoon the palace is relaxed and quiet (even on the busiest of days).

Information: The interactive map on their website gives a good visual orientation; recorded info toll-free tel. 0800-849-6500, www.blenheimpalace.com.

Tours: Guided tours are available for the state rooms (included in admission, 2/hour, 40 minutes, last tour 16:45, daily except Sun), the private apartments (£5, 2/hour, about 40 minutes, generally daily 11:00-16:30, most likely to run in summer, tickets are limited), and the gardens (included in admission).

Eating and Sleeping near the Palace: The Water Terraces Café at the garden exit is delightful for basic lunch and teatime treats. In the pleasant, posh town of Woodstock just outside the palace gates, **$ Hampers Deli** is a good place to pick up provisions for a picnic on the palace grounds (31 Oxford Street, tel. 01993/811-535, www.hampersfoodandwine.co.uk). If you need a bed, consider a room in the characteristic old half-timbered **$$ Blenheim Buttery** (7 Market Place, tel. 01865/811-950, www.theblenheimbuttery.co.uk, info@theblenheimbuttery.co.uk).

VISITING THE PALACE

From the parking lot, you'll enter through the Visitors Center (shop, café, and WCs). Pick up a free map and daily tour program, consider signing up at the welcome desk for tours of the private apartments and the gardens, and head through the small courtyard. You'll emerge into a grand courtyard in front of the palace's columned yellow facade.

Facing the palace's steps, consider your six options: the state rooms, the Winston Churchill Exhibition, a skippable multimedia exhibit called The Untold Story, the private apartments tour, the gardens, and the Churchills' Destiny exhibit. The first three of these depart from the Great Hall, directly ahead. The palace tour and Winston Churchill Exhibition are substantial and most important (allow 1.5 hours total for both). The private apartment tour, an excellent behind-the-scenes peek at the palace, requires a special ticket and meets in the corner of the courtyard to the left. The gardens, through the wing on the right, are simply enchanting. And the Churchills' Destiny exhibit, worth a 15-minute walk-through, is in the stables farther to the right.

State Rooms: Enter into the truly great Great Hall, where you'll be greeted and have your options explained. While you can go "free flow" (reading info plaques and talking with docents in each room), you'll get much more out of your visit by taking the included guided tour of the state rooms.

The state rooms are the fancy halls the dukes use to impress visiting dignitaries. These most sumptuous rooms in the palace are ornamented with fine porcelain, gilded ceilings, portraits of past dukes, photos of the present duke's family, and "chaperone" sofas designed to give courting couples just enough privacy...but not *too* much.

Enjoy the series of 10 Brussels tapestries that commemorate military victories of the First Duke of Marlborough, including the Battle of Blenheim. After winning that pivotal conflict, he scrawled a quick note on the back of a tavern bill notifying the queen of his victory (you'll see a replica). The tour offers insights into the quirky ways of England's fading nobility—for example, in exchange for this fine palace, the duke still pays "rent" to the Queen in the form of one ornamental flag per year.

Finish with the remarkable "long library"—with its tiers of books and stuccoed ceilings—before exiting through the chapel, near the entrance to the gardens.

Winston Churchill Exhibition: This is a fascinating display of letters, paintings, and other artifacts of the great statesman who was born here. You'll either be instructed to see this before touring the main state rooms or directed into this exhibition from the library—the last room of the state rooms tour—before leaving the palace.

A highlight of your visit, the exhibit gives you an appreciation for this amazing leader and how blessed Britain was to have him when it did. Along with lots of intimate artifacts from his life, you'll see the bed in which Sir Winston was born in 1874 (prematurely...his mother went into labor suddenly while attending a party here).

The Untold Story: Upstairs, to the left as you enter the Great Hall, is a modern, 45-minute, multimedia "visitors' experience" in a series of eight rooms (15 people go in every 5 minutes, included in your ticket). You'll travel from room to room—as doors open and close behind you every five minutes or so—guided through 300 years of history by a maid named Grace Ridley. (If you have limited time to spend at the palace, this is skippable.) If bored (which is likely), you can quietly push open the next door and fast-track your experience.

Private Apartments: For a more extensive visit, book a spot as soon as you arrive for a 30-minute guided walk through the private apartments of the duke. Tours leave at the top and bottom of each hour—when His Grace is not in; enter in the corner of courtyard to left of grand palace entry.

You'll see the chummy billiards room, luxurious china, the

servants quarters with 47 bells—one for each room to call the servants, private rooms, 18th-century Flemish tapestries, family photos, and so on.

Churchills' Destiny: In the "stables block" (under the gateway to the right as you face the main palace entrance) is an exhibit that traces the military leadership of two great men who shared the name Churchill: John, who defeated Louis XIV at the Battle of Blenheim in the 18th century, and in whose honor this palace was built; and Winston, who was born in this palace, and who won the Battle of Britain and helped defeat Hitler in the 20th century. It's remarkable that arguably two of the most important military victories in the nation's history were overseen by distant cousins. (Winston Churchill fans can visit his tomb, just over a mile away to the south in the Bladon town churchyard—the church is faintly visible from inside the palace. Look for the footpath across from the White House pub.)

Gardens: The palace's expansive gardens stretch nearly as far as the eye can see in every direction. Access them from the main courtyard by following signs through a little door (it's to the right as you face the main palace entrance). You'll emerge into the **Water Terraces;** from there, you can loop around to the left, behind the palace, to see (but not enter) the Italian Garden. Or, head down to the lake to walk along the waterfront trail; going left takes you to the rose gardens and arboretum, while turning right brings you to the Grand Bridge. You can explore on your own (using the map and good signposting), or join a free tour.

On the way out of the palace complex, stop in at the **kid-friendly pleasure garden,** where a lush and humid greenhouse flutters with butterflies. A kid zone includes a few second-rate games and the "world's largest symbolic hedge maze." The maze is worth a look if you haven't seen one and want some exercise. If you have a car, you'll pass these gardens as you drive down the road toward the exit; otherwise, you can take the tiny train from the palace parking lot to the garden (2/hour).

STRATFORD-UPON-AVON

Stratford is Shakespeare's hometown. To see or not to see? Stratford is a must for every big bus tour in England, and one of the most popular side-trips from London. English majors and actors are in seventh heaven here. Sure, it's touristy, and nonliterary types might find it's much ado about nothing. But nobody back home would understand if you skipped Shakespeare's house.

Shakespeare connection aside, the town's riverside and half-timbered charm, coupled with its hardworking tourist industry, make Stratford a fun stop. But the play's the thing to bring the Bard to life—and you've arrived just in time to see the Royal Shakespeare Company (the world's best Shakespeare ensemble) making the most of their state-of-the-art theater complex. If you'll ever enjoy a Shakespeare performance, it'll  be here...even if you flunked English Lit.

PLANNING YOUR TIME

If you're just passing through Stratford, it's worth a half-day—stroll the charming core, visit your choice of Shakespeare sights (Shakespeare's Birthplace is best and easiest), and watch the swans along the river. But if you can squeeze it in, it's worth it to stick around to see a play; in this case, you'll need to spend the night here or drive in from the Cotswolds (just 30 minutes away; see previous chapter).

By Train or Bus: It's easy to stop in Stratford for a wander or an overnight. Stratford is well-connected by train to London and Oxford, and linked by bus and train to nearby towns (Warwick and Coventry to the north, and Moreton in the Cotswolds to the south).

By Car: Stratford, conveniently located at the northern edge of the Cotswolds, is made to order for drivers connecting the Cotswolds with points north (such as Ironbridge Gorge or North Wales).

Orientation to Stratford

Stratford, with around 30,000 people, has a compact old town, with the TI and theater along the riverbank, and Shakespeare's Birthplace a few blocks inland; you can easily walk to everything except Mary Arden's Farm. The core of the town is lined with half-timbered houses. The River Avon has an idyllic yet playful feel, with a park along both banks, rowboats, swans, and a fun old crank-powered ferry.

TOURIST INFORMATION

The TI is in a small brick building on Bridgefoot, where the main street hits the river (Mon-Sat 9:00-17:30, Sun 10:00-16:00, tel. 01789/264-293, www.shakespeare-country.co.uk).

Combo-Tickets: The TI and the Shakespeare Birthplace Trust sights sell combo-tickets that cover the five trust sights. The TI also has a special "any-three" option covering your pick of three of the five (see "Shakespearean Sights," later, for details on both tickets).

Discounts: If you've taken a Stratford town walk (described under "Tours in Stratford," later), show your ticket stub to receive a discount at many sights, shops, and restaurants in town. Also, ask your B&B owner if they have any discount vouchers—they often do.

ARRIVAL IN STRATFORD

By Train: Don't get off at the Stratford Parkway train station—you want Stratford-upon-Avon. Once there, exit straight ahead from the train station, bear right up the stairs, then turn left and follow the main drag straight to the river. (For the Grove Road B&Bs, turn right at the first big intersection.)

By Car: If you're sleeping in Stratford, ask your B&B for arrival and parking details (many have a few free parking spaces, but it's best to reserve ahead). If you're just here for the day, you'll find plenty of lots scattered around town. The Bridgefoot garage is big, easy, and cheap—coming from the south (i.e., the Cotswolds), cross the big bridge and veer right, following *Through Traffic, P,* and

Stratford-upon-Avon

To Mary Arden's Farm

BIRMINGHAM RD.

SHAKESPEARE ST.

N

P

ARDEN ST.

TRAIN STATION

To Worcester via A-46

STATION RD.

ALCESTER RD.

MANSELL ST.

WINDSOR ST.

SHAKESPEARE'S BIRTHPLACE

18

4

MEER ST.

GREENHILL ST.

10 **20**

21 **11**

AMERICAN FOUNTAIN

Market Place

GROVE RD.

ELY ST.

16

ROTHER ST.

SCHOLARS LN.

1

2

SHAKESPEARE'S SCHOOLROOM & GUILDHALL

CHURCH ST.

CHESTNUT WALK

12

To Anne Hathaway's Cottage

HALL'S CROFT

OLD TOWN

BROAD ST.

BROAD WALK

BULL ST.

COLLEGE ST.

NARROW LN.

SANCTUS ST.

21

COLLEGE LN.

Accommodations

1 Adelphi, Ambleside & Salamander Guest Houses
2 Woodstock Guest House
3 Mercure Shakespeare Hotel
4 The Emsley Guest House
5 To Hemmingford House Hostel

Eateries

6 Le Bistro Pierre & Bear Free House
7 Edward Moon
8 Lambs & The Opposition
9 The Vintner Restaurant
10 Avon Spice
11 The Old Thatch Tavern
12 The Windmill Inn
13 The Garrick Inn
14 Grocery (2)
15 Barnaby's Fish & Chips
16 Kingfisher Fish & Chips
17 The Fourteas 1940s Tea Room
18 Bensons Restaurant & Tea Rooms

Other

19 Library (Internet)
20 Mailboxes Etc (Bag Storage)
21 Launderette (2)
22 Swan Fountain (Town Walks)
23 City Bus Tours
24 Boat Rental (2)
25 River Cruises
26 Chain Ferry

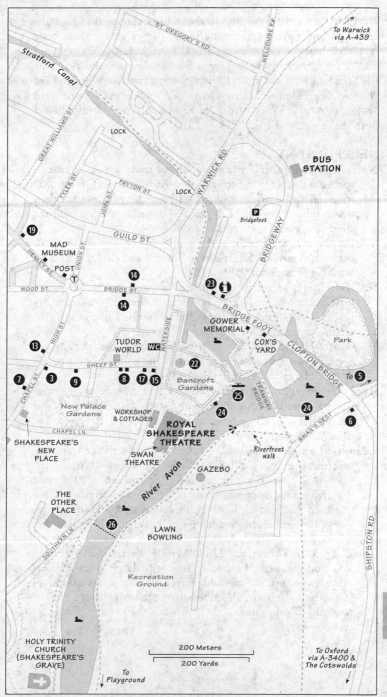

Wark (Warwick Road) signs. Go around the block—turning right and right and right—and enter the multistory garage; first hour free, £6/9 hours, £10/24 hours. The City Sightseeing bus stop and the TI are a block away. Parking is £1-3 at the park-and-ride near the Stratford Parkway train station, just off the A-46—from here you can ride a shuttle bus into town (£2 round-trip, 4/hour until 18:45, drops off at Wood Street NatWest Bank and Windsor Street near Shakespeare's Birthplace).

HELPFUL HINTS

Name That Stratford: If you're coming by train or bus, be sure to request a ticket for "Stratford-upon-Avon," not just "Stratford" (to avoid a mix-up with Stratford Langthorne, near London, which hosted the 2012 Olympics and now boasts a huge park where the games were held).

Market Days: A local crafts and food market runs along the park between the Royal Shakespeare Theater and Bridge Street on Sundays from about 9:00 to 16:00.

Festival: Every year on the weekend nearest to Shakespeare's birthday (traditionally considered to be April 23—also the day he died), Stratford celebrates. The town hosts free events, including activities for children.

Wi-Fi: You'll find free but spotty Wi-Fi hot spots throughout town. If you're in a pinch, the library has computers for public use (12 Henley Street, tel. 0300-555-8171).

Baggage Storage: Mailboxes Etc., a five-minute walk from the train station, can store your luggage (£2.50/bag, Mon-Fri 9:30-17:00, closed Sat-Sun, 12a Greenhill Street, tel. 01789/294-968).

Laundry: Laundry Quarter is on the road between the train station and the river (daily 8:00-20:00, 34 Greenhill Street, tel. 01789/417-766). The other option is **Sparklean,** a 10-minute walk from the city center, or about five minutes from the Grover Road B&Bs (daily 8:00-21:00, last wash at 20:00, full-service option sometimes available—call to check, 74 Bull Street, tel. 01789/269-075).

Taxis: Try **007 Taxis** (tel. 01789/414-007) or the taxi stand on Woodbridge, near the intersection with High Street. To arrange for a private car and driver, contact **Platinum Cars** (£250/half-day tour, also does airport transfers from Heathrow and Birmingham, tel. 01789/264-626, www.platinum-cars.co.uk).

Tours in Stratford

Stratford Town Walks

These entertaining, award-winning two-hour walks introduce you to the town and its famous playwright. Tours run daily year-round, rain or shine. Just show up at the

Swan fountain (on the waterfront, opposite Sheep Street) in front of the Royal Shakespeare Theatre and pay the guide (£6, ticket stub offers discounts to some sights and shops, daily at 11:00, Sat-Sun also at 14:00, mobile 07855-760-377, www.stratfordtownwalk.co.uk). They also run an evening ghost walk led by a professional magician (£7, Sat at 19:30, 1.5 hours, must book in advance).

City Sightseeing Bus Tours

Open-top buses constantly make the rounds, allowing visitors to hop on and hop off at all the Shakespeare sights. Given the far-flung nature of some of the Shakespeare sights, and the value of the fun commentary provided, this tour makes the town more manageable. The full 11-stop circuit takes about an hour and comes with a steady and informative commentary (£14, ticket valid 24 hours, discount with town walk ticket stub, buy tickets on bus or as you board; buses leave from the TI every 20 minutes 9:30-17:00 in high season, every 30 minutes and shorter hours off-season, some buses have live guides weekends April-Sept; tel. 01789/412-680, www.citysightseeing-stratford.com).

Shakespearean Sights

Stratford's five biggest Shakespeare sights are run by the Shakespeare Birthplace Trust (www.shakespeare.org.uk). While these sights are promoted like tacky tourist attractions—and designed to be crowd-pleasers rather than to tickle academics—they're well-run and genuinely interesting. Shakespeare's Birthplace, Shakespeare's New Place, and Hall's Croft are in town; Mary Arden's Farm and Anne Hathaway's Cottage are just outside Stratford. Each has a tranquil garden and helpful, eager docents who love to tell a story; and yet, each is quite different, so visiting all five gives you a well-rounded look at the Bard. (A sixth sight, Shakespeare's Schoolroom and Guildhall, is run by a separate organization, with a separate ticket.)

If you're here for Shakespeare sightseeing—and have time to

William Shakespeare (1564-1616)

To many, William Shakespeare is the greatest author, in any language, period. In one fell swoop, he expanded and helped define modern English—the unrefined tongue of everyday people—and granted it a beauty and legitimacy that put it on par with Latin. In the process, he gave us phrases like "one fell swoop," which we quote without knowing that no one ever said it before Shakespeare wrote it.

Shakespeare was born in Stratford-upon-Avon in 1564 to John Shakespeare and Mary Arden. Though his parents were probably illiterate, Shakespeare is thought to have attended Stratford's grammar school, finishing his education at age 14. When he was 18, he married 26-year-old Anne Hathaway (she was three months pregnant with their daughter Susanna).

The very beginnings of Shakespeare's writing career are shrouded in mystery: Historians have been unable to unearth any record of what he was up to in his early 20s. We only know that seven years after his marriage, Shakespeare was living in London as a budding poet, playwright, and actor. He soon hit the big time, writing and performing for royalty, founding (along with his troupe) the Globe Theatre (a functioning replica of which now stands along the Thames' South Bank— see page 132), and raking in enough dough to buy New Place, a swanky mansion back in his hometown. Around 1611, the rich-and-famous playwright retired from the theater and moved back to Stratford, where he died at the age of 52.

With plots that entertained both the highest and the lowest minds, Shakespeare taught the play-going public about human nature. His tool was an unrivaled linguistic mastery of English. Using borrowed plots, outrageous puns, and poetic language, Shakespeare wrote comedies (c. 1590—*Taming of the Shrew, As You Like It*), tragedies (c. 1600—*Hamlet, Othello, Macbeth, King Lear*), and fanciful combinations (c. 1610—*The Tempest*), explor-

venture to the countryside sights—you might as well buy a combo-ticket and drop into all five Shakespeare Birthplace Trust sights (described next). If your time is limited, visit only Shakespeare's Birthplace, which is the most convenient to reach (right in the town center) and offers the best historical introduction to the playwright.

Combo-Tickets: A combo-ticket that covers all five Shakespeare Birthplace Trust sights is called the **Full Story ticket**— a.k.a. the "five-house ticket"—and is sold at the TI and covered

ing the full range of human emotions and reinventing the English language.

Perhaps as important was his insight into humanity. His father was a glove-maker and wool merchant, and his mother was the daughter of a landowner from a Catholic family. Some scholars speculate that Shakespeare's parents were closet Catholics, practicing their faith during the rise of Protestantism. It is this tug-of-war between two worlds, some think, that helped enlighten Shakespeare's humanism. Think of his stock of great characters and great lines: Hamlet ("To be or not to be, that is the question"), Othello and his jealousy ("It is the green-eyed monster"), ambitious Mark Antony ("Friends, Romans, countrymen, lend me your ears"), rowdy Falstaff ("The better part of valor is discretion"), and the star-crossed lovers Romeo and Juliet ("But soft, what light through yonder window breaks"). Shakespeare probed the psychology of human beings 300 years before Freud. Even today, his characters strike a familiar chord.

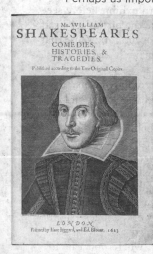

The scope of his brilliant work, his humble beginnings, and the fact that no original Shakespeare manuscripts survive raise a few scholarly eyebrows. Some have wondered if Shakespeare had help on several of his plays. After all, they reasoned, how could a journeyman actor with little education have written so many masterpieces? And he was surrounded by other great writers, such as his friend and fellow poet, Ben Jonson. Most modern scholars, though, agree that Shakespeare did indeed write the plays and sonnets attributed to him.

His contemporaries had no doubts about Shakespeare—or his legacy. As Jonson wrote in the preface to the First Folio, "He was not of an age, but for all time!"

sights (£22.50 if purchased at a covered sight, £22 at TI, £20.25 online).

Another option is the £16.95 **any-three combo-ticket,** sold only at the TI. This ticket lets you choose three of the five Shakespeare Birthplace Trust sights—for instance, the birthplace, Anne Hathaway's Cottage, and Mary Arden's Farm (buy at TI; you'll get a receipt, then show it at the first sight you visit to receive your three-sight card).

Booking online saves you 10 percent; tickets are valid for one year.

IN STRATFORD
▲▲Shakespeare's Birthplace

Touring this sight, you'll experience a modern exhibit before seeing Shakespeare's actual place of birth. While the birthplace itself is a bit underwhelming, the exhibit, helpful docents, and sense that Shakespeare's ghost still haunts these halls make it a good introduction to the Bard.

Cost and Hours: £17.50, covered by combo-tickets, daily 9:00-17:00, Nov-March 10:00-16:00, café, in town center on Henley Street, tel. 01789/204-016.

Visiting Shakespeare's Birthplace: You'll begin by touring an **exhibit** that provides an entertaining and easily digestible introduction (or, for some, review) about what made the Bard so great. The exhibit includes a timeline of his plays, movie clips of his works, and information about his upbringing in Stratford, his family life, and his career in London. Historical artifacts, including an original 1623 First Folio of Shakespeare's work, and less-significant pieces like a 19th-century visitors' book, are also on display.

You'll exit the exhibit into the garden, where you can follow signs to the **birthplace,** a half-timbered Elizabethan building where young William grew up. I find the old house a bit disappointing, as if millions of visitors have rubbed it clean of anything authentic. It was restored in the 1800s, and, while the furnishings seem tacky and modern, they're supposed to be true to 1575, when William was 11. To liven up the otherwise dead-feeling house, chat  up the well-versed, often-costumed attendants posted in many of the rooms, eager to engage with travelers and answer questions. You'll be greeted by a guide who offers an introductory talk, then set free to explore on your own. Look for the window etched with the names of decades of important visitors, from Walter Scott to actor Henry Irving.

Shakespeare's father, John—who came from humble beginnings, but bettered himself by pursuing a career in glove-making (you'll see the window where he sold them to customers on the street)—provided his family with a comfortable upper-middle-class existence. The guest bed in the parlor was a major status symbol: They must have been rich to afford such a nice bed that wasn't

STRATFORD-UPON-AVON

even used every day. This is also the house where Shakespeare and his bride, Anne Hathaway, began their married life together. Upstairs are the rooms where young Will, his siblings, and his parents slept (along with their servants). After Shakespeare's father died and William inherited the building, the thrifty playwright converted it into a pub to make a little money.

Exit into the fine **garden** where Shakespearean **actors** often perform brief scenes (they may even take requests). Pull up a bench and listen, imagining the playwright as a young boy stretching his imagination in this very place.

Shakespeare's New Place

While nothing remains of the house the Bard built when he made it big (it was demolished in the 18th century), its atmospheric grounds are a tranquil spot to soak up some history. Modern sculptures and traditional gardens now adorn the grounds of the mansion Shakespeare called home for nearly 20 years. At the least, the sight has nostalgic value—especially for fans who can picture him writing *The Tempest* on this very spot. Next door, Nash's House (which belonged to Shakespeare's granddaughter and her husband) hosts exhibits, including a large-scale model of Shakespeare's house, domestic artifacts, and displays of period clothing.

Cost and Hours: £12.50, covered by combo-tickets, daily 9:00-17:00, Nov-March 10:00-16:00, 22 Chapel Street, tel. 01789/338-536.

Hall's Croft

This former home of Shakespeare's eldest daughter, Susanna, is in Stratford town center. A fine old Jacobean house, it's the fanciest of the group. Since she married a doctor, the exhibits here are focused on 17th-century medicine. If you have time to spare and one of the combo-tickets, it's worth a quick pop-in. To make the exhibits interesting, ask the docent for the 15- to 20-minute introduction, or one of the large laminated self-guides, both of which help bring the plague—and some of the bizarre remedies of the time—to life.

Cost and Hours: £8.50, covered by combo-tickets, daily 10:00-17:00, Nov-March 11:00-16:00, on-site tearoom, between Church Street and the river on Old Town Street, tel. 01789/338-533.

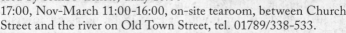

STRATFORD-UPON-AVON

Shakespearean Plays 101

Shakespeare's 38 plays span (and often intertwine) three genres: comedy, history, and tragedy. Brush up some of the Bard's greatest hits before enjoying a performance in Stratford.

Comedy

As You Like It: Two brothers, a banished duke, noblemen, and a duke's daughter (Rosalind) fight and fall in love in the Forest of Arden, contemplating life, love, and death.

Much Ado About Nothing: Soldier Claudio and a nobleman's daughter, Hero, fall in love and play matchmakers to their unsuspecting friends. Trickery, slander, and heartbreak are overcome in an ultimately happy ending.

A Midsummer Night's Dream: Four Athenian lovers, two eloping, follow each other into the woods, where fairy King Oberon enchants them with love potion. A mistaken identity leaves Lysander and Demetrius both pining after Helena, and Hermia without a groom.

The Tempest: Prospero, Duke of Milan, is overthrown by his brother and Alonso (the King of Naples) and dwells on an enchanted island with daughter Miranda. When his old enemies wash ashore, Prospero enlists island spirits to seek his revenge—and Miranda falls in love with Alonso's son Ferdinand.

History

The Henriad: A series of four plays chronicles the demise of England's King Richard II, the rule of successor King Henry IV, and his relationship with rebellious son Prince Harry (eventually King Henry V). War across England and France forms the backdrop for

Shakespeare's Grave

To see his final resting place, head to the riverside Holy Trinity Church. Shakespeare was a rector for this church when he died. While the church is surrounded by an evocative graveyard, the Bard is entombed in a place of honor, right in front of the altar inside. The church marks the ninth-century birthplace of the town, which was once a religious settlement.

Cost and Hours: £3 donation, Mon-Sat 8:30-17:40, Sun 12:30-16:40, Oct-March until at least 15:40; no access to grave 12:45-13:30; 10-minute walk past the theater—see its grace-

Shakespeare's exploration of honor, nationalism, and power.

Tragedy

Romeo and Juliet: Lovers from rival families seek to marry, but are torn apart by their families. When Juliet fakes her death to avoid an arranged marriage, misunderstanding breeds heartbreak.

Macbeth: Three witches prophesize Macbeth's ascension from nobility to the throne of Scotland, leading Macbeth, aided by his ambitious wife, to embark on a violent mission to become king. Plagued by paranoia and hallucinations, he commits heinous crimes to gain—and maintain—power.

Othello: General Othello promotes Cassio to lieutenant over officer Iago. After Othello elopes with senator Brabantio's daughter Desdemona, a bitter Iago seeks revenge, manipulating the couple and Cassio by pitting one against another.

Hamlet: Haunted by his father's ghost, Prince Hamlet plots to kill his father's murderer, King Claudius. But when Hamlet inadvertently causes his lover Ophelia's death, her brother Laertes vows to kill Hamlet, with Claudius' help. A climactic duel between Laertes and Hamlet leads to a bloodbath.

King Lear: King Lear banishes daughter Cordelia to France, while daughters Regan and Goneril secretly plot his death. Lear's ally the Earl of Gloucester, at odds with his own sons, warns Lear of the vengeful plot, and Lear drifts into madness. Both men succumb to the political chaos created by their families' greed and betrayal.

ful spire as you gaze down the river, tel. 01789/266-316, www.stratford-upon-avon.org.

Shakespeare's Schoolroom and Guildhall

From the 13th to mid-16th centuries, Stratford citizens relied on guilds (which functioned like trade associations) to build infrastructure (bridges and schools), provide social services (assistance for widows and the elderly), and foster good business and social connections. This sight includes a guild headquarters from 1420, along with a chapel (with medieval wall paintings), almshouses, and the highlight—Shakespeare's classroom, where you'll learn what it was like to be a student in the 1570s as you test a quill pen, play Tudor games, and learn some Latin.

Cost and Hours: £8, save 10 percent by booking online in advance, daily 10:00-17:00, Church Street, tel. 01789/203-170, www.shakespearesschoolroom.org.

JUST OUTSIDE STRATFORD

To reach either of these sights, it's best to drive or take the hop-on, hop-off bus tour (see "Tours in Stratford," earlier)—unless you're staying at one of the Grove Road B&Bs, which are an easy 20-minute walk from Anne Hathaway's Cottage. Both sights are well-signposted (with brown signs) from the major streets and ring roads around Stratford. If driving between the sights, ask for directions at the sight you're leaving.

▲▲Mary Arden's Farm

Along with Shakespeare's Birthplace, this is my favorite of the Shakespearean sights. Famous as the girlhood home of William's mom, this homestead is in Wilmcote (about three miles from Stratford). Built around two historic farmhouses, it's an open-air folk museum depicting 16th-century farm life...which happens to have ties to Shakespeare. The Bard is basically an afterthought here.

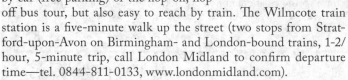

Cost and Hours: £15, also covered by combo-tickets, daily 10:00-17:00, everyone's shooed out at 17:30, closed Nov-mid-March, on-site café and picnic tables, tel. 01789/338-535.

Getting There: It's most convenient by car (free parking) or the hop-on, hop-off bus tour, but also easy to reach by train. The Wilmcote train station is a five-minute walk up the street (two stops from Stratford-upon-Avon on Birmingham- and London-bound trains, 1-2/hour, 5-minute trip, call London Midland to confirm departure time—tel. 0844-811-0133, www.londonmidland.com).

Visiting Mary Arden's Farm: The museum hosts many special **events,** including the falconry show described later. The day's events are listed on a chalkboard by the entry, or you can call ahead to find out what's on. There are always plenty of activities to engage kids: It's an active, hands-on place. Save some time for a walk: There are 23 acres of bucolic trails, orchards, and meadows to explore.

Pick up a map (and handful of organic animal feed) at the entrance and wander the grounds and buildings. Throughout the complex, you'll see period interpreters in Tudor costumes. They'll likely be going through the day's chores as people back then would have done—activities such as milking the sheep and cutting wood to do repairs on the house. They're there to answer questions and provide fun, gossipy insight into what life was like at the time.

Look out for typical farmyard animals including goats, woolly pigs, and friendly donkeys.

The first building, **Palmer's farm** (mistaken for Mary Arden's home for hundreds of years, and correctly identified in 2000), is furnished as it would have been in Shakespeare's day. Step into the kitchen to see food being prepared over an open fire—at 13:00 each day the "servants" (employees) sit down in the adjacent dining room for a traditional dinner.

Mary Arden actually lived in the neighboring **farmhouse,** covered in brick facade and seemingly less impressive. The house is filled with kid-oriented activities, including period dress-up clothes, board games from Shakespeare's day, and a Tudor alphabet so kids can write their names in fancy lettering.

Of the many events here, the most enjoyable is the **falconry demonstration,** with lots of mean-footed birds (daily, usually at 11:00, 12:30, 14:30, and 16:00). Chat with the falconers about their methods for earning the birds' trust. The birds' hunger sets them to flight (a round-trip earns the bird a bit of food; the birds fly when hungry—but don't have the energy if they're *too* hungry). Like Katherine, the wife described as "my falcon" in *The Taming of the Shrew*, these birds are tamed and trained with food as a reward. If things are slow, ask if you can feed one.

▲Anne Hathaway's Cottage

Located 1.5 miles out of Stratford (in Shottery), this home is a 12-room farmhouse where the Bard's wife grew up. William courted Anne here—she was 26, he was only 18—and his tactics proved successful. (Maybe a little too much, as she was several months pregnant at their wedding.) Their 34-year marriage produced two more children, and lasted until his death in 1616 at age

52. The Hathaway family lived here for 400 years, until 1911, and much of the family's 92-acre farm remains part of the sight.

Cost and Hours: £12.50, also covered by combo-tickets, daily 9:00-17:00, Nov-mid-March 10:00-16:00, on-site tearoom, tel. 01789/338-532.

Stratford Thanks America

Residents of Stratford are thankful for the many contributions Americans have made to their city and its heritage. Along with pumping up the economy day in and day out with tourist visits, Americans paid for half the rebuilding of the Royal Shakespeare Theatre after it burned down in 1926. The Swan Theatre renovation was funded entirely by American aid. Harvard University inherited—you guessed it—the Harvard House, and it maintains the house today. London's much-loved theater, Shakespeare's Globe, was the dream (and gift) of an American. And there's even an odd but prominent "American Fountain" overlooking Stratford's market square on Rother Street, which was given in 1887 to celebrate the Golden Jubilee of the rule of Queen Victoria.

Getting There: It's a 30-minute walk from central Stratford (20 minutes from the Grove Road B&Bs), a stop on the hop-on, hop-off tour bus, or a quick taxi ride from downtown Stratford (around £7). Drivers will find it well-signposted entering Stratford from any direction, with easy cheap parking.

Visiting Anne Hathaway's Cottage: After buying your ticket, turn right and head down through the garden to the thatched-roof **cottage,** which looks cute enough to eat. The house offers an intimate peek at life in Shakespeare's day. In some ways, it feels even more authentic than his birthplace, and it's fun to imagine the writer of some of the world's greatest romances wooing his favorite girl right here during his formative years. Docents provide meaning and answer questions; while most tourists just stampede through, you'll have a more informative visit if you pause to listen to their introduction in the parlor and commentary throughout the house. (If the place shakes, a tourist has thunked his or her head on the low beams.)

Maybe even more interesting than the cottage are the **gardens,** which have several parts (including a prizewinning "traditional cottage garden"). Follow the signs to the "Woodland Walk" (look for the music-note willow sculpture on your way), along with a fun sculpture garden littered with modern interpretations of Shakespearean characters (such as Falstaff's mead gut, and a great photo-op statue of the British Isles sliced out of steel). From April through June, the gardens are at their best, with birds chirping, bulbs in bloom, and a large sweet-pea display. You'll also find a music trail, a butterfly trail, and—likely—rotating exhibits, generally on a gardening theme.

THE ROYAL SHAKESPEARE COMPANY

The Royal Shakespeare Company (RSC), undoubtedly the best Shakespeare company on earth, performs year-round in Stratford and in London. Seeing a play here in the Bard's birthplace is a must for Shakespeare fans, and a memorable experience for anybody. Between its excellent acting and remarkable staging, the RSC makes Shakespeare as accessible and enjoyable as it gets.

The RSC makes it easy to take in a play, thanks to their very user-friendly website, painless ticket-booking system, and chock-a-block schedule that fills the summer with mostly big-name Shakespeare plays (plus a few more obscure titles to please the die-hard aficionados). Except in January and February, there's almost always something playing.

The RSC is enjoying renewed popularity after the update of its Royal Shakespeare Theatre. Even if you're not seeing a play, exploring this cleverly designed theater building is well worth your time. The smaller attached Swan Theatre hosts plays on a more intimate scale, with only about 400 seats.

▲▲▲Seeing a Play

Performances take place most days (Mon-Sat generally at 19:15 at the Royal Shakespeare Theatre or 19:30 at the Swan, matinees around 13:15 at the RST or 13:30 at the Swan, sporadic Sun shows). Shows generally last three hours or more, with one intermission; for an evening show, don't count on getting back to your B&B much before 23:00. There's no strict dress code—and people dress casually (nice jeans and short-sleeve shirts are fine)—but shorts are discouraged. You can buy a program for £4. If you're feeling bold, buy a £10 standing ticket and then slip into an open seat as the lights dim—if nothing is available during the play's first half, something might open up after intermission.

Getting Tickets: Tickets range from £10 (standing) to £75, with most around £45. Saturday-evening shows—the most popular—are the most expensive. You can book tickets as you like it: online (www.rsc.org.uk), by phone (tel. 01789/403-493), or in person at the box office (Mon-Sat 10:00-20:00, Sun until 17:00). Pay by credit card, get a confirmation number, then pick up your tickets at the theater 30 minutes before "curtain up." Because it's so easy to get tickets online or by phone, it makes absolutely no sense to pay extra to book tickets through any other source.

Tickets go on sale months in advance. Saturdays and very famous plays (such as *Romeo and Juliet* or *Hamlet*)—or any play with a well-known actor—sell out the fastest; the earlier in the week the performance is, the longer it takes to sell out (Thursdays sell out faster than Mondays, for example). Before your trip, check the schedule on their website, and consider buying tickets if something

The Look of Stratford

There's much more to Stratford than Shakespeare sights. Take time to appreciate the look of the town itself. While the main street goes back to Roman times, the key date for the city was 1196, when the king gave the town "market privileges." Stratford was shaped by its marketplace years. The market's many "departments" were located on logically named streets, whose names still remain: Sheep Street, Corn Street, and so on. Today's street plan—and even the 57' 9" width of the lots—survives from the 12th century. (Some of the modern storefronts in the town center are still that exact width.)

Starting in about 1600, three great fires gutted the town, leaving very few buildings older than that era. After those fires, tinderbox thatched roofs were prohibited—the Old Thatch Tavern on Greenhill Street is the only remaining thatched roof in town, predating the law and grandfathered in.

The town's main drag, Bridge Street, is the oldest street in town, but looks the youngest. It was built in the Regency style—a result of a rough little middle row of wattle-and-daub houses being torn down in the 1820s to double the street's width. Today's Bridge Street buildings retain that early 19th-century style.

Throughout Stratford, you'll see striking black-and-white half-timbered buildings, as well as half-timbered structures that were partially plastered over and covered up in the 19th century. During Victorian times, the half-timbered style was considered low-class, but in the 20th century—just as tourists came, preferring ye olde style—timbers came back into vogue, and the plaster was removed on many old buildings. But any black and white you see is likely to be modern paint. The original coloring was "biscuit yellow" and brown.

strikes your fancy. But demand is difficult to predict, and some tickets do go unsold. On a past visit, on a sunny Friday in June, the riverbank was crawling with tourists. I stepped into the RSC on a lark to see if they had any tickets. An hour later, I was watching King Lear lose his marbles.

Even if there aren't any seats available, you may be able to buy a returned ticket on the same day of an otherwise sold-out show. Also, the few standing-room tickets in the main theater are sold only on the day of the show. While you can check at the box office anytime during the day, it's best to go either when it opens at 10:00 (daily) or between 17:30 and 18:00 (Mon-Sat). Be prepared to wait.

Visiting the Theaters

▲▲The Royal Shakespeare Theatre

The RSC's main venue was updated head to toe in 2011, with both a respect for tradition and a sensitivity to the needs of contemporary theatergoers. You need to take a guided tour (explained later) to see the backstage areas, but you're welcome to wander the theater's public areas any time the building is open. Interesting tidbits of theater history and easy-to-miss special exhibits make this one of Stratford's most fascinating sights. If you're seeing a play here, come early to poke around the building. Even if you're not, step inside and explore.

Cost and Hours: Free entry, Mon-Sat 10:00-23:00, Sun until 17:00.

Guided Tours: Well-informed RSC volunteers lead entertaining, one-hour building tours. Some cover the main theater while others take you into behind the scenes spaces, such as the space-age control room (try for a £8.50 behind-the-scenes tour, but if those aren't running, consider a £6.50 front-of-the-house tour—which skips the backstage areas; tour schedule varies by

day, depending on performances, but there's often one at 9:15—call, check online, or go to box office to confirm schedule; best to book ahead, tel. 01789/403-493, www.rsc.org.uk/theatretours).

Background: The flagship theater of the RSC has an interesting past. The original Victorian-style theater was built in 1879 to honor the Bard, but it burned down in 1926. The big Art Deco-style building you see today was erected in 1932 and outfitted with a stodgy Edwardian "picture frame"-style stage, even though a more dynamic "thrust"-style stage—better for engaging the audience—was the actors' choice. (It would also have been closer in design to Shakespeare's original Globe stage, which jutted into the crowd.)

The latest renovation addressed this ill-conceived design, adding an updated thrust-style stage. They've left the shell of the 1930s theater, but given it an unconventional deconstructed-industrial style, with the seats stacked at an extreme vertical pitch. Though smaller, the redesigned theater can seat about the same size audience as before (1,048 seats), and now there's not a bad seat in the house—no matter what, you're no more than 50 feet from the stage (the cheapest "gallery" seats look down right onto Othello's bald spot). Productions are staged to play to all of the seats throughout the show. Those sitting up high appreciate different details from those at stage level, and vice versa.

Visiting the Theater: From the main lobby and box office/gift shop area, there's plenty to see. First head left. In the circular

atrium between the brick wall of the modern theater and fragments of the previous theater, notice the ratty old floorboards. These were pried up from the 1932 stage and laid down here—so as you wait for your play, you're treading on theater history. Upstairs on level 2, find the **Paccar Room,** with generally excellent temporary exhibits assembled from the RSC's substantial collection of historic costumes, props, manuscripts, and other theater memorabilia. Continue upstairs to level 3 to the Rooftop Restaurant (described later). High on the partition that runs through the restaurant, facing the brick theater wall, notice the four **chairs** affixed to the wall. These are original seats from the earlier theater, situated where the back row used to be (90 feet from the stage)—illustrating how much more audience-friendly the new design is.

Back downstairs, pass through the box office/gift shop area to find the **Swan Gallery**—an old, Gothic-style Victorian space that survives from the original 1879 Memorial Theatre and hosts rotating exhibitions.

Back outside, across the street from the theater, notice the building with the steep gable and huge door (marked *CFE 1887*). This was built as a **workshop** for building sets, which could be moved in large pieces to the main theater. To this day, all the sets, costumes, and props are made here in Stratford. The row of **cottages** to the right is housing for actors. The RSC's reputation exerts enough pull to attract serious actors from all over the UK and beyond, who live here for the entire season. The RSC uses a repertory company approach, where the same actors appear in multiple shows concurrently. Today's Lady Macbeth may be tomorrow's Rosalind.

Tower View: For a God's-eye view of all of Shakespeare's houses, ride the elevator to the top of the RSC's tower (£2.50, buy ticket at box office, closes 30 minutes before the theater). Aside from a few sparse exhibits, the main attraction here is the 360-degree view over the theater building, the Avon, and the lanes of Stratford.

The Food's the Thing: The main theater has a casual **$ café** with a terrace overlooking the river (sandwiches, daily 10:00-21:00), as well as the fancier **$$ Rooftop Restaurant**, which counts the Queen as a patron (Mon-Sat 11:30 until late, Sun 10:30-18:15, dinner reservations smart, tel. 01789/403-449, http://www.rsc.org.uk/rooftop).

The Swan Theatre

Adjacent to the RSC Theatre is the smaller (about 400 seats), Elizabethan-style Swan Theatre, named not for the birds that fill the park out front, but for the Bard's nickname—the "sweet swan of Avon." This galleried playhouse opened in 1986, thanks to an extremely generous donation from an American theater lover. It has a vertical layout and a thrust stage similar to the RSC Theatre, but its wood trim and railings give it a cozier, more traditional feel. The Swan is used for lesser-known Shakespeare plays and alternative works. Occasionally, the lowest level of seats is removed to accommodate "groundling" (standing-only) tickets, much like at the Globe Theatre in London.

The Other Place (Former Courtyard Theatre)

A two-minute walk down Southern Lane from the original Royal Shakespeare Theatre, the Courtyard Theatre (affectionately called the "rusty shed" by locals) was built as a replacement venue while the RSC was being renovated. Now called The Other Place, it serves as a space for rehearsal, research, and development, and educates theater buffs about play production through its "From Page to Stage" tours, where you'll learn about everything from rehearsals to costumes to props. The venue also hosts festivals of new work, a bar/café, plus monthly music nights, spoken-word nights, and family activities.

Cost and Hours: Music nights-free, tours-£8.50—book in advance online or by phone, café open Mon-Sat 9:30-21:00 or later, closed Sun, tel. 01789-403-493, www.rsc.org.uk/theatretours.

Other Stratford Sights

Avon Riverfront

The River Avon is a playground of swans and canal boats. The swans have been the mascots of Stratford since 1623, when, seven years after the Bard's death, Ben Jonson's poem in the First Folio dubbed him "the sweet swan of Avon."

For a nice **riverfront walk,** consider crossing over the Tramway Footbridge and following the trail to the right (west) along the south bank of the Avon. From here, you'll get a great view of the Royal Shakespeare Theater across the river. Continuing down the path, you'll pass the local lawn bowling club (guest players welcome, £4, Mon 18:00-20:00, Tue and Thu 14:00-16:00) and Lucy's Mill Weir, an area popular with fishers and kayakers, where you can turn around. On the way back, cross the river by chain ferry (described next) and return to the town center via the north bank for a full loop.

In the water you'll see colorful **canal boats.** These boats saw their workhorse days during the short window of time between the start of the Industrial Revolution and the establishment of the railways. Today they're mostly pleasure boats. The boats are long and narrow, so two can pass in the slim canals. There are 2,000 miles of canals in England's Midlands, built to connect centers of industry with seaports and provide vital transportation during the early days of the Industrial Revolution. Stratford was as far inland as you could sail on natural rivers from Bristol; it was the terminus of the man-made Birmingham Canal, built in 1816. Even today you can motor your canal boat all the way to London from here. Along the embankment, look for the signs indicating how many hours it'll take—and how many locks you'll traverse—to go by boat to various English cities.

For a little bit of mellow river action, rent a **rowboat** (£6/hour per person) or, for more of a challenge, pole yourself around on a Cambridge-style **punt** (the  canal is only 4-5 feet deep; same price as the rowboat and more memorable/embarrassing if you do the punting—don't pay £10 for a waterman to do the punting for you). You can rent boats at the Swan's Nest Boathouse across the Tramway Footbridge; another rental station, along the river, next to the theater, has higher prices but is more conveniently located.

You can also try a sleepy 40-minute **river cruise** (£6, includes commentary, Avon Boating, board boat in Bancroft Gardens near the RSC theater, tel. 01789/267-073, www.avon-boating.co.uk), or jump on the oldest surviving **chain ferry** (c. 1937) in Britain (£0.50), which shuttles people across the river just beyond the theater.

The old **Cox's Yard,** a riverside timber yard until the 1990s, is a rare physical remnant of the days when Stratford was an industrial port. Today, Cox's has been  taken over by a pricey, sprawling restaurant complex, with a café, lots of outdoor seating, and occasional live music. Upstairs is the Attic Theatre, which puts on fringe theater acts (www.treadtheboardstheatre.co.uk).

In the riverfront park, roughly between Cox's Yard and the TI, the **Gower Memorial** honors the Bard and his creations. Named for Lord Ronald Gower, the man who paid for and sculpted the memorial, this 1888 work shows Shakespeare up top ringed by four of his most indelible creations, each representing a human pursuit: Hamlet (philosophy), Lady Macbeth (tragedy), Falstaff (comedy), and Prince Hal (history). Originally located next to the theater, it was moved here after the 1932 fire.

▲MAD Museum

A refreshing change of pace in Bard-bonkers Stratford, this museum's name stands for "Mechanical Art and Design." It celebrates machines as art, showcasing a changing collection of skillfully constructed robots, gizmos, and Rube-Goldberg machines that spring to entertaining life with the push of a button. Engaging for kids, riveting for engineers, and enjoyable to anybody, it's pricey but conveniently located near Shakespeare's Birthplace.

Cost and Hours: £7.80, Mon-Fri 10:00-17:00, Sat-Sun until 17:30, 45 Hanley Street, tel. 01789/269-356, www.themadmuseum. co.uk.

Tudor World at the Falstaff Experience

This attraction is tacky, gimmicky, and more about entertainment than education. (And, while it's named for a Shakespeare character, the exhibit isn't about the Bard.) Filling Shrieve's House Barn with mostly kid-oriented exhibits (mannequins and descriptions, but few real artifacts), it sweeps through Tudor history from the plague to Henry VIII's privy chamber to a replica 16th-century tavern. If you're into ghost-spotting, their nightly ghost tours may be your best shot.

Cost and Hours: Museum-£6, daily 10:30-17:30; ghost tours-£7.50, daily at 18:00, additional tours possible Fri-Sat; 40 Sheep Street, tel. 01789/298-070, www.tudorworld.com.

Sleeping in Stratford

If you want to spend the night after you catch a show, options abound. Ye olde timbered hotels are scattered through the city center. Most B&Bs are a short walk away on the fringes of town, right on the busy ring roads that route traffic away from the center. (The recommended places below generally have double-paned windows for rooms in the front, but still get some traffic noise.)

In general, the weekend on or near Shakespeare's birthday (April 23) is particularly tight, but Fridays and Saturdays are busy throughout the season. This town is so reliant upon the theater for its business that some B&Bs have insurance covering their loss if the Royal Shakespeare Company ever stops performing in Stratford.

ON GROVE ROAD

These accommodations are at the edge of town on busy Grove Road, across from a grassy square, and come with free parking when booked in advance. From here, it's about a 10-minute walk either to the town center or to the train station (opposite directions).

$$ Adelphi Guest House is run by Shakespeare buffs Sue and Simon, who pride themselves on providing a warm welcome, homemade gingerbread, and original art in every room (RS%, 39 Grove Road, tel. 01789/204-469, www.adelphi-guesthouse.com, info@adelphi-guesthouse.com).

$$ Ambleside Guest House is run with quiet efficiency and attentiveness by owners Peter and Ruth. Each of the six rooms has been completely renovated, including the small but tidy bathrooms. The place has a homey, airy feel, with no B&B clutter (ground-floor rooms, family rooms, 41 Grove Road, tel. 01789/297-239, www.amblesideguesthouse.com, peter@amblesideguesthouse.com—include your phone number in your request, since they like to call you back to confirm with a personal touch).

$ Woodstock Guest House is a friendly, frilly, family-run, and flowery place with five comfortable rooms (RS%, ground-floor room, 30 Grove Road, tel. 01789/299-881, www.woodstock-house.co.uk, enquiries@woodstock-house.co.uk, owners Denis and bubbly Jackie).

$ Salamander Guest House, run by gregarious Frenchman Pascal and his wife, Anna, rents eight simple rooms that are a bit cheaper than their neighbors (family room, 40 Grove Road, tel. 01789/205-728, www.salamanderguesthouse.co.uk, p.delin@btinternet.com).

ELSEWHERE IN STRATFORD

$$ Mercure Shakespeare Hotel, centrally located in a black-and-white building just up the street from Shakespeare's New Place, has 78 business-class rooms, each one named for a Shakespearean play or character. Some of the rooms are old-style Elizabethan higgledy-piggledy (with modern finishes), while others are contemporary style—note your preference when you reserve (breakfast extra, pay parking, Chapel Street, tel. 02477/092-802, www.mercure.com, h6630@accor.com).

$$ The Emsley Guest House, with Victorian style and modern comfort, holds five bright rooms named after different counties in England—plus a cozy guest library (family rooms, no kids under 5, free off-street parking, 5 minutes from train station at 4 Arden Street, tel. 01789/299-557, www.theemsley.co.uk, stay@theemsley.co.uk, Liz and Chris).

¢ **Hostel:** Family-friendly **Hemmingford House** has 32 rooms, half of them en suite. It's a 10-minute bus ride from town (private rooms, family rooms, breakfast extra, take bus #X18 or #18 two miles to Alveston, tel. 01789/297-093, www.yha.org.uk/hostel/stratford upon avon, stratford@yha.org.uk).

Eating in Stratford

RESTAURANTS

Stratford's numerous restaurants vie for your pretheater business, with special hours and meal deals. (Most offer light two- and three-course menus before 19:00.) You'll find many hardworking places on Sheep Street and Waterside. Unfortunately, post-theater dinners are more challenging, as most places close early.

$$$ Le Bistro Pierre, across the river near the boating station, is a French eatery that's been impressing Stratford residents. They have indoor or outdoor seating and slow service (Mon-Fri 12:00-15:00 & 17:00-22:30, Sat until 16:00 & 23:00, Sun 12:30-16:30 & 18:00-22:00, Swan's Nest, Bridgefoot, tel. 01789/264-804). The pub next door, **Bear Free House,** is owned by the same people and shares the same kitchen, but offers a different menu.

$$$ Edward Moon is an upscale English brasserie serving signature dishes like steak-and-ale pies and roasted lamb shank in a setting reminiscent of *Casablanca* (Mon-Fri 12:00-14:30 & 17:00-21:30, Sat until 15:00 & 20:00, Sun until 15:00 & 21:00, 9 Chapel Street, tel. 01789/267-069, www.edwardmoon.com).

$$$ Sheep Street Eateries: The next three places, part of the same chain, line up along Sheep Street, offering trendy ambience and modern English cuisine at relatively high prices (all three have good-value pre-theater menus before 19:00): **Lambs** is intimate and serves meat, fish, and veggie dishes with panache. The upstairs feels dressy, under low half-timbered beams (Mon-Fri 17:00-21:30, Sat from 16:30, Sun 18:00-21:00, lunch served Tue-Sun, 12 Sheep Street, tel. 01789/292-554). **The Opposition,** next door, has a less formal "bistro" ambience (Mon-Thu 12:00-14:00 & 17:00-21:00, Fri-Sat until 22:30, closed Sun, tel. 01789/269-980; book in advance for post-theater dinner here Fri-Sat). **The Vintner,** just up the street, has the best reputation and feels even trendier than its

426 Rick Steves Great Britain

siblings, but still with old style. They're known for their burgers (daily 9:30-22:00, Sun until 21:30, 4 Sheep Street, tel. 01789/297-259).

Indian: $$ Avon Spice has a good reputation and good prices (daily 17:30-23:30, 7 Greenhill Street, tel. 01789/267-067).

PUBS

$$ The Old Thatch Tavern is, according to natives, the best place in town for beer, serving up London-based Fuller's brews. The atmosphere is cozy, and the food is a cut above what you'll get in other pubs; enjoy it either in the bar, in the tight, candlelit restaurant, or out on the quiet patio (food served daily 12:00-21:00, on Greenhill Street overlooking the market square, tel. 01789/295-216).

$$ The Windmill Inn serves decent, modestly priced fare in a 17th-century inn. It combines old and new styles, and—since it's a few steps beyond the heart of the tourist zone—actually attracts some locals as well. Order drinks and food at the bar, settle into a comfy chair or head out to the half-timbered courtyard, and wait for your meal (food served daily 11:00-21:00, Church Street, tel. 01789/297-687).

$$ The Garrick Inn bills itself as the oldest pub in town, and comes with a cozy, dimly lit restaurant vibe. Choose between the pub or table-service section; either way, you'll dine on bland, pricey pub grub (food served daily 11:00-23:00, 25 High Street, tel. 01789/292-186).

PICNICS

With its sprawling and inviting riverfront park, Stratford is a particularly pleasant place to picnic. Choose a bench and enjoy views of the river and vacation houseboats while munching your meal. It's a fine way to spend a midsummer night's eve. For groceries or prepared foods, find **Marks & Spencer** on Bridge Street (Mon-Sat 8:00-18:00, Sun 10:30-16:30, small coffee-and-sandwiches café upstairs, tel. 01789/292-430). Across the street, **Sainsbury's Local** stays open later than other supermarkets (daily 7:00-22:00).

For fish-and-chips, you have a couple of options: **$ Barnaby's** is a greasy fast-food joint near the waterfront—but convenient if you want takeout for the riverside park just across the street (daily 11:00-19:30, at Sheep Street and Waterside). For better food (but a less convenient location—closer to my recommended B&Bs than to the park), queue up with the locals at **$ Kingfisher,** then ask for the freshly battered haddock (Mon-Sat 11:30-13:45 & 17:00-22:00, closed Sun, a long block up at 13 Ely Street, tel. 01789/292-513).

TEAROOMS

$$ The FourTeas 1940s Tea Room transports diners to another era, with period details ranging from the servers' housedresses to the ration-card menu to the Glenn Miller-era soundtrack. There's even an air-raid shelter beyond the terrace garden. Don't be fooled by the theme: This place eludes kitsch with high-quality pastry, hearty sandwiches, all-day breakfast, and locally sourced ingredients (Mon-Sat 9:30-17:30, Sun 11:00-16:30, 24 Sheep Street, tel. 01789/293-908).

$$ Bensons Restaurant and Tea Rooms, across the street from Shakespeare's Birthplace, has indoor seating, outdoor tables right on the main pedestrian mall, and friendly service (teas available all day, daily 9:00-17:30, 40 Henley Street, tel. 01789/415-572). The same people run Bensons House of Tea & Gift Shop, just down the street (at #33).

Stratford Connections

Remember: When buying tickets or checking schedules, ask for "Stratford-upon-Avon," not just "Stratford." Notice that a single train (running about every 2 hours) connects most of these destinations: Warwick, Leamington Spa (change for Coventry or Oxford), then London.

From Stratford-upon-Avon by Train to: London (3/day direct, more with transfers, 2-2.5 hours, to Marylebone Station), **Moreton-in-Marsh** (almost hourly, 3 hours, 2-3 transfers, slow and expensive, better by bus). Train info: tel. 0345-748-4950, www.nationalrail.co.uk.

By Bus to: Cotswolds towns (bus #1 or #2, Mon-Sat 8/day, none on Sun, 35 minutes to **Chipping Campden,** 1.5 hours to **Moreton-in-Marsh;** some also stop at Broadway, Broad Campden, Blockley, and/or Bourton-on-the-Hill; Johnsons Coaches, tel. 01564/797-070, www.johnsonscoaches.co.uk). Most intercity buses stop on Stratford's Bridge Street (a block up from the TI). For bus info that covers all the region's companies, call Traveline at tel. 0871-200-2233 (www.travelinemidlands.co.uk).

By Car: Driving is easy and distances are short: **Chipping Campden** (12 miles), **Stow-on-the-Wold** (22 miles).

ROUTE TIPS FOR DRIVERS

These tips assume you're heading north from Stratford.

Leaving the Bridgefoot garage in downtown Stratford, circle to the right around the same block, but stay on "the Wark" (Warwick Road, A-439).

To the Northeast: Heading toward York, Durham, and other destinations northeast of Stratford, take the Wark to the A-46. Just past Coventry, it merges into the M-69 toward Leicester, which intersects with a major north-south route, the M-1.

To the Northwest: When heading toward Ironbridge Gorge, North Wales, Liverpool, or the Lake District, take A-46 toward Warwick then exit onto the M-40 north toward Birmingham. You want to avoid driving through Birmingham. After Warwick, take the M-42 to the west; the sign will read *The Southwest (M5), Birmingham (S & W), Redditch.* When the M-42 ends at the M-5, follow M-5 north, the sign will read *The Northwest, B'ham, Stour-bridge.*

After Birmingham, for Ironbridge Gorge, take the M-54 toward Telford. For specifics on getting to Ironbridge Gorge, see page 440. For other destinations, take the M-6.

IRONBRIDGE GORGE

The Industrial Revolution was born in the Severn River Valley. In its glory days, this valley—blessed with abundant deposits of iron ore and coal, and a river for transport—gave the world its first iron wheels, steam-powered locomotive, and cast-iron bridge (begun in 1779). Other industries flourished here, too—from mass-produced clay pipes to delicate porcelain and colorful decorative tiles. The museums in Ironbridge Gorge, which capture the flavor of the Victorian Age, take you back into the days when Britain was racing into the modern era, and pulling the rest of the West with her.

Near the end of the 20th century, the valley went through a second transformation: Photos taken just 30 years ago show an industrial wasteland. Today the Severn River Valley is lush and lined with walks and parkland. Even its bricks, while still smoke-stained, seem warmer and more inviting. Those who come for its "industrial" sights are pleasantly surprised to find an extremely charming corner of England—with wooded hillsides and tidy, time-warp brick villages.

PLANNING YOUR TIME

Without a car, Ironbridge Gorge isn't worth the headache for most (though I've included some tips at the end of this chapter). Drivers can slip it in between the Cotswolds/Stratford and points north (such as the Lake District or North Wales). Speed demons zip in for a midday tour of the Blists Hill Victorian Town, look at the famous Iron Bridge and quaint Industrial Age town that sprawls around it, and head out. For an overnight visit, arrive in the early evening to browse the town, see the bridge, and walk along the river. Spend the morning touring the Blists Hill Victorian Town, have lunch there, and head to your next destination.

Those with more time (or a healthy interest in the Industrial Revolution), can spend two nights and a leisurely day: 9:30-Iron Bridge and town stroll; 10:30-Museum of the Gorge; 11:30-Coalbrookdale Museum of Iron; 14:30-Blists Hill Victorian Town; then dinner at one of my recommended restaurants.

Orientation to Ironbridge Gorge

The village of Ironbridge is just a few blocks gathered around the Iron Bridge, which spans the peaceful, tree-lined River Severn.

While the smoke-belching bustle is long gone, knowing that this wooded, sleepy river valley was the "Silicon Valley" of the 19th century makes wandering its brick streets almost a pilgrimage. Other villages—including Coalbrookdale, Jackfield, and Coalport—are scattered along the valley, all within a short drive or a long walk. The museum sights are scattered over three miles. The modern cooling towers (for coal, not nuclear energy) that you'll see west of town, looming ominously over these red-brick remnants, seem strangely appropriate.

TOURIST INFORMATION

The TI is in the Museum of the Gorge, just west of the town center (daily 10:00-16:00, tel. 01952/433-424, www.ironbridge.org.uk or www.ironbridgeguide.info). In summer, you may also find an information desk inside the Iron Bridge tollbooth.

GETTING AROUND IRONBRIDGE GORGE

For connections from the Telford train or bus stations to the sights, see the end of this chapter.

By Bus: Gorge Connect buses link the area museums on busy summer weekends when school's out—including Easter and the two May Bank Holidays (Sat-Mon), plus every weekend from late July through mid-September (every 30 minutes 9:30-17:00, £2.20 day ticket—discounted to £1 with Passport Ticket—described in "Sights in Ironbridge Gorge"; see schedule at www.telford.gov.uk—search for "Gorge Connect"; tel. 01952/200-005). If you're waiting for the Gorge Connect bus on the main road by the bridge, or at a stop for one of the less-popular museums, make sure the driver sees you.

Bus **#9,** operated by Arriva, connects the Museum of Iron (stop: Coalbrookdale School Road) and the TI in Ironbridge, but runs infrequently (roughly hourly).

By Car: Routes to the attractions are well-signed, so driving is snap (museum parking described later).

By Taxi: Taxis will pick up at the museums and are a good option if you don't have a car and the bus is not convenient. Call Go Carz at tel. 01952/501-050.

Sights in Ironbridge Gorge

Ten museums clustered within a few miles focus on the Iron Bridge and all that it represents—but not all are worth your time. The Blists Hill Victorian Town is by far the best. The Museum of the Gorge attempts to give a historical overview, but the displays are humble—its most interesting feature is the 12-minute video, which helps give context to other area sights. The Coalbrookdale Museum of Iron is interesting to metalheads. Enginuity is just for kids. The original Abraham Darby Furnace (free to view, located across from the Museum of Iron) is a shrine to 18th-century technology. And the Jackfield Tile Museum, Coalport China Museum, and Broseley Pipeworks delve into industries that picked up the slack when the iron industry shifted away from the Severn Valley in the 1850s.

Cost: Individual admission charges vary (£4-17); the £25 **Passport Ticket** (families-£68) covers admission to all area sights and gives a discount on the Gorge Connect bus. Even if you visit only the Blists Hill Victorian Town and the Coalbrookdale Museum of Iron, the Passport Ticket pays for itself.

Hours: All museums open daily 10:00-16:00 unless otherwise noted; closed Mon Oct-mid-March.

Information: Tel. 01952/433-424, www.ironbridge.org.uk.

Parking: To see the most significant sights by car, you'll park three times: once in town (either in the pay-and-display lot just over the bridge or at the Museum of the Gorge—the Iron Bridge and Gorge Museum are connected by an easy, flat walk); once at the Blists Hill parking lot; and once outside the Coalbrookdale Museum of Iron (Enginuity is across the lot, and the Darby Houses are a three-minute uphill hike away). While you'll pay separately to park at the Museum of the Gorge, a single £3 ticket is good for pay-and-display lots at all other sights.

IRONBRIDGE GORGE

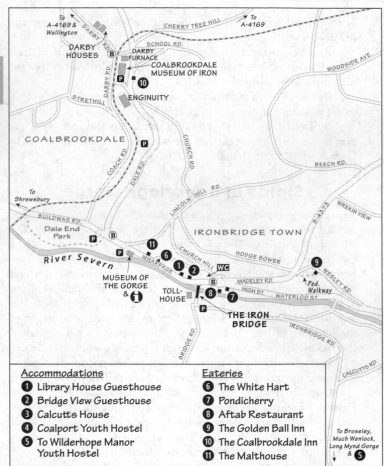

Accommodations
1. Library House Guesthouse
2. Bridge View Guesthouse
3. Calcutts House
4. Coalport Youth Hostel
5. To Wilderhope Manor Youth Hostel

Eateries
6. The White Hart
7. Pondicherry
8. Aftab Restaurant
9. The Golden Ball Inn
10. The Coalbrookdale Inn
11. The Malthouse

IRONBRIDGE VILLAGE
▲▲Iron Bridge

While England was at war with her American colonies, this first cast-iron bridge was built in 1779 to show off a wonderful new building material. Lacking experience with cast iron, the builders erred on the side of sturdiness and constructed it as if it were made of wood. Notice that the original construction used traditional timber-jointing techniques rather than rivets. (Rivets are from later repairs.) The valley's centerpiece is free, open all the time, and thought-provoking...cars still used it into the 1960s. Walk

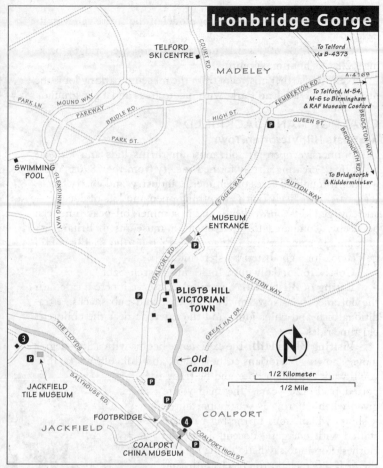

Ironbridge Gorge

TELFORD
SKI CENTRE

MADELEY

To Telford
via B-4373

COURT RD.

A-4169

KEMBERTON RD.

To Telford, M-54,
M-6 to Birmingham
& RAF Museum Cosford

PARK LN.
MOUND WAY
PARKWAY
BRIDLE RD.
PARK ST.

HIGH ST.

QUEEN ST.

BRIDGNORTH RD.

BROCKTON WAY

SWIMMING
POOL

GLENDINNING WAY

LEGGES WAY

To Bridgnorth
& Kidderminster

SUTTON WAY

MUSEUM
ENTRANCE

COALPORT RD.

BLISTS HILL
VICTORIAN
TOWN

SUTTON WAY

GREAT HAY DR.

THE LLOYDS

3

BALTHOUSE RD.

Old
Canal

1/2 Kilometer

1/2 Mile

JACKFIELD
TILE MUSEUM

FOOTBRIDGE

JACKFIELD

4

COALPORT

COALPORT HIGH ST.

COALPORT
CHINA MUSEUM

across the bridge to the tollhouse. Inside, read the fee schedule and notice the subtle slam against royalty. (England was not immune to the revolutionary sentiment inhabiting the colonies at this time.) Pedestrians paid half a penny to cross; poor people crossed cheaper by coracle—a crude tub-like wood-and-canvas shuttle ferry. Cross back to the town and enjoy a pleasant walk downstream along the towpath. Where horses once dragged boats laden with Industrial Age cargo, locals now walk their dogs.

Museum of the Gorge

Orient yourself to the valley at this simple museum, filling the Old Severn Warehouse. It's worthwhile merely for the 12-minute introductory movie (on a continuous loop), which lays the groundwork for what you'll see in the other museums. You'll also see exhibits on local geology and ecology, some of the items that were produced

IRONBRIDGE GORGE

here, and a well-explained, 30-foot model of the entire valley in its heyday.

Cost: £4.50, 500 yards upstream from the bridge, parking–£2.80 (3-hour maximum).

Nearby: Farther upstream from the museum parking lot is the fine riverside **Dale End Park,** with picnic areas and a playground.

COALPORT AND JACKFIELD
▲▲Blists Hill Victorian Town

This immersive open-air folk museum thrills kids and kids-at-heart by re-creating a fully formed society from the 1890s. You'll wander through 50 acres of commerce, industry, and chatty locals. It's particularly lively (with everything open and lots of docents—and engaged kids) on weekends and in summer; off-peak times can be sleepy. Compared to other open-air museums in Britain, it's refreshingly compact and manageable. Pick up the £5 Blists Hill guidebook for a good step-by-step rundown.

Cost: £16.25, daily until 16:30 mid-March-Sept.

Eating in Blists Hill: Several places serve lunch: a café near the entrance, the New Inn Pub for beer and pub snacks, a traditional fish-and-chips joint, and the cafeteria near the children's old-time rides.

Visiting Blists Hill: The experience begins with a 360-degree movie showing Victorians at (noisy, hot, and difficult) work. Then you'll walk through a door and be transported back 120 years. The map you're given when entering is very important—it shows which stops in the big park are staffed with energetic docents in period clothes. Pop in to say hello to the banker, the post office clerk, the blacksmith, and the girl in the candy shop. Maybe the boys are singing in the pub. It's fine to take photos. Asking questions and chatting with the villagers is encouraged. What's a shilling? How was the pay? How about 1800s health care?

Stop by the pharmacy and check out the squirm-inducing setup of the dentist's chair—it'll make you appreciate modern dental care. Check the hands-on activities in the barn across the way. Down the street, kids like watching a candle-maker at work, as he explains the process and tells how candles were used back in the day. You'll find out what a "spinning donkey" is, why candles have two wicks, and why miners used green candles instead of white ones.

Just as it would've had in Victorian days, the village has a working pub, a greengrocer's shop, a fascinating squatter's cottage, and a snorty, slippery pigsty. On your way down to the ironworks, drop in on the high-end mine manager's house, with a doctor's surgery tucked in the back. Don't miss the explanation of the "winding engine" at the Blists Hill Mine (demos throughout the day).

At the back of the park, you can hop aboard a train and enter a clay mine, complete with a sound-and-light show illustrating the dangers of working in this type of environment (£2, 15 minutes). Nearby, the Hay Inclined Plane was used to haul loaded tub boats between the river and the upper canal. Today, a passenger-operated lift hauls visitors instead (just press the button to call for it). At the top, you can walk along the canal back to the town.

Coalport China Museum

This museum fills an old porcelain factory directly downhill from Blists Hill, along the river. You'll see a few fine samples of china that was made here (the Caughley porcelain, at the end, is top-quality); walk through a long workshop, where workers demonstrate various aspects of porcelain production (molds, flowers, printing, glazing, painting, and gilding); peek into a working glassblower's shop; and walk around inside a cavernous "botte kiln." While a bit less engaging than most of Ironbridge's museums, it's informative and rounds out your look at the area.

Cost: £8.85.

▲Jackfield Tile Museum

While most area museums focus on the grit and brawn of the Industrial Revolution—iron, coal, that sort of thing—the Jackfield Tile Museum looks at the softer side of Severn Valley innovation. Located in the village of Jackfield (across the river from Ironbridge), here you can walk through several buildings in an old brick industrial complex where tiles are still produced. The highlight is seeing the wide range of uses and styles of tile—a material so versatile (and so beautiful) that it looks equally good in bathrooms and in churches, and even in London's Tube (much of the Underground tile came from right here). The modern Fusion facility next door suggests that tile's heyday isn't over.

Cost: £8.85.

COALBROOKDALE

Note that the Darby Houses close an hour before the other sights here; if visiting later in the day, go there first.

▲Coalbrookdale Museum of Iron and Abraham Darby's Old Furnace

The Coalbrookdale neighborhood is the birthplace of modern technology—locals like to claim it's where mass production was

How to Smelt Iron... and Change the World

The Severn Valley had an abundance of ingredients for big industry: iron ore, top-grade coal (known as coke), and water for power and shipping. And the person who finally put all the pieces together was a clever Quaker brassmaker from Bristol named Abraham Darby.

Before Darby's time, iron ore was laboriously melted by charcoal—they couldn't use coal because sulfur made the iron brittle. Darby experimented with higher-carbon coke instead. With huge waterwheel-powered bellows, Darby burned coke at super-hot temperatures and dumped iron ore into the furnace. Impurities floated to the top, while the pure iron sank to the bottom of a clay tub in the bottom of the furnace.

Twice a day, the plugs were knocked off, allowing the "slag" to drain away on the top and the molten iron to drain out on the bottom. The low-grade slag was used locally on walls and paths. The high-grade iron trickled into molds formed in the sand below the furnace. It cooled into pig iron (named because the molds look like piglets suckling their mother). The pig-iron "planks" were broken off by sledgehammers and shipped away.

The River Severn became one of Europe's busiest, shipping pig iron to distant foundries, where it was melted again and made into cast iron (for projects such as the Iron Bridge), or to forges, where it was worked like toffee into wrought iron.

Once Darby cracked the coke code, iron became *the* go-to building material. Versatile and ubiquitous, iron became the plastic of the Victorian age. To this day, many of the icons of Britain—post boxes, frilly benches, fences in front of tidy houses—are made of iron. All thanks to the innovation that took place 200 years ago, right here in the Severn Valley.

invented. The museum and furnace are located on either side of a parking lot, tucked under a rail trestle. There's a café on-site, and the Coalbrookdale Inn—a classic pub—is just up the hill in front of the museum.

Cost: Museum—£8.85, £9.25 combo-ticket includes the Darby Houses; Furnace—free, volunteers sometimes lead free guided walks to the furnace (ask at museum info desk for times).

Visiting the Museum: The fresh, well-presented museum works hard to explain all facets of iron—which has been used to make tools since ancient times, and makes up 95 percent of all industrial metal. You'll get a quick primer on the history of iron tools, then head up to the top floor and work your way down, chronologically, through the role iron played here in the Severn Valley. You'll see original items from Coalbrookdale's boom time (including a little three-legged pot created by Abraham Darby, c. 1714) and learn about the critical role Quakers (like Darby) played in the Industrial Revolution—several important individuals are profiled. You'll also see a detailed model of the Iron Bridge, and—on the middle floor—several Victorian Age items made possible by this innovation, from a gigantic cast-iron anchor to delicately crafted benches and sculptures.

Abraham Darby Furnace: Across from the museum, standing like a shrine to the Industrial Revolution, is Darby's blast furnace, sitting inside a big glass pyramid and surrounded by evocative Industrial Age ruins. It was here that in 1709 Darby first smelted iron, using coke as fuel. To me, "coke" is a drink, and "smelt" is the past tense of smell... but around here, these words recall the event that  kicked off the modern Industrial Age and changed the world (see the sidebar).

Enginuity

Enginuity is a hands-on funfest for kids. Riffing on Ironbridge's engineering roots, this converted 1709 foundry is full of entertaining-to-kids water contraptions, pumps, magnets, and laser games. Build a dam, try your hand at earthquake-proof construction, navigate a water maze, operate a remote-controlled robot, or power a turbine with your own steam. Mixed in among all this entertainment is a collection of vintage machines.

Cost: £8.85, across the parking lot from the Coalbrookdale Museum of Iron.

Darby Houses

Abraham Darby, who kicked off the Industrial Age when he figured out how to smelt iron in his big furnace, lived with his family

ily in these two homes up on a ridge overlooking the Coalbrookdale Museum (go under the rail bridge and head uphill). Although Quakers, they were the area's wealthiest residents by far. Touring their homes, you'll learn a bit about their lifestyles, and about Quakers in general.

The 18th-century Darby mansion, **Rosehill House,** is

decorated and furnished as the family home would have been in 1850. It features a collection of fine china, furniture, and trinkets from various family members. If the gilt-framed mirrors and fancy china seem a little ostentatious for wealth-shunning Quakers, keep in mind that these folks were rich beyond reason, and—as docents will assure you—considering their vast wealth, this was relatively modest. At the end of the tour is a collection of period clothes: You're welcome to dress up as a modest Quaker or a fashionable dandy.

Skip the adjacent **Dale House.** Dating from the 1710s, it's older than Rosehill, but almost completely devoid of furniture, and its exhibits are rarely open.

Cost and Hours: £5.50, £9.25 combo-ticket includes Coalbrookdale Museum of Iron, closes earlier than the other museums—at 15:00—and closed entirely Oct-mid-March.

MORE SIGHTS AND EXPERIENCES IN AND NEAR IRONBRIDGE GORGE
Skiing and Swimming
A small brush-covered **ski and snowboarding slope** with two Poma lifts is at Telford Snowboard and Ski Centre in Madeley, two miles from Ironbridge Gorge; you'll see signs for it as you drive into Ironbridge Gorge (open practice times vary by day—schedule posted online, tel. 01952/382-688, www.telfordandwrekinleisure. co.uk). A public **swimming pool,** the Abraham Darby Sports and Leisure Centre, is near Madeley (5-minute drive from town on Ironbridge Road, tel. 01952/382-770).

Royal Air Force (RAF) Museum Cosford
This Red Baron magnet displays more than 80 aircraft, from warplanes to rockets. Get the background on ejection seats and a primer on the principles of propulsion (free, daily 10:00-17:00, Nov-Feb until 16:00, last entry one hour before closing, parking-£3/3 hours, Shifnal, Shropshire, on the A-41 near junction with the M-54, tel. 01902/376-200, www.rafmuseum.org.uk/cosford).

More Sights
If you're looking for reasons to linger in Ironbridge Gorge, these sights are all within a short drive: the **medieval town** of Shrewsbury, the **abbey village** of Much Wenlock, the **scenic Long Mynd gorge** at Church Stretton, the **castle** at Ludlow, and the **steam railway** at the river town of Bridgnorth. Shoppers like Chester (en route to points north). **Brosely Pipeworks,** in the town of Brosley Wood, offers a fascinating look at the mass-production of clay pipes, but its opening hours are severely limited (£5.15, open mid-May-Sept 13:00-16:00, tours at 13:30 and 15:00, closed off-season).

IRONBRIDGE GORGE

Sleeping in Ironbridge Gorge

$$ Library House Guesthouse is *Town and Country*-elegant. Located in the town center, a half-block downhill from the bridge, it's a classy, friendly gem that once served as the village library. Each of its three rooms is a delight, and the public spaces are decorated true to the Georgian period. The Chaucer Room, which includes a small garden, is the smallest and least expensive. Tim and Sarah will make you feel right at home (free parking just up the road, 11 Severn Bank, tel. 01952/432-299, www.libraryhouse.com, info@libraryhouse.com).

$$ Bridge View Guesthouse rents seven tidy but uninspired rooms over a tearoom directly at the Iron Bridge; true to its name, four rooms have bridge views. While less personal than Library House or Calcutts, they may have a room when those are full (free parking nearby, 10 Tontine Hill, tel. 01952/432-541, www.ironbridgeview.co.uk, bookings@ironbridgeview.co.uk).

OUTSIDE OF TOWN

$$ Calcutts House rents seven rooms in an 18th-century ironmaster's home and adjacent coach house. Rooms in the main house are elegant, while the coach-house rooms are bright, modern, and less expensive. Their inviting garden is a plus. Ask the owners, James and Sarah Pittam, how the rooms were named (free parking, Calcutts Road, tel. 01952/882-631, www.calcuttshouse.co.uk, info@calcuttshouse.co.uk). From Calcutts House, it's a delightful 15-minute stroll down a former train track into town.

¢ Coalport Youth Hostel, plush for a hostel, fills an old factory at the China Museum in Coalport (reception open 7:30-23:00, no lockout, High Street, tel. 01952/588-755 or 0845-371-9325, www.yha.org.uk, coalport@yha.org.uk). Don't confuse this hostel with another area hostel, Coalbrookdale, which is only available for groups.

¢ Wilderhope Manor Youth Hostel, a beautifully remote Elizabethan manor house from 1586, is one of Europe's best hostels (it even has a bridal suite). On Sunday afternoons, tourists actually pay to see what hostelers get to sleep in (family rooms, reservations recommended, reception closed 10:00-15:00, restaurant open 18:00-20:30, tel. 0345-371-9149, www.yha.org.uk, wilderhope@yha.org.uk). It's in Longville-in-the-Dale, six miles from Much Wenlock, down the B-4371 toward Church Stretton.

Eating in Ironbridge Gorge

$$$$ **The White Hart** has a split personality—the woody pub section is Brit-rustic, while the two-level restaurant is white-tablecloth chic. Prices make this a splurge, but the food is creative and tasty (daily 11:00-22:00, food served until 21:00, reservations smart on weekends, 10 Wharfage, tel. 01952/432-901, www.whitehartironbridge.com).

$$$ **Pondicherry,** in a renovated former police station, serves Indian meals that gild the lily. The basement holding cells are now little plush lounges—a great option if you'd like your predinner drink "in prison" (daily 17:30-23:00, 57 Waterloo Street, tel. 01952/433-055). For cheaper (but still good) Indian food, look for $$ **Aftab**, a bit closer to the Iron Bridge.

$$ **The Golden Ball Inn** is a classic countryside pub high on the hill above Ironbridge. You can dine with the friendly local crowd in the "bar," eat in back with the 18th-century brewing gear in the quieter—and more formal—dining room, or munch out on the lush garden patio. This place is serious about their beer, listing featured ales daily (food served Mon-Sat 12:00-21:00, Sun until 19:00, reservations smart on weekends, 10-minute hike up Madeley Road from the town roundabout, look for sign to pedestrian shortcut, 1 Newbridge Road, tel. 01952/432-179, www.goldenballironbridge.co.uk).

$$ **The Coalbrookdale Inn** is filled with locals enjoying excellent ales and simple pub grub—nothing fancy. This former "best pub in Britain" has a tradition of offering free samples from a lineup of featured beers. Ask which real ales are available (Mon-Fri 16:00-23:00, Sat-Sun from 12:00, lively ladies' loo, across street from Coalbrookdale Museum of Iron, 1 mile from Ironbridge, 12 Wellington Road, tel. 01952/432-166).

$$ **The Malthouse,** located in an 18th-century beer house, is popular with local twentysomethings. The menu includes pub standards, plus a few pricier, high-end dishes (food served daily 11:30-22:00, near Museum of the Gorge, 5-minute walk from center, The Wharfage, tel. 01952/433-712). For nighttime action, The Malthouse is *the* vibrant spot in town, with live rock music and a fun crowd (generally Fri-Sat).

Ironbridge Gorge Connections

Ironbridge Gorge is five miles southwest of Telford, which has the nearest train station.

Getting Between Telford and Ironbridge Gorge: It's easiest to take a **taxi** from Telford train station to Ironbridge Gorge (about £5.50 to Blists Hill, £9 to the Iron Bridge; call Go Carz at tel.

01952/501-050). If the Gorge Connect bus is running (described earlier, under "Getting Around Ironbridge Gorge"), you could take **bus #4** (2-5/hour) from the Telford train station to High Street in the town of Madeley. This is where the Gorge Connect bus originates and ends. Hop on it to ride to one of the museums, the TI, or the bridge.

By Train from Telford to: Birmingham (2/hour, 45 minutes), **Stratford-upon-Avon** (2/hour, 2.5 hours, 1-2 changes), **Moreton-in-Marsh** (hourly, 2.5-3 hours, 2 transfers), **Conwy** in North Wales (3/day direct, 2.5 hours, more with transfer), **Keswick/Lake District** (hourly, 4 hours total; 3 hours to Penrith with 1-2 changes, then catch a bus to Keswick—see page 506). **Train info:** Tel. 0345-748-4950, www.nationalrail.co.uk.

ROUTE TIPS FOR DRIVERS

From the South to Ironbridge Gorge: From the Cotswolds and Stratford, you want to avoid going through Birmingham; see page 428 for the best route. After Birmingham, follow signs to *Telford* via the M-54. Leave the M-54 at the Telford/Ironbridge exit (Junction 4). Follow the brown *Ironbridge* signs through several roundabouts to Ironbridge Gorge. (Note: On maps, Ironbridge Gorge is often referred to as "Iron Bridge" or "Iron-Bridge.")

From Ironbridge Gorge to North Wales: The drive is fairly easy, with clear signs and good roads all the way. From Ironbridge Gorge, follow signs to the M-54. Get on the M-54 in the direction of Telford, and then Shrewsbury, as the M-54 becomes the A-5; then follow signs to North Wales. In Wales, the A-483 (direction Wrexham, then Chester) takes you to the A-55, which leads to Conwy.

LIVERPOOL

Wedged between serene North Wales and the even-more-serene Lake District, Liverpool provides an opportunity to sample the "real" England. It's the best look at urban England outside London.

Beatles fans flock to Liverpool to learn about the Fab Four's early days, but the city has much more to offer—most notably, a wealth of free and good museums, a pair of striking cathedrals, a dramatic skyline mingling old red-brick maritime buildings and glassy new skyscrapers, and—most of all—the charm of the Liverpudlians.

Sitting at the mouth of the River Mersey in the metropolitan county of Merseyside, Liverpool has long been a major shipping center. Its port played a key role in several centuries of world history—as a point in the "triangular trade" of African slaves, a gateway for millions of New World-bound European emigrants, and a staging ground for the British Navy's Battle of the Atlantic against the Nazi's U-boat fleet. But Liverpool was devastated physically by WWII bombs, and then economically by the advent of container shipping in the 1960s. Liverpudlians looked on helplessly as postwar recovery resources were steered elsewhere, the city's substantial wartime contributions seemingly ignored.

Despite the pride and attention garnered in the 1960s by a certain quartet of favorite sons, Liverpool continued to decline through the 1970s and '80s. The Toxteth Riots of 1981, sparked by the city's dizzyingly high unemployment, brought worldwide attention to Liverpool's troubles.

But, finally, things started to improve. The city's status as the 2008 European Capital of Culture spurred major gentrification, EU funding, and a cultural renaissance. And, with some 50,000

On the Scouse

Nicknamed "Scousers" (after a traditional local stew, originally brought here by Norwegian immigrants), the people of Liverpool have a reputation for being relaxed, easygoing, and welcoming to visitors. The Scouse dialect comes with a distinctive lilt and quick wit (the latter likely a means of coping with long-term hardship)—think of the Beatles' familiar accents, and all their famously sarcastic off-the-cuff remarks, and you get the picture. Many Liverpudlians attribute these qualities to the Celtic influence here: Liverpool is a melting pot of not only English culture, but also loads of Irish and Welsh, as well as arrivals from all over Europe and beyond (Liverpool's diverse population includes many of African descent). Liverpudlians are also famous for their passion for football (i.e., soccer), and the Liverpool FC team—as locals will be quick to tell you—is one of England's best.

students attending three universities in town, Liverpool is also a youthful city, with a pub or nightclub on every corner. Anyone who still thinks of Liverpool as a depressed industrial center is behind the times.

PLANNING YOUR TIME

Liverpool deserves at least a few hours, but those willing to give it a full day or more won't be disappointed.

For the quickest visit, focus your time around the Albert Dock area, home to The Beatles Story, Merseyside Maritime Museum, Tate Gallery (for contemporary art lovers), Museum of Liverpool, and the British Music Experience. If time allows, consider a Beatles bus tour (departs from the Albert Dock).

A full day buys you time either to delve into the rest of the city (the rejuvenated urban core, the cathedrals, and the Walker Art Gallery near the train station), to binge on more Beatles sights (the boyhood homes of John and Paul), or a bit of both.

If you're here just for the Beatles, you can easily fill a day with Fab Four sights: Do the tour of John's and Paul's homes in the morning, then return to the Albert Dock area to visit The Beatles Story and/or the British Music Experience. Take an afternoon bus tour from the Albert Dock to the other Beatles sights in town, winding up at the Cavern Quarter to enjoy a Beatles cover band in the reconstructed Cavern Club. (Beatles bus tours zip past the John and Paul houses from the outside, but visiting the interiors takes more time and should be reserved well in advance.)

International Beatles Week, celebrated in late August, is a very busy time in Liverpool, with lots of live musical performances.

Orientation to Liverpool

With nearly half a million people, Liverpool is Britain's fifth-biggest city. But for visitors, most points of interest are concentrated in the generally pedestrian-friendly downtown area. You can walk from one end of this zone to the other in about 25 minutes. Since interesting sights and colorful neighborhoods are scattered throughout this area, it's enjoyable to connect your sightseeing on foot. (Beatles sights, however, are spread far and wide—it's much easier to connect them with a tour.)

Tourist Information: Liverpool's TI is at the **Albert Dock** (daily 9:00-16:30, just inland from The Beatles Story, tel. 0151/707-0729, www.visitliverpool.com).

ARRIVAL IN LIVERPOOL

By Train: Most trains use the main **Lime Street train station.** The station has eateries, shops, and pay baggage storage (daily 7:00-21:00, weekends until 23:00, tel. 0151/909-3697, www.left-baggage.co.uk; most bus tours and private minivan/car tours are able to accommodate people with luggage). Regional trains also arrive in Liverpool at the much smaller **Central Station,** located just a few blocks south. Note that the greater Liverpool  area transit system is under renovation through at least 2019; trains may use other stations in surrounding areas and connect you with the city center via bus service. Plan ahead (check www.merseyrail.org or ask at the TI for travel advice) and leave plenty of time for your trip.

Getting to the Albert Dock: From Lime Street Station to the

Albert Dock is about a 20-minute walk or a quick trip by bus, subway, or taxi.

To **walk,** exit straight out the front door. On your right, you'll see the giant Neoclassical St. George's Hall; the Walker Art Gallery is just beyond it. To reach the Albert Dock, go straight ahead across the street, then head down the hill between St. George's Hall (on your right) and the big blob-shaped mall (on your left). Just after the mall, the Queen Square Bus Station is on the left at Roe Street/Hood Street. (The round pavilion with the yellow clock in the middle of the hub is the Travel Centre—see "Getting Around Liverpool," later.) From here, you can continue by bus (see later) or take a pleasant walk through Liverpool's spiffed-up central core: Head around the right side of the transit-info pavilion, then turn left onto Whitechapel Street, which soon becomes a slick pedestrian zone lined with shopping malls until you reach a traffic light. Cross Hanover Street and follow Liver Street all the way down to the waterfront, where you'll see the big red-brick warehouses of the Albert Dock.

To ride the **bus,** walk to Queen Square Bus Station (see directions above); for the most direct route to the Albert Dock, take bus #10A from stop A or bus #79 from stand 1 (every 10 minutes—see schedule posted next to stand; bus prices vary—from £2.30/ride, pay on bus; £3.90 for all-day ticket—available at Travel Centres only). Exit the bus at Liverpool One Bus Station. You can take the same buses back to the station.

You can also take a **subway** from Lime Street Station to James Street Station, then walk about five minutes to the Albert Dock (£2.30, also covered by BritRail pass). Note that some regional trains may pass through James Street Station before reaching Lime Street Station; if so, you can hop out here rather than riding to Lime Street.

A **taxi** from Lime Street Station to the Albert Dock costs about £6. Taxis wait outside either of the side doors of the station.

By Plane: Liverpool John Lennon Airport (tel. 0871-521-8484, www.liverpoolairport.com, airport code: LPL) is about eight miles southeast of downtown, along the river. Buses into town depart regularly from Liverpool One Bus Station. Bus #500 to the city center is quickest (2/hour, 35 minutes, £2.30, covered by all-day ticket). Buses #80A, #82A, and #86A also go from the airport to the Liverpool One Bus Station, but these take a bit longer and only #86A runs long hours (generally 5:30-23:00).

By Car: Drivers approaching Liverpool first follow signs to *City Centre* and *Waterfront,* then brown signs to *Albert Dock,* where you'll find a huge pay parking lot at the dock. If coming from Wales, take the toll tunnel under the River Mersey (£1.70) and follow signs for *Albert Dock.*

LIVERPOOL

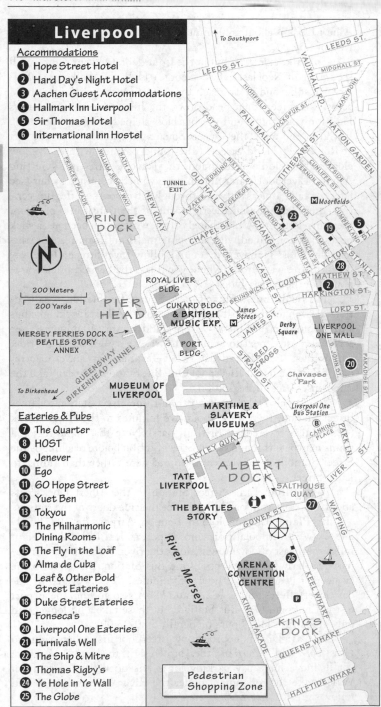

Liverpool

Accommodations
1. Hope Street Hotel
2. Hard Day's Night Hotel
3. Aachen Guest Accommodations
4. Hallmark Inn Liverpool
5. Sir Thomas Hotel
6. International Inn Hostel

Eateries & Pubs
7. The Quarter
8. HOST
9. Jenever
10. Ego
11. 60 Hope Street
12. Yuet Ben
13. Tokyou
14. The Philharmonic Dining Rooms
15. The Fly in the Loaf
16. Alma de Cuba
17. Leaf & Other Bold Street Eateries
18. Duke Street Eateries
19. Fonseca's
20. Liverpool One Eateries
21. Furnivals Well
22. The Ship & Mitre
23. Thomas Rigby's
24. Ye Hole in Ye Wall
25. The Globe

Pedestrian Shopping Zone

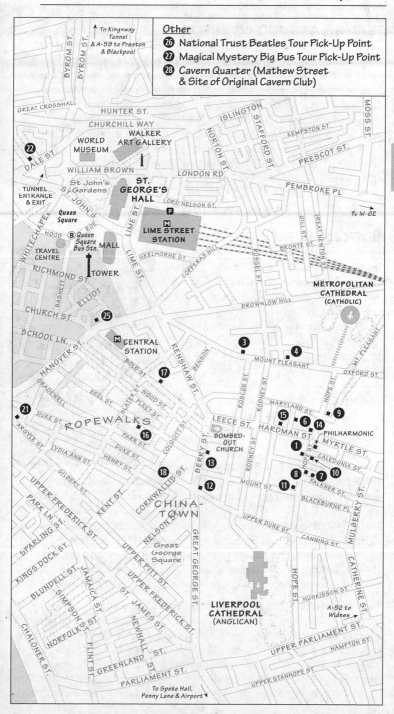

LIVERPOOL

Other

㉖ National Trust Beatles Tour Pick-Up Point

㉗ Magical Mystery Big Bus Tour Pick-Up Point

㉘ Cavern Quarter (Mathew Street
& Site of Original Cavern Club)

GETTING AROUND LIVERPOOL

The city is walkable (and fun to explore), so you may not need to take advantage of the local bus network. But if you're near the Lime Street Station and Queen Square Bus Station and need to get to the Cavern sights, Liverpool One mall, or the Albert Dock, you can take bus #10A or #79. For more public-transit information, visit a Merseytravel center—either at Queen Square Bus Station or at the Liverpool One Bus Station (1 Canning Place), across the busy street from the Albert Dock (centers open Mon-Sat 8:30-18:00, Sun 10:00-17:00, except Liverpool One closed Sun; tel. 0151-330-1000, www.merseytravel.gov.uk).

Tours in Liverpool

BEATLES BUS TOURS

If you want to see as many Beatles-related sights as possible in a short time, these tours are the way to go. Each drives by the houses where the Fab Four grew up (exteriors only), places they performed, and spots made famous by the lyrics of their hits ("Penny Lane," "Strawberry Fields," the Eleanor Rigby graveyard, and so on). Even lukewarm fans will enjoy the commentary and seeing the shelter on the roundabout, the barber who shaves another customer, and the banker who never wears a mack in the pouring rain. (Very strange.)

Magical Mystery Big Bus Tour

Beatles fans enjoy loading onto this old, psychedelically painted bus for a spin past Liverpool's main Beatles landmarks, with a few photo ops off the bus. With an enthusiastic live commentary and Beatles tunes cued to famous landmarks, it leaves people happy (£18, 5-8/day, fewer on Sun and in off-season, 2 hours, buses depart from the Albert Dock near The Beatles Story and TI, tel. 0151/703-9100, www.cavernclub.org). As these tours often fill up, you'd be wise to book at least a day ahead by phone or online.

Phil Hughes Minibus Beatles and Liverpool Tours

For something more extensive, fun, and intimate, consider a four-hour minibus Beatles tour from Phil Hughes. It's longer because it includes information on historic Liverpool, along with the Beatles stuff and a couple of *Titanic* and *Lusitania* sights. Phil organizes his tour to fit your schedule and will do his best to accommodate you (£125 for private group tour with 1-5 people; £25/person in peak season if he can assemble a group of 5-8 people; can coordinate tour to include pickup from end of National Trust tour of Lennon and McCartney homes or drop-off for late-day tour starting at Speke Hall, also does door-to-door service from your hotel or train station, 8-seat minibus, tel. 0151/228-4565, mobile 07961-511-223, www.tourliverpool.co.uk, tourliverpool@hotmail.com).

Jackie Spencer Private Tours

To tailor a visit to your schedule and interests, Jackie Spencer is at your service...just say when and where you want to go (up to 5 people in her chauffeur-driven minivan-£240, 3 hours, longer tours available, will pick you up at hotel or train station, mobile 0799-076-1478, www.beatleguides.com, jackie@beatleguides.com).

OTHER TOURS

City Bus Tour

Two different hop-on, hop-off bus tours cruise around town, offering a quick way to get an overview that links all the major sights. The options are **Liverpool City Sights** (£12, recorded commentary, 16 stops, tel. 0151/298-1253, www.liverpoolcitysights.co.uk) and **City Explorer** (£11, live guides, 13 stops, tel. 0151/933-2324, www.cityexplorerliverpool.co.uk). On either bus, your ticket is valid 24 hours and can be purchased from the driver (both run 2-3/hour daily April-Oct, generally 10:00-17:00; shorter hours and less frequent in winter).

Ferry Cruise

Mersey Ferries offers narrated cruises that depart from the Pier Head ferry terminal, a 5- to 10-minute walk north of the Albert Dock. The 50-minute cruise makes two brief stops on the other side of the river; you can hop off and catch the next boat back (£10 round-trip, leaves Pier Head at top of hour, daily 10:00-15:00, Sat-Sun until 18:00 in April-Oct, café, WCs onboard, tel. 0151/330-1000, www.merseyferries.co.uk).

Sights in Liverpool

ON THE WATERFRONT

In its day, Liverpool was England's greatest seaport, but trade declined after 1890, as the port wasn't deep enough for the big new ships. The advent of mega container ships in the 1960s put the final nail in the port's coffin, and by 1972 it was closed entirely.

But over the last couple of decades, this formerly derelict and dangerous area has been the focus of the city's rejuvenation efforts. Liverpool's waterfront is now a venue for some of the city's top attractions. Three zones interest tourists (from south to north): the Kings Dock, with Liverpool's futuristic new arena, conference

LIVERPOOL

Liverpool at a Glance

▲▲**Museum of Liverpool** Three floors of intriguing exhibits, historical artifacts, and fun interactive displays tracing the port city's history, culture, and contributions to the world. **Hours:** Daily 10:00-17:00. See page 456.

▲▲**British Music Experience** Immersive and interactive museum on the history of British music from 1945 to current times. **Hours:** Daily 9:00-19:00, Thu until 21:00. See page 458.

▲▲**Liverpool Cathedral** Huge Anglican house of worship—the largest cathedral in Great Britain—with cavernous interior and tower climb. **Hours:** Daily 8:00-18:00. See page 464.

▲**The Beatles Story** Well-done if overpriced exhibit about the Fab Four, with a great audioguide narrated by John Lennon's sister, Julia Baird. **Hours:** Daily 9:00-19:00, Nov-March 10:00-18:00. See page 451.

▲**Merseyside Maritime Museum and International Slavery Museum** Duo of thought-provoking museums exploring Liverpool's seafaring heritage and the city's role in the African slave trade. **Hours:** Daily 10:00-17:00. See page 452.

▲**Walker Art Gallery** Enjoyable, easy-to-appreciate collection of European paintings, sculptures, and decorative arts. **Hours:** Daily 10:00-17:00. See page 460.

▲**Metropolitan Cathedral of Christ the King** Striking, daringly modern Catholic cathedral with a story as fascinating as the building itself. **Hours:** Daily 7:30-18:00. See page 462.

▲**Lennon and McCartney Homes** Guided visit to their 1950s boyhood homes, with restored interiors. **Hours:** Tours run daily 4/day in peak season. See page 466.

center, and adjacent Ferris wheel; the red-brick Albert Dock complex, with some of the city's top museums and lively restaurants and nightlife; and Pier Head, with the Museum of Liverpool, ferries across the River Mersey, and buildings both old/stately and new/glassy. Below are descriptions of the main sights at the Albert Dock and Pier Head.

At the Albert Dock

Opened in 1852 by Prince Albert and enclosing seven acres of water, the Albert Dock is surrounded by five-story brick warehouses. A half-dozen trendy eateries are lined up here, protected from the rain by arcades and padded by lots of shopping mall-type distractions. There's plenty of pay parking.

▲The Beatles Story

It's sad to think the Beatles are stuck in a museum. Still, this exhibit—while overpriced and a bit small—is well done, the story's a fascinating one, and even an avid fan will pick up some new information. The Beatles Story has two parts: the original, main exhibit at the south end of the Albert Dock; and a much smaller branch in the Mersey Ferries terminal at Pier Head, near the Museum of Liverpool, just to the north. A free shuttle runs between the two locations every 30 minutes.

Cost and Hours: £16 covers both parts, tickets good for 48 hours, includes audioguide; daily 9:00-19:00, Nov-March 10:00-18:00, Pier Head exhibit has shorter hours, last entry one hour before closing; tel. 0151/709-1969, www.beatlesstory.com.

Visiting the Museum: Start in the **main exhibit** with a chronological stroll through the evolution of the Beatles, focusing on

their Liverpool years: meeting as schoolboys, performing at (and helping decorate) the Casbah Coffee Club, making a name for themselves in Hamburg's red light district, meeting their manager Brian Epstein, and the advent of worldwide Beatlemania (with some help from Ed Sullivan). There are many actual artifacts (from George Harrison's first boyhood guitar to John Lennon's orange-tinted "Imagine" glasses), as well as large dioramas celebrating landmarks in Beatles lore (a reconstruction of the Cavern Club, a life-size recreation of the *Sgt. Pepper* album cover, and a walk-through yellow submarine). The last rooms trace the members' solo careers, and the final few steps are reserved for reverence about John's peace work, including a replica of the white room he used while writing "Imagine." Rounding out the exhibits are a "Discovery Zone" for kids and (of course) the "Fab 4 Store," with an impressive pile of Beatles buyables.

The great audioguide, narrated by Julia Baird (John Lennon's little sister), captures the Beatles' charm and cheekiness in a way the stiff wax mannequins can't. You'll hear clips of interviews from the actual participants in the Beatles' story—their families, friends, and collaborators. Cynthia Lennon, John's first wife, still marvels at the manic power of Beatlemania, while producer George Martin explains why he wanted their original drummer dumped for Ringo.

While this is a fairly sanitized look at the Fab Four (LSD and Yoko-related conflicts are glossed over), the exhibits remind listeners of all that made the group earth-shattering—and even a little edgy—at the time. For example, performing before the Queen Mother, John Lennon famously quips: "Will the people in the cheaper seats clap your hands? And the rest of you, if you'll just rattle your jewelry." Surprisingly, there are no clips from Beatles movies or performances—not even the epic *Ed Sullivan Show* broadcast. You'll find that it's strong on Beatles' history, but you'll have to go elsewhere to understand why Beatlemania happened.

The **Pier Head exhibit** is less interesting, but since it's included with the ticket, it's worth dropping into if you have the time. You'll find it upstairs in the Mersey Ferries terminal at Pier Head—10-minute walk north (at the opposite end of the Albert Dock, then another 5 minutes across the bridge and past the Museum of Liverpool). The main attraction here is a corny "Fab 4D Experience," an animated movie that strings together Beatles tunes into something resembling a plot while mainly offering an excuse to play around with 3-D effects and other surprises (such as the smell of strawberries when you hear "Strawberry Fields Forever"). There are also rotating temporary exhibits here.

▲Merseyside Maritime Museum and International Slavery Museum

These museums tell the story of Liverpool, once the second city of the British Empire. The third floor covers slavery, while the first, second, and basement handle other maritime topics.

Cost and Hours: Free, donations accepted, daily 10:00-17:00, café, tel. 0151/478-4499, www.liverpoolmuseums.org.uk.

Background: Liverpool's port prospered in the 18th century as one corner of a commerce triangle with Africa and America. British shippers profited greatly through exploitation: About 1.5 million enslaved African people were taken to the Americas on Liverpool's ships (that's 10 percent of all African slaves). From Liverpool, the British exported manufactured goods to Africa in exchange for enslaved Africans; the slaves were then shipped to the Americas, where they were traded for raw material (cotton, sugar, and tobacco); and the goods were then brought back to Britain. While the merchants on all three sides made money, the big profit came home to England (which enjoyed substantial income from customs, duties, and a thriving smugglers' market). As Britain's economy boomed, so did Liverpool's.

After participation in the slave trade was outlawed in Britain in the early 1800s, Liverpool kept its port busy as a transfer point for emigrants. If your ancestors came from Scandinavia, Ukraine, or Ireland, they likely left Europe from this port. Between 1830 and 1930, nine million emigrants sailed from Liverpool to find their dreams in the New World.

Visiting the Museums: Begin by riding the elevator up to floor 3—we'll work our way back down.

On floor 3, three galleries make up the **International Slavery Museum.** First is a description of life in West Africa, which re-creates traditional domestic architecture and displays actual artifacts. Then comes a harrowing exhibit about enslavement and the Middle Passage. The tools of the enslavers—chains, muzzles, and a branding iron—and the intense film about the Middle Passage sea voyage to the Americas drive home the horrifying experience of being abducted from your home and taken in life-threatening conditions thousands of miles away to toil for a wealthy stranger. The exhibits don't shy away from how Liverpool profited from slavery; you can turn local street signs around to find out how they were named after slave traders—even Penny Lane has slavery connections. Finally, the museum examines the legacy of slavery—both the persistence of racism in contemporary society and the substantial positive impact that people of African descent have had on European and American cultures. Walls of photos celebrate important people of African descent, and a music station lets you sample songs from a variety of African-influenced genres.

Continue down the stairs to the **Maritime Museum,** on floor 2. This celebrates Liverpool's shipbuilding heritage and displays actual ship components, model boats, and a gallery of nautical paintings. Part of that heritage is covered in an extensive exhibit on the *Titanic.* The shipping line and its captain were based in Liverpool, and 89 of the crew members who died were from the city. The informative panels allow you to follow real people as they set off on the voyage and debunk many *Titanic* myths (no one ever said it was unsinkable).

Floor 1 shows footage and artifacts from another maritime disaster—the 1915 sinking of the *Lusitania,* which was torpedoed by a German U-boat. She sank off the coast of Ireland in under 20 minutes; 1,191 people died in the tragedy, including 405 crew members from Liverpool. The attack on an unarmed passenger ship sparked riots in Liverpool and almost thrust the US into the war. Also on this floor, an extensive exhibit traces the **Battle of the Atlantic** (during World War II, Nazi U-boats attacked merchant ships bringing supplies to Britain, in an attempt to cripple this

The Beatles in Liverpool

The most iconic rock-and-roll band of all time was made up of four Liverpudlians who spent their formative years amid the bombed-out shell of WWII-era Liverpool. The city has become a pilgrimage site for Beatlemaniacs, but even those with just a passing interest in the Fab Four are likely to find themselves humming their favorite tunes around town. Most Beatles sights in Liverpool relate to their early days, before the psychedelia, transcendental meditation, Yoko, and solo careers. Because these sights are so spread out, the easiest way to connect all of them in one go is by tour (see "Tours in Liverpool").

All four of the Beatles were born in Liverpool, and any tour of town glides by the **home** most identified with each one's childhood: John Lennon at "Mendips," Paul McCartney at 20 Forthlin Road, George Harrison at 12 Arnold Grove, and Ringo Starr (a.k.a. Richard Starkey) at 10 Admiral Grove.

Behind John's house at Mendips is a wooded area called **Strawberry Field** (he added the "s" for the song). This surrounds a Victorian mansion that was, at various times, a Salvation Army home and an orphanage. John enjoyed sneaking into the trees around the mansion to play. Today visitors pose in front of Strawberry Field's red gate (a replica of the original).

During the Beatles' formative years in the mid-1950s, skiffle music (American-inspired rockabilly/folk) swept through Liverpool. As a teenager, John formed a skiffle band called the Quarrymen. Paul met John for the first time when he saw the Quarrymen on July 6, 1957, at **St. Peter's Church** in Woolton. After the show, in the social hall across the street, Paul noted that John played only banjo chords (his mother had taught him to play on a banjo rather than a guitar—he didn't even know how to tune a guitar), and improvised many lyrics. John, two years older, realized he was a better improviser than a musician, so he was impressed when Paul borrowed a guitar, tuned it effortlessly, and played a note-perfect rendition of Eddie Cochran's "Twenty Flight Rock." Before long, Paul had joined the band.

In the St. Peter's Church graveyard is a headstone for a woman named **Eleanor Rigby.** But to this day, Paul swears that he never saw it, and made up the name for that famous song. Either he's lying, the name crept into his subconscious, or it's a truly remarkable coincidence.

The boys went to school on **Mount Street** in the center of Liverpool (near Hope Street, between the two cathedrals). John and his friend Stuart Sutcliffe attended the Liverpool College of Art, and Paul and his pal George Harrison went to Liverpool Institute High School for Boys. (When Paul introduced George to John as a possible new member for the band, John dismissed him as being too young...until he heard George play. He immediately became the lead guitarist.) Paul later bought his old school building and turned it into the Liverpool Institute for Performing Arts (LIPA)—nicknamed the "Fame Academy" for the similar school on the American TV series.

As young men, the boys rode the bus together to school—waiting at a bus stop in the **Penny Lane** neighborhood. Later they wrote a nostalgic song about the things they would observe while waiting there: the shelter by the roundabout, the barbershop, and so on. (While they also sing about the fireman with the clean machine, the firehouse itself is not actually on Penny Lane, but around the corner.)

After a series of lineup shuffles, by 1960 the group had officially become The Beatles: John Lennon, Paul McCartney, George

Harrison, and...Pete Best and Stu Sutcliffe. The quintet gradually built a name for themselves in Liverpool's "Merseybeat" scene, performing at local clubs. While the famous **Cavern Club** is gone (the one you see advertised is a reconstruction, but does offer similar ambience and good cover bands), the original **Casbah Coffee Club**—which the group felt more attached to—still exists and is open for tours (3.5 miles northwest of downtown in Pete Best's former basement, prebook by calling the TI at tel. 0151/707-0729 or online at www.petebest.com).

The group went to Hamburg, Germany, to cut their teeth in the thriving music scene there. They wound up performing as the backing band for Tony Sheridan's single "My Bonny." When this caught on back in Liverpool, promoter Brian Epstein took note, and signed the act. His shrewd management would eventually propel the Beatles to superstardom.

Many different people could be considered the "Fifth Beatle." John's friend Stu, who performed with the group in Hamburg, left to pursue his own artistic interests. Pete Best was the band's original drummer, but he was a loner and producers questioned his musical chops, so he was replaced with Ringo Starr. (John later said, "Pete Best was a great drummer, but Ringo was a Beatle.") Brian Epstein, the manager who marketed the Beatles brilliantly before his untimely death, is another candidate. But—in terms of long-term musical influence—it's hard to ignore the case for George Martin, who produced all the Beatles' albums except *Let It Be,* and was instrumental in both forging and developing the Beatles sound.

By early 1964, the Beatles were already world-famous—but, as evidenced by their songs about Penny Lane and Strawberry Fields, they never forgot their Merseyside home.

island nation). You'll see how crew members lived aboard merchant ships. The **Hello Sailor!** exhibit explains how gay culture flourished at sea at a time when it was taboo in almost every other walk of British life.

Make your way to the basement, where exhibits describe the tremendous wave of **emigration** through Liverpool's port. And the **Seized!** exhibit looks at the legal and illegal movement of goods through that same port, including thought-provoking displays on customs, taxation, and smuggling.

Tate Liverpool

This prestigious gallery of modern art is near the Maritime Museum. It won't entertain you as well as its London sister, the Tate Modern, but if you're into modern art, any Tate's great. Its two airy floors dedicated to the rotating collection of statues and paintings from the 20th century are free; the top and ground floors are devoted to special exhibits. The Tate also has an inexpensive recommended café.

Cost and Hours: Free, donations accepted, £10-12 for special exhibits, daily 10:00-18:00, tel. 0151/702-7400, www.tate.org.uk/visit/tate-liverpool.

At Pier Head, North of the Albert Dock

A five-minute walk across the bridge north of the Albert Dock takes you to the Pier Head area, with the following sights. Note that the Mersey Ferries terminal at Pier Head also hosts some exhibits from The Beatles Story.

▲▲Museum of Liverpool

This museum, in the blocky white building just across the bridge north of the Albert Dock, does a good job of fulfilling its goal to "capture Liverpool's vibrant character and demonstrate the city's unique contribution to the world." The museum is full of interesting items, fun interactive displays (great for kids), and fascinating facts that bring a whole new depth to your Liverpool experience.

Cost and Hours: Free, donations accepted, daily 10:00-17:00, guidebook-£1, café, Mann Island, Pier Head, tel. 0151/478-4545, www.liverpoolmuseums.org.uk.

Visiting the Museum: First, stop by the information desk to check on the show times for the museum's various videos. If you have kids age six and under, you can also get a free timed-entry ticket for the hands-on Little Liverpool exhibit on the ground floor.

Ground Floor: On this level, **The Great Port** details the story of Liverpool's defining industry and how it developed through the Industrial Revolution. On display is an 1838 steam locomotive that was originally built for the Liverpool and Manchester Railway. The **Global City** exhibit focuses on how Liverpool's status as a major British shipping center made it the gateway to a global empire and features a 20-minute video, *Power and the Glory,* about Liverpool's role within the British Empire.

First Floor: Don't miss the **Liverpool Overhead Railway** exhibit, which features the only surviving car from this 19th-century elevated railway. You can actually jump aboard and take a seat to watch 1897 movie footage shot from the train line. A huge interactive model shows the railway's route. Also on this floor is the **History Detectives** exhibit, which covers Liverpool's history and archaeology.

Second Floor: If you're short on time, spend most of it here. The **People's Republic** exhibit examines what it means to be a Liverpudlian (a.k.a. "Scouser") and covers everything from housing and health issues to military and religious topics. As industrialized Liverpool has long been a hotbed of the labor movement, exhibits here also detail the political side of the city, including child labor issues and women's suffrage.

One fascinating display is the re-creation of Liverpool's 19th-century court housing, which consisted of a series of tiny dwellings bunched around a narrow courtyard. With more than 60 people sharing two toilets, this was some of the most overcrowded and unsanitary housing in Britain at the time.

On the other side of the floor, the **Wondrous Place** exhibit celebrates the arts, cultural, and sporting side of Liverpool. An exhibit on the city's famous passion for soccer features memorabilia and the 17-minute video *Kicking and Screaming,* about the rivalry between the Everton and Liverpool football teams and the sometimes tragic history of the sport (such as when 96 fans were crushed to death at a Liverpool match).

Music is the other big focus here, with plenty of fun interactive stops that include quizzes, a karaoke booth, and listening stations featuring artists with ties to Liverpool (from Elvis Costello to Echo & the Bunnymen). And of course you'll see plenty of Beatles mania, including their famous suits, the original stage from St. Peter's Church (where John Lennon was performing the first time Paul McCartney laid eyes on him; located in the theater), and an eight-minute film on the band.

Finally, in the **Skylight Gallery,** look for Ben Johnson's painting *The Liverpool Cityscape, 2008,* a remarkable and fun-to-examine melding of old and new art styles. At first glance, it's a typical sky-line painting, but Johnson used computer models to create perfect depictions of each building before he put brush to canvas. This method allows for a photorealistic, highly detailed, but completely sanitized portrait of a city. Notice there are no cars or people.

The Three Graces

Three towering buildings near the Museum of Liverpool, rem-nants of a time of great seafaring prosperity, are known collectively as Liverpool's Three Graces: the double-clock-towered **Royal Liver Building**, with spires topped by the city's mythical mascot, the "Liver birds"; the relatively dull and boxy **Cunard Building** (now hosting the British Music Experience, described next); and the domed **Port of Liverpool Building**, which strains to evoke memories of St. Paul's Cathedral in London. A 2002 plan to create a Fourth Grace—a metallic, glassy, and yellow blob called The Cloud—never panned out, and that site is now home to the Mu-seum of Liverpool. While you can see the Three Graces from along the embank-ment—which is also lined with monu-

ments to important Liverpudlians—the best views are from across the River Mersey (see page 474 for details on riding the ferry).

▲▲British Music Experience

This new museum, located in the Cunard Building at Pier Head, goes beyond Liverpool's Beatlemania, immersing visitors in the history of British music of all genres from 1945 until today. The multimedia ex-hibits include costumes, instruments, recordings, and memorabilia from artists and bands such as David Bowie, Queen, Amy Winehouse, Coldplay, and Adele, plus the chance to

play professional-grade instruments in a sound studio. You could easily spend hours here, but plan for at least 90 minutes.

Cost and Hours: £16, includes multimedia guide, daily 9:00-19:00, Thu until 21:00, last entry 1.5 hours before closing; tel. 0344/335-0655, www.britishmusicexperience.com.

Visiting the Museum: As you enter, pause at the big video wall in the main hall to see music videos and a hologram show featuring Boy George (every 20 minutes). Then either follow the displays chronologically—beginning on your right and working counterclockwise—or pick your decades of interest.

Each section displays interesting facts about well-known artists, billboard art, costumes, instruments, and more. Your multimedia guide provides interviews, videos, and picture galleries. The first two sections (1945-1962, which covers jazz, skiffle, and rock 'n' roll, and 1962-1966, covering R&B, Merseybeat, and the Beatles) have well-done interactive tables explaining the origin of these music genres and how the UK and US music scenes influenced each other. Timelines throughout each section place the music in historical context, describing its relation to the politics and culture of each decade. Additional sections are dedicated to the history of music devices and TV/radio programs.

In the back is a studio where you can exercise your own musical skills—take interactive instrument lessons, record your singing, or learn dance moves that have been popular over the decades.

DOWNTOWN
Beatles Sights in the Cavern Quarter

The narrow, bar-lined Mathew Street, right in the heart of downtown, is ground zero for Beatles fans. The Beatles frequently performed in their early days together at the original Cavern Club, deep in a cellar along this street. While that's long gone, a mock-up of the historic nightspot (built with many of the original bricks) lives on a few doors down. Still billed as "the **Cavern Club**," this is worth a visit to see the reconstructed cellar that's often filled by Beatles cover bands. While touristy, dropping by in the afternoon for a live Beatles tribute act in the Cavern Club somehow just feels right. You'll have Beatles songs stuck in your head all day anyway, so you might as well see a  wannabe John and Paul strumming and harmonizing a close approximation of the original (open daily 10:00-24:00; live music daily from mid-afternoon until late evening, free admission most of the time, small entry fee Thu-Sun evenings; tel. 0151/236-9091, www.cavernclub.org).

Across the street and run by the same owners, the **Cavern Pub** lacks its sibling's troglodyte aura, but makes up for it with

LIVERPOOL

LIVERPOOL

walls lined with old photos and memorabilia from the Beatles and other bands who've performed here. Like the Cavern Club, the pub features frequent performances by Beatles cover bands and other acts (no cover, daily 11:00-24:00, tel. 0151/236-4041).

Out front is the Cavern's **Wall of Fame,** with a too-cool-for-school bronze John Lennon leaning up against a wall of bricks engraved with the names of musical acts that have graced the Cavern stage.

At the corner is the recommended **Hard Day's Night Hotel,** decorated inside and out to honor the Fab Four. Notice the statues of John, Paul, George, and Ringo on the second-story corners, and the Beatles gift shop (one of many in town) on the ground floor.

Museums near the Train Station
Both of these museums are just a five-minute walk from the Lime Street train station.

▲Walker Art Gallery
Though it has few recognizable works, Liverpool's main art gallery offers an enjoyable walk through an easy-to-digest collection of European (mostly British) paintings, sculpture, and decorative arts. There's no audioguide, but many of the works are well explained by posted descriptions.

Cost and Hours: Free, donations accepted, daily 10:00-17:00, William Brown Street, tel. 0151/478-4199, www.liverpoolmuseums.org.uk.

Visiting the Museum: The ground floor has an information desk, café, children's area, small decorative arts collection, and sculpture gallery focusing on British Neoclassical works from the 19th century. The sculpture gallery has many works by John Gibson, a Welshman who grew up in Liverpool and later studied under the Italian master Antonio Canova. Gibson's *Tinted Venus* (in the case in the middle) was considered scandalous to Victorian mores because of the nude sculpture's lifelike pinkish tint.

Upstairs is a concise 15-room painting gallery. For a general chronological spin, from the top of the stairs head straight back to find Room 1. Because of various special exhibits that rotate in and out, the following paintings may be located in other rooms or not on display.

Room 1 (actually two adjoining rooms) has a famous Nicholas Hilliard portrait of Queen Elizabeth I (nicknamed "The Pelican," for her brooch) and a well-known royal portrait of Henry VIII by Hans Holbein. Room 3 has bombastic Baroque works by Rubens and Murillo, Room 4 features a Rembrandt self-portrait, while Room 5 focuses on 18th-century English painting, including canvases by Gainsborough, Hogarth (find the painting of the great actor David Garrick in the role of Richard III), and lots of George Stubbs. Rooms 6-8 showcase a delightful array of Pre-Raphaelite works, among them Millias' evocative portrait of Isabella (Room 6). You'll find some Turners (a mushy landscape and a more sharp-focus Linlithgow Castle) in Room 7.

Room 10 makes the transition to the 20th century and Impressionism, while modern British art is displayed in Rooms 11-15. In Room 11, Bernard Fleetwood-Walker's *Amity* shows a pair of chaste but (apparently) sexually charged teenagers relaxing in the grass.

World Museum

This catchall family museum offers five floors of kid-oriented exhibits. You'll see dinosaurs, an aquarium, artifacts from the ancient world, a planetarium and theater (get free tickets at the info desk in the lobby for these), and more.

Cost and Hours: Free, donations accepted, daily 10:00-17:00, William Brown Street, tel. 0151/478-4393, www.liverpoolmuseums.org.uk.

Cathedrals

Liverpool has not one but two notable cathedrals—one Anglican, the other Catholic. (As the Spinners song puts it, "If you want a cathedral, we've got one to spare.") Both are huge, architecturally significant, and well worth visiting. Near the eastern edge of downtown, they're connected by a 10-minute, half-mile walk on pleasant Hope Street, which is lined with theaters and good restaurants (see "Eating in Liverpool," later).

Liverpudlians enjoy pointing out that they have not only the world's only Catholic cathedral designed by a Protestant architect, but also the only Protestant one designed by a Catholic. With its large Irish-immigrant population, Liverpool suffered from tension between its Catholic and Protestant communities for much of its history. But during the city's darkest stretch of the depressed 1970s, the bishops of each church—Anglican Bishop David Sheppard and Catholic Archbishop Derek Worlock—came together and worked hard to reconcile the two communities for the betterment of Liverpool. (Liverpudlians nicknamed this dynamic duo "fish and chips" because they were "always together, and always in the newspaper.") It worked: Liverpool is a bold new cultural center, and relations between the two faiths remain healthy here. Join in this ecumenical spirit by visiting both of their main churches.

▲Metropolitan Cathedral of Christ the King (Catholic)

This daringly modern building, a cone topped with a crowned cylinder, seems almost out of place in its workaday Liverpool neighborhood. But the cathedral you see today bears no resemblance to Sir Edwin Lutyens' original 1930s plans for a stately Neo-Byzantine cathedral, which was to take 200 years to build and rival St. Peter's Basilica in Vatican City. (Lutyens was desperate to one-up the grandiose plans of Sir Giles Gilbert Scott, who was building the Anglican Cathedral down the street.) The crypt for the ambitious church was excavated in the 1930s, but World War II (during which the crypt was used as an air-raid shelter) stalled progress for decades. In the 1960s, the plans were scaled back, and this smaller (but still impressive) house of worship was completed in 1967.

Cost and Hours: Cathedral—free entry but donations accepted, daily 7:30-18:00—but after 17:15 (during Mass), you won't be able to walk around; crypt—£3, Mon-Sat 10:00-16:00, closed Sun, last entry 45 minutes before closing, enter from inside church near organ; visitors center and café, Mount Pleasant, tel. 0151/709-9222, www.liverpoolmetrocathedral.org.uk.

Visiting the Cathedral: On the stepped plaza in front of the church, you'll see the entrance to the cathedral's visitors center and café (on your right). You're standing on a big concrete slab that provides a roof to the humongous Lutyens Crypt, underfoot. The existing cathedral occupies only a small part of the would-be cathedral's footprint. Imagine what might have been—"the greatest building never built." Because of the cathedral's tent-like appear-

ance and ties to the local Irish community, some Liverpudlians dubbed it "Paddy's Wigwam."

Climb up the stairs to the main doors, step inside, and let your eyes adjust to this magnificent dimly lit space. Unlike a typical nave-plus-transept cross-shaped church, this cathedral has a round footprint, with seating for a congregation of 3,000 fully surrounding the white marble altar. Like a theater in the round, it was designed to involve worshippers in the service. Suspended above the altar is a stylized crown of thorns.

Spinning off from the round central sanctuary are 13 smaller chapels, many of them representing different stages of Jesus' life. Each chapel is different. Explore, tuning into the symbolic details in each one. Also keep an eye out for the 14 exquisite bronze Stations of the Cross by local artist Sean Rice (on the wall).

The massive **Lutyens Crypt** (named for the ambitious original architect)—the only part of the originally planned cathedral to be completed—is massive, with huge vaults and vast halls lined with six million bricks. The crypt contains a chapel—with windows by Lutyens—that's still used for Sunday Mass, the tombs of three archbishops, a treasury, and an exhibit about the cathedral's construction.

Hope Street

The street connecting the cathedrals is the main artery of Liverpool's "uptown," a lively and fun-to-explore district loaded with dining and entertainment options. In addition to well-respected theaters, this street is home to the Philharmonic and its namesake pub (see "Eating in Liverpool," later). At the intersection with Mount Street is a monument consisting of concrete suitcases; just down this street are the high schools that Paul, George, and John attended (for details, see "The Beatles in Liverpool" sidebar, earlier).

▲▲Liverpool Cathedral (Anglican)

The largest cathedral in Great Britain, this gigantic house of worship hovers at the south end of downtown. Tour its cavernous interior and consider scaling its tower.

Cost and Hours: Free, £3 suggested donation, daily 8:00-18:00; £5.50 ticket includes tower climb (2 elevators and 108 steps), audioguide, and 10-minute *Great Space* film; tower—Mon-Sat 10:00-17:00 (Thu until sunset March-Oct), Sun 12:00-16:00 (changes possible depending on bell-ringing schedule); St. James Mount, tel. 0151/709-6271, www.liverpoolcathedral.org.uk.

Visiting the Cathedral: Over the main door is a modern *Risen Christ* statue by Elisabeth Frink. Liverpudlians, not thrilled with the featureless statue and always quick with a joke, have dubbed it **"Frinkenstein."**

Stepping inside, pick up a floor plan at the information desk, go into the main hall, and take in the size of the place. When Liverpool was officially designated a "city" (seat of a bishop), they wanted to build a huge house of worship as a symbol of Liverpudlian pride. Built in bold Neo-Gothic style (like London's Parliament), it seems to trumpet with modern bombast the importance of this city on the Mersey. Begun in 1904, the cathedral's construction was interrupted by the tumultuous 20th century and not completed until 1973.

Go to the big circular tile in the very center of the cathedral, under the highest tower. This is a plaque for the building's architect, **Sir Giles Gilbert Scott** (1880-1960). While the church you're surrounded by may seem like his biggest legacy, he also designed an icon that's synonymous with Britain: the classic red telephone box. Notice the highly detailed sandstone carvings flanking this aisle.

Take a counterclockwise spin around

the church interior. Head up the right aisle until you find the **model** of the original plan for the cathedral (press the button to light it up). Scott was a very young architect and received the commission with the agreement that he work closely under the wing of his more established mentor, George Bodley. These two architects' visions clashed, and Bodley usually won...until he died early in the planning stages, leaving Scott to pursue his own muse. If Bodley had survived, the cathedral would probably look more like this model. As it was, only one corner of the complex (the Lady Chapel, which we're about to see) was completed before Giles changed plans to create the version you see today.

Nearby, the **"whispering arch"** spanning the sarcophagus has remarkable acoustics, carrying voices from one end to the other. Try it.

Continuing down the church, notice the very colorful, modern painting of *The Good Samaritan* (by Adrian Wiszniewski,

1995), high above on the right. The naked crime victim (who has been stabbed in his side, like the Crucifixion wound of Jesus) has been ignored by the well-dressed yuppies in the foreground, but the female Samaritan is finally taking notice. The canvas is packed with symbolism (for example, the Swiss Army knife, in a pool of blood in the left foreground, is open in the 3 o'clock position—the time that Jesus was crucified). This contemporary work of art demonstrates that this is a new, living church. But the congregation has its limits. This painting used to hang closer to the front of the church, but now they've moved it here, out of sight.

Proceeding to the corner, you'll reach the entrance to the oldest part of the church (1910): the **Lady Chapel,** with stained-glass windows celebrating im-

portant women. (Sadly, the original windows were destroyed in World War II; these are replicas.)

Back up in the main part of the church, continue behind the main altar to the **Education Centre,** with a fun, sped-up video showing all of the daily work it takes to make this cathedral run.

Circling around the far corner of the church, you'll pass the children's chapel and chapterhouse, and then pass under another modern Wiszniewski painting *(The House Built on Rock)*. Across from that painting, go into the choir to get a good look at the Last Supper altarpiece above the **main altar.**

Continuing back up the aisle, you'll come to the **war memorial transept.** At its entrance is a book listing Liverpudlians lost in war. Battle flags fly high on the wall above.

You'll wind up at the gift shop, where you can buy a ticket to climb to the top of the tower. The cathedral's café is up the stairs, above the gift shop.

AWAY FROM THE CENTER
▲Lennon and McCartney Homes

John's and Paul's boyhood homes are now owned by the National Trust and have both been restored to how they looked during the lads' 1950s childhoods. While some Beatles bus tours stop here for photo ops, only the National Trust minibus tour gets you inside the homes. This isn't Graceland—you won't find an over-the-top rock-and-roll extravaganza here. If you don't know the difference between John and Paul, you'll likely be bored. But for die-hard Beatles fans who want to get a glimpse into the time and place that created these musical masterminds, the National Trust tour is worth ▲▲▲.

Famous musicians who perform in Liverpool often make the pilgrimage to these homes—Bob Dylan turned up on one tour disguised in a hoodie—and Paul himself occasionally drops by. Ask the guides about recent memorable visitors.

Because the houses are in residential neighborhoods—and still share walls with neighbors—the National Trust runs only a few tours per day, limited to 15 or so Beatlemaniacs each.

Cost: £23, £3 guidebooks available through preorder online or at John Lennon's home.

Reservations: Advance booking is strongly advised, especially in summer and on weekends or holidays. Book online or by phone as soon as you know your Liverpool plans—or at least two weeks ahead (tel. 0151/427-7231, www.nationaltrust.org.uk/beatles). At times you may be able to get tickets a couple of days ahead of time, but at others, such as during Beatles week in August, tours can book up months in advance. If you haven't reserved ahead, you can try to book a same-day tour (for the morning tours, call 0151/707-0729); the last tour of the day is least likely to be full.

Tour Options: Tours run daily from the Albert Dock at 10:00, 11:00, and 14:15 (tours do not run Mon-Tue in mid-Feb-mid-March and Nov; no tours at all Dec-mid-Feb). They depart from the Jurys Inn (south across the bridge from The Beatles Story, near the Ferris wheel—meet in hotel lobby) and follow a route that includes a quick pass, but no stop, by Penny Lane (ask driver to point it out to you).

An additional tour leaves at 15:00 from Speke Hall, an out-of-the-way National Trust property located eight miles southeast of Liverpool. Drivers should allow 30 minutes from the city center to Speke Hall—follow the brown *Speke Hall* signs through dozens of roundabouts, heading in the general direction of the airport. If you don't have a car, hop in a taxi.

From either starting point, the entire visit takes about 2.5 hours.

Visiting the Homes: A minibus takes you to the homes of John and Paul, with about 45 minutes inside each (no photos allowed inside either home). Each home has a caretaker who acts as your guide. These folks give an entertaining, insightful-to-fans talk that lasts about 30 minutes. You then have 10-15 minutes to wander through the house on your own. Ask lots of questions if their spiel peters out early—these docents are a wealth of information. Morning tours visit John's home first, while afternoon tours start with Paul's (where you can also find a WC).

Mendips (John Lennon's Home): Even though he sang about being a working-class hero, John grew up in the suburbs of Liverpool, surrounded by doctors, lawyers, and—beyond the back fence—Strawberry Field.

This was the home of John's Aunt Mimi, who raised him in this house from the time he was five years old and once told him, "A guitar's all right, John, but you'll never earn a living by it." (John later bought Mimi a country cottage with those fateful words etched over the fireplace.) John moved out at age 23, but his first wife, Cynthia, bunked here for a while when John made his famous first trip to America. Yoko Ono bought the house in 2002 and gave it as a gift to the National Trust (generating controversy among the neighbors). The house's stewards make this place come to life.

On the surface, it's just a 1930s house carefully restored to how it would have been in the past. But delve deeper. It's been lovingly

LIVERPOOL

cared for—restored to be the tidy, well-kept place Mimi would have recognized (down to dishtowels hanging in the kitchen). It's a lucky quirk of fate that the house's interior remained mostly unchanged after the Lennons left: The bachelor who owned it decades after them didn't upgrade much, so even the light switches are true to the time.

If you're a John Lennon fan, it's fun to picture him as a young boy drawing and imagining at his dining room table. His bedroom, with an Elvis poster and his favorite boyhood books, offers tantalizing hints at his later musical genius. Sing a song to yourself in the enclosed porch—John and Paul did this when they wanted an echo-chamber effect.

20 Forthlin Road (Paul McCartney's Home): In comparison to Aunt Mimi's house, the home where Paul grew up is simpler, much less "posh," and even a little ratty around the edges. Michael, Paul's brother, wanted it that way—their mother, Mary (famously mentioned in "Let It Be"), died when the boys were young, and it never had the tidiness of a woman's touch. It's been intentionally scuffed up around the edges to preserve the historical accuracy. Notice the differences—Paul has said that John's house was vastly different and more clearly middle class; at Mendips, there were books on the bookshelves— but Paul's father had an upright piano. He also rigged up wires and headphones that connected the boys' bedrooms to the living room radio so they could listen to rock 'n' roll on Radio Luxembourg.

More than a hundred Beatles songs were written in this house (including "I Saw Her Standing There") during days Paul and John spent skipping school. The photos from Michael, taken in this house, help make the scene of what's mostly a barren interior much more interesting. Ask your guide how Paul would sneak into the house late at night without waking up his dad.

Nightlife in Liverpool

Liverpool hops after hours, especially on weekends.

Ropewalks

The most happening zone is the area called Ropewalks, just east of the downtown shopping district and Albert Dock. Part of the protected historic area of Liverpool's docklands, the redeveloped Ropewalks area is now filled with pubs, nightclubs, and lounges—some of them rough around the edges, others posh and sleek. While this area is aimed primarily at the college-age crowd, it's still worth a stroll, and has a few eateries worth considering. **Furnivals Well** cocktail bar fills a circa-1850 police station with a lively pub atmosphere. Downstairs, past the bar, several jail cells have been converted into cozy seating areas, while another bar and dining area sprawl upstairs (closed Sun, 1 Campbell Square).

City Center

Liverpool also has a wide range of watering holes. The ones listed here are all in the city center and are best for serious drinkers and beer aficionados—the food is an afterthought.

The Ship and Mitre, overlooking an off-ramp at the edge of downtown, has perhaps Liverpool's best selection of beers—with 30-plus types on tap—as well as frequent beer festivals; it can get very crowded (133 Dale Street, tel. 0151/236-0859, see festival schedule at www.theshipandmitre.com).

Thomas Rigby's has hard-used wooden floors in the taproom that spill out into a rollicking garden courtyard. Its atmosphere is laid back, and chances are good you'll meet locals, especially after work hours (21 Dale Street).

Around the corner and much more sedate, **Ye Hole in Ye Wall** brags that it's Liverpool's oldest pub, from 1726. Notice the men's room on the ground floor—the women's room, required by law to be added in the 1970s, is upstairs (just off Dale Street on Hackins Hey).

A few blocks over, right in the heart of downtown and surrounded by modern mega-malls, is **The Globe**—a tight, cozy, local-feeling pub with five real ales and sloping floors (17 Cases Street).

Sleeping in Liverpool

Your best budget options in this thriving city are the boring, predictable, and central chain hotels—though I've listed a couple of more colorful options also worth considering. Many hotels, including the ones listed below, charge more on weekends (particularly Sat), especially when the Liverpool FC soccer team plays a home game. Rates shoot up even higher two weekends a year: during the Grand National horse race (long weekend in April) and during Beatles Week in late August—avoid these times if you can. Prices plummet on Sunday nights.

$$$$ Hope Street Hotel is a class act that sets the bar for Liverpool's hotels. Located across from the Philharmonic on Hope Street (midway between the cathedrals, in a fun dining neighborhood), this stylish and contemporary hotel has 89 luxurious rooms

LIVERPOOL

with lots of hardwood, exposed brick, and elegant little extras. An extension, located in the former School for the Blind, has 50 additional rooms, a roof garden, a spa with a pool, and a cinema (breakfast extra—book ahead, elevator, some rooms handicap accessible, pay parking, 40 Hope Street, tel. 0151/709-3000, www. hopestreethotel.co.uk, sleep@hopestreethotel.co.uk).

$$$ Hard Day's Night Hotel is the ideal splurge for Beatles pilgrims. Located in a carefully restored old building smack in the heart of the Cavern Quarter, its contemporary decor is purely Beatles, from its public spaces (lobby, lounge, bar, restaurant) to its 110 rooms, each with a different original Beatles portrait by New York artist Shannon. There's often live music in the afternoons in the lobby bar—and it's not all Beatles covers. What could have been a tacky travesty is instead tasteful, with a largely black-and-white color scheme and subtle nods to the Fab Four (breakfast extra, elevator, Internet-enabled TVs with music playlists, pay parking, Central Building, North John Street,

tel. 0151/236-1964, www.harddaysnighthotel.com, enquiries@ harddaysnighthotel.com).

$$ Aachen Guest Accommodations has 15 modern, straightforward rooms in an old Georgian townhouse on a pleasant street just uphill from the heart of downtown (includes breakfast, 89 Mount Pleasant, tel. 0151/709-3477, www.aachenhotel.co.uk, enquiries@aachenhotel.co.uk).

$$ Hallmark Inn Liverpool, nearly next door in a stately old Georgian building, has tight hallways and 82 small rooms with mod decor and amenities (breakfast extra—prebook, no elevator and six floors, pay parking, 115 Mount Pleasant, tel. 0330/028-3426, www.hallmarkhotels.co.uk, liverpoolinn@hallmarkhotels. co.uk).

$$ Sir Thomas Hotel is a centrally located hotel that was once a bank. The lobby has been redone in trendy style, and the 39 rooms are comfortable. As windows are thin and it's a busy neighborhood, ask for a quieter room (some rates include breakfast, elevator, pay parking, 10-minute walk from station, 24 Sir Thomas Street at the corner of Victoria Street, tel. 0151/236-1366, www.sirthomashotel. co.uk, reservations@sirthomashotel.co.uk).

Other Chain Hotels: At the Albert Dock, you'll find a **Premier Inn** and **Holiday Inn Express.** Premier Inn has several other central branches, including downtown on Vernon Street and near the Liverpool One mall on Hanover Street.

¢ **Hostel:** Run by the daughter of the Beatles' first manager, **International Inn Hostel** rents 100 budget beds in a former Victorian warehouse (includes sheets, all rooms have bathrooms, guest kitchen with free toast and tea/coffee available 24 hours, laundry room, game room/TV lounge, video library, 24-hour reception, 4 South Hunter Street, tel. 0151/709-8135, www.internationalinn. co.uk, info@internationalinn.co.uk). From the Lime Street Station, the hostel is an easy 15-minute walk; if taking a taxi, tell them it's on South Hunter Street near Hardman Street.

Eating in Liverpool

Liverpool has an exciting and quickly evolving culinary scene; as a rollicking, youthful city, it's a magnet for creative chefs as well as upscale chain restaurants. I've arranged my listings by neighborhood. Consider my suggestions, but also browse the surrounding streets. This is a city where restaurant-finding is a joy rather than a chore. Note that many places tend to close down a bit earlier on Sundays—arrive an hour or two before my listed closing times.

ON AND NEAR HOPE STREET

Hope Street, which connects the two cathedrals, is also home to several excellent restaurants. The Quarter, HOST, and 60 Hope Street—which cluster near the corner of Hope and Falkner streets—are owned by brothers.

$$ The Quarter serves up Mediterranean food at rustic tables that sprawl through several connected houses. It's trendy but cozy. They also serve breakfast and have carryout coffee, cakes, pasta, and sandwiches in their attached deli (daily 9:00-23:00, 7 Falkner Street, tel. 0151/707-1965).

$$ HOST (short for "Hope Street") features Asian fusion dishes in a casual, colorful, modern atmosphere. There are gluten-free and vegan options here (daily 11:00-23:00, 31 Hope Street, tel. 0151/708-5831).

$$ Jenever is a little one-room bistro specializing in tapas and 65 varieties of gin. While there's also beer and wine, you can't help but try one of their gin cocktails or splurge on a four-flight gin tasting menu (food served Wed-Sun 12:00-21:00, closed Mon-Tue, bar open later, 29a Hope Street, tel. 0151/707-7888).

$$$ Ego offers Moroccan, Spanish, and Greek dishes in a cozy and relaxing atmosphere. Their "Lunch Rapido" (Mon-Sat until 16:00) comes with a drink—including wine or beer—and is a great option when visiting the cathedrals on Hope Street (food served daily 12:00-22:00, next to the Philharmonic on Hope Street, tel. 0151/706-0707).

$$$$ 60 Hope Street has modern English cuisine made

with "as locally sourced as possible" ingredients in an upscale atmosphere. While the prices are high, their two- and three-course meals are a good deal (afternoon tea, open Mon-Sat 12:00-14:30 & 17:00-22:30, Sun 12:00-20:00, reservations smart—especially on weekends, 60 Hope Street, tel. 0151/707-6060, www.60hopestreet.com).

$$ Chinatown: A few blocks southwest of Hope Street is Liverpool's thriving Chinatown neighborhood, with the world's

biggest Chinese arch. Lots of enticing options dishing up Chinese grub line up along Berry Street in front of the arch and Cornwallis Street behind it. Among these, **Yuet Ben** is one of the most established (Tue-Sun 17:00-23:00, closed Mon, facing the arch at 1 Upper Duke Street, tel. 0151/709-5772). Or you can line up with the Liverpudlians at **Tokyou,** featuring tasty noodle and rice dishes (Cantonese, Japanese, Malaysian, etc.), with service that's fast and furious (daily 12:00-23:00, 7 Berry Street, tel. 0151/708-6286).

Pubs near Hope Street

$$ The Philharmonic Dining Rooms, kitty-corner from the actual Philharmonic, is actually a pub—but what a pub. This place

wins the "atmosphere award" for its old-time elegance. The bar is a work of art, the marble urinals are downright genteel, and the three sitting areas on the ground floor (including the giant hall) are an enticing place to sip a pint. This is a better place to drink than to eat, as food is usually served in the less-atmospheric upstairs. John Lennon once said that his biggest regret about fame was "not being able to go to the Phil for a drink" (food served daily 11:00-22:00, bar open until late, corner of Hope and Hardman streets, tel. 0151/707-2837).

$ The Fly in the Loaf has a classic pub exterior and interior, with efficient service, eight hand-pulls for real ales, and good food (food served daily 12:00-18:45, bar open until late, 13 Hardman Street, tel. 0151/708-0817).

ROPEWALKS

While primarily a nightlife zone, this gentrified area also has a smattering of unique restaurants.

$$$ Alma de Cuba is housed in the former Polish Catholic Church of St. Peter's with a trendy bar (downstairs, in the nave and altar area) and restaurant (upstairs, looking down into the nave). While the food (an eclectic international mix) is an afterthought, the "hedonists' church" atmosphere is nothing short of remarkable—at least to those who don't find it all a bit sacrilegious. To keep out the stag parties, no male groups of five or more are allowed to enter (food served daily 12:00-22:00, tapas until 17:00, bar stays open later; live music Tue and Thu from 22:30, live DJ with flower-petal shower and samba dancers Fri-Sat from 23:00, gospel brunch with small gospel choir Sun 13:30-17:00; Seel Street, tel. 0151/702-7394).

Bold Street: Liverpool's food scene is starting to percolate on this street between the pedestrian shopping zone and the Hope Street neighborhood. Look for trendy tapas, Middle Eastern, and Italian eateries. Check out **$$ Leaf,** which started as a teahouse and now offers a range of inventive breakfast, lunch, and dinner menus (vegetarian options, daily 9:00-22:00, 65 Bold Street, tel. 0151/707-7747, www.thisisleaf.co.uk).

Duke Street: A few big, modern, popular, chain-feeling restaurants—Japanese, Mexican, Italian, and more—line up along Duke Street in the heart of the Ropewalks area (concentrated on the block between Kent Street and the Chinatown arch). While not high cuisine, these crowd-pleasers are close to the nightlife action.

DOWNTOWN

$$ Fonseca's is a casual bistro serving high-quality British, Mediterranean, and international cuisine (Tue-Fri 17:00-21:00, Sat 12:00-22:00, closed Sun-Mon, 12 Stanley Street, tel. 0151/255-0808). They also have a bar downstairs.

Liverpool One: This shopping center, right in the heart of town, is nirvana for British chain restaurants. The upper Leisure Terrace has a row of some popular chains, all with outdoor seating. If you want to dine on predictable mass-produced food, you'll have a wide selection here.

AT THE ALBERT DOCK

The eateries at the Albert Dock aren't high cuisine, but they're handy to your sightseeing. A slew of trendy restaurants come alive with club energy at night, but are sedate and pleasant in the afternoon and early evening. For lunch near the sights, consider the **$ Tate Gallery Café** (daily 10:00-16:30).

Liverpool Connections

BY TRAIN

Note that many connections from Liverpool transfer at the Wigan North Western Station, which is on a major north-south train line.

From Liverpool by Train to: Keswick/Lake District (train to Penrith—roughly hourly with change in Wigan and possibly elsewhere, 2.5 hours; then bus to Keswick), **York** (at least hourly, 2.5 hours, more with transfer), **Edinburgh** (1-2/hour, 4.5 hours, most change in Wigan or Manchester), **Glasgow** (1-2/hour, 4 hours, change in Wigan and possibly elsewhere), **London**'s Euston Station (at least hourly, 2.5 hours, more with changes), **Crewe** (3/hour, 45 minutes), **Chester** (3/hour, 45 minutes). Train info: Tel. 0345-748-4950, www.nationalrail.co.uk.

BY FERRY

By Ferry to Dublin, Republic of Ireland: P&O Irish Sea Ferries runs a car ferry only—no foot passengers (1-3/day, 7.5-hour trip, prices vary widely—roughly £150 for car and 2 passengers, overnight ferry includes berth and meals, 20-minute drive north of the city center at Liverpool Freeport—Gladstone dock, check in 1-2 hours before departure, tel. 0800-130-0030, www.poirishsea.com). Those without cars can take a ferry to Dublin via the Isle of Man (runs mid-June-Aug, www.steam-packet.com), or ride the train to North Wales and catch the Dublin ferry from Holyhead (www.stenaline.co.uk).

By Ferry to Belfast, Northern Ireland: Ferries sail from nearby Birkenhead roughly twice a day (8.5 hours, fares vary widely, tel. 0844-770-7070, www.stenaline.co.uk). Birkenhead's dock is a 15-minute walk from Hamilton Square Station on Merseyrail's Wirral Line.

LIVERPOOL

THE LAKE DISTRICT

Keswick and the North Lake District • Ullswater Lake
• South Lake District

In the pristine Lake District, William Wordsworth's poems still shiver in trees and ripple on ponds. Nature rules this land, and humanity keeps a wide-eyed but low profile. Relax, recharge, take a cruise or a hike, and maybe even write a poem. Renew your poetic license at Wordsworth's famous Dove Cottage.

The Lake District, about 30 miles long and 30 miles wide, is nature's lush green playground. Explore it by foot, bike, bus, or car. Locals are fond of declaring that their mountains are older than the Himalayas and were once as tall, but have been worn down by the ages (Scafell Pike, the tallest peak in England, is only 3,206 feet). There's a walking-stick charm about the way nature and the culture mix here. Hiking along a windblown ridge or climbing over a rock fence to look into the eyes of a ragamuffin sheep, even tenderfeet get a chance to feel very outdoorsy. The tradition of staying close to the land remains true—albeit in an updated form—in the 21st century; restaurants serve organic food and you'll see stickers in home windows advocating for environmental causes.

Dress in layers, and expect rain mixed with brilliant "bright spells" (pubs offer atmospheric shelter at every turn). Drizzly days can be followed by delightful evenings.

Plan to spend the majority of your time in the unspoiled North Lake District. In this chapter, I focus on the town of Keswick, the lake called Derwentwater, and the vast, time-passed Newlands Valley. The North Lake District works great by car or by bus (with easy train access via Penrith), delights nature lovers, and has good accommodations to boot.

The South Lake District—slightly closer to London—is famous primarily for its Wordsworth and Beatrix Potter sights, and gets the promotion, the tour crowds, and the tackiness that comes with them. While the slate-colored towns (Ambleside, Windermere, Bowness-on-Windermere, and so on) are cute, they're also touristy—which means crowded and overpriced. I strongly recommend that you buck the trend and focus on the north. Ideally, enter the region from the north, via Penrith. Make your home base in or near Keswick, and side-trip from here into the South Lake District only if you're interested in the Wordsworth and Beatrix Potter sights. Dipping into the South Lake District also works well en route if you're driving between Keswick and points south.

PLANNING YOUR TIME

I'd suggest spending two days and two nights in this area. Penrith is the nearest train station, just 45 minutes by bus or car from Keswick. Those without a car will use Keswick as a springboard: Cruise the lake and take a hike in the Catbells area, or hop on a minibus tour. If great scenery is commonplace in your life, the Lake District can be more soothing (and rainy) than exciting. If you're rushed, you could make this area a one-night stand—or even a quick drive-through. But since the towns themselves are unexceptional, a visit here isn't worth it unless you have time to head up into the hills or out on the water at least once.

Two-Day Driving Plan: Here's the most exciting way for drivers coming from the south—who'd like to visit South Lake District sights en route to the North Lake District—to max out their time here:

Day 1: Leave the motorway at Kendal by 10:30; drive along Windermere, the lake, and through the town of Ambleside.

11:30   Tour Dove Cottage and the Wordsworth Museum.

13:00   Backtrack to Ambleside, where a small road leads up and over the dramatic Kirkstone Pass (far more scenic northbound than southbound—get out and bite the wind) and down to Glenridding on Lake Ullswater.

15:00   Catch the next Ullswater boat and ride to Howtown. Hike six miles (3-4 hours) from Howtown back to Glenridding. Or, for a shorter Ullswater experience, hike up to the Aira Force waterfall (1 hour) or up and around Lanty's Tarn (2 hours).

19:00   Drive to your Keswick hotel or farmhouse B&B near Keswick, with a stop as the sun sets at Castlerigg Stone Circle.

Day 2: Spend the morning (3-4 hours) splicing the Catbells high-ridge hike into a circular boat trip around Derwentwater. In the afternoon, make the circular drive from Keswick through the Newlands Valley, Buttermere, Honister Pass, and Borrowdale. You could tour the Honister Slate Mine en route (last tour at 15:30) and/or pitch-and-putt nine holes in Keswick before a late dinner.

GETTING AROUND THE LAKE DISTRICT
By Car

Nothing is very far from Keswick and Derwentwater. Pick up a good map (any hotel can loan you one), get off the big roads, and leave the car, at least occasionally, for some walking. In summer, the Keswick-Ambleside-Windermere-Bowness corridor (A-591) suffers from congestion. Back lanes are far less trampled and lead you through forgotten villages, where sheep outnumber people and stone churchyards are filled with happily permanent residents.

To **rent a car** here, try Enterprise in Penrith. They'll pick you up in Keswick and drive you back to their office to get the car, and also drive you back to Keswick after you've dropped it off (Mon-Fri 8:00-18:00, Sat 9:00-12:00, closed Sun, requires drivers license and second ID, reserve a day in advance, located at the David Hayton Peugeot dealer, Haweswater Road, tel. 01768/893-840). Larger outfits are more likely to have a branch in Carlisle, which is a bit to the north but well-served by train (on the same Glasgow-Birmingham line as Penrith) and only a few minutes farther from the Keswick area.

Parking is tight throughout the region. It's easiest to park in the pay-and-display lots (generally about £3/2-3 hours, £5/4-5 hours, and £8/12 hours; have coins on hand; most machines don't make change or won't take credit cards without a chip). If you're parking for free on the roadside, don't block vital turnouts. Never park on double yellow lines.

Without a Car

Those based in Keswick without a car manage fine. Because of the region's efforts to "green up" travel and cut down on car traffic, the bus service is quite efficient for hiking and sightseeing. (Consider leaving your car in town and using the bus for many sightseeing and hiking agendas.)

By Bus: Keswick has no real bus station; buses stop at a turnout in front of the Booths supermarket. Local buses take you quickly and easily (if not always frequently) to all nearby points of interest. Check the schedule carefully to make sure you can catch the

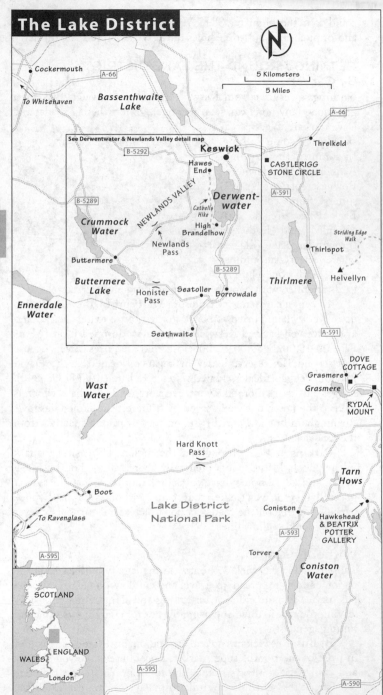

The Lake District

5 Kilometers

5 Miles

LAKE DISTRICT

Cockermouth

A-66

To Whitehaven

Bassenthwaite Lake

A-66

Threlkeld

See Derwentwater & Newlands Valley detail map

B-5292

Keswick

Hawes End

CASTLERIGG STONE CIRCLE

A-591

B-5289

NEWLANDS VALLEY

Catbells Hike

Derwent-water

Striding Edge Walk

Crummock Water

High Brandelhow

Thirlspot

Newlands Pass

B-5289

Buttermere

Thirlmere

Helvellyn

Ennerdale Water

Buttermere Lake

Honister Pass

Seatoller

Borrowdale

A-591

Seathwaite

DOVE COTTAGE

Grasmere

Grasmere

RYDAL MOUNT

Wast Water

Hard Knott Pass

Tarn Hows

Boot

Lake District National Park

Coniston

Hawkshead & BEATRIX POTTER GALLERY

To Ravenglass

A-593

A-595

Torver

Coniston Water

SCOTLAND

ENGLAND

WALES

London

A-595

A-590

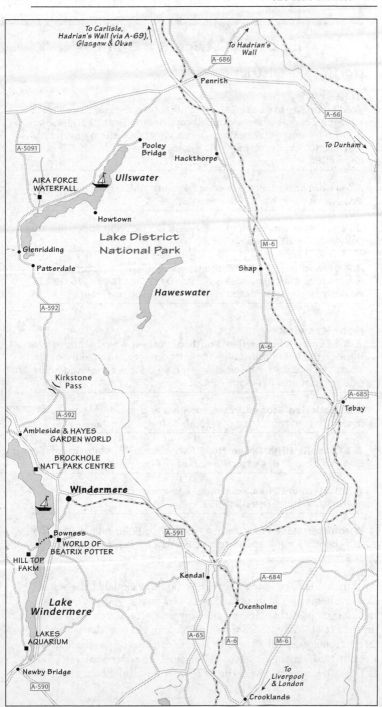

The Lake District at a Glance

North Lake District

In Keswick

▲▲**Theatre by the Lake** Top-notch theater a pleasant stroll from Keswick's main square. **Hours:** Shows generally at 19:30, also at 14:00 on Wed and Sat, winter times vary; box office open daily 9:30-20:00 on performance days, other days until 18:00. See page 498.

▲**Derwentwater Lake** immediately south of Keswick, with good boat service and trails. See page 488.

▲**Pencil Museum** Paean to graphite-filled wooden sticks. Hours: Daily 9:30-17:00. See page 489.

▲**Pitch-and-Putt Golf** Cheap, easygoing nine-hole course in Keswick's Hope Park. **Hours:** Daily from 10:00, last start at 18:00 but possibly later in summer, closed Nov-Feb. See page 490.

Near Keswick

▲▲▲**Scenic Circle Drive South of Keswick** Hour-long drive through the best of the Lake District's scenery, with plenty of fun stops (including the fascinating Honister Slate Mine) and short side-trip options. See page 494.

▲▲**Castlerigg Stone Circle** Evocative and extremely old (even by British standards) ring of Neolithic stones. See page 490.

▲▲**Catbells High Ridge Hike** Two-hour hike along dramatic ridge southwest of Keswick. See page 491.

▲▲**Buttermere Hike** Four-mile, low-impact lakeside loop in a gorgeous setting. See page 493.

▲**Honister Slate Mine Tour** A 1.5-hour guided hike through a 19th-century mine at the top of Honister Pass. **Hours:** Daily at

last bus home. The *Lakes Connection* booklet explains the schedules (available at TIs or on any bus). On board, you can purchase an Explorer pass that lets you ride any Stagecoach bus throughout the area (£11/1 day, £25/3 days), or you can get one-day passes for certain routes (described below); tickets can also be purchased with a credit card via the Stagecoach Bus app. The Derwentwater Bus & Boat all-day pass covers the #77/#77A bus and a boat cruise on

10:30, 12:30, and 15:30; also at 14:00 in summer; Dec-Jan 12:30 tour only. See page 496.

Ullswater Lake Area

▲▲**Ullswater Hike and Boat Ride** Long lake best enjoyed via steamer boat and seven-mile walk. **Hours:** Boats generally daily 9:45-16:55, 6-9/day April-Oct, fewer off-season. See page 507.

▲▲**Lanty's Tarn and Keldas Hill** Moderately challenging 2.5-mile loop hike from Glenridding with sweeping views of Ullswater. See page 507.

▲**Aira Force Waterfall** Easy uphill hike to thundering waterfall. See page 508.

South Lake District

▲▲**Dove Cottage and Wordsworth Museum** The poet's humble home, with a museum that tells the story of his remarkable life. **Hours:** Daily 9:30-17:30, Nov-Feb 10:00-16:30 except closed Jan and for events in Dec and Feb (call ahead). See page 509.

▲**Rydal Mount** Wordsworth's later, more upscale home. **Hours:** Daily 9:30-17:00; Nov and Feb 11:00-16:00 and closed Mon-Tue; closed Dec-Jan. See page 511.

▲**Hill Top Farm** Beatrix Potter's painstakingly preserved cottage. **Hours:** June-Aug daily 10:00-17:30; mid-Feb-May and Sept-Oct until 16:30 and closed Fri; Nov-Dec until 15:30 and closed Mon-Thu; closed Jan-mid-Feb; often a long wait to visit—call ahead. See page 513.

▲**Beatrix Potter Gallery** Collection of artwork by and background on the creator of Peter Rabbit. **Hours:** Daily 10:30-16:00, closed Nov-mid-Feb. See page 514.

Derwentwater. For bus and rail info, visit www.stagecoachbus.com and set your location for Keswick.

Buses **#X4** and **#X5** connect Penrith train station to Keswick (hourly, every 2 hours on Sun Nov-April, 45 minutes).

Bus **#77/#77A**, the Honister Rambler, makes the gorgeous circle from Keswick around Derwentwater, over Honister Pass, through Buttermere, and down the Whinlatter Valley (5-7/day clockwise, 4/day "anticlockwise," daily Easter-Oct, 1.75-hour loop). Bus **#78,** the Borrowdale Rambler, goes topless in the summer, affording a wonderful sightseeing experience in and of itself, heading from Keswick to Lodore Hotel, Grange, Rosthwaite, and Seatoller at the base of Honister Pass (hourly, daily Easter-Oct, 2/hour July-Sept, 30 minutes each way). Both of these routes are covered by the £8 Keswick and Honister Dayrider all-day pass.

Bus **#508,** the Kirkstone Rambler, runs between Penrith and Glenridding (near the bottom of Ullswater), stopping in Pooley Bridge (5/day, more frequent June-Aug with open-top buses, 50 minutes). Bus #508 also connects Glenridding and Windermere (1 hour). The £15 Ullswater Bus & Boat all-day pass covers bus #508 as well as steamers on Ullswater.

Bus **#505,** the Coniston Rambler, connects Windermere with Hawkshead (about hourly, daily Easter-Oct, 35 minutes).

Bus **#555** connects Keswick with the south (hourly, more frequent in summer, 1 hour to Windermere).

Bus **#599,** the open-top Lakeland Experience, runs along the main Windermere corridor, connecting the big tourist attractions in the south: Grasmere and Dove Cottage, Rydal Mount, Ambleside, Brockhole (National Park Visitors Centre), Windermere, and lake cruises from Bowness Pier (3/hour June-Sept, 2/hour May and Oct, 50 minutes each way, £8 Central Lakes Dayrider all-day pass).

By Bike: Keswick works well as a springboard for several fine days out on a bike; consider a three-hour loop trip up Newlands Valley. Ask about routes at the TI or your bike rental shop.

Several shops in Keswick rent road and mountain bikes (£20-25/day) and e-bikes (£30-50/day); rentals come with helmets and advice for good trips. Try **Whinlatter Bikes** (Mon-Sat 10:00-17:00, Sun until 16:00; free touring maps, 82 Main Street, tel. 017687/73940, www.whinlatterbikes.com); **e-venture** (daily 9:00-17:30, Elliot Park, tel. 0778/382 2722, www.e-venturebikes.co.uk); or **Keswick Bikes** (daily 9:00-17:30, 133 Main Street, tel. 017687/73355, www.keswickbikes.co.uk).

By Boat: A circular boat service glides you around Derwentwater, with several hiker-aiding stops along the way (for a cruise/hike option, see "Derwentwater Lakeside Walk" on page 489).

By Foot: Hiking information is available everywhere. Don't hike without a good, detailed map (wide selection at Keswick TI and at the many outdoor gear stores, or borrow one from your B&B). Helpful fliers at TIs and B&Bs describe the most popular routes. For an up-to-date weather report, ask at a TI or call 0844-846-2444. Wear suitable clothing and footwear (you can rent boots in town; B&Bs can likely loan you a good coat or an umbrella if weather looks threatening). Plan for rain. Watch your footing. Injuries are common. Every year, several people die while hiking in the area (some from overexertion; others are blown off ridges).

By Tour: For organized bus tours that run the roads of the Lake District, see "Tours in Keswick," later.

Keswick and the North Lake District

As far as touristy Lake District towns go, Keswick (KEZ-ick, population 5,000) is far more enjoyable than Windermere, Bowness, or Ambleside. Many of the place names around Keswick have Norse origins, inherited from the region's 10th-century settlers. Notice that most lakes in the region end in either *water* (e.g., Derwentwater) or *mere* (e.g., Windermere), which is related to the German word for lake, *Meer*.

LAKE DISTRICT

An important mining center for slate, copper, and lead through the Middle Ages, Keswick became a resort in the 19th century. Its fine Victorian buildings recall those Romantic days when city slickers first learned about "communing with nature." Today, the compact town is lined with tearooms, pubs, gift shops, and hiking-gear shops. The lake called Derwentwater is a pleasant 10-minute walk from the town center.

Orientation to Keswick

Keswick is an ideal home base, with plenty of good B&Bs, an easy bus connection to the nearest train station at Penrith, and a prime location near the best lake in the area, Derwentwater. In Keswick, everything is within a 10-minute walk of everything else: the pedestrian town square, the TI, recommended B&Bs, grocery stores, the wonderful municipal pitch-and-putt golf course, the main bus stop, a lakeside boat dock, and a central parking lot. Thursdays and Saturdays are market days in the town square, but the square is lively every day throughout the summer.

Keswick town is a delight for wandering. Its centerpiece, Moot Hall (meaning "meeting hall"), was a 16th-century copper warehouse upstairs with an arcade below (closed after World War II; most Lake District towns and villages have similar meeting halls).

"Keswick" means "cheese farm"—a legacy from the time when the town square was the spot to sell cheese. When the town square went pedestrian-only, locals were all abuzz about people tripping over the curbs. (The English, seemingly thrilled by ever-present danger, are endlessly warning visitors to "watch your head," "duck or grouse," "watch the step," and "mind the gap.")

Keswick and the Lake District are popular with English holidaymakers who prefer to travel with their dogs. The town square in Keswick can look like the Westminster Dog Show, and the recommended Dog and Gun pub, where "well-behaved dogs are welcomed," is always full of patient pups. If you are shy about connecting with people, pal up to an English pooch—you'll often find they're happy to introduce you to their owners.

TOURIST INFORMATION

The National Park Visitors Centre/TI is in Moot Hall, right in the middle of the town square (daily 9:30-17:30, Nov-Easter until 16:30, tel. 017687/72645, www. lakedistrict.gov.uk and www. keswick.org). Staffers are pros at advising you about hiking routes. They can also help you figure out public transportation to outlying sights and tell you about the region's various adventure activities.

The TI sells theater tickets, Keswick Launch tickets (at a £1 discount), fishing licenses, and brochures and maps that outline nearby hikes (£1.25-2.50, including a very simple and driver-friendly *Lap Map* featuring sights, walks, and a mileage chart). The TI also has books and maps for hikers, cyclists, and drivers (more books are sold at shops all over town).

Check the boards inside the TI's foyer for information about walks, talks, and entertainment. You can also pick up the *Events and Guided Walks* guide. The daily weather forecast is posted just outside the front door (weather tel. 0844-846-2444). For information about the TI's guided walks, see "Tours in Keswick," later.

HELPFUL HINTS

Book in Advance: It's smart to book ahead if you'll be visiting during the summer or over a bank-holiday weekend (see "Holidays and Festivals" in the appendix). Please honor your bookings—the B&B proprietors here lose out on much-needed business if you don't show up.

A sampling of events: The Keswick Jazz Festival mel-

LAKE DISTRICT

lows out the town in mid-May (www.keswickjazzfestival.
co.uk), followed by the Mountain Festival (www.
keswickmountainfestival.co.uk), and a beer festival in June
(www.keswickbeerfestival.co.uk). The Keswick Convention packs the town with 4,000 evangelical Christians
for three weeks each summer (late July-mid-Aug, www.
keswickministries.org).

If you have trouble finding a room (or a B&B that accepts
small children), try www.keswick.org to search for available
rooms.

Laundry: The town's launderette is on Bank Street, just up the
side street from the post office (full- and self-service; Mon-Fri
8:00-19:00, Sat-Sun 9:00-18:00; coin-op soap dispenser, free
Wi-Fi, tel. 017687/75448, see Keswick map, later, for location).

Midges: Tiny biting insects called midges—similar to no-see-
ums—might bug you in this region from late May through
September, particularly at dawn and dusk. The severity depends on the weather since wind and sunshine can deter them,
and insect repellant fends them off: Ask the locals what works
if you'll be hiking.

Local Candy: Be sure to try Kendal mint cakes, which are basically flat, mint-flavored sugar cubes. You'll find them in area
supermarkets and gift stores.

Tours in Keswick

BY FOOT

KR Guided Walks offers private guided hikes of varying difficulty levels. The local guides also provide transportation from Keswick to the trailhead (£80/day, Easter-Oct, wear suitable clothing
and footwear, bring lunch and water, must book in advance, tel.
017687/71302, mobile 0734-263-7813, keswickrambles.blogspot.
co.uk, armstrongps1@gmx.com).

TIs throughout the region also offer **free walks** led by "Voluntary Rangers" several times a month in summer (depart from
Keswick TI; check schedule in the *Events and Guided Walks* guide,
optional contribution welcome at end of walk).

ON WHEELS

Bus tours are great for people with bucks who'd like to wring maximum experience out of their limited time and see the area without
lots of hiking or messing with public transport. For a cheaper alternative, take public buses.

Mountain Goat Tours is the region's dominant tour company. Unfortunately, they run their minibus tours out of Wind-

LAKE DISTRICT

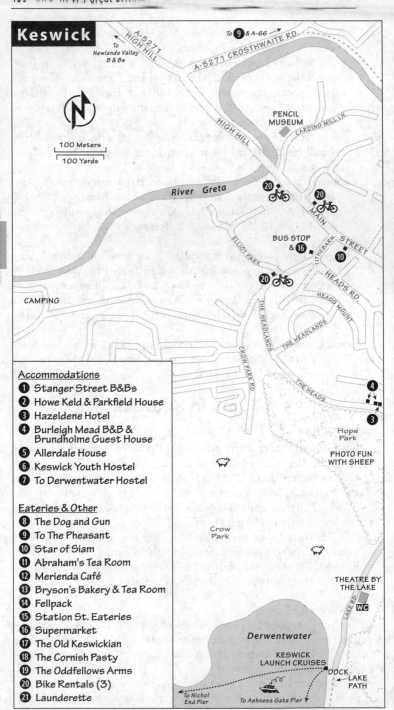

Keswick

LAKE DISTRICT

To **9** & A-66 →

A-5271 HIGH HILL

To Newlands Valley B & Bs

A-5271 CROSTHWAITE RD.

HIGH HILL

N

100 Meters
100 Yards

PENCIL MUSEUM

CARDING MILL LN.

River Greta

20

20

MAIN STREET

ELLIOT PARK

BUS STOP & **16**

TITHEBARN STREET

10

20

HEADS RD.

HEADS MOUNT

CAMPING

THE HEADLANDS

THE HEADLANDS

THE HEADS

CROW PARK RD.

4

3

Hope Park

PHOTO FUN WITH SHEEP

Crow Park

THEATRE BY THE LAKE

LAKE RD.

WC

Derwentwater

KESWICK LAUNCH CRUISES

DOCK

LAKE PATH

To Nichol End Pier

To Ashness Gate Pier

Accommodations
1 Stanger Street B&Bs
2 Howe Keld & Parkfield House
3 Hazeldene Hotel
4 Burleigh Mead B&B & Brundholme Guest House
5 Allerdale House
6 Keswick Youth Hostel
7 To Derwentwater Hostel

Eateries & Other
8 The Dog and Gun
9 To The Pheasant
10 Star of Siam
11 Abraham's Tea Room
12 Merienda Café
13 Bryson's Bakery & Tea Room
14 Fellpack
15 Station St. Eateries
16 Supermarket
17 The Old Keswickian
18 The Cornish Pasty
19 The Oddfellows Arms
20 Bike Rentals (3)
21 Launderette

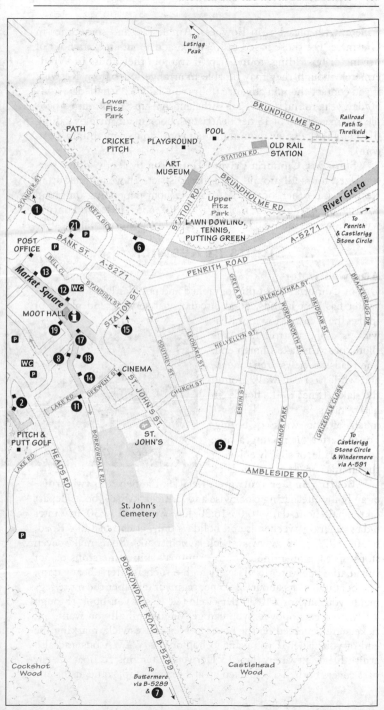

ermere, with pick-ups in Bowness, Ambleside, and sometimes in Grasmere. For those based in Keswick, add about an extra hour of driving or bus riding, round-trip (if you join their tours in Windermere), though they may be able to arrange tours from Keswick if you contact them in advance (tours run daily, £25/half-day, £44-50/day, year-round if there are sufficient sign-ups, minimum 4 people to a maximum of 16 per hearty bus, book in advance by calling 015394/45161, www.mountain-goat.com, tours@mountain-goat.com).

Show Me Cumbria Private Tours, run by Andy, offers personalized tours all around the Lake District. They can pick up in Keswick and other locations (from £35/hour depending on group size, tel. 01768/864-825, mobile 0780-902-6357, based in Penrith, www.showmecumbria.co.uk, andy@showmecumbria.co.uk).

Sights in Keswick

▲Derwentwater

One of Cumbria's most photographed and popular lakes, Derwentwater has four islands, good circular boat service, and plenty of trails. The pleasant town of Keswick is a short stroll from the shore, near the lake's north end. The roadside views aren't much, and while you can walk around the lake (fine trail, floods in heavy rains, 9 miles, 4 hours), much of the walk is boring. You're better off mixing a hike and boat ride, or simply enjoying the circular boat tour of the lake.

Boating on Derwentwater: Keswick Launch runs two **cruises** an hour, alternating clockwise and "anticlockwise" (boats depart on the half-hour, daily 10:00-16:30, July-Aug until 17:30, in winter 6/day generally weekends and holidays only, at end of Lake Road, tel. 017687/72263, www.keswick-launch.co.uk). Boats make seven stops on each 50-minute round-trip (may skip some stops or not run at all if the water level is very high—such as after a heavy rain). The boat trip costs about £2.25 per segment (cheaper the more segments you buy) or £10.50 per circle (£1 less if you book through TI) with free stopovers; you can get on and off all you want, but tickets are collected on the boat's last leg to Keswick, marking the end of your ride. If you want to hop on a #77/#77A bus and also cruise Derwentwater, the £13 Derwentwater Bus & Boat all-day pass covers both. To be picked up at a certain stop, stand at the end of the pier Gilligan-style, or the boat may not stop. See the map on page 494 for an overview of all the boat stops.

Keswick Launch also has a delightful **evening cruise** (see page 498) and rents **rowboats** for up to three people (£8/30 minutes, £12/hour, open Easter-Oct, larger rowboats and motor boats available).

Derwentwater Lakeside Walk: A marked trail runs all along Derwentwater, but much of it (especially the Keswick-to-Hawes End stretch) is not that interesting. The best hour-long section is the 1.5-mile path between the docks at High Brandelhow and Hawes End, where you'll stroll a level trail through peaceful trees. This walk works best in conjunction with the lake boat described above.

▲Pencil Museum

Graphite was first discovered centuries ago in Keswick. A hunk of the stuff proved great for marking sheep in the 15th century. In 1832, the first crude Keswick pencil factory opened, and the rest is history (which is what you'll learn about here). While you can't tour the 150-year-old factory where the famous Derwent pencils were made, you can enjoy the smell of thousands of pencils getting sharpened for the first time. The adjacent charming and kid-friendly museum is a good way to pass a rainy hour; you may even catch an artist's demonstration. Take a look at the exhibit on "war pencils," which were made for WWII bomber crews (filled with tiny maps and compasses). Relax in the theater with a 10-minute video on the pencil-manufacturing process, followed by dull company and product videos.

Cost and Hours: £4.95, daily 9:30-17:00, last entry one hour before closing, humble café, 3-minute walk from town center, signposted off Main Street, tel. 017687/73626, www.pencilmuseum.co.uk.

Fitz Park

An inviting grassy park stretches alongside Keswick's tree-lined, duck-filled River Greta. There's a playground and plenty of room for kids to burn off energy. Consider an after-dinner stroll on the footpath. You may catch men in white (or frisky schoolboys in uniform) playing a game of cricket. There's the serious bowling green (where you're welcome to watch the experts play and enjoy the cheapest cuppa—i.e., tea—in town), and the public one where tourists are welcome to give lawn bowling a go. You can try tennis on a grass court or enjoy the putting green. Find the rental pavilion across the road from the art gallery (open daily Easter-Sept 10:00-17:30, longer hours July-Aug, mobile 07976-573-785).

LAKE DISTRICT

▲Golf

A nine-hole pitch-and-putt golf course near the lush gardens in Hope Park separates the town from the lake and offers a classy, cheap, and convenient chance to golf near the birthplace of the sport. This is a great, fun, and inexpensive experience—just right after a day of touring and before dinner (£5 for pitch-and-putt, £3.25 for putting, £3.95 for 18 tame holes of "obstacle golf," daily from 10:00, last round starts around 18:00, possibly later in summer, closed Nov-Feb, café, tel. 017687/73445, www.hopeleisure. com).

Swimming

While the leisure center lacks a serious adult pool, it does have an indoor pool kids love, with a huge waterslide and wave machine (swim times vary by day and by season—call or check website, no towels or suits for rent, lockers-£1 deposit, 10-minute walk from town center, follow Station Road past Fitz Park and veer left, tel. 017687/72760, www.better.org.uk—search for "Keswick").

NEAR KESWICK

▲▲Castlerigg Stone Circle

For some reason, 70 percent of England's stone circles are here in Cumbria. Castlerigg is one of the best and oldest in Britain, and an easy stop for drivers. The circle—90 feet across and 5,000 years old—has 38 stones mysteriously laid out on a line between the two tallest peaks on the horizon. They served as a celestial calendar for ritual celebrations. Imagine the ambience here, as ancient people filled this clearing in spring to celebrate fertility, in late summer to commem-

orate the harvest, and in the winter to celebrate the winter solstice and the coming renewal of light. Festival dates were dictated by how the sun rose and set in relation to the stones. The more that modern academics study this circle, the more meaning they find in the placement of the stones. The two front stones face due north, toward a cut in the mountains. The rare-for-stone-circles "sanctuary" lines up with its center stone to mark where the sun rises on May Day. (Party!) For maximum "goose pimples" (as they say here), show up at sunset (free, open all the time, 1-mile hike from town; by car it's a 3-mile drive east of Keswick—follow brown signs, 3 minutes off the A-66, easy parking; see map on page 494).

Hikes and Drives in the North Lake District

FROM KESWICK

For an easy, flat stroll, consider the trail that runs alongside Derwentwater (see page 488). More involved options are described next.

▲▲Catbells High Ridge Hike

For a great "king of the mountain" feeling, 360-degree views, and a close-up look at the weather blowing over the ridge, hike above

Derwentwater about two hours from Hawes End up along the ridge to Catbells (1,480 feet) and down to High Brandelhow. Because the mountaintop is basically treeless, you're treated to dramatic panoramas the entire way up. From High Brandelhow, you can catch the boat back to Keswick or take the easy path along the shore of Derwentwater to your Hawes End starting point. (Extending the hike farther around the lake to Lodore takes you to a waterfall, rock climbers, a fine café, and another boat dock for a convenient return to Keswick—see page 494). Note: When the water level is very high (for example, after a heavy rain), boats can't stop at Hawes End—ask at the TI or boat dock before setting out.

Catbells is probably the most dramatic family walk in the area (but wear sturdy shoes, bring a raincoat, and watch your footing). From Keswick, the lake, or your farmhouse B&B, you can see silhouetted figures hiking along this ridge.

Getting There: To reach the trailhead from Keswick, catch the "anticlockwise" boat (see "Boating on Derwentwater," earlier) and ride for 10 minutes to the second stop, Hawes End. (You can also ride to High Brandelhow and take this walk in the other direction, but I don't recommend it—two rocky scrambles along the way are easier and safer to navigate going uphill from Hawes End.) Note the schedule for your return boat ride. Drivers can park free at Hawes End, but parking is limited and the road can be hard to find—get very clear directions in town before heading there. (Hardcore hikers can walk to the foot of Catbells from Keswick via Portinscale, which takes about 40 minutes—ask your B&B or the TI for directions). The Keswick TI sells a *Catbells* brochure about the hike.

The Route: The path is not signposted, but it's easy to follow, and you'll see plenty of other walkers. From Hawes End, walk away from the lake through a kissing gate to the turn just before the car park. Then turn left and go up, up, up. After about 20 minutes, you'll hit the first of two short scrambles (where the trail vanishes into a cluster of steep rocks), which leads to a bluff. From the first little summit (great for a picnic break), and then along the ridge, you'll enjoy sweeping views of the lake on one side and of Newlands Valley on the other. The bald peak in the distance is Catbells. Broken stones crunch under each step, wind buffets your ears, clouds prowl overhead, and the sheep baa comically. To anyone looking up from the distant farmhouse B&Bs, you are but a stick figure on the ridge. Just below the summit, the trail disintegrates into another short, steep scramble. Your reward is just beyond: a magnificent hilltop perch.

After the Catbells summit, descend along the ridge to a saddle ahead. The ridge continues much higher, and while it may look like your only option, at its base a small, unmarked lane with comfortable steps leads left. Unless you're up for extending the hike (see "Longer Catbells Options," next), take this path down to the lake. To get to High Brandelhow Pier, take the first left fork you come across down through a forest to the lake. When you reach Abbot's Bay, go left through a swinging gate, following a lakeside trail around a gravelly bluff, to the idyllic High Brandelhow Pier, a peaceful place to wait for your boat back to Keswick. (You can pay your fare when you board.)

Longer Catbells Options: Catbells is just the first of a series of peaks, all connected by a fine ridge trail. Hardier hikers continue up to nine miles along this same ridge, enjoying valley and lake views as they arc around the Newlands Valley toward (and even down to) Buttermere. After High Spy, you can descend an easy path into Newlands Valley. The ultimate, very full day-plan would be to take a bus to Buttermere, climb Robinson, and follow the ridge around to Catbells and back to Keswick.

Latrigg Peak

For the easiest mountain-climbing sensation around, take the short drive to the Latrigg Peak parking lot just north of Keswick, and hike 15 minutes to the top of the 1,200-foot-high hill, where you'll be rewarded with a commanding view of the town, lake, and valley, all the way to the next lake over (Bassenthwaite). At the traffic circle just outside Keswick, take the A-591 Carlisle exit, then an immediate right (direction: Ormathwaite/Underscar). Take the next right, a hard right, at the *Skiddaw* sign, where a long, steep, one-lane road leads to the Latrigg car park at the end of the lane. With more time, you can walk all the way from your Keswick B&B to Latrigg and back (it's a popular evening walk for locals).

Railway Path

The four-mile Railway Path from downtown Keswick follows an old train track and the river to the village of Threlkeld (with two pubs). However, parts of the path are indefinitely closed following a 2015 flood. Until the path is restored, walkers (but not cyclists) can take a detour through Brundholme Woods (just past Low Briery) to Brundholme Road and into Threlkeld (expect some uphill segments; ask at TI for detour updates). You can either walk back along the same path, or loop back via the Castlerigg Stone Circle (described earlier, roughly eight miles total). The Railway Path starts behind the leisure center (as you face the center, head right and around back).

Walla Crag

From your Keswick B&B, a fine two-hour walk to Walla Crag offers great fell (mountain) walking and a ridge-walk experience without the necessity of a bus or car. Start by strolling along the lake to the Great Wood parking lot (or drive to this lot), and head up Cat Ghyl (where "fell runners"—trail-running enthusiasts—practice) to Walla Crag. You'll be treated to great panoramic views over Derwentwater and surrounding peaks—especially beautiful when the heather blossoms in the summer. You can do a shorter version of this walk from the parking lot at Ashness Packhorse Bridge.

HIKES OUTSIDE KESWICK
▲▲Buttermere Hike

The ideal little lake with a lovely circular four-mile stroll offers nonstop, no-sweat Lake District beauty. If you're not a hiker but wish you were, take this walk. If you're short on time, at least stop here and get your shoes dirty.

Buttermere is connected with Borrowdale and Derwentwater by a great road that runs over rugged Honister Pass. Buses #77/#77A make a 1.75-hour round-trip loop between Keswick and Buttermere that includes a trip over this pass. The two-pub hamlet of Buttermere has a pay-and-display parking lot and free parking along the roadside. There's also a pay parking lot at the Honister Pass end of the lake (at Gatesgarth Farm). The Syke Farm in Buttermere is popular for its homemade ice cream.

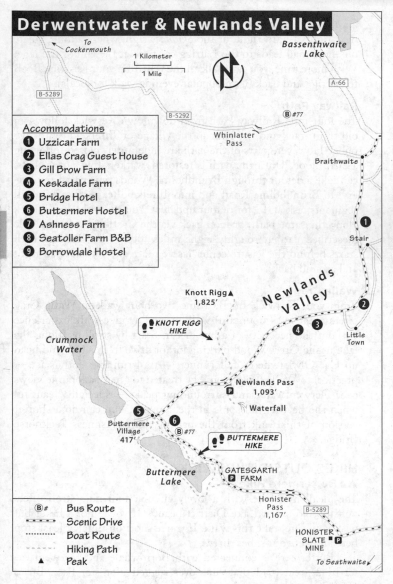

Derwentwater & Newlands Valley

To Cockermouth

Bassenthwaite Lake

1 Kilometer
1 Mile

B-5289

B-5292

Ⓑ #77

Whinlatter Pass

A-66

Braithwaite

Accommodations
1 Uzzicar Farm
2 Ellas Crag Guest House
3 Gill Brow Farm
4 Keskadale Farm
5 Bridge Hotel
6 Buttermere Hostel
7 Ashness Farm
8 Seatoller Farm B&B
9 Borrowdale Hostel

1
Stair

2

Little Town

Knott Rigg▲
1,825'

Newlands Valley

4   3

KNOTT RIGG HIKE

Crummock Water

Newlands Pass
1,093'

🅿

Waterfall

5

6

Ⓑ #77

BUTTERMERE HIKE

Buttermere Village
417'

Buttermere Lake

GATESGARTH FARM
🅿

Honister Pass
1,167'

B-5289

HONISTER SLATE MINE 🅿

To Seathwaite

Ⓑ #   Bus Route
━✕━✕━ Scenic Drive
········· Boat Route
─ ─ ─ Hiking Path
▲   Peak

LAKE DISTRICT

CAR HIKING
▲▲▲Scenic Circle Drive South of Keswick
This hour-long drive, which includes Newlands Valley, Buttermere, Honister Pass, and Borrowdale, offers the North Lake District's best scenery. (To do a similar route without a car from Keswick, take loop bus #77/#77A.) Distances are short, roads are narrow and

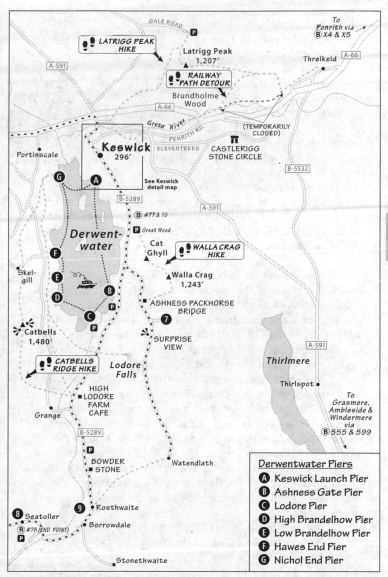

have turnouts, and views are rewarding. Get a good map and ask your B&B host for advice.

From Keswick, leave town on Crosthwaite Road, then, at the roundabout, head west on Cockermouth Road (A-66, following *Cockermouth* and *Workington* signs). Don't take the first Newlands Valley exit, but do take the second one (through Braithwaite), and follow signs up the majestic Newlands Valley (also signed for *Buttermere*).

If the **Newlands Valley** had a lake, it would be packed with tourists. But it doesn't—and it isn't. The valley is dotted with 500-year-old family-owned farms. Shearing day is reason to rush home from school. Sons get school out of the way ASAP and follow their dads into the family business. Neighbor girls marry those sons and move in.

Grandparents retire to the cottage next door. With the price of wool depressed, most of the wives supplement the family income by running B&Bs (virtually every farm in the valley rents rooms). The road has one lane, with turnouts for passing. From the Newlands Pass summit, notice the glacial-shaped wilds, once forested, now not.

From the parking lot at **Newlands Pass,** at the top of Newlands Valley (unmarked, but you'll see a waterfall on the left), an easy 300-yard hike leads to a little waterfall. On the other side of the road, an easy one-mile hike climbs up to **Knott Rigg,** which probably offers more TPCB (thrills per calorie burned) than any walk in the region. If you don't have time for even a short hike, at least get out of the car and get a feel for the setting.

After Newlands Pass, descend to **Buttermere** (scenic lake, tiny hamlet with pubs and an ice-cream store—see "Buttermere Hike," earlier), turn left, drive the length of the lake, and climb over rugged **Honister Pass**—strewn with glacial debris, remnants from the old slate mines, and curious shaggy Swaledale sheep (looking more like goats with their curly horns). The U-shaped valleys you'll see are textbook examples of those carved out by glaciers. Look high on the hillsides for "hanging valleys"—small glacial-shaped scoops cut off by the huge flow of the biggest glacier, which swept down the main valley.

The **Honister Slate Mine,** England's last still-functioning slate mine (and worth ▲), stands at the summit of Honister Pass. The youth hostel next to it was originally built to house miners in the 1920s. The mine offers worthwhile tours (perfect for when it's pouring outside): You'll put on a hard hat, load onto a bus for a short climb, then hike into a shaft to learn about the region's slate industry. It's a long, stooped hike into the mountain,

made interesting by the guide and punctuated by the sound of your helmet scraping against low bits of the shaft. Standing deep in the mountain, surrounded by slate scrap and the beams of 30 head-lamps fluttering around like fireflies, you'll learn of the hardships of miners' lives and how "green gold" is trendy once again, making the mine viable. Even if you don't have time to take the tour, stop here for its slate-filled shop (£13.50, 1.5-hour tour; departs daily at 10:30, 12:30, and 15:30; additional tour at 14:00 in summer; Dec-Jan 12:30 tour only; call ahead to confirm times and to book a spot, helmets and lamps provided, wear good walking shoes and bring warm clothing even in summer, café and nice WCs, tel. 017687/77230, www.honister.com).

After stark and lonely Honister Pass, drop in to sweet and homey **Borrowdale,** with a few lonely hamlets and fine hikes from Seathwaite. Circling back to Keswick past Borrowdale, the B-5289 (a.k.a. the Borrowdale Valley Road) takes you past the following popular attractions.

A set of stairs leads to the top of the house-size **Bowder Stone** (signposted, a few minutes' walk off the main road). For a great lunch or snack, including tea and homemade quiche and cakes, drop in to the much-loved **$ High Lodore Farm Café** (daily 9:00-18:00, closed Nov-Easter, short drive uphill from the main road and over a tiny bridge, tel. 017687/77221). Farther along, **Lodore Falls** is a short walk from the road, behind Lodore Hotel (a nice place to stop for tea and beautiful views). **Shepherds Crag,** a cliff overlooking Lodore, was made famous by pioneer rock climbers. (Their descendants hang from little ridges on its face today.) This is serious climbing, with several fatalities a year.

A very hard right off the B-5289 (signposted *Ashness Bridge, Watendlath*) and a steep half-mile climb on a narrow lane takes you to the postcard-pretty **Ashness Packhorse Bridge,** a quintessen-tial Lake District scene (parking lot just above on right). A half-mile farther up, park the car and hop out (parking lot on left, no sign). You'll be startled by the "surprise view" of Derwentwater—great for a lakes photo op. Continuing from here, the road gets extremely narrow en  route to the hamlet of **Watendlath,** which has a tiny lake and lazy farm animals.

Return to the B-5289 and head back to Keswick. If you have

LAKE DISTRICT

yet to see it, cap your drive with a short detour from Keswick to the Castlerigg Stone Circle (described earlier).

Nightlife in Keswick

For a small and remote town, Keswick has lots going on in the evening. Remember, at this latitude it's light until 22:00 in midsummer.

▲▲Theatre by the Lake

Keswickians brag that they enjoy "London theater quality at Keswick prices." Their theater offers events year-round and a wonderful rotation of six plays from late May through October (plays vary throughout the week, with music concerts on Sun in summer). There are two stages: The main one seats 400, and the smaller "studio" theater seats 100 (and features edgier plays that may involve rough language and/or nudity). Attending a play here is a fine opportunity to enjoy a classy night out.

Cost and Hours: £10-32, discounts for old and young; shows generally at 19:30, also at 14:00 on Wed and Sat, winter schedule varies; café, restaurant (pretheater dinners start at 17:30 and must be booked 24 hours ahead by calling 017687/81102), parking at the adjacent lot is free after 19:00. It's smart to buy tickets in advance—book at box office (daily 9:30-20:00 on performance days, other days until 18:00), by phone (tel. 017687/74411), at TI, or at www.theatrebythelake.com.

Hope Park

Along with the Theatre by the Lake (described above), you can do some early evening **golfing** (fine course, pitch-and-putt, goofy golf, or just enjoy the putting green—see page 490) or **walk** among the grazing sheep as the sun gets ready to set (between the lake and the golf course, access from just above the beach, great photo ops on balmy evenings).

Keswick Launch's **evening lake cruise** comes with a glass of wine and a midlake stop for a short commentary. You're welcome to bring a picnic dinner and munch scenically as you cruise (£10.75, £25 family ticket, 1 hour, daily mid-July-Aug at 18:30 and 19:30—weather permitting and if enough people show up).

Pub Events

To socialize with locals, head to a pub for one of their special evenings: There's **quiz night** at The Dog and Gun (21:30 on most Thu; £1, proceeds go to Keswick's Mountain Rescue team, which rescues hikers and the occasional sheep). At a quiz night, tourists are more than welcome. Drop in, say you want to join a team, and you're in. If you like trivia, it's a great way to get to know people here.

The Oddfellows Arms has free **live music** (often classic rock) just about every night in summer (April-Oct, from 21:30).

Keswick Street Theatre

This theatrical walk through Keswick and its history takes place on Tuesday evenings in summer (£3, 1.5 hours, usually starts at 19:30, weekly late May-early July, details at TI).

Movies

The Lonsdale Alhambra Cinema is a restored old-fashioned movie theater a few minutes' walk from the town center (St. Johns Street, tel. 017687/72195, www.keswick-alhambra.co.uk).

Sleeping in Keswick

The Lake District abounds with attractive B&Bs, guesthouses, and hostels. It needs them all when the summer hordes threaten the serenity of this Romantic mecca.

Reserve your room in advance in high season. From November through March, you should have no trouble finding a room, but to get a particular place (especially on Saturdays), book ahead. If you're using public transportation, sleep in Keswick. If you're driving, staying outside Keswick is your best chance for a remote farmhouse experience. Lakeland hostels offer inexpensive beds and come with an interesting crowd of all ages.

For Keswick, I've featured B&Bs and small hotels mainly on two streets, each within three blocks of the bus station and town square. Stanger Street, a bit humbler but quiet and handy, has smaller homes and more moderately priced rooms. The Heads is a classier area lined with proud Victorian houses, close to the lake and theater, overlooking the golf course. In addition to these two streets, Keswick abounds with many other options that are equally good.

Many of my Keswick listings charge extra for a one-night stay and most won't book one-night stays on weekends (but if you show up and they have a bed free, it's yours). Most don't welcome young children. None have elevators and all have lots of stairs—ask about a ground-floor unit if steps are a problem. Owners are enthusiastic about offering advice to get you on the right walking trail. Most accommodations have inviting lounges with libraries of books on the region and loaner maps.

This is still the countryside—expect huge breakfasts (often with a wide selection, including vegetarian options) and shower systems that might need to be switched on to get hot water. Parking is generally easy.

LAKE DISTRICT

ON STANGER STREET

This street, quiet but just a block from Keswick's town center, is lined with B&Bs situated in Victorian slate townhouses. Each of these places is small and family-run. They are all good, offering comfortably sized rooms, free parking, and a friendly welcome.

$$ Ellergill Guest House has four spic-and-span rooms with an airy, contemporary feel—several with views (2 percent surcharge for credit cards, 2-night minimum, no children under age 10, 22 Stanger Street, tel. 017687/73347, www.ellergill.co.uk, stay@ellergill.co.uk, Clare and Robin Pinkney).

$$ Badgers Wood B&B, at the top of the street, has six modern, bright, unfrilly view rooms, each named after a different tree (3 percent surcharge for credit cards, 2-night minimum, no children under age 12, special diets accommodated, 30 Stanger Street, tel. 017687/72621, www.badgers-wood.co.uk, enquiries@badgers-wood.co.uk, chatty Scotsman Andrew and his charming wife Anne).

$$ Abacourt House, with a daisy-fresh breakfast room, has five pleasant doubles (3 percent surcharge for credit cards, 2-night minimum, no children, sack lunches available, 26 Stanger Street, tel. 017687/72967, www.abacourt.co.uk, abacourt.keswick@btinternet.com, John and Heather).

$ Dunsford Guest House rents four updated rooms at bargain prices. Stained glass and wooden pews give the blue-and-cream breakfast room a country-chapel vibe (RS%, cash only, 16 Stanger Street, tel. 017687/75059, www.dunsfordguesthouse.co.uk, info@dunsfordguesthouse.co.uk, Deb and Keith).

ON THE HEADS

The classy area known as The Heads has B&Bs with bigger and grander Victorian architecture and great views overlooking the pitch-and-putt range and out into the hilly distance. The golf-course side of The Heads has free parking, if you can snare a spot (easy at night). A single yellow line on the curb means you're allowed to park there for free, but only overnight (16:00-10:00).

$$$ Howe Keld has the polished feel of a boutique hotel, but offers all the friendliness of a B&B. Its 12 contemporary-posh rooms are spacious and tastefully decked out in native woods and slate. It's warm, welcoming, and family-run, with an à la carte breakfast cooked to order by chef Jerome (cash and 2-night minimum preferred, sack lunches available, bike garage in basement, tel. 017687/72417 or toll-free 0800-783-0212, www.howekeld.co.uk, laura@howekeld.co.uk, run with care by Laura and Jerome Bujard).

$$ Parkfield House, thoughtfully run and decorated by John and Susan Berry, is a big Victorian house with a homey lounge. Its six rooms, some with fine views, are bright and classy (RS%, 2-night minimum, no children under age 16, free parking, tel. 017687/72328, www.parkfieldkeswick.co.uk, parkfieldkeswick@hotmail.co.uk).

$$ Burleigh Mead B&B is a slate mansion from 1892 with wild carpeting. Gill (pronounced "Jill," short for Gillian) rents seven lovely rooms and offers a friendly welcome, as well as a lounge and peaceful front-yard sitting area that's perfect for enjoying the view (cash only, no children under age 8, tel. 017687/75935, www.burleighmead.co.uk, info@burleighmead.co.uk).

$$ Hazeldene Hotel, on the corner of The Heads, rents 10 spacious rooms, many with commanding views. There's even a "boot room" that doubles as a guest rec room with a ping-pong table. It's run with care by delightful Helen and Howard (one ground-floor unit available, free parking, tel. 017687/72106, www.hazeldene-hotel.co.uk, info@hazeldene-hotel.co.uk).

$$ Brundholme Guest House has four bright and comfy rooms, most with sweeping views at no extra charge—especially from the front side—and a friendly and welcoming atmosphere (minifridge, free parking, tel. 017687/73305, mobile 0773-943-5401, www.brundholme.co.uk, bazaly@hotmail.co.uk, Barry and Allison Thompson).

ON ESKIN STREET

The area just southeast of the town center has several streets (Eskin, Blencathra, and Helvellyn) lined with good B&Bs. Though this neighborhood is a few minutes farther than the areas listed above, it's still within easy walking distance of downtown and the lake and has easier parking.

$$ Allerdale House, a classy, nicely decorated stone mansion, holds six rooms and is well-run by Barbara and Paul (RS%, 3 percent surcharge for credit cards, free parking, 1 Eskin Street, tel. 017687/73891, www.allerdale-house.co.uk, reception@allerdale-house.co.uk).

HOSTELS IN AND NEAR KESWICK

The Lake District's inexpensive hostels, mostly located in great old buildings, are handy sources of information and social fun.

¢ Keswick Youth Hostel, with a big lounge and a great riverside balcony, fills a converted mill. Travelers of all ages feel at home here, but book ahead—family rooms book up July through

September (breakfast extra, pay guest computer, café, bar, office open 7:00-23:00, center of town just off Station Road before river, tel. 017687/72484, www.yha.org.uk, keswick@yha.org.uk).

¢ **Derwentwater Hostel,** in a 220-year-old mansion on the shore of Derwentwater, is two miles south of Keswick (breakfast extra, family rooms, 23:00 curfew; follow the B-5289 from Keswick—entrance is 2 miles along the Borrowdale Valley Road about 150 yards after Ashness exit—look for cottage and bus stop at bottom of the drive; tel. 017687/77246, www.derwentwater.org, contact@derwentwater.org).

WEST OF KESWICK, IN THE NEWLANDS VALLEY

If you have a car, drive 10 minutes past Keswick down the majestic Newlands Valley (described earlier, under "Scenic Circle Drive South of Keswick"). Each place offers easy parking, grand views, and perfect tranquility. Most of these rooms tend to be plainer and more dated than the B&Bs in town and come with steep and gravelly roads, plenty of dogs, and an earthy charm. Don't expect mobile-phone service—even your B&B's satellite Wi-Fi can be spotty—but living off the grid is why you came here. Traditionally, farmhouses lacked central heating, and while they are now heated, you can still request a hot-water bottle to warm up your bed.

Getting to the Newlands Valley: Leave Keswick via the roundabout at the end of Crosthwaite Road, and then head west on Cockermouth Road (A-66). Take the second Newlands Valley exit through Braithwaite, and follow signs through Newlands Valley (drive toward Buttermere). All my recommended B&Bs are on this road: Uzzicar Farm (under the shale field, which local kids love hiking up to glissade down; a 10-minute drive from Keswick), Ellas Crag Guest House, then Gill Brow Farm, and finally—the last house before the stark summit—Keskadale Farm (about four miles before Buttermere at the top of the valley; 15-minute drive from Keswick). The one-lane road can be intimidating, but it has turnouts for passing.

$$ Ellas Crag Guest House, with three rooms—each with a great view—is a comfortable stone house with a contemporary feel and tranquil terrace overlooking the valley. This homey B&B offers a good mix of modern and traditional decor, including beautifully tiled bathrooms (RS%, singles available Mon-Thu only, 2-night minimum, local free-range meats and eggs for breakfast, sack lunches available, huge DVD library, laundry, tel. 017687/78217, www.ellascrag.co.uk, info@ellascrag.co.uk, run by friendly Jane and Ed Ma).

$ Keskadale Farm is another good farmhouse experience, with Ponderosa hospitality. One of the valley's oldest, the house—with two guest rooms and a cozy lounge—is made from 500-year-old ship beams. This working farm is an authentic slice of Lake District life and is your chance to get to know lots of curly-horned sheep and the dogs that herd them. While her husband and sons work in the fields, Margaret Harryman runs the B&B (cash only, sack lunches available, closed Dec-Feb, tel. 017687/78544, www.keskadalefarm.co.uk, info@keskadalefarm.co.uk). They also rent a one-bedroom apartment that sleeps two (£450/week).

$ Uzzicar Farm is a big, rustic place with two comfy guest rooms in a low-ceilinged 16th-century farmhouse—watch out for ducks. It's a particularly intimate and homey setting, where you'll feel like part of the family (family rooms, cash or check preferred, PayPal possible, continental breakfast only, tel. 017687/78026, www.uzzicarfarm.co.uk, stay@uzzicarfarm.co.uk, Helen, David, and three daughters).

$ Gill Brow Farm is a rough-hewn working farmhouse more than 300 years old where Anne Wilson rents two simple but fine rooms, one with an en-suite bathroom, the other with a private bathroom down the hall (self-catering cottage that sleeps up to 6 also available, tel. 017687/78270, www.gillbrow-keswick.co.uk, info@gillbrow-keswick.co.uk).

SOUTHWEST OF KESWICK, IN BUTTERMERE

$$$$ Bridge Hotel, just beyond Newlands Valley at Buttermere, offers 21 beautiful rooms—most of them quite spacious—and a classic Old World countryside-hotel experience. On Fridays and Saturdays, dinner is required (apartments available, minimum 2-night stay on weekends, Wi-Fi in lobby, tel. 017687/70252, www.bridge-hotel.com, enquiries@bridge-hotel.com). There are no shops within 10 miles—only peace and quiet a stone's throw from one of the region's most beautiful lakes. The hotel has a dark-wood pub/restaurant on the ground floor.

¢ Buttermere Hostel, a quarter-mile south of Buttermere village on Honister Pass Road, has good food and a peacefully rural setting (family rooms, breakfast extra, inexpensive dinners and packed lunches, office open 8:30-10:00 & 17:00-22:00, 23:00 curfew, reservation tel. 0345-371-9508, www.yha.org.uk, buttermere@yha.org.uk).

SOUTH OF KESWICK, NEAR BORROWDALE

$$ Ashness Farm, ruling its valley high above Derwentwater, immerses guests in farm sounds and lakeland beauty. On this 750-acre working farm, now owned by the National Trust, people have raised sheep and cattle for centuries. Today Anne and her family are "tenant farmers," keeping this farm operating and renting five rooms to boot (cozy lounge, farm-fresh eggs and sausage for breakfast, sack lunches available, just above Ashness Packhorse

Bridge, tel. 017687/77361, www.ashnessfarm.co.uk, enquiries@ashnessfarm.co.uk).

$$ Seatoller Farm B&B is a rustic 16th-century house on another working farm owned by the National Trust. Christine Simpson rents three rooms in her B&B, one of five buildings in this hamlet. The old windows are small, but the abundant flower boxes keep things bright (cottage available, closed Dec-mid-Jan, tel. 017687/77232, www.seatollerfarm.co.uk, info@seatollerfarm.co.uk).

¢ Borrowdale Hostel, in secluded Borrowdale Valley just south of Rosthwaite, is a well-run place surrounded by many ways to immerse yourself in nature. The hostel offers cheap dinners and sack lunches (family rooms, breakfast extra, office open 7:00-23:00, 23:00 curfew, reservation tel. 0845-371-9624, hostel tel. 017687/77257, www.yha.org.uk, borrowdale@yha.org.uk). To reach this hostel from Keswick by bus, take #78, the Borrowdale Rambler. Note that the last bus from Keswick departs around 18:00 most of year (see page 477 for bus details).

Eating in Keswick

Keswick has a variety of good, basic eateries, but nothing particularly outstanding. Most stop serving by 21:00.

$$ The Dog and Gun serves good pub food (I love their rump of lamb) with great pub ambience. Upon arrival, muscle up to the bar to order your beer and/or meal. Then snag a table as soon as one opens up. Mind your head and tread carefully: Low ceilings and wooden beams loom overhead, while paws poke out from under tables below, as Keswick's canines wait patiently for their masters to finish their beer (food served daily 12:00-21:00, famous goulash, dog treats, 2 Lake Road, tel. 017687/73463).

$$ The Pheasant is a walk outside town, but locals trek here regularly for the food. The menu offers Lake District pub standards (fish pie, Cumbrian sausage, guinea fowl), as well as more inventive choices. Check the walls for caricatures of pub regulars, sketched at these tables by a Keswick artist. There's a small restaurant section, but I much prefer eating in the bar (food served daily 12:00-14:00 & 18:00-21:00, bar open until 23:00, Crosthwaite Road, tel. 017687/72219). From the town square, walk past the Pencil Museum, hang a right onto Crosthwaite Road, and walk 10 minutes. For a more scenic route, cross the river into Fitz Park, go left along the riverside path until it ends at the gate to Crosthwaite Road, turn right, and walk five minutes.

$$ Star of Siam serves authentic Thai dishes in a tasteful dining room (daily 12:00-14:30 & 17:30-22:30, 89 Main Street, tel. 017687/71444).

$ **Abraham's Tea Room,** popular with townspeople, is a fine value for lunch. It's tucked away on the upper floor of the giant George Fisher outdoor store (gluten-free options; Mon-Sat 10:00-17:00, Sun 10:30-16:30, on the corner where Lake Road turns right, tel. 017687/71811).

$$ **Merienda Café** has a friendly staff and a small selection of tasty, reasonably priced fare along with wine and beer in a contemporary, inviting space (daily 9:00-21:00, 10 Main Street, tel. 017687/72024).

$$ **Bryson's Bakery and Tea Room** has an enticing ground-floor bakery, with sandwiches and light lunches. The upstairs is a popular tearoom. Order lunch to-go from the bakery, or for a few pence more, eat there, either sitting on stools or at a couple of sidewalk tables. Consider their two-person Cumberland Cream Tea made with local ingredients; it's a good deal for what most would consider "afternoon tea," with sandwiches, scones, and little cakes served on a three-tiered platter (daily 9:00-17:00, 42 Main Street, tel. 017687/72257).

$ **Fellpack** serves wraps, salads, and local dishes—all available to enjoy in their small café, or to-go for a picnic (daily 9:00-18:00, 19 Lake Road, tel. 017687/71177).

Eateries on Station Street: The street leading from the town square to the leisure center has several restaurants, including $$ **Casa Bella,** a popular and packed Italian place that's good for families—reserve ahead (daily 12:00-15:30 & 17:00-21:00, 24 Station Street, tel. 017687/75575). Across the street is $$ **Lakes Bar & Bistro,** with burgers, meat pies, and good fixed-price meal deals (daily 10:00-22:30, 25 Station Street, tel. 017687/74080).

Picnic Food: The fine **Booths supermarket** is right where all the buses arrive (Mon-Sat 8:00-21:00, Sun 9:30-16:00, Tithebarn Street). The recommended **Bryson's Bakery** does good sandwiches to go (described earlier). $ **The Old Keswickian,** on the town square, serves up old-fashioned fish-and-chips to go (daily 11:00-19:30, tel. 017687/73861). Just around the corner, $ **The Cornish Pasty** offers an enticing variety of fresh meat pies to go (daily 9:00-17:00 or until the pasties are all gone, across from The Dog and Gun on Borrowdale Road, tel. 017687/72205).

IN THE NEWLANDS VALLEY

The farmhouse B&Bs of Newlands Valley don't serve dinner, so their guests have two good options: Go into Keswick, or take the lovely 10-minute drive to Buttermere for an evening meal at $$ **The Fish Inn** pub, which has fine indoor and outdoor seating, but takes no reservations (food served daily 12:00-14:00 & 18:00-21:00, family-friendly, good fish and daily specials with fresh vegetables, tel. 017687/70253). The neighboring $$ **Bridge Hotel Pub** is a bit cozier and serves "modern-day nibbles and good classic pub grub" (food served daily 9:00-21:30, tel. 017687/70252). For lunch, also consider the **$ Croft House Farm Café,** which serves freshly made soups and sandwiches to eat on their sunny deck or to take away (daily 10:00-17:00, tel. 017687/70235).

Keswick Connections

The nearest train station to Keswick is in Penrith (no lockers). For train and bus info, check at a TI, visit www.traveline.org.uk, or call 0345-748-4950 (for train), or 0871-200-2233. Most routes run less frequently on Sundays.

From Keswick by Bus: For connections, see page 477.

From Penrith by Bus to: Keswick (hourly, every 2 hours on Sun in Nov-April, 45 minutes, pay driver, Stagecoach bus #X4 or #X5), **Ullswater** and **Glenridding** (5/day, more frequent June-Aug with open-top buses, 50 minutes, bus #508). The Penrith bus stop is just outside the train station (bus schedules posted inside and outside station).

From Penrith by Train to: Liverpool (hourly, 2.5 hours, change in Wigan or Preston), **Durham** (hourly, 3 hours, change in Carlisle and Newcastle), **York** (roughly 2/hour, 4 hours, 1-2 transfers), **London**'s Euston Station (hourly, 4 hours), **Edinburgh** (9/day direct, 2 hours), **Glasgow** (hourly, 1.5 hours), **Oban** (5/day, 6 hours, transfer in Glasgow).

ROUTE TIPS FOR DRIVERS

From Points South (such as Liverpool and North Wales) to the Lake District: The direct, easy way to Keswick is to leave the M-6 at Penrith and take the A-66 motorway for 16 miles to Keswick. For a scenic sightseeing drive through the south lakes to Keswick, exit the M-6 on the A-590/A-591 through the towns of Kendal and Windermere to reach Brockhole National Park Visitors Centre. From Brockhole, the A-road to Keswick is fastest, but the high road—the tiny road over Kirkstone Pass to Glenridding and lovely Ullswater—is much more dramatic.

Coming from (or Going to) the West: Only 1,300 feet above sea level, Hard Knott Pass is still a thriller, with a narrow, winding, steeply graded road. Just over the pass are the scant but evocative remains of the Hard Knott Roman fortress. The great views can come with miserable rainstorms, and it can be very slow and frustrating when the one-lane road with turnouts is clogged by traffic. Avoid it on summer weekends.

Ullswater Lake Area

For advice on the Ullswater area, visit the **TI** at the pay parking lot in the heart of the lakefront village of Glenridding (daily 9:30-17:30, Nov-March until 15:30, tel. 017684/82414, www.visiteden.co.uk).

▲▲Ullswater Hike and Boat Ride

Long, narrow Ullswater, which some consider the loveliest lake in the area, offers eight miles of diverse and grand Lake District scenery. While you can drive it or cruise it, I'd ride the boat from the south tip halfway up (to Howtown—which is nothing more than a dock) and hike back. Or walk first, then enjoy an easy ride back.

An old-fashioned **"steamer" boat** (actually diesel-powered) leaves Glenridding regularly for Howtown (departs daily generally

9:45-16:55, 6-9/day April-Oct, fewer off-season, 40 minutes; £6.80 one-way, £10.80 round-trip, £14.20 round-the-lake ticket lets you hop on and off, covered by Ullswater Bus & Boat day pass, family rates, drivers can use safe pay-and-display parking lot, by public transit take bus #508 from Penrith, café at dock, £4 walking route map, tel. 017684/82229, www.ullswater-steamers.co.uk).

From Howtown, spend three to four hours hiking and dawdling along the well-marked path by the lake south to Patterdale, and then along the road back to Glenridding. This is a serious seven-mile walk with good views, varied terrain, and a few bridges and farms along the way. For a shorter hike from Howtown Pier, consider a three-mile loop around Hallin Fell. A rainy-day plan is to ride the covered boat up and down the lake to Howtown and Pooley Bridge at the northern tip of the lake (2 hours). Boats don't run in bad weather—call ahead if it looks iffy.

▲▲Lanty's Tarn and Keldas Hill

If you like the idea of an Ullswater-area hike, but aren't up for the long huff from Howtown, consider this shorter (but still moderately challenging and plenty scenic) loop that leaves right from the TI's pay parking lot in Glenridding (about 2.5 miles, allow 2 hours; before embarking, buy the well-described leaflet for this walk in the TI).

From the parking lot, head to the main road, turn right to cross the river, then turn right again immediately and follow the

LAKE DISTRICT

river up into the hills. After passing a row of cottages, turn left, cross the wooden bridge, and proceed up the hill through the swing gate. Just before the next swing gate, turn left (following *Grisedale* signs) and head to yet another gate. From here you can see the small lake called Lanty's Tarn.

While you'll eventually go through this gate and walk along the lake to finish the loop, first you can detour to the top of the adjacent hill, called Keldas, for sweeping views over the near side of Ullswater (to reach the summit, climb over the step gate and follow the faint path up the hill). Returning to—and passing through— the swing gate, you'll walk along Lanty's Tarn, then begin your slow, steep, and scenic descent into the Grisedale Valley. Reaching the valley floor (and passing a noisy dog breeder's farm), cross the stone bridge, then turn left and follow the road all the way back to the lakefront, where a left turn returns you to Glenridding.

▲Aira Force Waterfall

At Ullswater, there's a delightful little park with parking, a ranger trailer, and easy trails leading half a mile uphill to a powerful 60-foot-tall waterfall. You'll read about how Wordsworth was inspired to write three poems here...and after taking this little walk, you'll know why. The pay-and-display car park is just where the Troutbeck road from the A-66 hits the lake, on the A-592 between Pooley Bridge and Glenridding.

Helvellyn

Considered by many the best high-mountain hike in the Lake District, this breathtaking round-trip route from Glenridding includes the spectacular Striding Edge—about a half-mile along the ridge. Be careful; do this six-hour hike only in good weather, since the wind can be fierce. While it's not the shortest route, the Glenridding ascent is best. Get advice from the Ullswater TI in Glenridding or look for various books on this hike at any area TI.

South Lake District

The South Lake District has a cheesiness that's similar to other popular English resort destinations. Here, piles of low-end vacationers suffer through terrible traffic, slurp ice cream, and get candy floss caught in their hair. The area around Windermere is worth a drive-through if you're a fan of Wordsworth or Beatrix Potter, but you'll still want to spend the majority of your Lake District time (and book your accommodations) up north.

GETTING AROUND THE SOUTH LAKE DISTRICT

By Car: Driving is your best option to see the small towns and sights clustered in the South Lake District; consider combining your drive with the bus trip mentioned below. If you're coming to or leaving the South Lake District from the west, you could take the Hard Knott Pass for a scenic introduction to the area.

By Bus: Buses #599 and #555 are a fine and stress-free way to lace together this gauntlet of sights in the congested Lake Windermere neighborhood. Consider leaving your car at Grasmere and enjoying the breezy and extremely scenic bus #599, hopping off and on as you like (see page 477 for details).

Sights in the South Lake District

LAKE DISTRICT

WORDSWORTH SIGHTS

William Wordsworth was one of the first writers to reject fast-paced city life. During England's Industrial Age, hearts were muzzled and brains ruled. Science was in, machines were taming nature, and factory hours were taming humans. In reaction to these brainy ideals, a rare few—dubbed Romantics—began to embrace untamed nature and undomesticated emotions.

Back then, nobody climbed a mountain just because it was there—but Wordsworth did. He'd "wander lonely as a cloud" through the countryside, finding inspiration in "plain living and high thinking." He soon attracted a circle of like-minded creative friends.

The emotional highs the Romantics felt weren't all natural. Wordsworth and his poet friends Samuel Taylor Coleridge and Thomas de Quincey got stoned on opium and wrote poetry, combining their generation's standard painkiller drug with their tree-hugging passions (Coleridge's opium scale is on view in Dove Cottage). Today, opium is out of vogue, but the Romantic movement thrives as visitors continue to inundate the region.

▲▲Dove Cottage and Wordsworth Museum

For poets, this two-part visit is the top sight of the Lake District. Take a short tour of William Wordsworth's humble cottage, and get inspired in its excellent museum, which displays original writings, sketches, personal items, and fine paintings.

The poet whose appreciation of nature and a back-to-basics lifestyle put this area on the map spent his most productive years

Wordsworth at Dove Cottage

William Wordsworth (1770-1850) was a Lake District home-boy. Born in Cockermouth (in a house now open to the public), he was schooled in Hawkshead. In adulthood, he married a local girl, settled down in Grasmere and Ambleside, and was buried in Grasmere's St. Oswald's churchyard.

But the 30-year-old man who moved into Dove Cottage in 1799 was not the carefree lad who'd once roamed the district's lakes and fields. At Cambridge University, he'd been a C student, graduating with no job skills and no interest in a nine-to-five career. Instead, he and a buddy hiked through Europe, where Wordsworth had an epiphany of the "sublime" atop Switzerland's Alps. He lived a year in France, watching the Revolution rage. It stirred his soul. He fell in love with a Frenchwoman who bore his daughter, Caroline. But lack of money forced him to return to England, and the outbreak of war with France kept them apart.

Pining away in London, William hung out in the pubs and coffeehouses with fellow radicals, where he met poet Samuel Taylor Coleridge. They inspired each other to write, edited each other's work, and jointly published a groundbreaking book of poetry.

In 1799, his head buzzing with words and ideas, William and his sister (and soul mate), Dorothy, moved into the white-washed, slate-tiled former inn now known as Dove Cottage. He came into a small inheritance, and dedicated himself to poetry full time. In 1802, with the war temporarily over, William returned to France to finally meet his daughter. (He wrote of the rich experience: "It is a beauteous evening, calm and free... / Dear child! Dear Girl! that walkest with me here, / If thou appear untouched by solemn thought, / Thy nature is not therefore less divine.")

Having achieved closure, Wordsworth returned home to marry a former kindergarten classmate, Mary. She moved into Dove Cottage, along with an initially jealous Dorothy. Three of their five children were born here, and the cottage was also home to Mary's sister, the family dog Pepper (a gift from Sir Walter Scott; see Pepper's portrait), and frequent houseguests who bedded down in the pantry: Scott, Coleridge, and Thomas de Quincey, the Timothy Leary of opium.

The time at Dove Cottage was Wordsworth's "Golden Decade," when he penned his masterpieces. But after almost nine years here, Wordsworth's family and social status had outgrown the humble cottage. They moved first to a house in Grasmere before settling down in Rydal Hall. Wordsworth was changing. After the Dove years, he would write less, settle into a regular government job, quarrel with Coleridge, drift to the right politically, and endure criticism from old friends who branded him a sellout. Still, his poetry—most of it written at Dove—became increasingly famous, and he died honored as England's Poet Laureate.

(1799-1808) in this well-preserved stone cottage on the edge of Grasmere. After functioning as the Dove and Olive Bow pub for almost 200 years, it was bought by his family. This is where Wordsworth got married, had kids, and wrote much of his best poetry. Still owned by the Wordsworth family, the furniture was his, and the place comes with some amazing artifacts, including the poet's passport and suitcase (he packed light). Even during his lifetime, Wordsworth was famous, and Dove Cottage was turned into a museum in 1891—it's now protected by the Wordsworth Trust.

Cost and Hours: £8.95, daily 9:30-17:30, Nov-Feb 10:00-16:30 except closed Jan and for events in Dec and Feb (call ahead), café, bus #555 from Keswick, bus #555 or #599 from Windermere, tel. 015394/35544, www.wordsworth.org.uk. Pay parking in the Dove Cottage lot off the main road (A-591), 50 yards from the site.

Visiting the Cottage and Museum: Even if you're not a fan, Wordsworth's appreciation of nature, his Romanticism, and the ways his friends unleashed their creative talents with such abandon are appealing. The 25-minute cottage tour (which departs regularly—you shouldn't have to wait more than 30 minutes) and adjoining museum, with lots of actual manuscripts handwritten by Wordsworth and his illustrious friends, are both excellent. In dry weather, the garden where the poet was much inspired is worth a wander. (Visit this after leaving the cottage tour and pick up the description at the back door. The garden is closed when wet.) Allow 1.5 hours for this visit.

Poetry Readings: The Wordsworth Trust puts on shared poetry readings of Wordsworth's works written at Dove Cottage. Readings are held in the museum library in a relaxed and friendly setting (£5, every second Tue at 18:30, generally April-Oct, confirm schedule in advance, same contact info as above).

▲Rydal Mount

Located just down the road from Dove Cottage, this sight is worthwhile for Wordsworth fans. The poet's final, higher-class home, with a lovely garden and view, lacks the humble charm of Dove Cottage, but still evokes the time and creative spirit of the literary giant who lived here for 37 years. His family repurchased it in 1969 (after a 100-year gap), and his great-great-great-granddaughter still calls it home on occasion, as shown by recent family photos sprinkled throughout the house. After a short intro by the attendant,

LAKE DISTRICT

Wordsworth's Poetry at Dove

At Dove Cottage, Wordsworth was immersed in the beauty of nature and the simple joy of his young, growing family. It was here that he reflected on both his idyllic childhood and his troubled 20s. The following are select lines from two well-known poems from this fertile time.

Ode: Intimations of Immortality

There was a time when meadow, grove, and stream,
The earth, and every common sight, to me did seem
Apparelled in celestial light,
The glory and the freshness of a dream.
It is not now as it hath been of yore;—
Turn wheresoe'er I may,
By night or day,
The things which I have seen I now can see no more.

I Wandered Lonely as a Cloud (Daffodils)

I wandered lonely as a cloud
That floats on high o'er vales and hills,
When all at once I saw a crowd,
A host, of golden daffodils;
Beside the lake, beneath the trees,
Fluttering and dancing in the breeze . . .
. . . .
For oft, when on my couch I lie
In vacant or in pensive mood,
They flash upon that inward eye
Which is the bliss of solitude,
And then my heart with pleasure fills,
And dances with the daffodils.

you'll be given an explanatory flier and are welcome to roam. Wander through the garden William himself designed, which has changed little since then. Surrounded by his nature, you can imagine the poet enjoying them with you. "O happy garden! Whose seclusion deep hath been so friendly to industrious hours; and to soft slumbers, that did gently steep our spirits, carrying with them dreams of flowers, and wild notes warbled among leafy bowers."

Cost and Hours: £7.50; daily 9:30-17:00, Nov and Feb 11:00-16:00 and closed Mon-Tue, closed all of Dec-Jan; occasionally closed for private functions—check website; tearoom, 1.5 miles north of Ambleside, well-signed, free and easy parking, bus #555 from Keswick, tel. 015394/33002, www.rydalmount.co.uk.

BEATRIX POTTER SIGHTS

Of the many Beatrix Potter commercial ventures in the Lake District, there are two serious Beatrix Potter sights: her farm (Hill Top Farm) and her husband's former office, which is now the Beatrix Potter Gallery, filled with her sketches and paintings. The sights are two miles apart: Beatrix Potter Gallery is in Hawkshead, a cute but extremely touristy town that's a 20-minute drive south of Ambleside; Hill Top Farm is south of Hawkshead, in Near Sawrey village.

On busy summer days, the wait to get into Hill Top Farm can last several hours (only 8 people are allowed in every 5 minutes, and the timed-entry tickets must be bought in person). If you like quaint towns engulfed in Potter tourism (Hawkshead), this extra waiting time can be a blessing. Otherwise, you'll wish you were in the woods somewhere with Wordsworth.

To reach Hawkshead from Windermere, take bus #505 or catch the little 15-car ferry from Bowness (runs constantly except when it's extremely windy, 10-minute trip, £4.40 car fare includes all passengers). If you have questions, visit the Hawkshead TI inside the Ooh-La-La gift shop right across from the parking lot (tel. 015394/36946). To reach Hill Top Farm, see the directions below.

▲Hill Top Farm

A hit with Beatrix Potter fans (and skippable for others), this dark and intimate cottage, swallowed up in the inspirational and rough

nature around it, provides an enjoyable if quick experience. The six-room farm was left just as it was when she died in 1943. At her request, the house is set as if she had just stepped out—flowers on the tables, fire on, low lights. While there's no printed information here, guides in each room are eager to explain things. Fans of her classic *The Tale of Samuel Whiskers* will recognize the home's rooms, furniture, and views—the book and its illustrations were inspired by an invasion of rats when she bought this place.

Cost and Hours: Farmhouse-£10.90, tickets often sell out by 14:00 or even earlier during busy times; gardens-free; June-Aug daily 10:00-17:30; mid-Feb-May and Sept-Oct until 16:30 and

LAKE DISTRICT

Beatrix Potter (1866-1943)

As a girl growing up in London, Beatrix Potter vacationed in the Lake District, where she became inspired to write her popular children's books. Unable to get a publisher, she self-published the first two editions of *The Tale of Peter Rabbit* in 1901 and 1902. When she finally landed a publisher, sales of her books were phenomenal. With the money she made, she bought Hill Top Farm, a 17th-century cottage, and fixed it up, living there sporadically from 1905 until she married in 1913. Potter was more than a children's book writer; she was a fine artist, an avid gardener, and a successful farmer. She married a lawyer and put her knack for business to use, amassing a 4,000-acre estate. An early conservationist, she used the garden-cradled cottage as a place to study nature. She willed it—along with the rest of her vast estate—to the National Trust, which she enthusiastically supported.

closed Fri; Nov-Dec until 15:30 and closed Mon-Thu; closed Jan-mid-Feb; tel. 015394/36269, www.nationaltrust.org.uk/hill-top.

Buying Tickets: You must buy tickets in person. To beat the lines, get to the ticket office when it opens—15 minutes before Hill Top starts its first tour. If you can't make it early, call the farm for the current wait times (if no one answers, leave a message for the administrator; someone will call you back).

Getting There: Mountain Goat Tours runs a shuttle bus from across the Hawkshead TI to the farm every 40 minutes (tel. 015394/45161). Drivers can take the B-5286 and B-5285 from Ambleside or the B-5285 from Coniston—be prepared for extremely narrow roads with no shoulders that are often lined with stone walls. Park and buy tickets 150 yards down the road, and walk back to tour the place.

▲Beatrix Potter Gallery

Located in the cute but extremely touristy town of Hawkshead, this gallery fills Beatrix's husband's former law office with the wonderful and intimate drawings and watercolors that she did to illustrate her books. Each year the museum highlights a new theme and brings out a different set of her paintings, drawings, and other items. Unlike Hill Top, the gallery has plenty of explanation about her life and work, including touchscreen displays and information panels. Even non-Potter fans will find this museum rather charming and her art surprisingly interesting.

Cost and Hours: £6.50, daily 10:30-16:00, closed Nov-mid-Feb, Main Street, drivers use the nearby pay-and-display lot and walk 200 yards to the town center, tel. 015394/36355, www.nationaltrust.org.uk/beatrix-potter-gallery.

Hawkshead Grammar School Museum

This interesting museum, just across from the pay-and-display parking lot, was founded in 1585 and is where William Wordsworth studied from 1779 to 1787. It shows off old school benches and desks whittled with penknife graffiti.

Cost and Hours: £2.50 includes guided tour; Mon-Sat 10:00-13:00 & 13:30-17:00, Oct until 16:30, closed Sun and Nov-March; tel. 015394/36735, www.hawksheadgrammar.org.uk.

The World of Beatrix Potter

This exhibit, a hit with children, is gimmicky, with all the historical value of a Disney ride. The 45-minute experience features a four-minute video trip into the world of Mrs. Tiggywinkle and company, a series of Lake District tableaux starring the same imaginary gang, and an all-about-Beatrix section, with an eight-minute video biography.

Cost and Hours: £7.50, kids-£3.95, daily 10:00-17:30, tearoom, on Crag Brow in Bowness-on-Windermere, tel. 015394/88444, www.hop-skip-jump.com.

MORE SIGHTS AT LAKE WINDERMERE
Brockhole National Park Visitors Centre

Look for a stately old lakeside mansion between Ambleside and Windermere on the A-591. Set in a nicely groomed lakeside park, the center offers a free video on life in the Lake District, an information desk, organized walks (see the park's free *Visitor Guide*), exhibits, a shop (excellent selection of maps and guidebooks), a cafeteria, gardens, and nature walks. It's also a great place to bring kids for its free indoor play space and fun adventure playground with slides, swings, nets, and swinging bridges. Other family activities, including an aerial treetop trek, a zip line, mini golf, and pony rides, have a fee. Boat and bike rentals are also available.

Cost and Hours: Free entry; daily 10:00-17:00, Nov-March until 16:00; pay-when-you-leave parking (online option up to 48 hours after), bus #555 from Keswick, bus #599 from Windermere, tel. 015394/46601, www.lakedistrict.gov.uk.

Cruise: For a joyride around famous Lake Windermere, you can catch the Brockhole "Green" cruise here (£8.25, runs daily April-Oct 10:00-17:00, hourly, 2/hour in summer, 50-minute circle, scant narration, passengers can hop on and off on one ticket, tel. 015394/43360, www.windermere-lakecruises.co.uk).

Lakes Aquarium

Get a glimpse of the natural history of Cumbria via exhibits describing the local wildlife living in lake and coastal environments, including otters, eels, pike, and sharks. A rainforest exhibit features reptiles and marmoset monkeys. Experts give various talks throughout the day.

Cost and Hours: £9, £6 for kids under age 16, cheaper online, family deals, daily 9:00-18:00, until 17:00 in winter, last entry one hour before closing, in Lakeside, one mile north of Newby Bridge, at south end of Lake Windermere, tel. 015395/30153, www.lakesaquarium.co.uk.

Hayes Garden World

This extensive gardening center, a popular weekend excursion for locals, offers garden supplies, a bookstore, a playground, and gorgeous grounds. Gardeners could wander this place all afternoon. Upstairs is a fine cafeteria-style restaurant (open Mon-Sat 9:00-18:00, Sun 11:00-17:00, at south end of Ambleside on main drag, see *Garden Centre* signs, located at north end of Lake Windermere, tel. 015394/33434, www.hayesgardenworld.co.uk).

YORK

Historic York is loaded with world-class sights. Marvel at the York Minster, England's finest Gothic church. Ramble The Shambles, York's wonderfully preserved medieval quarter. Enjoy a walking tour led by an old Yorker. Hop a train at one of the world's greatest railway museums, travel to the 1800s in the York Castle Museum, head back 1,000 years to Viking times at the Jorvik Viking Centre, or dig into the city's buried past at the Yorkshire Museum.

York has a rich history. In A.D. 71 it was Eboracum, a Roman provincial capital—the northernmost city in the empire. Constantine was proclaimed emperor here in A.D. 306. In the fifth century, as Rome was toppling, the Roman emperor sent a letter telling England it was on its own, and York—now called Eoforwic—became the capital of the Anglo-Saxon kingdom of Northumbria.

The city's first church was built in 627, and the town became an early Christian center of learning. The Vikings later took the town, and from the 9th through the 11th century, it was a Danish trading center called Jorvik. The invading and conquering Normans destroyed and then rebuilt the city, fortifying it with a castle and the walls you see today.

Medieval York, with 9,000 inhabitants, grew rich on the wool trade and became England's second city. Henry VIII used the city's fine Minster as the northern capital of his Anglican Church. (In today's Anglican Church, the Archbishop of York is second only to the Archbishop of Canterbury.)

In the Industrial Age, York was the railway hub of northern England. When it was built, York's train station was the world's largest. During World War II, Hitler chose to bomb York by picking the city out of a travel guidebook (not this one).

Today, York's leading industry is tourism. It seems like everything that's great about Britain finds its best expression in this manageable town. While the city has no single claim to fame, York is more than the sum of its parts. With its strollable cobbles and half-timbered buildings, grand cathedral and excellent museums, thriving restaurant scene and welcoming locals, York delights.

PLANNING YOUR TIME

After London, York is the best sightseeing city in England. On even a 10-day trip through Britain, it deserves two nights and a day. For the best 36 hours, follow this plan: Arrive early enough to catch the 17:15 evensong service at the Minster, then take the free city walking tour at 18:15 (evening tours offered June-Aug only). Splurge on dinner at one of the city's bistros. The next morning at 9:00, take my self-guided walk, interrupting it midway with a tour of the Minster. Finish the walk and grab lunch. To fill your afternoon, choose among the town's many important sights (such as the York Castle Museum or the Railway Museum). Spend the evening enjoying a ghost walk of your choice and another memorable dinner.

This is a packed day; as you review this chapter, you'll see that there are easily two days of sightseeing fun in York.

Orientation to York

There are roughly 200,000 people in York and its surrounding area; about one in ten is a student. But despite the city's size, the sightseer's York is small. Virtually everything is within a few minutes' walk: sights, train station, TI, and B&Bs. The longest walk a visitor might take (from a B&B across the old town to the York Castle Museum) is about 25 minutes.

Bootham Bar, a gate in the medieval town wall, is the hub of your York visit. (In York, a "bar" is a gate and a "gate" is a street. Blame the Vikings.) At Bootham Bar and on Exhibition Square, you'll find the starting points for most walking tours and bus tours, handy access to the medieval town wall, a public WC, and Bootham Street (which leads to my recommended B&Bs). To find your way around York, use the Minster's towers as a navigational landmark, or follow the strategically placed signposts, which point out all places of interest to tourists.

TOURIST INFORMATION

York's TI is a block in front of the Minster (Mon-Sat 9:00-17:00, Sun 10:00-16:00, 1 Museum Street, tel. 01904/550-099, www. visityork.org).

York Pass: The TI sells an expensive pass that covers the major sights in York, the City Sightseeing bus, and a few regional sights. You'd have to be a very busy sightseer to make this pass worth the cost (£38/1 day, multiday options available, www.yorkpass.com).

ARRIVAL IN YORK

By Train: The train station is a 10-minute walk from downtown. Day-trippers can pay to store baggage at the small hut next to the Europcar office just off Queen Street—as you exit the station, turn right and walk along a bridge to the first intersection, then turn right (cash only, daily until 20:00).

Recommended B&Bs are a 5- to 15-minute walk (depending on where you're staying) or a £7-9 taxi ride from the station. For specific walking directions to the B&Bs, see page 551.

To walk downtown from the station, exit straight, crossing the street through the bus stops, and turn left down Station Road, keeping the wall on your right. At the first intersection, turn right through the gap in the wall and then left across the river, and follow the crowd toward the Gothic towers of the Minster. After the bridge, a block before the Minster, you'll see the TI on your right.

By Car: Driving and parking in York is maddening. Those day-tripping here should follow signs to one of several park-and-ride lots ringing the perimeter. At these lots, parking is free, and shuttle buses go every 10 minutes into the center.

If you're sleeping here, park your car where your B&B advises and walk. As you near York (and your B&B), you'll hit the A-1237 ring road. Follow this to the A-19/Thirsk roundabout (next to river on northwest side of town). From the roundabout, follow signs for *York*, traveling through Clifton into Bootham. All recommended B&Bs are four or five blocks before you hit the medieval city gate (see neighborhood map on page 553). If you're approaching York from the south, take the M-1 until it becomes the A-1M, exit at junction 45 onto the A-64, and follow it for 10 miles until you reach York's ring road (A-1237), which allows you to avoid driving through the city center. If you have more time, the A-19 from Selby is a slower and more scenic route into York.

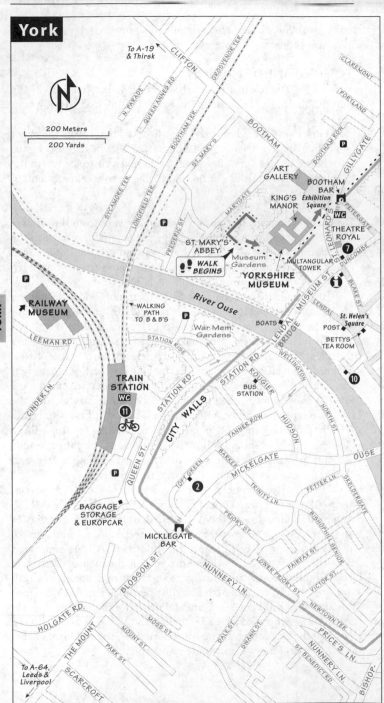

York

To A-19 & Thirsk

CLIFTON

CLAREMONT

PORTLAND

BOOTHAM ROW

GILLYGATE

N. PARADE

QUEEN ANNE'S RD.

GROSVENOR TER.

BOOTHAM TER.

ST. MARY'S

BOOTHAM

ART GALLERY

KING'S MANOR

BOOTHAM BAR

Exhibition Square

WC

PETERGATE

SYCAMORE TER.

LONGFIELD TER.

FREDERIC ST.

MARYGATE

ST. MARY'S ABBEY

Museum Gardens

Multangular Tower

YORKSHIRE MUSEUM

ST. LEONARD'S

THEATRE ROYAL

7

DUNCOMBE

MUSEUM ST.

BLAKE ST.

i

LENDAL

WALK BEGINS

River Ouse

200 Meters

200 Yards

P

RAILWAY MUSEUM

P

WALKING PATH TO B & B'S

P

War Mem. Gardens

BOATS

LENDAL BRIDGE

St. Helen's Square

POST

BETTYS TEA ROOM

LEEMAN RD.

Station Rise

STATION RISE

STATION RD.

WELLINGTON

10

CINDER LN.

TRAIN STATION

WC

11

STATION RD.

CITY WALLS

STATION RD.

ROUGIER

BUS STATION

NORTH ST.

OUSE

QUEEN ST.

TOFT GREEN

BARKER

TANNER ROW

MICKELGATE

HUDSON

FETTER LN.

SKELDERGATE

2

TRINITY LN.

BISHOPHILL SENIOR

P

BAGGAGE STORAGE & EUROPCAR

MICKLEGATE BAR

PRIORY ST.

LOWER PRIORY ST.

FAIRFAX ST.

VICTOR ST.

NUNNERY LN.

BLOSSOM ST.

HOLGATE RD.

THE MOUNT

PARK ST.

MOUNT ST.

MOSS ST.

DALE ST.

SWANN ST.

NUNNERY LN.

NEWTOWN TER.

PRICE'S LN.

ST. BENEDICT RD.

BISHOP-

SCARCROFT

To A-64, Leeds & Liverpool

YORK

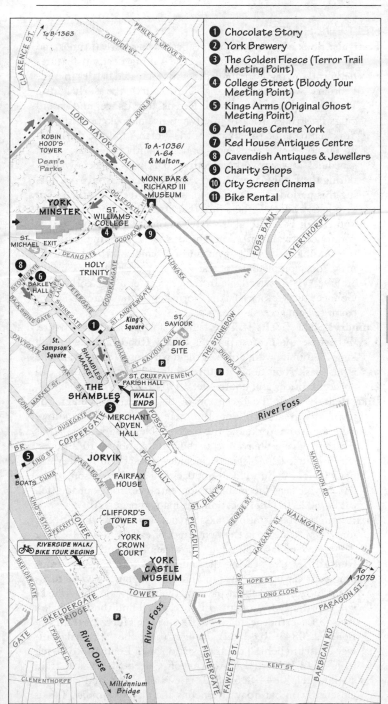

1 Chocolate Story
2 York Brewery
3 The Golden Fleece (Terror Trail Meeting Point)
4 College Street (Bloody Tour Meeting Point)
5 Kings Arms (Original Ghost Meeting Point)
6 Antiques Centre York
7 Red House Antiques Centre
8 Cavendish Antiques & Jewellers
9 Charity Shops
10 City Screen Cinema
11 Bike Rental

YORK

HELPFUL HINTS

Festivals: Book a room well in advance during festival times and on weekends any time of year. The **Viking Festival** features *lur* horn-blowing, warrior drills, and re-created battles in mid-February (www.jorvik-viking-centre.co.uk). The **Early Music Festival** (medieval minstrels, Renaissance dance, and so on) zings its strings in early July (www.ncem.co.uk/yemf.shtml). York claims to be the "Ascot of the North," and the town fills up on horse-race weekends (once a month May-Oct, check schedules at www.yorkracecourse.co.uk); it's especially busy during the **Ebor Races** in mid-August. (Many avoid York during this period, as prices go up and the streets are filled with drunken revelers. Others find that attractive.) The **York Food and Drink Festival** takes a bite out of late September (www.yorkfoodfestival.com). And the St. Nicholas Fair Christmas market jingles its bells from mid-November through Christmas. For a complete list of festivals, see YorkFestivals.com.

Wi-Fi: Free Wi-Fi is available in the city center using York's City Connect network (select the "form" option and create an account to gain access).

Laundry: Some B&Bs will do laundry for a reasonable charge. Otherwise the nearest place is **Haxby Road Launderette,** a long 15-minute walk north of the town center (or you can take a bus—ask your B&B for directions, 124 Haxby Road, call ahead for prices and hours—tel. 01904/623-379).

Bike Rental: With the exception of the pedestrian center, the town's not great for biking. But there are several fine countryside rides from York, and the riverside New Walk bike path is pleasant. **Cycle Heaven** is at the train station (£10/2 hours, £15/5 hours, £20/24 hours, includes helmet and lock, Mon-Sat 9:00-17:30, Sun 11:00-16:00, closed Sun off-season, to the left as you face the main station entrance from outside, tel. 01904/622-701). For location, see map on page 520.

Taxi: From the train station, taxis zip new arrivals to their B&Bs for £7-9. Queue up at the taxi stand, or call 01904/638-833 or 01904/659-659; cabbies don't start the meter until you get in.

Car Rental: If you're nearing the end of your trip, consider dropping your car upon arrival in York. The money saved by turning it in early just about pays for the train ticket that whisks you effortlessly to London. In York, you'll find these agencies: **Avis** (3 Layerthorpe, tel. 0844-544-6117); **Hertz** (at train station, tel. 0843-309-3082); **Budget** (near the National Railway Museum behind the train station at 75 Leeman Road, tel. 01904/644-919); and **Europcar** (off Queen Street near train station, tel. 0844-846-0872). Beware: Car-rental agencies close early on Saturday afternoons and all day Sunday. This is

YORK

OK when dropping off, but picking up at these times is possible only by prior arrangement (and for an extra fee).

Tours in York

▲▲▲WALKING TOURS
Free Walks with Volunteer Guides
Charming locals give energetic, entertaining, and free two-hour walks through York (April-Oct daily at 10:15 and 14:15, June-Aug also at 18:15; Nov-March daily at 10:15 and 13:15; depart from Exhibition Square in front of the art gallery, tel. 01904/550-098, www.avgyork.co.uk). These tours often go long because the guides love to teach and tell stories. You're welcome to cut out early—but let them know, or they'll worry, thinking they've lost you.

Yorkwalk Tours
These are more serious 1.5- to 2-hour walks with a history focus. They do four different walks—Essential York, Roman York, Secret York, and The Snickelways of York—as well as a variety of "special walks" on more specific topics (£6, daily at 10:30 and 14:15, no tours Dec-Jan, depart from Museum Gardens Gate, just show up, tel. 07970/848-709, www.yorkwalk.co.uk—check website, ask TI, or call to confirm schedule). Tours go rain or shine, with as few as two participants.

Ghost Walks
Each evening, the old center of York is crawling with creepy ghost walks. These are generally 1.5 hours long, cost £5, and go rain or shine. There are no reservations (you simply show up) and no tickets (just pay at the start). At the advertised time and place, your black-clad guide appears, and you follow him or her to the first stop. Your guide gives a sample of the entertainment you have in store, humorously collects the "toll," and you're off.

You'll see fliers and signboards all over town advertising the many ghost walks. Companies come and go, but I find there are three general styles of walks: historic, street theater, and storytelling. Here are three reliably good walks, one for each style (ask about RS%, limit two "victims").

The **Terror Trail Walk** is more historic, "all true," and a bit more intellectual (daily at 18:45, meet at The Golden Fleece at bottom of The Shambles, www.yorkterrortrail.co.uk).

The **Bloody Tour of York,** led by Mad Alice (an infamous figure in York lore), is an engaging walk with tales of history, violence, and mayhem (Thu-Sat at 18:00, also at 20:00 in April-Oct, no tours Sun-Wed, Dec-Jan by reservation only, meet outside St. Williams College behind the Minster on College Street, www.thebloodytourofyork.co.uk).

YORK

The **Original Ghost Walk** was the first of its kind, dating back to the 1970s, and is more classic spooky storytelling rather than comedy (daily at 20:00, meet at The Kings Arms at Ouse Bridge, www.theoriginalghostwalkofyork.co.uk).

HOP-ON, HOP-OFF BUS TOUR

City Sightseeing's half-enclosed, double-decker, hop-on, hop-off buses circle York, taking tourists past secondary sights that the city walking tours skip—the mundane perimeter of town. While you can hop on and off all day, York is so compact that these have no real transportation value. If taking a bus tour, I'd catch either one at Exhibition Square (near Bootham Bar) and ride it for an orientation all the way around. Consider getting off at the National Railway Museum, skipping the last five minutes. In the summer, several departures come with a live guide (£13, ticket good for £2 off York Boat cruise—described next, pay driver, cash only, ticket valid 24 hours, Easter-Oct departs every 10-15 minutes, daily 9:00-17:30, less frequent off-season, about 1 hour, tel. 01904/633-990, www.yorkbus.co.uk).

BOAT CRUISE

York Boat does a lazy, narrated 45-minute lap along the River Ouse (£8.50, ticket good for £3 off City Sightseeing bus tours—see earlier, April-Sept runs every 30 minutes, daily 10:30-15:00, off-season 4/day, no cruises Dec-Jan; leaves from Lendal Bridge and King's Staith landings, near Skeldergate Bridge; also 1.5-hour evening cruise at 21:15 for £9.50, leaves from King's Staith; tel. 01904/628-324, www.yorkboat.co.uk).

York Walk

Get a taste of Roman and medieval York on this easy, self-guided stroll. The walk begins in the gardens just in front of the Yorkshire Museum, covers a stretch of the medieval city walls, and then cuts through the middle of the old town. Start at the ruins of St. Mary's Abbey in the Museum Gardens.

St. Mary's Abbey

This abbey dates to the age of William the Conqueror—whose harsh policies (called the "Harrowing of the North") consisted of massacres and destruction, including the burning of York's main

York at a Glance

▲▲▲**York Minster** York's pride and joy, and one of England's finest churches, with stunning stained-glass windows, textbook Decorated Gothic design, and glorious evensong services. **Hours:** Mon-Sat 9:00-18:30, Sun 12:30-18:30; shorter hours for tower and undercroft; evensong services Tue-Sat and some Mon at 17:15, Sun at 16:00. See page 531.

▲▲▲**Walking Tours** Variety of guided town walks and evening ghost walks covering York's history. **Hours:** Various times daily; fewer off-season. See page 523.

▲▲**Yorkshire Museum** Sophisticated archaeology and natural history museum with York's best Viking exhibit, plus Roman, Saxon, Norman, and Gothic artifacts. **Hours:** Daily 10:00-17:00. See page 538.

▲▲**Jorvik Viking Centre** Entertaining and informative Disney-style exhibit/ride exploring Viking lifestyles and artifacts. **Hours:** Daily 10:00-17:00, Nov-March until 16:00. See page 542.

▲▲**York Castle Museum** Far-ranging collection displaying everyday objects from Victorian times to the present. **Hours:** Daily 9:30-17:00. See page 544.

▲▲**National Railway Museum** Train buff's nirvana, tracing the history of all manner of rail-bound transport. **Hours:** Daily 10:00-18:00. See page 545.

▲**The Shambles** Atmospheric old butchers' quarter, with colorful, tipsy medieval buildings. See page 530.

▲**Ouse Riverside Walk** Bucolic path along river to a mod pedestrian bridge. See page 547.

▲**York Brewery** Honest, casual tour through an award-winning microbrewery with the guy who makes the beer. **Hours:** Mon-Sat at 12:30, 14:00, 15:30, and 17:00. See page 547.

▲**Fairfax House** Glimpse into an 18th-century Georgian family house, with enjoyably chatty docents. **Hours:** Tue-Sat 10:00-16:30, Sun 11:00-15:30, Mon by tour only at 11:00 and 14:00, closed Jan-mid-Feb. See page 543.

YORK

church. His son Rufus, who tried to improve relations in the 11th century, established a great church here. The church became an abbey that thrived from the 13th century until the Dissolution of the Monasteries in the 16th century. The Dissolution, which accompanied the Protestant Reformation and break with Rome, was a power play by Henry VIII. The king wanted much more than just a divorce: He wanted the land and riches of the monasteries. Upset with the pope, he demanded that his subjects pay him taxes rather than give the Church tithes. (For more information, see the sidebar on page 534.)

As you gaze at this ruin, imagine magnificent abbeys like this scattered throughout the realm. Henry VIII destroyed most of them, taking the lead from their roofs and leaving the stones to scavenging townsfolk. Scant as they are today, these ruins still evoke a time of immense monastic power. The one surviving wall was the west half of a very long, skinny nave. The tall arch marked the start of the transept. Stand on the nearby plaque that

reads *Crossing beneath central tower*, and look up at the air that now fills the space where a huge tower once stood. (Fine carved stonework from the ruined abbey is on display in a basement room of the adjacent Yorkshire Museum.)

Beyond the abbey, you'll see a bowling green and the abbey's original wall (not part of the city walls).

• *With your back to the abbey, see the fine Neoclassical building housing the* **Yorkshire Museum** *(well worth a visit and described later, under "Sights in York"). Walk past this about 30 yards and turn left, following signs to the York Art Gallery. Ahead to the right is a corner of the city's* **Roman wall***. A tiny lane on the right leads through the garden (past a yew tree) and under a small, gated arch (may be locked), giving a peek into the ruined tower.*

Multangular Tower

This 12-sided tower (c. A.D. 300) was likely a catapult station built to protect the town from enemy river traffic. The red ribbon of bricks was a Roman trademark—both structural and decorative. The lower stones are Roman, while the upper (and bigger) stones are medieval. After Rome fell, York suffered through two centuries of a dark age. Then, in the ninth century, the Vikings ruled. They built with wood, so almost nothing from that period remains. The Normans came in 1066 and built in stone, generally atop Roman structures (like this wall). The wall that defined the ancient

Roman garrison town worked for the Norman town, too. But after the English Civil War in the 1600s and Jacobite rebellions in the 1700s, fortified walls were no longer needed in England's interior.

• *Now, return 10 steps down the lane and turn right, walking between the museum and the Roman wall. Continuing straight, the lane goes between the abbot's palace and the town wall. This is a "snickelway"—a small, characteristic York lane or footpath. The snickelway pops out on...*

Exhibition Square

With Henry VIII's Dissolution of the Monasteries, the abbey was destroyed and the Abbot's Palace became the **King's Manor** (from

the snickelway, make a U-turn to the left and through the gate). Enter the building under the coat of arms of Charles I, who stayed here during the English Civil War in the 1640s. Today, the building is part of the University of York. Because the northerners were slow to embrace the king's reforms, Henry VIII came here to enforce the Dissolution. He stayed 17 days in this mansion and brought along 1,000 troops to make his determination clear. You can wander into the grounds and building. An onsite café serves cheap cakes, soup, and sandwiches to students, professors, and visitors like you (Mon-Fri 9:30-15:00, closed Sat-Sun).

Exhibition Square is the departure point for various walking and bus tours. You can see the towers of the Minster in the distance. Travelers in the Middle Ages could see the Minster from miles away as they approached the city. Across the street is a pay WC and **Bootham Bar**—one of the fourth-century Roman gates in York's wall—with access to the best part of the city walls (free, walls open 8:00-dusk).

• *Climb up the bar.*

Walk the Wall

Hike along the top of the wall behind the Minster to the first corner. Just because you see a padlock on an entry gate, don't think it's locked—give it a push, and you'll probably find it's open. York's 13th-century walls are three miles long.

This stretch follows the original Roman wall. Norman kings built the walls to assert control over northern England. Notice the pivots in the crenellations (square notches at the top of a medieval wall), which once held wooden hatches to provide cover for archers. The wall was extensively renovated in the 19th century (Victorians added Romantic arrow slits).

At the corner with the benches—**Robin Hood's Tower**—you can lean out and see the moat outside. This was originally the Roman ditch that surrounded the fortified garrison town. Continue walking for a fine view of the Minster, with its truncated main tower and the pointy rooftop of its chapter house.

Continue on to the next gate, **Monk Bar.** This fine medieval gatehouse is the home of the overly slick **Richard III Museum** (described later, under "Sights in York").

• *Descend the wall at Monk Bar, and step past the portcullis behind you (last lowered in 1953 for the Queen's coronation) to emerge outside the city's protective wall. Take 10 paces and gaze up at the tower. Imagine 10 archers behind the arrow slits. Keep an eye on the 17th-century guards, with their stones raised and primed to protect the town.*

Return through the city wall. After a short block, turn right on Ogleforth. ("Ogle" is the Norse word for owl, hence our word "ogle"—to look at something fiercely.)

York's Old Town

Walking down Ogleforth, ogle (on your left) a charming little brick house from the 17th century called the **Dutch House.** It was designed by an apprentice architect who was trying to show off for his master, and was the first entirely brick house in town—a sign of opulence. Next, also of brick, is a former brewery, with a 19th-century industrial feel.

Ogleforth jogs left and becomes **Chapter House Street,** passing the Treasurer's House to the back side of the Minster. Circle around the left side of the church, past the stonemasons' lodge (where craftsmen are chiseling local limestone for the church, as has been done here since the 13th century), to the statue of Roman Emperor Constantine and an ancient Roman column.

Step up to lounging **Constantine.** Five emperors visited York when it was the Roman city of Eboracum. Constantine was here when his father died. The troops declared him the Roman emperor in A.D. 306 at this site, and six years later, he went to Rome to claim his throne. In

A.D. 312, Constantine legalized Christianity, and in A.D. 314, York got its first bishop.

The **ancient column,** across the street from Constantine, is a reminder that the Minster sits upon the site of the Roman headquarters, or *principia*. The city placed this column here in 1971, just before celebrating the 1,900th anniversary of the founding of Eboracum—a.k.a. York. Take a hard look at the column—the town accidentally erected it upside down.

• *If you want to visit the **York Minster** now, find the entrance on its west side, ahead and around the corner (see description on page 531). Otherwise, head into the town center. From opposite the Minster's south transept door (the door by Constantine), take a narrow pedestrian walkway—which becomes Stonegate—into the tangled commercial center of medieval York. Walk straight down Stonegate, a street lined with fun and inviting cafés, pubs, and restaurants. Just before the Ye Old Starre Inne banner hanging over the street, turn left down the snickelway called Coffee Yard. (It's marked by a red devil.) Enjoy strolling York's...*

"Snickelways"

This is a made-up York word combining "snicket" (a passageway between walls or fences), "ginnel" (a narrow passageway between buildings), and "alleyway" (any narrow passage)—snickelway. York—with its population packed densely inside its protective walls—has about 50 of these public passages. In general, when exploring the city, you should duck into these—both for the adventure and to take a shortcut. While some of York's history has been bulldozed by modernity, bits of it hide and survive in the snickelways.

Coffee Yard leads past Barley Hall, popping out at the corner of Grape Lane and Swinegate. Medieval towns named streets for the business done there. Swinegate, a lane of pig farmers, leads to the market. Grape Lane is a polite version of that street's original crude name, Gropec*nt Lane. If you were here a thousand years ago, you'd find it lined by brothels. Throughout England, streets for prostitutes were called by this graphic name. Today, if you see a street named Grape Lane, that's usually its heritage.

Skip Grape Lane and turn right down Swinegate to a market (which you can see in the distance). The recently upgraded **Shambles Market,** popular for cheap produce and clothing, was created in the 1960s with the demolition of a bunch of colorful medieval lanes.

• *In the center of the market, tiny "Little Shambles" lane (on the left) dead-ends into the most famous lane in York.*

The Shambles

This colorful old street (rated ▲) was once the "street of the butchers." The name was derived from "shammell"—a butcher's bench upon which he'd cut and display his meat. In the 16th century, this lane was dripping with red meat. Look for the hooks under the eaves; these were once used to hang rabbit, pheasant, beef, lamb, and pigs' heads. Fresh slabs were displayed on the fat sills, while people lived above the shops. All the garbage and sewage flushed down the street to a mucky pond at the end—a favorite hangout for the town's cats and dogs. Tourist shops now fill these fine, half-timbered Tudor buildings. Look above the modern crowds and storefronts to appreciate the classic old English architecture. Unfortunately, the soil here isn't great for building; notice how the structures have settled in the absence of a solid foundation.

Turn right and slalom down The Shambles. Just past the tiny sandwich shop at #37, pop in to the snickelway and look for very old **woodwork.** Study the 16th-century carpentry: mortise-and-tenon joints with wooden plugs rather than nails.

Next door (on The Shambles) is the **shrine of St. Margaret Clitherow,** a 16th-century Catholic crushed by Protestants under her own door (as was the humiliating custom when a city wanted to teach someone a lesson). She was killed for hiding priests in her home. Step into the tiny shrine for a peaceful moment to ponder Margaret, who in 1970 was sainted for her faith.

At the bottom of The Shambles is the cute, tiny **St. Crux Parish Hall,** which charities use to raise funds by selling light meals (see "Eating in York," later). Take some time to chat with the volunteers.

With blood and guts from The Shambles' 20 butchers all draining down the lane, it's no wonder The Golden Fleece, just below, is considered the most haunted pub in town.

• *Your town walk is finished. From here, you're just a few minutes from plenty of fun: street entertainment and lots of cheap eating options on King's Square, good restaurants on Fossgate, the York Castle Museum (a few blocks farther downhill), and the starting point for my Ouse Riverside Walk.*

Sights in York

▲▲▲YORK MINSTER

The pride of York, this largest Gothic church north of the Alps (540 feet long, 200 feet tall) brilliantly shows that the High Middle Ages were far from dark. The word "minster" means an important church chartered with a mission to evangelize. As it's the seat of a bishop, York Minster is also a cathedral. While Henry VIII destroyed England's great abbeys, this was not part of a monastery and was therefore left standing. It seats 2,000 comfortably; on Christmas and Easter, at least 4,000 worshippers pack the place. Today, more than 250 employees and 500 volunteers work to preserve its heritage and welcome 1.3 million visitors each year.

Cost: £10, includes guided tour, undercroft museum, and crypt; free for kids under age 16.

Hours: The cathedral is open for sightseeing Mon-Sat 9:00-18:30, Sun 12:30-18:30. It opens for worship daily at 7:30. Closing time flexes with activities, but last entry is generally at 17:00—call or look online to confirm. Sights within the Minster have shorter hours (listed below). The Minster may close for special events (check calendar on website).

Information: Tel. 01904/557-217 or 0844-393-0011, www.yorkminster.org.

Visitor Information: You'll get a free map with your ticket. For more information, pick up the inexpensive *York Minster Short Guide*. Helpful Minster guides stationed throughout are happy to answer your questions.

Tower Climb: It costs £5 for 30 minutes of exercise (275 steps) and forgettable views. The tower opens at 10:00 (13:00 on Sun), with ascents every 45 minutes; the last ascent is generally at 17:30—later in peak season and earlier in winter (no children under 8, not good for acrophobes, closes in extreme weather). Be sure to get your ticket upon arrival, as only 50 visitors are allowed up at once; you'll be assigned an entry time. It's a tight, spiraling, claustrophobic staircase with an iron handrail. You'll climb about 150 steps to the top of the transept, step outside to cross a narrow

York Minster

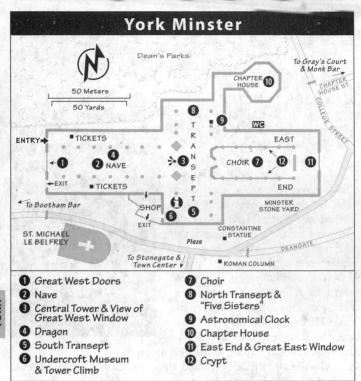

1 Great West Doors
2 Nave
3 Central Tower & View of Great West Window
4 Dragon
5 South Transept
6 Undercroft Museum & Tower Climb
7 Choir
8 North Transept & "Five Sisters"
9 Astronomical Clock
10 Chapter House
11 East End & Great East Window
12 Crypt

walkway, then go back inside for more than 100 steps to the top of the central tower. From here, you'll have caged-in views of rooftops and the flat countryside.

Undercroft Museum: This museum focuses on the history of the site and its origins as a Roman fortress (Mon-Sat 10:00-17:00, Sun 13:00-16:00).

Tours: Free guided tours depart from the ticket desk every hour on the hour (Mon-Sat 10:00-15:00, can be more frequent during busy times, none on Sun, one hour, they run even with just one or two people). You can join a tour in progress, or if none is scheduled, request a departure.

Evensong: To experience the cathedral in musical and spiritual action, attend an evensong (Tue-Sat at 17:15, Sun at 16:00). On Mondays, visiting choirs fill in about half the time (otherwise it's a spoken service, also at 17:15). Visiting choirs also perform when the Minster's choir is on summer break (mid-July-Aug, confirm at church or TI). Arrive 15 minutes early and wait just outside the choir in the center of the church. You'll be ushered in and can sit in one of the big wooden stalls. As evensong is a worship service, attendees enter the church free of charge. For more on evensong, see page 163.

Church Bells: If you're a fan of church bells, you'll experience ding-dong ecstasy Sunday morning at about 10:00 and during the Tuesday practice session between 19:00 and 22:00. These performances are especially impressive, as the church holds a full carillon of 35 bells (it's the only English cathedral to have such a range). Stand in front of the church's west portal and imagine the gang pulling on a dozen ropes (halfway up the right tower—you can actually see the ropes through a little window) while one talented carillonneur plays 22 more bells with a keyboard and foot pedals.

❍ Self-Guided Tour

Enter the great church through the west portal (under the twin towers). Upon entering, decide whether you're climbing the tower. If so, get a ticket (with an assigned time). Also consider visiting the undercroft museum (described later) if you want to get a comprehensive history and overview of the Minster before touring the church.

• *Entering the church, turn 180 degrees and look back at the...*

❶ Great West Doors: These are used only on special occasions. Flanking the doors is a list of archbishops (and other church offi-

cials) that goes unbroken back to the 600s. The statue of Peter with the key and Bible is a reminder that the church is dedicated to St. Peter, and the key to heaven is found through the word of God. While the Minster sits on the remains of a Romanesque church (c. 1100), today's church was begun in 1220 and took 250 years to complete. Up above, look for the female, headless "semaphore saints," using semaphore flag code to spell out a message with golden discs: "Christ is here."

• *Grab a chair and enjoy the view down the...*

❷ Nave: Your first impression might be of its spaciousness and brightness. One of the widest Gothic naves in Europe, it was built between 1280 and 1360— the middle period of the Gothic style, called "Decorated Gothic." Rather than risk a stone roof, builders spanned the space

England's Anglican Church

The Anglican Church (a.k.a. the Church of England) came into existence in 1534 when Henry VIII declared that he, and not Pope Clement VII, was the head of England's Catholics. The pope had refused to allow Henry to divorce his wife to marry his mistress Anne Boleyn (which Henry did anyway, resulting in the birth of Elizabeth I). Still, Henry regarded himself as a faithful Catholic—just not a *Roman* Catholic—and made relatively few changes in how and what Anglicans worshipped.

Henry's son, Edward VI, later instituted many of the changes that Reformation Protestants were bringing about in continental Europe: an emphasis on preaching, people in the pews actually reading the Bible, clergy being allowed to marry, and a more "Protestant" liturgy in English from the revised Book of Common Prayer (1549). The next monarch, Edward's sister Mary I, returned England to the Roman Catholic Church (1553), earning the nickname "Bloody Mary" for her brutal suppression of Protestant elements. When Elizabeth I succeeded Mary (1558), she soon broke from Rome again. Today, many regard the Anglican Church as a compromise between the Catholic and Protestant traditions. In the US, Anglicans split off from the Church in England after the American Revolution, creating the Episcopal Church that still thrives today.

Ever since Henry VIII's time, the York Minster has held a special status within the Anglican hierarchy. After a long feud over which was the leading church, the archbishops of Canterbury and York agreed that York's bishop would have the title "Primate of England" and Canterbury's would be the "Primate of All England," directing Anglicans on the national level.

with wood. Colorful shields on the arcades are the coats of arms of nobles who helped tall and formidable Edward I, known as "Longshanks," fight the Scots in the 13th century.

The coats of arms in the clerestory (upper-level) glass represent the nobles who helped his son, Edward II, in the same fight. There's more medieval glass in this building than in the rest of England combined. This precious glass survived World War II—hidden in stately homes throughout Yorkshire.

Walk to the very center of the church, under the ❸ **central tower.** Look up. An exhibit in the undercroft explains how gifts and skill saved this 197-foot tower from collapse. Use the neck-saving mirror to marvel at it.

Look back at the west end to marvel at the **Great West Window,** especially the stone tracery. While its nickname is the "Heart of Yorkshire," it represents the sacred heart of Christ, meant to remind people of his love for the world.

Find the ❹ **dragon** on the right of the nave (two-thirds of the way up the wall, affixed to the top of a pillar). While no one is sure of its purpose, it pivots and has a hole through its neck—so it was likely a mechanism designed to raise a lid on a baptismal font.

• *Facing the altar, turn right and head into the...*

❺ **South Transept:** Look up. The new "bosses" (carved medallions decorating the point where the ribs meet on the ceiling) are a reminder that the roof of this wing of the church was destroyed by fire in 1984, caused when lightning hit an electricity box. Some believe the lightning was God's angry response to a new bishop, David Jenkins, who questioned the literal truth of Jesus' miracles. (Jenkins had been interviewed at a nearby TV studio the night before, leading locals to joke that the lightning occurred "12 hours too late, and 17 miles off-target.") Regardless, the entire country came to York's aid. *Blue Peter* (England's top kids' show) conducted a competition among their young viewers to design new bosses. Out of 30,000 entries, there were six winners (the blue ones—e.g., man on the moon, feed the children, save the whales).

Two other sights can be accessed through the south transept: the ❻ **Undercroft Museum** (explained later) and the **tower climb** (explained earlier). But for now, stick with this tour; we'll circle back to the south transept at the end, before exiting the church.

• *Head back into the middle of the nave and face the front of the church. You're looking at the...*

❼ **Choir:** Examine the choir screen—the ornate wall of carvings separating the nave from the choir. It's lined with all the English kings from William I (the Conqueror) to Henry VI (during whose reign it was carved, in 1461). Numbers indicate the years each reigned. It is indeed "slathered in gold leaf," which sounds impressive, but the gold is very thin...a nugget the size of a sugar cube is pounded into a sheet the size of a driveway.

Step into the choir, where a service is held daily. All the carving was redone after an 1829 fire, but its tradition of glorious evensong services (sung by choristers from the Minster School) goes all the way back to the eighth century.

• *To the left as you face the choir is the...*

❽ **North Transept:** In this transept, the grisaille windows—dubbed the **"Five Sisters"**—are dedicated to British servicewomen who died in wars. Made in 1260, before colored glass was produced in England, these contain more than 100,000 pieces of glass.

The 18th-century ❾ **astronomical clock** is worth a look (the sign helps you make sense of it). It's dedicated to the heroic Allied

aircrews from bases here in northern England who died in World War II (as Britain kept the Nazis from invading in its "darkest hour"). The Book of Remembrance below the clock contains 18,000 names.

• *A corridor leads to the Gothic, octagonal...*

❿ Chapter House: This was the traditional meeting place of the governing body (or chapter) of the Minster. On the pillar in the middle of the doorway, the Virgin holds Baby Jesus while standing on the devilish serpent. The Chapter House, without an interior support, is remarkable (almost frightening) for its breadth. The fanciful carvings decorating the canopies above the stalls date from 1280 (80 percent are originals) and are some of the Minster's finest. Stroll slowly around the entire room and imagine that the tiny sculpted heads are a 14th-century parade—a fun glimpse of medieval society. Grates still send hot air up robes of attendees on cold winter mornings. A model of the wooden construction illustrates the impressive 1285 engineering.

The Chapter House was the site of an important moment in England's parliamentary history. Fighting the Scots in 1295, Edward I (the "Longshanks" we met earlier) convened the "Model Parliament" here, rather than down south in London. (The Model Parliament is the name for its early version, back before the legislature was split into the Houses of Commons and Lords.) The government met here through the 20-year reign of Edward II, before moving to London during Edward III's rule in the 14th century.

• *Go back out into the main part of the church, turn left, and continue all the way down the nave (behind the choir) to the...*

⓫ East End: This part of the church is square, lacking a semicircular apse, typical of England's Perpendicular Gothic style (15th century). Monuments (almost no graves) were once strewn throughout the church, but in the Victorian Age, they were gathered into the east end, where you see them today.

The **Great East Window,** the size of a tennis court, may still be under restoration when you visit. In the area beneath the win-

dow, the exhibit "Let There Be Light" gives an intimate look at Gothic stone and glasswork.

The exhibit explains the significance of the window and the scope of the conservation project. It illustrates the pains-taking process of removing, dismantling, cleaning, and re-storing each of the 311 panels. Interactive displays let you zoom in on each panel, read about the stories depicted in them, and explore the codes and symbols that are hidden in the window.

Because of the Great East Window's immense size, the east end has an extra layer of supportive stonework, parts of it wide enough to walk along. In fact, for special occasions, the choir has been known to actually sing from the walkway halfway up the win-dow. But just as the window has deteriorated over time, so too has the stone. Nearly 3,500 stones need to be replaced or restored. On some days, you may even see masons in action in the stone yard behind the Minster.

• *Below the choir (on either side), steps lead down to the...*

⓬ Crypt: Here you can view the boundary of the much small-er, but still huge, Norman church from 1100 that stood on this spot (look for the red dots, marking where the Norman church ended, and note how thick the wall was). You can also see some of the old columns and additional remains from the Roman fortress that once stood here, the tomb of St. William of York (actually a Roman sarcophagus that was reused), and the modern concrete save-the-church foundations (much of this church history is covered in the undercroft museum).

• *You'll exit the church through the gift shop in the south transept. If you've yet to climb the **tower**, the entrance is in the south transept before the exit. Also before leaving, look for the entrance to the...*

Undercroft Museum: Well-described exhibits follow the his-tory of the site from its origins as a Roman fortress to the founding of an Anglo-Saxon/Viking church, the shift to a Norman place of worship, and finally the construction of the Gothic structure that stands today. Videos re-create how the fortress and Norman struc-ture would have been laid out, and various artifacts and remains provide an insight into each period. The museum fills a space that was excavated following the near collapse of the central tower in 1967.

Highlights include the actual remains of the Roman fort's ba-silica, which are viewable through a see-through floor. There are

also patches of Roman frescoes from what was the basilica's anteroom. One remarkable artifact is the Horn of Ulf, an intricately carved elephant's tusk presented to the Minster in 1030 by Ulf, a Viking nobleman, as a symbol that he was dedicating his land to God and the Church. Also on view is the York Gospels manuscript, a thousand-year-old text containing the four gospels. Made by Anglo-Saxon monks at Canterbury, it's the only book in the Minster's collection that dates prior to the Norman Conquest. It is still used to this day to swear in archbishops. Your last stop in the undercroft is a small and comfortable theater where you can enjoy three short videos (10 minutes total) showing the Minster in action. One is about Roman Emperor Constantine and the rise of Christianity, another covers a day in the life of the cathedral (skippable), and the final video explores hidden treasures of the Minster.
• *This finishes your visit. Before leaving, take a moment to just be in this amazing building. Then, go in peace.*

Nearby: As you leave through the south transept, notice the people-friendly plaza created here and how effectively it ties the church in with the city that stretches before you. To your left are the Roman column from the ancient headquarters, which stood where the Minster stands today (and from where Rome administered the northern reaches of Britannia 1,800 years ago); a statue of Emperor Constantine (for more details, see page 528); and the covered York Minster Stone Yard, where masons are chiseling stone—as they have for centuries—to keep the religious pride and joy of York looking good.

OTHER SIGHTS INSIDE YORK'S WALLS

I've listed these roughly in geographical order, from near the Minster at the northwest end of town to the York Castle Museum at the southeast end.

Note that several of York's glitzier and most heavily promoted sights (including Jorvik Viking Centre, Dig, and Barley Hall) are run by the York Archaeological Trust (YAT). While rooted in real history, YAT attractions are geared primarily for kids and work hard (some say too hard) to make the history entertaining. If you like their approach and plan to visit several, ask about the various combo-ticket options.

▲▲Yorkshire Museum

Located in a lush, picnic-perfect park next to the stately ruins of St. Mary's Abbey (described in my "York Walk," earlier), the Yorkshire Museum is the city's serious "archaeology of York" museum. You can't dig a hole in York without hitting some remnant of the city's long past, and most of what's found ends up here. While the hordes line up at Jorvik Viking Centre, this museum has no crowds and provides a broader historical context, with more real artifacts. The three main collections—Roman, medieval, and natural history—are well described, bright, and kid-friendly.

Cost and Hours: £7.50, kids under 16 free with paying adult, daily 10:00-17:00, within Museum Gardens, tel. 01904/687-687, www.yorkshiremuseum.org.uk.

Visiting the Museum: At the entrance, you're greeted by an original, early-fourth-century A.D. Roman statue of the god Mars. If he could talk, he'd say, "Hear me, mortals. There are three sections here: Roman (on this floor), medieval (downstairs), and natural history (a kid-friendly wing on this floor). Start first with the 10-minute video for a sweeping history of the city."

The **Roman** collection surrounds a large map of the Roman Empire, set on the floor. You'll see slice-of-life exhibits about Roman baths, a huge floor mosaic, and skulls accompanied by artists' renderings of how the people originally looked. (One man was apparently killed by a sword blow to the head—making it graphically clear that the struggle between Romans and barbarians was a violent one.) These artifacts are particularly interesting when you consider that you're standing in one of the farthest reaches of the Roman Empire.

The **medieval** collection is in the basement. During the Middle Ages, York was England's second city. One large room is dominated by ruins of the St. Mary's Abbey complex (described on page 524; one wall still stands just out front—be sure to see it before leaving). In the center of the ruins is the Vale of York Hoard, displaying a silver cup and the accompanying treasures it held—more than 600 silver coins as well as silver bars and jewelry. A father and son team discovered the hoard (thought to have been buried by Vikings in 927) while out for a day of metal detecting in 2007. You'll also see old weapons, glazed vessels, and a well-preserved 13th-century leather box.

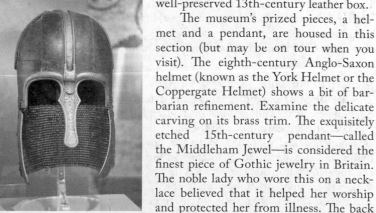

The museum's prized pieces, a helmet and a pendant, are housed in this section (but may be on tour when you visit). The eighth-century Anglo-Saxon helmet (known as the York Helmet or the Coppergate Helmet) shows a bit of barbarian refinement. Examine the delicate carving on its brass trim. The exquisitely etched 15th-century pendant—called the Middleham Jewel—is considered the finest piece of Gothic jewelry in Britain. The noble lady who wore this on a necklace believed that it helped her worship and protected her from illness. The back of the pendant, which rested near her heart, shows the Nativity. The front shows the Holy Trinity crowned by a sapphire (which people believed put their prayers at the top of God's to-do list).

In addition to the Anglo-Saxon pieces, the Viking collection is one of the best in England. Looking over the artifacts, you'll find that the Vikings (who conquered most of the Anglo-Saxon lands) wore some pretty decent shoes and actually combed their hair. The Cawood Sword, nearly 1,000 years old, is one of the finest surviving swords from that era (also may be on tour during your visit).

The **natural history** exhibit (titled Extinct) is back upstairs, showing off skeletons of the extinct dodo and ostrich-like moa birds, as well as an ichthyosaurus.

Barley Hall

Uncovered behind a derelict office block in the 1980s, this medieval house has been restored to replicate a 1483 dwelling. It's designed to resurrect the Tudor age for visiting school groups, but feels soulless to adults.

Cost and Hours: £6, kids under 5-free, combo-tickets with Jorvik Viking Centre and/or Dig, daily 10:00-17:00, Nov-March until 16:00, 2 Coffee Yard off Stonegate, tel. 01904/615-505, www.barleyhall.co.uk.

Holy Trinity Church

Built in the late Perpendicular Gothic style, this church has windows made of precious clear and stained glass from the 13th to 15th century. It holds rare box pews, which rest atop a floor that is sinking as bodies rot and coffins collapse. Enjoy its peaceful picnic-friendly gardens.

Cost and Hours: Free, daily 12:00-16:00, 70 Goodramgate, www.holytrinityyork.org.

Richard III Museum

The last king of England's Plantagenet dynasty got a bad rap from Shakespeare (the Tudors took over after Richard was killed in 1485, so Shakespeare followed the party line and demonized him as a hunchbacked monster). With the discovery of Richard's remains in Leicester in 2013, interest in him has skyrocketed, and the company who runs the Jorvik Viking Centre (described later) took over an amateurish museum inside the Monk Bar's gatehouse and turned it into a hands-on, high-tech extravaganza. It tries to excite visitors with all the blood and gore of that era, but it lacks any historic artifacts. If you're not a Richard III groupie, skip it.

Cost and Hours: £5, daily 10:00-17:00, Monk Bar, tel. 01904/615-505, http://richardiiiexperience.com.

King's Square

This lively people-watching zone, with its inviting benches, once hosted a church. Then it was the site for the town's gallows. Today, it's prime real estate for buskers and street performers. Just hanging out here can be very entertaining. Beyond is the most characteristic and touristy street in old York: The Shambles. Within sight of this lively square are plenty of cheap eating options (for tips, see "Eating in York," later).

York's Chocolate Story

Though known mainly for its Roman, Viking, and medieval past, York also has a rich history in chocolate-making. Throughout the 1800s and 1900s, York was home to three major confectionaries—including Rowntree's, originators of the venerable Kit Kat. However, this chocolate "museum" is childish and overpriced. The building has no significance, and there are almost no historic artifacts. If you visit, you'll join a tour, which pairs generous samples with the history of York's confectionary connections—and you'll have a chance to make your own chocolate lolly.

Cost and Hours: £11.50, one-hour tours run every 15 minutes daily starting at 10:00, last tour at 16:00, King's Square, tel. 01904-527-765, www.yorkchocolatestory.com.

Dig

This hands-on, kid-oriented archaeological site gives young visitors an idea of what York looked like during Roman, Viking, medieval, and Victorian eras. Sift through "dirt" (actually shredded tires), dig up reconstructed Roman wall plaster, and take a look at what archaeologists have found recently. Entry is possible only with a one-hour guided tour (departures every 30 minutes); pass any waiting time by looking at the exhibits near the entry. The exhibits fill the haunted old St. Saviour's Church.

Cost and Hours: £6.50, kids under 5 free, combo-tickets with Jorvik Viking Centre and/or Barley Hall, daily 10:00-17:00, last tour departs one hour before closing, Saviourgate, tel. 01904/615-505, www.digyork.com.

Merchant Adventurers' Hall

Claiming to be the finest surviving medieval guildhall in Britain (from 1357-1361), this vast half-timbered building with marvelous exposed beams contains about 15 minutes' worth of interesting displays about life and commerce in the Middle Ages. You'll see three original, large rooms that are still intact: the great hall itself, where meetings took place; the undercroft, which housed a hospital and almshouse; and a chapel. Several smaller rooms are filled with exhibits about old York. Sitting by itself in its own little park, this classic old building is worth a stop even just to see it from the outside. Remarkably, the hall is still owned by

the same Merchant Adventurers society that built it 660 years ago (now a modern charitable organization).

Cost and Hours: £6, includes audioguide, Sun-Fri 10:00-16:30, Sat until 13:30, south of The Shambles between Fossgate and Piccadilly, tel. 01904/654-818, www.merchantshallyork.org.

▲▲Jorvik Viking Centre

Take the "Pirates of the Caribbean," sail them northeast and back in time 1,000 years, sprinkle in some real artifacts, and you get Jorvik (YOR-vik). Between 1976 and 1981, more than 40,000 artifacts were dug out of the peat bog right here in downtown York—the UK's largest archaeological dig of Viking-era artifacts. When the archaeologists were finished, the dig site was converted into this attraction, opened in 1984 and renovated following a flood in 2015.

Jorvik blends museum exhibits with a 16-minute ride on theme-park-esque "time capsules" that glide through the re-created Viking street of Coppergate as it looked circa the year 975. Animatronic characters and modern-day interpreters bring the scenes to life. Innovative when it first opened, the commercial success of Jorvik inspired copycat rides/museums all over England. Some love Jorvik, while others call it gimmicky and overpriced. If you think of it as Disneyland with a splash of history, Jorvik's fun. To me, Jorvik is a commercial venture designed for kids, with too much emphasis on its gift shop. But it's also undeniably entertaining, and—if you take the time to peruse its exhibits—it can be quite informative.

Cost and Hours: £10.25, various combo-tickets with Dig and/or Barley Hall, daily 10:00-17:00, Nov-March until 16:00, these are last-entry times, hours may vary for special events, tel. 01904/615-505, www.jorvik-viking-centre.co.uk.

Crowd-Beating Tips: This popular attraction can come with long lines. At the busiest times (roughly 11:00-15:00), you may have to wait an hour or more—especially on school holidays. For £2 extra, you can book a slot in advance, either over the phone or on their website. Or you can avoid the worst lines by coming early or late in the day (when you'll more likely wait just 10-15 minutes).

▲Fairfax House

This well-furnished home, supposedly the "first Georgian townhouse in England," is perfectly Neoclassical inside. Each room is staffed by pleasant docents eager to talk with you. They'll explain how the circa-1760 home was built as the dowry for an aristocrat's daughter. The house is compact and bursting with stunning period furniture (the personal collection of a local chocolate magnate), gorgeously restored woodwork, and lavish stucco ceilings that offer clues as to each room's purpose. For example, stuccoed philosophers look down on the library, while the goddess of friendship presides over the drawing room. Taken together, this house provides fine insights into aristocratic life in 18th-century England.

Cost and Hours: £7.50, Tue-Sat 10:00-16:30, Sun 11:00-15:30, Mon by guided tour only at 11:00 and 14:00—the one-hour tours are worthwhile, closed Jan-mid-Feb, near Jorvik Viking Centre at 29 Castlegate, tel. 01904/655-543, www.fairfaxhouse.co.uk.

Clifford's Tower

Perched high on a knoll across from the York Castle Museum, this ruin is all that's left of York's 13th-century castle—the site of the gruesome 1190 mass-suicide of local Jews (they locked themselves inside and set the castle afire rather than face death at the hands of the bloodthirsty townspeople; read the whole story on the sign at the base of the hill). If you go inside, you'll see a model of the original cas-

tle complex as it looked in the Middle Ages, and you can climb up to enjoy fine city views from the top of the ramparts—but neither is worth the cost of admission.

Cost and Hours: £5, daily 10:00-18:00, closes earlier off-season, may close for renovation in 2018, tel. 01904/646-940, www.english-heritage.org.uk

YORK

▲▲York Castle Museum

This fascinating social-history museum is a Victorian home show, possibly the closest thing to a time-tunnel experience England has to offer. The one-way plan en-sures that you'll see everything, including remakes of rooms from the 17th to 20th century, a re-creation of a Victorian street, a heartfelt WWI exhibit, and some eerie prison cells.

Cost and Hours: £10, kids under 16 free with paying adult, daily 9:30-17:00, roaming guides will happily answer your questions (no audioguide), cafeteria at en-trance, tel. 01904/687-687, www.yorkcastlemuseum.org.uk. It's at the bottom of the hop-on, hop-off bus route. The museum can call you a taxi (worthwhile if you're hurrying to the National Railway Museum, across town).

Visiting the Museum: The exhibits are divided between two wings: the North Building (to the left as you enter) and the South Building (to the right).

Follow the one-way route through the complex, starting in the **North Building.** You'll first visit the Period Rooms, illuminating Yorkshire lifestyles during different time periods (1600s-1950s) and among various walks of life, and Toy Stories—an enchant-ing review of toys through the ages. Next is the Shaping the Body exhibit, detailing diet and fashion trends over the last 400 years. Check out the codpieces, bustles, and corsets that used to "en-hance" the human form, and wonder over some of the odd diet fads that make today's paleo diet seem normal. For foodies and chefs, the exhibit showcasing fireplaces and kitchens from the 1600s to the 1980s is especially tasty.

Next, stroll down the museum's re-created Kirkgate, a street from the Victorian era, when Britain was at the peak of its power.

It features old-time shops and storefronts, including a phar-macist, sweet shop, school, and grocer for the working class, along with roaming live guides in period dress. Around the back is a slum area depicting how the poor lived in those times.

Circle back to the entry and cross over to the **South Building.** In the WWI exhibit, erected to mark the war's centennial, you can follow the lives of five York citizens as they experience the horrors and triumphs of the war years. One room plunges you into the gruesome world of trench warfare, where the average life expectancy was six weeks (and if you fell asleep during sentry duty, you'd be shot). A display about the home front notes that York suffered from Zeppelin attacks in which six died. At the end you're encouraged to share your thoughts in a room lined with chalkboards.

Exit outside and cross through the castle yard. A detour to the left leads to a flour mill (open sporadically). Otherwise, your tour continues through the door on the right, where you'll find another reconstructed historical street, this one capturing the spirit of the

swinging 1960s—"a time when the cultural changes were massive but the cars and skirts were mini." Slathered with DayGlo colors, this street scene examines fashion, music, and television (including clips of beloved kids' shows and period news reports).

Finally, head into the York Castle Prison, which recounts the experiences of actual people who were thrown into the clink here. Videos, eerily projected onto the walls of individual cells, show actors telling tragic stories about the cells' one-time inhabitants.

ACROSS THE RIVER
▲▲National Railway Museum
If you like model railways, this is train-car heaven. The thunderous museum—displaying 200 illustrious years of British railroad history—is one of the biggest and best railroad museums anywhere.

Cost and Hours: Free but £5 suggested donation, daily 10:00-18:00, café, restaurant, tel. 0844-815-3139, www.nrm.org.uk.

Getting There: It's about a 15-minute walk from the Minster (southwest of town, up the hill behind the train station). From the train station itself, the fastest approach is to go all the way to the back of the station (using the overpass to cross the tracks), exit out the back door, and turn right up the hill. To skip the walk, a cute little "road train" shuttles you more quickly between the Minster and the Railway Museum (£3 one-way, runs daily Easter-Oct, leaves museum every 30 minutes 11:00-16:00 at :00 and :30 past each hour; leaves town—from Duncombe Place, 100 yards in front of the Minster—at :15 and :45 past each hour).

Visiting the Museum: Pick up the floor plan to locate the various exhibits, which sprawl through several gigantic buildings on both sides of the street. Throughout the complex, red-shirted "explainers" are eager to talk trains.

The museum's most impressive room is the **Great Hall** (head right from the entrance area and take the stairs to the underground passage). Fanning out from this grand roundhouse is an array of historic cars and engines, starting with the very first "stagecoaches on rails," with a crude steam engine from 1830. You'll trace the evolution of steam-powered transportation, from a replica of the Rocket (one of the first successful steam locomotives) to the era of the aerodynamic Mallard (famous as the first train to travel at a startling two miles per minute—a marvel back in 1938) and the striking Art Deco-style Duchess of Hamilton. (Certain trains may not be on display, as they are sometimes on loan

or under maintenance—ask an explainer if you can't find something.) The collection spans to the present day, with a replica of the Eurostar (Chunnel) train and the Shinkansen Japanese bullet train. Other exhibits include a steam engine that's been sliced open to show its cylinders, driving wheels, and smoke box, as well as a working turntable that's put into action twice a day. The Mallard Experience simulates a ride on the Mallard.

The Works is an actual workshop where engineers scurry about, fixing old trains. Live train switchboards show real-time rail traffic on the East Coast Main Line. Next to the diagrammed screens, you can look out to see the actual trains moving up and down the line. **The Warehouse** is loaded with more than 10,000 items relating to train travel (including dinnerware, signage, and actual trains). Exhibits feature dining cars, post cars, sleeping cars, train posters, and info on the Flying Scotsman (the first London-Edinburgh express rail service, now running again).

Crossing back to the entrance side, continue to the **Station Hall,** with a collection of older trains, including ones that the royals have used to ride the rails (including Queen Victoria's lavish royal car and a WWII royal carriage reinforced with armor). Behind that are the South Yard and the Depot, with actual working trains in storage.

▲York Brewery

This intimate, tactile, and informative 45-minute-long tour gives an enjoyable look at how this charming little microbrewery produces 5,700 pints per batch. Their award-winning Ghost Ale is strong, dark, and chocolaty. You can sample their beer throughout town, but to get it as fresh as possible, drink it where it's birthed, in their cozy Tap Room.

Cost and Hours: £8, includes four tasters of the best beer—ale not lager—in town; tours Mon-Sat at 12:30, 14:00, 15:30, and 17:00—just show up, none on Sun; cross the river on Lendal Bridge and walk 5 minutes to Toft Green just below Micklegate, tel. 01904/621-162, www.york-brewery.co.uk.

OUTSIDE TOWN

▲Ouse Riverside Walk or Bike Ride

The New Walk is a mile-long, tree-lined riverside lane created in the 1730s as a promenade for York's dandy class to stroll, see, and be seen—and is a fine place for today's visitors to walk or bike. This hour-long walk is a delightful way to enjoy a dose of countryside away from York. It's paved, illuminated in the evening, and a popular jogging route any time of day.

Start from the riverside under Skeldergate Bridge (near the York Castle Museum), and walk south away from town for a mile. Notice modern buildings across the river, with their floodwalls. Shortly afterward, you cross the tiny River Foss on Blue Bridge, originally built in 1738. The easily defended confluence of the Foss and the Ouse is the reason the Romans founded York in A.D. 71. Look back to see the modern floodgate (built after a flood in 1979) designed to stop the flooding Ouse from oozing up the Foss. At the bridge, a history panel describes this walk to the Millennium Bridge.

Stroll until you hit the striking, modern **Millennium Bridge.** Sit a bit on its reclining-lounge-chair fence and enjoy the vibrations of bikes and joggers as they pass. There's a strong biking trend in Britain these days. The British have won many Olympic gold medals in cycling. In 2012, Bradley Wiggins became Sir Bradley Wiggins by winning the Tour de France; his countryman Chris Froome won it in several subsequent years. You'll see lots of locals riding fancy bikes and wearing high-tech gear while getting into better shape. (Energetic bikers can continue past the Millennium Bridge 14 miles to the market town of Selby.)

Cross the river and walk back home, passing **Rowntree Park.** After the skateboard court, enter the park through its fine old gate. This park was financed by Joseph Rowntree, a wealthy chocolate baron with a Quaker ethic of contributing to his community. In the 19th century, life for the poor was a Charles Dickens-like

YORK

struggle. A rich man building a park for the working class, which even had a swimming pool, was quite progressive. Victorian England had a laissez-faire approach to social issues. Then, like now, many wealthy people believed things would work out for the poor if the government just stayed out of it. However, others, such as the Rowntree family, felt differently. Their altruism contributed to the establishment of a society that now takes care of its workers and poor much better.

Walk directly into the park toward the evocative Industrial Age housing complex capping the hill beyond the central fountain. In the park's brick gazebo are touching memorial plaques to WWI and WWII deaths. Rowntree also gave this park to York to remember those lost in the "Great War." Stroll along the delightful, duck-filled pond near the Rowntree Park Café, return to the riverside lane, and continue back into York. You're almost home.

Shopping in York

With its medieval lanes lined with classy as well as tacky little shops, York is a hit with shoppers. I find two kinds of shopping in York particularly interesting: antique malls and charity shops.

Antique Malls: Three places within a few blocks of each other are filled with stalls and cases owned by antique dealers from the countryside (all open daily). The malls, a warren of rooms on three floors with cafés buried deep inside, sell the dealers' bygones on commission. Serious shoppers do better heading for the country, but York's shops are a fun browse: The **Antiques Centre York** (41 Stonegate, www.theantiquescentreyork.co.uk), the **Red House Antiques Centre** (a block from the Minster at Duncombe Place, www.redhouseyork.co.uk), and **Cavendish Antiques and Jewellers** (44 Stonegate, www.cavendishjewellers.co.uk).

Charity Shops: In towns all over Britain, it seems one low-rent street is lined with charity shops, allowing locals to both donate their junk and buy the junk of others in the name of a good cause. (Talk about a win-win.) It's great for random shopping. And, as the people working there are often volunteers involved in that cause, it can lead to some interesting conversations. In York, on Goodramgate (stretching a block or so in from the town wall), you'll find "thrift shops" run by the British Heart Foundation, Mind, and Oxfam. Good deals abound on clothing, purses, accessories, children's toys, books, CDs, and maybe even a guitar. If you buy something, you're getting a bargain and at the same time helping the poor, mentally ill, elderly, or even a pet in need of a vet (stores generally open between 9:00 and 10:00 and close between 16:00 and 17:00, with shorter hours on Sun).

Nightlife in York

PUBS

Even more than chocolate, York likes its beer. It has its own award-winning microbrewery, the York Brewery (which offers fine tours—see page 547), along with countless atmospheric pubs for memorable and convivial eating or drinking. Many pubs serve inexpensive plates at lunch, and then focus on selling beer in the evening. Others offer lunch and early dinner. You can tell by their marketing how enthusiastic they are about cooking versus drawing pints.

The York Brewery Tap Room, a private club, feels like a fraternity of older men. But if you drop in, you can be an honorary guest. It's right at the microbrewery, with five beloved varieties on tap as fresh as you'll find anywhere (14 Toft Green, just below Micklegate, tel. 01904/621-162, www.york-brewery.co.uk).

The Maltings, just over Lendal Bridge, has classic pub ambience and serves good meals at lunch only. Local beer purists swear by this place (cross the bridge and look down and left to Tanners Moat, tel. 01904/655-387).

The Blue Bell is one of my favorites for old-school York vibes. This tiny, traditional establishment with a time-warp Edwardian interior is the smallest pub in York. It has two distinct and inviting little rooms (east end of town at 53 Fossgate, tel. 01904/654-904).

The House of the Trembling Madness is another fine watering hole with a cozy atmosphere; it sits above a "bottle shop" that sells a stunning variety of beers by the bottle to go (48 Stonegate; also described later, under "Eating in York").

Evil Eye Lounge, a hit with York's young crowd, is a creaky, funky, hip space famous for its strong cocktails and edgy ambience. There are even beds to drink in. You can order downstairs at the bar (with a small terrace out back), or head upstairs (42 Stonegate, tel. 01904/640-002).

The Golden Fleece is a sloppy, dingy place with tilty floors that make you feel drunk even if you aren't. Its wooden frame has survived without foundations for 500 years. Originally owned by wool traders, it's considered the oldest and most haunted coaching inn in York (16 Pavement, across the street from the southern end of The Shambles, tel. 01904/625-171).

The Last Drop is a solid, basic pub—no game machines, no children, Pub Quiz on Wednesdays, and live music twice a week. It's owned by the York Brewery, so it always has their ales on tap (27 Colliergate facing King's Square, tel. 01904/621-951).

The Hop is the most modern pub I've listed, with a spacious, brick-nouveau interior, four house ales and another five local York beers plus half a dozen international options on tap, and a proper pizzeria (11 Fossgate; restaurant described later, under "Eating in York").

Student Pub Crawl: The **"Micklegate Run"** is a ritual for students all over Yorkshire. As this pub crawl starts just below the train station, students ride the train into York and then have a pint in each pub or club along Micklegate. You'll pass at least eight pubs as the street runs downhill from Micklegate Bar to the river. It can be lowbrow and sloppy. You'll see lots of hen-party and stag-party spectacles, and what local guys rudely call "mutton dressed as lamb"—older women trying to look young.

Riverside Eating and Drinking: On sunny days, there are several pubs with riverside tables just below Ouse Bridge, starting with **The Kings Arms,** which boasts flood marks inside its door and has a rougher local crowd than other recommended pubs. For a cheap thrill, grab a pint indoors and sit outside at their rustic picnic tables (3 King's Staith, tel. 01904/659-435).

ENTERTAINMENT

Theatre Royal

This recently spiffed-up theater offers a full variety of dramas, comedies, and works by Shakespeare. The locals are proud of the high-tech main theater and little 100-seat theater-in-the-round (£10-22 tickets, shows usually Tue-Sun at 19:30, tickets easy to get, on St. Leonard's Place near Bootham Bar and a 5- to 10-minute walk from recommended B&Bs, booking tel. 01904/623-568, www.yorktheatreroyal.co.uk). Those under 18 and students of any age can get tickets for £8-12.

Ghost Tours

You'll see fliers, signs, and promoters hawking a variety of entertaining after-dark tours. For a rundown on this scene, see page 523.

Movies

The centrally located **City Screen Cinema,** right on the river, plays both art-house and mainstream flicks. They also have an enticing café/bar overlooking the river that serves good food (13 Coney Street, tel. 0871-902-5726).

Sleeping in York

July through October are the busiest (and usually most expensive) months. B&Bs often charge more for weekends and sometimes turn away one-night bookings, particularly for peak-season Saturdays. (York is worth two nights anyway.) Prices may spike for horse races and Bank Holidays (about 20 nights a season). Remember to book ahead during festival times (see "Helpful Hints" on page 522) and weekends year-round.

B&BS AND GUESTHOUSES

These places are all small and family-run. They come with plenty of steep stairs (and no elevators) but no traffic noise. Rooms can be tight; if maneuverability is important, say so when booking. For a good selection, contact them well in advance. Most have permits to lend for street parking.

The handiest B&B neighborhood is the quiet residential area just outside the old town wall's Bootham gate, along the road called Bootham. All of these are within a 10-minute walk of the Minster and TI, and a 5- to 15-minute walk from the station. If driving, head for the cathedral and follow the medieval wall to the gate called Bootham Bar. The street called Bootham leads away from Bootham Bar.

Getting There: Here's the most direct way to walk to this B&B area from the train station: Head to the north end of the station, to the area between platforms 2 and 4. Shoot through the gap between the men's WC and the York Tap pub, past some racks of bicycles, and into the short-stay parking lot. Walk to the end of the lot to a pedestrian ramp, and zigzag your way down. At the bottom, head left, following the sign for the riverside route. When you reach the river, cross over on the footbridge—you'll have to carry your bags up and down two-dozen steps. At the far end of the bridge, the Abbey Guest House is a few yards to your right, facing the river. To reach The Hazelwood (closer to the town wall), walk from the bridge along the river until just before the short ruined tower, then turn inland up onto Marygate. For other B&Bs, at the bottom of the footbridge, turn left immediately onto a path that skirts the big parking lot (parallel to the train tracks). At the end of the parking lot, you'll turn depending on your B&B: for the places on or near Bootham Terrace, turn left and go under the tracks; for B&Bs on St. Mary's Street, take the short stairway on your right.

On or near Bootham Terrace

$$ At **St. Raphael Guesthouse,** the veteran husband-and-wife team of Al and Les understand a traveler's needs. You'll be instant friends. Their son's graphic design training brings a dash of class to the seven comfy rooms, each themed after a different York street, and each lovingly accented with a fresh rose (RS%, free drinks and ice in their guests' fridge, family rooms, 44 Queen Annes Road, tel. 01904/645-028, www.straphaelguesthouse.co.uk, info@straphaelguesthouse.co.uk).

$$ **Alcuin Lodge,** run by Darren and Mark, is a cozy place, with five rooms that feel personal (look for Darren's grandmother's

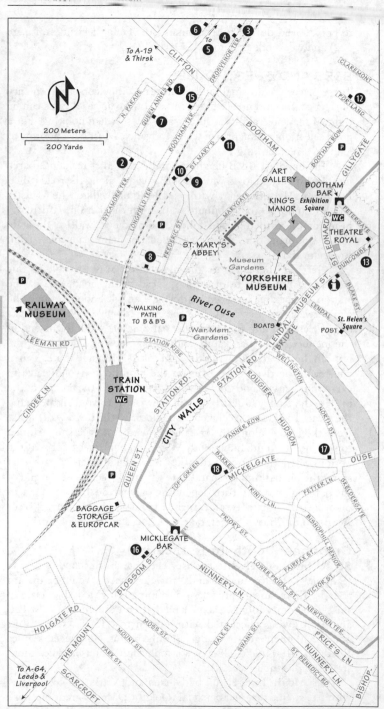

York

To A-19 & Thirsk

CLIFTON

CLAREMONT

PORTLAND

To
6
5
4
3
GROSVENOR TER.

N

200 Meters
200 Yards

R. PARADE
QUEEN ANNE'S RD.
1
15
7

BOOTHAM TER.

BOOTHAM

12
GILLYGATE
BOOTHAM ROW
P

ST. MARY'S
11

SYCAMORE TER.
LONGFIELD TER.
2
10
9

MARYGATE

ART
GALLERY

KING'S
MANOR

BOOTHAM
BAR
Exhibition
Square
WC

PETERGATE

ST. LEONARD'S

P

FREDERICK ST.

8

ST. MARY'S
ABBEY

Museum
Gardens

YORKSHIRE
MUSEUM

THEATRE
ROYAL
DUNCOMBE
13

RAILWAY
MUSEUM

P

River Ouse

WALKING
PATH
TO B & B'S

MUSEUM ST.
BLAKE ST.
LENDAL

i

BOATS

LENDAL
BRIDGE

St. Helen's
Square
POST

LEEMAN RD.

P

War Mem.
Gardens

STATION RISE

STATION RD.

WELLINGTON

CINDER LN.

TRAIN
STATION
WC

STATION RD.

ROUGIER

CITY WALLS

TANNER ROW

HUDSON

NORTH ST.

OUSE

17

QUEEN ST.

TOFT GREEN

BARKER

MICKLEGATE
18

FETTER LN.

SKELDERGATE

BAGGAGE
STORAGE
& EUROPCAR

P

TRINITY LN.

PRIORY ST.

BISHOPHILL SENIOR

MICKLEGATE
BAR
16

BLOSSOM ST.

NUNNERY LN.

LOWER PRIORY ST.
FAIRFAX ST.
VICTOR ST.

NEWTOWN TER.

NUNNERY LN.

PRICE'S LN.

HOLGATE RD.

THE MOUNT

MOSS ST.

MOUNT ST.

PARK ST.

DALE ST.

SWANN ST.

ST. BENEDICT RD.

BISHOP.

To A-64,
Leeds &
Liverpool

SCARCROFT

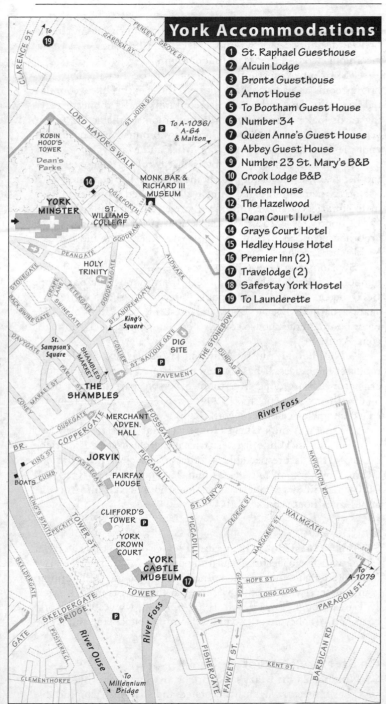

York Accommodations

1. St. Raphael Guesthouse
2. Alcuin Lodge
3. Bronte Guesthouse
4. Arnot House
5. To Bootham Guest House
6. Number 34
7. Queen Anne's Guest House
8. Abbey Guest House
9. Number 23 St. Mary's B&B
10. Crook Lodge B&B
11. Airden House
12. The Hazelwood
13. Dean Court Hotel
14. Grays Court Hotel
15. Hedley House Hotel
16. Premier Inn (2)
17. Travelodge (2)
18. Safestay York Hostel
19. To Launderette

YORK

vase and dresser) yet up to date (one room with private WC in the hallway just outside; 15 Sycamore Place, tel. 01904/629-837, www.alcuinlodge.com, darren@alcuinlodge.com).

$$ Bronte Guesthouse is a modern B&B with five airy, bright rooms and a lovely back garden. Little extras like a communal fridge stocked with water, ice, and milk and a room for playing cards make it easy to relax (family room available, 22 Grosvenor Terrace, tel. 01904/621-066, www.bronte-guesthouse.com, enquiries@bronte-guesthouse.com, Mick and Mandy).

$$ Arnot House, run by a hardworking daughter-and-mother team, is old-fashioned, homey, and lushly decorated with Victorian memorabilia. The three well-furnished rooms even have little libraries (2-night minimum preferred, no children, huge DVD library, 17 Grosvenor Terrace, tel. 01904/641-966, www.arnothouseyork.co.uk, kim.robbins@virgin.net, Kim and her cats Pickle and Tabitha).

$$ Bootham Guest House features creamy walls and contemporary furniture that are a break from more traditional York B&B decor. Of the eight rooms, six are en suite, while two share a bath (RS%, 56 Bootham Crescent, tel. 01904/672-123, www.boothamguesthouse.co.uk, boothamguesthouse1@hotmail.com, Andrew).

$ Number 34, run by Amy and Jason, has five simple, light rooms at fair prices. It has a clean, uncluttered feeling, with modern decor (RS%, ground-floor room, 5-person apartment next door, 34 Bootham Crescent, tel. 01904/645-818, www.number34york.co.uk, enquiries@number34york.co.uk).

$ Queen Anne's Guest House has nine basic rooms in two adjacent houses. While it doesn't have the plushest beds or richest decor, this is a respectable, affordable, and clean place to sleep (RS%, family room, lounge, 24 and 26 Queen Annes Road, tel. 01904/629-389, www.queen-annes-guesthouse.co.uk, info@queen-annes-guesthouse.co.uk, Phil).

On the River

$$ Abbey Guest House is a peaceful refuge overlooking the River Ouse, with five cheerful, beautifully updated, contemporary-style rooms and a cute little garden. The riverview rooms will ramp up your romance with York (RS%, free parking, pay laundry service, 13 Earlsborough Terrace, tel. 01904/627-782, www.abbeyghyork.co.uk, info@abbeyghyork.co.uk, welcoming couple Jane and Kingsley).

On St. Mary's Street

$$ Number 23 St. Mary's B&B, run by Simon and his helpful staff, has nine extravagantly decorated and spaciously comfortable rooms, plus a classy lounge and all the doily touches (discount for longer stays, family room, honesty box for drinks and snacks, lots of stairs, 23 St. Mary's, tel. 01904/622-738, www.23stmarys.co.uk, stmarys23@hotmail.com).

$ Crook Lodge B&B, with six tight but elegantly charming rooms, serves breakfast in an old Victorian kitchen. The 21st-century style somehow fits this old house (one ground-floor room, free parking, quiet, 26 St. Mary's, tel. 01904/655-614, www.crooklodgeguesthouseyork.co.uk, crooklodge@hotmail.com, David and Caroline).

$ Airden House rents 10 nice, mostly traditional rooms, though the two basement-level rooms are more mod—one has a space-age-looking hot tub and a separate room with twin bed (RS%, lounge, free parking, 1 St. Mary's, tel. 01904/638-915, www.airdenhouse.co.uk, info@airdenhouse.co.uk, Emma and Heather).

Closer to the Town Wall

$$ The Hazelwood, more formal than a B&B, rents 14 rooms sharing a garden patio and pleasant basement lounge complete with a guest fridge. The "standard" rooms have bright, cheery decor and small bathrooms, while the bigger "superior" rooms come with newer bathrooms and handcrafted furniture—and everyone gets homemade biscuits on arrival (two-bedroom apartment also available, free laundry service for Rick Steves readers if you book directly with the hotel, free parking, 24 Portland Street, tel. 01904/626-548, www.thehazelwoodyork.com, reservations@thehazelwoodyork.com; Ian and Carolyn, along with Sharon and Emma).

HOTELS

$$$$ Dean Court Hotel, a Best Western facing the Minster, is a big stately hotel with classy lounges and 37 comfortable rooms. It has a great location and friendly vibe for a business-class establishment. A few rooms have views for no extra charge—try requesting one (elevator, restaurant, Duncombe Place, tel. 01904/625-082, www.deancourt-york.co.uk, sales@deancourt-york.co.uk).

$$$$ Grays Court Hotel is a historic mansion—the home of dukes and archbishops since 1091—that now rents nine rooms and two suites to tourists. While its public spaces and gardens are lavish, its rooms are elegant yet modest. The creaky, historic nature of the place makes for a memorable stay. If it's too pricey for lodging, consider coming here for its recommended tearoom (Chapter House Street, tel. 01904/612-613, www.grayscourtyork.com).

$$$ Hedley House Hotel, well run by a wonderful family, has 30 clean and spacious rooms. The outdoor hot tub and sauna

YORK

are a fine way to end your day, or you can sign up for yoga or Pilates (ask for a deal with stay of three or more nights, family rooms, good two-course evening meals, in-house massage and beauty services, free parking, 3 Bootham Terrace, tel. 01904/637-404, www.hedleyhouse.com, greg@hedleyhouse.com, Greg and Louise Harrand). They also have nine luxury studio apartments—see their website for details.

Budget Chain Hotels: If looking for something a little less spendy than the hotels listed above, consider several chains, with central locations in town. These include **Premier Inn** (two branches side-by-side) and **Travelodge** (one location near the York Castle Museum at 90 Piccadilly; second location on Micklegate).

HOSTEL

¢ Safestay York is a boutique hostel on a rowdy street (especially on Fridays and Saturdays). Located in a big old Georgian house, they rent 158 beds in 4- to 12-bed rooms, with great views, private prefab "pod" bathrooms, and reading lights for each bed. They also offer fancier, hotel-quality doubles (family room for up to four, includes sheets, continental breakfast extra, 4 floors, no elevator, air-con, Wi-Fi in public areas only, self-service laundry, TV lounge, game room, bar, lockers, no curfew, 5-minute walk from train station at 88 Micklegate, tel. 01904/627-720, www.safestay.com/ss-york-micklegate.html, bookings@safestay.com).

Eating in York

York is a great food city, with a wide range of ethnic options and lots of upscale foodie bistros. Thanks to the local high-tech industry, the university, and tourism, there's a demand that sustains lots of creative and fun eateries.

If you're in a hurry or on a tight budget, picnic and light-meals-to-go options abound, and it's easy to find a churchyard, bench, or riverside perch where you can munch. On a sunny day, perhaps the best picnic spot in town is under the evocative 12th-century ruins of St. Mary's Abbey in the Museum Gardens (near Bootham Bar).

Upscale Bistros: As these trendy, pricey eateries are a York forte, I've listed several of my favorites: Café No. 8, Café Concerto, The Star Inn the City, and Bistro Guy. These places are each romantic, laid-back, and popular with locals (so reservations are wise for dinner). They also have good-quality, creative vegetarian options. Most offer economical lunch specials and early dinners. After 19:00 or so, main courses cost £16-26 and fixed-price meals (two or three courses) go for around £25. On Friday and Saturday evenings, many offer special, more expensive menus.

CITY CENTER
Cheap Eats Around King's Square

King's Square is about as central as can be for sightseers. And from here, you can actually see several fine quick-and-cheap lunch options. After buying your takeout food, sit on the square and enjoy the street entertainers. Or, for a peaceful place to eat more prayerfully, find the Holy Trinity Church yard, with benches amid the old tombstones on Goodramgate (half a block to the right of York Roast Company).

$ York Roast Company is a local fixture, serving delicious and hearty pork sandwiches with applesauce, stuffing, and "crackling" (roasted bits of fat and skin). Other meats are also available. You can even oversee the stuffing of your own Yorkshire pudding. If Henry VIII wanted fast food, he'd eat here (corner of Low Petergate and Goodramgate, order at counter then dine upstairs or take away, daily 10:00-23:00, 74 Low Petergate, tel. 01904/629-197, second location at 4 Stonegate).

$ Drakes Fish & Chips across the street from York Roast Company, is a local favorite chippy (daily 11:00-22:30, 97 Low Petergate, tel. 01904/624-788).

$ The Cornish Bakery, facing King's Square, cooks up pasties to eat in or take away (30 Colliergate, tel. 01904/671-177).

$ Shambles Market has many food stalls and street food vendors offering fun and nutritious light meals. The once-frumpy, recently renovated market is wedged between The Shambles and Parliament Street (daily 7:00-17:00, until 16:00 in winter).

$ St. Crux Parish Hall is a medieval church now used by a medley of charities that sell tea, homemade cakes, and light meals. They each book the church for a day, often a year in advance (usually open Tue-Sat 10:00-16:00, closed Sun-Mon, at bottom of The Shambles at its intersection with Pavement, tel. 01904/621-756).

For a nice finish, consider the **$ Harlequin Café,** a charming place loved by locals for its good coffee and homemade cakes, as well as its light meals. It's up a creaky staircase overlooking the square (Mon-Sat 10:00-16:00, Sun 11:00-15:00, 2 King's Square, tel. 01904/630-631).

On or near Swinegate

$$ Strolling this street, you can just take your pick of the various tempting bars and eateries. Some are trendy, with thumping music, while others are tranquil; some have elaborately decorated dining rooms, while others emphasize heated courtyards. This corner of town has two similar American-style bar/brasserie/lounges (both open daily): **Oscar's,** right on Swinegate, has a mod interior and good burgers; **Stonegate Yard,** around the corner on Little Stone-

York Restaurants

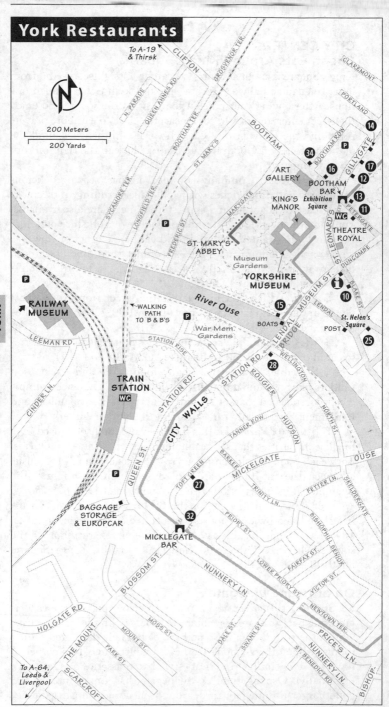

YORK

To A-19
& Thirsk

CLIFTON

CLAREMONT

N

200 Meters

200 Yards

N. PARADE

QUEEN ANNE'S RD.

GROSVENOR TER.

BOOTHAM

BOOTHAM ROW

GILLYGATE

PORTLAND

14

34

16

17

12

ART
GALLERY

BOOTHAM
BAR

13

KING'S
MANOR

Exhibition
Square

11

WC

PETERGATE

THEATRE
ROYAL

ST. LEONARD'S

SYCAMORE TER.

LONGFIELD TER.

ST. MARY'S

BOOTHAM TER.

MARYGATE

FREDERIC ST.

P

ST. MARY'S
ABBEY

Museum
Gardens

YORKSHIRE
MUSEUM

DUNCOMBE

MUSEUM ST.

P

RAILWAY
MUSEUM

P

River Ouse

← WALKING
PATH
TO B & B'S

P

War Mem.
Gardens

15

BOATS

LENDAL
BRIDGE

Lendal

i

10

BLAKE ST.

St. Helen's
Square

POST

25

LEEMAN RD.

CINDER LN.

Station Rise

STATION RISE

STATION RD.

TRAIN
STATION

WC

STATION RD.

CITY WALLS

28

WELLINGTON

ROUGIER

HUDSON

NORTH ST.

OUSE

TANNER ROW

BARKER

MICKLEGATE

FETTER LN.

SKELDERGATE

QUEEN ST.

TOFT GREEN

27

TRINITY LN.

BISHOPHILL SENIOR

P

32

PRIORY ST.

FAIRFAX ST.

BAGGAGE
STORAGE
& EUROPCAR

MICKLEGATE
BAR

BLOSSOM ST.

NUNNERY LN.

LOWER PRIORY ST.

VICTOR ST.

NEWTOWN TER.

PRICE'S LN.

NUNNERY LN.

BISHOP'

HOLGATE RD.

THE MOUNT

PARK ST.

MOUNT ST.

MOSS ST.

DALE ST.

SWANN ST.

ST. BENEDICT RD.

To A-64,
Leeds &
Liverpool

SCARCROFT

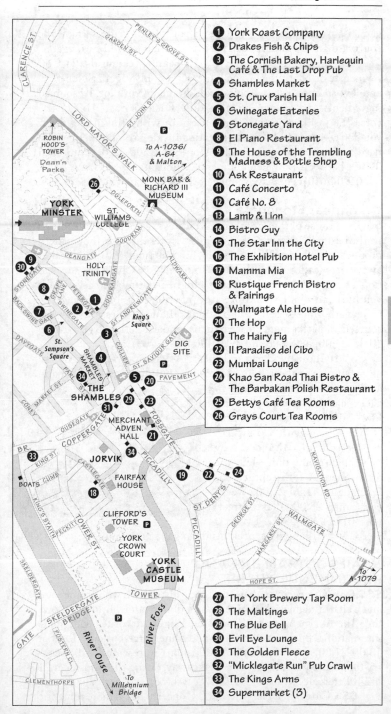

1 York Roast Company
2 Drakes Fish & Chips
3 The Cornish Bakery, Harlequin Café & The Last Drop Pub
4 Shambles Market
5 St. Crux Parish Hall
6 Swingate Eateries
7 Stonegate Yard
8 El Piano Restaurant
9 The House of the Trembling Madness & Bottle Shop
10 Ask Restaurant
11 Café Concerto
12 Café No. 8
13 Lamb & Lion
14 Bistro Guy
15 The Star Inn the City
16 The Exhibition Hotel Pub
17 Mamma Mia
18 Rustique French Bistro & Pairings
19 Walmgate Ale House
20 The Hop
21 The Hairy Fig
22 Il Paradiso del Cibo
23 Mumbai Lounge
24 Khao San Road Thai Bistro & The Barbakan Polish Restaurant
25 Bettys Café Tea Rooms
26 Grays Court Tea Rooms

27 The York Brewery Tap Room
28 The Maltings
29 The Blue Bell
30 Evil Eye Lounge
31 The Golden Fleece
32 "Micklegate Run" Pub Crawl
33 The Kings Arms
34 Supermarket (3)

YORK

gate, is in a delightful ivy-covered courtyard. Others enjoy the courtyard and Mediterranean food at **Lucia** (daily, 12 Swinegate).

Vegetarian: The popular **$$ El Piano Restaurant,** just off Swinegate on charming Grape Lane, serves only vegan, gluten-free, and low-sodium dishes. Their meals are made with locally sourced ingredients and Indian/Asian/Middle Eastern/East African flavors. The inside ambience is bubble gum with blinking lights. If you don't want to feel that you're eating inside a sombrero, they also have a pleasant patio out back (Mon-Sat 12:00-22:00, Sun until 20:00, between Low Petergate and Swinegate at 15 Grape Lane, tel. 01904/610-676). Save money at the takeaway window.

On or near Stonegate

$$ The House of the Trembling Madness, considered by some to be the best pub in town, is easy to miss. Enter through The Bottle, a ground-floor shop selling an astonishing number of different takeaway beers (called a "bottle shop" in England). Climb the stairs to find a small but cozy pub beneath a high, airy timbered ceiling. It's youthful and a bit fashion-forward, yet still accessible to all ages—come early since seating can be tight. The food tries to be locally sourced and is far more creative than standard York pub grub (daily 10:30-24:00, 48 Stonegate, tel. 01904/640-009).

$$ Italian: The cheap and cheery **Ask Restaurant** is an Italian chain similar to those found in historic buildings all over Britain.

York's version lets you dine in the majestic Neoclassical yellow hall of its Grand Assembly Rooms, lined with Corinthian marble columns. The food may be Italian-chain dull—but the atmosphere is 18th-century deluxe (daily 11:00-22:00, weekends until 23:00; Blake Street, tel. 01904/637-254). Even if you're just walking past, peek inside to gape at the interior.

NEAR BOOTHAM BAR AND RECOMMENDED B&BS

$$$ Café Concerto, a casual and cozy bistro with wholesome food and a charming musical theme, has an understandably loyal following. The fun menu features updated English favorites with some international options (vegetarian and gluten-free options; Tue-Sat 13:00-21:00, Sun-Mon until 17:00, smart to reserve for dinner—try for a window seat, also offers takeaway, facing the Minster at 21 High Petergate, tel. 01904/610-478, www.cafeconcerto.biz).

$$$ Café No. 8 feels like Café Concerto but is more romantic and modern, with hardworking headwaiter Christopher bringing it all together. Grab one of the tables in front or in the sunroom, or enjoy a shaded little garden out back if the weather's good. Chef Chris Pragnell uses what's fresh in the market to shape his simple, elegant, and creative menu (daily 12:00-22:00, 8 Gillygate, tel. 01904/653-074, www.cafeno8.co.uk).

Lamb & Lion serves local ales alongside a classy **$$$ pub menu** in their wood-cozy bistro, back room snugs, and casual outdoor garden, or elegant **$$$$ dinners** in their country-cute parlor restaurant (Mon-Sat 12:00-21:00, restaurant open only for dinner from 17:00, closed Sun, 2 High Petersgate, tel. 01904/654-112, www.lambandlionyork.com).

$$$$ At **Bistro Guy,** chef Guy Whapples serves breakfast and lunch daily, and dinner—with a fancier modern English and international "bistro" tasting menu—three nights a week. Choose between seven cute tables in front or a delightful garden under the town wall out back (daily 10:00-15:00, also open for dinner Thu-Sat 18:30-21:00—deposit required for dinner reservation, 40 Gillygate, tel. 01904/652-500, www.bistroguy.co.uk).

$$$$ The Star Inn the City is an offshoot of Chef Andrew Pern's Michelin-star-rated restaurant in the Yorkshire countryside—The Star Inn. He excels in showing off local meats and produce, creating memorable combinations such as chicken breasts in a beet-vegetable broth or duck with rhubarb and sweet potato fondant. Dine outside along the river or in the mod eatery that looks out over the Museum Gardens (daily 9:00-22:00, reservations smart, next to the river in Lendal Engine House, Museum Street, tel. 01904/619-208, www.starinnthecity.co.uk).

$$ The Exhibition Hotel pub has a classic pub interior, as well as a glassed-in conservatory and beer garden out back that's great for kids. While the food is nothing special, it's conveniently located near my recommended B&Bs (food served daily 12:00-15:00 & 17:00-21:00, bar open late, facing Bootham Bar at 19 Bootham Street, tel. 01904/641-105).

Italian: For functional, affordable food, **$$ Mamma Mia** is a popular choice. The casual, garlicky eating area features a tempting gelato bar, and in nice weather the back patio is *molto bello* (daily 11:30-14:00 & 17:30-23:00, 20 Gillygate, tel. 01904/622-020).

Supermarkets: For picnic provisions, **Sainsbury's Local** is handy and open late (long hours daily, 50 yards outside Bootham Bar, on Bootham; another location is at the opposite end of town on Picadilly). There's also a **Marks & Spencer** food hall a block away from Shambles Market on Parliament Street (Mon-Sat 8:00-18:30, Sun 10:30-17:00).

YORK

AT THE EAST END OF TOWN

This neighborhood is across town from my recommended B&Bs, but still central (and a short walk from the York Castle Museum). These places are all hits with local foodies; reservations are smart for all.

$$$ Rustique French Bistro has one big room of tight tables and walls decorated with simple posters. The place has good prices and is straight French—right down to the welcome (daily 12:00-22:00, across from Fairfax House at 28 Castlegate, tel. 01904/612-744, www.rustiqueyork.co.uk).

$$$ Walmgate Ale House is a fun and casual place to eat. This homey, spacious, youthful restaurant (combining old timbers and mod tables) serves up elegantly simple traditional and international meals, all with a focus on local ingredients. The seating sprawls on several floors: ground-floor pub, upstairs bistro, and top-floor loft (Tue-Sun until 22:30, closed Mon, just past Fossgate at 25 Walmgate, tel. 01904/629-222).

$$ Pairings is a stylish wine bar with small bites and an extensive list of drinks. Two travelers can make a light lunch out of the £22 deli platter, and their £13 white or red pairing board—three wines plus three meats or cheeses carefully selected for each glass—is a fun way to start or cap your night (daily 12:00-23:00, 28 Castlegate, tel. 01904/848-909).

$$ The Hop is a local favorite for its simple approach and winning combo: pizza and beer. The pub pulls real ales in the front, serves woodfire pies in an inviting space in the back, and offers live music Wed-Sun at 21:00 (daily 12:00-23:00, food served until 21:00—Sun until 20:00, 11 Fossgate, tel. 01904/541-466).

$$ At **The Hairy Fig** try grabbing one of four tables in the quaint lunchtime café (simple soups, salads, toasties, and a £5 cream tea), or assemble a picnic out of freshly prepared pies, quiches, breads, and high-quality meat and cheese from their delicatessen (deli open Mon-Sat 9:00-17:30, café open 11:30-15:00, closed Sun, 39 Fossgate, tel. 01904/677-074).

Italian: The restaurant/pizzeria **$$$ Il Paradiso del Cibo** just feels special. It's a small place with tight seating, no tourists, and a fun bustle, run by a Sardinian with attitude (cash only, daily 12:00-15:00 & 18:00-22:00, 40 Walmgate, tel. 01904/611-444).

Indian: The lively **$$ Mumbai Lounge** (named for its top-floor lounge) is considered the best place in town for Indian food, so it's very popular. The space is big and high-energy, with a hardworking team of waiters in black T-shirts. I'd call to reserve a table on the ground floor—but avoid the basement (daily 12:00-14:00 & 17:30-23:30, 47 Fossgate, tel. 01904/654-155, www.mumbailoungeyork.co.uk).

$$-$$$ Ethnic on Walmgate: The emerging bohemian-chic

street called Walmgate has several quality restaurants with a local, untouristy energy: **Khao San Road Thai Bistro** (52 Walmgate, tel. 01904/635-599) and **The Barbakan Polish Restaurant** (58 Walmgate, tel. 01904/672-474).

TEAROOMS

York is famous for its elegant teahouses. These two places serve traditional afternoon tea as well as light meals in memorable settings. In both cases, the food is pricey and comes in small portions—I'd come here at 16:00 for tea and cakes, but dine elsewhere. It's permissible for travel partners on a budget to enjoy the experience for about half the price by having one person order "full tea" (with enough little sandwiches and sweets for two to share) and the other a simple cup of tea.

$$ Bettys Café Tea Rooms is a destination restaurant for many ladies. Choose between a Yorkshire Cream Tea (tea and scones with clotted Yorkshire cream and strawberry jam) or a full traditional English afternoon tea (tea, delicate sandwiches, scones, and sweets). Your table is so full of doily niceties that the food is served on a little three-tray tower. While you'll pay a little extra here (and the food's nothing special), the ambience and people-watching are hard to beat. When there's a line, it moves quickly (except at dinnertime). They'll offer to seat you sooner in the bigger and less atmospheric basement, but I'd be patient and wait for a place upstairs—ideally by the window (daily 9:00-21:00, "afternoon tea" served all day; on weekends the special £33 afternoon tea includes fresh-from-the-oven scones served 12:30-17:00 in upstairs room with pianist—must reserve ahead; piano music nightly 18:00-21:00 and Sun 10:00-13:00, tel. 01904/659-142, www.bettys.co.uk, St. Helen's Square, fine view of street scene from a window seat on the main floor). Near the WC downstairs is a mirror signed by WWII bomber pilots—read the story. For those just wanting to buy a pastry to go, it's fine to skip the lines and go directly to the bakery counter.

$$ Grays Court, tucked away behind the Minster, holds court over its own delightful garden just inside the town wall. (You'll look down into its inviting oasis as you walk along the top of the wall.) For centuries, this was the residence of the Norman Treasurers of York Minster. Today it's home to a pleasant tearoom, small hotel, restaurant, and bar. In summer, you can sit outside, at tables scattered in the pleasant garden, or inside, in their elegant dining room or Jacobean gallery—a long wood-paneled hall with comfy sofas (two-person "afternoon tea" served 14:00-17:00, daily 11:00-21:00, Chapter House Street, tel. 01904/612-613, www.grayscourtyork.com).

York Connections

From York by Train to: Durham (3-4/hour, 45 minutes), **London**'s King's Cross Station (2/hour, 2 hours), **Bath** (hourly with change in Bristol, 5 hours, more with additional transfers), **Cambridge** (hourly, 2.5 hours, transfer in Peterborough), **Keswick/Lake District** (train to Penrith: roughly 2/hour, 3.5 hours, 1-2 transfers; then bus, allow about 4.5 hours total), **Manchester Airport** (2/hour, 2 hours), **Edinburgh** (2/hour, 2 hours). Train info: Tel. 0345-748-4950, www.nationalrail.co.uk.

Connections with London's Airports: Heathrow (allow 4 hours minimum; from airport take Heathrow Express train to London's Paddington Station, transfer by Tube to King's Cross, then take train to York; for details on cheaper but slower Tube or bus option from airport to London King's Cross, see page 206), **Gatwick** (allow 4 hours minimum; from Gatwick South, catch First Capital Connect train to London's St. Pancras International Station; from there, walk to neighboring King's Cross Station, and catch train to York).

DURHAM & NORTHEAST ENGLAND

Durham • Beamish Museum • Hadrian's Wall

Northeast England harbors some of the country's best historical sights. Go for a Roman ramble at Hadrian's Wall, a reminder that Britain was an important Roman colony 2,000 years ago. Marvel at England's greatest Norman church—Durham's cathedral—and enjoy an evensong service there. At the excellent Beamish Museum, travel back in time to the 19th and early 20th centuries.

PLANNING YOUR TIME

For **train** travelers, Durham is the most convenient overnight stop in this region. But it's problematic to see en route to another destination since there's no baggage storage in Durham: Either stay overnight, or do Durham as a day trip from York. If you like Roman ruins, visit Hadrian's Wall (tricky but doable by public transportation). The Beamish Museum is an easy day trip from Durham (less than an hour by bus).

By **car,** you can easily visit everything in this chapter. Spend a night in Durham and a night near Hadrian's Wall, stopping at the Beamish Museum on your way to Hadrian's Wall.

For the best quick visit to Durham, arrive by midafternoon, in time to tour the cathedral and enjoy the evensong service (Tue-Sat at 17:15, Sun at 15:30; limited access and no tours during June graduation ceremonies). Sleep in Durham. Visit Beamish the next morning before continuing on to your next destination.

Durham

Without its cathedral, Durham would hardly be noticed. But this magnificently situated structure is hard to miss (even if you're zooming by on the train). Seemingly happy to go nowhere, Durham sits along the tight curve of its river, snug below its castle and famous church. It has a medieval, cobbled atmosphere and a scraggly peasant's indoor market just off the main square. Durham is home to England's third-oldest university, with a student vibe jostling against its lingering working-class mining-town feel. You'll see tattooed and pierced people in search of job security and a good karaoke bar. Yet Durham has a youthful liveliness and a small-town warmth that shines—especially on sunny days, when most everyone is out licking ice-cream cones.

Orientation to Durham

As it has for a thousand years, tidy little Durham (pop. 50,000) clusters everything safely under its castle, within the protective hairpin bend of the River Wear.

Because of the town's hilly topography, going just about anywhere involves a lot of up and down...and back up again. The main spine through the middle of town (Framwellgate Bridge, Silver Street, and Market Place) is level to moderately steep, but walking in any direction from that area involves some serious uphill climbing. Take advantage of the handy Cathedral Bus to avoid the tiring elevation changes—especially up to the cathedral and castle area, or to the train station (perched high on a separate hill).

TOURIST INFORMATION

Durham does not have a physical TI, but the town does maintain a call center and website (calls answered Mon-Sat 9:30-17:30, Sun 11:00-16:00, tel. 03000-262-626, www.thisisdurham.com, visitor@thisisdurham.com).

During the summer, a group of 60 volunteers called **Durham Pointers** staff a tourist information cart in Market Place near the equestrian statue. They hand out free maps of the city and offer unbiased advice on Durham attractions—tell them Rick Steves sent you (late May-early Oct Mon-Sat 9:30-15:30, Sun 11:00-15:00, mobile 0758-233-2621, www.durhampointers.co.uk).

DURHAM & NE ENGLAND

Though not an official TI, the **Durham World Heritage Site Visitor Centre,** near the Palace Green, can offer some guidance, including brochures on things to see and a short video on the town. They also sell tickets to tour the castle (center open daily April-Sept 9:30-17:00, July-Aug until 18:00, Oct-March until 16:30, 7 Owengate, tel. 0191/334-3805, www.durhamworldheritagesite.com).

ARRIVAL IN DURHAM

By Train: From the train station, the fastest and easiest way to reach the cathedral is to hop on the **Cathedral Bus** (described later, under "Getting Around Durham"). But the town's setting—while steep in places—is enjoyable to stroll through (and you can begin my self-guided walk halfway through, at the Framwellgate Bridge).

To **walk** into town, follow the *walkway route to Durham city* signs exiting the station and head along the road downhill to the second pedestrian turnoff (the spiral one within sight of the railway bridge), which leads almost immediately over a bridge above busy road A-690. From here, you can bypass the bridge and continue straight down the hill to some of my recommended accommodations (using this chapter's map—and the giant rail bridge as a handy landmark), or cross the pedestrian bridge and take North Road into town to reach other hotels, the river, and the cathedral.

By Car: Drivers simply surrender to the wonderful 400-space Prince Bishops Shopping Centre parking lot (coming from the A-1/M-1 exit, you'll run right into it at the roundabout at the base of the old town). It's perfectly safe, with 24-hour access. An elevator deposits you right in the heart of Durham (£3.30/up to 4 hours, £11.50/over 6 hours, £1.50/overnight 18:00-8:00, must enter license plate number to use payment machines, cash or credit card with chip, a short block from Market Place, tel. 0191/375-0416, www.princebishops.co.uk).

HELPFUL HINTS

Markets: The main square, known as Market Place, has an indoor market (generally Mon-Sat 9:00-17:00, closed Sun) and hosts outdoor markets (Sat retail market generally 9:30-16:30, farmers' market third Thu of each month 9:30-15:30, tel. 0191/384-6153, www.durhammarkets.co.uk).

Tours: Blue Badge guides offer 1.5-hour city walking tours on Saturdays at 14:00 in peak season (£4, meet at Durham World Heritage Site Visitor Centre, contact TI call center to confirm schedule, tel. 03000-262-626). **David Butler,** the town historian, gives excellent private tours (reasonable prices, tel. 0191/386-1500, www.dhent.co.uk, dhent@dhent.co.uk).

DURHAM & NE ENGLAND

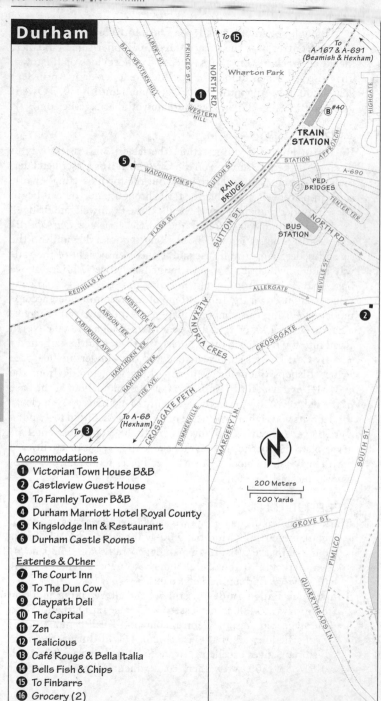

Durham

To 15

To
A-167 & A-691
(Beamish & Hexham)

Wharton Park

WESTERN HILL

B #40

TRAIN STATION

STATION APPROACH

A-690

PED. BRIDGES

TENTER TER.

RAIL BRIDGE

BUS STATION

NORTH RD.

ALLERGATE

NEVILLE ST.

CROSSGATE

REDHILLS LN.

MISTLETOE ST.

LAWSON TER.

LABURNUM AVE.

HAWTHORN TER.

THE AVE.

ALEXANDRIA CRES.

To A-68
(Hexham)

CROSSGATE PETH

SUMMERVILLE

MARGERY LN.

GROVE ST.

PIMLICO

QUARRYHEADS LN.

SOUTH ST.

To 3

N

200 Meters
200 Yards

Accommodations
1. Victorian Town House B&B
2. Castleview Guest House
3. To Farnley Tower B&B
4. Durham Marriott Hotel Royal County
5. Kingslodge Inn & Restaurant
6. Durham Castle Rooms

Eateries & Other
7. The Court Inn
8. To The Dun Cow
9. Claypath Deli
10. The Capital
11. Zen
12. Tealicious
13. Café Rouge & Bella Italia
14. Bells Fish & Chips
15. To Finbarrs
16. Grocery (2)

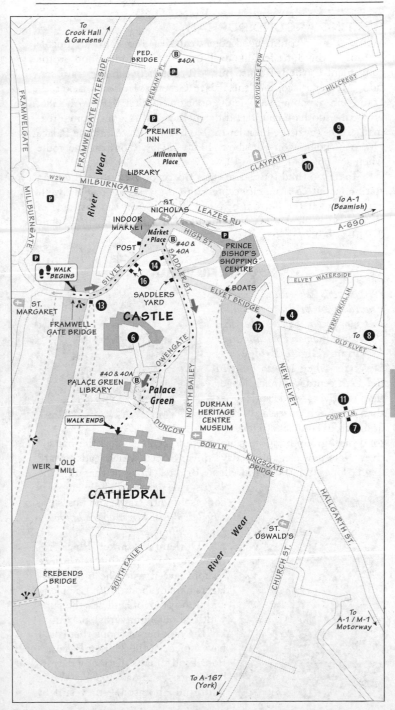

To Crook Hall
& Gardens

PED.
BRIDGE

B #40A

FRAMWELGATE WATERSIDE

FREEMAN'S PL.

HILLCREST

PROVIDENCE ROW

PREMIER
INN

Millennium
Place

CLAYPATH

9

10

LIBRARY

River Wear

W2W

MILBURNGATE

To A-1
(Beamish)

A-690

FRAMWELGATE

MILBURNGATE

ST.
NICHOLAS

LEAZES RD.

INDOOR
MARKET

Market
Place

HIGH ST.

POST

B #40 &
40A

PRINCE
BISHOP'S
SHOPPING
CENTRE

P

WALK
BEGINS

SILVER

14

SADDLER ST.

ELVET WATERSIDE

16

BOATS

ELVET BRIDGE

SADDLERS
YARD

ST.
MARGARET

13

CASTLE

4

12

TERRITORIAL LN.

To
8

FRAMWELL-
GATE BRIDGE

6

OWENGATE

OLD ELVET

NORTH BAILEY

NEW ELVET

#40 & 40A

PALACE GREEN
LIBRARY

B

Palace
Green

11

COURT LN.

7

WALK ENDS

DUNCOW

DURHAM
HERITAGE
CENTRE
MUSEUM

BOW LN.

KINGSGATE
BRIDGE

WEIR

OLD
MILL

HALLGARTH ST.

CATHEDRAL

SOUTH BAILEY

River Wear

ST.
OSWALD'S

CHURCH ST.

PREBENDS
BRIDGE

To
A-1 / M-1
Motorway

To A-167
(York)

DURHAM & NE ENGLAND

GETTING AROUND DURHAM

While all my recommended hotels, eateries, and sights are doable by foot, if you don't feel like walking Durham's hills, hop on the convenient **Cathedral Bus.** Bus #40 runs between the train station, Market Place, and the Palace Green (£1 all-day ticket, 3/hour Mon-Sat about 9:00-17:00, none on Sun; tel. 0191/372-5386, www.thisisdurham.com). A different bus #40A goes from Freeman's Place (near the Premier Inn) to Market Place and the Palace Green (2/hour Mon-Sat about 10:00-15:45). Confirm the route when you board.

Taxis zip tired tourists to their B&Bs or back up to the train station (about £5 from city center, wait on west side of Framwellgate Bridge at the bottom of North Road or on the east side of Elvet Bridge). If you need to call a taxi, try Polly's Taxis, mobile 07910-179-397.

Durham Walk

• *Begin this self-guided walk at Framwellgate Bridge (down in the center of town, halfway between the train station and the cathedral).*

Framwellgate Bridge was a wonder when it was built in the 12th century—much longer than the river is wide and higher than seemingly necessary. It was designed to connect stretches of solid high ground and to avoid steep descents toward the marshy river. Note how elegantly today's Silver Street (which leads toward town) slopes into the Framwellgate Bridge. (Imagine that until the 1970s, this people-friendly lane was congested with traffic and buses.)

• *Follow Silver Street up the hill to the town's main square.*

Durham's **Market Place** retains the same plotting the prince bishop gave it when he moved villagers here in about 1100. Each long and skinny plot of land was the same width (about eight yards), maximizing the number of shops that could have a piece of the Market Place action. Find today's distinctly narrow buildings (Thomas Cook, Whittard, and Thomson)—they still fit

DURHAM & NE ENGLAND

the 900-year-old plan. The widths of the other buildings fronting the square are multiples of that original shop width.

Examine the square's **statues.** Coal has long been the basis of this region's economy. The statue of Neptune was part of an ill-

fated attempt by a coal baron to bribe the townsfolk into embracing a canal project that would make the shipment of his coal more efficient. The statue of the fancy guy on the horse is of Charles Stewart Vane, the Third Marquess of Londonderry. He was an Irish aristocrat and a general in Wellington's army who married a local coal heiress. A clever and aggressive businessman, he managed to create a vast business empire by controlling every link in the coal business chain—mines, railroads, boats, harbors, and so on.

In the 1850s throughout England, towns were moving their markets off squares and into Industrial Age iron-and-glass market halls. Durham was no exception, and today its funky 19th-century **indoor market** (which faces Market Place) is a delight to explore (closed Sun). There are also outdoor markets here on Saturdays and the third Thursday of each month.

Do you enjoy the sparse traffic in Durham's old town? It was the first city in England to institute a "congestion fee." When drivers enter the town Monday through Saturday, a camera snaps a photo of their car's license plate, and the driver must pay £2 that day or face a £50 fine by mail. This has cut downtown traffic by more than 50 percent. Locals brag that London (which now has a similar congestion fee) was inspired by their success.

• *Head up the hill on Saddler Street toward the cathedral, stopping where you reach the chunk of wall at the top of a stairway. On the left, you'll see a bridge.*

A 12th-century construction, **Elvet Bridge** led to a town market over the river. Like Framwellgate, it's very long (17 arches) and designed to avoid riverside muck and steep inclines. Even today, Elvet Bridge leads to an unusually wide road—once swollen to accommodate the market action. Shops lined the right-hand side of Elvet Bridge in the 12th century, as they do today. An alley separated the bridge from the buildings on the left. When the bridge was widened, it met the upper stories of the buildings on the left, which became "street level."

Turn back to look at the chunk of **wall** by the top of the stairs— a reminder of a once-formidable fortification. The Scots, living just 50 miles from here, were on the rampage in the 14th century. After their victory at Bannockburn in 1314, they pushed farther south and actually burned part of Durham. Wary of this new threat, Durham built thick city walls. As people settled within the walls, the population density soared. Soon, open lanes were covered by residences and became tunnels (called "vennels"). A classic vennel leads to Saddlers Yard, a fine little 16th-century courtyard (opposite the wall, look for the yellow Vennels Café sign). While the vennels are cute today, centuries ago they were Dickensian nightmares—the filthiest of hovels.

• *Continue up Saddler Street. Just before the fork at the top of the street, duck through the purple door below the* Georgian Window *sign. You'll see a bit of the medieval wall incorporated into the brickwork of a newer building and a turret from an earlier wall. Back on Saddler Street, you can see the ghost of the old wall (picture it standing exactly the width of the building now housing the Salvation Army.) Veer right at Owengate*

as you continue uphill to the Palace Green. (The Durham World Heritage Site Visitor Centre is near the top of the hill, on the left.)

The **Palace Green** was the site of the original 11th-century Saxon town, filling this green between the castle and an earlier church. Later, the town made way for 12th-century Durham's defenses, which now enclose the green. With the threat presented by the Vikings, it's no wonder people found comfort in a spot like this.

The **castle** still stands—as it has for a thousand years—on its motte (man-made mound). Like Oxford and Cambridge, Durham University is a collection of colleges scattered throughout the town, and even this castle is now part of the school. Look into the old courtyard from the castle gate. It traces the very first and smallest bailey (protected area). As future bishops expanded the castle, they left their coats of arms as a way of "signing" the

wing they built. Because the Norman kings appointed prince bishops here to rule this part of their realm, Durham was the seat of power for much of northern England. The bishops had their own army and even minted their own coins. The castle is accessible with a 45-minute guided tour, which includes the courtyard, kitchens, great hall, and chapel (£5, open most days when school is in session—but schedule varies so call ahead, buy tickets at Durham

Durham's Early Years

Durham's location, tucked inside a tight bend in the River Wear, was practically custom-made for easy fortifications. But it wasn't settled until A.D. 995, with the arrival of St. Cuthbert's body (buried in Durham Cathedral). Shortly after that, a small church and fortification were built upon the site of today's castle and church to house the relic. The castle was a classic "motte-and-bailey" design (with the "motte," or mound, providing a lookout tower for the stockade encircling the protected area, or "bailey"). By 1100, the prince bishop's bailey was filled with villagers—and he wanted everyone out. This was *his* place! He provided a wider protective wall, and had the town resettle below (around today's Market Place). But this displaced the townsfolk's cows, so the prince bishop constructed a fine stone bridge (today's Framwellgate) to connect the new town to grazing land he established across the river. The bridge had a defensive gate, with a wall circling the peninsula and the river serving as a moat.

World Heritage Site Visitor Centre or Palace Green Library—described next, ask about possible self-guided tour in summer only, tel. 0191/334-2932, www.dur.ac.uk/durham.castle).

• *Turning your back to the castle and facing the cathedral, on the right is the university's Palace Green Library.*

The **Palace Green Library** has a free permanent exhibit—*Living on the Hills*—that chronicles 10,000 years of human history on the site of Durham. It also hosts temporary exhibits in both its Wolfson Gallery and Dennyson Stoddart Gallery on everything from rare books to robots. Pop in or check online for current exhibits (temporary exhibits—generally £5, Tue-Sun 10:00-16:45, Mon 12:00-16:45, Palace Green, tel. 0191/334-2932, www.dur.ac.uk/library/asc).

• *This walk ends at Durham's stunning **cathedral**, described next.*

Sights in Durham

▲▲▲DURHAM'S CATHEDRAL

Built to house the much-venerated bones of St. Cuthbert from Lindisfarne (known today as Holy Island), Durham's cathedral offers the best look at Norman architecture in England. ("Norman" is British for "Ro-

manesque.") In addition to touring the cathedral, try to fit in an evensong service.

Cost: Entry to the cathedral itself is free, though a £3 donation is suggested, and you must pay to climb the tower and to enter the new *Open Treasure* exhibit.

Hours: The cathedral is open to visitors Mon-Sat 9:30-18:00, Sun 12:30-18:00, daily until 20:00 mid-July-Aug, sometimes closes for special services, opens daily at 7:15 for worship and prayer. Access is limited for a few days in June, when the cathedral is used for graduation ceremonies (check online).

Information: The £1 pamphlet, *A Short Guide to Durham Cathedral,* is informative but dull. Tel. 0191/386-4266, www.durhamcathedral.co.uk.

Evensong: For a thousand years, this cradle of English Christianity has been praising God. To really experience the cathedral, attend an evensong service. Arrive early and ask to be seated in the choir. It's a spiritual Oz, as the choristers (12 men and 40 youngsters—now girls as well as boys) sing psalms—a red-and-white-robed pillow of praise, raised up by the powerful pipe organ. If you're lucky and the service goes well, the organist will run a spiritual musical victory lap as the congregation breaks up (Tue-Sat at 17:15, Sun at 15:30, 1 hour, sometimes sung on Mon; visiting choirs nearly always fill in when choir is off on school break mid-July-Aug; tel. 0191/386-4266). For more on evensong, see page 163.

Organ Recitals: The organ plays most Wednesday evenings in July and August (£8, 19:30).

Tower Climb: The view from the tower will cost you 325 steps and £5 (Mon-Sat 10:00-16:00, closes at 15:00 in winter, sometimes open Sun outside of services; closed during services, events, and bad weather; must be at least eight years old, no high heels or backless shoes; enter through south transept).

Open Treasure Exhibit: This collection of the church's rare artifacts is housed in the former monks' quarters (£7.50, Mon-Sat 10:00-17:00, Sun from 12:30, last entry one hour before closing).

Tours: Regular tours run Monday through Saturday. If one is already in session, you're welcome to join (£5; tours start at 10:30, 11:00, and 14:00; fewer in winter, call or check website to confirm schedule).

Visitor Services: A shop, café, and WC are tucked away in the cloister.

❍ Self-Guided Tour

Begin your visit outside the cathedral. From the Palace Green, notice how this fortress of God stands boldly opposite the Norman keep of Durham's fortress of man.

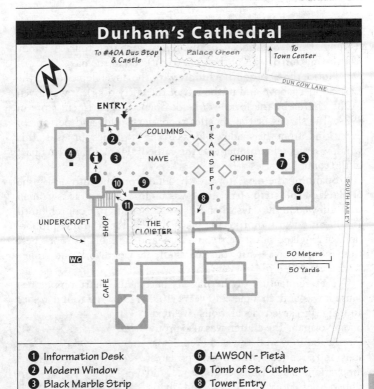

Durham's Cathedral

To #40A Bus Stop & Castle · Palace Green · To Town Center

DUN COW LANE

ENTRY

COLUMNS

T R A N S E P T

NAVE · CHOIR

UNDERCROFT

SHOP

THE CLOISTER

WC

CAFÉ

SOUTH BAILEY

50 Meters
50 Yards

❶ Information Desk
❷ Modern Window
❸ Black Marble Strip
❹ Galilee Chapel &
   Tomb of the Venerable Bede
❺ Chapel of the Nine Altars
❻ LAWSON - Pietà
❼ Tomb of St. Cuthbert
❽ Tower Entry
❾ Miners' Memorial
❿ Cloister Entry
⓫ Stairs to Open Treasure Exhibit

Look closely: The **exterior** of this awe-inspiring cathedral has a serious skin problem. In the 1770s, as the stone was crumbling,

they crudely peeled it back a few inches. The scrape marks give the cathedral a bad complexion to this day. For proof of this odd "restoration," study the masonry 10 yards to the right of the door. The L-shaped stones in the corner would normally never be found in a church like this—they only became L-shaped when the surface was cut back.

At the cathedral **door,** check out the big, bronze, lion-faced knocker (this is a replica of the 12th-century original, which is in the Open Treasure exhibit). The knocker was used by criminals seeking sanctuary (read the explanation).

Inside, purple-robed church attendants are standing by to happily answer questions. Ideally, follow a church tour. A handy ❶ **information desk** is at the back (right) end of the nave.

Notice the ❷ **modern window** with the novel depiction of the Last Supper (above and to the left of the entry door). It was given to the church by the local Marks & Spencer department store in 1984. The shapes of the apostles represent worlds and persons of every kind, from the shadowy Judas to the brightness of Jesus. This window is a good reminder that the cathedral remains a living part of the community.

Spanning the nave (toward the altar from the info desk), the ❸ **black marble strip** on the floor was as close to the altar as women were allowed in the days when this was a Benedictine church (until 1540). Sit down (ignoring the black line) and let the fine proportions of England's best Norman nave—and arguably Europe's best Romanesque nave—stir you. All the frilly woodwork and stonework were added in later centuries.

The architecture of the **nave** is particularly harmonious because it was built in a mere 40 years (1093-1133). The round arches and zigzag-carved decorations are textbook·Norman. The church was also proto-Gothic, built by well-traveled French masons and architects who knew the latest innovations from Europe. Its stone and ribbed roof, pointed arches, and flying buttresses were revolutionary in England. Notice the clean lines and simplicity. It's not as cluttered as other churches for several reasons: For centuries—out of respect for St. Cuthbert—no one else was buried here (so it's not filled with tombs). During Reformation times, sumptuous Catholic decor was removed. Subsequent fires and wars destroyed what Protestants didn't.

Head to the back of the nave and enter the ❹ **Galilee Chapel** (late Norman, from 1175). Find the smaller altar just to the left of the main altar. The paintings of St. Cuthbert and St. Oswald (seventh-century king of Northumbria) on the side walls of the niche are rare examples of Romanesque (Norman) paintings. Facing this altar, look above to your right to see more faint paintings on the upper walls above the columns. On the right side of the chapel, the upraised tomb topped with a black slab contains the remains of the **Venerable Bede,** an eighth-century Christian scholar who wrote the first history of England. The Latin reads, "In this tomb are the bones of the Venerable Bede."

Back in the main church, stroll down the nave to the center, under the highest **bell tower** in Europe (218 feet). Gaze up. The ropes turn wheels upon which bells are mounted. If you're stirred by the cheery ringing of church bells, tune in to the cathedral on Sunday (9:15-10:00 & 14:30-15:30) or Thursday (19:30-21:00 practice, trained bell ringers welcome, www.durhambellringers.org.uk), when the resounding notes tumble merrily through the entire town.

Continuing east (all medieval churches faced east), enter the **choir.** Monks worshipped many times a day, and the choir in the center of the church provided a cozy place to gather in this vast, dark, and chilly building. Mass has been said daily here in the heart of the cathedral for 900 years. The fancy wooden benches are from the 17th century. Behind the altar is the delicately carved Neville Screen from 1380 (made of Normandy stone in London, shipped to Newcastle by sea, then brought here by wagon). Until the Reformation, the niches contained statues of 107 saints. Exit the choir from the far right side (south). Look for the stained-glass window (to your right) that commemorates the church's 1,000th anniversary in 1995. The colorful scenes depict England's history, from coal miners to cows to computers.

Step down behind the high altar into the east end of the church, which contains the 13th-century ❺ **Chapel of the Nine Altars.** Built later than the rest of the church, this is Gothic—taller, lighter, and relatively more extravagant than the Norman nave. On the right, see the powerful modern ❻ **pietà** made of driftwood, with brass accents by local sculptor Fenwick Lawson.

Climb a few steps to the ❼ **tomb of St. Cuthbert.** An inspirational leader of the early Christian Church in north England, St. Cuthbert lived in the Lindisfarne monastery (100 miles north of Durham, today called Holy Island). He died in 687. Eleven years later, his body was exhumed and found to be miraculously preserved. This stoked the popularity of his shrine, and pilgrims came in growing numbers. When Vikings raided Lindisfarne in 875, the monks fled with his body (and the famous illuminated Lindisfarne Gospels, now in the British Library in London). In 995, after 120 years of roaming, the monks settled in Durham on an easy-to-defend tight bend in the River Wear. This cathedral was built over Cuthbert's tomb.

Throughout the Middle Ages, a shrine stood here and was visited by countless pilgrims. In 1539, during the Reformation—whose proponents advocated focusing on God rather than saints—the shrine was destroyed. But pilgrims still come, especially on St. Cuthbert's feast day (March 20).

Turn around and walk back the way you came. In the **south transept** (to your left) is the ❽ **tower entry** (tower described earlier), as well as an astronomical clock and the Chapel of the Durham Light Infantry, a regiment of the British Army (1881-1968). The old flags and banners hanging above were actually carried into battle.

Return along the left side of the nave toward the entrance. Across from the entry is the door to the cloister. Along the wall by the door to the cloister, notice the ❾ **memorial honoring coal miners** who died, and those who "work in darkness and danger in those pits today." (This message is a bit dated—Durham's coal mines closed down in the 1980s.) The nearby book of remembrance lists mine victims. As an ecclesiastical center, a major university town, and a gritty, blue-collar coal-mining town, Durham's population has long been a complicated mix: priests, academics, and the working class.

After exiting the church, act like a monk and make a circuit of the Gothic ❿ **cloister** (made briefly famous in a scene from the Harry Potter film *The Sorcerer's Stone,* in which Harry walks with his owl through a snowy courtyard). This area provides a fine view back up to the church towers.

Enter the newly opened, £9-million ⓫ **Open Treasure exhibit** from the cloister, going up some stairs to the Monks' Dormitory, a long, impressive room that stretches out under an original 14th-century timber roof. Formerly the monks' sleeping quarters, the room now holds artifacts from the cathedral treasury and monks' library. At the far end of the hall you'll find a door leading to the new Collections Gallery. The double set of glass doors allows the cathedral to display more of its treasures in a climate-controlled environment—sometimes including a copy of the Magna Carta from 1216—as well as items from the Norman/medieval period (when the monks of Durham busily copied manuscripts), the Reformation, and the 17th century. The exhibit continues through the cloister's Great Kitchen, where the actual relics from St. Cuthbert's tomb are on view—his coffin, vestments, and cross—and ends in the undercroft, where you'll find a **shop** and a **café.**

MORE SIGHTS IN DURHAM

There's little to see in Durham beyond its cathedral, but it's a pleasant place to go for a stroll and enjoy its riverside setting.

Durham Heritage Centre Museum

Situated in the old Church of St. Mary-le-Bow near the cathedral, this modest, somewhat hokey little museum does its best to illuminate the city's history, but it's worthwhile only on a rainy day. The exhibits, which are scattered willy-nilly throughout the old nave, include a reconstructed Victorian-era prison cell; a look at Durham industries past and present, especially coal mining (in Victorian times, the river was literally black from coal); and a 10-minute movie about 20th-century Durham. In the garden on the side of the church are two modern sculptures by local artist Fenwick Lawson, whose work is also in the cathedral.

Cost and Hours: £2.50; July-Sept daily 11:00-16:30, weekend afternoons only in off-season, closed Nov-March; corner of North Bailey and Bow Lane, tel. 0191/384-5589, www.durhamheritagecentre.org.uk.

Riverside Path

For a 20-minute woodsy escape, walk Durham's riverside path from busy Framwellgate Bridge to sleepy Prebends Bridge.

Boat Cruise and Rental

Hop on the *Prince Bishop* for a relaxing one-hour narrated cruise of the river that nearly surrounds Durham (£8, Easter-Oct; for schedule, call 24-hour info line at 0191/386-9525, check their website, or go down to the dock at Brown's Boat House at Elvet Bridge, just east of old town; www.princebishoprc.co.uk). Sailings vary based on weather and tides. For some exercise with identical scenery, you can rent a rowboat at the same pier (£6.50/hour per person, £10 deposit, late-March-Oct daily 10:00-18:00, last rental at 17:00, tel. 0191/386-3779).

Crook Hall and Gardens

While most English gardens are in the countryside, Crook Hall

is only a 10-minute walk from the city center, making it a convenient sight for travelers without a car. It has all the elements you'd expect in a classic English garden—walled "secret" gardens, a maze, a pool, and plenty of moss-covered statues. A map and witty signs take you on a self-guided tour.

Cost and Hours: £7.50, £5.50 off-season, April-Sept Sun-Wed 10:00-17:00, shorter hours off-season, closed Thu-Sat for weddings; café open daily 9:30-17:00, pay parking; from the city center, walk across the river and head north along the riverside path—it's just past the Radisson Hotel on Frankland Lane; tel. 0191/384-8028, www.crookhallgardens.co.uk.

Sleeping in Durham

Close-in pickings are slim in Durham. Because much of the housing is rented to students, there are only a handful of B&Bs. Otherwise, there are a few hotels within easy walking distance of the town center. During graduation (typically the last two weeks of June), everything books up well in advance and prices increase dramatically. Rooms can be tight on weekends any time of year.

B&BS

$$$ Victorian Town House B&B offers three spacious, boutique-like rooms in an 1853 townhouse. It's in a nice residential area just down the hill from the train station and is handy to the town center. This is your best B&B option in Durham (family room, cash only, 2-night minimum preferred April-Oct, some view rooms, check-in 16:00-19:00 or by prior arrangement, 2 Victoria Terrace, 10-minute walk from train or bus station, tel. 0191/370-9963, www.durhambedandbreakfast.com, stay@durhambedandbreakfast.com, friendly Jill and Andy).

$$$ Castleview Guest House rents five airy, restful rooms in a well-located, 250-year-old guesthouse next door to a little church. If it's sunny, guests relax in the Eden-like backyard. Located on a charming cobbled street, it's just above Silver Street and the Framwellgate Bridge—take the stairs just after the church (cash preferred, free street-parking permit, 4 Crossgate, tel. 0191/386-8852, www.castle-view.co.uk, info@guesthousesdurham.co.uk, Anne and Mike Williams).

$$ Farnley Tower, a decent but impersonal B&B, has 13 large rooms and a quirky staff. On a quiet street at the top of a hill, it's a 15-minute hike up from the town center. Though you won't find the standard B&B warmth and service, this is a suitable alternative when the central hotels are booked (some rooms with cathedral view, family room, 2 percent fee for credit cards, easy free parking, inviting yard, The Avenue—hike up this steep street and look for the sign on the right, tel. 0191/375-0011, www.farnley-tower.co.uk, enquiries@farnley-tower.co.uk, Raj and Roopal Naik). The Naiks also run the inventive fine-dining restaurant in the same building.

HOTELS

If the B&Bs are full, Durham could be a good place to resort to a bigger chain hotel, such as the Marriott (see below) or the centrally located **Premier Inn** (on Freemans Place).

$$$ Durham Marriott Hotel Royal County scatters its 150 posh, four-star but slightly scruffy rooms among several buildings sprawling across the river from the city center. The Leisure Club has a pool, sauna, hot tub, spa, and fitness equipment (breakfast included in some rates, elevator, free Wi-Fi in public areas, pay Wi-Fi in rooms, restaurant, bar, parking-£5/overnight, Old Elvet, tel. 0191/386-6821 or tel. 0870-400-7286, www.marriott.co.uk).

$$ Kingslodge Inn & Restaurant is a slightly worn but comfortable 21-room place with charming terraces, an attached restaurant, and a pub. Located in a pleasantly wooded setting, it's convenient for train travelers (family room, free parking, Waddington Street, Flass Vale, tel. 0191/370-9977, http://kingslodgeinn.co.uk, enquiries@kingslodgeinn.co.uk).

STUDENT HOUSING OPEN TO ANYONE

$$$ Durham Castle, a student residence actually on the castle grounds facing the cathedral, rents rooms during the summer break (generally July-Sept). Request a room in the stylish main building, which is more appealing than the modern dorm rooms (includes breakfast in an elegant dining hall, Palace Green, tel. 0191/334-4106, www.dur.ac.uk/university.college, durham.castle@durham.ac.uk). Note that the same office also rents rooms in other university buildings, but most are far less convenient to the city center—make sure to request the Durham Castle location when booking.

Eating in Durham

Durham is a university town with plenty of lively, inexpensive eateries, but except for Finbarrs, there's not much to get excited about. Especially on weekends, the places downtown are crowded with noisy college kids and rowdy townies. Stroll down North Road, across Framwellgate Bridge, up through Market Place, and up Saddler Street, and consider the options suggested below. The better choices are about a five-minute walk from this main artery—or a long hike to the suburbs—and worth the trek.

Pubs Across the Elvet Bridge: Two good options are within a five-minute walk of the Elvet Bridge (just east of the old town). **$$ The Court Inn** offers an eclectic menu of pub grub and an open, lively atmosphere (food served daily 11:00-22:00; cross the Elvet Bridge, turn right, walk several blocks, and then look left; Court Lane, tel. 0191/384-7350). For beer and ales, locals favor **The Dun Cow.** There's a cozy "snug bar" up front and a more spacious lounge in the back. Read the legend behind the pub's name on the wall along the outside corridor. More sedate than the student-oriented places in the town center, this pub serves only snacks and light meals—come here to drink and nibble, not to feast (daily 11:00-

23:00; from the Elvet Bridge, walk five minutes straight ahead to Old Elvet 37; tel. 0191/386-9219).

Deli Lunch: Creative **$ Claypath Delicatessen** is worth the five-minute uphill walk above Market Place. Not just any old sandwich shop, this place assembles fresh ingredients and homemade bread into tasty sandwiches, salads, sampler platters, and more. They pride themselves on their killer espresso. While carryout is possible, most people eat in the casual, comfortable café setting (Tue-Fri 10:00-17:00, Sat 10:00-16:00, closed Sun-Mon; from Market Place, cross the bridge and walk up Claypath to #57; tel. 0191/340-7209).

Indian: For well-executed Indian food in a contemporary setting, try **$$ The Capital,** a five-minute uphill walk above Market Place, near the Claypath Deli (daily 18:00-23:30, 69 Claypath, tel. 0191/386-8803).

Thai: Trendy **$$ Zen** is a modern, dark-wood place serving curries, noodles, fried rice, and other Asian fare. It's popular with students, so it's best to book a table or go early and sit in the bar (daily 11:00-22:00, Court Lane, tel. 0191/384-9588, www.zendurham.co.uk).

Afternoon Tea: At **$ Tealicious,** mother-and-daughter team Alison and Jenny bake homemade cakes and scones for their all-day tea, as well as prepare fresh soups and sandwiches. Look for a tall, skinny teahouse at the end of Elvet Bridge (Tue-Sat 10:00-16:00, Sun from 12:00, closed Mon, 88 Elvet Bridge, tel. 0191/340-1393).

Chain Restaurants with a Bridge View: Two chain places (that you'll find in every British city) are worth considering in Durham only because of their delightful setting right at the old-town end of the picturesque Framwellgate Bridge. **$$ Café Rouge** has French-bistro food and decor (daily 9:00-22:30, 21 Silver Street, tel. 0191/384-3429). **$$ Bella Italia,** next door and down the stairs, has a terrace overlooking the river and surprisingly good food (Mon-Fri 11:30-22:30, Sat-Sun 9:00-23:00, reservations recommended, 20 Silver Street, tel. 0191/386-1060).

Fish-and-Chips: A standby for carryout fish-and-chips, **$ Bells** is just off Market Place toward the cathedral. I'd skip their fancier dining room (hours vary but likely Mon-Thu 11:00-21:00, Fri-Sat 11:00-24:00, Sun 12:00-16:00).

Splurge Outside the Town Center: One of Durham's top restaurants, **$$$$ Finbarrs** is an untouristy splurge serving sophisticated meat and seafood dishes. You'll find inventive twists on regional standards—such as roasted venison or duck breast—and daily fish selections. More than a mile from the city center, it's practical only for drivers or hardy walkers staying near the train station who don't mind a 20-minute hike. The early-evening fixed-price meals are one of the best deals in town (lunch and dinner specials available, open Mon-Sat 12:00-14:00 & 17:30-22:00, Sun 12:00-15:00, reservations smart on weekends, northwest of town, Aykley Heads, tel. 0191/307-7033, www.finbarrsrestaurant.co.uk).

Supermarket: Marks & Spencer is in the old town, just off Market Place (Mon-Sat 8:00-18:00, Sun 11:00-17:00, 4 Silver Street, across from post office). Next door is a **Tesco Metro** (Mon-Sat 7:00-22:00, Sun 11:00-17:00). You can **picnic** on Market Place, or on the benches and grass outside the cathedral entrance (but not on the Palace Green, unless the park police have gone home).

Durham Connections

From Durham by Train to: York (4/hour, 45 minutes), **Keswick/ Lake District** (train to Penrith—hourly, 3 hours, change in Newcastle and Carlisle; then bus to Keswick), **London** (hourly direct, 3 hours, more with transfers), **Hadrian's Wall** (take train to Newcastle—4/hour, 20 minutes, then a train/bus or train/taxi combination to Hadrian's Wall—see "Getting Around Hadrian's Wall" on page 591), **Edinburgh** (hourly direct, 2 hours, more with changes, less frequent in winter). Train info: Tel. 0345-748-4950, www.nationalrail.co.uk.

ROUTE TIPS FOR DRIVERS

As you head north from Durham on the A-1 motorway, you'll pass a famous bit of public art: **The Angel of the North,** a modern, rusted-metal angel standing 65 feet tall with a wingspan of 175 feet (wider than a Boeing 757). While initially controversial when it was erected in 1998, it has since become synonymous with Northeast England, and is a beloved local fixture.

DURHAM & NE ENGLAND

Beamish Museum

This huge, 300-acre open-air museum, which recreates life in northeast England during the 1820s, 1900s, and 1940s, is England's best museum of its type. It takes at least three hours to explore its four sections: Pit Village (a coal-mining settlement with an actual mine), The Town (a 1913 street lined with actual shops), Pockerley Old Hall (a "gentleman farmer's" manor house),

Near Durham

To Edinburgh
Eyemouth
Burnmouth
SCOTLAND
To Edinburgh
Berwick-upon-Tweed
Duns
Swinton
Note: Road submerged at high tide
Earlston
Melrose
Coldstream
Holy Island
(Lindisfarne)
Beal
Flodden
Bamburgh BAMBURGH CASTLE
Kelso
Belford
Seahouses
Kalemouth
Warenford
Beadnell
Ancrum
Wooler
B-1339
Jedburgh
A-697
Embleton
A-1
Longhoughton
Alnwick
Rugley
Alnmouth
Southdean
Catcleugh
Amble
Felton
Broomhill
Rochester
Weldon
Widdrington
A-1
A-189
Otterburn
Ashington
N. Tyne
A-68
Morpeth
Bellingham
Ridsdale
Bedlington
Blyth
Wark
A-696
Roadhead
HADRIAN'S WALL
A-1
A-19
Haltwhistle
B-6318
Newcastle
South Shields
To Amsterdam
A-69
Tyne
A-196
Hexham
ANGEL OF THE NORTH
A-194
Brampton
VINDOLANDA ROMAN FORT
HOUSESTEADS ROMAN FORT
A-68
Sunderland
See Detail Map
Consett
A-693
Houghton-le-Spring
A-1
Alston
A-689
BEAMISH MUSEUM
Durham
A-690
Wearhead
Brandon
Melmerby
Spennymoor
A-1
Hartlepool
ENGLAND
Penrith
Bishop Auckland
Shildon
To Keswick
M-6
A-66
A-688
To York
Middlesbrough

North Sea

10 Kilometers
10 Miles

SCOTLAND
ENGLAND
WALES
London

DURHAM & NE ENGLAND

and Home Farm (a preserved farm and farmhouse). This isn't a wax museum. If you touch the exhibits, they may smack you. Attendants at each stop happily explain everything. In fact, the place is only really interesting if you talk to the attendants—who make it worth ▲▲▲.

GETTING THERE

By **car,** the museum is five minutes off the A-1/M-1 motorway (one exit north of Durham at Chester-le-Street/Junction 63, well-signposted, 12 miles, 25-minute drive northwest of Durham).

Getting to Beamish from Durham by **bus** is a snap on peak-season Saturdays via direct bus #128 (8/day, 30 minutes, runs April-Oct only, stops at Durham train and bus stations). Otherwise, catch bus #21, #X21, or #50 from the Durham bus station (3-4/hour, 25 minutes) and transfer at Chester-le-Street to bus #8, #8A, or #28, which takes you right to the museum entrance (2/hour Mon-Sat, hourly Sun, 15 minutes, leaves from central bus kiosk a half-block away, tel. 0191/420-5050, www.simplygo.com). Show your bus ticket for a 25 percent museum discount.

ORIENTATION TO BEAMISH MUSEUM

Cost and Hours: £19, children 5-16-£11, under 5-free; open Easter-Oct daily 10:00-17:00; off-season until 16:00, weekends only Dec-mid-Feb, and only The Town and Pit Village are open with vintage trams still running; check events schedule on chalkboard as you enter, last tickets sold at 15:00 year-round, tel. 0191/370-4000, www.beamish.org.uk.

Getting Around the Museum: Pick up a free map at the entry to help navigate the four zones; while some are side-by-side, others are up to a 15-minute walk apart. Vintage trams and cool, circa-1910 double-decker buses shuttle visitors around the grounds, and their attendants are helpful and knowledgeable. Signs on  the trams advertise a variety of 19th-century products, from "Borax, for washing everything" to "Murton's Reliable Travelling Trunks."

Eating: Several eateries are scattered around Beamish, including a pub and tearooms (in The Town), a fish-and-chips stand (in the Pit Village), and various cafeterias and snack stands. Or bring a picnic.

VISITING THE MUSEUM

I've described the four areas in counterclockwise order from the entrance.

From the entrance building, bear left along the road, then watch for the turnoff on the right to the **Pit Village.** This is a company town built around a coal mine, with a schoolhouse, a Methodist chapel, and a row of miners' homes with long, skinny pea-patch gardens out front. Poke into some of the homes to see their modest interiors. In the Board School, explore the different classrooms, and look for the interesting poster with instructions for avoiding consumption (a.k.a. tuberculosis, a huge public-health crisis back then).

Next, cross to the adjacent **Colliery** (coal mine), where you can take a fascinating—if claustrophobic—20-minute tour into the drift mine (check in at the "lamp camp"—tours depart when enough people gather, generally every 5-10 minutes). Your guide will tell you stories about beams collapsing, gas exploding, and flooding; after that cheerful speech, you'll don a hard hat as you're led into the mine. Nearby (across the tram tracks) is the fascinating **engine works,** where you can see the actual steam-powered winding engine used to operate the mine elevator. The "winderman" demonstrates how he skillfully eases both coal and miners up and down the tight shaft of the mine. This delicate, high-stakes job was one of the most sought-after at the entire Colliery—passed down from father to son—and the winderman had to stay in this building for his entire shift (the seat of his chair flips up to reveal a built-in WC).

A path leads through the woods to Georgian-era **Pockerley,** which has two parts. First you'll see the **Waggonway,** a big barn filled with steam engines, including the re-created, first-ever passenger train from 1825. (Occasionally this train takes modern-day visitors for a spin on 1825 tracks—a hit with railway buffs.)

Then, climb the hill to **Pockerley Old Hall,** the manor house of a gentleman farmer and his family. The house dates from the

1820s, and—along with the farmhouse described later—is Beamish's only vintage building still on its original site (other buildings at Beamish were relocated from elsewhere and reconstructed here). While not extremely wealthy, the farmer who lived here owned large tracts of land and could afford to hire help to farm it for him. This rustic home is no palace, but it was comfortable for the period. Costumed docents in the kitchen often bake delicious cookies from old recipes...and hand out samples.

The small garden terrace out front provides beautiful views across the pastures. From the garden, turn left and locate the narrow stairs up to the "old house." Actually under the same roof as the gentleman farmer's home, this space consists of a few small rooms that were rented by some of the higher-up workers to shelter their entire families of up to 15 children (young boys worked on the farm, while girls were married off early). While the parents had their own bedroom, the children all slept in the loft up above (notice the ladder in the hall).

From the manor house, hop on a vintage tram or bus or walk 10 minutes to the Edwardian-era **The Town** (c. 1913). This bus-

tling street features several working shops and other buildings that are a delight to explore. In the Masonic Hall, ogle the grand high-ceilinged meeting room, and check out the fun, old metal signs inside the garage. Across the street, poke into the courtyard to find the stables, which are full of carriages. The heavenly-smelling candy store sells old-timey sweets and has an actual workshop in back with trays of free samples. The newsagent sells stationery, cards, and old toys, while in the grocery, you can see old packaging and the scales used for weighing out products. Other buildings include a clothing store, a working pub (The Sun Inn, don't expect 1913 prices), Barclays Bank, and a hardware store featuring a variety of "toilet sets" (not what you think).

For lunch, try the Tea Rooms cafeteria (upstairs); or, if the weather is good, picnic in the grassy park with the gazebo next to the tram stop. The row of townhouses includes both homes and offices (if the dentist is in, chat with him to hear some harrowing stories about pre-Novocain tooth extraction). At the circa-1913 railway station at the far end of The Town, you can stand on the bridge over the tracks to watch old steam engines go back and forth—along with a carousel of "steam gallopers." Nearby, look for the "Westoe netty," a circa-1890 men's public urinal. This loo became famous in 1972 as the subject in a nostalgic Norman Rockwell–style painting of six miners and a young boy doing their business while they read the graffiti.

Finally, walk or ride a tram or bus to the **Home Farm.** (This

is the least interesting section—if you're running short on time, it's skippable.) Here you'll get to experience a petting zoo and see a "horse gin" (a.k.a. "gin gan")—where a horse walking in a circle turned a crank on a gear to amplify its "horsepower," helping to replace human hand labor. Near the cafeteria, you can cross a busy road (carefully) to the old farmhouse, still on its original site, where attendants sometimes bake goodies on a coal fire.

Hadrian's Wall

Cutting across the width of the isle of Britain, this ruined Roman wall is one of England's most thought-provoking sights. Once a towering 20-foot-tall fortification, these days "Hadrian's Shelf," as some cynics call it, is only about three feet wide and three to six feet high. (The conveniently precut stones of the wall were carried away by peasants during the post-Rome Dark Ages and now form the foundations of many local churches, farmhouses, and other structures.) In most places, what's left of the wall has been covered over by centuries of sod...making it effectively disappear into the landscape. But for those intrigued by Roman history, Hadrian's Wall provides a fine excuse to take your imagination for a stroll. These are the most impressive Roman ruins in Britain. Pretend you're a legionnaire on patrol in dangerous and distant Britannia, at the empire's northernmost frontier...with nothing but this wall protecting you from the terrifying, bloodthirsty Picts just to the north.

Today, several restored chunks of the wall, ruined forts, and museums thrill history buffs. While a dozen Roman sights cling along the wall's route, I've focused my coverage on an easily digestible six-mile stretch right in the middle, where you'll find the best museums and some of the most enjoyable-to-hike stretches of the wall. Three top sights are worth visiting: Housesteads Roman Fort shows you where the Romans lived; Vindolanda's museum shows you how they lived; and the Roman Army Museum explains the empire-wide military organization that brought them here.

A breeze for drivers, this area can also be seen fairly easily in summer by bus for those good at studying timetables (see "Getting Around Hadrian's Wall," later).

Hadrian's Wall is in vogue as a destination for multiday hikes through the pastoral English countryside. The Hadrian's Wall National Trail runs 84 miles, following the wall's route from coast to coast (for details, go to www.nationaltrail.co.uk/HadriansWall).

The History of Hadrian's Wall

In about A.D. 122, during the reign of Emperor Hadrian, the Romans constructed this great stone wall. Stretching 73 miles coast to coast across the narrowest stretch of northern England, it was built and defended by some 20,000 troops. Not just a wall, it was a military complex with forts, ditches, settlements, and roads. At every mile of the wall, a castle guarded a gate, and two turrets stood between each castle. The milecastles are numbered (80 covering 73 miles, because a Roman mile was shorter than our mile).

In cross-section, Hadrian's Wall consisted of a stone wall—around 15 to 20 feet tall—with a ditch on either side. The flat-bottomed ditch on the south side of the wall, called the vallum, was flanked by earthen ramparts and likely demarcated the "no-man's land" beyond which civilians were not allowed to pass. Between the vallum and the wall ran a service road called the Military Way. Another less-elaborate ditch ran along the north side of the wall. In some areas—including the region that I describe—the wall was built upon a volcanic ridgeline that provided a natural fortification.

The wall's actual purpose is still debated. While Rome ruled Britain for 400 years, it never quite ruled its people. The wall may have been used for any number of reasons: to protect Roman Britain from invading Pict tribes from the north (or at least cut down on pesky border raids); to monitor the movement of people as a show of Roman strength and superiority; or to simply give an otherwise bored army something to do. (Emperors understood that nothing was more dangerous than a bored army.) Or perhaps the wall represented Hadrian's tacit admission that the empire had reached its maximum extent; Hadrian was known for consolidating his territory, in some cases giving up chunks of land that had been conquered by his predecessor, Trajan, to create an easier-to-defend (if slightly smaller) empire. His philosophy of "defense before expansion" is embodied by the impressive wall that still bears his name.

Through-hikers (mostly British) can walk the wall's entire length in four to ten days. You'll see them bobbing along the ridgeline, drying out their socks in your B&B's mudroom, and recharging at local pubs in the evening. For those with less time, the brief ridge walk next to the wall from Steel Rigg to Sycamore Gap to Housesteads Roman Fort gives you a perfect taste of the scenery and history.

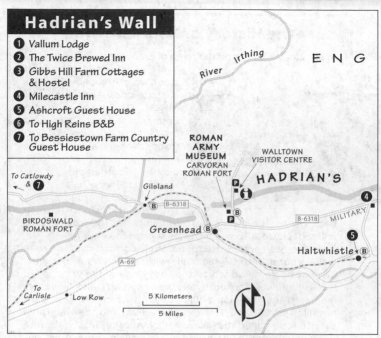

Hadrian's Wall

1 Vallum Lodge
2 The Twice Brewed Inn
3 Gibbs Hill Farm Cottages
   & Hostel
4 Milecastle Inn
5 Ashcroft Guest House
6 To High Reins B&B
7 To Bessiestown Farm Country
   Guest House

DURHAM & NE ENGLAND

Orientation to Hadrian's Wall

The area described in this section is roughly between the midsize towns of Bardon Mill and Haltwhistle, which are located along the busy A-69 highway. Each town has a train station and some handy B&Bs, restaurants, and services. However, to get right up close to the wall, you'll need to head a couple of miles north to the adjacent villages of Once Brewed and Twice Brewed (along the B-6318 road).

TOURIST INFORMATION

For an overview of your options, visit the Hadrian's Wall Country website at www.hadrianswallcountry.co.uk.

Portions of the wall are in Northumberland National Park. The **Walltown Visitor Centre** lies along the Hadrian's Wall bus #AD122 route and has information on the area, including walking guides to the wall (Easter-Oct daily 9:30-17:00, closed Nov-Easter, just off the B-6318 next to the Roman Army Museum, follow signs to *Walltown Quarry*, pay parking, tel. 01434/344-396, www.nnpa.org.uk).

Visitor information may also be found at **The Sill National Landscape Discovery Centre,** next to the recommended Twice Brewed Inn and about a half-mile from the Steel Rigg trailhead.

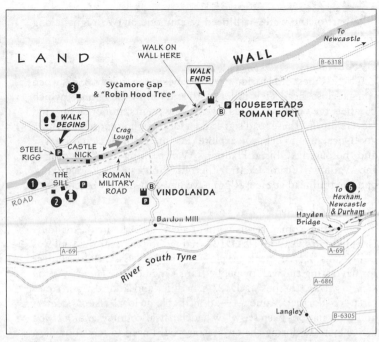

The Sill, with its unique grassland roof, also features interactive exhibits about the surrounding landscape and includes a local crafts shop, a café, and an 86-bed hostel (daily April-Oct 9:30-18:00, Nov-March 10:00-16:00, pay parking, served by bus #AD122, on the B-6318 near Bardon Mill, tel. 01434/341-200, www.thesill. org.uk).

The helpful TI in Haltwhistle, a block from the train station inside the library, has a good selection of maps and guidebooks and schedule information for Hadrian's Wall bus #AD122 (year-round Mon-Fri 10:00-13:00 & 13:30-16:30, Sat 10:00-13:00, closed Sun, The Library, Westgate, tel. 01434/321-1863, www. visitnorthumberland.com).

GETTING AROUND HADRIAN'S WALL

Hadrian's Wall is anchored by the big cities of Newcastle to the east and Carlisle to the west. Driving is the most convenient way to see Hadrian's Wall. If you're coming by train, consider renting a car for the day at either Newcastle or Carlisle; otherwise, you'll need to rely on trains and a bus to connect the sights, hire taxis, or book a private guide with a car. If you're just passing through for the day using public transportation, it's challenging to stop and see more than just one or two of the sights—study the schedules carefully and prioritize. Nondrivers who want to see everything—or even hike part of the wall—will need to stay one or two nights along the bus route.

By Car

Zip to this "best of Hadrian's Wall" zone on the speedy A-69; when you get close, head a few miles north and follow the B-6318, which parallels the wall and passes several viewpoints, minor sights, and "severe dips." (These road signs add a lot to a photo portrait.) Buy a good local map to help you explore this interesting area more easily and thoroughly. Official Hadrian's Wall parking lots (including at the Walltown Visitor Centre, The Sill, Housesteads Roman Fort, and the trailhead at Steel Rigg) have pay-and-display machines.

Without a Car

To reach the Roman sights without a car, take the made-for-tourists Hadrian's Wall **bus #AD122** (named for the year the wall was built; runs only in peak season—see below). Essential resources for navigating the wall by public transit include the *Hadrian's Wall Country Map,* the bus #AD122 schedule, and a local train timetable for Northern Line #4—all available at local visitors centers and train stations (also see www.hadrianswallcountry.co.uk). If you arrive by train during the off-season, you'll need to rely on taxis, a private guide, or long walks to visit the wall (see "Off-Season Options," later).

By Bus: Bus #AD122 connects the Roman sights (and several recommended accommodations) with train stations in **Haltwhistle** and **Hexham** (from £2/ride, £12.50 unlimited Day Rover ticket, buy tickets on board).

The bus runs between Haltwhistle and Hexham (8/day in each direction Easter-Sept, no service Oct-Easter). If you're coming from Carlisle or Newcastle, you'll need to take the train to Haltwhistle or Hexham and pick up the bus there. The bus used to run between Carlisle and Newcastle, and there's talk of restoring extended service in the future. If you're planning to take this bus, it's smart to confirm whether it'll be running during your visit (tel. 01434/322-002, www.gonortheast.co.uk/ad122).

By Train: Northern Line's train route #4 runs parallel to and a few miles south of the wall much more frequently than the bus. While the train stops at stations in larger towns—including (west to east) **Carlisle, Haltwhistle, Hexham,** and **Newcastle**—it doesn't take you near the actual Roman sights. You can catch bus #AD122 at Hexham and Haltwhistle (no bus service off-season; train runs hourly; Carlisle to Haltwhistle—30 minutes; Haltwhistle to Hexham—20 minutes; Hexham to Newcastle—40 minutes; www.northernrail.org).

By Taxi: These Haltwhistle-based taxi companies can help you connect the dots: Sprouls (tel. 01434/321-064, mobile 07712-321-064) or Diamond (mobile 07597/641-222). It costs about £14 one-way from Haltwhistle to Housesteads Roman Fort (arrange for return pickup or have museum staff call a taxi). Note that on school days, all of these taxis are busy shuttling rural kids to class in the morning (about 8:00-10:00) and afternoon (about 14:30-16:30), so you may have to wait.

By Private Tour: Peter Carney, a former history teacher who waxes eloquently on all things Roman, offers tours with his car and also leads guided walks around Hadrian's Wall, including an all-day seven-mile hike that starts at the Roman Army Museum and connects Vindolanda and Housesteads. He can also customize tours to suit your time frame and interests and is happy to pick you up from your B&B or the train station (£125/day for up to 5 people, £70/half-day, does not include museum admission, £40 extra for pick-up at Carlisle or Newcastle train stations, mobile 07585-139-016 or 07810-665/733, www.hadrianswall-walk.com, petercarney@hadrianswall-walk.com). Peter also offers tours of medieval Durham.

Off-Season Options: Bus #AD122 doesn't run off-season (Oct-Easter), so you can only get as far as the train will take you (i.e., Haltwhistle)—from there, you'll have to take a taxi or hire a local guide to take you to the sights. Or, if you're a hardy hiker, take the Northern Line train to Bardon Mill, then walk about 2 miles to Vindolanda and another 2.5 miles to Housesteads Roman Fort.

Baggage Storage: It's difficult to bring your luggage along with you. If you're day-tripping, you can store your luggage in **Carlisle** (ask at the train station or try across the street at Bar Solo, call for price and hours, tel. 01228/631-600) or in **Newcastle** at the Eldon Square Shopping Center, a five-minute walk north of the train station (tel. 01912/611-891, www.intu.co.uk/eldonsquare). If you must travel with luggage, Housesteads Roman Fort and Vindolanda will most likely let you leave your bags at the sight entrance while you're inside. If you want to walk the wall, various baggage-courier services will send your luggage ahead to your next B&B in the region for about £6 per bag (contact Hadrian's Haul, mobile 07967-564-823, www.hadrianshaul.com; or Walkers', tel. 0871-423-8803, www.walkersbags.co.uk).

Sights at Hadrian's Wall

▲▲Hiking the Wall

It's enjoyable to hike along the wall speaking Latin, even if only for a little while. Note that park rangers forbid anyone from actually walking on top of the wall, except along a very short stretch at Housesteads. On the following hike, you'll walk alongside the wall.

For a good, craggy, three-mile, one-way, up-and-down walk along the wall, hike between Steel Rigg and Housesteads Roman Fort. For a shorter hike, begin at  Steel Rigg (where there's a pay parking lot) and walk a mile to Sycamore Gap, then back again (described next; the Still and Walltown visitor centers hand out a free sheet outlining this walk). These hikes are moderately strenuous and are best for those in good shape. You'll need sturdy shoes and a windbreaker to comfortably overcome the often blustery environment.

To reach the trailhead for the short hike from **Steel Rigg to Sycamore Gap,** take the little road off the B-6318 near the Twice  Brewed Inn and park in the pay-and-display parking lot on the right at the crest of the hill. Walk through the gate to the shoulder-high stretch of wall, go to the left, and follow the wall running steeply down the valley below you. Ahead of you are dramatic cliffs, creating a natural boundary made to order for this Roman fortification. Walk down the steep slope into the valley, then back up the other side (watch your footing on the stone stairs). Following the wall, you'll do a similar up-and-down routine three more times, like a slow-motion human roller coaster. In the second gap is one of the best-preserved milecastles, #39 (called Castle Nick because it sits in a nick in a crag).

Soon after, you'll reach the third gap, called Sycamore Gap for the large symmetrical tree in the middle. (Do you remember the 1991 Kevin Costner movie  *Robin Hood: Prince of Thieves*? Locals certainly do—this tree was featured in it, and tourists frequently ask for directions to the "Robin Hood Tree.") You can either hike back the way you came or cut down toward the main road to find the less strenuous Roman Military Way path, which skirts the bottom of the ridge (rather than following the wall); this leads back to the base of the Steel Rigg hill, where you can huff back up to your car.

If you continue on to Housesteads, you'll pass a traditional Northumbrian sheep farm, windswept lakes, and more ups and downs. The farther you go, the fewer people you'll encounter, making this hike even more magical. As you close in on Housesteads, you'll be able to actually walk on top of the wall.

▲▲Housesteads Roman Fort

With its respectable museum, powerful scenery, and the best-preserved segment of the wall, this is your best single stop at Hadrian's

Wall. It requires a steep hike up from the parking lot, but once there it's just you, the bleating sheep, and memories of ancient Rome.

Cost and Hours: £7.50 for site and museum; daily April-Sept 10:00-18:00, Oct until 17:00, Nov-March until 16:00; last entry 45 minutes before closing, pay parking, bus #AD122 stops here.

Services and Information: At the parking lot is a visitors center with WCs, a snack bar, and a gift shop. They sell a £3.50 guidebook about the fort or a £5 guidebook covering the entire wall. If you're traveling by bus and want to leave your luggage, ask at the visitors center if they'll stow it for a bit. (Museum tel. 01434/344-363, info tel. 0870-333-1181, gift shop tel. 01434/344-525, www.english-heritage.org.uk/housesteads.)

Visiting the Museum and Fort: From the visitors center, head outside and hike about a half-mile uphill to the fort. At the top of the hill, duck into the **museum** (on the left) before touring the site. While smaller and housing fewer artifacts than the museum at Vindolanda, it's interesting nonetheless. Look for the giant Victory statue, which once adorned the fort's East Gate; her foot is stepping on a globe, serving as an intimidating reminder to outsiders of the Romans' success in battle. A good seven-minute film shows how Housesteads (known back then as Vercovicium) would have operated.

Artifacts offer more insights into those who lived here. A cooking pot from Frisia (Northern Holland) indicates the presence of women, showing that soldiers came with their families in tow. A tweezer, probe, spoons, and votive foot (that would have been offered to the gods in exchange for a cure for a foot ailment) reveal the type of medical care you could expect. And a weighted die and a coin mold—perhaps used to make counterfeit money—show what may have been the less-than-savory side of life at the fort.

After exploring the museum, head out to the sprawling ruins of the **fort.** Interpretive signs and illustrations explain what you're seeing. All Roman forts were the same rectangular shape and design, containing a commander's headquarters, barracks, and latrines (Housesteads has the best-preserved Roman toilets found anywhere—look for them at the lower-right corner). This fort even had a hospital. The fort was built right up to the wall, which runs along its upper end. Even if you're not a hiker, take some time to walk the wall here. (This is the one place along the wall where you're actually allowed to get up and walk on top of it for a photo op.) Visually trace the wall to the left to see how it disappears into a bank of overgrown turf.

▲▲Vindolanda

This larger Roman fort (which actually predates the wall by 40 years) and museum are just south of the wall. Although Housesteads has better ruins and the wall, Vindolanda has the more impressive museum, packed with artifacts that reveal intimate details of Roman life.

Cost and Hours: £7, £11 combo-ticket includes Roman Army Museum, daily April-Sept 10:00-18:00, mid-Feb-March and Oct until 17:00, Nov-Dec until 16:00, closed Jan-mid-Feb, last entry one hour before closing, call first during bad weather, free parking with entry, bus #AD122 stops here, café.

Information: A guidebook is available for £4; tel. 01434/344-277, www.vindolanda.com.

Tours: Guided tours run twice daily on weekends only (typically at 10:45 and 14:00); in high season, archaeological talks and tours may be offered on weekdays as well. Both are included in your ticket.

Archaeological Dig: The Vindolanda site is an active dig—from Easter through September, you'll see the excavation work in progress (usually Mon-Fri, weather permitting). Much of the work is done by volunteers, including armchair archaeologists from the US.

Visiting the Site and Museum: After entering, stop at the model of the entire site as it was in Roman times (c. A.D. 213-276). Notice that the site had two parts: the fort itself, and the town just outside that helped to supply it.

Head out to the **site,** walking through 500 yards of grassy parkland decorated by the foundation stones of the Roman fort and a full-size replica chunk of the wall. Over the course of 400 years, at least nine forts were built on this spot. The Romans, by lazily sealing the foundations from each successive fort, left modern-day archaeologists with a 20-foot-deep treasure trove of remarkably well-preserved artifacts: keys, coins, brooches, scales, pottery, glass, tools, leather shoes, bits of cloth, and even a wig. Many of these are now displayed in the

museum, well-described in English, German, French, and...Latin.

At the far side of the site, pass through the pleasant riverside garden area on the way to the museum. The well-presented **museum** pairs actual artifacts with insightful explanations—such as a collection of Roman shoes with a description about what each one tells us about its wearer. The weapons (including arrowheads and spearheads) and fragments of armor are a reminder that Vindolanda was an important outpost on Rome's northern boundary—look for the Scottish skull stuck on a pike to discourage rebellion.

Thanks to Vindolanda's boggy grounds, trash tossed away by the Romans was preserved in an airless environment. You'll see the world's largest collection of Roman leather; tools that were used for building and expanding the fort; locks and keys (the fort had a password that changed daily—jotting it on a Post-It note wasn't allowed); a large coin collection; items imported here from the far corners of the vast empire (such as fragments of French pottery and amphora jugs from the Mediterranean); beauty aids such as combs, tools for applying makeup, and hairpins; and religious pillars and steles.

But the museum's main attraction is its collection of writing tablets. A good video explains how these impressively well-preserved examples of early Roman cursive were discovered here in 1973. Displays show some of the actual letters—written on thin pieces of wood—alongside the translations. These letters bring Romans to life in a way that ruins alone can't. The most famous piece (described but not displayed here) is the first known example of a woman writing to a woman (an invitation to a birthday party).

Finally, you'll pass through an exhibit about the history of the excavations, including a case featuring the latest discoveries, on your way to the shop and cafeteria.

▲▲Roman Army Museum

This museum, a few miles farther west at Greenhead (near the site of the Carvoran Roman fort), has cutting-edge, interactive exhibits illustrating the structure of the Roman Army that built and monitored this wall, with a focus on the everyday lifestyles of the Roman soldiers stationed here. Bombastic displays, life-size figures, and several different films—but few actual artifacts—make this entertaining museum a good complement to the archaeological emphasis of Vindolanda. If you're visiting all three Roman sights, this is a good one to start at, as it sets the stage for what you're about to see.

Cost and Hours: £5.75, £11 combo-ticket includes Vindolanda, April-Sept daily 10:00-18:00, mid-Feb-March and Oct daily until 17:00, Nov-Dec Sat-Sun only until 16:00, closed Jan-mid-Feb; free parking with entry, bus #AD122 stops here. Tel. 01697/747-485; if no answer, call Vindolanda tel. 01434/344-277; www.vindolanda.com.

Visiting the Museum: In the first room, a video explains the complicated structure of the Roman Army—legions, cohorts, centuries, and so on. While a "legionnaire" was a Roman citizen, an "auxiliary" was a noncitizen specialist recruited for their unique skills (such as horsemen and archers). A video of an army-recruiting officer delivers an "Uncle Caesar wants YOU!" speech to prospective soldiers. A timeline traces the history of the Roman Empire, especially as it related to the British Isles.

The good 20-minute *Edge of Empire* 3-D movie offers an evocative look at what life was like for a Roman soldier marking time on the wall, and digital models show reconstructions of the wall and forts. In the exhibit on weapons, shields, and armor (mostly replicas), you'll learn how Roman soldiers trained with lead-filled wooden swords, so that when they went into battle, their metal swords felt light by comparison. Another exhibit explains the story of Hadrian, the man behind the wall, who stopped the expansion of the Roman Empire, declaring that the age of conquest was over.

Sleeping and Eating near Hadrian's Wall

If you want to spend the night in this area, set your sights on the adjacent villages of Once Brewed and Twice Brewed, with a few accommodations options, a good pub, and easy access to the most important sights. I've also listed some other accommodations scattered around the region.

IN AND NEAR ONCE BREWED AND TWICE BREWED

These two side-by-side villages, each with a handful of houses, sit at the base of the volcanic ridge along the B-6318 road. (While the mailing address for these hamlets is "Bardon Mill," that town is actually about 2.5 miles away, across the busy A-69 highway.) The Twice Brewed Inn and Milecastle Inn are reachable with Hadrian's Wall bus #AD122. Bus drivers can drop you off at Vallum Lodge by request (but they won't pick you up).

$$ Vallum Lodge is a cushy, comfortable, nicely renovated base situated near the vallum (the ditch that forms part of the fortification a half-mile from the wall itself). Its six cheery rooms are all on the ground floor, along with a guest lounge, and a separate guesthouse called the Snug has one bedroom and a kitchen. It's just up the road from The Twice Brewed Inn—a handy dinner option (pay laundry service, Military Road, tel. 01434/344-248, www.vallum-lodge.co.uk, stay@vallum-lodge.co.uk, Clare and Michael). , Clare and Michael).

$$ The Twice Brewed Inn, two miles west of Housesteads and a half-mile from the wall, rents 16 basic, workable rooms; all are en-suite and most have been recently renovated (ask for a room away from the road, Military Road, tel. 01434/344-534, www. twicebrewedinn.co.uk, info@twicebrewedinn.co.uk). The inn's friendly **$$ pub** serves as the community gathering place (free Wi-Fi) and is a hangout for hikers and the archaeologists digging at the nearby sites. It serves real ales and large portions of good pub grub (vegetarian options, fancier restaurant in back with same menu, food served daily 12:00-21:00, Sun until 20:00).

Rural and Remote, North of the Wall: $$ Gibbs Hill Farm Cottages and Hostel is a friendly, working sheep-and-cattle farm set on 700 acres in the stunning valley on the far side of the wall (only practical for drivers). The three 6-bed dorm rooms are in a restored hay barn (breakfast extra, packed lunch-£6, coin-op laundry facilities, 5-minute drive from Twice Brewed Inn or 30-minute walk from Steel Rigg trailhead, tel. 01434/344-030, www. gibbshillfarm.co.uk,val@gibbshillfarm.co.uk, warm Val). They also rent two self-catering cottages for two to four people by the week or occasionally shorter periods.

Eating West of Once/Twice Brewed: $$ Milecastle Inn, two miles to the west, cooks up all sorts of exotic game and offers the best dinner around, according to hungry national park rangers. You can order food at the counter and sit in the pub, or take a seat in the table-service area (food served daily Easter-Sept 12:00-20:45, Oct-Easter 12:00-14:30 & 18:00-20:30, smart to reserve in summer, North Road, tel. 01434/321-372).

IN HALTWHISTLE

The larger town of Haltwhistle has a train station, along with stops for Hadrian's Wall bus #AD122 (at the train station and a few blocks east, at Market Place). It also has a helpful TI (see "Tourist Information" on page 590), a launderette, several eateries, and a handful of B&Bs, including this one.

$$ Ashcroft Guest House, a large Victorian former vicarage, is 400 yards from the Haltwhistle train station and 200 yards from the Market Place bus stop. It has seven big, luxurious rooms, huge

DURHAM & NE ENGLAND

terraced gardens, and views from the comfy lounge, along with a two-bedroom apartment with kitchen, and ample free parking. If you want to indulge yourself after hiking the wall, this is the place (2-night minimum for apartment, 1.5 miles from the wall, Lanty's Lonnen, tel. 01434/320-213, www.ashcroftguesthouse. co.uk, info@ashcroftguesthouse.co.uk, helpful Geoff and Christine James).

NEAR HEXHAM
$$ High Reins offers four rooms in a stone house built by a shipping tycoon in the 1920s. The rooms are cushy and comfortable—there's a cozy feeling all over the place (cash only, 2-bedroom apartment also available in the house, lounge, 1 mile south of train station on the western outskirts of Hexham, Leazes Lane, tel. 01434/603-590, walton45@hotmail.com, Jan and Peter Walton). They also rent an apartment in the town center; ask for details.

NEAR CARLISLE
$$ Bessiestown Farm Country Guest House, located far northwest of the Hadrian sights, is convenient for drivers connecting the Lake District and Scotland. It's a quiet and soothing stop in the middle of sheep pastures, with four bedrooms in the main house and two 2-bedroom apartments in the former stables. One apartment is on the ground floor and has a handicapped-accessible bath (discount with 3-night stay, honesty bar; in Catlowdy, midway between Gretna Green and Hadrian's Wall, 20-minute drive north of Carlisle; tel. 01228/577-219, www.bessiestown.co.uk, info@ bessiestown.co.uk, gracious Margaret and Jack Sisson).

WALES

WALES

Croeso! Welcome to Wales, a country with 750 miles of scenic, windswept coastline jutting out of the west coast of the Isle of Britain into the Irish Sea. Shaped somewhat like a miniature Britain, Wales is longer than it is wide (170 miles by 60 miles) and is roughly the size of Massachusetts. The north is mountainous, rural, and sparsely populated. It's capped by 3,560-foot Mount Snowdon, taller than any mountain in England. The south, with a less-rugged topography, is where two-thirds of the people live (including 350,000 in the capital of Cardiff).

The Welsh are proud of their, well, Welshness. Despite centuries of English imperialism, the Welsh language (a.k.a. Cymraeg,

pronounced kum-RAH-ig) remains alive and well—more so than its nearly dead Celtic cousin in Scotland, Gaelic. Though everyone in Wales speaks English, one in five can also speak the native tongue; for many, it's their first language. In the northwest, well over half the population is fluent in Welsh and uses it in everyday life. Listen in.

Most certainly *not* a dialect of English, the Celtic Welsh tongue sounds to foreign ears like Elvish from *The Lord of the Rings*. One of Europe's oldest languages, Welsh has been written down since about A.D. 600, and it was spoken 300 years before French or German. Today, the Welsh language is protected by law from complete English encroachment—the country is officially bilingual, and signs display both languages (e.g., *Cardiff/Caerdydd*). In schools, it's either the first or the required second language; in many areas, English isn't used in classes at all until middle school.

Though English has been the dominant language in Wales for many years (and most newspapers and media are in English), the Welsh people cherish their linguistic heritage as something that

Speaking Welsh

Welsh pronunciation is tricky. The common "ll" combination sounds roughly like "thl" (pronounced as if you were ready to make an "l" sound and then blew it out; it can also sound like "cl" or "tl"). As in Scotland, "ch" is a soft, guttural k, pronounced in the back of the throat. The Welsh "dd" sounds like the English "th," f = v, ff = f, w = the "u" in "push," y = i. Non-Welsh people often make the mistake of trying to say a long Welsh name too fast, and inevitably trip themselves up. A local tipped me off: Slow down and say each syllable separately, and it'll come out right. For example, Llangollen

is thang-GOTH-lehn. But it gets harder. Some words are a real mouthful, like Llanfairpwllgwyngyllgogerychwyrndrobwllllantysiliogogogoch, the 58-character name for a small town on the island of Angelsey (it's the longest single-word place name in Europe).

Although there's no need to learn any Welsh (because everyone also speaks English), without too much effort you can make friends and impress the locals by learning a few polite phrases. In a pub, toast the guy who just bought your drink with *Diolch* and *Yeach-hid dah* (YECH-id dah, "Good health to you").

English	Welsh
Hello	**Helo** (hee-LOH)
Good-bye	**Hwyl** (hoo-il)
Please	**Os gwelwch yn dda** (os GWELL-uck UN thah)
Thank you	**Diolch** (dee-olkh)
Wales	**Cymru** (KUM-ree)
England	**Lloegr** (THLOY-ger)

sets them apart. In fact, a line of the Welsh national anthem goes, "Oh, may the old language survive!"

You can psychoanalyze the English-Welsh relationship through the word for Wales. The Anglo-Saxon word for "enemy" is "wealas" (which became "Wales"), and that's what they called this wild and historically unrulable part of their island (from their point of view). By contrast, the Celtic word for Wales, "Cymru," means "comrade" in Welsh—the opposite of what eventually became the English name for this region.

Wales has some traditional foods worth looking for, particularly lamb dishes and leek soup *(cawl)*. In fact, the national

Wales

To Dublin
Holyhead

To Blackpool
& Lake District

Anglesey

Llandudno • Liverpool

BEAUMARIS

IRELAND

Llanfairpwll
Caernarfon

Conwy

Bangor

• Chester

Betws-
y-coed

Ruthin

Mt.
Snowdon

CRICCIETH

Irish
Sea

Llangollen

HARLECH

Cardigan
Bay

Welshpool •

N

ENGLAND

Aberystwyth •

WALES

To Rosslare
Harbor

Cardigan •

• Fishguard

Hay-on-Wye •

• St. Davids

To
Ironbridge
Gorge

To
Rosslare
Harbor

• Pembroke

BIG PIT NAT'L
COAL MUSEUM

Monmouth •

Swansea •

TINTERN ABBEY

Chepstow

Gower
Peninsula

CAERPHILLY

Cardiff

• Newport

River

Severn

Atlantic
Ocean

ST. FAGAN'S
NATIONAL
HISTORY MUSEUM

• Bristol

50 Kilometers

50 Miles

Bristol
Channel

Bath •

WALES

symbol is the leek, ever since medieval warriors—who wore the vegetable on their helmets in battle—saved the land from Saxon invaders. Melted cheese on toast—kind of an open-faced grilled cheese sandwich—is known as "Welsh rarebit" (or "Welsh rabbit"; the name is a throwback to a time when the poor Welsh couldn't afford much meat in their diet). At breakfast, you might get some "Welsh cakes," basically a small squashed scone. Cockles and seaweed bread were once common breakfast items—but don't expect your B&B to serve them.

Wales' three million people are mostly white and Christian (Presbyterian, Anglican, or Catholic). Like their English and Scottish counterparts, they enjoy football (soccer), but rugby is the unofficial Welsh sport, more popular in Wales than in any country outside of New Zealand. Other big sports are cricket and snooker (similar to billiards).

The Welsh flag features a red dragon on a field of green and white. The dragon has been a symbol of Wales since at least the ninth century. According to legend, King Arthur's men carried the dragon flag to battle.

Welsh history stretches back into the mists of prehistoric Britain. In A.D. 43, Romans invaded Britain. Arriving in Wales about A.D. 50, they met stiff resistance from indigenous Welsh guerillas who harassed the Romans for 30 years. The Romans built a string of forts (each 12 miles—or a half-day's march—apart) along a military road, today's A-48 highway. You'll notice towns along this route that are still 12 miles apart.

The Welsh in South Wales ultimately became Romanized and Christian. When Rome checked out as the Empire fell, the Celts assumed power, adopting the Roman style of defense and the fortifications they left behind. (The dragon on the Welsh flag may originally have been a Roman military symbol.)

Saxon (Germanic) tribes like the Angles then stepped into the power vacuum, conquering what they renamed "Angle-land"—but they failed to penetrate Wales. Brave Welsh warriors, mountainous terrain, and the 177-mile manmade ditch-and-wall known as Offa's Dyke helped preserve the country's unique Celt-ic/Roman heritage.

A fixed border dividing England and Wales was established in about A.D. 780. Behind that border, Wales was a mosaic of small independent kingdoms. When the Normans beat the English at the Battle of Hastings in 1066, they moved rapidly to con-solidate greater Norman rule, and Wales sank into three centu-ries of war with generations of Norman warlords.

In 1216, Wales' medieval kingdoms unified under Llywelyn Fawr ("the Great"). But in 1282, King Edward I of England in-vaded and conquered, putting an end to Wales' one era as a uni-fied, sovereign nation. To solidify his hold on the country, Edward built a string of castles (see sidebar on page 624). He then named his son and successor the "Prince of Wales," starting the tradi-tion of granting that ceremonial title to the heir to the English throne.

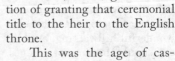

This was the age of cas-tles—man-made earthen mounds crowned by wooden forts, eventually becoming the evocative stone wonders we climb through today. The big castles you can see through-

WALES

out Wales were designed to keep the angry Welsh locals under control. Just as the Normans built the Tower of London in their capital, they built castles in Cardiff, Conwy, and Caernarfon to protect their foothold in Wales. English settlers were imported to live within the walls of the garrison town (with gardens behind their houses) and to give the place a tax base. The indigenous Welsh people, outside the walls, were called "piss poor"—back then, very poor people sold their own urine (used to soak leather in Norman tanneries) to earn a few pennies.

Despite an unsuccessful rebellion in 1400, led by Owen Glendower (Owain Glyndwr), Wales has remained under English rule ever since Edward's invasion. In 1535, the annexation was formalized under Henry VIII.

By the 19th century, Welsh coal and iron stoked the engines of Britain's Industrial Revolution, and its slate was exported to shingle roofs throughout Europe. Wales became the first country on earth with the majority of its people working in industry. That's why the Welsh didn't emigrate to North America in droves like the Scottish and Irish. Rather, the big people movement here during that era was from villages and farms to mining valleys and seaports.

While this was a lucrative boom time for wealthy industrialists, the common working people of Wales toiled under very difficult conditions. The stereotype of the Welsh as poor, grimy-faced miners continued into the 20th century. Their economy has been slow to transition from mining, factories, and sheep farming to the service-and-software model of the global world.

In recent decades, the Welsh have consciously tried to preserve their local traditions and language. In 1999, Wales was granted its own parliament, the National Assembly, with powers to distribute its portion of the UK's national budget. Though still ruled by the UK government in London, Wales now has a measure of independence and self-rule. The Plaid Cymru party, which advocates for Welsh independence, has a small percentage of Welsh seats in parliament.

Less urbanized and less wealthy than England, Wales consists of miles of green land where sheep graze (because the soil is too poor for crops). It makes for wonderful hillwalking, but hikers should beware of midges. From late May through September, these tiny biting insects are very interested in dawn, dusk, dampness, and you— bring insect repellent along on any hike.

WALES

Singing the Praises of Welsh Choirs

The Welsh love their choirs. Nearly every town has a choir (men's or mixed) that practices weekly. Visitors are usually welcome to observe the session (lasting about 1.5-2 hours), and sometimes the choir heads to the pub afterward for a good old-fashioned, beer-lubricated sing-along that you can join.

As these choir rehearsals have become something of a tourist attraction, many choirs ask attendees for a small donation—fair enough. Note that some towns have more than one choir, and schedules are subject to change (especially in Aug, when most choirs take a break from practicing); confirm the schedule with a TI or your B&B before making the trip. Additionally, many choirs regularly perform concerts—inquire for the latest schedule.

Here are choir practices that occur in or near towns I recommend visiting: **Llandudno Junction,** near **Conwy** (men's choir Mon at 19:30 except Aug, tel. 01248/681-159, www.cormaelgwn.cymru); **Caernarfon** (men's choir Tue at 19:45, arrive by 19:30 in summer to guarantee a seat, no practice in Aug, in the Galeri Creative Enterprise Centre at Victoria Dock, tel. 01286/677-404, www.cormeibioncaernarfon.org/eng); **Llangollen** (men's choir Fri at 19:30 at Hand Hotel, 21:30 pub singsong afterward, hotel tel. 01978/860-303); **Ruthin** (mixed choir Thu at 20:00 except Aug at Pwllglas Village Hall, three miles south of Ruthin in Pwllglas, mobile tel. 07724/112-984, www.corrhuthun.co.uk); and **Betws-y-Coed** (men's choir twice a month in summer, Sun at 14:00, www.cantoriongogleddcymru.co.uk; other choruses most other Sun July-Sept at 20:00; St. Anne's Church, book ahead at TI).

Because Wales is an affordable weekend destination for many English, the country is popular among avid English drinkers, who pour over the border on Friday nights for cheap beer before stumbling home on Sunday. Expect otherwise-sleepy Welsh border towns to be rowdy on Saturday nights.

I've focused most of my coverage of Wales on the north, which has the highest concentration of castles, natural beauty, and attractions. But I've also covered a few important sights in South Wales that are easy to combine with a visit to Bath or the Cotswolds (or as a quick stopover between them), including the

Welsh capital of Cardiff, its nearby top-notch open-air museum, and the picturesque Tintern Abbey.

Try to connect with Welsh culture on your visit. Clamber over a castle, eat a leek, count sheep in a field, catch a rugby match, or share a pint of bitter with a baritone. Open your ears to the sound of words as old as the legendary King Arthur. "May the old language survive!"

NORTH WALES

Conwy • Near Conwy • Caernarfon • Snowdonia National
Park • Northeast Wales

Wales' top historical, cultural, and natural wonders are found in its north. From towering Mount Snowdon to lush forests to desolate moor country, North Wales is a poem written in landscape. For sightseeing thrills and diversity, North Wales is Britain's most interesting slice of the Celtic crescent. And it's remarkably compact: In a single day you can lie on a beach, conquer a castle, spelunk in a slate mine, hike on a mountain slope, ogle a grand garden, and settle in for dinner at one of Britain's most pleasant small towns, Conwy.

Wales is wonderful, but smart travelers sort through their options carefully. Tourism dominates the local economy, and sales pitches can be aggressive. Be careful not to be waylaid by the many gimmicky sights and bogus "best of" lists.

When choosing where to sleep, the most logical options are Conwy and Caernarfon—each an old walled town attached to a castle (the two best in Wales). Conwy, the more charming of the two, makes the region's best home base, with appealing B&Bs and restaurants, a fun-to-explore townscape within mighty walls, and manageable connections to many nearby sights. Caernarfon is bigger, more blue-collar, and slightly better-connected.

At Conwy's doorstep are sumptuous Bodnant Garden and the interesting Trefriw Woolen Mills. And if two castles aren't enough, you have several more to choose from (I've also described Beaumaris, Harlech, and Criccieth).

Close by, Snowdonia National Park plunges you into some of Wales' top scenery—you can ride a train from Llanberis to the top of Mount Snowdon, learn more about the local industry at Llanberis' National Slate Museum, and explore the huggable villages

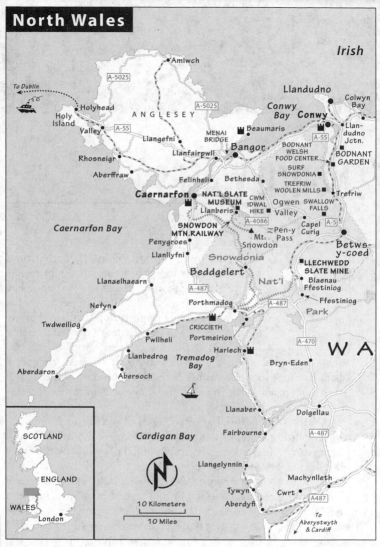

North Wales

Irish

Amlwch

To Dublin

A-5025

Holyhead   Llandudno   Colwyn Bay
Holy Island   A N G L E S E Y   Conwy Bay   Conwy   Llan-dudno Jctn.
Valley   A-55   A-5025
Rhosneigr   Llangefni   MENAI BRIDGE   Beaumaris   A-55   BONDANT WELSH FOOD CENTER   BODNANT GARDEN
Aberffraw   Llanfairpwll   Bangor   SURF SNOWDONIA
Felinheli   Bethesda   TREFIW WOOLEN MILLS   Trefriw
Caernarfon   NAT'L SLATE MUSEUM   CWM IDWAL HIKE   Ogwen Valley   SWALLOW FALLS
Llanberis   A-4086   Capel Curig   A-5
Caernarfon Bay   SNOWDON MTN. RAILWAY   Pen-y Pass   Betws-y-coed
Penygroes   Mt. Snowdon
Llanllyfni   *Snowdonia*   LLECHWEDD SLATE MINE
Beddgelert   Nat'l   Blaenau Ffestiniog
Llanaelhaearn   A-487   Ffestiniog
Nefyn   Porthmadog   A-487   *Park*
Twdweiliog   CRICCIETH   A-470
Pwllheli   Portmeirion   W A
Llanbedrog   Harlech
Aberdaron   *Tremadog Bay*   Bryn-Eden
Abersoch

Llanaber
Dolgellau
Cardigan Bay   Fairbourne   A-487

SCOTLAND

Llangelynnin
Machynlleth
ENGLAND   Tywyn   Cwrt   A487
Aberdyfi
WALES   London
To Aberystwyth & Cardiff

10 Kilometers
10 Miles

of Beddgelert and Betws-y-Coed. The tongue-twisting industrial town of Blaenau Ffestiniog invites you to tour an actual slate mine. And on the way back to England are the appealing towns of Llangollen, strikingly set in a gorge, and Ruthin, with a relaxing market-town vibe.

There's so much variety in this region—and it's all so close—that there's no single "best plan" for seeing it all. Peruse this chapter, make a wish list, and weave together a North Wales itinerary that suits your interests.

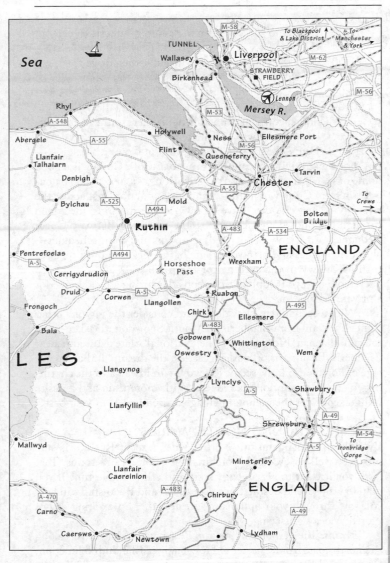

PLANNING YOUR TIME

The absolute minimum is two nights and a day; if you can spare the time, you won't regret adding an extra night (or two).

With two nights in Conwy, use your arrival and departure days to see the town and its castle, leaving your full day for side-tripping. For a "best of" North Wales itinerary, **drivers** can try this:

    9:30   Leave after breakfast.

  10:00   Visit Bodnant Garden.

12:00   Drive the gorgeous Pen-y-Pass to Llanberis (lunch on the way).

13:00   Tour the National Slate Museum, then drive to Caernarfon.

16:00   Tour Caernarfon Castle.

17:00   Scenic drive to Conwy via Beddgelert (allow 1.5 hours; consider dinner in Beddgelert) or head straight back to Conwy (45 minutes).

19:00   Dinner or my self-guided walk in Conwy.

For those relying on **public transportation,** Conwy is a good home base. Most of the region's destinations can be reached by bus or train from Conwy or nearby Llandudno Junction, just across the river. With just one day, leave Conwy in the morning for a loop through the Snowdonia sights (possibly including Betws-y-Coed, Beddgelert, or Llanberis, depending on bus and train schedules— check timetables and plan your route before heading out), then return to Conwy in the evening for the town walk and dinner. To pack more into your limited time, consider hiring a local guide for a private driving tour.

With a second day, slow down and consider the region's other sights: the train from Llanberis up Mount Snowdon, the slate-mine tour in Blaenau Ffestiniog or the National Slate Museum near Llanberis, Beaumaris or Harlech castles, the dreamy Italianate village of Portmeirion, the scenic hike to Cwm Idwal, and the charming towns of Ruthin or Llangollen. With more time and a desire to hike, consider the mountain village of Beddgelert as your base.

GETTING AROUND NORTH WALES

By Public Transportation: North Wales (except Ruthin) is surprisingly well covered by a combination of buses and trains. That said, you'll want to get an early start and allow ample time if you plan to visit several destinations. Local TIs and B&B staff can help you sort through your options to lace together an exciting day of North Wales sightseeing.

Trains: The main train line, run by Arriva Wales, travels along the north coast from Chester to Holyhead via Llandudno Junction, Conwy, and Bangor, with nearly hourly departures (tel. 0345-748-4950, www.nationalrail.co.uk or www.arrivatrainswales.co.uk; note that Virgin Trains to Holyhead do not stop in Conwy).

There are also several intersecting, scenic spur lines. From Llandudno Junction, the **Conwy Valley line** goes south to Betws-y-Coed and Blaenau Ffestiniog (5/day Mon-Sat, 3/day Sun in summer, no Sun trains in winter, www.conwyvalleyrailway.co.uk). The old-fashioned **Welsh Highland Railway** steam train goes from Caernarfon to Beddgelert (2-3 trips/day, most days late March-Oct, 1.5 hours), then loops back to the coast and Porthmadog.

North Wales at a Glance

▲▲**Conwy Castle** North Wales' best castle, in its most charming town, with stunning 360-degree views. **Hours:** Daily 9:30-17:00, July-Aug until 18:00; Nov-Feb Mon-Sat 10:00-16:00, Sun from 11:00. See page 623.

▲▲**Plas Mawr** Oldest house in Wales with a rare glimpse into 16th-century life within Conwy's walls. **Hours:** Daily 9:00-17:00, Oct 9:30-16:00, closed Nov-March. See page 623.

▲▲**Caernarfon Castle** North Wales' best-known castle, with fine exhibits, and where Welsh princes are invested. **Hours:** Daily 9:30-17:00, July-Aug until 18:00; Nov-Feb Mon-Sat 10:00-16:00, Sun from 11:00. See page 640.

▲▲**Snowdon Mountain Railway** Britain's only rack-and-pinion railway chugs up to Mount Snowdon from Llanberis. **Hours:** Weather-dependent but several daily late March-Oct generally 9:00-17:30, 10/day peak season. See page 649.

▲▲**National Slate Museum** 19th-century industrial workshop converted into an excellent museum. **Hours:** Daily 10:00-17:00; Nov-Easter Sun-Fri until 16:00, closed Sat. See page 650.

▲▲**Llechwedd Slate Caverns** Descend 400 feet into a working slate mine to learn harrowing tales of Victorian-era miners. **Hours:** Daily 9:00-17:30. See page 652.

▲▲**Plas Newydd** Tour the ornate manor home of two upper-class Irish women who ran off together and lived here in the 18th century. **Hours:** Wed-Mon 10:30-17:00, closed Tue except June-Aug; house interior closed Nov-March—but gardens open. See page 657.

▲**Bodnant Garden** One of Britain's best gardens, with 80 acres of flora amidst a craggy mountain backdrop. **Hours:** Daily 10:00-17:00, Wed until 20:00 May-Aug; Nov-Feb daily until 16:00. See page 632.

▲**Harlech Castle** Compact castle built by Edward I, with expansive sea views. **Hours:** Daily 9:30-17:00, July-Aug until 18:00; Nov-Feb Mon-Sat 10:00-16:00, Sun from 11:00. See page 653.

▲**Portmeirion** Fun faux-Italian Riviera village that's a pastel-colored, flower-filled folly. **Hours:** Daily 9:30-19:30, Nov-March until 17:30. See page 654.

NORTH WALES

Porthmadog is a terminus for the **Ffestiniog Railway** steam train (2-6/day, more in Aug, 1.25 hours), which heads into the mountains to Blaenau Ffestiniog, where it meets the Conwy Valley line.

Buses: Public buses (run by various companies) pick up where trains leave off. Get the *Public Transport Information* booklet at any TI. Certain bus lines—dubbed "Sherpa" routes (bus numbers begin with #S)—circle Snowdonia National Park with the needs of hikers in mind (www.gwynedd.gov.uk, search "Snowdon Sherpa" for timetables).

Schedules get sparse late in the afternoon and on Sundays; plan ahead and confirm times carefully at local TIs and at bus and train stations. For questions about public transportation, call the Wales Travel Line at tel. 0871-200-2233, or check www.traveline. cymru.

Your choices for money-saving public-transportation **passes** are confusing. The Red Rover Ticket—the simplest and probably the best bet for most travelers—covers all buses west of Llandudno, including Sherpa buses (£6.80/day, buy from driver). Sort through your choices at the TI to find the best deal for your itinerary.

By Car: Driving and parking throughout North Wales is easy and allows you to cover more ground. If you need to rent a car here, see "Helpful Hints," later.

By Private Tour: Mari Roberts, a Welsh guide based in Ruthin, leads driving tours of the area tailored to your interests. Tours in her car are generally out of Conwy, but she will happily pick you up in Ruthin or Holyhead (£30/hour, 4-hour minimum, £180/day, tel. 01824/702-713, marihr@talktalk.net). **Donna Goodman** leads private day trips of North Wales and walking tours of Conwy, Caernarfon, or Beaumaris, including the castles (from £180/day, book in advance, tel. 01286/677-059, mobile 07946-163-906, www. turnstone-tours.co.uk, info@turnstone-tours.co.uk).

Conwy

Along with Conwy Castle, this garrison town was built in the 1280s to give Edward I a toe-hold in Wales. As there were no real cities in 13th-century Wales, this was an English town, planted with settlers for the king's political purposes. What's left today are the best medieval walls in Britain, surrounding a humble town crowned by the bleak and barren hulk of a castle that was awesome in its day (and still is). Conwy's charming High Street leads down to a fishy harbor that permitted Edward to restock his castle safely. Because the modern highway was tunneled under the town, Conwy has a strolling ambience. I find it the perfect size—big enough to have a real vitality, but small enough to be cozy. It's one of the most purely delightful towns of its size in Britain.

Orientation to Conwy

Conwy is an enjoyably small community of 4,000 people. The walled old town center is compact and manageable. Lancaster Square marks the center, where you'll find the bus "station" (a blue-and-white bus shelter), the unstaffed train kiosk (the little white hut at the end of a sunken parking lot), and the start of the main drag—High Street—and my self-guided walk.

TOURIST INFORMATION

Conwy's TI is located across from the castle's short-stay parking lot on Rose Hill Street (Mon-Sat 9:30-17:00, Sun until 16:30, free Wi-Fi, pay WCs, tel. 01492/577-566, www.visitllandudno.org.uk). Because Conwy's train and bus "stations" are unstaffed, ask at the TI about train or bus schedules. Don't confuse the TI with the uninformative Conwy Visitors Centre, a big gift shop near the station.

ARRIVAL IN CONWY

By Bus or Train: Whether taking the bus or train, you need to tell the driver or conductor you want to stop at Conwy. Milk-run trains stop here only upon request; major trains don't stop here at all (instead, they stop at nearby Llandudno Junction—see later). For additional train info in town, ask at the TI, call tel. 0871-200-2233, or see www.traveline.cymru. If you're leaving Conwy by train, you can buy your ticket on board with no penalty.

For more frequent trains, use **Llandudno Junction,** visible a mile away beyond the bridges (to get into Conwy from here, catch the bus, take a £5 taxi, or simply walk a mile if you've packed light—it's quite scenic, especially in good weather). Make sure to ask for trains that stop at Llandudno Junction, not Llandudno proper, which is a seaside resort farther from Conwy.

By Car: The easiest parking option for day-trippers is the pay lot just behind the castle, facing the TI.

HELPFUL HINTS

Festivals: The town is eager to emphasize its medieval history, with several events and festivals annually: Pirate Weekend

(May, www.conwypirates.co.uk), the River Festival (Aug, www.conwyriverfestival.org), and a food festival, which includes a laser light show projected onto the castle (Oct, www.conwyfeast.co.uk). The town also shuts down two days a year to host a pair of 700-year-old markets: the Seed Fair (March) and the Honey Fair (Sept). Ask the TI or your B&B what might be going on during your visit.

Car Rental: Several car-rental agencies in the city of Llandudno (a mile north of Llandudno Junction) can generally deliver to you in Conwy; the Conwy TI has a list. The closest ones, in Llandudno Junction, are **Avis,** a 10-minute walk from Conwy (113a Conwy Road, tel. 0844-544-6075) and **Enterprise** (tel. 01492/593-380). Both close early on Saturday and all day Sunday.

Bike Rental: Conwy lacks its own bike-rental outfit, but **Gog-Cogs** in nearby Porth Eirias (on Colwyn Bay) can deliver a bike to you in Conwy for an extra charge (tel. 07423/010-638, www.gogcogs.co.uk).

Harbor Cruise: Two tour boats depart nearly hourly from the Conwy harborfront (£6.50/30 minutes, £9/1 hour, pay on boat, early Feb-Oct daily 10:30-17:00 or 18:00, may be cancelled for low tides, mobile 07917-343-058, www.sightseeingcruises.co.uk).

Conwy Walk

This brief self-guided orientation walk introduces you to essential Conwy in about an hour. As the town walls are open late, you can do this walk any time—evening is fine. For a shorter stroll, skip ahead to the harborfront's promenade, which is perfect for a peaceful half-mile shoreline walk (start at the Smallest House in Great Britain—listed later, under "Harborfront").

• *Start at the top of High Street on the main square.*

Lancaster Square: The square's centerpiece is a **column** honoring the town's red-cloaked founder, the Welsh prince Llywelyn the Great. Looking downhill, past the blue-and-white bus stop, find the cute pointed archway built into the medieval wall so the train could get through. Turning 180 degrees and looking uphill, you can see Bangor Gate, built by the British engineer Thomas Telford in 1826 to accommodate traffic from his suspension bridge.

• *Walk uphill on York Place, past the recommended Alfredo Restaurant, to the end of the lane.*

Slate Memorials: This wall of various memorials includes one recalling the 1937 coronation of King George VI (the father of today's Queen Elizabeth II). Also find one offering a Welsh-language lesson, donated to the town by a citizen who never learned to read and wanted to inspire others to avoid his fate. It lists, in Welsh, the counties (shires, or *sir*), months (a few are vaguely recognizable), days, numbers, and the Welsh alphabet with its unique letters (CH, DD, FF, NG, LL, PH, and TH). Much has changed since this memorial was posted. Today more people speak Welsh, and all local children are taught Welsh in school until age 12.

• *Turn left and walk uphill on Upper Gate Street all the way to the wall, where steps lead to the ramparts. At the top of the stairs, head left and continue climbing to the very top of the town's tallest turret.*

Tallest Tower and Walls: You're standing atop the most complete set of medieval town walls in Britain. In 1283, workers started to build them in conjunction with the castle. Four years later, they sent a message to London declaring, "Castle habitable, town defensible." Edward then sent in English settlers. Enjoy the view from the top all the way down to Conwy Castle, at the opposite corner of town (and the end point of this walk). From up here, guards could spot ships approaching by sea.

• *Continue downhill around the ramparts.*

Ramparts: The turrets you see were positioned about every 50 yards, connected by ramparts, and each one had a drawbridge that could be raised to bottle up any breach. Passing the second turret, notice that its wall is cracked. When they tunneled underneath this turret for the train, the construction accidentally undermined the foundation, effectively taking the same tactic that invading armies would have. The huge crack makes plain why undermining was such a popular technique in medieval warfare. (Unlike the town walls, Conwy Castle was built upon solid rock, so it couldn't be undermined.)

• *At the first opportunity (just after walking above Bangor Gate), take the steps back down to street level. Then leave the old town by passing through Bangor Gate, heading downhill, and crossing the street for the best wide view of the walls.*

The Walls (from Outside): You are walking down Town Ditch Road, named for the dry moat that was the first line of defense from the highest tower down to the riverbank. As was the case with most walled towns, there was a clear swath of "dead ground" outside the walls, so no one could sneak up. Once England centralized and consolidated its rule, there was no longer a use for all the walls and castles in Britain. Most fell into disrepair—ravaged by time and by scavengers who used them as quarries. During the Napoleonic Wars, English aristocrats were unable to make their Grand Tour of the Continent, so they explored the far reaches of their own land. That's when ruined castles such as this one were "discovered" and began to be appreciated for their romantic allure.

• *Stroll downhill to the bottom of Town Ditch Road. At the elderly-crossing sign (which also serves as a reminder to stand up straight), re-*

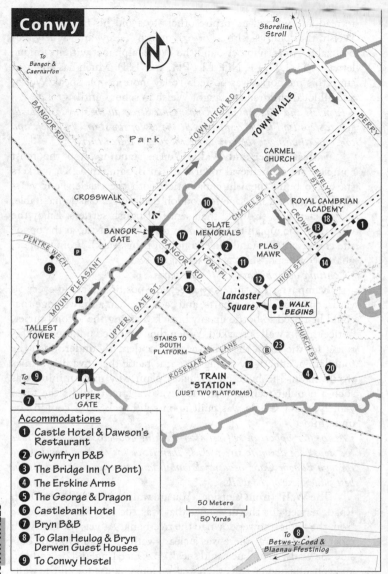

Conwy

To Shoreline Stroll

To Bangor & Caernarfon

BANGOR RD.

TOWN DITCH RD.

TOWN WALLS

BERRY

Park

CARMEL CHURCH

CROSSWALK

LLEWELYN ST.

ROYAL CAMBRIAN ACADEMY

BANGOR GATE

SLATE MEMORIALS

CHAPEL ST.

CROWN LN.

13 **18** **1**

PENTRE WECH

17

10

2

PLAS MAWR

11

HIGH ST.

14

MOUNT PLEASANT

6

19

BANGOR RD.

YORK PL.

12

21

Lancaster Square

WALK BEGINS

TALLEST TOWER

UPPER GATE ST.

STAIRS TO SOUTH PLATFORM

CHURCH ST.

B **23**

To **9**

ROSEMARY LANE

TRAIN "STATION" (JUST TWO PLATFORMS)

20

4

7

UPPER GATE

50 Meters

50 Yards

To **8**
Betws-y-Coed & Blaenau Ffestiniog

Accommodations

1 Castle Hotel & Dawson's Restaurant
2 Gwynfryn B&B
3 The Bridge Inn (Y Bont)
4 The Erskine Arms
5 The George & Dragon
6 Castlebank Hotel
7 Bryn B&B
8 To Glan Heulog & Bryn Derwen Guest Houses
9 To Conwy Hostel

enter the old town—crossing through a hole cut in the wall by a modern mayor who wanted better access from his land—and walk down Berry Street. Originally called "Burial Street," it was a big ditch for mass burials during a 17th-century plague. After one block, turn right, climbing up Chapel Street to an austere stone structure.

Carmel Church: This Presbyterian church is a fine example of stark "statement architecture"—stern, no-frills, and typical of churches built in the early 20th century. Even very small Welsh

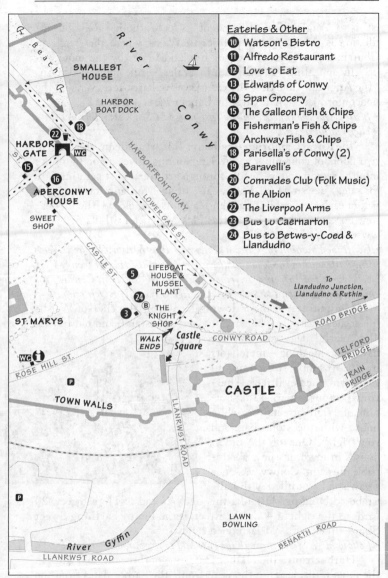

Eateries & Other

⑩ Watson's Bistro
⑪ Alfredo Restaurant
⑫ Love to Eat
⑬ Edwards of Conwy
⑭ Spar Grocery
⑮ The Galleon Fish & Chips
⑯ Fisherman's Fish & Chips
⑰ Archway Fish & Chips
⑱ Parisella's of Conwy (2)
⑲ Baravelli's
⑳ Comrades Club (Folk Music)
㉑ The Albion
㉒ The Liverpool Arms
㉓ Bus to Caernarfon
㉔ Bus to Betws-y-Coed & Llandudno

NORTH WALES

towns tend to have churches for several Christian denominations. (The Welsh have a reputation for nonconformity, even contentiousness—as the saying goes, "Get two Welshmen together, and you'll have an argument. Get three together, and you'll have a fight.") In the 18th and 19th centuries, Welsh Christians who didn't want to worship in the official, English-style Anglican Church joined "nonconformist" congregations, such as Methodists, Congregationalists, Quakers, or Presbyterians. You could say "nonconformist" is to "Anglican" as "Protestant" is to "Catholic." Religious affiliation is closely tied to politics in Wales, where the Anglican Church, a.k.a. "The Church of England," goes by the more politically appealing "The Church in Wales." Still, many Welsh say, "The Anglican Church is the Conservative Party at prayer, and the nonconformist churches are the Labour Party at prayer."

• *Just beyond the church (on the left, just past Sea View Terrace), in a modern building, is...*

The Royal Cambrian Academy: This art academy, showing off two floors of contemporary Welsh painting, gives a good glimpse into the region and its people through art (free, most paintings are for sale; Tue-Sat 11:00-17:00, closed Sun-Mon and for one week before each new exhibition, shorter hours and closed Tue off-season; on Crown Lane just above Plas Mawr, tel. 01492/593-413, www.rcaconwy.org).

• *Continue downhill on Crown Lane past **Plas Mawr**. The first Welsh house built within the town walls, it dates from the time of Henry VIII (well worth touring, and described later, under "Sights in Conwy"; the entrance is a few steps to the right, up High Street). Turn left onto...*

High Street: Wander downhill, enjoying this slice-of-Welsh-life scene—tearooms, bakery, butcher, newsstand, and old timers.

The colorful flags you may see have no meaning—merchants fly them simply to pump up the town's medieval feel. **Aberconwy House** marks the bottom of High Street (the white house with the stone base, on your right). One of the oldest houses in town, it's now a skippable museum. Conwy was once a garrison town filled with half-

timbered buildings just like this one. At end of High Street, 20 yards to the right at 4 Castle Street, is the **Penny Farthing Sweet Shop**—filled with old-fashioned candy.

• *Follow High Street through the gate and to the harbor.*

Harborfront: The Harbor Gate, one of three original gates in the town walls, leads to the waterfront. The harbor dates from the 13th century, when it served Edward's castle and town. (The harborfront street is still called King's Quay.) Conwy was once a busy slate port. Slate, barged downstream to here, was loaded onto big three-masted ships and transported to the Continent. Back when much of Europe was roofed with Welsh slate, Conwy was a boomtown. All the mud is new—the modern bridge caused this part of the river to silt up.

The actions of the European Union have had a mixed effect on this waterfront. EU money helped pay for the recently built promenade, but hygiene laws have forced Conwy's fishermen out: Now that fish must be transported in refrigerated vehicles, the fishermen had to set up shop a few miles away (since refrigerator trucks can't fit through the stone gate).

Conwy's harbor is now a laid-back area that locals treat like a town square. On summer evenings, the action is on the quay (pronounced "key"). The scene is mellow, multigenerational, and perfectly Welsh. It's a small town, and everyone is here enjoying the local cuisine—"chips," ice cream, and beer—and savoring that great British pastime: torturing little crabs. (If you want to do more than photograph the action, rent gear from the nearby lifeboat house. Mooch some bacon from others for bait, and join in. It's catch-and-release.)

The benches and knee-high walls all along here are ideal for a picnic (two recommended fish-and-chips shops are back through the gate). Just be wary of those noisy gulls taking an interest in your food: They're notorious for swooping in and stealing your lunch while you're distracted.

Just next to the Harbor Gate is **The Liverpool Arms** pub, built by a captain who ran a ferry service to Liverpool in the 19th century. Today it remains a salty and characteristic hangout—one of the few thriving pubs in town. In 1900, Conwy had about 40 pubs. Back when this harbor was busy with quarrymen shipping their slate, mussel men carting their catch, and small farmers with their goods, Conwy's pubs were all thriving. Today, times are tough on the pubs, and this one depends on tourism.

• *Facing the harbor in front of The Liverpool Arms, turn left and walk along the promenade.*

It's easy to miss the **Smallest House in Great Britain.** It's red, 72 inches wide, 122 inches high, and worth £1 to pop in and listen to the short audioguide tour. No WC—but it did have a bedpan (April-Oct daily 10:00-16:00, closed Nov-March, mobile 07925-049-786).

• *Now do an about-face and walk along the promenade in the opposite direction, toward the bridges and castle.*

About 100 yards down, on your right, you'll find a **mussel processing plant.** Mussels, historically a big "crop" for Conwy, are processed "in the months with an R." If there's a fresh catch, you'll find a little shop here; you can read information panels about mussels anytime.

NORTH WALES

The nearby **lifeboat house** welcomes visitors. Each coastal town has a house like this one, outfitted with a rescue boat suited to the area—in the shallow waters around Conwy, inflatable boats work best. You'll see *Lifeboats* stickers around town, marking homes of people who donate to the valuable cause of the Royal National Lifeboat Institution (RNLI)—Britain's all-volunteer and totally donation-funded answer to the Coast Guard.

Check out the striking **sculpture** on the quay—a giant clump of mussels carved from dark-gray limestone.

• *Walk past the sculpture and head up the stairs by the huge red-and-white buoy to the big street for a view of the castle and bridges. You can cross the road for a closer look at the...*

Bridges: Three bridges cross the river, side by side. Behind the modern 1958 highway bridge is the historic 1826 Telford Suspension Bridge. This was an engineering marvel in its day, part of a big infrastructure project to better connect Ireland with the rest of the realm (and, as a result, have more control over Ireland). In those days, Dublin was the number-two city in all of Britain. These two major landmarks—the castle and 19th-century bridge—are both symbols of English imperialism. Just beyond that is Robert Stephenson's tube bridge for the train line (built in 1848). These days, 90 percent of traffic passes Conwy underground, unseen and unheard, in a modern tunnel.

• *On the town side of the big road, follow the sidewalk away from the water, past the ivy and through an arch, to a tiny park around a well. Facing that square is...*

The Knight Shop: If you're in the market for a battle-axe or perhaps some chainmail, pop in here. Even if you're not, it's a fun place to browse. The manager, Toby, is evangelical about mead, an ancient drink made from honey. Most travelers just get the cheap stuff at tourist shops, but Toby offers free tastes to help you appreciate quality mead (daily 10:00-17:00, Castle Square, tel. 01492/596-142, www.theknightshop.com).

• *Now, with a belly full of mead, set your bleary eyes on the...*

View of Conwy Castle: Imagine this castle when it was newly built. Its eight mighty drum towers were brightly whitewashed, a statement of power from the English king to the Welsh—who had no cities and little more than bows and arrows to fight with. The castle is built upon solid rock—making it impossible for invaders to tunnel underneath the walls. The English paid dearly for its construction, through heavy taxes. And today, with the Welsh flag proudly flying from its top, the English pay again just to visit. Notice the remains of the castle entry, which was within the town walls. There was once a steep set of stairs (designed so no horse could approach) up to the drawbridge. The castle is by far the town's top sight (described next).

Sights in Conwy

▲▲Conwy Castle

Dramatically situated on a rock overlooking the sea with eight linebacker towers, this castle has an interesting story to tell. Finished

in just four years, it had a water gate that allowed safe entry for English boats in a land of hostile Welsh subjects. This is my favorite of the many castles in North Wales—it's compact, fun to explore, and has the best views.

Cost and Hours: £8.95, £10.80 combo-ticket with Plas Mawr; daily 9:30-17:00, July-Aug until 18:00; Nov-Feb Mon-Sat 10:00-16:00, Sun from 11:00; guidebook-£5, tel. 01492/592-358, www.cadw.wales.gov.uk.

Visiting the Castle: The exhibits are paltry, so just enjoy exploring the place and climbing its ramparts and towers. Entering the main courtyard, head to the far end (past the 91-foot-deep, spring-fed well) and go through the Middle Gate to access the main courtyard. Of the four perfectly round towers here, you can climb to the very top of three of them—each one with stunning 360-degree views over the entire area. In the base of the Chapel Tower is a scale model of the town as it might have looked around the year 1312. Heading up a flight of stairs, you'll find a small chapel (with reconstructed stained-glass windows) and—up another flight of stairs—the king's "watching chamber" (for observing chapel services by himself...complete with a private toilet).

▲City Walls

Most of the walls, with 22 towers and castle and harbor views, can be walked for free. Start at Upper Gate (the highest point) or Berry Street (the lowest), or you can do the small section at the castle entrance. (My favorite stretch is described on my "Conwy Walk," earlier.) In the evening, most of the walkways stay open, though the section located near the castle closes 30 minutes before the castle does.

▲▲Plas Mawr

A rare house from 1580, built during the reign of Elizabeth I, Plas Mawr was the first Welsh home to be built within Conwy's walls. (The Tudor family had Welsh roots—and therefore relations between Wales and England warmed.) Billed as "the oldest house in Wales," it offers a delightful look at 16th-century domestic life, with gorgeous plasterwork throughout. Historically accurate household

King Edward's Castles

The castles of Wales hover in the mist as mysterious reminders of the country's hard-fought history. In the 13th century, the Welsh, unified by two great princes named Llywelyn, created a united and independent Wales. The English king, Edward I, fought hard to end this Welsh sovereignty. In 1282, Llywelyn the Last was killed (and went "where everyone speaks Welsh"). King Edward spent the next 20 years building or rebuilding 17 great castles to consolidate his English foot-hold in troublesome North Wales. The greatest of these (such as Conwy Castle) were masterpieces of medieval en-gineering, with round towers

(tough to undermine), castle-within-a-castle defenses (giving defenders a place to retreat and wreak havoc on the advancing enemy...or just wait for reinforcements), and sea access (safe to restock from England).

These castles were English islands in the middle of angry Wales. Most were built with a fortified grid-plan town attached and then filled with English settlers. (With this blatant abuse of Wales, you have to wonder, where was Greenpeace 700 years ago?) Edward I was arguably England's most successful mon-arch. By establishing and consolidating his realm (adding Wales to England), he made his kingdom big enough to compete with other rising European powers.

Edward I's "big five" border castles—listed next—are all with-in about an hour's drive of each other. Doing all five is overkill for most visitors. When choosing your castle, consider the town at-tached to each. Compared to Caernarfon, Conwy is more quaint, with a higgledy-piggledy medieval vibe and a modern workaday heart and soul. Conwy also has more accommodations and good eateries than Caernarfon, making it a better home base.

items bring the rooms to life, as does the refreshing lack of velvet ropes—you're free to wander as you imagine life in this house. Un-like the austere Welsh castles, here you'll feel like you're visiting a home where the 16th-century owner has just stepped out for a minute.

Cost and Hours: £6.50, £10.80 combo-ticket with Conwy Castle, includes audioguide; daily 9:00-17:00, Oct 9:30-16:00, closed Nov-March; last entry 45 minutes before closing, tel. 01492/580-167, www.cadw.wales.gov.uk.

Visiting the House: At the entry, pick up the included au-

The castles themselves are mostly variations on the same theme, with modest, mildly interesting exhibits and lots of stony stairs to climb. You'll hike to the top of towers, stroll along ramparts, and peer into grassy, open courtyards. To help you choose, here's a quick rundown—listed roughly in my order of preference:

▲▲ **Conwy** is my favorite castle in North Wales. It's a bit more ruined and less slick than Caernarfon, but in a way, that makes it more evocative. It's compact and has the best views (see page 623).

▲▲ **Caernarfon** is the most famous of the castles. With several entertaining exhibits inside, it's probably the best presented (see page 640).

▲ **Harlech** has perhaps the most dramatic setting, perched on a hillside next to the cute town of Blaenau Ffestiniog, with sweeping views (see page 653).

▲ **Beaumaris,** surrounded by a moat on the Isle of Anglesey, is the last and largest of Edward's castles. It was never finished, but would've been the quintessential medieval castle if it had been (see page 636).

Criccieth (KRICK-ith), the smallest of the five, is perched on a hilltop over the sea near Snowdonia National Park. The views *from* the castle are magnificent, but there's very little to see inside (see page 655).

If you have a big appetite for castles, a car and two days gives you one of Europe's best castle tours. All five castles are operated by Cadw (KAH-dew), the Welsh version of England's National Trust, and share similar opening hours (daily 9:30-17:00, July-Aug until 18:00; Nov-Feb Mon-Sat 10:00-16:00, Sun from 11:00). Criccieth has slightly shorter hours (see listing).

If you're visiting at least three of the castles, consider Cadw's three-day Explorer Pass, which covers the castles plus many other sights in Wales (£17.50, £27 for 2 people, £37 for a family; 7-day pass available; buy at castle ticket offices). For more information on the castles and other Welsh historic monuments, see www.cadw.wales.gov.uk.

NORTH WALES

dioguide—it's engagingly narrated by family members who lived here. Docents, who are posted in some rooms, are happy to answer your questions—take advantage of their enthusiasm.

Guests stepping into the house in the 16th century were wowed by the heraldry over the fireplace. This symbol, now repainted in its original bright colors, proclaimed the family's rich lineage and princely stock. The kitchen came with all the circa-1600 conveniences: hay on the floor to add a little warmth and soak up spills; a hanging bread cage to keep food safe from wandering critters; and a good supply of fresh meat in the pantry. Inside the parlor, an interactive display lets you take a closer virtual look at the different parts of the house. The brewhouse is where the family made their own ale.

Upstairs, the lady of the house's bedroom doubled as a sitting room—with a finely carved four-poster bed and a foot warmer by the chair. At night, the bedroom's curtains were drawn to keep in warmth. In the great chamber next door, hearty evening feasting was followed by boisterous gaming, dancing, and music. And fixed above all this extravagant entertainment was...more heraldry, pronouncing those important—if unproven—family connections, and leaving a powerful impact on impressed guests. On the same floor is a well-done exhibit on health and hygiene in medieval Britain—you'll be grateful you were born a few centuries later.

Don't bother climbing the many stairs to the top of the tower—the views from the castle and town wall are better.

St. Mary's Parish Church

Sitting lonely in the town center, Conwy's church was the centerpiece of a Cistercian abbey that stood here a century before the town or castle. The Cistercians were French monks who built their abbeys in places "far from the haunts of man." Popular here because they were French—that is, not English—the Cistercians taught locals farming and mussel-gathering techniques. Edward moved the monks 12 miles upstream but kept the church for his town. Out in the churchyard, find the tombstone of a survivor of the 1805 Battle of Trafalgar who died in 1860 (two feet left of the north transept). On the other side of the church, a tomb containing seven brothers and sisters is marked "We Are Seven." It inspired William Wordsworth to write his poem of the same name. The slate tombstones look new even though many are hundreds of years old; slate weathers better than marble.

Cost and Hours: Free, church generally open Mon-Fri 10:00-12:00 & 14:00-16:00, closed Sat-Sun though you can try visiting before or after the Sunday services at 11:00, tel. 01492/593-402, www.stmarysconwy.org.uk.

JUST BEYOND CONWY
Hill Climb

For lovely views across the bay to Llandudno, take a pleasant walk (40 minutes one-way) along the footpath up Conwy Mount (follow

NORTH WALES

Sychnant Pass Road past the recommended Bryn B&B, look for fields on the right and a sign with a stick figure of a walker).

For an even more satisfying, extended version of this hike, begin at the top of the pass. Drivers should look for the pull-out on the left with hiking signs, just past the Pensychnant Conservation Centre. Or, so that you don't have to backtrack to fetch your car later, take a taxi or bum a ride from a friendly local (such as your B&B host). From the parking lot, it's about an hour-long walk along a lovely ridgeline with gorgeous 360-degree views. After about 10 minutes, the official Wales Coastal Trail veers to the right; at this point, bear left and follow the gravel path over the peaks for a higher vantage point. Eventually you'll rejoin the official path and pop out into the suburbs of Conwy. The hike is easy to moderate, with a bit of steep climbing up and down on loose-gravel trails.

Llandudno

This genteel Victorian beach resort, a few miles away, is much bigger and better known than Conwy. It was built after the advent of railroads, which made the Welsh seacoast easily accessible to the English industrial heartland. In the 1800s, the notion that bathing in seawater was good for your health was trendy, and the bracing sea air was just what the doctor ordered. These days, Llandudno remains popular with the English, but you won't see many other foreigners strolling its long pleasure pier and line of old-time hotels. If the weather is nice, it's worth checking out if only to see how middle-class Brits like to holiday.

Nightlife in Conwy

No one goes to Conwy for wild nightlife. But you will find some typically Welsh diversions here.

In Town: The **Conwy Folk Music Club** plays at the Comrades Club off Church Street Mondays at 20:30. Note that this isn't local, Welsh-language folk music, but amateurs performing a variety of folk tunes from every region and era (free, doors open at 20:00, www.conwyfolkclub.org.uk).

To sample local brews, including some made in Conwy, head to **The Albion.** Managed by a coalition of four local breweries, the Albion has real ales and a fun communal pub atmosphere (Sun-Thu 12:00-23:00, Fri-Sat until 24:00, Upper Gate Street, tel. 01492/582-484, www.conwybrewery.co.uk). The same people run **The Bridge (Y Bont)** at the other end of town, near the castle (this location—unlike the Albion—also has food; Rose Hill Street, tel. 01492/572-974).

Near Conwy: For an authentic Welsh experience, catch a performance of the **local choir.** The Maelgwn men's choir from nearby

Llandudno Junction rehearses weekly, and visitors are welcome to watch (free, Mon 19:30-21:00 except Aug, call ahead to confirm, at Awel y Mynydd School, Pen Dyffryn, Llandudno Junction, tel. 01492/534-115, www.cormaelgwn.cymru).

Several churches in Llandudno hold regular **choir concerts** in summer. Concerts at St. John's Church feature a rotation of visiting choirs (£7, May-Oct Tue and Thu at 20:00, between the two Marks & Spencer stores at 53 Mostyn Street, tel. 01492/860-439, www.stjohnsllandudno.org). The Llanddulas Choir performs weekly concerts at Gloddaeth Church (£5, April-Sept most Tue at 20:00, corner of Chapel Street and Gloddaeth Street, www.llanddulaschoir.co.uk).

Llandudno also has the **beach fun** you'd expect at a Coney-Island-type coastal resort.

Sleeping in Conwy

Conwy's hotels are overpriced, but its B&Bs include some good-value gems. Nearly all have free parking (ask when booking). There's no launderette; the closest one is in Llandudno Junction, a short drive (or bus or taxi ride) away.

INSIDE CONWY'S WALLED OLD TOWN

Note that on summer weekends, bar-hoppers and revelers can make the Old Town a bit noisy: Ask for a quieter room or pack earplugs.

$$$ Castle Hotel, along the main drag, rents 28 dated but comfortable rooms where Old World antique furnishings mingle with modern amenities (RS%, High Street, tel. 01492/582-800, www.castlewales.co.uk, castle@innmail.co.uk, Joe Lavin).

$$ Gwynfryn B&B is located dead center in town, a few steps off Lancaster Square. The five rooms in their main house are bright and airy, each with eclectic decor, and there's a plush shared lounge. In the old chapel next door, they've converted the vestry into four utilitarian, less-charming but well-designed rooms. The main part of the church is now a striking breakfast room, with pews and a big organ looming overhead (one cheaper room with private bathroom down the hall, no children under 15, free parking nearby, self-catering cottage for 4 available, 4 York Place, on the lane off Lancaster Square, tel. 01492/576-733, mobile 07947-272-821, www.bedandbreakfastconwy.co.uk, info@gwynfrynbandb.co.uk, energetic Monica and Colin).

Rooms in Pubs: While I'd opt for one of the fine B&Bs listed here, if they're full you can usually get a room at a pub in town. **$$ The Bridge Inn (Y Bont),** with six straightforward rooms close to the castle, has lots of stairs, and its location on a busy roundabout makes traffic noise unavoidable (Rose Hill Street, tel. 01492/572-

974, www.bridgeinnconwy.co.uk). **$$ The Erskine Arms,** a newer place, rents 10 rooms (10 Church Street, tel. 01492/593-535, www. erskinearms.co.uk). **$$$ The George and Dragon** has seven modern rooms in the heart of town; while comfortable, they're not the best value (21 Castle Street, tel. 01492/584-232, www. georgeanddragonconwy.com).

JUST OUTSIDE THE WALL

These options are just a few paces from Conwy's old town wall.

$$ Castlebank Hotel feels old-time plush, with nine exuberantly decorated rooms—some quite spacious, a small bar, and an inviting lounge with a wood-burning fireplace that makes the Welsh winter warmer (RS%, family rooms, DVD library, easy parking, closed first 3 weeks in Jan, just outside town wall at Mount Pleasant, tel. 01492/593-888, www.castlebankhotel.co.uk, bookings@castlebankhotel.co.uk, Jo and Henrique).

$$ Bryn B&B offers four large, tastefully decorated rooms (and one small one) with castle or mountain views in a big 19th-century house with the city wall literally in the backyard. Owner Alison Archard runs the place with style and energy, providing all the thoughtful touches—a library of regional guides and maps, a glorious garden, granny's Welsh cakes for breakfast, and a very warm welcome (one room with private bathroom next door, ground-floor room available, private parking, just outside Upper Gate of wall on Sychnant Pass Road, tel. 01492/592-449, www.bryn.org.uk, stay@bryn.org.uk).

BEYOND THE OLD TOWN

The first two places, both good-value options with free parking, share a building overlooking Llanrwst Road on the way to Betws-y-Coed, about a 10-minute walk from the center.

$ Glan Heulog Guest House offers seven bright rooms and a pleasant, enclosed sun porch (one room with private bathroom downstairs, family suite, will pick you up at the train station, tel. 01492/593-845, www.conwy-bedandbreakfast.co.uk, stay@conwy-bedandbreakfast.co.uk, Richard and Jenny Nash).

$ Bryn Derwen Guest House rents six modern rooms that feel tidy and contemporary (family rooms, tel. 01492/596-134, www. conwybrynderwen.co.uk, info@conwybrynderwen.co.uk, Andrew and Jill).

¢ Conwy Hostel, welcoming travelers of any age, has super views from all 25 rooms and a spacious garden. The airy dining hall and glorious rooftop lounge and deck make you feel like you're in the majestic midst of Wales (breakfast extra, laundry, lockers, packed lunches, dinners, bar, elevator, parking, staffed 24 hours, check-in at 15:00, Sychnant Pass Road in Larkhill, tel. 01492/593-

NORTH WALES

571, www.yha.org.uk, conwy@yha.org.uk). It's a 10-minute uphill walk from the Upper Gate of Conwy's wall.

Eating in Conwy

All of these places are inside Conwy's walled old town. For dinner, consider strolling down High Street, comparing the cute teahouses and workaday eateries. With limited options for a good sit-down meal, Conwy gets booked up on summer weekends: Reserve ahead on Friday or Saturday night.

$$$$ Watson's Bistro, tucked away on Chapel Street, serves freshly prepared modern and traditional Welsh cuisine in a warm wood-floor-and-exposed-beam setting. Dishes are made from locally sourced ingredients and well worth the splurge. It's more affordable if you get the early-bird special, served weekdays before 18:30 (open Tue 17:30-20:00, Wed-Sun 12:00-14:00 & 17:30-20:30, until later Fri-Sat, closed Mon, reservations smart, tel. 01492/596-326, www.watsonsbistroconwy.co.uk).

$$$ Dawson's Restaurant, in the recommended Castle Hotel, has a good selection of seafood and other dishes. The same menu is served in both the dressy restaurant and the more casual bar (daily 12:00-21:30, High Street, tel. 01492/582-800, www.castlewales.co.uk).

$$ Alfredo Restaurant, a thriving and family-friendly place right on Lancaster Square, serves decent, reasonably priced Italian food (daily 18:00-22:00, York Place, tel. 01492/592-381, Christine).

$ Love to Eat dishes up cheap, hearty daily specials, salads, and homemade sweets in a cheery setting (daily 9:00-17:00, until 16:30 in winter, 26 High Street, tel. 01492/596-445).

Pub Food: Conwy doesn't have a proper gastropub, but a few pubs serve up the standards. **$$ The Bridge (Y Bont)** is probably your best bet (food served daily 12:00-14:00 & 17:30-20:30, Rose Hill Street, tel. 01492/572-974). **$$$ The Erskine Arms,** at the top of Rose Hill Street, has a classy setting with good food (daily 11:30-23:00, 10 Church Street, tel. 01492/593-535).

Takeaway and Picnics: A well-respected butcher right on High Street, **$ Edwards of Conwy** has a deli counter serving top-quality and affordably priced meals to go, including hot or cold sandwiches and curries (Mon-Sat 7:00-17:30, closed Sun, 18 High Street, tel. 01492/581-111). The **Spar** grocery is conveniently located and well-stocked (daily 7:00-23:00, middle of High Street).

At the bottom of High Street, on the intersecting Castle Street, are two **$** chippies—**The Galleon** (daily 12:00-19:00 in summer, until 15:00 off-season weekdays, closed Nov-mid-March, mobile 07899-901-637) and **Fisherman's** (daily 11:30-20:00, closes earlier off-season, small sit-down area, tel. 01492/593-792).

$$ Archway Fish & Chips, at the top of town just inside Bangor Gate, is open later and has both a restaurant and takeaway service (takeout daily 11:30-22:00, restaurant daily until 20:00, 10 Bangor Road, tel. 01492/592-458). Consider taking your fish-and-chips down to the harbor and sharing it with the noisy seagulls.

Sweets: Parisella's of Conwy has some of the best ice cream I've enjoyed in Britain, including some unusual flavors. They have locations on High Street and along the harborfront (both typically daily 10:00-19:30 in summer). Near Lancaster Square, **Baravelli's** makes their own top-end chocolates, which have earned a national reputation (Mon-Sat 10:00-17:00, Sun 11:00-16:00, 13 Bangor Road, tel. 01492/330-0540).

Conwy Connections

If you want to leave Conwy by train, be sure the schedule indicates the train can stop there, then wave as it approaches; for more frequent trains, go to Llandudno Junction (see "Arrival in Conwy," earlier). Train schedules are posted at street level before you descend to the platforms. There's no ticket machine on the Conwy platform; buy your ticket from the conductor. For train info, call 0871-200-2233, or see www.traveline.cymru. If hopping around by bus, simply buy the £6.80 Red Rover Ticket from the driver, and you're covered for the entire day on buses running west of Llandudno. Remember, all connections are less frequent on Sundays.

From Conwy by Bus to: Llandudno Junction (4/hour, 5 minutes), **Caernarfon** (2-4/hour, 1.5 hours, transfer in Bangor), **Betws-y-Coed** (hourly, 45 minutes, fewer on Sun), **Blaenau Ffestiniog** (8/day, none on Sun, 1 hour, transfer in Llandudno Junction to bus #X1, also stops in Betws-y-Coed; train is better—see later), **Beddgelert** (6/day Mon-Sat, none on Sun, 2 hours total, requires 2 transfers—in Bangor and Caernarfon).

From Conwy by Train to: Llandudno Junction (nearly hourly, 5 minutes), **Chester** (nearly hourly, 1 hour), **Holyhead** (nearly hourly, 1 hour), **Llangollen** (7/day, 2 hours; take train to Ruabon, then change to bus #5), **London's Euston Station** (nearly hourly, 3.5 hours, transfer in Chester).

From Llandudno Junction by Train to the Conwy Valley: Take the train to Llandudno Junction, where you'll board the scenic little Conwy Valley line, which runs up the pretty Conwy Valley to **Betws-y-Coed** and **Blaenau Ffestiniog** (5/day Mon-Sat, 3/day on Sun in summer, no Sun trains in winter, 30 minutes to Betws-y-Coed, 1 hour to Blaenau Ffestiniog, www.conwyvalleyrailway.co.uk). If your train from Conwy to Llandudno Junction is late and you miss the Conwy Valley connection, tell a station employee at Llandudno Junction, who can arrange a taxi for you. Your taxi is free, as long as the missed connection is the Conwy train's fault *and* the next train doesn't leave for more than an hour (common on the infrequent Conwy Valley line).

From Llandudno Junction by Train to: Chester (3/hour, 1 hour), **Birmingham** (3/day direct, 2.5 hours, more with transfers), **London**'s Euston Station (5/day direct, 3 hours, many more with transfers).

Near Conwy

SOUTH OF CONWY

These sights are on the route to Betws-y-Coed and Snowdonia National Park. Note that Bodnant Garden is on the east side of the River Conwy, on the A-470, while Trefriw and Surf Snowdonia are on the west side, along the B-5106. To see sights on both sides, you'll drive about 20 minutes and cross the river at Tal-y-Cafn.

▲Bodnant Garden

This sumptuous 80-acre display of floral color six miles south of Conwy is one of Britain's best gardens—it's worth ▲▲▲ for gar-

deners and nature lovers. Originally the private garden of the stately Bodnant Hall, this lush landscape was donated by the Aberconway family (who still live in the house) to the National Trust in 1949. The map you receive upon entering helps you navigate the sprawling grounds. The highlight for many is the famous Laburnum Arch—a 180-foot-long canopy made of bright-yellow laburnum, hanging like stalactites over the heads of garden lovers who stroll beneath it (just inside the entry, blooms late May through early June). The garden is also famous for its magnolias, rhododendrons, camellias, and roses—and for the way that the buildings of the estate complement the carefully planned landscaping—all with a backdrop of rolling hills and craggy Welsh mountains. The wild English-style plots seem to spar playfully with the more formal rose gardens along the terrace. Victorian explorers donated rare species to the owners—try to find an American redwood tree and Himalayan poppies. Consider your visit an extravagantly beautiful nature hike, and walk all the way to the old mill and waterfall. If you're going to devote substantial time to any garden in Britain, this one deserves serious consideration.

Cost and Hours: £12; daily 10:00-17:00, Wed until 20:00 May-Aug; Nov-Feb daily until 16:00; multiple cafés, WCs in parking lot and inside garden, best in spring, check online to see what's blooming and get a schedule of guided walks, tel. 01492/650-460, www.nationaltrust.org.uk/bodnant-garden.

Getting There: To reach the garden by public transportation from Conwy, first take a bus or train to Llandudno Junction, then catch bus #25 (6/day Mon-Sat, 30 minutes, direction: Eglwysbach; on Sun take bus #X19, 4/day, 20 minutes, direction: Betws-y-Coed or Dolwyddelan).

Nearby: About 1.5 miles south of Bodnant Garden off the A-470, the **Bodnant Welsh Food Centre** has a farm shop selling mostly food produced in Wales, a restaurant, an underwhelming tearoom, and a cooking school (Mon-Sat 9:30-17:00, Sun 10:00-16:00, tel. 01492/651-100, www.bodnant-welshfood.co.uk). It's also the home of the National Beekeeping Centre, which features an interesting exhibit on bees and honey production and offers paid tours of its beehives in nice weather (closed Mon, tel. 01492/651-106, www.beeswales.co.uk).

Surf Snowdonia

The world's largest simulated wave pool is improbably located in a tranquil Welsh valley, where surfers and amateurs alike can pay to ride perfect waves in the "wave garden." They offer lessons for beginners, or experienced surfers can simply rent time in the pool (check website for specifics, and to book ahead). Even if you're not looking to surf, this can be a good spot to grab lunch while you watch the lagoon action. They also have a kids' activity pool, as well as "glamping" pods for a unique overnight experience.

Cost and Hours: Surf lessons -£55, one hour of time for experienced surfers-£50, rentable boards and wetsuits, daily 8:30-23:00—waves run until sunset, 3 miles north of Trefriw in the village of Dolgarrog, tel. 01492/353-123, www.surfsnowdonia. com.

Trefriw Woolen Mills

At Trefriw (TREV-roo), five miles north of Betws-y-Coed, you can peek into a working woolen mill. It's surprisingly interesting and rated ▲ if the machines are running (weekdays Easter-Oct).

Cost and Hours: Free, variable hours for different parts of mill (see below), tel. 01492/640-462, www.t-w-m.co.uk.

Getting There: Bus #19 goes from Conwy and Llandudno Junction right to Trefriw (hourly Mon-Sat, fewer on Sun, 30 minutes).

Visiting the Mill: This mill turns British wool (and some from New Zealand) into bedspreads, rugs, and tweeds. The highlight is the **mill museum** (Mon-Fri 10:00-13:00 & 14:00-17:00, closed Sat-Sun, closed Nov-Easter due to lack of heat). Pick up the self-guided tour brochure, then walk through both levels of the mill, following the 11 stages of wool transformation: blending, carding, spinning, doubling, hanking, spanking, warping, weaving, and so on (some, but not all, machines are likely running at any one time). Follow a matted glob of fleece on its journey to becoming a fashionable cap or scarf. It's impressive that this Rube Goldberg-type process was so ingeniously designed and coordinated in an age before computers (mostly the 1950s and 1960s)—each machine seems to "know" how to do its rattling, clattering duty with amazing precision (In the summer, the **rug-making and hand-spinning house** (next to the WC) has a charming spinster as well as yarn and knitted goods for sale (only open Tue-Thu June-Sept).

You can peruse the finished products in the **shop** (June-Sept Mon-Sat 9:30-17:30, Sun 11:00-17:00; Oct-May Mon-Sat 10:00-17:00, closed Sun). The whole complex creates its own hydroelectric power; the **"turbine house"** in the cellar lets you glance at enormous, fiercely spinning turbines dating from the 1930s and 1940s, powered by streams that flow down the hillside above the mill (same hours as shop). Watch the **weaving looms,** with bobbin-loaded shuttles flying to and fro, to see a bedspread being created (mid-Feb-mid-Dec Mon-Fri 10:00-13:00 & 14:00-17:00).

Nearby: The grade school next door is busy with rambunctious Welsh-speaking kids—fun to listen to at recess.

ISLE OF ANGLESEY

The huge Isle of Anglesey ("Ynys Môn" in Welsh) looms just offshore, about a 40-minute drive west from Conwy (connected by bridge to the mainland), and a short detour from the route to Caernarfon. While Anglesey—and its port-town Holyhead—is known primarily as the jumping-off point for ferries to Dublin (see page

Thrill-Seeking in Wales

To further immerse yourself in North Wales' natural beauty—and inject some adrenaline in your travels—you can pick from a variety of outdoor activities. These are becoming increasingly popular with travelers, particularly those with teenagers.

Zipline courses at two old slate mines—in Blaenau Ffestiniog and Bethesda—let you speed high above piles of discarded slate scraps; the same company also runs a zipline course through the woods near Betws-y-Coed (www.zipworld.co.uk).

High-speed **RIB** (rigid inflatable boat) tours depart from the Isle of Anglesey, racing across the waters of the Menai Strait and nearby (www.ribride.co.uk).

At **Surf Snowdonia,** tucked in idyllic Welsh countryside just south of Conwy, the surf's always up—thanks to an artificial surf machine (described on page 632).

Whitewater rafting is another fun way to get up close and personal with Welsh nature (www.canoewales.com or www.ukrafting.co.uk).

663), from a sightseeing perspective it has one real sight: Beaumaris Castle.

Menai Suspension Bridge

The Isle of Anglesey is connected to the mainland by one of the engineering marvels of its day, the Menai Suspension Bridge. With the Act of Union of 1800, London needed to be better connected to Dublin. And, as the economy of the island of Anglesey was mainly cattle farming (cows had to literally swim the Straits of Menai to get to market), there was a local need for this bridge. Designed by Thomas Telford and finished in 1826, at 580 feet it was the longest bridge of that era. It was built to be 100 feet above sea level at high tide—high enough to let Royal Navy ships sail beneath. When it opened, the bridge cut the travel time from London to Holyhead from 36 to 27 hours. Most drivers today take the modern A-55 highway bridge, but the historic bridge still handles local traffic (on the A-5).

Beaumaris

This charming town originated, like other castle towns, as an English "green zone" in the 13th century, surrounded by Welsh guerrillas. Today, it feels workaday Welsh, with a fine harborfront, a simple pleasure pier (advertising boat trips around the bird sanctuary at Puffin Island), lots of colorful shops and eateries, a mothballed Victorian prison (now a museum), and the remains of an idyllic castle. Around the castle are putt-putt-type amusements for the family, including a fine little picnic-and-playground area tucked right against the castle wall.

Beaumaris' small, simple **TI** is staffed entirely by volunteers, and is stocked with helpful maps and brochures, even if no one's there to answer questions (hours vary, in the town hall on Castle Street, next to the Buckeley Hotel, www.visitanglesey.co.uk).

Getting There: If driving, simply follow signs for *Holyhead*. Immediately after crossing the big bridge onto the island, take the small coastal A-545 highway for 15 lovely minutes into Beaumaris. There's a vast, grassy pay-and-display lot at the point just beyond the end of town (and the castle).

▲Beaumaris Castle

Begun in 1295, Beaumaris was the last link in King Edward's "Iron Chain" of castles to enclose Gwynedd, the rebellious former kingdom of North Wales.
The site has no natural geological constraints like those that encumbered the castle designers at Caernarfon and Conwy, so its wall-within-a-wall design is almost perfectly concentric. If completed, the result would have been one of Britain's most beautiful castles, and medieval castle

engineering at its best—four rings of defense, a moat, and a fortified dock. But problems in Scotland changed the king's priorities, construction stopped in 1330, and the castle was never finished. Today it looks ruined (and rather squat), but it was never ransacked or destroyed—it's simply unfinished. The site was overgrown until the last century, but now it's been uncovered and cleaned up to act as a park, with pristine lawns and a classic moat. Because it's harder to get here than the big, famous castles in Conwy and Caernarfon, it's less crowded—making your visit more enjoyable. In the south gatehouse (near where you enter), you can watch a brief film about the castle's history. The rest is mostly unexplained, with a few small information plaques and several hands-on activities for kids.

Cost and Hours: £6.50; daily 9:30-17:00, July-Aug until 18:00; Nov-Feb Mon-Sat 10:00-16:00, Sun from 11:00; tel. 01248/810-361, www.beaumaris.com.

Beaumaris Gaol

The jail opened in 1829 as a result of new laws designed to give prisoners more humane treatment; it remained in use until 1878. Under this "modern" ethic, inmates had their own cells, women prisoners were kept separate and attended by female guards, and prisoners worked to pay for their keep rather than suffer from jail-

NORTH WALES

crs bilking their families for favors. This new standard of incarceration is the subject of this museum, where you'll see the prisoners' quarters, work yard, punishment cells, whipping rack, treadmill, and chapel. Explanations are limited, but it's interesting to explore the old space. (Ruthin has a similar but more engaging prison exhibit—see page 660.)

Cost and Hours: £5.40; Sat-Thu 10:30-17:00, closed Fri, weekends only in Oct, closed most days Oct-Easter; to reach the jail, head down the main street from the castle, go right on Steeple Lane, then left on Bunkers Hill; tel. 01248/810-921.

Llanfairpwllgwyngyllgogerychwyrndrobwllllantysiliogogogoch

Proud owner of the second-longest place name in the world, this village is called "Llanfairpwll Gwyngyll" for short. To reach it, take

the first exit after crossing the A-55 bridge—it's well-marked. Follow the A-5, which leads past a Volvo dealership with a very long sign, to the train station, a popular place to take photos of the platform sign. The town itself is otherwise wholly unexceptional—but the "long name" gimmick is a huge draw for visitors. Next to the train station is the James Pringle Weavers shop, a souvenir superstore catering to big-bus tours. (You can ask nicely inside if they'll stamp your passport with the village name.) It's tacky, but fun to see such a fuss made over a town name, and it's an easy detour from Beaumaris.

Caernarfon

The small, salty town of Caernarfon (kah-NAR-von) is famous for its striking castle—the place where the Prince of Wales is "invested" (given his title). Like Conwy, it has an Edward I garrison town marching out from the castle; it still follows the original medieval grid plan laid within its well-preserved ramparts.

Caernarfon is mostly a 19th-century town. In those days, the most important thing in town wasn't the castle or the adjacent walled town, but the seafront that sprawled below the castle (now a parking lot). This was once a booming slate port, shipping tidy bundles of the rock from North Wales mining towns to roofs all over Europe.

The statue of local boy David Lloyd George looks over the town square. A member of Parliament from 1890 to 1945, he was the most important politician Wales ever sent to London, and ultimately became Britain's prime minister during the last years of World War I. Young Lloyd George began his career as a noisy nonconformist Liberal advocating Welsh rights. He ended up an eloquent spokesperson for the nation of Great Britain, convincing his slate-mining constituents that only as part of the Union would their industry boom.

Caernarfon bustles with shops, cafés, and people. It's fun to explore—but compared to Conwy, it's noticeably scruffier. Locals, who seem self-conscious about their rival town, told me, "we're poor cousins to Conwy." But in many ways, Caernarfon's blue-collar vibe gives it an appealing authenticity.

Orientation to Caernarfon

The small walled old town of Caernarfon (pop. 10,000) spreads out from its waterfront castle, its outer flanks fringed with modern sprawl. The main square, called Castle Square ("Y Maes" in Welsh), is fronted by the castle. Public WCs are off the main square, on the road down to the riverfront and parking lot, where you'll find a bike-rental shop.

Funding for the **TI,** which faces the castle entrance, is in flux; it may be closed when you visit.

ARRIVAL IN CAERNARFON

If you arrive by **bus,** walk straight ahead up to the corner at Bridge Street, turn left, and walk two short blocks until you hit the main square and the castle. **Drivers** can park in the pay-and-display lot along the riverfront quay below the castle; other pay parking lots fill the moat-like area along Greengate Street. If lots in the center are full (or you prefer to park on the outskirts and avoid traffic), there's a big pay lot below the Morrisons Supermarket, near Victoria Dock.

HELPFUL HINTS

Market Day: Caernarfon's big main square hosts a market of varying size on Saturdays year-round; a smaller, sleepier market yawns on Mondays from late May to September.

Laundry: Pete's Launderette hides at the end of Skinner Street,

Caernarfon

Accommodations

1. Celtic Royal Hotel
2. Victoria House B&B
3. Caer Menai B&B
4. Totters Hostel

Eateries & Other

5. Hole-in-the-Wall Street Eateries
6. Palace Street Eateries
7. Castell Pub
8. J&C's Fish & Chips
9. Ainsworth's Fish & Chips
10. The Anglesey Arms
11. Supermarket (3)
12. Launderette
13. Bike Rental
14. Na-Nog Shop

Menai Strait

Victoria Dock

GALERI

To Bangor & Conwy

BALACLAVA RD.

BANGOR ST.

A-487

P

TURKEY SHORE

PRIORY TERRACE

1

LON TWTHILL

To Harlech,
Mt. Snowdon via A-4086
& Segontium via A-4085

FFORDD PAFLIWN

WC

P

P

CROWN ST.

GLAN MOR

BANK QUAY

MARKET ST.

NORTHGATE ST.

CHURCH ST.

TWLL YN Y WAL

TOWN WALLS

3

2

OLD

HIGH ST.

SHIREHALL ST.

4

TOWN

CASTLE ST.

PALACE ST.

6

5

GREENGATE

NORTH PENRALLT

SOUTH PENRALLT

9

Buses to/from Conwy

B

PENLLYN

11

WC

P

POOL SIDE

From
A-487

THE PROMENADE

10

CASTLE DITCH

i

P

12

BRIDGE ST.

14

POOL HILL

POOL ST.

8

POOL ST.

To A-487

EAGLE TOWER

NE TOWER

CASTLE

STATUE

WC

Castle Square

7

POOT

NEW ST.

CHAPEL ST.

ABER BRIDGE

CHAMB. TOWER

CASTLE HILL

FFORDD SANTES HELEN

11

13

SEGONTIUM TERRACE

QUEEN'S TOWER

P

SLATE QUAY

HARBOR CRUISES

ST. HELEN'S RD.

Seiont River

TRAIN STATION
WELSH HIGHLAND RAILWAY

N

100 Meters
100 Yards

NORTH WALES

a narrow lane branching off the main square (same-day full-service, Mon-Thu 9:00-18:00, Fri-Sat until 17:30, Sun 11.00-16:00, tel. 01286/678-395, Pete and Monica).

Bike Rental: Near the start of a handy bike path, **Beics Menai Cycles** rents good bikes on the riverfront (daily 9:00-17:00, closed off-season Sun-Mon, 1 Slate Quay—across the parking lot from the lot's payment booth, tel. 01286/676-804, mobile 07436-797-969, www.beicsmenai.co.uk). One of their suggested routes is 12 miles down an old train track—now a bike path—through five villages to Bryncir and back (figure 4 hours for the 24-mile round-trip).

Harbor Cruise: Narrated cruises on the **Queen of the Sea** run daily in summer (£8; late May-late Sept 11:30-17:30 or 18:30—depending on weather, tides, and demand; 40 minutes, castle views, mobile 07979-593-483, www.menaicruises.co.uk).

Welsh Choir: If you're spending a Tuesday night here, you can attend the weekly practice of the local men's choir (Tue at 19:45 in Galeri Creative Enterprise Centre at Victoria Dock, no practice in Aug, arrive by 19:30 in summer—practices can be crowded, just outside the old town walls, tel. 01286/677-404, www.cormeibioncaernarfon.org/eng; best to reserve a spot by phone or online).

A Taste of Wales: For a store selling all things Welsh—books, movies, music, and more—check out **Na-Nog** on the main square (Mon-Sat 9:00-17:00, closed Sun, 16 Castle Square, tel. 01286/676-946).

Horseback Riding: To ride a pony or horse, try **Snowdonia Riding Stables** (must book in advance, 3 miles from Caernarfon, off the road to Beddgelert, bus #S4 from Caernarfon, tel. 01286/479-435, www.snowdoniaridingstables.co.uk).

Crabs on the Quay: As is the case in neighboring harbor towns, a popular family activity is capturing, toying with, then releasing little crabs (under the castle, along the harbor).

Sights in Caernarfon

▲▲Caernarfon Castle

Edward I built this impressive castle 700 years ago to establish English rule over North Wales. Rather than being purely defensive, it also had elements of a palace—where Edward and his family could stay on visits to Wales. Modeled after the striped, angular walls of ancient Constantinople, the castle, though impressive, was never finished and never really used. From the inner courtyard, you can see the notched walls ready for more walls—which were never built.

The castle's fame derives from its physical grandeur and its association with the Prince of Wales. Edward got the angry Welsh to agree that if he presented them with "a prince, born in Wales, who spoke not a word of English," they would submit to the Crown. In time, Edward had a son born in Wales (here in Caernarfon), who spoke not a word of English, Welsh, or any other language—as an infant. In modern times, as another political maneuver, the Prince of Wales has been "invested" (given his title) here. This "tradition" actually dates only from the 20th century, and only

two of the 21 Princes of Wales (Prince Charles, the current prince, and King Edward VIII) have taken part.

Cost and Hours: £8.95; daily 9:30-17:00, July-Aug until 18:00; Nov-Feb Mon-Sat 10:00-16:00, Sun from 11:00; tel. 01286/677-617, www.cadw.wales.gov.uk.

Tours: Local guide **Martin de Lewandowicz** gives mind-bending tours of the castle (tel. 01286/674-369).

Visiting the Castle: In the huge **Eagle Tower** (to the far right as you enter), see the "Princes of Wales" exhibit, featuring a chess-board of Welsh and English princes as life-size chess pieces. You'll also see a model of the original castle, and a video clip from the investiture of Prince Charles in 1969. The next level's skimpy exhibit covers the life of Eleanor of Castile, wife of Edward I. Be sure to climb the tower for a great view.

The **Chamberlain's Tower** and **Queen's Tower** (ahead and to the right as you enter the castle) house the mildly interesting Museum of the Royal Welsh Fusiliers—a military branch made up entirely of Welshmen. The museum shows off medals, firearms, uniforms, and information about various British battles and military strategies.

The **Northeast Tower,** at the opposite end of the castle (to the left as you enter), has an eight-minute video covering the history of the castle. Nearby, the **Black Tower** has a small exhibit that psychoanalyzes Edward's decision to build such an important castle here—which, some believe, is rooted in a legend surrounding a Roman emperor who dreamed of marrying a Welsh princess...and then did. And you can step out onto the little balcony overlooking the seaside parking lot, where Prince Charles addressed the crowd moments after his royal investiture (an event that locals still recall fondly).

JUST BEYOND CAERNARFON
Narrow-Gauge Steam Train

The Welsh Highland Railway steam train billows scenically through the countryside south from Caernarfon along the original line that served a slate quarry, crossing the flanks of Mount Snowdon en route. The trip to Beddgelert makes a fine joyride; to save time, ride the train one-way, look around, and catch bus #S4 back to Caernarfon. Steam-train enthusiasts will want to ride all the way to Porthmadog—and can even loop from there back up to Conwy with a ride on the Ffestiniog Railway steam train from Porthmadog to Blaenau Ffestiniog, and then the Conwy Valley line from Blaenau Ffestiniog to Conwy (Caernarfon to Beddgelert—£21 one-way, £31 round-trip, 1.5 hours; Caernarfon to Porthmadog—£27 one-way, £40 round-trip, 2.5 hours; trains run 2-3 times per day on most days late March-Oct, tel. 01766/516-000, www.festrail.co.uk).

Segontium Roman Fort

Dating from A.D. 77, this ruin is the westernmost Roman fort in Britain. It was manned for more than 300 years to keep the Welsh and the coast quiet. Little is left but foundations (the stone was plundered to help build Edward I's castle at Caernarfon), and any artifacts that are found end up in Cardiff. This is only worth seeing if you have an unusual appetite for the footprints of Roman buildings (free, gate generally unlocked daily 12:30-16:30, 20-minute walk from town, atop a hill on the A-4085—drivers follow signs to *Beddgelert*).

Sleeping in Caernarfon

These choices (except the Celtic Royal) line a cozy, sleepy, narrow street just inside the town's seawall—you can't get more central. If you're looking for a bigger hotel farther out, try the Celtic Royal or—cheaper—Caernarfon's branches of **Premier Inn** (www.premierinn.com) or **Travelodge** (www.travelodge.co.uk).

$$$ Celtic Royal Hotel rents 110 large, comfortable rooms and includes a restaurant, gym, pool, hot tub, and sauna; some top-floor rooms have castle views. Its grand, old-fashioned look comes with modern-day conveniences—but it's still overpriced (on Bangor Street, tel. 01286/674-477, www.celtic-royal.co.uk, reservations@celtic-royal.co.uk).

$$ Victoria House B&B rents four airy, fresh, large-for-Britain rooms with nice natural-stone bathrooms. Generous breakfasts are served in a pleasant woody room, and the lounge has a fridge stocked with free soft drinks. Stairs from the courtyard lead to the top of the castle wall for a fine view (13 Church Street, tel.

01286/678-263, mobile 07748/098-928, www.thevictoriahouse. co.uk, jan@thevictoriahouse.co.uk, friendly Jan Baker).

$ Caer Menai B&B ("Fort of the Menai Strait") rents seven modern, classy-for-the-price rooms (try requesting the one seaview room, 15 Church Street, tel. 01286/672-612, www.caermenai. co.uk, info@caermenai.co.uk, Karen and Mark).

¢ Totters Hostel is a creative little hostel run by Bob and Henryette. They have dorms as well as private rooms, including some in a building across the street (includes continental breakfast, cash only, open 24 hours, inviting living room, kitchen, 2 High Street, tel. 01286/672-963, www.totters.co.uk, totters.hostel@ gmail.com).

Eating in Caernarfon

The streets near Caernarfon's castle teem with inviting eateries. The lineup seems to change often; rather than recommending specifics, here are some streets worth browsing.

In the Old Town: "Hole-in-the-Wall Street" (just inside the back wall of town) is a trendy strip lined with several charming cafés and bistros. **Palace Street,** a block toward the water, also has several choices (including the well-established, extremely atmospheric, but questionably named **$$ Black Boy** pub).

Near Palace Square: In nice weather, several places on the main square have outside tables from which you can watch the people scene while munching your toasted sandwich. **$$ Castell,** a big and bright pub inside Castle Hotel facing Palace Square, dishes up good food. Across the square, the pedestrianized but grubby **Pool Street** offers several budget options, including the popular **$ J&C's** fish-and-chips joint. A couple of blocks away, **$ Ainsworth's** has arguably better fish-and-chips, but the wait can be longer.

Along the Waterfront: $ The Anglesey Arms is a rough, old, characteristic pub serving basic pub grub at picnic benches on the harborfront (the only eating or drinking place along the water). It's lively in the evening with darts and well-lubricated locals; they host live folk music on some Fridays from about 21:00 (Harbour Front, tel. 01286/672-158).

Picnics: For groceries, you'll find a small **Spar** supermarket on the main square, an **Iceland** supermarket near the bus stop, and a huge **Morrisons** supermarket a five-minute walk from the city center on Bangor Street.

NORTH WALES

Caernarfon Connections

Caernarfon is a handy hub for buses into Snowdonia National Park (such as to Llanberis, Beddgelert, and Betws-y-Coed). Bus info: tel. 0871-200-2233, www.gwynedd.gov.uk/bwsgwynedd. And the narrow-gauge steam train provides both sightseeing and transport from Caernarfon to **Beddgelert** (described earlier).

From Caernarfon by Bus to: Conwy (4/hour, 1.5 hours, transfer in Bangor), **Llanberis** (2/hour, 20 minutes, bus #88), **Beddgelert** (bus #S4, 7/day Mon-Sat, 2/day on Sun, 30 minutes), **Betws-y-Coed** (hourly, 1-1.5 hours, 1 transfer), **Blaenau Ffestiniog** (hourly, 1.5 hours, change in Porthmadog).

Snowdonia National Park

This is Britain's second-largest national park, and its centerpiece— the tallest mountain in Wales or England—is Mount Snowdon. Each year, half a million people ascend one of seven different paths to the top of the 3,560-foot mountain. Hikes take from five to seven hours; if you're fit and the weather's good, it's an exciting day. Trail info abounds (local TIs sell maps and guidebooks, including the small £3 book *The Ascent of Snowdon*, by E. G. Bowland, which describes the routes). Even if you're not a hiker, the park offers plenty of cute towns and sights—and

stunning scenery—to fill up a day. As you explore, notice the slate roofs—the local specialty—then visit the National Slate Museum and the Llechwedd Slate Caverns to learn about the up-and-down role the industry played in Welsh life. The towns of Beddgelert and Blaenau Ffestiniog are quintessentially Welsh.

Betws-y-Coed

The resort center of Snowdonia National Park, Betws-y-Coed (BET-oos-uh-coyd), bursts with tour buses and souvenir shops. This picturesque town is cuddled by wooded hills, made cozy by generous trees, and situated along a striking waterfall-rippled stretch of the River Conwy. It verges on feeling overly manicured, with uniform checkerboard-stone houses yawning at each other from across a broad central green. There's little to do here except wander along the waterfalls (don't miss the old stone bridge—just up the river from the green—with the best waterfall views), have a snack or meal, and go for a walk in the woods.

Trains and buses arrive at the village green; with your back to the station, the TI is to the right of the green. There's also a short-stay pay-and-display parking lot along the green.

Betws-y-Coed's good **National Park Centre/TI** sells a variety of good maps for hiking in Snowdonia, including the handy £3 *Forest Walks* map, outlining five different walks you can do from here (daily Easter-Oct 9:30-17:00, Nov-Easter 9:30-12:30 & 13:30-16:00, tel. 01690/710-426, www.snowdonia-npa.gov.uk). They show a free 13-minute video with bird's-eye views of the park, and offer a free downloadable audioguide tour of the park on their website (with maps and navigational aids). In summer, you might catch some live entertainment in the TI's courtyard.

Walks: Most of the "hikes" in Betws-y-Coed are along rivers and through woodland—certainly pleasant, but I'd rather save my time and energy for more dramatic mountain hikes. One easy stroll in town is the **Pont y Pair boardwalk** that begins just over the old stone bridge in the center of town (pay-and-display lot and WCs nearby) and runs a half-mile along the river; you'll return the same way. Another easy and enjoyable option is the **"two rivers walk,"** which begins through the white gate (marked *Private Road—Royal Oak Farm*) just outside the TI. You'll follow the Afon Llugwy river up to the confluence with the River Conwy, which you'll then follow back to St. Michael's Church and across the suspension bridge into town; most of this walk is through woods, circling the town golf course (allow about 45 minutes round-trip).

Music: St. Anne's Church, in the middle of town, hosts performances of the local men's chorus, Cantorion Gogledd Cymru, twice monthly in summer (June-Sept Sun at 14:00, www.cantoriongogleddcymru.co.uk). Most other Sunday evenings in summer, the church hosts a variety of other choruses (Sun at 20:00, book ahead with the TI).

Nearby: If you drive west out of town on the A-5 (toward Beddgelert or Llanberis), after two miles you'll see the parking lot for scenic **Swallow Falls,** a pleasant five-minute walk from the road (overpriced at £1.50/person; best views are from the top of the steep trail—not the bottom). A half-mile past the falls on the right is **The Ugly House** (with a café, see photo on previous page), built overnight to take advantage of a 15th-century law that let any quickie building avoid fees and taxes.

Betws-y-Coed Connections: Betws-y-Coed is connected by the Conwy Valley train line to **Llandudno Junction** near Conwy (north, 30 minutes) and **Blaenau Ffestiniog** (south, 30 minutes; 5/day Mon-Sat, 3/day Sun in summer, no Sun trains in winter). Buses connect Betws-y-Coed with **Conwy** (bus #19, hourly, 45 minutes, fewer on Sun), **Llanberis** (bus #S2, 7/day, more in summer, 40 minutes), **Beddgelert** (4/day, 1-1.5 hours; bus #S2 to Pen-y-Pass, then transfer to bus #S97 to Beddgelert), **Blaenau Ffestiniog** (bus #X1, 8/day, none on Sun, 20 minutes), and **Caernarfon** (hourly, 1-1.5 hours; ride bus #S2 to Llanberis, noted above, then transfer to frequent Caernarfon-bound bus).

▲Ogwen Valley (Dyffryn Ogwen)

Leaving Betws-y-Coed, road A-5 continues toward the village of Capel Curig. Here, most visitors peel off on the A-4086 toward Beddgelert or Llanberis, but I'd continue on A-5 through the just-as-dramatic, less-touristed Ogwen Valley—a gorgeous glacial groove filled by the lake called Llyn Ogwen. The surrounding mountains are peppered with stone walls, stray sheep, and lonely farms.

One of my favorite easy-to-moderate Snowdonia hikes—called **Cwm Idwal**—begins from the pay-and-display lot at the far end of Llyn Ogwen (by a hostel and a café). From 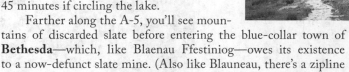 the parking lot, follow the flagstone path that leads up to the left of the café. You'll hike about 15-20 minutes with some uphill sections (on an uneven but well-tended stone path) to the gorgeous mountain lake called Llyn Idwal, hemmed in on three sides—like a natural amphitheater—by sheer cliff walls. From here, you can either head back the way you came, or with more time, circle clockwise around the entire lake. Plan on about an hour to hike to the lake and back; add about 45 minutes if circling the lake.

Farther along the A-5, you'll see mountains of discarded slate before entering the blue-collar town of **Bethesda**—which, like Blaenau Ffestiniog—owes its existence to a now-defunct slate mine. (Also like Blauneau, there's a zipline course that sends you soaring over all that slate, www.zipworld.co.uk.)

Dropping down from Bethesda, you eventually rejoin the A-55, which zips you east to Conwy or west to Caernarfon.

▲▲Beddgelert

This quintessential Snowdon village, 17 miles from Betws-y-Coed, packs a scenic mountain punch without the tourist crowds. Beddgelert (BETH-geh-lert) is a cluster of stone houses lining a babbling brook in the shadow of Mount Snowdon and her sisters. The stony homes, surrounding a stony bridge, seem to rise straight up from the Welsh landscape. (In a sense, they do.) Cute

as a hobbit, Beddgelert will have you looking for The Shire around the next bend. Thanks to the fine variety of hikes from its doorstep and its decent bus service, Beddgelert is the ideal stop for those wanting to experience the peace of Snowdonia.

Getting There: The Welsh Highland Railway train serves Beddgelert. This narrow-gauge joyride (12 miles and 1.5 hours to or from Caernarfon) is a popular excursion (for details, see page 642). Most people ride the train one-way and return by bus (see "Beddgelert Connections," later).

Orientation: The village doesn't have real "sights," but it's a starting place for some great walks—ask locals for tips, or stop at the **National Park Centre/TI** at the far end of town (daily 9:30-17:00, along the main road a couple of blocks from the bridge toward Porthmadog, tel. 01766/890-615, www.snowdonia-npa.gov.uk). For town info, see www.beddgelerttourism.com.

Activities: For an easy stretch-your-legs **stroll**, simply take the path along the river and follow signs to "Gelert's Grave" (*Beddgelert* in Welsh). In about 10 minutes, you'll reach a small grove of trees in a field marking the spot where the 13th-century Prince Gelert honored the dog, Gelert, who saved his infant son from a wolf attack. To extend your walk, follow the flat path beside the river as far as you like (it's 3 miles round-trip if you go all the way to the end and back).

For a more serious **hike,** you can trek along the cycle path that goes from the center of Beddgelert, through the forest to the village of Rhyd-Ddu (4.5 miles); walk down the river and around the hill (3 hours, 6 miles, 900-foot gain, via Cwm Bycham); hike along (or around) Llyn Gwynant Lake and four miles back to Beddgelert (ride the bus to the lake); or try the dramatic ridge walks on Moel Hebog (Hawk Hill).

For **mountain-bike rentals,** try Beddgelert Bikes (directly under Welsh Highland Railway station, tel. 01766/890-434, www. beddgelertbikes.co.uk).

Sleeping in Beddgelert: This little village has a few choices, mostly clustering around the bridge in the heart of town.

$$ Saracens Head is a newer, upmarket pub with 11 of the town's plushest rooms (tel. 01766/890-329, www.saracens-head.co.uk).

$$ Tanronnen Inn is an older choice, with seven rooms above a pub that's been renovated from its interior medieval timbers to its exterior stone walls (tel. 01766/890-347, www.tanronnen.co.uk, guestservice@tanronnen.co.uk, Alan and Jill).

$$ Plas Gwyn Guest House rents six rooms in a cozy, cheery, 19th-century townhouse with a comfy lounge (RS%, cash only, tel. 01766/890-215, mobile 07815-549-708, www.plas-gwyn.com, stay@plas-gwyn.com).

$ Colwyn Guest House has five tight but slick and new-feeling rooms (RS%, 2-night minimum on weekends, cash only, tel. 01766/890-276, mobile 07774/002-637, www.beddgelertguesthouse.co.uk, colwynguesthouse@tiscali.co.uk, Colleen).

Sleeping near Beddgelert: Mountaineers appreciate that Sir Edmund Hillary and Sherpa Tenzing Norgay practiced here before the first successful ascent of Mount Everest. They slept at **$$ Pen-y-Gwryd Hotel,** at the base of the road leading up to the Pen-y-Pass by Mount Snowdon, and today the bar is strewn with fascinating memorabilia from Hillary's 1953 climb. The 18 rooms, with dingy old furnishings and crampon ambience, are a poor value—aside from the impressive history (old-time-elegant public rooms, some double rooms share museum-piece Victorian tubs and showers, natural pool and sauna for guests, dinners, closed Jan-Feb, tel. 01286/870-211, www.pyg.co.uk, reserve by phone).

Eating in Beddgelert: $$ Caffi Colwyn, just across the bridge from the B&Bs, serves nicely done home cookin' at good prices in a cozy one-room bistro, or in their back garden (daily 9:00-14:00 & 18:00-20:30, mid-Sept-Easter 10:00-18:00 except closed Jan, tel. 01766/890-374). The **$$ Tanronnen Inn** serves up tasty food in an inviting pub setting, with several cozy, atmospheric rooms (food served daily 12:30-14:00 & 19:00-20:30, tel. 01766/890-347). **$$$ Saracens Head** is an upscale choice, with a classy dining room and equally classy pub food (food served daily 12:00-15:00 & 17:00-20:30, tel. 01766/890-329).

For something sweet, the **Glaslyn Homemade Ice Cream** shop (up the road from the Tanronnen Inn) offers good quality and selection.

Beddgelert Connections: Beddgelert is connected to **Caernarfon** by the scenic Welsh Highland Railway (2-3/day on most days late March-Oct, 1.5 hours) and handy bus #S4 (7/day Mon-Sat, 2/day Sun, 30 minutes). Bus connections to **Betws-y-Coed** are much less convenient (4/day, 1-1.5 hours, 1 transfer). To reach **Conwy**, you'll need to transfer in Caernarfon and Bangor (6/day Mon-Sat, none on Sun, 2 hours total). Buses to **Blaenau Ffestiniog** involve one or two transfers (7/day Mon-Sat, fewer on Sun, 1-2.5 hours).

Llanberis

Llanberis (THLAN-beh-ris) is a long, skinny, rugged, and functional town that feels like a frontier village. It's surrounded by dramatic, bald Welsh mountains—several of which are gouged by huge slate quarries. With 2,000 people and just as many tourists on a sunny day, Llanberis is a popular base for Snowdon activities. Most people prefer to take the train from here to the  Snowdon summit, but Llanberis is also loaded with hikers, as it's the launchpad for the longest (five miles) but least strenuous hiking route to the summit. (Routes from the nearby Pen-y-Pass, between here and Beddgelert, are steeper and even more scenic.)

Drivers approaching Llanberis will find pricey pay parking lots throughout town, including one next to the Electric Mountain/TI and another along the lake.

The **TI,** a desk inside the Electric Mountain visitors center, sells maps and offers tips for ascending Snowdon (Fri-Tue 10:00-15:00, closed Wed-Thu and Oct-Easter, tel. 01286/870-765, www.visitsnowdonia.info).

Getting There: Llanberis is easiest to reach from Caernarfon (2/hour, 20 minutes, bus #88) or Betws-y-Coed (7/day, more in summer, 40 minutes); from Conwy, transfer in one of these towns (Caernarfon is generally best). While it's a quick 30-minute drive from Beddgelert to Llanberis, the bus connection is more complicated, requiring a transfer at Caernarfon or Pen-y-Pass, on the high road around Mount Snowdon (9/day, 1-1.5 hours).

▲▲Snowdon Mountain Railway

This is the easiest and most popular ascent of Mount Snowdon. You'll travel five miles from Llanberis to the summit on Britain's only rack-and-pinion railway (from 1896), climbing a total of 3,500 feet. Along with the views, there's a mountaintop visitors center and a café. You can take a diesel or steam train: the diesel-powered train with a 70-person car, or the steam train, carrying 34 passengers in a rebuilt Victorian carriage. Either trip takes 2.5 hours (one hour up, one hour down, 30 minutes free time at the summit).

Don't confuse this with the Welsh Highland Railway (described on page 642) or the Llanberis Lake Railway, a different (and far less appealing) "Thomas the Tank Engine"-type steam train that fascinates kids and runs to the end of Padarn Lake and back.

Cost and Hours: Diesel train—£29 round-trip, £23 early-bird special for 9:00 departure (must book in advance); steam train—£37 round-trip. The first departure is often at 9:00, and the last trip can be as late as 17:30 in peak season (July-Aug). While the schedule flexes with weather and demand, several trips generally run each day from late March through October, with up to 10/day in peak season (steam train up to 4/day). Until May (or in bad weather), the train may not run all the way to the summit (tickets are partially refunded or sold at a reduced rate).

Buying Tickets: On sunny summer days—especially weekends, and any day in July and August—trains fill up fast. Originally designed for Victorian gentry, these days the train is overrun with commoners, and it's smart to reserve ahead. You can buy tickets in advance either online or by calling after 13:00 the day before (£3.50 fee/per group, tel. 01286/870-223, www.snowdonrailway.co.uk). Same-day tickets are only available in person. Show up early: The office opens at 8:30, and on very busy (read: sunny) days, tickets can sell out by midmorning; even if you get one, you may have to wait until afternoon for your scheduled departure time.

Getting There: The train departs from Llanberis Station, along the main road at the south end of Llanberis' town center. The closest parking lots are the pay-and-display lot located behind the station (off Victoria Terrace) or the pricier car park at Royal Victoria Hotel (across the street from the station). You can also park at one of the other pay lots in town (cheaper, about a 10-minute walk).

▲▲National Slate Museum

Across the lake from Llanberis yawns a giant slate quarry, which was a critical local industry until 1969. Slate from the hillsides above Llanberis was transported to the harbor in Caernarfon, where it was shipped all over the world. Today, the 19th-century industrial workshops have been converted into an excellent and free museum, where you can learn more about processing slate. The highlight is the 30-minute slate-splitting demo—try to plan your visit around one (starts at :15 past each hour, may not run at 12:15).

This museum is a nice complement to the Llechwedd Slate Caverns in Blaenau Ffestiniog (described next): While that experience focuses on the lifestyles of the people who worked in underground mines (and is of general interest), this museum is primarily about the aboveground workshops (and is particularly thrilling for engineers).

Cost and Hours: Free, daily 10:00-17:00; Nov-Easter Sun-Fri until 16:00, closed Sat; last entry one hour before closing, pay-and-display parking, tel. 02920/573-700, www.museumwales.ac.uk/en/slate.

Visiting the Museum: Entering the courtyard, note the time of the next slate-splitting demonstration, then work your way

clockwise around the exhibits. A poetic 12-minute film provides context. Nearby, the "caban" is where workers would gather to socialize. Head through the passage at the far end of the courtyard to find a little row of impossibly modest quarrymen's houses from different eras—offering a thought-provoking glimpse into their hardy lifestyle. Nearby, look for the stairs or elevator up to take a look at a gigantic, 50-foot-high waterwheel, which turns a shaft that runs throughout the workshop. Walk through the different parts of the shop—the foundry, the blacksmiths' forge, the machine shop—noticing how that one shaft powers all the various belt-driven machinery. Stepping out of the museum, peer up at the gouged-out mountainside—and tip your hardhat to the 3,000 people who once worked here.

Electric Mountain

This visitors center (with free WCs, a café, and a TI desk) offers tours into a power plant burrowed into Elidir Mountain. After a 10-minute video, you'll board a bus and venture underground into Europe's biggest hydroelectric power station for a one-hour guided tour.

Cost and Hours: Visitors center-free, tour-£8.50, daily 9:30-17:30, tours run Easter-Oct about hourly (every 30 minutes when busy); Sept-May open 10:00-16:30, 3-5 tours/day—call or check online for times; wear warm clothes and sturdy shoes, reserve ahead online, no children under 4, tel. 01286/870-636, www.electricmountain.co.uk.

NORTH WALES

Blaenau Ffestiniog

High on a mountaintop, Blaenau Ffestiniog (BLEH-nigh FES-tin-yog) is a quintessential Welsh slate-mining town. The town seems to struggle on, oblivious to the tourists who nip in and out. Though it's tucked amidst a pastoral Welsh landscape, Blaenau Ffestiniog is surrounded by a gunmetal-gray wasteland of "tips," huge mountain-like piles of excess slate. While not technically inside the national park (thanks to its heavy industry and those giant slate heaps), Blaenau Ffestiniog is surrounded by Snowdonia on all sides, and is a short drive from the idyll of Betws-y-Coed or Beddgelert.

Take a walk. The shops are right out of the 1950s. Long rows of humble "two-up and two-down" houses (four rooms) feel a bit grim. The train station, bus stop, and parking lot all cluster along a one-block stretch in the heart of town. There's no TI.

Getting There: Blaenau Ffestiniog is conveniently connected by the Conwy Valley train to Betws-y-Coed and Conwy (5/day Mon-Sat, 3/day Sun in summer, no Sun trains in winter, 30 minutes to Betws-y-Coed, 1 hour to Conwy via Llandudno Junction) and by bus #X1 (8/day, none on Sun, 20 minutes to Betws-y-Coed, 1 hour to Llandudno Junction near Conwy). By bus, it's possible to connect with Beddgelert (7/day Mon-Sat, fewer on Sun, 1-2.5 hours, 1-2 transfers) or Caernarfon (hourly, 1.5 hours, transfer in Porthmadog).

▲▲Llechwedd Slate Caverns

Slate mining played a blockbuster role in Welsh heritage, and this working slate mine on the northern edge of Blaenau Ffestiniog does an excellent job of explaining the mining culture of Victorian Wales. The Welsh mined and split most of the slate roofs of Europe. When done right, a quality Welsh slate roof could last for up to 300 years. But it was hard work: 10 tons of slate were mined for every one ton of usable slate extracted. Miners would work 12-hour shifts, six days a week, with one 30-minute break every day. They'd latch themselves to the cliff face at an angle and slowly, one tap at a time, use a long metal rod to chip out four-foot-deep holes to fill with gunpowder. The guided tour will give you a new appreciation for all those slate roofs you'll see in your travels. Dress warmly—I mean it. You'll freeze underground without a sweater or jacket (you can borrow a coverall). Lines are longer when rain drives in the hikers.

Cost and Hours: £20, daily 9:00-17:30, tours run every 15-30 minutes depending on demand—first tour usually at 9:30, last tour generally at 17:00 (16:30 off-season); cafeteria, pub, tel. 01766/830-306, www.llechwedd-slate-caverns.co.uk.

Getting There: The slate mine is about a mile from the town center. Bus #X1 leaves from the Blaenau Ffestiniog rail station and drops you off near the mine (8/day Mon-Sat, none on Sun, Express Motors). You can also walk 30 minutes to the mine or take a taxi (about £5, reserve in advance, tel. 01766/762-465 or 01766/831-781).

Visiting the Mine: The one-hour tour takes you into the mine with a live guide. You'll descend on a cable railway about 400 feet into the mountain for an audiovisual dramatization, set in the 1860s and centered around several relatives who work in the mine. You'll walk through several chambers, learning about the miners' primitive techniques and their (virtually nonexistent) safety measures. You'll find out why they preferred using chains to ropes, why they'd set off the gunpowder at the end of a shift, and why the "danger man" had the

most harrowing—and most important—job of the lot. Sadly, despite the reassurances of doctors during that age, inhaling slate dust caused often-fatal cases of silicosis...where the inside of a miner's lung became coated with tiny chips of slate. You'll get to heft their tools (such as the pointed and weighted rod, called a "jumper") and watch a brief slate-splitting demonstration. The tour requires a half-mile of walking through tunnels and caves with 60-plus stairs and some uneven footing.

▲Ffestiniog Railway
This 13-mile narrow-gauge train line was built in 1836 for small horse-drawn wagons to transport slate from the Ffestiniog mines to the port of Porthmadog. In the 1860s, horses gave way to steam trains. Today, hikers and tourists enjoy these tiny titans (tel. 01766/516-000, www.festrail.co.uk). This line connects to the narrow-gauge Welsh Highland Railway from Caernarfon via Porthmadog (see page 642). This is a novel steam-train experience, but the full-size Conwy Valley line from Llandudno to Blaenau Ffestiniog is more scenic and works a little better for hikers (see page 612).

Near Blaenau Ffestiniog
▲Harlech Castle
Dramatically situated 14 miles south of Blaenau Ffestiniog, Harlech Castle is compact and fun to explore. When it was built by Edward I in 1283, the sea lapped at the base of the castle wall (you can see the jagged dike since built in the distance, along with an

old stone staircase that led down
to the former water level, now
the train tracks). During the
War of the Roses, Queen Mary
of Anjou hid out here for a time,
and it was the last castle in Britain to fall (after a nine-month
siege) during the Civil War. Before crossing the bridge to the
castle, watch the seven-minute

introductory film. At the gatehouse (where you enter the castle),
climb to the top of the southwest tower, with panoramic views to
the sea. Back down in the central courtyard, you can climb either
tower flanking the gatehouse to reach the lower wall-top walkway
and hike all the way around. The village of Harlech is cute and
worth a wander.

Cost and Hours: £6.50; daily 9:30-17:00, July-Aug until
18:00; Nov-Feb Mon-Sat 10:00-16:00, Sun from 11:00; in the village of Harlech, just above the A-496; pay-and-display lot at castle
entry, tel. 01766/780-552, www.cadw.wales.gov.uk.

Near Snowdonia National Park

Tucked between Snowdonia and the North Sea is a sweeping,
sandy tidal estuary called Tremadog Bay, with a faux Italian town
(Portmeirion) and yet another castle, Criccieth. The sights here—
about a half-hour's drive from Beddgelert, Blaenau Ffestiniog,
or Caernarfon—can help round out a busy day exploring North
Wales. The area's main town, Porthmadog, is the end point of two
of the area's scenic rail lines (the Ffestiniog Railway and the Welsh
Highland Railway). Portmeirion and Criccieth Castle are both
within a 15-minute drive of Porthmadog, in different directions.

▲Portmeirion

File this under "Britain's offbeat sights." Tucked into a balmy
microclimate, a short drive from the slag heaps of Blaenau Ffestiniog or the hobbit town of
Beddgelert, is a faux-Italian
Riviera village modeled after
Portofino. This flower-filled fantasy is extravagant: Surrounded
by lush Welsh greenery and a
windswept mudflat at low tide,
Portmeirion is an artistic glob
of palazzo arches, fountains,
gardens, and promenades filled

with cafés, souvenir shops, two hotels, and local tourists who always wanted to go to Italy.

In 1925, Sir Clough Williams-Ellis began building this grand-scale folly—a pastel world of Italianate architecture. Soon this retreat began to attract celebrities seeking both novelty and privacy: H.G. Wells, Noel Coward, Prince Charles, and Beatles manager Brian Epstein were all repeat guests. The 1960s British TV series *The Prisoner*—which still has a big cult following—was filmed here, adding to the town's fame.

You'll pay admission at the tollhouse, then you're free to wander and explore. Free and helpful 20-minute orientation tours leave from the entrance every 30 minutes (10:30-15:30). Two 45-minute trails—the "Woodland Walk" and the "Coastal Walk"—provide structure for your meanderings, and a shuttle bus passes along the village and the Woodland trail every 20 minutes or so. If you'd like to completely forget you're in Wales...this is the place.

Cost and Hours: £12, cheaper after 15:15 or if you buy online, daily 9:30-19:30, Nov-March until 17:30, tel. 01766/770-000, www.portmeirion-village.com.

Criccieth Castle

Perched on a grassy bluff over the pretty seafront town of the same name, Criccieth (KRICK-ith) is the smallest, least historic,

and least impressive of the "big five" border castles. Built by the Welsh around 1230, it was later seized, beefed up, and added to the castle ring by the English. The modern visitors center at the base of the hill has a small but well-presented exhibit on the castle's history...but there's not much to say. You can hike up and prowl the ruins, with great 360-degree views over Tremadog Bay and deep into Snowdonia. On a nice day, you can see all the way to Harlech Castle. Of the five Edward castles, this is the one where the views from the castle are better than the interior of the castle itself.

Cost and Hours: £5; daily 10:00-17:00; Nov-March Fri-Sat 9:30-16:00, Sun from 11:00, closed Mon-Thu; on the A-497 in the village of Criccieth; a few free street-parking spaces right in front of the ticket office, tel. 01766/522-227, www.cadw.wales.gov.uk.

NORTH WALES

Northeast Wales

If you're driving between North Wales and England, the Denbigh-shire towns of Llangollen and Ruthin are worth a stop. Llangollen is more engaging, with a dramatic setting and lots of ways to spend a few minutes or a few hours. Ruthin is appealing simply for its salt-of-the-earth character; while it has some good sights and a fine hotel, it's more of a place to melt into small-town Welsh life. Neither town is particularly well-connected by public transportation, so they're effectively just for drivers. You can squeeze either or both into the drive from North Wales to England, but with more time, spend a night...or two.

While you're in the Denbighshire area, look for the free, engaging, wryly written "Town Trail" maps, detailing self-guided walks in Llangollen, Ruthin, and other towns (free at TIs).

Llangollen

Llangollen (thlang-GOTH-lehn) is a red-brick riverside town that's strikingly set in a gorge with a rushing river. It has an impressive history (thanks to its clever canal, a symbol of the Industrial Revolution) and a handful of great sights, including the fascinating manor house called Plas Newydd. It's also a popular launch pad for hikes, boat trips, and steam-train journeys. The town is famous for its weeklong International Musical Eisteddfod, a very popular and crowded festival held every July, with dance competitions and evening concerts (tel. 01978/862-001, www.international-eisteddfod. co.uk). The town feels equal parts blue-collar and touristy.

Orientation to Llangollen

With about 3,600 people, little Llangollen is easy to navigate. It has a big pay parking lot on Market Street, well-signed as you enter town, and a handy and helpful **TI** just around the corner on Castle Street (Mon-Sat 9:30-17:00, Sun until 16:00, shorter hours Oct-May, tel. 01978/860-828, www.llangollen.org.uk). A couple of blocks north, a bridge scenically crosses the River Dee, with the steam railway station and the canal just beyond. To

the south, the aptly named Hill Street climbs steeply up to a residential zone, where you'll find the town's best sight, Plas Newydd.

Sights in Llangollen

Llangollen Canal

At the turn of the 18th century, famed engineers Thomas Telford and William Jessop built this remarkable industrial canal, with a horse-drawn towpath for hauling cargo running its entire length. (It was originally intended to connect to a network of canals linking all the way to the big port at Liverpool, but the entire run was never completed.) The ingenious design—which begins at the River Dee's Horseshoe Falls two miles west of town, and crosses the towering Pontcysyllte Aqueduct four miles east of town—was engineered to drop less than 20 inches over its entire 11-mile length.

Today it's a tourist attraction (to find it, cross the bridge from the town center and head up the hill). You can go for an easy, level stroll along its towpath, or take a lazy **canal-boat cruise.** The classic choice is by horse-drawn boat—either the basic, 45-minute version (£7, July-Aug 2/hour daily 11:00-16:30, shorter hours and less frequent rest of the year) or the full-blown two-hour version all the way to Horseshoe Falls (£12.50, Easter-Oct Sat-Sun at 11:30, may run on some weekdays—confirm details at TI for either boat trip; tel. 01978/860-702, www.horsedrawnboats.co.uk). A two-hour motorized canal-boat trip goes all the way to—and across—the Pontcysyllte Aqueduct (£14, Easter-Oct daily at 12:15 and 13:45, sometimes also at 10:00 or 11:30). As the longer tours (both horse-drawn and motorized) can sell out, it's smart to book ahead.

▲▲Plas Newydd

This is the manor home (pronounced "plass NEW-eth") of two 18th-century upper-class Irish women who ran off together and

lived here as a couple for 50 years. Known as the "Ladies of Llangollen," Lady Eleanor Butler and Sarah Ponsonby escaped from their families and settled here in 1778, causing a sensation in Georgian society. The rich and famous—inspired by the way the ladies' relationship epitomized the Romantic Age—beat a path to their door, including the Duke of Wellington, Josiah Wedgwood, William Wordsworth, and Sir Walter Scott. While historians say it's not possible to confirm whether they were lesbians, the pair slept in the same bed, cut their hair short, and liked to wear "mannish" riding habits. They were avid collectors of fine woodwork, which they incorporated into both the exterior and interior of their "cottage." These ornate wood carvings cover seemingly every surface of the many cozy rooms you'll see—living room, library, bedroom, guest room—which also display some of their personal belongings. Out front is the well-tended topiary garden. While there are plenty of old British manor houses to tour, this one is uniquely fascinating. Invest £1.50 in the essential audioguide, and take time to listen to its complete story.

Cost and Hours: £6; Wed-Mon 10:30-17:00, closed Tue except June-Aug; house interior closed Nov-March—but gardens open; 10-minute walk from TI on Hill Street, free parking, café, tel. 01978/862-834, www.plasnewyddllangollen.co.uk.

Other Experiences in Llangollen

You'll see a steady stream of serious walkers huffing through town. Llangollen is a popular launch pad for both short and long-distance **walks** in the Welsh countryside. For an easy stroll, wander along the canal's towpath in either direction (Horseshoe Falls is 2 miles away). For a sturdier hike, head for Valle Crucis Abbey. (The falls and abbey are both described later.) Another popular choice is the steep huff up to Castell Dinas Brân, the ruined castle capping the bald mountain over the canal side of town (visible from various points in Llangollen). The TI can give advice on any of these hikes.

The **men's choir** practices traditional Welsh songs weekly on Friday nights (19:30 at the Hand Hotel on Bridge Street, 21:30 pub sing-along afterward, hotel tel. 01978/860-303).

Llangollen has its own little **steam-train line,** the Llangollen Railway, which putters up and down the Dee Valley to the town of Corwen and back (about 30 minutes each way, www.llangollen-railway.co.uk).

The humble, endearingly cluttered **town museum** fills a circular, bunker-like building between the TI and the river (on Parade Street, free, daily 10:00-16:00). It's worth ducking in on a rainy day. The centerpiece is a replica of the ninth-century Eliseg's Pillar (you can see the original on the way up to the Horseshoe Pass—see "Route Tips for Drivers," later).

Sleeping and Eating in Llangollen

$ Glasgwm B&B rents four spacious rooms in a Victorian townhouse—it's tidy, updated, and centrally located (evening meals and sack lunches available by request, cash only, free parking, Abbey Road, tel. 01978/861-975, www.glasgwm-llangollen.co.uk, glasgwm@llangollen.co.uk, friendly John and Heather). **$$ Manorhaus** is a luxurious boutique option with eight rooms, run by the owners of the recommended Manorhaus hotel in Ruthin (Hill Street, tel. 01978/860-775, www.manorhaus.com, post@manorhaus.com).

You'll find no shortage of options for a quick lunch downtown. Several vendors sell savory pastries, called oggies. **Chatwins** (a local bakery/coffee shop chain) sells tasty, filling, made-to-order sandwiches, and the **Spar** on the main drag is good for picnic supplies. A couple blocks away, **$$ The Corn Mill** is a lively and tempting pub in an historic stone building along the water (a short walk upstream from the bridge). If the weather's nice, grab a seat on the deck hanging over the rapids (food served daily 12:00-21:30, Dee Lane, tel. 01978/869-555).

Llangollen Connections

By Bus/Train: To reach **Conwy,** you can take bus #5 to Ruabon (every 10 min Mon-Sat, fewer on Sun), where you can transfer to a train (5/day; 2 hours total).

Route Tips for Drivers (Between Llangollen and Ruthin): It's a fast (30 minutes), scenic, and satisfying drive between Llangollen and Ruthin on the A-542 over the Horseshoe Pass. Allow more time if you stop on the way at the falls, abbey, or pillar.

From Llangollen's town center, cross the bridge and turn left on Abbey Road (A-542). About two miles out of town, watch for the Horseshoe Falls turnoff on the left. Follow this road and park in a pay-and-display lot, then walk five minutes steeply downhill through a meadow to reach **Horseshoe Falls** (and, nearby, the starting point of the Llangollen Canal).

Back on the main road, about a mile farther along on the right is the turn-off for Valle Crucis Abbey. This lovely Cistercian abbey, from 1201, was one of many "dissolved" by King Henry VIII. While not as striking as others—especially the much more famous and evocative Tintern Abbey in South Wales—it's worth stopping if it's your best chance to see a ruined abbey (£4, daily 10:00-17:00, closed Nov-March but free access to grounds, tel. 01978/860-326, www.cadw.wales.gov.uk).

A few hundred yards farther along the main road, looking right for a green mound topped by **Eliseg's Pillar**— a weathered nub of a monument placed here by a Welsh king in the ninth century.

From here, over the next few miles you'll ascend past the tree line, zoom by an old slate mine (with a roadside mountain of unwanted slate fragments), and dodge some roadside sheep to reach the top of **Horseshoe Pass** (1,367 feet), with sweeping views of the countryside. The scenery eventually changes from sheep to cows as you wind your way down to Ruthin.

NORTH WALES

Ruthin

Ruthin (RITH-in; "Rhuthun" in Welsh) is a low-key market town with charm in its ordinary Welshness. The people are the sights, and admission is free if you start the conversation.

Ruthin (pop. 5,000) is situated atop a gentle hill surrounded by undulating meadows. In this crossroads town, the central round-about (at the former medieval marketplace, St. Peter's Square) is a busy pinwheel, with cars spinning off in every direction. The market square, jail, museum, arts center, bus station, and in-town accommodations are all within five blocks of one another. The town is so untouristy that it has no official TI (though the rec-ommended Craft Center has handy brochures).

▲Ruthin Gaol

Get a glimpse into crime and punishment in 17th- to early-20th-century Wales in this 100-cell prison. First, you'll head down to the cellar to explore the "dark" and condemned cells, give the dreaded hand-crank a whirl, and learn about the men, women, and children who did time here be-fore the prison closed in 1916. The audioguide—partly narrated by a jovial "prisoner" named Will—is very good, informative, and engaging. You'll find out why pris-

on kitchens came with a cat, why the bathtubs had a severe case of ring-around-the-tub, how they got prisoners to sit still for their mug shots (and why these photos often included the prisoners' hands). Fi-nally, you'll head up into the bright and eerie "panopticon"—a design all British prisons adopted in the late 19th century to allow all prisoners to be watched at the same time.

Cost and Hours: £5, includes essential audioguide, Wed-Mon 10:00-17:00, closed Tue and Oct-March, last entry one hour before closing, Clwyd Street, tel. 01824/708-281, www.ruthingaol.co.uk.

Nantclwyd y Dre

This Elizabethan-era "oldest timbered townhouse in Wales"—a white-and-brown half-timbered house between the castle and the

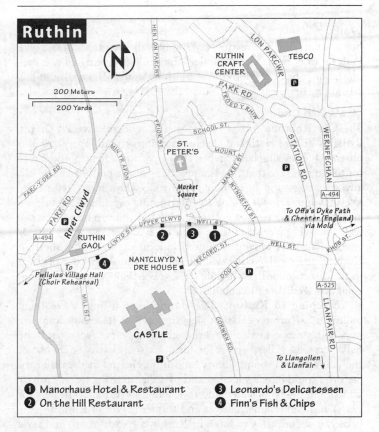

Ruthin

- **1** Manorhaus Hotel & Restaurant
- **2** On the Hill Restaurant
- **3** Leonardo's Delicatessen
- **4** Finn's Fish & Chips

market square—underwent an award-winning £600,000 renovation (funded partly by the EU) to convert it into a museum. Seven decorated rooms give visitors a peek into the history of the house, which was built in 1435.

Cost and Hours: £5; June-Aug Sat-Wed 11:00-15:00 or later, closed Thu-Fri; April-May and Sept Sat-Mon 11:00-15:00 or later, closed Tue-Fri; closed Oct-March; last entry 45 minutes before closing, call ahead or check website to confirm hours; Castle Street, tel. 01824/709-822, www.denbighshire.gov.uk.

Ruthin Craft Center

This state-of-the-art facility, hosting contemporary art, overlooks a busy roundabout at the base of Ruthin's hill. Inside, you'll find an information desk (stocked with brochures about Ruthin and the surrounding region), as well as a series of galleries and studio spaces for Welsh artists.

Cost and Hours: Free, daily 10:00-17:30, café, Park Road, tel. 01824/704-774, www.ruthincraftcentre.org.uk.

Walks

For a scenic and interesting one-hour walk, try the Offa's Dyke Path to Moel Famau (the "Jubilee Tower," a 200-year-old war memorial on a peak overlooking stark moorlands). The trailhead is a 10-minute drive east of Ruthin on the A-494.

▲▲Welsh Choir

The Côr Rhuthun mixed choir usually rehearses weekly at the Pwllglas Village Hall, and welcomes visitors to pull up a chair and observe. ("They sing better when they have an audience," the director told me.) Note that this is a practice—not a performance—but anyone who's sung in a choir (or anyone who's interested in the Welsh language) will find it an entertaining evening. The songs—and the instruction—are entirely in Welsh; you can be a fly on the wall for living Welsh culture (Thu at 20:00 except Aug, call or email in advance to confirm practice; located three miles south of Ruthin in the village of Pwllglas—follow the A-494 out of town in the direction of Blas; mobile 07724/112-984, www.corrhuthun.co.uk, cor@corrhuthun.co.uk).

Sleeping in Ruthin: $$ Manorhaus, filling a Georgian building, is Ruthin's classiest sleeping option. Its eight rooms are impeccably appointed with artsy-contemporary decor, and the halls serve as gallery space for local artists. Guests enjoy use of the sauna, steam room, library, and mini cinema in the cellar. In fact, you could have a vacation and never leave the place. It's run by Christopher (who played piano in London's West End theaters for years) and Gavin (an architect and former mayor of Ruthin)—together, it seems, they've brought Ruthin a splash of fun and style (no children under 9, recommended restaurant, Well Street, tel. 01824/704-830, www.manorhaus.com, post@manorhaus.com).

Eating in Ruthin: $$$ On the Hill serves hearty lunches and dinners—mostly made with fresh, local ingredients—to an enthusiastic crowd. The Old World decor complements the quality cuisine (lunch served Mon-Sat 11:45-14:00; dinner served Mon-Thu 18:30-21:00, Fri-Sat from 17:00; closed Sun, 1 Upper Clwyd Street, tel. 01824/707-736). **$$$ Manorhaus,** in a recommended hotel, serves inventive and locally-sourced dinners in a mod art-gallery space. Eating here—especially when in the care of Christopher or Gavin—is an experience in itself (daily 18:30-21:00, reservations recommended, Well Street, tel. 01824/704-830). **$ Leonardo's Delicatessen** is *the* place to buy a top-notch gourmet picnic (made-to-order sandwiches, small salad bar, Mon-Sat 9:00-16:00, closed Sun, just off the main square at 4 Well Street, tel. 01824/707-161). **$ Finn's** is the local favorite for takeaway fish-and-chips (daily 11:30-14:00 & 16:30-21:30, near Ruthin Gaol at the bottom of Clwyd Street, tel. 01824/702-518).

North Wales Connections

Two major transfer points out of (or into) North Wales are Crewe and Chester. Figure out your complete connection at www.nationalrail.co.uk.

From Crewe by Train to: London's Euston Station (4/hour direct, 2 hours), Bristol, near **Bath** (2/hour, 3 hours, 1 transfer), **Cardiff** (hourly direct, 2.5 hours, more with transfer), **Holyhead** (5/day direct, 2 hours, more with transfer), **Blackpool** (hourly, 1.5 hours, transfer in Preston), **Keswick** in the Lake District (every 2 hours direct, 1.5 hours to Penrith, more with transfer; then bus to Keswick, 45 minutes), **Birmingham** (3/hour direct, 1 hour, more with transfer), **Glasgow** (roughly hourly direct, 3 hours, more with transfer).

From Chester by Train to: London's Euston Station (hourly, 2 hours direct, more with transfer), **Liverpool** (4/hour direct, 45 minutes), points in North Wales via **Llandudno Junction** (2-3/hour, 1 hour).

FERRY CONNECTIONS BETWEEN NORTH WALES AND IRELAND

Two companies make the crossing between Holyhead (in North Wales, beyond Caernarfon) and Dublin: **Stena Line** (www.stenaline.co.uk) and **Irish Ferries** (www.irishferries.com; both roughly 4/day, 3-4 hours, book online for best fares).

Sleeping near Holyhead Dock: On the Isle of Anglesey, the fine **$ Monravon B&B** has five rooms a 15-minute uphill walk from the dock (includes continental breakfast, cooked breakfast-£4, Porth-Y-Felin Road, tel. 01407/762-944, www.monravon.co.uk, monravon@yahoo.co.uk, John and Joan).

SOUTH WALES

Cardiff • The Wye Valley

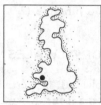

South Wales offers a taste of Welsh flavor just an hour from major English destinations such as Bath and the Cotswolds. While the dramatic castles and scenery that many find quintessentially Welsh are in the north, spunky South Wales leaves you with great memories—from the revitalized capital city of Cardiff with its own castle ruins, to the lush Wye Valley with the romantic Tintern Abbey.

Cardiff—like so many Industrial Age giants—became a rundown rust-belt city, but has now reemerged with fresh vigor. Its castle has medieval intrigue as well as Victorian bling, its downtown is ruddy yet vibrant, and its port—which shipped 20 percent of the world's fuel when coal was king—is now a delightful place to stroll.

Just outside Cardiff, St. Fagans open-air museum celebrates the unheralded Welsh culture. The towns of Chepstow and Caerphilly both have stout castles designed by the British to keep the natives of this feisty little country in line. And the beloved Tintern Abbey, frequently immortalized in verse and on canvas, is the most spectacular of Britain's many ruined abbeys.

PLANNING YOUR TIME

South Wales could fill two or three days (overnight in Cardiff or near Tintern Abbey). To learn about Welsh history and culture, spend a few hours at the St. Fagans National History Museum; for an urban Welsh experience, visit Cardiff. Castle lovers and romantics should consider seeing Tintern Abbey and the castles of Caerphilly and Chepstow (Caerphilly is best).

For a targeted visit, cherry-pick the best sights on a busy day between Bath and the Cotswolds:

9:00   Leave Bath for South Wales.

10:30   Tour St. Fagans (or visit Cardiff).

14:30   Head to Tintern Abbey and/or a castle of your choice, then drive to the Cotswolds.

18:00   Set up in your Cotswolds home base.

Cardiff

The Welsh capital of Cardiff (pop. 350,000) feels underrated. It has a fine castle, a freshly revitalized pedestrian core, a smattering of museums, and an impressively modern waterfront. While rugby and soccer fans know Cardiff as the home of Millennium Stadium, and sci-fi fans know it as the place where *Doctor Who* is filmed, the Welsh proudly view the city as their political and cultural capital.

SOUTH WALES

South Wales at a Glance

▲▲**Cardiff Bay** People-friendly, rejuvenated harborfront brimming with attractions, striking architecture, entertainment, and dining options. See page 677.

▲▲**St. Fagans National History Museum** One hundred acres dedicated to Welsh folk life, including a museum, castle, and more than 40 reconstructed houses demonstrating bygone Welsh ways. **Hours:** Daily 10:00-17:00. See page 680.

▲▲**Caerphilly Castle** Britain's second-largest castle, featuring a leaning tower inhabited by a heartbroken ghost. **Hours:** Daily 9:30-17:00, July-Aug until 18:00; Nov-Feb Mon-Sat 10:00-16:00, Sun from 11:00. See page 683.

▲▲**Tintern Abbey** Remains of a Cistercian abbey that once inspired William Wordsworth and J. M. W. Turner. **Hours:** Daily 9:30-17:00, July-Aug until 18:00; Nov-Feb Mon-Sat 10:00-16:00, Sun from 11:00. See page 690.

▲**Cardiff Castle** Sumptuous castle with a fanciful Victorian-era makeover, plus WWII tunnels, museum, and expansive walled grounds. **Hours:** Daily 9:00-18:00, Nov-Feb until 17:00. See page 673.

PLANNING YOUR TIME

If you're just passing through, Cardiff can be seen in a few hours: Visit the castle, follow my self-guided town walk, take a quick look at the Cardiff Bay waterfront, then be on your way. But it's also worth considering as an overnight home base for exploring more of South Wales. Just outside Cardiff are two sights well worth visiting: St. Fagans National History Museum (open-air folk museum) to the west, and Caerphilly (with its sturdy castle) to the north—all doable with just one night and a busy day on either side. If you're seeing other ruined castles in North Wales, Caerphilly is skippable (consider Tintern Abbey instead).

Orientation to Cardiff

Compact Cardiff can be seen quickly, with two main sightseeing zones: the castle and adjacent city center, and Cardiff Bay (a short bus or taxi ride away).

TOURIST INFORMATION

A small TI is inside the Old Library downtown, sharing a building with The Cardiff Story exhibit (Mon-Sat 9:00-17:00, Sun 10:00-

Cardiff's Rise, Fall, and Rise

Modern Cardiff, built as a coal port, was made a "city" only in 1905, but its local history goes back to ancient times. In A.D. 55, the Romans established Cardiff as a fort that could garrison

up to 6,000 men, to help subdue the indigenous Welsh. The castle was further fortified (for much the same reason) by King Edward I of England, in the late 13th century. (For more on the early history of Wales, see page 602.)

In 1800, Cardiff had fewer than 2,000 residents (two dozen other Welsh towns were bigger). But that all changed when the steam-powered Industrial Revolution hit, and fuel-hungry factories recognized Welsh coal as the world's finest. (Welsh coal provided more heat per ton, with less smoke and ash.) Cardiff built a suitable port to export the mainstay of Wales' new economy. By 1900 Cardiff was nicknamed "Coalopolis," and the old town was suddenly industrialized. (There's little for the modern visitor to see that predates this building boom.)

Eventually, Britain began looking east for coal. Modern container ports on England's east coast (facing the continent), coupled with a Europe-wide emphasis on free trade, prompted Britain to begin importing its coal rather than using coal from Wales. (Today, the port of Hull in eastern England imports nearly the same tonnage of coal as Cardiff exported in 1900.)

In 1964, the last shipment of coal left Cardiff, marking the end of its industrial port. Like many blue-collar British towns, Cardiff's economy slumped severely in the 1970s and 1980s as its steelworks and other heavy industry were shuttered.

Cardiff experienced a rebound in the 1990s and 2000s. Once a gloomy industrial wasteland, Cardiff's docklands were revitalized with state-of-the-art facilities (such as the impressive Wales Millennium Centre for the performing arts) that sit side by side with restored historic buildings and futuristic government centers. Formerly traffic-choked downtown streets were pedestrianized and are today filled with modern shopping centers.

Cardiff's transformation echoes that of many "second cities" in Britain and beyond that have emerged from dark economic times to a brighter future. And here, on the south coast of Wales, it comes with a lilting Welsh accent.

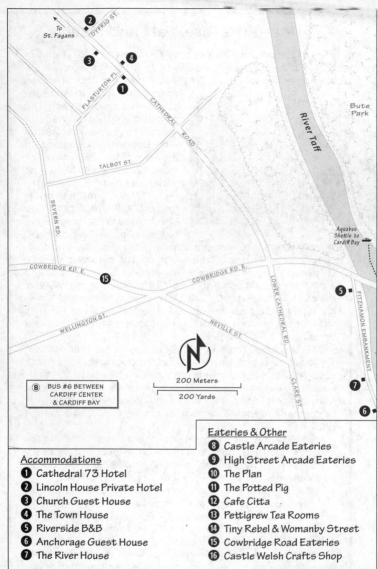

To St. Fagans

DYFRIG ST.

Bute Park

River Taff

FLASTURTON PL.

CATHEDRAL ROAD

TALBOT ST.

SEVERN RD.

Aquabus Shuttle to Cardiff Bay

COWBRIDGE RD. E

COWBRIDGE RD. E.

LOWER CATHEDRAL RD.

FITZHAMON EMBANKMENT

WELLINGTON ST.

NEVILLE ST.

CLARE ST.

N

200 Meters

200 Yards

Ⓑ BUS #6 BETWEEN CARDIFF CENTER & CARDIFF BAY

Eateries & Other
⑧ Castle Arcade Eateries
⑨ High Street Arcade Eateries
⑩ The Plan
⑪ The Potted Pig
⑫ Cafe Citta
⑬ Pettigrew Tea Rooms
⑭ Tiny Rebel & Womanby Street
⑮ Cowbridge Road Eateries
⑯ Castle Welsh Crafts Shop

Accommodations
① Cathedral 73 Hotel
② Lincoln House Private Hotel
③ Church Guest House
④ The Town House
⑤ Riverside B&B
⑥ Anchorage Guest House
⑦ The River House

16:00, The Hayes); there's also a branch at Cardiff Bay, inside the Wales Millennium Centre (daily 10:00-18:00, Bute Place, tel. 029/2087-7927, www.visitcardiff.com).

ARRIVAL IN CARDIFF

By Train: Cardiff Central train station (with the bus station across the street) is at the southern edge of the town center. From here, it's

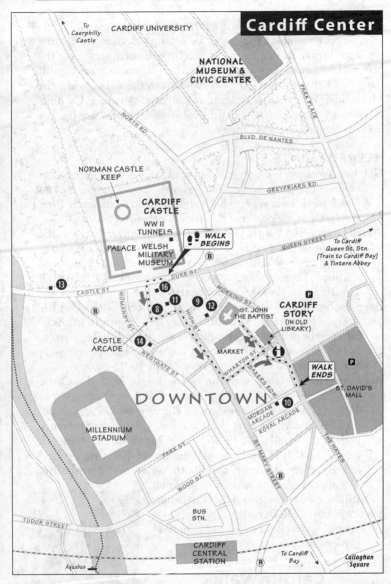

Cardiff Center

To Caerphilly Castle

CARDIFF UNIVERSITY

NATIONAL MUSEUM & CIVIC CENTER

NORTH RD.

PARK PLACE

BLVD. DE NANTES

GREYFRIARS RD.

NORMAN CASTLE KEEP

CARDIFF CASTLE

WW II TUNNELS

PALACE

WELSH MILITARY MUSEUM

QUEEN STREET

To Cardiff Queen St. Stn. (Train to Cardiff Bay) & Tintern Abbey

WALK BEGINS

B

DUKE ST.

CASTLE ST.

WOMANBY ST.

WORKING ST.

13

16

8 **11** **9** **12**

HIGH ST.

ST. JOHN THE BAPTIST

CARDIFF STORY (IN OLD LIBRARY)

P

B

CASTLE ARCADE

14

WESTGATE ST.

MARKET

WHARTON ST.

BAKERS ROW

i

WALK ENDS

P

ST. DAVID'S MALL

D O W N T O W N

10

MORGAN ARCADE

ROYAL ARCADE

THE HAYES

MILLENNIUM STADIUM

PARK ST.

WOOD ST.

ST. MARY STREET

B

BUS STN.

TUDOR STREET

CARDIFF CENTRAL STATION

B

To Cardiff Bay

Callaghan Square

Aquabus

about a 15-minute walk to the castle: Exit the station to the right, then bear left when you hit busy St. Mary Street. Follow this as it becomes High Street, which runs right into Cardiff Castle. The train station has no lockers; you can walk 10 minutes to the Old Library and use the lockers there (see "Helpful Hints," later).

By Car: Cardiff's city center has multiple parking garages. The most convenient, spacious, and reasonably priced are associated with St. David's mall, just southeast of the castle area. To get as close as possible to the castle for a targeted visit, try finding pay-and-display street parking in the Civic Center area (near the National Museum, just east of the castle). If heading for Cardiff Bay, the Pierhead Street garage is handiest to the sights, while the Mermaid Quay garage is closer to restaurants. Warning: Cardiff's ridiculously high and jagged curbs seem designed to damage any car that challenges them...trust me.

HELPFUL HINTS

Getting Around: The only public transit you'll likely need is to connect the castle and downtown with the port zone. **Bus #6** and a small **boat service** both shuttle people efficiently from the castle to the port. For details, see page 676.

Welsh Crafts: The **Castle Welsh Crafts Shop** (directly across the street from the castle entrance) is an insanely touristy place offering every Welsh cliché, plus an impressive exhibition of traditional carved wooden love spoons (Mon-Sat 9:00-18:00, Sun 10:30-16:30, 1-3 Castle Street).

Baggage Storage: You'll find pay storage lockers in the **Old Library,** which hosts The Cardiff Story (see "Sights in Cardiff," later) in the pedestrian core of town, just behind the big church. It's a 5-minute walk from Cardiff Castle and a 10-minute walk from the train station (lockers open daily 10:00-16:00).

Walking Tours: Handy **walking tours** depart from the Castle Welsh Crafts Shop (described above) about every other day at 11:00 (£7/person, 2 hours, covers the city but not the castle, schedule posted in craft shop window, call to confirm dates and time, mobile 07849-067-449). Many of the tours are guided by **Bill O'Keefe,** a walking encyclopedia well-versed in the history of Cardiff and South Wales, and a passionate, nonstop teacher. You can also book Bill for a private tour (£100/half-day, £200/day, £250/day with car for up to 4 people, www.planetwales.co.uk, tours@ planetwales.co.uk).

Cardiff Walk

Ideally, visit the castle first (see "Sights in Cardiff," later). Then follow this brief self-guided orientation walk from the castle, past just about everything worth seeing in the town center, and ending near a bus stop for Cardiff Bay. Allow about an hour.

• *We'll begin at the castle gate, with the castle to your back. Look across the busy street to the start of High Street.*

Cardiff was a garrison town back when Wales was an English-ruled apartheid society. The English lived within the walls (now long gone), and the indigenous Welsh who lived beyond made the English thankful they had those walls. The medieval city was mostly built over during Cardiff's Victorian boom times. Pedestrianized **High Street** (which becomes St. Mary Street) is the spine, running from the castle's entrance through the center.

• *We'll head down High Street...eventually. But first, take a little detour. Cross the busy street and bear right (past the Castle Welsh Crafts Shop) to the entrance of the...*

Castle Arcade: This is the most impressive of the many Victorian-era arcades burrowing through the city center. During

the late 1800s, when Cardiff was booming, there emerged a class of wealthy women who demanded climate-controlled, London-quality shopping. The city answered by developing several arcades with glass roofs, ensuring the ladies stayed warm in the winter, and didn't get a "working-class" tan in the summer. (The term "blue blooded" refers to the fact that their wrists were so lily white that the blue of the veins popped.) These long, narrow Victorian arcades—echoing the shape of farm plats from the days when people lived and farmed within the town's protective walls—were state-of-the-art when first constructed, with some of the first electric lighting anywhere.

Today, the joy of visiting these arcades lies in their characteristic shops and little cafés, the majority of which are family-run rather than chain stores. Stroll through Castle Arcade, noticing the fun liquid nitrogen ice cream being made at **Science Cream,** and (at the bend in the arcade) the recommended **Madame Fromage,** an upscale cheese-and-wine bar—one of many places on this walk ideal for a Welsh lunch. Look above to see the upper gallery (accessed via well-marked staircases).

• *Exiting out the far end of Castle Arcade, you'll pop out along...*

High Street (Heol Fawr): Cardiff's main street was pedestrianized in 2007, making it a delightful walking zone. Turn right and stroll down the street.

At the first corner with Quay Street, look right to glimpse a small corner (and the big, white, sail-like riggings) of gigantic **Millennium Stadium** (also called Principality Stadium). This is the main sports venue for all of Wales, and it seems to dwarf the city.

Nicknamed "The Dragon's Den" (after the national symbol and sports mascot of Wales), it serves as the home pitch of the Welsh national rugby (WRU) and soccer teams, hosted soccer matches during the 2012 London Summer Olympics, and is *the* place for big rock concerts in Wales. The stadium boasts the largest retractable roof in Europe. Even if you don't join 74,500 screaming spectators for a rugby or soccer match, you can pay for a guided tour of the building (see www.principalitystadium.wales).

• *A half-block farther down High Street, watch on the left for a big, white clock with the date 1891 in the stone threshold, marking the entrance to the...*

Cardiff Market (Marchnad Caerdydd): Like Cardiff itself, this lively market does its best to cater to tourists...but is predominantly used by locals. Spend some time exploring this all-purpose space (open Mon-Sat 8:00-17:30, closed Sun). You'll find plenty of butchers, fishmongers, fruits and veggies, and sweets. And you'll find more practical items, from hardware and vintage menswear ("Traders to the Dandy") to jewelry, greeting cards, and hair extensions. Mixed in are some tempting food stalls, ranging from basic snack stands to gourmet cheese counters (The Cheese Pantry) and healthy lunches (Migli Market). Upstairs is a top-notch vintage record store (Kelly's) and a few bric-a-brac shops. For a tasty treat, find Bakestones (under the clock tower in the middle of the main floor), where a big griddle cooks up an endless supply of cheap, fresh, piping-hot Welsh cakes.

• *Exit out the far end of the market, turn left, and hook around to the base of the church tower to enter the church of...*

St. John the Baptist: This Anglican church is the most important church in Cardiff's city center (open to visitors Mon-Sat 10:00-15:00, closed Sun). Built in 1180, then rebuilt in the 15th century after damage sustained during a rebellion against English rule, St. John the Baptist is one of the oldest buildings in Cardiff. Step inside to enjoy the Victorian stained glass and the Herbert family tomb (in the chapel to the left of the main altar). The Herberts ran the town in the 16th century like gangster Medicis.

As you face the altar, exit the church through the door on your right, emerging into the churchyard. Look for the tall, well-worn nub of a medieval **preaching cross**. Originally standing on High Street, this cross marked the site of official announcements and special preaching (e.g., "Join in on the newest crusade!").

• *With the church at your back, exit the churchyard through the gate, then continue past the fenced park to...*

The Old Library (Yr Hen Lyfrgell): This fine building dates from Cardiff's Victorian glory days—back when city leaders wanted to be sure the general public had access to good books. Today it contains a TI, a fine shop full of classy Welsh souvenirs, lockers for baggage storage, WCs, and a museum exhibit.

As you enter the library, turn left to find the gorgeously preserved, colorfully tiled **Victorian corridor**—evoking the spare-no-expense gentility of Cardiff's boom era.

The building houses a free, engaging exhibit called **The Cardiff Story** (daily 10:00-16:00, www.cardiffstory.com). Step into its one large room for a concise, vividly illustrated look at the full sweep of Cardiff's history—including a big model of its sprawling port circa 1913. More exhibits are in the basement, including a children's dress-up area and a reading nook with comfy couches and lots of Cardiff and Wales-related books to choose from.

• *Beyond the Old Library, at a plaza with tall trees, the street widens into a pedestrian boulevard called...*

The Hayes (Yr Aes): Like High Street, The Hayes was revitalized (in 2006) and transformed into the city's finest shopping zone. The trees mark a small food court called Hayes Island, with a venerable snack stand, fish-and-chips shop, and a noodle bar. Stroll beyond that, noticing the vast, sprawling, modern St. David's mall on your left. For more local browsing, watch on your right for the entrance to the **Morgan Arcade**—another classic Victorian shopping gallery. Step inside and poke your way into the center, where you'll find **The Plan Café,** one of Cardiff's best coffee shops...and a good place to unwind at the end of this walk.

• *To continue to Cardiff's other main sightseeing zone—Cardiff Bay— you're not far from a handy bus stop. Walk through Morgan Arcade to the far end. You'll pop out on St. Mary' Street, the southern part of High Street. Turn left and walk two blocks to the curve of a busy road. Here you'll see bus stops—hop on bus #6 or the "Baycar" for a ride to Cardiff Bay.*

Sights in Cardiff

IN THE CENTER
▲Cardiff Castle

Cardiff Castle (Castell Caerdydd in Welsh) is one of the town's top sights—a fun complex that contains within its big medieval wall bits of several fortresses erected here since Roman times. You'll ramble its ramparts, climb an impressive Norman keep built on a man-made mound, see a WWII bomb shelter, visit an impressive

Welsh military museum, and tour a romantically rebuilt Victorian-era palace that is less than historic but dazzling just the same.

Cost and Hours: £12.50, includes audioguide; daily 9:00-18:00, Nov-Feb until 17:00, last entry one hour before closing, café, tel. 029/2087-8100, www. cardiffcastle.com.

Tours: For a 45-minute tour of the 19th-century palace, pay £3.25 extra as you enter and reserve a time. Tours depart at the top of each hour and cover the rooms you can see on your own plus a handful of otherwise inaccessible rooms (the nursery, bedroom, and rooftop garden).

Visiting the Castle: Your visit includes the following stops, which you can tour in any order. All are well explained in the included audioguide.

The **entrance building** has the ticket office, shop, café, and WCs. Upstairs are the audioguide pick-up and a brief movie about the castle. Downstairs is a fine exhibit called "Firing Line: Museum of the Welsh Soldier." Illustrated with plenty of artifacts (uniforms, medals, and weapons), the exhibit zigzags chronologically through the cellar, from conflict to conflict. You'll learn why a goat always leads Welsh regiments into battle.

Stepping out into the main courtyard, on your right (near the catapult) is a long, two-level stretch of passageways—the **battlements and WWII tunnels.** The old battlements are above, and underneath them is a tunnel that was used during WWII air-raids as a bomb shelter. Cardiff was an important military port (20 percent of all American GIs who fought in Europe landed here), which made it a target of Nazi bombers. While the port was hit hard, the city center got off pretty lightly.

Dominating the castle grounds is the **keep,** a classic Norman motte-and-bailey construction, with a stout fortress on top of a man-made hill. The original structure, made of wood, was built by William the Conqueror in 1081. He was returning from what he called a "pilgrimage" to St. David's—a cathedral town in western Wales—which clearly included a little scouting for future military action. You can ascend the very steep steps into the keep's courtyard, then even more steps to reach the (empty) inner chamber, the (empty) jail, and the rest of this mostly empty shell.

Finally, on the left is the most interesting interior in the castle complex: the **Castle Apartments**. This Neo-Gothic fantasy palace was rebuilt by John Crichton-Stuart, third marquess of Bute, whose income from the thriving coal trade flowing through his dock-

 lands made him one of Europe's wealthiest men in the late 1860s. He spared no expense. With his funds and architect William Burges' know-how, the castle was turned into a whimsical, fantastical take on the Middle Ages. It's the Welsh equivalent of "Mad" King Ludwig's fairy-tale castles in Bavaria (built in the same romantic decade). In 1947, the family donated it to the city of Cardiff.

Heading upstairs, peek into the glittering **Arab Room,** slathered in gold, including a gold-leaf stalactite ceiling. Then you'll step into the highlight of the complex, the breathtaking **Banqueting Hall**—with every surface covered in the highly detailed, gilded imagery of medieval symbolism. This hall grandly evokes the age of chivalry, right down to the raised minstrel's gallery (where musicians could perform overhead but remain unseen). Farther along, the **small dining room** has a table designed for a grapevine to grow up through a hole in the middle—so that guests could pick their own dessert. And the **library** boasts rows of leather-bound books and desks that double as radiators.

Nearby: The lush Bute Park—the largest urban park in Britain (as big as New York's Central Park)—runs from the castle to the open valley beyond Cardiff. It offers a world of escapes for relaxing locals—formal gardens, rugby and cricket pitches, and a riverside path that leads through natural surroundings from the castle into the hills. On the River Taff, at the southeast end of the park (nearest the castle), you'll find the dock for the shuttle boats to the port. For more about the shuttle boat, see "Getting to Cardiff Bay" later.

National Museum and Civic Center

The **National Museum** focuses not on Welsh culture and history—that's at St. Fagans (see "Near Cardiff," later)—but on art (with a particularly strong Impressionist collection), natural history (dinosaurs and mammoths), and archaeology (scant fragments of prehistoric Wales). The imposing **Civic Center**—a gathering of stately buildings—was erected just before Cardiff reached the end of its boom. A leading citizen sold the city some prime land at a great price on one condition: Grand London-class structures made of Portland stone must be built here, and remain forever open to the public. So, in 1910 the city built its Edwardian City Hall, law courts, National Museum, and the University of Wales just north of the castle on North Road.

Cost and Hours: Free, Tue-Sun 10:00-17:00, closed Mon,

Cathays Park, tel. 0300-111-2333, www.museumwales.ac.uk/cardiff.

CARDIFF BAY

Cardiff Bay (worth ▲▲) was the city's industrial engine during its golden age—and its most miserable corner during its era of precipitous decline. But today

the bay has bounced back, with lots of new construction and some thoughtful refurbishment of historical sights. It's worth the short bus or boat ride from downtown to this lively area to get a glimpse of Cardiff's past, present, and future, and to see how a once-flailing city can right the ship.

Getting to Cardiff Bay: It's about 15 minutes by **bus** from downtown. While various routes get you close, your best bet is bus #6 (or another service, called the "Baycar," that follows the same route; if bus #X8 comes by, that will also get you here). You can catch bus #6 at various points from downtown: try the Wyndham Arcade stop (southern end of St. Mary Street, near the end of my self-guided walk); or the Kingsway stop in front of the Hilton Hotel, across the street from the side wall of Cardiff Castle (£1.80, exact change only; about every 10 minutes, www.cardiffbus.com). Hop off at the East Bute Street stop, just behind the Wales Millennium Centre (walk through the Millennium Centre—and past the TI—to pop out on Roald Dahl Plass). For the return trip, you can catch the bus at the more convenient Millennium Centre stop, facing Roald Dahl Plass.

You can also get here by slightly-slower-yet-scenic **boat.** Two companies (Aquabus and Princess Katharine) leave from a dock in Bute Park not far from the castle, below the Castle Street bridge and Pettigrew Tea Rooms (£4, each company goes hourly—alternating on the half-hour, 25 minutes, www.cardiffboat.com).

Background: Cardiffians love to brag that in its heyday, the port of Cardiff shipped almost a quarter of the world's coal. Valleys rich with the best coal deposits anywhere funneled the black gold of the 19th century right into Cardiff. Capitalizing on the Industrial Revolution demand for steam power, the city built a massive port, ultimately with about 200 miles of train tracks lining its shipping piers. (There are none of the vast brick warehouses you'd expect in a 19th-century port; rather than being warehoused, the coal was simply piled next to the tracks and shipped almost immediately upon arrival.)

But with the advent of imported coal and oil, Cardiff's port

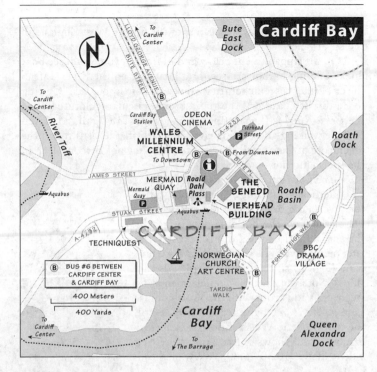

declined. A generation ago, the port was derelict—a place no tourist would dream of visiting. But in the late 1980s, city leaders hatched a scheme for the "Cardiff Bay Barrage," designed to seal off the mouth of the port and create a permanent high-tide waterline. Their goal was to attract developers with the promise of an inviting new people-zone on the waterfront. It worked. Today, as with rusty old ports all over Europe, Cardiff Bay is thriving—packed with sparkling bold architecture, sightseeing attractions, and fun entertainment.

▲▲Cardiff Bay Visual Tour

There's a lot to see at Cardiff Bay. Fortunately, you can see almost all of it with a strategic sweep of the head. To get your bearings, plant yourself on the little bridge at the harbor end of Roald Dahl Plass, and survey the bay.

• *Begin by facing straight out to sea.*

Cardiff Bay and the Barrage: Before 2002, one of biggest tides in the world literally emptied this bay twice a day. Now, the mouth of the harbor is dammed by "The Barrage" (BAH-rahzh), a high-tech dam marked by the grassy slope in the distance. While locks let in boats and a fish ladder lets in fish, the tide is kept out, and Cardiff Bay has become an inviting tourist zone. The bluff called Penarth Head (right of the Barrage) is a desirable residential zone, and on a clear day, you can spot the hills of West England in the far distance.

On the embankment below and in front of you, you'll see **boat docks** offering harbor cruises, or a boat ride up the River Taff to the city center (a scenic return if you came here by bus; see "Getting to Cardiff Bay," earlier). The giant, bronze circular sculpture (called the *Celtic Ring*) is the starting point for the **Taff Trail,** a beloved 55-mile walking and cycling riverside path that leads through the green core of Cardiff all the way to the village of Brecon, deep in the Welsh interior.

• *The stately, red-brick building on your left is the...*

Pierhead Building: Sometimes called the "Welsh Big Ben," this landmark is a symbol of the city. The building was originally the port authority for Cardiff Bay, which was later merged with the Cardiff Railway Company (logical, since this is where rails met ships). Note the evocative relief celebrating steamships and trains with the Welsh phrase *wrth ddŵr a thân* ("by water and fire")—still the motto of the Welsh railways. A history exhibit inside shows a free and interesting video (daily 10:30-16:30, www.pierhead. org).

Behind the Pierhead—but not visible from here—is the Welsh National Assembly (more on this later).

• *Looking just to the right from the Pierhead, you'll see a white shiplap church that seems like it would be more at home on a fjord. This is the...*

Norwegian Church Art Centre: This was originally built as a seamen's mission by the Norwegian merchant marines, in properly austere Lutheran style, during Cardiff's Industrial-Age boom. Originally, it sat where the Wales Millennium Centre is today, but in the 1970s and 1980s—when the docklands were a dangerous, derelict no-man's land—the church was literally disassembled and mothballed for future use. Over the last couple of decades, it has been reassembled, reconsecrated, refurbished, and repurposed as a successful arts center (free, daily 11:00-16:00, café, www. norwegianchurchcardiff.com).

• *Beyond the Norwegian Church are a handful of other sights.*

More Bay Sights: Many popular BBC television shows are filmed in Cardiff, including the astoundingly long-running science-fiction series *Doctor Who.* Until recently, the giant, curved **blue-gray building** housed the Doctor Who Experience, with show props and costumes. While it closed in 2017, local fans are hoping the exhibit might reopen, or be replaced by another Doctor Who-related sight in Cardiff. Ask around.

Behind the blue-gray building, on Roath Lock, sprawls the **BBC Drama Village,** the studio lot where shows such as *Doctor Who, Casualty,* and the Welsh-language soap opera *Pobol y Cwm,* are filmed. *Torchwood* and the 2010-12 version of *Upstairs Downstairs* also filmed here.

In the bay beyond here, notice the rotting **wooden pilings** in the harbor. Nicknamed "dolphins," these were used to brace ships caught here by falling tides before the construction of the Barrage. (Captains would tie their boats to a dolphin and gently settle onto mud without toppling.)

• *Now turn with your back to the bay. You're looking right at the huge plaza at the center of this area called...*

Roald Dahl Plass: Visitors congregate on this expansive bowl-shaped main plaza named for the Cardiff-born children's author who has many fans worldwide. You can see a seated statue of him on the right. (The Norwegian term plass—"square"—honors Dahl's Norwegian ancestry.) As this area was once a coal port, it angles down to the water. The pillars are illuminated with a light show after dark, and the 70-foot-tall silver water tower is always trickling.

• *On the left side of the square is **Mermaid Quay,** a sprawling outdoor-dining zone loaded with mostly chain restaurants. On the right side of the square is the dramatic...*

Wales Millennium Centre: Wales, a land famous for its love of music, had no national opera house until 2004. The Welsh fixed that with gusto when they built the 2,000-seat Wales Millennium Centre. It's a cutting-edge venue housing opera and theater, among other performances (funded mostly by lottery money). The enormous opera house anchors the entire Cardiff Bay district. Its facade—dominated by slate and steel, two important Welsh resources that have kept this small country humming—is carved with the words of one-time Welsh national poet Gwyneth Lewis: the English phrase "In these stones horizons sing," and the Welsh phrase *Creu gwir fel gwydr o ffwrnais awen* ("Creating truth like glass from the furnace of inspiration"). The expansive lobby holds shops, an enticing food court, a TI, and lots of activities, including occasional free lunch concerts (tel. 029/2063 6464, www.wmc.org.uk).

• *One more important sight nearby is not visible from here. Facing the water, walk to the left along the railing. Looking to your left, soon you'll see the big, modern...*

Senedd, The National Assembly of Wales: With its huge overhanging roof, this is essentially the Welsh capitol. While Wales—like Scotland and Northern Ireland—has a degree of autonomy from the United Kingdom, many matters are still decided in London. The National Assembly was created in 1999, moved

into these new digs in 2006, and gained more authority in 2007. The building, with vast walls of glass symbolizing the ideal of an open and transparent government, was designed by prominent architect Richard Rogers (best known for London's Millennium Dome and Lloyd's Building, and—with frequent collaborator Renzo Piano—Paris' Pompidou Centre).

In front of the Senedd, notice the modern sculpture that resembles the hull of a ship—but notice that its prow has the ghostly features of a human head. This is the **Merchant Marine Memorial,** built to remember the sailors who died keeping Britain supplied during the WWII Battle of the Atlantic.

• *Our tour is over. We've covered the main landmarks, but there's much more to see and do around this bay: bikes and boats for rent, a hands-on science museum (Techniquest), fake-yet-thrilling whitewater rafting, an open-air exhibit of boats from around the world, a multiplex (with Wales' only IMAX screen), and the nearby International Sports Village (with an ice arena and swimming pool). Enjoy!*

NEAR CARDIFF
▲▲St. Fagans National History Museum

The best look anywhere at traditional Welsh folk life, St. Fagans is a 100-acre open-air museum with more than 40 carefully re-constructed and fully furnished historic buildings from all corners of Wales, as well as a "castle" (actually a Tudor-era manor house) that offers a glimpse of how the other half lived. Also known as *Amgueddfa Werin Cymru* (Museum of Welsh Life), its workshops feature busy craftsmen eager to demonstrate their skills. Each house comes

equipped with a local expert warming up beside a toasty fire, happy to tell you anything you want to know about life in this old cottage. Ask questions.

Cost and Hours: Free, parking-£5 (cash only), daily 10:00-17:00, tel. 030/0111-2333, www.museumwales.ac.uk/en/stfagans.

Information: Pick up the essential £0.30 map, which helps you navigate your way through the park. Plaques by each building do an exceptional job of succinctly explaining where the building came from, its role in Welsh culture, and how it came to be here, all illustrated by a helpful timeline. Docents posted throughout can tell you more. For more detail, buy the £4 museum guidebook.

Expect Changes: The museum is in the midst of a £30 million renovation. The main entrance building has reopened with a new café and gift shop, but don't be surprised if the changes displace some of the exhibits mentioned next.

Getting There: From Cardiff's bus station (across the street from Cardiff Central train station), catch **bus #32A** (which stops right at the museum entrance; bus #320 takes you to St. Fagans village, a 5-minute walk to the museum; buses run hourly, 25 minutes, tel. 0871-200-2233, www.traveline-cymru.info). **Drivers** leave the M-4 at Junction 33 and follow the brown signs to *Museum of Welsh Life*. Leaving the museum, jog left on the freeway, take the first exit, and circle back, following signs to the M-4.

Getting Around: While large, the sprawling grounds are walkable. But if you want to take it easy, a small train trundles among the exhibits from Easter to October (five stops, £0.50/stop, whole circuit takes 30 minutes).

Eating at St. Fagans: Within the park are plenty of snack stands, as well as two bigger eateries: the Gwalia Tea Room in the heart of the traditional building zone, and The Buttery inside the castle (may be closed when you visit). Derwen Bakehouse sells snacks and traditional fruit-studded bread, which is tasty and warm out of the oven. Back in the real world, The Plymouth Arms pub, just outside the museum, serves the best food.

Visiting the Museum: Buy the map and pick up the list of today's activities. Once in the park, you'll find most of the traditional buildings to your left, while to the right are the castle and its surrounding gardens. Here's a rough framework for seeing the highlights:

First, head left and do a clockwise spin around the traditional buildings, starting with the circa-1800, red-and-white **Kennixton Farmhouse.** Then swing left, go down past the mill, and hook left again down the path to the fine **Lywyn-yr-eos Farmhouse.** Along with the castle, this is the only building at the museum that stands in its original location. It's furnished as it would have been at the end of World War I—complete with "welcome home" banner and patriotic portraits of stiff-upper-lip injured troops. From here you can side-trip five minutes to two Celtic **round houses,** which were farmhouses back in the Iron Age.

Head back up the main path and continue deeper into the park, turning left at the fork (toward *Church* and *Y Garieg Fawr*). Passing another farmhouse, then a small mill (used for grinding gorse—similar to scotch broom—into animal feed) and a Tudor-era trader's house, continue through the woods to **St. Teilos' Church,**

surrounded by a whitewashed stone
fence. The interior has been restored
to the way it looked around 1520—
including vibrantly colorful illustrations of Bible stories on all the walls.

Leaving the church, turn left
and continue ahead to the **Oakdale
Workmen's Institute**—basically a
leisure club and community center for hardworking miners and
their families. Poking around the building—from the library,
reading room, and meeting hall downstairs to the concert hall upstairs—you can imagine how a space like this provided a humble
community with a much-needed social space.

Next up, just past the tall red box (a **telephone booth** from
the 20th century, where people would make "telephonic" calls) are
the **Gwalia Stores,** a village general store where you could buy just
about anything imaginable (poke around to see what locals may
have shopped for). One section of the store still sells canned goods,
local cheeses, sweets, and ice cream; upstairs is a full-service tearoom.

Pass the olde-tyme portrait studio on your way up to the museum's highlight, the **Rhyd-y-Car** terrace of row houses, which displays ironworker cottages as they might have looked in 1805, 1855,
1895, 1925, 1955, and 1985—offering a fascinating zip through
Welsh domestic life from hearths to microwaves. Notice the pea
patches in front, the outhouse, and the chicken coops in the back.

Just past the row houses is a large grassy expanse (with a penny
arcade and period rides on the far side). Turn right and step into the
one-room **St. Mary's Board Schoolhouse,** where the docent can
explain the various items used to punish ill-behaved kids in the late
19th century. What looks like a wooden version of brass knuckles
was used to force lefties to write right. The "Welsh not" was worn as
a badge of shame by any student heard speaking Welsh rather than
the required English. Students could pass it on to other kids they
heard speaking Welsh, and whoever was wearing it at day's end was
caned (spanked with a stick). On the day of my visit, I overheard
a present-day schoolkid loudly complaining that his teachers force
him to speak *Welsh* instead of English.

After exiting the schoolhouse, take a hard right at the tollhouse to reach the **bakery.** This is a fine place to break for coffee and cake—they sell *bara brith* (speckled bread), a kind of fruit
bread, hot out of the oven. Sitting on the picnic benches, you can
enjoy all the family fun around you. Listen for parents talking to
their kids in Welsh.

Head back past the entrance area and continue to the castle
and gardens. You'll dip down past a series of terraced ponds, then

climb steeply up to the misnamed **"castle"**—so-called because it was built on the remains of a real, Norman-era castle that once stood here. This circa-1580 Elizabethan manor house boasts a stately interior decorated with antique, period furnishing. It feels like the perfect setting for a murder mystery or a ghost tale. Pick up the information paddles in each room, and ask the docents questions. Entering, you'll walk through The Hall (a reception room for visitors), The Study (where the master of the house carried out his business), and The Drawing Room (where the ladies would convene for a post-dinner chat, à la *Downton Abbey*). Climb the funhouse stairs up to the long gallery, where you can dip into a series of bedrooms.

Leaving the castle, if it's nice out, turn left and explore the expansive manicured **gardens** that stretch out across the grounds. Near the far end is a woolen mill.

▲▲Caerphilly Castle

This impressive but gutted old castle—evocative but with no actual artifacts—is surrounded by lakes, gently rolling hills, and the town of Caerphilly. It's the most visit-worthy I've seen in South Wales—but if you're heading to the great castles of North Wales (such as Conwy and Caernarfon) a visit here is redundant.

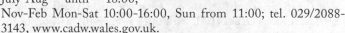

Cost and Hours: £7.95; daily 9:30-17:00, July-Aug until 18:00; Nov-Feb Mon-Sat 10:00-16:00, Sun from 11:00; tel. 029/2088-3143, www.cadw.wales.gov.uk.

Information: Scant explanations are offered by a few posted plaques; if you want the full story, invest in the £4 guidebook. Across the moat, Caerphilly's helpful town **TI** happily answers questions. It also has free Wi-Fi with comfortable seating overlooking the castle, and sells a variety of locally-sourced, nontacky Welsh souvenirs, from hand-carved heart spoons to gifty edibles (daily 10:00-17:30, tel. 029/2088-0011, www.visitcaerphilly.com).

Getting There: The castle is located right in the center of the town of Caerphilly, nine miles north of Cardiff. To get there, take the **train** from Cardiff to Caerphilly (4/hour Mon-Sat, hourly Sun, 20 minutes) and walk five minutes. It's 20 minutes by **car** from St. Fagans (exit 32, following signs from the M-4). Once in town, follow signs to park in the pay lot right next to the TI (described above), facing the castle.

Background: Spread over 30 acres, Caerphilly is the second-largest castle in Britain after Windsor. English Earl Gilbert de Clare erected this squat behemoth to try to establish a stronghold in Wales. With two concentric walls, it was considered to be a brilliant arrangement of defensive walls and moats. Attackers had to negotiate three drawbridges and four sets of doors and portcullises just to reach the main entrance. For the record, there were no known successful enemy forays beyond the current castle's inner walls. Later, this castle understandably became a favorite of Romantics, who often painted it in the shimmering Welsh mist. And in modern times, during the Great Depression of the 1930s, the castle's owner undertook a restoration of the then-mostly ruined structure (as a sort of private stimulus package), restoring it at least partway to its previous glory. Today it's surrounded by a picturesque, picnic-perfect park.

Visiting the Castle: Cross the first moat and enter the outer gate to buy your ticket. Then head across the second moat to reach the central keep of the castle.

You'll enter through the **Inner East Gatehouse,** with a short introductory video on the ground floor, and unfurnished but still stately residential halls upstairs. The top-floor terrace offers great views between the crenellations of the castle complex and the town. On the way up and down, look for the little bathrooms. No need to flush—the chute beneath the hole drops several stories directly into the moat below. (Just one more disincentive for would-be attackers thinking of crossing that moat.)

From there, head into the **Inner Ward**—the central yard (or "bailey") that's ringed by thick walls and stout towers. The tower across the Inner Ward to the right features another short video about the castle. To the left as you enter the Inner Ward is the restored, cavernous **Great Hall,** with thick stony walls, a wood-beam ceiling, and a man-sized fireplace. This space helps you imagine a great medieval feast. (If you'd like to do more than imagine, you can rent out the hall for a banquet of your own.)

Hiding behind the Great Hall is the icon of the castle—a half-destroyed listing **tower** (which, they like to brag, "out-leans Pisa's"). Following the English Civil War, the Parliament decreed that many castles like this one be destroyed as a preventive measure; this tower was a victim. Some believe that the adjacent **Braose Gallery** has a resident ghost: Legend has it that de Clare, after learning of his wife Alice's infidelity, exiled her back to France and had her lover killed. Upon discovering her paramour's fate, Alice died of a broken heart. Since then, the "Green Lady," named for her husband's jealousy, has reportedly roamed the ramparts.

Before leaving, be sure to visit the strip of yard that stretches out in front of the ticket office (along the inner moat). The first tower has a replica (complete with sound effects) of the **latrines** that were used by the soldiers—again, these dumped right into the moat. Just beyond that tower is a collection of life-size replica **siege engines**—ingenious catapult-like devices and oversized crossbows designed to deter attackers (each one is well described).

Big Pit National Coal Museum

To learn just how important the coal industry was to the economic development of South Wales, venture 30 miles north of Cardiff to a former coal mine in Blaenavon. Now part of the National Museum of Wales, the mine operated from 1860 to 1980. You can wander the grounds to see machinery and visit old buildings and exhibits. The highlight is the hour-long miner-guided tour 300 feet underground (hard hats and headlamps provided).

Cost and Hours: Free, parking-£3, daily 9:30-17:00, underground tours run 10:00-15:30, shorter hours off-season, last entry one hour before closing, café and coffee shop; in Blaenavon on the A-4043, tel. 0300-111-2333, www.museumwales.ac.uk/bigpit.

Sleeping in Cardiff

ALONG CATHEDRAL ROAD

This pleasant (but busy) tree-lined street—a one-mile walk or quick bus ride from the city center—feels classic and upscale, with rows of tidy Victorian homes...several of which host B&Bs. Expect some street noise. Street parking here is free but tight; I've noted places that offer private parking.

$$ Cathedral 73 Hotel is plush but loosely run, with eight rooms above a classy, contemporary lobby area (breakfast extra, free parking, 73 Cathedral Rd, tel. 029/2023-5005, www.cathedral73.com, stay@cathedral73.com).

$$ Lincoln House Private Hotel feels classic and classy. Its 21 rooms are traditionally decorated and neatly maintained, and the public spaces—from a plush lounge to a convivial bar—are appealing (free parking, 118-120 Cathedral Rd, tel. 029/2039-5558, www.lincolnhotel.co.uk, reservations@lincolnhotel.co.uk).

$ Church Guest House rents nine straightforward rooms with simple, contemporary style (includes continental breakfast, 109 Cathedral Road, tel. 029/2034-0881, www.churchguesthouse.co.uk, enquiries@churchguesthouse.co.uk, David Church).

$ The Town House has eight nondescript rooms and a big, shared breakfast table (free parking, 70 Cathedral Road, tel. 029/2023-9399, www.thetownhousecardiff.co.uk, thetownhouse@msn.com, Charles and Paula).

FACING MILLENNIUM STADIUM

A quiet middle-class neighborhood of row houses lines up across the river from Millennium Stadium. It's a shorter walk to the center than the Cathedral Road options (about 10 minutes to the castle), and generally less "posh" and more affordable—making it a smart budget choice.

$ Riverside B&B, carefully run by Irena, has one en-suite double and three top-floor rooms that share a bathroom. Everything is neat as a pin, and guests gather around a big shared breakfast table (free parking, 1 Coldstream Terrace, tel. 029/2021-0378, mobile 0774-591-9300, www.riversidebandb.co.uk, irenahinc@yahoo.co.uk).

$ Anchorage Guest House feels impersonal—there's no 24-hour reception, and you'll use a key code to come and go. The public spaces are a bit dated and scuffed, but its 14 rooms are comfortable, and the price is right (cheaper rooms with shared bath, includes continental breakfast, pay-and-display street parking, 45-47 Fitzhamon Embankment, tel. 029/2240-1888, www.anchorageguesthouse.co.uk, anchorageguesthousecardiff@gmail.com).

¢ The River House is a delightful hostel/backpackers' hotel, conscientiously run by brother-and-sister team Charlie and Abi. Their 12 rooms include doubles, as well as four- and six-bed dorms (all with shared bath). They pride themselves on offering good value and a welcoming, mellow home base in Cardiff. There's a shared kitchen, a small lounge, and delightful back garden. No wonder they've been voted best hostel in Wales (59 Fitzhamon Embankment, tel. 029/2039-9810, www.riverhousebackpackers.com).

CHAIN HOTELS IN THE CENTER

Cardiff's city center—where you'll be spending most of your sightseeing time—is full of big chain hotels at every price point. Mid-range options include **$ Jurys Inn** (1 Park Place), **$ Travelodge** (St. Mary Street), **$ Ibis** (near the Queen Street train station on Churchill Way), and **$ Premier Inn** (also near the Queen Street train station, 10 Churchill Way). Generally, these are a good deal in a convenient location; when it's busy (such as when there's a big rugby match), prices skyrocket and the city center can feel rowdy. Either way, parking can be pricey.

Eating in Cardiff

All of my recommendations, except those on except Cowbridge Road, are in the city center. Many are deep inside Cardiff's delightful shopping arcades, and most are lunch-only. If looking for a meal on Cardiff Bay, simply peruse the restaurants at Mermaid

Quay (Pizza Pronto and Moksh Indian restaurant are both well-regarded nonchain options).

In Castle Arcade: $$ Madame Fromage, right at the bend of the arcade, is a tempting choice for mostly cheese-focused light meals, such as Welsh rarebit (Mon-Sat 10:00-17:00, closed Sun, 21 Castle Arcade, tel. 029/2064-4888). **$$ Barkers** is a sprawling-yet-cozy café, good for tea or a light meal either inside or out on the arcade (Mon-Sat 8:30-17:30, Sun 10:30-16:30).

In High Street Arcade: $ New York Deli dishes up good sandwiches (Mon-Sat 9:30-16:30, Sun 11:00-15:30...or until they run out of bread, 19 High Street Arcade, tel. 029/2038-8388). **$$ Barkers Tea Rooms** is an outpost of the popular Barkers described above, with a similar menu (daily 9:00-17:00, 8-12 High Street Arcade, tel. 029/2034-1390).

In Morgan Arcade: $$ The Plan may be Cardiff's most appealing coffee shop, filling a woody two-story space in a genteel arcade (light meals, Mon-Sat 8:45-17:00, Sun 10:00-16:00, food until one hour before closing, 28-29 Morgan Arcade, tel. 029/2039-8764).

Near the Castle: $$$$ The Potted Pig is *the* place for a fancy meal downtown. It's in a cellar with straightforward decor that doesn't compete with the menu: locally sourced, seasonal, and artfully composed modern Welsh dishes with French influences. Reservations are smart at dinnertime. While pricey to order à la carte, their lunch special—just £12 for two courses—is affordable (Tue-Sat 12:00-14:00 & 19:00-21:30, Sun 12:00-14:30 only, closed Mon, directly in front of Cardiff Castle at 27 High Street, tel. 029/2022-4817, www.thepottedpig.com).

$$ Cafe Citta, in the pedestrian zone in front of the castle, is clearly the local favorite for Italian food. Tight and cozy (reserve ahead), the first language spoken here is Italian—and the food is authentically delicious (Mon-Sat 12:00-23:00, closed Sun, 4 Church Street, tel. 029/2022-4040).

Tea in the Park: $ Pettigrew Tea Rooms is a cozy space just inside Bute Park that feels like a visit to grandma's (Mon-Fri 8:30-17:30, Sat-Sun 9:00-18:00, between the castle and the river, tel. 029/2023-5486, www.pettigrew-tearooms.com).

Local Brews: An outpost of a brewery in nearby Newport, **$$ Tiny Rebel** fills a striking, classic red-brick building near the stadium. With youthful-but-mellow ambience and a basic menu of burgers and bar food, this is a good place to sample Welsh brews (flights available, long hours daily, food served Mon-Sat until 20:00, Sun until 16:00, 25 Westgate Street). Tiny Rebel also marks the start of **Womanby Street,** a lively after-hours zone where bars and clubs fill formerly abandoned industrial buildings.

Cowbridge Road: This street just west of the river (and south of my recommended Cathedral Road hotels) is lined with a mish-mash of blue-collar businesses and ethnic eateries. **$ Chai Street** (#153) serves Indian street food on silver thali platters, while **$ Got Beef** (#161) is a local favorite for its gourmet hamburgers.

Cardiff Connections

From Cardiff by Train to: Caerphilly (2-4/hour, 20 minutes), **Bath** (hourly, 1-1.5 hours), **Birmingham** (1/hour direct, more with change in Bristol, 2 hours), **London**'s Paddington Station (2/hour, 2 hours), **Chepstow** (2/hour, 35 minutes; then bus #69 to **Tintern**—runs every 1-2 hours, 20 minutes). Train info: tel. 0871-200-2233, www.traveline-cymru.info.

By Car: For driving directions from Bath to Cardiff, see "Route Tips for Drivers" at the end of this chapter.

The Wye Valley

From Chepstow, on the mouth of the River Severn, the River Wye cuts north, marking the border between Wales (Monmouthshire, on the west bank) and England (Gloucestershire, on the east bank). While everything covered here is in Wales, it's all within sight of England—just over the river.

This land is lush, mellow, and historic. Local tourist brochures explain the area's special dialect, its strange political autonomy, and its oaken ties to Trafalgar and Admiral Nelson (who harvested timbers for his ships in the Forest of Dean). The valley is home to the legendary Tintern Abbey, the ruined skeleton of a glorious church that's well worth a quick stop. The abbey sits partway between two pleasant, workaday towns with interesting sights of their own: Chepstow (with a fine castle) and Monmouth (a market town with some quirky sights). Just to the east of the river, in England, is the romantic-sounding but disappointing Forest of Dean.

If you've always dreamed of visiting Tintern Abbey—and wouldn't mind a quick taste of a stout castle and a couple of charming Welsh towns—the riverside A-466 traces the Wye and makes a detour between Bath and the Cotswolds that's worth considering (adding about an hour of driving compared with the less scenic, more direct route). I've listed these sights in the order you'll reach them as you move north up the Wye.

Chepstow

This historic burg enjoys a strategic location, for the same reason it may be your first stop in Wales: It marks the natural boundary between England and Wales. Driving into town, you'll pass through the town gate where, in medieval times, folks arriving to sell goods or livestock were hit up for tolls.

Park in the pay-and-display lot just below the castle, which is also conveniently close to the TI, museum, and free WCs. Everything worth seeing is within a short walk. To explore more of the town, buy the *Chepstow Town Trail* guide at the TI (daily 9:30-17:00, mid-Oct-Easter until 15:30, Bridge Street, tel. 01291/623-772, www.visitmonmouthshire.com) or Chepstow Museum. St. Mary's Street is lined with appealing little lunch spots (try the Lime Tree Café).

Chepstow Castle

Perched on a riverside ridge overlooking the pleasant village of Chepstow on one side and the River Wye on the other, this castle is worth a short

stop for drivers heading for Tintern Abbey, or it's a 10-minute walk from the Chepstow train station (follow signs; uphill going back). The stone-built Great Tower, dating from 1066, was among the first castles the Normans plunked down to secure their turf in Wales, and it remained in use through 1690. While many castles of the time were built first in wood, Chepstow, then a key foothold on the England-Wales border, was built from stone from the start for durability. You'll work your way up through various towers and baileys (inner yards); a few posted plaques provide details, but you're mostly on your own. As you clamber along the battlements (with great views to town and over the river to England), you'll find architectural evidence of military renovations through the centuries, from Norman to Tudor right up through Cromwellian additions. You can tell which parts date from Norman days—they're the ones built from yellow sandstone instead of the grayish limestone that makes up the rest of the castle. While the castle would benefit from more exhibits (it's basically an empty shell), with a little imagination you can resurrect the skeletons of buildings and appreciate how formidable and strategic it must have been in its heyday.

Cost and Hours: £6.50; daily 9:30-17:00, July-Aug until 18:00; Nov-Feb Mon-Sat 10:00-16:00, Sun from 11:00; guidebook-£4.50, in Chepstow village a half-mile from train station, tel. 01291/624-065, www.cadw.wales.gov.uk.

SOUTH WALES

▲Chepstow Museum

Highlighting Chepstow's history, this museum is in an 18th-century townhouse across the street from the castle. Endearingly earnest, jammed with artifacts, and well presented, it says just about everything that could possibly be said about this small town. Upstairs, the 1940 machine for giving women permanents will be etched in your memory forever.

Cost and Hours: Free; daily 10:30-17:30; March-June and Oct Mon-Sat 11:00-17:00, Sun 14:00-17:00; Nov-Feb daily 11:00-16:00; tel. 01291/625-981.

Riverfront Park

From the TI and parking lot, walk one block down Bridge Street to the River Wye. The river is spanned by a graceful, white cast-iron bridge. If you walk across it to the ornate decorations in the middle (at the *Gloucester/Monmouth* sign), you can stand with one foot in Wales and the other in England (notice the *Gloucestershire* sign across the bridge). From the bridge, you'll also have great views back to the castle. Beneath your feet, the River Wye's banks and water are muddy because this is a tidal river, which can rise and fall about 20 feet twice a day.

Back in Wales, stroll 100 yards along the riverside park (with the river on your left), noticing that the English bank sits on a chalk cliff—into which has been painted a Union Jack (to celebrate King George V's Silver Jubilee in 1935). Near the standing stones is a large circular plaque marking the beginning of the Welsh Coast Path; from here, you can walk 870 miles all the way along the coast of Wales. Nearby is the 176-mile Offa's Dyke Path, which roughly traces the border between Wales and England. Together, these two paths go almost all the way around the country.

▲▲Tintern Abbey

Inspiring monks to prayer, William Wordsworth to poetry, J. M. W. Turner to a famous painting, and rushed tourists to a thought-ful moment, this verse-worthy ruined-castle-of-an-abbey merits a five-mile detour off the motorway. Founded in 1131 on a site chosen by Norman monks for its tranquility, it functioned as an austere Cistercian abbey until its dissolution in 1536. The monks followed a strict schedule. They rose several hours after  midnight for the first of eight daily prayer sessions and spent the rest of their time studying, working the surrounding farmlands, and meditating. Dissolved under Henry VIII's Act of Suppression in 1536, the magnificent church moldered in relative obscurity until tourists in the Romantic era (late-18th century) discovered the wooded Wye Valley and abbey ruins. J. M. W. Turner made his first sketches in 1792, and William Wordsworth penned "Lines Composed a Few Miles Above Tintern Abbey..." in 1798.

With all the evocative ruined abbeys dotting the British landscape, why all the fuss about this one? Because few are as big, as remarkably intact, and as picturesquely situated. Most of the external walls of the 250-foot-long, 150-foot-wide church still stand, along with the exquisite window tracery and outlines of the sacristy, chapter house, and dining hall. The daylight that floods through the roofless ruins highlights the Gothic decorated arches—in those days a bold departure from Cistercian simplicity. While the guidebook (described next) narrates a very detailed, architecture-oriented tour, the best visit is to simply stroll the cavernous interior and let your imagination roam, like the generations of Romantics before you.

In summer, the abbey is flooded with tourists, so visit early or late to miss the biggest crowds. The shop sells Celtic jewelry and other gifts. Take an easy 15-minute walk up to St. Mary's Church (on the hill above town) for a view of the abbey, River Wye, and England just beyond.

Cost and Hours: £6.50; daily 9:30-17:00, July-Aug until 18:00; Nov-Feb Mon-Sat 10:00-16:00, Sun from 11:00; occasional summertime concerts in the cloisters (check website for schedule or ask at the TI), tel. 01291/689-251, www.cadw.wales.gov.uk.

Information: Sparse informational plaques clearly identify and explain each part of the complex. The dry, extensive £4.50 guidebook may be too much information—but if you're looking to redeem your £3 parking fee (see next), it brings the cost down to just £1.50, and makes the guidebook a fine souvenir.

Getting There: Drivers park in the pricey pay lot right next to the abbey (£3, refundable if you buy anything in the official shop or at The Anchor restaurant). By public transportation from Cardiff, catch a 35-minute train to Chepstow; from there, take bus #69

(every 1-2 hours, 20 minutes) or a taxi (about £10 one-way) the final six miles to the abbey.

Near Tintern Abbey: The villages of **Tintern** and **Tintern Parva** cluster in wide spots along the main riverside road, just north of the abbey. A couple of miles north, just beyond the last of the inns, you'll find

SOUTH WALES

the **Old Station**—a converted train station with old rail cars that house a regional TI, gift shop, and an exhibit on the local railway (closed Nov-March, pay parking lot, tel. 01291/689-566, www. visitmonmouthshire.com). Surrounding the train cars are a fine riverside park, a café, and a few low-key, kid-friendly attractions.

Monmouth

Another bustling market town—bookending the valley of the River Wye with Chepstow—Monmouth has a pleasant square, a few offbeat museums, and an impressive roster of past residents. The main square is called **Agincourt Square,** after the famous battle won by a king who was born right here: Henry V (you'll see a statue of him in the niche on the big building). The stately building on that square, which houses the TI, is **Shire Hall,** the historic home of the courts and town council. This was the site of a famous 1840 trial of John Frost, a leader of the Chartist movement (championing the rights of the working class in Victorian Britain).

Standing in front of Shire Hall is a statue of **Charles Rolls** (1877-1910), contemplating a model airplane. This descendant of a noble Monmouth family was a pioneer of ballooning and aviation, and—together with his business partner, Frederick Royce—revolutionized motoring with the creation of their company, Rolls-Royce. The airplane he's holding, which he purchased from the Wright Brothers, helped him become the first person to fly over the English Channel and back, in 1910. (Just over a month later, he also became the first British person to die in a plane crash, when that same Wright Flyer lost its tail midflight.)

Across the street from Shire Hall, angle right up the lane to the Regimental Museum and the scant ruins of **Monmouth Castle,** where Henry V was born in 1386. While there's not much to see, the site may wring out a few goose bumps for historians.

A block up Priory Street is the endearing **Nelson Museum** (a.k.a. Monmouth Museum). Admiral Horatio Nelson, who was considered in Victorian times (and still today, by many) to be the savior of England for his naval victories in the Napoleonic Wars, was a frequent visitor to Monmouth. This remarkable collection of Nelson-worship began as the personal collection of local noblewoman Lady Georgiana Llangattock, who was also the mother of Charles Rolls. You'll see several of Nelson's personal effects, a replica of his uniform, the actual sword he wore in the Battle of Trafalgar (as well as the two swords surrendered by the French and Spanish commanders), and some 800 letters by or to him (pull out the drawers to see them). There are also a few small exhibits about other aspects of town history, including the Rolls family (www. monmouthshire.gov.uk).

A few blocks downhill in the opposite direction (down Monnow Street from Agincourt Square) is the picturesque, 13th-century **Monnow Bridge,** with its graceful arches and stout defensive tower in the middle.

Forest of Dean

East of Monmouth and the River Wye is this heavily promoted, 43-square-mile patch of rare "ancient woodland" (what Americans call "old-growth forest"). While the name alone is enough to conjure fantasies of primeval forests, King Arthur, and Robin Hood, the reality is underwhelming if you come from a region with a forested area of any significant size. You could drive to the visitors center at Beechenhurst Lodge to pay too much for parking and get advice for a local hike, but I'd rather skip this forest entirely. Both England and Wales have far more interesting natural areas that are deserving of your time.

Sleeping in the Wye Valley

If you're seduced into spending the night in this charming area, you'll find plenty of B&Bs near Tintern Abbey or in the castle-crowned town of Chepstow, located just down the road (a one-hour drive from Bath). The two places I've listed are near the abbey.

$$ Parva Farmhouse has eight old-fashioned rooms in a 400-year-old building right along the main road through Tintern. While a bit dated, it comes with Welsh charm and is within walking distance of the abbey, village, and local pubs (Monmouth Road, tel. 01291/689-411, www.parvafarmhouse.co.uk, parvahoteltintern@hotmail.co.uk, Roger and Marta).

¢ St. Briavels Castle Youth Hostel is housed in an 800-year-old Norman castle used by King John in 1215 (the year he signed the Magna Carta). The hostel is comfortable (as castles go), friendly, and in the center of the quiet village of St. Briavels just north of Tintern Abbey. Nonguests are welcome to poke around the courtyard; if you're in town and the gates are open, step inside (breakfast extra, private rooms possible, Nov-March open to groups only, reception open daily 8:00-10:00 & 17:00-22:00, no curfew but ask for door code, modern kitchen and medieval banquet hall, brown-bag lunches and evening meals available, tel. 0345-371-9042, www.yha.org.uk, stbriavels@yha.org.uk). The village of St. Briavels sits in a forest high above the river. From Tintern, head north on the A-466, watch for the St. Briavels turnoff on the right, and switchback up the steep road into town.

South Wales Connections

ROUTE TIPS FOR DRIVERS

Bath to Cardiff and St. Fagans: Leave Bath following signs for the A-4, then the M-4. It's 10 miles north (on the A-46 past a village called Pennsylvania) to the M-4 freeway. Zip westward, crossing a huge suspension bridge over the Severn, into Wales (£6.50 toll westbound only). Stay on the M-4 (not the M-48) past Cardiff, take exit 33, and follow the brown signs south to *St. Fagans National History Museum/Amgueddfa Werin Cymru/Museum of Welsh Life.*

Bath to Tintern Abbey: Follow the directions above to the M-4. Take the M-4 to exit 21 and get on the M-48. After crossing the northern bridge (£6.50 toll) into Wales, take exit 2 for the A-466 for six miles (follow signs to *Chepstow,* then *Tintern*). You'll see the Abbey on your right.

Cardiff to the Cotswolds via Forest of Dean: On the Welsh side of the big suspension bridge, take the Chepstow exit and follow signs up the A-466 to *Tintern Abbey* and the *Wye River Valley.* Carry on to Monmouth, and follow the A-40 and the M-50 to the Tewkesbury exit, where small roads lead to the Cotswolds.

SCOTLAND

SCOTLAND

One of the three countries that make up Great Britain, rugged, feisty, colorful Scotland stands apart. Whether it's the laid-back, less-organized nature of the people, the stony architecture, the unmanicured landscape, or simply the haggis, go-its-own-way Scotland is distinctive.

Scotland encompasses about a third of Britain's geographical area (30,400 square miles), but has less than a tenth of its population (about 5.4 million). This sparsely populated chunk of land stretches to Norwegian latitudes. Its Shetland Islands, at about 60°N (similar to Anchorage, Alaska), are the northernmost point of the British Isles. You may see Scotland referred to as "Caledonia" (its ancient Roman name) or "Alba" (its Gaelic name). Scotland's fortunes were long tied to the sea; all of its leading cities are located along firths (estuaries), where major rivers connect to ocean waters.

The southern part of Scotland, called the Lowlands, is relatively flat and urbanized. The northern area—the Highlands—features a wild, severely undulating terrain, punctuated by lochs (lakes) and fringed by sea lochs (inlets) and islands.

The Highland Boundary Fault that divides Scotland geologically also divides it culturally. Historically, there were two distinct identities: rougher Highlanders in the northern wilderness and the more refined Lowlanders in the southern flatlands and cities. Highlanders represented the stereotypical image of "true Scots," speaking Gaelic, wearing kilts, and playing bagpipes, while Lowlanders spoke languages of Saxon origin and wore trousers. After the Scottish Reformation, the Lowlanders embraced Protestantism, while most Highlanders stuck to Catholicism. Although this Lowlands/Highlands division has faded over time, some Scots still cling to it.

The Lowlands are dominated by a pair of rival cities: Edinburgh (on the east coast's Firth of Forth) and Glasgow (on the west

Scotland

Orkney Islands
John O'Groats
Durness
Thurso · Wick

OUTER HEBRIDES
Lewis

Harris

50 Kilometers

50 Miles

Ullapool

Isle of Skye

North Atlantic
Portree · Applecross

Inverness
· CULLODEN
· CLAVA CAIRNS

Loch Ness

INNER HEBRIDES
Mallaig
Fort William
▲ Ben Nevis

H I G H L A N D S
BALMORAL
■ Ballater

Aberdeen

Glencoe

· Pitlochry

North Sea

Iona
Mull
· Oban

Loch Lomond

Stirling
FALKIRK
WHEEL

Dundee

· St. Andrews

Glasgow **Edinburgh**

Arran

L O W L A N D S

Irish Sea

· Ayr

· Jedburgh

NORTHERN IRELAND

· Cairnryan

· Dumfries

Newcastle

Belfast ·

ENGLAND

coast's Firth of Clyde) mark the endpoints of Scotland's 75-mile-long "Central Belt," where three-quarters of the country's population resides. Edinburgh, the old royal capital, teems with Scottish history and is the country's most popular tourist attraction. Glasgow, once a gloomy industrial city, is becoming a hip, laid-back city of art, music, and architecture. In addition to these two cities—both of which warrant a visit—the Lowlands' highlights include the medieval university town and golf mecca of St. Andrews, the small city of Stirling (with its castle

and many nearby historic sites), and selected countryside stopovers.

The Highlands provide your best look at traditional Scotland. The sights are subtle, but the vivid traditional culture and friendly

people are engaging. The Highlands are more rocky and harsh
than other parts of the British
Isles. Most of the "Munros"—
Scotland's 282 peaks over 3,000
feet—are concentrated in the
Highlands. It's no wonder that
many of the exterior scenes of
Hogwarts' grounds in the *Harry*

Potter movies were filmed in this moody, spooky landscape (see
page 1024). Keep an eye out for shaggy Highland cattle (adorable
"hairy coos," with their bangs falling in their eyes); bring bug spray
in summer to thwart the tiny mosquitoes called midges, which can
make life miserable; and plan your trip around trying to attend a
Highland game (see sidebar on page 918).

Generally, the Highlands are hungry for the tourist dollar,
and everything overtly Scottish is exploited to the kilt; you need
to spend some time here to get to know the area's true character.
You can get a feel for the Highlands with a quick drive to Oban,
through Glencoe, then up the Caledonian Canal to Inverness.
With more time, the Isles of Iona, Staffa, and Mull (an easy day
trip from Oban); and countless brooding countryside castles will
flesh out your Highlands experience.

At these northern latitudes, cold and drizzly weather isn't
uncommon—even in midsummer. The blazing sun can quickly be
covered over by black clouds and howling wind. Your B&B host
will warn you to prepare for "four seasons in one day." Because
Scots feel personally responsible for bad weather, they tend to be
overly optimistic about forecasts. Take any Scottish promise of "sun
by the afternoon" with a grain of salt—and bring your raincoat, just
in case.

The major theme of Scottish history is the drive for independence, especially from England. (Scotland's rabble-rousing national motto is *Nemo me impune lacessit*—"No one provokes me with
impunity.") Like Wales, Scotland is a country of ragtag Celts sharing an island with wealthy and powerful Anglo-Saxons. Scotland's
Celtic culture is a result of its remoteness—the invading Romans
were never able to conquer this rough-and-tumble people, and even
built Hadrian's Wall to lock off this distant corner of their empire.
The Anglo-Saxons, and their descendants the English, fared little
better than the Romans did. Even King Edward I—who so successfully dominated Wales—was unable to hold on to Scotland for
long, largely thanks to the relentlessly rebellious William Wallace
a.k.a. "Braveheart" (see page 744).

Failing to conquer Scotland by the blade, England eventually absorbed it politically. In 1603, England's Queen Elizabeth I

died without an heir, so her closest royal relative—Scotland's King James VI—took the throne, becoming King James I of England. It took another century or so of battles, both military and diplomatic, but the Act of Union in 1707 definitively (and controversially) unified the Kingdom of Great Britain. Meanwhile, the English parliament overthrew the grandson of James I when he became a Catholic, replacing him with a line of Protestant monarchs. In 1745, Bonnie Prince Charlie attempted to reclaim the throne on behalf of the deposed Stuarts, but his army was slaughtered at the Battle of Culloden (see page 976). This cemented English rule over Scotland, and is seen by many Scots as the last gasp of the traditional Highlands clan system. Bagpipes, kilts, the Gaelic language, and other symbols of the Highlands were briefly outlawed.

Scotland has been joined—however unwillingly—to England ever since, and the Scots have often felt oppressed by their English countrymen (see sidebar). During the Highland Clearances in the 18th and 19th centuries, landowners (mostly English) decided that vast tracks of land were more profitable as grazing land for sheep than as farmland for people. Many Highlanders were forced to abandon their traditional homes and lifestyles and seek employment elsewhere, moving to the cities to work in Industrial Revolution-era factories. Large numbers ended up in North America, especially parts of eastern Canada, such as Prince Edward Island and Nova Scotia (literally, "New Scotland").

Americans and Canadians of Scottish descent enjoy coming "home" to Scotland. If you're Scottish, your surname will tell you which clan your ancestors likely belonged to. The prefix "Mac" (or "Mc") means "son of"—so "MacDonald" means the same thing as "Donaldson." Tourist shops everywhere are happy to help you track down your clan's tartan (distinctive plaid pattern). For more on how these "clan tartans" don't go back as far as you might think, see the sidebar on page 720.

Scotland shares a monarchy with the rest of the United Kingdom, though to Scots, Queen Elizabeth II is just "Queen Elizabeth"; the first Queen Elizabeth ruled England, but not Scotland. (In this book, I use England's numbering.) Scotland is not a sovereign state, but it is a "nation" in that it has its own traditions, ethnic identity, languages (Gaelic and Scots), and football league. To some extent, it even has its own government.

Recently, Scotland has enjoyed its greatest measure of political autonomy in centuries—a trend called "devolution." In 1999, the

SCOTLAND

Scottish parliament convened in Edinburgh for the first time in almost 300 years; in 2004, it moved into its brand-new building near the foot of the Royal Mile. Though the Scottish parliament's powers are limited (most major decisions are still made in London), the Scots are enjoying the refreshing breeze of increased self-governance. In a 2014 independence referendum, the Scots favored staying in the United Kingdom by a margin of 10 percent. The question of independence will likely remain a pivotal issue in Scotland for many years to come.

Scotland even has its own currency...sort of. Scots use the same coins as England, Wales, and Northern Ireland, but Scotland

also prints its own bills (featuring Scottish, rather than English people, and landmarks). Just to confuse tourists, three different banks print Scottish pound notes, each with a different design. In the Lowlands (around Edinburgh and Glasgow), you'll receive both Scottish and English pounds from ATMs and in change. But in the Highlands, you'll almost never see English pounds. Bank of England notes are legal and widely used; Northern Ireland bank notes are legal but less common.

The Scottish flag—a diagonal, X-shaped white cross on a blue field—represents the cross of Scotland's patron saint, the Apostle Andrew (who was crucified on an X-shaped cross). You may not realize it, but you see the Scottish flag every time you look at the Union Jack: England's flag (the red St. George's cross on a white field) superimposed on Scotland's (a blue field with a white diagonal cross). The diagonal red cross (St. Patrick's cross) over Scotland's white one represents Northern Ireland. (Wales gets no love on the Union Jack.)

Here in "English-speaking" Scotland, you may still encounter a language barrier. First is the lovely, lilting Scottish accent—which may take you a while to understand. You may also hear an impenetrable dialect of Scottish English that many linguists consider to be a separate language, called "Scots." You may already know several Scots words: lad, lassie, wee, bonnie, glen, loch, aye. On menus, you'll see neeps and tatties (turnips and potatoes). And in place names, you'll see ben (mountain), brae (hill), firth (estuary), and kyle (strait).

British, Scottish, and English

Scotland and England have been tied together politically for more than 300 years, since the Act of Union in 1707. For a century and a half afterward, Scottish nationalists rioted for independence in Edinburgh's streets and led rebellions ("uprisings") in the Highlands. In this controversial union, history is clearly seen through two very different filters.

If you tour a British-oriented sight, such as Edinburgh's National War Museum Scotland, you'll find things told in a "happy union" way, which ignores the long history of Scottish resistance—from the ancient Picts through the time of Robert the Bruce. The official line: In 1706-1707, it was clear to England and certain parties in Scotland (especially landowners from the Lowlands) that it was in their mutual interest to dissolve the Scottish government and fold it into the United Kingdom, to be ruled from London.

But talk to a cabbie or your B&B host, and you may get a different spin. Scottish independence is still a hot-button issue. Since 2007, the Scottish National Party (SNP) has owned the largest majority in the Scottish Parliament. During a landmark referendum in September 2014, the Scots voted to remain part of the union—but many polls, right up until election day, suggested that things could easily have gone the other way.

The rift shows itself in sports, too. While the English may refer to a British team in international competition as "English," the Scots are careful to call it "British." If a Scottish athlete does well, the English call him "British." If he screws up... he's a clumsy Scot.

Second is Gaelic (pronounced "gallic" here; Ireland's closely related Celtic language is pronounced "gaylic")—the ancient Celtic language of the Scots. While only one percent of the population speaks Gaelic, it's making a comeback—particularly in the remote and traditional Highlands.

While soccer ("football") is as popular here as anywhere, golf

is Scotland's other national sport. But in Scotland, it's not necessarily considered an exclusively upper-class pursuit; you can generally play a round at a basic course for about £15. While Scotland's best scenery is along the west coast, its best golfing is on the east coast—home to many prestigious golf courses. Most of these are links courses, which use natural sand from the beaches for the bunkers. For tourists, these links are more authentic, more challenging, and more fun than

SCOTLAND

Haggis and Other Traditional Scottish Dishes

Scotland's most unique dish, **haggis,** began as a peasant food. Waste-conscious cooks wrapped the heart, liver, and lungs of a sheep in its stomach lining, packed in some oats and spices, and then boiled the lot to create a hearty, if slightly palatable, meal. Traditionally served with "neeps and tatties" (turnips and potatoes), haggis was forever immortalized thanks to Robbie Burns' *Address to a Haggis.*

Today haggis has been refined almost to the point of high cuisine. You're likely to find it on many menus, including at breakfast. You can dress it up with anything from a fine whisky cream sauce to your basic HP brown sauce. To appreciate this iconic Scottish dish, think of how it tastes—not what it's made of.

The king of Scottish **black puddings** (blood sausage) is made in the Hebrides Islands. Called Stornoway, it's so famous that the European Union has granted it protected status to prevent imitators from using its name. A mix of beef suet, oatmeal, onion, and blood, the sausage is usually served as part of a full Scottish breakfast, but it also appears on the menus of top-class restaurants.

Be on the lookout for other traditional Scottish taste treats. **Cullen skink** is Scotland's answer to chowder: a hearty, creamy fish soup, often made with smoked haddock. A **bridie** (or Forfar bridie) is a savory meat pastry similar to a Cornish pasty, but generally lighter (no potatoes). A **Scotch pie**—small, double-crusted, and filled with minced meat, is a good picnic food; it's a common snack at soccer matches and outdoor events. **Crowdie** is a dairy spread that falls somewhere between cream cheese and cottage cheese.

And for dessert, **cranachan** is similar to a trifle, made with whipped cream, honey, fruit (usually raspberries), and whisky-soaked oats. Another popular dessert is the **Tipsy Laird,** served at "Burns Suppers" on January 25, the annual celebration of national poet Robert Burns. It's essentially the same as a trifle but with whisky or brandy and Scottish raspberries.

the regular-style courses (with artificial landforms) farther inland. If you're a golfer, St. Andrews—on the east coast—is a pilgrimage worth making.

Scottish cuisine is down-to-earth, often with an emphasis on local produce. Both seafood and "land food" (beef, chicken, lamb, and venison) are common. One Scottish mainstay—eaten more by tourists than by Scots these days—is the famous haggis, tastier than it sounds and worth trying...even before you've tucked into the whisky. Also look for cullen skink, a satisfying, chowder-like cream soup with smoked fish (see sidebar).

The "Scottish Breakfast" is similar to the English version, but they often add a potato scone (like a flavorless, soggy potato pancake) and haggis (best when served with poached eggs and HP brown sauce).

Breakfast, lunch, or dinner, the Scots love their whisky—and touring one of the country's many distilleries is a sightseeing treat. The Scots are fiercely competitive with the Irish when it comes to this peaty spirit. Scottish "whisky" is typically distilled twice, whereas Irish "whiskey" adds a third distillation (and an extra *e*). Some distilleries roast their barley over peat fires, giving many Scottish whiskies a smokier flavor than their Irish cousins. Also note that what we call "scotch"—short for "scotch whisky"—is just "whisky" here. I've listed a few of the most convenient and interesting distilleries to visit, but if you're a whisky connoisseur, make a point of tracking down and touring your favorite.

Outside of the main cities, Scotland's sights are subtle, but its misty glens, brooding countryside castles, and warm culture are plenty engaging. Whether toasting with beer, whisky, or Scotland's favorite soft drink Irn-Bru, enjoy meeting the Scottish people. It's easy to fall in love with the irrepressible spirit and beautiful landscape of this faraway corner of Britain.

EDINBURGH

Edinburgh is the historical, cultural, and political capital of Scotland. For nearly a thousand years, Scotland's kings, parliaments, writers, thinkers, and bankers have called Edinburgh home. Today, it remains Scotland's most sophisticated city.

Edinburgh (ED'n-burah—only tourists pronounce it like "Pittsburgh") is Scotland's showpiece and one of Europe's most entertaining cities. It's a place of stunning vistas—nestled among craggy bluffs and studded with a prickly skyline of spires, towers, domes, and steeples. Proud statues of famous Scots dot the urban landscape. The buildings are a harmonious yellow-gray, all built from the same local sandstone.

Culturally, Edinburgh has always been the place where Lowland culture (urban and English) met Highland style (rustic and Gaelic). Tourists will find no end of traditional Scottish clichés: whisky tastings, kilt shops, bagpipe-playing buskers, and gimmicky tours featuring Scotland's bloody history and ghost stories.

Edinburgh is two cities in one. The Old Town stretches along the Royal Mile, from the grand castle on top to the palace on the bottom. Along this colorful labyrinth of cobbled streets and narrow lanes, medieval skyscrapers stand shoulder to shoulder, hiding peaceful courtyards.

A few hundred yards north of the Old Town lies the New Town. It's a magnificent planned neighborhood (from the 1700s). Here, you'll enjoy upscale shops, broad boulevards, straight streets, square squares, circular circuses, and Georgian mansions decked out in Greek-style columns and statues.

Today's Edinburgh is big in banking, scientific research, and scholarship at its four universities. Since 1999, when Scotland regained a measure of self-rule, Edinburgh reassumed its place as home of the Scottish Parliament. The city hums with life. Students and professionals pack the pubs and art galleries. It's especially lively in August, when the Edinburgh Festival takes over the town. Historic, monumental, fun, and well organized, Edinburgh is a tourist's delight.

PLANNING YOUR TIME

While the major sights can be seen in a day, I'd give Edinburgh two days and three nights.

Day 1: Tour the castle, then consider catching a city bus tour for a one-hour loop (departing from a block below the castle at the Hub/Tolbooth Church; you could munch a sandwich from the top deck if you're into multitasking). Back near the castle, take my self-guided Royal Mile walk, stopping in at shops and museums that interest you (Gladstone's Land is tops but you can only visit it by booking a tour). At the bottom of the Mile, consider visiting the Scottish Parliament, the Palace of Holyroodhouse, or both. If the weather's good, you could hike back to your B&B along the Salisbury Crags.

Day 2: Visit the National Museum of Scotland. After lunch (several great choices nearby, on Forrest Road), stroll through the Princes Street Gardens and the Scottish National Gallery. Then follow my self-guided walk through the New Town, visiting the Scottish National Portrait Gallery and the Georgian House—or squeeze in a quick tour of the good ship *Britannia* (check last entry time before you head out).

Evenings: Options include various "haunted Edinburgh" walks, literary pub crawls, or live music in pubs. Sadly, full-blown traditional folk performances are just about extinct, surviving only in excruciatingly schmaltzy variety shows put on for tour-bus groups. Perhaps the most authentic evening out is just settling down in a pub to sample the whisky and local beers while meeting the locals...and attempting to understand them through their thick Scottish accents (see "Nightlife in Edinburgh," page 790).

Orientation to Edinburgh

A VERBAL MAP

With 490,000 people (835,000 in the metro area), Edinburgh is Scotland's second-biggest city (after Glasgow). But the tourist's Edinburgh is compact: Old Town, New Town, and the B&B area south of the city center.

Edinburgh's **Old Town** stretches across a ridgeline slung between two bluffs. From west to east, this "Royal Mile" runs from the Castle Rock—which is visible from anywhere—to the base of the 822-foot extinct volcano called Arthur's Seat. For visitors, this east-west axis is the center of the action. Just south of the Royal Mile are the university and the National Museum of Scotland; farther to the south is a handy B&B neighborhood that lines up along **Dalkeith Road** and **Mayfield Gardens.** North of the Royal Mile ridge is the **New Town,** a neighborhood of grid-planned streets and elegant Georgian buildings.

In the center of it all—in a drained lake bed between the Old and New Towns—sit the Princes Street Gardens park and Waverley Bridge, where you'll find the Waverley train station, TI, Waverley Mall, bus info office (starting point for most city bus tours), Scottish National Gallery, and a covered dance-and-music pavilion.

TOURIST INFORMATION

The crowded TI is as central as can be, on the rooftop of the Waverley Mall and Waverley train station (Mon-Sat 9:00-17:00, Sun from 10:00, June daily until 18:00, July-Aug daily until 19:00; tel. 0131-473-3868, www.visitscotland.com). While the staff is helpful, be warned that much of their information is skewed by tourism payola (and booking seats on bus tours seems to be a big priority). There's also a TI at the airport (tel. 0131-344-3120).

For more information than what's included in the TI's free map, buy the excellent *Collins Discovering Edinburgh* map (which comes with opinionated commentary and locates almost every major sight). If you're interested in evening music, ask for the comprehensive entertainment listing, *The List.* Also consider buying Historic Scotland's Explorer Pass, which can save you some money if you visit the castles at both Edinburgh and Stirling, or are also visiting the Orkney Islands (for details, see page 1025).

ARRIVAL IN EDINBURGH

By Train: Arriving by train at Waverley Station puts you in the city center and below the TI. Taxis line up outside, on Market Street or Waverley Bridge. For the TI or bus stop, follow signs for Princes Street and ride up several escalators. From here, the TI is to your left, and the city bus stop is two blocks to your right (for bus directions from here to my recommended B&Bs, see "Sleeping in Edinburgh," later).

By Bus: Scottish Citylink, Megabus, and National Express buses use the bus station (with luggage lockers) in the New Town, two blocks north of the train station on St. Andrew Square.

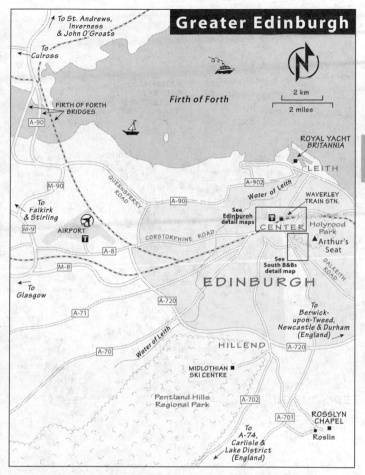

By Car: If you're arriving from the north, rather than drive through downtown Edinburgh to my recommended B&Bs, circle the city on the A-720 City Bypass road. Approaching Edinburgh on the M-9, take the M-8 (direction: Glasgow) and quickly get onto the A-720 City Bypass (direction: Edinburgh South). After four miles, you'll hit a roundabout. Ignore signs directing you into *Edinburgh North* and stay on the A-720 for 10 more miles to the next and last roundabout, named *Sheriffhall*. Exit the roundabout at the first left *(A-7 Edinburgh)*. From here it's four miles to the B&B neighborhood. After a while, the A-7 becomes Dalkeith Road (you'll pass the Royal Infirmary hospital complex). If you see the huge Royal Commonwealth Pool, you've gone a couple of blocks too far (avoid this by referring to the map on page 795).

If you're driving in on the A-68 from the south, first follow

EDINBURGH

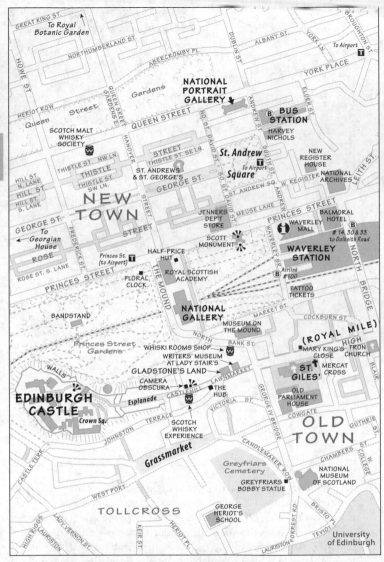

signs for *Edinburgh South & West* (A-720), then exit at *A-7(N) /Edinburgh* and follow the directions above.

By Plane: Edinburgh's airport is eight miles and a 25-minute taxi ride from downtown. For information, see "Edinburgh Connections," at the end of this chapter.

HELPFUL HINTS

Sunday Activities: Many Royal Mile sights close on Sunday (except in Aug), but other major sights and shops are open. Sun-

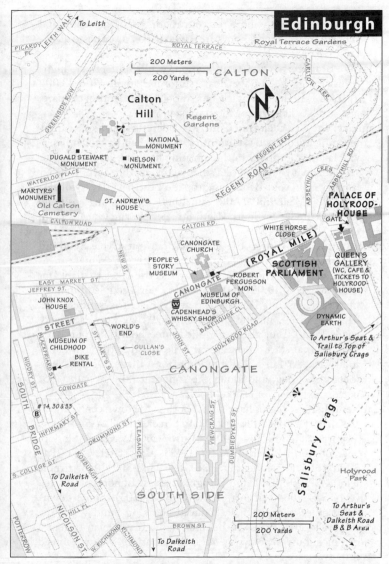

Edinburgh

To Leith

PICARDY PL.

LEITH WALK

ROYAL TERRACE

Royal Terrace Gardens

GREENSIDE ROW

CALTON

200 Meters

200 Yards

Calton Hill

Regent Gardens

N

CARLTON TERR.

DUGALD STEWART MONUMENT

NATIONAL MONUMENT

NELSON MONUMENT

REGENT TERR.

WATERLOO PLACE

REGENT ROAD

ABBEYHILL CRES.

ABBEYHILL RD.

MARTYRS' MONUMENT

Old Calton Cemetery

ST. ANDREW'S HOUSE

PALACE OF HOLYROOD-HOUSE

GATE

CALTON ROAD

CALTON RD.

WHITE HORSE CLOSE

QUEEN'S GALLERY (WC, CAFE & TICKETS TO HOLYROOD-HOUSE)

NEW ST.

CANONGATE CHURCH

(ROYAL MILE)

SCOTTISH PARLIAMENT

EAST MARKET ST.

JEFFREY ST.

PEOPLE'S STORY MUSEUM

CANONGATE

ROBERT FERGUSSON MON.

JOHN KNOX HOUSE

MUSEUM OF EDINBURGH

CADENHEAD'S WHISKY SHOP

HOLYROOD ROAD

DYNAMIC EARTH

STREET

WORLD'S END

BAKEHOUSE CL.

To Arthur's Seat & Trail to Top of Salisbury Crags

BLACKFRIARS ST.

ST. MARY'S ST.

MUSEUM OF CHILDHOOD

GULLAN'S CLOSE

ST. JOHN ST.

BIKE RENTAL

CANONGATE

NIDDRY ST.

COWGATE

SOUTH BRIDGE

14, 30 & 35

B

VIEWCRAIG ST.

DUMBIEDYKES ST.

Salisbury Crags

S. INFIRMARY ST.

DRUMMOND ST.

PLEASANCE

ROXBURGH PL.

To Dalkeith Road

S. COLLEGE ST.

HILL PL.

Holyrood Park

SOUTH SIDE

To Arthur's Seat & Dalkeith Road B & B Area

POTTERROW

NICOLSON ST.

HILL FL.

W. RICHMOND

RICHMOND

BROWN ST.

200 Meters

200 Yards

To Dalkeith Road

EDINBURGH

day is a good day to catch a guided walking tour along the Royal Mile or a city bus tour (buses go faster in light traffic). The slopes of Arthur's Seat are lively with hikers and picnickers on weekends.

Festivals: August is a crowded, popular month to visit Edinburgh thanks to the multiple festivals hosted here, including the official Edinburgh International Festival, the Fringe Festival, and the Military Tattoo. Book ahead for hotels, events, and restaurant dinners if you'll be visiting in August, and expect to pay significantly more for your room. Many museums and shops have extended hours in August. For more festival details, see page 783.

Baggage Storage: At the train station, you'll find pricey, high-security luggage storage near platform 2 (daily 7:00-23:00). There are also lockers at the bus station on St. Andrew Square, just two blocks north of the train station.

Laundry: The **Ace Cleaning Centre** launderette is located near my recommended B&Bs south of town. You can pay for full-service laundry (drop off in the morning for same-day service) or stay and do it yourself. For a small extra fee, they'll collect your laundry from your B&B and drop it off the next day (Mon-Fri 8:00-20:00, Sat 9:00-17:00, Sun 10:00-16:00, along bus route to city center at 13 South Clerk Street, opposite Queens Hall, tel. 0131/667-0549).

Bike Rental and Tours: The laid-back crew at **Cycle Scotland** happily recommends good bike routes with your rental (prices starting at £20/3 hours or £30/day, electric bikes available for extra fee, daily 10:00-18:00, may close for a couple of months in winter, just off Royal Mile at 29 Blackfriars Street, tel. 0131/556-5560, mobile 07796-886-899, www.cyclescotland. co.uk, Peter). They also run guided three-hour bike tours daily at 11:00 that start on the Royal Mile and ride through Holyrood Park, Arthur's Seat, Duddingston Village, Doctor Neil's (Secret) Garden, and along the Innocent railway path (£45/person, extra fee for e-bike, book ahead).

Car Rental: These places have offices both in the town center and at the airport: **Avis** (24 East London Street, tel. 0844-544-6059, airport tel. 0844-544-6004), **Europcar** (Waverley Station, near platform 2, tel. 0871-384-3453, airport tel. 0871-384-3406), **Hertz** (10 Picardy Place, tel. 0843-309-3026, airport tel. 0843-309-3025), and **Budget** (24 East London Street, tel. 0844-544-9064, airport tel. 0844-544-4605). Some downtown offices close or have reduced hours on Sunday, but the airport locations tend to be open daily. If you plan to rent a car, pick it up on your way out of Edinburgh—you won't need it in town.

Dress for the Weather: Weather blows in and out—bring your sweater and be prepared for rain.

GETTING AROUND EDINBURGH

Many of Edinburgh's sights are within walking distance of one another, but **buses** come in handy—especially if you're staying at a B&B south of the city center. Double-decker buses come with fine views upstairs. It's easy once you get the hang of it: Buses come by frequently (screens at bus stops show wait times) and have free, fast

Wi-Fi on board. The only hassle is that you must pay with exact change (£1.60/ride, £4/all-day pass). As you board, tell your driver where you're going (or just say "single ticket") and drop your change into the box. Ping the bell as you near your stop. You can pick up a route map at the TI or at the transit office at Old Town end of Waverley Bridge (tel. 0131/555-6363, www.lothianbuses.com). Edinburgh's single **tram** line (also £1.60/ride) is designed more for locals than tourists; it's most useful for reaching the airport (see "Edinburgh Connections" at the end of this chapter).

The 1,300 **taxis** cruising Edinburgh's streets are easy to flag down (ride between downtown and the B&B neighborhood costs about £7; rates go up after 18:00 and on weekends). They can turn on a dime, so hail them in either direction. **Uber** also works well here.

Tours in Edinburgh

Royal Mile Walking Tours

Walking tours are an Edinburgh specialty; you'll see groups trailing entertaining guides all over town. Below I've listed good all-purpose walks; for **literary pub crawls** and **ghost tours,** see "Nightlife in Edinburgh" on page 790.

Edinburgh Tour Guides offers a good historical walk (without all the ghosts and goblins). Their Royal Mile tour is a gentle two-hour downhill stroll from the castle to the palace (£16.50; daily at 9:30 and 19:00; meet outside Gladstone's Land, near the top of the Royal Mile—see map on page 719, must reserve ahead, mobile 0785-888-0072, www.edinburghtourguides.com, info@edinburghtourguides.com).

Mercat Tours offers a 1.5-hour "Secrets of the Royal Mile" walk that's more entertaining than intellectual (£13; £30 includes optional, 45-minute guided Edinburgh Castle visit; daily at 10:00 and 13:00, leaves from Mercat Cross on the Royal Mile, tel. 0131/225-5445, www.mercattours.com). The guides, who enjoy making a short story long, ignore the big sights and take you behind the scenes with piles of barely historical gossip, bully-pulpit Scottish pride, and fun but forgettable trivia. They also offer other tours, such as ghost walks, tours of 18th-century underground vaults on the southern slope of the Royal Mile, and *Outlander* sights (see their website for a rundown).

Sandemans New Edinburgh runs "free" tours multiple times a day; you won't pay upfront, but the guide will expect a tip (check schedule online, 3 hours, meet in front of Starbucks by Tron Kirk on High Street, www.neweuropetours.eu).

The **Voluntary Guides Association** offers free two-hour walks, but only during the Edinburgh Festival. You don't need a

EDINBURGH

reservation—just show up (check website for times, generally depart from City Chambers across from St. Giles' Cathedral on the Royal Mile, www.edinburghfestivalguides.org). You can also hire their guides (for a small fee) for private tours outside of festival time.

Blue Badge Local Guides

The following guides charge similar prices and offer half-day and full-day tours: **Jean Blair** (a delightful teacher and guide, £190/day without car, £430/day with car, mobile 0798-957-0287, www.travelthroughscotland.com, scotguide7@gmail.com); **Sergio La Spina** (an Argentinean who adopted Edinburgh as his hometown more than 20 years ago, £250/day, tel. 0131/664-1731, mobile 0797-330-6579, www.vivaescocia.com, sergiolaspina@aol.com); **Ken Hanley** (who wears his kilt as if pants don't exist, £130/half-day, £250/day, extra charge if he uses his car—seats up to six, tel. 0131/666-1944, mobile 0771-034-2044, www.small-world-tours.co.uk, kennethhanley@me.com); and **Liz Everett** (walking tours only—no car; £165/half-day, £230/day, mobile 07821-683-837, liz.everett@live.co.uk).

Hop-On, Hop-Off Bus Tours

The following one-hour hop-on, hop-off bus tour routes, all run by the same company, circle the town center, stopping at the major sights. **Edinburgh Tour** (green buses) focuses on the city center, with live guides. **City Sightseeing** (red buses, focuses on Old Town) has recorded commentary, as does the **Majestic Tour** (blue-and-yellow buses, includes a stop at the *Britannia* and Royal Botanic Garden). You can pay for just one tour (£15/24 hours), but most people pay a few pounds more for a ticket covering all buses (£20; buses run April-Oct roughly 9:00-19:00, shorter hours off-season; every 10-15 minutes, buy tickets on

board, tel. 0131/220-0770, www.edinburghtour.com). On sunny days the buses go topless, but come with increased traffic noise and exhaust fumes. For £52, the Royal Edinburgh Ticket covers two days of unlimited travel on all three buses, as well as admission (and line-skipping privileges) at Edinburgh Castle, the Palace of Holyroodhouse, and *Britannia* (www.royaledinburghticket.co.uk).

The **3 Bridges Tour** combines a hop-on, hop-off bus to South Queensferry with a boat tour on the Firth of Forth (£20, 3 hours total).

Weekend Tour Packages for Students

Andy Steves (Rick's son) runs Weekend Student Adventures (WSA Europe), offering 3-day and 10-day budget travel packages across Europe including accommodations, skip-the-line sightseeing, and unique local experiences. Locally guided and DIY options are available for student and budget travelers in 13 of Europe's most popular cities, including Edinburgh (guided trips from €199, see www.wsaeurope.com for details). Check out Andy's tips, resources, and podcast at www.andysteves.com.

Day Trips from Edinburgh

Many companies run a variety of day trips to regional sights, as well as multiday and themed itineraries. (Several of the local guides listed earlier have cars, too.)

The most popular tour is the all-day **Highlands trip.** The standard Highlands tour gives those with limited time a chance to experience the wonders of Scotland's wild and legend-soaked Highlands in a single long day (about £50, roughly 8:00-20:00). Itineraries vary but you'll generally visit/pass through the Trossachs, Rannoch Moor, Glencoe, Fort William, Fort Augustus on Loch Ness (some tours offer an optional boat ride), and Pitlochry. To save time, look for a tour that gives you a short glimpse of Loch Ness rather than driving its entire length or doing a boat trip. (Once you've seen a little of it, you've seen it all.)

Larger outfits, typically using bigger buses, include **Timberbush Highland Tours** (tel. 0131/226-6066, www.timberbushtours.com), **Gray Line** (tel. 0131/555-5558, www.graylinescotland.com), **Highland Experience** (tel. 0131/226-1414, www.highlandexperience.com), **Highland Explorer** (tel. 0131/558-3738, www.highlandexplorertours.com), and **Scotline** (tel. 0131/557-0162, www.scotlinetours.co.uk). Other companies pride themselves on keeping group sizes small, with 16-seat minibuses; these include **Rabbie's** (tel. 0131/212-5005, www.rabbies.com) and **Heart of Scotland Tours: The Wee Red Bus** (10 percent Rick Steves discount on full-price day tours—mention when booking, does not apply to overnight tours or senior/student rates, occasionally canceled off-season if too few sign up—leave a contact number, tel. 0131/228-2888, www.heartofscotlandtours.co.uk, run by Nick Roche).

For young backpackers, **Haggis Adventures** runs day tours plus overnight trips of up to 10 days (tel. 0131/557-9393, www.haggisadventures.com).

At **Discreet Scotland,** Matthew Wight and his partners specialize in tours of greater Edinburgh and Scotland in spacious SUVs—good for families (£360/2 people, 8 hours, mobile 0798-941-6990, www.discreetscotland.com).

Edinburgh at a Glance

▲▲▲**Royal Mile** Historic road—good for walking—stretching from the castle down to the palace, lined with museums, pubs, and shops. See page 716.

▲▲▲**Edinburgh Castle** Iconic hilltop fort and royal residence complete with crown jewels, Romanesque chapel, memorial, and fine military museum. **Hours:** Daily 9:30-18:00, Oct-March until 17:00. See page 738.

▲▲▲**National Museum of Scotland** Intriguing, well-displayed artifacts from prehistoric times to the 20th century. **Hours:** Daily 10:00-17:00. See page 763.

▲▲**Gladstone's Land** Seventeenth-century Royal Mile merchant's residence. **Hours:** Daily 10:30-16:00 by tour only, closed Nov-March. See page 749.

▲▲**St. Giles' Cathedral** Preaching grounds of Scottish Reformer John Knox, with spectacular organ, Neo-Gothic chapel, and distinctive crown spire. **Hours:** Mon-Fri 9:00-19:00, Sat until 17:00; Oct-April Mon-Sat 9:00-17:00; Sun 13:00-17:00 year-round. See page 751.

▲▲**Scottish Parliament Building** Striking headquarters for parliament, which returned to Scotland in 1999. **Hours:** Mon-Sat 10:00-17:00, longer hours Tue-Thu when parliament is in session (Sept-June), closed Sun year-round. See page 759.

▲▲**Palace of Holyroodhouse** The Queen's splendid official residence in Scotland, with lavish rooms, 12th-century abbey, and gallery with rotating exhibits. **Hours:** Daily 9:30-18:00, Nov-March until 16:30, closed during royal visits. See page 760.

▲▲**Scottish National Gallery** Choice sampling of European masters and Scotland's finest. **Hours:** Daily 10:00-17:00, Thu until 19:00; longer hours in Aug. See page 767.

▲▲**Scottish National Portrait Gallery** Beautifully displayed

Who's Who of Scottish history. **Hours:** Daily 10:00-17:00. See page 772.

▲▲**Georgian House** Intimate peek at upper-crust life in the late 1700s. **Hours:** Daily 10:00-17:00, March and Nov 11:00-16:00, closed Dec-Feb. See page 775.

▲▲**Royal Yacht *Britannia*** Ship for the royal family with a history of distinguished passengers, a 15-minute trip out of town. **Hours:** Daily 9:30-16:30, Oct until 16:00, Nov-March 10:00-15:30 (these are last entry times). See page 775.

▲**Scotch Whisky Experience** Gimmicky but fun and educational introduction to Scotland's most famous beverage. **Hours:** Generally daily 10:00-18:00. See page 748.

▲**The Real Mary King's Close** Tour of underground street and houses last occupied in the 17th century, viewable by guided tour. **Hours:** Daily 10:00-21:00, Nov-March Sun-Thu until 17:00 (these are last tour times). See page 757.

▲**Museum of Childhood** Five stories of historic fun. **Hours:** Thu-Mon 10:00-17:00 except Sun from 12:00, closed Tue-Wed. See page 758.

▲**People's Story Museum** Everyday life from the 18th to 20th century. **Hours:** Wed-Sat 10:00-17:00 except Sun from 12:00, closed Mon-Tue. See page 758.

▲**Museum of Edinburgh** Historic mementos, from the original National Covenant inscribed on animal skin to early golf balls. **Hours:** Thu-Mon 10:00-17:00 except Sun from 12:00, closed Tue-Wed. See page 759.

▲**Rosslyn Chapel** Small 15th-century church chock-full of intriguing carvings a short drive outside of Edinburgh. **Hours:** Mon-Sat 9:30-17:00, June-Aug until 18:00, Sun 12:00-16:45 year-round. See page 777.

EDINBURGH

EDINBURGH

Walks in Edinburgh

I've outlined two walks in Edinburgh: along the Royal Mile, and through the New Town. Many of the sights we'll pass on these walks are described in more detail later, under "Sights in Edinburgh."

THE ROYAL MILE

The Royal Mile is one of Europe's most interesting historic walks—it's worth ▲▲▲. The following self-guided stroll is also available as a 🎧 downloadable Rick Steves audio tour; see page 30.

Overview

Start at Edinburgh Castle at the top and amble down to the Palace of Holyroodhouse. Along the way, the street changes names—Castlehill, Lawnmarket, High Street, and Canongate—but it's a straight, downhill shot totaling just over one mile. And nearly every step is packed with shops, cafés, and lanes leading to tiny squares.

The city of Edinburgh was born on the easily defended rock at the top, where the castle stands today. Celtic tribes (and maybe the Romans) once occupied this site. As the town grew, it spilled downhill along the sloping ridge that became the Royal Mile. Because this strip of land is so narrow, there was no place to build but up. So in medieval times, it was densely packed with multistory "tenements"—large edifices under one roof that housed a number of tenants.

As you walk, you'll be tracing the growth of the city—its birth atop Castle Hill, its Old Town heyday in the 1600s, its expansion in the 1700s into the Georgian New Town (leaving the old quarter an overcrowded, disease-ridden Victorian slum), and on to the 21st century at the modern Scottish parliament building (2004).

In parts, the Royal Mile feels like one long Scottish shopping mall, selling all manner of kitschy souvenirs (known locally as "tartan tat"), shortbread, and whisky. But the streets are also packed with history, and if you push past the postcard racks into one of the many side alleys, you can still find a few surviving rough edges of the old city. Despite the drizzle, be sure to look up—spires, carvings, and towering Gothic "skyscrapers" give this city its unique urban identity.

This walk covers the Royal Mile's landmarks, but skips the many museums and indoor attractions along the way. These and other sights are described in walking order under "Sights in Edinburgh" on page 738. You can stay focused on the walk (which takes about 1.5 hours, without entering sights), then return later to visit the various indoor attractions; or review the sight descriptions beforehand and pop into those that interest you as you pass them.

• *We'll start at the Castle Esplanade, the big parking lot at the entrance to...*

EDINBURGH

➊ Edinburgh Castle

Edinburgh was born on the bluff—a big rock—where the castle now stands. Since before recorded history, people have lived on this strategic, easily defended perch.

The **castle** is an imposing symbol of Scottish independence. Flanking the entryway are statues of the fierce warriors who battled English invaders, William Wallace (on the right) and Robert the Bruce (left). Between them is the Scottish motto, *Nemo me impune lacessit*—roughly, "No one messes with me and gets away with it." (For a self-guided tour of Edinburgh Castle, see page 740.)

The esplanade—built as a military parade ground (1816)—is now the site of the annual Military Tattoo. This spectacular massing

of regimental bands fills the square nightly for most of August. Fans watch from temporary bleacher seats to see kilt-wearing bagpipers marching against the spectacular backdrop of the castle. TV crews broadcast the spectacle to all corners of the globe.

When the bleachers aren't up, there are fine views in both directions from the esplanade. Facing north, you'll see the body of water called the Firth of Forth, and Fife beyond that. (The Firth of Forth is the estuary where the River Forth flows into the North Sea.) Still facing north, find the lacy spire of the Scott Monument and two Neoclassical buildings housing art galleries. Beyond them, the stately buildings of Edinburgh's New Town rise. (For a self-guided walk of the New Town, see page 731.) Panning to the right, find the Nelson Monument and some faux Greek ruins atop Calton Hill (see page 781).

The city's many bluffs, crags, and ridges were built up by volcanoes, then carved down by glaciers—a city formed in "fire and ice," as the locals say. So, during the Ice Age, as a river of glaciers swept in from the west (behind today's castle), it ran into the super-hard volcanic basalt of Castle Rock and flowed around it, cutting valleys on either side and leaving a tail that became the Royal Mile you're about to walk.

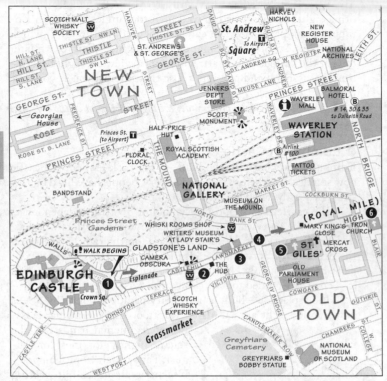

At the bottom of the esplanade, where the square hits the road, look left to find a plaque on the wall above the tiny **witches' well** (now a planter). This memorializes 300 women who were accused of witchcraft and burned here. Below was the Nor' Loch, the swampy lake where those accused of witchcraft (mostly women) were tested: Bound up, they were dropped into the lake. If they sank and drowned, they were innocent. If they floated, they were guilty, and were burned here in front of the castle, providing the city folk a nice afternoon out. The plaque shows two witches: one good and one bad. Tickle the serpent's snout to sympathize with the witches. (I just made that up.)

• *Start walking down the Royal Mile. The first block is a street called...*

❷ Castlehill

You're immediately in the tourist hubbub. The big tank-like building on your left was the Old Town's **reservoir.** You'll see the wellheads it served all along this walk. While it once held 1.5 million gallons of water, today it's filled with the touristy Tartan Weaving Mill and Exhibition. While it's interesting to see the mill at work, you'll have to twist your way down through several floors of tartan-

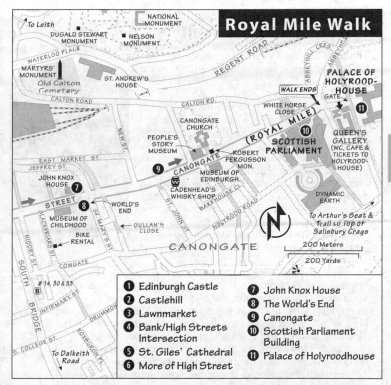

Royal Mile Walk

To Leith

DUGALD STEWART MONUMENT

NATIONAL MONUMENT

NELSON MONUMENT

WATERLOO PLACE

REGENT ROAD

ABBEYHILL CRES.

ABBEYHILL

MARTYRS' MONUMENT

Old Calton Cemetery

ST. ANDREW'S HOUSE

PALACE OF HOLYROOD-HOUSE

CALTON ROAD

CALTON RD.

WALK ENDS

WHITE HORSE CLOSE

GATE

CANONGATE CHURCH

NEW ST.

PEOPLE'S STORY MUSEUM

SCOTTISH PARLIAMENT

QUEEN'S GALLERY (WC, CAFE & TICKETS TO HOLYROOD-HOUSE)

EAST MARKET ST.

JEFFREY ST.

CANONGATE (ROYAL MILE)

ROBERT FERGUSSON MON.

MUSEUM OF EDINBURGH

JOHN KNOX HOUSE

CADENHEAD'S WHISKY SHOP

ST. JOHN ST.

BAKEHOUSE CL.

DYNAMIC EARTH

STREET

BLACKFRIARS ST.

WORLD'S END

ST. MARY'S ST.

GULLAN'S CLOSE

HOLYROOD ROAD

To Arthur's Seat & Trail to Top of Salisbury Crags

MUSEUM OF CHILDHOOD

BIKE RENTAL

NIDDRY ST.

COWGATE

CANONGATE

200 Meters

200 Yards

#14, 30 & 33

SOUTH BRIDGE

INFIRMARY ST.

DRUMMOND

S. COLLEGE ST.

ROXBURGH PL.

To Dalkeith Road

EDINBURGH

1. Edinburgh Castle
2. Castlehill
3. Lawnmarket
4. Bank/High Streets Intersection
5. St. Giles' Cathedral
6. More of High Street
7. John Knox House
8. The World's End
9. Canongate
10. Scottish Parliament Building
11. Palace of Holyroodhouse

ry and Chinese-produced Scottish kitsch to reach it at the bottom level.

The black-and-white tower ahead on the left has entertained visitors since the 1850s with its **camera obscura,** a darkened room where a mirror and a series of lenses capture live images of the city surroundings outside. (Giggle at the funny mirrors as you walk fatly by.) Across the street, filling the old Castlehill Primary School, is a gimmicky-if-intoxicating whisky-sampling exhibit called the **Scotch Whisky Experience** (a.k.a. "Malt Disney"). Both of these are described later, under "Sights in Edinburgh."

• *Just ahead, in front of the church with the tall, lacy spire, is the old market square known as...*

EDINBURGH

The Kilt

The kilt, Scotland's national dress, is intimately tied to the country's history. The six-foot-by-nine-foot bolt of fabric originated in the 1500s as a multipurpose robe, toga, tent, poncho, and ground cloth. A wearer would lay it on the ground to scrunch up pleats, then wrap it around the waist and belt it. Extra fabric was thrown over the shoulder or tucked into the belt, creating both a rakish sash and a rucksack-like pouch.

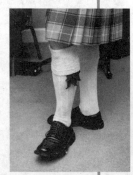

The kilt was standard Highlands dress and became a patriotic statement during conflicts with England. After the tragic-for-Scotland Battle of Culloden in 1746, the British government wanted to end the Scottish clan system. Wearing the kilt, speaking Gaelic, and playing the bagpipes were all outlawed.

In 1782, kilts were permitted again, but had taken on an unrefined connotation, so many Scots no longer wanted to wear one. This changed in 1822 when King George IV visited Edinburgh, wearing a kilt to send the message that he was king of Scotland. Scottish aristocrats were charmed by the king's pageantry, and the kilt was in vogue once more.

During the king's visit, Sir Walter Scott organized a Highland festival that also helped change the image of traditional Scottish culture, giving it a newfound respectability. A generation later, Queen Victoria raised the image of Scottish culture even higher. She loved Scotland and wallpapered her palace at Balmoral with tartan patterns.

The colors and patterns of the original kilts were determined by what dyes were available and who wove them. Because members of one clan tended to live in the same areas, they often wore similar patterns—but the colors were muted, and the patterns weren't necessarily designed to represent a single clan. The "clan tartans" you'll see in Scottish souvenir shops—with a specific, brightly colored design for each family—started as a scam by fabric salesmen in Victorian times. Since then, tartanry has been embraced as if it were historic. (By the way, Scots use these key terms differently than Americans do: "Tartan" is the pattern itself, while "plaid" is the piece of cloth worn over the shoulder with a kilt.)

As Highlanders moved to cities and took jobs in factories, the smaller kilt, or philibeg, replaced the traditional kilt, which could become dangerously snagged by modern machinery. Half the weight of old-style kilts, the practical philibeg is more like a wraparound skirt.

Other kilt-related gear includes the sporran, the leather pouch worn around the waist, and the sgian dubh ("black knife"), the short blade worn in the top of the sock. If you're in the market for a kilt, see page 788.

❸ Lawnmarket

During the Royal Mile's heyday, in the 1600s, this intersection was bigger and served as a market for fabric (especially "lawn," a linen-like cloth). The market would fill this space with bustle, hustle, and lots of commerce. The round white hump in the middle of the roundabout is all that remains of the official weighing beam called the Butter Tron—where all goods sold were weighed for honesty and tax purposes.

Towering above Lawnmarket, with the tallest spire in the city, is the former **Tolbooth Church.** This impressive Neo-Gothic

structure (1844) is now home to the Hub, Edinburgh's festival-ticket and information center. The world-famous Edinburgh Festival fills the month of August with cultural action. The various festivals feature classical music, traditional and fringe theater (especially comedy), art, books, and more. Drop inside the building to get festival info (see also page 783). This is a handy stop for its WC, café, and free Wi-Fi.

In the 1600s, this—along with the next stretch, called High Street—was the city's main street. At that time, Edinburgh was bursting with breweries, printing presses, and banks. Tens of thousands of citizens were squeezed into the narrow confines of the Old Town. Here on this ridge, they built **tenements** (multiple-unit residences) similar to the more recent ones you see today. These tenements, rising 10 stories and more, were some of the tallest domestic buildings in Europe. The living arrangements shocked class-conscious English visitors to Edinburgh because the tenements were occupied by rich and poor alike—usually the poor in the cellars and attics, and the rich in the middle floors.

• *Continue a half-block down the Mile.*

Gladstone's Land (at #477b, on the left), a surviving original tenement, was acquired by a wealthy merchant in 1617. Stand in front of the building and look up at this centuries-old skyscraper. This design was standard for its time: a shop or shops on the ground floor, with columns and an arcade, and residences on the floors above. Because window glass was expensive, the lower halves of window openings were made of cheaper wood, which swung out like shutters for ventilation—and were convenient for tossing out garbage. (Gladstone's Land can be seen by tour only and is closed Nov-March—consider dropping in and booking ahead for a spot. For details, see listing on page 749.) Out front, you may also see trainers with live birds of prey. While this

EDINBURGH

is mostly just a fun way to show off for tourists (and raise donations for the Just Falconry center), docents explain the connection: The building's owner was named Thomas Gledstanes—and *gled* is the Scots word for "hawk."

Branching off the spine of the Royal Mile are a number of narrow alleyways that go by various local names. A "wynd" (rhymes with "kind") is a narrow, winding lane. A "pend" is an arched gateway. "Gate" is from an Old Norse word for street. And a "close" is a tiny alley between two buildings (originally with a door that "closed" at night). A "close" usually leads to a "court," or courtyard.

To explore one of these alleyways, head into **Lady Stair's Close** (on the left, 10 steps downhill from Gladstone's Land). This alley pops out in a small courtyard, where you'll find the **Writers' Museum** (described on page 749). It's well worth a visit for fans of Scotland's holy trinity of writers (Robert Burns, Sir Walter Scott, and Robert Louis Stevenson), but it's also a free glimpse of what a typical home might have looked like in the 1600s. Burns actually lived for a while in this neighborhood, in 1786, when he first arrived in Edinburgh.

Opposite Gladstone's Land (at #322), another close leads to **Riddle's Court.** Wander through here and imagine Edinburgh in the 17th and 18th centuries, when tourists came here to marvel at its skyscrapers. Some 40,000 people were jammed into the few blocks between here and the World's End pub (which we'll reach soon). Visualize the labyrinthine maze of the old city, with people scurrying through these back alleyways, buying and selling, and popping into taverns.

No city in Europe was as densely populated—or perhaps as filthy. Without modern hygiene, it was a living hell of smoke, stench, and noise, with the constant threat of fire, collapse, and disease. The dirt streets were soiled with sewage from bedpans emptied out windows. By the 1700s, the Old Town was rife with poverty and cholera outbreaks. The smoky home fires rising from tenements and the infamous smell (or "reek" in Scottish) that wafted across the city gave it a nickname that sticks today: "Auld Reekie."

• *Return to the Royal Mile and continue down it a few steps to take in some sights at the...*

❹ Bank/High Streets Intersection

A number of sights cluster here, where Lawnmarket changes its name to High Street and intersects with Bank Street and George IV Bridge.

Begin with **Deacon Brodie's Tavern.** Read the "Doctor Jekyll and Mr. Hyde" story of this pub's notorious namesake on the wall facing Bank Street. Then, to see his spooky split personality, check out both sides of the hanging signpost. Brodie—a pillar of the community by day but a burglar by night—epitomizes the divided personality of 1700s Edinburgh. It was a rich, productive city—home to great philosophers and scientists, who actively contributed to the Enlightenment. Meanwhile, the Old Town was riddled with crime and squalor. The city was scandalized when a respected surgeon—driven by a passion for medical research and needing corpses—was accused

of colluding with two lowlifes, named Burke and Hare, to acquire freshly murdered corpses for dissection. (In the next century, in the late 1800s, novelist Robert Louis Stevenson would capture the dichotomy of Edinburgh's rich-poor society in his *Strange Case of Dr. Jekyll and Mr. Hyde.*)

In the late 1700s, Edinburgh's upper class moved out of the Old Town into a planned community called the New Town (a quarter-mile north of here). Eventually, most tenements were torn down and replaced with newer **Victorian buildings.** You'll see some at this intersection.

Look left down Bank Street to the green-domed **Bank of Scotland.** This was the headquarters of the bank, which had practiced modern capitalist financing since 1695. The building now houses the Museum on the Mound, a free exhibit on banking history (see page 751), and it's also the Scottish headquarters for Lloyds Banking Group—which swallowed up the Bank of Scotland after the financial crisis of 2008.

If you detour left down Bank Street toward the bank, you'll find the recommended **Whiski Rooms Shop.** If you head in the opposite direction, down George IV Bridge, you'll reach the excellent **National Museum of Scotland,** the famous Greyfriars Bobby statue, restaurant-lined Forrest Road, and photogenic Victoria Street, which leads to the pub-lined Grassmarket square (all described later in this chapter).

Otherwise, continue along the Royal Mile. As you walk, be careful crossing the streets along the Mile. Edinburgh drivers—

EDINBURGH

especially cabbies—have a reputation for being impatient with jaywalking tourists. Notice and heed the pedestrian crossing signals, which don't always turn at the same time as the car signals.

Across the street from Deacon Brodie's Tavern is a seated green statue of hometown boy **David Hume** (1711-1776)—one of the most influential thinkers not only of Scotland, but in all of Western philosophy. The atheistic Hume was one of the towering figures of the Scottish Enlightenment of the mid-1700s. Thinkers and scientists were using the experimental method to challenge and investigate everything, including religion. Hume questioned cause and effect in thought puzzles such as this: We can see that when one billiard ball strikes another, the second one moves, but how do we know the collision "caused" the movement? Notice his shiny toe: People on their way to trial (in the high court just

behind the statue) or students on their way to exams (in the nearby university) rub it for good luck.

Follow David Hume's gaze to the opposite corner, where a **brass H** in the pavement marks the site of the last public execution in Edinburgh in 1864. Deacon Brodie himself would have been hung about here (in 1788, on a gallows whose design he had helped to improve—smart guy).

• *From the brass H, continue down the Royal Mile, pausing just before the church square at a stone wellhead with the pyramid cap.*

All along the Royal Mile, **wellheads** like this (from 1835) provided townsfolk with water in the days before buildings had plumbing. This neighborhood well was served by the reservoir up at the castle. Imagine long lines of people in need of water standing here, gossiping and sharing the news. Eventually buildings were retrofitted with water pipes—the ones you see running along building exteriors.

• *Ahead of you (past the Victorian statue of some duke), embedded in the pavement near the street, is a big heart.*

The **Heart of Midlothian** marks the spot of the city's 15th-century municipal building and jail. In times past, in a nearby open space, criminals were hanged, traitors were decapitated, and witches were burned. Citizens hated the rough justice doled out here. Locals still spit on the heart in the pavement. Go ahead...do as the locals do—land one right in the heart of the heart. By the way, Edinburgh has two soccer teams—Heart of Midlothian (known as "Hearts") and Hibernian ("Hibs"). If you're a Hibs fan, spit again.

• *Make your way to the entrance of the church.*

❺ St. Giles' Cathedral

This is the flagship of the Church of Scotland (Scotland's largest denomination)—called the "Mother Church of Presbyterianism." The interior serves as a kind of Scottish Westminster Abbey, filled with monuments, statues, plaques, and stained-glass windows dedicated to great Scots and moments in history.

A church has stood on this spot since 854, though this structure is an architectural hodgepodge, dating mostly from the 15th through 19th century. In the 16th century, St. Giles' was a kind of national stage on which the drama of the Reformation was played out. The reformer John Knox (1514-1572) was the preacher here. His fiery sermons helped turn once-Catholic Edinburgh into a bastion of Protestantism. During the Scottish Reformation, St. Giles' was transformed from a Catholic cathedral to a Presbyterian church. The spacious interior is well worth a visit, and described in my self-guided tour on page 751.

• *Facing the church entrance, curl around its right side, into a parking lot.*

Sights Around St. Giles'

The grand building across the parking lot from St. Giles' is the **Old Parliament House.** Since the 13th century, the king had ruled a rubber-stamp parliament of nobles and bishops. But the Protestant Reformation promoted democracy, and the parliament gained real power. From the early 1600s until 1707, this building evolved to become the seat of a true parliament of elected officials. That came to an end in 1707, when Scotland signed an Act of Union, joining what's known today as the United Kingdom and giving up their right to self-rule. (More on that later in the walk.) If you're curious to peek inside, head through the door at #11 (free, described on page 756).

The great reformer **John Knox** is buried—with appropriate austerity—under parking lot spot #23. The statue among the cars shows King Charles II riding to a toga party back in 1685.

• *Continue on through the parking lot, around the back end of the church.*

Every Scottish burgh (town licensed by the king to trade) had three standard features: a "tolbooth" (basically a Town Hall, with a courthouse, meeting room, and jail); a "tron" (official weighing scale); and a "mercat" (or market) cross. The **mercat cross** stand-

ing just behind St. Giles' Cathedral has a slender column decorated with a unicorn holding a flag with the cross of St. Andrew. Royal proclamations have been read at this mercat cross since the 14th century. In 1952, a town crier heralded the news that Britain had a new queen—three days after the actual event (traditionally the time it took for a horse to speed here from London). Today, Mercat Cross is the meeting point for many of Edinburgh's walking tours—both historic and ghostly.

• *Circle around to the street side of the church.*

The statue to **Adam Smith** honors the Edinburgh author of the pioneering *Wealth of Nations* (1776), in which he laid out the economics of free market capitalism. Smith theorized that an "invisible hand" wisely guides the unregulated free market. Stand in front of Smith and imagine the intellectual energy of Edinburgh in the mid-1700s, when it was Europe's most enlightened city. Adam Smith was right in the center of it. He and David Hume were good friends. James Boswell, the famed biographer of Samuel Johnson, took classes from Smith. James Watt, inventor of the steam engine, was another proud Scotsman of the age. With great intellectuals like these, Edinburgh helped create the modern world. The poet Robert Burns, geologist James Hutton (who's considered the father of modern geology), and the publishers of the first *Encyclopedia Britannica* all lived in Edinburgh. Steeped in the inquisitive mindset of the Enlightenment, they applied cool rationality and a secular approach to their respective fields.

• *Head on down the Royal Mile.*

❻ More of High Street

A few steps downhill, at #188 (on the right), is the **Police Information Center.** This place provides a pleasant police presence (say that three times) and a little local law-and-order history to boot. Ask the officer on duty about the impact of modern technology and budget austerity on police work today. Seriously—drop in and discuss whatever law-and-order issue piques your curiosity.

Continuing down this stretch of the Royal Mile, which is traffic-free most of the day (notice the bollards that raise and lower for permitted traffic), you'll see the Fringe Festival office (at #180), street musicians, and another wellhead (with horse "sippies," dating from 1675).

Notice those **three red boxes.** In the 20th century, people used these to make telephone calls to each other. (Imagine that!) These cast-iron booths are produced for all of Britain here in Scotland. As phone booths are decommissioned, some are finding new use as tiny shops, ATMs, and even showing up in residential neighborhoods as nostalgic garden decorations.

At the next intersection, on the left is **Cockburn Street** (pronounced "COE-burn"). This was cut through High Street's dense wall of medieval skyscrapers in the 1860s to give easy access to the Georgian New Town and the train station. Notice how the sliced buildings were thoughtfully capped with facades that fit the aesthetic look of the Royal Mile. In the Middle Ages, only tiny lanes (like Fleshmarket Close just uphill from Cockburn Street) interrupted the long line of Royal Mile buildings. These days, Cockburn Street has a reputation for its eclectic independent shops and string of trendy bars and eateries.

• *When you reach the* **Tron Church** *(17th century, currently housing shops), you're at the intersection of* **North and South Bridge streets.** *These major streets lead left to Waverley Station and right to the Dalkeith Road B&Bs. Several handy bus lines run along here.*

This is the halfway point of this walk. Stand on the corner diagonally across from the church. Look up to the top of the Royal Mile at the Hub and its 240-foot spire. Notwithstanding its turret and 16th-century charm, the **Radisson Blu Hotel** just across the street is entirely new construction (1990), built to fit in. The city is protecting its historic look. The **Inn on the Mile** next door was once a fancy bank with a lavish interior. As modern banks are moving away from city centers, sumptuous buildings like these are being converted into ornate pubs and restaurants.

In the next block downhill are three **characteristic pubs,** side by side, that offer free traditional Scottish and folk music in the evenings. Notice the chimneys. Tenement buildings shared stairways and entries, but held individual apartments, each with its own chimney. Take a look back at the spire of St. Giles' Cathedral—inspired by the Scottish crown and the thistle, Scotland's national flower.

• *Go down High Street another block, passing near the Museum of Childhood (on the right, at #42, and worth a stop; see page 758) and a fragrant fudge shop a few doors down, where you can sample various flavors (tempting you to buy a slab).*

Directly across the street, just below another wellhead, is the...

❼ John Knox House

Remember that Knox was a towering figure in Edinburgh's history, converting Scotland to a Calvinist style of Protestantism. His religious bent was "Presbyterianism," in which parishes are governed by elected officials rather than appointed bishops. This more democratic brand of Christianity also spurred Scotland toward political democracy. If you're interested in Knox or the Reformation, this sight is worth a visit (see page 758). Full disclosure: It's not certain that Knox ever actually lived here. Attached to the Knox House is the Scottish Storytelling Centre, where locals with the gift of gab perform regularly; check the posted schedule.

• *A few steps farther down High Street, at the intersection with St. Mary's and Jeffrey streets, you'll reach...*

❽ The World's End

For centuries, a wall stood here, marking the end of the burgh of Edinburgh. For residents within the protective walls of the city,

this must have felt like the "world's end," indeed. The area beyond was called Canongate, a monastic community associated with Holyrood Abbey. At the intersection, find the brass bricks in the street that trace the gate (demolished in 1764). Look to the right down St. Mary's Street about 200 yards to see a surviving bit of that old wall, known as the **Flodden Wall.** In the 1513 Battle of Flodden, the Scottish king James IV made the disastrous decision to invade northern England. James and 10,000 of his Scotsmen were killed. Fearing a brutal English counterattack, Edinburgh scrambled to reinforce its broken-down city wall. To the left, down Jeffrey Street, you'll see Scotland's top tattoo parlor, and a supplier for a different kind of tattoo (the Scottish Regimental Store).

• *Continue down the Royal Mile—leaving old Edinburgh—as High Street changes names to...*

❾ Canongate

About 10 steps down Canongate, look left down Cranston Street (past the train tracks) to a good view of the Calton Cemetery up on **Calton Hill.** The obelisk, called Martyrs' Monument, remembers a group of 18th-century patriots exiled by London to Australia for their reform politics. The round building to the left is the grave of philosopher David Hume. And the big, turreted building to the right was the jail master's house. Today, the main reason to

go up Calton Hill is for the fine views (described on page 781).

The giant, blocky building that dominates the lower slope of the hill is **St. Andrew's House,** headquarters of the Scottish Government—including the office of the first minister of Scotland. According to locals, the building has also been an important base for MI6, Britain's version of the CIA. Wait a minute—isn't James Bond Scottish? Hmmm...

• *A couple of hundred yards farther along the Royal Mile (on the right at #172) you reach Cadenhead's, a serious place to learn about and buy whisky (see page 785). About 30 yards farther along, you'll pass two worthwhile and free museums, the People's Story Museum (on the left, in the old tollhouse at #163) and Museum of Edinburgh (on the right, at #142; for more on both, see page 758). But our next stop is the church just across from the Museum of Edinburgh.*

The 1688 **Canongate Kirk** (Church)—located not far from the royal residence of Holyroodhouse—is where Queen Elizabeth II and her family worship when-

ever they're in town. (So don't sit in the front pew, marked with her crown.) The gilded emblem at the top of the roof, high above the door, has the antlers of a stag from the royal estate of Balmoral. The Queen's granddaughter married here in 2011.

The church is open only when volunteers have signed up to welcome visitors (and closed in winter). Chat them up and borrow the description of the place. Then step inside the lofty blue and red interior, renovated with royal money; the church is filled with light and the flags of various Scottish regiments. In the narthex, peruse the photos of royal family events here, and find the list of priests and ministers of this parish—it goes back to 1143 (with a clear break with the Reformation in 1561).

Outside, turn right as you leave the church and walk up into the graveyard. The large, gated grave (abutting the back of the People's Story Museum) is the affectionately tended tomb of **Adam Smith,** the father of capitalism. (Throw him a penny or two.)

Just outside the churchyard, the statue on the sidewalk is of the poet **Robert Fergusson.** One of the first to write verse in the Scots language, he so inspired Robert Burns that Burns paid for Fergusson's tombstone in the Canongate churchyard and composed his epitaph.

Now look across the street at the **gabled house** next to the Museum of Edinburgh. Scan the facade to see shells put there in the 17th century to defend against the evil power of witches yet to be drowned.

• *Walk about 300 yards farther along. In the distance you can see the*

Palace of Holyroodhouse (the end of this walk) and soon, on the right, you'll come to the modern Scottish parliament building.

Just opposite the parliament building is **White Horse Close** (on the left, in the white arcade). Step into this 17th-century courtyard. It was from here that the Edinburgh stagecoach left for London. Eight days later, the horse-drawn carriage would pull into its destination: Scotland Yard. Note that bus #35 leaves in two directions from here—downhill for the Royal Yacht *Britannia,* and uphill along the Royal Mile (as far as South Bridge) and on to the National Museum of Scotland.

• *Now walk up around the corner to the flagpoles (flying the flags of Europe, Britain, and Scotland) in front of the...*

❿ Scottish Parliament Building

Finally, after centuries of history, we reach the 21st century. And finally, after three centuries of London rule, Scotland has a parlia-

ment building...in Scotland. When Scotland united with England in 1707, its parliament was dissolved. But in 1999, the Scottish parliament was reestablished, and in 2004, it moved into this striking new home. Notice how the eco-friendly build-

ing, by the Catalan architect Enric Miralles, mixes wild angles, lots of light, bold windows, oak, and native stone into a startling complex. (People from Catalunya—another would-be breakaway nation—have an affinity for Scotland.) From the front of the parliament building, look in the distance at the rocky Salisbury Crags, with people hiking the traverse up to the dramatic next summit called Arthur's Seat. Now look at the building in relation to the craggy cliffs. The architect envisioned the building as if it were rising right from the base of Arthur's Seat, almost bursting from the rock.

Since it celebrates Scottish democracy, the architecture is not a statement of authority. There are no statues of old heroes. There's not even a grand entry. You feel like you're entering an office park. Given its neighborhood, the media often calls the Scottish Parliament "Holyrood" for short (similar to calling the US Congress "Capitol Hill"). For details on touring the building and seeing parliament in action, see page 759.

• *Across the street is the* **Queen's Gallery,** *where she shares part of her amazing personal art collection in excellent revolving exhibits (see page 762). Finally, walk to the end of the road (Abbey Strand), and step up to the impressive wrought-iron gate of the Queen's palace. Look up at the stag with its holy cross, or "holy rood," on its forehead, and peer into the palace grounds. (The ticket office and palace entryway, a fine café, and a handy WC are just through the arch on the right.)*

⓫ Palace of Holyroodhouse

EDINBURGH

Since the 16th century, this palace has marked the end of the Royal Mile. An abbey—part of a 12th-century Augustinian monastery—

originally stood in its place. While most of that old building is gone, you can see the surviving nave behind the palace on the left. According to one legend, it was named "holy rood" for a piece of the cross, brought here as a relic by Queen (and later Saint) Margaret. (Another version of the story is that King David I, Margaret's son, saw the image of a cross upon a stag's head while hunting here and took it as a sign that he should build an abbey on the site.) Because Scotland's royalty preferred living at Holyroodhouse to the blustery castle on the rock, the palace grew over time. If the Queen's not visiting, the palace welcomes visitors (see page 760 for details).

• *Your walk—from the castle to the palace, with so much Scottish history packed in between—is complete. And, if your appetite is whetted for more, don't worry; you've just scratched the surface. Enjoy the rest of Edinburgh.*

BONNIE WEE NEW TOWN WALK

Many visitors, mesmerized by the Royal Mile, never venture to the New Town. And that's a shame. With some of the city's finest Georgian architecture (from its 18th-century boom period), the New Town has a completely different character than the Old Town. This self-guided walk—worth ▲▲—gives you a quick orientation in about one hour.

• *Begin on Waverley Bridge, spanning the gully between the Old and New towns; to get there from the Royal Mile, just head down the curved Cockburn Street near the Tron Church (or cut*

EDINBURGH

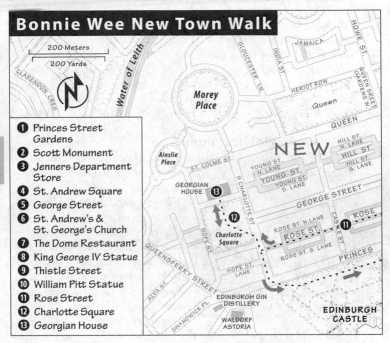

Bonnie Wee New Town Walk

200 Meters
200 Yards

1 Princes Street Gardens
2 Scott Monument
3 Jenners Department Store
4 St. Andrew Square
5 George Street
6 St. Andrew's & St. George's Church
7 The Dome Restaurant
8 King George IV Statue
9 Thistle Street
10 William Pitt Statue
11 Rose Street
12 Charlotte Square
13 Georgian House

down any of the "close" lanes opposite St. Giles' Cathedral). Stand on the bridge overlooking the train tracks, facing the castle.

View from Waverley Bridge: From this vantage point, you can enjoy fine views of medieval Edinburgh, with its 10-story-plus "skyscrapers." It's easy to imagine how miserably crowded this area was, prompting the expansion of the city during the Georgian period. Pick out landmarks along the Royal Mile, most notably the open-work steeple of St. Giles'.

A big lake called the **Nor' Loch** once was to the north (nor') of the Old Town; now it's a valley between Edinburgh's two towns. The lake was drained around 1800 as part of the expansion. Before that, the lake was the town's water reservoir...and its sewer. Much has been written about the town's infamous stink (a.k.a. the "flowers of Edinburgh"). The town's nickname, "Auld Reekie," referred to both the smoke of its industry and the stench of its squalor.

The long-gone loch was also a handy place for drowning witches. With their thumbs tied to their ankles, they'd be lashed to dunking stools. Those who survived the ordeal were considered "aided by the devil" and burned as witches. If they died, they were innocent and given a good Christian burial. Edinburgh was Europe's witch-burning mecca—any perceived "sign," including a small birthmark, could condemn you. Scotland burned more witches per capita than any other country—17,000 souls between 1479 and 1722.

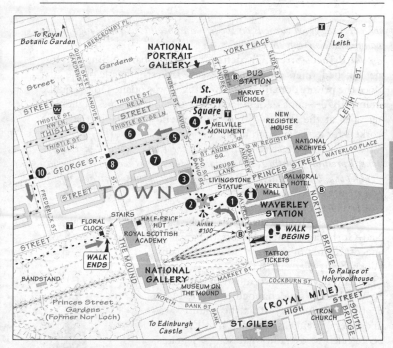

Visually trace the train tracks as they disappear into a tunnel below the **Scottish National Gallery** (with lesser-known paintings by great European artists; you can visit it during this walk—see page 767). The two fine Neoclassical buildings of the National Gallery date from the 1840s and sit upon a mound that's called, well, **The Mound.** When the New Town was built, tons of rubble from the excavations were piled here (1781-1830), forming a dirt bridge that connected the new development with the Old Town to allay merchant concerns about being cut off from the future heart of the city.

Turning 180 degrees (and facing the ramps down into the train station), notice the huge, turreted building with the clock tower. **The Balmoral** was one of the city's two grand hotels during its glory days (its opposite bookend, the **Waldorf Astoria Edinburgh,** sits at the far end of the former lakebed—near the end of this walk). Aristocrats arriving by train could use a hidden entrance to go from the platform directly up to their plush digs. (Today The Balmoral is known mostly as the place where J. K. Rowling completed the final Harry Potter book.)

• *Now walk across the bridge toward the New Town. Before the cor-*

ner, enter the gated gardens on the left, and head toward the big, pointy monument. You're at the edge of...

❶ **Princes Street Gardens:** This grassy park, filling the former lakebed, offers a wonderful escape from the bustle of the city. Once the private domain of the wealthy, it was opened to the public around 1870—not as a democratic gesture, but in hopes of increasing sales at the Princes Street department stores. Join the office workers for a picnic lunch break.

• *Take a seat on the bench indicated by the Livingstone (Dr. Livingstone, I presume?) statue. (The Victorian explorer is well equipped with a guidebook, but is hardly packing light—his lion skin doesn't even fit in his rucksack carry-on.)*

   Look up at the towering...

❷ **Scott Monument:** Built in the early 1840s, this elaborate Neo-Gothic monument honors the great author Sir Walter Scott, one of Edinburgh's many illustrious sons.

When Scott died in 1832, it was said that "Scotland never owed so much to one man." Scott almost singlehandedly created the Scotland we know. Just as the country was in danger of being assimilated into England, Scott celebrated traditional songs, legends, myths, architecture, and kilts, thereby reviving the Highland culture and cementing a national identity. And, as the father of the Romantic historical novel, he contributed to Western literature in general. The 200-foot monument shelters a marble statue of Scott and his favorite pet, Maida, a deerhound who was one of 30 canines this dog lover owned during his lifetime. They're surrounded by busts of 16 great Scottish poets and 64 characters from his books. Climbing the tight, stony spiral staircase of 287 steps earns you a peek at a tiny museum midway, a fine city view at the top, and intimate encounters going up and down (£5, daily 10:00-19:00, Oct-March until 16:00, tel. 0131/529-4068). For more on Scott, see page 757.

• *Exit the gate near Livingstone and head across busy Princes Street to the venerable...*

❸ **Jenners Department Store:** As you wait for the light to change (and wait...and wait...), notice how statues of women support the building—just as real women support the business. The arrival of new fashions here was such a big deal in the old days that they'd announce it by flying flags on the Nelson Monument atop Calton Hill.

Step inside and head upstairs into the grand, skylit atrium. The central space—filled with a towering tree at Christmas—is classic Industrial Age architecture. The Queen's coat of arms high on the wall indicates she shops here.

• *From the atrium, turn right and exit onto South St. David Street. Turn left and follow this street uphill one block up to...*

❹ **St. Andrew Square:** This green space is dedicated to the patron saint of Scotland. In the early 19th century, there were no

shops around here—just fine residences; this was a private garden for the fancy people living here. Now open to the public, the square is a popular lunch hangout for workers. The Melville Monument honors a powermonger member of parliament who, for four decades (around 1800), was nicknamed the "uncrowned king of Scotland."

One block up from the top of the park is the excellent **Scottish National Portrait Gallery,** which introduces you to all of the biggest names in Scottish history (described later, under "Sights in Edinburgh").

• *Follow the Melville Monument's gaze straight ahead out of the park. Cross the street and stand at the top of...*

❺ **George Street:** This is the main drag of Edinburgh's grid-planned New Town. Laid out in 1776, when King George III was busy putting down a revolution in a troublesome overseas colony, the New Town was a model of urban planning in its day. The architectural style is "Georgian"—British for "Neoclassical." And the street plan came with an unambiguous message: to celebrate the union of Scotland with England into the United Kingdom. (This was particularly important, since Scotland was just two decades removed from the failed Jacobite uprising of Bonnie Prince Charlie.)

St. Andrew Square (patron saint of Scotland) and Charlotte Square (George III's queen) bookend the New Town, with its three main streets named for the royal family of the time (George, Queen, and Princes). Thistle and Rose streets—which we'll see near the end of this walk—are named for the national flowers of Scotland and England.

The plan for the New Town was the masterstroke of the 23-year-old urban designer James Craig. George Street—20 feet wider than the others (so a four-horse carriage could make a U-turn)—was the main drag. Running down the high spine of the area, it afforded grand, unobstructed views (thanks to the parks on either side) of the River Forth in one direction and the Old Town in the other. As you stroll down the street, you'll notice that Craig's grid is a series of axes designed to connect monuments new and old; later architects made certain to continue this harmony. For example, notice that the Scott Monument lines up perfectly with this first intersection.

• *Halfway down the first block of George Street, on the right, is...*

❻ **St. Andrew's and St. George's Church:** Designed as part of the New Town plan in the 1780s, the church is a product of the Scottish Enlightenment. It has an elliptical plan (the first in Britain) so that all can focus on the pulpit. If it's open, step inside. A fine leaflet tells the story of the church, and a handy cafeteria downstairs serves cheap and cheery lunches.

Directly across the street from the church is another temple, this one devoted to money. This former bank building (now housing the recommended restaurant ❼ **The Dome**) has a pediment filled with figures demonstrating various ways to make money, which they do with all the nobility of classical gods. Consider scurrying across the street and ducking inside to view the stunning domed atrium.

Continue down George Street to the intersection with a ❽ statue commemorating the visit by **King George IV.** Notice the particularly fine axis formed by this cross-street: The National Gallery lines up perfectly with the Royal Mile's skyscrapers and the former Tolbooth Church, creating a Gotham City collage.

• *By now you've gotten your New Town bearings. Feel free to stop this walk here: If you were to turn left and head down Hanover Street, in a block you'd run into the Scottish National Gallery; the street behind it curves back up to the Royal Mile.*

But to see more of the New Town—including the Georgian House, offering an insightful look inside one of these fine 18th-century homes—stick with me for a few more long blocks, zigzagging through side streets to see the various personalities that inhabit this rigid grid.

Turn right on Hanover Street; after just one (short) block, cross over and go down...

❾ **Thistle Street:** Of the many streets in the New Town, this has perhaps the most vivid Scottish character. And that's fitting, as it's named after Scotland's national flower. At the beginning and end of the street, also notice that Craig's street plan included tranquil cul-de-sacs within the larger blocks. Thistle Street seems sleepy, but holds characteristic boutiques and good restaurants (see "Eating in Edinburgh," later). Halfway down the street on the left, Howie Nicholsby's shop 21st Century Kilt updates traditional Scottish menswear.

You'll pop out at Frederick Street. Turning left, you'll see a ❿ statue of **William Pitt,** prime minister under King George III. (Pitt's father gave his name to the American city of Pittsburgh— which Scots pronounce as "Pitts-burrah"...I assume.)

• *For an interesting contrast, we'll continue down another side street. Pass the statue of Pitt (heading toward Edinburgh Castle), and turn right onto...*

⓫ **Rose Street:** As a rose is to a thistle, and as England is to Scotland, so is brash, boisterous Rose Street to sedate, thoughtful

Thistle Street. This stretch of Rose Street feels more commercialized, jammed with chain stores; the second block is packed with pubs and restaurants. As you walk, keep an eye out for the cobbled Tudor rose embedded in the brick sidewalk. When you cross the aptly named Castle Street, linger over the grand views to Edinburgh Castle. It's almost as if they planned it this way... just for the views.

• *Popping out at the far end of Rose Street, across the street and to your right is...*

⓬ **Charlotte Square:** The building of the New Town started cheap with St. Andrew Square, but finished well with this stately space. In 1791, the Edinburgh town council asked the prestigious Scottish architect Robert Adam to pump up the design for Charlotte Square. The council hoped that Adam's plan would answer criticism that the New Town buildings lacked innovation or ambition—and they got what they wanted. Adam's design, which raised the standard of New Town architecture to "international

class," created Edinburgh's finest Georgian square.

• *Along the right side of Charlotte Square, at #7 (just left of the pointy pediment), you can visit the* ⓭ **Georgian House,** *which gives you a* *great peek behind all of these harmonious Neoclassical facades (see page 775).*

When you're done touring the house, you can head back through the New Town grid, perhaps taking some different streets than the way you came. Or, for a restful return to our starting point, consider this...

Return Through Princes Street Gardens: From Charlotte Square, drop down to busy Princes Street (noticing the red building to the right—the grand Waldorf Astoria Hotel and twin sister of The Balmoral at the start of our walk). But rather than walking along the busy bus-and-tram-lined shopping drag, head into **Princes Street Gardens** (cross Princes Street and enter the gate on the left). With the castle looming overhead, you'll pass a playground, a fanciful Victorian fountain, more monuments to great Scots, war memorials, and a bandstand (which hosts Scottish country dancing—see page 791—as well as occasional big-name acts). Finally you'll reach a staircase up to the Scottish National Gallery; notice the oldest **floral clock** in the world on your left as you climb up.

• *Our walk is over. From here, you can tour the gallery; head up Bank Street just behind it to reach the Royal Mile; hop on a bus along Princes Street to your next stop (or B&B); or continue through another stretch of the Princes Street Gardens to the Scott Monument and our starting point.*

Sights in Edinburgh

▲▲▲EDINBURGH CASTLE

The fortified birthplace of the city 1,300 years ago, this imposing symbol of Edinburgh sits proudly on a rock high above you. The

home of Scotland's kings and queens for centuries, the castle has witnessed royal births, medieval pageantry, and bloody sieges. Today it's a complex of various buildings, the oldest dating from the 12th century, linked by cobbled roads that survive from its more recent use as a military garrison. The castle—with expansive views, plenty of history, and the stunning crown jewels of Scotland—is a fascinating and multifaceted sight that deserves several hours of your time.

Cost and Hours: £17, daily 9:30-18:00, Oct-March until 17:00, last entry one hour before closing, tel. 0131/225-9846, www.edinburghcastle.gov.uk.

Avoiding Lines: The castle is usually less crowded after 14:00

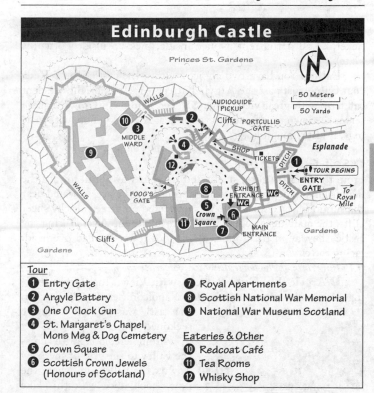

Edinburgh Castle

Princes St. Gardens

AUDIOGUIDE PICKUP

Cliffs PORTCULLIS GATE

WALLS

MIDDLE WARD

SHOP

Esplanade

TICKETS

DITCH

TOUR BEGINS

ENTRY GATE

EXHIBIT ENTRANCE

WC

WC

FOOG'S GATE

WALLS

To Royal Mile

Crown Square

MAIN ENTRANCE

Gardens

Cliffs

Gardens

50 Meters

50 Yards

EDINBURGH

Tour
1 Entry Gate
2 Argyle Battery
3 One O'Clock Gun
4 St. Margaret's Chapel, Mons Meg & Dog Cemetery
5 Crown Square
6 Scottish Crown Jewels (Honours of Scotland)
7 Royal Apartments
8 Scottish National War Memorial
9 National War Museum Scotland

Eateries & Other
10 Redcoat Café
11 Tea Rooms
12 Whisky Shop

or so; if planning a morning visit, the earlier the better. To avoid ticket lines (worst in Aug), book online and print your ticket at home. You can also pick up your prebooked ticket at machines just inside the entrance or at the Visitor Information desk a few steps

uphill on the right. You can also skip the ticket line with a Historic Scotland Explorer Pass (see page 1025 for details).

Getting There: Simply walk up the Royal Mile (if arriving by bus from the B&B area south of the city, get off at South Bridge and huff up the Mile for about 15 minutes). Taxis get you closer, dropping you a block below the esplanade at the Hub/Tolbooth Church.

Tours: Thirty-minute introductory **guided tours** are free with admission (2-4/hour, depart from Argyle Battery, see clock for next departure; fewer off-season). The informative **audioguide** provides four hours of descriptions, including the National War Museum Scotland (£3 if you purchase with your ticket; £3.50 if you rent it once inside, pick up inside Portcullis Gate).

Eating: You have two choices within the castle. The **$ Redcoat Café**—just past the Argyle Battery—is a big, bright, efficient cafeteria with great views. The **$$ Tea Rooms** in Crown Square serves sit-down meals and afternoon tea. A whisky shop, with tastings, is just through Foog's Gate.

⊙ Self-Guided Tour

From the ❶ **entry gate**, start winding your way uphill toward the main sights—the crown jewels and the Royal Palace—located near the summit. Since the castle was protected on three sides by sheer cliffs, the main defense had to be here at the entrance. During the castle's heyday in the 1500s, a 100-foot tower loomed overhead, facing the city.

• *Passing through the portcullis gate, you reach the...*

❷ **Argyle (Six-Gun) Battery, with View:** These front-loading, cast-iron cannons are from the Napoleonic era (c. 1800), when the castle was still a force to be reckoned with.

From here, look north across the valley to the grid of the New Town. The valley sits where the Nor' Loch once was; this lake was drained and filled in when the New Town was built in the late 1700s, its swamps replaced with gardens. Later the land provided sites for the Greek-temple-esque Scottish National Gallery and Waverley Station. Looking farther north, you can make out the port town of Leith with its high-rises and cranes, the Firth of Forth, the island of Inchkeith, and—in the far, far distance (to the east)—the cone-like mountain of North Berwick Law, a former volcano.

Now look down. The sheer north precipice looks impregnable. But on the night of March 14, 1314, 30 armed men silently scaled this rock face. They were loyal to Robert the Bruce and determined to recapture the castle, which had fallen into English hands. They caught the English by surprise, took the castle, and—three months later—Bruce defeated the English at the Battle of Bannockburn.

• *A little farther along, near the café, is the...*

❸ **One O'Clock Gun:** Crowds gather for the 13:00 gun blast, a tradition that gives ships in the bay something to set their navigational devices by. Before the gun, sailors set their clocks with help from the Nelson Monument—that's the tall pillar in the distance on Calton Hill. The monument has a "time ball" affixed to the cross on top, which drops precisely at the top of the hour. But on foggy days, ships couldn't see the ball, so the cannon shot was instituted instead (1861). The tradition stuck, every day at 13:00. (Locals joke that the frugal Scots don't fire it at high noon, as that would cost 11 extra rounds a day.)

• *Continue uphill, winding to the left and passing through Foog's Gate. At the very top of the hill, on your left, is...*

❹ St. Margaret's Chapel: This tiny stone chapel is Edinburgh's oldest building (around 1120) and sits atop its highest point

(440 feet). It represents the birth of the city.

In 1057, Malcolm III murdered King Macbeth (of Shakespeare fame) and assumed the Scottish throne. Later, he married Princess Margaret, and the family settled atop this hill. Their marriage united Malcolm's Highland Scots with Margaret's Lowland Anglo-Saxons—the cultural mix that would define Edinburgh.

Step inside the tiny, unadorned church—a testament to Margaret's reputed piety. The style is Romanesque. The nave is wonderfully simple, with classic Norman zigzags decorating the round arch that separates the tiny nave from the sacristy. You'll see a facsimile of St. Margaret's 11th-century gospel book. The small (modern) stained-glass windows feature St. Margaret herself, St. Columba, and St. Ninian (who brought Christianity to Scotland in A.D. 397), St. Andrew (Scotland's patron saint), and William Wallace (the defender of Scotland). These days, the place is popular for weddings. (As it seats only 20, it's particularly popular with brides' parents.)

Margaret died at the castle in 1093, and her son King David I built this chapel in her honor (she was sainted in 1250). David expanded the castle and also founded Holyrood Abbey, across town. These two structures were soon linked by a Royal Mile of buildings, and Edinburgh was born.

Mons Meg, in front of the church, is a huge and once-upon-a-time frightening 15th-century siege cannon that fired 330-pound stones nearly two miles. Imagine. It was a gift from Philip the Good, duke of Burgundy, to his great-niece's husband King James II of Scotland.

Nearby, belly up to the banister and look down to find the **Dog Cemetery,** a tiny patch of grass with a sweet little line of doggie tombstones, marking the graves of soldiers' faithful canines in arms.

• *Continue on, curving downhill into...*

❺ **Crown Square:** This courtyard is the center of today's Royal Castle complex. Get oriented. You're surrounded by the crown jewels, the Royal Palace (with its Great Hall), and the Scottish National War Memorial.

The castle has evolved over the centuries, and Crown Square is relatively "new." After the time of Malcolm and Margaret, the castle was greatly expanded by David II (1324-1371), complete with tall towers, a Great Hall, dungeon, cellars, and so on. This served as the grand royal residence for two centuries. Then, in 1571-1573, the Protestant citizens of Edinburgh laid siege to the castle and its Catholic/monarchist holdouts, eventually blasting it to smithereens. (You can tour the paltry remains of the medieval castle in nearby **David's Tower.**) The palace was rebuilt nearby—around what is today's Crown Square.

• *We'll tour the buildings around Crown Square. First up: the crown jewels. Look for two entrances. The one on Crown Square, only open in peak season, deposits you straight into the room with the crown jewels but usually comes with a line. The other entry, around the side (near the WCs), takes you—often at a shuffle—through the interesting, Disney-esque "Honours of Scotland" exhibition, which tells the story of the crown jewels and how they survived the harrowing centuries, but lacks any actual artifacts.*

❻ **Scottish Crown Jewels (Honours of Scotland):** For centuries, Scotland's monarchs were crowned in elaborate rituals involving three wondrous objects: a jewel-studded crown, scepter, and sword. These objects—along with the ceremonial Stone of Scone (pronounced "skoon")—are known as the "Honours of Scotland." Scotland's crown jewels may not be as impressive as England's, but they're treasured by locals as a symbol of Scottish nationalism. They're also older than England's; while Oliver Cromwell destroyed England's jewels, the Scots managed to hide theirs.

History of the Jewels: The Honours of Scotland exhibit that leads up to the Crown Room traces the evolution of the jewels, the ceremony, and the often turbulent journey of this precious regalia. Here's the SparkNotes version:

In 1306, Robert the Bruce was

crowned with a "circlet of gold" in a ceremony at Scone—a town 40 miles north of Edinburgh, which Scotland's earliest kings had claimed as their capital. Around 1500, King James IV added two new items to the coronation ceremony—a scepter (a gift from the pope) and a huge sword (a gift from another pope). In 1540, James V had the original crown augmented by an Edinburgh goldsmith, giving it the imperial-crown shape it has today.

These Honours were used to crown every monarch: nine-month-old Mary, Queen of Scots (she cried); her one-year-old son James VI (future king of England); and Charles I and II. But the days of divine-right rulers were numbered.

In 1649, the parliament had Charles I (king of both England and Scotland) beheaded. Soon Cromwell's rabid English antiroyalists were marching on Edinburgh. Quick! Legend says two women scooped up the crown and sword, hid them in their skirts and belongings, and buried them in a church far to the northeast until the coast was clear.

When the monarchy was restored, the regalia were used to crown Scotland's last king, Charles II (1660). Then, in 1707, the Treaty of Union with England ended Scotland's independence. The Honours came out for a ceremony to bless the treaty, and were then locked away in a strongbox in the castle. There they lay for over a century, until Sir Walter Scott—the writer and great champion of Scottish tradition—forced a detailed search of the castle in 1818. The box was found...and there the Honours were, perfectly preserved. Within a few years, they were put on display, as they have been ever since.

The crown's most recent official appearance was in 1999, when it was taken across town to the grand opening of the reinstated parliament, marking a new chapter in the Scottish nation. As it represents the monarchy, the crown is present whenever a new session of parliament opens. (And if Scotland ever secedes, you can be sure that crown will be in the front row.)

The Honours: Finally, you enter the Crown Room to see the regalia itself. The four-foot steel **sword** was made in Italy under orders of Pope Julius II (the man who also commissioned Michelangelo's Sistine Chapel and St. Peter's Basilica). The **scepter** is made of silver, covered with gold, and topped with a rock crystal and a pearl. The gem- and pearl-encrusted **crown** has an imperial arch topped with a cross. Legend says the band of gold in the center is the original crown that once adorned the head of Robert the Bruce.

The **Stone of Scone** (a.k.a. the "Stone of Destiny") sits plain and strong next to the jewels. It's a rough-hewn gray slab of sandstone, about 26 by 17 by 10 inches. As far back as the ninth century, Scotland's kings were crowned atop this stone, when it stood at the medieval capital of Scone. But in 1296, the invading army of Ed-

William Wallace (c. 1270-1305)

In 1286, Scotland's king died without an heir, plunging the prosperous country into a generation of chaos. As Scottish nobles bickered over naming a successor, the English King Edward I—nicknamed "Longshanks" because of his long legs—invaded and assumed power (1296). He placed a figurehead on the throne, forced Scottish nobles to sign a pledge of allegiance to England (the "Ragman's Roll"), moved the British parliament north to York, and took the highly symbolic Stone of Scone to London, where it would remain for centuries.

WILLIAM WALLACE.

A year later, the Scots rose up against Edward, led by William Wallace (popularized in the film *Braveheart*). A mix of history and legend portrays Wallace as the son of a poor-but-knightly family that refused to sign the Ragman's Roll. Exceptionally tall and strong, he learned Latin and French from two uncles, who were priests. In his teenage years, his father and older brother were killed by the English. Later, he killed an English sheriff to avenge the death of his wife, Marion. Wallace's rage inspired his fellow Scots to revolt.

In the summer of 1297, Wallace and his guerrillas scored a series of stunning victories over the English. On September 11, a well-equipped English army of 10,000 soldiers and 300 horsemen began crossing Stirling Bridge. Wallace's men attacked, and in the chaos, the bridge collapsed, splitting the English ranks in two. The ragtag Scots drove the confused English into the river. The Battle of Stirling Bridge was a rout, and Wallace was knighted and appointed guardian of Scotland.

All through the winter, King Edward's men chased Wallace, continually frustrated by the Scots' hit-and-run tactics. Finally, at the Battle of Falkirk (1298), they drew Wallace's men out onto the open battlefield. The English with their horses and archers easily destroyed the spear-carrying Scots. Wallace resigned in disgrace and went on the lam, while his successors negotiated truces with the English, finally surrendering unconditionally in 1304. Wallace alone held out.

In 1305, the English tracked him down and took him to London, where he was convicted of treason and mocked with a crown of oak leaves as the "king of outlaws." On August 23, they stripped him naked and dragged him to the execution site. There he was strangled to near death, castrated, and dismembered. His head was stuck on a spike atop London Bridge, while his body parts were sent on tour to spook would-be rebels. But Wallace's martyrdom only served to inspire his countrymen, and the torch of independence was picked up by Robert the Bruce (see page 747). Despite the *Braveheart* movie, Robert the Bruce, not Wallace, was considered the original "Braveheart." (For the full story, see page 876.)

ward I of England carried the stone off to Westminster Abbey. For the next seven centuries, English (and subsequently British) kings and queens were crowned sitting on a coronation chair with the Stone of Scone tucked in a compartment underneath.

In 1950, four Scottish students broke into Westminster Abbey on Christmas Day and smuggled the stone back to Scotland in an act of foolhardy patriotism. But what could they do with it? After three months, they abandoned the stone, draped in Scotland's national flag. It was returned to Westminster Abbey, where (in 1953) Queen Elizabeth II was crowned atop it. In 1996, in recognition of increased Scottish autonomy, Elizabeth agreed to let the stone go home, on one condition: that it be returned to Westminster Abbey for all British coronations. One day, the next monarch of the United Kingdom—Prince Charles is first in line—will sit atop it, re-enacting a coronation ritual that dates back a thousand years.

• *Exit the crown jewel display, heading down the stairs. But just before exiting into the courtyard, turn left through a door that leads into the...*

❼ Royal Apartments: Scottish royalty lived in the Royal Palace only when safety or protocol required it (they preferred the

Palace of Holyroodhouse at the bottom of the Royal Mile). Here you can see several historic but unimpressive rooms. The first one, labeled **Queen Mary's Chamber,** is where Mary, Queen of Scots (1542-1587), gave birth to James VI of Scotland, who later became King James I of England. Nearby **Laich Hall** (Lower Hall) was the dining room of the royal family.

The **Great Hall** (through a separate entrance on Crown Square) was built by James IV to host the castle's official banquets and meetings. It's still used for such purposes today. Most of the interior—its fireplace, carved walls, pikes, and armor—is Victorian. But the well-constructed wood ceiling is original. This hammer-beam roof (constructed like the hull of a ship) is self-supporting.

The complex system of braces and arches distributes the weight of the roof outward to the walls, so there's no need for supporting pillars or long crossbeams. Before leaving, look for the big iron-barred peephole above the fireplace, on the right. This allowed the king to spy on his subjects while they partied.

• *Across the Crown Square courtyard is the...*

EDINBURGH

❽ Scottish National War Memorial: This commemorates the 149,000 Scottish soldiers lost in World War I, the 58,000 who died in World War II, and the nearly 800 (and counting) lost in British battles since. This is a somber spot (stow your camera and phone). Paid for by public donations, each bay is dedi-

cated to a particular Scottish regiment. The main shrine, featuring a green Italian-marble memorial that contains the original WWI rolls of honor, sits on an exposed chunk of the castle rock. Above you, the archangel Michael is busy slaying a dragon. The bronze frieze accurately shows the attire of various wings of Scotland's military. The stained glass starts with Cain and Abel on the left, and finishes with a celebration of peace on the right. To appreciate how important this place is, consider that Scottish soldiers died at twice the rate of other British soldiers in World War I.

• *Our final stop is worth the five-minute walk to get there. Backtrack to the café (and One O'Clock Gun), then head downhill to the War Museum. The statue in the courtyard in front of the museum is* **Field Marshall Sir Douglas Haig**—*the Scotsman who commanded the British Army through the WWI trench warfare of the Battle of the Somme and in Flanders Fields.*

❾ National War Museum Scotland: This thoughtful museum covers four centuries of Scottish military history. Instead of

the usual musty, dusty displays of endless armor, there's a compelling mix of videos, uniforms, weapons, medals, mementos, and eloquent excerpts from soldiers' letters.

Here you'll learn the story of how the fierce and courageous Scottish warrior changed from being a symbol of resistance against Britain to being a champion of that same empire. Along the way, these military men received many decorations for valor and did more than their share of dying in battle. But even when fighting alongside—rather than against—England, Scottish regiments still promoted their romantic, kilted-warrior image.

Queen Victoria fueled this ideal throughout the 19th century. She was infatuated with the Scottish Highlands and the culture's

Robert the Bruce (1274-1329)

In 1314, Robert the Bruce's men attacked Edinburgh's Royal Castle, recapturing it from the English. It was just one of many intense battles between the oppressive English and the plucky Scots during the Wars of Independence.

In this era, Scotland had to overcome not only its English foes but also its own divisiveness—and no one was more divided than Robert the Bruce. As earl of Carrick, he was born with blood ties to England and a long-standing family claim to the Scottish throne.

When England's King Edward I ("Longshanks") conquered Scotland in 1296, the Bruce family welcomed it, hoping Edward would defeat their rivals and put Bruce's father on the throne. They dutifully signed the "Ragman's Roll" of allegiance—and then Edward chose someone else as king.

Twentysomething Robert the Bruce (the "the" comes from his original family name of "de Bruce") then joined William Wallace's revolt against the English. As legend has it, he was the one who knighted Wallace after the victory at Stirling Bridge. When Wallace fell from favor, Bruce became a guardian of Scotland (caretaker ruler in the absence of a king) and continued fighting the English. But when Edward's armies again got the upper hand in 1302, Robert—along with Scotland's other nobles—diplomatically surrendered and again pledged loyalty.

In 1306, Robert the Bruce murdered his chief rival and boldly claimed to be king of Scotland. Few nobles supported him. Edward crushed the revolt and kidnapped Bruce's wife, the Church excommunicated him, and Bruce went into hiding on a distant North Sea island. He was now the king of nothing. Legend says he gained inspiration by watching a spider patiently build its web.

The following year, Bruce returned to Scotland and wove alliances with both nobles and the Church, slowly gaining acceptance as Scotland's king by a populace chafing under English rule. On June 24, 1314, he decisively defeated the English (now led by Edward's weak son, Edward II) at the Battle of Bannockburn. After a generation of turmoil (1286-1314), England was finally driven from Scotland, and the country was united under Robert I, king of Scotland.

As king, Robert the Bruce's priority was to stabilize the monarchy and establish clear lines of succession. His descendants would rule Scotland for the next 400 years, and even today, Bruce blood runs through the veins of Queen Elizabeth II, Prince Charles, princes William and Harry, and wee George and Charlotte.

untamed, rustic mystique. Highland soldiers, especially officers, went to great personal expense to sport all their elaborate regalia, and the kilted men fought best to the tune of their beloved bagpipes. For centuries the stirring drone of bagpipes accompanied Highland soldiers into battle—raising their spirits and announcing to the enemy that they were about to meet a fierce and mighty foe.

This museum shows the human side of war as well as the cleverness of government-sponsored ad campaigns that kept the lads enlisting. Two centuries of recruiting posters make the same pitch that still works today: a hefty signing bonus, steady pay, and job security with the promise of a manly and adventurous life—all spiked with a mix of pride and patriotism.

Stepping outside the museum, you're surrounded by cannons that no longer fire, stony walls that tell an amazing story, dramatic views of this grand city, and the clatter of tourists (rather than soldiers) on cobbles. Consider for a moment all the bloody history and valiant struggles, along with British power and Scottish pride, that have shaped the city over which you are perched.

SIGHTS ON AND NEAR THE ROYAL MILE

Camera Obscura

A big deal when it was built in 1853, this observatory topped with a mirror reflected images onto a disc before the wide eyes of people

who had never seen a photograph or a captured image. Today, you can climb 100 steps for an entertaining 20-minute demonstration (3/hour). At the top, enjoy the best view anywhere of the Royal Mile. Then work your way down through five floors of illusions, holograms, and early photos. This is a big hit with kids, but very overpriced. (It's less impressive on cloudy days.)

Cost and Hours: £15, daily 9:30-19:00, July-Aug until 21:00, Sept-Oct until 20:00, tel. 0131/226-3709, www.camera-obscura. co.uk.

▲The Scotch Whisky Experience

This attraction seems designed to distill money out of your pocket. The 50-minute experience consists of a "Malt Disney" whisky-barrel ride through the production process followed by an explanation and movie about Scotland's five main whisky regions. Though gimmicky, it does succeed in providing an entertaining yet informative orientation to the creation of Scottish firewater (things get pretty psychedelic when you hit the yeast stage). Your ticket also includes sampling a wee dram and the chance to stand amid the world's largest Scotch whisky collection (almost 3,500 bottles). At the end, you'll find yourself in the bar, with a fascinating wall of un-usually shaped whisky bottles. Serious connoisseurs should

stick with the more substantial shops in town, but this place can be worthwhile for beginners. (See sidebar for more on whisky and whisky tastings.)

Cost and Hours: £15 "silver tour" includes one sample, £26 "gold tour" includes samples from each main region, generally daily 10:00-18:00, tel. 0131/220-0441, www.scotchwhiskyexperience. co.uk.

▲▲Gladstone's Land

This is a typical 16th- to 17th-century merchant's "land," or tene-ment building. These multistory structures—in which merchants

ran their shops on the ground floor and lived upstairs—were typical of the time (the word "tenement" didn't have the slum connota-tion then that it has today). At six stories, this one was still just half the height of the tallest "skyscrapers."

Gladstone's Land, which you'll visit via one-hour guided tour, comes complete with an almost-lived-in, furnished interior and 400-year-old Renaissance painted ceil-ing. The downstairs cloth shop and upstairs kitchen and living quarters are brought to life by your guide. Keep this place in mind

as you stroll the rest of the Mile, imagining other houses as if they still looked like this on the inside. (For a comparison of life in the Old Town versus the New Town, also visit the Georgian House, described later.)

Cost and Hours: £7, tours run daily 10:30-16:00, 3-8 tours/ day, must book ahead by phone or in person; closed Nov-March, tel. 0131/226-5856, www.nts.org.uk/Visit/Gladstones-Land.

Writers' Museum at Lady Stair's House

This aristocrat's house, built in 1622, is filled with well-described manuscripts and knickknacks of Scotland's three greatest literary figures: Robert Burns, Robert Louis Stevenson, and Sir Walter Scott. If you'd like to see Scott's pipe and Burns' snuffboxes, you'll love this little museum. You'll wind up steep staircases through a

EDINBURGH

Whisky 101

Whisky is high on the experience list of most visitors to Scotland—even for teetotalers. Whether at a distillery, a shop, or a pub, be sure to try a few drams. (From the Gaelic word for "drink," a dram isn't necessarily a fixed amount—it's simply a small slug.) While touring a distillery is a sss Scottish experience, many fine whisky shops (including Cadenhead's in Edinburgh) offer guided tastings and a chance to have a small bottle filled from the cask of your choice.

Types of Whisky

Scotch whiskies come in two broad types: **"single malt,"** meaning that the bottle comes from a single batch made by a single distiller; and **"blends,"** which master blenders mix and match from various whiskies into a perfect punch of booze. While single malts get the most attention, blended whiskies represent 90 percent of all whisky sales. They tend to be light and mild—making them an easier way to tiptoe into the whisky scene.

There are more than 100 distilleries in Scotland, each one proud of its unique qualities. The **Lowlands,** around Edinburgh, produce light and refreshing whiskies—more likely to be taken as an aperitif. Whiskies from the **Highlands** and **Islands** range from floral and sweet (vanilla or honey) to smoky (peaty) and robust. **Speyside,** southeast of Inverness, is home to half of all Scottish distilleries. Mellow and fruity, Speyside whiskies can be the most accessible for beginners. The **Isle of Islay** is just the opposite, specializing in the peatiest, smokiest whiskies—not for novices. Only a few producers remain to distill the smoky and pungent **Campbeltown** whiskies in the southwest Highlands, near Islay.

Tasting Whisky

Tasting whisky is like tasting wine; you'll use all your senses. First, swirl the whisky in the glass and observe its color and "legs"—the trail left by the liquid as it runs back down the side of the glass (quick, thin legs indicate light, young whisky; slow, thick legs mean it's heavier and older one). Then take a deep sniff—do you smell smoke and peat? And finally, taste it (sip!). Adding a few drops of water is said to "open up the taste"—look for a little glass of water with a dropper standing by, and try tasting your whisky before and after.

A whisky's flavor is most influenced by three things: whether the malt is peat-smoked; the shape of the stills; and the composition of the casks. Even local climate can play a role; some island distilleries tout the salty notes of their whiskies, as the sea air permeates their casks.

maze of rooms as you peruse first editions and keepsakes of these celebrated writers. Edinburgh's high society gathered in homes like this in the 1780s to hear the great poet Robbie Burns read his work—it's meant to be read aloud rather than to oneself (stop in the Burns room to hear his poetry).

Cost and Hours: Free, Wed-Sat 10:00-17:00, Sun from 12:00, closed Mon-Tue, tel. 0131/529-4901, www.edinburghmuseums. org.uk.

Museum on the Mound

Located in the basement of the grand Bank of Scotland building, this exhibit tells the story of the bank, which was founded in 1695 (making it only a year younger than the Bank of England, and the longest operating bank in the world). Featuring displays on cash production, safe technology, and bank robberies, this museum struggles mightily to make banking interesting (the case holding £1 million is cool). It's worth popping in if you have extra time or find the subject appealing.

Cost and Hours: Free, Tue-Fri 10:00-17:00, closed Sat-Mon, down Bank Street from the Royal Mile—follow the street around to the left and enter through the gate, tel. 0131/243-5464, www. museumonthemound.com.

▲▲St. Giles' Cathedral

This is Scotland's most important church. Its ornate spire—the Scottish crown steeple from 1495—is a proud part of Edinburgh's skyline. The fascinating interior contains nearly 200 memorials honoring distinguished Scots through the ages.

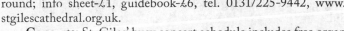

Cost and Hours: Free but £3 donation encouraged; Mon-Fri 9:00-19:00, Sat until 17:00; Oct-April Mon-Sat 9:00-17:00; Sun 13:00-17:00 year-round; info sheet-£1, guidebook-£6, tel. 0131/225-9442, www. stgilescathedral.org.uk.

Concerts: St. Giles' busy concert schedule includes free organ recitals and visiting choirs (frequent events at 12:15 and concerts

Sun at 18:00, also sometimes Wed, Thu, or Fri at 20:00, see schedule or ask for *Music at St. Giles'* pamphlet at welcome desk or gift shop).

❷ Self-Guided Tour: Today's facade is 19th-century Neo-Gothic, but most of what you'll see inside is from the 14th and 15th centuries.

EDINBURGH

Robert Burns (1759–1796)

Robert Burns, Scotland's national poet, holds a unique place in the heart of the Scottish people—a heart that still beats loud and proud thanks, in large part, to Burns himself.

Born on a farm in southwestern Scotland, Robbie (or "Rabbie," as Scots affectionately call him) was the oldest of seven children. His early years were full of backbreaking farm labor, which left him with a lifelong stoop. Though much was later made of his ascendance to literary acclaim from a rural, poverty-stricken upbringing, he was actually quite well educated (per Scottish tradition), equally as familiar with Latin and French as he was with hard work.

He started writing poetry at 15, but didn't have any published until age 28—to finance a voyage to the West Indies. When that first volume, *Poems, Chiefly in the Scottish Dialect*, became a sudden and overwhelming success, he reconsidered his emigration. Instead, he left his farm for Edinburgh, living just off the Royal Mile. He spent a year and a half in the city, schmoozing with literary elites, who celebrated this "heaven taught" farmer from the Hinterlands as Scotland's "ploughman poet."

His poetry, written primarily in the Scots dialect, drew on his substantial familiarity with both Scottish tradition and Western literature. By using the language of the common man to create works of beauty and sophistication, he found himself wildly popular among both rural folk and high society. Hearty poems such as "To a Mouse," "To a Louse," and "The Holy Fair" exalted the virtues of physical labor, romantic love, friendship, natural beauty, and drink—all of which he also pursued with vigor in real life. This further endeared him to most Scots, though considerably less so to Church fathers, who were particularly displeased with his love

Engage the cathedral guides in conversation; you'll be glad you did.

Just inside the entrance, turn around to see the modern stained-glass ❶ **Robert Burns window,** which celebrates Scotland's favorite poet (see sidebar). It was made in 1985 by the Icelandic artist Leifur Breidfjord. The green of the lower level symbolizes the natural world—God's creation. The middle zone with the circle shows the brotherhood of man—Burns was a great internationalist. The top is a rosy red sunburst of creativity, reminding Scots of Burns' famous line, "My love is like a red, red rose"—part of a song near and dear to every Scottish heart.

To the right of the Burns window is a fine ❷ **Pre-Raphaelite**

life (of Burns' dozen children, nine were by his eventual wife, the others by various servants and barmaids).

After achieving fame and wealth, Burns never lost touch with the concerns of the Scottish people, championing such radical ideas as social equality and economic justice. Burns bravely and loudly supported the French and American revolutions, which inspired one of his most beloved poems, "A Man's a Man for A' That," and even an ode to George Washington—all while other writers were being shipped off to Australia for similar beliefs. While his social causes cost him some aristocratic friends, it cemented his popularity among the masses, and not just within Scotland (he became, and remains, especially beloved in Russia).

Intent on preserving Scotland's rich musical and lyrical traditions, Burns traveled the countryside collecting traditional Scottish ballads. If it weren't for Burns, we'd have to come up with a different song to sing on New Year's Eve—he's the one who found, reworked, and popularized "Auld Lang Syne." His championing of Scottish culture came at a critical time: England had recently and finally crushed Scotland's last hopes of independence, and the Highland clan system was nearing its end. Burns lent the Scots dialect a new prestige, and the scrappy Scottish people a reinvigorated identity. (The official Burns website, www.robertburns.org, features a full collection of his works.)

Burns died at 37 of a heart condition likely exacerbated by so much hard labor (all the carousing probably hadn't helped, either). By that time, his fortune was largely spent, but his celebrity was going strong—around 10,000 people attended his burial. Even the Church eventually overcame its disapproval, installing a window in his honor at St. Giles' Cathedral. In 2009, his nation voted Burns "Greatest Ever Scot" in a TV poll. And every January 25 (the poet's birthday), on Burns Night, Scots gather to recite his songs and poems, tuck into some haggis ("chieftain o' the puddin' race," according to Burns), and raise their whisky to friendship and Scotland.

window. Like most in the church, it's a memorial to an important patron (in this case, John Marshall). From here stretches a great swath of war memorials.

As you walk along the north wall, find ❸ **John Knox's statue** (standing like a six-foot-tall bronze chess piece). Look into his eyes for 10 seconds from 10 inches away, and think of the Reformation struggles of the 16th century. Knox, the great religious reformer and founder of austere Scottish Presbyterianism, first preached here in 1559. His insistence that every person should be able to personally read the word of God—notice that he's pointing to a book—gave Scotland an educational system 300 years ahead of the rest of Europe (for more on Knox, see "The Scottish Reformation"

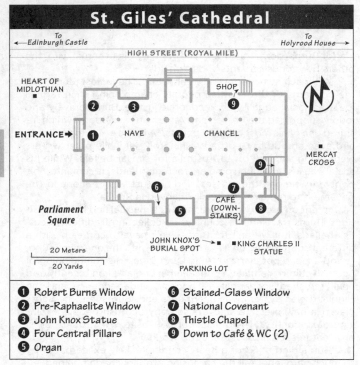

St. Giles' Cathedral

← To Edinburgh Castle

To Holyrood House →

HIGH STREET (ROYAL MILE)

HEART OF MIDLOTHIAN ■

SHOP

2   **3**   **9**

ENTRANCE → **1**   NAVE   **4**   CHANCEL

■ MERCAT CROSS

9

Parliament Square

6   **5**   **7**   CAFÉ (DOWN-STAIRS)   **8**

20 Meters
20 Yards

JOHN KNOX'S → ■   ■ KING CHARLES II
BURIAL SPOT   STATUE

PARKING LOT

1 Robert Burns Window
2 Pre-Raphaelite Window
3 John Knox Statue
4 Four Central Pillars
5 Organ

6 Stained-Glass Window
7 National Covenant
8 Thistle Chapel
9 Down to Café & WC (2)

EDINBURGH

on page 890). Thanks partly to Knox, it was Scottish minds that led the way in math, science, medicine, and engineering. Voltaire called Scotland "the intellectual capital of Europe."

Knox preached Calvinism. Consider that the Dutch and the Scots both embraced this creed of hard work, frugality, and strict ethics. This helps explain why the Scots are so different from the English (and why the Dutch and the Scots—both famous for their thriftiness and industriousness—are so much alike).

The oldest parts of the cathedral—the **4 four massive central pillars**—are Norman and date from the 12th century. They supported a mostly wooden superstructure that was lost when an invading English force burned it in 1385. The Scots rebuilt it bigger and better than ever, and in 1495 its famous crown spire was completed.

During the Reformation—when Knox preached here (1559-

1572)—the place was simplified and whitewashed. Before this, when the emphasis was on holy services provided by priests, there were lots of little niches. With the new focus on sermons rather than rituals, the grand pulpit took center stage.

Knox preached against anything that separated you from God, including stained glass (considered the poor man's Bible, as illiterate Christians could learn from its pictures). Knox had the church's fancy medieval glass windows replaced with clear glass, but 19th-century Victorians took them out and installed the brilliantly colored ones you see today.

Cross over to the ➎ **organ** (1992, Austrian-built, one of Europe's finest) and take in its sheer might. (To light it up, find the button behind the organ to the right of the glass.)

Immediately to the right of the organ (as you're facing it) is a tiny chapel for silence and prayer. The dramatic ➏ **stained-glass**

window above shows the commotion that surrounded Knox when he preached. The bearded, fiery-eyed Knox had a huge impact on this community. Notice how there were no pews back then. The church was so packed, people even looked through clear windows from across the street. With his hand on the holy book, Knox seems to conduct divine electricity to the Scottish faithful.

Find a copy of the ➐ **National Covenant** (in the corner to the far left of the organ as you face it). It was signed in blood in 1638 by Scottish heroes who refused to compromise their religion for the king's. Most who signed were martyred (their monument is nearby in Grassmarket). You can see the original National Covenant in the Edinburgh Museum, described later.

Head toward the east (back) end of the church, and turn right to see the Neo-Gothic ➑ **Thistle Chapel** (£3 donation requested, volunteer guide is a wealth of information). The interior is filled with intricate wood carving. Built in two years (1910-1911), entirely with Scottish materials and labor, it is the private chapel of the Order of the Thistle, the only Scottish chivalric order. It's used several times a year for the knights to gather (and, if one dies, to inaugurate a new member). Scotland recognizes its leading citizens by bestowing a membership upon them. The Queen presides over the ritual from her fancy stall, marked by her Scottish coat of arms—a heraldic zoo of symbolism. Are there bagpipes in heaven? Find the tooting stone angel at the top of a window to the left of the altar, and the wooden one to the right of the doorway where you entered.

➒ **Downstairs** you'll find handy public WCs and an inviting

EDINBURGH

Scotland's Literary Greats

Edinburgh was home to Scotland's three greatest literary figures, pictured above: Robert Burns (left), Robert Louis Stevenson (center), and Sir Walter Scott (right).

Robert Burns (1759-1796), known as "Rabbie" in Scotland and quite possibly the most famous and beloved Scot of all time, moved to Edinburgh after achieving overnight celebrity with his first volume of poetry (staying in a house on the spot where Deacon Brodie's Tavern now stands). Even though he wrote in the rough Scots dialect and dared to attack social rank, he was a favorite of Edinburgh's high society, who'd gather in fine homes to hear him recite his works. For more on Burns, see the sidebar, earlier.

One hundred years later, **Robert Louis Stevenson** (1850-1894) also stirred the Scottish soul with his pen. An avid traveler who always packed his notepad, Stevenson created settings that are vivid and filled with wonder. Traveling through Scotland, Europe, and around the world, he distilled his adventures into Romantic classics, including *Kidnapped* and *Treasure Island* (as well as *The Strange Case of Dr. Jekyll and Mr. Hyde*). Stevenson, who

$ café—a good place for paupers to munch prayerfully (simple, light lunches, coffee and cakes; Mon-Sat 9:00-17:00, Sun from 11:00, in basement on back side of church, tel. 0131/225-5147).

Old Parliament House

The building now holds the civil law courts, so you'll need to go through security first. Peruse the info panels in the grand hall, with its fine 1639 hammer-beam ceiling and stained glass. This space housed the Scottish parliament until the Act of Union in 1707. The biggest stained-glass window depicts the initiation of the first Scottish High Court in 1532. The building now holds the civil law courts and is busy with wigged and robed lawyers hard at work in the old library (peek through the door) or pacing the hall deep in

was married in San Francisco and spent his last years in the South Pacific, wrote, "Youth is the time to travel—both in mind and in body—to try the manners of different nations." He said, "I travel not to go anywhere...but to simply go." Travel was his inspiration and his success.

Sir Walter Scott (1771-1832) wrote the *Waverley* novels, including *Ivanhoe* and *Rob Roy*. He's considered the father of the Romantic historical novel. Through his writing, he generated a worldwide interest in Scotland, and reawakened his fellow countrymen's pride in their heritage. His novels helped revive interest in Highland culture—the Gaelic language, kilts, songs, legends, myths, the clan system—and created a national identity. An avid patriot, he wrote, "Every Scottish man has a pedigree. It is a national prerogative, as unalienable as his pride and his poverty." Scott is so revered in Edinburgh that his towering Neo-Gothic monument dominates the city center. With his favorite hound by his side, Sir Walter Scott overlooks the city that he inspired, and that inspired him.

The best way to learn about and experience these literary greats is to visit the Writers' Museum at Lady Stair's House (see page 749) and to take Edinburgh's Literary Pub Tour (see page 790).

While just three writers dominate your Edinburgh sightseeing, consider also the other great writers with Edinburgh connections: J. K. Rowling (who captures the "Gothic" spirit of Edinburgh with her Harry Potter series); current resident Ian Rankin (with his "tartan noir" novels); J. M. Barrie (who attended University of Edinburgh and later created Peter Pan); Sir Arthur Conan Doyle (who was born in Edinburgh, went to medical school here, and is best known for inventing Sherlock Holmes); and James Boswell (who lived 50 yards away from the Writers' Museum, in James Court, and is revered for his biography of Samuel Johnson).

discussion. The basement café is literally their supreme court's restaurant (open to public until 14:30).

Cost and Hours: Free, public welcome Mon-Fri 9:00-16:30, closed Sat-Sun, no photos, enter behind St. Giles' Cathedral at door #11; open-to-the-public trials are just across the street at the High Court—the doorman has the day's docket.

▲The Real Mary King's Close

For an unusual peek at Edinburgh's gritty, plague-ridden past, join a costumed performer on an hour-long trip through an excavated underground street and buildings on the northern slope of the Royal Mile. Tours cover the standard goofy, crowd-pleasing ghost stories, but also provide authentic and historical insight into a part of town entombed by later construction. It's best to book

EDINBURGH

ahead (online up to the day before, or by phone or in person for a same-day booking)—even though tours leave every 15-30 minutes, groups are small and the sight is popular.

Cost and Hours: £15; daily 10:00-21:00, Nov-March Sun-Thu until 17:00; these are last tour times, across from St. Giles' at 2 Warriston's Close—but enter through well-marked door facing High Street, tel. 0845-070-6244, www.realmarykingsclose.com.

▲Museum of Childhood

This five-story playground of historical toys and games is rich in nostalgia and history. Each well-signed gallery is as jovial as a Norman Rockwell painting, highlighting the delights and simplicity of childhood. The museum does a fair job of representing culturally relevant oddities, such as ancient Egyptian, Peruvian, and voodoo dolls, and displays early versions of toys it's probably best didn't make the final cut (such as a grim snake-centered precursor to the popular board game Chutes and Ladders).

Cost and Hours: Free, Thu-Mon 10:00-17:00 except Sun from 12:00, closed Tue-Wed, 42 High Street.

John Knox House

Intriguing for Reformation buffs, this fine medieval house dates back to 1470 and offers a well-explained look at the life of the great 16th-century reformer. Although most contend he never actu-
ally lived here, preservationists called
it "Knox's house" to save it from the
wrecking ball in the 1840s. Regardless, the place has good information
on Knox and his intellectual spar-
ring partner, Mary, Queen of Scots.
Imagine the Protestant firebrand
John Knox and the devout Catholic

Mary sitting face-to-face in old rooms like these, discussing the most intimate matters of their spiritual lives as they decided the course of Scotland's religious future. The sparsely furnished house contains some period furniture, an early 1600s hand-painted ceiling, information on the house and its resident John Mossman (goldsmith to Mary, Queen of Scots), and exhibits on printing—an essential tool for early reformers.

Cost and Hours: £5, Mon-Sat 10:00-18:00, closed Sun except in July-Aug 12:00-18:00, 43 High Street, tel. 0131/556-9579, www.tracscotland.org.

▲People's Story Museum

This engaging exhibit traces the working and social lives of ordinary people through the 18th, 19th, and 20th centuries. You'll see tools, products, and objects related to important Edinburgh trades (printing, brewing), a wartime kitchen, and a circa-1989 trip to the

movies. On the top floor, a dated but endearing 22-minute film offers insight into the ways people have lived in this city for generations. On the ground floor, peek into the former jail, an original part of the historic building (the Canongate Tolbooth, built in 1591).

EDINBURGH

Cost and Hours: Free, Wed-Sat 10:00-17:00 except Sun from 12:00, closed Mon-Tue, 163 Canongate, tel. 0131/529-4057, www.edinburghmuseums.org.uk.

▲Museum of Edinburgh

Another old house full of old stuff, this one is worth a stop for a look at its early Edinburgh history (and its handy ground-floor WC). Be sure to see the original copy of the National Covenant—written in 1638 on animal skin. Scottish leaders signed this, refusing to adopt the king's religion—and were killed because of it. Exploring the rest of the collection, keep an eye out for Robert Louis Stevenson's antique golf ball, James Craig's architectural plans for the Georgian New Town, an interactive kids' area with dress-up clothes, a sprawling top-floor exhibit on Edinburgh-born Field Marshall Sir David Haig (who led the British Western Front efforts in World War I and later became Earl Haig), and locally made glass and ceramics.

Cost and Hours: Free, Thu-Mon 10:00-17:00 except Sun from 12:00, closed Tue-Wed, 142 Canongate, tel. 0131/529-4143, www.edinburghmuseums.org.uk.

▲▲Scottish Parliament Building

Scotland's parliament originated in 1293 and was dissolved when Scotland united with England in 1707. But after the Scottish elec-

torate and the British parliament gave their consent, in 1997 it was decided that there should again be "a Scottish parliament guided by justice, wisdom, integrity, and compassion." Formally reconvened by Queen Elizabeth II in 1999, the Scottish parliament now enjoys self-rule in many areas (except for matters of defense, foreign policy, immigration, and taxation). The current government, run by the Scottish Nationalist Party (SNP), is pushing for even more independence.

The innovative building, opened in 2004, brought together all the functions of the fledgling parliament in one complex. It's a people-oriented structure (conceived by Catalan architect Enric Miralles). Signs are written in both English and Gaelic (the Scots' Celtic tongue).

For a peek at the building and a lesson in how the Scottish parliament works, drop in, pass through security, and find the visitors' desk. You're welcome in the public parts of the building, including a small ground-floor exhibit on the parliament's history and function and, up several flights of stairs, a viewing gallery overlooking the impressive Debating Chambers.

Cost and Hours: Free; Mon-Sat 10:00-17:00, Tue-Thu 9:00-18:30 when parliament is in session (Sept-June), closed Sun year-round. For a complete list of recess dates or to book tickets for debates, check their website or call their visitor services line, tel. 0131/348-5200, www.parliament.scot.

Tours: Free worthwhile hour-long tours covering history, architecture, parliamentary processes, and other topics are offered by proud locals. Tours generally run throughout the day Mon and Fri-Sat in session (Sept-June) and Mon-Sat in recess (July-Aug). While you can try dropping in, these tours can book up—it's best to book ahead online or over the phone.

Seeing Parliament in Session: The public can witness the Scottish parliament's hugely popular debates (usually Tue-Thu 14:00-18:00; book ahead online, over the phone, or at the info desk).

On Thursdays from 11:40 to 12:45 the First Minister is on the hot seat and has to field questions from members across all parties (reserve ahead for this popular session over the phone a week in advance; spots book up quickly—call at 9:00 sharp on Thu for the following week).

▲▲Palace of Holyroodhouse

Built on the site of the abbey/monastery founded in 1128 by King David I, this palace was the true home, birthplace, and coronation spot of Scotland's Stuart kings in their heyday (James IV; Mary, Queen of Scots; and Charles I). It's particularly memorable as the site of some dramatic moments from the short reign of Mary, Queen of Scots—including the murder of her personal secretary, David Rizzio, by agents of her jealous husband. Today, it's one of Queen Elizabeth II's official residences. She usually manages her Scottish affairs here during Holyrood Week, from late June to early July (and generally stays at Balmoral in August). Holyrood is open to the public outside of the Queen's visits. Touring the interior offers a more polished contrast to Edinburgh Castle, and is particularly worth considering if you don't plan to go to Balmoral. The one-way audioguide route leads you through the fine apartments and tells some of the notable stories that played out here.

Cost: £12.50, includes quality one-hour audioguide; £17.50 combo-ticket includes the Queen's Gallery; £21.50 combo-ticket adds guided tour of palace gardens (April-Oct only); tickets sold in Queen's Gallery to the right of the castle entrance (see next listing).

Hours: Daily 9:30-18:00, Nov-March until 16:30, last entry 1.5 hours before closing, tel. 0131/556-5100, www.royalcollection.org.uk. It's still a working palace, so it's closed when the Queen or other VIPs are in residence.

Visiting the Palace: The building, rich in history and decor, is filled with elegantly furnished Victorian rooms and a few darker, older rooms with glass cases of historic bits and Scottish pieces

that locals find fascinating. Bring the palace to life with the audioguide. The tour route leads you into the grassy inner courtyard, then up to the royal apartments: dining rooms, *Downton Abbey*-style drawing rooms, and royal bedchambers. Along the way, you'll learn the story behind the 96 portraits of Scottish leaders (some real, others imaginary) that line the Great Gallery; why the king never slept in his official "state bed"; why the exiled Comte d'Artois took refuge in the palace; and how the current Queen puts her Scottish subjects at ease when she receives them here. Finally you'll twist up a tight spiral staircase to the private chambers of Mary, Queen of Scots, where conspirators stormed in and stabbed her secretary 56 times.

After exiting the palace, you're free to stroll through the evocative **ruined abbey** (destroyed by the English during the time of

Mary, Queen of Scots, in the 16th century) and the **palace gardens** (closed Nov-March except some weekends). Some 8,000 guests—including many honored ladies sporting fancy hats—gather here every July when the Queen hosts a magnificent tea party. (She gets help pouring.)

Nearby: Hikers, note that the wonderful trail up Arthur's Seat starts just across the street from the gardens (see page 779 for details).

(see page 779 for details)

EDINBURGH

Queen's Gallery

This small museum features rotating exhibits of artwork from the royal collection. For more than five centuries, the royal family has amassed a wealth of art treasures. While the Queen keeps most in her many private palaces, she shares an impressive load of it here, with exhibits changing about every six months. Though the gallery occupies just a few rooms, its displays can be exquisite. The entry fee includes an excellent audioguide, written and read by the curator.

Cost and Hours: £7, £17.50 combo-ticket includes Palace of Holyroodhouse, daily 9:30-18:00, Nov-March until 16:30, last entry one hour before closing, café, on the palace grounds, to the right of the palace entrance, www.royalcollection.org.uk. Buses #35 and #36 stop outside, saving you a walk to or from Princes Street/North Bridge.

Our Dynamic Earth

Located about a five-minute walk from the Palace of Holyroodhouse, this immense exhibit tells the story of our planet, filling

several underground floors under a vast, white Gore-Tex tent. It's pitched, appropriately, at the base of the Salisbury Crags. The exhibit is designed for younger kids and does the same thing an American science exhibit would do—but with a charming Scottish accent. You'll learn about the Scottish geologists who pioneered the discipline, then step into a "time machine" to watch the years rewind, from cave dwellers to dinosaurs to the Big Bang. After viewing several short films on stars, tectonic plates, ice caps, and worldwide weather (in a "4-D" exhibit), you're free to wander past salty pools and a re-created rain forest.

Cost and Hours: £15, kids-£9.50, daily 10:00-17:30, July-Aug until 18:00, closed Mon-Tue Nov-March, last entry 1.5 hours before closing, on Holyrood Road, between the palace and mountain, tel. 0131/550-7800, www.dynamicearth.co.uk.

SIGHTS SOUTH OF THE ROYAL MILE
▲▲▲National Museum of Scotland

This huge museum has amassed more historic artifacts than every other place I've seen in Scotland combined. It's all wonderfully displayed, with fine descriptions offering a best-anywhere hike through the history of Scotland.

Cost and Hours: Free, daily 10:00-17:00; two long blocks south of St. Giles' Cathedral and the Royal Mile, on Chambers Street off George IV Bridge, tel. 0131/247-4422, www.nms.ac.uk.

Tours: Free one-hour general tours are offered daily at 11:00 and 13:00; themed tours at 15:00 (confirm tour schedule at info desk or on TV screens). The National Museum of Scotland Highlights app provides thin coverage of select items but is free and downloadable using their free Wi-Fi.

Eating: A **$$ brasserie** is on the ground floor near the information desks, and a **$ café** with coffee, tea, cakes, and snacks is on the level 3 balcony overlooking the Grand Gallery. On the museum's fifth floor, the dressy and upscale **$$$ Tower restaurant** serves good food with a castle view (lunch/early bird special, afternoon tea, three-course dinner specials; daily 10:00-22:00—use Tower entry if eating after museum closes, reservations recommended, tel. 0131/225-3003, www.tower-restaurant.com). A number of good eating options are within a couple of blocks of the museum (see page 803).

Overview: The place gives you two museums in one. One wing houses the Natural World galleries (T. Rex skeletons and other animals), the Science and Technology galleries, and a fashion exhibit. (The museum's Ancient Egypt and East Asia collections are currently under renovation.) With time and interest, these are all worth a look. But we'll focus on the other wing, which sweeps you through Scottish history covering Roman and Viking times, Edinburgh's witch-burning craze and clan massacres, the struggle for Scottish independence, the Industrial Revolution, and right up to Scotland in the 21st century.

⊘ Self-Guided Tour: Get oriented on level 1, in the impressive glass-roofed Grand Gallery right above the entrance hall. Just outside the Grand Gallery is the **millennium clock,** a 30-foot high clock with figures that move to a Bach concerto on the hour from 11:00 to 16:00. The clock has four parts (crypt, nave, belfry, and spire) and represents the turmoil of the 20th century, with a pietà at the top.

• *To reach the Scottish history wing, exit the Grand Gallery at the far right end, under the clock and past the statue of James Watt.*

On the way, you'll pass through the science and technology wing. While walking through, look for **Dolly the sheep**—the world's first cloned mammal—born in Edinburgh and now stuffed and on display. Continue into Hawthornden Court (level 1), where our tour begins. (It's possible to detour downstairs from here to level -1 for Scotland's prehistoric origins—geologic formation, Celts, Romans, Vikings.)

• *Enter the door marked...*

Kingdom of the Scots (c. 1300-1700): From its very start, Scotland was determined to be free. You're greeted with proud quotes from what's been called the Scottish Declaration of Independence—the Declaration of Arbroath, a defiant letter written to the pope in 1320. As early as the ninth century, Scotland's patron saint, Andrew (see the small statue in the next room), had—according to legend—miraculously intervened to help the Picts and Scots of Scotland remain free by defeating the Angles of England. Andrew's X-shaped cross still decorates the Scottish flag today.

Enter the first room on your right, with imposing swords and other objects related to Scotland's most famous patriots—William Wallace and Robert the Bruce. Bruce's descendants, the Stuarts, went on to rule Scotland for the next 300 years. Eventually, James VI of Scotland (see his baby cradle) came to rule England as well (as King James I of England).

In the next room, a big guillotine recalls the harsh justice meted out to criminals, witches, and "Covenanters" (17th-century

political activists who opposed interference of the Stuart kings in affairs of the Presbyterian Church of Scotland). Nearby, also check out the tomb (a copy) of Mary, Queen of Scots, the 16th-century Stuart monarch who opposed the Presbyterian Church of Scotland. Educated and raised in Renaissance France, Mary brought refinement to the Scottish throne. After she was imprisoned and then executed by Elizabeth I of England in 1587, her supporters rallied each other by invoking her memory. Pendants and coins with her portrait stoked the irrepressible Scottish spirit (see display case near tomb).

Browse the rest of level 1 to see everyday objects from that age: carved panels, cookware, and clothes.

• *Backtrack to Hawthornden Court and head up to level 3.*

Scotland Transformed (1700s): You'll see artifacts related to Bonnie Prince Charlie and the Jacobite rebellions as well as the ornate Treaty of Union document, signed in 1707 by the Scottish parliament. This act voluntarily united Scotland with England under the single parliament of the United Kingdom. For some Scots, this move was an inevitable step in connecting to the wider world, but for others it symbolized the end of Scotland's existence.

Union with England brought stability and investment to Scotland. In this same era, the advances of the Industrial Revolu-

tion were making a big impact on Scottish life. Mechanized textile looms (on display) replaced hand craftsmanship. The huge Newcomen steam-engine water pump helped the mining industry to develop sites with tricky drainage. Nearby is a model of a coal mine (or "colliery"); coal-rich Scotland exploited this natural resource to fuel its textile factories.

How the parsimonious Scots financed these new, large-scale enterprises is explained in an exhibit on the Bank of Scotland. Powered by the Scottish work ethic and the new opportunities that came from the Industrial Revolution, the country came into relative prosperity. Education and medicine thrived. With the dawn of the modern age came leisure time, the concept of "healthful sports," and golf—a popular Scottish pastime. On display (near the back, behind the machinery) are some early golf balls, which date from about 1820, made of leather and stuffed with feathers.

• *Journey up to level 5.*

Industry and Empire (1800s): Turn right and do a counterclockwise spin around this floor to survey Scottish life in the 19th century. Industry had transformed the country. Highland farmers left their land to find work in Lowland factories and foundries. Modern inventions—the phonograph, the steam-powered train, the kitchen range—revolutionized everyday life. In Glasgow near the turn of the century, architect Charles Rennie Mackintosh helped to define Scottish Art Nouveau. Scotland was at the forefront of literature (Robert Burns, Sir Walter Scott, Robert Louis Stevenson), science (Lord Kelvin, James Watt, Alexander Graham Bell...he was born here, anyway!), world exploration (John Kirk in Africa, Sir Alexander Mackenzie in Canada), and whisky production.

• *Climb the stairs to level 6.*

Scotland: A Changing Nation (1900s): Turn left and do a clockwise spin through this floor to bring the story to the present day. The two world wars decimated the population of this already wee nation. In addition, hundreds of thousands emigrated, especially to Canada (where one in eight Canadians has Scottish origins). Other exhibits include Scots in the world of entertainment (from early boy-band Bay City Rollers to actor-comedian Billy Connolly); a look at the recent trend of devolution from the United Kingdom (1999 opening of Scotland's own parliament and the landmark 2014 referendum on Scottish independence); and a sports Hall of Fame (from golfer Tom Morris to auto racers Jackie Stewart and Jim Clark).

• *Finish your visit on level 7, the rooftop.*

Garden Terrace: The well-described roof garden features grasses and heathers from every corner of Scotland and spectacular views of the city.

Greyfriars Bobby Statue and Greyfriars Cemetery

This famous **statue** of Edinburgh's favorite dog is across the street from the National Museum of Scotland. Every business nearby, it seems, is named for this Victorian Skye terrier, who is reputed to have stood by his master's grave in Greyfriars Cemetery for 14 years. The story was immortalized in a 1960s Disney flick, but recent research suggests that 19th-century businessmen bribed a stray to hang out in the cemetery to attract sightseers. If it was a ruse, it still works.

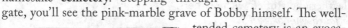

Just behind Bobby is the entrance to his namesake **cemetery**. Stepping through the gate, you'll see the pink-marble grave of Bobby himself. The well-

tended cemetery is an evocative place to stroll, and a nice escape from the city's bustle. Harry Potter fans could turn it into a scavenger hunt: J. K. Rowling sketched out her saga just around the corner at The Elephant House Café—and a few of the cemetery's weather-beaten headstones bear familiar names, including McGonagall and Thomas Riddell. Beyond the cemetery fence are the frilly Gothic spires of posh George Heriot's School, said to have inspired Hogwarts. And just a few short blocks to the east is a street called...Potterrow.

Grassmarket

Once Edinburgh's site for hangings (residents rented out their windows—above the rudely named "Last Drop" pub—for the

view), today Grassmarket is a people-friendly piazza. It was originally the city's garage, a depot for horses and cows (hence the name). It's rowdy here at night—a popular place for "hen dos" and "stag dos" (bachelorette and bachelor parties). In the early evening, the Literary Pub Tour departs

from here (see page 790). Some good shopping streets branch off from Grassmarket: Victoria Street, built in the Victorian Age, is lined with colorful little shops and eateries; angling off in the other direction, Candlemaker's Row has a few interesting artisan shops (and leads, in just a couple of minutes' walk, up to Greyfriars Bobby and the National Museum; for more shopping tips in this area, see page 784).

At the top of Grassmarket is the round monument to the "Covenanters." These strict 17th-century Scottish Protestants were killed for refusing to accept the king's Episcopalian prayer book. To this day, Scots celebrate their national church's emphatically democratic government. Rather than big-shot bishops (as in the Anglican or Roman Catholic Church), they have a low-key "moderator" who's elected each year.

MUSEUMS IN THE NEW TOWN

These sights are linked by the "Bonnie Wee New Town Walk" on page 731.

▲▲Scottish National Gallery

This delightful, small museum has Scotland's best collection of paintings. In a short visit, you can admire well-described works

by Old Masters (Raphael, Rembrandt, Rubens), Impressionists (Monet, Degas, Gauguin), and a few underrated Scottish painters. (Scottish art is better at the National Portrait Gallery, described next.) Although there are no iconic masterpieces, it's

a surprisingly enjoyable collection that's truly world-class.

Cost and Hours: Free; daily 10:00-17:00, Thu until 19:00, longer hours in Aug; café downstairs, The Mound (between Princes and Market streets), tel. 0131/624-6200, www.nationalgalleries.org.

Expect Changes: The museum is undergoing major renovation to increase the space of its Scottish collection and build a grand main entrance from Princes Street Gardens. As a result, certain exhibits may be closed, and pieces may be relocated, on loan, or in storage. Ask one of the friendly tartan-sporting attendants or at the info desk downstairs (near the WCs and gallery shop) if you can't find a particular item.

Next Door: The skippable **Royal Scottish Academy** hosts temporary art exhibits and is connected to the Scottish National Gallery at the Gardens level (underneath the gallery) by the Weston Link building (same hours as gallery, fine café and restaurant).

Visiting the Museum: Start at the gallery entrance (at the north end of the building). Climb the stairs to the upper level (north end), and take a left. You'll run right into...

Van der Goes, *The Trinity Panels*, c. 1473-1479: For more than five centuries, these two double-sided panels have remained

here—first in a church, then (when the church was leveled to build Waverley train station) in this museum. The panels likely were the wings of a triptych, flanking a central scene of the Virgin Mary that was destroyed by Protestant vandals during the Reformation.

In one panel is the Trinity: God the Father, in a rich red robe, cradles a spindly, just-crucified Christ, while the dove of the Holy Spirit hovers between them. (This is what would have been seen when the triptych was closed.) The flip side of the Christ panel depicts Scotland's king and queen, who are best known to history as the parents of the boy kneeling alongside them. He grew up to become James IV, the Renaissance king who made Edinburgh a cultural capital. On the other panel, the church's director (the man who commissioned the painting from the well-known Flemish painter) kneels and looks on while an angel plays a hymn on the church organ. On the opposite side is Margaret of Denmark, Queen of Scots, being presented by a saint.

In typically medieval fashion, the details are meticulous—expressive faces, intricate folds in the robes, Christ's pallid skin, observant angels. The donor's face is a remarkable portrait, with realistic skin tone and a five-o'clock shadow. But the painting lacks true 3-D realism—God's gold throne is overly exaggerated, and Christ's cardboard-cutout body hovers weightlessly.

• *Go back across the top of the skylight, to a room where the next two paintings hang.*

Botticelli, *The Virgin Adoring the Sleeping Christ Child*, c. 1485: Mary looks down at her baby, peacefully sleeping in a flower-filled garden. It's easy to appreciate Botticelli's masterful style: the precisely drawn outlines, the Virgin's pristine skin, the translucent glow. Botticelli creates a serene world in which no shadows are cast. The scene is painted on canvas—unusual at a time when wood panels were the norm. For the Virgin's rich cloak, Botticelli used ground-up lapis lazuli (a very pricey semiprecious stone), and her hem is decorated with gold leaf.

Renaissance-era art lovers would instantly catch the symbolism. Mary wears a wispy halo and blue cloak that recalls the sky blue of heaven. The roses without thorns and enclosed garden are both symbols of virginity, while the violet flowers (at bottom) represent humility. Darker symbolism hints at what's to come. The strawberries (lower right) signify Christ's blood, soon to be shed, while the roses—though thornless now—will become the Crown of Thorns. For now, Mary can adore her sleeping, blissful baby in a peaceful garden. But in a few decades she'll be kneeling again to weep over the dead, crucified Messiah.

Raphael, *Holy Family with a Palm Tree*, 1506-1507: Mary, Joseph, and the Christ Child fit snugly within a round frame (a tondo), their pose symbolizing geometric perfection and the perfect family unit. Joseph kneels to offer Jesus flowers. Mary curves toward him. Baby Jesus dangles in between, linking the family together. Raphael also connects the figures through eye contact: Mary eyes Joseph, who locks onto Jesus, who gazes precociously back. Like in a cameo, we see the faces incised

in profile, while their bodies bulge out toward us.

• *Back downstairs at ground level is the main gallery space. Circle around the collection chronologically, watching for works by Bellini, Titian, Velázquez, and El Greco. In Room 7, look for the next two paintings.*

Rubens, *Feast of Herod*, c. 1635-1638: All eyes turn to watch the dramatic culmination of the story of John the Baptist. Salome

EDINBURGH

(standing in center) presents John's severed head on a platter to a horrified King Herod, who clutches the tablecloth and buries his hand in his beard to stifle a gag. Meanwhile, Herod's wife—who cooked up the nasty plot—pokes spitefully at John's head with a fork. A dog tugs at Herod's foot like a nasty conscience. The canvas—big, colorful, full of motion and drama—is totally Baroque. Some have suggested that the features of Herod's wife and Salome are those of Rubens' wife and ex-wives, and the head is Rubens himself.

Rembrandt, *Self-Portrait, Aged 51*, c. 1657: At 51, Rembrandt has just declared bankruptcy. Besides financial hardship and the auctioning-off of his personal belongings, he's also facing social stigma and behind-his-back ridicule. Once Holland's most renowned painter, he's begun a slow decline into poverty and obscurity.

His face says it all. Holding a steady gaze, he stares with matter-of-fact acceptance, with his lips pursed. He's dressed in dark clothes against a dark background, with the only spot of light shining on the worry lines of his forehead. Get close enough to the canvas to see the thick paste of paint he used for the wrinkles around his eyes—a study in aging.

• *In Room 11, find...*

Gainsborough, *The Honorable Mrs. Graham*, 1775-1777: The slender, elegant, lavishly dressed woman was the teenage bride of a wealthy Scottish landowner. She leans on a column, ostrich feather in hand, staring off to the side (Thoughtfully? Determinedly? Haughtily?). Her faultless face and smooth neck stand out from the elaborately ruffled dress and background foliage. This 18th-century woman wears a silvery dress that echoes 17th-century style—Gainsborough's way of showing how, though she was young, she was classy. Thomas ("Blue Boy") Gainsborough—the product of a clothes-making father and a flower-painting mother—  uses aspects of both in this lush portrait. The ruby brooch on her bodice marks the center of this harmonious composition.

• *Climb the stairs to the upper level (south end, opposite from where you entered) and turn right for the Impressionists and Post-Impressionists.*

Impressionist Collection: The gallery has a smattering of (mostly smaller-scale) works from all the main artists of the Impressionist and Post-Impressionist eras. You'll see Degas' ballet scenes, Renoir's pastel-colored family scenes, Van Gogh's peasants, and Seurat's pointillism.

• *Keep an eye out for these three paintings.*

Monet's *Poplars on the River Epte* (1891) was part of the artist's famous "series" paintings. He set up several canvases in a floating studio near his home in Giverny. He'd start on one canvas in the morning (to catch the morning light), then move to the next as the light changed. This particular canvas captures a perfect summer day, showing both the poplars on the riverbank and their mirror image in the still water. The subject matter begins to dissolve into a pure pattern of color, anticipating abstract art.

Gauguin's *Vision of the Sermon* (1888) shows French peasant women imagining the miraculous event they've just heard preached about in church—when Jacob wrestles with an angel. The painting is a watershed in art history, as Gauguin throws out the rules of "realism" that had reigned since the Renaissance. The colors are surreal, there are no shadows, the figures are arranged almost randomly, and there's no attempt to make the wrestlers appear distant. The diagonal tree branch is the only thing separating the everyday world from the miraculous. Later, when Gauguin moved to Tahiti (see his *Three Tahitians* nearby), he painted a similar world, where the everyday and magical coexist, with symbolic power.

Sargent's *Lady Agnew of Lochnaw* (1892) is the work that launched the career of this American-born portrait artist. Lady Agnew—the young wife of a wealthy old Scotsman—lounges back languidly and gazes out self-assuredly. The Impressionistic smudges of paint on her dress and the chair contrast with her clear skin and luminous eyeballs. Her relaxed pose (one arm hanging down the side) contrasts with her intensity: head tilted slightly down while she gazes up, a corner of her mouth askew, and an eyebrow cocked seductively.

Scottish Collection: The museum is undergoing a major renovation to build a larger and better home for this collection. Until then, look for the following artists scattered around the main gallery.

Allan Ramsay, the son of the well-known poet of the same name, painted portraits of curly-wigged men of the Enlightenment era (the philosopher David Hume, King George III) as well as likenesses of his two wives. Ramsay's portrait of the duke of Argyll—

founder of the Royal Bank of Scotland—appears on the front of notes printed by this bank.

Sir Henry Raeburn chronicled the next generation: Sir Walter Scott, the proud kilt-wearing Alastair Macdonell, and the ice-skating Reverend Robert Walker, minister of the Canongate Church.

Sir David Wilkie's forte was small-scale scenes of everyday life. *The Letter of Introduction* (1813) captures Wilkie's own experience of trying to impress skeptical art patrons in London; even the dog is sniffing the Scotsman out. *Distraining for Rent* (1815) shows the plight of a poor farmer about to lose his farm—a common occurrence during 19th-century industrialization.

William Dyce's *Francesca da Rimini* (1837) depicts star-crossed lovers—a young wife and her husband's kid brother—who can't help but indulge their passion. The husband later finds out and kills her; at the far left, you see his ominous hand.

William McTaggart's impressionistic landscape scenes from the late 1800s provide a glimpse of the unique light, powerful clouds, and natural wonder of the Highlands.

▲▲Scottish National Portrait Gallery

Put a face on Scotland's history by enjoying these portraits of famous Scots from the earliest times until today. From its Neo-Gothic facade to a grand entry hall featuring a *Who's Who* of Scotland, to galleries highlighting the great Scots of each age, this impressive museum will fascinate anyone interested in Scottish culture. The gallery also hosts temporary exhibits highlighting the work of more contemporary Scots. Because of its purely Scottish focus, many travelers prefer this to the (pan-European) main branch of the National Gallery.

Cost and Hours: Free, daily 10:00-17:00, good $ cafeteria serving healthy meals, 1 Queen Street, tel. 0131/624-6490, www.nationalgalleries.org.

Visiting the Gallery: In the stirring **entrance hall** you'll find busts of great Scots and a full-body statue of Robbie "Rabbie" Burns, as well as (up above) a glorious frieze showing a parade of historical figures and murals depicting important events in Scottish history. (These are better viewed from the first floor and its mezzanine—described later.) We'll start on the **second floor**, right into the thick of the struggle between Scotland and England over who should rule this land.

Reformation to Revolution (gallery 1): The collection starts with a portrait of **Mary, Queen of Scots** (1542-1587), her cross and rosary prominent. This controversial ruler set off two centuries of strife. Mary was born with both Stuart blood (the ruling family of Scotland) and the Tudor blood of England's monarchs (Queen Elizabeth I was her cousin). Catholic and French-educated, Mary felt alienated from her own increasingly Protestant homeland. Her tense conversations with the reformer John Knox must have been epic. Then came a series of scandals: She married unpopular Lord Darnley, then (possibly) cheated on him, causing Darnley to (possibly) murder her lover, causing

Mary to (possibly) murder Darnley, then (possibly) run off with another man, and (possibly) plot against Queen Elizabeth.

Amid all that drama, Mary was forced by her own people to relinquish her throne to her infant son, **James VI.** Find his portraits as a child and as a grown-up. James grew up to rule Scotland, and when Queen Elizabeth (the "virgin queen") died without an heir, he also became king of England (James I). But James' son, **Charles I,** after a bitter civil war, was arrested and executed in 1649: See the large *Execution of Charles I* painting high on the far wall, his blood-dripping head displayed to the crowd; nearby is a portrait of Charles in happier times, as a 12-year-old boy. His son, Charles II, restored the Stuarts to power. He was then succeeded by his Catholic brother James VII of Scotland (II of England), who was sent into exile in France. There the Stuarts stewed, planning

a return to power, waiting for someone to lead them in what would come to be known as the Jacobite rebellions.

The Jacobite Cause (gallery 4): One of the biggest paintings in the room is *The Baptism of Prince Charles Edward Stuart.* Born in 1720, this Stuart heir to the thrones of Great Britain and Ireland is better known to history as "Bonnie Prince Charlie." (See his bonnie features in various portraits nearby, as a child, young man, and grown man.) Charismatic

Charles convinced France to invade Scotland and put him back on the throne there. In 1745, he entered Edinburgh in triumph. But he was defeated at the tide-turning Battle of Culloden (1746). The Stuart cause died forever, and Bonnie Prince Charlie went into exile, eventually dying drunk and wasted in Rome, far from the land he nearly ruled.

• *The next few rooms (galleries 5-6) contain special exhibits that swap out every year or two—they're worth a browse.*

The Age of Improvement (gallery 7): The faces portrayed here belonged to a new society whose hard work and public spirit

achieved progress with a Scottish accent. Social equality and the Industrial Revolution "transformed" Scotland—you'll see portraits of the great poet Robert Burns, the son of a farmer (Burns was heralded as a "heaven-taught ploughman" when his poems were first published), and the man who perfected the steam engine, James Watt.

Central Atrium (first floor): Great Scots! The atrium is decorated in a parade of late 19th-century Romantic Historicism. The

frieze (working counterclockwise) is a visual encyclopedia, from an ax-wielding Stone Age man and a druid, to the early legendary monarchs (Macbeth), to warriors William Wallace and Robert the Bruce, to many kings (James I, II, III, and so on), to great thinkers, inventors, and artists (Allan Ramsay, Flora MacDonald, David Hume, Adam Smith, James Boswell, James Watt), the three greatest Scottish writers (Robert Burns, Sir Walter Scott, Robert Louis Stevenson), and culminating with the historian Thomas Carlyle, who was the driving spirit (powered by the fortune of a local newspaper baron) behind creating this portrait gallery.

Around the first-floor mezzanine are large-scale **murals** depicting great events in Scottish history, including the landing of St. Margaret at Queensferry in 1068, the Battle of Stirling Bridge in 1297, the Battle of Bannockburn in 1314, and the marriage procession of James IV and Margaret Tudor through the streets of Edinburgh in 1503.

• *Also on this floor you'll find the...*

Modern Portrait Gallery: This space is dedicated to rotating art and photographs highlighting Scots who are making an impact in the world today, such as Annie Lennox, Alan Cumming, and physicist Peter Higgs (theorizer of the Higgs boson, the so-called God particle). Look for the *Three Oncologists*, a ghostly painting depicting the anxiety and terror of cancer and the dedication of those working so hard to conquer it.

▲▲Georgian House

This refurbished Neoclassical house, set on Charlotte Square, is a trip back to 1796. It recounts the era when a newly gentrified and

well-educated Edinburgh was nicknamed the "Athens of the North." Begin on the second floor, where you'll watch an interesting 16-minute video dramatizing the upstairs/downstairs lifestyles of the aristocrats and servants who lived here. Try on some Georgian outfits, then head downstairs to tour period rooms and even peek into the fully stocked medicine cabinet. Info sheets are available in each room, along with volunteer guides who share stories and trivia, such as why Georgian bigwigs had to sit behind a screen while enjoying a fire. A walk down George Street after your visit here can be fun for the imagination.

Cost and Hours: £7.50, daily 10:00-17:00, March and Nov 11:00-16:00, closed Dec-Feb, last entry 45 minutes before closing; 7 Charlotte Square, tel. 0131/226-3318, www.nts.org.uk.

SIGHTS NEAR EDINBURGH
▲▲Royal Yacht *Britannia*

This much-revered vessel, which transported Britain's royal family for more than 40 years on 900 voyages (an average of once

around the world per year) before being retired in 1997, is permanently moored in Edinburgh's port of Leith. Queen Elizabeth II said of the ship, "This is the only place I can truly relax." Today it's open to the curious public, who have access to its many decks—from engine rooms to drawing rooms—and offers a fascinating time-warp look into the late-20th-century lifestyles of the rich and royal. It's worth the 20-minute bus or taxi ride from the center; figure on spending about 2.5 hours total on the outing.

Cost and Hours: £15.50, includes 1.5-hour audioguide, daily 9:30-16:30, Oct until 16:00, Nov-March 10:00-15:30, these are last entry times, tearoom; at the Ocean Terminal Shopping Mall, on Ocean Drive in Leith; tel. 0131/555-5566, www.royalyachtbritannia.co.uk.

Getting There: From central Edinburgh, catch Lothian bus #11 or #22 from Princes Street (just above Waverley Station), or #35 from the bottom of the Royal Mile (alongside the parliament building) to Ocean Terminal (last stop). From the B&B neighborhood, you can either bus to the city center and transfer to one of the buses mentioned, or take bus #14 from Dalkeith Road to Mill Lane, then walk about 10 minutes. The Majestic Tour hop-on, hop-off bus stops here as well. Drivers can park free in the blue parking garage. Take the shopping center elevator to level E, then follow the signs.

Visiting the Ship: First, explore the **museum,** filled with engrossing royal-family-afloat history. You'll see lots of family photos that evoke the fine times the Windsors enjoyed on the *Britannia*, as well as some nautical equipment and uniforms. Then, armed with your audioguide, you're welcome aboard.

This was the last in a line of royal yachts that stretches back to 1660. With all its royal functions, the ship required a crew of more than 200. Begin in the captain's bridge, which feels like it's been preserved from the day it was launched in 1953. Then head down a deck to see the officers' quarters, then the garage, where a Rolls Royce was hoisted aboard to use in places where the local transportation wasn't up to royal standards. The Veranda Deck at the back of the ship was the favorite place for outdoor entertainment. Ronald Reagan, Boris Yeltsin, Bill Clinton, and Nelson Mandela all sipped champagne here. The Sun Lounge, just off the back Veranda Deck, was the Queen's favorite, with Burmese teak and the same phone system she was used to in Buckingham Palace. When she wasn't entertaining, the Queen liked it quiet. The crew wore sneakers, communicated in hand signals, and (at least near the Queen's quarters) had to be finished with all their work by 8:00 in the morning.

Take a peek into the adjoining his-and-hers bedrooms of the Queen and the Duke of Edinburgh (check out the spartan twin beds), and the honeymoon suite where Prince Charles and Lady Di began their wedded bliss.

Heading down another deck, walk through the officers' lounge (and learn about the rowdy games they played) and past the galleys (including custom cabinetry for the fine

china and silver) on your way to the biggest room on the yacht, the state dining room. Now decorated with gifts given by the ship's many noteworthy guests, this space enabled the Queen to entertain a good-size crowd. The drawing room, while rather simple (the Queen specifically requested "country house comfort"), was perfect for casual relaxing among royals. Princess Diana played the piano, which is bolted to the deck. Note the contrast to the decidedly less plush crew's quarters, mail room, sick bay, laundry, and engine room.

▲Rosslyn Chapel

This small but fascinating countryside church, about a 20-minute drive outside Edinburgh, is a riot of carved iconography. The pat-

terned ceiling and walls have left scholars guessing about the symbolism for centuries.

Cost and Hours: £9, Mon-Sat 9:30-17:00, June-Aug until 18:00, Sun 12:00-16:45 year-round, located in Roslin Village, tel. 0131/440-2159, www.rosslynchapel.org.uk.

Getting There: Ride Lothian bus #37 from Princes Street (stop PJ), North Bridge, or Newington Road in the B&B neighborhood (1-2/hour, 45 minutes). By car, take the A-701 to Penicuik/Peebles, and follow signs for *Roslin;* once you're in the village, you'll see signs for the chapel.

Background: After it was featured in the climax of Dan Brown's 2003 bestseller *The Da Vinci Code,* the number of visitors to Rosslyn Chapel more than quadrupled. But the chapel's allure existed well before the books, and will endure long after they move from bargain bin to landfill. Founded in 1446 as the private mausoleum of the St. Clair family—who wanted to be buried close to God—the church's interior is carved with a stunning mishmash of Christian, pagan, family, Templar, Masonic, and other symbolism. After the Scottish Reformation, Catholic churches like this fell into disrepair. But in the 18th and 19th centuries, Romantics such as Robert Burns and Sir Walter Scott discovered these evocative old ruins, putting Rosslyn Chapel back on the map. Even Queen Victoria visited, and gently suggested that the chapel be restored to its original state. Today, after more than a century of refits and refurbishments, the chapel transports visitors back to a distant and mysterious age.

Visiting the Chapel: From the ticket desk and visitors center, head to the chapel itself. Ask about docent lectures (usually at the top of the hour). If you have time to kill, pick up the good laminated descriptions for a clockwise tour of the carvings. In the crypt—where the stonemasons worked—you can see faint architectural drawings engraved in the wall, used to help them plot out their master design.

Elsewhere, look for these fun details: In the corner to the left of the altar, find the angels playing instruments—including one with bagpipes. Nearby, you'll see a person dancing with a skeleton. This "dance of death" theme—common in the Middle Ages—is a reminder of mortality: We'll all die eventually, so we might as well whoop it up while we're here. On the other side of the nave are carvings of the seven deadly sins and the seven acts of mercy. One inscription reads: "Wine is strong. Kings are stronger. Women are stronger still. But truth conquers all."

Flanking the altar are two carved columns that come with a legend: The more standard-issue column, on the left, was executed by a master mason, who soon after (perhaps disappointed in his lack of originality) went on a sabbatical to gain inspiration. While he was gone, his ambitious apprentice carved the beautiful corkscrew-shaped column on the right. Upon returning, the master flew into an envious rage and murdered the apprentice with his carving hammer.

Scattered throughout the church, you'll also see the family's symbol, the "engrailed cross" (with serrated edges). Keep an eye out for the more than one hundred "green men"—chubby faces with leaves and vines growing out of their orifices, symbolizing nature. This paradise/Garden of Eden theme is enhanced by a smattering of exotic animals (monkey, elephant, camel, dragon, and a lion fighting a unicorn) and some exotic foliage: aloe vera, trillium, and corn. That last one (framing a window to the right of the altar) is a mystery: It was carved well before Columbus sailed the ocean blue, at a time when corn was unknown in Europe. Several theories have been suggested—some far-fetched (the father of the man who built the chapel explored the New World before Columbus), and others more plausible (the St. Clairs were of Norse descent, and the Vikings are known to have traveled to the Americas well before Columbus). Others simply say it's not corn at all—it's stalks of wheat. After all these centuries, Rosslyn Chapel's mysteries still inspire the imaginations of historians, novelists, and tourists alike.

Royal Botanic Garden

Britain's second-oldest botanical garden (after Oxford) was established in 1670 for medicinal herbs, and this 70-acre refuge is now one of Europe's best. A visitors center has temporary exhibits.

Cost and Hours: Gardens-free, greenhouse-£6.50, daily 10:00-18:00, Feb and Oct until 17:00, Nov-Jan until 16:00, greenhouse last entry one hour before closing, café and restaurant, a mile north of the city center at Inverleith Row, tel. 0131/248-2909, www.rbge.org.uk.

Getting There: It's a 10-minute bus ride from the city center: Take bus #8 from North Bridge, or #23 or #27 from George IV Bridge (near the National Museum) or The Mound. The Majestic Tour hop-on, hop-off bus also stops here.

Scottish National Gallery of Modern Art

This museum, set in a beautiful parkland, houses Scottish and international paintings and sculpture from 1900 to the present, including works by Matisse, Duchamp, Picasso, and Warhol. The grounds include a pleasant outdoor sculpture park and a café.

Cost and Hours: Free, daily 10:00-17:00, 75 Belford Road, tel. 0131/624-6336, www.nationalgalleries.org.

Getting There: It's about a 20-minute walk west from the city center. Or take the shuttle bus, which runs about hourly between this museum and the Scottish National Gallery (£1 donation requested, confirm times on website).

Experiences in Edinburgh

URBAN HIKES

▲▲Holyrood Park: Arthur's Seat and the Salisbury Crags

Rising up from the heart of Edinburgh, Holyrood Park is a lush green mountain squeezed between the parliament/Holyroodhouse (at the

bottom of the Royal Mile) and my recommended B&B neighborhood. For an exhilarating hike, connect these two zones with a moderately strenuous 30-minute walk along the Salisbury Crags—reddish cliffs with sweeping views over the city. Or, for a more serious climb, make the ascent to the summit of Arthur's Seat, the 822-foot-tall remains of an extinct volcano. You can run up like they did in *Chariots of Fire,* or just stroll—at the summit, you'll be rewarded with commanding views of the town and surroundings. On May Day, be on the summit at dawn and wash your face in the morning dew to commemorate the Celtic holiday of Beltane, the celebration of spring. (Morning dew is supposedly very good for your complexion.)

You can do this hike either from the bottom of the Royal Mile, or from the B&B neighborhood.

From the Royal Mile: Begin in the parking lot below the Palace of Holyroodhouse. Facing the cliff, you'll see two trailheads. For the easier hike along the base of the **Salisbury Crags,** take the trail to the right. At the far end, you can descend into the Dalkeith Road area or—if you're up for more hiking—continue steeply up the switchbacked trail to the Arthur's Seat summit. If you know you'll want to ascend **Arthur's Seat** from the start, take the wider path on the left from the Holyroodhouse parking lot (easier grade, through the abbey ruins and "Hunter's Bog").

From the B&B Neighborhood: If you're sleeping in this area, enjoy a pre-breakfast or late-evening hike starting from the other

side (in June, the sun comes up early, and it stays light until nearly midnight). From the Commonwealth Pool, take Holyrood Park Road, bear left at the first round-about, then turn right at the second roundabout (onto Queen's Drive). Soon you'll see the trailhead, and make your choice: Bear right up the steeper "Piper's Walk" to **Arthur's Seat** (about a 20-minute hike from here, up a steeply switchbacked trail). Or bear left for an easier ascent up the "Radial Road" to the **Salisbury Crags,** which you can follow—with great views over town—all the way to Holyroodhouse Palace.

By Car: If you have a car, you can drive up most of the way to Arthur's Seat from behind (follow the one-way street from the palace, park safely and for free by the little lake, and hike up).

Duddingston Village and Dr. Neil's Garden

This low-key, 30-minute walk goes from the B&B neighborhood to Duddingston Village—a former village that got absorbed by the city but still retains its old, cobbled feel, local church, and great old-time pub, the recommended Sheep Heid Inn. Also here is Dr. Neil's Garden, a peaceful, free garden on a loch.

Walk behind the Commonwealth Pool along Holyrood Park Road. Before the roundabout, just after passing through the wall/gate, take the path to your right. This path runs alongside the Duddingston Low Road all the way to the village and garden. Ignore the road traffic and enjoy the views of Arthur's Seat, the golf course, and eventually, Duddingston Loch. When you reach the cobbled road, you're in Duddingston Village, with the church on your right and the Sheep Heid Inn a block down on your left. Another 100 feet down the main road is a gate labeled *"The Manse"* with the number 5—enter here for the garden.

Dr. Neil's Garden (also known as the Secret Garden) was started by doctors Nancy and Andrew Neil, who traveled through-out Europe in the 1960s gathering trees and plants. They brought them back here, planted them on this land, and tended to them with the help of their patients. Today it offers a quiet, secluded break from the city, where you can walk among flowers and trees and over quaint bridges, get inspired by quotes written on chalkboards, or sit on a bench overlooking the loch (free, daily 10:00-dusk, mobile 07849-187-995, www.drneilsgarden.co.uk).

▲Calton Hill

For an easy walk for fine views over all of Edinburgh, head up to Calton Hill—the monument-studded bluff that rises up from the eastern end of the New Town. From the Waverley Station area, simply head east on Princes Street (which becomes Waterloo Place).

About five minutes after passing North Bridge, watch on the right for the gated entrance to the **Old Calton Cemetery**—worth a quick walk-through for its stirring monuments to great Scots. The can't-miss-it round monument honors the philosopher David Hume; just next to that is a memorial topped by Abraham Lincoln, honoring Scottish-American troops who were killed in combat. The obelisk honors political martyrs.

The views from the cemetery are good, but for even better ones, head back out to the main road and continue a few more min-

utes on Waterloo Place. Across the street, steps lead up into **Calton Hill.** Explore. Informational plaques identify the key landmarks. At the summit of the hill is the giant, unfinished replica of the Parthenon, honoring those lost in the Napoleonic Wars. Donations to finish it never materialized, leaving it with the nickname "Edinburgh's Disgrace." Nearby, the old observatory is filled with an avant-garde art gallery, and the back of the hillside boasts sweeping views over the Firth of Forth and Edinburgh's sprawl. Back toward the Old Town, the tallest tower celebrates Admiral Horatio Nelson—the same honoree of the giant pillar on London's Trafalgar Square. The best views are around the smaller, circular Dugald Stewart Monument, with postcard panoramas overlooking the spires of the Old Town and the New Town.

More Hikes

You can hike along the river (called the Water of Leith) through Edinburgh. Locals favor the stretch between Roseburn and Dean Village, but the 1.5-mile walk from Dean Village to the Royal Botanic Garden is also good. For more information on these and other hikes, ask at the TI or your B&B.

EDINBURGH

WHISKY AND GIN TASTING

Whisky Tasting

One of the most accessible places to learn about whisky is at the **Scotch Whisky Experience** on the Royal Mile, an expensive but informative overview to whisky, including a tasting (see page 748). To get more into sampling whisky, try one of the early-evening tastings at the recommended **Cadenhead's Whisky Shop** (see page 785).

Serious whisky drinkers can check out **The Scotch Malt Whisky Society** in the New Town. Formerly a private club, it recently opened the Kaleidoscope bar to the public, serving glasses from anonymous, numbered bottles of single malts from all over Scotland and beyond. In this "blind tasting" approach, you have to read each number's tasting notes to make your choice...or enlist the help of the bartender, who will probe you on what kind of flavor profile you like. While this place's shrouded-in-mystery pretense could get lost on novices, aficionados enjoy it (daily 11:00-23:00, bar serves light dishes, on-site restaurant, 28 Queen Street, tel. 0131/220-2044, www.smws.com).

Gin Distillery Tours

The residents of Edinburgh drink more gin per person than any other city in the United Kingdom, and the city is largely responsible for the recent renaissance of this drink, so it's only appropriate that you visit a gin distillery while in town. Two distilleries right in the heart of Edinburgh offer hourlong tours with colorful guides who discuss the history of gin, show you the stills involved in the production process, and ply you with libations. Both tours are popular and fill up; book ahead on their websites.

Pickering's is located in a former vet school and animal hospital at Summerhall, halfway between the Royal Mile and the B&B neighborhood—you'll still see cages lining the walls (£10, 3/day Thu-Sun, meet at the Royal Dick Bar in the central courtyard at 1 Summerhall, tel. 0131/290-2901, www.pickeringsgin.com).

Edinburgh Gin is in the New Town, next to the Waldorf Astoria Hotel. Besides the basic tour, there's a connoisseur tour with more tastings and a gin-making tour (basic tour £10, 3/day daily, 1A Rutland Place, tel. 0131/656-2810, www.edinburghgin.com). If you can't get on to one of their tours, visit their Heads & Tales bar to taste their gins (daily 17:00-24:00).

LEISURE ACTIVITIES

Several enjoyable activities cluster near the B&B area around Dalkeith Road. For details, check their websites.

The **Royal Commonwealth Pool** is an indoor fitness and activity complex with a 50-meter pool, gym/fitness studio, and kids' soft play zone (daily, tel. 0131/667-7211, www.edinburghleisure. co.uk).

The **Prestonfield Golf Club,** also an easy walk from the B&Bs, has golfers feeling like they're in a country estate (dress code, 6 Priestfield Road North, tel. 0131/667-9665, www.prestonfieldgolf. co.uk).

Farther out at **Midlothian Snowsports Centre** (a little south of town in Hillend; better for drivers), try skiing without any pesky snow. It feels like snow-skiing on a slushy day, even though you're schussing over matting misted with water. Four new tubing runs offer fun even for nonskiers (Mon-Fri 9:30-21:00, Sat-Sun until 19:00, tel. 0131/445-4433, http://ski.midlothian.gov.uk).

EDINBURGH'S FESTIVALS

Every summer, Edinburgh's annual festivals turn the city into a carnival of the arts. The season begins in June with the international-

al film festival (www.edfilmfest.org. uk); then the jazz and blues festival in July (www.edinburghjazzfestival. com).

In August a riot of overlapping festivals known collectively as the **Edinburgh Festival** rages simulta-neously—international, fringe, book, and art, as well as the Military Tat-too. There are enough music, dance, drama, and multicultural events to make even the most jaded traveler giddy with excitement. Every day is jammed with formal and spontaneous fun. Many city sights run on extended hours. It's a glorious time to be in Edinburgh...*if* you have (and can afford) a room.

If you'll be in town in August, book your room and tickets for major events (especially the Tattoo) as far ahead as you can lock in dates. Plan carefully to ensure you'll have time for festival activi-ties as well as sightseeing. Check online to confirm dates; the best overall website is www.edinburghfestivals.co.uk. Several publica-tions—including the festival's official schedule, the *Edinburgh Fes-tivals Guide Daily, The List, Fringe Program,* and *Daily Diary*—list and evaluate festival events.

The official, more formal **Edinburgh International Festival** is the original. Major events sell out well in advance (ticket office at the Hub, in the former Tolbooth Church near the top of the Royal Mile, tel. 0131/473-2000, www.hubtickets.co.uk or www. eif.co.uk).

The less formal **Fringe Festival,** featuring edgy comedy and theater, is huge—with 2,000 shows—and has eclipsed the original festival in popularity (ticket/info office just below St. Giles' Cathedral on the Royal Mile, 180 High Street, bookings tel. 0131/226-0000, www.edfringe.com). Tickets may be available at the door, and half-price tickets for some events are sold on the day of the show at the Half-Price Hut, located at The Mound, near the Scottish National Gallery.

The **Military Tattoo** is a massing of bands, drums, and bagpipes, with groups from all over the former British Empire and beyond. Displaying military finesse with a stirring lone-piper finale, this grand spectacle fills the Castle Esplanade (nightly during most of Aug except Sun, performances Mon-Fri at 21:00, Sat at 19:30 and 22:30, £25-63, booking starts in Dec, Fri-Sat shows sell out first, all seats generally sold out by early summer, some scattered same-day tickets may be available; office open Mon-Fri 10:00-16:30, closed Sat-Sun, during Tattoo open until show time and closed Sun; 32 Market Street, behind Waverley Station, tel. 0131/225-1188, www.edintattoo.co.uk). Some performances are filmed by the BBC and later broadcast as a big national television special.

The **Festival of Politics,** adding yet another dimension to Edinburgh's festival action, is held in August in the Scottish parliament building. It's a busy weekend of discussions and lectures on environmentalism, globalization, terrorism, gender, and other issues (www.festivalofpolitics.org.uk).

Other summer festivals cover books (mid-late Aug, www.edbookfest.co.uk) and art (late July-Aug, www.edinburghartfestival.com).

Shopping in Edinburgh

Edinburgh is bursting with Scottish clichés for sale: kilts, shortbread, whisky...if they can slap a tartan on it, they'll sell it. Locals dismiss the touristy trinket shops, which are most concentrated along the Royal Mile, as "tartan tat." Your challenge is finding something a wee bit more authentic. If you want to be sure you are taking home local merchandise, check if the labels read: "Made in Scotland." "Designed in Scotland" actually means "Made in China." Shops are usually open around 10:00-18:00 (later on Thu, shorter hours or closed on Sun). Tourist shops are open longer hours.

SHOPPING STREETS AND NEIGHBORHOODS

Near the Royal Mile: The Royal Mile is intensely touristy, mostly lined with interchangeable shops selling made-in-China souvenirs. I've listed a few worthwhile spots along here later, under "What to Shop For." But in general, the area near Grassmarket, an easy stroll from the top of the Royal Mile, offer more originality. **Victoria**

Street, which climbs steeply downhill from the Royal Mile (near the Hub/Tolbooth Church) to Grassmarket, has a fine concentration of local chain shops, including I.J. Mellis Cheesemonger and Walker Slater for designer tweed (both described later), plus Calzeat (scarves, throws, and other textiles), a Harry Potter store, and more clothing and accessory shops. **Candlemaker Row,** exiting Grassmarket opposite Victoria Street, is a little more artisan, with boutiques selling hats (everything from dapper men's caps to outrageous fascinators), jewelry, art, design items, and even fossils. The street winds a couple of blocks up toward the National Museum; Greyfriars Bobby awaits you at the top of the street (see page 766).

In New Town: For mass-market shopping, you'll find plenty of big chain stores along **Princes Street.** In addition to Marks & Spencer, H&M, Zara, Primark, and a glitzy Apple Store, you'll also see the granddaddy of Scottish department stores, Jenners (generally daily 9:30-18:30, open later on Thu, shorter hours on Sun; described on page 734). Parallel to Princes Street, **George Street** has higher-end chain stores (including many from London, such as L.K. Bennett, Molton Brown, and Karen Millen). Just off St. Andrew Square is a branch of the high-end London department store Harvey Nichols.

For more local, artisan shopping, check out **Thistle Street,** lined with some fun eateries and a good collection of shops. You'll see some fun boutiques selling jewelry, shoes, and clothing. This is also the home of Howie Nicolsby's 21st Century Kilts, which attempts to bring traditional Scottish menswear into the present day (described later).

WHAT TO SHOP FOR
Whisky
You can order whisky in just about any bar in town, and whisky shops are a dime a dozen around the Royal Mile. But the places I've listed here distinguish themselves by their tradition and helpful staff. Before sampling or buying whisky, read all about Scotland's favorite spirit on page 750.

Cadenhead's Whisky Shop is not a tourist sight—don't expect free samples. Founded in 1842, this firm prides itself on bottling good whisky straight from casks at the distilleries, without all the compromises that come with profitable mass production (coloring with sugar to fit the expected look, wa-

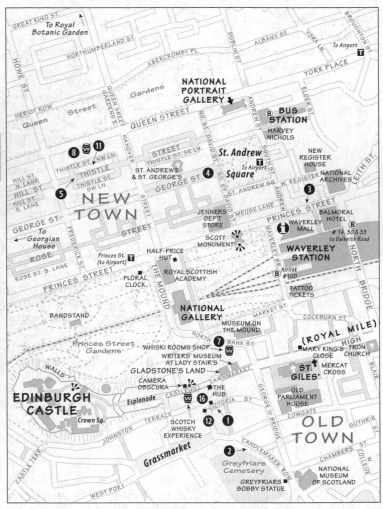

tering down to reduce the alcohol tax, and so on). Those drinking from Cadenhead-bottled whiskies will enjoy the pure product as the distilleries' owners themselves do, not as the sorry public does. The staff explains the sometimes-complex whisky board and talks you through flavor profiles. Buy the right bottle to enjoy in your hotel room night after night (prices start around £14 for about 7 ounces)—unlike wine, whisky has a long shelf life after it's opened. The bottles are extremely durable; ask them to demonstrate (Mon-Sat 10:30-17:30, closed Sun, 172 Canongate, tel. 0131/556-5864, www.wmcadenhead.com). They host hour-long whisky tastings during the week—a hit with aficionados (£25, Mon-Fri at 17:45, best to arrange in advance in peak season).

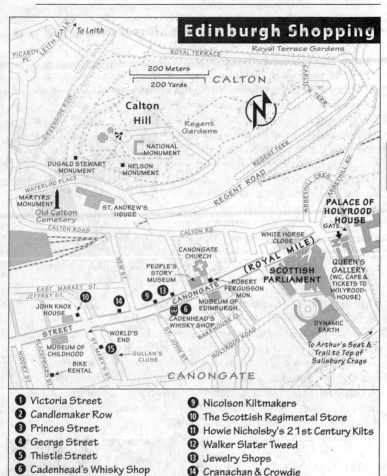

Edinburgh Shopping

1. Victoria Street
2. Candlemaker Row
3. Princes Street
4. George Street
5. Thistle Street
6. Cadenhead's Whisky Shop
7. Whiski Rooms Shop
8. The Scotch Malt Whisky Society
9. Nicolson Kiltmakers
10. The Scottish Regimental Store
11. Howie Nicholsby's 21st Century Kilts
12. Walker Slater Tweed
13. Jewelry Shops
14. Cranachan & Crowdie
15. Pinnies & Poppy Seeds
16. I.J. Mellis Cheesemonger

Whiski Rooms Shop, just off the Royal Mile, comes with a knowledgeable, friendly staff that happily assists novices and experts alike to select the right bottle. Their adjacent bar usually has about 400 open bottles: Serious purchasers can get a sample. Even better, try one of their tastings. You have two options: You can order a flight in the bar, which comes with written information about each whisky you're sampling (variety of options starting around £25, available anytime the bar is open). Or you can opt for a guided tasting (£22.50 introductory tasting, £40 premium tasting with the really good stuff, chocolate and cheese pairings also available; takes about one hour, reserve ahead). If you're doing a flight or a tasting, you'll get a small discount voucher for buying a bottle in the store (shop open daily 10:00-18:00, bar until 24:00, both open later in Aug, 4 North Bank Street, tel. 0131/225-1532, www.whiskirooms.com).

Near the B&B Neighborhood: Perhaps the most accessible place to learn about local whiskies is conveniently located in the B&B area south of the city center. **WoodWinters** has a passion both for traditional spirits and for the latest innovations in Edinburgh's booze scene. It's well stocked with 300 whiskies and gins (a trendy alternative to Scotch), as well as wines and local craft beers. Manager Rob invites curious browsers to sample a wee dram; he loves to introduce customers to something new (Mon-Tue 10:00-19:00, Wed-Sat until 21:00, Sun  13:00-17:00, 91 Newington Road, www.woodwinters.com, tel. 0131/667-2760). For location, see the map on page 795.

Kilts and Other Traditional Scottish Gear

Many of the kilt outfitters you'll see along the Royal Mile are selling cheap knock-offs, made with printed rather than woven tartan material. If you want a serious kilt—or would enjoy window-shopping for one—try one of the places below. These have a few off-the-rack options, but to get a kilt in your specific tartan and size, they'll probably take your measurements, custom-make it, and ship it to you. For a good-quality outfit (kilt, jacket, and accessories), plan on spending in the neighborhood of £1,000.

Nicolson Kiltmakers has a respect for tradition and quality. Owner Gordon enlists and trains local craftspeople who specialize in traditionally manufactured kilts and accessories. He prides himself on keeping the old ways alive (in the face of deeply discounted "tartan tat") and actively cultivates the next generation  of kiltmakers (daily 9:30-17:30, 189 Canongate, tel. 0131/558-2887, www.nicolsonkiltmakers.co.uk).

The Scottish Regimental Store, run by Nigel, is the official outfitter for military regiments. They sell top-of-the-line, formal kiltwear, as well as medals and pins that can be a more affordable souvenir (Mon-Thu 10:00-16:00, Fri-Sat until 17:00, closed Sun, 9 Jeffrey Street, tel. 0131/557-0249, www.scottishregimentalstore.co.uk).

Howie Nicholsby's 21st Century Kilts, in the New Town,

brings this traditional craft into the present day. It's fun to peruse his photos of both kilted celebrities (from Alan Cumming to Vin Diesel) and wedding albums—which make you wish you were Scottish, engaged, and wealthy enough to hire Howie to outfit your bridal party (Howie asks that you make an appointment, though you're welcome to drop in if he happens to be there; closed Sun-Mon and Wed, 48 Thistle Street, send text to 07774-757-222, www.21stcenturykilts.com, howie@21stcenturykilts.com).

Tweed

Several places around town sell the famous Harris Tweed (the authentic stuff is handwoven on the Isle of Harris). **Walker Slater**

is the place to go for top-quality tweed at top prices. They have three locations on Victoria Street, just below the Royal Mile near Grassmarket: menswear (at #16), womenswear (#44), and a sale shop (#5). You'll find a rich interior and a wide variety of gorgeous jackets, scarves, bags, and more. This place feels elegant and exclusive (Mon-Sat 10:00-18:00, Sun 11:00-17:00, www.walkerslater.com).

Jewelry

Jewelry with Celtic designs, mostly made from sterling silver, is a popular and affordable souvenir. While you'll see these sold around town, two convenient shops face each other near the bottom of the Royal Mile: **Hamilton and Young,** which has a line of *Outlander*-inspired designs (173 Canongate), and **Celtic Design** (156 Canongate).

Food and Treats

Cranachan & Crowdie collects products (mostly edibles, some crafts) from more than 200 small, independent producers all over Scotland. The selection goes well beyond the mass-produced clichés, and American Beth and Scottish Fiona love to explain the story behind each item. They also offer up Scottish gin samples upon request (daily 11:00-18:00, on the Royal Mile at 263 Canongate, tel. 07951/587-420).

Pinnies & Poppy Seeds is a small, artisan bakery selling handmade shortbread made fresh daily from local, organic ingredients. Besides traditional all-butter shortbread, they have a rotating selection of 35 other flavors including chocolate hazelnut, rose pistachio, and cardamom white chocolate. They can package it for you to take home (lasts a month). They also sell other Scottish-made treats, both their own and from other local artisans, such as their Ballantyne Toffee from an old family recipe, gourmet marsh-mallows, shortbread truffles, and scented candles to match their shortbread flavors (Mon-Sat 10:00-17:30, closed Sun and in Jan, 26 St Mary's Street, tel. 0131/261-7012, run by American Jennifer).

I.J. Mellis Cheesemonger, tucked down Victoria Street just off the top of the Royal Mile, stocks a wide variety of Scottish, English, and international cheeses. They're as knowledgeable about cheese as they are generous with samples (Mon-Sat 9:30-19:00, Sun 11:00-18:00, 30A Victoria Street, tel. 0131/226-6215).

Nightlife in Edinburgh

▲▲Literary Pub Tour

This two-hour walk is interesting even if you think Sir Walter Scott won an Oscar for playing General Patton. You'll follow the witty dialogue of two actors as they debate whether the great literature of Scotland was high art or the creative re-creation of fun-loving louts fueled by a passion for whisky. You'll wander from the Grassmarket over the Old Town and New Town, with stops in three pubs, as your guides share their takes on Scotland's literary greats. The tour meets at the Beehive Inn on Grassmarket (£14, book online and save £2, May-Sept nightly at 19:30, April and Oct Thu-Sun, Jan-March Fri and Sun, Nov-Dec Fri only, tel. 0800-169-7410, www.edinburghliterarypubtour.co.uk).

▲Ghost Walks

A variety of companies lead spooky walks around town, providing an entertaining and affordable night out (offered nightly, most around 19:00 and 21:00, easy socializing for solo travelers). These two options are the most established.

The theatrical and creatively staged **The Cadies & Witchery Tours,** the most established outfit, offers two different 1.25-hour walks: "Ghosts and Gore" (April-Aug only, in daylight and following a flatter route) and "Murder and Mystery" (year-round, after dark, hillier, more surprises and scares). The cost for either tour is the same (£10, includes book of stories, leaves from top of Royal Mile, outside the Witchery Restaurant, near Castle Esplanade, reservations required, tel. 0131/225-6745, www.witcherytours.com).

Auld Reekie Tours offers a scary array of walks daily and nightly (£12-16, 60-90 minutes, leaves from front steps of the Tron Church building on Cockburn Street, tel. 0131/557-4700, www.auldreekietours.com). Auld Reekie focuses on the paranormal, witch covens, and pagan temples, taking groups into the "haunted vaults" under the old bridges "where it was so dark, so crowded, and so squalid that the people there knew each other not by how they looked, but by how they sounded, felt, and smelt." If you want more, there's plenty of it (complete with screaming Gothic "jumpers").

Scottish Folk Evenings

A variety of £35-40 dinner shows, generally for tour groups intent on photographing old cultural clichés, are held in the huge halls of expensive hotels. (Prices are bloated to include 20 percent commissions.) Your "traditional" meal is followed by a full slate of swirling kilts, blaring bagpipes, and Scottish folk dancing with an old-time music hall emcee. If you like Lawrence Welk, you're in for a treat. But for most travelers, these are painfully cheesy. You can sometimes see the show without dinner for about two-thirds the price. The TI has fliers on all the latest venues.

Prestonfield House, a luxurious venue near the Dalkeith Road B&Bs, offers its kitschy "Taste of Scotland" folk evening with or without dinner Sunday to Friday. For £50, you get the show with two drinks and a wad of haggis; £65 buys you the same, plus a three-course meal and a half-bottle of wine (be there at 18:45, dinner at 19:00, show runs 20:00-22:00, April-Oct only). It's in the stables of "the handsomest house in Edinburgh," which is now home to the recommended Rhubarb Restaurant (Priestfield Road, a 10-minute walk from Dalkeith Road B&Bs, tel. 0131/225-7800, www.scottishshow.co.uk).

For something more lowbrow—and arguably more authentic—in summer, you can watch the **Princes Street Gardens Dancers** perform a range of Scottish country dancing. The volunteer troupe will demonstrate each dance, then invite spectators to give it a try (£5, June-July Mon 19:30-21:30, at Ross Bandstand in Princes Street Gardens—in the glen just below Edinburgh Castle, tel. 0131/228-8616, www.princesstreetgardensdancing.org.uk). The same group offers summer programs in other parts of town (see website for details).

Theater

Even outside festival time, Edinburgh is a fine place for lively and affordable theater. Pick up *The List* for a complete rundown of what's on (free at TI; also online at www.list.co.uk).

▲▲Live Music in Pubs

While traditional music venues have been eclipsed by beer-focused student bars, Edinburgh still has a few good pubs that can deliver a traditional folk-music fix. The monthly *Gig Guide* (free at TI, accommodations, and various pubs, www.gigguide.co.uk) lists several places each night that have live music, divided by genre (pop, rock, world, and folk).

South of the Royal Mile: Sandy Bell's is a tight little pub with live folk music nightly from 21:30 (near National Museum of Scotland at 25 Forrest Road, tel. 0131/225-2751). Food is very simple (toasted sandwiches and pies), drinks are cheap, tables are small, and the vibe is local. They also have a few sessions earlier in the day (Sat at 14:00, Sun at 16:00, Mon at 17:30).

Captain's Bar is a cozy, music-focused pub with live sessions of folk and traditional music nightly around 21:00—see website for lineup (4 South College Street, http://captainsedinburgh.webs.com).

The **Royal Oak** is another good—if small—place for a dose of folk and blues (just off South Bridge opposite Chambers Road at 1 Infirmary Street, tel. 0131/557-2976).

The **Grassmarket** neighborhood (below the castle) bustles with live music and rowdy people spilling out of the pubs and into what was (once upon a time) a busy market square. While it used to be a mecca for Scottish folk music, today it's more youthful with a heavy-drinking, rockin' feel. It's fun to just wander through this area late at night and check out the scene. Thanks to the music and crowds, you'll know where to go...and where not to. Have a beer and follow your ear to places like **Biddy Mulligans** or **White Hart Inn** (both on Grassmarket). **Finnegans Wake,** on Victoria Street (which leads down to Grassmarket), also has live music in a variety of genres each night.

On the Royal Mile: Three characteristic pubs within a few steps of each other on High Street (opposite Radisson Hotel) offer a fun setting, classic pub architecture and ambience, and live music for the cost of a beer: **Whiski Bar** (mostly trad and folk; nightly at 22:00), **Royal Mile** (variety of genres; nightly at 22:00), and **Mitre Bar** (acoustic pop/rock with some trad; Fri-Sun at 21:30).

Just a block away (on South Bridge) is **Whistlebinkies Live Music Bar.** While they rarely do folk or Scottish trad, this is the most serious of the music pubs, with an actual stage and several acts nightly (schedule posted inside the door makes the genre clear; most nights music starts at 19:00 or 21:30, young crowd, fun energy, sticky floors, no cover, tel. 0131/557-5114). **No. 1 High Street** is an accessible little pub with a love of folk and traditional music (Wed-Thu from about 21:00, 1 High Street, tel. 0131/556-5758). **World's End,** across the street, also has music starting about 21:00 (trad on Thu, other genres Fri-Sat, 4 High Street, tel. 0131/556-3628).

In the New Town: All the beer drinkers seem to head for the pedestrianized Rose Street, famous for having the most pubs per square inch anywhere in Scotland—and plenty of live music.

Pubs near the B&B Neighborhood

The pubs in the B&B area don't typically have live music, but some are fun evening hangouts. **Leslie's Bar,** sitting between a working-class and an upper-class neighborhood, has two sides. Originally, the gang would go in on the right to gather around the great hardwood bar, glittering with a century of *Cheers* ambience. Meanwhile, the more delicate folks would slip in on the left, with its discreet doors, plush snugs (cozy private booths), and ornate ordering windows. Since 1896, this Victorian classic has been appreciated for both its real ales and its huge selection of fine whiskies (listed on a lengthy menu). Dive into the whisky mosh pit on the right, and let them show you how whisky can become "a very good friend." (daily 12:00-24:00, 49 Ratcliffe Terrace, tel. 0131/667-7205.)

Other good pubs in this area include **The Old Bell** (uphill from Leslie's, popular and cozy, with big TV screens) and **The Salisbury Arms** (bigger, more sprawling, feels upscale); both are described later, under "Eating in Edinburgh."

Sleeping in Edinburgh

To stay in the city center, you'll likely have to stay in a larger hotel or more impersonal guesthouse. For the classic B&B experience, look to the area south of town. A number of B&Bs cluster along Dalkeith Road and on side streets just off of it (south of the Royal Commonwealth Pool), and also along the parallel street Mayfield Gardens (which leads directly to South Bridge in the center). From either area, it's a long walk to the city center (about 25 minutes) or a quick bus or taxi/Uber ride.

While many of my B&B listings are not cheap (generally around £90-130), most come with friendly hosts and great cooked breakfasts. And they're generally cheaper than staying at a city-center hotel.

Note that during the Festival in August, prices skyrocket and most places do not accept bookings for one- or even two-night stays. If coming in August, book far in advance. Conventions, rugby matches, school holidays, and weekends can make finding a room tough at other times of year, too. In winter, when demand is light, some B&Bs close, and prices at all accommodations get soft.

For some travelers, short-term Airbnb-type rentals can be a good alternative to hotels; search for places in my recommended hotel and B&B neighborhoods. See page 1034 for more information.

B&BS SOUTH OF THE CITY CENTER

At these not-quite-interchangeable places, character is provided by the personality quirks of the hosts and sometimes the decor. In general, cash is preferred and can lead to discounted rates. Book direct—you will pay a much higher rate through a booking service.

Near the B&Bs, you'll find plenty of fine eateries (see "Eating

EDINBURGH

Accommodations

1. Gil Dun Guest House
2. Gifford House
3. AmarAgua Guest House
4. Hotel Ceilidh-Donia
5. Ard-Na-Said B&B
6. Dunedin Guest House
7. Airdenair Guest House
8. 23 Mayfield Guest House & Glenalmond House
9. Kingsway Guest House
10. Barony House
11. Sonas Guest House

Eateries & Other

12. The Salisbury Arms Pub

in Edinburgh," later) and some good, classic pubs (see "Nightlife in Edinburgh," earlier). A few places have their own private parking; others offer access to easy, free street parking (ask when booking— or better yet, don't rent a car for your time in Edinburgh). The nearest launderette is Ace Cleaning Centre (which picks up and drops off; see page 710).

Taxi or Uber fare between the city center and the B&Bs is about £7. If taking the bus from the B&Bs into the city, hop off at

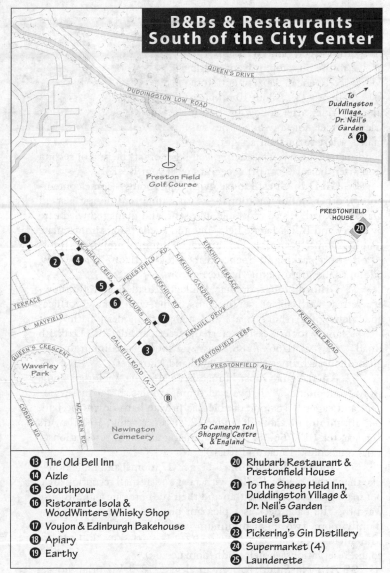

B&Bs & Restaurants South of the City Center

- **13** The Old Bell Inn
- **14** Aizle
- **15** Southpour
- **16** Ristorante Isola & WoodWinters Whisky Shop
- **17** Voujon & Edinburgh Bakehouse
- **18** Apiary
- **19** Earthy
- **20** Rhubarb Restaurant & Prestonfield House
- **21** To The Sheep Heid Inn, Duddingston Village & Dr. Neil's Garden
- **22** Leslie's Bar
- **23** Pickering's Gin Distillery
- **24** Supermarket (4)
- **25** Launderette

the South Bridge stop for the Royal Mile (£1.60 single ride, £4 day ticket, use exact change; see below for more bus specifics).

Near Dalkeith Road

Most of my B&Bs near Dalkeith Road are located south of the Royal Commonwealth Pool. This comfortable, safe neighborhood is a ten-minute bus ride from the Royal Mile.

To get here from the train station, catch the bus around the

corner on North Bridge: Exit the station onto Princes Street, turn right, cross the street, and walk up the bridge to the bus stop in front of the Marks & Spencer department store (#14, #30, or #33). About 10 minutes into the ride, after following South Clerk Street for a while, the bus makes a left turn, then a right. Depending on where you're staying, you'll get off at the first or second stop after the turn (confirm specifics with your B&B).

$$ Gil Dun Guest House, with eight rooms—some contemporary, others more traditional—is on a quiet cul-de-sac just off Dalkeith Road. It's comfortable, pleasant, and managed with care by Gerry and Bill; Maggie helps out and keeps things immaculate (family rooms, two-night minimum in summer preferred, limited off-street parking, 9 Spence Street, tel. 0131/667-1368, www.gildun.co.uk, gildun.edin@btinternet.com).

$$ Gifford House, on busy Dalkeith Road, is a bright, flowery retreat with six peaceful rooms (some with ornate cornices and views of Arthur's Seat) and compact, modern bathrooms (RS%, family rooms, cash preferred, street parking, 103 Dalkeith Road, tel. 0131/667-4688, www.giffordhouseedinburgh.com, giffordhouse@btinternet.com, David and Margaret).

$$ AmarAgua Guest House is an inviting Victorian home away from home, with five welcoming rooms, a Japanese garden, and eager hosts (one double has private bath down the hall, 2-night minimum, no kids under 12, street parking, 10 Kilmaurs Terrace, tel. 0131/667-6775, www.amaragua.co.uk, reservations@amaragua.co.uk, Lucia and Kuan).

$$ Hotel Ceilidh-Donia is bigger (17 rooms) and more hotel-like than other nearby B&Bs, with a bar and a small reception area, but managers Kevin and Susan and their staff provide a guesthouse warmth. The back deck is a pleasant place to sit on a warm day (family room, two-night minimum on peak-season weekends, 14 Marchhall Crescent, tel. 0131/667-2743, www.hotelceilidh-donia.co.uk, reservations@hotelceilidh-donia.co.uk).

$$ Ard-Na-Said B&B, in an elegant 1875 Victorian house, has seven bright, spacious rooms with modern bathrooms, including one ground-floor room with a pleasant patio (two-night minimum preferred in summer, off-street parking, 5 Priestfield Road, tel. 0131/283-6524, mobile 07476-606-202, www.ardnasaid.co.uk, info@ardnasaid.co.uk, Audrey Ballantine and her son Steven).

$$ Dunedin Guest House (dun-EE-din) is bright and plush, with seven well-decorated rooms, an angelic atrium, and a spacious breakfast room/lounge with TV (family rooms, one room with private bath down the hall, includes continental breakfast, extra charge for cooked breakfast, limited off-street parking, 8 Priestfield Road, tel. 0131/468-3339, www.dunedinguesthouse.co.uk, reservations@dunedinguesthouse.co.uk, Mary and Tony).

$ Airdenair Guest House is a hands-off guesthouse, with no formal host greeting (you'll get an access code to let yourself in) and a self-serve breakfast buffet. But the price is nice and the five simple rooms are well-maintained (29 Kilmaurs Road, tel. 0131/468-0173, http://airdenair-edinburgh.co.uk, contact@airdenair-edinburgh.co.uk, Duncan).

On or near Mayfield Gardens

These places are just a couple of blocks from the Dalkeith Road options, along the busy Newington Road (which turns in to Mayfield Gardens). All have private parking. To reach them from the center, hop on bus #3, #7, #8, #29, #31, #37, or #49. Note: Some of these buses depart from the second bus stop, a bit farther along North Bridge. To ride from these guesthouses to the city center, simply hop on any bus (except #47).

$$$ At 23 Mayfield Guest House, Ross and Kathleen (with their wee helpers Ethan and Alfie) rent seven splurge-worthy, thoughtfully appointed rooms complete with high-tech bathrooms (rain showers and motion-sensor light-up mirrors). Little extras—such as locally sourced gourmet breakfasts, an inviting guest lounge outfitted with leather-bound Sir Arthur Conan Doyle books, an "honesty bar," and classic black-and-white movie screenings—make you feel like royalty (RS% if you pay cash, family room for up to 4, two-night minimum preferred in summer, 23 Mayfield Gardens, tel. 0131/667-5806, www.23mayfield.co.uk, info@23mayfield.co.uk). They also rent an apartment (details on website).

$$$ Glenalmond House, run by Jimmy and Fiona Mackie, has nine elegantly decorated rooms featuring elaborately carved mahogany pieces (RS% if you pay cash, family room, no kids under 5, 25 Mayfield Gardens, tel. 0131/668-2392, www.glenalmondhouse.com, enquiries@glenalmondhouse.com).

$$ Kingsway Guest House, with seven stylish rooms, is owned by conscientious, delightful Gary and Lizzie, who have thought of all the little touches, such as DVD library and in-room Internet radios, and offer good advice on neighborhood eats (RS% if you pay cash, family room, one room with private bath down the hall, 5 East Mayfield, tel. 0131/667-5029, www.edinburgh-guesthouse.com, booking@kingswayguesthouse.com).

$$ Barony House is run with infectious enthusiasm by Aussies Paul and Susan. Their eight doubles are each named and themed, and lovingly decorated by Susan, who's made the beautiful fabric headboards and created some of the art (she also bakes welcome pastries for guests). Two of the rooms are next door, in a former servants quarters, now a peaceful retreat with access to a shared kitchen (three-night minimum preferred in summer, no kids under 9, 20 Mayfield Gardens, tel. 0131/662-9938, www.baronyhouse. co.uk, booknow@baronyhouse.co.uk).

$$ Sonas Guest House is nothing fancy—just a simple, easygoing place with seven rooms, six of which have bathtubs (family room, 3 East Mayfield, tel. 0131/667-2781, www.sonasguesthouse. com, info@sonasguesthouse.com, Irene and Dennis).

HOTELS IN THE CITY CENTER

While a B&B generally provides more warmth, character, and lower prices, a city-center hotel gives you more walkability and access to sights and Edinburgh's excellent restaurant and pub scene. Prices are very high in peak season and drop substantially in off-season (a good time to shop around). In each case, I'd skip the institutional breakfast and eat out. You'll generally pay about £10 a day to park near these hotels.

$$$$ Macdonald Holyrood Hotel is a four-star splurge, with 157 rooms up the street from the parliament building and Holyroodhouse Palace. With its classy marble-and-wood decor, fitness center, spa, and pool, it's hard to leave. On a gray winter day in Edinburgh, this could be worth it (pricey breakfast, elevator, pay valet parking, near bottom of Royal Mile, across from Dynamic Earth, 81 Holyrood Road, tel. 0131/528-8000, www.macdonaldhotels. co.uk, newres@macdonald-hotels.co.uk).

$$$$ The Inn on the Mile is your trendy, central option, filling a renovated old bank building right in the heart of the Royal Mile (at North Bridge/South Bridge). The nine bright and stylish rooms are an afterthought to the busy upmarket pub, which is where you'll check in. If you don't mind some noise (from the pub and the busy street) and climbing lots of stairs, it's a handy home base (breakfast extra, complimentary drink, 82 High Street, tel. 0131/556-9940, www.theinnonthemile.co.uk, info@ theinnonthemile.co.uk).

$$$$ The Inn Place, part of a small chain, fills the former headquarters of *The Scotsman* newspaper—a few steep steps below the Royal Mile—with 41 characterless, minimalist rooms ("bunk rooms" for 6-8 people, best deals on weekdays, breakfast extra, elevator, 20 Cockburn Street, tel. 0131/526-3780, www. theinnplaceedinburgh.co.uk, reception@theinnplaceedinburgh. co.uk).

$$$ Grassmarket Hotel's 42 rooms are quirky and fun, from the Dandy comic-book wallpaper to the giant wall map of Edinburgh equipped with planning-your-visit magnets. The hotel is in a great location right on Grassmarket overlooking the Covenanters Memorial and above Biddy Mulligans Bar (family rooms, two-night minimum on weekends, elevator only serves half the rooms, 94 Grassmarket, tel. 0131/220-2299, www.grassmarkethotel. co.uk).

$$$ The Place Hotel, sister of the Inn Place listed above, has a fine New Town location 10 minutes north of the train station. It occupies three grand Georgian townhouses, with no elevator and long flights of stairs leading up to the 47 contemporary, no-frills rooms. Their outdoor terrace with retractable roof and heaters is a popular place to unwind (save money with a smaller city double, 34 York Place, tel. 0131/556-7575, www.yorkplace-edinburgh.co.uk, frontdesk@yorkplace-edinburgh.co.uk).

$$ Motel One Edinburgh Royal, part of a stylish German budget hotel chain, is between the train station and the Royal Mile; it feels upscale and trendy for its price range (208 rooms, pay more for a park view or less for a windowless "budget" room with skylight, breakfast extra, elevator, 18 Market Street, tel. 0131/220-0730, www.motel-one.com, edinburgh-royal@motel-one.com; second location in the New Town/shopping zone at 10 Princes Street).

Chain Hotels in the Center: Besides my recommendations above, you'll find a number of cookie-cutter chain hotels close to the Royal Mile, including **Jurys Inn** (43 Jeffrey Street), **Ibis Hotel** (two convenient branches: near the Tron Church and another around the corner along the busy South Bridge), **Holiday Inn Express** (two locations: just off the Royal Mile at 300 Cowgate and one in the New Town), and **Travelodge Central** (just below the Royal Mile at 33 St. Mary's Street; additional locations in the New Town).

HOSTELS

¢ **Baxter Hostel** is your boutique hostel option. Occupying one floor of a Georgian townhouse (up several long, winding flights of stairs and below two more hostels), it has tons of ambience: tartan wallpaper, wood paneling, stone walls, decorative tile floors, and a beautifully restored kitchen/lounge that you'd want in your own house. Space is tight—hallways are snug, and five dorms (42 beds) share one bathroom. Another room, with four beds, has its own en-suite bathroom (includes scrambled egg breakfast; small fee for towel, travel adapters, and locks; 5 West Register Street, tel. 0131/503-1001, www.thebaxter.eu, info@thebaxter.eu).

¢ **Edinburgh Central Youth Hostel** rents 251 beds in 72 rooms accommodating three to six people (all with private bathrooms and lockers). Guests can eat cheaply in the cafeteria, or cook for the cost of groceries in the members' kitchen (private rooms available, pay laundry, 15-minute downhill walk from Waverley

EDINBURGH

EDINBURGH

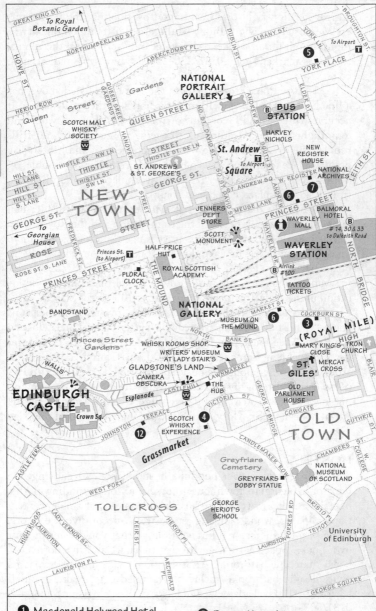

1 Macdonald Holyrood Hotel
2 The Inn on the Mile
3 The Inn Place
4 Grassmarket Hotel
5 The Place Hotel
6 Motel One Edinburgh (2)

7 Baxter Hostel
8 To Edinburgh Central Youth Hostel
9 SafeStay Edinburgh Hostel
10 High Street Hostel
11 Royal Mile Backpackers Hostel
12 Castle Rock Hostel

EDINBURGH

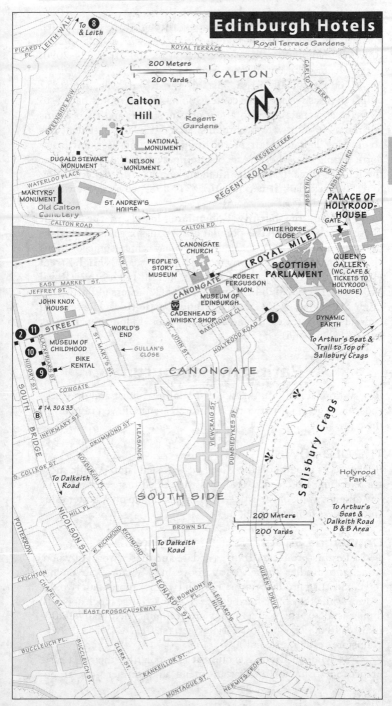

Edinburgh Hotels

To 8
& Leith

LEITH WALK

PICARDY PL.

GREENSIDE ROW

ROYAL TERRACE

Royal Terrace Gardens

CALTON

200 Meters
200 Yards

Calton
Hill

CARLTON TERR.

Regent
Gardens

N

NATIONAL
MONUMENT

DUGALD STEWART
MONUMENT

NELSON
MONUMENT

REGENT TERR.

REGENT ROAD

ABBEYHILL CRES.

ABBEYHILL RD.

WATERLOO PLACE

MARTYRS'
MONUMENT

Old Calton
Cemetery

ST. ANDREW'S
HOUSE

PALACE OF
HOLYROOD-
HOUSE

GATE

CALTON ROAD

CALTON RD.

NEW ST.

WHITE HORSE
CLOSE

CANONGATE
CHURCH

PEOPLE'S
STORY
MUSEUM

(ROYAL MILE)

QUEEN'S
GALLERY
(WC, CAFE &
TICKETS TO
HOLYROOD-
HOUSE)

SCOTTISH
PARLIAMENT

EAST MARKET ST.
JEFFREY ST.

CANONGATE

ROBERT
FERGUSSON
MON.

MUSEUM OF
EDINBURGH

JOHN KNOX
HOUSE

ST. MARY'S ST.

CADENHEAD'S
WHISKY SHOP

BAKEHOUSE CL.

DYNAMIC
EARTH

WORLD'S
END

STREET

1

HOLYROOD ROAD

To Arthur's Seat &
Trail to Top of
Salisbury Crags

11

2

BLACKFRIARS ST.

MUSEUM OF
CHILDHOOD

GULLAN'S
CLOSE

ST. JOHN ST.

10

NIDDRY ST.

BIKE
RENTAL

9

CANONGATE

SOUTH

COWGATE

14, 30 & 33

B

INFIRMARY ST.

BRIDGE

DRUMMOND ST.

PLEASANCE

VIEWCRAIG ST.

DUMBIEDYKES RD.

Salisbury Crags

S. COLLEGE ST.

ROXBURGH PL.

To Dalkeith
Road

SOUTH SIDE

HILL PL.

Holyrood
Park

To Arthur's
Seat &
Dalkeith Road
B & B Area

NICOLSON ST.

W. RICHMOND

RICHMOND

BROWN ST.

200 Meters
200 Yards

POTTERROW

CRICHTON

CHAPEL ST.

RICHMOND

To Dalkeith
Road

ST. LEONARD'S ST.

HILL

QUEEN'S DRIVE

EAST CROSSCAUSEWAY

BUCCLEUCH PL.

BUCCLEUCH ST.

CLERK ST.

RANKEILLOR ST.

BOWMONT PL.

ST. LEONARD'S

MONTAGUE ST.

HERMITS CROFT

Station—head down Leith Walk, pass through two roundabouts, hostel is on your left—or take Lothian bus #22 or #25 to Elm Rowe, 9 Haddington Place off Leith Walk, tel. 0131/524-2090, www.syha.org.uk, central@syha.org.uk).

¢ **SafeStay Edinburgh,** just off the Royal Mile, rents 272 bunks in pleasing purple-accented rooms. Dorm rooms have 4 to 12 beds, and there are also a few private singles and twin rooms (all rooms have private bathrooms). Bar 50 in the basement has an inviting lounge. Half of the rooms function as a university dorm during the school year, becoming available just in time for the tourists (breakfast extra, kitchen, laundry, free daily walking tour, 50 Blackfriars Street, tel. 0131/524-1989, www.safestay.com, reservations-edi@safestay.com).

¢ **Cheap and Scruffy Bohemian Hostels in the Center:** These three sister hostels—popular crash pads for young, hip backpackers—are beautifully located in the noisy center (some locations also have private rooms, www.macbackpackers.com): **High Street Hostel** (140 beds, 8 Blackfriars Street, just off High Street/Royal Mile, tel. 0131/557-3984); **Royal Mile Backpackers** (40 beds, 105 High Street, tel. 0131/557-6120); and **Castle Rock Hostel** (300 beds, just below the castle and above the pubs, 15 Johnston Terrace, tel. 0131/225-9666).

Eating in Edinburgh

Reservations for restaurants are essential in August and on weekends, and a good idea anytime. Children aren't allowed in many of the pubs.

THE OLD TOWN
Pricey places abound on the Royal Mile (listed later). While those are tempting, I prefer the two areas described first, each within a few minutes' walk of the Mile—just far enough to offer better value and a bit less touristy crush.

On Victoria Street, Near Grassmarket
$$$$ Grainstore Restaurant, a sedate and dressy world of wood, stone, and candles tucked away above busy Victoria Street, has served Scottish produce with a French twist for more than two decades. While they have inexpensive £14 two-course lunch specials, dinner is à la carte. Reservations are recommended (daily 12:00-14:30 & 18:00-21:30, 30 Victoria Street, tel. 0131/225-7635, www. grainstore-restaurant.co.uk).

$$$ Maison Bleue Restaurant is popular for their à la carte French/Scottish/North African menu and dinner special before 18:30 (18:00 on Fri-Sat; open daily 12:00-22:00, 36 Victoria Street, tel. 0131/226-1900).

$ Oink carves from a freshly roasted pig each afternoon for sandwiches that come in "oink" or "grunter" sizes. Watch the pig shrink in the front window throughout the day (daily 11:00-18:00 or whenever they run out of meat, cash only, 34 Victoria Street, tel. 01890/761-355). There's another location at the bottom end of the Royal Mile, near the parliament building (at 82 Canongate).

Near the National Museum

These restaurants are happily removed from the Royal Mile melee and skew to a youthful clientele with few tourists. After passing the Greyfriars Bobby statue and the National Museum, fork left onto Forrest Road.

$ Union of Genius is a creative soup kitchen with a strong identity. They cook up a selection of delicious soups with fun foodie twists each morning at their main location in Leith, then deliver them to this shop by bicycle (for environmental reasons). These are supplemented with good salads and fresh-baked breads. The "flight" comes with three small cups of soup and three types of bread. Line up at the counter, then either take your soup to go or sit in the cramped interior, with a couple of tables and counter seating (Mon-Fri 10:00-16:00, Sat from 12:00, closed Sun, 8 Forrest Road, tel. 0131/226-4436).

$$ Mums is a kitschy diner serving up comfort food just like mum used to make. The menu runs to huge portions of heavy, greasy Scottish/British standards—bangers (sausages), meat pies, burgers, and artery-clogging breakfasts (served until 12:00)—all done with a foodie spin, including vegetarian options (Mon-Sat 9:00-22:00, Sun from 10:00, 4A Forrest Road, tel. 0131/260-9806).

$$ Ting Thai Caravan, just around the corner from the above listings, is a casual, industrial-mod, food-focused eatery selling adventurous Thai street food (daily 11:30-22:00, Fri-Sat until 23:00, 8 Teviot Place, tel. 0131/225-9801).

Dessert: The **Frisky** frozen yogurt shop, on Forrest Road, makes for a fun treat.

Along the Royal Mile

Though the eateries along this most-crowded stretch of the city are invariably touristy, the scene is fun. Sprinkled in this list are some places a block or two off the main drag offering better values and maybe fewer tourists.

EDINBURGH

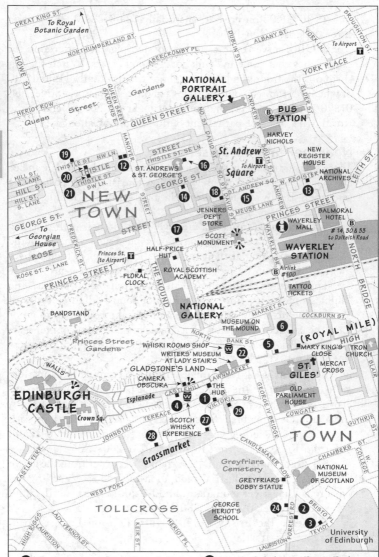

1 Grainstore, Maison Bleue & Oink
2 Union of Genius, Mums & Frisky
3 Ting Thai Caravan
4 The Witchery by the Castle
5 Angels with Bagpipes
6 Devil's Advocate
7 Wedgwood Restaurant
8 David Bann
9 Edinburgh Larder
10 Mimi's Bakehouse Picnic Parlour
11 Clarinda's Tea Room
12 Hendersons (3)
13 Café Royal
14 The Dome Restaurant
15 Dishoom
16 St. Andrew's & St. George's
   Church Undercroft Café
17 Marks & Spencer Food Hall
18 Sainsbury's

EDINBURGH

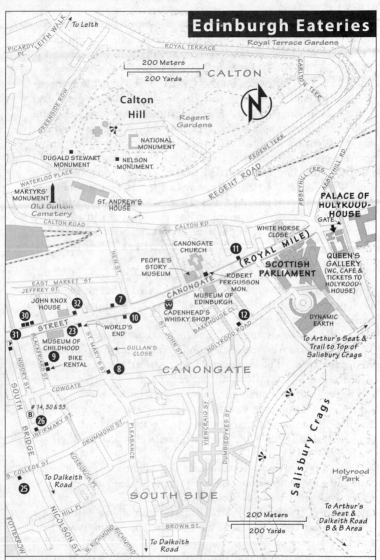

Edinburgh Eateries

19 Le Café St. Honoré
20 The Bon Vivant
21 El Cartel

Pubs & Nightlife
22 Deacon Brodie's Tavern
23 The World's End Pub
24 Sandy Bell's Pub
25 Captain's Bar

26 The Royal Oak Pub
27 Biddy Mulligans
28 White Hart Inn
29 Finnegans Wake
30 Whiski Bar, Royal Mile & Mitre Bar
31 Whistlebinkies Bar
32 No. 1 High Street Pub

Sit-Down Restaurants

These are listed roughly in downhill order, starting at the castle. You'll have more success getting into any of these with a reservation, especially on weekends.

$$$$ The Witchery by the Castle is set in a lushly decorated 16th-century building just below the castle on the Royal Mile, with wood paneling, antique candlesticks, tapestries, and opulent red leather upholstery. Frequented by celebrities, tourists, and locals out for a splurge, the restaurant's emphasis is on pricey Scottish meats and seafood. Their Secret Garden dining room, in a separate building farther back, is also a special setting—down some steps and in a fanciful room with French doors opening on to a terrace. Reserve ahead for either space, dress smartly, and bear in mind you're paying a premium for the ambience (two-course lunch specials—also available before 17:30 and after 22:30, three-course dinner menu, daily 12:00-23:30, tel. 0131/225-5613, www.thewitchery.com).

$$$ Angels with Bagpipes, conveniently located across from St. Giles' Cathedral, serves sophisticated Scottish staples in its dark, serious, plush interior (two- and three-course lunches, tasting menus at dinner, daily 12:00-21:30, 343 High Street, tel. 0131/220-1111, www.angelswithbagpipes.co.uk).

$$$ Devil's Advocate is a popular gastropub that hides down the narrow lane called Advocates Close, directly across the Royal Mile from St. Giles'. With an old cellar setting—exposed stone and heavy beams—done up in modern style, it feels like a mix of old and new Edinburgh. Creative whisky cocktails kick off a menu that dares to be adventurous, but with a respect for Scottish tradition (daily 12:00-22:00, later for drinks, 8 Advocates Close, tel. 0131/225-4465).

$$$$ Wedgwood Restaurant is romantic, contemporary, chic, and as gourmet as possible with no pretense. Paul Wedgwood cooks while his wife Lisa serves with appetizing charm. The cuisine: creative, modern Scottish with an international twist and a whiff of Asia. The pigeon and haggis starter is scrumptious. Paul and Lisa believe in making the meal the event of the evening—don't come here to eat and run. I like the ground level with the Royal Mile view, but the busy kitchen ambience in the basement is also fine (fine wine by the glass, daily 12:00-15:00 & 18:00-22:00, reservations advised, 267 Canongate on Royal Mile, tel. 0131/558-8737, www.wedgwoodtherestaurant.co.uk).

$$$ David Bann is a worthwhile stop for well-heeled vegetarians in need of a break from the morning fry-up. While vegetarian as can be, this place doesn't have even a hint of hippie. It's upscale (it has a cocktail bar), sleek, minimalist, and stylish (gorgeously presented dishes), serious about quality, and organic. Reserve ahead (decadent desserts, Mon-Fri 12:00-22:00, Sat-Sun from 11:00, vegan and gluten-free options, just off the Royal Mile at 56 St. Mary's Street, tel. 0131/556-5888, www.davidbann.co.uk).

Quick, Easy, and Cheap Lunch Options

$ **Edinburgh Larder** promises "a taste of the country" in the center of the city. They focus on high-quality, homestyle breakfast and lunches made from seasonal, local ingredients. The café, with table service, is a convivial space with rustic tables filled by local families. The takeaway shop next door has counter service and a few dine-in tables (Mon-Fri 8:00-16:00, Sat-Sun from 9:00, 15 Blackfriars Street, tel. 0131/556-6922).

$ **Mimi's Bakehouse Picnic Parlour,** a handy Royal Mile outpost of a prizewinning bakery, serves up baked goods—try the scones—and sandwiches in their cute and modern shop (daily 9:00-18:00, 250 Canongate, tel. 0131/556-6632).

$ **Clarinda's Tea Room,** near the bottom of the Royal Mile, is a charming and girlish time warp—a fine and tasty place to relax after touring the Mile or the Palace of Holyroodhouse. Stop in for a quiche, salad, or soup lunch. It's also great for sandwiches and tea and cake anytime (Mon-Sat 9:00-16:30, Sun from 10:00, 69 Canongate, tel. 0131/557-1888).

$$ **Hendersons** is a bright and casual local chain with good vegetarian dishes to go or eat in (daily 9:00-17:00, 67 Holyrood Road—three minutes off Royal Mile near Scottish Parliament end, tel. 0131/557-1606; for more details, see the Hendersons listing later, under "The New Town").

Historic Pubs Along the Mile

To drink a pint or grab some forgettable pub grub in historic surroundings, consider one of the landmark pubs described on my self-guided walk: $$ **Deacon Brodie's Tavern,** at a dead-center location on the Royal Mile (a sloppy pub on the ground floor with a sloppy restaurant upstairs) or $$ **The World's End Pub,** farther down the Mile at Canongate (a colorful old place dishing up hearty meals from a creative menu in a fun, dark, and noisy space, 4 High Street). Both serve pub meals and are open long hours daily.

THE NEW TOWN

In the Georgian part of town, you'll find a bustling world of office workers, students, and pensioners doing their thing. All of these eateries are within a few minutes' walk of the TI and Waverley Station.

Elegant Spaces near Princes Street

These places provide a staid glimpse at grand old Edinburgh. The ambience is generally better than the food.

Café Royal is a movie producer's dream pub—the perfect *fin de siècle* setting for a coffee, beer, or light meal. (In fact, parts of *Chariots of Fire* were filmed here.) Drop in, if only to admire the 1880 tiles featuring famous inventors (daily 12:00-14:30 & 17:00-21:30, bar food available all day, two blocks from Waverley Mall on 19 West Register Street, tel. 0131/556-1884, www.caferoyaledinburgh.co.uk). There are two eateries here: the noisy **$$ pub** and the dressier **$$$ restaurant,** specializing in oysters, fish, and game (reserve for dinner—it's quite small and understandably popular).

$$$$ The Dome Restaurant, in what was a fancy bank, serves modern international cuisine around a classy bar and under the elegant 19th-century skylight dome. With soft jazz and chic, white-tablecloth ambience, it feels a world apart. Come here not for the food, but for the opulent atmosphere (daily 12:00-23:00, food served until 21:30, reserve for dinner, open for a drink any time under the dome; the adjacent, more intimate Club Room serves food Mon-Thu 10:00-16:00, Fri-Sat until 21:30, closed Sun; 14 George Street, tel. 0131/624-8624, www.thedomeedinburgh.com).

Casual and Cheap near St. Andrew Square

$$ Dishoom, in the New Town, is the first non-London outpost of this popular Bombay café. You'll enjoy upscale Indian cuisine in a bustling, dark, 1920s dining room on the second floor overlooking St. Andrew Square. You can also order from the same menu in the basement bar at night (daily 9:00-23:00, 3A St. Andrew Square, tel. 0131/202-6406).

$ St. Andrew's and St. George's Church Undercroft Café, in the basement of a fine old church, is the cheapest place in town for lunch. Your tiny bill helps support the Church of Scotland (Mon-Fri lunch only, closed Sat-Sun, at 13 George Street, just off St. Andrew Square, tel. 0131/225-3847).

Supermarkets: Marks & Spencer Food Hall offers an assortment of tasty hot foods, prepared sandwiches, fresh bakery items, a wide selection of wines and beverages, and plastic utensils at the checkout queue. It's just a block from the Scott Monument and the picnic-perfect Princes Street Gardens (Mon-Sat 8:00-19:00, Thu until 20:00, Sun 11:00-18:00, Princes Street 54—separate stairway next to main M&S entrance leads directly to food hall, tel. 0131/225-2301). **Sainsbury's** supermarket, a block off Princes Street, also offers grab-and-go items (daily 7:00-22:00, on corner of Rose Street on St. Andrew Square, across the street from Jenners).

Hip Eateries on and near Thistle Street

For something a little more modern and food-focused, head a few more minutes deeper into the New Town to find Thistle Street. This strip and its surrounding lanes are packed with more enticing eateries than the rest of the New Town put together. Browse the options here, but tune into these favorites.

$$$ Le Café St. Honoré, tucked away like a secret bit of old Paris, is a charming place with friendly service and walls lined by wine bottles. It serves French-Scottish cuisine in tight, Old World, cut-glass elegance to a dressy crowd (three-course lunch and dinner specials, daily 12:00-14:00 & 17:30-22:00, reservations smart—ask to sit upstairs, down Thistle Street from Hanover Street, 34 Northwest Thistle Street Lane, tel. 0131/226-2211, www.cafesthonore. com).

$$$ The Bon Vivant is woody, youthful, and candlelit, with a rotating menu of French/Scottish dishes, a good cocktail list, and a companion wine shop next door. They have fun tapas plates and heartier dishes, served either in the bar up front or in the restaurant in back (daily 12:00-22:00, 55 Thistle Street, tel. 0131/225-3275, www.bonvivantedinburgh.co.uk).

$$ Hendersons has fed a generation of New Town vegetarians hearty cuisine and salads. Even carnivores love this place for its delectable salads, desserts, and smoothies. Henderson's has two separate eateries: Their main restaurant, facing Hanover Street, is self-service by day but has table service after 17:00. Each evening after 19:00, they have pleasant live music—generally guitar or jazz (Mon-Sat 9:00-22:00, Sun 10:30-16:00, between Queen and George streets at 94 Hanover Street, tel. 0131/225-2131). Just around the corner on Thistle Street, **Henderson's Vegan** has a strictly vegan menu and feels a bit more casual (daily 12:00-21:30, tel. 0131/225-2605).

$ El Cartel is a youthful place serving up good tacos and other Mexican dishes in a cramped, edgy atmosphere. Enjoy a drink at their sister restaurant the Bon Vivant (see earlier) while waiting for a table to open up (daily 12:00-22:00, 64 Thistle Street, tel. 0131/226-7171).

IN THE B&B NEIGHBORHOOD

Nearly all of these places (except for The Sheep Heid Inn) are within a 10-minute walk of my recommended B&Bs. For locations, see the map on page 795. For a cozy drink after dinner, visit the recommended pubs in the area (see "Nightlife in Edinburgh," earlier).

Pub Grub

$$ The Salisbury Arms Pub, with a nice garden terrace and separate restaurant area, serves upscale, pleasing traditional classics with yuppie flair in a space that exudes more Martha Stewart and Pottery Barn than traditional public house (book ahead for restaurant, food served daily 12:00-22:00, across from the pool at 58 Dalkeith Road, tel. 0131/667-4518, www.thesalisburyarmsedinburgh. co.uk).

$$ The Old Bell Inn, with an old-time sports-bar ambience—fishing, golf, horses, televisions—serves pub meals. This is a classic "snug pub"—all dark woods and brass beer taps, littered with evocative knickknacks. It comes with sidewalk seating and a mixed-age crowd (bar tables can be reserved, food served daily until 21:15, 233 Causewayside, tel. 0131/668-1573, http://oldbelledinburgh.co.uk).

Other Eateries

$$$$ Aizle is a delicious night out. They serve a set £45 five-course tasting menu based on what's in season—ingredients are listed on the chalkboard (with notice, they can accommodate dietary restrictions). The restaurant is intimate but unpretentious, and they only serve 36 people a night to keep the experience special and unrushed (dinner only Wed-Sun, this is not a walk-in type of place—book ahead at least a week, 107 St. Leonard's Street—five minutes past the Royal Commonwealth Pool, tel. 0131/662-9349, www.aizle. co.uk).

$$ Southpour is a nice place for a local beer, craft cocktail, or a reliable meal from a menu of salads, sandwiches, meat dishes, and other comfort foods. The brick walls, wood beams, and giant windows give it a warm and open vibe (daily 10:00-22:00, 1 Newington Road, tel. 0131/650-1100).

$$ Ristorante Isola is a calm and casual place with 15 tables surrounding a bright yellow bar. They serve pizzas, pastas, and meat or seafood *secondi* with an emphasis on Sardinian specialties (Mon-Tue 17:00-22:30, Wed-Sun 12:00-22:30, 85 Newington Road, tel. 0131/662-9977).

$$ Voujon Restaurant serves a fusion menu of Bengali and Indian cuisines. Vegetarians appreciate the expansive yet inexpensive offerings (daily 17:00-23:00, 107 Newington Road, tel. 0131/667-5046).

$$ Apiary has an inviting, casual interior and a hit-or-miss, eclectic menu that mingles various international flavors (daily 10:00-15:00 & 17:30-21:00, 33 Newington Road, tel. 0131/668-4999).

Fast Eats

At **$ Edinburgh Bakehouse,** award-winning baker James Lynch makes £1-2 fresh breads, sweets, and meat pies from scratch in this laid-back, nondescript shop. Locals line up for his morning rolls—which earned him the title "baker of the year." Stop by to see the friendly staff and open kitchen in action and judge for yourself (cash only, daily 7:00-16:00 or whenever the goods sell out, open

24 hours from Fri until Sun afternoon to cater to the weekend pub crowd, 101 Newington Road).

$ Earthy is an organic, farm-fresh café and grocery store with a proudly granola attitude. Order from the counter, with its appealing display of freshly prepared salads, sandwiches, and baked goods. Sit in the industrial-mod interior, with rustic picnic benches, or out in the ragtag back garden. In the well-stocked store, assemble a pricey but top-quality picnic (café daily 9:00-17:00, store open until 19:00, 33 Ratcliffe Terrace, tel. 0131/667-2967).

Groceries: Several grocery stores are on the main streets near the restaurants, including Sainsbury's Local and Co-op on South Clerk Road, and Tesco Express and another Sainsbury's Local one block over on Causewayside (all open late—until at least 22:00). Cameron Toll Shopping Centre, about a half-mile south on your way out of town, houses a Sainsbury's superstore for more substantial supplies and gasoline.

Memorable Meals Farther Out

$$$$ Rhubarb Restaurant specializes in Old World elegance. It's in "Edinburgh's most handsome house"—an over-the-top riot of antiques, velvet, tassels, and fringes. The plush dark-rhubarb color theme reminds visitors that this was the place where rhubarb was first grown in Britain. It's a 10-minute walk past the other recommended eateries behind Arthur's Seat, in a huge estate with big, shaggy Highland cattle enjoying their salads al fresco. At night, it's a candlelit wonder. Most spend a wad here. Reserve in advance and dress up if you can (two-course lunch and three-course dinner, daily 12:00-14:00 & 18:00-22:00, afternoon tea served daily 12:00-19:00, in Prestonfield House, Priestfield Road, tel. 0131/662-2303, www.prestonfield.com). For details on their schmaltzy Scottish folk evening, see "Nightlife in Edinburgh," earlier.

$$ The Sheep Heid Inn, Edinburgh's oldest and most inviting public house, is equally notable for its history, date-night appeal, and hearty portions of affordable, classy dishes. It's either a short cab ride or pleasant 30-minute walk from the B&B neighborhood (see page 780), but it's worth the effort to dine in this dreamy setting in the presence of past queens and kings—choose between the bar downstairs, dining room upstairs, or outside in the classic garden courtyard (food served Mon-Fri 12:00-21:00, Sat-Sun 12:00-21:30, 43 The Causeway, tel. 0131/661-7974, www.thesheepheidedinburgh.co.uk).

EDINBURGH

Edinburgh Connections

BY TRAIN OR BUS

From Edinburgh by Train to: Glasgow (10/hour, 50 minutes), **St. Andrews** (train to Leuchars, 2/hour, 1 hour, then 10-minute bus into St. Andrews), **Stirling** (2/hour, 1 hour), **Inverness** (6/day direct, 3.5 hours, more with transfer), **Oban** (5/day, 4.5 hours, change in Glasgow), **York** (3/hour, 2.5 hours), **London** (2/hour, 4.5 hours), **Durham** (hourly direct, 2 hours, less frequent in winter), **Keswick/Lake District** (8/day to Penrith—more via Carlisle, 2 hours, then 40-minute bus ride to Keswick). **Train info:** Tel. 0345-748-4950, www.nationalrail.co.uk.

By Bus: Edinburgh's bus station is in the New Town, just off St. Andrew Square, two blocks north of the train station. Direct buses go to **Glasgow** (Citylink bus #900, 4/hour, 1.5 hours), **Inverness** (express #G90, 2/day, 3.5 hours; slower #M90, 6/day, 4 hours), **Stirling** (every 2 hours on Citylink #909, 1 hour). To reach other destinations in the Highlands—including **Oban, Fort William,** or **Glencoe**—you'll have to transfer. It's usually fastest to take the train to Glasgow and change to a bus there. For details, see "Getting Around the Highlands" on page 906. For bus info, stop by the station or call Scottish Citylink (tel. 0871-266-3333, www.citylink.co.uk). Additional long-distance routes may be operated by National Express (www.nationalexpress.com) or Megabus (www.megabus.com).

BY PLANE

Edinburgh Airport is located eight miles northwest of the center (airport code: EDI, tel. 0844-481-8989, www.edinburghairport.com). **Taxis** or **Uber rides** between the airport and city center are about £20-25 (25 minutes to downtown or Dalkeith Road). The airport is also well connected to central Edinburgh by tram and bus. Just follow signs outside; the tram tracks are straight ahead, and the bus stop is to the right, along the main road in front of the terminal. **Trams** make several stops in town, including along Princes Street and at St. Andrew Square (£5.50, buy ticket from machine, runs every 10 minutes from early morning until 23:30, 35 minutes, www.edinburghtrams.com).

The Lothian **Airlink bus #100** drops you at Waverley Bridge (£4.50, £7.50 round-trip, runs every 10 minutes, 30 minutes, tel. 0131/555-6363, http://lothianbuses.co.uk). Whether you take the tram or bus to the center, to continue on to my recommended B&Bs south of the city center, you can either take a taxi (about £7) or hop on a city bus (for directions, see "Sleeping in Edinburgh," earlier). To get from the B&Bs *to* the Airlink or tram stops downtown, you can take a taxi...or ride a city bus to North Bridge, turn left at the grand Balmoral Hotel, and walk a short distance down Princes Street. Turn right up St. Andrew Street to catch the tram at St. Andrew Square, or continue up to the next bridge, Waverley, for the Airlink bus.

ROUTE TIPS FOR DRIVERS HEADING SOUTH

It's 100 miles south from Edinburgh to Hadrian's Wall; to Durham, it's another 50 miles.

To Hadrian's Wall: From Edinburgh, Dalkeith Road leads south and eventually becomes the A-68 (handy Cameron Toll supermarket with cheap gas is on the left as you leave Edinburgh Town, 10 minutes south of Edinburgh; gas and parking behind store). The A-68 road takes you to Hadrian's Wall in 2.5 hours. You'll pass Jedburgh and its abbey after one hour. (For one last shot of Scotland shopping, there's a coach tour's delight just before Jedburgh, with kilt makers, woolens, and a sheepskin shop.) Across from Jedburgh's lovely abbey is a free parking lot, a good visitors center, and pay toilets. The England/Scotland border is a fun, quick stop (great view, ice cream, and tea caravan). Just after the turn for Colwell, turn right onto the A-6079, and roller-coaster four miles down to Low Brunton. Then turn right onto the B-6318, and stay on it by turning left at Chollerford, following the Roman wall westward.

To Durham: If you're heading straight to Durham, you can take the scenic coastal route on the A-1 (a few more miles than the A-68, but similar time), which takes you near Holy Island and Bamburgh Castle.

GLASGOW

Glasgow (GLAS-goh)—astride the River Clyde—is a surprising city. In its heyday, Glasgow was one of Europe's biggest cities and the second-largest in Britain, right behind London. A century ago it had 1.2 million people, twice the size (and with twice the importance) of today. It was an industrial power-house producing 25 percent of the world's oceangoing ships. But in the mid-20th century, tough times hit Glasgow, giving it a rough edge and a run-down image.

At the city's low point during the Margaret Thatcher years (1980s), its leaders embarked on a systematic rejuvenation designed to again make Glasgow appealing to businesses, tourists...and locals. Today the city feels revitalized and goes out of its way to offer a warm welcome. Glaswegians (rhymes with "Norwegians") are some of the chattiest people in Scotland—and have the most entertaining (and impenetrable) accent.

Many travelers give Glasgow a miss, but that's a shame: I consider it Scotland's most underrated destination. Glasgow is a workaday Scottish city as well as a cosmopolitan destination, with an unpretentious friendliness, an energetic dining and nightlife scene, top-notch museums (most of them free), and a unique flair for art and design. It's also a pilgrimage site for architecture buffs, thanks to a cityscape packed with Victorian facades, early

20th-century touches, and bold and glassy new construction. Most beloved are the works by hometown boy Charles Rennie Mackintosh, the visionary—and now very trendy—architect who left his mark all over Glasgow at the turn of the 20th century.

Many more tourists visit Edinburgh, a short train trip away. But for a more complete look at urban Scotland, be sure to stop off in Glasgow. Edinburgh may have the royal aura, but Glasgow has down-to-earth appeal. In Glasgow, there's no upper-crust history, and no one puts on airs. In Edinburgh, people identify with the quality of the school they attended; in Glasgow, it's their soccer team allegiance. One Glaswegian told me, "The people of Glasgow have a better time at a funeral than the people of Edinburgh have at a wedding." Here, friendly locals do their best to introduce you to the fun-loving, laid-back Glaswegian way of life.

PLANNING YOUR TIME

While many visitors blitz Glasgow as a day trip from Edinburgh or Stirling (and a single day in Glasgow is certainly more exciting than a fourth day in Edinburgh), the city can easily fill two days of sightseeing.

On a quick visit, follow my "Get to Know Glasgow" self-guided walk of the city center, tying together the most important sights in the city's core. If your time is short, the interiors most worth considering are the Tenement House and the Kelvingrove Museum.

With additional time, your options open up. Follow my West End Walk to get a taste of Glasgow's appealing residential zone, which has some of the city's best restaurants as well as a number of worthwhile sights. Fans of Art Nouveau and Charles Rennie Mackintosh can lace together a busy day's worth of sightseeing (the TI has a brochure laying it out). At a minimum, those interested in Mackintosh should visit the Mackintosh House at the Hunterian Gallery (in the West End) and the Mackintosh exhibit at the Kelvingrove Museum.

Regardless of how long you're staying, consider the two-hour hop-on, hop-off bus tour, which is convenient for getting the bigger picture and reaching three important sights away from the center (the Cathedral Precinct, the Riverside Museum, and the Kelvingrove Museum).

Day Trip from Edinburgh: For a full day, catch the 9:30 train to Glasgow (morning trains every 10 minutes; discount for same-day round-trip if leaving after 9:15 or on weekend); it arrives at Queen Street Train Station before 10:30. To fill your Glasgow hours smartly, I'd do the entire hop-on, hop-off bus tour circuit (two hours), then follow my self-guided walk through downtown

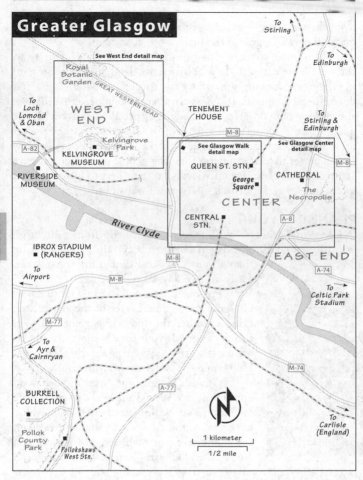

Greater Glasgow

To Stirling

To Edinburgh

See West End detail map

Royal Botanic Garden

GREAT WESTERN ROAD

To Loch Lomond & Oban

WEST END

TENEMENT HOUSE

To Stirling & Edinburgh

A-82

Kelvingrove Park

M-8

See Glasgow Center detail map

M-8

KELVINGROVE MUSEUM

See Glasgow Walk detail map

QUEEN ST. STN.

CATHEDRAL

RIVERSIDE MUSEUM

George Square

The Necropolis

CENTER

River Clyde

CENTRAL STN.

A-8

IBROX STADIUM (RANGERS)

M-8

EAST END

To Airport

M-8

A-74

To Celtic Park Stadium

M-77

To Ayr & Cairnryan

BURRELL COLLECTION

A-77

M-74

N

To Carlisle (England)

Pollok County Park

Pollokshaws West Stn.

1 kilometer

1/2 mile

GLASGOW

(finishing with the Tenement House). Next, check out the Kelvingrove Museum and have dinner nearby (in the Finnieston area). Catch a train that leaves around 21:00 to return to Edinburgh (evening trains depart every 10-20 minutes).

Orientation to Glasgow

Although it's often thought of as a "second city," Glasgow is actually Scotland's biggest (pop. 600,000, swelling to 1.2 million within Greater Glasgow—that's one out of every five Scots).

The tourist's Glasgow has two parts: the businesslike downtown (train stations, commercial zone, and main shopping drag) and the residential West End (B&Bs, restaurants, and nightlife).

When the Great Ships of the World Were "Clyde-Built"

Glasgow's River Clyde shipyards were the mightiest in the world, famed for building the largest moving man-made objects on earth. The shipyards, once 50 strong, have dwindled to just three. Yet a few giant cranes still stand to remind locals and visitors that from 1880 to 1950, a quarter of the world's ships were built here and "Clyde-built" meant reliability and quality. For 200 years, shipbuilding was Glasgow's top employer—as many as 100,000 workers at its peak, producing a new ship every two days. The glamorous Cunard ships were built here—from the *Lusitania* in 1906 (infamously sunk by a German U-boat in World War I, which almost brought the US into the war) to the *Queen Elizabeth II* in 1967. People still talk about the day when over 200,000 Glaswegians gathered for the launch, the Queen herself smashed the champagne bottle on the prow, and the magnificent ship slid into the harbor. To learn lots more about shipbuilding in Glasgow, visit the excellent Riverside Museum (described under "Sights in Glasgow").

GLASGOW

Both areas have good sights, and both are covered in this chapter by self-guided walks.

Glasgow's **downtown** is a tight grid of boxy office buildings and shopping malls, making it feel more like a midsized American city than a big Scottish one—like Cincinnati or Pittsburgh, but with shorter skyscrapers made of Victorian sandstone rather than glass and steel. The walkable city center has two main drags, both lined with shops and crawling with shoppers: Sauchiehall Street (pronounced "Suckyhall," running west to east) and Buchanan Street (running north to south). These two pedestrian malls—part of a shopping zone nicknamed the Golden Zed—make a big zig and zag through the heart of town (the third street of the Zed, Argyle Street, is busy with traffic and less appealing).

The **West End** is a posh suburb, with big homes, upscale apartment buildings, and lots of green space. The area has three pockets of interest: near the Hillhead subway stop, with a lively restaurant scene and the Botanic Gardens; the University of Glasgow campus, with its stately buildings and fine museums; and, just downhill through a sprawling park, the area around the Kelvingrove Museum, with a lively nearby strip of trendy bars and restaurants (Finnieston).

TOURIST INFORMATION

The TI is inside the Gallery of Modern Art on Royal Exchange Square, downstairs. They hand out a good, free map and brochures

on Glasgow and the rest of Scotland (daily 10:00-17:00, www.visitscotland.com).

ARRIVAL IN GLASGOW

By Train: Glasgow, a major Scottish transportation hub, has two main train stations, which are just a few blocks apart in the heart of town: **Central Station** (with a grand, genteel interior under a vast steel-and-glass Industrial Age roof) and **Queen Street Station** (more functional, with better connections to Edinburgh—take the exit marked *Buchanan Street* to reach the main shopping drag). Both stations have pay WCs and baggage storage. If going between the stations to change trains, you can walk five minutes or take the roundabout "RailLink" bus #398 (free with train ticket, otherwise £1.20, 5/hour; also goes to bus station).

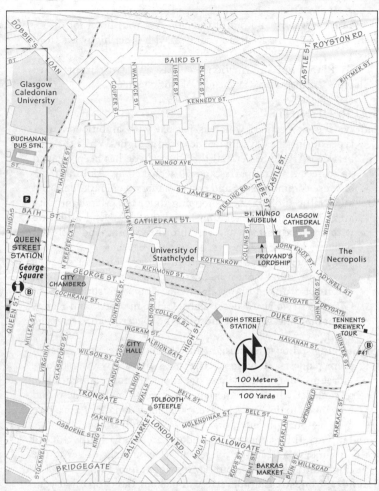

By Bus: Buchanan bus station is at Killermont Street, two blocks up the hill behind Queen Street Station (luggage lockers; travel center open daily 9:00-17:00).

By Car: Glasgow's downtown streets are steep, mostly one-way, congested with buses and pedestrians, and a horrible place to drive. Parking downtown is a hassle: Metered street parking is expensive (£3/hour) and limited to two hours during the day; garages are even more expensive (figure £25 for 24 hours). Ideally, do Glasgow without a car—for example, tour Edinburgh and Glasgow by public transit, then pick up your rental car on your way out of town. If you are stuck with a car in Glasgow, try to sleep in the West End, where driving and parking are easier (and use public transportation or taxis as necessary).

The M-8 motorway, which slices through downtown Glasgow,

is the easiest way in and out of the city. Ask your hotel for directions to and from the M-8, and connect with other highways from there.

By Plane: For information on Glasgow's two airports, see "Glasgow Connections," at the end of this chapter.

HELPFUL HINTS

Safety: The city center, which is packed with ambitious career types during the day, can feel deserted at night. While the area between Argyle Street and the River Clyde has been cleaned up in recent years, parts can still feel sketchy. As in any big city, use common sense and don't wander down dark, deserted alleys. The Golden Zed shopping drag, the Merchant City area (east of the train stations), and the West End all bustle with crowded restaurants well into the evening and feel well populated in the wee hours.

    If you've picked up a football (soccer) jersey or scarf as a souvenir, don't wear it in Glasgow; passions run very high, and most drunken brawls in town are between supporters of Glasgow's two rival soccer clubs: Celtic in green, and Rangers in blue and red. (For more on the soccer rivalry, see page 824.)

Sightseeing: Almost every sight in Glasgow is free, but most of them request a donation between £3 and £5 (www.glasgowmuseums.com). While these donations are not required, I like to consider what the experience was worth and decide if and how much to donate as I leave. (Voluntary donations are a nice option—but will only work if people actually donate.)

Sunday Travel: Bus and train schedules are dramatically reduced on Sundays and in the off-season. (If you want to get to the Highlands by bus on a Sunday in winter, forget it.)

Laundry: Majestic Launderette will pick up and drop off at your B&B or hotel (call to arrange); they also have a launderette near the Kelvingrove Museum in the West End (self-serve or full-serve, Mon-Fri 8:00-18:00, Sat until 16:00, Sun 10:00-16:00, 1110 Argyle Street, tel. 0141/334-3433).

GETTING AROUND GLASGOW

By City Bus: Most city-center routes are operated by First Bus Company (£2.20/ride, £4.50 for all-day ticket on First buses, buy tickets from driver, exact change required). Buses run every few minutes down Glasgow's main thoroughfares (such as Sauchiehall Street) to the downtown core (train stations). You can also get around the city via hop-on, hop-off bus (see "Tours in Glasgow," next).

By Taxi: Taxis are affordable, plentiful, and often come with nice, chatty cabbies (if your driver has an impenetrable Glaswegian accent, just smile and nod). Most taxi rides within the downtown area cost about £6; to the West End is about £8.

By Uber: Uber works particularly well in Glasgow and lets you make quick connections for about £5.

By Subway: Glasgow's cute little single-line subway system, nicknamed The Clockwork Orange, makes a six-mile circle that has 15 stops. While simple today, when it opened in 1896 it was a wonder (it's the world's third-oldest subway system, after those in London and Budapest). Though the subway is useless for connecting city-center sightseeing (Buchanan Street and St. Enoch are the only downtown stops), it's ideal for reaching sights farther out, including the Kelvingrove Museum (Kelvinhall stop) and West End restaurant/nightlife neighborhood (Hillhead stop). Ticket options are: £1.65 single trip, £4 for all-day ticket, or frequent riders can get a £3 Bramble card, which is reloadable and reduces your single-ride cost to £1.45 (subway runs Mon-Sat 6:30-23:15, Sun 10:00-18:00, www.spt.co.uk/subway).

Tours in Glasgow

Hop-On, Hop-Off Bus

CitySightseeing connects Glasgow's far-flung historic sights in a two-hour loop and lets you hop on and off as you like for two days. Buses are frequent (every 10-20 minutes, 9:30-18:20, service ends earlier in off-season) and alternate between live guides and recorded narration (both are equally good). The route covers the city very well, and the guide does a fine job of describing activities at each stop. While the first stop is on George Square, you can hop on and pay the driver anywhere along the route (£15, tel. 0141/204-0444, www.citysightseeingglasgow.co.uk).

Walking Tours

Walking Tours in Glasgow was started by Jenny and Liv, two recent University of Glasgow graduates who love their city. The city center tour starts in George Square and covers about 3.5 miles in 2.5 hours (daily 10:30 and 14:00; off-season tours by request). They also run a West End tour at 14:30 that requires advance booking (£10, www.walkingtoursin.com, walkingtoursinglasgow@gmail.com).

Trainspotters may enjoy the guided, behind-the-scenes tours of **Central Station,** including a spooky, abandoned Victorian train platform (book ahead, www.glasgowcentraltours.co.uk).

Those with a specific interest in **Mackintosh** architecture should consider the 2.25-hour Mackintosh-themed city walking tours given by students of the Glasgow School of Art (£20, 4/week, see page 838).

Local Guides

Joan Dobbie, a native Glaswegian and registered Scottish Tourist Guide, will give you the insider's take on Glasgow's sights (£135/half-day, £200/day, tours on foot or by public transit—no tours by car, tel. 01355/236-749, mobile 07773-555-151, joan.leo@lineone.net).

Ann Stewart is a former high-school geography teacher turned Blue Badge guide who is excited to show you around Glasgow or take you on an excursion outside the city (£150/4 hours, £220/8 hours, mobile 07716-358-997, www.comeseescotland.com, ann@comeseescotland.com).

Highlands Day Trips

Most of the same companies that do Highlands side-trips from Edinburgh also operate trips from Glasgow. If you'd like to spend an efficient day away from the city, skim the descriptions and listings on page 713, and then check each company's website or browse the brochures at the TI for details.

Glasgow Walks

These two self-guided walks introduce you to Glasgow's most interesting (and very different) neighborhoods: the downtown zone and the residential and university sights of the West End.

GET TO KNOW GLASGOW: THE DOWNTOWN CORE

Glasgow isn't romantic, but it has an earthy charm, its people are a joy to chat with, and architecture buffs love it. The more time you spend here, the more you'll appreciate the edgy, artsy vibe and the quirky, fun-loving spirit. Be sure to look up—above the chain restaurants and mall stores—and you'll discover a wealth of imaginative facades, complete with ornate friezes and expressive sculptures. These buildings transport you to the heady days around the turn of the 20th century—when the rest of Britain was enthralled by Victorianism, but Glasgow set its own course, thanks largely to the artistic bravado of Charles Rennie  Mackintosh and his Art Nouveau friends (the "Glasgow Four"). This walking tour takes about 1.5 hours (plus sightseeing stops along the way).

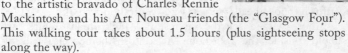

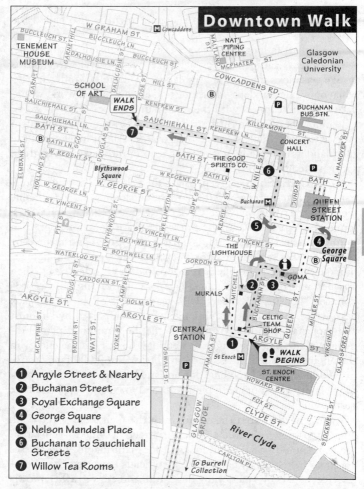

Downtown Walk

1. Argyle Street & Nearby
2. Buchanan Street
3. Royal Exchange Square
4. George Square
5. Nelson Mandela Place
6. Buchanan to Sauchiehall Streets
7. Willow Tea Rooms

• Start at the St. Enoch subway station, at the base of the pedestrian shopping boulevard, Buchanan Street. (This is a short walk from Central Station, or a longer walk or quick cab ride from Queen Street Station.) Stand at the intersection of Argyle and Buchanan, where the square hits the street (with your back to the glassy subway entry). Take a moment to get oriented.

❶ Argyle Street and Nearby

The grand pedestrian boulevard, Buchanan Street, leads uphill to the Royal Concert Hall. This is the start of the "Golden Zed"—the nickname for a Z-shaped pedestrian boulevard made of three streets: Buchanan, Sauchiehall, and Argyle. Always coming up with marketing slogans to goose the shopping metabolism of the city, this district (with the top shops in town) is also called the "Style Mile."

Look left (a long block away) to where Central Station (with its huge glass facade) makes a bridge over Argyle Street. This bridge was nicknamed "The Highlanders' Umbrella" from the days when poor Highlanders, who came to Glasgow to find work, would gather here to connect with their community.

Before heading up Buchanan Street, take a quick detour down Argyle to see a couple slices of Glasgow life. About half-way to the Highlanders' Umbrella on the right, step into the extremely green sports store (at #154).

The **Celtic Shop** is green. That's the color of Glasgow's dominant (for now) soccer team. It's hard for outsiders to fathom the intensity of the rivalry between Glasgow's Celtic and Rangers. Celtic, founded by an Irish Catholic priest to raise money for poor Irish immigrants in the East End, is—naturally—green and favored by Catholics. (For reasons no one can explain, the Celtic team name is pronounced "sell-tic"—like it is in Boston; in all other cases, such as when referring to music, language, or culture, this word is pronounced "kell-tic.") Rangers, with team colors of the Union Jack (red, white, and blue), are more likely to be supported by Unionist and Protestant families. Wander into the shop (minimizing or hiding any red or blue you might be wearing). Check out the energy in the photos and shots of the stadium filled with 60,000 fans. You're in a world where red and blue don't exist. Upstairs, tucked in a back room, is a trophy room with photos of the 1967 team, considered the best in club history.

Now head around the corner from the Celtic Shop and walk a few steps down the alley (Mitchell Street). While it seems a bit seedy, it should be safe...but look out for giant magnifying glasses and taxis held aloft by balloons. City officials have cleverly co-opted street artists by sanctioning huge, fun, and edgy **graffiti murals** like these. (You'll see even more if you side-trip down alleys along the Style Mile.) The girl with the magnifying glass is painted by graffiti artist Smug (see the girl's necklace). In the taxi painting, the driver is actually the artist and the license plate alludes to his tag name: Rogue-One. (By the way, there are no actual bricks on that wall.) Glasgow produces a free booklet called City Center Mural Trail (also available at www.citycentremuraltrail.co.uk), which explains all this fun art around town.

• *Now return to the base of...*

GLASGOW

❷ Buchanan Street

Buchanan Street has a friendly Ramblas-style vibe with an abundance of street musicians. As you stroll uphill, keep an eye out for a few big landmarks: **Frasers** (#45, on the left) is a vast and venerable department store, considered the "Harrods of Glasgow." The **Argyll Arcade** (#30, opposite Frasers), dating from 1827 with a proud red-sandstone facade, is the oldest arcade in town. It's filled most-

ly with jewelry and comes with security guards dressed in Victorian-era garb. **Princes Square** (at #48, just past Argyll Arcade) is a classic old building dressed with a modern steel peacock and foliage. Step inside to see the delightfully modernized Art Nouveau atrium.

At #97 (50 yards up, on the left) is one of two Mackintosh-designed **Willow Tea Rooms** (the other location, described later in this walk, is the original). This central location is designed to capitalize on the trendiness of Mackintosh.

• *Just past the tearooms, turn down the alley on the right, called Exchange Place. You'll pass the recommended Rogano restaurant on your right before emerging onto...*

❸ Royal Exchange Square

The centerpiece of this square—which marks the entrance to the shopping zone called Merchant City—is a stately, Neoclassical, bank-like building. This was once the **private mansion** of one of the tobacco lords, the super-rich businessmen who reigned here through the 1700s, stomping through the city with gold-tipped canes. During the port's heyday, these entrepreneurs helped Glasgow become Europe's sixth-biggest city—number two in the British Empire.

Today the mansion houses the **Glasgow Gallery of Modern Art,** nicknamed GoMA. Circle around the building to the main

entry (at the equestrian statue of the Duke of Wellington, often creatively decorated as Glasgow's favorite conehead), and step back to take in the full Neoclassical facade. On the pediment, notice the funky, mirrored mosaic celebrating the miracles of St. Mungo—an example of how Glasgow refuses to take itself too seriously. The temporary exhibits inside

GoMA are generally forgettable, but the museum does have an unusual charter: It displays only the work of living artists (free, £2 suggested donation, daily 10:00-17:00, TI inside and downstairs).

• *Facing the fanciful GoMA facade, turn right up Queen Street. Within a block, you'll reach...*

GLASGOW

❹ George Square

This square, the centerpiece of Glasgow, is filled with statues and lined with notable buildings, such as the Queen Street train station and the Glasgow City Chambers. (It's the big Neoclassical building standing like a secular church to the east; pop in to see its grand ground floor.) In front of the City Chambers stands a monument to Glaswegians killed fighting in the World Wars. The square is decorated with a *Who's Who* of statues depicting great Glaswegians. Find James Watt (the only

guy with a chair; he perfected the steam engine that helped power Europe into the Industrial Age), as well as Scotland's two top literary figures: Robert Burns and Sir Walter Scott (capping the tallest pillar in the center). The twin equestrian statues are of Prince Albert and a skinny Queen Victoria—a rare image of her in her more svelte youth.

• *Just past skinny Vic and Robert Peel, turn left onto West George Street, and cross Buchanan Street to the tall church in the middle of...*

❺ Nelson Mandela Place

This first public space named for Nelson Mandela honors the man who, while still in prison, helped bring down apartheid in South Africa. The square was renamed in the 1980s while apartheid was still in place—and when the South African consulate was on it. Subsequently, anyone sending the consulate a letter had to address it with the name of the man who embodied the anti-apartheid spirit: Mandela. (Glasgow, nicknamed Red Clyde Side for its socialist politics and empathy for the working class, has been quick to jump on progressive causes.)

The area around St. George's Church features some interesting bits of architectural detail. Facing the church's left side are the three circular friezes of the former **Stock Exchange** (with a Neo-Gothic facade, built in 1875). These idealized heads represent the industries that made Glasgow prosperous during its prime: building, engineering, and mining.

Around the back of the church, find the **Athenaeum,** the sandy-colored building at #8 (notice the low-profile label over the door). Now a law office, this was founded in 1847 as a school and city library during Glasgow's Golden Age. (Charles Dickens gave the building's inaugural address.) Like Edinburgh, Glasgow was at the forefront of the 18th-century Scottish Enlightenment, a celebration of education and intellectualism. The Scots were known for their extremely practical brand of humanism; all members of society, including the merchant and working classes, were expected to be well educated. Look above the door to find the symbolic statue of a reader sharing books with young children, an embodiment of this ideal.

• *Return to the big, pedestrianized Buchanan Street in front of the church. Head uphill.*

❻ Buchanan Street to Sauchiehall Street (More of the Golden Zed)

A short distance uphill is the glass entry to Glasgow's subway. Soon after, on the right, you'll pass the Buchanan Galleries, an indoor mall that sprawls through several city blocks (filled with shopping temptations and offering a refuge in rainy weather).

Whisky Side-trip: For a fun education in whisky, take a little detour. At Buchanan Galleries, head left down Bath Street 1.5 blocks to #23, where stairs lead down into **The Good Spirits Company**. This happy world of whisky is run by two young aficionados (Shane and Matthew) and their booze-geek staff. They welcome you to taste and learn (Mon-Sat 10:00-19:00, Sun 12:00-17:00, tel. 0141/258-8427).

• *Returning to Buchanan Street, continue uphill to the top.*

At the top of Buchanan Street stands the **Glasgow Royal Concert Hall.** Its steps are a favorite perch where local office workers munch lunch and enjoy the street scene. The statue is of **Donald Dewar,** who served as Scotland's first ever "First Minister" after the Scottish Parliament reconvened in 1999 (previously they'd been serving in London—as part of the British Parliament—since 1707).

• *From here, the Golden Zed zags left, Buchanan Street becomes Sauchiehall Street, and the shopping gets cheaper and less elegant. While*

Charles Rennie Mackintosh (1868-1928)

Charles Rennie Mackintosh brought an exuberant Art Nouveau influence to the architecture of his hometown. His designs challenged the city planners of this otherwise practical, working-class port city to create beauty in the buildings they commissioned.

As a student traveling in Italy, Mackintosh ignored the paintings inside museums and set up his easel to paint the exteriors of churches and buildings instead. He rejected the architectural traditions of ancient Greece and Rome. In Venice and Ravenna, he fell under the spell of Byzantine design, and in Siena he saw a unified, medieval city design he would try to import—but with a Scottish flavor and palette—to Glasgow.

When Mackintosh was at the Glasgow School of Art, the Industrial Age dominated life. Factories belched black soot as they burned coal and forged steel. Mackintosh and his artist friends drew inspiration from nature and created some of the first Art Nouveau buildings, paintings, drawings, and furniture. His first commission came in 1893, to design an extension to the Glasgow Herald building. More work followed, including the Glasgow School of Art and the Willow Tea Rooms.

A radical thinker, Mackintosh shared credit with his artist wife, Margaret MacDonald (who specialized in glass and metalwork). He once famously said, "I have the talent...Margaret has the genius." The two teamed up with another husband-and-wife duo—Herbert MacNair and Margaret's sister, Frances MacDonald—to define a new strain of Scottish Art Nouveau, called the "Glasgow Style." These influential couples were known as

there's little of note to see, it's still an entertaining stroll. Walk a few blocks, passing "Pound Shops" (the equivalent of "dollar stores"), newspaper hawkers, beggars, buskers, souvenir shops, and a good bookstore. Enjoy the people-watching. Just before the end of the pedestrian zone, on the left side (at #217), are the...

❼ Willow Tea Rooms

Tearooms were hugely popular during the industrial boom of the late 19th century. As Glasgow grew, more people moved to the suburbs, meaning that office workers couldn't easily return home for lunch. And during this age of Victorian morals, the temperance movement was trying to discourage the consumption of alcohol.

"the Glasgow Four."

Mackintosh's works show a strong Japanese influence, particularly in his use of black-and-white contrast to highlight the idealized forms of nature. He also drew inspiration from the Arts and Crafts movement, with an eye to simplicity, clean lines, respect for tradition, and an emphasis on precise craftsmanship over mass production. While some of his designs appear to be repeated, no two motifs are exactly alike—just as nothing is exactly the same in nature.

Mackintosh insisted on designing every element of his commissions—even the furniture, curtains, and cutlery. As a furniture and woodwork designer, Mackintosh preferred to use cheaper materials, then paint them with several thick coats, hiding seams and imperfections and making the piece feel carved rather than built. His projects often went past deadline and over budget, but resulted in unusually harmonious spaces.

Mackintosh inspired other artists, such as painter Gustav Klimt and Bauhaus founder Walter Gropius, but his vision was not appreciated in his own time as much as it is now; he died poor. Now, a century after Scotland's greatest architect set pencil to paper, his hometown is at last celebrating his unique vision.

In Glasgow, there are four main Mackintosh sights (listed in order of importance and all described in this chapter): The Mackintosh House (a reconstruction of his 1906 home filled with his actual furniture, on the University of Glasgow campus); the Kelvingrove Art Gallery (with a wonderful exhibit of his work along with the other three of the "Glasgow Four"); the Willow Tea Rooms (a functioning tearoom entirely furnished in the Mackintosh style); and the Glasgow School of Art (the building is his design but it was gutted by fire and is closed until 2019). For the mildly interested traveler, the easiest way to "experience" Mackintosh is to focus on the Kelvingrove Art Gallery exhibit and perhaps pop into the Willow Tea Rooms.

Tearooms were designed to be an appealing alternative to eating in pubs.

These tearooms, opened in 1903, are also an Art Nouveau masterpiece by Charles Rennie Mackintosh. Mackintosh made

his living from design commissions, including multiple tearooms for businesswoman Kate Cranston. Mackintosh designed everything here—down to the furniture, lighting, and cutlery. He took his theme for the café from the name of the street it's on—*saugh* is Scots for willow.

In the design of these tearooms, there was a meeting of the (very modern) minds. In addition to giving office workers an alternative to pubs, Cranston also wanted a place where women could gather while unescorted—in a time when traveling solo could give a woman a less-than-desirable reputation. An ardent women's rights supporter, Cranston requested that the rooms be bathed in white, the suffragettes' signature color.

At the Willows, you can have tea or just browse the exhibits showcasing his designs along with Mackintosh-inspired jewelry. The almost-hidden Room de Luxe dining room (upstairs) appears just as it did in Mackintosh's day, though most features are reproductions, such as the chairs and the doors, which were too fragile to survive (for details, see listing on page 842).

• *Our walk ends here. Within a few minutes' stroll are three more interesting sights. One of those is the Glasgow School of Art, which was gutted by a 2014 fire. Before the fire, this building, designed by 28-year-old Charles Rennie Mackintosh, attracted architects from far and wide. Now it's closed for a few years for repairs. Until it reopens, there are better Mackintosh sights for his fans to visit.*

Two additional sights (described later) lie within a five-minute stroll (in different directions). The remarkably preserved Tenement House offers a fascinating glimpse into Glasgow lifestyles in the early 1900s. And the National Piping Centre goes beyond the clichés and provides a better appreciation for the history and musicality of Scotland's favorite instrument.

WEST END WALK

Glasgow's West End—just a quick subway, bus, or taxi ride from downtown—is the city's top residential neighborhood. (Since this walk is most worthwhile as a scenic way to connect several important museums, be sure to do this when they're open.) As in so many British cities, the western part of town—upwind of industrial pollution—was the most desirable. This area has great restaurants and nightlife (see "Eating in Glasgow" and "Nightlife and Entertainment in Glasgow," later) and fine accommodations (see "Sleeping in Glasgow," later). This walk begins at the Hillhead subway stop, meanders through dining and residential zones, explores some grand old university buildings (and related museums), and ends with a wander through the park to the Kelvingrove Museum—Glasgow's top museum. To trace the route, see the map on page 832.

• *Start at the Hillhead subway station. Exiting the station, turn right and walk four short blocks up...*

Byres Road: A *byre* is a cowshed. So back when this was farmland outside the big city, cattle were housed along here. Today, Byres Road is a main thoroughfare through a trendy district. A block before the big intersection, notice the **Waitrose** supermarket on the left. In Britain, this upscale grocery is a sure sign of a posh neighborhood.

Approaching the corner with Great Western Road, you'll see a church spire on the right. Dating from 1862, this church was converted into a restaurant and music venue called **Òran Mòr** (Gaelic for "The Great Music"). Step into the entryway to see the colorful murals (by Alasdair Gray, a respected Glaswegian artist and novelist). Consider a drink or meal in their pub (try some whisky—they have more than 300 varieties). Also check what's on while you're in town, as this is a prime music and theater venue.

• *If the weather's good, cross Great Western Road and head into the...*

Glasgow Botanic Gardens: This inviting parkland is the

Glaswegians' favorite place to enjoy a break from the bustling city. And, like so many things in Glasgow, it's free. Locals brag about their many parks, claiming that—despite their industrial reputation—they have more green space per capita than any other city in Europe. And even

the city's name comes from the Gaelic for "the dear green place."

Before going into the park, pause at the red-brick entrance gate. On the gate on the left, look for Glasgow's quite busy **city seal,** which honors St. Mungo, the near-legendary town founder. The jumble of symbols (a bird, a tree, a bell, and a salmon with a ring in its mouth) recall Mungo's four key miracles. Ask any Glaswegian to tell you the tales of St. Mungo—they learn it all by heart. The city motto, "Let Glasgow Flourish," is apt—particularly given its recent rejuvenation following a long, crippling period of industrial rot. Glasgow's current renaissance was kicked off with an ambitious 1989 garden festival in a disused former shipyard. Now the city is one of Europe's trendiest success stories. Let Glasgow flourish, indeed.

Head into the park. If the sun's out, it'll be jammed with people enjoying some rare rays. Young lads wait all winter for the day when they can cry, "Sun's oot, taps aff!" and pull off their shirts to make the most of it.

In addition to the finely landscaped gardens, the park has two inviting greenhouse pavilions—both free and open to the public. The big white one on the right (from 1873, open 10:00-18:00) is the most elegant, with classical statues scattered among the palm fronds (but beware the killer plants, to

GLASGOW

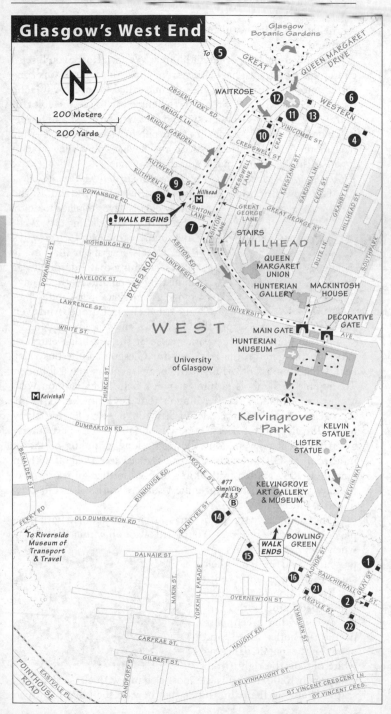

Glasgow's West End

N

200 Meters

200 Yards

Glasgow Botanic Gardens

To 5

GREAT

QUEEN MARGARET DRIVE

WESTERN

WAITROSE

OBSERVATORY RD.

ARHOLE LN.

ARHOLE GARDEN

6

12

11 13

CRAN

VINICOMBE ST.

10

4

CRESSWELL ST.

CRESSWELL LANE

KERSLAND ST.

SARDINIA LN.

CECIL ST.

GRANBY LN.

HILLHEAD ST.

RUTHVEN ST.

RUTHVEN LN.

DOWANSIDE RD.

9

8

Hillhead M

WALK BEGINS

ASHTON LANE

ASHTON LANE

7

GREAT GEORGE LANE

GREAT GEORGE ST.

STAIRS

HILLHEAD

BUTE LN.

SOUTHPARK

HIGHBURGH RD.

HAVELOCK ST.

LAWRENCE ST.

WHITE ST.

DOWANHILL ST.

BYRES ROAD

ASHTON RD.

UNIVERSITY AVE.

QUEEN MARGARET UNION

HUNTERIAN GALLERY

MACKINTOSH HOUSE

UNIVERSITY

W E S T

University of Glasgow

CHURCH ST.

M Kelvinhall

DUMBARTON RD.

MAIN GATE

HUNTERIAN MUSEUM

DECORATIVE GATE

AVE.

Kelvingrove Park

KELVIN STATUE

LISTER STATUE

BENALDER ST.

FERRY RD.

To Riverside Museum of Transport & Travel

BUNHOUSE RD.

OLD DUMBARTON RD.

ARGYLE ST.

BLANTYRE ST.

#77 SimpliCity #2 & 3
B

KELVINGROVE ART GALLERY & MUSEUM

14

KELVIN WAY

KELVIN ST.

WALK ENDS

BOWLING GREEN

15

16

1

DALNAIR ST.

NARIN ST.

YORKHILL PARADE

HAUGH RD.

OVERNEWTON ST.

RADNOR ST.

GRAY ST.

SAUCHIEHALL ST.

ARGYLE ST.

LYMBURN ST.

21

2

22

GARFRAE ST.

SANDFORD ST.

GILBERT ST.

EASTVALE PL.

POINTHOUSE ROAD

KELVINHAUGHT ST.

ST. VINCENT CRESCENT LN.

ST. VINCENT CRES.

GLASGOW

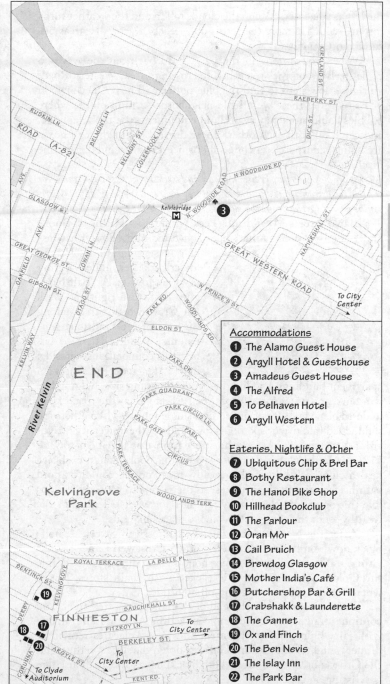

ROAD (A-82)

RUSKIN LN.

BELMONT LN.

COLEBROOK LN.

BELMONT ST.

AVE.

GLASGOW ST.

AVE.

OAKFIELD

GREAT GEORGE ST.

GIBSON ST.

OTAGO ST.

COWAN LN.

Kelvinbridge M

N WOODSIDE ROAD

N. WOODSIDE RD.

3

RAEBERRY ST.

DICK ST.

KIRKLAND ST.

NAPIERSHALL ST.

GREAT WESTERN ROAD

W. PRINCE'S ST.

To City
Center

ELDON ST.

PARK RD.

WOODLANDS RD.

KELVIN WAY

River Kelvin

E N D

PARK DR.

PARK QUADRANT

PARK CIRCUS LN.

PARK GATE

PARK CIRCUS

PARK TERRACE

WOODLANDS TERR.

Kelvingrove
Park

ROYAL TERRACE

LA BELLE PL.

BENTINCK ST.

KELVINGROVE

19

DERBY

SAUCHIEHALL ST.

17

FINNIESTON

FITZROY LN.

18

20

To
City Center

CORUNNA

ARGYLE ST.

BERKELEY ST.

To
City Center

To Clyde
Auditorium

KENT RD.

Accommodations
1. The Alamo Guest House
2. Argyll Hotel & Guesthouse
3. Amadeus Guest House
4. The Alfred
5. To Belhaven Hotel
6. Argyll Western

Eateries, Nightlife & Other
7. Ubiquitous Chip & Brel Bar
8. Bothy Restaurant
9. The Hanoi Bike Shop
10. Hillhead Bookclub
11. The Parlour
12. Òran Mòr
13. Cail Bruich
14. Brewdog Glasgow
15. Mother India's Café
16. Butchershop Bar & Grill
17. Crabshakk & Launderette
18. The Gannet
19. Ox and Finch
20. The Ben Nevis
21. The Islay Inn
22. The Park Bar

the left as you enter). When the clouds roll in and the weather turns rotten—which is more the status quo—these warm, dry areas become quite popular.

When you're done in the park, head back out the way you came in. Back on the street, before crossing Great Western Road, go right a few steps to find the blue **police call box.** Once an icon of British life, these were little neighborhood mini offices where bobbies could store paperwork and equipment, use the telephone, and catch up with each other. These days, some of the call boxes are being repurposed as coffee shops, ice-cream stands, and time machines.

• *Cross back over Great Western Road and backtrack (past the Òran Mòr church/restaurant) one block down Byres Road. Turn left down Vinicombe Street (across from the Waitrose). Now we'll explore...*

Back-Streets West End: Peek inside the **Hillhead Bookclub**—a former cinema that's been converted into a hipster bar/res-

taurant serving affordable food (described later, under "Eating in Glasgow"). A half-block after that, turn right and walk (on Crawnworth Street) along the row of red-sandstone **tenements.** While that word has negative connotations stateside, here a "tenement" is simply an apartment building. And judging from the grand size, bulging bay windows, and prime location of these, it's safe to say they're far from undesirable. Many are occupied by a single family, while others are subdivided into five or six rooms for students (the university is right around the corner). Across the street from this tenement row (at #12) is a **baths club**—a private swimming pool, like an exclusive health club back home. Historically, most people couldn't afford bathing facilities in their homes, so they came to central locations like this one to get clean every few days (or weeks). Today, it's the wealthy—not the poor—who come to places like this.

After the baths, turn right down Cresswell Street. A half-block down on the right, turn left down **Cresswell Lane**—an inviting, traffic-free, brick-floored shopping and dining zone. While the Golden Zed downtown is packed with chain stores, this is where you'll find charming one-off boutiques.

Browse your way to the end of the lane, cross the street, and continue straight to the even more appealing **Ashton Lane,** strung with fairy lights. Scout this street and pick a place to return for dinner tonight. Fancy a film? Halfway down the street on the right, the Grosvenor Cinema shows both blockbusters and art-house fare (see listing on page 849).

• *When you reach the end of the lane, take a very sharp left up the stairs (with the beer garden for Brel on your left). At the top of the stairs, turn right along the road. You're now walking through the modern part of the...*

University of Glasgow Campus: Founded in 1451, this is Scotland's second-oldest university (after St. Andrews). Its 24,000 students sprawl through the West End. Unlike the fancy "old university" buildings, this area is gloomy and concrete. The ugly, gray building on your left is the Queen Margaret Union, with a music venue that has hosted several big-name bands before they were famous—from Nirvana to Franz Ferdinand. (If you think Franz Ferdinand is an Austrian archduke rather than a Scottish alternative rock band...you've been out of college too long.)

• *Eventually you'll reach a wide cross street, University Avenue. Turn left up this street and walk two more blocks uphill. At the traffic light, the Hunterian Gallery and Mackintosh House are just up the hill on your left, and the Hunterian Museum is across the street on the right.*

Hunterian Gallery and Mackintosh House: First, stop in at the Hunterian Gallery to tour the Mackintosh House. In the morning, visits are by tour only; later you can free flow (admission is limited). Ask if there's a wait, and if so, spend your time either in the adjacent gallery, the wonderful university cafeteria (across the lane, cheap and cheery lunch), or the Hunterian Museum across the street. All three sights (the Mackintosh House, Hunterian Gallery, and Hunterian Museum) are important if you have the time and energy (for details, see page 842).

• *When you're done here, head for the Hunterian Museum in the university's big old main building across University Avenue. Instead of going through the main gate, go to the left end of the building facing the street to find a more interesting decorative gate.*

University of Glasgow Main Building: Take a good look at the gate, which is decorated with the names of illustrious alums. Pick out the great Scots you're familiar with: James Watt, King James II, Adam Smith, Lord Kelvin, William Hunter (the namesake of the university's museums), and Donald Dewar, a driving force behind devolution who became Scotland's first "First Minister" in 1999.

Go through the gate and face the main university building. Stretching to the left is Graduation Hall, where commencement takes place. Head straight into the building, ride the elevator to floor 4, and enjoy the **Hunterian Museum.**

After you visit the Hunterian Museum, find the grand staircase down (in the room with the Antonine Wall exhibit). You'll

emerge into one of the twin quads enclosed by the enormous ensemble of university buildings. Veer right to find your way into the atmospheric, Neo-Gothic **cloisters** that support the wing separating the two quads. These are modeled after the Gothic cloisters in the lower chapel of Glasgow Cathedral, across town. On the other side, you'll pop out into the adjoining quad. Enjoy pretending you're a student for a few minutes, then head out the door at the bottom of the quad.

Leaving the university complex, head for the tall flagpole on a bluff overlooking a grand view. The turreted building just below is the Kelvingrove Museum, where this walk ends. (If you get turned around in the park, just head for those spires.)

• *From the flagpole, turn left and head to the end of the big building. Head down the stairs leading through the woods on your right (marked* James Watt Building). *When you reach the busy road, turn right along it for a short distance, then—as soon as you can—angle to the right back into the green space of...*

Kelvingrove Park: Another of Glasgow's favorite parks, this originated in the Victorian period, when there was a renewed focus on trying to get people out into green spaces. One of the first things you'll come to is a big statue of **Lord Kelvin** (1824-1907). Born William Thomson, he chose to take the name of the River Kelvin, which runs through Glasgow (and gives its name to many other things here, including the museum we're headed to). One of the most respected scientists of his time, Kelvin was a pioneer in the field of thermodynamics, and gave his name (or, actually, the river's) to a new, absolute unit of temperature measurement designed to replace Celsius and Fahrenheit.

Just past Kelvin, bear left at the statue of **Joseph Lister** (1827-1912, of "Listerine" fame—he pioneered the use of antiseptics to remove infection-causing germs from the surgical environment), and take the bridge across the River Kelvin. Once across the bridge, turn right toward the museum. You'll walk along a pleasant bowling green that was built for the Commonwealth Games that Glasgow hosted in 2014. They keep it free and open to anyone—hoping to create a popular interest in this very old and genteel sport (see page 845 for details).

Now's the time to explore the Kelvingrove Museum, described on page 844.

• *When you're finished at the museum, exit out the back end, toward the busy road. Several recommended restaurants are ahead and to the left, in the Finnieston neighborhood (see page 857). Or, if you'd like to hop on the subway, just turn right along Argyle Street and walk five minutes to the Kelvinhall station.*

Sights in Glasgow

DOWNTOWN
▲▲Tenement House

Here's a chance to drop into a perfectly preserved 1930s-era middle-class residence. The National Trust for Scotland bought this otherwise ordinary row home, located in a residential neighborhood, because of the peculiar tendencies of Miss Agnes Toward (1886-1975). For five decades, she kept her home essentially unchanged. The kitchen calendar is still set for 1935, and canisters of licorice powder (a laxative) still sit on the bathroom shelf. It's a time-warp experience, where Glaswegian old-timers enjoy coming to reminisce about how they grew up.

Cost and Hours: £6.50, April-Oct daily 13:00-17:00, July-Aug from 11:00, closed Nov-March, guidebook-£3, 145 Buccleuch Street (pronounced "ba-KLOO"), down from the top of Garnethill, tel. 0141/333-0183, www.nts.org.uk.

Visiting the House: Buy your ticket on the main floor, and poke around the little museum. You'll learn that in Glasgow, a "tenement" isn't a slum—it's simply an apartment house. In fact, tenements like these were typical for every class except the richest. Then head upstairs to the apartment, which is staffed by caring volunteers. Ring the doorbell to request entrance. Explore the four little rooms. Imagine a world without electricity (Miss Toward was a late adapter, making the leap to electricity only in 1960). Ask about the utility of the iron stove. Ponder the importance of that drawer full of coal and how that stove heated her entire world. Ask why the bed is in the kitchen. As you look through the rooms laced with Victorian trinkets—such as the ceramic dogs on the living room's fireplace mantle—consider how different they are from Mackintosh's stark, minimalist designs from the same period.

▲National Piping Centre

If you consider bagpipes a tacky Scottish cliché, think again. At this small but insightful museum, you'll get a scholarly lesson in the proud and fascinating history of the bagpipe. For those with a healthy attention span for history or musical instruments—ideally both—it's fascinating. On Thursdays, Fridays, and Saturdays at 11:00 and 14:00 a piper is on hand to perform, answer questions, and show you around the collection. At other times, if it's quiet, ask the ticket-sellers to tell you more—some are bagpipe students at the music school across the street. The center also offers a shop, lessons, a restaurant, and accommodations.

Cost and Hours: £4.50, includes audioguide, Mon-Thu 9:00-19:00, Fri until 17:00, Sat until 15:00, closed Sun, 30 McPhater Street, tel. 0141/353-5551, www.thepipingcentre.co.uk.

Visiting the Museum: The collection is basically one big room packed with well-described exhibits, including several historic bagpipes. You'll learn that bagpipes

from as far away as Italy, Spain, and Bohemia predated Scottish ones; that Lowlands bagpipes were traditionally bellows-blown rather than lung-powered; and why bagpipes started being used to inspire Scottish soldiers on the battlefield. At the back of the room, look for the hand-engraved, backward printing plates for bagpipe sheet music (which didn't exist until the 19th century). The thoughtful, beautifully produced audioguide—which mixes a knowledgeable commentary with sound bites of bagpipes being played and brief interviews with performers—feels like a 40-minute audio-documentary on the BBC. The 15-minute film shown at the end of the room sums up the collection helpfully. They also have a basket of chanters and a practice set of bagpipes in case you want to try your hand. The chanter fingering is easy if you play the recorder, but keeping the bag inflated is exhausting.

Glasgow School of Art

When he was just 28 years old—and still a no-name junior draughtsman for a big architectural firm—Charles Rennie Mackintosh won the contest to create a new home for the Glasgow School of Art. He threw himself into the project, designing every detail of the building, inside and out. Remember that this work was the Art Nouveau original, and that Frank Lloyd Wright, the Art Deco Chrysler Building, and everything that resembles it came well after Charles Rennie Mack's time.

Unfortunately, the building was badly damaged by a fire in May 2014. It likely won't open again until 2019 at the earliest. For now, you can join the underwhelming tour of the **Reid Building,** which includes insight about the architecture of the School of Art and a visit to a small room full of furniture designed by Mackintosh and his wife, Margaret MacDonald. Or you can visit the small, free exhibition about Mackintosh, including an impressive model of the School of Art (shop, exhibition, and tour desk open daily during renovation 10:00-16:30).

Tours: Tours are £7 and last 45 minutes; 6/day in peak season, 4/day in off-season, check times online (tel. 0141/353-4526, www. gsa.ac.uk/tours). Serious admirers can ask about the 2.25-hour Mackintosh-themed city walking tours given by students (£20, 4/ week).

CATHEDRAL PRECINCT, WITH A HINT OF MEDIEVAL GLASGOW

Very little remains of medieval Glasgow, but a visit to the cathedral and the area around it is a visit to the birthplace of the city. The first church was built here in the seventh century. Today's towering cathedral is mostly 13th century—the only great Scottish church to survive the Reformation intact. In front of the cathedral (near the street), you'll see an attention-grabbing statue of **David Livingstone** (1813-1873). Livingstone—the Scottish missionary, explorer, and cartographer who discovered a huge waterfall in Africa and named it in honor of his queen, Victoria—was born eight miles from here.

Nearby, the Provand's Lordship is Glasgow's only secular building dating from the Middle Ages. The St. Mungo Museum of Religious Life and Art, built on the site of the old Bishop's Castle, is a unique exhibit covering the spectrum of religions. And the Necropolis, blanketing the hill behind the cathedral, provides an atmospheric walk through a world of stately Victorian tombstones. From there you can scan the city and look down on the brewery where Tennent's Lager (a longtime Glasgow favorite) has been made since 1885. And, if the spirit moves you, hike on down and tour the brewery (described later).

The following sights are within close range of each other. As you face the cathedral, the St. Mungo Museum is on your right (with handy public WCs), the Provand's Lordship is across the street from St. Mungo, and the Necropolis is behind the cathedral and to the right. The brewery is a 10-minute walk away.

To reach these sights from Buchanan Street, turn east on Bath Street, which soon becomes Cathedral Street, and walk about 15 minutes (or hop a bus along the main drag—try bus #38, or #57, confirm with driver that the bus stops at the cathedral). To head to

the Kelvingrove Museum after your visit, from the cathedral, walk
two blocks up Castle Street and catch bus #19 (on the cathedral
side).

▲Glasgow Cathedral

This blackened, Gothic cathedral is a rare example of an intact
pre-Reformation Scottish cathedral. (It was once known as "the

Pink Church" for the tone of
its stone, but with Industrial
Age soot and modern pollution, it blackened. Cleaning
would damage the integrity
of the stone structure, so it
was left black.) The zealous
Reformation forces of John
Knox ripped out the stained
glass and ornate chapels of
the Catholic age, but they left the church standing. The church
is aching to tell its long and fascinating story and volunteers are
standing by to do just that.

Cost and Hours: Free, £3 suggested donation; Mon-Sat 9:30-
17:30, Sun 13:00-17:00; Oct-March until 16:00; request a free
tour or join one in progress; near junction of Castle and Cathedral
Streets, tel. 0141/552-8198, www.glasgowcathedral.org.uk.

Visiting the Cathedral: Inside, look up to see the wooden
barrel-vaulted ceiling, and take in the beautifully decorated section

over the choir ("quire"). The choir
screen is the only pre-Reformation
screen surviving in Scotland. It
divided the common people from
the priests and big shots of the day,
who got to worship closer to the religious action. The cathedral's glass
dates mostly from the 19th century.
One window on the right side of

the choir, celebrating the 14 trades of Glasgow (try to find them),
dates from 1951. Left of that is a set of three windows that tell the
story of St. Mungo retrieving a ring from the mouth of a fish (it's
a long story).

Step into the choir and enjoy the east end with the four evan-
gelists presiding high above in stained glass. Two seats (with high
backs, right of altar) are reserved for Queen Elizabeth II and her
husband Prince Philip, the Duke of Edinburgh.

Step into the lower church (down stairs on right as you face the
choir), where the central altar sits upon St. Mungo's tomb. Mungo
was the seventh-century Scottish monk and mythical founder of

Glasgow who established the first wooden church on this spot and gave Glasgow its name. Notice the ceiling bosses (decorative caps where the ribs come together) with their colorfully carved demons, dragons, and skulls.

Nearby: On Cathedral Square, you'll find the cute Empire Coffee Box, where Rocco is ready to caffeinate you from this old-style police call box.

▲Necropolis

From the cathedral, a lane leads over the "bridge of sighs" into the park filled with grand tombstones. Glasgow's huge burial hill has a wistful, ramshackle appeal. A stroll among the tombstones of the eminent Glaswegians of the 19th century gives a glimpse of Victorian Glasgow and a feeling for the confidence and wealth of the second city of the British Empire in its glory days.

With the Industrial Age (in the early 1800s), Glasgow's population tripled to 200,000. The existing churchyards were jammed and unhygienic. The city needed a beautiful place in which to bury its beautiful citizens, so this grand necropolis was established. Because Presbyterians are more into simplicity, the statuary is simpler than in a Catholic cemetery. Wandering among the disintegrating memorials to once-important people, I thought about how, someday, everyone's tombstone will fall over and no one will care.

The highest pillar in the graveyard is a memorial to John Knox. The Great Reformer (who's actually buried in Edinburgh) looks down at the cathedral he wanted to strip of all art, and even tear down. (The Glaswegians rallied to follow Knox, but saved the church.) If the cemetery's main black gates are closed, see if you can get in and out through a gate off the street to the right.

▲St. Mungo Museum of Religious Life and Art

This secular, city-run museum, just in front of the cathedral, aims to promote religious understanding. Built in 1990 on the site of the old Bishop's Castle, it provides a handy summary of major and minor world religions, showing how each faith handles various rites of passage across the human life span: birth, puberty, marriage, death, and everything in between and after. Start with the 10-minute video overview on the first floor, and finish with a great view from the top floor of the cathedral and Necropolis. Ponder the Zen Buddhist garden out back as you leave.

Cost and Hours: Free, £3 suggested donation, Tue-Thu and Sat 10:00-17:00, Fri and Sun from 11:00, closed Mon, free

WCs downstairs, cheap ground-floor café, 2 Castle Street, tel. 0141/276-1625, www. glasgowmuseums.com.

Nearby: To view a modern-day depiction of St. Mungo, walk two minutes down High Street from the museum to a building-sized mural by the artist Smug.

Provand's Lordship

With low beams and medieval decor, this creaky home—supposedly the "oldest house in Glasgow"—is the only secular building surviving in Glasgow from the Middle Ages. On three floors it displays the *Lifestyles of the Rich and Famous*...circa 1471. First, sit down and watch the 10-minute video (ground floor). The interior, while sparse and stony, shows off a few pieces of furniture from the 16th, 17th, and 18th centuries. Out back, explore the St. Nicholas Garden, which was once part of a hospital that dispensed herbal remedies. The plaques in each section show the part of the body each plant is used to treat.

Cost and Hours: Free, small donation requested, Tue-Thu and Sat 10:00-17:00, Fri and Sun from 11:00, closed Mon, across the street from St. Mungo Museum at 3 Castle Street, tel. 0141/552-8819, www.glasgowmuseums.com.

▲▲Tennent's Brewery Tour

Tennent's, founded in 1740, is now the biggest brewery in Scotland, spanning 18 acres. They give serious hour-long tours showing how they make "Scotland's favorite pint," and how they fill 700 kegs per hour and 1,000 bottles per minute (you'll see more action Mon-Fri). It's hot and sweaty inside, with 100 steps to climb on your tour. When you're done (surrounded by "the Lager Lovelies"—cans from 1965 to 1993 that were decorated with cover girls), you'll enjoy three samples followed by a pint of your choice (£10, tours depart daily at 10:00, 12:00, 14:00, 16:00, & 18:00; call or book online; 161 Duke Street, 0141/202-7145, www.tennentstours.com). To head back downtown, bus #41 stops in front of the brewery on Duke Street and goes to George Square.

THE WEST END

These sights are linked by my West End Walk on page 830.

▲Hunterian Gallery and Mackintosh House

Here's a sightseeing twofer: an art gallery offering a good look at some Scottish artists relatively unknown outside their homeland, and the chance to take a guided tour through the reconstructed home of Charles Rennie Mackintosh, decorated exactly the way he liked it. For Charles Rennie Mack fans—or anyone fascinated by the unique habitats of artists—it's well worth a visit.

Cost and Hours: Gallery—free, Tue-Sat 10:00-17:00, Sun 11:00-16:00, closed Mon, across University Avenue from the main university building, tel. 0141/330-4221, www.gla.ac.uk/hunterian. Mackintosh House—£5, same hours as gallery, last entry 45 minutes before closing. The Mackintosh House is open weekday mornings by 30-minute tour only (Tue-Fri 10:00-12:30, departs every 30 minutes). After 13:00, and all day Sat-Sun, the house is open without a tour, but only 12 people are allowed at a time, so there may be a short wait.

Visitor Information: First, check in at the reception desk to sign up for a tour of the Mackintosh House or see if there's a wait to get in. You'll also need to check any bags (free lockers available). Spend your waiting time visiting the gallery, or, with a longer wait, head across the street to the Hunterian Museum (described later). If it's lunchtime, eat at **$ Food,** a cheap, healthy, fast, and modern student cafeteria across the lane from the museum that's open to the public.

Mackintosh House: In 1906, Mackintosh and his wife, Margaret MacDonald, moved into the end unit of a Victorian row house. Mackintosh gutted the place and redesigned it to his own liking—bathing the interior in his trademark style, a mix of curving, organic lines and rigid, proto-Art Deco functionalism. They moved out in 1914, and the house was demolished in the 1960s—but the university wisely documented the layout and carefully removed and preserved all of Mackintosh's original furnishings. In 1981, when respect for Mackintosh was on the rise, they built this replica house and reinstalled everything just as Mackintosh had designed it. You'll see the entryway, dining room, drawing room, and bedroom—each one offering glimpses into the minds of these great artists. You'll see original furniture and decorations by Mackintosh and MacDonald, providing insight into their creative process.

Hunterian Art Gallery: The adjacent gallery is manageable and worth exploring. Circling one floor, you'll enjoy three thoughtfully described sections. One highlight is the modern Scottish art (1850-1960), focusing on two groups: the "Glasgow Boys," who traveled to France to study during the waning days of Realism (1880s), and, a generation later, the Scottish Colourists, who found a completely different inspiration in circa-1910

France—bright, bold, with an almost Picasso-like exuberance. The gallery also has an extensive collection of portraits by American artist James Whistler—Whistler's wife was of Scottish descent, as was Whistler's mother. (Hey, that has a nice ring to it.) The painter always found great support in Scotland, and his heir donated his estate to the University of Glasgow.

▲Hunterian Museum

The oldest public museum in Scotland was founded by William Hunter (1718-1783), a medical researcher. Today his natural science collection is housed in a huge and gorgeous space inside the university's showcase building. Everything is well presented and well explained. You'll see a perceptive exhibit on the Antonine Wall (the lesser-known cousin of Hadrian's Wall), built in A.D. 142 to seal off the Picts from the Roman Empire. Ancient Roman artifacts on display include leather shoes, plumbing, weapons, and carved reliefs. The eclectic collection also includes musical instruments, a display on the Glasgow-built *Lusitania*, and a fine collection of fossils, including the aquatic dinosaur called plesiosaur (possibly a distant ancestor of the Loch Ness monster). But to some, most fascinating are the many examples of deformities—two-headed animals, body parts in jars, and so on (main hall, left of Romans). Ever the curious medical researcher, Hunter collected these for study, and these intrigue, titillate, and nauseate visitors to this day.

Cost and Hours: Free, Tue-Sat 10:00-17:00, Sun 11:00-16:00, closed Mon, Gilbert Scott Building, University Avenue, tel. 0141/330-4221, www.gla.ac.uk/hunterian.

▲▲Kelvingrove Art Gallery and Museum

This "Scottish Smithsonian" displays everything from a stuffed elephant to paintings by the great masters and what, for me, is the city's best collection of work by Charles Rennie Mackintosh. The well-described contents are impressively displayed in a grand, 100-year-old, Spanish Baroque-style building. The Kelvingrove claims to be one of the most-visited museums in Britain—presumably because of all the field-trip groups you'll see here. Watching all the excited Scottish kids—their imaginations ablaze—is as much fun as the collection itself.

Cost and Hours: Free, £5 suggested donation, Mon-Thu and Sat 10:00-17:00, Fri and Sun from 11:00, free tours at 11:00 and 14:30, Argyle Street, tel. 0141/276-9599, www.glasgowmuseums. com.

Getting There: My self-guided West End Walk leads you here from the Hillhead subway stop, or you can ride the **subway** to the Kelvinhall stop. When you exit, turn left and walk five minutes. **Buses** #2 and #3 run from Hope Street downtown to the museum. It's also on **the hop-on, hop-off bus** route. No matter how you arrive, just look for the huge, turreted red-brick building.

Organ Concerts: At the top of the main hall, the huge pipe organ booms with a daily 30-minute recital at 13:00 (15:00 on Sunday).

Visiting the Museum: Built in 1901 to house the city collection, the museum is divided into two sections: Art ("Expression") and Natural ("Life"), each with two floors. The symmetrical floor plan can be confusing. Pick up a map and plan your strategy.

The "Expression" section, in the East Court, is marked by a commotion of heads—each with a different expression—raining down from the ceiling. This half of the museum focuses on artwork, including Dutch, Flemish, French, and Scottish Romanticism from the late 19th century. The exhibits on "Scottish Identity in Art" let you tour the country's scenic wonders and its history on canvas. The Mackintosh section, a highlight for many, demonstrates the Art Nouveau work of the "Glasgow Four," including Charles Rennie Mackintosh. Unfortunately, the museum's star painting, Salvador Dalí's *Christ of St. John of the Cross,* will be on the road until 2020.

The "Life" section, in the West Court, features a menagerie of stuffed animals (including a giraffe, kangaroo, ostrich, and moose) with a WWII-era Spitfire fighter plane hovering overhead. Branching off are halls with exhibits ranging from Ancient Egypt to "Scotland's First People" to weaponry ("Conflict and Consequence").

Kelvingrove Lawn Bowling

For a fun and free activity surrounded by relaxed locals, try your hand at lawn bowling. There's a mission behind the perfectly manicured greens next to the Kelvingrove Museum (made beautiful to host the 2014 Commonwealth Games): Keep young people interested in the traditional sport. They'll provide balls (4 per person) and a court time. It's all free and tourists are welcome. While sunny weekends may be too busy, you'll always find a court on a cloudy weekday. It's a fine evening activity; you can bowl rain or shine (April-Sept Mon-Fri 9:00-21:00, Sat-Sun until 18:00, mobile 07920-048-945). Lawn bowling is a lot like *petanque* (popular in France); the object and scoring are the same. The balls are bigger

GLASGOW

and "biased" (lopsided on purpose to let experts throw curves). Let the attendant explain the rules if necessary. (They also rent tennis gear for the adjacent courts.) An efficient plan would be to end your sightseeing day at the huge Kelvingrove Museum (closes at 17:00), play an hour of "bowls," and have dinner a couple blocks away at a recommended Finnieston restaurant of your choice. You could cap your night with a beer and live music at a Gaelic pub.

AWAY FROM THE CENTER
▲▲Riverside Museum

Located along the River Clyde, this high-tech, extremely kid-friendly museum—nostalgic and modern at the same time—is dedicated to all things transportation-related. Named the European museum of the year in 2013, visiting is a must for anyone interested in transportation and how it has shaped society.

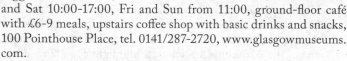

Cost and Hours: Free, £5 suggested donation, Mon-Thu and Sat 10:00-17:00, Fri and Sun from 11:00, ground-floor café with £6-9 meals, upstairs coffee shop with basic drinks and snacks, 100 Pointhouse Place, tel. 0141/287-2720, www.glasgowmuseums.com.

Getting There: It's on the riverfront promenade, two miles west of the city center. **Bus #100** runs between the museum and George Square (2/hour, last departure from George Square at 15:02, operated by McColl's), or you can take a **taxi** (£6-8, 10-minute ride from downtown). The museum is also included on the **hop-on, hop-off sightseeing bus** route (described earlier, under "Getting Around Glasgow").

Visiting the Museum: Most of the collection is strewn across one huge, wide-open floor. Upon entering, visit the info desk (to the right as you enter, near the shop) to ask about today's free tours and activities—or just listen for announcements. Also pick up a map from the info desk, as the museum's open floor plan can feel a bit like a traffic jam at rush hour.

Diving in, explore the vast collection: stagecoaches, locomotives, double-decker trolleys, and an entire wall stacked with vintage automobiles and another with motorcycles. Learn about the opening of Glasgow's old-timey subway (Europe's third oldest). Explore the collections of old toys and prams, and watch a film about 1930s cin-

ema. Stroll the re-creation of a circa-1900 main street, with video clips bringing each shop to life (there's one about a little girl who discovers her daddy was selling things to the pawn shop to pay the rent).

Don't miss the much smaller upstairs section, with great views over the River Clyde (cross the footbridge over the trains), additional exhibits about ships built here in Glasgow, and what may be the world's oldest bicycle. The description explains how two different inventors have tried to take credit for the bike—and both of them are Scottish.

Nearby: Be sure to head to the River Clyde directly behind the museum (just step out the back door). The *Glenlee*, one of five remaining tall ships built in Glasgow in the 19th century (1896), invites visitors to come aboard (free, daily 10:00-17:00, Nov-Feb until 16:00, tel. 0141/357-3699, www.thetallship.com). Good exhibits illustrate what it was like to live and work aboard  the ship. Explore the officers' living quarters, then head below deck to the café and more exhibits. Below that, the cargo hold has kids' activities and offers the chance to peek into the engine room. As you board, note the speedboat river tour that leaves from here each afternoon (£10, 20 minutes).

Burrell Collection

This eclectic art collection of a wealthy local shipping magnate—which includes sculpture from Roman to Rodin, stained glass, tapestries, furniture, Asian and Islamic works, and halls of paintings starring Cézanne, Renoir, Degas, and a Rembrandt self-portrait—is closed for renovation until at least 2020 (three miles outside the city center in Pollok Country Park, tel. 0141/287-2550, www. glasgowmuseums.com).

Shopping in Glasgow

Downtown, the **Golden Zed**—a.k.a. "Style Mile"—has all the predictable chain stores, with a few Scottish souvenir stands mixed in. For more on this, see the start of my self-guided "Get to Know Glasgow" walk. The Glasgow Modern Art Museum (GoMA) has a quirky gift shop that many find enticing.

The West End also has some appealing shops. Many are concentrated on **Cresswell Lane** (covered in my self-guided West End Walk). Browsing here, you'll find an eclectic assortment of gifty shops, art galleries, design shops, hair salons, record stores, home-decor shops, and lots of vintage bric-a-brac. Be sure to poke into De Courcy's Arcade, a two-part warren of tiny offbeat shops.

Nightlife and Entertainment in Glasgow

Glasgow has a youthful vibe, and its nightlife scene is renowned. The city is full of live music acts and venues. Walking through the city center, you'll pass at least one club or bar on every block.

PUBS AND CLUBS

Downtown: Glasgow's central business and shopping district is pretty sleepy after hours, but there are a few pockets of activity—each with its own personality. **Bath Street's** bars and clubs are focused on young professionals as well as students; the recommended Pot Still is a perfect place to sample Scotch whisky (see "Eating in Glasgow," later). Nearby, running just below the Glasgow School of Art, **Sauchiehall Street** is younger, artsier, and more student-oriented. The recently revitalized **Merchant City** zone, stretching just east of the Buchanan Street shopping drag, has a slightly older crowd and a popular gay scene.

West End: You'll find fun bars and music venues in **Hillhead**, on Ashton Lane and surrounding streets. **Finnieston,** just below the Kelvingrove Museum, is packed with trendy bars and restaurants. But it also has an old-school selection of spit-and-sawdust Gaelic pubs, some of which have live music in the evenings (see next).

LIVE MUSIC

Glasgow has a great music scene, on its streets (talented buskers) and in its bars and clubs (including trad sessions). For the latest, *The Skinny* is Glasgow's information-packed alternative weekly (www.theskinny.co.uk). Or check out *The List* (www.list.co.uk) or the *Gig Guide* (www.gigguide.co.uk). All three are also available in print around town. Or check out what's going on at these bars:

Finnieston

The following pubs line up along Argyle Street.

The Ben Nevis hosts lively, toe-tapping sessions three times a week. It's a good scene—full of energy but crowded. Show up early to grab a seat in this tiny pub, or be ready to stand (Wed, Thu, and Sun at 21:00, no food service—just snacks, #1147).

The Islay Inn has bands twice weekly—some traditional, some doing contemporary covers. On nonmusic nights you'll find televisions blasting sports (music Fri and Sat at 21:00, food available, #1256, at corner with Radnor).

At **The Park Bar,** you'll find live music several nights a week, including traditional Scottish bands and sessions on Thursdays (Thu-Sun around 21:00, food available, #1202).

Hillhead

The **Òran Mòr** (a former church, www.oran-mor.co.uk) and **Hillhead Bookclub** (a former cinema, www.hillheadbookclub.co.uk) are popular live music venues (both recommended later, under "Eating in Glasgow").

Jinty McGuinty's has acoustic music every night, ranging from chart hits to Irish classics to soul and blues (daily at 21:30, 29 Ashton Lane).

Downtown

Twice weekly at **Babbity Bowster,** musicians take over a corner of this cute pub (under a recommended B&B) for a trad session. The music, energy, and atmosphere are top-notch (Wed and Sat at 15:00, solid pub grub, 16 Blackfriars Street).

Sloans, hidden away through a muraled tunnel off Argyle Street, is a fun pub with outdoor tables filling an alley. They have live traditional music on Wednesdays (21:00) and *ceilidh* dancing instruction on Fridays (£10, starts at 20:30, book ahead, food available, 108 Argyle Street, www.sloansglasgow.com).

Waxy O'Connor's is a massive, multilevel Irish bar featuring a maze of dark, atmospheric rooms, a tree climbing up a wall, and lots of live music (usually acoustic—check their website for days/times) and trad sessions on Sundays at 15:00 (food available, 44 West George Street, www.waxyoconnors.co.uk).

MOVIES

The Grosvenor Cinema, right on Ashton Lane in the heart of the bustling West End restaurant scene, is an inviting movie theater, with cushy leather seats in two theaters showing films big and small (most movies £10) and lots of special events. Wine and beer are available at the theater, or you can order cocktails and warm food at the bar next door and have it delivered to your seat (21 Ashton Lane, tel. 0845-166-6002, www.grosvenorcinema.co.uk).

Sleeping in Glasgow

For accommodations, choose between downtown (bustling by day, nearly deserted at night, close to main shopping zone and some major sights, very expensive parking and one-way streets that cause headaches for drivers) and the West End (neighborhoody, best variety of restaurants, easier parking, easy access to West End sights and parks but a bus or subway ride from the center and train station).

DOWNTOWN

These accommodations are scattered around the city center. For locations, see the map on page 852. Glasgow also has all the predictable chains—**Ibis, Premier Inn, Travelodge, Novotel, Mercure, Jurys Inn, EasyHotel**—check online for deals.

$$$ Pipers' Tryst has eight simple rooms enthusiastically done up in good tartan style above a restaurant in the National Piping Centre (described on page 838). It's in a grand, old former church building overlooking a busy intersection, across the street from the downtown business, shopping, and entertainment district. The location is handy, if not romantic, and it's practically a pilgrimage for fans of bagpipes (30 McPhater Street, tel. 0141/353-5551, www.thepipingcentre.co.uk, hotel@thepipingcentre.co.uk).

$$$ Z Hotel, part of a small "compact luxury" chain, offers 104 sleek, stylish rooms (some are very small and don't have windows). It's welcoming and handy to Queen Street Station, just a few steps off George Square (breakfast extra, air-con, elevator, free wine-and-cheese buffet each afternoon, 36 North Frederick Street, tel. 0141/212-4550, www.thezhotels.com, glasgow@thezhotels.com).

$$ Grasshoppers is a cheerful, above-it-all retreat on the sixth floor of a building overlooking Central Station. The street level entry is minimal, but popping out of the elevator, you know you've arrived. The 29 rooms are tight, with small "efficiency" bathrooms, but the welcome is warm and there's 24-hour access to fresh cupcakes, shortbread, and ice cream (free breakfast to those booking direct, optional buffet dinner, elevator, 87 Union Street, tel. 0141/222-2666, www.grasshoppersglasgow.com, info@grasshoppersglasgow.com).

$$ Motel One, part of a stylish German budget hotel chain, has 374 rooms and is located conveniently, right next to Central Station (corner of Oswald and Argyle streets, www.motel-one.com).

$ Babbity Bowster, named for a traditional Scottish dance, is a pub and restaurant renting five simple, mod rooms up top. It's located in the trendy Merchant City area on the eastern fringe of downtown, near several clubs and restaurants (no breakfast, lots of stairs and no elevator, 10-minute walk from either station, 16 Blackfriars Street, tel. 0141/552-5055, www.babbitybowster.com, info@babbitybowster.com). The ground-floor **$$** pub serves good grub (daily 12:00-22:00) and has twice-weekly sessions (see "Nightlife and Entertainment in Glasgow").

¢ The huge **Euro Hostel** (over 400 beds) is a well-run and well-located option for those on a tight budget (private rooms, family rooms, all rooms have en-suite bathrooms, breakfast extra, kitchen, bar, very central on the River Clyde near Central Station, 318 Clyde Street, tel. 0845-539-9956, www.eurohostels.co.uk, glasgow@eurohostels.co.uk).

IN THE WEST END

For a more appealing neighborhood experience, bunk in the West End—the upper-middle-class neighborhood just a few subway stops (or a 15-minute, £8 taxi ride) from downtown. As this is also one of the city's best dining zones, you'll likely come here for dinner anyway—so why not sleep here? My favorites in this area are the Alamo and Amadeus, which have the most personality. For locations, see the map on page 832.

Finnieston

These places are in an inviting residential area near the Kelvingrove Museum (not as handy to the subway, but easy by bus). They're close to the lively Argyle Street scene, with good restaurants and fun Gaelic pubs.

$$ The Alamo Guest House, energetically run by Steve and Emma, faces the bowling green and tennis court. It has rich, lavishly decorated public spaces and 10 comfortable rooms, including two luxury suites with bathtubs (family room, some rooms with bathroom down the hall, 2- or 3-night minimum stay on weekends in peak season, 46 Gray Street, tel. 0141/339-2395, www.alamoguesthouse.com, info@alamoguesthouse.com).

At the **$$ Argyll Hotel and Guesthouse** you won't forget you're in Scotland. Each room is accessorized with a different tartan and has info on the associated clan, while the halls are adorned with symbols of Scotland (bagpipes, thistle, local landmarks, etc.). The hotel has an elevator, breakfast room, and higher prices than the guesthouse (guesthouse customers must cross the street for breakfast and deal with stairs). Otherwise the rooms are just as nice and a bit larger in the guesthouse (family rooms, save money by skipping breakfast, 973 Sauchiehall Street, tel. 0141/337-3313, www.argyllhotelglasgow.co.uk, info@argyllhotelglasgow.co.uk).

Near Kelvinbridge

$$ Amadeus Guest House, a classy refuge just north of the large Kelvingrove Park, has nine modern rooms and artistic flourishes. It hides down a quiet street yet is conveniently located near the Kelvinbridge subway stop—just a 10-minute walk or one subway stop from the restaurant zone (includes continental breakfast, 411 North

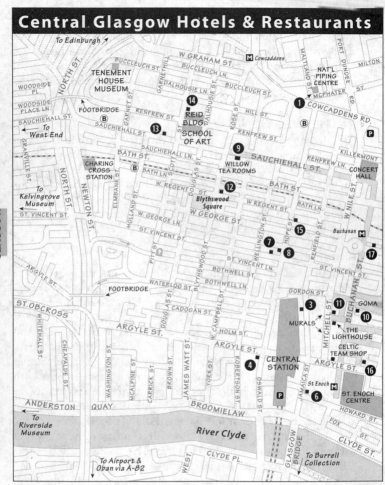

Central Glasgow Hotels & Restaurants

Woodside Road, tel. 0141/339-8257, www.amadeusguesthouse.
co.uk, reservations@amadeusguesthouse.co.uk, Alexandra).

Hillhead

These places, overlooking the busy Great Western Road, are close
to the Botanic Gardens and Hillhead restaurant scene but farther
from the center (10-minute walk to Hillhead subway stop or catch
bus to center from Great Western Road).

$$ The Alfred, run by the landmark Òran Mòr restaurant/
pub (located in the former church just up the street), brings a con-
temporary elegance to the neighborhood, with 14 new-feeling,
stylish rooms (family room, includes continental breakfast, 1 Al-
fred Terrace, tel. 0141/357-3445, www.thealfredhotelglasgow.
co.uk, alfred@thealfredhotelglasgow.co.uk).

Accommodations
1. Pipers' Tryst
2. Z Hotel
3. Grasshoppers
4. Motel One
5. Babbity Bowster
6. Euro Hostel

Eateries & Nightlife
7. Martha's
8. Mussel Inn
9. Willow Tea Rooms
10. Rogano
11. Tabac
12. Two Fat Ladies
13. CCA Saramago Bar & Courtyard Vegetarian Café
14. The Vic
15. The Pot Still
16. Sloans
17. Waxy O'Connor's

$$ Belhaven Hotel, a little farther out (about 10 minutes past Byres Road), has 18 rooms in an elegant four-floor townhouse with a pretty, tiled atrium (save money by skipping breakfast, bar in breakfast room serves drinks to guests, no elevator, 15 Belhaven Terrace, tel. 0141/339-3222, www.belhavenhotel.com, info@belhavenhotel.com).

$ Argyll Western, with 17 sleek and tartaned Scottish-themed rooms, feels modern, efficient, and a bit impersonal (breakfast extra, 6 Buckingham Terrace, tel. 0141/339-2339, www.argyllwestern.co.uk, info@argyllwestern.co.uk, same family runs the Argyll Hotel, listed earlier).

Eating in Glasgow

DOWNTOWN

$ Martha's is ideal for hungry, hurried sightseers (and local office workers) in search of a healthy and satisfying lunch. They serve a seasonal menu of wraps, rice boxes, soups, and other great meals made with Scottish ingredients but with eclectic, exotic, international flavors (Indian, Thai, Mexican, and so on). It's understandably popular: Just line up (it moves fast), order at the counter, and then find a table or take your food to go (Mon-Fri 7:30-18:00, closed Sat-Sun, 142A St. Vincent Street, tel. 0141/248-9771).

$$$ Mussel Inn offers light, good-value fish dinners and seafood plates in an airy, informal environment. The restaurant is a cooperative, owned and run by shellfish farmers. Their "kilo pot" of Scottish mussels is popular with locals and big enough to share ("lunchtime quickie" deals, daily specials, daily 12:00-14:30 & 17:00-22:00, 157 Hope Street, tel. 0141/572-1405).

$$ The **Willow Tea Rooms,** designed by Charles Rennie Mackintosh, has a diner-type eatery and a classy Room de Luxe. The cheap and cheery menu covers both dining areas (afternoon tea, Mon-Sat 9:00-17:00, Sun from 10:30, reservations smart, 217 Sauchiehall Street, tel. 0141/332-0521, www.willowtearooms. co.uk).

Rogano is a time-warp Glasgow institution that retains much of the same classy Art Deco interior it had when it opened in 1935. The restaurant has three distinct sections: **$$ The Rogano Bar** in front is an Art Deco diner with dressy outdoor seating and serves soups, sandwiches, and simple dishes; **$$$$ The Rogano Restaurant,** a fancy dining room at the back of the main floor which smacks of the officers' mess on the *Queen Mary*, focuses on seafood, classic Scottish dishes, and afternoon tea (their early menu—until 19:00—is a good deal); **$$$ The Rogano Café,** a more casual yet still dressy bistro in the cellar, is filled with 1930s-Hollywood posters and offers a similar menu to the fancy restaurant, but cheaper (daily 12:00-16:00 & 18:00-21:30, 11 Exchange Place—just before giant Merchant City archway just off Buchanan Street, reservations smart, tel. 0141/248-4055, www.roganoglasgow.com).

$$ Tabac is a dark, mod, and artsy cocktail bar with spacious seating on a narrow lane just off Buchanan Street. They serve pizza, burgers, and big salads (daily 12:00-24:00, food served until 21:00, across from "The Lighthouse" at 10 Mitchell Lane, tel. 0141/572-1448).

$$$ Two Fat Ladies is a hard-working and dressy little place with a focus on food rather than atmosphere and a passion for white fish (early-bird menu until 18:15 a great value, daily 12:00-14:30 & 17:00-22:00, 118 Blythswood Street, tel. 0141/847-0088).

$$ CCA Saramago Bar and Courtyard Vegetarian Café, located on the first floor of Glasgow's edgy contemporary art museum, charges art-student prices for its designer, animal-free food. An 18th-century facade, discovered when the site was excavated to build the gallery, looms over the atrium restaurant (food served daily 12:00-22:00, free Wi-Fi, 350 Sauchiehall Street, tel. 0141/332-7959).

$ The Vic is a student hangout within the Glasgow School of Art itself. Face the modern Reid Building and hook around the left side to find the easy-to-miss entrance to this funky bar/café with starving-artist fare from an eclectic, international menu (Mon-Sat 12:00-21:00, closed Sun).

For Your Whisky: The Pot Still is an award-winning malt whisky bar dating from 1835 that's also proud of its meat pies. You'll see locals of all ages sitting in its leathery interior, watching football (soccer), and discussing their drinks. Give the friendly bartenders a little background on your beverage tastes, and they'll narrow down a good choice for you from their long list (daily 11:00-24:00, 154 Hope Street, tel. 0141/333-0980, Frank has the long beard).

IN THE WEST END

This hip, lively residential neighborhood/university district is worth exploring, particularly in the evening. The restaurant scene focuses on two areas (at opposite ends of my West End Walk): near the Hillhead subway stop and, farther down, in the Finnieston neighborhood near the Kelvingrove Museum. For locations, see the map on page 832. It's smart to book ahead at any of these places for weekend evenings.

Near Hillhead

There's a fun concentration of restaurants on the streets that fan out from the Hillhead subway stop (£8 taxi ride from downtown).

If it's a balmy evening, several have convivial gardens designed to catch the evening sun. Before choosing a place, take a stroll and scout the Ashton Lane scene, which has the greatest variety of places (including Ubiquitous Chip and Brel Bar, recommended below). Tucked away on Ruthven Lane (opposite the subway station) are Bothy Restaurant and The Hanoi Bike Shop. And a couple blocks away (near the Botanic Gardens) are Hillhead Bookclub, The Parlour, Òran Mòr, and Cail Bruich.

$$$$ Ubiquitous Chip, a.k.a. "The Chip," is a beloved local landmark with a couple inviting pubs and two great restaurant options. On the ground floor is their fine restaurant with beautifully presented contemporary Scottish dishes in a garden atrium. Their early-bird menu (order by 18:30) is a great value. Upstairs (looking down on the scene) is the less-formal, less-expensive, but still very nice brasserie (daily 11:00-22:00, 12 Ashton Lane, tel. 0141/334-5007, www.ubiquitouschip.co.uk).

$$ Brel Bar is a fun-loving place with a happy garden and a menu with burgers, mussels, and quality bar food. On a nice evening, its backyard beer garden is hard to beat (daily 12:00-24:00, 37 Ashton Lane, tel. 0141/342-4966).

$$$ Bothy Restaurant is a romantic place offering tasty, traditional Scottish fare served by waiters in kilts. Sit outside in the inviting alleyway or in the rustic-contemporary dining room (daily 12:00-22:00, down the lane opposite the subway station to 11 Ruthven Lane, tel. 0141/334-4040).

$$ The Hanoi Bike Shop, a rare-in-Scotland Vietnamese "street food" restaurant, serves Asian tapas that are healthy and tasty, using local produce. With tight seating and friendly service, the place has a fun energy (daily 12:00-23:00, 8 Ruthven Lane, tel. 0141/334-7165).

$$ Hillhead Bookclub is a historic cinema building cleared out to make room for fun, disco, pub grub, and lots of booze. It's a youthful and quirky art-school scene, with lots of beers on tap, creative cocktails, retro computer games, ping-pong, and theme evenings like "drag queen bingo" night. The menu: meat pies, fish and chips, burgers, and salads (daily 10:00-21:30, 17 Vinicombe Street, tel. 0141/576-1700).

$$ The Parlour, across from the Hillhead Bookclub, gets all the evening sun on its terrace seating. In bad weather, the spacious interior is warmed by an open fire. It's young, fun, and pub-like, with pizza, tacos, burgers, and creative cocktails (daily 11:00-21:30, 28 Vinicombe Street, mobile 07943-852-973).

$$ Òran Mòr fills a converted church from the 1860s with a classic pub. They offer basic pub grub either inside or on the front-porch beer garden (daily 10:00-21:00, later on weekends, across from the Botanic Gardens at 731 Great Western Road, tel. 0141/357-600).

$$$$ Cail Bruich serves award-winning classic Scottish dishes with an updated spin in an elegant and romantic setting. Reservations are smart (classy tasting menus for £35-45, lunch Wed-Sun 12:00-14:00, dinner Mon-Sat 18:00-21:00, 725 Great Western Road, tel. 0141/334-6265, www.cailbruich.co.uk).

Facing the Kelvingrove Museum

These three places are immediately across from the Kelvingrove

Museum (which is likely to leave you hungry). They're more basic and less trendy than the Finnieston places (a few blocks away, listed next) that will leave you with better memories.

$$ Brewdog Glasgow is a beer-and-burgers joint. It's a great place to sample Scottish microbrews—from their own brewery in Aberdeen, as well as guest brews—in an industrial-mod setting reminiscent of American brewpubs (daily 12:00-24:00, 1397 Argyle Street, tel. 0141/334-7175, www.brewdog.com).

$$ Mother India's Café serves basic Indian and is a good stop if you crave Scotland's national dish: "a good curry." The menu features small plates designed to enjoy family style (about two plates per person makes a meal, daily 12:00-22:30, 1355 Argyle Street, tel. 0141/339-9145).

$$$ Butchershop Bar & Grill is a casual, rustic, American-style steak house, but featuring Scottish products—focusing on dry-aged Scottish steaks (lunch and early-bird deals, daily 12:00-22:00, 1055 Sauchiehall Street, tel. 0141/339-2999, www.butchershopglasgow.com).

Trendy Finnieston Eateries on and near Argyle Street

This trendy, up-and-coming neighborhood—with a hipster charm in this hipster city—stretches east from in front of the Kelvingrove Museum (a 10-minute walk from the Kelvinhall or Kelvinbridge subway stops). Each of these are likely to require a reservation. The Crabshakk started things off here and today it anchors a strip of similarly funky, foodie eateries.

$$ Crabshakk, specializing in fresh, beautifully presented seafood, is a foodie favorite, with a very tight bar-and-mezzanine seating area and tables spilling out onto the sidewalk. It's casual but still respectable, and worth reserving ahead (daily 12:00-22:00, 1114 Argyle Street, tel. 0141/334-6127, www.crabshakk.com).

$$$ The Gannet emphasizes Scottish ingredients with a modern spin. It's relaxed and stylish but the owners/chefs are serious about the food (lunch Thu-Sat 12:00-14:00, dinner Tue-Sat 17:00-21:30, Sun 13:00-19:30, closed Mon, 1155 Argyle Street, tel. 0141/204-2081, www.thegannetgla.com).

$$ Ox and Finch, with a romantic setting, open kitchen, and smart clientele, serves modern international cuisine. It features small plates in an upscale, rustic, wood-meets-industrial atmosphere (daily 12:00-22:00, 920 Sauchiehall Street, tel. 0141/339-8627, www.oxandfinch.com).

Glasgow Connections

Traveline Scotland has a journey planner that's linked to all of Scotland's train and bus schedule info. Go online (www. travelinescotland.com), call them at tel. 0871-200-2233, or use the individual websites listed below. If you're connecting with Edinburgh, note that the train is faster but the bus is cheaper.

BY TRAIN

From Glasgow's Queen Street Station by Train to: Oban (5/day, 3 hours), **Fort William** (3/day, 4 hours), **Inverness** (5/day direct, 3 hours, more with change in Perth), **Edinburgh** (6/hour, 50 minutes), **Stirling** (3/hour, 45 minutes).

From Glasgow's Central Station by Train to: Keswick in England's Lake District (hourly, 1.5 hours to Penrith, then catch a bus to Keswick, 45 minutes), **Cairnryan** for ferry to Belfast (take train to Ayr, 2/hour, 1 hour; then ride bus to Cairnryan, 1 hour), **Liverpool** (2/hour, 4 hours, change in Wigan or Preston), **Durham** (2/hour, 3 hours, may require change in Edinburgh), **York** (hourly, 4 hours, more with change in Edinburgh), **London** (2/hour, 5 hours direct). Train info: Tel. 0345-748-4950, www. nationalrail.co.uk.

BY BUS

Glasgow's Buchanan bus station is a hub for reaching the Highlands. If you're coming from Edinburgh, you can take the bus to Glasgow and transfer here. Or, for a speedier connection, zip to Glasgow on the train, then walk a few short blocks to the bus station. (Ideally, try to arrive at Glasgow's Queen Street Station, which is closer to the bus station.) For more details on these connections, see "Getting Around the Highlands" on page 906.

From Glasgow by Bus to: Edinburgh (Citylink bus #900, 4/hour, 1.5 hours), **Oban** (Citylink buses #976 and #977; 5/day, 3 hours), **Fort William** (Citylink buses #914, #915, and #916; 8/day, 3 hours), **Glencoe** (Citylink buses #914, #915, and #916; 8/day, 2.5 hours), **Inverness** (5/day on Citylink express bus #G10, 3 hours; 1/day direct on National Express #588, 4 hours), **Portree** on the Isle of Skye (Citylink buses #915 and #916, 3/day, 7 hours), **Stirling** (hourly on Citylink #M8, 45 minutes). Citylink: tel. 0871-266-3333, www.citylink.co.uk. National Express: tel. 0871-781-8181, www.nationalexpress.com.

BY PLANE

Glasgow International Airport: Located eight miles west of the city, this airport (code: GLA) has currency-exchange desks, a TI, luggage storage, and ATMs (tel. 0844-481-5555, www.

glasgowairport.com). Taxis connect downtown to the airport for about £25. Your hotel can likely arrange a private taxi service for £15, or you can take Uber.

Bus #500 zips to central Glasgow (every 10 minutes, 5:00-23:00, £7.50/one-way, £10/round-trip, 25 minutes to both train stations and the bus station, catch at bus stop #1). Slow bus #77 goes to the West End, stopping at the Kelvingrove Museum and rolling along Argyle Street (departs every 30 minutes, £5/one-way, 50 minutes).

Prestwick Airport: A hub for Ryanair, this airport is 30 miles southwest of the city center (code: PIK, tel. 0871-223-0700, ext. 1006, www.glasgowprestwick.com). The best connection is by train, which runs between the airport and Central Station (3/ hour, 50 minutes, half-price with Ryanair ticket, trains also run to Edinburgh Waverley Station—about 2/hour, 2 hours). Stagecoach buses link the airport with Buchanan Bus Station (£10, 1-2/hour, 50 minutes, www.stagecoachbus.com).

ROUTE TIPS FOR DRIVERS

From England's Lake District to Glasgow: From Keswick, take the A-66 for 18 miles to the M-6 and speed north nonstop (via Penrith and Carlisle), crossing Hadrian's Wall into Scotland. The road becomes the M-74 just north of Carlisle. To slip through Glasgow quickly, leave the M-74 at Junction 4 onto the M-73, following signs to *M-8/Glasgow*. Leave the M-73 at Junction 2, exiting onto the M-8. Stay on the M-8 west through Glasgow, exit at Junction 30, cross Erskine Bridge, and turn left on the A-82, following signs to *Crianlarich* and *Loch Lomond*. (For a scenic drive through Glasgow, take exit 17 off the M-8 and stay on the A-82 toward Dumbarton.)

STIRLING & NEARBY

Stirling • Wallace Monument • Bannockburn • Falkirk • Culross • Doune

The historic city of Stirling is the crossroads of Scotland: Equidistant from Edinburgh and Glasgow (less than an hour from both), and rising above a plain where the Lowlands meet the Highlands, it's no surprise that Stirling has hosted many of the biggest names (and biggest battles) of Scottish history. Everyone from Mary, Queen of Scots to Bonnie Prince Charlie has passed through the gates of its stately, strategic castle.

From the cliff-capping ramparts of Stirling Castle, you can see where each of the three pivotal battles of Scotland's 13th- and 14th-century Wars of Independence took place: the Battle of Stirling Bridge, where against all odds, the courageous William Wallace defeated the English army; the Battle of Falkirk, where Wallace was toppled by a vengeful English king; and the Battle of Bannockburn, when—in the wake of Wallace's defeat—Robert the Bruce rallied to kick out the English once and for all (well, at least for a few generations). The Wallace Monument and Bannockburn Heritage Centre—on the outskirts of Stirling, in opposite directions—are practically pilgrimage sites for patriotic Scots.

Stirling itself is sleepy, but it's a good home base for a variety of side-trips. In Falkirk, take a spin in a fascinating Ferris wheel for boats, and ogle the gigantic horse heads called The Kelpies. Sitting on the nearby estuary known as the Firth of Forth—on the way to Edinburgh or St. Andrews—is the gorgeously preserved time-warp village of Culross. To the north, fans of Monty Python and *Outlander* flock to Doune Castle.

Stirling Area

5 Kilometers
5 Miles

Crieff
Gleneagles
Strathyre
Muthill
Auchterarder
To Perth & Pitlochry
Loch Katrine
Brig o'Turk
Callander
Braco
A-9
To Inveraray & Oban
Ben Lomond
Forth R.
DOUNE
DEANSTON
Drumvaich
Doune
WALLACE MONUMENT
The Trossachs
Tarbet
Aberfoyle
Lake of Menteith
A-84
A-91
Stirling
Conic Hill
Buchlyvie
Luss
Balmaha
BANNOCKBURN
See detail map
M-9
THE KELPIES
Culross
Loch Lomond
A-82
M-80
M-876
Bo'ness
Helensburgh
HILL HOUSE
Balloch
Forth & Clyde Canal
Bonnybridge
Falkirk
Firth of Clyde
Dumbarton
Kirkintilloch
M-80
FALKIRK WHEEL
Cumbernauld
Union Canal
To Edinburgh
A-8
Clydebank
Bathgate

PLANNING YOUR TIME

You'll likely pass near Stirling at least once as you travel through Scotland. Skim this chapter to learn about your options and select the stops that interest you. If you can't fit it all in on a pass-through, spend the night. Just as Stirling was ideally situated for monarchs and armies of the past, it's handy for present-day visitors: It's much smaller, and arguably even more conveniently located, than Edinburgh or Glasgow, and it has a variety of good accommodations. You'd need a solid three days to see all the big sights within an hour's drive of Stirling—but most people are (and should be) more selective.

Stirling

Every Scot knows the city of Stirling (pop. 41,000) deep in their bones. This patriotic heart of Scotland is like Bunker Hill, Gettysburg, and the Alamo, all rolled into one. Stirling perches on a ridge overlooking Scotland's most history-drenched plain: a flat expanse—cut through by the twisting River Forth and the meandering stream called Bannockburn—that divides the Lowlands from the Highlands. And capping that ridge is Stirling's formidable castle, the seat of the final kings of Scotland.

From a traveler's perspective, Stirling

is a pleasant mini-Edinburgh, with a steep spine leading up to that grand castle. It's busy with tourists by day, but sleepy at night. The town, and its castle, may lack personality—but both are striking and strategic.

Orientation to Stirling

Stirling's old town is situated along a long, narrow, steep hill. At its base are the train and bus stations and a thriving (but characterless) commercial district; at its apex is the castle. The old town feels like a steeper, shorter, less touristy, and far less characteristic version of Edinburgh's Royal Mile.

Tourist Information: The TI is a five-minute walk below the castle, just inside the gates of the Old Town Jail (daily 10:00-17:00, free Wi-Fi, St. Johns Street, tel. 01786/475-019).

Getting Around: While the sights within Stirling nestle together at the top of the town, the Wallace Monument and Bannockburn Heritage Centre are an easy bus or taxi ride, or short drive away.

Sights in Stirling

▲▲STIRLING CASTLE

"He who holds Stirling, holds Scotland." These fateful words have been proven, more often than not, to be true. Stirling Castle's prized

position—perched on a volcanic crag overlooking a bridge over the River Forth, the primary passage between the Lowlands and the Highlands—has long been the key to Scotland. This castle was the preferred home of Scottish kings and queens in the Middle Ages; today it's one of the most historic—and most popular—castles in Scotland. While its interiors are pretty empty and new-feeling, the castle still has plenty to offer: spectacular views over a gentle countryside, tales of the dynamic Stuart monarchs, and several exhibits that try to bring the place to life.

Cost and Hours: £15, daily April-Sept 9:30-18:00, Oct-March until 17:00, last entry 45 minutes before closing, Regimental Museum closes one hour before castle, good café, tel. 01786/450-000, www.stirlingcastle.gov.uk.

Tours: The included 40-minute **guided tour** helps you get your bearings—both to the castle, and to Scottish history (generally on the hour 10:00-16:00, often on the half-hour too, departs

STIRLING & NEARBY

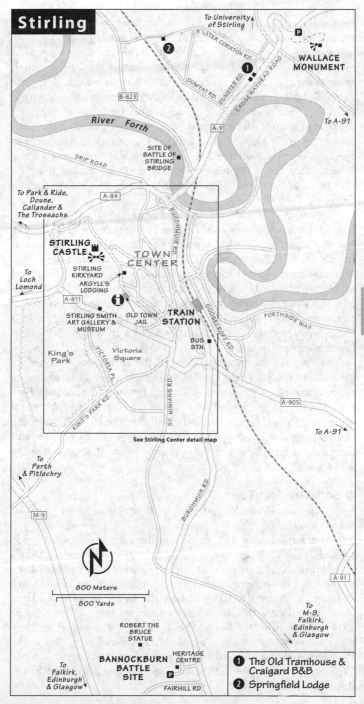

Stirling

To University of Stirling

MASTER CORNTON RD.

2

WALLACE MONUMENT

DUMYAT RD.

DUNSTER RD.

1

CAUSEWAYHEAD ROAD

B-823

River Forth

A-9

To A-91

DRIP ROAD

SITE OF BATTLE OF STIRLING BRIDGE

To Park & Ride, Doune, Callander & The Trossachs

A-84

BURGHMUIR RD.

TOWN CENTER

STIRLING CASTLE

STIRLING KIRKYARD

ARGYLL'S LODGING

To Loch Lomond

A-811

STIRLING SMITH ART GALLERY & MUSEUM

OLD TOWN JAIL

TRAIN STATION

GOOSECROFT RD.

FORTHSIDE WAY

BUS STN.

King's Park

VICTORIA PL.

Victoria Square

KING'S PARK RD.

ST. NINIAN'S RD.

A-905

To A-91

See Stirling Center detail map

To Perth & Pitlochry

M-9

BURGHMUIR RD.

A-91

N

800 Meters

800 Yards

ROBERT THE BRUCE STATUE

HERITAGE CENTRE

To M-9, Falkirk, Edinburgh & Glasgow

BANNOCKBURN BATTLE SITE

P

To Falkirk, Edinburgh & Glasgow

FAIRHILL RD.

1 The Old Tramhouse & Craigard B&B

2 Springfield Lodge

STIRLING & NEARBY

from inside the main gate near the well). Docents posted throughout can tell you more, and you can rent a £3 **audioguide.**

Getting There: Stirling Castle sits at the very tip of a steep old town. Drivers should follow the *Stirling Castle* signs uphill through town to the esplanade and park at the £4 lot just outside the castle gate. Without a car, you can hike the 20-minute uphill route from the train or bus station to the castle, or take a taxi (about £5).

Background: The first real castle was built here in the 12th century by King David I. But Stirling Castle's glory days were in the 16th century, when it became the primary residence of the Stuart (often spelled "Stewart") monarchs, who turned it into a showpiece of Scotland—and a symbol of one-upmanship against England.

The 16th century was a busy time for royal intrigues here: James IV married the sister of England's King Henry VIII, thereby knitting together the royal families of Scotland (the Stuarts) and England (the Tudors). Later, James V further expanded the castle. Mary (who became the Queen of Scots) spent her early childhood at the castle before being raised in France. As queen and as a Catholic, she struggled against the rise of Protestantism in her realm. But when Mary's son, King James VI, was crowned King James I of England, he took his royal court with him away from Stirling to London—never to return.

During the Jacobite rebellions of the 18th century, the British military took over the castle—bulking it up and destroying its delicate beauty. Even after the Scottish threat had subsided, it remained a British garrison, home base of the Argyll and Sutherland regiments. (You'll notice the castle still flies the Union Jack of the United Kingdom.) Today, while Stirling Castle is fully restored and gleaming, it feels new and fairly empty—with almost no historic artifacts.

❷ Self-Guided Tour

Begin on the esplanade, just outside the castle entrance, with its grand views.

The Esplanade: The castle's esplanade, a military parade ground in the 19th century, is a tour-bus parking lot today. As you survey this site, remember that Stirling Castle bore witness to some of the most important moments in Scottish history. To the right as you face the castle, **King Robert the Bruce** looks toward the plain called Bannockburn, where he defeated the English army in 1314. Squint off to the horizon on Robert's left to spot the pointy stone monument capping the hill called Abbey Craig. This is the **Wallace Monument,** marking the spot where the Scottish warrior William Wallace surveyed the battlefield before his victory in the Battle of Stirling Bridge (1297).

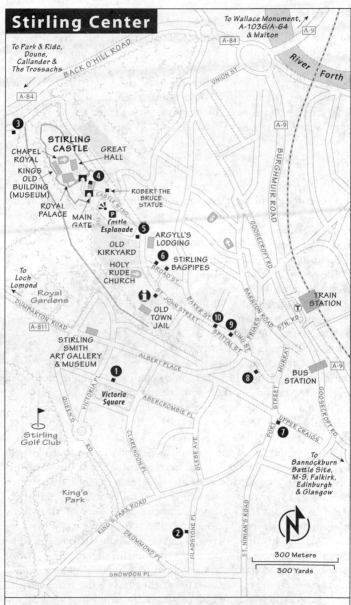

Stirling Center

To Wallace Monument,
A-1036/A-64
& Malton

A-9

River Forth

To Park & Ride,
Doune,
Callander &
The Trossachs

A-84

BACK O'HILL ROAD

UNION ST.

A-84

A-9

BURGHMUIR ROAD

GOOSECROFT RD.

STIRLING CASTLE

CHAPEL ROYAL

GREAT HALL

KINGS OLD BUILDING (MUSEUM)

ROYAL PALACE

MAIN GATE

CASTLE WYND

ROBERT THE BRUCE STATUE

Castle Esplanade

ARGYLL'S LODGING

OLD KIRKYARD

STIRLING BAGPIPES

HOLY RUDE CHURCH

BROAD ST.

BAKER ST.

BARNTON ROAD

ST. JOHN STREET

FRIARS ST.

KING ST.

SPITTAL ST.

OLD TOWN JAIL

TRAIN STATION

STN. RD.

To Loch Lomond

Royal Gardens

DUMBARTON ROAD

A-811

STIRLING SMITH ART GALLERY & MUSEUM

ALBERT PLACE

VICTORIA PL.

Victoria Square

ABERCROMBIE PL.

CLARENDON PL.

GLEBE AVE.

QUEEN'S RD.

MURRAY

PORT STREET

UPPER CRAIGS

BUS STATION

A-9

GOOSECROFT RD.

Stirling Golf Club

King's Park

KING'S PARK ROAD

DRUMMOND PL.

GLADSTONE PL.

ST. NINIAN'S ROAD

SNOWDON PL.

To Bannockburn Battle Site, M-9, Falkirk, Edinburgh & Glasgow

N

300 Meters

300 Yards

STIRLING & NEARBY

Accommodations
1 Victoria Square Guest House
2 Number Ten
3 Castlecroft B&B

Eateries
4 Unicorn Cafeteria

5 The Portcullis
6 Hermann's
7 Blue Lagoon Fish & Chips
8 Maharaja
9 Brea
10 Nicky-Tams Bar & Bothy

These great Scots helped usher in several centuries of home rule. In 1315, Robert the Bruce's daughter married into an on-the-rise noble clan called the Stuarts, who had distinguished themselves fighting at Bannockburn. When their son Robert became King Robert II of Scotland in 1371, he kicked off the Stuart dynasty. Over the next few generations, their headquarters—Stirling Castle—flourished. The fortified grand entry showed all who approached that James IV (r. 1488-1513) was a great ruler with a powerful castle.

• *Head through the first gate into Guardroom Square, where you can buy your ticket, check tour times, and consider renting the audioguide. Then continue up through the inner gate.*

Gardens and Battlements: Once through the gate, follow the passage to the left into a delightful grassy courtyard called the **Queen Anne Garden.** This was the royal family's playground in the 1600s. Imagine doing a little lawn bowling with the queen here.

In the casemates lining the garden is the **Castle Exhibition.** Its "Come Face to Face with 1,000 Years of History"

exhibit provides an entertaining and worthwhile introduction to the castle. You'll meet each of the people who left their mark here, from the first Stuart kings to William Wallace and Robert the Bruce. The video leaves you thinking that re-enactors of Jacobite struggles are even more spirited than our Civil War re-enactors.

Leave the garden the way you came and make a sharp U-turn up the ramp to the top of the **battlements.** From up here, this castle's strategic position is evident: Defenders had a 360-degree view of enemy armies approaching from miles away. These battlements were built in 1710, long after the castle's Stuart glory days, in response to the early Jacobite rebellions (from the Latin word for "James"). By this time, the successes of William Wallace and Robert the Bruce were a distant memory; and through the 1707 Act of Union, Scotland had become welded to England. Bonnie Prince Charlie—descendant of those original Stuart "King Jameses" who built this castle—later staged a series of uprisings to try to reclaim the throne of Great Britain for the Stuart line, frightening England enough for it to further fortify the castle. And sure enough, Bonnie Prince Charlie found himself—ironically—laying siege to the fortress that his own ancestors had built: Facing the main gate (with its two round towers below the UK flag), notice the pockmarks from Jacobite cannonballs in 1746.

• *Now head back down to the ramp and pass through that main gate, into the...*

Outer Close: As you enter this courtyard, straight ahead is James IV's yellow **Great Hall.** To the left is his son **James V's**

royal palace, lined with finely carved Renaissance statues. In 1540, King James V, inspired by French Renaissance châteaux he'd seen, had the castle covered with about 200 statues and busts to "proclaim the peace, prosperity, and justice of his reign" and to validate his rule. Imagine the impression all these classical gods and goddesses made on visitors. The message: James' rule was a Golden Age for Scotland.

The **guided tours** of the castle depart from just to your right, near the well. Beyond that is the Grand Battery, with its cannons and rampart views and, underneath that, the Great Kitchens. We'll see both at the end of this tour.

• *Hike up the ramp between James V's palace and the Great Hall (under the crenellated sky bridge connecting them). You'll emerge into the...*

Inner Close: Standing at the center of Stirling Castle, you're surrounded by Scottish history. This courtyard was the core of the 12th-century castle. From here, additional buildings were added—each by a different monarch. Facing downhill, you'll see the Great Hall. To the left is the Chapel Royal—where Mary, Queen of Scots was crowned in 1543. Opposite that, to the right, is the royal palace (containing the Royal Apartments)—notice the "I5" monogram above the windows (for the king who built it: James, or Iacobus in Latin, V). Upstairs in this same palace is the Stirling Heads Gallery. And behind you is the Regimental Museum.

• *We'll visit each of these in turn. First, at the far-left end of the gallery with the coffee stand, step into...*

The Great Hall: This is the largest secular space in medieval Scotland. Dating from 1503, this was a grand setting for the great banquets of Scotland's Renaissance kings. One such party, to which all the crowned heads of Europe were invited, reportedly went on for three full days. This was also where kings and queens would hold court, earning it the nickname "the parliament." The impressive hammerbeam roof is a modern reconstruction, modeled on the early 16th-century roof at Edinburgh Castle. It's made of 400 local oak trees, joined by wooden pegs. If you flipped it over, it would float.

• *At the far end of the hall, climb a few stairs and walk across the sky bridge into James V's palace. Here you can explore...*

The Royal Apartments: Six ground-floor apartments are colorfully done up as they might have looked in the mid-16th century,

when James V and his queen, Mary of Guise, lived here. Costumed performers play the role of palace attendants, happy to chat with you about medieval life. You'll begin in the King's Inner Hall, where he received guests. Notice the 60 carved and colorfully painted oak medallions on the ceiling. The medallions are carved with the faces of Scottish and European royalty. These are copies, painstakingly reconstructed after expert research. You'll soon see the originals up close (and upstairs) in the Stirling Heads Gallery.

Continue (left of the fireplace) into the other rooms (each with actors in costumes who love to interact): the King's Bedchamber, with a four-poster bed supporting a less-than-luxurious rope mattress; and then the Queen's Bedchamber, the Inner Hall, and the Outer Hall, offering a more vivid example of what these rich spaces would have looked like.

• *From the queen's apartments, you'll exit into the top corner of the Inner Close. Directly to your left, up the stairs, is the...*

Stirling Heads Gallery: This is, for me, the castle's highlight—a chance to see the originals of the elaborately carved and painted portrait medallions that

decorated the ceiling of the king's presence chamber. Each one is thoughtfully displayed and lovingly explained. Don't miss the video at the end of the hall.

• *If you were to leave this gallery through the intended exit, you'd wind up back down in the Queen Anne Garden. Instead, backtrack and exit the way you came in to return to the Inner Close, and visit the two remaining sights.*

The Chapel Royal: One of the first Protestant churches built in Scotland, the Chapel Royal was constructed in 1594 by James VI for the baptism of his first son, Prince Henry. The faint painted frieze high up survives from Charles I's coronation visit to Scotland in 1633. Clearly the holiness of the chapel ended in the 1800s when the army moved in.

Regimental Museum: At the top of the Inner Close, in the King's Old Building, is the excellent **Argyll and Sutherland Highlanders Museum.** Another highlight of the castle, it's barely mentioned in castle promotional material because it's run by a different organization. With lots of tartans, tassels, and swords, it shows how the fighting spirit of Scotland was absorbed by Britain. The two regiments, established in the 1790s to defend Britain in the Napoleonic age and combined in the 1880s, have served with distinction in British military campaigns for more than two centuries. Their pride shows here in the building that has served as their headquarters since 1881. The "In the Trenches" exhibit is a powerful look at World War I, with accounts from the battlefield. Up the spiral stairs, the exhibit continues through World War II and conflicts in the Middle East to the present day.

• *When you're ready to move on, consider the following scenic route back to the castle exit.*

Rampart Walk to the Kitchen: The skinny lane between church and museum leads to the secluded Douglas Garden at the rock's highest point. Belly up to the ramparts for a commanding view, including the Wallace Monument. From here you can walk the ramparts downhill to the Grand Battery, with its cannon rampart back at the Outer Close. The Outer Close was the service zone, with a well and the kitchen (below the cannon rampart). The great banquets of James VI didn't happen all by themselves, as you'll appreciate when you explore the fine medieval kitchen exhibit (where mannequin cooks oversee medieval recipes); to find it, head down the ramp and look for the *Great Kitchens* sign.

• *Your castle visit ends here, but your castle ticket includes Argyll's Lodging, a fortified noble mansion. Or, for a scenic route down into town, consider a detour through an old churchyard cemetery (both described next).*

MORE SIGHTS IN STIRLING
Old Kirkyard Stroll

Stirling has a particularly evocative old cemetery in the kirkyard (churchyard) just below the castle. For a soulful stroll, sneak down the stairs where the castle meets the esplanade parking lot (near the statue of the Scotsman fighting in the South African War).

From here, you can wander through the tombstones—Celtic crosses, Victorian statues, and faded headstones—from centuries gone by. The rocky crag in the middle of the graveyard is a fine viewpoint. Work your way over to the Church of the Holy Rude (well worth a visit), where you can re-enter the town. From here, Argyll's Lodging and the castle parking lot are just to the left, and the Old Town Jail (also housing the TI) is just to the right.

Argyll's Lodging

Just below the castle esplanade is this 17th-century nobleman's fortified mansion. European aristocrats wanted to live near power—making this location, where the Earl of Argyll's family resided for about a century, prime real estate. You'll get oriented with a historical display on the first floor, and then see the kitchens, dining room, drawing room, and bedchambers. Pick up the descriptions in each room, or ask the docents if you have any questions. Argyll's Lodging is less sterile than the castle and worth a few minutes.

Cost and Hours: Included in castle ticket, daily 12:45-17:30.

▲Historic and Haunted Walks

David Kinnaird, a local actor/historian, gives history walks by day and haunted walks by night in Stirling. Each walk meets at the TI (inside the gates of the Old Town Jail), lasts 75 minutes, and cost £4 for readers of this book (tel. 01592/874-449, www.stirlingghostwalk.com). Just show up and pay him directly. David's historic walks (May-Sept Fri-Sun at 12:00, 14:00, and 16:00) tell the story of Stirling as you wander through town. His "Happy Hangman" haunted walks through the old kirkyard cemetery involve more storytelling (July-Aug Tue-Sat at 20:30, Sept-June Fri-Sat at 20:00).

Old Town Jail

Stirling's jail was built during the Victorian Age, when the purpose of imprisonment was shifting from punishment to rehabilitation. While there's little to see today, theatrical 30-minute tours entertain families with a light and funny walk through one section of the jail. You'll end at the top of the tower for a Q&A with a commanding view of the surrounding countryside.

Cost and Hours: £6.50, July-Sept only, tours every 30 minutes daily 10:15-17:15, St. John Street, www.destinationstirling.com.

▲Stirling Bagpipes

This fun little shop, just a block below the castle on Broad Street, is worth a visit for those curious about bagpipes. Owner Alan refurbishes old bagpipes here, but also makes new ones from scratch, in a workshop on the premises. The pleasantly cluttered shop, which is a bit of a neighborhood hangout, is littered with bagpipe components—chanters, drones, bags, covers, and cords. If he's not too busy, Alan can answer your questions. He'll explain how the most expensive parts of the bagpipe are the "sticks"—the chanter and drones, carved from blackwood—while the bag and cover are cheap. A serious set costs £700...beginners should instead consider a £40 starter kit that includes a practice chanter (like a recorder) with a book of sheet music and a CD. Alan hopes to open a wee museum next door to show off his collection of historic bagpipes.

Cost and Hours: Free, Mon-Sat 10:00-18:00, closed Sun, 8 Broad Street, tel. 01786/448-886, www.stirlingbagpipes.com.

Nearby: On the wide street in front of the shop, look for Stirling's **mercat cross** ("market cross"). A standard feature of any medieval Scottish market town, this was the place where townsfolk would gather for the market, and where royal proclamations were read and executions took place. Today the commercial metabolism of this once-thriving street is at a low ebb. Locals joke that every 100 years, the shopping bustle moves one block farther down the road. These days, it's squeezed into the modern shopping mall between the old town and the river.

Stirling Smith Art Gallery and Museum

Tucked at the edge of the grid-planned, Victorian Age neighborhood just below the castle, this endearing and eclectic museum is a hodgepodge of artifacts from Stirling's past: art gallery (where you can meet historical figures with connections to this proud little town), pewter collection, local history exhibits, a steam-powered carriage, the mutton bone shard removed in the world's first documented tracheotomy (1853), and a 19th-century executioner's cloak and ax. The museum's prized piece is what they claim is the world's oldest surviving soccer ball—a 16th-century stitched-up pig's bladder that restorers found stuck in the rafters of Stirling Castle. The building is surrounded by a garden filled with public art.

Cost and Hours: Free, Tue-Sat 10:30-17:00, Sun from 14:00, closed Mon, Dumbarton Road, tel. 01786/471-917.

Sleeping in Stirling

NEAR THE TOWN CENTER

These places are all in large, spacious homes with easy parking.

In the Victorian Town, South of the Castle

When Stirling expanded beyond its old walls during the Victorian Age, a modern, grid-planned town sprouted just to the south. Today, this posh-feeling area holds a few B&Bs that are within a (long) walk of Stirling's old town and castle.

$$$ Victoria Square Guest House has 10 plush rooms in a beautiful location facing a big, grassy park. While the prices are high, it's neat as a pin, and Kari and Phil keep things running smoothly. It's about a 10-minute walk to the lower part of town, or 20 minutes up to the castle (no kids under 12, minifridges, 12 Victoria Square, tel. 01786/473-920, www.victoriasquareguesthouse. com, info@vsgh.co.uk).

$ Number Ten rents three nice, traditional rooms in a Scottish-feeling home with tartan carpets blanketing the halls and a lovely garden out back (no kids under 5, 10 Gladstone Place, tel. 01786/472-681, www.cameron-10.co.uk, cameron-10@tinyonline. co.uk, Carol and Donald Cameron).

Just Under the Castle

$$ Castlecroft B&B is well cared for by Laura, who keeps everything immaculate, bakes her own bread, and welcomes guests with tea/coffee and shortbread upon arrival. Just under the castle and overlooking a field with "hairy coos," it's a 10-minute walk down a path to the town center. Two of the five rooms come with their own patios, and anyone can make use of the living room and deck (Ballengeich Road, tel. 01786/474-933, www.castlecroft-uk.co.uk, castlecroft@gmail.com).

ALONG AND NEAR CAUSEWAYHEAD ROAD, NORTH OF THE CASTLE

A number of B&Bs offering slightly lower prices line Causewayhead Road, a busy thoroughfare that connects Stirling to the Wallace Monument. From here, it's a long walk into town (or the Wallace Monument), but the location is handy for drivers (each place has free parking). While this modern residential area lacks charm, it's convenient.

$$ The Old Tramhouse is the frilliest of the bunch, with five rooms elegantly decorated with a delicate charm (family room, 42 Causewayhead Road, tel. 01786/449-774, mobile 0759-054-0604, www.theoldtramhouse.com, enquiries@theoldtramhouse.com, Alison Cowie). They also have an apartment for up to five people.

$ Craigard B&B has three small, modern, tidy, and proper rooms that offer good value and a shared breakfast table (40 Causewayhead Road, tel. 01786/460-540, mobile 0784-040-1551, www. craigardstirling.co.uk, craigard@hotmail.co.uk, Liz).

$ Springfield Lodge sits at the back end of the residential zone that lines up along Causewayhead Road. It's across the street from farm fields, giving it a countryside feeling. The four neat rooms fill a spacious modern house (no kids under 6, Easter Cornton Road, tel. 01786/474-332, mobile 0795-469-2412, www. springfieldlodgebandb.co.uk, springfieldlodgebandb@gmail.com, Kim and Kevin).

STIRLING & NEARBY

Eating in Stirling

Stirling isn't a place to go looking for high cuisine; eateries here tend to be barely satisfying but functional. All of these are open daily unless otherwise noted.

UP NEAR THE CASTLE

$$ Unicorn Cafeteria, tucked under the casemates inside the castle, is a decent place for lunch if touring the grounds (same hours as castle).

$$ The Portcullis, just below the castle esplanade, is a pub that aches with history, from its dark, wood-grained bar area to its stony courtyard. The food, like the setting, is old-school. If the restaurant is full, you can also eat at the bar (01786/472-290, 12:00-15:00 & 17:30-20:30).

$$$$ Hermann's, a block below the castle esplanade, is more dressy, spacious, and homey with a sunny conservatory out back. It serves a mix of Scottish and Austrian food—perfect when you've got a hankering for haggis, but your travel partner wants Wiener schnitzel (lunch and dinner, top of Broad Street, tel. 01786/450-632, www.hermanns-restaurant.co.uk).

LOWER DOWN IN THE TOWN

Dumbarton Road, at the bottom of town, has a line of cheap eateries (Indian, Asian, cheap buffets) including **Blue Lagoon Fish & Chips** (11:00-23:00, at Port Street). Among a group of chain pubs and ethnic eateries (Thai and Italian), these three are within about a block of Stirling's clock tower near King Street in the old town center:

$$ Maharaja is popular for its "authentic Indian cuisine" served in a dressy dining room (39 King Street, tel. 01786/470-728).

$$$ Brea, which means "love" in Gaelic, has a nice Scottish theme from the menu to the decor, to the pop music playing. It's unpretentious and popular for its modern and tasty dishes. Consider treating first courses like tapas and eating family style (12:00-21:00, closed for lunch Mon, 5 Baker Street, tel. 01786/446-277).

$$ Nicky-Tams Bar and Bothy is a fun little hangout with an Irish pub-ambience, providing a great place to chat up a local and enjoy some good, basic pub grub. They serve meals from 12:00 to 20:00, then make way for drinking and, often, live music (29 Baker Street, tel. 01786/472-194).

STIRLING & NEARBY

Stirling Connections

From Stirling by Train to: Edinburgh (2/hour, 1 hour), **Glasgow** (3/hour, 45 minutes), **Inverness** (6/day direct, 3 hours, more with transfer in Perth). Train info: Tel. 0345-748-4950, www.nationalrail.co.uk.

By Bus to: Glasgow (hourly on #M8, 45 minutes), **Edinburgh** (every 2 hours on #909, 1 hour). Citylink: tel. 0871-266-3333, www.citylink.co.uk.

Near Stirling

The Wallace Monument and the Bannockburn Heritage Centre are just outside of town. Sights within side-trip distance include The Kelpies horse-head sculptures, the Falkirk Wheel boat "elevator," the stuck-in-time village of Culross, and Doune Castle.

JUST OUTSIDE OF STIRLING
▲Wallace Monument
Commemorating the Scottish hero better known to Americans as "Braveheart," this sandstone tower—built during a wave of Scottish nationalism in the mid-19th century—marks the Abbey Craig hill on the outskirts of Stirling. This is where, in 1297, William Wallace gathered forces and secured his victory against England's King Edward I at the Battle of Stirling Bridge. The victory was a huge boost to the Scottish cause, but England came back to beat the Scots the next year. (For more on Wallace, see page 744.)

Cost and Hours: £10, daily July-Aug 9:30-18:00, April-June and Sept-Oct until 17:00, Nov-March 10:30-16:00, last entry 45 minutes before closing, café at visitors center, tel. 01786/472-140, www.nationalwallacemonument.com. The £1 audioguide basically repeats the posted information.

Getting There: The monument is two miles northeast of Stirling on the A-9, signposted from the city center. Frequent public buses go from the Stirling bus station to the roundabout below the monument (15-minute ride). From there, it's about a 15-minute hike up to the visitors center, then an additional hike up to the monument. Taxis cost about £8 one-way. From the visitors center parking lot, you'll need to hike (a steep 10 minutes) or hop on the shuttle bus up the hill to the monument itself (free, departs every 10 minutes).

Visiting the Monument: Buy your ticket either at the visitors center below or the monument above. Then hike or ride the shuttle bus up to the monument's base. Gazing up, think about how this fanciful 19th-century structure, like so many around Europe in that age, was created and designed to evoke (and romanticize) earlier architectural styles—in this case, medieval Scottish castles. The crown-shaped top—reminiscent of St. Giles' on the Royal Mile in Edinburgh—and the dynamic sculpture of William Wallace are patriotic to the max.

Climb the tight stone spiral staircases a total of 246 steps, stopping at each of the three levels to see museum displays. The first level, the Hall of Arms, tells the story of William Wallace and the Battle of Stirling Bridge. Second is the Hall of Heroes, adorned with busts of great Scots—suggesting the debt this nation owes to Wallace. In the middle of the room, ogle Wallace's five-foot-long broadsword. But it's not all just hero worship: A thoughtful video presentation on the first level considers the role of Wallace in both Scottish and English history, and raises the point that one person's freedom fighter is another person's terrorist. The third level's exhibits are about the monument itself: why and how it was built.

Finally, you reach the top with stunning views over Stirling, its castle, the winding River Forth, and Stirling Bridge—a 500-year-old stone version that replaced the original wooden one. Looking out from the same vantage point as Wallace, imagine how the famous battle played out. But if you find yourself picturing *Braveheart*—with  berserker Scots, their faces painted blue, running across a field to take on the English cavalry—you have the wrong idea. While that portrayal was cinematically powerful, in reality the battle took place on a bridge in a narrow valley (see sidebar).

Bannockburn Heritage Centre

Just south of Stirling is the Bannockburn Heritage Centre, commemorating what many Scots view as their nation's most significant military victory over the invading English: the Battle of Bannockburn, won by a Scottish army led by Robert the Bruce against England's King Edward II in 1314. The battle memorial is free and always open. The Heritage Centre "Battle Game" is an

Debunking *Braveheart*

The 1995 multiple-Oscar-winner movie *Braveheart* informs many travelers' impressions of William Wallace and the battles near Stirling. But Mel Gibson's much-assailed Scottish accent may very well be the most authentic thing about the film.

In the 1297 Battle of Stirling Bridge, William Wallace and his ragtag Scottish forces hid out in the forest overlooking the bottleneck bridge, waiting until the perfect moment to ambush the English. Thanks to the tight quarters and the element of surprise, the Scots won an unlikely victory. *Braveheart* serves up an entirely different version of events: armies lining up across an open field, with blue-faced, kilted Highlanders charging at top speed toward heavily armored English troops. The filmmakers left out the bridge entirely, calling it simply "The Battle of Stirling." And the blue face paint? Never happened. A millennium before William Wallace, the ancient Romans did encounter war-painted fighters in Scotland, whom they called the Picts ("painted ones"). But painting faces in the late 13th century would be like WWII soldiers suiting up in chain mail.

Braveheart takes many other liberties with history. William Wallace was *not* the rugged-born Highlander depicted in the movie—he was born in Elderslie, next to Paisley, in the Lowlands. Wallace did *not* vengefully kill Andrew de Moray for deserting him at Falkirk (Moray fought valiantly by Wallace's side at Stirling, and died from battle wounds). Robert the Bruce did *not* betray Wal-

interactive techy experience, with 3-D screens and a re-creation that basically reduces the battle to a video game.

Cost and Hours: Memorial—free, always open. Heritage Centre and "Battle Game"—£11.50, daily 10:00-17:30, Nov-Feb until 17:00, café, tel. 0844/493-2139, www.battleofbannockburn.com. If interested in the 3D experience, call or visit the website to book a time.

Getting There: Bannockburn is two miles south of Stirling on the A-872, off the M-80/M-9. For nondrivers, it's an easy bus ride from the Stirling bus station (8/hour, 15 minutes).

Background: In simple terms, Robert the Bruce—who was first and foremost a politician—found himself out of political options after years of failed diplomatic attempts to make peace with the strong-arming English. William Wallace's execution left a vacuum in military leadership, and eventually Robert stepped in, waging

lace to the English. And William Wallace most certainly did *not* impregnate the future King Edward II's French bride...who was 10 years old, not yet married to Edward, and still living in France at the time of Wallace's death.

Also, the modern concept of national "Freee-dooooom!" was essentially unknown during the divine-right Middle Ages. Wallace wasn't fighting for "democracy" or "liberty"; he simply wanted to trade one authoritarian, aristocratic ruler (from London) for another authoritarian, aristocratic ruler (from Scotland).

Even the film's title is a falsehood: No Scottish person ever referred to Wallace as "Braveheart," which was actually the nickname of one of the film's villains, Robert the Bruce. After Robert's death, his heart was taken (in a small casket) on a crusade to the Holy Land by his friend Sir James Douglas. During one battle, Douglas threw the heart at an oncoming army and shouted, "Lead on, brave heart, I will follow thee!" Gibson's title is a bit like naming a film about Abraham Lincoln *Old Hickory*.

Scottish people have mixed feelings about *Braveheart*. They appreciate the boost it gave to their underdog nation's profile—and to its tourist industry—juuust enough that they're willing to overlook the film's historical gaffes. For travelers, it can be enjoyable to watch *Braveheart* to prep for your trip...as entertainment. Then go to Stirling and get the real story. (For a fact-based account of Wallace's life, see the sidebar on page 744.)

STIRLING & NEARBY

a successful guerrilla campaign that came to a head as young Edward's army marched to Stirling. Although the Scots were greatly outnumbered, their strategy and use of terrain at Bannockburn—with its impossibly twisty stream presenting a natural barrier for the invading army—allowed them to soundly beat the English and drive Edward out of Scotland...for the time being. (For more about Robert the Bruce, see page 747.)

Visiting the Heritage Centre: There are no historic artifacts here. First, you'll spend 30 minutes learning about the emerging battle from the perspective of both sides, and getting familiar with the characters and weaponry. Then, when your time arrives, you enter the "battle room," huddling with a dozen or so others (divided into two sides—English and Scots) around a large interactive 3D map of the battleground. On screen, the "Battle Master" leads the group, but you get to call the shots as the battle unfolds.

Monument and Statue of Robert the Bruce: Leaving the center, hike out into the field behind, where you can see a monument to those lost in the fight. Nearby, on a plinth, stands an equestrian statue of Robert the Bruce.

FALKIRK

Two engaging landmarks sit just outside the town of Falkirk, 12 miles south of Stirling. Taken together, The Kelpies and the Falkirk Wheel offer a welcome change of pace from Scottish countryside kitsch. These flank Falkirk's otherwise unexciting town center, about a 5-mile, 20-minute drive apart. Driving between the two is a riddle of roundabouts. Think of it as fun: Carefully follow the brown signs and you'll eventually get there. (Ask for a flier illustrating directions between them at either site.)

▲The Kelpies

Unveiled in 2014 and standing over a hundred feet tall, these two giant steel horse heads have quickly become a symbol of this town and region. They may seem whimsical, but they're rooted in a mix of mythology and real history: Kelpies are magical, waterborne, shape-shifting sprites of Scottish lore, who often took the form of a horse. And historically, horses—the ancestors of today's Budweiser Clydesdales—were used as beasts of burden to power Scotland's industrial output. These statues stand over old canals where hardworking horses towed heavily laden barges. But if you prefer, you can just forget all that and ogle the dramatic, energy-charged statues (particularly thrilling to Denver Broncos fans) that make for an entertaining photo op. A café nearby sells drinks and light meals, and a free visitors center shows how the heads were built. A 30-minute guided tour through the inside of one of the great beasts shows how they're supported by a sleek steel skeleton: 300 tons of steel apiece, sitting upon a foundation of 1,200 tons of steel-reinforced concrete, and gleaming with 990 steel panels.

Cost and Hours: Always open and free to view (£3 to park); visitors center open daily 9:30-17:00. Tours—£7.50, daily at the bottom of every hour 10:30-16:30, fewer tours Oct-March, tel. 01324/506-850, www.thehelix.co.uk.

Getting There: The Kelpies are in a park called The Helix, just off the M-9 motorway—you'll spot them looming high over the motorway as if inviting you to exit. For a closer look, exit the M-9 for the A-905 (Falkirk/Grangemouth), then follow *Falkirk/A-904* and brown *Helix Park & Kelpies* signs.

▲▲Falkirk Wheel

At the opposite end of Falkirk stands this remarkable modern incarnation of Scottish technical know-how. You can watch the beautiful, slow-motion contraption as it spins—like a nautical

Ferris wheel—to efficiently shuttle ships between two canals separated by 80 vertical feet.

Cost and Hours: Wheel is free to view, visitors center open daily 10:00-17:30, park open until 20:00, shorter hours Nov-mid-March; cruises run about hourly and cost £13, call or go online to check schedule and book your seat, tel. 0870-050-0208, www.thefalkirkwheel.co.uk.

Getting There: Exit the M-876 motorway for *A-883/Falkirk/Denny,* then follow brown *Falkirk Wheel* signs. Parking is free and a short walk from the wheel.

Background: Scotland was a big player in the Industrial Revolution, thanks partly to its network of shipping canals (including the famous Caledonian Canal—see page 985). Using dozens of locks to lift barges up across Scotland's hilly spine, these canals were effective...but slow.

The 115-foot-tall Falkirk Wheel, opened in 2002, is a modern take on this classic engineering challenge: linking the Forth and Clyde Canal below with the aqueduct of the Union Canal, 80 feet above. Rather than using rising and lowering water through several locks, the wheel simply picks boats up and—ever so slowly—takes them where they need to go, like a giant waterborne elevator. In the 1930s, it took half a day to ascend or descend through 11 locks; now it takes only five minutes.

The Falkirk Wheel is the critical connection in the Millennium Link project, an ambitious £78 million initiative to restore the long-neglected Forth and Clyde and Union canals connecting Edinburgh and Glasgow. Today this 70-mile-long aquatic connection between Scotland's leading cities is a leisurely traffic jam of pleasure craft, and canalside communities have been rejuvenated.

Visiting the Wheel: Twice an hour, the wheel springs (silently) to life: Gates rise up to seal off each of the water-filled gondolas, and then the entire structure slowly rotates a half-turn to swap the positions of the lower and upper boats—each of which stays comfortably upright. The towering structure is not only functional, but beautiful: The wheel's elegantly sweeping shape—with graceful cogs and pointed tips that slice into the water as they spin. It's strangely exciting to witness this.

The **visitors center** has a cafeteria (with a fine view of the wheel) and a shop, but no information about the wheel. The Falkirk

TI is just steps away. The park around the canal is cluttered with trampolines, laser tag, and other family amusements.

Riding the Wheel: Each hour, a barge takes 96 people (listening to a recorded narration explaining everything) into the Falkirk Wheel for the slow and graceful ride. Once at the top, the barge cruises a bit of the canal. The slow-motion experience lasts 50 minutes.

▲CULROSS

This time warp of a village, sitting across the Firth of Forth from Edinburgh (about a 30-minute drive from Stirling), is a perfectly

preserved artifact from the 17th and 18th centuries. If you're looking to let your pulse slow, stroll through a steep and sleepy village, and tour a creaky old manor house, Culross is your place. Filmmakers often use Culross to evoke Scottish villages of yore (you've seen it in everything from *Captain America: The First Avenger* to *Outlander*). While

not worth a long detour, it's a workable stop for drivers connecting Edinburgh to either the Stirling area or St. Andrews (free parking lots flank the town center—an easy, 5-minute waterfront stroll away).

The story of Culross (which locals pronounce KOO-russ) is the story of Sir George Bruce, who, in the late 16th century, figured out a way to build coal mines beneath the waters of the Firth of Forth. The hardworking town flourished, Bruce built a fine mansion, and the town was granted coveted "royal burgh" status by the king. But several decades later, with Bruce's death and the flooding of the mines, the town's fortunes tumbled—halting its development and trapping it as if in amber for centuries. Rescued and rehabilitated by the National Trust for Scotland, today the entire village feels like one big open-air folk museum.

The main sightseeing attraction here is the misnamed **Culross "Palace,"** the big-but-creaky, half-timbered home of George Bruce (£10.50, daily 11:00-17:00 in summer, Sat-Mon only in off-season, closed Nov-March, tel. 01383/880-359, www.nts.org.uk/culross). Buy your ticket at the office under the Town Hall's clock tower, pick up the included audioguide, then head a few doors down to the ochre-

colored palace. Following a 10-minute orientation film, you'll walk through several creaky floors to see how a small town's big shots lived four centuries ago. Docents in each room are happy to answer questions. You'll see the great hall, the "principal stranger's bedchamber" (guest room for VIPs), George Bruce's bedroom and stone strong room (where he stored precious—and flammable—financial documents), and the highlight, the painted chamber. The wood slats of its barrel-arched ceiling are painted with whimsical scenes illustrating Scottish virtues and pitfalls. You can also poke around the densely planted, lovingly tended garden out back.

A 45-minute **guided town walk** takes place for a small fee (3/ day, check palace website for schedule).

The only other real sight, a steep hike up the cobbled lanes to the top of town, is the partially ruined **abbey.** While there are far more evocative ruins in Scotland, it's fun to poke into the stony, mysterious-feeling interior of this church. But the stroll up the town's cobbled streets past pastel houses, with their carefully tended flower boxes, is even better than the church itself.

DOUNE

The village of Doune (pronounced "doon") is just a 15-minute drive north of Stirling. While there's not much to see in town, on its outskirts are a pair of attractions: a castle and a distillery. In the village of Doune itself, notice the town seal: a pair of crossed pistols. Aside from its castle and whisky, the town is known for its historic pistol factory. Locals speculate that the first shot of the American Revolution was fired with a Doune pistol.

Getting There: Bus #59 runs from Stirling to Doune and the distillery (just outside Doune). Drivers head to Doune, then follow castle signs on pretty back roads from there.

Doune Castle

Doune Castle is worth considering for its pop-culture connections: Most recently, Doune stands in for Castle Leoch in the TV series *Outlander.* But well before that, parts of *Monty Python and the Holy Grail* were filmed here. And, while the castle may underwhelm *Outlander* fans (only some exterior scenes were shot here), Python fans—and anyone who appreciates British comedy—will be tickled by the included audioguide,

narrated by Python troupe member Terry Jones (featuring sound clips from the film). The audioguide also has a few stops featuring Sam Heughan of *Outlander*. (If you're not into Python or *Outlander*, Scotland has better castles to visit.)

Cost and Hours: £6, daily April-Sept 9:30-17:30, Oct-March 10:00-16:00, tel. 01786/841-742.

Visiting the Castle: Buy your ticket and pick up the 45-minute audioguide, which explains that the castle's most important resident was not Claire Randall or the Knights Who Say Ni, but Robert Stewart, the Duke of Albany (1340-1420)—a man so influential he was called the "uncrowned king of Scotland." You'll see the cellars, ogle the empty-feeling courtyard, then scramble through the two tall towers and the great hall that connects them. The castle rooms are almost entirely empty, but they're brought to life by the audioguide. You'll walk into the kitchen's ox-sized fireplace to peer up the gigantic chimney, and visit the guest room's privy to peer down the medieval toilet. You'll finish your visit at the top of the main tower, with 360-degree views that allow you to fart in just about anyone's general direction.

Deanston Distillery

This big, attractive red-brick industrial complex (formerly a cotton mill) sits facing the river just outside of Doune. While Deanston has been long respected for its fruity, slightly spicy Highland single-malt whisky, the 2012 movie *The Angels' Share*, filmed partly at this distillery, helped put it on the map for tourists. The complex boasts a slick visitors center that's open for tours. On the 50-minute visit, you'll see the equipment used to make the whisky and enjoy a sample. (For more on whisky and the distillation process, see page 750.) A bit more corporate-feeling than some of my favorite Scottish distilleries, Deanston has the advantage of being handy to Stirling.

Cost and Hours: £9 or £12 depending on number of tastings, tours depart at the top of each hour daily 10:00-16:00 (last tour), best to call ahead to reserve, tel. 01786/843-010, www.deanstonmalt.com.

ST. ANDREWS

St. Andrews is synonymous with golf. But there's much more to this charming town than its famous links. Dramatically situated at the edge of a sandy bay, St. Andrews is the home of Scotland's most important university—think of it as the Scottish Cambridge. And centuries ago, the town was the religious capital of the country.

In its long history, St. Andrews has seen two boom periods. First, in the early Middle Ages, the relics of St. Andrew made the town cathedral one of the most important pilgrimage sites in Christendom. The faithful flocked here from all over Europe, leaving the town with a medieval all-roads-lead-to-the-cathedral street plan that survives today. But after the Scottish Reformation, the cathedral rotted away and the town became a forgotten backwater. A new wave of visitors arrived in the mid-19th century, when a visionary mayor (with the on-the-nose surname Playfair) began to promote the town's connection with the newly in-vogue game of golf. Most buildings in town date from this Victorian era.

Today St. Andrews remains a popular spot for students, golf devotees (from amateurs to professional golfers to celebrities), and occasionally Britain's favorite royal couple, Will and Kate (college sweethearts, U. of St. A. class of '05). With vast sandy beaches, golfing opportunities for pros and novices alike, playgrounds of castle and cathedral ruins, and a fun-loving student vibe, St. Andrews is an appealing place to take a vacation from your busy vacation.

PLANNING YOUR TIME

St. Andrews, hugging the east coast of Scotland, is a bit off the main tourist track. But it's well connected by train to Edinburgh (via bus from nearby Leuchars), making it a worthwhile day trip from the capital. Better yet, spend a night (or more, if you're a golfer) to enjoy this university town after dark.

If you're not here to golf, this is a good way to spend a day: Follow my self-guided walk, which connects the golf course, the university quad, the castle, and the cathedral. Dip into the Golf Museum, watch the golfers on the Old Course, and play a round at "the Himalayas" putting green, or walk along the West Sands beach.

Orientation to St. Andrews

St. Andrews (pop. 16,000, plus several-thousand more students during term) is situated at the tip of a peninsula next to a broad bay. The town retains its old medieval street plan: Three main streets (North, Market, and South) converge at the cathedral, which overlooks the sea at the tip of town. The middle street—Market Street—has the TI and many handy shops and eateries. North of North Street, the seafront street called The Scores connects the cathedral with the golf scene, which huddles along the West Sands beach at the base of the old town. St. Andrews is compact: You can stroll across town—from the cathedral to the historic golf course—in about 15 minutes.

TOURIST INFORMATION

St. Andrews' helpful TI is on Market Street, about two blocks in front of the cathedral (Mon-Sat 9:15-17:00, Sun from 10:00, closed Sun in winter; free Wi-Fi, 70 Market Street, tel. 01334/472-021, www.visitscotland.com).

ARRIVAL IN ST. ANDREWS

By Train and Bus: The nearest train station is in the village of Leuchars, five miles away. From there, a 10-minute bus ride takes you right into St. Andrews (buy ticket from driver, buses meet most trains—see schedule at bus shelter for next bus to St. Andrews; while waiting, read the historical info under the nearby flagpole). St. Andrews' bus station is near the base of Market Street—a short walk from most B&Bs and the TI. A taxi from Leuchars into St. Andrews costs about £14.

By Car: For a short stay, drivers can park anywhere along the street in the town center (pay-and-display, coins only, 2-hour limit, monitored Mon-Sat 9:00-17:00, Sun from 13:00). For longer stays, you can park for free along certain streets near the center (such as the small lot near the B&B neighborhood around Murray Place, and along The Scores), or use one of the pay-and-display lots near the entrance to town.

HELPFUL HINTS

Golf Events: Every five years, St. Andrews is swamped with about 100,000 visitors when it hosts the British Open (officially called "The Open Championship"; the next one will be the 150th in 2021). The town also fills up every year in early October for the Alfred Dunhill Links Championship. Unless you're a golf pilgrim, avoid the town at these times (as room rates skyrocket).

School Term: The University of St. Andrews has two terms: spring semester ("Candlemas"), from mid-February through May; and fall semester ("Martinmas"), from mid-September until December. St. Andrews has a totally different vibe in the summer, when most students leave and are replaced by upper-crust golfers and tourists.

Sand Surfing and Adventure Activities: Nongolfers who want to stay busy while their travel partners play the Old Course may enjoy some of the adventure activities offered by **Blown Away**—including "land yachting" (zipping across the beach in wind-powered go-carts), kayaking, and paddle boarding. Brothers Guy and Jamie McKenzie set up shop at the northern tip of the West Sands beach (sporadic hours—call first, mobile 07784-121-125, www.blownaway.co.uk, ahoy@blownaway.co.uk).

Theater: The **Byre Theatre** regularly hosts concerts, shows, dance, and opera. Check their website or stop in to see what's on (tickets about £10-25, Abbey Street, tel. 01334/475-000, www.byretheatre.com).

Ghost Tours: Richard Falconer, who has researched and written books on paranormal activity in the area, gives 1.5-hour tours mixing St. Andrews history with ghost stories (£12, tours at 16:00, 17:30, 19:30, and 21:00, must book ahead, text 0746-296-3163 or visit www.standrewsghosttours.com).

St. Andrews Walk

This walk links all of St. Andrews' must-see sights and takes you down hidden medieval streets. Allow a couple of hours, or more if you detour for the sights along the way.

• *Start at the base of the seaside street called The Scores, overlooking the famous golf course.*

ST. ANDREWS

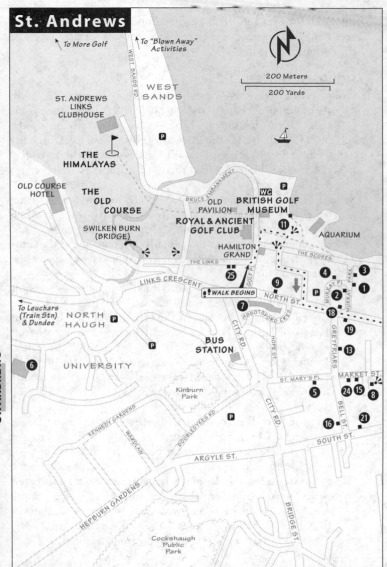

▲The Old Course

You're looking at the mecca of golf. The 18th hole of the world's first golf course is a few yards away, on your left (for info on playing the course, see "Golfing in St. Andrews," later).

The gray Neoclassical building to the right of the 18th hole is the clubhouse of the **Royal and Ancient Golf Club**—"R&A" for short. R&A is a private club with membership by invitation only;

Accommodations

1. Glenderran Guest House & Cameron House
2. Hoppity House
3. Montague Guest House & Lorimer House
4. Doune Guest House
5. St. Andrews Tourist Hostel
6. Agnes Blackadder Hall
7. McIntosh Hall

Eateries & Other

8. Forgan's
9. Playfair's
10. The Doll's House
11. The Seafood Ristorante
12. Little Italy
13. Kazoku
14. Cromars
15. Tailend
16. Aikmans
17. The Central
18. Greyfriars
19. Taste
20. Luvians Bottle Shop
21. I. J. Mellis Cheesemonger
22. Fisher and Donaldson
23. B. Jannettas
24. Supermarket (2)
25. Tom Morris & Old Course Shops

it was men-only until 2014, but now—finally!—women are also allowed to join. (In Scotland, men-only clubs lose tax benefits, which is quite costly, but they generally don't care about expenses because their membership is wealthy.) The shop (across the street from the 18th hole, next to Tom Morris—the oldest golf shop in the world) is a great spot to buy a souvenir for the golf lover back home. Even if you're not golfing, watch the action for a while. (Serious fans can walk around to the low-profile stone bridge across the creek called the Swilken Burn, with golf's single most iconic view: back over the 18th hole and the R&A Clubhouse.)

Overlooking the course is the big red-sandstone **Hamilton Grand,** an old hotel that was turned into university dorms and then swanky apartments (rumor has it Samuel L. Jackson owns one). According to town legend, the Hamilton Grand was originally built to upstage the R&A Clubhouse by an American upset over being declined membership to the exclusive club.

Between Hamilton Grand and the beach is the low-profile British Golf Museum (described later, under "Golfing in St. Andrews").

• *Turn your back to the golf course and walk through the park toward the obelisk (along the street called The Scores). Stop at the top of the bluff.*

Beach Viewpoint

The broad, two-mile-long sandy beach that stretches below the golf course is the **West Sands.** It's a wonderful place for a relaxing and/or invigorating walk. Or do a slo-mo jog, humming the theme to *Chariots of Fire*—this is the beach on which the characters run in the movie's famous opening scene.

From the bluff look at the **cliffs** on your right. The sea below was once called "Witches' Lake" because of all the women and men pushed off the cliff on suspicion of witchcraft.

The big obelisk is a **martyrs' monument,** commemorating all those who died for their Protestant beliefs during the Scottish Reformation. (We'll learn more about that chapter of St. Andrews history farther along this walk.)

The Victorian bandstand **gazebo** (between here and the Old Course) recalls the town's genteel heyday as a seaside resort, when the train line ran all the way to town.

• *Just opposite the obelisk, across The Scores and next to Alexander's Restaurant, walk down the tiny alley called...*

Gillespie Wynd

This winds through the back gardens of the city's stone houses. Notice how the medieval platting gave each landowner a little bit of street front and a long back garden. St. Andrews' street plan typifies that of a medieval pilgrimage town: All main roads lead to the cathedral; only tiny lanes, hidden alleys, and twisting "wynds" (rhymes with "minds") such as this one connect the main east-west streets.

• *The wynd pops you out onto North Street. Head left, past the cinema toward the church tower with the red clock face. It's on the corner of North Street and Butts Wynd. For some reason, this street sign often goes missing.*

St. Salvator's College

The tower with the red clock marks the entrance to St. Salvator's College. If you're a student, be careful not to stand on the **initials PH** in the reddish cobbles in front of the gate. These mark the spot where St. Andrews alum and professor Patrick Hamilton—the Scottish Reformation's most famous martyr—was burned at the stake. According to student legend, as he suffered in the flames, Hamilton threatened that any students who stood on this spot would fail their exams.

Now enter the grounds by walking through the arch under the tower. (If the entrance is closed, you can go halfway down Butts

Wynd and enter, or at least look, through the gate to the green square.) This grassy square, known to students as **Sally's Quad,** is the heart of the university. As most of the university's classrooms, offices, and libraries are spread out across the medieval town, this quad is the one focal point for student gatherings. It's where graduation is held every July, where the free-for-all food fight of Raisin Monday takes place in November (see sidebar on page 892), and where almost the entire student body gathered on the wedding day of their famous alumni couple Prince William and Kate Middleton for a celebration complete with military flybys.

On the outside wall of St. Salvator's Chapel, under the arcade, are **display cases** holding notices and university information; if you're here in spring, you might see students nervously clustered here, looking to see if they've passed their exams.

Go through the simple wooden door and into the **chapel.** Dating from 1450, this is the town's most beautiful medieval church. It's a Gothic gem, with a wooden ceiling, 19th-century stained glass, a glorious organ, and what's supposedly the pulpit of reformer John Knox.

Stroll around Sally's Quad counterclockwise. On the east (far) side, stop to check out the crazy faces on the heads above the second-floor windows. Find the **university's shield** over the door marked *School 6.* The diamonds are from the coat of arms of the bishop who issued the first university charter in 1411; the crescent moon is a shout-out to Pope Benedict XIII, who gave the OK in

The Scottish Reformation

It's easy to forget that during the 16th-century English Reformation—when King Henry VIII split with the Vatican and formed the Anglican Church (so he could get an officially recognized divorce)—Scotland was still its own independent nation. Like much of northern Europe, Scotland eventually chose a Protestant path, but it was more gradual and grassroots than Henry VIII's top-down, destroy-the-abbeys approach. While the English Reformation resulted in the Church of England (a.k.a. the Anglican Church, called "Episcopal" outside of England), with the monarch at its head, the Scottish Reformation created the Church of Scotland, which had groups of elected leaders (called "presbyteries" in church jargon).

One of the leaders of the Scottish Reformation was John Knox (1514-1572), who studied under the great Swiss reformer John Calvin. Returning to Scotland, Knox hopped from pulpit to pulpit, and his feverish sermons incited riots of "born-again" iconoclasts who dismantled or destroyed Catholic churches and abbeys (including St. Andrew's Cathedral). Knox's newly minted Church of Scotland gradually spread from the Lowlands to the Highlands. The southern and eastern part of Scotland, around St. Andrews—just across the North Sea from the Protestant countries of northern Europe—embraced the Church of Scotland long before the more remote and Catholic-oriented part of the country to the north and west. Today about 40 percent of Scots claim affiliation with the Church of Scotland, compared with 20 percent who are Catholic (still mostly in the western Highlands). Glasgow and western Scotland are more Catholic partly because of the Irish immigrants who settled there after fleeing the potato famine in the 1840s.

1413 to found the university (his given name was Peter de Luna); the lion is from the Scottish coat of arms; and the X-shaped cross is a stylized version of the Scottish flag (a.k.a. St. Andrew's Cross). On the next building to the left, facing the chapel, is St. Andrew himself (above door of building labeled *Lower & Upper College Halls*).

• *Exit the square and make your way back to Butts Wynd. Walk to the end; you're back at The Scores. Across the street and a few steps to the right is the...*

Museum of the University of St. Andrews (MUSA)

This free museum is worth a quick stop. The first room has some well-explained medieval artifacts. Find the copy of the earliest-known map of the town, made in 1580—back when the town walls led directly to the countryside and the cathedral was intact. Notice that the street plan within the town walls has remained the same—but no golf course. The next room has some exhibits on student life, including the "silver arrow competition" (which determined the best archer on campus from year to year) and several of the traditions explained in the "Student Life in St. Andrews" sidebar. The next room displays scientific equipment, great books tied to the school, and an exhibit on the Scottish Reformation. The final room has special exhibits. For a great view of the West Sands, climb to the rooftop terrace.

Cost and Hours: Free; Mon-Sat 10:00-17:00, Sun 12:00-16:00, shorter hours and closed Mon-Wed in winter; 7 The Scores, tel. 01334/461-660, www.st-andrews.ac.uk/musa.

• *Leaving the museum, walk left toward the castle. The turreted stone buildings along here (including one fine example next door to the museum) are built in the Neo-Gothic Scottish Baronial style, and most are academic departments. About 100 yards further along, the grand building on the right is St. Salvator's Hall, the most prestigious of the university residences and former dorm of Prince William.*

Just past St. Salvator's Hall on the left are the remains of...

St. Andrews Castle

Overlooking the sea, the castle is an evocative empty shell—another casualty of the Scottish Reformation. With a small museum

and good descriptions, it offers a quick king-of-the-castle experience in a striking setting.

Cost and Hours: £6, £9 combo-ticket includes cathedral exhibit, daily April-Sept 9:30-17:30, Oct-March 10:00-16:00, tel. 01334/477-196, www.historic-scotland.gov.uk.

Visiting the Castle: Your visit starts with a colorful, kid-friendly exhibit about the history of the castle. Built by a bishop to entertain visiting diplomats in the late 12th century, the castle was home to the powerful bishops, archbishops, and cardinals of St. Andrews. In 1546, the cardinal burned a Protestant preacher at the stake in front of the castle. In retribution, Protestant reformers took the castle and killed the cardinal. In 1547, the French came to attack the castle on behalf of their Catholic ally, Mary, Queen of Scots. During the ensuing siege, a young Protestant refugee named John Knox was captured and sent to France to row on a galley ship. Eventually he traveled to Switzerland and met the Swiss Protestant ringleader, John Calvin. Knox brought Calvin's ideas back home and became Scotland's greatest reformer.

Next, head outside to explore. The most interesting parts are

Student Life in St. Andrews

St. Andrews is first and foremost a university town. Scotland's most prestigious university, founded in 1411, is the third-oldest in the English-speaking world after Oxford and Cambridge. While U. of St. A. is sometimes called "England's northernmost university" due to the high concentration of English students—as numerous as the Scottish ones—a quarter of the 6,000 undergrads and 1,000 grad students hail from overseas.

Some Scots resent the preponderance of upper-crust English students (disparagingly dubbed "Yahs" for the snooty way they say "yes"). However, these southerners pay the bills—they are on the hook for tuition, unlike Scots and most EU citizens. And no one seems to mind that the school's most famous graduates, Prince William and Kate Middleton (class of '05), are the definition of upper-class. Soon after "Wills" started studying art history here, the number of female art history majors skyrocketed. (He later switched to geography.)

As with any venerable university, St. Andrews has its share of quirky customs. Most students own traditional red academic "gowns" (woolen robes) to wear on special occasions, such as graduation. In medieval times, however, they were the daily uniform—supposedly so students could be easily identified in brothels and pubs. (In a leap of faith, divinity students—apparently beyond temptation—wear black.) The way the robe is worn indicates the student's status: First-year students (called "bejants") wear them normally, on the shoulders; second-years ("semi-bejants") wear them slightly off the shoulders; third-years ("tertians") wear them off one shoulder (right for "scientists," left for "artists"); and fourth-years ("magistrands") wear them off both shoulders.

The best time to see these robes is during the Pier Walk on Sundays during the university term. After church services (around noon), gown-clad students parade out to the end of the lonesome pier beyond the cathedral ruins. The tradition dates so far back that no one's sure how it started (probably to bid farewell to a visiting dignitary). Today, students just enjoy being a part of the visual spectacle of a long line of red robes flapping in the North Sea wind.

Another age-old custom is a social-mentoring system in which underclass students choose an "academic family." On Raisin Monday, in mid-November, students give their upperclass "parents" treats—traditionally raisins, but these days more often indulgences like wine and lingerie. Then the "parents" dress up their "children" in outrageous costumes and parade them through town. The underclass students are obliged to carry around "receipts" for their gifts—written on unlikely or unwieldy objects like plastic dinosaurs, microwave ovens, or even refrigerators—and to sing the school song in Latin on demand. This oddball scenario invariably degenerates into a free-for-all food fight on Sally's Quad.

underground: the "bottle dungeon," where prisoners were sent, never to return (peer down into it in the Sea Tower); and the tight "mine" and even tighter "counter-mine" tunnels (follow the signs, crawling is required to reach it all; go in as far as your claustrophobia allows). This shows how the besieging pro-Catholic Scottish government of the day dug a mine to take (or "undermine") the castle—but were followed at every turn by the Protestant counterminers.

Nearby: Just below the castle is a small beach called the **Castle Sands,** where university students take a traditional and chilly morning dip on May 1. Supposedly, doing this May Day swim is the only way to reverse the curse of having stepped on Patrick Hamilton's initials (explained earlier).

> • *Leaving the castle, turn left and continue along the bluff on The Scores, which soon becomes a pedestrian lane leading directly to the gate to the cathedral graveyard. Enter it to stand amid the tombstone-strewn ruins of...*

▲St. Andrews Cathedral

Between the Great Schism and the Reformation (roughly the 14th-16th centuries), St. Andrews was the ecclesiastical capital of Scotland—and this was its showpiece church. Today the site features the remains of the cathedral and cloister (with walls and spires pecked away by centuries of scavengers), a graveyard, and a small exhibit and climbable tower.

Cost and Hours: Cathedral ruins-free, exhibit and tower-£5, £9 combo-ticket includes castle; daily April-Sept 9:30-17:30, Oct-March 10:00-16:00, tel. 01334/472-563, www.historic-scotland.gov.uk.

Background: It was the relics of the Apostle Andrew that first put this town on the map and gave it its name. There are numerous legends associated with the relics. According to one version, in the fourth century, St. Rule was directed in a dream to bring the relics northward from Constantinople. When the ship wrecked offshore from here, it was clear that this was a sacred place. Andrew's bones (an upper arm, a kneecap, some fingers, and a tooth) were kept on this site, and starting in 1160, the cathedral was built and pilgrims began to arrive. Since St. Andrew had a direct connection to Jesus, his relics were believed to possess special properties, making them worthy of pilgrimages on par with St. James' relics in Santiago de Compostela, Spain (of Camino de Santiago fame). St. Andrew became Scotland's patron saint; in fact, the white "X" on the blue Scottish flag evokes the diagonal cross on which St. Andrew was crucified (he chose this type of cross because he felt unworthy to die as Jesus had).

Visiting the Cathedral: You can stroll around the cathedral

ruins—the best part of the complex—for free. First, walk between the two ruined but still towering ends of the church, which used to be the apse (at the sea end, where you entered) and the main entry (at the town end). Visually trace the gigantic footprint of the former church in the ground, including the bases of columns—like giant sawed-off tree trunks. Plaques identify where elements of the church once stood.

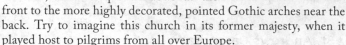

Looking at the one wall that's still standing, you can see the architectural changes that were made over the 150 years the cathedral was built—from the rounded, Romanesque windows at the

front to the more highly decorated, pointed Gothic arches near the back. Try to imagine this church in its former majesty, when it played host to pilgrims from all over Europe.

The church wasn't destroyed all at once, like all those ruined abbeys in England (demolished in a huff by Henry VIII when he broke with the pope). Instead, because the Scottish Reformation was more gradual, this church was slowly picked apart over time. First just the decorations were removed from inside the cathedral. Then the roof was pulled down to make use of its lead. Without a roof, the cathedral fell further and further into disrepair, and was quarried by locals for its handy precut stones (which you'll still find in the walls of many old St. Andrews homes). The elements—a big storm in the 1270s and a fire in 1378—also contributed to the cathedral's demise.

The surrounding **graveyard,** dating from the post-Reformation Protestant era, is much more recent than the cathedral. In this

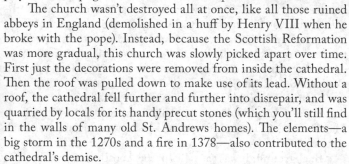

golf-obsessed town, the game even infiltrates the cemeteries: Many notable golfers from St. Andrews are buried here, including four-time British Open winner Young Tom "Tommy" Morris.

Go through the surviving wall into the former **cloister,** marked by a gigantic grassy

square in the center. You can still see the cleats up on the wall, which once supported beams. Imagine the cloister back in its heyday, its passages filled with strolling monks.

At the end of the cloister is a small **exhibit** (entry fee required), with a relatively dull collection of old tombs and other carved stone relics that have been unearthed on this site. Your ticket also includes entry to the surviving **tower of St. Rule's Church** (the rectangular tower beyond the cathedral ruins that was built to hold the precious relics of St. Andrew about a thousand years ago). If you feel like hiking up the 157 very claustrophobic steps for the view over St. Andrews' rooftops, it's worth the price. Up top, you can also look out to sea to find the pier where students traditionally parade in their robes (see sidebar on page 892).

• *Leave the cathedral grounds on the town side of the cathedral. Angling right, head down North Street. Just ahead, on the left, is the adorable...*

▲St. Andrews Preservation Trust Museum and Garden

Filling a 17th-century fishing family's house that was protected from developers, this museum is a time capsule of an earlier, simpler era. The house itself seems built for Smurfs, but it once housed 20 family members. The ground floor features replicas of a grocer's shop and a "chemist's" (pharmacy), using original fittings from actual stores. Upstairs are temporary exhibits. Out back is a tranquil garden (dedicated to the memory of a beloved professor) with "great-grandma's washhouse," featuring an exhibit about the history of soap and washing. Lovingly presented, this quaint, humble house provides a nice contrast to the big-money scene around the golf course at the other end of town.

Cost and Hours: Free but donation requested, generally open June-Sept daily 14:00-17:00, closed off-season, 12 North Street, tel. 01334/477-629, www.standrewspreservationtrust.org.

• *From the museum, hang a left around the next corner to South Castle Street. Soon you'll reach...*

Market Street

At the top of Market Street—one of the most atmospheric old streets in town—look for the tiny white house on your left, with the cute curved staircase. What's that chase scene on the roof?

Now turn right down Market Street (which leads directly to the town's center, but we'll take a curvier route). Notice how the streets and even the buildings are smaller at this oldest end of town, as if the whole city is shrinking as the streets close in on the cathedral. Homeowners along Market Street are particularly proud of their address, and recently pooled their money to spiff up the cobbles and sidewalks.

Passing an antique bookstore on your right, take a left onto Baker Lane, a.k.a. Baxter Wynd. You'll pass a tiny and inviting public garden on your right before landing on South Street.

ST. ANDREWS

• *Turn right and head down South Street. After 50 yards, cross the street and enter a gate marked by a cute gray facade and a university insignia.*

St. Mary's College

This is the home of the university's School of Divinity (theology). If the gate's open, find the peaceful quad, with its gnarled tree that was purportedly planted by Mary, Queen of Scots. To get a feel of student life from centuries past, try poking your nose into one of the old classrooms.

• *Back on South Street, continue to your left. Some of the plainest buildings on this stretch of the street have the most interesting history—several of them were built to fund the Crusades. Turn right on Church Street. You can end this walk at charming Church Square—perhaps while enjoying a decadent pastry from the recommended Fisher and Donaldson bakery. Or if you continue a few more yards down Church Street, you'll spill onto Market Street and the heart of town.*

Golfing in St. Andrews

St. Andrews is the Cooperstown of golf. While St. Andrews lays claim to founding the sport (the first record of golf being played here was in 1553), nobody knows exactly where and when people first hit a ball with a stick for fun. In the Middle Ages, St. Andrews traded with the Dutch; some historians believe they picked up a golf-like Dutch game played on ice and translated it to the bonnie rolling hills of Scotland's east coast. Since the grassy beachfront

strip just outside St. Andrews was too poor to support crops, it was used for playing the game—and, centuries later, it still is. Why do golf courses have 18 holes? Because that's how many fit at the Old Course—golf's single most famous site. When you putt-er around, keep in mind this favorite Scottish say-it-aloud joke: "Balls," said the queen. "If I had two, I'd be king." The king laughed—he had to.

The Old Course

The Old Course hosts the British Open every five years (next in 2021). At other times it's open to the public for golfing. The famous Royal and Ancient Golf Club (R&A) doesn't actually own the course, which is public and managed by the St. Andrews Links Trust. Drop by the St. Andrews Links Clubhouse, overlooking the beach near the Old Course (open long hours daily). They have a well-stocked shop, a restaurant, and a rooftop garden with nice views over the Old Course.

Old Course Tours: One-hour guided tours visit the 1st, 17th, and 18th holes (£10, daily April-May at 11:00, June-Sept at 11:00 and 14:00, leaves from the St. Andrews Links Clubhouse, tel. 01334/466-666, www.standrews.com).

Teeing Off at the Old Course: Playing at golf's pinnacle course is pricey (£175/person, less off-season), but open to the public—subject to lottery drawings for tee times and reserved spots by club members. You can play the Old Course only if you have a handicap of 24 (men) or 36 (women and juniors) or better; bring along your certificate or card. If you don't know your handicap—or don't know what "handicap" means—then you're not good enough to play here (they want to keep the game moving). If you play, you'll do nine holes out, then nine more back in—however, all but four share the same greens.

Reserving a Tee Time: To ensure a specific tee time at the Old Course, reserve a year ahead during a brief window between late August and early September (fill out form at www.standrews.com). Otherwise, some tee times are determined each day by a lottery called the "daily ballot." Enter your name on their website, in person, or by calling 01334/466-666—by 14:00 two days before (2 players minimum, 4 players max). They post the results online at 16:00. Note that no advance reservations are taken on Saturdays or in September, and the courses are closed on Sundays—which is traditionally the day reserved for townspeople to stroll.

Singleton Strategies: Single golfers aren't eligible to reserve or ballot. If you're golfing solo, you could try to team up with someone (ask your B&B for tips). Otherwise, each day, a few single golfers fill out a two- or three-golfer group by showing up in person at the Old Pavilion (in front of the R&A Clubhouse). It's first-come, first-served, and a very long shot, so get there early. The starter generally arrives at 6:00, but die-hard golfers start lining up several hours before or even camp out overnight (especially in peak season). Swing by the day before, when they should have a sense of how likely a spot is to open up and can recommend just how early to arrive.

Other Courses: Two of the seven St. Andrews Links courses are right next to the Old Course—the New Course and the Jubilee Course. And the modern cliff-top Castle Course is just outside the city. These are cheaper, and it's much easier to get a tee time (£75 for New and Jubilee, £120 for Castle Course, much less for others). It's usually possible to get a tee time for the same day or next day (if you want a guaranteed reservation, make it at least 2 weeks in advance). The Castle Course has great views overlooking the town, but even more wind to blow your ball around.

Club Rental: You can rent decent-quality clubs around town for about £30. The **Auchterlonies** shop has a good reputation (on Golf Place—a few doors down from the R&A Clubhouse, tel. 01334/473-253, www.auchterlonies.com); you can also rent clubs from the St. Andrews Links Clubhouse for a few pounds more.

▲The Himalayas

The St. Andrews Ladies' Putting Club, better known as "The Himalayas" (for its dramatically hilly terrain), is basically a very classy (but still relaxed) game of minigolf.

The course presents the perfect opportunity for nongolfers (female or male) to say they've played the links at St. Andrews—for less than the cost of a Coke. It's remarkable how this cute little patch of undulating grass can present even more challenging obstacles than the tunnels, gates, and distractions of a miniature golf course back home. Flat shoes are required (no high heels). You'll see it on the left as you walk toward the St. Andrews Links Clubhouse from the R&A Clubhouse.

Cost and Hours: £3 for 18 holes. The putting green is open to nonmembers (tourists like you) Mon-Fri 10:30-18:30, Sat until 18:00, Sun from 12:00, weekends only Oct and March, closed in winter, tel. 01334/475-196, www.standrewsputtingclub.com.

British Golf Museum

This exhibit, which started as a small collection in the R&A Clubhouse across the street, is the best place in Britain to learn about the Scots' favorite sport. It's fascinating for golf lovers.

Cost and Hours: £8, April-Oct Mon-Sat 9:30-17:00, Sun from 10:00; Nov-March daily 10:00-16:00; last entry 45 minutes before closing; café upstairs; Bruce Embankment, in the blocky modern building squatting behind the R&A Clubhouse by the Old Course, tel. 01334/460-046, www.britishgolfmuseum.co.uk.

Visiting the Museum: The compact, one-way exhibit reverently presents a meticulous survey of the game's history. Start with the film, then follow the counterclockwise route to learn about the evolution of golf—from the monarchs who loved and hated golf (including the king who outlawed it because it was distracting men from church and archery practice), to Tom Morris and Bobby Jones, all the way up to the "Golden Bear" and a randy Tiger. Along the way, you'll see plenty of old clubs, balls, medals, and trophies, and learn about how the earliest "feathery" balls and wooden clubs were made. Touchscreens invite you to learn more, and you'll also see a "hall of fame" with items donated by today's biggest golfers. Finally, you'll have a chance to dress up in some old-school golfing duds and try out some of that antique equipment for yourself.

Sleeping in St. Andrews

Owing partly to the high-roller golf tourists flowing through the town, St. Andrews' accommodations are quite expensive. During graduation week in June, hotels often require a four-night stay and book up quickly. All of the guesthouses I've listed are on the streets called Murray Park and Murray Place, between North Street and The Scores in the old town. If you need to find a room on the fly, look around in this same neighborhood, which has far more options than just the ones I've listed below.

$$$ Glenderran Guest House offers five plush rooms (including two true singles) and a few nice breakfast extras (no kids under 12, pay same-day laundry, 9 Murray Park, tel. 01334/477-951, www.glenderran.com, info@glenderran.com, Ray and Maggie).

$$ Hoppity House is a bright and contemporary place, with attention to detail and fun hosts Gordon and Heather, who are helpful and generous with travel tips. There's a lounge and kitchen for guest use and a storage closet for golf equipment. You may find a stuffed namesake bunny or two hiding out among its four impeccable rooms (cash or PayPal only, fridges in rooms, 4 Murray Park, tel. 01334/461-116, mobile 07701-099-100, www.hoppityhouse.co.uk, enquiries@hoppityhouse.co.uk).

$$ Cameron House has five clean and simple rooms around a beautiful stained-glass atrium (two-night minimum in summer, 11 Murray Park, tel. 01334/472-306, www.cameronhouse-sta.co.uk, info@cameronhouse-sta.co.uk, Donna).

$$ Montague Guest House has richly furnished public spaces—with a cozy, leather-couches lounge/breakfast room—and eight nice rooms (21 Murray Park, tel. 01334/479-287, www.montaguehouse.com, info@montagueguesthouse.com, Raj and Judith).

$$ Lorimer House has six comfortable, tastefully decorated rooms, including one on the ground floor (two-night minimum preferred, no kids under 12, 19 Murray Park, tel. 01334/476-599, www.lorimerhouse.com, info@lorimerhouse.com, Mick and Chris).

$$ Doune Guest House's seven rooms provide a more impersonal but perfectly comfortable place to stay in St. Andrews (breakfast extra, two-night minimum preferred in summer, 5 Murray Place, tel. 01334/475-195, www.dounehouse.com, info@dounehouse.com).

ST. ANDREWS

¢ **St. Andrews Tourist Hostel** has 44 beds in colorful 5- to 8-bed rooms about a block from the base of Market Street. The high-ceilinged lounge is a comfy place for a break, and the friendly staff is happy to recommend their favorite pubs (kitchen, St. Mary's Place, tel. 01334/479-911, www.hostelsstandrews.com, info@hostelsstandrews.com).

UNIVERSITY ACCOMMODATIONS

In the summer (early June-Aug), some of the University of St. Andrews' student-housing buildings are tidied up and rented out to tourists. I've listed the most convenient options below (website for both: www.discoverstandrews.com; pay when reserving). Both of these include breakfast and Wi-Fi. Because true single rooms are rare in St. Andrews' B&Bs, these dorms are a good option for solo travelers.

$ **Agnes Blackadder Hall** has double beds and private bathrooms; it's more comfortable, but also more expensive and less central (North Haugh, tel. 01334/467-000, agnes.blackadder@st-andrews.ac.uk).

$ **McIntosh Hall** is cheaper and more central, but it only has twin beds and shared bathrooms (Abbotsford Crescent, tel. 01334/467-035, mchall@st-andrews.ac.uk).

Eating in St. Andrews

RESTAURANTS

$$$ **Forgan's** is tempting and popular, tucked back in a huge space behind Market Street in what feels like a former warehouse. It's done up country-kitschy, with high ceilings, cool lanterns, and a fun energy. It serves up hearty food and offers a tempting steak selection (daily 12:00-22:00, reservations smart, 110 Market Street, tel. 01334/466-973, www.forgansstandrews.co.uk). On Friday and Saturday nights after 22:30, they have live *ceilidh* (traditional Scottish) music, and everyone joins in the dancing; consider reserving a booth for a late dinner, then stick around for the show. They also have live acoustic music on Thursday evenings.

$$$ **Playfair's,** a restaurant and steakhouse downstairs in the Ardgowan Hotel between the B&B neighborhood and the Old Course, has a cozy/classy interior and outdoor seating at rustic tables set just below the busy street. Their bar next door also serves food (daily 12:00-22:00, off-season weekdays open for dinner only, 2 Playfair Terrace on North Street, tel. 01334/472-970).

$$$ **The Doll's House** serves dressed-up Scottish cuisine in a stone-and-wood interior or at tables on the square in front, complete with fur throws on the chairs (daily 10:00-22:00, across from Holy Trinity Church at 3 Church Square, tel. 01334/477-422).

$$$$ The Seafood Ristorante, in a modern glassy building overlooking the beach near the Old Course, is like dining in an aquarium. They serve high-end Italian with a focus on seafood in a formal space with floor-to-ceiling windows providing unhindered views (minimum £20/person food order at dinner, daily 12:00-14:30 & 18:00-21:30, reservations a must on weekends and in summer, The Scores, tel. 01334/479-475, www.theseafoodristorante. com).

$$ Little Italy is a crowded Italian joint with all the clichés—red-and-white checkered tablecloths, replica Roman busts, a bit of freneticism, and even a moped in the wall. But the food is authentically good and the menu is massive. It's popular—make reservations (daily 12:30-22:30, 2 Logies Lane, tel. 01334/479-299).

$$ Kazoku is a casual and satisfying sushi bar that also serves some hot Japanese dishes (seared scallops on a bed of haggis, anyone?). It's a family business—the name means "family" in Japanese (daily 12:00-14:30 & 17:00-21:30, 6A Greyfriars Gardens, tel. 01334/477-750).

Fish-and-Chips: $ Cromars is a local favorite for takeaway fish-and-chips (and burgers). At the counter, you can order yours to go, or—in good weather—enjoy it at the sidewalk tables; farther in is a small **$$** sit-down restaurant with more choices (both open daily 11:00-22:00, at the corner of Union and Market, tel. 01334/475-555). **Tailend** also has a **$** takeaway counter up front (fish-and-chips) and a **$$** restaurant with a bigger selection in the back (daily 11:30-22:00, 130 Market Street, tel. 01334/474-070).

BEER, COFFEE, AND WHISKY

Pubs: There's no shortage in this college town. These aren't "gastropubs," but they all serve straightforward pub fare (all open long hours daily).

Aikmans, run by Barbara and Malcolm (two graduates from the university who couldn't bring themselves to leave), features a cozy wood-table ambience, a focus on ales, live music (usually Fri-Sat), and simple soups, sandwiches, and snacks (32 Bell Street, tel. 01334/477-425). **The Central,** right along Market Street, is a St. Andrews standby, with old lamps and lots of brass (77 Market Street, tel. 01334/478-296). **Greyfriars,** with forgettable food, is in a classy, modern hotel near the Murray Park B&Bs (129 North Street, tel. 01334/474-906).

Coffee: $ Taste, a little café just across the street from the B&B neighborhood, has the best coffee in town and a laid-back, borderline-funky ambience that feels like a big-city coffeehouse back home. It also serves cakes and light food (daily 7:00-18:00 in summer, open later when students are back, 148 North Street, tel. 01334/477-959).

Whisky: Luvians Bottle Shop—run by three brothers (Luigi, Vincenzo, and Antonio)—is a friendly place to talk, taste, and purchase whisky. Distilleries bottle unique single-cask vintages exclusively for this shop to celebrate the British Open every five years (ask about the 21-year-old Springbank they received in 2015 to commemorate the tournament). With nearly 50 bottles open for tastings, a map of Scotland's whisky regions, and helpful team members, this is a handy spot to learn about whisky. They also sell fine wines and a wide range of microbrews (Mon-Sat 10:00-22:00, Sun from 12:30, 66 Market Street, tel. 01334/477-752).

PICNIC FOOD AND SWEETS
Cheese: I.J. Mellis Cheesemonger, the excellent Edinburgh cheese shop with a delectable array of Scottish, English, and international cheeses, has a St. Andrews branch (Mon-Sat 9:00-19:00, Sun 10:00-17:00, 149 South Street, tel. 01334/471-410).

Pastries: Fisher and Donaldson is beloved for its rich, affordable pastries and chocolates. Listen as the straw-hatted bakers chat with their regular customers, then try their Coffee Tower—like a giant cream puff filled with rich, lightly coffee-flavored cream—or their number-one seller, the fudge doughnut (Mon-Sat 6:00-17:00, closed Sun, just around the corner from the TI at 13 Church Street, tel. 01334/472-201).

Gelato: You'll see many people walking around licking cones from **B. Jannettas,** which has been around for more than a century. While waiting in line, ponder what you want from their range of 50-plus gelato flavors (daily 9:00-22:00, 31 South Street, tel. 01334/473-285).

Supermarkets: You can stock up for a picnic at **Tesco** or **Sainsbury's Local** on Market Street.

St. Andrews Connections

Trains don't go into St. Andrews—instead, use the Leuchars station (5 miles from St. Andrews, connected by buses coordinated to meet most trains, 2-4/hour, see "Arrival in St. Andrews" on page 884).

From Leuchars by Train to: Edinburgh (1-2/hour, 1 hour), **Glasgow** (2/hour, 2 hours, transfer in Haymarket), **Inverness** (roughly hourly, 3.5 hours, 1-2 changes). Trains run less frequently on Sundays. Train info: Tel. 0345-748-4950, www.nationalrail.co.uk.

OBAN & THE INNER HEBRIDES

*Oban • Isles of Mull, Iona, and Staffa • Near Oban
(Inveraray and Kilmartin Glen)*

For a taste of Scotland's west coast, the port town of Oban is equal parts endearing and functional. This busy little ferry-and-train terminal has no important sights, but makes up the difference in character, in scenery (with its low-impact panorama of overlapping islets and bobbing boats), and with one of Scotland's best distillery tours. But Oban is also convenient: It's midway between the Lowland cities (Glasgow and Edinburgh) and the Highland riches of the north. And it's the "gateway to the isles," with handy ferry service to the Hebrides Islands.

If time is tight and serious island-hopping is beyond the scope of your itinerary, Oban is ideally situated for a busy and memorable full-day side-trip to three of the most worthwhile Inner Hebrides: big, rugged Mull; pristine little Iona, where buoyant clouds float over its historic abbey; and Staffa, a remote, grassy islet inhabited only by sea birds. Sit back, let someone else do the driving, and enjoy a tour of the Inner Hebrides.

This chapter also includes a few additional sights near Oban, handy for those connecting the dots: the most scenic route between Glasgow and Oban (along the bonnie, bonnie banks of Loch Lomond and through the town of Inveraray, with its fine castle); and the faint remains of Kilmartin Glen, the prehistoric homeland of the Scottish people.

PLANNING YOUR TIME

If you're on a speedy blitz tour of Scotland, Oban is a strategic and pleasant place to spend the night. But you'll need two nights to enjoy Oban's main attraction: the side-trip to Mull, Iona, and Staffa. There are few actual sights in Oban itself, beyond the distillery tour, but—thanks to its manageable size, scenic waterfront setting, and great restaurants—the town is an enjoyable place to linger.

Oban

Oban (pronounced OH-bin) is a low-key resort. Its winding promenade is lined by gravel beaches, ice-cream stands, fish-and-chip joints, a tourable distillery, and a good choice of restaurants. Everything in Oban is close together, and the town seems eager to please its many visitors: Wool and tweed are perpetually on sale, and posters announce a variety of day tours to Scotland's wild and wildlife-strewn western islands. When the rain clears, sun-starved Scots sit on benches along the Esplanade, leaning back to catch some rays. Wind, boats, gulls, layers of islands, and the promise of a wide-open Atlantic beyond give Oban a rugged charm.

Orientation to Oban

Oban, with about 10,000 people, is where the train system of Scotland meets the ferry system serving the Hebrides Islands. As "gateway to the isles," its center is not a square or market, but its harbor. Oban's business action, just a couple of streets deep, stretches along the harbor and its promenade.

TOURIST INFORMATION

Oban's TI, located at the North Pier, sells bus and ferry tickets, is well stocked with brochures, and has free Wi-Fi (generally daily July-Aug 9:00-19:00; April-June 9:00-17:30; Sept-March 10:00-17:00; 3 North Pier, tel. 01631/563-122, www.oban.org.uk).

HELPFUL HINTS

Bookstore: Waterstones, a huge bookstore overlooking the harborfront, offers maps and a fine collection of books on Scotland (Mon-Sat 9:00-17:30, Sun 11:00-17:00, longer hours in July-Aug, 12 George Street, tel. 0843/290-8529).

Baggage Storage: The train station has pay luggage lockers, but is open limited hours (Mon-Sat 5:00-20:30, Sun 10:45-18:00)—confirm the closing time before committing.

Laundry: You'll find **Oban Quality Laundry** tucked a block behind the main drag just off Stevenson Street (same-day drop-off service, no self-service, Mon-Fri 9:00-17:00, Sat until 13:00, closed Sun, tel. 01631/563-554). The recommended **Backpackers Plus Hostel** (page 917) will also do laundry for nonguests.

Supermarket: The giant **Tesco** is a five-minute walk from the train station (Mon-Sat until 24:00, Sun until 20:00, walk through Argyll Square and look for entrance to large parking lot on right, Lochside Street

Bike Rental: Oban Cycles is on the main drag (£25/day, Tue-Sat 10:00-17:00, closed Sun-Mon, 87 George Street, tel. 01631/566-033).

Bus Station: The "station" is just a pullout, marked by a stubby clock tower, at the roundabout in front of the train station. In peak season, it's wise to prebook bus tickets the day before—either at the TI, or at the West Coast Tours office (see next).

Bus and Island Tour Tickets: West Coast Tours, a block from the train station in the bright-red building along the harbor, sells bus and island tour tickets (Tue-Sat 6:30-17:30, Sun-Mon 8:30-17:30, 17 George Street, tel. 01631/566-809, www.westcoasttours.co.uk).

Highland Games: Oban hosts its touristy Highland Games every August (www.obangames.com), and the more local-oriented Lorne Highland Games each June (www.lorne-highland-games.org.uk). Nearby Taynuilt, a 20-minute drive east, hosts their sweetly small-town Highland Games in mid-July (www.taynuilthighlandgames.com). For more about the Highland Games, see page 918.

Tours from Oban

For the best day trip from Oban, tour the islands of Mull, Iona, and/or Staffa (offered daily Easter-Oct, described later)—or consider staying overnight on remote and beautiful Iona. With more time or other interests, consider one of many other options you'll see advertised.

Wildlife Tours

If you just want to go for a boat ride, the easiest option is the one-hour seal-watching tour (£10, various companies—look for signs at the harbor). But to really get a good look at Scottish coastal wildlife, several groups—including **Coastal Connection** (based in Oban) and **Sealife Adventures** and **SeaFari** (based in nearby

Getting Around the Highlands

By Car: The Highlands are made for joyriding. There are a lot of miles, but they're scenic, the roads are good, and the traffic is light. Drivers enjoy flexibility and plenty of tempting stopovers. Be careful, but don't be too timid about passing; otherwise, diesel fumes and large trucks might be your main memory of driving in Scotland. The farther north you go, the more away-from-it-all you'll feel, with few signs of civilization. Even on a sunny weekend, you can go miles without seeing another car. Don't wait too long to gas up—village gas stations are few and far between, and can close unexpectedly. Get used to single-lane roads: While you can make good time when they're empty (as they often are), don't let your guard down, and slow down on blind corners—you never know when an oncoming car (or a road-blocking sheep) is right around the bend. If you do encounter an oncoming vehicle, un-spoken rules of the road dictate that the driver closest to a pullout will use it—even if they have to back up. A little "thank-you" wave (or even just an index finger raised off the steering wheel) is the customary end to these encounters.

By Public Transportation: Glasgow is the gateway to this re-gion (so you'll most likely have to transfer there if coming from Edinburgh). The **train** zips from Glasgow to Fort William and Oban in the west; and up to Stirling and Inverness in the east. For more remote destinations (such as Glencoe), the bus is better.

Most of the **buses** are operated by Scottish Citylink. You can pay the driver in cash when you board. But in peak season—when these buses fill up—it's smart to buy tickets at least a day in ad-vance: Book at www.citylink.co.uk, call 0871-216-3333, or stop by a bus station or TI.

Glasgow's Buchanan Station is the main Lowlands hub for

coastal towns)—run whale-watching tours that seek out rare minke whales, basking sharks, bottlenose dolphins, and porpoises. For an even more ambitious itinerary, the holy grail is Treshnish Island (out past Staffa), which brims with puffins, seals, and other sea crit-ters. Options abound—check at the TI for information.

Open-Top Bus Tours

If the weather is good and you don't have a car, you can go by bus for a spin out of Oban for views of nearby castles and islands, plus a stop near McCaig's Tower with narration by the driver (£7, departs train station 4/day June-Sept only, 1.5 hours, www.citysightseeingoban.com).

reaching Highlands destinations. From Edinburgh, it's best to transfer in Glasgow (fastest by train, also possible by bus)—though there are direct buses from Edinburgh to Inverness, where you can connect to Highlands buses. Once in the Highlands, Inverness and Fort William serve as the main bus hubs.

Note that bus frequency can be substantially reduced on Sundays and in the off-season (Oct-mid-May). Unless otherwise noted, I've listed bus information for summer weekdays. Always confirm schedules locally.

These buses are particularly useful for connecting the sights in this book:

Buses **#976** and **#977** connect Glasgow with Oban (5/day, 3 hours).

Buses **#914, #915,** and **#916** go from Glasgow to Fort William, stopping at Glencoe (8/day, 2.5 hours to Glencoe, 3 hours total to Fort William).

Bus **#918** goes from Oban to Fort William, stopping en route at Ballachulish near Glencoe (2/day, 1 hour to Ballachulish, 1.5 hours total to Fort William).

Bus **#44** (operated by Stagecoach) is a cheaper alternative for connecting Glencoe to Fort William (hourly Mon-Sat, fewer on Sun, www.stagecoachbus.com).

Buses **#19** and **#919** connect Fort William with Inverness (7/day, 2 hours).

Buses **#M90** and **#G90** run from Edinburgh to Inverness (express #G90, 2/day, 3.5 hours; slower #M90, 6/day, 4 hours).

Bus **#G10** is an express connecting Inverness and Glasgow (5/day, 3 hours). National Express **#588** also goes direct (1/day, 4 hours, www.nationalexpress.com).

Sights in Oban

▲The Burned-Out Sightseer's Visual Tour from the Pier

If the west coast weather permits, get oriented to the town while taking a break: Head out to the North Pier, just past the TI, and find the benches that face back toward town (in front of the recommended Piazza restaurant). Take a seat and get to know Oban.

Scan the harborfront from left to right, surveying the mix of grand Victorian sandstone buildings and humbler modern storefronts. At the far-right end of town is the **ferry terminal** and—very likely—a huge ferry loading or unloading. Oban has always been on the way to somewhere, and today is no different. (A recent tourism slogan: Oban...it's closer than you think.) The townscape seems dominated by Caledonian-MacBrayne, Scotland's biggest ferry company. CalMac's 30 ships serve 24 destinations and transport

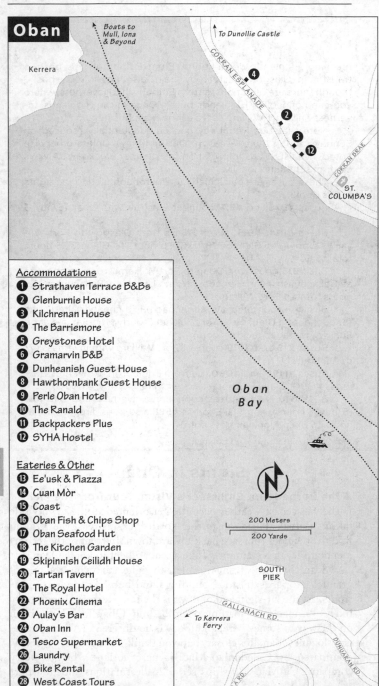

Oban

OBAN & INNER HEBRIDES

Kerrera

Boats to Mull, Iona & Beyond

To Dunollie Castle

CORRAN ESPLANADE

GORRAN BRAE

ST. COLUMBA'S

Oban Bay

200 Meters
200 Yards

SOUTH PIER

GALLANACH RD.

To Kerrera Ferry

VILLA RD.

DUNUARAN RD.

Accommodations
1 Strathaven Terrace B&Bs
2 Glenburnie House
3 Kilchrenan House
4 The Barriemore
5 Greystones Hotel
6 Gramarvin B&B
7 Dunheanish Guest House
8 Hawthornbank Guest House
9 Perle Oban Hotel
10 The Ranald
11 Backpackers Plus
12 SYHA Hostel

Eateries & Other
13 Ee'usk & Piazza
14 Cuan Mòr
15 Coast
16 Oban Fish & Chips Shop
17 Oban Seafood Hut
18 The Kitchen Garden
19 Skipinnish Ceilidh House
20 Tartan Tavern
21 The Royal Hotel
22 Phoenix Cinema
23 Aulay's Bar
24 Oban Inn
25 Tesco Supermarket
26 Laundry
27 Bike Rental
28 West Coast Tours (Day Trips, Bus Tickets)

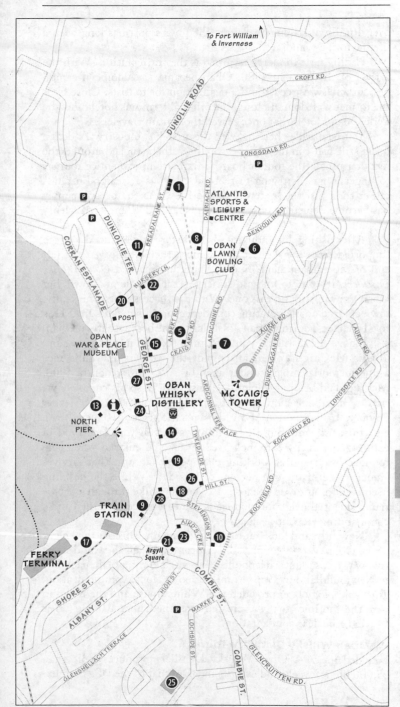

over 4 million passengers a year. The town's port has long been a lifeline to the islands.

Hiding near the ferry terminal is the **train station.** With the arrival of the train in 1880, Oban became the unofficial capital of Scotland's west coast and a destination for tourists. Close by is the former Caledonian Hotel, the original terminus hotel (now the Perle Oban Hotel) that once served those train travelers.

Tourism aside, herring was the first big industry. A dozen boats still fish commercially—you'll see them tucked around the ferry terminal. The tourist board, in an attempt to entice tourists to linger longer, is trying to rebrand Oban as a "seafood capital" rather than just the "gateway to the isles." As the ocean's supply has become depleted, most local fish is farmed. There's still plenty of shellfish.

After fishing, big industries here historically included tobacco (imported from the American colonies), then whisky. At the left end of the embankment, find the building marked *Oban Whisky Distillery*. It's rare to find a distillery in the middle of a town, but Oban grew up around this one. With the success of its whisky, the town enjoyed an invigorating confidence, optimism, and, in 1811, a royal charter. Touring Oban's distillery is the best activity in Oban.

Above the distillery, you can't miss the odd mini-Colosseum. This is **McCaig's Tower,** an employ-the-workers-and-build-me-a-fine-memorial project undertaken by an Oban tycoon in 1900. McCaig died before completing the structure, so his complete vision for it remains a mystery. This is an example of a "folly"—that uniquely British notion of an idiosyncratic structure erected by a colorful aristocrat. Building a folly was an in-your-face kind of extravagance many extremely wealthy people enjoyed when surrounded by struggling working-class people (an urge that survives among some of the one percent to this day). While the building itself is nothing to see up close, a 10-minute hike through a Victorian residential neighborhood leads you to a peaceful garden and a commanding view (nice at sunset).

Now turn and look out to sea, and imagine this: At the height of the Cold War, Oban played a critical role when the world's first two-way transatlantic telephone cable was laid from Gallanach Bay to Newfoundland in 1956—a milestone in global communication. This technology later provided the White House and the Kremlin with the "hotline" that was created after the Cuban Missile Crisis to avoid a nuclear conflagration.

▲▲Oban Whisky Distillery Tours

Founded in 1794, Oban Whisky Distillery produces more than 25,000 liters a week, and exports much of that to the US. Their exhibition (upstairs, free to all) gives a quick, whisky-centric history of Oban and Scotland.

The distillery offers serious and fragrant one-hour tours explaining the process from start to finish, with two smooth samples of their signature product: Oban whisky is moderately smoky ("peaty") and characterized by notes of sea salt, citrus, and honey. You'll also receive a whisky glass and a discount coupon for the shop. This is the handiest whisky tour you'll encounter—just a block off the harbor—and one of the best. Come 10 minutes before your tour starts to check out the exhibition upstairs. Then your guide will walk you through each step of the process: malting, mashing, fermentation, distillation, and maturation. Photos are not allowed inside. For more on whisky, including how to taste it, see page 750.

Cost and Hours: Tours cost £10, are limited to 16 people and depart every 20 to 30 minutes. Tours fill up, so book in advance by phone, online, or in person to get a firm spot. Unless it's really a busy day, you should be able to drop in and pay for a tour leaving in the next hour or so, then easily pass time in the town center. Generally open July-Sept Mon-Fri 9:30-19:30, Sat-Sun until 17:00; March-June and Oct-Nov daily 9:30-17:30; Dec-Feb daily 12:30-16:00; last tour 1.25 hours before closing, Stafford Street, tel. 01631/572-004, www.discovering-distilleries.com.

Serious Tasting: Connoisseurs can ask about their "exclusive tour," which adds a visit to the warehouse and four premium tastings in the manager's office (£40, 2 hours, likely July-Sept, Mon, Wed, and Fri at 16:00 only, reservation required).

Oban War & Peace Museum

Opened in 1995 on the 50th anniversary of Victory in Europe Day, this charming little museum focuses on Oban's experience during World War II. But it covers more than just war and peace. Photos show Oban through the years, and a 15-minute looped video gives a simple tour around the town and region. Volunteer staffers love to chat about the exhibit—or anything else on your mind (free; May-Oct Mon-Sat 10:00-18:00, Sun until 16:00; off-season daily until 16:00; next to Regent Hotel on the promenade, tel. 01631/570-007, www.obanmuseum.org.uk).

Dunollie Castle and Museum

In a park just a mile up the coast, a ruined castle and an old house hold an intimate collection of clan family treasures. This spartan, stocky castle with 10-foot walls offers a commanding, windy view of the harbor—a strategic spot back in the days when transport was mainly by water. For more than a thousand years, clan chiefs ruled this region from this ancestral home of Clan MacDougall, but the castle was abandoned in 1746. The adjacent house, which dates from 1745, shows off the MacDougall clan's heritage with a handful of rooms filled with a humble yet fascinating trove of treasures. While the exhibit won't dazzle you, the family and clan pride in the display, their "willow garden," and the walk from Oban make the visit fun.

To get there, head out of town along the harborfront promenade. At the war memorial (with inviting seaview benches), cross the street. A gate leads to a little lane, lined with historic and nature boards along the way to the castle.

Cost and Hours: £5.50, April-Oct Mon-Sat 10:00-16:00, Sun from 13:00, closed Nov-March, free tours given most days at 11:00 and 14:00, tel. 01631/570-550, www.dunollie.org.

ACTIVITIES IN OBAN
Atlantis Leisure Centre
This industrial-type sports center is a good place to get some exercise on a rainy day or let the kids run wild for a few hours. It has a rock-climbing wall, tennis courts, indoor "soft play centre" (for kids under 5), and an indoor swimming pool with a big water slide. The outdoor playground is free and open all the time (pool only-£4.20, no rental towels or suits, fees for other activities; open Mon-Fri 6:30-21:30, Sat-Sun 9:00-18:00; on the north end of Dalriach Road, tel. 01631/566-800, www.atlantisleisure.co.uk).

Oban Lawn Bowling Club
The club has welcomed visitors since 1869. This elegant green is the scene of a wonderfully British spectacle of old men tiptoeing wishfully after their balls. It's fun to watch, and—if there's no match scheduled and the weather's dry—anyone can rent shoes and balls and actually play (£5/person; informal hours, but generally daily 10:00-12:00 & 14:00-16:00 or "however long the weather lasts"; just south of sports center on Dalriach Road, tel. 01631/570-808, www.obanbowlingclub.com).

ISLANDS NEAR OBAN
The isles of Mull, Iona, and Staffa are farther out, require a full day to visit, and are described later in this chapter. For a quicker glimpse at the Inner Hebrides, consider these two options.

Isle of Kerrera
Functioning like a giant breakwater, the Isle of Kerrera (KEH-reh-rah) makes Oban possible. Just offshore from Oban, this stark but very green island offers a quick, easy opportunity to get that romantic island experience. While it has no proper roads, it offers nice hikes, a ruined castle, and a few sheep farms. It's also a fine place to bike (ask for advice at bike rental shop). You may see the Kerrera ferry filled with sheep heading for Oban's livestock market.

Getting There: You have two options for reaching the island.

A boat operated by the Oban Marina goes from Oban's North Pier to the Kerrera Marina in the northern part of the island (£5 round-trip, every two hours, book ahead at tel. 01631/565-333, www.obanmarina.com).

A ferry departs from Gallanach (two miles south of Oban) and goes to the middle of the island. This is the best option if you want to hike to Kerrera's castle (passengers only, £4.50 round-trip, bikes free, runs 10:30-18:00 with a break 12:30-14:00, none in off-season, 5-minute ride, tel. 01475/650-397, www.calmac.co.uk. To reach Gallanach, drive south, following the coast road past the ferry terminal (parking available).

Eating and Sleeping on Kerrera: $$ Waypoint Bar & Grill has a laid-back patio with a simple menu of steak, burgers, and seafood; on a nice day the open-air waterside setting is unbeatable (late May-Sept Tue-Sun 18:00-21:00, bar opens at 17:00, closed Mon and in winter, reservations highly recommended, tel. 01631/565-333, www.obanmarina.com). For lodging, your only option is the **$ Kerrera Bunkhouse,** a refurbished 18th-century stable that can sleep up to seven people in a small, cozy space (1 double and 5 single bunks, 2-night minimum, includes bedding but not towels, open Easter-Oct but must book ahead, kitchen, tel. 01631/566-367, www.kerrerabunkhouse.co.uk, info@kerrerabunkhouse.co.uk, Martin and Aideen). They also run a tea garden that serves meals (Easter-Sept daily 10:30-16:30, closed Oct-Easter).

Isle of Seil

Enjoy a drive, a walk, some solitude, and the sea. Drive 12 miles south of Oban on the A-816 to the B-844 to the Isle of Seil (pronounced "seal"), connected to the mainland by a bridge (which, locals like to brag, "crosses the Atlantic"...well, maybe a small part of it).

Just over the bridge on the Isle of Seil is a pub called **Tigh-an-Truish** ("House of Trousers"). After the Jacobite rebellions, a new law forbade the wearing of kilts on the mainland. Highlanders on the island used this pub to change from kilts to trousers before they made the crossing. The pub serves great meals and good seafood dishes to those either in kilts or pants (pub generally open daily—call ahead, tel. 01852/300-242).

Seven miles across the island, on a tiny second island and facing the open Atlantic, is **Easdale,** a historic, touristy, windblown little slate-mining town—with a slate-town museum and an egomaniac's incredibly tacky "Highland Arts" shop (shuttle ferry goes the 300 yards). Expensive wildlife/nature tours plus tours to Iona and Staffa also run from Easdale (www.seafari.co.uk).

Nightlife in Oban

Little Oban has a few options for entertaining its many visitors; check www.obanwhatson.co.uk. Fun low-key activities may include open-mic, disco, or quiz theme nights in pubs; occasional Scottish folk shows; coffee meetings; and—if you're lucky—duck races. On Wednesday nights, the Oban Pipe Band plays in the square by the train station. Here are a few other ways to entertain yourself while in town.

Music and Group Dancing: On many summer nights, you can climb the stairs to the **Skipinnish Ceilidh House,** a sprawling venue on the main drag for music and dancing (the owners are professional musicians Angus and Andrew). There's *ceilidh* (KAY-lee) dancing a couple of times per week, where you can learn some group dances to music performed by a folk band (including, usually, a piper). These group dances are a lot of fun—wallflowers and bad dancers are warmly welcomed, and the staff is happy to give you pointers (£8, May-Sept Mon & Thu at 21:00). They also host concerts by folk and traditional bands (check website for schedule, 34 George Street, tel. 01631/569-599, www.skipinnishceilidhhouse. com).

Traditional Music: Various pubs and hotels in town have live traditional music in the summer; as specifics change from year to year, ask your B&B host or the TI for the latest. Try the **Tartan Tavern,** a block off the waterfront at 3 Albany Terrace or **The Royal Hotel,** just above the train station on Argyll Square.

Cinema: The **Phoenix Cinema** closed down for two years and then was saved by the community. It's now volunteer-run and booming (140 George Street, tel. 01631/562-905, www. obanphoenix.com).

Characteristic Pubs: Aulay's Bar, with decor that shows off Oban's maritime heritage, has two sides, each with a different personality (I like the right-hand side). Having a drink here invariably comes with a good "blether" (conversation), and the gang is local (daily 11:00-24:00, 8 Airds Crescent, just around the corner from the train station and ferry terminal). The **Oban Inn,** right on the harborfront, is also a fun and memorable place for a pint and possibly live music.

Sleeping in Oban

Oban's B&Bs offer a much better value than its hotels.

ON STRATHAVEN TERRACE

The following B&Bs line up on a quiet, flowery street that's nicely located two blocks off the harbor, three blocks from the center, and a 10-minute walk from the train station. Rooms here are more compact than those on the Esplanade and don't have views, but the location can't be beat.

By car, as you enter town from the north, turn left immediately after King's Knoll Hotel, and take your first right onto Breadalbane Street. ("Strathaven Terrace" is actually just the name for this row of houses on Breadalbane Street.) The alley behind the buildings has tight, free parking for all of these places.

$$ Rose Villa Guest House has six crisp and cheery rooms (at #5, tel. 01631/566-874, stuartcameronsmith@yahoo.co.uk, Stuart and Jacqueline).

$ Raniven Guest House has five simple, tastefully decorated rooms and gracious, fun-loving hosts Moyra and Stuart (cash only, 2-night minimum in summer, continental breakfast, at #1, tel. 01631/562-713, www.ranivenoban.com, bookings@ranivenoban.com).

$ Sandvilla B&B rents five pleasant, polished rooms (2-night minimum in summer, at #4, tel. 01631/564-483, www.holidayoban.co.uk, sandvilla@holidayoban.co.uk, Josephine and Robert).

ALONG THE ESPLANADE

These are along the Corran Esplanade, which stretches north of town above a cobble beach; they are a 10-minute walk from the center. For the most part, they offer much more spacious rooms than places in town (and many rooms have beautiful bay views). Walking from town, you'll reach them in this order: Kilchrenan, Glenburnie, and Barriemore. stately Victorian home, has an elegant breakfast room over the bay. Its 12 spacious, comfortable, classy rooms feel a plush living rooms. There's a nice lounge and a tiny sunroo'/562-089, www.glenburnie.co.uk, stay@glenburnie.co with a stuffed "hairy coo" head (closed mid-Nov-March, te.eme).

$$ Glenburnie Housng the bay.

$$ Ki' **House,** the turreted former retreat of a textile magnate rooms, most with bay views. The stunning room and #15 are worth the few extra pounds, while the "st rooms in the newer annex are a good value (2-night in summer, welcome drink of whisky or sherry, dif-breakfast special" every day, family rooms, closed Nov-tel. 01631/562-663, www.kilchrenanhouse.co.uk, info@renanhouse.co.uk, Colin and Frances).

$$ The Barriemore, at the very end of Oban's grand water-Esplanade, is a welcome refuge after a day of exploration. well-appointed rooms come with robes, sherry, etc. It has a nt patio, spacious breakfast room, and glassed-in sunporch with a view of the water (family suite, tel. 01631/566-356, www.barriemore.co.uk, info@barriemore.co.uk, Jan and Mark).

ABOVE THE TOWN CENTER

These places perch on the hill above the main waterfront zone—a short (but uphill) walk from all of the action. Many rooms come with views, and are priced accordingly.

$$$ Greystones is an enticing splurge. It fills a big, stately, turreted mansion at the top of town with five spacious rooms that mix Victorian charm and sleek gray-and-white minimalism. Built as the private home for the director of Kimberley Diamond Mine, it later became a maternity hospital, and today Mark and Suzanne have turned it into a stylish and restful retreat. The lounge and breakfast room offer stunning views over Oban and the offshore isles (closed Nov-mid-Feb, 13 Dalriach Road, tel. 01631/358-653, www.greystonesoban.co.uk, stay@greystonesoban.co.uk).

$$ Gramarvin B&B feels a little more homey and personal, with just two rooms and warm host Mary. Window seats in each room provide a lovely view over Oban, but be warned—the climb up from town and then up their stairs is steep (skip breakfast to save a few pounds, cash only, 2-night minimum in summer preferred, on-street parking, Benvoulin Road, tel. 01631/564-622, www.gramarvin.co.uk, mary@gramarvin.co.uk, Mary and Joe).

$$ Dunheanish Guest House offers six pleasant rooms (two on the ground floor) and wide-open views from its perch above town, which you can enjoy from the front stone patio, breakfast room, and several guest rooms (parking, Alconnel Road, tel. 01631/566-556, www.dunheanish.com, info@dunheanish.com, William and Linda).

$ Hawthornbank Guest House fills a big Victorian sandstone house with seven traditional rooms. Half of the rooms face bay views, and the others overlook the town's lawn bowling green (2-night minimum in summer, Dalriach Road, tel. 01631/562-041, www.hawthornbank.co.uk, info@hawthornbank.co.uk).

HOTELS IN THE TOWN CENTER

A number of hotels are in the center of town along the main drag—but you'll pay heavily for the convenience.

$$$$ Perle Oban Hotel is your luxury base. Right across from the harbor, it has 59 super-sleek, calming sea-color walls, decorative bath tile floors, and large, comfortable beds (suites, fancy restaurant, bar with light bites, pay parking, Station Square, tel. 01631/700-301, www.perleoban.com, info@perleoban.com).

$$$ The Ranald is a modern change of pace from the dated scene in Oban. This narrow, 17-room, three-floor hotel

budget-boutique vibe going (family rooms, bar, no elevator, street or off-site parking, a block behind the Royal Hotel at 41 Stevenson Street, tel. 01631/562-887, www.theranaldhotel.com, info@ theranaldhotel.com).

HOSTELS

¢ **Backpackers Plus** is central, laid-back, and fun. It fills part of a renovated old church with a sprawling public living room, 47 beds, and a staff generous with travel tips. Check out the walls as you go up to the reception desk—they're covered with graffiti messages from guests (includes breakfast, great shared kitchen, pay laundry service, 10-minute walk from station, on Breadalbane Street, tel. 01631/567-189, www.backpackersplus.com, info@ backpackersplus.com, Peter). They have two other locations nearby with private rooms.

¢ The official **SYHA hostel**, on the scenic waterfront Esplanade, is in a grand building with 87 beds and smashing views of the harbor and islands from the lounges and dining rooms. While institutional, this place is quite nice (all rooms en suite, private rooms available, also has family rooms and 8-bed apartment with kitchen, breakfast extra, pay laundry, kitchen, tel. 01631/562-025, www. syha.org.uk, oban@syha.org.uk).

Eating in ~~~~an~~~~

Oban brags that it is the "seafood ~~~~~~~~~l of Scot~~~~nd," and indeed its sit-down restaurants (listed f~~~~~~~~more cas~~~~," consider a fish-for such a small town. For some~~~~~~~~~~~~~~~ surpris~~~~gly high quality and-chips joint.

SIT-DOWN RESTAU~~~~~~~~~~~~~~~~~~~~ on week~~~~ds. To ensure getting
These fill up in summer ~~~~~~~~~. The firs~~~~our are generally open a table, you'll want to~~~~lic for "fi") is a popular, stylish, daily from 12:00-1~~~~ts a casua~~~~thic, yacht-clubby atmo-

$$$ Ee'usk~~~~~~~~~assy inter~~~~or and sweeping views on place on the ~~~~~~~~g the ferr~~~~s come and go. They some-sphere, wit~~~~ecial until ~~~~8:45, and their seafood plat-three side~~~~h s are recommended (no kids under age times of~~~~r, tel. 01631/565-666, www.eeusk.com,

ters ~~~~~~~~~s a popular, casual restaurant that combines
12 ~~~~a~~~~ food with modern flair—both in its crowd-N~~~~nd in its furnishings, made of wood, stone, ~~~~~~~~~ged from the beaches of Scotland's west coast

Scottish Highland Games

Throughout the summer, Highland communities host traditional festivals of local sport and culture. These Highland Games (sometimes called Highland Gatherings) combine the best elements of a track meet and a county fair. They range from huge and glitzy (such as Braemar's world-famous games, which the Queen attends, or the Cowal Highland Gathering, Scotland's biggest) to humble and small-town. Some of the more modern games come with loud pop music and corporate sponsorship, but still manage to celebrate the Highland spirit.

Most Highland Games take place between mid-June and late August (usually on Saturdays, but occasionally on weekdays). The games are typically a one-day affair, kicking off around noon and winding down in the late afternoon. At smaller games, you'll pay a nominal admission fee (typically around £5-7). Events are rain or shine (so bring layers) and take place in a big park ringed by a running track, with the heavy events and Highland dancing stage at opposite ends of the infield. Surrounding the whole scene are junk-food stands, a few test-your-skill carnival games, and local charities raising funds by selling hamburgers, fried sausage sandwiches, baked goods, and bottles of beer and Irn-Bru. The emcee's running commentary is a delightful opportunity to just sit back and enjoy a lilting Scottish voice.

The day's events often kick off with a **pipe band** parading through town, ending with a lap around the field — led by the local clan chieftain—and ending with a lap around the field local clan chieftain—and ending

In the **heavy events** the sporting events begin. These kilted athletes test their abilities of Highland strength—brawny, in shapes and sizes that are as varied various objects of awkward tors spin like ballerinas as they hurl the weight throw, competitors on a chain. The hammer throw (hurling a 28- or 56-pound ball 26-pound ball on a long stick) has adopted a similar technique with a pound ball) has been adopted a similar technique with a

In the "weight over the bar" one put (with a 20- to 25-weight over a horizontal bar such sports as the shot put. at closer to 15 feet. (That's like swing a 56-pound double-decker bus.) And, of of 9 feet high and ends up a giant log (the caber), get a year-old child over a over-end with enough force to flip caber toss: Pick way over and land at the 12 o'clock release it end-wind up closer to 6.) caber flip all the

Meanwhile, the **track events** competitors

the muscl

the 90-meter dash, the 1,600-meter, and so on. The hill race adds a Scottish spin: Combine a several-mile footrace with the ascent of a nearby summit. The hill racers begin with a lap in the stadium before disappearing for about an hour. Keep an eye on nearby hillsides to pick out their colorful jerseys bobbing up and down a distant peak. This custom supposedly began when an 11th-century king staged a competition to select his personal letter carrier. After about an hour—when you've forgotten all about them—the hill racers start trickling back into the stadium to cross the finish line.

The **Highland dancing** is a highlight. Accompanied by a lone piper, the dancers (in groups of two to four) toe their routines

with intense concentration. Dancers remain always on the balls of their feet, requiring excellent balance and stamina. While some men participate, most competitors are female—from wee lassies barely out of nappies, all the way to poised professionals. Common steps are the Highland fling (in which the goal is to keep the feet as close as possible to one spot), sword dances (in which the dancers step gingerly over crossed swords on the stage), and a variety of national dances.

Other events further enliven the festivities. A pipe band periodically assembles to play a few tunes, while marching around the track (giving the runners a bagpipe and drumming competitions. You may also see reenactments of medieval battles, herd dog demonstrations, or dog shows (grooming and obedience). Haggis hurling—a relatively new event in which participants stand on a whisky barrel and attempt to throw a cooked haggis as far as possible—has caught on recently. And many small-town events end with the grand finale of a town-wide tug-of-war, during which everybody gets bruised, muddy, and hysterical.

If you're traveling to Scotland in the summer, before locking in your itinerary, check online schedules to see if you'll be near any Highland Games. Rather than target the big, famous gatherings, I make a point of visiting the smaller clan games. One helpful website—listing dates for most but not all of the games around Scotland—is www.shga.co.uk. For many travelers to Scotland, attending a Highland Games can be a trip-capping highlight. And, of course, many communities in the US and Canada also host their own Highland Games.

(brewery in back, 60 George Street, tel. 01631/565-078). Its harborside tables on the sidewalk are popular when it's warm.

$$$$ Coast proudly serves fresh local fish, meat, and veggies in a mod pine-and-candlelight atmosphere. As everything is cooked to order and presented with care by husband-and-wife team Richard and Nicola—who try to combine traditional Scottish elements in innovative new ways—this is no place to dine and dash (two- and three-course specials, closed Sun for lunch, 104 George Street, tel. 01631/569-900, www.coastoban.co.uk).

$$ Piazza, next door to Ee'usk, is a casual, family-friendly place serving basic Italian dishes with a great harborfront location. They have some outdoor seats and big windows facing the sea (smart to reserve ahead July-Aug, tel. 01631/563-628, www.piazzaoban.com).

$$ Oban Fish and Chips Shop—run by Lewis, Sammy, and their family—serves praiseworthy haddock and mussels among other tasty options in a cheery cabana-like dining room. Consider venturing away from basic fish-and-chips into a world of more creative seafood dishes—like their tiny squat lobster. You can bring your own wine for no charge (daily, sit-down restaurant closes at 21:00, takeaway available later, 116 George Street, tel. 01631/567-000).

LUNCH

$ Oban Seafood Hut, in a green shack near the ferry dock, is a finger-licking festival of cheap and fresh seafood. John and Marion regularly get fresh deliveries from local fish. and this is the best spot to pick up a seafood sandwich or a snack. sell smaller bites (such as cold sandwiches), as well as some big froud platters and a few hot dishes (picnic tables nearby, daily until the boat unloads from Mull around 18:00).

$ The Kitchen Garden is fine for soup, salad, or sanc It's a deli and gourmet-foods store with a charming café up (daily 9:00-17:30, 14 George Street, tel. 01631/566-332).

Oban Connections

By Train from Oban: Trains link Oban to the nearest transportation hub in **Glasgow** (6/day, fewer on Sun, 3 hours); to get to **Edinburgh,** you'll have to transfer in Glasgow (5/day, 4.5 hours). To reach **Fort William** (a transit hub for the Highlands), you'll take the same Glasgow-bound train, but transfer in Crianlarich (3/day, 4 hours)—the direct bus is easier (see next). Oban's small train station has a ticket window and lockers (both open Mon-Sat 5:00-20:30, Sun 10:45-18:00, train info tel. 0845-748-4950, www.nationalrail.co.uk).

By Bus: Bus #918 passes through Ballachulish—a half-mile from **Glencoe**—on its way to **Fort William** (2/day, 1 hour to Ballachulish, 1.5 hours total to Fort William). Take this bus to Fort William, then transfer to reach **Inverness** (4 hours). A different bus (#976 or #977) connects Oban with **Glasgow** (5/day, 3 hours), from where you can easily connect by bus or train to **Edinburgh** (figure 4.5 hours). Buses arrive and depart from a roundabout, marked by a stubby clock tower, just before the entrance to the train station (tel. 0871-266-3333, www.citylink.co.uk). You can buy bus tickets at the West Coast shop near the bus stop, or at the TI across the harbor. Book in advance during peak times.

By Boat: Ferries fan out from Oban to the **southern Hebrides** (see information on the islands of Iona and Mull, later). Caledonian MacBrayne Ferry info: Tel. 01631/566-688, free booking tel. 0800-066-5000, www.calmac.co.uk.

ROUTE TIPS FOR DRIVERS

From Glasgow to Oban via Loch Lomond and Inveraray: For details on the most scenic route from Glasgow to Oban, see "Near Oban" at the end of this chapter.

From Oban to Glencoe and Fort William: It's an easy one-hour drive from Oban to Glencoe. From Oban, follow the coastal A-828 toward Fort William. After about 20 miles—as you leave the village of Appin—you'll see the photogenic **Castle Stalker** marooned on a lonely island (you can pull over at the Castle Stalker View Café for a good photo from just below its parking lot). At North Ballachulish, you'll reach a bridge spanning Loch Leven; rather than crossing the bridge, turn off and follow the A-82 into the Glencoe Valley for about 15 minutes. (For tips on the best views and hikes in Glencoe, see the next chapter.) After exploring the dramatic valley, make a U-turn and return through Glencoe village. To continue on to Fort William, backtrack to the bridge at North Ballachulish (great view from bridge) and cross it, following the A-82 north.

For a scenic shortcut directly back to Glasgow or Edinburgh, continue south on the A-82 after Glencoe via Rannoch Moor and Tyndrum. Crianlarich is where the road splits, and you'll either continue on the A-82 toward Loch Lomond and Glasgow or pick up the A-85 and follow signs for Stirling, then Edinburgh.

OBAN & INNER HEBRIDES

Isles of Mull, Iona, and Staffa

For the easiest one-day look at a good sample of the dramatic and historic Inner Hebrides (HEB-rid-eez) islands, take a tour from Oban to Mull, Iona, and Staffa. Though this trip is spectacular when it's sunny, it's worthwhile in any weather (but if rain or rough seas are expected, I'd skip the Staffa option).

GETTING AROUND THE ISLANDS
Visiting Mull and Iona

To visit Mull and ultimately Iona, you'll take a huge ferry run by Caledonian MacBrayne (CalMac) from Oban to the town of Craignure on Mull (45 minutes).

From there, you'll ride a bus or drive across Mull to its westernmost ferry terminal, called Fionnphort (1.25 hours), where you can catch the ferry to Iona (10 minutes). It's a long journey, but it's all incredibly scenic; you also get about two hours of free time on Iona. There are several ways to do this.

By Tour (Easiest): If you book a tour with **West Coast Tours,** all of the transportation is included. The CalMac ferry leaves from the Oban pier daily at 9:50 (as schedule can change from year to year, confirm times locally; board at least 20 minutes before departure). You can buy tickets online at www.westcoasttours.co.uk, from the West Coast Tours office, or from the Tour Shop Oban at the ferry building (tel. 01631/562-244, tourshop@calmac.co.uk). Book as far in advance as possible for July and August (tickets can sell out). When you book their tour, you'll receive a strip of tickets—one for each leg; if you book online, go to the West Coast Tours office and collect tickets in person (£35; April-Oct only, no tours Nov-March).

Tour Tips: The best inside seats on the **Oban-Mull ferry**—with the biggest windows—are in the sofa lounge on the "observation deck" (level 4) at the back end of the boat. (Follow signs for the toilets, and look for the big staircase to the top floor). The ferry has a fine cafeteria with hot meals and packaged sandwiches, a small snack bar on the top floor (hot drinks and basic sandwiches), and a bookshop. If it's a clear day, ask a local or a crew member to point out Ben Nevis, the tallest mountain in Britain. Five minutes before landing on Mull, you'll see the striking 13th-century Duart Castle on the left.

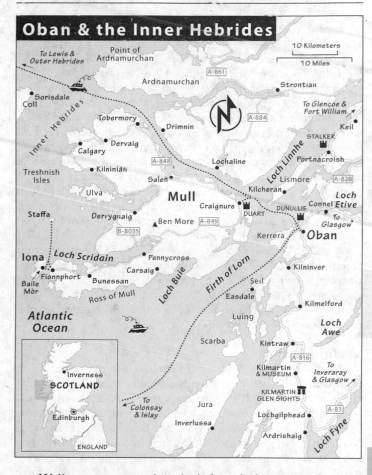

Walk-on passengers disembark from deck 3, across from the bookshop (port side). Upon arrival in Mull, find your **bus** for the entertaining and informative ride across the Isle of Mull. The right (driver's) side offers better sea views during the second half of the journey to Fionnphort, while the left side has fine views of Mull's rolling wilderness. The driver spends the entire ride chattering away about life on Mull, slowing to point out wildlife, and sharing adages like, "If there's no flowers on the gorse, snogging's gone out of fashion." These hardworking locals make historical trivia fascinating—or at least fun. At Fionnphort, you'll board a small, rocking **ferry to Iona.** You'll have about two hours to roam freely around the island before returning to Oban (arrives around 18:00).

By Public Transit: If you want an early start (and want to avoid some crowds), would like more time on Iona (includin: spending the night—see "Sleeping and Eating on Iona"), or dor

OBAN & INNER HEBRIDES

get a space on the tour described above, you can take the early ferry and public bus across Mull, paying individually per leg (Tue-Sat only; approximate round-trip prices: £7 for Oban-Mull ferry, £15 for public bus across Mull, £3.50 for Mull-Iona ferry).

Take the first boat of the day (departs about 7:30, buy ticket at Oban ferry terminal), then connect at Mull to bus #496 to Fionnphort (departs 8:25, 80 minutes, buy ticket from driver, no tour narration, no guarantee you'll get to sit), then hop on the Iona ferry (every 30 minutes, buy ticket from small trailer ferry office; if closed, purchase ticket from ferry worker at the dock; cash or credit/debit cards accepted; leaving Iona, do the same, as there's no ferry office). You'll have about four hours on Iona and will need to return to Fionnphort in time for the bus back (15:15). It's important to confirm all of these times locally (just pop in to the West Coast Tours office or the ferry terminal Tour Shop).

By Car: You can do this trip on your own by driving your car onto the ferry to Mull, but space is limited so book way in advance. Because of tight ferry timings, you'll wind up basically following the tour buses anyway, you'll miss all of the commentary, and no visitor cars are allowed on Iona (£26 round-trip for the car, plus passengers, www.calmac.co.uk).

Visiting Staffa

With two extra hours, you can add a side-trip to Staffa along with your Mull/Iona visit. Like above, you'll ferry from Oban to Mull, take a bus across Mull to Fionnphort, then board a **Staffa Tours** boat (35-minute trip, about an hour of free time on Staffa). From Staffa you'll head to Iona for about two hours before returning to Mull for the bus then ferry back to Oban. You can either depart on the 9:50 ferry, returning around 20:05 (£60) or do the "early bird" tour (£55, Tue-Sat only, depart at 7:30, return 18:00; book through West Coast Tours or Staffa Tours—mobile 07831-885-985, www.staffatours.com).

For a bit more of a relaxed schedule, **Staffa Trips** offers a guided tour with the same route as the one above, but with more time on Staffa and Iona (£60, Tue-Sat only, depart at 7:30, return 19:10, tel. 01681/700-358, www.staffatrips.co.uk).

Turus Mara offers nature/wildlife tours to just Staffa or Staffa and the small island of Ulva, departing from Oban (book at Tour Shop at Oban ferry terminal or contact Turus Mara—tel. 01688/400-242, www.turusmara.com).

Mull

The Isle of Mull, the second largest of the Inner Hebrides (after Skye), has nearly 300 scenic miles of coastline and castles and a

3,169-foot-high mountain, one of Scotland's Munros. Called Ben More ("Big Mountain" in Gaelic), it was once much bigger. At 10,000 feet tall, it made up the entire island of Mull—until a volcano erupted. Things are calmer now, and, similarly, Mull has a noticeably laid-back population. My bus driver reported that there are no deaths from stress, and only a few from boredom.

With steep, fog-covered hillsides topped by cairns (piles of stones, sometimes indicating graves) and ancient stone circles, Mull has a gloomy, otherworldly charm. Bring plenty of rain protection and wear layers in case the sun peeks through the clouds. As my driver said, Mull is a place of cold, wet, windy winters and mild, wet, windy summers.

On the far side of Mull, the caravan of tour buses unloads at Fionnphort, a tiny ferry town. The ferry to the island of Iona takes about 200 walk-on passengers. Confirm the return time with your bus driver, then hustle to the dock to make the first trip over (otherwise, it's a 30-minute wait; on very busy days, those who dillydally may not fit on the first ferry). At the dock, there's a small ferry-passenger building with a meager snack bar and a pay WC; a more enticing seafood bar is across the street. After the 10-minute ride, you wash ashore on sleepy Iona (free WC on this side), and the ferry mobs that crowded you on the boat seem to disappear up the main road and into Iona's back lanes.

The **About Mull Tours and Taxi** service can get you around Mull (tel. 01681/700-507 or mobile 0788-777-4550, www.aboutmull.co.uk). They also do day tours of Mull, focusing on local history and wildlife (half-day tours also available, or ask about shorter Mull tour combined with drop-off and pick-up at Fionnphort ferry dock for quick Iona trip, minimum 2 people, must book ahead).

Iona

The tiny island of Iona, just 3 miles by 1.5 miles, is famous as birthplace of Christianity in Scotland. If you're on a day trip, you have about two hours here on your own before you retrace

OBAN & INNER HEBRIDES

steps (your bus driver will tell you which return ferry to take back to Mull).

A pristine quality of light and a thoughtful peace pervades the stark, (nearly) car-free island and its tiny community. With buoyant clouds bouncing playfully off distant bluffs, sparkling-white crescents of sand, and lone tourists camped thoughtfully atop huge rocks just looking out to sea, Iona is a place that's perfect for meditation. To experience Iona, it's important to get out and take a little hike; you can follow some or all of my self-guided walk outlined below. And you can easily climb a peak—nothing's higher than 300 feet above the sea.

Orientation to Iona

The ferry arrives at the island's only real village, Baile Mòr, with shops, a restaurant/pub, a few accommodations, and no bank (get cash back with a purchase at the grocery store). The only taxi on Iona is **Iona Taxi** (mobile 07810-325-990, www.ionataxi.co.uk). Up the road from the ferry dock is a little **Spar** grocery with free island maps). Iona's official website (www.isle-of-iona.net) has good information about the island.

Iona Walk

Here's a basic self-guided route for exploring Iona on foot (since no private cars are permitted unless you're a resident or have a permit). With the standard two hours on Iona that a day trip allows, you will have time for a visit to the abbey (with a guided tour and/or audioguide) and then a light stroll; or do the entire walk described below, but skip the abbey (unless you have time for a quick visit on your way back).

Nunnery Ruins: From the ferry dock, head directly up the single paved road that passes through the village and up a small hill to visit one of Britain's best-preserved medieval nunneries (free).

Immediately after the nunnery, turn right on North Road. You'll curve up through the fields—passing the parish church.

Heritage Center: This little museum, tucked behind the church (watch for signs), is small but well done, with displays on al and natural history and a tiny tearoom (free but donation re- sted, closed Sun and in off-season, tel. 01681/700-576, www. heritage.co.uk).

History of Iona

St. Columba (521-597), an Irish scholar, soldier, priest, and founder of monasteries, got into a small war over the posses-

sion of an illegally copied psalm book. Victorious but sickened by the bloodshed, Columba left Ireland, vowing never to return. According to legend, the first bit of land out of sight of his homeland was Iona. He stopped here in 563 and established an abbey.

Columba's monastic community flourished, and Iona became the center of Celtic Christianity. Missionaries from Iona spread the gospel throughout Scotland and northern England, while scholarly monks established Iona as a center of art and learning. The *Book of Kells*—perhaps the finest piece of art from "Dark Ages" Europe—was probably made on Iona in the eighth century.

The island was so important that it was the legendary burial place for ancient Scottish clan chieftains and kings (including Macbeth, of Shakespeare fame) and even some Scandinavian monarchs.

Slowly, the importance of Iona ebbed. Vikings massacred 68 monks in 806. Fearing more raids, the monks evacuated most of Iona's treasures to Ireland (including the *Book of Kells,* which is now in Dublin). Much later, with the Reformation, the abbey was abandoned, and most of its finely carved crosses were destroyed. In the 17th century, locals used the abbey only as a handy quarry for other building projects.

Iona's population peaked at about 500 in the 1830s. In the 1840s, a potato famine hit, and in the 1850s, a third of the islanders emigrated to Canada or Australia. By 1900, the population was down to 210, and today it's only around 200.

But in our generation, a new religious community has given the abbey fresh life. The Iona Community is an ecumenical gathering of men and women who seek new ways of living the Gospel in today's world, with a focus on worship, peace and justice issues, and reconciliation (http://iona.org.uk).

St. Oran's Chapel and Iona Abbey: Continue on North Road. After the road swings right, you'll soon see **St. Oran's Chapel,** in the graveyard of the Iona Abbey. This chapel is the oldest church building on the island. Inside you'll find a few grave slabs carved in the distinctive Iona School style, which was developed by local stone-carvers in the 14th century. On these tall, skinny headstones, look for the depictions of medieval warrior aristocrats with huge swords. Many more of these carvings have been moved to the abbey, where you can see them in its cloister and museum.

It's free to see the graveyard and chapel; the ▲**Iona Abbey** itself has an admission fee, but it's worth the cost just to sit in the stillness of its lovely, peaceful interior courtyard (£7.50, tel. 01681/700-512, www.historicenvironment.scot—search for "Iona Abbey").

The abbey marks the site of Christianity's arrival in Scotland. You'll see Celtic crosses, the original shrine of St. Columba, a big church slathered with medieval carvings, a tranquil cloister, and an excellent museum with surviving fragments of this site's fascinating layers of history. While the present abbey, nunnery, and graveyard go back to the 13th century, much of what you'll see was rebuilt in the 20th century. Be sure to read the "History of Iona" sidebar to prepare for your visit.

At the entrance building, pick up your included audioguide, and ask about the good 30-minute guided tours (4/day and well worthwhile). Then head toward the church. You'll pass two faded **Celtic crosses** (and the base of a third); the originals are in the museum at the end of your visit. Some experts believe that Celtic crosses—with their distinctive shape so tied to Christianity on the British Isles—originated right here on Iona.

Facing the entrance to the church, you'll see the original **shrine to St. Columba** on your left—a magnet for pilgrims.

Head inside the **church.** It feels like an active church—with hymnals neatly stacked in the pews—because it is, thanks to the Iona Community. While much of this space has been rebuilt, take a moment to look around. Plenty of original medieval stone carving (especially the capitals of many columns) still survives. To see a particularly striking example, stand near the pulpit in the middle of the church and look back to the entrance. Partway up the left span of the pointed arch framing the transept, look for the eternally screaming face. While interpretations vary, this may have been a reminder for the priest not to leave out the fire-and-brimstone parts of his message. Some of the newer features of the church—including the base of the baptismal font near the entrance, and the main altar—are carved from locally quarried Iona marble: white with green streaks. In the right/south transept is the tomb of George Campbell—the Eighth Duke of Argyll, who donated this property in 1900, allowing it to be restored.

When you're ready to continue, find the poorly marked door to the **cloister.** (As you face the altar, it's about halfway down

the nave on the left, before
the transept.) This space
is filled with harmoni-
ous light, additional finely
carved capitals (these are
modern re-creations),
and—displayed along the
walls—several more of the
tall, narrow tombstones
like the ones displayed in

St. Oran's Chapel. On these, look for a couple of favorite motifs:
the long, intimidating sword (indicating a warrior of the Highland
clans) and the ship with billowing sails (a powerful symbol of this
seafaring culture).

Around the far side of the cloister is the shop. But before leaving, don't overlook the easy-to-miss **museum.** (To find it, head
outside and walk around the left side of the abbey complex, toward
the sea.) This modern, well-presented space exhibits a remarkable
collection of original stonework from the abbey—including what's
left of the three Celtic crosses out front—all eloquently described.

Iona Community's Welcome Centre: Just beyond and across
the road from the abbey is the Iona Community's Welcome Centre (free WCs), which runs the abbey with Historic Scotland and
hosts modern-day pilgrims who come here to experience the birthplace of Scottish Christianity. (If you're staying longer, you could
attend a worship service at the abbey—check the schedule here;
tel. 01681/700-404, www.iona.org.uk.) Its gift shop is packed with
books on the island's important role in Christian history.

Views: A 10-minute walk on North Road past the welcome
center brings you to the footpath for **Dùn Ì,** a steep but short climb
with good views of the abbey looking back toward Mull.

North Beach: Returning to the main road, walk another
20-25 minutes to the end of the paved road, where you'll arrive at
a gate leading through a sheep- and cow-strewn pasture to Iona's
pristine white-sand beach. Dip your toes in the Atlantic and ponder what this Caribbean-like alcove is doing in Scotland. Be sure to
allow at least 40 minutes to return to the ferry dock.

Sleeping and Eating on Iona

For a chance to really experience peaceful, idyllic Iona, spend
night or two (Scots bring their kids and stay on this tiny island f
a week). To do so, you'll have to buy each leg of the ferry-bus-fe
(and return) trip separately (see "By Public Transit," earlier). Th
accommodations are listed roughly in the order you'll reach the
you climb the main road from the ferry dock. The first two b

listed have **$$$** restaurants that are open to the public for lunch, tea, and dinner and closed in winter. For more accommodation options, see www.isle-of-iona.net/accommodation.

$$ Argyll Hotel, built in 1867, proudly overlooks the waterfront, with 17 cottage-like rooms and pleasingly creaky hallways lined with bookshelves. Of the two hotels, it feels classier (reserve far in advance for summer, comfortable lounge and sunroom, tel. 01681/700-334, www.argyllhoteliona.co.uk, reception@argyllhoteliona.co.uk).

$$$$ St. Columba Hotel, a bit higher up in town and situated in the middle of a peaceful garden with picnic tables, has 27 institutional rooms and spacious lodge-like common spaces—such as a big, cushy seaview lounge (closed Nov-March, next door to abbey on road up from dock, tel. 01681/700-304, www.stcolumba-hotel.co.uk, info@stcolumba-hotel.co.uk).

$ Calva B&B, a five-minute walk past the abbey, has three spacious rooms (second house on left past the abbey, look for sign in window and gnomes on porch, tel. 01681/700-340; friendly Janetta and Ken).

Staffa

Those more interested in nature than in church history will enjoy the trip to the wildly scenic Isle of Staffa. Completely uninhabited (except for seabirds), Staffa is a knob of rock draped with a vibrant green carpet of turf. Remote and quiet, it feels like a Hebrides nature preserve.

Most day trips give you an hour on Staffa—barely enough time to see its two claims to fame: The basalt columns of Fingal's Cave, and (in summer) a colony of puffins. To squeeze in both, be ready to hop off the boat and climb the staircase. Partway up to the left, you can walk around to the cave (about 7 minutes). Or continue up to the top, then  turn right and walk across the spine of the grassy island (about 10-15 minutes) to the cove where the puffins gather. (Your captain should point out both options and let you know how active the puffins have been.)

Fingal's Cave

Staffa's shore is covered with bizarre, mostly hexagonal basalt columns that stick up at various heights. It's as if the earth were offering God his choice of thousands of six-sided cigarettes. (The

island's name likely came from the Old Norse word for "stave"—the building timbers these columns resemble.) This is the other end of Northern Ireland's popular Giant's Causeway. You'll walk along the uneven surface of these columns, curling around the far side of the island, until you can actually step inside the gaping mouth of a cave—where floor-to-ceiling columns and crashing waves combine to create a powerful experience. Listening to the water and air flowing through this otherworldly space inspired Felix Mendelssohn to compose his overture, *The Hebrides*.

While you're ogling the cave, consider this: Geologists claim these unique formations were created by volcanic eruptions more than 60 million years ago. As the surface of the lava flow quickly cooled, it contracted and crystallized into columns (resembling the caked mud at the bottom of a dried-up lakebed, but with deeper cracks). As the rock later settled and eroded, the columns broke off into the many stair-like steps that now honeycomb Staffa.

Of course, in actuality, these formations resulted from a heated rivalry between a Scottish giant named Fingal, who lived on Staffa, and an Ulster warrior named Finn MacCool, who lived across the sea on Ireland's Antrim Coast. Knowing that the giant was coming to spy on him, Finn had his wife dress him as a sleeping infant. The giant, shocked at the infant's size, fled back to Scotland in terror of whomever had sired this giant baby. Breathing a sigh of relief, Finn tore off the baby clothes and prudently knocked down the bridge.

▲▲Puffins

A large colony of Atlantic puffins settles on Staffa each spring and summer during mating season (generally early May through early August). The puffins tend to scatter when the boat arrives. But after the boat pulls out and its passengers hike across the island, the very tame puffins' curiosity gets the better of them. First you'll see them flutter up from the offshore rocks, with their distinctive, bobbin

OBAN & INNER HEBRIDES

Puffins

The Atlantic puffin (Fratercula arctica) is an adorably stout, tuxedo-clad seabird with a too-big orange beak and beady black eyes. Puffins live most of their lives on the open Atlantic, coming to land only to breed. They fly north to Scotland between mid-May and early June, raise their brood, then take off again late in August. Puffins mate for life and typically lay just one egg each year, which the male and female take turns caring for. A baby puffin is called—wait for it—a puffling.

To feed their pufflings, puffins plunge as deep as 200 feet below the sea's surface to catch sand eels, herring, and other small fish. Their compact bodies, stubby wings, oil-sealed plumage, and webbed feet are ideal for navigating underwater. Famously, puffins can stuff several small fish into their beaks at once, thanks to their agile tongues and uniquely hinged beaks. This evolutionary trick lets puffins stock up before returning to the nest.

Stocky, tiny-winged puffins have a distinctive way of flying. To take off, they either beat their wings like crazy (on sea) or essentially hurl themselves off a cliff (on land). Once aloft, they beat their wings furiously—up to 400 times per minute—to stay airborne. Coming in for a smooth landing on a rocky cliff is a challenge (and highly entertaining to watch): They choose a spot, swoop in at top speed on prevailing currents, then flutter their wings madly to brake as they try to touch down. At the moment of truth, the puffin decides whether to attempt to stick the landing; more often than not, he bails out and does another big circle on the currents...and tries again...and again...and again.

flight. They'll zip and whirl around, and finally they'll start to land on the lip of the cove. Sit quietly, move slowly, and be patient, and

soon they'll get close. (If any seagulls are nearby, shoo them away—puffins are undaunted by humans, who do them no harm, but they're terrified of predator seagulls.)

In the waters around Staffa—on your way to and from the other islands—also keep an eye out for a variety of **marine life,** including seals, dolphins, porpoises, and the occasional minke whale, fin whale, or basking shark (a gigantic fish that hinges open its enormous jaw to drift-net plankton).

Near Oban

The following sights are worth considering for drivers. The first section outlines the best driving route from Glasgow to Oban, including the appealing pit stop at Inveraray. And the second section covers a longer route through one of Scotland's most important prehistoric sites, Kilmartin Glen.

GLASGOW TO OBAN DRIVE

The drive from Glasgow (or Edinburgh) to Oban via Inveraray provides dreamy vistas and your first look at the dramatic landscapes of the Highlands, as well as historic sites and ample opportunity to stop for a picnic.

• *Leaving Glasgow on the A-82, you'll soon be driving along the west bank of...*

Loch Lomond

The first picnic turnout has the best views of this famous lake, benches, a park, and a playground. Twenty-four miles long and speckled with islands, Loch Lomond is Great Britain's biggest lake by surface area, and second in volume only to Loch Ness. Thanks largely to its easy proximity to Glasgow (about 15 miles away), this scenic lake is a favorite retreat for Scots as well as foreign tourists. The southernmost of the Munros, Ben Lomond (3,196 feet), looms over the eastern bank.

Loch Lomond's biggest claim to fame is its role in a beloved folk song: "Ye'll take the high road, and I'll take the low road, and I'll be in Scotland afore ye...For me and my true love will never meet again, on the bonnie, bonnie banks of Loch Lomond." As you'll now be humming that all day (you're welcome), here's one interpretation of the song's poignant meaning: Celtic culture believes that fairies return the souls of the deceased to their homeland through the soil. After the disastrous Scottish loss at the Battle of Culloden, Jacobite ringleaders were arrested and taken for trial in faraway London. In some cases, accused pairs were given a choice: One of you will die, and the other will live. The song is a bittersweet reassurance, sung from the condemned to the survivor, that the soon-to-be-deceased will take the spiritual "low road" back to his Scottish homeland—where his soul will be reunited with the living, who will return on the physical "high road" (over land).

You're driving over an isthmus between Loch Lomond and a sea inlet. Halfway up the loch, you'll find the town of Tarbet—the Viking word for isthmus, a common name on Scottish maps. Imagine, a thousand years ago, Vikings dragging their ships across this narrow stretch of land to reach Loch Lomond.

• *At Tarbet, the road forks. The signs for Oban keep you on the direct route along A-82. For the scenic option that takes you past Loch Fyne to Inveraray (about 30 minutes longer to drive), keep left for the A-83 (toward Campbeltown).*

Highland Boundary Fault

You'll pass the village of **Arrochar,** and then drive along the banks of Loch Long. The scenery crescendos as you pull away from the loch and twist up over the mountains and through a pine forest, getting your first glimpse of bald Highlands mountains—it's clear that you've just crossed the **Highland Boundary Fault.** Enjoy the waterfalls, and notice that the road signs are now in English as well as Gaelic. As you climb into more rugged territory—up the valley called Glen Croe—be mindful that the roads connecting the Lowlands with the Highlands (like the one down in the glen below) were originally a military project designed to facilitate government quelling of the Highland clans.

• *At the summit, watch for the large parking lot with picnic tables on your left (signed for Argyll Forest Park). Stretch your legs at what's aptly named...*

Rest-and-Be-Thankful Pass

The colorful name comes from the 19th century, when just reaching this summit was exhausting. At the top of the military road, just past the last picnic table, there's actually a stone dated 1814 that was put there by the military with that phrase.

As you drive on, enjoy the dramatic green hills. You may see little bits of hillside highlighted by sunbeams. Each of these is a "soot" (Sun's Out Over There). Look for soots as you drive further north into the Highlands.

• *Continue twisting down the far side of the pass. You'll drive through Glen Kinglas and soon reach...*

Loch Fyne

This saltwater "sea loch" is famous for its shellfish (keep an eye out for oyster farms and seafood restaurants). In fact, Loch Fyne is the namesake of a popular UK restaurant chain with 40 locations across the UK. While a chain restaurant is a chain restaurant, this is different: **$$$$ Loch Fyne Seafood Restaurant and Deli** in the big white building at the end of the loch is the original. It's a famous stop for locals—an elegant seafood restaurant and oyster

The Irish Connection

The Romans called the people living in what is now Ireland the "Scoti" (meaning pirates). When the Scoti crossed the narrow Irish Sea and invaded the land of the Picts 1,500 years ago, that region became known as Scoti-land. Ireland and Scotland were never fully conquered by the Romans, and they retained similar clannish Celtic traits. Both share the same Gaelic branch of the linguistic tree.

On clear summer days, you can actually see Ireland—just 17 miles away—from the Scottish coastline. The closest bit to Scotland is the boomerang-shaped Rathlin Island, part of Northern Ireland. Rathlin is where Scottish leader Robert the Bruce retreated in 1307 after defeat at the hands of the English. Legend has it that he hid in a cave on the island, where he observed a spider patiently rebuilding its web each time a breeze knocked it down. Inspired by the spider's perseverance, Bruce gathered his Scottish forces once more and finally defeated the English at the decisive battle of Bannockburn (see page 747).

Flush with confidence from his victory, Robert the Bruce decided to open a second front against the English...in Ireland. In 1315, he sent his brother Edward over to enlist their Celtic Irish cousins in an effort to thwart the English. After securing Ireland, Edward hoped to move on and enlist the Welsh, thus cornering England with their pan-Celtic nation. But Edward's timing was bad: Ireland was in the midst of famine. His Scottish troops had to live off the land and began to take food and supplies from the starving Irish. Some of Ireland's crops may have been intentionally destroyed to keep it from being used as a colonial "breadbasket" to feed English troops. The Scots quickly wore out their welcome, and Edward the Bruce was eventually killed in battle near Dundalk in 1318.

It's interesting to imagine how things might be different today if Scotland and Ireland had been permanently welded together as a nation 700 years ago. You'll notice the strong Scottish influence in Northern Ireland when you ask a local a question and he answers, "Aye, a wee bit." And in Glasgow—on Scotland's west coast, closest to Ireland—an Ireland-like division between royalist Protestants and republican Catholics survives today in the form of soccer team allegiances. In big Scottish cities (like Glasgow and Edinburgh), you'll even see "orange parades" of protesters marching in solidarity with their Protestant Northern Irish cousins. The Irish—always quick to defuse tension with humor—joke that the Scots are just Irish people who couldn't swim home.

bar worth traveling for (open daily from noon, last order 18:45, no reservations, tel. 01499/600-482, www.lochfyne.com). Even if you're not eating, it's fun to peruse their salty deli (tasty treats to go, picnic tables outside, good coffee).

• *Looping around Loch Fyne, you approach Inveraray. As you get close, keep an eye on the right (when crossing the bridge, have your camera ready) for the dramatic...*

▲Inveraray Castle

This residence of the Duke of Argyll comes with a dramatic, turreted exterior (one of Scotland's most striking) and a lavishly decorated interior that feels spacious, lived in, and neatly tended. Histori-cally a stronghold of one of the more notorious branches of the Campbell clan, it's filled with precious-if-you're-a-Campbell artifacts and fun to tour.

Roam from room to room, reading the laminated descrip-tions and asking questions of the gregarious docents. The highlight is the Armory Hall that fills the main atrium, where swords and rifles are painstakingly arrayed in starburst patterns. The rifles were actually used when the Camp-bells fought with the British at the Battle of Culloden in 1746.

Upstairs a room is dedicated to *Downton Abbey*. Public televi-sion fans may recognize this as "Duneagle Castle" (a.k.a. Uncle Shrimpy's pad) from one of the *Downton Abbey* Christmas spe-cials—big photos of the Grantham and MacClare clans decorate the genteel rooms.

As with many such castles, the aristocratic clan still lives here (*private* signs mark rooms where the family resides). Another up-stairs room is like an Argyll family scrapbook; for example, see photos of the duke playing elephant polo—the ultimate aristocratic sport. The kids attend school in London, but spend a few months here each year; in the winter, the castle is closed to the public and they have the run of the place. After touring the interior, do a loop through the finely manicured gardens (£11, April-Oct daily 10:00-17:45, closed Nov-March, last entry 45 minutes before closing, nice café in the basement, buy tickets at the car park booth, tel. 01499/302-203, www.inveraray-castle.com).

• *After visiting the castle, spend some time exploring...*

▲Inveraray Town

Nearly everybody stops at this lovely, seemingly made-for-tourists town on Loch Fyne. Browse the main street—lined with touristy shops and cafés all the way to the church at its top. As this is the geological and demographic border between the Highlands and the Lowlands, traditionally church services here were held in both Scots and Gaelic. Just before the church is Loch Fyne Whiskies with historic bottles on its ceiling.

There's free parking on the main street and plenty of pay-and-display parking near the pier (TI open daily, on Front Street, tel. 01499/302-063; public WCs at end of nearby pier).

The **Inveraray Jail** is the main site in town—an overpriced, corny, but mildly educational former jail converted into a museum. This "living 19th-century prison" includes a courtroom where mannequins argue the fate of the accused. Then you'll head outside and explore the various cells of the outer courtyard. The playful guards may lock you up for a photo op, while they explain how Scotland reformed its prison system in 1839—you'll see both "before" and "after" cells in this complex (£11.50, includes 75-minute audioguide, open daily, tel. 01499/302-381, www.inverarayjail.co.uk).

• *To continue directly to Oban from Inveraray (about an hour), leave town through the gate at the woolen mill and get on the A-819, which takes you through Glen Aray and along Loch Awe. A left turn on the A-85 takes you into Oban.*

But if you have a healthy interest in prehistoric sites, you can go to Oban by way of Kilmartin Glen (adds about 45 minutes of driving). To get there, head straight up Inveraray's main street and get on the waterfront A-83 (marked for Campbeltown); after a half-hour, in Lochgilphead, turn right onto the A-816, which takes you through Kilmartin Glen and all the way up to Oban. (To avoid backtracking, be ready to stop at the prehistoric sites lining the A-816 between Lochgilphead and Kilmartin village.)

Kilmartin Glen

Except for the Orkney Islands, Scotland isn't as rich with prehistoric sites as South England is, but the ones in Kilmartin Glen, while faint, are some of Scotland's most accessible—and most important. This wide valley, clearly imbued with spiritual and/or strategic power, contains reminders of several millennia worth of inhabitants. Today it's a playground for those who enjoy tromping through grassy fields while daydreaming about who moved these giant stones here so many centuries

ago. This isn't worth a long detour, unless you're fascinated by prehistoric sites.

Four to five thousand years ago, Kilmartin Glen was inhabited by Neolithic people who left behind fragments of their giant, stony monuments. And 1,500 years ago, this was the seat of the kings of the Scoti, who migrated here from Ireland around A.D. 500, giving rise to Scotland's own branch of Celtic culture. From this grassy valley, the Scoti kings ruled their empire, called Dalriada (also sometimes written Dál Riata), which encompassed much of Scotland's west coast, the Inner Hebrides, and the northern part of Ireland. The Scoti spoke Gaelic and were Christian; as they overtook the rest of the Highlands—eventually absorbing their rival Picts—theirs became a dominant culture, which is still evident in pockets of present-day Scotland. Today, Kilmartin Glen is scattered with burial cairns, standing stones, and a hill called Dunadd—the fortress of the Scoti kings.

Visiting Kilmartin Glen: Sites are scattered throughout the valley, including some key locations along or just off the A-816 south of Kilmartin village. If you're coming from Inveraray, you'll pass these *before* you reach the village and museum itself. Each one is explained by good informational signs.

Dunadd: This bulbous hill sits just west of the A-816, about four miles north of Lochgilphead and four miles south of Kilmartin village (watch for blue, low-profile *Dunadd Fort* signs). A fort stood here since the time of Christ, but it was the Scoti kings—who made it their primary castle from the sixth to ninth centuries—that put Dunadd on the map. Park in the big lot at its base and hike through the faint outlines of terraces to the top, where you can enjoy sweeping views over all of Kilmartin Glen; this southern stretch is a marshland called "The Great Moss" (Moine Mhor). Look for carvings in the rock: early Celtic writing, the image of a boar, and a footprint (carved into a stone crisscrossed with fissures). This "footprint of fealty" (a replica) recalls the inauguration ceremony in which the king would place his foot into the footprint, symbolizing the marriage between the ruler and the land.

Dunchraigaig Cairn: About two miles farther north on the A-816, brown *Dunchraigaig* signs mark a parking lot where you can cross the road to the 4,000-year-old, 100-foot-in-diameter Dunchraigaig Cairn—the burial place for 10 Neolithic VIPs. Circle around to find the opening, where you can still crawl into a small recess. This is one of at least five such cairns that together created a mile-and-a-half-long "linear cemetery" up the middle of Kilmartin Glen.

From this cairn, you can walk five minutes to several more prehistoric structures: Follow signs through the gate, and walk to a farm field with **Ballymeanoch**—an avenue of two stone rows (with six surviving stones), a disheveled old cairn, and a stone circle.

Sites near Kilmartin Burn: About one more mile north on the A-816, just off the intersection with the B-8025 (toward *Tayvallich*), is the small Kilmartin Burn parking lot. From here, cross the stream to a field where the five **Nether Largie Standing Stones** have stood in a neat north-south line for 3,200 years. Were these stones designed as an astronomical observatory? Burial rituals or other religious ceremonies? Sporting events? Or just a handy place for sheep to scratch themselves? From here, you can hike the rest of the way through the field (about 10 minutes) to the **Nether Largie South Cairn** and the **Temple Wood Stone Circles** (which don't have their own parking). The larger, older of these circles dates to more than 5,000 years ago, and both were added onto and modified over the millennia.

Kilmartin Museum: To get the big picture, head for the Kilmartin Museum, in the center of Kilmartin village. The cute stone house has a ticket desk, bookshop, and café; the museum—with exhibits explaining this area's powerful history—fills the basement of the adjacent building (though a new home for the exhibit is in the works). The modest but modern museum features handy explanations, a few original artifacts, and lots of re-creations (£6.50, daily except closed Christmas-Feb, tel. 01546/510-278, www.kilmartin.org).

From the museum, you can look out across the fields to see **Glebe Cairn,** one of the five cairns of the "linear cemetery." Another one, the **Nether Largie North Cairn,** was reconstructed in the 1970s and can actually be entered (a half-mile south of the museum; ask for directions at museum).

Many, many more prehistoric sites fill Kilmartin Glen (more than 800 within a six-mile radius); the museum sells in-depth guidebooks for the curious, and can point you in the right direction for what you're interested in.

OBAN & INNER HEBRIDES

GLENCOE & FORT WILLIAM

Scotland is a land of great natural wonders. And some of the most spectacular—and most accessible—are in the valley called Glencoe, just an hour north of Oban and on the way to Fort William, Loch Ness, or Inverness. The evocative "Weeping Glen" of Glencoe aches with both history and natural beauty. Beyond that, Fort William anchors the southern end of the Caledonian Canal, offering a springboard to more Highlands scenery. This is where Britain's highest peak, Ben Nevis, keeps its head in the clouds.

PLANNING YOUR TIME

On a quick visit, this area warrants just a few hours between Oban and Inverness: Wander through Glencoe village, tour its modest museum, then drive up Glencoe valley for views before continuing on your way north. But if you have only a day or two to linger in the Highlands, Glencoe is an ideal place to do it. Settle in for a night (or more) to make time for a more leisurely drive and to squeeze in a hike or two—I give an overview of the best options, from easy strolls to challenging ascents.

Beyond Glencoe, Fort William—a touristy and overrated transportation hub—is skippable, but can be a handy lunch stop.

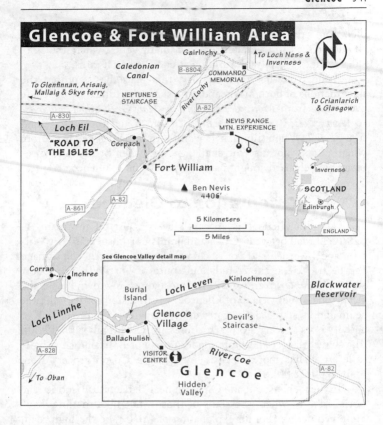

Glencoe & Fort William Area

Gairlochy

To Loch Ness & Inverness

Caledonian Canal

B-8804

COMMANDO MEMORIAL

To Glenfinnan, Arisaig, Mallaig & Skye ferry

NEPTUNE'S STAIRCASE

River Lochy

A-82

To Crianlarich & Glasgow

A-830

Loch Eil

"ROAD TO THE ISLES"

Corpach

NEVIS RANGE MTN. EXPERIENCE

Fort William

Inverness

SCOTLAND

Edinburgh

ENGLAND

▲ Ben Nevis 4406'

A-861

A-82

5 Kilometers

5 Miles

See Glencoe Valley detail map

Corran

Inchree

Burial Island

Loch Leven

Kinlochmore

Blackwater Reservoir

Glencoe Village

Devil's Staircase

Loch Linnhe

Ballachulish

A-828

VISITOR CENTRE

River Coe

A-82

To Oban

G l e n c o e

Hidden Valley

Glencoe

This valley is the essence of the wild, powerful, and stark beauty of the Highlands. Along with its scenery, Glencoe offers a good dose of bloody clan history: In 1692, government Redcoats (led by a local Campbell commander) came to the valley, and they were sheltered and fed for 12 days by the MacDonalds—whose leader had been late in  swearing an oath to the British monarch. Then, on the morning of February 13, the soldiers were ordered to rise up early and kill their sleeping hosts, violating the rules of Highland hospitality and earning the valley the nickname "The Weeping Glen." Thirty-eight men were killed outright; hundreds more fled through a blizzard, and some 40 additional villagers (mostly women and children)

GLENCOE & FORT WILLIAM

died from exposure. It's fitting that such an epic, dramatic incident should be set in this equally epic, dramatic valley, where the cliff-sides seem to weep (with running streams) when it rains.

Aside from its tragic history, this place has captured the imaginations of both hikers and artists. Movies filmed here include everything from *Monty Python and the Holy Grail* and *Highlander* to *Harry Potter and the Prisoner of Azkaban* and the James Bond film *Skyfall*. When filmmakers want a stunning, rugged backdrop; when hikers want a scenic challenge; and when Scots want to remember their hard-fought past...they all think of Glencoe.

Orientation to Glencoe

The valley of Glencoe is an easy side-trip just off the main A-828/A-82 road between Oban and points north (such as Fort William and Inverness). If you're coming from the north, the signage can be tricky—at the roundabout south of Fort William, follow signs to *Crianlarich* and *A-82*. The most appealing town here is the sleepy one-street village of Glencoe, worth a stop for its folk museum and its status as the gateway to the valley. The town's hub of activity is its grocery store, which has an ATM (daily 8:00-19:30). The slightly larger and more modern town of Ballachulish (a half-mile away) has more services, including a Co-op grocery store (daily 7:00-22:00).

In the loch just outside Glencoe (near Ballachulish), notice the burial island—where the souls of those who "take the low road" are piped home. (For an explanation of "Ye'll take the high road, and I'll take the low road," see page 933.) The next island was the Island of Discussion—where those in dispute went until they found agreement.

TOURIST INFORMATION

Your best source of information (especially for walks and hikes) is the **Glencoe Visitor Centre,** described later. The nearest **TI** is in the next town, Ballachulish (buried inside a huge gift shop, daily 9:00-17:00, Nov-Easter 10:00-16:00, tel. 01855/811-866, www.glencoetourism.co.uk). For more information on the area, see www.discoverglencoe.com.

Bike Rental: At **Crank It Up Gear,** Davy rents road and mountain bikes, and can offer plenty of suggestions for where to pedal in the area (£15/half-day, £25/all day, just off the main street to the left near the start of town, 20 Lorn Drive, mobile 07746-860-023, www.crankitupgear.com, best to book ahead in summer).

Sights in Glencoe

Glencoe Village

Glencoe village is just a line of houses sitting beneath the brooding mountains. The only real sight in town is the folk museum (described below). But walking the main street gives a good glimpse of village Scotland. From the free

parking lot at the entrance to town, go for a stroll. You'll pass lots of little B&Bs renting two or three rooms, the stony Episcopal church,

the folk museum, the town's grocery store, and the village hall.

At the far end of the village, on the left just before the bridge, a Celtic cross **World War I** memorial stands on a little hill. Even this wee village lost 11 souls during that war—a reminder of Scotland's disproportionate contribution to Britain's war effort. You'll see memorials like this (usually either a Celtic cross or a soldier with bowed head) in virtually every town in Scotland.

If you were to cross the little bridge, you'd head up into Glencoe's wooded parklands, with some easy hikes (described later). But for one more landmark, turn right just before the bridge and walk about five minutes. Standing on a craggy bluff on your right is another memorial—this one to the **Glencoe Massacre,** which still haunts the memories of people here and throughout Scotland.

Glencoe and North Lorn Folk Museum

This gathering of thatched-roof, early 18th-century croft houses is a volunteer-run community effort. It's jammed with local his-

tory, creating a huggable museum filled with humble exhibits gleaned from the town's old closets and attics. When one house was being rethatched, its owner found a cache of 200-year-old swords and pistols hidden there from

the government Redcoats after the disastrous Battle of Culloden. You'll also see antique toys, boxes from old food products, sports paraphernalia, a cabinet of curiosities, evocative old black-and-white photos, and plenty of information on the MacDonald clan. Be sure to look for the museum's little door that leads out back, where additional, smaller buildings are filled with everyday items (furniture, farm tools, and so on) and exhibits on the Glencoe Massacre and a beloved Highland doctor. You can listen to an interview with the late Arthur Smith, a local historian, about the valley and its story in the "Scottish Highlands" program available on my Rick Steves Audio Europe app—for details, see page 30 (£3, Easter-Sept Mon-Sat 10:00-16:30, closed Sun and off-season, tel. 01855/811-664, www.glencoemuseum.com).

Glencoe Visitor Centre

This modern facility, a mile past Glencoe village up the A-82 into the dramatic valley, is designed to resemble a *clachan*, or traditional Highland settlement. The information desk inside the shop at the ranger desk is your single best resource for advice (and maps or guidebooks) about local walks and hikes (several of which are outlined later in this chapter). At the back of the complex you'll find a viewpoint with a handy 3-D model of the hills for orientation. There's also a pricey exhibition about the surrounding landscape, the region's history, wildlife, mountaineering, and conservation. It's worth the time to watch the more-interesting-than-it-sounds two-minute video on geology and the 14-minute film on the Glencoe Massacre, which thoughtfully traces the events leading up to the tragedy rather than simply recycling romanticized legends (free, exhibition-£6.50; April-Oct daily 9:30-17:30; Nov-March Thu-Sun 10:00-16:00, closed Mon-Wed; free Wi-Fi, café, tel. 01855/811-307, www.glencoe-nts.org.uk).

Glencoe Valley Driving Tour

If you have a car, spend an hour or so following the A-82 through the valley, past the Glencoe Visitor Centre, up into the desolate moor beyond, and back again. You'll enjoy grand views, dramatic craggy hills, and, if you're lucky, a chance to hear a bagpiper in the wind: Roadside Highland buskers often set up here on good-weather summer weekends. (If you play the recorder—and the piper's not swarmed with other tourists—ask to finger a tune while he does the hard work.)

Here's a brief explanation of the route. Along the way, I've pointed out sometimes easy-to-miss trailheads, in case you're up for a hike (hikes described in the next section).

➔ **Self-Guided Driving Tour:** Leaving Glencoe village

on the A-82, it's just a mile to the **Glencoe Visitor Centre** (on the right, described earlier). Soon after, the road pulls out of the forested hills and gives you unobstructed views of the U-shaped valley.

About a mile after the visitors center, on the left, is a parking lot for **Signal Rock and An Torr,** a popular place for low-impact forested hikes. Just beyond, also on the left, is a single-track road leading to the recommended **Clachaig Inn,** a classic hikers'. The hillsides above the inn were the setting for Hagrid's hut in the third Harry Potter movie (though nothing remains from filming).

Continuing along the A-82, you'll hit a straight stretch, passing a lake (Loch Achtriochtan), and then a small farm, both on the right. After the farm, the valley narrows a bit as you cut through Glencoe Pass. On the right, you'll pass two small parking lots. Pull into the second one for perhaps the best viewpoint of the entire valley, with point-blank views (directly ahead) of the steep ridge-like mountains known as the **Three Sisters.** Hike about 100 feet away from the pullout to your own private bluff to enjoy the view alone—it makes a big difference. This is also the starting point for the challenging **Hidden Valley hike,** which leads between the first and second sisters.

As you continue, you'll pass a raging waterfall in a canyon—the Tears of the MacDonalds—on the right. After another mile

or so—through more glorious waterfall scenery—watch on the left for the **Coffin Cairn,** which looks like a stone igloo (parking is just across the road if you want a photo op). Just after the cairn, look on the left for pullout parking for the hike to **The Study,** a viewpoint overlooking the road you just drove down (described later).

After this pullout, you'll hit a straightaway for about a mile, followed by an S-curve. At the end of the curve, look for the pullout parking on the left, just before the stand of pine trees. This is the trailhead for the **Devil's Staircase** hike, high into the hills.

Continuing past here, you're nearing the end of the valley. The intimidating peak called the Great Shepherd of Etive (on the right) looms like a dour watchman, guarding the far end of the valley. Soon you'll pass the turnoff (on the right) for **Glen Etive,** an even more remote-feeling valley. (This was the setting for the final scenes of *Skyfall*. Yes, this is where James Bond grew up.) Continuing past that, the last sign of civilization (on the right) is the Glencoe Ski Centre. And from here, the terrain flattens out as you

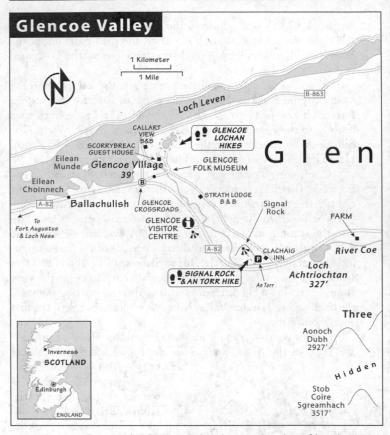

Glencoe Valley

1 Kilometer

1 Mile

N

Loch Leven   B-863

CALLART
VIEW
B&B   GLENCOE
LOCHAN
HIKES

SCORRYBREAC
GUEST HOUSE

Eilean
Munde   Glencoe Village   GLENCOE
39'   FOLK MUSEUM   G l e n

Eilean
Choinnech

B   STRATH LODGE
A-82   B & B   Signal
Ballachulish   GLENCOE   Rock   FARM
CROSSROADS

GLENCOE
To   VISITOR
Fort Augustus   CENTRE   River Coe
& Loch Ness   A-82   CLACHAIG
P   INN   Loch
SIGNAL ROCK   Achtriochtan
& AN TORR HIKE   An Torr   327'

Three

Aonoch
SCOTLAND   Dubh
Inverness   2927'
Hidden

Edinburgh   Stob
Coire
ENGLAND   Sgreamhach
3517'

enter the vast **Rannoch Moor**—50 bleak square miles of heather,
boulders, and barely enough decent land to graze a sheep. Robert
Louis Stevenson called it the "Highland Desert."

You could keep driving as far as you like—but the moor looks
pretty much the same from here on out. Turn around and head
back through Glencoe...it's scenery you'll hardly mind seeing
twice.

Hiking in Glencoe

Glencoe is made for hiking. Many routes are not particularly well
marked, so it's essential to get very specific instructions (from the
rangers at the Glencoe Visitor Centre, or other knowledgeable locals) and equip yourself with a good map (the Ordnance Survey
Explorer Map #384, sold at the center). Below, I've suggested a few
of the most enticing walks and hikes. These vary from easy, level
strolls to challenging climbs. Either way, equip yourself with prop-

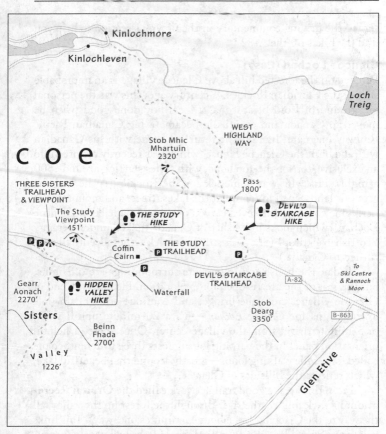

Kinlochmore

Kinlochleven

Loch Treig

c o e

Stob Mhic
Mhartuin
2320'

WEST
HIGHLAND
WAY

Pass
1800'

THREE SISTERS
TRAILHEAD
& VIEWPOINT

The Study
Viewpoint
451'

**THE STUDY
HIKE**

**DEVIL'S
STAIRCASE
HIKE**

Coffin
Cairn

THE STUDY
TRAILHEAD

Gearr
Aonach
2270'

**HIDDEN
VALLEY
HIKE**

Waterfall

DEVIL'S STAIRCASE
TRAILHEAD

A-82

To
Ski Centre
& Rannoch
Moor

Sisters

Stob
Dearg
3350'

B-863

Beinn
Fhada
2700'

Valley
1226'

Glen Etive

er footwear (even the easy trails can get swamped in wet weather) and rain gear—you never know when a storm will blow in.

I've listed these roughly in order of how close they are to Glencoe village, and given a rough sense of difficulty for each. Some of them (including the first two) are more forested, but the ones out in the open—which really let you feel immersed in the wonders of Glencoe—are even better.

While you can walk to the first two areas from Glencoe village, the rest are best for drivers. Some of these trailheads are tricky to find; remember, I've de-

signed the driving commentary in the previous section to help you find the hikes off the A-82.

Glencoe Lochan (Easy)

Perched on the forested hill above Glencoe village is an improbable slice of the Canadian Rockies. A century ago, this was the personal playground of Lord Strathcona, a local boy done good when he moved to Canada and eventually became a big Canadian Pacific Railway magnate. In 1894, he returned home with his Canadian wife and built the Glencoe House (which was recently restored into an exclusive, top-of-the-top hotel, with suites starting around £500 a night). His wife was homesick for the Rockies, so he had the grounds landscaped to represent the lakes, trees, and mountains of her home country. They even carved out a manmade lake (Glencoe Lochan), which looks like a slice of Canada tucked under a craggy Scottish backdrop. (She was still homesick—they eventually returned to Canada.)

Today, the house and immediate surroundings are off-limits, but the rest of the area is open for exploration. Head to the end of Glencoe village, cross the bridge, and continue straight up (following signs for *Glencoe Lochan*)—it's a 20-minute uphill walk, or 5-minute drive, from the village center. Once there, a helpful orientation panel in the parking lot suggests three different, color-coded, one-mile walking loops—mostly around that beautiful lake, which reflects the hillsides of Glencoe.

From this area, a good trail network called the **Orbital Recreational Track** follows the river through the forest up the valley, all the way to the Clachaig Inn (about 45 minutes one-way). This links you to the Signal Rock and An Torr areas (described next). Eventually they hope to extend this trail system across the valley and back to the Glencoe Visitor Centre, which would allow a handy loop hike around the valley floor.

Signal Rock and An Torr (Easy to Moderate)

This forested area has nicely tended trails and gives you a better chance of spotting wildlife than the more desolate hikes described later. To explore this area, park at the well-marked lot just off of the A-82 and go for a walk. A well-described panel at the trailhead narrates three options: easy yellow route to the Clachaig Inn; longer blue route to Signal Rock; and strenuous black route along the hillsides of An Torr. The Signal Rock route brings you to a panoramic point overlooking the valley—so named because a fire could be lit here to alert others in case of danger.

Hidden Valley (Challenging)

Three miles east of Glencoe village, this aptly named glen is tucked between two of the dramatic Three Sisters mountains. Also called the Lost Valley (Coire Gabhail in Gaelic), this was supposedly where the MacDonalds hid stolen cattle from their rivals, the Campbells (who later massacred them). This is the most challenging of the hikes I describe—it's strenuous and has stretches with uneven footing. Expect to scramble a bit over rocks, and to cross a river on stepping stones (which may be underwater after a heavy rain). As the rocks can be slippery when wet, skip this hike in bad weather. Figure about two-and-a-half to three hours round-trip (with an ascent of more than 1,000 feet).

Begin at the second parking lot at Glencoe Pass (on the right when coming from Glencoe), with views of the Three Sisters. You're aiming to head between the first and second Sisters (counting from the left). Hike down into the valley between the road and the mountains. Bear left, head down a metal staircase, and cross the bridge over the river. (Don't cross the bridge to the right of the parking lots—a common mistake.) Once across, you'll start the treacherous ascent up a narrow gorge. Some scrambling is required, and at one point a railing helps you find your way. The next tricky part is where you cross the river. You're looking for a pebbly beach and a large boulder; stepping stones lead across the river, and you'll see the path resume on the other side. But if the water level is high, the stones may be covered—though still passable with good shoes and steady footing. (Don't attempt to scramble over the treacherous slopes on the side of the river with the loose rocks called scree.) Once across the stepping stones, keep on the trail, hiking further up into the valley.

Much Easier Alternative: If you'd simply enjoy the feeling of walking deep in Glencoe valley—with peaks and waterfalls overhead—you can start down from the parking lot toward the Hidden Valley trail, and then simply stroll the old road along the valley floor as far as you want in either direction.

The Study (Easy to Moderate)

For a relatively easy, mostly level hike through the valley with a nice viewpoint at the end, consider walking to the flat rock called "The Study" and back. It takes about 45-60 minutes round-trip. The walk essentially parallels the main highway, but on the old road a bit higher up. You'll park just beyond the Three Sisters and the Coffin Cairn. From there, cut through the field of stone and marshy turf to the old road—basically two gravel tire ruts—and

follow them to your left. You'll hike above the modern road, passing several modest waterfalls, until you reach a big, flat rock with stunning views of the Three Sisters and the valley beyond. (Fellow hikers have marked the spot with a pile of stones.)

The Devil's Staircase (Strenuous but Straightforward)

About eight miles east of Glencoe village, near the end of the valley, you can hike this brief stretch of the West Highland Way. It was built by General Wade, the British strategist who came to Scotland after the 1715 Jacobite rebellion to help secure government rule here. Designed to connect Glencoe valley to the lochside town of Kinlochmore, to the north, it's named for its challenging switchbacks. Most hikers simply ascend to the pass at the top (an 800-foot gain), then come back down to Glencoe. It's challenging, but easier to follow and with more comfortable footing than the Hidden Valley hike. Figure about 45-60 minutes up, and 30 minutes back down (add 45-60 minutes for the optional ascent to the summit of 2,320-foot Stob Mhic Mhartuin).

From the parking lot, a green sign points the way. It's a steep but straightforward hike up, on switchback trails, until you reach the pass—marked by a cairn (pile of stones). From here, you can return back down into the valley. Or, if you have stamina left, consider continuing higher—head up to the peak on the left, called **Stob Mhic Mhartuin.** The 30-40-minute hike to the top (an additional gain of 500 feet) earns you even grander views over the entire valley.

For an even longer hike, it is possible to carry on down the other side of the staircase to **Kinlochmore** (about 2 hours descent)—but your car will still be in Glencoe. Consider this: Leave your car in Glencoe village. Take a taxi to the trailhead. Hike across to Kinlochmore. Then take the hourly Stagecoach bus #44 back to Glencoe and your car (see "Glencoe Connections," later).

Sleeping in Glencoe

Glencoe is an extremely low-key place to spend the night between Oban or Glasgow and the northern destinations. You'll join two kinds of guests: one-nighters just passing through and outdoorsy types settling in for several days of hiking.

B&BS IN GLENCOE VILLAGE

The following B&Bs are along or just off the main road through the middle of the village.

$$ Beechwood Cottage B&B is a shoes-off, slippers-on, whisky-honor-bar kind of place where Jackie rents three lovely rooms and Ian pursues his rock-garden dreams in the yard (look for the sign at the church on Main Street, tel. 01855/811-062, www. beechwoodcottage.scot, stay@beechwoodcottage.scot).

$$ Heatherlea B&B is at the far end of the village, with a relaxed atmosphere, hotel-meets-country-home rooms, and a serene grassy garden with berry bushes (which they harvest for homemade jam). Hosts Jo and Helen are fun, outdoorsy types who opened a guesthouse because they "wanted to get out of the rat race" (four rooms—one a single with private bath down the hall, pack lunches available for small fee, tel. 01855/811-519, mobile 07815-042-505, www.heatherleaglencoe.com, info@heatherleaglencoe.com).

$ Ghlasdruim B&B, behind the Glencoe Café and set back from the A-82, has three large and cozy ground-floor rooms, spacious bathrooms, a homey dining room with a fireplace, and one big table for conversational breakfasts (cash only, closed in winter, tel. 01855/811-593, http://ghlasdruim.co.uk, ghlasdruim@gmail. com, Maureen and Ken).

OUTSIDE OF TOWN

These options are a bit outside of town, with good proximity to both the village and the valley. Strath Lodge and Clachaig Inn are on the back road that runs through the forest parallel to the A-82 (best-suited for drivers). Scorrybreac is on a hill above the village, and Callart View is along the flat road that winds past Loch Leven. Strathassynt Guest House is in the center of Ballachulish.

$$ Strath Lodge, energetically run by Ann and Dan (who are generous with hiking tips and maps), brings a fresh perspective to Glencoe's sometimes stodgy accommodations scene. Their four rooms, in a modern, light-filled, lodge-like home, are partway down the road to the Clachaig Inn (2-3 night minimum preferred, no kids under 16, tel. 01855/811-337, www.strathlodgeglencoe. com, stay@strathlodgeglencoe.com). Take the road up through the middle of Glencoe village, cross the bridge, and keep right following the river for a few minutes; it's on the right.

$$ Clachaig Inn, which runs two popular pubs on site, also rents 23 rooms, all with private bath. It's a family-friendly place surrounded by a dramatic setting that works well for hikers seeking a comfy mountain inn (recommended pub, tel. 01855/811-252, 3 miles from Glencoe, www.clachaig.com, frontdesk@clachaig. com). Follow the directions for the Strath Lodge above, and drive another three miles past campgrounds and hostels—the Clachaig Inn is on the right.

$ Scorrybreac Guest House enjoys a secluded forest setting and privileged position next to the restored Glencoe House (now an exclusive luxury hotel). From here, walks around the Glencoe Lochan wooded lake park are easy, and it's about a 10-minute walk down into the village. Emma and Graham rent five homey rooms and serve a daily breakfast special that goes beyond the usual offerings (family room, 2-3 nights preferred in peak season, tel. 01855/811-354, www.scorrybreacglencoe.com, scorrybreac@ btinternet.com). After crossing the bridge at the end of the village, head left up the hill and follow signs.

$ **Callart View B&B** offers four rooms, quilted-home comfort, and a peaceful spot overlooking Loch Leven, less than a mile outside the village and close to the wooded trails of the Glencoe Lochan. You'll be spoiled by Lynn's homemade shortbread (family room, self-catering cottages, pack lunches available, tel. 01855/811-259, www.callart-view.co.uk, callartview@hotmail.com, Lynn and Geoff). Turn off from the main road for Glencoe village but instead of turning right into the village, keep left and drive less than a mile along the loch.

$ **Strathassynt Guest House** sits in the center of Ballachulish, across from the recommended Laroch Bar & Bistro. Some parts of the house may feel dated (it's a work in progress—they call it "modern vintage"), but the six bedrooms are all fresh and nicely modernized (family rooms, closed Nov-Feb, tel. 01855/811-261, www.strathassynt.com, info@strathassynt.com, Neil and Katya).

Eating in Glencoe

Choices around Glencoe are slim—this isn't the place for fine dining. But the following options offer decent food a short walk or drive away. For evening fun, take a walk or ask your B&B host where to find music and dancing.

In Glencoe: The only real restaurant is $$$ **The Glencoe Gathering,** with lovely dining areas and a large outdoor deck, and specializing in seafood with a Scottish twist. Choose between the quirky, fun pub or the fancier restaurant (food served daily 8:00-22:00, at junction of A-82 and Glencoe village, tel. 01855/811-265). The adjacent hotel has a more subdued and formal restaurant called **The Glencoe Inn.**

The $ **Glencoe Café,** also in the village, is just right for soups and sandwiches, and Deirdre's homemade baked goods—especially the carrot loaf—are irresistible (soup and *panini* lunch combo, daily 10:00-17:00, last order at 16:15, free Wi-Fi, Alan).

Near Glencoe: Set in a stunning valley a few miles from Glencoe village, $$ **Clachaig Inn** serves solid pub grub all day long to a clientele that's half locals and half tourists. This unpretentious and very popular social hub features billiards, live music, and a wide range of whiskies and hand-pulled ales. There are two areas, sharing the same menu: The Bidean Lounge feels a bit like an upscale ski lodge while the Boots Bar has a spit-and-sawdust, pub-around-an-open-fire atmosphere (open daily for lunch and dinner, music Sat from 21:00, Sun open-mike folk music, see hotel listing earlier for driving directions, tel. 01855/811-252, no reservations).

In Ballachulish: Trying to bring some modern class to this sleepy corner of Scotland, **$$$$ The Laroch Bar & Bistro** offers a choice between the fancier bistro (pricey, more sophisticated menu, reservations smart) or the cozy bar (lighter fare, no reservations) with big-screen TVs and video games (Tue-Sun 12:00-15:00 & 18:00-21:00, closed Mon, tel. 01855/811-940, www.thelarochrestaurantandbar.co.uk). Drive three minutes from Glencoe into Ballachulish village, and you'll see it on the left. There's also a simple **$ fish-and-chips** joint next door (open until 21:30).

Glencoe Connections

Buses don't actually drive down the main road through Glencoe village, but they stop nearby at a place called **"Glencoe Crossroads"** (a short walk into the village center). They also stop in the town of **Ballachulish,** which is just a half-mile away (or a £3 taxi ride). Tell the bus driver where you're going ("Glencoe village") and ask to be let off as close as possible.

Citylink buses #914, #915, or #916 stop at Glencoe Crossroads and Ballachulish, heading north to **Fort William** (8/day, 30 minutes) or south to **Glasgow** (3 hours). Another option is Stagecoach bus #44, which runs from either Glencoe Crossroads or Ballachulish to **Fort William** (hourly, fewer on Sun). From Ballachulish, you can take Citylink bus #918 to **Oban** (2/day, 1 hour).

To reach **Inverness,** transfer in Fort William. To reach **Edinburgh,** transfer in Glasgow.

Bus info: Citylink tel. 0871-266-3333, www.citylink.co.uk; Stagecoach tel. 01397/702-373, www.stagecoachbus.com.

Fort William

Fort William—after Inverness, the second biggest town in the Highlands (pop. 10,000)—is Glencoe's opposite. While Glencoe

is a humble one-street village, appealing to hikers and nature-lovers, Fort William's glammed-up car-free main drag feels like one big Scottish shopping mall (with souvenir stands and outdoor stores touting perpetual "70 percent off" sales). The town is clogged with a United Nations of tourists trying to get out of the rain. Big bus tours drive through Glencoe...but they sleep in Fort William.

While Glencoe touches the Scottish soul of the Highlands, Fort William was a steely and intimidating headquarters of the British counter-insurgency movement—in many ways designed to crush that same Highland spirit. After the English Civil War (early 1650s), Oliver Cromwell built a fort here to control his rebellious Scottish subjects. This was beefed up (and named for King William III) in 1690. And following the Jacobite uprising in 1715, King George I dispatched General George Wade to coordinate and fortify the crown's Highland defenses against further Jacobite dissenters. Fort William was the first of a chain of intimidating bastions (along with Fort Augustus on Loch Ness, and Fort George near Inverness) stretching the length of the Great Glen. But Fort William's namesake fortress is long gone, leaving precious little tangible (except a tiny bit of rampart in a park near the train station) to help today's visitors imagine its militaristic past.

With the opening of the Caledonian Canal in 1822, the first curious tourists arrived. Many more followed with the arrival of the train in 1894, and grand hotels were built. Today, sitting at the foot of Ben Nevis, the tallest peak in Britain, Fort William is considered the outdoors capital of the United Kingdom.

Orientation to Fort William

Given its strategic position—between Glencoe and Oban in the south and Inverness in the east—you're likely to pass through Fort William at some point during your Highlands explorations. And, while "just passing through" is the perfect plan here, Fort William can provide a good opportunity to stock up on whatever you need (last supermarket before Inverness), grab lunch, and get any questions answered at the TI.

Arrival in Fort William: You'll find pay parking lots flanking the main pedestrian zone, High Street. The train and bus stations sit side by side just north of the old town center, where you'll find a handy pay parking lot.

Tourist Information: The TI is on the car-free main drag (daily July-Aug 9:30-18:30, Sept-June 9:00-17:00; free Wi-Fi, 15 High Street, tel. 01397/701-801). Free public WCs are up the street, next to the parking lot.

Sights in Fort William

Fort William's High Street

Enjoy an hour-long stroll up and down the length of Fort William's main street for lots of Scottish clichés, great people watching, and a shop at #125 (near the south end) called Aye2Aye, which favors a new referendum on Scottish independence.

▲West Highland Museum

Fort William's only real sight is its humble but well-presented museum. It's a fine opportunity to escape the elements, and—if you take the time to linger over the exhibits—genuinely insightful about local history and Highland life (free, £3 suggested donation, guidebook-£1.50, Mon-Sat 10:00-17:00, and maybe Sun in high season; Nov-Dec and March until 16:00, closed Sun; closed Jan-Feb; midway down the main street on Cameron Square, tel. 01397/702-169, www.westhighlandmuseum.org.uk).

Follow the suggested one-way route through exhibits on two floors. You'll begin by learning about the WWII green beret commandos, who were trained in secrecy near here (see "Commando Memorial" listing, later). Then you'll see the historic Governor's Room, decorated with the original paneling from the room in which the order for the Glencoe Massacre was signed. The ground floor also holds exhibits on natural history (lots of stuffed birds and other critters), mountaineering (old equipment), and archaeology (stone and metal tools).

Upstairs, you'll see a selection of old tartans and a salacious exhibit about Queen Victoria and John Brown (her Scottish servant... and, possibly, suitor). The Jacobite exhibit gives a concise timeline of that complicated history, from Charles I to Bonnie Prince Charlie, and displays a selection of items emblazoned with the prince's bonnie face—including a clandestine portrait that you can only see by looking in a cylindrical mirror. Finally, the Highland Life exhibit collects a hodgepodge of tools, musical instruments (some fine old harps that were later replaced by the much louder bagpipes as the battlefield instrument of choice), and other bric-a-brac.

NEAR FORT WILLIAM
Ben Nevis

From Fort William, take a peek at Britain's highest peak, Ben Nevis (4,406 feet). Thousands walk to its summit each year. On a clear day, you can admire it from a distance. Scotland's only mountain cable cars—at the **Nevis Range Mountain Experience**—can take you to a not-very-lofty 2,150-foot perch on the slopes of Aonach Mòr for a closer look (£14, 15-minute ride, generally open daily but closed in high winds and winter—call ahead, signposted on the A-82 north of Fort William, tel. 01397/705-825, www.nevisrange.co.uk).

▲Commando Memorial

This powerful bronze ensemble of three stoic WWII commandos, standing in an evocative mountain setting, is one of Britain's most beloved war memorials. During World War II, Winston Churchill decided that Britain needed an elite military corps. He created the British Commandos, famous for wearing green berets (an accessory—and name—later borrowed by elite fighting forces in the US and other countries). The British Commandos trained in the Lochaber region near Fort William, in the windy shadow of Ben Nevis. Many later died in combat, and this memorial—built in 1952—remembers those fallen British heroes.

Nearby is the Garden of Remembrance, honoring British Commandos who died in more recent conflicts, from the Falkland Islands to Afghanistan. It's also a popular place to spread Scottish military ashes. Taken together, these sights are a touching reminder that the US is not alone in its distant wars. Every nation has its share of honored heroes willing to sacrifice for what they believe to be the greater good.

Getting There: The memorial is about nine miles outside of Fort William, on the way to Inverness (just outside Spean Bridge); see "Route Tips for Drivers."

Sleeping and Eating in Fort William

Sleeping: The Hobbit-cute **$ Gowan Brae B&B** ("Hill of the Big Daisy") has an antique-filled dining room and three rooms with loch or garden views (one room has private bath down the hall, cash only, 2-night minimum July-Aug, on Union Road—a 5-minute walk up the hill above High Street, tel. 01397/704-399, www.gowanbrae.co.uk, gowan_brae@btinternet.com, Jim and Ann Clark).

Eating: These places are on traffic-free High Street, near the start of town. For lunch and picnics, try **$ Deli Craft,** with good, made-to-order deli sandwiches and other prepared foods (61 High Street, tel. 01397/698-100), or **$ Hot Roast Company,** which sells beef, turkey, ham, or pork sandwiches topped with some tasty extras, along with soup, salad, and coleslaw (127 High Street, tel. 01397/700-606).

For lunch or dinner, **$$ The Grog & Gruel** serves real ales, good pub grub, and Tex-Mex and Cajun dishes, with some unusual choices such as burgers made from boar and haggis or Highland venison. There's also a variety of "grog dogs" (66 High Street, tel. 01397/705-078).

GLENCOE & FORT WILLIAM

Fort William Connections

Fort William is a major transit hub for the Highlands, so you'll likely change buses here at some point during your trip.

From Fort William by Bus to: Glencoe or **Ballachulish** (all Glasgow-bound buses—#914, #915, and #916; 8/day, 30 minutes; also Stagecoach bus #44, hourly, fewer on Sun), **Oban** (bus #918, 2/day, 1.5 hours), **Inverness** (buses #19 and #919, 7/day, 2 hours), **Glasgow** (buses #914, #915, and #916; 8/day, 3 hours). To reach **Edinburgh,** take the bus to Glasgow, then transfer to a train or bus (figure 5 hours total). Citylink: tel. 0871-266-3333, www.citylink.co.uk. Stagecoach: tel. 01397/702-373, www.stagecoachbus.com.

ROUTE TIPS FOR DRIVERS

From Fort William to Loch Ness and Inverness: Head north out of Fort William on the A-82. After about eight miles, in the village of Spean Bridge, take the left fork (staying on the A-82). About a mile later, on the left, keep an eye out for the **Commando Memorial** (described earlier and worth a quick stop). From here, the A-82 sweeps north and follows the Caledonian Canal, passing through **Fort Augustus** (a good lunch stop, with its worthwhile Caledonian Canal Visitor Centre), and then follows the north side of Loch Ness on its way to Inverness. Along the way, the A-82 passes **Urquhart Castle** and two **Loch Ness Monster exhibits** in Drumnadrochit (described in the Inverness & Loch Ness chapter).

From Oban to Fort William via Glencoe: See page 921 in the Oban chapter.

GLENCOE & FORT WILLIAM

INVERNESS & LOCH NESS

Inverness • Culloden Battlefield • Clava Cairns
• Loch Ness

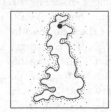

Inverness, the Highlands' de facto capital, is an almost-unavoidable stop on the Scottish tourist circuit. It's a pleasant town and an ideal springboard for some of the country's most famous sights. Hear the music of the Highlands in Inverness and the echo of muskets at Culloden, where government troops drove Bonnie Prince Charlie into exile and conquered his Jacobite supporters. Ponder the mysteries of Scotland's murky prehistoric past at Clava Cairns, and enjoy a peek at Highland aristocratic life at Cawdor Castle. Just to the southwest of Inverness, explore the locks and lochs of the Caledonian Canal while playing hide-and-seek with the Loch Ness monster.

PLANNING YOUR TIME

Though it has little in the way of sights, Inverness does have a workaday charm and is a handy spot to spend a night or two between other Highland destinations. With two nights, you can find a full day's worth of sightseeing nearby.

Note that Loch Ness is between Inverness and Oban or Glencoe. If you're heading to or from one of those places, it makes sense to see Loch Ness en route, rather than as a side-trip from Inverness.

GETTING AROUND THE HIGHLANDS

With a car, the day trips around Inverness are easy. Without a car, you can get to Inverness by train (better from Edinburgh, Stirling, or Glasgow) or by bus (better from Oban and Glencoe), then side-trip to Loch Ness, Culloden, and other nearby sights by public bus or with a package tour.

Inverness

Inverness is situated on the River Ness at the base of a castle (now used as a courthouse, but with a public viewpoint). Inverness' charm is its normalcy—it's a nice, midsize Scottish city that gives you a palatable taste of the "urban" Highlands and a contrast to cutesy tourist towns. It has a disheveled, ruddy-cheeked grittiness and is well located for enjoying the surrounding countryside sights. Check out the bustling, pedestrianized downtown, or meander the picnic-friendly riverside paths and islands—best at sunset, when the light hits the castle and couples hold hands while strolling along the water and over its footbridges.

Orientation to Inverness

Inverness, with about 70,000 people, has been one of the fastest-growing areas of Scotland in recent years. Marked by its castle, Inverness clusters along the River Ness. The TI is on High Street, an appealing pedestrian shopping zone a few blocks away from the river; nearby are the train and bus stations. Most of my recommended B&Bs huddle atop a gentle hill behind the castle (a 10-minute uphill walk from the city center).

TOURIST INFORMATION

At the TI, you can pick up the self-guided *City Centre Trail* walking-tour leaflet and the *What's On* weekly events sheet (June-Sept Mon-Sat 8:45-18:30, shorter hours on Sun and off-season, free Wi-Fi, 36 High Street, tel. 01463/252-401, www.inverness-scotland.com).

HELPFUL HINTS

Charity Shops: Inverness is home to several pop-up charity shops. Occupying vacant rental spaces, these are staffed by volunteers who are happy to talk about their philanthropy. You can pick

Inverness

ABBAN ST.

FRIARS BRIDGE

River Ness

FRIARS ST.

To A-862

TELFORD ST.

WELLS ST.

TELFORD GARDENS

LOCHALSH RD.

CELT ST.

WALK ENDS

"BOUNCY BRIDGE" (FOOT BRIDGE)

QUEEN ST.

19

HARROWDEN RD.

ROSS AVE.

ARDADALE RD.

KENNETH ST.

GREIG ST.

20

KING ST.

FAIRFIELD RD.

PLANEFIELD RD.

KENNETH ST.

MONTAGUE ROW

TOMNAHURICH ST.

ARDROSS ST.

GLENURQUHART RD.

EDEN COURT THEATRE

BISHOP'S RD.

BALLIFEARY RD.

NESS WALK

To A-82, Loch Ness (West), Caledonian Canal, Fort William, & Oban

BALLIFEARY LN.

To Bught Park

Accommodations

1. Ardconnel House & Crown Hotel Guest House
2. Craigside Lodge B&B
3. Eildon Guesthouse
4. Dionard Guest House
5. Lynver Guest House
6. Rossmount Guest House
7. Strathness House
8. Castle View Guest House
9. Heathmount Hotel
10. Waterside Inverness
11. Inverness Student Hotel & Bazpackers Hostel

Eateries & Other

12. Café 1
13. Number 27
14. La Tortilla
15. The Mustard Seed
16. Hootananny
17. Aspendos
18. Rocpool Restaurant
19. River House
20. The Kitchen Brasserie
21. Catch of the Day
22. The Gellions Pub
23. SoBar
24. Malt Room
25. Black Isle Brewery
26. Co-op Supermarket
27. Leakey's Bookshop
28. Launderettes (2)
29. Inverness Bike Tours

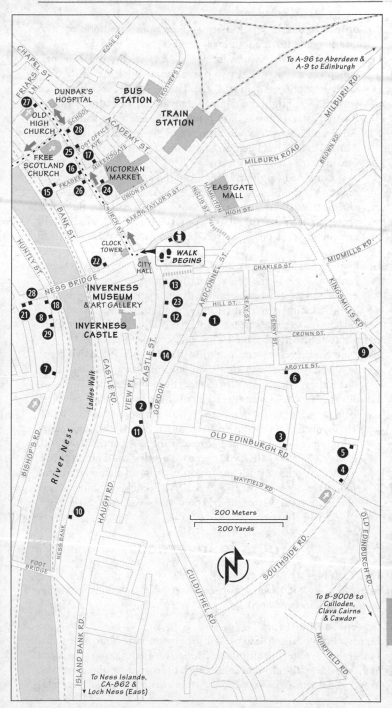

To A-96 to Aberdeen &
A-9 to Edinburgh

CHAPEL ST.

ROSE ST.

FRIARS' LN.

DUNBAR'S
HOSPITAL

BUS
STATION

STROTHER'S LN.

TRAIN
STATION

MILBURN RD.

27

OLD
HIGH
CHURCH

SCHOOL

28

ACADEMY ST.

BROWN RD.

MILBURN ROAD

POST OFFICE AVE.

25

17

QUEENSGATE

FREE
SCOTLAND
CHURCH

16

FRASER ST.

VICTORIAN
MARKET

EASTGATE
MALL

15

26

24

BANK ST.

UNION ST.

CHURCH ST.

BARON TAYLOR'S ST.

INGLIS ST.

HAMILTON ST.

HIGH ST.

HUNTLY ST.

CLOCK
TOWER

22

WALK
BEGINS

CITY HALL

ARDCONNEL ST.

CHARLES ST.

MIDMILLS RD.

NESS BRIDGE

INVERNESS
MUSEUM
& ART GALLERY

13

23

HILL ST.

REAY ST.

KINGSMILLS RD.

28

18

21

8

12

1

DENNY ST.

29

INVERNESS
CASTLE

CROWN ST.

9

7

CASTLE ST.

14

ARGYLE ST.

6

Ladies Walk

CASTLE RD.

VIEW PL.

GORDON

2

11

OLD EDINBURGH RD.

3

5

4

BISHOP'S RD.

River Ness

HAUGH RD.

MAYFIELD RD.

200 Meters

200 Yards

NESS BANK

10

N

OLD EDINBURGH RD.

FOOT
BRIDGE

ISLAND BANK RD.

CULDUTHEL RD.

SOUTHSIDE RD.

MURFIELD RD.

To B-9008 to
Culloden,
Clava Cairns
& Cawdor

To Ness Islands,
CA-862 &
Loch Ness (East)

INVERNESS & LOCH NESS

up a memorable knickknack, adjust your wardrobe for the weather, and learn about local causes.

Festivals and Events: The summer is busy with special events, which can make it tricky to find a room. Book far ahead during these times, including the Etape Loch Ness bike race (early June), Highland Games (late June), Belladrum Tartan Heart Festival (music, late July), Black Isle farm show (early Aug), and Loch Ness Marathon (late Sept). The big RockNess Music Festival has been on hiatus due to budget cuts, but may return.

For a real Highland treat, catch a **shinty match** (a combination of field hockey, hurling, and American football—but without pads). Inverness Shinty Club plays at Bught Park, along Ness Walk (the TI or your B&B can tell you if there are any matches on, or search online for the Inverness Shinty Club.

Bookstore: Leakey's Bookshop, located in a converted church built in 1649, is the place to browse through teetering towers of musty old books and vintage maps, warm up by the wood-burning stove, and climb the spiral staircase to the loft for views over the stacks (Mon-Sat 10:00-17:30, closed Sun, Church Street, tel. 01463/239-947, Charles Leakey).

Baggage Storage: The train station has lockers (open Mon-Sat 6:40-20:30, Sun from 10:40), or you can leave your bag at the bus station's ticket desk (small fee, daily until 17:30).

Laundry: New City Launderette is near the west end of the Ness Bridge (self-service or same-day full-service, Mon-Sat 8:00-18:00, until 20:00 Mon-Fri in summer, Sun 10:00-16:00 year-round, last load one hour before closing, 17 Young Street, tel. 01463/242-507). **Thirty Degrees Laundry** on Church Street is another option (full-service only, drop off before 10:00 for same-day service, Mon-Sat 8:30-17:30, closed Sun, a few blocks beyond Victorian Market at 84 Church Street, tel. 01463/710-380).

Tours in Inverness

IN TOWN

Skip the City Sightseeing hop-on, hop-off bus tour (this format doesn't work in Inverness).

Inverness Bike Tours

Hard-working Alison leads small groups on two-hour bike tours. Her six-mile route is nearly all on traffic-free paths along canals and lochs outside of the city and comes with light guiding along the way. You'll pedal through Ness Island, stop at the Botanical Gardens, ride along the Caledonian Canal with its system of locks (you may even catch a boat passing through the locks), and cycle through a nature preserve (£21, no kids under 14, 10-person max; daily in season at 10:00, 13:00, and 16:00; best to book spot in advance online, goes even in light rain, meet near west end of Ness Bridge at Prime restaurant at 5 Ness Walk, call or text mobile 07443-866-619, www. invernessbiketours.co.uk, info@invernessbiketours.co.uk). Arrive a bit early to size up your bike and helmet.

EXCURSIONS FROM INVERNESS

While thin on sights of its own, Inverness is a great home base for day trips. A variety of tour companies offer day trips to other Highlands destinations, including many not covered by this book—details and tickets are available at the TI. While the big sellers among Inverness day-trips are the many Loch Ness tours (because the monster is on every bucket list), I far prefer an Isle of Skye all-day joyride—which gives you a good look at Loch Ness and its famous castle along the way. Study the various websites for comparative details. For Isle of Skye and Orkney Island tours in summer, it's a good idea to book about a week in advance.

Loch Ness

The famous lake is just a 20-minute drive from Inverness. Tours will often include a short boat ride, a visit to the Urquhart Castle, and a stop at the Loch Ness monster exhibits. The lake is not particularly scenic. The castle, while scenic, is just a shell. And the monster is mostly a promotional gimmick. Still, if you have no car, this can be the most efficient way to check this off your list. **Jacobite Tours** focuses on trips that include Loch Ness, from a one-hour basic boat ride to a 6.5-hour extravaganza. Their four-hour "Sensation" tour includes a guided bus tour with live narration, a half-hour Loch Ness cruise, and visits to Urquhart Castle and the Loch Ness exhibits (£35, for more options see www.jacobite.co.uk, tel. 01463/233-999).

Isle of Skye

Several companies do good day tours to the Isle of Skye. They travel 110 miles (a 2.5 hour drive) to the heart of Skye (Portree). With about six hours of driving, and one hour for lunch in Portree, that leaves two or three hours for a handful of quick and scenic photo stops. All travel along Loch Ness so you can see Urquhart Castle and try for a monster sighting. And all stop for a view of Eilean Donan Castle. The longer rides loop around the Trotternish Peninsula. Websites explain the exact itineraries.

Wow Scotland's ambitious 12-hour itinerary goes in a big bus. They depart at 8:30 from the Inverness bus station and include short but smart and adequate stops all along the way (£77,

5/week June-Aug, fewer departures in April-May and Sept, none Oct-March, tel. 01808/511-773, www.wowscotlandtours.com). I'd pay the extra for the £99 front row.

Highland Experience Tours runs another, shorter Isle of Skye itinerary in 24-seat buses (daily April-Oct, less off-season, 10 hours) but doesn't make it as far north as the Trotternish Peninsula (£55, tel. 01463/719-222, www.highlandexperience.com). They offer a variety of other daylong tours, including to the far north with John O'Groats, or a trip to Royal Deeside and the Speyside Whisky Trail.

Happy Tours Scotland organizes daily minibus tours on a 10-hour joy ride (getting all the way to Quiraing) with top-notch guides (£70, 8 people per minibus, daily at 8:30, leaves from 7 Ness Walk at Columba Hotel, mobile 07828-154-683, book at www.happy-tours.biz, run by Cameron). They also do other tours including itineraries focusing on Loch Ness, the *Outlander* books and TV series, a Speyside whisky tour, and private minibus tours.

Rabbie's Small Group Tours does 12-hour trips to Skye in its 16-seater buses for £52 nearly daily from Inverness. Their website explains their busy program (www.rabbies.com).

Iona Highland Tours takes eight people on several different Isle of Skye itineraries, including one that allows hiking time at the Fairy Pools (£70, 9 hours, tel. 01463/250-457, www.ionahighlandtours.com).

By Train Then Tour: To avoid a long bus ride or skip the sights along the way to Skye, take the train from Inverness to Kyle of Lochalsh, where a Skye-based tour company will pick you up and take you around. Try **Skye Tours** (tel. 01471/822-716, www.skye-tours.co.uk) or **Tour Skye** (tel. 01478/613-514, www.tourskye.com). The train leaves Inverness before 9:00 and arrives around 11:30; the return train is around 17:15 (covered by BritRail Pass).

Orkney Islands

For a very ambitious itinerary, John O'Groats Ferries offers an all-day tour that departs Inverness at 7:15, drives you up to John O'Groats to catch the 40-minute passenger ferry, then a second bus takes you on a whistle-stop tour of Orkney's main attractions (with an hour in the town of Kirkwall) before returning you to Inverness by 21:00. While it's a long day, it's an efficient use of your time if you're determined to see Orkney (£74, daily June-Aug only, tel. 01955/611-353, www.jogferry.co.uk).

Inverness Walk

Humble Inverness has meager conventional sights, but its fun history and quirky charm become clear as you take this short self-guided walk. To trace the route, see the map earlier in this chapter.

• *Start at the clock tower.*

Clock Tower: Notice the **Gaelic language** on directional and street signs all around you. While nobody speaks Gaelic as a first language (and only about 60,000 Scottish people speak it fluently), this old Celtic language symbolizes the strength of Scottish Highland culture.

The clock tower looming 130 feet above you is all that remains of a tollbooth building erected in 1791. This is the highest spire in town, and for generations was a collection point for local taxes. Here, four streets—Church, Castle, Bridge, and High—come together, integrating God, defense, and trade—everything necessary for a fine city.

About 800 years ago, a castle was built on the bluff overhead and the town of Inverness coalesced right about here. For centuries, this backwater town's economy was based on cottage industries. Artisans who made things also sold them. In 1854, the train arrived, injecting energy and money from Edinburgh and Glasgow, and the Victorian boom hit. With the Industrial Age came wholesalers, distributors, mass production, and affluence. Much of the city was built during this era, in Neo-Gothic style—over-the-top and fanciful, like the City Hall (from 1882, kitty-corner to the clock tower). With the Victorian Age also came tourism.

Look for the **Bible quotes** chiseled into the wall across the street from the City Hall. A civic leader, tired of his council members being drunkards, edited these Bible verses for maximum impact, especially the bottom two.

Hiding just up the hill (behind the eyesore concrete home of the Inverness Museum and Art Gallery) is **Inverness Castle.** While the "castle" is now a courthouse, there is a small exhibition and a chance to climb to the top of the tower (£5). It's worth hiking up to the castle at some point during your visit to enjoy some of the best views of Inverness and its river. The courthouse in the castle doesn't see a lot of action. In the last few decades, there have been only two murders to prosecute. As locals like to say, "no guns, no problems." While hunters can own a gun, gun ownership in Scotland is complicated and tightly regulated.

• Walk a few steps away from the river (toward McDonald's)...

Mercat Cross and Old Town Center: Standing in front of the City Hall is a well-worn mercat cross, which designated the market in centuries past. This is where the townspeople gathered to hear important proclamations, share news, watch hangings, gossip, and so on. The scant remains of a prehistoric stone at the base of the cross are what's left of Inverness' "Stone of Destiny." According to tradition, whenever someone moved away from Inverness, they'd take a tiny bit of home with them in the form of a chip of this stone—so it's been chipped and pecked almost to oblivion.

The yellow **Caledonian** building faces McDonald's at the base of High Street. (Caledonia was the ancient Roman name for Scotland.) It was built in 1847, complete with Corinthian columns and a Greek-style pediment, as the leading bank in town, back when banks were designed to hold the money of the rich and powerful... and intimidate working blokes. Notice how nicely pedestrianized High Street welcomes people and seagulls...but not cars.

• *Next we'll head up Church Street, which begins between the clock tower and The Caledonian.*

Church Street: The street art you'll trip over at the start of Church Street is called *Earthquake*— a reminder of the quake that hit Inverness in 1816. As the slabs explain, the town's motto is "Open Heartedness, Insight, and Perseverance."

Stroll down Church Street. Look up above the modern storefronts to see Old World facades. **Union Street** (the second corner on the right)—stately, symmetrical, and Neoclassical—was the fanciest street in the Highlands when it was built in the 19th century. Its buildings had indoor toilets. That was big news.

Midway down the next block of Church Street (on the right), an alley marked by an ugly white canopy leads to the **Victorian Market.** Venturing down the alley, you'll pass **The Malt Room** (a small and friendly whisky bar eager to teach you to appreciate Scotland's national tipple; see "Nightlife in Inverness") and **The Old Market Bar** (a dive bar worth a peek). Stepping into the Victorian Market, you'll find a gallery of shops under an iron-

and-glass domed roof dating from 1876. The first section seems abandoned, but delve deeper to find some more active areas, where local shops mix with tacky "tartan tat" souvenir stands. If you're seriously into bagpipes, look for **Cabar Fèidh,** where American expat Brian sells CDs and sheet music, and repairs and maintains the precious instruments of local musicians.

Go back out of the market the way you came in, and continue down Church Street. At the next corner you come to **Hootananny,** famous locally for its live music (pop in to see what's on tonight). Just past that is **Abertarff House,** the oldest house in Inverness. It was the talk of the town in 1593 for its "turnpike" (spiral staircase) connecting the floors.

Continue about a block farther along Church Street. The lane on the left leads to the **"Bouncy Bridge"** (where we'll finish this walk). Opposite that lane (on the right) is **Dunbar's Hospital,** with four-foot-thick walls. In 1668, Alexander Dunbar was a wealthy landowner who built this as a poor folks' home. You can almost read the auld script in his coat of arms above the door.

A few steps farther up Church Street, walk through the iron gate on the left and into the churchyard (we're focusing on the shorter church on the right—ignore the bigger one on the left). Looking at the WWI and WWII memorials on the church's wall, it's clear which war hit Scotland harder. While no one famous is buried here, many tombstones go back to the 1700s. Being careful not to step on a rabbit, head for the bluff overlooking the river and turn around to see...

Old High Church: There are a lot of churches in Inverness (46 Protestant, 2 Catholic, 2 Gaelic-language, and one offering a Mass in Polish), but these days, most are used for other purposes. This one, dating from the 11th century, is the most historic (but is generally closed). It was built on what was likely the site of a pagan holy ground. Early Christians called upon St. Michael to  take the fire out of pagan spirits, so it only made sense that the first Christians would build their church here and dedicate the spot as St. Michael's Mount.

In the sixth century, the Irish evangelist monk St. Columba brought Christianity to northern England, the Scottish islands (at Iona), and the Scottish Highlands (in Inverness). He stood here amongst the pagans and preached to King Brude and the Picts.

Study the bell tower from the 1600s. The small door to nowhere (one floor up) indicates that back before the castle offered protection, this tower was the place of last refuge for townsfolk under attack. They'd gather inside and pull up the ladder. The church became a prison for Jacobites after the Battle of Culloden, and executions were carried out in the churchyard.

Every night at 20:00, the bell in the tower rings 100 times. It has rung like this since 1730 to remind townsfolk that it's dangerous to be out after dinner.

• *From here, you can circle back to the lane leading to the "Bouncy Bridge" and then hike out onto the bridge. Or you can just survey the countryside from this bluff.*

The River Ness: Emptying out of Loch Ness and flowing seven miles to the sea (a mile from here), this is one of the shortest rivers in the country. While it's shallow (you can almost walk across it), there are plenty of fish in it. A 64-pound salmon was once pulled out of the river right here. In the 19th century, Inverness was smaller, and across the river stretched nothing but open fields. Then, with the Victorian boom, the suspension footbridge (a.k.a. "Bouncy Bridge") was built in 1881 to connect new construction across the river with the town.

• *Your tour is over. Inverness is yours to explore.*

Sights in Inverness

Inverness Museum and Art Gallery

This free, likable town museum is worth poking around on a rainy day to get a taste of Inverness and the Highlands. The ground-floor exhibits on geology and archaeology peel back the layers of Highland history: Bronze and Iron ages, Picts (including some carved stones), Scots, Vikings, and Normans. Upstairs you'll find the "social history" exhibit (everything from Scottish nationalism to hunting and fishing) and temporary art exhibits.

Cost and Hours: Free, April-Oct Tue-Sat 10:00-17:00, shorter hours off-season, closed Sun-Mon year-round, cheap café, in the ugly modern building on the way up to the castle, tel. 01463/237-114, www.highlifehighland.com.

Inverness Castle

Aside from nice views from the front lawn, a small exhibition on the ground floor, and a tower climb, Inverness' biggest nonsight is not open to the public. A wooden fortress that stood on this spot was replaced by a stone structure in the 15th century. In 1715, that castle was named Fort George to assert English control over the area. In 1745, it was destroyed by Bonnie Prince Charlie's Jacobite army and remained a ruin until the 1830s, when the present castle was built. The statue outside (from 1899) depicts Flora MacDonald, who helped Bonnie Prince Charlie escape from the English (see page 976). The castle was built as the courthouse, and when trials are in session, loutish-looking men hang out here, waiting for their bewigged barristers to arrive. For £5 you can climb to the top of the tower for a commanding city view. In a few years, the castle will host what promises to be a top-notch new museum.

River Walks

As with most European cities, where there's a river, there's a walk. Inverness, with both the River Ness and the Caledonian Canal, does not disappoint. Consider an early-morning stroll along the Ness Bank to capture the castle at sunrise, or a postdinner jaunt to Bught Park for a local shinty match (see "Helpful Hints—Festivals and Events," earlier). The path is lit at night. The forested islands in the middle of the River Ness—about a 10-minute walk south of the center—are a popular escape from the otherwise busy city.

Here's a good plan for your Inverness riverside constitutional: From the Ness Bridge, head along the riverbank under the castle (along the path called "Ladies Walk"). As you work your way up the river, you'll see the architecturally bold Eden Court Theatre (across the river), pass a white pedestrian bridge, see a WWI memorial, and peek into the gardens of several fine old Victorian sandstone riverfront homes. Nearing the tree-covered islands, watch for fly-fishers in hip waders on the pebbly banks. Reaching the first, skinny little island, take the bridge with the wavy, wrought-iron railing and head down the path along the middle of the island. Notice that this is part of the Great Glen Way, a footpath that stretches from here all the way to Fort William (79 miles). Enjoy this little nature break, with gurgling rapids—and, possibly, a few midges. Reaching the bigger bridge, cross it and enjoy strolling through tall forests. Continue upriver. After two more green-railinged bridges, traverse yet another island, and find one last white-iron bridge that takes you across to the opposite bank. You'll pop out at the corner of Bught Park, the site of shinty practices and games—are any going on today?

From here, you can simply head back into town on this bank. If you'd like to explore more, you could continue farther south. It's not as idyllic or as pedestrian-friendly, but in this zone you'll find minigolf, a skate park, the Highland Archive building, the free Botanic Gardens (daily 10:00-17:00, until 16:00 Nov-March), and the huge Active Inverness leisure center, loaded with amusements including a swimming pool with adventure slides, a climbing wall, a sauna and steam area, and a gym (www.invernessleisure.co.uk).

Continuing west from these leisure areas, you'll eventually hit the Caledonian Canal; to the south, this parallels the River Ness, and to the north is where it meets Beauly Firth, then Moray Firth and the North Sea. From the Tomnahurich Bridge, paths on either bank allow you to walk along the Great Glen Way until you're ready to turn around.

Nightlife in Inverness

Scottish Folk Music

While you can find traditional folk music sessions in pubs and hotel bars anywhere in town, two places are well established as *the* music pubs. Neither charges a cover for the music, unless a bigger-name band is playing.

The Gellions has live folk and Scottish music nightly (from 21:30). It has local ales on tap and brags it's the oldest bar in town (14 Bridge Street, tel. 01463/233-648, www.gellions.co.uk).

Hootananny is an energetic place with several floors of live rock, blues, or folk music, and drinking fun nightly. It's rock (upstairs) and reel (ground floor). Music in the main bar (ground floor) usually begins about 21:30 (traditional music sessions Sun-Wed, trad bands on weekends; also a daytime session on Sat afternoon at 14:30). On Friday and Saturday nights only, upstairs is the Mad Hatter's nightclub, complete with a cocktail bar (67 Church Street, tel. 01463/233-651, www.hootananny.co.uk).

Billiards and Darts

SoBar is a sprawling pub with dartboards (free but £5 deposit), pool tables (£7.50 per hour), a museum worth of sports memorabilia, and the biggest TV screens in town (popular on big game nights). It's a fine place to hang out and meet locals if you'd rather not have live music (just across from the castle at 55 Castle Street, tel. 01463/229-780).

Whisky Tastings and Brew Pubs

For a whisky education, or just a fine cocktail, drop in to the intimate **Malt Room,** with whiskies ranging from £4 to £75. The whisky-plus-chocolate flight makes for a fun nightcap (just off Church Street in the alley leading to the Victorian Market, 34 Church Street, tel. 01463/221-888, Lee and Matt).

At the **Black Isle Brewery,** you can sample their local organic beers and ciders. Choose from 26 beers on tap (including some non-Black Isle brews), all listed on the TV screen over the bar (wood-fired pizzas, 68 Church Street, tel. 01463/229-920).

Sleeping in Inverness

B&BS NEAR THE TOWN CENTER

These B&Bs are popular; book ahead for June through August (and during the peak times listed in "Helpful Hints," earlier), and be aware that some require a two-night minimum during busy times. The places I list are a 10- to 15-minute walk from the train station and town center. To get to the B&Bs, either catch a taxi (£5) or walk: From the train and bus stations, go left on Academy Street. At the first stoplight (the second if you're coming from the bus station), veer right onto Inglis Street in the pedestrian zone. Go up the Market Brae steps. At the top, turn right onto Ardconnel Street.

On or near Ardconnel Street

These places line up above Castle Street (with several recommended restaurants).

$$ **Ardconnel House** is a classic, traditional place offering a nice, large guest lounge, along with six spacious and comfortable rooms (family room, two-night minimum preferred in summer, no children under 10, 21 Ardconnel Street, tel. 01463/240-455, www.ardconnel-inverness.co.uk, ardconnel@gmail.com, John and Elizabeth).

$ **Craigside Lodge B&B** has five large rooms with tasteful modern flair, nice tartan touches, and fun stuffed-animal door-stoppers. The breakfast room is a nice place to soak up city views (family room, no kids under 8, just above Castle Street at 4 Gordon Terrace, tel. 01463/231-576, www.craigsideguesthouse.co.uk, enquiries@craigsideguesthouse.co.uk, hospitable Paul and Mandy).

$ **Crown Hotel Guest House** has seven pleasant rooms (two with private bath down the hall) and is a bargain if you're willing to put up with a few quirks—some dated elements and owners who are still learning the ins and outs of running a guesthouse (family room, 19 Ardconnel Street, tel. 01463/231-135, www.crownhotel-inverness.co.uk, crownhotelguesthouse@gmail.com, Munawar and Asia).

Around Old Edinburgh Road and Southside Road

These places are just a couple of minutes farther out from Castle Street and the places on Ardconnel.

$$ **Eildon Guesthouse,** set on a quiet corner, offers five tranquil rooms with spacious baths. The cute-as-a-button 1890s countryside brick home exudes warmth and serenity from the moment you open the gate (family rooms, 2-night minimum in summer, no kids under 10, in-room fridges, parking, 29 Old Ed-

inburgh Road, tel. 01463/231-969, www.eildonguesthouse.co.uk, eildonguesthouse@yahoo.co.uk, Jacqueline).

$$ Dionard Guest House, wrapped in a fine hedged-in garden, has cheerful common spaces, six lovely rooms, some fun stag art, and lively hosts Gail and Anne—best friends turned business partners (family suite, in-room fridges, they'll do guest laundry for free, 39 Old Edinburgh Road, tel. 01463/233-557, www.dionardguesthouse.co.uk, enquiries@dionardguesthouse.co.uk).

$$ Lynver Guest House will make you feel spoiled, with three large, boutiquey rooms (all with sitting areas), a backyard stone patio that catches the sun, and veggie and fish options at breakfast (2-night minimum preferred in summer, no kids under 10, in-room fridges, 30 Southside Road, tel. 01463/242-906, www.lynver.co.uk, info@lynver.co.uk, Michelle and Brian).

$$ Rossmount Guest House feels like home, with its curl-up-on-the-couch lounge space, unfussy rooms (five in all), and friendly hosts (two rooms share a bath and are cheaper, 2-night minimum in summer, Argyle Street, tel. 01463/229-749, www.rossmount.co.uk, mail@rossmount.co.uk, Ruth and Robert).

B&BS ACROSS THE RIVER

$$$ Strathness House has a prime spot on the river a block from Ness Bridge. Formerly a hotel, it's a bigger place, with 12 rooms and a large ground-floor lounge, but comes with the same intimate touches of a guesthouse. They cater to all diets at breakfast, including vegan, gluten-free, halal, and kosher (family room for 3, no kids under 5, street or off-site parking, 4 Ardross Terrace, tel. 01463/232-765, www.strathnesshouse.co.uk, info@strathnesshouse.com, Joan and Javed).

$$ Castle View Guest House sits right along the River Ness at the Ness Bridge—and, true to its name, it owns smashing views of the castle. Its five big and comfy rooms (some with views) are colorfully furnished, and the delightful place is lovingly run by Eleanor (2A Ness Walk, tel. 01463/241-443, www.castleviewguesthouseinverness.com, enquiries@castleviewguesthouseinverness.com).

HOTELS

Inverness has a number of big chain hotels. These tend to charge a lot when Inverness is busy but may be worth a look if the B&Bs are full or if it's outside the main tourist season. Options include the Inverness Palace Hotel & Spa (a Best Western fancy splurge right on the river with a pool and gym), Premier Inn (River Ness location), and Mercure. The following hotels are smaller and more local.

$$$ Heathmount Hotel's understated facade hides a chic retreat for comfort-seeking travelers. Its eight elegant rooms come with unique decoration, parking, and fancy extras (family room, no elevator, restaurant, Kingsmill Road, tel. 01463/235-877, www. heathmounthotel.com, info@heathounthotel.com,).

$$$ Waterside Inverness, in a nice, peaceful location along the River Ness, has 35 crisp rooms and a riverview restaurant (parking, 19 Ness Bank, tel. 01463/233-065, www.thewatersideinverness. co.uk, info@thewatersideinverness.co.uk).

HOSTELS

For funky and cheap dorm beds near the center and the recommended Castle Street restaurants, consider these friendly side-by-side hostels, geared toward younger travelers. They're about a 12-minute walk from the train station.

¢ **Bazpackers Hostel,** a stone's throw from the castle, has a quieter, more private feel for a hostel. There are 34 beds in basic dorms (private rooms with shared bath available, reception open 7:30-23:00, no curfew, pay laundry service, 4 Culduthel Road, tel. 01463/717-663, www.bazpackershostel.co.uk, info@ bazpackershostel.co.uk). They also rent a small apartment nearby (sleeps up to 4).

¢ **Inverness Student Hotel** has 57 thin-mattressed beds in nine brightly colored rooms and a laid-back lounge with a bay window overlooking the River Ness. The knowledgeable, friendly staff welcomes any traveler over 18. Dorms are a bit grungy, but each bunk has its own playful name (breakfast extra, free tea and coffee, pay laundry service, kitchen, 8 Culduthel Road, tel. 01463/236-556, www.invernessstudenthotel.com, info@invernessstudenthotel. com).

Eating in Inverness

BY THE CASTLE

The first three eateries line Castle Street, facing the back of the castle.

$$$ Café 1 serves up high-quality modern Scottish and international cuisine with trendy, chic bistro flair. Fresh meat from their own farm adds to an appealing menu (lunch and early-bird dinner specials until 18:45, open Mon-Fri 12:00-14:30 & 17:00-21:30, Sat from 13:00 & 18:00, closed Sun, reservations smart, 75 Castle Street, tel. 01463/226-200, www.cafe1.net).

$$ Number 27 has a straightforward, crowd-pleasing menu that offers something for everyone—burgers, pastas, and more. The food is surprisingly elegant for this price range (daily 12:00-15:00 & 17:00-21:00, generous portions, local ales on tap, 27 Castle Street, tel. 01463/241-999).

$$ La Tortilla has Spanish tapas, including spicy king prawns (the house specialty). It's an appealing, colorfully tiled, and vivacious dining option that feels like Spain. With the tapas format, three family-style dishes make about one meal (daily 12:00-22:00, 99 Castle Street, tel. 01463/709-809).

IN THE TOWN CENTER

$$$$ The Mustard Seed serves Scottish food with a modern twist in an old church with a river view. It's a lively place with nice outdoor tables over the river when sunny (early specials before 19:00, daily 12:00-15:00 & 17:30-22:00, reservations smart, on the corner of Bank and Fraser Streets, 16 Fraser Street, tel. 01463/220-220, www.mustardseedrestaurant.co.uk, Matthew).

$$ Hootananny is a spacious pub with a hardwood-and-candlelight vibe and a fun menu featuring dishes one step above pub grub (food served Mon-Sat 12:00-15:00 & 17:00-20:30, dinner only on Sun). The kitchen closes early to make way for the live music scene that takes over each night after 21:30 (see "Nightlife in Inverness," earlier).

$$ Aspendos serves up freshly prepared, delicious Turkish dishes in a spacious, dressy, and exuberantly decorated dining room (daily 12:00-21:30, 26 Queensgate, tel. 01463/711-950).

Picnic: There's a Co-op market with plenty of cheap picnic grub at 59 Church Street (daily until 22:00).

ACROSS THE RIVER

$$$$ Rocpool Restaurant is a hit with locals, good for a splurge, and perhaps the best place in town. Owner/chef Steven Devlin serves creative modern European food to a smart clientele in a sleek, contemporary dining room (early-bird weekday special until 18:45, open Mon-Sat 12:00-14:30 & 17:45-22:00, closed Sun, reservations essential; across Ness Bridge at 1 Ness Walk, tel. 01463/717-274, www.rocpoolrestaurant.com).

$$$$ River House, a classy, sophisticated, but unstuffy riverside place, is the brainchild of Cornishman Alfie—who prides himself on melding the seafood know-how of both Cornwall and Scotland, with a bit of Mediterranean flair (Mon-Sat 15:00-21:30, closed Mon off-season and Sun year-round, reservations smart, 1 Greig Street, tel. 01463/222-033, www.riverhouseinverness.co.uk).

$$$ The Kitchen Brasserie is a modern building overlooking the river, popular for their homemade comfort food—pizza, pasta, and burgers (early-bird special until 19:00, daily 12:00-15:00 & 17:00-22:00, 15 Huntly Street, tel. 01463/259-119, www.kitchenrestaurant.co.uk, Christine).

Fish and Chips: Consider the $ Catch of the Day chippy for a nicely presented sit-down meal or to go (daily 12:00-14:00

& 16:30-22:00, closed Sun at lunch, a block over Ness Bridge on Young Street, mobile 07909-966-525).

Inverness Connections

From Inverness by Train to: Edinburgh (hourly, 4 hours, some with change in Perth), **Glasgow** (11/day, 3 hours, 4 direct, others change in Perth). The Caledonian Sleeper provides overnight service to **London** (www.sleeper.scot). Train info: tel. 0345-748-4950, www.nationalrail.co.uk.

By Bus: For destinations in western Scotland, you'll first head for **Fort William** (bus #19 or #919, 8/day, 2 hours). For connections onward to **Oban** (figure 4 hours total) or **Glencoe** (3 hours total), see "Fort William Connections" on page 957. Inverness is also connected by direct bus to **Edinburgh** (express bus #G90, 2/day, 3.5 hours; slower bus #M90, 6/day, 4 hours) and **Glasgow** (5/day on Citylink express bus #G10, 3 hours; 1/day direct on National Express #588, 4 hours). Scottish Citylink: www.citylink.co.uk.

Tickets are sold in advance online, by phone at tel. 0871-266-3333, or in person at the Inverness bus station (daily 7:45-18:15, baggage storage, 2 blocks from train station on Margaret Street, tel. 01463/233-371). For bus travel to England, check National Express (www.nationalexpress.com) or Megabus (http://uk.megabus.com).

ROUTE TIPS FOR DRIVERS

Inverness to Edinburgh (160 miles, 3.25 hours minimum): Leaving Inverness, follow signs to the A-9 (south, toward Perth). If you haven't seen the Culloden Battlefield yet (described later), it's an easy detour: Just as you leave Inverness, head four miles east off the A-9 on the B-9006. Back on the A-9, it's a wonderfully speedy, scenic highway (A-9, M-90, A-90) all the way to Edinburgh.

Inverness to Fort William (65 miles, 1.5 hours): This city, southwest of Inverness via the A-82, is a good gateway to Oban and Glencoe. See page 957.

Near Inverness

Inverness puts you in the heart of the Highlands, within easy striking distance of several famous and worthwhile sights: Commune with the Scottish soul at the historic Culloden Battlefield, where British history reached a turning point. Wonder at three mysterious Neolithic cairns, which remind visitors that Scotland's story goes back thousands of years. And enjoy a homey country castle at

Cawdor. Loch Ness—with its elusive monster—is another popular and easy day trip.

CULLODEN BATTLEFIELD

Jacobite troops under Bonnie Prince Charlie were defeated at Culloden (kuh-LAW-dehn) by supporters of the Hanover dynasty (King George II's family) in 1746. Sort of the "Scottish Alamo," this last major land battle fought on British soil spelled the end of Jacobite resistance and the beginning of the clan chiefs' fall from power. Wandering the desolate, solemn battlefield, you sense that something terrible occurred here. Locals still bring white roses and speak of "The '45" (as Bonnie Prince Charlie's entire campaign is called) as if it just happened. The

battlefield at Culloden and its high-tech visitors center together are worth ▲▲▲.

Orientation to Culloden

Cost and Hours: £11, £5 guidebook; daily 9:00-17:30, June-Aug until 18:00, Nov-March 10:00-16:00, closed Jan; café, tel. 01463/796-090, http://www.nts.org.uk/culloden.

Tours: The included **audioguide** leads you through both the exhibition and the battlefield. There are several free tours daily along with costumed events (see schedule posted at entry).

Getting There: It's a 15-minute **drive** east of Inverness. Follow signs to *Aberdeen,* then *Culloden Moor*—the B-9006 takes you right there (well-signed on the right-hand side). Parking is £2. Public **buses** leave from Inverness' Queensgate Street and drop you off in front of the entrance (£5 round-trip ticket, bus #5, roughly hourly, 40 minutes, ask at TI for route/schedule updates). A **taxi** costs around £15 one-way.

Length of This Tour: Allow 2 hours.

Background

The Battle of Culloden (April 16, 1746) marks the steep decline of the Scottish Highland clans and the start of years of cruel repression of Highland culture by the British. It was the culmination of a year's worth of battles, and at the center of it all was the charismatic, enigmatic Bonnie Prince Charlie (1720-1788).

Charles Edward Stuart, from his first breath, was raised with a single purpose—to restore his family to the British throne. His grandfather was King James II (VII of Scotland), deposed in 1688 by the English Parliament for his tyranny and pro-Catholic bias. The Stuarts remained in exile in France and Italy, until 1745, when young Charlie crossed the Channel from France to retake the throne in the name of his father (James VIII and III to his supporters). He landed on the west coast of Scotland and rallied support for the Jacobite cause. Though Charles was not Scottish-born, he was the rightful heir directly down the line from Mary, Queen of Scots—and why so many Scots joined the rebellion out of resentment at being ruled by a "foreign" king (King George II, who was born in Germany, couldn't even speak English).

Bagpipes droned, and "Bonnie" (handsome) Charlie led an army of 2,000 tartan-wearing, Gaelic-speaking Highlanders across Scotland, seizing Edinburgh. They picked up other supporters of the Stuarts from the Lowlands and from England. Now 6,000 strong, they marched south toward London—quickly advancing as far as Derby, just 125 miles from the capital—and King George II made plans to flee the country. But anticipated support for the Jacobites failed to materialize in the numbers they were hoping for (both in England and from France). The Jacobites had so far been victorious in their battles against the Hanoverian government forces, but the odds now turned against them. Charles retreated to the Scottish Highlands, where many of his men knew the terrain and could gain an advantage when outnumbered. The English government troops followed closely on his heels.

Against the advice of his best military strategist, Charles' army faced the Hanoverian forces at Culloden Moor on flat, barren terrain that was unsuited to the Highlanders' guerrilla tactics. The Jacobites— many of them brandishing only broadswords, targes (wooden shields covered in leather and studs), and dirks (long daggers)— were mowed down by  King George's cannons and horsemen. In less than an hour, the government forces routed the Jacobite army, but that was just the start. They spent the next weeks methodically hunting down ringleaders and sympathizers (and many others in the Highlands who had nothing to do with the battle), ruthlessly killing, imprisoning, and banishing thousands.

Charles fled with a £30,000 price on his head (an equivalent of millions of today's pounds). He escaped to the Isle of Skye, hidden by a woman named Flora MacDonald (her grave is on the Isle of Skye, and her statue is outside Inverness Castle). Flora dressed Charles in women's clothes and passed him off as her maid. Later,

Flora was arrested and thrown in the Tower of London before being released and treated like a celebrity.

Charles escaped to France. He spent the rest of his life wandering Europe trying to drum up support to retake the throne. He drifted through short-lived romantic affairs and alcohol, and died in obscurity, without an heir, in Rome.

Though usually depicted as a battle of the Scottish versus the English, in truth Culloden was a civil war between two opposing dynasties: Stuart (Charlie) and Hanover (George). However, as the history has faded into lore, the battle has come to be remembered as a Scottish-versus-English standoff—or, in the parlance of the Scots, the Highlanders versus the Strangers.

The Battle of Culloden was the end of 60 years of Jacobite rebellions, the last major battle fought on British soil, and the final stand of the Highlanders. From then on, clan chiefs were deposed; kilts, tartans, and bagpipes were outlawed; and farmers were cleared off their ancestral land, replaced by more-profitable sheep. Scottish culture would never fully recover from the events of the campaign called "The '45."

◉ Self-Guided Tour

Your tour takes you through two sections: the exhibit and the actual battlefield.

The Exhibit

As you pass the ticket desk, note the **family tree:** Bonnie Prince Charlie ("Charles Edward Stuart") and George II were distant cousins. Then the exhibit's shadowy-figure **touchscreens** connect you with historical figures who give you details from both the Hanoverian and Jacobite perspectives. A **map** shows the other power struggles happening in and around Europe, putting this fight for political control of Britain in a wider context. This battle was no

small regional skirmish, but rather a key part of a larger struggle between Britain and its neighbors, primarily France, for control over trade and colonial power. In the display case are **medals** from the early 1700s, made by both sides as propaganda.

From here, your path through this building is cleverly designed to echo the course of the Jacobite army. Your short march (with lots of historic artifacts) gets under way as Charlie sails from France to Scotland, then finagles the support of

Highland clan chiefs. As he heads south with his army to take London, you, too, are walking south. Along the way, maps show the movement of troops, and wall panels cover the buildup to the attack, as seen from both sides. Note the clever division of information: To the left and in red is the story of the "government" (a.k.a. Hanoverians/Whigs/English, led by the Duke of Cumberland); to the right, in blue, is the Jacobites' perspective (Prince Charlie and his Highlander/French supporters).

But you, like Charlie, don't make it to London—in the dark room at the end, you can hear Jacobite commanders arguing over whether to retreat back to Scotland. Pessimistic about their chances of receiving more French support, they decide to U-turn, and so do you. Heading back up north, you'll get some insight into some of the strategizing that went on behind the scenes.

By the time you reach the end of the hall, it's the night before the battle. Round another bend into a dark passage, and listen to the voices of the anxious troops. While the English slept soundly in their tents (recovering from celebrating the Duke's 25th birthday), the scrappy and exhausted Jacobite Highlanders struggled through the night to reach the battlefield (abandoning their plan of a surprise night attack at Nairn and instead retreating back toward Inverness).

At last the two sides meet. As you wait outside the theater for the next showing, study the chart depicting how the forces were arranged on the battlefield. Once inside the theater, you'll soon be surrounded by the views and sounds of a windswept moor. An impressive four-minute **360° movie** projects the re-enacted battle with you right in the center of the action.  The movie drives home just how outmatched the Jacobites were.

The last room has **period weapons,** including ammunition and artifacts found on the battlefield, as well as **historical depictions** of the battle. You'll also find a section describing the detective work required to piece together the story from historical evidence. Be sure to tour the **aftermath corridor,** which talks about the nearly genocidal years following the battle and the cultural wake of this event to this day. Be sure to examine the **huge map,** with narration explaining the combat you've just experienced while giving you a bird's-eye view of the field through which you're about to roam.

The Battlefield

Leaving the visitors center, survey the battlefield (which you'll tour with the help of your audioguide). In the foreground is a cottage used as a makeshift hospital during the conflict. Red flags show the front line of the government army (8,000 troops). This is where most of the hand-to-hand fighting took place. The blue flags in the distance are where the Jacobite army (5,500 troops) lined up.

As you explore the battlefield, notice how uneven and boggy the ground is in parts, and imagine trying to run across this hummocky terrain with all your gear, toward almost-certain death.

The old stone memorial cairn, erected in 1881, commemorates the roughly 1,500 Jacobites buried in in this field. It's known as the Graves of the Clans. As you wander the battlefield, following the

audioguide, you'll pass by other **mass graves,** marked by small headstones, and ponder how entire clans fought, died, and were buried here.

Heading back to the parking lot, notice the wall of protruding bricks. Each represents a soldier who died. The handful of Hanoverian casualties is on the left (about 50); the rest of the long wall's raised bricks represent the multitude of dead Jacobites.

CLAVA CAIRNS

Scotland is littered with reminders of prehistoric peoples—especially in Orkney and along the coast of the Moray Firth—but the Clava Cairns, worth ▲, are among the best-preserved, most interesting, and easiest to reach. You'll find them nestled in the spooky countryside just beyond Culloden Battlefield.

Cost and Hours: Free, always open; just after passing Culloden Battlefield on the B-9006 coming from Inverness, signs on the right point to *Clava Cairns.* Follow this twisty road a couple miles, over the "weak bridge" and to the free parking lot by the stones. Skip the cairns if you don't have a car.

Visiting the Cairns: These "Balnauran of Clava" are Neolithic burial chambers dating from 3,000 to 4,000 years ago. Although they appear to be just some giant piles of rocks in a sparsely forested clearing, a closer look will help you appreciate the prehistoric logic behind them. (The site is explained by an information plaque near the entry.) There are three structures: a central "ring cairn" with an open space in the center but no access to it, flanked by two "passage cairns," which were once buried under turf-covered mounds. The entrance shaft in each passage cairn lines up with the setting sun at the winter solstice. Each cairn is surrounded by a stone circle, and the entire ensemble is framed by evocative trees—injecting this site with even more mystery.

Enjoy the mystery of the site: Were the stone circles part of a celestial calendar system? Or did they symbolize guardians? Why were the clamshell-sized hollows carved into the stones facing the chambers? Was the soul of the deceased transported into the next life by the ray of sunlight on that brief moment that it filled the inner chamber? No one knows.

CAWDOR CASTLE

Homey, intimate, and worth ▲, this castle is still the residence of the Dowager (read: widow) Countess of Cawdor, a local aristocratic branch of the Campbell family. While many associate the castle with Shakespeare's *Macbeth* (because "Cawdor" is mentioned more than a dozen times in the play), there is no actual connection with Shakespeare. *Macbeth* is set 300 years

before the castle was even built. The castle is worth a visit simply because it's historic and beautiful in its own right—and because the woman who owns it flies a Buddhist flag from its tower. She is from Eastern Europe and was the Earl's second wife.

Cost and Hours: £11, good £5 guidebook explains the family and the rooms, May-Sept daily 10:00-17:30, closed Oct-April, tel. 01667/404-401, www.cawdorcastle.com.

Getting There: It's on the B-9090, just off the A-96, about

15 miles east of Inverness (6 miles beyond Culloden and Clava Cairns). In recent years, public transportation to the castle has been nonexistent—but ask at the Inverness TI just in case it has resumed.

Visiting the Castle: You'll follow a one-way circuit around the castle with each room explained with posted explanations written by the countess' late husband, the sixth Earl of Cawdor. His notes bring the castle to life and make you wish you'd known the old chap. Cawdor feels very lived in because it is. While the Dowager Countess moves out during the tourist season, for the rest of the year this is her home. You can imagine her stretching out in front of the fireplace with a good book. Notice her geraniums in every room.

The drawing room (for "with-drawing" after dinner) is lined with a family tree of portraits looking down. In the Tapestry Bedroom you'll see the actual marriage bed of Sir Hugh Campbell from 1662 and 17th-century tapestries warming the walls. In the Yellow Room, a flat-screen TV hides inside an 18th-century cabinet (ask a docent to show you). In the Tartan Passage, lined with modern paintings, find today's dowager—Lady Angelika—in a beautiful 1970 pastel portrait, staring at her late husband's predecessors. Notice how their eyes follow you creepily down the hall—but hers do not.

A spiral stone staircase near the end of the tour leads down to the castle's proud symbol: a holly tree dating from 1372. According to the beloved legend, a donkey leaned against this tree to mark the spot where the castle was to be built...and it was, around the tree.

The **gardens,** included with the ticket, are worth exploring, with some 18th-century linden trees and several surprising species (including sequoia and redwood). Note the hedge maze crowned by a minotaur (not open to the public) and surrounded by a laburnum arbor (dripping with yellow blossoms in May and June).

The nine-hole **golf course** on the castle grounds provides a quick and affordable way to have a Scottish golfing experience. The course is bigger than pitch-and-putt and fun even for nongolfers (£18/person with clubs). You're welcome to try the putting green for £4.

Nearby: The close but remote-feeling **village of Cawdor**—with a few houses, a village shop, and a tavern—is also worth a look if you've got time to kill.

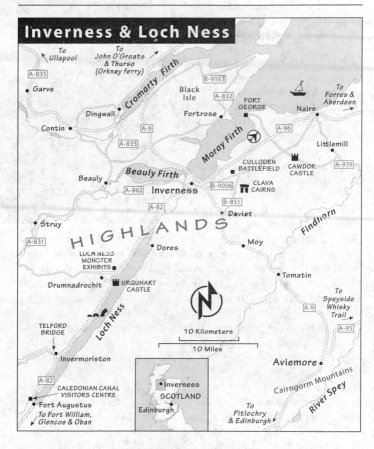

Inverness & Loch Ness

Loch Ness

I'll admit it: I had my zoom lens out and my eyes on the water. The local tourist industry thrives on the legend of the Loch Ness monster. It's a thrilling thought, and there have been several seemingly reliable "sightings" (by monks, police officers, and sonar imaging). But even if you ignore the monster stories, the loch is impressive: 23 miles long, less than a mile wide, 754 feet deep, and containing more water than all of the freshwater bodies of England and Wales combined. It's essentially the vast chasm of a fault line, filled with water.

Getting There: The Loch Ness sights are a 20-minute drive southwest of Inverness. To drive the full length of Loch Ness takes about 45 minutes. Fort William-bound buses #19 and #919 make stops at Urquhart Castle and Drumnadrochit (8/day, 40 minutes).

Sights on Loch Ness

In July 1933, a couple swore they saw a giant sea monster shimmy across the road in front of their car by Loch Ness. Within days, ancient legends about giant monsters in the lake (dating as far back as the sixth century) were revived— and suddenly everyone was spotting "Nessie" poke its head above the waters of Loch Ness. Further sightings and photographic "evidence" have bolstered the claim that there's something mysterious living in this unthinkably deep and murky lake.

(Most sightings take place in the deepest part of the loch, near Urquhart Castle.) Most witnesses describe a waterbound dinosaur (resembling the real, but extinct, plesiosaur). Others cling to the slightly more plausible theory of a gigantic eel. And skeptics figure the sightings can be explained by a combination of reflections, boat wakes, and mass hysteria. The most famous photo of the beast (dubbed the "Surgeon's Photo") was later discredited—the "monster's" head was actually attached to a toy submarine. But that hasn't stopped various cryptozoologists from seeking photographic, sonar, and other proof.

And that suits the thriving local tourist industry just fine. The Nessie commercialization is so tacky that there are two different monster exhibits within 100 yards of each other, both in the town of Drumnadrochit. Of the two competing sites, Nessieland is pretty cheesy while the Loch Ness Centre and Exhibition (described later) is surprisingly thoughtful. Each has a tour-bus parking lot and more square footage devoted to their kitschy shops than to the exhibits. While Nessieland is a tourist trap, the Loch Ness Centre may appease that small part of you that knows the *real* reason you wanted to see Loch Ness.

▲Loch Ness Centre & Exhibition

This exhibit has two parts: First you make six stops in a series of video rooms, and then you enter the exhibition explaining the history of the Great Glen and Loch Ness. It's spearheaded by Adrian Shine, a naturalist fond of saying "I like mud," who has spent many years researching lake ecology and scientific phenomena. With video presentations and special effects, this exhibit explains the geological and historical environment that bred the monster story, as well as the various searches that have been conducted. Refreshingly, it retains an air of healthy skepticism instead of breathless monster-chasing. It also has some artifacts related to the search,

The Caledonian Canal

Two hundred million years ago, two tectonic plates collided, creating the landmass we know as Scotland and leaving a crevice of thin lakes slashing diagonally across the country. This Great Glen Fault, from Inverness to Oban, is easily visible on any map.

British engineer Thomas Telford connected the lakes 200 years ago with a series of canals so ships could avoid the long trip around the north of the country. The Caledonian Canal runs 62 miles from Scotland's east to west coasts; 22 miles of it is manmade. Telford's great feat of engineering took 19 years to complete, opening in 1822 at a cost of one million pounds.

But bad timing made the canal a disaster commercially. Napoleon's defeat in 1815 meant that ships could sail the open seas more freely. And by the time the canal opened, commercial ships were too big for its 15-foot depths. Just a couple of decades after the Caledonian Canal opened, trains made the canal almost useless...except for Romantic Age tourism. From the time of Queen Victoria (who cruised the canal in 1873), the canal has been a popular tourist attraction. To this day the canal is a hit with vacationers, recreational boaters, and lock-keepers who compete for the best-kept lock.

The scenic drive from Inverness along the canal is entertaining, with Drumnadrochit (Nessie centers), Urquhart Castle, Fort Augustus (five locks), and Fort William (under Ben Nevis, with the eight-lock "Neptune's Staircase"). As you cross Scotland, you'll follow Telford's work—22 miles of canals and locks between three lochs, raising ships from sea level to 51 feet (Ness), 93 feet (Lochy), and 106 feet (Oich).

While Neptune's Staircase, a series of eight locks near Fort William, has been cleverly named to sound intriguing, the best lock stop is midway, at Fort Augustus, where the canal hits the south end of Loch Ness. In Fort Augustus, the **Caledonian Canal Visitor Centre,** overlooking the canal just off the main road, gives a good rundown on Telford's work (described later). Stroll past several shops and eateries to the top for a fine view.

Seven miles north, in the town of **Invermoriston,** is another Telford structure: a stone bridge, dating from 1805, which spans the Morriston Falls as part of the original road. Look for a small parking lot just before the junction at A-82 and A-887, on your right as you drive from Fort Augustus. Carefully cross the A-82 and walk three minutes back the way you came. The bridge, which took eight years to build and is still in use, is on your right.

such as a hippo-foot ashtray used to fake monster footprints and the *Viperfish*—a harpoon-equipped submarine used in a 1969 Nessie search. You'll also learn how in 1952 record-seeker John Cobb died going 200 mph in his speed boat on the loch.

Cost and Hours: £8, ask about RS%, daily Easter-Oct 9:30-17:45, July-Aug until 18:45, Nov-Easter 10:00-16:15, last entry 45 minutes before closing, in the big stone mansion right on the main road to Inverness, tel. 01456/450-573, www.lochness.com.

▲Urquhart Castle

The ruins at Urquhart (UR-kurt), just up the loch from the Nessie exhibits, are gloriously situated with a view of virtually the entire lake and create a traffic jam of tourism on busy days.

The visitors center has a tiny exhibit with interesting castle artifacts and an eight-minute film taking you on a sweep through a thousand years of tumultuous history—from St. Columba's visit to the castle's final destruction in 1689. The castle itself, while dramatically situated and fun to climb through, is an empty shell. After its owners (who supported the crown) blew it up to keep the Jacobites from taking it, the largest medieval castle in Scotland (and the most important in the Highlands) wasn't considered worth rebuilding or defending, and was abandoned. Well-placed, descriptive signs help you piece together this once-mighty fortress. As

you walk toward the ruins, take a close look at the trebuchet (a working replica of one of the most destructive weapons of English King Edward I), and ponder how this giant catapult helped Edward grab almost every castle in the country away from the native Scots.

Cost and Hours: £9, guidebook-£5, daily April-Sept 9:30-18:00, Oct until 17:00, Nov-March until 16:30, last entry 45 minutes before closing, café, tel. 01456/450-551, www.historic-scotland.gov.uk).

Loch Ness Cruises

Cruises on Loch Ness are as popular as they are pointless. The lake is scenic, but far from Scotland's prettiest—and the time-consuming boat trips show you little more than what you'll see from the road. As it seems that Loch Ness cruises are a mandatory part of every "Highlands Highlights" day tour, there are several options, leaving from the top, bottom, and middle of the loch. The basic one-hour loop costs around £14 and includes views of Urquhart Castle and lots of legends and romantic history (Jacobite is the dominant outfit of the many cruise companies, www.jacobite. co.uk). I'd rather spend my time and money at Fort Augustus or Urquhart Castle.

▲Fort Augustus

Perhaps the most idyllic stop along the Caledonian Canal is the little lochside town of Fort Augustus. It was founded in the 1700s—before there was a canal here—as part of a series of garrisons and military roads built by the English to quell the Highland clansmen, even as the Jacobites kept trying to take the throne in London. Before then, there were no developed roads in the Highlands—and without roads, it's hard to keep indigenous people down.

From 1725 to 1733, the English built 250 miles of hard roads and 40 bridges to open up the region; Fort Augustus was a central Highlands garrison at the southern tip of Loch Ness, designed to awe clansmen. It was named for William Augustus, Duke of Cumberland—notorious for his role in destroying the clan way of life in the Highlands. (When there's no media and no photographs to get in the way, ethnic cleansing has little effect on one's reputation.)

Fort Augustus makes for a delightful stop if you're driving through the area. Parking is easy. There are plenty of B&Bs, charming eateries, and an inviting park along the town's five locks. You can still see the capstans, surviving from the days when the locks were cranked open by hand.

The fine little **Caledonian Canal Visitor Centre** tells the story of the canal's construction (free, daily Easter-Oct, tel. 01320/366-493). Also, consider the pleasant little canalside stroll out to the head of the loch.

Eating in Fort Augustus: You can eat reasonably at a string of eateries all lining the same side of the canal. Consider **The Little Neuk,** a good café serving filled rolls and homemade soups; **The Lock Inn,** cozy and pub-like with great canalside tables, ideal if it's sunny; **The Bothy,** another pub with decent food; and the **Canalside Chip Shop** offering fish and chips to go (no seating, but plenty of nice spots on the canal). A small grocery store is at the gas station, next to the TI, which is a few steps from the canal just after crossing the River Oich (also housing the post office, a WC, and an ATM).

BRITAIN: PAST & PRESENT

To fully appreciate the many fascinating sights you'll encounter in your travels, learn the basics of the sweeping story of this land and its people. (Generally speaking, the fascinating stories you'll hear from tour guides are not true...and the boring ones are.)

Regardless of the revolution we had more than 240 years ago, many American travelers feel that they "go home" to Britain. This most popular tourist destination has a strange influence and power over us. The more you know of Britain's roots, the better you'll get in touch with your own.

This chapter starts with a once-over of Britain's illustrious history. It's speckled throughout with more in-depth information about current issues and this great country's future.

British History

ORIGINS (2000 B.C.-A.D. 500)

When Julius Caesar landed on the misty and mysterious isle of Britain in 55 B.C., England entered the history books. He was met by primitive Celtic tribes whose druid priests made human sacrifices and worshipped trees. (Those Celts were themselves immigrants, who had earlier conquered the even more mysterious people who built Stonehenge.) The Romans eventually settled in England (A.D. 43) and set about building towns and roads and establishing their capital at Londinium (today's London).

But the Celtic natives—consisting of Gaels, Picts, and Scots—

were not easily subdued. Around A.D. 60, Boadicea, a queen of the Isle's indigenous people, defied the Romans and burned Londinium before the revolt was squelched. Some decades later, the Romans built Hadrian's Wall near the Scottish border as protection against their troublesome northern neighbors. Even today, the Celtic language and influence are strongest in these far reaches of Britain.

Londinium became a bustling Roman river-and-sea trading port. The Romans built the original London Bridge and a city wall, encompassing one square mile, which set the city boundaries for 1,500 years. By A.D. 200, London was a thriving, Latin-speaking capital of Roman-dominated England.

DARK AGES (500-1000)

As Rome fell, so fell Roman Britain—a victim of invaders and internal troubles. Barbarian tribes from Germany, Denmark, and northern Holland, called Angles, Saxons, and Jutes, swept through the southern part of the island, establishing Angle-land. These were the days of the real King Arthur, possibly a Christianized Roman general who fought valiantly—but in vain—against invading barbarians.

In 793, England was hit with the first of two centuries of savage invasions by barbarians from Norway, called the Vikings or Norsemen. King Alfred the Great (849-899) liberated London from Danish Vikings, reunited England, reestablished Christianity, and fostered learning. Nevertheless, for most of this 500-year period, the island was plunged into a dark age—wars, plagues, and poverty—lit only by the dim candle of a few learned Christian monks and missionaries trying to convert the barbarians. Today, visitors see little from this Anglo-Saxon period.

WARS WITH FRANCE, WARS OF THE ROSES (1000-1500)

Modern England began with yet another invasion. In 1066, William the Conqueror and his Norman troops crossed the English Channel from France. William crowned himself king in Westminster Abbey (where all subsequent coronations would take place). He began building the Tower of London, as well as Windsor Castle, which would become the residence of many monarchs to come.

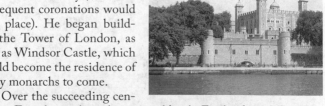

Over the succeeding centuries, French-speaking kings would rule England, and English-speaking kings invaded France as the two budding nations defined

PAST & PRESENT

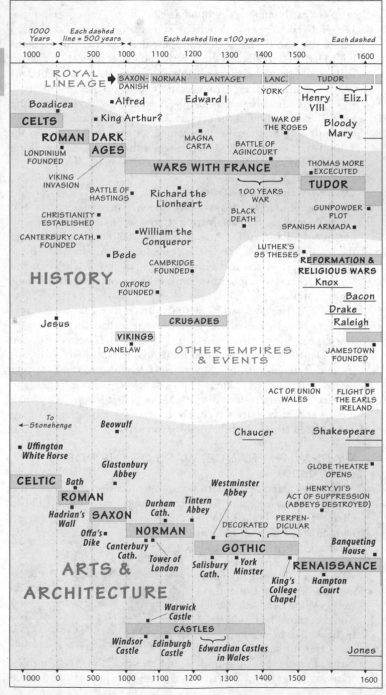

British History & Art Timeline

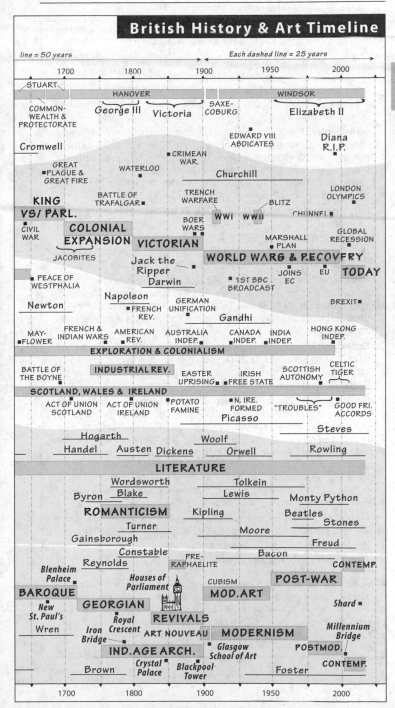

line = 50 years | Each dashed line = 25 years

1700 — 1800 — 1900 — 1950 — 2000

STUART

HANOVER — WINDSOR

COMMON-WEALTH & PROTECTORATE | George III | Victoria | SAXE-COBURG | Elizabeth II

Cromwell

EDWARD VIII ABDICATES

Diana R.I.P.

GREAT PLAGUE & GREAT FIRE | WATERLOO | CRIMEAN WAR.

Churchill

BATTLE OF TRAFALGAR | TRENCH WARFARE | BLITZ

LONDON OLYMPICS

KING VS/ PARL.

BOER WARS | WWI WWII | CHUNNEL

CIVIL WAR | COLONIAL EXPANSION | VICTORIAN

MARSHALL PLAN | GLOBAL RECESSION

JACOBITES

Jack the Ripper | WORLD WARS & RECOVERY

PEACE OF WESTPHALIA | Darwin | 1ST BBC BROADCAST | JOINS EC | EU | TODAY

Newton | Napoleon | GERMAN UNIFICATION

BREXIT

FRENCH REV.

MAY-FLOWER | FRENCH & INDIAN WARS | AMERICAN REV. | AUSTRALIA INDEP. | CANADA INDEP. | INDIA INDEP. | HONG KONG INDEP.

Gandhi

EXPLORATION & COLONIALISM

BATTLE OF THE BOYNE | INDUSTRIAL REV. | EASTER UPRISING | IRISH FREE STATE | SCOTTISH AUTONOMY | CELTIC TIGER

SCOTLAND, WALES & IRELAND

ACT OF UNION SCOTLAND | ACT OF UNION IRELAND | POTATO FAMINE | N. IRE. FORMED | "TROUBLES" | GOOD FRI. ACCORDS

Picasso

Steves

Hogarth | Woolf

Handel | Austen | Dickens | Orwell | Rowling

LITERATURE

Wordsworth | Tolkein

Byron | Blake | Lewis

Kipling | Monty Python

ROMANTICISM | Beatles

Turner | Stones

Moore

Gainsborough | Freud

Constable | Bacon

Reynolds | PRE-RAPHAELITE | CONTEMP.

Blenheim Palace | Houses of Parliament | CUBISM | POST-WAR

BAROQUE | MOD.ART

New St. Paul's | GEORGIAN | Shard

Wren | Royal Crescent | REVIVALS

Iron Bridge | ART NOUVEAU | MODERNISM | Millennium Bridge

IND.AGE ARCH. | Glasgow School of Art | POSTMOD.

Brown | Crystal Palace | Blackpool Tower | Foster | CONTEMP.

1700 — 1800 — 1900 — 1950 — 2000

Britain Almanac

Official Name: The United Kingdom of Great Britain and Northern Ireland (locals say "the UK" or "Britain").

Size: Britain's 64 million people inhabit one large island and a chunk of another, totaling 95,000 square miles (about the size of Michigan).

Geography: Most of the British Isles consists of low hills and rolling plains, with a moderate climate. The country's highest point is 4,410-foot Ben Nevis in western Scotland. Britain's two longest rivers are the Severn (flowing 220 miles east from Wales and then south) and the Thames (running 215 miles through southern England, including London).

Latitude and Longitude: 54°N and 2°W. The latitude is similar to Alberta, Canada.

Biggest Cities: London is the capital, with 10 million people. Industrial Birmingham has about 2.5 million, Glasgow 1.2 million, Edinburgh 500,000, and the port of Liverpool 870,000.

People: Britain's population includes a sizable and growing minority of immigrants, largely from Asia and Eastern Europe. Six in ten Brits call themselves Christian (half of those are Anglican), but in any given week, more Brits visit a mosque than an Anglican church.

Economy: The Gross Domestic Product is $2.7 trillion and the GDP per capita is $41,200. Moneymakers include banking, insurance, agriculture, shipping, and trade. Heavy industry—which drove the Industrial Revolution—is in decline.

Government: Queen Elizabeth II officially heads the country, but in practice it's the prime minister, who leads the majority party in Parliament. Conservative leader Theresa May became prime minister in 2016 in the wake of the "Brexit" referendum that triggered Britain's exit from the European Union (which will take years). In 1999, Scotland, Wales, and Northern Ireland were each granted their own Parliament, a move that provided some autonomy but failed to quash independence movements, particularly in Scotland.

Flag: The "Union Jack" has three crosses on a field of blue: the English cross of St. George, the Irish cross of St. Patrick, and the Scottish cross of St. Andrew.

The Average Brit: Eats 35 pounds of pizza and 25 pounds of chocolate a year, and weighs 12 stone (170 pounds). He or she is 40 years old, has 1.9 children, and will live to age 81. He/she drinks 8 cups of tea and 2.5 glasses of wine a week. He/she has free health care, and gets 28 vacation days a year (versus 13 in the US). He/she sleeps 7.5 hours a night, speaks one language, loves soccer, and enjoys talking about the weather.

their modern borders. Richard the Lionheart (1157-1199) ruled as a French-speaking king who spent most of his energy on distant Crusades. This was the time of the legendary (and possibly real) Robin Hood, a bandit who robbed from the rich and gave to the poor—a populace that felt neglected by its francophone rulers. In 1215, King John (Richard's brother), under pressure from England's barons, was forced to sign the Magna Carta, establishing the principle that even kings must follow the rule of law.

London asserted itself as England's trade center. London Bridge—the famous stone version, topped with houses—was built (1209), and Old St. Paul's Cathedral was finished (1314).

Then followed two centuries of wars, chiefly the Hundred Years' War with France (1337-1443), in which France's Joan of Arc rallied the French to drive English forces back across the Channel. In 1348, the Black Death (bubonic plague) killed half of London's population.

In the 1400s, noble families duked it out for the crown. The York and Lancaster families fought the Wars of the Roses, so-called because of the white and red flowers the combatants chose as their symbols. Rife with battles and intrigues, and with kings, nobles, and ladies imprisoned and executed in the Tower, it's a wonder the country survived its rulers.

THE TUDOR RENAISSANCE (1500s)

England was finally united by the "third-party" Tudor family. Henry VIII, a Tudor, was England's Renaissance king. Powerful, charismatic, handsome, athletic, highly sexed, a poet, a scholar, and a musician, Henry VIII thrust England onto the world stage. He was also arrogant, cruel, gluttonous, and paranoid. He went through six wives in 40 years, divorcing, imprisoning, or executing them when they no longer suited his needs. (To keep track of each one's fate, British kids learn this rhyme: "Divorced, beheaded, died; divorced, beheaded, survived.")

When the Pope refused to grant Henry a divorce so he could marry his mistress Anne Boleyn, Henry "divorced" England from the Catholic Church. He established the Protestant Church of England (the Anglican Church), thus setting in motion a century of bitter Protestant/Catholic squabbles. Henry's own daughter, "Bloody" Mary, was a staunch Catholic who presided over the burning of hundreds of prominent Protestants. (For more on Henry VIII, see the sidebar on page 122.)

Mary was followed by another daughter of Henry's daughters (by Anne Boleyn)—Queen Elizabeth I. She reigned for 45 years, making England a great trading and naval power (defeating the Spanish Armada) and treading diplomatically over the Protestant/Catholic divide. Elizabeth presided over a cultural renaissance

known (not surprisingly) as the "Elizabethan Age." Playwright William Shakespeare moved from Stratford-upon-Avon to London, beginning a remarkable career as the earth's greatest playwright. Sir Francis Drake circumnavigated the globe. Sir Walter Raleigh explored the Americas, and Sir Francis Bacon pioneered the scientific method. London's population swelled.

But Elizabeth—the "Virgin Queen"—never married or produced an heir. So the English Parliament invited Scotland's King James (Elizabeth's first cousin twice removed) to inherit the English throne. The two nations have been tied together ever since, however fitfully.

KINGS VS. PARLIAMENT (1600s)

The enduring quarrel between England's kings and Parliament's nobles finally erupted into the Civil War (1642). The war pitted (roughly speaking) the Protestant Puritan Parliament against the Catholic aristocracy. Parliament forces under Oliver Cromwell defeated—and beheaded—King Charles I. After Cromwell died, Parliament invited Charles' son to take the throne—the "restoration of the monarchy." To emphasize the point, Cromwell's corpse was subsequently exhumed and posthumously beheaded.

This turbulent era was followed by back-to-back disasters—the Great Plague of 1665 (which killed 100,000) and the Great Fire of 1666 (which incinerated London). London was completely rebuilt in stone, centered around New St. Paul's Cathedral, which was built by Christopher Wren. With a population more than 200,000, London was now Europe's largest city. At home, Isaac Newton watched an apple fall from a tree, leading him to discover the mysterious force of gravity.

In the war between kings and Parliament, Parliament finally got the last word, when it deposed Catholic James II and imported the Dutch monarchs William and Mary in 1688, guaranteeing a Protestant succession.

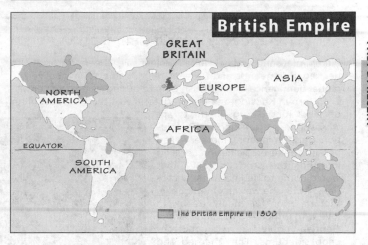

British Empire

GREAT
BRITAIN

NORTH
AMERICA

EUROPE

ASIA

AFRICA

EQUATOR

SOUTH
AMERICA

The British Empire in 1900

COLONIAL EXPANSION (1700s)

Britain grew as a naval superpower, colonizing and trading with all parts of the globe. Eventually, Britannia ruled the waves, exploiting the wealth of India, Africa, and Australia. (And America...at least until they lost its most important colony when those ungrateful Yanks revolted in 1776 in the "American War.") Throughout the century, the country was ruled by the German Hanover family, including four kings named George.

The "Georgian Era" was one of great wealth. London's population was now half a million, and one in seven Brits lived in London. The nation's first daily newspapers hit the streets. The cultural scene was refined: painters (like William Hogarth, Joshua Reynolds, and Thomas Gainsborough), theater (with actors like David Garrick), music (Handel's *Messiah*), and literature (Samuel Johnson's dictionary). Scientist James Watt's steam engines laid the groundwork for a coming Industrial Revolution.

In 1789, the French Revolution erupted, sparking decades of war between France and Britain. Britain finally prevailed in the early 1800s, when Admiral Horatio Nelson defeated Napoleon's fleet at the Battle of Trafalgar and the Duke of Wellington stomped Napoleon at Waterloo. (Nelson and Wellington are memorialized by many arches, columns, and squares throughout England.)

By war's end, Britain had emerged as Europe's top power.

Queen Victoria (1819-1901)

Plump, pleasant, and not quite five feet tall, Queen Victoria, with her regal demeanor and 64-year reign, came to symbolize the global dominance of the British Empire during its greatest era.

Born in Kensington Palace, Victoria was the granddaughter of "Mad" King George III, the tyrant who sparked the American Revolution. Her domineering mother raised her in sheltered seclusion, drilling into her the strict morality that would come to be known as "Victorian." At 18, she was crowned queen. Victoria soon fell madly, deeply in love with Prince Albert, a handsome German nobleman with mutton-chop sideburns. They married and set up house in Buckingham Palace (the first monarchs to do so) and at Windsor Castle. Over the next 17 years, she and Albert had nine children, whom they eventually married off to Europe's crowned heads. Victoria's royal descendants include Kaiser Wilhelm II of Germany (who started World War I); the current monarchs of Spain, Norway, Sweden, and Denmark; and England's Queen Elizabeth II, who is Victoria's great-great-granddaughter.

Victoria and Albert promoted the arts and sciences, organizing a world's fair in Hyde Park (1851) that showed off London as *the* global capital. Just as important, they were role models for an entire nation; this loving couple influenced several generations with their wholesome middle-class values and devoted parenting. Though Victoria is often depicted as dour and stuffy—she supposedly coined the phrase "We are not amused"—in private she was warm, easy to laugh, plainspoken, thrifty, and modest, with a talent for sketching and journal writing.

In 1861, Victoria's happy domestic life ended. Her mother's death was soon followed by the sudden loss of her beloved Albert to typhoid fever. A devastated Victoria dressed in black for the funeral—and for her remaining 40 years never again wore any other color. She hunkered down at Windsor with her family. Critics complained she was an absentee monarch. Rumors swirled that her kilt-wearing servant, John Brown, was not only her close friend but also her lover. For two decades, she rarely appeared in public.

Over time, Victoria emerged from mourning to assume her role as one of history's first constitutional monarchs. She had inherited a crown with little real power. But beyond her ribbon-cutting ceremonial duties, Victoria influenced events behind the scenes. She studiously learned politics from powerful mentors (especially Prince Albert and two influential prime ministers) and kept well-informed on what Parliament was doing. Thanks to Victoria's personal modesty and honesty, the British public never came to disdain the monarchy, as happened in other countries.

Victoria gracefully oversaw the peaceful transfer of power from the nobles to the people. The secret ballot was introduced during her reign, and ordinary workers acquired voting rights (though this applied only to men—Victoria opposed women's suffrage). The traditional Whigs and Tories morphed into today's Liberal and Conservative parties. Victoria personally promoted progressive charities, and even paid for her own crown.

Most of all, Victoria became the symbol of the British Empire, which she saw as a way to protect and civilize poorer peoples. Britain enjoyed peace at home, while its colonial possessions included India, Australia, Canada, and much of Africa. Because it was always daytime someplace under Victoria's rule, it was often said that "the sun never sets on the British Empire."

The Victorian era saw great changes. The Industrial Revolution was in full swing. When Victoria was born, there were no trains. By 1842, when she took her first train trip (with much fanfare), railroads crisscrossed Europe. The telegraph, telephone, and newspapers further laced the world together. The popular arts flourished—it was the era of Dickens novels, Tennyson poems, Sherlock Holmes stories, Gilbert and Sullivan operettas, and Pre-Raphaelite paintings. Economically, Britain saw the rise of the middle class. Middle-class morality dominated—family, hard work, honor, duty, and sexual modesty.

By the end of her reign, Victoria was wildly popular, both for her personality and as a focus for British patriotism. At her Golden Jubilee (1887), she paraded past adoring throngs to Westminster Abbey. For her Diamond Jubilee (1897), she did the same at St. Paul's Cathedral. Cities, lakes, and military medals were named for her. When she passed away in 1901, it was literally the end of an era.

PAST & PRESENT

VICTORIAN GENTILITY AND THE INDUSTRIAL REVOLUTION (1800s)

Britain reigned supreme, steaming into the Industrial Age with her mills, factories, coal mines, gas lights, and trains. By century's end, there was electricity, telephones, and the first Underground.

In 1837, eighteen-year-old Victoria became queen. She ruled for 64 years, presiding over an era of unprecedented wealth, peace, and middle-class ("Victorian") values. Britain was at its zenith of power, with a colonial empire that covered one-fifth of the world (for more on Victoria and her Age, see sidebar on page 141).

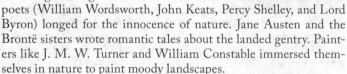

Meanwhile, there was another side to Britain's era of superiority and industrial might. A generation of Romantic poets (William Wordsworth, John Keats, Percy Shelley, and Lord Byron) longed for the innocence of nature. Jane Austen and the Brontë sisters wrote romantic tales about the landed gentry. Painters like J. M. W. Turner and William Constable immersed themselves in nature to paint moody landscapes.

The gritty modern world was emerging. Popular novelist Charles Dickens brought literature to the masses, educating them about Britain's harsh social and economic realities. Rudyard Kipling critiqued the colonial system. Charles Darwin questioned the very nature of humanity when he articulated the principles of natural selection and evolution. Jack the Ripper, a serial killer of prostitutes, terrorized east London and was never caught. Not even by Sherlock Holmes—a fictional detective living at 221B Baker Street who solved fictional crimes that the real Scotland Yard couldn't.

WORLD WARS AND RECOVERY (20th Century)

The 20th century was not kind to Britain. Two world wars and economic struggles whittled Britain down from a world empire to an island chain struggling to compete in a global economy.

In World War I, Britain joined France and other allies to battle Germany in trench warfare. A million British men died. Meanwhile, after decades of rebellion, Ireland finally gained its independence—except for the Protestant-leaning Northern Ireland, which remained tied to Britain. This division of the Emerald Isle would result in decades of bitter strife, protests, and terrorist attacks known as "The Troubles."

In the 1920s, London was home to a flourishing literary scene, including T. S. Eliot (American-turned-British), Virginia Woolf, and E. M. Forster. In 1936, the country was rocked and scandalized when King Edward VIII abdicated to marry a divorced American commoner, Wallis Simpson. He was succeeded by his brother, George VI—"Bertie" of *The King's Speech* fame, and father of Queen Elizabeth II.

In World War II, the Nazi Blitz (aerial bombing campaign) reduced much of London to rubble, sending residents into Tube stations for shelter and the government into a fortified bunker (now the Churchill War Rooms). Britain was rallied through its darkest hour by two leaders: Prime Minister Winston Churchill, a remarkable orator, and King George VI, who overcame a persistent stutter. Amid the chaos of war, the colonial empire began to dwindle to almost nothing, and Britain emerged from the war as a shell of its former superpower self.

The postwar recovery began, aided by the United States. Many cheap, concrete (ugly) buildings rose from the rubble.

Culturally, Britain remained world-class. Oxford professor J. R. R. Tolkien wrote *The Lord of the Rings* and his friend C. S. Lewis wrote *The Chronicles of Narnia*. In the 1960s, "Swinging London" became a center for rock music, film, theater, youth culture, and Austin Powers-style joie de vivre. America was conquered by a "British Invasion" of rock bands (The Beatles, The Rolling Stones, and The Who, followed later by Led Zeppelin, Elton John, David Bowie, and others), and James Bond ruled the box office.

The 1970s brought massive unemployment, labor strikes, and recession. A conservative reaction followed in the 1980s and '90s, led by Prime Minister Margaret Thatcher—the "Iron Lady." As proponents of traditional Victorian values—community, family, hard work, thrift, and trickle-down economics—the Conservatives took a Reaganesque approach to Britain's serious social and economic problems. They cut government subsidies to old-fashioned heavy industries (closing many factories, earning working-class ire), as they tried to nudge Britain toward a more modern economy.

In 1981, the world was captivated by the spectacle of Prince Charles marrying Lady Diana in St. Paul's Cathedral. Their children, Princes William and Harry, grew up in the media spotlight, and when Diana died in a car crash (1997), the nation—and the world—mourned.

The 1990s saw Britain finally emerging from decades of economic stagnation and social turmoil. An energized nation prepared for the new millennium.

EARLY 2000s

London celebrated the millennium with a new Ferris wheel (the London Eye), the Millennium Bridge, and the Millennium Dome exhibition (now "The O2"). Britain was now ruled by a Labour (left-of-center) government under Prime Minister Tony Blair. But Blair's popularity was undermined when he joined the US invasion of Iraq. On "7/7" in 2005, London was rocked by a terrorist attack—a harbinger of others to come.

Britain suffered mightily in the global recession of the early 2000s. British voters turned for answers to the Conservative party under Prime Minister David Cameron. Cameron's austerity measures—cutting government spending and benefits while raising taxes—had mixed results and remains a topic of great debate.

Thankfully, one hot spot—Northern Ireland—was healed. In the spring of 2007, ultra-nationalists sat down with ultra-unionists and arrived at an agreement. After almost 40 years of the "Troubles," the British Army withdrew from Northern Ireland.

In 2011, Prince William married commoner Catherine "Kate" Middleton in a lavish ceremony that stirred renewed enthusiasm for the monarchy. The couple's two children, George (born in 2013) and Charlotte (2015), round out the picture-perfect royal family. (See the "Royal Families: Past and Present" sidebar, later.)

In 2012, in a one-two punch of festivity, the Brits hosted two huge events: the London Olympics and the Queen's Diamond Jubilee, celebrating 60 years on the throne. A flurry of renovation turned former urban wastelands and industrial waterfronts into hip, thriving people zones, and left the country looking better than ever.

Britain Today

The Britain you visit today is vibrant and alive. It's smaller, and no longer the superpower it once was, but it's still a cultural and economic powerhouse.

WHAT'S SO GREAT ABOUT BRITAIN?

Think of it. At its peak in the mid-1800s, Britain owned one-fifth of the world and accounted for more than half the planet's industrial output. Today, the Empire is down to the Isle of Britain itself and a few token scraps (the Falklands, Gibraltar, Northern Ireland) and a loose association of former colonies (Canada, Australia) called the "British Commonwealth."

Get It Right

Americans tend to use "England," "Britain," and the "United Kingdom" (or "UK") interchangeably, but they're not quite the same.

- **England** is the country occupying the center and south-east part of the island.
- **Britain** is the name of the island.
- **Great Britain** is the political union of the island's three countries: England, Scotland, and Wales.
- The **United Kingdom** (UK) adds a fourth country, Northern Ireland.
- The **British Isles** (not a political entity) also includes the independent Republic of Ireland.
- The **British Commonwealth** is a loose association of possessions and former colonies (including Canada, Australia, and India) that profess at least symbolic loyalty to the Crown.

You can call the modern nation either the United Kingdom ("the UK"), "Great Britain," or simply "Britain."

Geographically, the Isle of Britain is small—smaller than the state of Oregon—and its highest mountain (Ben Nevis in Scotland at 4,410 feet) is a foothill by US standards. The population is a fifth that of the United States.

It's small, but Britain is still Great.

Economically, Great Britain's industrial production is about 5 percent of the world's total. Ethnically, it's become quite diverse. It's a mix of Celtic (the natives of Scotland, Ireland, Wales, and Cornwall), Anglo-Saxon (the former "barbarians" from Dark Age times), the conquering Normans, and the many recent immigrants from around the world.

The Britain you visit today remains a global superpower of heritage, culture, and tradition. It's a major exporter of actors, movies, and theater; of rock and classical music; and of writers, painters, and sculptors. It's the perfect place for you to visit and make your own history.

CURRENT ISSUES AND POLITICAL LANDSCAPE

Britain is ruled by the House of Commons, with some guidance from the mostly figurehead Queen and House of Lords. Just as the United States Congress is dominated by Democrats and Republicans, Britain's Parliament has traditionally been dominated by two parties: left-leaning Labour and right-leaning Conservative ("Tories"). In recent elections, the Scottish National Party became the third-largest party in the House of Commons, securing 56 of Scotland's 59 seats—many of these taken from the Labour Party. Other

Royal Families: Past and Present

Royal Lineage

802-1066	Saxon and Danish kings
1066-1154	Norman invasion (William the Conqueror), Norman kings
1154-1399	Plantagenet (kings with French roots)
1399-1461	Lancaster
1462-1485	York
1485-1603	Tudor (Henry VIII, Elizabeth I)
1603-1649	Stuart (civil war and beheading of Charles I)
1649-1653	Commonwealth, no royal head of state
1653-1659	Protectorate, with Cromwell as Lord Protector
1660-1714	Restoration of Stuart dynasty
1714-1901	Hanover (four Georges, William IV, Victoria)
1901-1910	Saxe-Coburg (Edward VII)
1910-present	Windsor (George V, Edward VIII, George VI, Elizabeth II)

The Royal Family Today

It seems you can't pick up a British newspaper without some mention of the latest event, scandal, or oddity involving the royal family. Here is the cast of characters:

Queen Elizabeth II wears the traditional crown of her great-great grandmother Victoria, who ruled for 63 years, 7 months, and 2 days. In September 2015, Queen Elizabeth officially overtook Victoria as England's longest-reigning monarch, and in April 2016 she became the first UK sovereign to reach 90 years old. Elizabeth's husband is Prince Philip, who's not considered king.

Their son, Prince Charles (the Prince of Wales), is next in line to become king—and already holds the title as the longest "heir in waiting."

But it's Prince Charles' sons who generate the tabloid buzz. The older son, Prince William (b. 1982), is a graduate of Scotland's St. Andrews University and served as a search-and-rescue helicopter pilot with the Royal Air Force. In 2011, when William married Catherine "Kate" Middleton, the TV audience was estimated at one-quarter of the world's population—more than two billion people. Kate—a commoner William met at university—is now the Duchess of Cambridge and will eventually become Britain's queen.

Their son, Prince George Alexander Louis, born in 2013—and voted the most powerful and influential person in London by a poll in the *Evening Standard* two months later—will ultimately succeed William as sovereign. (A conveniently timed change in the law ensured that William and Kate's firstborn would inherit the throne, regardless of gender.) In 2015, the royal couple welcomed the arrival of their second child, daughter Princess Charlotte Elizabeth Diana.

William's brother, redheaded Prince Harry (b. 1984), has mostly shaken his earlier reputation as a bad boy: He's proved his mettle as a career soldier, completing a tour in Afghanistan, doing charity work in Africa, and serving as an Apache aircraft commander pilot with the Army Air Corps. Harry's romances and high-wire party antics used to be popular tabloid topics, but his marriage to American actress Meghan Markle is now the main headline fodder.

For years, their parents' love life was also fodder for the British press: Charles' 1981 marriage to Princess Di, their bitter divorce, Diana's dramatic death in 1997, and the ongoing drama with Charles' longtime girlfriend—and now wife—Camilla Parker Bowles. Camilla, trying to gain the respect of the Queen and the public, doesn't call herself a princess—she uses the title Duchess of Cornwall. (And even when Charles becomes king, she will not be Queen Camilla—instead she plans to call herself the "Princess Consort.")

Charles' siblings are occasionally in the news: Princess Anne, Prince Andrew (who married and divorced Sarah "Fergie" Ferguson), and Prince Edward (who married Di look-alike Sophie Rhys-Jones).

Royal Sightseeing

You can see the trappings of royalty at Buckingham Palace (the Queen's London residence) with its Changing of the Guard; Kensington Palace—with a wing that's home to Will, Kate, and kids, and a cottage that serves as Harry's bachelor pad; Clarence House, the London home of Prince Charles and Camilla; Althorp Estate (80 miles from London), the childhood home and burial place of Princess Diana; Windsor Castle, a royal country home near London; and the crown jewels in the Tower of London.

Your best chances to actually see the Queen are on three public occasions: State Opening of Parliament (on the first day of a new parliamentary session), Remembrance Sunday (early November, at the Cenotaph), or Trooping the Colour (one Saturday in mid-June, parading down Whitehall and at Buckingham Palace).

Otherwise, check www.royal.gov.uk, where you can search for royal events.

Being in Britain During Brexit

In 2016 Britain voted to leave the European Union, rocking Europe's political landscape as much as the election of Donald Trump rocked ours. While it means a lot to British citizens, who will have more control over trade and immigration—but will not be playing ball so freely with the rest of Europe—it means very little to travelers. Britain won't formally leave the EU until 2019, so for now the border between Northern Ireland and the Republic of Ireland remains totally open, and both sides want to keep it that way (even though the Republic is an EU member). The biggest change so far affects your pocketbook. Because of the economic uncertainty—and because Great Britain will likely become a more isolationist "Lesser Britain"—the British pound has dropped by about 15 percent. The entire UK is currently on sale for American visitors—everything from beer to B&Bs to bagpipes just got cheaper. And while American tourists are enjoying the bargains, the price the British people will pay for their hasty exit from the European Union remains to be seen.

parties also attract votes (e.g., the center-left Liberal Democrats), and whoever rules must occasionally form some kind of coalition to remain strong.

Strangely, Britain's "constitution" is not one single document; the government's structures and policies are based on centuries of tradition, statutes, and doctrine, and much of it is not actually in writing. While this might seem potentially troublesome—if not dangerous—the British body politic takes pride in its ethos of civility and mutual respect, which has long made this arrangement work.

The prime minister is the chief executive but is not elected directly by voters; rather, he or she assumes power as the head of the party that wins a majority in parliamentary elections. While historically the prime minister could dissolve Parliament at will to make way for new elections, a law passed in 2011 now requires parliamentary elections to be held every five years, unless two-thirds of the members approve an earlier vote.

The single biggest issue facing Britain today is dealing with the repercussions of the "Brexit"—the 2016 referendum in which 52 percent of Brits voted to leave the European Union. As a result, Conservative Prime Minister David Cameron (who supported remaining in the EU) resigned and was replaced by the Conservative Party's Theresa May (also a "Remain" supporter), who became Britain's first female prime minister since Margaret Thatcher left office in 1990. The Brexit vote stunned Britain, throwing it into uncharted territory with no clear path forward.

The Brexit vote demands a split with the EU. But it remains to be seen exactly what that will mean. Many Brits want to maintain trade deals and close relationships with their neighbors on the Continent. Young British people have grown up in a world where they can travel freely and live anywhere in Europe. The Brexit also upset the traditional political order. In the past, the Labour Party was always pro-EU while Conservatives were the Euro-skeptics. Now it's a brave new world for all involved.

No country has ever left the EU—the process could take years. Politicians will need to hammer out the details, trying to keep what has worked with the EU while steering the path to independence.

The Brexit also fueled new worries that pro-EU Scotland may demand independence after all. Although Scotland rejected an independence referendum in 2014, that was before the Brexit, in which Scottish voters came down overwhelmingly on the "Remain" side. Nationalists insist a free Scotland would be rich (on oil reserves) and free from the "shackles" of London-based problems.

All of this comes against a backdrop of a sluggish British economy and concerns about immigration and terrorism. The 2008 global downturn hurt Britain enormously, and it's been a long slog back. The Brexit vote only compounded things, sending the pound into a tailspin and raising economic uncertainty. The dividing lines are similar to those in the States: Should government nurture the economy through spending on social programs (Labour's platform) or cut programs and taxes to allow businesses to thrive (as Conservatives say)?

Britain has a large immigrant population (nearly 4 million). While 9 out of 10 Brits are white, the country has large minority groups, mainly from Britain's former colonies: India, Pakistan, Bangladesh, and parts of Africa and the Caribbean. For the most part Britain is relatively integrated, with minorities represented in most (if not all) walks of life. A large Muslim population is just one thread in the tapestry of today's Britain.

You'll also see many Eastern Europeans (mostly Poles, Slovaks, and Lithuanians) working in restaurants, cafés, and B&Bs. These transplants—who started arriving after their home countries joined the EU in 2004—can make a lot more money working here than back home. But the "Leave" Brexit campaign was fueled in part by complaints about the EU's open-border policy, and concerns that immigrants are taking British jobs, diluting British culture, and receiving overgenerous financial aid.

Like the US, Britain has suffered a number of terrorist threats and attacks. Brits are stunned that many terrorists (like the notorious "Jihadi John" of ISIS) speak the Queen's English and were born and raised in Britain. It raises the larger questions: Just how well is the nation assimilating its many immigrants? And how to balance security with privacy concerns? The British have surveillance cameras everywhere—you'll frequently see signs warning you that you're being recorded.

Among social issues, binge-drinking is a serious problem. Since 2003, pubs can stay open past the traditional 23:00 closing time. An unintended consequence is that (according to one study) one-in-three British men and one-in-five British women routinely drinks to excess, carousing at pubs and sometimes in the streets.

Wealth inequality is also a hot button. The global recession sharpened unemployment and slashed programs for the working class, resulting in protests and riots that pitted poor young men against the police.

Then there's the eternal question of the royals. Is having a monarch (who's politically irrelevant) and a royal family (who can fill the tabloids with their scandals and foibles) worth it? In decades past, many Brits wanted to toss the whole lot of them. But the recent marriage of the popular William and Kate and the birth of their two cute kids have boosted royal esteem. According to pollsters, four out of five Brits want to keep their Queen and let the tradition live on.

BRITISH TV

Although it has its share of lowbrow reality programming, much British television is still so good—and so British—that it deserves a mention as a sightseeing treat. After a hard day of castle climbing, watch the telly over tea in your B&B.

For many years there were only five free channels, but now nearly every British television can receive a couple of dozen. BBC television is government-regulated and commercial-free. Broadcasting of its eight channels (and of the five BBC radio stations) is funded by a mandatory £147-per-year-per-household television and radio license (hmmm, 53 cents per day to escape commercials and public-broadcasting pledge drives...not bad). Channels 3, 4, and 5 are privately owned, are a little more lowbrow, and have commercials—but those "adverts" are often clever and sophisticated, providing a fun look at British life. About 60 percent of households pay for cable or satellite television.

Whereas California "accents" fill US airwaves 24 hours a day, homogenizing the way our country speaks, Britain protects and promotes its regional accents by its choice of TV and radio announcers. See if you can tell where each is from (or ask a local for help).

Commercial-free British TV, while looser than it used to be, is still careful about what it airs and when. But after the 21:00 "watershed" hour, when children are expected to be in bed, some nudity and profanity are allowed, and may cause you to spill your tea.

American programs (such as *Game of Thrones, CSI, Family Guy*, and trash-talk shows) are very popular. But the visiting viewer should be sure to tune the TV to more typically British shows, including a dose of British situation- and political-comedy fun, and the top-notch BBC evening news. British comedies have tickled the American funny bone for years, from sketch comedy *(Monty Python's Flying Circus)* to sitcoms (*Fawlty Towers, Blackadder, Red Dwarf, Absolutely Fabulous*, and *The Office*). Quiz shows and reality shows are taken very seriously here (*American Idol, America's Got Talent, Dancing with the Stars, Who Wants to Be a Millionaire?*, and *The X Factor* are all based on British shows). Jonathan Ross is the Jimmy Fallon of Britain for sometimes-edgy late-night talk. Other popular late-night "chat show" hosts include Graham Norton and Alan Carr. For a tear-filled, slice-of-life taste of British soaps dealing in all the controversial issues, see the popular and remarkably long-running *Emmerdale, Coronation Street,* or *EastEnders*. The costume drama *Downton Abbey,* the long-running sci-fi serial *Doctor Who,* the small-town dramedy *Doc Martin,* and the modern crime series *Sherlock* have all become hits on both sides of the Atlantic.

NOTABLE BRITS OF TODAY AND TOMORROW

Only history can judge which British names will stand the test of time, but these days big names in the UK include politicians (Theresa May, David Cameron, Boris Johnson, Jeremy Corbyn, Nicola Sturgeon), actors (Helen Mirren, Emma Thompson, Helena Bonham Carter, Jude Law, Stephen Fry, Ricky Gervais, James Corden, Daniel Radcliffe, Kate Winslet, Benedict Cumberbatch, Martin Freeman, Peter Capaldi, Colin Firth), musicians (Adele, Chris Martin of Coldplay, James Arthur, Ellie Goulding, One Direction, Ed Sheeran, Sam Smith), writers (J. K. Rowling, E. L. James, Hilary Mantel, Tom Stoppard, Nick Hornby, Ian McEwan, Zadie Smith), artists (Damien Hirst, Rachel Whiteread, Tracey Emin, Anish Kapoor), athletes (David Beckham, Bradley Wiggins, Andy Murray), entrepreneurs (Sir Richard Branson, Lord Alan Sugar)... and, of course, William, Kate, and their children, George and Charlotte.

Architecture in Britain

From Stonehenge to Big Ben, travelers are storming castle walls, climbing spiral staircases, and snapping the pictures of 5,000 years of architecture. Let's sort it out.

The oldest ruins—mysterious and prehistoric—date from before Roman times back to 3000 B.C. The earliest sites, such as Stonehenge and Avebury, were built during the Stone and Bronze ages. The remains from these periods are made of huge stones or mounds of earth, even man-made hills, and were created as celestial calendars and for worship or burial. Britain is criss-crossed with imaginary lines said to connect these mysterious sights (ley lines). Iron Age people (600 B.C.-A.D. 50) left desolate stone forts. The Romans thrived in Britain from A.D. 50 to 400, building cities, walls, and roads. Evidence of Roman greatness can be seen in lavish villas with ornate mosaic floors, temples uncovered beneath great English churches, and Roman stones in medieval city walls. Roman roads sliced across the island in straight lines. Today, unusually straight rural roads are very likely laid directly on these ancient roads.

As Rome crumbled in the fifth century, so did Roman Britain. Little architecture survives from Dark Ages England, the Saxon period from 500 to 1000. Architecturally, the light was switched on with the Norman Conquest in 1066. As William earned his title "the Conqueror," his French architects built churches and castles in the European Romanesque style.

English Romanesque is called Norman (1066-1200). Norman churches had round arches, thick walls, and small windows; Durham Cathedral and the Chapel of St. John in the Tower of London are prime examples. The Tower of London, with its square keep, small windows, and spiral stone stairways, is a typical Norman castle. You can see plenty of Norman castles around England—all built to secure the conquest of these invaders from Normandy.

Gothic architecture (1200-1600) replaced the heavy Norman style with light, vertical buildings, pointed arches, soaring spires, and bigger windows. English Gothic is divided into three stages. Early English Gothic (1200-1300) features tall, simple spires; beautifully carved capitals; and elaborate chapter houses (such as the Wells Cathedral). Decorated Gothic (1300-1400) gets fancier, with more elaborate tracery, bigger windows, and ornately carved pinnacles, as you see at Westminster Abbey. Finally, the Perpendicular Gothic style (1400-1600, also called "rectilinear") returns to square towers and emphasizes straight, uninterrupted vertical lines from ceiling to floor, with vast windows and exuberant decoration, including fan-vaulted ceilings (King's College Chapel at Cambridge). Through this evolution, the structural ribs (arches meeting at the top of the ceilings) became more and more decorative and fanciful (the most fancy being the star vaulting and fan vaulting of the Perpendicular style).

As you tour the great medieval churches of Britain, remember that almost everything is symbolic. For instance, on the tombs of knights, if the figure has crossed legs, he was a Crusader. If his feet rest on a dog, he died at home; but if his legs rest on a lion, he died in battle. Local guides and books help us modern pilgrims understand at least a little of what we see.

Wales is particularly rich in English castles, which were needed to subdue the stubborn Welsh. Edward I built a ring of powerful castles in North Wales, including Conwy and Caernarfon.

Gothic houses were a simple mix of woven strips of thin wood, rubble, and plaster called wattle and daub. The famous black-and-white Tudor (or "half-timbered") look came simply from filling in heavy oak frames with wattle and daub.

The Tudor period (1485-1560) was a time of relative peace (the Wars of the Roses were finally over), prosperity, and renaissance. But when Henry VIII broke with the Catholic Church and disbanded its monasteries, scores of Britain's greatest churches were left as gutted shells. These hauntingly beautiful abbey ruins (Glastonbury, Tintern, Whitby, Rievaulx, Battle, St. Augustine's in Canterbury, St. Mary's in York, and lots more), surrounded by lush lawns, are now pleasant city parks.

Although few churches were built during the Tudor period, this was a time of house and mansion construction. Heating a home was becoming popular and affordable, and Tudor buildings featured small square windows and many chimneys. In towns, where land was scarce, many Tudor houses grew up and out, getting wider with each overhanging floor.

The Elizabethan and Jacobean periods (1560-1620) were followed by the English Renaissance style (1620-1720). English architects mixed Gothic and classical styles, then Baroque and classical styles. Although the ornate Baroque never really grabbed Britain, the classical style of the Italian architect Andrea Palladio did. Inigo Jones (1573-1652), Christopher Wren (1632-1723), and those they inspired plastered Britain with enough columns, domes, and symmetry to please a Caesar. The Great Fire of London (1666) cleared the way for an ambitious young Wren to put his mark on London forever with a grand rebuilding scheme, including the great St. Paul's Cathedral and more than 50 other churches.

The celebrants of the Boston Tea Party remember Britain's

Typical Church Architecture

History comes to life when you visit a centuries-old church. Even if you wouldn't know your apse from a hole in the ground, learning a few simple terms will enrich your experience. Note that not every church has every feature, and that a "cathedral" isn't a type of church architecture, but rather a designation for a church that's a governing center for a local bishop.

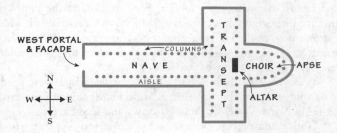

Aisles: The long, generally low-ceilinged arcades that flank the nave.

Altar: The raised area with a ceremonial table (often adorned with candles or a crucifix), where the priest prepares and serves the bread and wine for Communion.

Apse: The space beyond the altar, often bordered with small chapels.

Barrel Vault: A continuous round-arched ceiling that resembles an extended upside-down U.

Choir ("quire" in British English): A cozy area, often screened off, located within the church nave and near the high altar where services are sung in a more intimate setting.

Cloister: Covered hallways bordering a square or rectangular open-air courtyard, traditionally where monks and nuns got fresh air.

Facade: The exterior surface of the church's main (west) entrance, viewable from outside and usually highly decorated.

Groin Vault: An arched ceiling formed where two equal barrel vaults meet at right angles. Less common usage: term for a medieval jock strap.

Narthex: The area (portico or foyer) between the main entry and the nave.

Nave: The long, central section of the church (running west to east, from the entrance to the altar) where the congregation sits or stands through the service.

Transept: In a traditional cross-shaped floor plan, the transept is one of the two parts forming the "arms" of the cross. The transepts run north-south, perpendicularly crossing the east-west nave.

West Portal: The main entry to the church (on the west end, opposite the main altar).

Typical Castle Architecture

Castles were fortified residences for medieval nobles. Castles come in all shapes and sizes, but knowing a few general terms will help you understand them.

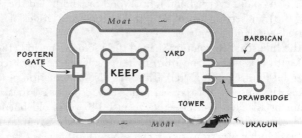

Barbican: A fortified gatehouse, sometimes a stand-alone building located outside the main walls.

Crenellation: A gap-toothed pattern of stones atop the parapet.

Drawbridge: A bridge that could be raised or lowered using counterweights or a chain and winch.

Great Hall: The largest room in the castle, serving as throne room, conference center, and dining hall.

Hoardings (or Gallery or Brattice): Wooden huts built onto the upper parts of the stone walls. They served as watchtowers, living quarters, and fighting platforms.

The Keep (or Donjon): A high, strong stone tower in the center of the castle complex; the lord's home and refuge of last resort.

Loopholes (or Embrasures): Narrow wall slits through which soldiers could shoot arrows.

Machicolation: A stone ledge jutting out from the wall, with holes through which soldiers could drop rocks or boiling oil onto wall-scaling enemies below.

Moat: A ditch encircling the wall, often filled with water.

Motte-and-Bailey: A type of early English castle, with a hilltop fort (motte) and an enclosed, fortified yard (bailey).

Parapet: Outer railing of the wall walk.

Portcullis: A heavy iron grille that could be lowered across the entrance.

Postern Gate: A small, unfortified side or rear entrance from which to launch attacks or escape.

Towers: Tall structures with crenellated tops or conical roofs serving as lookouts, chapels, living quarters, or dungeons.

Turret: A small lookout tower rising up from the top of the wall.

Wall Walk (or Allure): A pathway atop the wall where guards could patrol and where soldiers stood to fire at the enemy.

The Yard (or Bailey): An open courtyard inside the castle walls.

Georgian period (1720-1840) for its lousy German kings. But in architectural terms, "Georgian" is English for "Neoclassical." Its architecture was rich and showed off by being very classical. Grand ornamental doorways, fine cast-ironwork on balconies and railings, Chippendale furniture, and white-on-blue Wedgwood ceramics graced rich homes everywhere. John Wood Sr. and Jr. led the way, giving the trendsetting city of Bath its crescents and circles of aristocratic Georgian row houses.

The Industrial Revolution shaped the Victorian period (1840-1890) with glass, steel, and iron. Britain had a huge new erector set (so did France's Mr. Eiffel). This was also a Romantic period, reviving the "more Christian" Gothic style. London's Houses of Parliament are Neo-Gothic—they're just 140 years old but look 700, except for the telltale modern precision and craftsmanship. Whereas Gothic was stone or concrete, Neo-Gothic was often red brick. These were Britain's glory days, and there was more building in this period than in all previous ages combined.

The architecture of the mid-20th century obeyed the formula "form follows function"—it worried more about your needs than your eyes. But more recently, the dull "international style" has been nudged aside by a more playful style, thanks to cutting-edge architects such as Lord Norman Foster and Renzo Piano. In the last several years, London has added several creative buildings to its skyline: the City Hall (nicknamed "The Armadillo"), 30 St. Mary Axe ("The Gherkin"), 20 Fenchurch ("The Walkie-Talkie"), and the tallest building in Western Europe, the pointy Shard London Bridge (called simply, "The Shard").

Even as it sets trends for the 21st century, Britain treasures its heritage and takes great pains to build tastefully in historic districts and to preserve its many "listed" (government-protected) buildings. With a booming tourist trade, these quaint reminders of its past—and ours—are becoming a valuable part of the British economy.

For more about British history, consider Europe 101: History and Art for the Traveler *by Rick Steves and Gene Openshaw, available at www.ricksteves.com.*

PRACTICALITIES

This chapter covers the practical skills of European travel: how to get tourist information, pay for purchases, sightsee efficiently, find good-value accommodations, eat affordably but well, use technology wisely, and get between destinations smoothly. To round out your knowledge, check out "Resources from Rick Steves." For more information on these topics, see www.ricksteves.com/travel-tips.

Tourist Information

Before your trip, start with the Visit Britain website, which contains a wealth of knowledge on destinations, activities, accommodations, and transport in Great Britain. Families will especially appreciate the "Britain for Kids & Families" travel suggestions. Maps, airport transfers, sightseeing tours, and theater tickets can be purchased online (www.visitbritain.com, www.visitbritainshop.com/usa for purchases).

    In Britain, a good first stop is generally the tourist information office (abbreviated **TI** in this book and locally as **TIC,** for "tourist information centre"). In London, the **City of London Information Centre,** near St. Paul's Cathedral, is helpful (see page 42).

TIs are in business to help you enjoy spending money in their town. While this corrupts much of their advice—and you can get plenty of information online—I still make a point to swing by to confirm sightseeing plans, pick up a city map, and get information on public transit, walking tours, special events, and nightlife. Prepare a list of questions and a proposed plan to double-check. Some TIs have information on the entire country or at least the region, so try to pick up maps and printed information for destinations you'll be visiting later in your trip.

Due to funding constraints, some of Britain's TIs are struggling; village TIs may be staffed by volunteers who need to charge you for maps and informational brochures.

Travel Tips

Emergency and Medical Help: Dial 999 or 112 for police help or a medical emergency. If you get sick, do as the locals do and go to a pharmacy and see a "chemist" (pharmacist) for advice. Or ask at your hotel for help—they'll know of the nearest medical and emergency services. In London, St. Thomas' Hospital, across the river from Big Ben, has a fine reputation.

Theft or Loss: To replace a passport, you'll need to go in person to a US embassy (see page 1073). If your credit and debit cards disappear, cancel and replace them (see "Damage Control for Lost Cards" on page 1019). File a police report, either on the spot or within a day or two; you'll need it to submit an insurance claim for lost or stolen rail passes or travel gear, and it can help with replacing your passport or credit and debit cards. For more information, see www.ricksteves.com/help.

Time Zones: Britain, which is one hour earlier than most of continental Europe, is five/eight hours ahead of the East/West Coasts of the US. The exceptions are the beginning and end of Daylight Saving Time: Britain and Europe "spring forward" the last Sunday in March (two weeks after most of North America), and "fall back" the last Sunday in October (one week before North America). For a handy online time converter, see www.timeanddate.com/worldclock.

Business Hours: Most stores are open Monday through Saturday (roughly 9:00 or 10:00 to 17:00 or 18:00). In cities, some stores stay open later on Wednesday or Thursday (until 19:00 or 20:00). Some big-city department stores are open later throughout the week (Mon-Sat until about 21:00). Sundays have the same pros and cons as they do for travelers in the US: Sightseeing attractions are generally open, many street markets are lively with shoppers,

PRACTICALITIES

banks and many shops are closed, public transportation options are fewer (for example, no bus service to or from smaller towns), and there's no rush hour. Friday and Saturday evenings are lively; Sunday evenings are quiet.

Watt's Up? Britain's electrical system is 220 volts, instead of North America's 110 volts. Most newer electronics (such as laptops, battery chargers, and hair dryers) convert automatically, so you won't need a converter, but you will need an adapter plug with three square prongs, sold inexpensively at travel stores in the US. Avoid bringing older appliances that don't automatically convert voltage; instead, ask to borrow one from your B&B or buy a cheap replacement locally. Low-cost hairdryers and other small appliances are sold at Superdrug and Boots (ask your hotelier for the closest branch). Or pop into a department store or grocery "superstore."

Discounts: Discounts (called "concessions" or "concs" in Britain) for sights are generally not listed in this book. However, many sights, buses, and trains offer discounts to youths (up to age 18), students (with proper identification cards, www.isic.org), families, seniors (loosely defined as retirees or those willing to call themselves seniors), and groups of 10 or more. Always ask. Some discounts are available only for British citizens.

Money

Here's my basic strategy for using money in Europe:
- Upon arrival, head for a cash machine (ATM) at the airport and load up on local currency, using a debit card with low international transaction fees.
- Withdraw large amounts at each transaction (to limit fees) and keep your cash safe in a money belt.
- Pay for most items with cash.
- Pay for larger purchases with a credit card with low (or no) international fees.

PLASTIC VERSUS CASH

Although credit cards are widely accepted in Europe, day-to-day spending is generally more cash-based than in the US. I find cash is the easiest—and sometimes only—way to pay for cheap food, taxis, tips, and local guides. Some businesses (especially smaller ones,

Exchange Rate

1 British pound (£1)=about $1.40

Britain uses the pound sterling. The British pound (£), also called a "quid," is broken into 100 pence (p). Pence means "cents." You'll find coins ranging from 1p to £2 and bills from £5 to £50.

Scotland and Northern Ireland issue their own currency in pounds, worth the same as an English pound. English, Scottish, and Northern Ireland's Ulster pound notes are technically interchangeable in each region, although Scottish and Ulster pounds are considered "undesirable" and sometimes not accepted in England. Banks in any of the three regions will convert your Scottish or Ulster pounds into English pounds for no charge. Don't worry about the coins, which are the same throughout the UK.

To convert prices from pounds to dollars, add about 40 percent: £20=about $28, £50=about $70. (Check www.oanda.com for the latest exchange rates.)

such as B&Bs and mom-and-pop cafés and shops) may charge you extra for using a credit card—or might not accept credit cards at all. Having cash on hand helps you out of a jam if your card randomly doesn't work.

I use my credit card to book and pay for hotel reservations, to buy advance tickets for events or sights, and to cover major expenses (such as car rentals or plane tickets). It can also be smart to use plastic near the end of your trip, to avoid another visit to the ATM.

WHAT TO BRING

I pack the following and keep it all safe in my money belt.

Debit Card: Use this at ATMs to withdraw local cash.

Credit Card: Use this to pay for larger items (at hotels, larger shops and restaurants, travel agencies, car-rental agencies, and so on).

Backup Card: Some travelers carry a third card (debit or credit; ideally from a different bank), in case one gets lost, demagnetized, eaten by a temperamental machine, or simply doesn't work.

US Dollars: I carry $100-200 US dollars as a backup. While you won't use it for day-to-day purchases, American cash in your money belt comes in handy for emergencies, such as if your ATM card stops working.

What NOT to Bring: Resist the urge to buy pounds before your trip or you'll pay the price in bad stateside exchange rates. Wait until you arrive to withdraw money. I've yet to see a European airport that didn't have plenty of ATMs.

BEFORE YOU GO

Use this pretrip checklist.

Know your cards. Debit cards from any major US bank will work in any standard European bank's ATM (ideally, use a debit card with a Visa or MasterCard logo).

Newer credit and debit cards have chips that authenticate and secure transactions. In Europe, the cardholder inserts the chip card into the payment machine slot, then enters a PIN. (In the US, you provide a signature to verify your identity.)

Any American card, whether with a chip or an old-fashioned magnetic stripe, will work at Europe's hotels, restaurants, and shops. I've been inconvenienced a few times by self-service payment machines in Europe that wouldn't accept my card, but it's never caused me serious trouble.

If you're concerned, ask if your bank offers a true chip-and-PIN card. Cards with low fees and chip-and-PIN technology include those from Andrews Federal Credit Union (www.andrewsfcu.org) and the State Department Federal Credit Union (www.sdfcu.org).

Report your travel dates. Let your bank know that you'll be using your debit and credit cards in Europe, and when and where you're headed.

Know your PIN. Make sure you know the numeric, four-digit PIN for each of your cards, both debit and credit. Request it if you don't have one and allow time to receive the information by mail.

Adjust your ATM withdrawal limit. Find out how much you can take out daily and ask for a higher daily withdrawal limit if you want to get more cash at once. Note that European ATMs will withdraw funds only from checking accounts; you're unlikely to have access to your savings account.

Ask about fees. For any purchase or withdrawal made with a card, you may be charged a currency conversion fee (1-3 percent), a Visa or MasterCard international transaction fee (1 percent), and—for debit cards—a $2-5 transaction fee each time you use a foreign ATM (some US banks partner with European banks, allowing you to use those ATMs with no fees—ask).

If you're getting a bad deal, consider getting a new debit or credit card. Reputable no-fee cards include those from Capital One, as well as Charles Schwab debit cards. Most credit unions and some airline loyalty cards have low-to-no international transaction fees.

IN EUROPE
Using Cash Machines

European cash machines work just like they do at home—except they spit out local currency instead of dollars, calculated at the day's standard bank-to-bank rate.

PRACTICALITIES

In most places, ATMs are easy to locate—in Britain ask for a "cashpoint." When possible, withdraw cash from a bank-run ATM located just outside that bank. Ideally, use it during the bank's opening hours; if your card is munched by the machine, you can go inside for help.

If your debit card doesn't work, try a lower amount—your request may have exceeded your withdrawal limit or the ATM's limit. If you still have a problem, try a different ATM or come back later—your bank's network may be temporarily down.

Avoid "independent" ATMs, such as Travelex, Euronet, Moneybox, Cardpoint, and Cashzone. These have high fees, can be less secure than a bank ATM, and may try to trick users with "dynamic currency conversion" (see below).

Exchanging Cash

Avoid exchanging money in Europe; it's a big rip-off. In a pinch you can always find exchange desks at major train stations or airports—convenient but with crummy rates. Banks in some countries may not exchange money unless you have an account with them.

Using Credit Cards

European cards use chip-and-PIN technology, while most cards issued in the US use a chip-and-signature system. But most European card readers can automatically generate a receipt for you to sign, just as you would at home. If a cashier is present, you should have no problems. Some card readers will instead prompt you to enter your PIN (so it's important to know the code for each of your cards).

At self-service payment machines (transit-ticket kiosks, parking, etc.), results are mixed, as US chip-and-signature cards aren't configured for unattended transactions. If your card won't work, look for a cashier who can process your card manually—or pay in cash.

Drivers Beware: Be aware of potential problems using a credit card to fill up at an unattended gas station, enter a parking garage, or exit a toll road. Carry cash and be prepared to move on to the next gas station if necessary. When approaching a toll plaza, use the "cash" lane.

Dynamic Currency Conversion

Some European merchants and hoteliers cheerfully charge you for converting your purchase price into dollars. If it's offered, refuse this "service" (called dynamic currency conversion, or DCC). You'll pay extra for the expensive convenience of seeing your charge in dollars. Some ATM machines also offer DCC, often in confusing or misleading terms. If an ATM offers to "lock in" or "guarantee" your conversion rate, choose "proceed without conversion." Other prompts might state, "You can be charged in dollars: Press YES for dollars, NO for pounds." Always choose the local currency.

Security Tips

Even in "Jollie Olde Britain," pickpockets target tourists. To safeguard your cash, wear a money belt—a pouch with a strap that you buckle around your waist like a belt and tuck under your clothes. Keep your cash, credit cards, and passport secure in your money belt, and carry only a day's spending money in your front pocket or wallet.

Before inserting your card into an ATM, inspect the front. If anything looks crooked, loose, or damaged, it could be a sign of a card-skimming device. When entering your PIN, carefully block other people's view of the keypad.

Don't use a debit card for purchases. Because a debit card pulls funds directly from your bank account, potential charges incurred by a thief will stay on your account while the fraudulent use is investigated by your bank.

While traveling, to access your accounts online, be sure to use a secure connection (see page 1052).

Damage Control for Lost Cards

If you lose your credit or debit card, report the loss immediately to the respective global customer-assistance centers. Call these 24-hour US numbers collect: Visa (tel. 303/967-1096), MasterCard (tel. 636/722-7111), and American Express (tel. 336/393-1111). In Britain, to make a collect call to the US, dial 0-800-89-0011. Press zero or stay on the line for an operator. European toll-free numbers (listed by country) can be found at the websites for Visa and MasterCard.

You'll need to provide the primary cardholder's identification-verification details (such as birthdate, mother's maiden name, or Social Security number). You can generally receive a temporary card within two or three business days in Europe (see www.ricksteves.com/help for more).

If you report your loss within two days, you typically won't be responsible for unauthorized transactions on your account, although many banks charge a liability fee of $50.

TIPPING

Tipping in Britain isn't as automatic and generous as it is in the US. For special service, tips are appreciated, but not expected. As in the US, the proper amount depends on your resources, tipping philosophy, and the circumstances, but some general guidelines apply.

Restaurants: It's not necessary to tip if a service charge is included in the bill (common in London—usually 12.5 percent). Otherwise, it's appropriate to tip about 10-12 percent for good service. See page 1037).

Taxis: For a typical ride, round up your fare a bit, but not more than 10 percent (for instance, if the fare is £7.40, pay £8). If the cabbie hauls your bags and zips you to the airport to help you catch your flight, you might want to toss in a little more. But if you feel like you're being driven in circles or otherwise ripped off, skip the tip.

Services: In general, if someone in the tourism or service industry does a super job for you, a small tip of a pound or two is appropriate...but not required. If you're not sure whether (or how much) to tip, ask a local for advice.

GETTING A VAT REFUND

Wrapped into the purchase price of your British souvenirs is a Value-Added Tax (VAT) of about 20 percent. You're entitled to get most of that tax back if you purchase more than £30 (about $40) worth of goods at a store that participates in the VAT-refund scheme (although individual stores can require that you spend more—Harrods, for example, won't process a refund unless you spend £50). Typically, you must ring up the minimum at a single retailer—you can't add up your purchases from various shops to reach the required amount. (If the store ships the goods to your US home, VAT is not assessed on your purchase.)

Getting your refund is straightforward...and worthwhile if you spend a significant amount on souvenirs.

Get the paperwork. Have the merchant completely fill out the necessary refund document (either an official VAT customs form, or the shop or refund company's own version of it). You'll have to present your passport at the store. Get the paperwork done before you leave the shop to ensure you'll have everything you need (including your original sales receipt).

Get your stamp at the border or airport. Process your VAT document at your last stop in the European Union (such as at the airport) with the customs agent who deals with VAT refunds. Arrive an additional hour early before you need to check in to allow time to find the customs office—and to stand in line. Some customs desks are positioned before airport security; confirm the location before going through security.

It's best to keep your purchases in your carry-on. If they're too large or dangerous to carry on (such as knives), pack them in your checked bags and alert the check-in agent. You'll be sent (with your tagged bag) to a customs desk outside security; someone will examine your bag, stamp your paperwork, and put your bag on the belt. You're not supposed to use your purchased goods before you leave.

If you show up at customs wearing your new Wellingtons, officials might look the other way—or deny you a refund.

Collect your refund. Many merchants work with a service that has offices at major airports, ports, or border crossings (at Heathrow, Travelex counters and customs desks are located before and after security in terminals 2-5). These services, which extract their own fee (usually around 4 percent), can refund your money immediately in cash or credit your card (within two billing cycles). Other refund services may require you to mail the documents from home, or more quickly, from your point of departure (using an envelope you've prepared in advance or one that's been provided by the merchant). You'll then have to wait—it can take months.

CUSTOMS FOR AMERICAN SHOPPERS

You can take home $800 worth of items per person duty-free, once every 31 days. Many processed and packaged foods are allowed, including vacuum-packed cheeses, dried herbs, jams, baked goods, candy, chocolate, oil, vinegar, mustard, and honey. Fresh fruits and vegetables and most meats are not allowed, with exceptions for some canned items. As for alcohol, you can bring in one liter duty-free (it can be packed securely in your checked luggage, along with any other liquid-containing items).

To bring alcohol (or liquid-packed foods) in your carry-on bag on your flight home, buy it at a duty-free shop at the airport. You'll increase your odds of getting it onto a connecting flight if it's packaged in a "STEB"—a secure, tamper-evident bag. But stay away from liquids in opaque, ceramic, or metallic containers, which usually cannot be successfully screened (STEB or no STEB).

For details on allowable goods, customs rules, and duty rates, visit http://help.cbp.gov.

Sightseeing

Sightseeing can be hard work. Use these tips to make your visits to Britain's finest sights meaningful, fun, efficient, and painless.

MAPS AND NAVIGATION TOOLS

A good map is essential for efficient navigation while sightseeing. The maps in this book are concise and simple, designed to help you locate recommended destinations, sights, and local TIs, where you can pick up more in-depth maps. Maps with even more detail are sold at newsstands and bookstores. The *Rick Steves Britain, Ireland & London City Map* is useful for planning ($9, www.ricksteves.com). For those visiting London, *Bensons London Street Map*—sold at many newsstands and bookstores—is my favorite for efficient sightseeing and might be the best £4 you'll spend. I also

PRACTICALITIES

like the *Handy London Map and Guide* version, which shows every little lane and all the sights, and comes with a transit map. Many Londoners, along with obsessive-compulsive tourists, rely on the highly detailed *London A-Z* map book (generally £5-7, called "A to Zed" by locals, available at newsstands).

You can also use a mapping app on your mobile device. Be aware that pulling up maps or looking up turn-by-turn walking directions on the fly requires an Internet connection: To use this feature, it's smart to get an international data plan (see page 1048). With Google Maps or City Maps 2Go, it's possible to download a map while online, then go offline and navigate without incurring data-roaming charges, though you can't search for an address or get real-time walking directions. A handful of other apps—including Apple Maps, OffMaps, and Navfree—also allow you to use maps offline.

PLAN AHEAD

Set up an itinerary that allows you to fit in all your must-see sights. For a one-stop look at opening hours, see the "At a Glance" sidebars for London, Bath, the Cotswolds, Liverpool, the Lake District, York, North Wales, South Wales, and Edinburgh. Most sights keep stable hours, but you can easily confirm the latest by checking with the TI or visiting museum websites.

Don't put off visiting a must-see sight—you never know when a place will close unexpectedly for a holiday, strike, or royal audience. Many museums are closed or have reduced hours at least a few days a year, especially on holidays such as Christmas, New Year's, and Bank Holiday Mondays in May and August. A list of holidays is on page 1074; check online for possible museum closures during your trip. Off-season, many museums have shorter hours.

Given how precious your vacation time is, I recommend getting reservations for any must-see sight that offers them (see page 29). Going at the right time helps avoid crowds. This book offers tips on the best times to see specific sights. Try visiting popular sights very early or very late. Evening visits (when possible) are usually peaceful, with fewer crowds.

If you plan to hire a local guide, reserve ahead by email. Popular guides can get booked up.

Study up. To get the most out of the self-guided tours and sight descriptions in this book, read them before you visit. The British Museum rocks if you understand the significance of the Rosetta Stone.

AT SIGHTS

Here's what you can typically expect:

Entering: Be warned that you may not be allowed to enter if you arrive less than 30 to 60 minutes before closing time. And guards start ushering people out well before the actual closing time, so don't save the best for last.

Many sights have a security check, where you must open your bag or send it through a metal detector. Allow extra time for these lines in your planning. Some sights require you to check daypacks and coats. (If you'd rather not check your daypack, try carrying it tucked under your arm like a purse as you enter.)

At ticket desks, you may see references to "Gift Aid"—a tax-deduction scheme that benefits museums—but this only concerns UK taxpayers.

Photography: If the museum's photo policy isn't clearly posted, ask a guard. Generally, taking photos without a flash or tripod is allowed. Some sights ban selfie sticks; others ban photos altogether.

Temporary Exhibits: Museums may show special exhibits in addition to their permanent collection. An extra fee, which may not be optional, might be assessed for these shows.

Expect Changes: Artwork can be on tour, on loan, out sick, or shifted at the whim of the curator. Pick up a floor plan as you enter, and ask museum staff if you can't find a particular item.

Audioguides and Apps: Many sights rent audioguides, which generally offer excellent recorded descriptions (about £5). If you bring your own earbuds, you can enjoy better sound. To save money, bring a Y-jack and share one audioguide with your travel partner. Museums and sights often offer free apps that you can download to your mobile device (check their websites). And, I've produced free, downloadable audio tours for London's Westminster Walk, the British Museum, the British Library, St. Paul's Cathedral, and Historic London: The City Walk and for Edinburgh's Royal Mile; look for the 🎧 symbol in this book. For more on my audio tours, see page 30.

Guided tours are most likely to occur during peak season (either for free or a small fee—figure £5-10—and widely ranging in quality). Some sights also run short introductory videos featuring their highlights and history. These are generally well worth your time and a great place to start your visit.

Services: Important sights and cathedrals may have a reasonably priced on-site café or cafeteria (usually a handy place to rejuvenate during a long visit—try a cheap "cream tea" to pick up your energy in midafternoon, like Brits do). The WCs at sights are free and generally clean.

Before Leaving: At the gift shop, scan the postcard rack or thumb through a guidebook to be sure that you haven't overlooked something that you'd like to see.

Every sight or museum offers more than what is covered in this

Harry Potter Sights

Harry Potter's story is set in a magical, largely fictional Britain, but you can visit many real locations used in the film series. Other settings, like Diagon Alley, exist only at Leavesden Film Studios (north of London; see page 152).

London
Harry first realizes his wizard powers in *The Sorcerer's Stone* (2001) when talking with a snake at the **London Zoo**'s Reptile House. Later, Harry shops for school supplies in the glass-roofed **Leadenhall Market.**

In *The Chamber of Secrets* (2002), Harry catches the train to Hogwarts wizarding school at **King's Cross Station** from the fictional Platform 9¾. (For a fun photo-op, head to King's Cross Station's track 9 to find the *Platform 9¾* sign, the luggage cart that looks like it's disappearing into the wall, a Harry Potter gift shop...and a 30-minute wait in line to snap a photo.)

In *The Prisoner of Azkaban* (2004), a three-decker bus dumps Harry at the Leaky Cauldron pub, shot on rough-looking Stoney Street at the southeast edge of **Borough Market.**

When the Order takes to the night sky on broomsticks in *The Order of the Phoenix* (2007), they pass over plenty of identifiable landmarks, including the **London Eye, Big Ben,** and **Buckingham Palace.** The **Millennium Bridge** collapses into the Thames in the dramatic finale to *The Half-Blood Prince* (2009). The real govern-

book. Use the information in this book as an introduction—not the final word.

SIGHTSEEING PASSES
Many sights in Britain are managed by English Heritage, the National Trust, Cadw (a Welsh organization), or Historic Scotland; the sights don't overlap. Each organization has a combo-deal that can save some money for busy sightseers.

Membership in **English Heritage** includes free entry to more than 400 sights in England and discounted or free admission to about 100 more sights in Scotland and Wales. For most travelers, the **Overseas Visitor Pass** is a better choice than the pricier one-year membership (Visitor Pass: £31/9 days, £37/16 days, discounts for couples and families, www.english-heritage.org.uk/ovp; membership: £54 for one person, £96 for two, discounts for families, se-ment offices of **Whitehall** serve as exteriors for the Ministry of Magic.

Elsewhere in England

Near Bath: In *The Sorcerer's Stone,* Harry is chosen for Gryffindor's Quidditch team in the halls of the 13th-century **Lacock Abbey.** Harry attends Professor Snape's class in one of the abbey's peeling-plaster rooms.

Oxford: Christ Church College provided the model for Hogwarts' Great Hall. In *The Sorcerer's Stone,* Harry sneaks under a cloak of invisibility into the Hogwarts Library (really Duke Humfrey's Library), and he awakens in the Hogwarts infirmary (the big-windowed Divinity School of the Bodleian Library).

Northeast England: In *The Sorcerer's Stone,* Harry walks with his white owl, Hedwig, through a snowy courtyard in Durham's Cathedral.

Scotland

Glencoe was the main location for outdoor filming in *The Prisoner of Azkaban* and *The Half-Blood Prince,* and many shots of the Hogwarts grounds were filmed in the Fort William and Glencoe areas. The *Hogwarts Express* that carries Harry, Ron, and Hermione to school each year runs along the actual **Jacobite Steam Train** line (between Fort William and Mallaig).

In *The Prisoner of Azkaban* and *The Goblet of Fire,* **Loch Shiel, Loch Eilt,** and **Loch Morar** (near Fort William) were the stand-ins for the Great Lake. **Steal Falls,** at the base of Ben Nevis, is the locale for the Triwizard Tournament in *The Goblet of Fire.*

niors, and students, children under 19 free, www.english-heritage. org.uk/membership; tel. 0370-333-1181).

Membership in the **National Trust** is best suited for garden-and-estate enthusiasts, ideally those traveling by car. It covers more than 350 historic houses, manors, and gardens throughout Great Britain, including 100 properties in Scotland. From the US, it's easy to join online through the Royal Oak Foundation, the National Trust's American affiliate (one-year membership: $65 for one person, $95 for two, family and student memberships, www. royal-oak.org). For more on National Trust properties, see www. nationaltrust.org.uk.

Cadw's Explorer Pass covers many sights in Wales (3-day pass: £21 for one person, £33 for two, £44 for a family; 7-day pass available; buy at castle ticket desks, www.cadw.wales.gov.uk).

Historic Scotland's Explorer Pass covers its 77 properties, including Edinburgh Castle, Stirling Castle, and several sights on

Orkney (£31/3 days out of any 5, £42/7 days out of any 14, www. historic-scotland.gov.uk/explorer). This pass allows you to skip the ticket-buying lines at Edinburgh and Stirling castles.

Factors to Consider: An advantage to these deals is that you'll feel free to dip into lesser sights without considering the cost of admission. But remember that your kids already get in free or cheaply at most places, and people over 60 get discounted prices at many sights. If you're traveling by car and can get to the remote sights, you're more likely to get your money's worth out of a pass or membership, especially during peak season (Easter-Oct), when all the sights are open.

Sleeping

I favor hotels and restaurants that are handy to your sightseeing activities. In Britain, small bed-and-breakfast places (B&Bs) generally provide the best value, though I also include some bigger hotels. Rather than list accommodations scattered throughout a city, I choose places in my favorite neighborhoods. My recommendations run the gamut, from dorm beds to fancy rooms with all the comforts. Outside of pricey big cities, you can expect to find good doubles for £80-120 (about $105-155), including cooked breakfasts and tax. Bigger cities, swanky splurge B&Bs, and big hotels generally cost significantly more.

Extensive and opinionated listings of good-value rooms are a major feature of this book's Sleeping sections. I like places that are clean, central, relatively quiet at night, reasonably priced, friendly, small enough to have a hands-on owner and stable staff, and run with a respect for British traditions. I'm more impressed by a convenient location and a fun-loving philosophy than flat-screen TVs and a fancy gym. Most places I recommend fall short of perfection. But if I can find a place with most of these features, it's a keeper.

Britain has a rating system for hotels and B&Bs. Its stars are supposed to imply quality, but I find they mean only that the place is paying dues to the tourist board. Rating systems often have little to do with value.

Book your accommodations as soon as your itinerary is set, especially if you want to stay at one of my top listings or if you'll be traveling during busy times. See page 1074 for a list of major holidays and festivals; for tips on making reservations, see the sidebar, later.

Some people make reservations as they travel, calling hotels and B&Bs a few days to a week before their arrival. If you anticipate crowds (worst weekdays at business destinations and weekends at tourist locales) on the day you want to check in, call hotels at about 9:00 or 10:00, when the receptionist knows who'll be check-

---

Sleep Code

Hotels are classified based on the average price of a typical en suite double room with breakfast in high season.

$$$$	**Splurge:**	Most rooms over £160
$$$	**Pricier:**	£120-160
$$	**Moderate:**	£80-120
$	**Budget:**	£40-80
¢	**Backpacker:**	Under £40
RS%	**Rick Steves discount**	

Unless otherwise noted, credit cards are accepted and free Wi-Fi is available. Comparison-shop by checking prices at several hotels (on each hotel's own website, on a booking site, or by email). For the best deal, *always book directly with the hotel.* Ask for a discount if paying in cash; if the listing includes **RS%,** request a Rick Steves discount.

---

ing out and which rooms will be available. Some apps—such as HotelTonight.com—specialize in last-minute rooms, often at business-class hotels in big cities.

RATES AND DEALS

I've categorized my recommended accommodations based on price, indicated with a dollar-sign rating (see sidebar). The price ranges suggest an estimated cost for a one-night stay in a typical en suite double room with a private toilet and shower in high season, and assume you're booking directly with the hotel (not through a booking site, which extracts a commission). Room prices can fluctuate significantly with demand and amenities (size, views, room class, and so on), but relative price categories remain constant. City taxes are generally insignificant (a dollar or two per person, per night). For most places, the rates they quote include the 20 percent VAT tax—but it's smart to ask when you book your room.

While B&B prices tend to be fairly predictable, room rates are especially volatile at larger hotels that use "dynamic pricing" to set rates. Prices can skyrocket during festivals and conventions, while business hotels can have deep discounts on weekends when demand plummets. Of the many hotels I recommend, it's difficult to say which will be the best value on a given day—until you do your homework.

Once your dates are set, check the specific price for your preferred stay at several hotels. You can do this either by comparing prices on Hotels.com or Booking.com, or by checking the hotels' own websites. To get the best deal, contact my family-run places directly by phone or email. When you go direct, the owners avoid the 20 percent commission, giving them wiggle room to offer you a discount, a nicer room, or a free breakfast if it's not already included (see sidebar). If you prefer to book online or are considering a hotel chain, it's in your advantage to use the hotel's website.

Some accommodations offer a discount to those who pay cash or stay longer than three nights. To cut costs further, try asking for a cheaper room (for example, with a shared bathroom or no window) or offer to skip breakfast (if included). For recommendations on finding online hotel deals in London, as well as using auction-type sites, see page 165.

Additionally, some accommodations offer a special discount for Rick Steves readers, indicated in the listing by the abbreviation "**RS%**." Discounts vary: Ask for details when you reserve. Generally, to qualify you must book direct (that is, not through a booking site), mention this book when you reserve, show this book upon arrival, and sometimes pay cash or stay a certain number of nights. In some cases, you may need to enter a discount code (which I've provided in the listing) in the booking form on the hotel's website. Rick Steves discounts apply to readers with ebooks as well as printed books. Understandably, discounts do not apply to promotional rates.

Staying in B&Bs and small hotels can save money over sleeping in big hotels. Chain hotels can be even cheaper, but they don't include breakfast. When comparing prices between chain hotels and B&Bs, remember you're getting two breakfasts (about a £25 value) for each double room at a B&B.

When establishing prices, confirm if the charge is per person or per room (if a price is too good to be true, it's probably per person). Because many places in Britain charge per person, small groups often pay the same for a single and a double as they would for a triple. In this book, I've categorized hotels based on the per room price, not per person.

TYPES OF ACCOMMODATIONS
Hotels

In cities, you'll find big, Old-World elegant hotels with modern amenities, as well as familiar-feeling business-class and boutique hotels no different from what you might experience at home. But you'll also find hotels that are more uniquely European.

A "twin" room has two single beds; a "double" has one double bed. If you'll take either, let the hotel know, or you might be needlessly turned away. Some hotels can add an extra bed (for a small charge) to turn a double into a triple, and some offer larger rooms for four or more people (I call these "family rooms" in the listings). If there's space for an extra cot, they'll cram it in for you. In general, a triple room is cheaper than the cost of a double and a single. Three or four people can economize by requesting one big room.

Hotels vs. Booking Websites vs. Consumers

In the last decade it's become almost impossible for independent-minded, family-run hotels to survive without playing the game as dictated by the big players in the online booking world. Priceline's Booking.com and Expedia's Hotels.com take roughly 80 percent of this business. Hoteliers note that without this online presence, "We become almost invisible." Online booking services demand about a 20 percent commission. And in order to be listed, a hotel must promise that its website does not undercut the price on the third-party's website. Without that restriction, hoteliers could say, "Sure, sell our rooms for whatever markup you like, and we'll continue to offer a fair rate to travelers who come to us directly"—but that's not allowed.

Here's the work-around: For independent and family-run hotels, book direct by email or phone, in which case hotel owners are free to give you whatever price they like. Research the price online, and then ask for a room without the commission mark-up. You could ask them to split the difference—the hotel charges you 10 percent less but pockets 10 percent more. Or you can ask for a free breakfast (if not included) or upgrade.

If you do book online, be sure to use the hotel's website (you'll likely pay the same price as via a booking site, but your money goes to the hotel, not agency commissions).

As consumers, remember: Whenever you book with an online booking service, you're adding a needless middleman who takes roughly 20 percent. If you'd like to support small, family-run hotels whose world is more difficult than ever, book direct.

An "en suite" room has a bathroom (toilet and shower/tub) attached to the room; a room with a "private bathroom" can mean that the bathroom is all yours, but it's across the hall. If you want your own bathroom inside the room, request "en suite." If money's tight, ask about a room with a shared bathroom. You'll almost always have a sink in your room, and as more rooms go en suite, the hallway bathroom is shared with fewer guests.

Note that to be called a "hotel," a place technically must have certain amenities, including a 24-hour reception (though this rule is loosely applied).

Modern Hotel Chains: Chain hotels—common in bigger cities all over Great Britain—can be a great value (£60-100, depending on location and season; more expensive in London). These hotels are about as cozy as a Motel 6, but they come with private showers/WCs, elevators, good security, and often an attached res-

Making Hotel Reservations

Reserve your rooms as soon as you've pinned down your travel dates. For busy national holidays, it's wise to reserve far in advance (see page 1074).

Requesting a Reservation: For family-run hotels, it's generally cheaper to book your room direct via email or a phone call. For business-class hotels, or if you'd rather book online, reserve directly through the hotel's official website (not a booking agency's site). For complicated requests, send an email.

Here's what the hotelier wants to know:

- type(s) of rooms you need and size of your party
- number of nights you'll stay
- your arrival and departure dates, written European-style as day/month/year (for example, 18/06/19 or 18 June 2019)
- special requests (such as en suite bathroom vs. down the hall, cheapest room, twin beds vs. double bed, quiet room)
- applicable discounts (such as a Rick Steves reader discount, cash discount, or promotional rate)

Confirming a Reservation: Most places will request a credit-card number to hold your room. If you're using an online reservation form, look for the *https* or a lock icon at the top of your browser. If you book direct, you can email, call, or fax this information.

Canceling a Reservation: If you must cancel, it's courteous—and smart—to do so with as much notice as possible, especially for smaller family-run places. Cancellation policies can be strict;

taurant. Branches are often located near the train station, on major highways, or outside the city center.

This option is especially worth considering for families, as kids often stay for free. While most of these hotels have 24-hour reception and elevators, breakfast and Wi-Fi generally cost extra, and the service lacks a personal touch (at some, you'll check in at a self-service kiosk). When comparing your options, keep in mind that for about the same price, you can get a basic room at a B&B that has less predictable comfort but more funkiness and friendliness in a more enjoyable neighborhood.

Room rates change from day to day with volume and vary depending on how far ahead you book. The best deals generally must be prepaid a few weeks ahead and may not be refundable—read the fine print carefully.

The biggest chains are **Premier Inn** (www.premierinn.com, toll reservations tel. 0871-527-9222) and **Travelodge** (www. travelodge.co.uk, toll reservations tel. 0871-984-8484). Both have attractive deals for prepaid or advance bookings. Other chains operating in Britain include the Irish **Jurys Inn** (www.jurysinns.com)

From: rick@ricksteves.com
Sent: Today
To: info@hotelcentral.com
Subject: Reservation request for 19-22 July

Dear Hotel Central,

I would like to stay at your hotel. Please let me know if you have a room available and the price for:
• 2 people
• Double bed and en suite bathroom in a quiet room
• Arriving 19 July, departing 22 July (3 nights)

Thank you!
Rick Steves

read the fine print or ask about these before you book. Many discount deals require prepayment, with no cancellation refunds.

Reconfirming a Reservation: Always call or email to reconfirm your room reservation a few days in advance. For B&Bs or very small hotels, I call again on my day of arrival to tell my host what time to expect me (especially important if arriving late—after 18:00).

Phoning: For tips on calling hotels overseas, see page 1050.

and the French-owned **Ibis** (www.ibishotel.com). Couples can consider **Holiday Inn Express,** which generally allow only two people per room. It's like a Holiday Inn lite, with cheaper prices and no restaurant (make sure Express is part of the name or you'll be paying more for a regular Holiday Inn, www.hiexpress.co.uk).

Arrival and Check-In: Many of my recommended hotels have three or more floors of rooms and steep stairs. Older properties often do not have elevators. If stairs are an issue, ask for a ground-floor room or choose a hotel with a lift (elevator). Air-conditioning isn't a given (I've noted which of my listings have it), but most places have fans. On hot summer nights, you'll want your window open—and in a big city, street noise is a fact of life. Bring earplugs or request a room on the back side. If you suspect night noise will be a problem (if, for instance, your room is over a noisy pub), ask for a quieter room on an upper floor.

If you're arriving in the morning, your room probably won't be ready. Check your bag safely at the hotel and dive right into sightseeing.

In Your Room: More pillows and blankets are usually in the closet or available on request. Towels and linens aren't always re-placed every day. Hang up your towel to dry.

TVs are standard in rooms, but may come with limited chan-nels (no cable). Note that all of Britain's accommodations are non-smoking. Most hotels have free Wi-Fi (although the Wi-Fi signal doesn't always make it to the rooms; sometimes it's only available in the lobby). There's sometimes a guest computer with Internet access in the lobby.

Electrical outlets may have switches that turn the current on or off; if your appliance isn't working, flip the switch at the outlet.

To guard against theft in your room, keep valuables out of sight. Some rooms come with a safe, and other hotels have safes at the front desk. I've never bothered using one and in a lifetime of travel, I've never had anything stolen from my room.

Breakfast: Your room cost usually includes a traditional full cooked breakfast (fry-up) or a lighter, healthier continental break-fast.

Checking Out: While it's customary to pay for your room upon departure, it can be a good idea to settle your bill the day before, when you're not in a hurry and while the manager's in. That way you'll have time to discuss and address any points of conten-tion.

Hotelier Help: Hoteliers can be a good source of advice. Most know their city well, and can assist you with everything from pub-lic transit and airport connections to finding a good restaurant, the nearest launderette, or a late-night pharmacy.

Hotel Hassles: Even at the best places, mechanical break-downs occur: Sinks leak, hot water turns cold, toilets may gurgle or smell, the Wi-Fi goes out, or the air-conditioning dies when you need it most. Report your concerns clearly and calmly at the front desk. For more complicated problems, don't expect instant results. Above all, keep a positive attitude. Remember, you're on vacation. If your hotel is a disappointment, spend more time out enjoying the place you came to see.

B&Bs and Small Hotels

B&Bs and small hotels are generally family-run places with fewer amenities but more character than a conventional hotel. They range from large inns with 15-20 rooms to small homes renting out a spare bedroom. Places named "guesthouse" or "B&B" typically have eight or fewer rooms. The philosophy of the management de-termines the character of a place more than its size and amenities. I avoid places run as a business by absentee owners. My top listings are run by people who enjoy welcoming the world to their breakfast table.

Compared to hotels, B&Bs and guesthouses give you double

the cultural intimacy for half the price. While you may lose some of the conveniences of a hotel—such as fancy lobbies, in-room phones, and frequent bedsheet changes—I happily make the trade-off for the personal touches, whether it's joining my hosts for afternoon tea or relaxing by a common fireplace at the end of the day. If you have a reasonable but limited budget, skip hotels and go the B&B way.

B&B proprietors are selective about the guests they invite in for the night. Many do not welcome children. If you'll be staying for more than one night, you are a "desirable." In popular weekend-getaway spots, you're unlikely to find a place to take you for Saturday night only. If my listings are full, ask for guidance. Mentioning this book can help. Owners usually work together and can call up an ally to land you a bed. Many B&B owners are also pet owners. If you're allergic, ask about resident pets when you reserve.

Rules and Etiquette: B&Bs and small hotels come with their own etiquette and quirks. Keep in mind that owners are at the whim of their guests—if you're getting up early, so are they; if you check in late, they'll wait up for you. Most B&Bs have set check-in times (usually in the late afternoon). If arriving outside that time, they will want to know when to expect you (call or email ahead). Most will let you check in earlier if the room is available (or they'll at least let you drop off your bag).

Most B&Bs and guesthouses serve a hearty cooked breakfast of eggs and much more (for details on breakfast, see the Eating section, later). Because the owner is often also the cook, breakfast hours are usually abbreviated. Typically the breakfast window lasts for 1 or 1.5 hours (make sure you know when it is before you turn in for the night). Some B&Bs ask you to fill in your breakfast order the night before. It's an unwritten rule that guests shouldn't show up at the very end of the breakfast period and expect a full cooked breakfast. If you do arrive late (or need to leave before breakfast is served), most establishments are happy to let you help yourself to cereal, fruit, juice, and coffee.

B&Bs and small hotels often come with thin walls and doors, and sometimes creaky floorboards, which can make for a noisy night. If you're a light sleeper, bring earplugs. And please be quiet in the halls and in your rooms at night...those of us getting up early will thank you for it.

Treat these lovingly maintained homes as you would a
friend's house. Be careful maneuvering your bag up narrow
staircases with fragile walls and
banisters. And once in the room,
use the luggage rack—putting
bags on the bed can damage nice
comforters.

In the Room: Every B&B
offers "tea service" in the room—
an electric kettle, cups, tea bags, coffee packets, and a pack of
biscuits.

Your bedroom probably won't include a phone, but nearly
every B&B has free Wi-Fi. However, the signal may not reach all
rooms; you may need to sit in the lounge to access it.

You're likely to encounter unusual bathroom fixtures. The
"pump toilet" has a flushing handle or button that doesn't kick in
unless you push it just right: too hard or too soft, and it won't go.
(Be decisive but not ruthless.) Most B&B baths have an instant
water heater. This looks like an electronic box under the shower-
head with dials and buttons: One control adjusts the heat, while
another turns the flow off and on (let the water run for a bit to moderate the temperature before you hop in). If the hot water doesn't
work, you may need to flip a red switch (often located just outside
the bathroom). If the shower looks mysterious, ask your B&B host
for help...*before* you take off your clothes.

Paying: Many B&Bs take credit cards, but may add the card
service fee to your bill (about 3 percent). If you do need to pay cash
for your room, plan ahead to have enough on hand when you check
out.

Short-Term Rentals

A short-term rental—whether an apartment (or "flat"), house, or
room in a local's home—is an increasingly popular alternative, especially if you plan to settle in one location for several nights. For
stays longer than a few days, you can usually find a rental that's
comparable to—and even cheaper than—a hotel room with similar
amenities. Plus, you'll get a behind-the-scenes peek into how locals
live.

Many places require a minimum night stay, and compared
to hotels, rentals usually have less-flexible cancellation policies.
Also you're generally on your own: There's no hotel reception desk,
breakfast, or daily cleaning service.

Finding Accommodations: Aggregator websites such as
Airbnb, FlipKey, Booking.com, and the HomeAway family of sites

(HomeAway, VRBO, and VacationRentals) let you browse properties and correspond directly with European property owners or managers. If you prefer to work from a curated list of accommodations, consider using a rental agency such as InterhomeUSA.com or RentaVilla.com. Agency-represented apartments typically cost more, but this method often offers more help and safeguards than booking direct. For a list of rental agencies for London, see page 182.

Before you commit, be clear on the details, location, and amenities. I like to virtually "explore" the neighborhood using the Street View feature on Google Maps. Also consider the proximity to public transportation, and how well-connected the property is with the rest of the city. Ask about amenities (elevator, air-conditioning, laundry, Wi-Fi, parking, etc.). Reviews from previous guests can help identify trouble spots.

Think about the kind of experience you want: Just a key and an affordable bed...or a chance to get to know a local? There are typically two kinds of hosts: those who want minimal interaction with their guests, and hosts who are friendly and may want to interact with you. Read the promotional text and online reviews to help shape your decision.

Apartments and Rental Houses: If you're staying somewhere for four nights or longer, it's worth considering an apartment or house (shorter stays aren't worth the hassle of arranging key pickup, buying groceries, etc.). Apartments and rental houses can be especially cost-effective for groups and families. European apartments, like hotel rooms, tend to be small by US standards. But they often come with laundry machines and small, equipped kitchens, making it easier and cheaper to dine in. If you make good use of the kitchen (and Europe's great produce markets), you'll save on your meal budget. Also, determine how close the nearest public transit stop is, and factor transportation costs into the overall price.

Private and Shared Rooms: Renting a room in someone's home is a good option for those traveling alone, as you're more likely to find true single rooms—with just one single bed, and a price to match. Beds range from air-mattress-in-living-room basic to plush-B&B-suite posh. Some places allow you to book for a single night; if staying for several nights, you can buy groceries just as you would in a rental house. While you can't expect your host to also be your tour guide—or even to provide you with much info—some may be interested in getting to know the travelers who come through their home.

Other Options: Swapping homes with a local works for people with an appealing place to offer, and who can live with the idea of having strangers in their home (don't assume where you live is not interesting to Europeans). A good place to start is HomeEx-

The Good and Bad of Online Reviews

User-generated review sites and apps such as Yelp, Booking.com, and TripAdvisor can give you a consensus of opinions about everything from hotels and restaurants to sights and nightlife. If you scan reviews of a hotel and see several complaints about noise or a rotten location, it tells you something important that you'd never learn from the hotel's own website.

But as a guidebook writer, my sense is that there is a big difference between the uncurated information on a review site and a guidebook. A user-generated review is based on the experience of one person, who likely stayed at one hotel in a given city and ate at a few restaurants there (and who doesn't have much of a basis for comparison). A guidebook is the work of a trained researcher who, year after year, visits many alternatives to assess their relative value. I recently checked out some top-rated user-reviewed hotel and restaurant listings in various towns; when stacked up against their competitors, some were gems, while just as many were duds.

Both types of information have their place, and in many ways, they're complementary. If something is well-reviewed in a guidebook, and also gets good ratings on one of these sites, it's likely a winner.

change. To sleep for free, Couchsurfing.com is a vagabond's alternative to Airbnb. It lists millions of outgoing members, who host fellow "surfers" in their homes.

Confirming and Paying: Many places require you to pay the entire balance before your trip. It's easiest and safest to pay through the site where you found the listing. Be wary of owners who want to take your transaction offline to avoid fees; this gives you no recourse if things go awry. Never agree to wire money (a key indicator of a fraudulent transaction).

Hostels

Britain has hundreds of hostels of all shapes and sizes. Choose your hostel selectively. Hostels can be historic castles or depressing tenements, serene and comfy or overrun by noisy school groups.

A hostel provides cheap beds in dorms where you sleep alongside strangers for about £20-30 per night. Travelers of any age are welcome if they don't mind dorm-style accommodations and meeting other travelers. Most hostels offer kitchen facilities, guest computers, Wi-Fi, and a self-service laundry. Hostels almost always provide bedding, but the towel's up to you (though you can usually rent one for a small fee). Family and private rooms are often available.

Independent hostels tend to be easygoing, colorful, and informal (no membership required; www.hostelworld.com). You may pay slightly less by booking direct with the hostel.

Official hostels are part of Hostelling International (HI) and share an online booking site (www.hihostels.com). HI hostels typically require that you be a member or pay extra per night. In Britain, these official hostels are run by the Youth Hostel Association (YHA, www.yha.org.uk); in Scotland they're run by the Scottish Youth Hostel Association (SYHA, also known as Hostelling Scotland, www.syha.org.uk). HI hostels typically require that you be a member or pay extra per night.

Eating

These days, the stereotype of "bad food in Britain" is woefully dated. Britain has caught up with the foodie revolution, and I find it's easy to eat very well here.

British cooking has embraced international influences and local, seasonal ingredients, making "modern British" food quite delicious. While some dreary pub food still exists, you'll generally find the cuisine scene here innovative and delicious (but expensive). Basic pubs are more likely to dish up homemade, creative dishes than microwaved pies, soggy fries, and mushy peas. Even traditional pub grub has gone upmarket, with gastropubs that serve locally sourced meats and fresh vegetables.

All of Britain is smoke-free. Expect restaurants and pubs to be nonsmoking indoors, with smokers occupying patios and doorways outside. You'll find the Brits eat at about the same time of day as Americans do.

When restaurant-hunting, choose a spot filled with locals, not tourists. Venturing even a block or two off the main drag leads to higher-quality food for a better price. Locals eat better at lower-rent locales. Rely on my recommendations in the various eating sections throughout this book.

Tipping: At pubs and places where you order at the counter, you don't have to tip. Regular customers ordering a round sometimes say, "Add one for yourself" as a tip for drinks ordered at the bar—but this isn't expected. At restaurants and fancy pubs with waitstaff, it's not necessary to tip if a service charge is already included in the bill (common in London—usually 12.5 percent). Otherwise, it's appropriate to tip about 10-12 percent; you can add a bit more for finer dining or extra good service. Tip only what you think the service warrants (if it isn't already added to your bill), and be careful not to tip double.

Restaurant Code

I've assigned each eatery a price category, based on the average cost of a typical main course. Drinks, desserts, and splurge items (steak and seafood) can raise the price considerably.

$$$$	**Splurge:** Most main courses over £20
$$$	**Pricier:** £15-20
$$	**Moderate:** £10-15
$	**Budget:** Under £10

In Great Britain, carryout fish-and-chips and other takeout food is **$;** a basic pub or sit-down eatery is **$$;** a gastropub or casual but more upscale restaurant is **$$$;** and a swanky splurge is **$$$$**.

RESTAURANT PRICING

I've categorized my recommended eateries based on price, indicated with a dollar-sign rating (see sidebar). The price ranges suggest the average price of a typical main course—but not necessarily a complete meal. Obviously, expensive items (such as steak and seafood), fine wine, appetizers, and dessert can significantly increase your final bill.

The dollar-sign categories also indicate the overall personality and "feel" of a place:

$ Budget eateries include street food, takeaway, order-at-the-counter shops, basic cafeterias, bakeries selling sandwiches, and so on.

$$ Moderate eateries are typically nice (but not fancy) sit-down restaurants, ideal for a straightforward, fill-the-tank meal. A majority of my listings fall in this category—great for getting a good taste of the local cuisine on a budget.

$$$ Pricier eateries are a notch up, with more attention paid to the setting, service, and cuisine. These are ideal for a memorable meal that's still relatively casual and doesn't break the bank. This category often includes affordable "destination" or "foodie" restaurants.

$$$$ Splurge eateries are dress-up-for-a-special-occasion-swanky—Michelin star-type restaurants, typically with an elegant setting, polished service, pricey and intricate cuisine, and an expansive (and expensive) wine list.

I haven't categorized places where you might assemble a picnic, snack, or graze: supermarkets, delis, ice-cream stands, cafés or bars specializing in drinks, chocolate shops, and so on.

BREAKFAST (FRY-UP)

The traditional fry-up or full English/Scottish/Welsh breakfast—generally included in the cost of your room—is famous as a hearty way to start the day. Also known as a "heart attack on a plate," your standard fry-up comes with your choice of eggs, Canadian-style bacon and/or sausage, a grilled tomato, sautéed mushrooms, baked beans, and sometimes potatoes, kippers (herring), or fried

bread (sizzled in a greasy skillet). Expect regional variations, such as black pudding (a blood sausage; northern England and Scotland) and a dense potato scone or haggis (Scotland). Toast comes in a rack (to cool quickly and crisply) with butter and marmalade. The meal typically comes with your choice of tea or coffee. Many B&B owners offer alternatives, such as porridge, as well as vegetarian, organic, gluten-free, or other creative variations on the traditional breakfast.

As much as the full breakfast fry-up is a traditional way to start the morning, these days most places serve a healthier continental breakfast as well—with a buffet of yogurt, cereal, fruit, and pastries. At some hotels, the buffet may also include hot items, such as eggs and sausage.

LUNCH AND DINNER ON A BUDGET

Even in pricey cities, plenty of inexpensive choices are available: pub grub, daily lunch and early-bird dinner specials, ethnic restaurants, cafeterias, fast food, picnics, greasy-spoon cafés, cheap chain restaurants, and pizza.

I've found that portions are huge, and with locals feeling the economic pinch, **sharing plates** is generally just fine. Ordering two drinks, a soup or side salad, and splitting a £10 meat pie can make a good, filling meal. If you're on a limited budget, share a main course in a more expensive place for a nicer eating experience.

Pub grub is the most atmospheric budget option. You'll usually get hearty lunches and dinners priced reasonably at £8-15 under ancient timbers (see "Pubs," later). Gastropubs, with better food, are more expensive.

Classier restaurants have some affordable deals. Lunch is usually cheaper than dinner; a top-end, £30-for-dinner-type restaurant often serves the same quality two-course lunch deals for about half the price.

Many restaurants have **early-bird** or **pre-theater specials** of

PRACTICALITIES

two or three courses, often for a significant savings. They are usually available only before 18:30 or 19:00 (and sometimes on weekdays only), but are good for bargain hunters willing to eat a bit earlier.

Ethnic restaurants add spice to Britain's cuisine scene. Eating Indian, Bangladeshi, Chinese, or Thai is cheap (even cheaper if you do takeout). Middle Eastern shops sell gyro sandwiches, falafel, and *shwarmas* (grilled meat in pita bread). An Indian samosa (greasy, flaky meat-and-vegetable turnover) costs about £2 and makes a very cheap, if small, meal. (For more, see "Indian Cuisine," later.) You'll find inexpensive, quick Asian options (often Chinese), such as all-you-can-eat buffets and takeaway places serving up standard dishes in to-go boxes.

Fish-and-chips are a heavy, greasy, but tasty British classic. Every town has at least one "chippy" selling takeaway fish-and-chips in a cardboard box or (more traditionally) wrapped in paper for about £5-7. You can dip your fries in ketchup, American-style, or "go British" and drizzle the whole thing with malt vinegar and fresh lemon.

Most large **museums** (and many historic **churches**) have handy, moderately priced cafeterias with forgettably decent food.

Picnicking saves time and money. Fine park benches and polite pigeons abound in most towns and city neighborhoods. You can easily get prepared food to go. The modern chain eateries on nearly every corner often have simple seating but are designed for takeout. Bakeries serve a wonderful array of fresh sandwiches and pasties (savory meat pastries). Street markets, generally parked in pedestrian-friendly zones, are fun and colorful places to stock up for a picnic (see page 154 for suggestions on street markets in London).

Open-air markets and supermarkets sell produce in small quantities. The corner grocery store has fruit, drinks, fresh bread, tasty British cheese, meat, and local specialties. Supermarkets often have good deli sections, even offering Indian dishes, and sometimes salad bars. Decent packaged sandwiches (£3-4) are sold everywhere. Munch a relaxed "meal on wheels" picnic during your open-top bus tour or river cruise to save 30 precious minutes for sightseeing.

PUBS

Pubs are a fundamental part of the British social scene, and whether you're a teetotaler or a beer guzzler, they should be a part of your travel here. "Pub" is short for "public house." It's an extended common room where, if you don't mind the stickiness, you can feel the local pulse. Smart travelers use pubs to eat, drink, get out of the rain, watch sporting events, and  make new friends. Unfortunately, many city pubs have been afflicted with an excess of brass, ferns, and video slot machines. The most traditional atmospheric pubs are in the countryside and in smaller towns.

It's interesting to consider the role pubs filled for Britain's working class in more modest times: For workers with humble domestic quarters and no money for a vacation, a beer at the corner pub was the closest they'd get to a comfortable living room, a place to entertain, and a getaway. And locals could meet people from far away in a pub—today, that's you!

Though hours vary, pubs generally serve beer daily from 11:00 to 23:00, though many are open later, particularly on Friday and Saturday. (Children are served food and soft drinks in pubs, but you must be 18 to order a beer.) As it nears closing time, you'll hear shouts of "last orders." Then comes the 10-minute warning bell. Finally, they'll call "Time!" to pick up your glass, finished or not, when the pub closes.

A cup of darts is free for the asking. People go to a public house to be social. They want to talk. Get vocal with a local. This is easiest at the bar, where people assume you're in the mood to talk (rather than at a table, where you're allowed a bit of privacy). The pub is the next best thing to having relatives in town. Cheers!

Pub Grub: For £8-15, you'll get a basic budget hot lunch or dinner in friendly surroundings. In high-priced London, this is your best indoor eating value. (For something more refined, try a **gastropub,** which serves higher-quality meals for £12-20.) The *Good Pub Guide* is an excellent resource (www.thegoodpubguide. co.uk). Pubs that are attached to restaurants, advertise their food, and are crowded with locals are more likely to have fresh food and a chef—and less likely to sell only lousy microwaved snacks.

Pubs generally serve traditional dishes, such as fish-and-chips, roast beef with Yorkshire pudding (batter-baked in the oven), and assorted meat pies, such as steak-and-kidney pie or shepherd's pie (stewed lamb topped with mashed potatoes) with cooked vegetables. Side dishes include salads, vegetables, and—invariably— "chips" (French fries). "Crisps" are potato chips. A "jacket potato" (baked potato stuffed with fillings of your choice) can almost be a meal in itself. A "ploughman's lunch" is a traditional British meal of bread, cheese, and sweet pickles. These days, you'll likely find more pasta, curried dishes, and quiche on the menu than traditional fare.

Meals are usually served from 12:00 to 14:00 and again from 18:00 to 20:00—with a break in the middle (rather than serving straight through the day). Since they make more money selling beer, many pubs stop food service early in the evening—especially on weekends. There's generally no table service. Order at the bar, and then take a seat. Either they'll bring the food when it's ready or you'll pick it up at the bar. Pay at the bar (sometimes when you order, sometimes after you eat). It's not necessary to tip unless it's a place with full table service. Servings are hearty, and service is quick. A beer, cider, or dram of whisky adds another couple of pounds. Free tap water is always available. For details on ordering beer and other drinks, see the "Beverages" section, later. For a list of recommended historic pubs in London, see page 192.

GOOD CHAIN RESTAURANTS

I know—you're going to Britain to enjoy characteristic little hole-in-the-wall pubs, so mass-produced food is the furthest thing from your mind. But several excellent chains with branches across the UK offer long hours, reasonable prices, reliable quality, and a nice break from pub grub. My favorites are Pret, Wasabi, and Eat. Expect to see these familiar names wherever you go:

$ Pret (a.k.a. Pret à Manger) is perhaps the most pervasive of these modern convenience eateries. Some are takeout only, and others have seating ranging from simple stools to restaurant-quality tables. The service is fast, the price is great, and the food is healthy and fresh. Their slogan: "Made today. Gone today. No 'sell-by' date, no nightlife."

$$ Côte Brasserie is a contemporary French chain serving good-value French cuisine in reliably pleasant settings (early dinner specials).

$$ Le Pain Quotidien is a Belgian chain serving fresh-baked bread and hearty meals in a thoughtfully designed modern-rustic atmosphere.

$$ Byron Hamburgers, an upscale-hamburger chain with hip interiors, is worth seeking out if you need a burger fix. While British burgers tend to be a bit overcooked by American standards, Byron's burgers are your best bet.

$$ Wagamama Noodle Bar, serving pan-Asian cuisine (udon noodles, fried rice, and curry dishes), is a noisy, organic slurpathon. Portions are huge and splittable. There's one in almost every mid-size city in Britain, usually located in sprawling halls filled with long shared tables and busy servers who scrawl your order on the placemat.

$$$ Loch Fyne Fish Restaurant is a Scottish chain that raises its own oysters and mussels. Its branches offer an inviting, lively atmosphere with a fine fishy energy and no pretense (early-bird specials).

$ Marks & Spencer department stores have inviting deli sections with cheery sit-down eating (along with their popular sandwiches-to-go section). M&S food halls are also handy if you're renting a city flat and want to prepare your own meals.

$$ Busaba Eathai is a hit in several cities for its snappy (sometimes rushed) service, boisterous ambience, and good, inexpensive Thai cuisine.

$$$ Thai Square is a dependable Thai option with a nice atmosphere (salads, noodle dishes, curries, meat dishes, and daily lunch box specials). Most branches are in London.

$$ Masala Zone is a London chain providing a good, predictable alternative to the many one-off, hole-in-the-wall Indian joints around town. Try a curry-and-rice dish, a *thali* (platter with several small dishes), or their street food specials. Each branch has its own personality.

$$ Ask and **Pizza Express** serve quality pasta and pizza in a pleasant, sit-down atmosphere that's family-friendly. **$$ Jamie's Italian** (from celebrity chef Jamie Oliver) is hipper and pricier.

$$ Japanese: Three popular chains serve fresh and inexpensive Japanese food. **Itsu** and **Wasabi** are two bright and competitive chains that let you assemble your own plate in a fun and efficient way, while **Yo! Sushi** lets you pick your dish off a conveyor belt and pay according to the color of your plate. If you're in the mood for sushi, all are great.

Carry-Out Chains: While the following may have some seating, they're best as places to grab prepackaged food on the run.

Major supermarket chains have smaller, offshoot branches that specialize in sandwiches, salads, and other prepared foods to go. These can be a picnicker's dream come true. Some shops are stand-alone, while others are located inside a larger store. The most prevalent—and best—is **M&S Simply Food** (an offshoot of Marks & Spencer; there's one in every major train station). **Sainsbury's Local** grocery stores also offer decent prepared food; **Tesco Express** and **Tesco Metro** run a distant third.

Some "cheap and cheery" chains provide office workers with good, healthful sandwiches, salads, and pastries to go. These include **Pod** and **Eat** (with slightly higher-quality food and higher prices).

INDIAN CUISINE

Eating Indian food is "going local" in cosmopolitan, multiethnic Britain. You'll find Indian restaurants in most cities, and even in small towns. Take the opportunity to sample food from Britain's former colony. Indian cuisine is as varied as the country itself. In general, it uses more exotic spices than British or American cuisine—some hot, some sweet. Indian food is very vegetarian-friendly, offering many meatless dishes.

For a simple meal that costs about £10-12, order one dish with rice and naan (Indian flatbread). Generally, one order is plenty for two people to share. Many Indian restaurants offer a fixed-price combination that offers more variety, and is simpler and cheaper than ordering à la carte. For about £20, you can make a mix-and-match platter out of several shareable dishes, including dal (simmered lentils) as a starter, one or two meat or vegetable dishes with sauce (for example, chicken curry, chicken *tikka masala* in a creamy tomato sauce, grilled fish tandoori, chickpea *chana masala*, or a spicy vindaloo dish), *raita* (a cooling yogurt that's added to spicy dishes), rice, naan, and an Indian beer (wine and Indian food don't really mix) or chai (cardamom/cinnamon-spiced tea, usually served with milk). An easy way to taste a variety of dishes is to order a thali—a sampler plate, generally served on a metal tray, with small servings of various specialties.

AFTERNOON TEA

Once the sole province of genteel ladies in fancy hats, afternoon tea has become more democratic in the 21st century. These days, people of leisure punctuate their day with an afternoon tea at a tearoom. Tearooms, which often serve appealing light meals, are usually open for lunch and close at about 17:00, just before dinner.
[A: Insert image]
[Image Tea.tif]

The cheapest "tea" on the menu is generally a "cream tea"; the most expensive is the "champagne tea." **Cream tea** is simply a pot of tea and a homemade scone or two with jam and thick clotted cream. (For maximum pinkie-waving taste per calorie, slice your scone thin like a miniature loaf of bread.) **Afternoon tea**—what many Americans would call "high tea"—is a pot of tea, small finger foods (such as sandwiches with the crusts cut off), scones, an assortment of small pastries, jam, and thick clotted cream. **Champagne tea** includes all of the goodies, plus a glass of bubbly. **High tea** to the English generally means a more substantial late afternoon or early evening meal, often served with meat or eggs.

British Chocolate

My chocoholic readers are enthusiastic about British chocolates. As with other dairy products, chocolate seems richer
and creamier here than it does in the US, so even standbys
such as Mars, Kit Kat (which was actually invented in York—see
page 541), and Twix have a different taste. Some favorites
include Cadbury Gold bars (filled with liquid caramel), Cadbury Crunchie bars, Nestlé's Lion bars (layered wafers covered
in caramel and chocolate), Cadbury's Boost bars (a shortcake
biscuit with caramel in milk chocolate), Cadbury Flake (crum-
bly folds of melt-in-your-mouth chocolate), Aero bars (with
"aerated" chocolate filling), and Galaxy chocolate bars (especially the ones with hazelnuts). Thornton shops (in larger train
stations) sell a box of sweets called the Continental Assortment, which comes with a tasting guide. (The highlight is the
mocha white-chocolate truffle.) British M&Ms, called Smarties,
are better than American ones. Many Brits feel that the ultimate treat is a box of either Nestlé Quality Street or Cadbury
Roses—assortments of filled chocolates in colorful wrappers.
(But don't mention the Kraft takeover of Cadbury in 2010—
many Brits believe the American company changed the recipe
for their beloved Dairy Milk bars, and they're not happy about
it). At ice-cream vans, look for the beloved traditional "99p"—
a vanilla soft-serve cone with a small Flake bar stuck right into
the middle.

DESSERTS (SWEETS)

To the British, the traditional word for dessert is "pudding," although it's also referred to as "sweets" these days. Sponge cake,
cream, fruitcake, and meringue are key players.

Trifle is the best-known British concoction, consisting of
sponge cake soaked in brandy or sherry (or orange juice for children), then covered with jam and/or fruit and custard cream.
Whipped cream can sometimes put the final touch on this "light"
treat.

The British version of custard is a smooth, yellow liquid.
Cream tops most everything that custard does not. There's single
cream for coffee. Double cream is really thick. Whipped cream is
familiar, and clotted cream is the consistency of whipped butter.

Fool is a dessert with sweetened pureed fruit (such as rhubarb,
gooseberries, or black currants) mixed with cream or custard and
chilled. Elderflower is a popular flavoring for sorbet.

Flapjacks here aren't pancakes, but are dense, sweet oatmeal
cakes (a little like a cross between a granola bar and a brownie).
They come with toppings such as toffee and chocolate.

Scones are tops, and many inns and restaurants have their

secret recipes. Whether made with fruit or topped with clotted cream, scones take the cake.

BEVERAGES

Beer: The British take great pride in their beer. Many locals think that drinking beer cold and carbonated, as Americans do, ruins the taste. Most pubs will have **lagers** (cold, refreshing, American-style beer), **ales** (amber-colored, cellar-temperature beer), **bitters** (hop-flavored ale, perhaps the most typical British beer), and **stouts** (dark and somewhat bitter, like Guinness).

At pubs, long-handled pulls (or taps) are used to draw the traditional, rich-flavored "real ales" up from the cellar. These are the connoisseur's favorites and often come with fun names. Served straight from the brewer's cask at cellar temperature, real ales finish fermenting naturally and are not pasteurized or filtered, so they must be consumed within two or three days after the cask is tapped. Naturally carbonated, real ales have less gassiness and head; they vary from sweet to bitter, often with a hoppy or nutty flavor.

Short-handled pulls mean colder, fizzier, mass-produced, and less interesting keg beers. Mild beers are sweeter, with a creamy malt flavoring. Irish cream ale is a smooth, sweet experience. Try the draft cider (sweet or dry)...carefully.

Order your beer at the bar and pay as you go, with no need to tip. An average beer costs about £4. Part of the experience is standing before a line of hand pulls, and wondering which beer to choose.

As dictated by British law, draft beer and cider are served by the pint (20-ounce imperial size) or the half-pint (9.6 ounces). (It's almost feminine for a man to order just a half; I order mine with quiche.) In 2011, the government sanctioned an in-between serving size—the schooner, or two-thirds pint (it's become a popular size for higher alcohol-content craft beers). Proper English ladies like a **shandy** (half beer and half 7-Up).

Whisky: While bar-hopping tourists generally think in terms of beer, many pubs are just as enthusiastic about serving whisky (common throughout Britain, but especially popular in Scotland, where much of it is produced). If you are unfamiliar with whisky (what Americans call "Scotch" and the Irish call "whiskey"), it's a great conversation starter. Many pubs have dozens of whiskies available. Lists describe their personalities (peaty, heavy iodine finish, and so on), which are much easier to discern than most wine flavors.

A glass of basic whisky generally costs around £2.50. Let a local teach you how to drink it "neat," then add a little water. Make a friend, buy a few drams, and learn by drinking. Keep experimenting until you discover the right taste for you.

The British Accent

In the olden days, an British person's accent indicated his or her social standing. Eliza Doolittle had the right idea—elocution could make or break you. Wealthier families would send their kids to fancy private schools to learn proper pronunciation. But these days, in a sort of reverse snobbery that has gripped the nation, accents are back. Politicians, newscasters, and movie stars are favoring deep accents over the Queen's English. While it's hard for American ears to pick out the variations, most Brits can determine where a person is from based on their accent...not just the region, but often the village, and even the part of town.

Consider going beyond the single-malt whisky rut. Like microbrews, small-batch, innovative Scottish spirits are trendy right now. Blends can be surprisingly creative—even for someone who thinks they're knowledgeable about whisky—and non-whisky alternatives are pushing boundaries. For example, you'll find gin that's aged in whisky casks, taking off the piney edge and infusing a bit of that distinctive whisky flavor.

Distilleries throughout Scotland offer tours, but you'll often only learn about that one type of whisky. At a good whisky shop, the knowledgeable staff offer guided tastings (for a fee and typically by pre-arrangement), explaining four or five whiskies to help you develop your palate. If you don't care for a heavy, smoky whisky, ask for something milder. Some shops have several bottles open and will let you try a few wee drams to narrow down your options. Be aware: If they're providing samples, they're hoping you'll buy a bottle at the end.

But the easiest and perhaps best option for sampling Scotland's national drink is to find a local pub with a passion for whisky that's filled with locals who share that passion.

For much more about whisky, see the "Whisky 101" sidebar on page 750.

Other Alcoholic Drinks: Many pubs also have a good selection of wines by the glass and a fully stocked bar for the gentleman's "G and T" (gin and tonic). **Pimm's** is a refreshing and fruity summer liqueur, traditionally popular during Wimbledon. It's an upper-class drink—a rough bloke might insult a pub by claiming it sells more Pimm's than beer.

Non-Alcoholic Drinks: Teetotalers can order from a wide variety of soft drinks—both the predictable American sodas and other more interesting bottled drinks, such as ginger beer (similar to ginger ale but with more bite), root beers, or other flavors (Fentimans brews some unusual options that are stocked in many pubs). Note that in Britain, "lemonade" is lemon-lime soda (like 7-Up).

Staying Connected

One of the most common questions I hear from travelers is, "How can I stay connected in Europe?" The short answer is: more easily and cheaply than you might think.

The simplest solution is to bring your own device—mobile phone, tablet, or laptop—and use it just as you would at home (following the tips below, such as connecting to free Wi-Fi whenever possible). Another option is to buy a European SIM card for your mobile phone—either your US phone or one you buy in Europe. Or you can use European landlines and computers to connect. Each of these options is described below, and more details are at www.ricksteves.com/phoning. For a very practical one-hour talk covering tech issues for travelers, see www.ricksteves.com/mobile-travel-skills.

USING A MOBILE PHONE IN EUROPE

Here are some budget tips and options.

Sign up for an international plan. Using your cellular network in Europe on a pay-as-you-go basis can add up (about $1.70/minute for voice calls, 50 cents to send text messages, 5 cents to receive them, and $10 to download one megabyte of data). To stay connected at a lower cost, sign up for an international service plan through your carrier. Most providers offer a simple bundle that includes calling, messaging, and data. Your normal plan may already include international coverage (T-Mobile's does).

Before your trip, call your provider or check online to confirm that your phone will work in Europe, and research your provider's international rates. Activate the plan a day or two before you leave, then remember to cancel it when your trip's over.

Use free Wi-Fi whenever possible. Unless you have an unlimited-data plan, you're best off saving most of your online tasks for Wi-Fi. You can access the Internet, send texts, and even make voice calls over Wi-Fi.

Most accommodations in Europe offer free Wi-Fi, but some—especially expensive hotels—charge a fee. Many cafés (including Starbucks and McDonald's) have free hotspots for customers; look for signs offering it and ask for the Wi-Fi password when you buy something. You'll also often find Wi-Fi at TIs, city squares, major museums, public-transit hubs, airports, and aboard trains and buses. In Britain, another option is to sign up for Wi-Fi access through a company such as BT (one hour-£4, one day-£10, www.

btwifi.co.uk) or The Cloud (free though sometimes slow, www. skywifi.cloud).

Minimize the use of your cellular network. Even with an international data plan, wait until you're on Wi-Fi to Skype, download apps, stream videos, or do other megabyte-greedy tasks. Using a navigation app such as Google Maps over a cellular network can take lots of data, so do this sparingly or use it offline.

Limit automatic updates. By default, your device constantly checks for a data connection and updates apps. It's smart to disable these features so your apps will only update when you're on Wi-Fi, and to change your device's email settings from "auto-retrieve" to "manual" (or from "push" to "fetch").

When you need to get online but can't find Wi-Fi, simply turn on your cellular network just long enough for the task at hand. When you're done, avoid further charges by manually turning off data roaming or cellular data (either works) in your device's Settings menu. Another way to make sure you're not accidentally using data roaming is to put your device in "airplane" mode (which also disables phone calls and texts), and then turn your Wi-Fi back on as needed.

It's also a good idea to keep track of your data usage. On your device's menu, look for "cellular data usage" or "mobile data" and reset the counter at the start of your trip.

Use Wi-Fi calling and messaging apps. Skype, Viber, FaceTime, and Google+ Hangouts are great for making free or low-cost voice and video calls over Wi-Fi. With an app installed on your phone, tablet, or laptop, you can log on to a Wi-Fi network and contact friends or family members who use the same service. If you buy credit in advance, with some of these services you can call any mobile phone or landline worldwide for just pennies per minute.

Many of these apps also allow you to send messages over Wi-Fi to any other person using that app. Be aware that some apps, such as Apple's iMessage, will use the cellular network if Wi-Fi isn't available: To avoid this possibility, turn off the "Send as SMS" feature.

USING A EUROPEAN SIM CARD

With a European SIM card, you get a European mobile number and access to cheaper rates than you'll get through your US carrier. This option works well for those who want to make a lot of voice calls or needing faster connection speeds than their US carrier provides. Fit the SIM card into a cheap phone you buy in Europe (about $40 from phone shops anywhere), or swap out the SIM card in an "unlocked" US phone (check with your carrier about unlocking it).

SIM cards are sold at mobile-phone shops, department-store

How to Dial

International Calls

Whether phoning from a US landline or mobile phone, or from a number in another European country, here's how to make an international call. I've used one of my recommended London hotels as an example (tel. 020/7730-8191).

Initial Zero: Drop the initial zero from international phone numbers—except when calling Italy.

Mobile Tip: If using a mobile phone, the "+" sign can replace the international access code (for a "+" sign, press and hold "0").

US/Canada to Europe

Dial 011 (US/Canada international access code), country code (44 for Britain), and phone number.

▸ To call the London hotel from home, dial 011-44-20/7730-8191.

Country to Country Within Europe

Dial 00 (Europe international access code), country code, and phone number.

▸ To call the London hotel from Spain, dial 00-44-20/7730-8191.

Europe to the US/Canada

Dial 00, country code (1 for US/Canada), and phone number.

▸ To call from Europe to my office in Edmonds, Washington, dial 00-1-425-771-8303.

Domestic Calls

To call within Britain (from one British landline or mobile phone to another), simply dial the phone number, including the initial 0 if there is one.

▸ To call the London hotel from Edinburgh, dial 020/7730-8191.

More Dialing Tips

British Phone Numbers: Numbers beginning with 071 through 079 are mobile numbers, which are more expensive to call than a landline.

electronics counters, some newsstands, and vending machines. Costing about $5-10, they usually include prepaid calling/messaging credit, with no contract and no commitment. Expect to pay $20-40 more for a SIM card with a gigabyte of data. If you travel with this card to other countries in the European Union, there may be extra roaming fees.

I like to buy SIM cards at a phone shop where there's a clerk to help explain the options. Certain brands—including Lebara and Lycamobile, both of which are available in multiple European countries—are reliable and especially economical. Ask the clerk to

Toll and Toll-Free Calls: Numbers starting with 0800 and 0808 are toll-free. Those beginning with 084, 087, and 03 are generally inexpensive toll numbers (£0.15/minute from a landline, £0.20-.40/minute from a mobile). Numbers beginning with 09 are pricey toll lines. If you have questions about a prefix, call 100 for free help. International rates apply to US toll-free numbers dialed from Britain—they're not free.

More Phoning Help: See www.howtocallabroad.com.

European Country Codes		Ireland & N. Ireland	353 / 44
Austria	43	Italy	39
Belgium	32	Latvia	371
Bosnia-Herzegovina	387	Montenegro	382
Croatia	385	Morocco	212
Czech Republic	420	Netherlands	31
Denmark	45	Norway	47
Estonia	372	Poland	48
Finland	358	Portugal	351
France	33	Russia	7
Germany	49	Slovakia	421
Gibraltar	350	Slovenia	386
Great Britain	44	Spain	34
Greece	30	Sweden	46
Hungary	36	Switzerland	41
Iceland	354	Turkey	90

help you insert your SIM card, set it up, and show you how to use it. In some countries, you'll be required to register the SIM card with your passport as an antiterrorism measure (which may mean you can't use the phone for the first hour or two).

Find out how to check your credit balance. When you run out of credit, you can top it up at newsstands, tobacco shops, mobile-phone stores, or many other businesses (look for your SIM card's logo in the window), or online.

PRACTICALITIES

Tips on Internet Security

Make sure that your device is running the latest versions of its operating system, security software, and apps. Next, ensure that your device and key programs (like email) are password- or passcode-protected. On the road, use only secure, password-protected Wi-Fi hotspots. Ask the hotel or café staff for the specific name of their Wi-Fi network, and make sure you log on to that exact one.

If you must access your financial info online, use a banking app rather than accessing your account via a browser. A cellular connection is more secure than Wi-Fi. Avoid logging onto personal finance sites on a public computer.

Never share your credit-card number (or any other sensitive information) online unless you know that the site is secure. A secure site displays a little padlock icon, and the URL begins with *https* (instead of the usual *http*).

PUBLIC PHONES AND COMPUTERS

It's possible to travel in Europe without a mobile device. You can make calls from your hotel (or the increasingly rare public phone), and check email or browse websites using public computers.

Most **hotels** charge a fee for placing calls—ask for rates before you dial. You can use a prepaid international phone card (available at post offices, newsstands, street kiosks, tobacco shops, and train stations) to call out from your hotel. Dial the toll-free access number, enter the card's PIN code, then dial the number.

If there's no phone in your **B&B** room, and you have an important, brief call to make, politely ask your hosts if you can use their personal phone. Use a cheap international phone card with a toll-free access number, or offer to pay your host for the call.

Public pay phones are hard to find in Britain, and they're expensive. To use one, you'll pay with a major credit card (minimum charge-£1.20) or coins (minimum charge-£0.60).

Most hotels have **public computers** in their lobbies for guests to use; otherwise you may find them at Internet cafés or public libraries (ask your hotelier or the TI for the nearest location). On a European keyboard, use the "Alt Gr" key to the right of the space bar to insert the extra symbol that appears on some keys. If you can't locate a special character (such as @), simply copy it from a Web page and paste it into your email message.

MAIL

You can mail one package per day to yourself worth up to $200 duty-free from Europe to the US (mark it "personal purchases"). If you're sending a gift to someone, mark it "unsolicited gift." For details, visit www.cbp.gov, select "Travel," and search for "Know Before You Go."

The British postal service works fine, but for quick transatlantic delivery (in either direction), consider services such as DHL (www.dhl.com). For postcards, get stamps at the neighborhood post office, newsstands within fancy hotels, and some minimarts and card shops.

Transportation

If you're debating between using public transportation and renting a car, consider these factors: Cars are best for three or more traveling together (especially families with small kids), those packing heavy, and those delving into the countryside—a tempting plan for this region. Trains and buses are best for solo travelers, blitz tourists, city-to-city travelers, and those who don't want to drive. While a car gives you more freedom, trains and buses zip you effortlessly and scenically from city to city, usually dropping you in the center, often near a TI. Cars are an expensive headache in places like London, but necessary for remote destinations not well-served by public transport.

In Britain, my choice is to connect big cities by train and to explore rural areas (the Cotswolds, North Wales, the Lake District, and the Scottish Highlands) footloose and fancy-free by rental car. The mix works quite efficiently (e.g., London, Bath, York, and Edinburgh by train, with a rental car for the rest).

TRAINS
Regular tickets on Britain's great train system (15,000 departures from 2,400 stations daily) are the most expensive per mile in all of Europe. For the greatest savings, book online in advance and leave after rush hour (after 9:30 weekdays).

Since Britain's railways have been privatized, a single train route can be operated by multiple companies. However, one website covers all train lines (www.nationalrail.co.uk), and another covers all bus and train routes (www.traveline.org.uk for information, not ticket sales). Another good resource, which also has schedules for trains throughout Europe, is German Rail's timetable (www.bahn.com).

As with airline tickets, British train tickets can come at many different prices for the same journey. A clerk at any station can figure out the cheapest fare for your trip.

While generally not required, reservations are free and can normally be made well in advance. They are an especially good idea for long journeys or for travel on Sundays or holidays. Make reservations at any train station, by phone, or online when you buy your

PRACTICALITIES

Public Transportation Routes in Britain

······	Rail
———	Eurostar
+++++	Bus
- - - (8H)	Ferry with crossing time

Orkney Islands
Stromness
Scrabster · Gill · John O' Groats
Thurso
Lewis

Skye
Portree · Inverness
Kyle · Culloden
Loch · Aviemore
Ness
Mallaig · Elgin
Fort William
SCOTLAND · Aberdeen
Pitlochry
Mull · Perth · Dundee
Iona · Oban · Leuchars
Stirling · St. Andrews

Edinburgh
Glasgow · Berwick

Holy Island

(2H)
Larne · Cairnryan · Hexham
(2.5H) · Stranraer · Newcastle · To Amsterdam (15H)
Belfast · Carlisle · Durham · North Sea
NORTHERN · Penrith · Whitby
IRELAND · Keswick
(8H) · Windermere · Settle · Danby · Scarborough
Isle · ENGLAND
of Man · York · To Zeebrugge (10H)
Irish · Blackpool · Preston · Hull
Sea · Leeds · Grimsby
Dublin · (7H) · Liverpool · Manchester · Lincoln
(2-3H) · Holyhead · Conwy · Chester
REPUBLIC · Bangor · Betws-y-Coed · Stoke · Peter- · King's
OF · Caernarfon · Blaenau · Derby · borough · Lynn · Norwich
IRELAND · Bed. · Ffest. · Telford · Wolv. · Ely
Pwllheli · Harlech · Birmingham · Cambridge
Aberystwyth · Ironbridge · Coventry
(3.5H) · Gorge · Warwick · Harwich
Rosslare · WALES · Stratford
· Chelt. · Stow · Moreton · To Hoek (6H)
Fishguard · Carmarthen · Newport · Oxford · Ebbs-fleet
Swansea · STONE- · Windsor · Canterbury
Cardiff · Bath · Reading · HENGE · Ashford · Dover (7.5H)
Bristol · Wells · West- · Salisbury · Brighton · Calais
Glastonbury · bury · Southampton · Newhaven
Atlantic · Exeter · Portsmouth · (4H) · Dieppe
Ocean · Dartmoor · English Channel · To Paris & Brussels
St. Ives · Truro · Plymouth
Penzance · Falmouth · To St-Malo (11H)
To Roscoff (6H)
FRANCE
Caen (Ouistreham)

N

50 Kilometers
50 Miles

ticket. With a point-to-point ticket, you can reserve as late as two hours before train time, but rail-pass holders should book seats at least 24 hours in advance (see below for more on rail passes). You must reserve in advance for Caledonian Sleeper overnight trains between London and Scotland (www.sleeper.scot).

For information on the high-speed Eurostar train through the "Chunnel" to Paris or Brussels, see page 213.

Rail Passes

Since Britain's pay-as-you-go train tickets are some of the most expensive in Europe, BritRail passes can pay for themselves quickly, especially if you ride a long-distance train (for example, between London and Scotland). A rail pass offers hop-on flexibility and no need to lock in reservations, except for overnight sleeper cars.

The BritRail pass (covering England, Scotland, and Wales) and the BritRail England-only pass come in "consecutive day" and "flexi" versions, with price breaks for youths, seniors, off-season travelers, and groups of three or more. Most allow one child under 16 to travel free with a paying adult. If you're exploring the backcountry with a BritRail pass, second class is a good choice since many of the smaller train lines don't even offer first-class cars.

Other BritRail options include England-only passes, Scotland-only passes, "London Plus" passes (good for travel in most of southeast England but not in London itself), and South West passes (good for the Cotswolds, Bath, Dorset, Devon, Cornwall, plus part of South Wales).

BritRail passes cannot be purchased locally; buy your pass through an agent before leaving the US. Make sleeper reservations in advance; you can also make optional, free seat reservations (recommended for busy weekends) at staffed train stations.

For more detailed advice on figuring out the smartest rail-pass options for your train trip, visit www.ricksteves.com/rail.

Buying Tickets

In Advance: The best fares go to those who book their trips well in advance of their journey. Savings can be significant. For a London-York round-trip (standard class), the peak "anytime" fare is about £245 (usually paid by business travelers) and up to £106 for "off-peak." However, if you book online at least a day ahead, off-peak and advance-purchase discounts can combine for a rate closer to £50. An "advance" fare for the same ticket booked a couple of months out can cost as little as £30.

The cheapest fares (minimum 7-day advance purchase) sell out fast. Especially in summer, it's often necessary to book six to eight weeks ahead. Keep in mind that "return" (round-trip) fares are not always cheaper than buying two "single" (one-way) tickets—but

PRACTICALITIES

Rail Passes and Train Travel in Great Britain

Rick Steves' GUIDE TO Eurail Passes

How to choose and use the rail pass that best fits your trip—and your budget

A **BritRail Pass** lets you travel by train in Scotland, England, and Wales for three to eight days within a one-month period, 15 days within two months, or for continuous periods of up to one month. In addition, BritRail sells England-only and other regional passes. Discounted rates are offered for children, youths, seniors, or for three or more people traveling together.

BritRail passes are sold only outside Europe (through travel agents or Rick Steves' Europe). For more on the ins and outs of rail passes, including prices, download my **free guide to Eurail Passes** (www.ricksteves.com/rail-guide) or go to www.ricksteves.com/rail.

If you're taking just a couple of train rides, individual **point-to-point train tickets** may save you money over a pass. Use this map to add up approximate pay-as-you-go fares for your itinerary, and compare that to the price of a rail pass. Keep in mind that significant discounts on point-to-point tickets may be available with advance purchase.

Map shows approximate costs, in US$, for one-way, second-class tickets at off-peak rates.

To Orkney

Thurso

Portree   Kyle   25
Armadale   Inverness
Mallaig   30   40   Aberdeen
   15   .15   30   25
        Ft.
Oban   15 William 30
Mull   35 40   25
           Glasgow   Edinburgh
Cairnryan 30   15
To   65   Durham
Belfast   30
              Penrith   30
Liverpool   York
Holyhead Conwy 65
To   20 10 Chester 60   175
Dublin   25
Aberystwyth 70
To   85 55 110   110
Rosslare   Cardiff
Fishguard 40   Cambridge 20 Norwich
           25   Bath   20   40 Harwich
Barnstaple   40 50 London   To
      15   40   Holland
   30 45 Salisbury   35
Exeter   25 40   25 Dover
Penzance   20   25
        Portsmouth Brighton To
              To   Calais
           Normandy To Paris & Paris
                   (via Eurostar)

PRACTICALITIES

Sample Train Journey

Here is a typical example of a personalized train schedule printed out at a British train station (also online at www. nationalrail.co.uk). At the Salisbury station, I told the clerk that I wanted to leave after 16:15 for Moreton-in-Marsh in the Cotswolds. Even though the trip involved two transfers, this schedule allowed me to easily navigate the rails.

Travel by	Leaving	From	Platform	To	Arriving	Platform	Duration
Train	16:21	Salisbury [SAL]	2	Basingstoke [BSK]	16:55	3	0h 34m
		South West Trains service from Exeter St David's to London Waterloo					
Train	17:04	Basingstoke [BSK]	5	Reading [RDG]	17:28	2	0h 24m
		First Great Western service from Basingstoke to Reading					
Train	17:50	Reading [RDG]	9	Moreton-in-Marsh [MIM]	18:54	1	1h 04m
		First Great Western service from London Paddington to Hereford					

Often the conductor on your previous train can tell you which platform your next train will depart from, but it's wise to confirm. Scrolling overhead screens on the platforms often show arrivals, departures, and intermediate stops; some list train departures by their final destination only. If you are traveling to an intermediate stop and aren't sure which platform you need, ask any conductor or at the info desk. For example, after checking with the conductor, I know that I'll need to look for *Oxford* to catch the train for Moreton-in-Marsh.

Britain's train system can experience delays, so don't schedule your connections too tightly if you need to reach your destination at a specific time.

National Rail's website will automatically display this option if it's the lowest fare. Cheap advance tickets often come with the toughest refund restrictions, so be sure to nail down your travel plans before you reserve.

To book ahead, go in person to any station, look online at www.nationalrail.co.uk, or call 0345-748-4950 (from the US, dial 011-44-20-7278-5240, phone answered 24 hours) to find out the schedule and best fare for your journey; you'll then be referred to the appropriate vendor—depending on the particular rail company—to book your ticket. If you order online, be sure you know what you want; it's tough to reach a person who can change your online reservation. You'll pick up your ticket at the station, or you may be able to print it at home. (BritRail pass holders, however, cannot make online seat reservations.)

A company called **Megabus** (through their subsidiary Megatrain) sells some discounted train tickets well in advance on a few specific routes, though their focus is mainly on selling bus tickets (info tel. 0871-266-3333, www.megatrain.com).

Buying Train Tickets as You Travel: If you'd rather have the flexibility of booking tickets as you go, you can save a few pounds by buying a round-trip ticket, called a "return ticket" (a same-day round-trip, called a "day return," is particularly cheap); buying before 18:00 the day before you depart; traveling after the morning rush hour (this usually means after 9:30 Mon-Fri); and going standard class instead of first class. Preview your options at www.nationalrail.co.uk.

Senior, Youth, Partner, and Family Deals: To get a third off the price of most point-to-point rail tickets, seniors can buy a Senior Railcard (ages 60 and up), younger travelers can buy a 16-25 Railcard (ages 16-25, or full-time students 26 and older), and two people traveling together can buy a Two Together Railcard (ages 16 and over). A Family and Friends Railcard gives adults about 33 percent off for most trips and 60 percent off for their kids age 5 to 15 (maximum 4 adults and 4 kids). Each Railcard costs £30; see www.railcard.co.uk. These cards are valid for a year on almost all trains, including special runs such as the Heathrow Express, but are not valid on the Eurostar to Paris or Brussels (fill out application at station, brochures on racks in info center, need to show passport; passport-type photo needed for 16-25 Railcard).

BUSES

Although buses are about a third slower than trains, they're also a lot cheaper. And buses go many places that trains don't. Most domestic buses are operated by **National Express** (tel. 0871-781-8181, www.nationalexpress.com); their international departures are called **Eurolines** (www.eurolines.co.uk). Note that Brits distinguish between "buses" (for in-city travel with lots of stops) and "coaches" (long-distance cross-country runs)—though for simplicity in this book, I call both "buses."

A smaller company called **Megabus** undersells National Express with deeply discounted promotional fares—the further ahead you buy, the less you pay (some trips for just £1.50, toll tel. 0900-160-0900, www.megabus.com). While Megabus can be much cheaper than National Express, they tend to be slower than their competitor and their routes mainly connect cities, not smaller towns. They also sell discounted train tickets on selected routes.

Most long-haul domestic routes in Scotland are operated by **Scottish Citylink.** In peak season, it's worth booking your seat on popular routes at least a few days in advance (at the bus station or TI, online at www.citylink.co.uk, or by calling 0871-266-3333). At slower times, you can just hop on the bus and pay the driver.

Try to avoid bus travel on Friday and Sunday evenings, when weekend travelers are more likely to make buses sell out.

To ensure getting a ticket—and to save money with special

promotions—book your ticket in advance online or over the phone. The cheapest prepurchased tickets can usually be changed (for a £5 fee), but not refunded. Check if the ticket is only "amendable" or also "refundable" when you buy. If you have a mobile phone, you can order online and have a "text ticket" sent right to your phone for a small fee.

Round-trip bus tickets usually cost less than two one-way fares. Budget travelers can save a wad with a bus pass. National Express sells a **Skimmer pass** to non-UK citizens for unlimited travel on consecutive days (£69/7 days, £119/14 days, £199/28 days, best to buy online, tel. 0871-781-8178, www.nationalexpress.com). Check their website to learn about online deals; senior/youth/family cards and fares; and discounts for advance booking. If you're taking a lot of buses **in Scotland,** consider Citylink's Explorer pass (£49/3 days in 5-day period, £74/5 days in 10-day period, £99/8 days in 16-day period).

If you want to take a bus from your last destination to the nearest airport, you'll find that National Express often offers **airport buses.** Bus stations are normally at or near train stations (in London, the main bus station is a block southwest of Victoria Station).

RENTING A CAR

Rental companies in Britain require you to be at least 21 years old and to have held your license for one year. Drivers under the age of 25 may incur a young-driver surcharge, and some rental companies will not rent to anyone 75 or older. If you're considered too young or old, look into leasing (covered later), which has less-stringent age restrictions.

Research car rentals before you go. It's cheaper to arrange most car rentals from the US. Consider several companies to compare rates. Most of the major US rental agencies (including Avis, Budget, Enterprise, Hertz, and Thrifty) have offices throughout Europe. Also consider the two major Europe-based agencies, Europcar and Sixt. It can be cheaper to use a consolidator, such as Auto Europe/Kemwel (www.autoeurope.com—or the often cheaper www.autoeurope.eu), which compares rates at several companies to get you the best deal—but because you're working with a middleman, it's especially important to ask in advance about add-on fees and restrictions.

Always read the fine print or query the agent carefully for add-on charges—such as one-way drop-off fees, airport surcharges, or mandatory insurance policies—that aren't included in the "total price."

For the best deal, rent by the week with unlimited mileage. I normally rent the smallest, least expensive model with a stick shift

PRACTICALITIES

British Radio

Local radio broadcasts can be a treat for drivers sightseeing in Britain. Many British radio stations broadcast nationwide; your car radio automatically detects the local frequency a station plays on and displays its name.

The BBC has five nationwide stations, which you can pick up in most of the country. These government-subsidized stations have no ads.

BBC Radio 1: Pop music, with youthful DJs spinning top 40 hits and interviewing big-name bands.

BBC Radio 2: The highest-rated station nationwide, aimed at a more mature audience, with adult contemporary, retro pop, and other "middle of the road" music.

BBC Radio 3: Mostly classical music, with some jazz and world music.

BBC Radio 4: All talk—current events, entertaining chat shows, special-interest topics such as cooking and gardening, and lots of radio plays.

(generally cheaper than automatic). Almost all rentals are manual by default, so if you need an automatic, request one in advance. An automatic makes sense for most American drivers: With a manual transmission in Britain, you'll be sitting on the right side of the car, and shifting with your left hand...while driving on the left side of the road. When selecting a car, chose a smaller model; they're more maneuverable on narrow, winding roads.

Figure on paying roughly $250 for a one-week rental. Allow extra for supplemental insurance, fuel, tolls, and parking. For trips of three weeks or more, leasing can save you money on insurance and taxes.

Picking Up Your Car: Big companies have offices in most cities, but small local rental companies can be cheaper. If you pick up your car in a smaller city or at an airport (rather than downtown), you'll more likely survive your first day on the road. Be aware that Brits call it "hiring a car," and directional signs at airports and train stations will read *Car Hire*.

Compare pickup costs (downtown can be less expensive than the airport) and explore drop-off options. For a trip covering both Britain and Ireland, you're better off with two separate car rentals. Always check the hours of the location you choose: Many rental offices close from midday Saturday until Monday morning and, in smaller towns, at lunchtime.

When selecting a location, don't trust the agency's description of "downtown" or "city center." In some cases, a "downtown" branch can be on the outskirts of the city—a long, costly taxi ride

PRACTICALITIES

BBC Radio 5 Live: Sporting events as well as news and sports talk programs.

You'll encounter regional variations of BBC stations, such as BBC London, Radio York, BBC Scotland, and BBC Gaelic. At the top of the hour, many BBC stations broadcast the famous "pips" (indicating Greenwich Mean Time) and a short roundup of the day's news.

Beyond the BBC offerings, several private stations broadcast music and other content with "adverts" (commercials). Some are nationwide, including **XFM** (alternative rock), **Classic FM** (classical), **Absolute Radio** (pop), and **Capital FM** (pop).

Traffic Alerts: Ask your rental-car company about turning on automatic traffic alerts that play on the car radio. Once these are enabled (look for the letters *TA* or *TP* on the radio readout), traffic reports for the area you are driving in will periodically interrupt programming.

from the center. Before choosing, plug the addresses into a mapping website. You may find that the "train station" location is handier. Returning a car at a big-city train station or downtown agency can be tricky; get precise details on the car drop-off location and hours, and allow ample time to find it.

When you pick up the rental car, check it thoroughly and make sure any damage is noted on your rental agreement. Rental agencies in Europe tend to charge for even minor damage, so be sure to mark everything. Before driving off, find out how your car's lights, turn signals, wipers, radio, and fuel cap function, and know what kind of fuel the car takes (diesel vs. unleaded). When you return the car, make sure the agent verifies its condition with you. Some drivers take pictures of the returned vehicle as proof of its condition.

The AA: The services of Britain's Automobile Association are included with most rentals (www.theaa.com), but check for this when booking to be sure you understand its towing and emergency road-service benefits.

Car Insurance Options

When you rent a car, you are liable for a very high deductible, sometimes equal to the entire value of the car. Limit your financial risk with one of these three options: Buy Collision Damage Waiver (CDW) coverage with a low or zero deductible from the car-rental company, get coverage through your credit card (free, if your card automatically includes zero-deductible coverage), or get collision insurance as part of a larger travel-insurance policy.

Basic **CDW** includes a very high deductible (typically $1,000-1,500), costs $15-30 a day (figure roughly 30-40 percent extra) and reduces your liability, but does not eliminate it. When you reserve or pick up the car, you'll be offered the chance to "buy down" the basic deductible to zero (for an additional $10-30/day; this is sometimes called "super CDW" or "zero-deductible coverage").

If you opt for **credit-card coverage,** you'll technically have to decline all coverage offered by the car-rental company, which means they can place a hold on your card (which can be up to the full value of the car). In case of damage, it can be time-consuming to resolve the charges with your credit-card company. Before you decide on this option, quiz your credit-card company about how it works.

If you're already purchasing a **travel-insurance policy** for your trip, adding collision coverage is an option. For example, Travel Guard (www.travelguard.com) sells affordable renter's collision insurance as an add-on to its other policies; it's valid everywhere in Europe except the Republic of Ireland, and some Italian car-rental companies refuse to honor it, as it doesn't cover you in case of theft.

For more on car-rental insurance, see www.ricksteves.com/cdw.

Leasing

For trips of three weeks or more, consider leasing (which automatically includes zero-deductible collision and theft insurance). By technically buying and then selling back the car, you save lots of money on tax and insurance. Leasing provides you a brand-new car with unlimited mileage and a 24-hour emergency assistance program. You can lease for as little as 21 days to as long as five-and-a-half months. Car leases must be arranged from the US. One of the many companies offering affordable lease packages is Auto Europe.

Navigation Options

If you'll be navigating using your phone or a GPS unit from home, remember to bring a car charger and device mount.

Your Mobile Device: The mapping app on your mobile phone works fine for navigation in Europe, but for real-time turn-by-turn directions and traffic updates, you'll generally need Internet access. And driving all day while online can be very expensive. Helpful exceptions are Google Maps, Here WeGo, and Navmii, which provide turn-by-turn voice directions and recalibrate even when they're offline.

Download your map before you head out—it's smart to select a large region. Then turn off your cellular connection so you're not

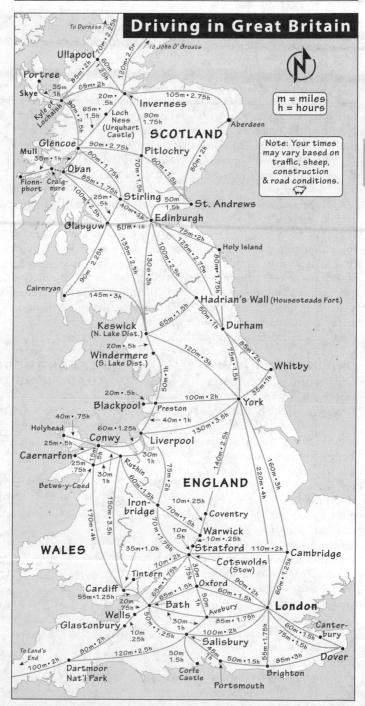

Driving in Great Britain

PRACTICALITIES

m = miles
h = hours

Note: Your times may vary based on traffic, sheep, construction & road conditions.

To Durness • 70m • 2.25h

To John O'Groats

Ullapool
60m • 2.5h
120m • 2.5h

Portree
35m • 1h
85m • 2h
Skye
Kyle of Lochalsh
65m • 2h
90m • 2.5h
65m • 1.5h

20m • .5h
Inverness
105m • 2.75h
Loch Ness (Urquhart Castle)
90m 1.75h

Aberdeen

SCOTLAND

80m • 2h

Glencoe
90m • 2.75h
Pitlochry
60m • 1.5h
Mull
35m • 1h
Oban
80m • 1.75h
70m • 1.5h
Fionn-phort
Craig-nure
85m • 1.75h
Stirling
50m 1.5h
St. Andrews
100m 2.5h
25m .5h
40m • 1h
Glasgow
Edinburgh
50m • 1h
75m • 2h
Holy Island
135m • 2.5h
125m • 2.7h
130m • 3h
80m • 1.75h
90m 2.25h
100m • 2.5h

Cairnryan
145m • 3h
Hadrian's Wall (Housesteads Fort)
65m • 1.5h
50m • 1h
Durham
Keswick (N. Lake Dist.)
20m • .5h
120m • 3h
75m • 1.5h
85m • 2h
Windermere (S. Lake Dist.)
Whitby
50m • 1h
35m • 1h
100m • 2h
York
20m • .5h
Blackpool
Preston
40m • 1h
130m • 3.5h
40m • .75h
60m • 1.25h
Liverpool
140m • 2.5h
160m • 3h
Holyhead
25m • .5h
Conwy
30m 1h
Caernarfon
25m .75h
Ruthin
75m • 2h
30m 1h
220m • 4h
Betws-y-Coed
60m • 1.5h
ENGLAND
150m • 3.5h
Iron-bridge
10m • .25h
Coventry
170m • 4h
70m • 1.5h
Warwick
10m .5h
35m • 1.0h
10m • 1.75h
Stratford
110m • 2h
Cambridge
WALES
70m • 2h
Cotswolds (Stow)
Tintern
75m
60m • 1.25h
65m • 1.5h
Oxford
90m • 2.5h
Cardiff
55m • 1.25h
20m .75h
Bath
65m • 1.5h
50m
60m • 1.5h
London
Wells
50m 1.25h
Avebury
85m • 1.75h
Glastonbury
10m .25h
30m 1h
100m • 2h
60m • 1.25h
Canterbury
55m • 1.75h
To Land's End
80m • 2h
120m • 2.5h
Salisbury
45m 1h
75m • 1.5h
100m • 2h
50m 1.5h
Dover
Dartmoor Nat'l Park
Corfe Castle
50m • 1.5h
85m • 3h
Portsmouth
Brighton

charged for data roaming. Call up the map, enter your destination, and you're on your way. View maps in standard view (not satellite view) to limit data demands.

GPS Devices: If you prefer the convenience of a dedicated GPS unit, known as a "satnav" in Britain, consider renting one with your car ($10-30/day). These units offer real-time turn-by-turn directions and traffic without the data requirements of an app. Note that the unit may only come loaded with maps for its home country; if you need additional maps, ask.

A less-expensive option is to bring a GPS device from home. Be aware that you'll need to buy and download European maps before your trip.

Maps and Atlases: Even when navigating primarily with a mobile app or GPS, I always make it a point to have a paper map. It's invaluable for getting the big picture, understanding alternate routes, and filling in when my phone runs out of juice. Several good road atlases cover all of Britain. Ordnance Survey, Collins, AA, and Bartholomew editions are all available at tourist information offices, gas stations, and bookstores. The tourist-oriented Collins Touring maps do a good job of highlighting the many roadside attractions you might otherwise drive right past. Before you buy a map, look at it to be sure it has the level of detail you want.

DRIVING IN BRITAIN

Driving here is basically wonderful—once you remember to stay on the left and after you've mastered the roundabouts. Every year, however, I get a few notes from traveling readers advising me that, for them, trying to drive in Britain was a nerve-racking and regrettable mistake. If you want to get a little slack on the roads, drop by a gas station or auto shop and buy a green *P* (probationary driver with license) sign to put in your car window (don't get the red *L* sign, which means you're a learner driver without a license and thus prohibited from driving on motorways).

Many Yankee drivers find the hardest part isn't

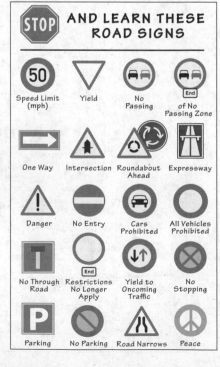

driving on the left, but steering from the right. Your instinct is to put yourself on the left side of your lane, which means you may spend your first day or two drifting into the left shoulder or curb. It helps to remember that the driver always stays close to the center line.

Road Rules: Be aware of Britain's rules of the road. Seat belts are mandatory for all, and kids under age 12 (or less than about 4.5 feet tall) must ride in an appropriate child-safety seat. It's illegal to use a mobile phone while driving—pull over or use a hands-free device. In Britain, you're not allowed to turn left on a red light unless a sign or signal specifically authorizes it. For more information about driving in Britain, ask your car-rental company, read the Department for Transport's *Highway Code* (www.direct.gov.uk—click on "Driving and transport" and look for "The Highway Code" link), or check the US State Department website (www.travel.state.gov, click on "International Travel," then specify your country of choice and click "Traffic Safety and Road Conditions").

Speed Limits: Speed limits are in miles per hour: 30 mph in town, 70 mph on the motorways, and 60 or 70 mph elsewhere (though, as back home, many British drivers consider these limits advisory). The national sign for the maximum speed is a white circle with a black slash. Motorways have electronic speed limit signs; posted speeds can change depending on traffic or the weather. Follow them accordingly.

Note that road-surveillance cameras strictly enforce speed limits. Any driver (including foreigners renting cars) photographed speeding will get a nasty bill in the mail. (Cameras—in foreboding gray boxes—flash on rear license plates to respect the privacy of anyone sharing the front seat with someone he or she shouldn't.) Signs (an image of an old-fashioned camera) alert you when you're entering  a zone that may be monitored by these "camera cops." Heed them.

Roundabouts: Don't let a roundabout spook you. After all, you routinely merge into much faster traffic on American highways back home. Traffic flows clockwise, and cars already in the roundabout have the right-of-way; entering traffic yields (look to your right as you merge). You'll probably encounter "double-roundabouts"—figure-eights where you'll slingshot from one roundabout directly into another. Just go with the flow and track signs carefully. When approaching an especially complex roundabout, you'll first pass a diagram showing the layout and the various exits. And

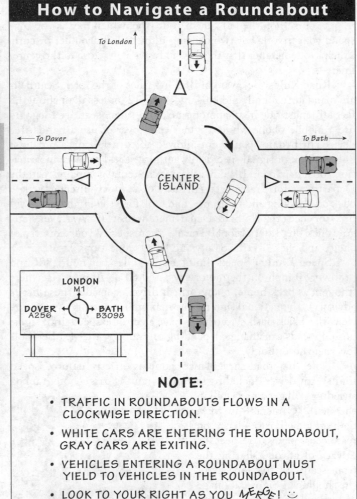

How to Navigate a Roundabout

To London

To Dover →

To Bath →

CENTER ISLAND

LONDON
M1

DOVER ←
A256

BATH →
B3098

NOTE:

- TRAFFIC IN ROUNDABOUTS FLOWS IN A CLOCKWISE DIRECTION.
- WHITE CARS ARE ENTERING THE ROUNDABOUT, GRAY CARS ARE EXITING.
- VEHICLES ENTERING A ROUNDABOUT MUST YIELD TO VEHICLES IN THE ROUNDABOUT.
- LOOK TO YOUR RIGHT AS YOU MERGE! ☺

in many cases, the pavement is painted to indicate the lane you should be in for a particular road or town.

Freeways (Motorways): The shortest distance between any two points is usually the motorway (what we'd call a "freeway"). In Britain, the smaller the number, the bigger the road. For example, the M-4 is a freeway, while the B-4494 is a country road.

Motorway road signs can be confusing, too few, and too late. Miss a motorway exit and you can lose 30 minutes. Study your map before taking off. Know the cities you'll be lacing together, since road numbers are inconsistent. British road signs are rarely marked with compass directions (e.g., *A-4 West*); instead, you need to know what major town or city you're heading for *(A-4 Bath)*. The driving directions in this book are intended to be used with a good map. Get a road atlas, easily purchased at gas stations in Britain, or download digital maps before your trip (see page 1062).

Unless you're passing, always drive in the "slow" lane on motorways (the lane farthest to the left). The British are very disciplined about this; ignoring this rule could get you a ticket (or into a road-rage incident). Remember to pass on the right, not the left.

Rest areas are called "services" and often have amenities, such as restaurants, cafeterias, gas stations, shops, and motels.

Fuel: Gas (petrol) costs about $5.50 per gallon and is self-serve. Pump first and then pay. Diesel costs about the same. Diesel rental cars are common; make sure you know what kind of fuel your car takes before you fill up. Unleaded pumps are usually green. Note that self-service gas pumps and automated tollbooths and parking garages often accept only cash or a chip-and-PIN credit card (see page 1018).

Driving in Cities: Whenever possible, avoid driving in cities. Be warned that London assesses a congestion charge if you're driving in the city center. Most cities have modern ring roads to skirt the congestion. Follow signs to the parking lots outside the city core—most are a 5- to 10-minute walk to the center—and avoid what can be an unpleasant grid of one-way streets (as in Bath) or roads that are restricted to public transportation during the day.

Driving in Rural Areas: Outside the big cities and except for the motorways, British roads tend to be narrow. In towns, you may have to cross over the center line just to get past parked cars. Adjust your perceptions of personal space: It's not "my side of the road" or "your side of the road," it's just "the road"—and it's shared as a cooperative adventure. If the road's wide enough, traffic in both directions  can pass parked cars simultaneously, but frequently you'll have to take turns—follow the locals' lead and drive defensively.

Narrow country lanes are often lined with stone walls or woody hedges—and no shoulders. Some are barely wide enough for one car. Go slowly, and if you encounter an oncoming car, look for the nearest pullout (or "passing place")—the driver who's closest to one is expected to use it, even if it means backing up to reach it. If another car pulls over and blinks its headlights, that means, "Go ahead; I'll wait to let you pass." British drivers—arguably the most

PRACTICALITIES

courteous on the planet—are quick to offer a friendly wave to thank you for letting them pass (and they appreciate it if you reciprocate). Pull over frequently—to let faster locals pass and to check the map.

Parking: Pay attention to pavement markings to figure out where to park. One yellow line marked on the pavement means no parking Monday through Saturday during work hours. Double yellow lines mean no parking at any time. Broken yellow lines mean short stops are OK, but you should always look for explicit signs or ask a passerby. White lines mean you're free to park.

In towns, rather than look for street parking, I generally just pull into the most central and handy pay-and-display parking lot I can find. To pay and display, feed change into a machine, receive a timed ticket, and display it on the dashboard or stick it to the driver's-side window. Rates are reasonable by US standards, and locals love to share stickers that have time remaining. If you stand by the machine, someone on their way out with time left on their sticker will probably give it to you. Most machines in larger towns accept credit cards with a chip, but it's smart to keep coins handy for machines that don't.

In some municipalities, drivers will see signs for "disc zone" parking. This is free, time-limited parking. But to use it, you must obtain a clock parking disc from a shop and display it on the dashboard (set the clock to show your time of arrival). Return within the signed time limit to avoid being ticketed.

Some parking garages (a.k.a. car parks) are totally automated and record your license plate with a camera when you enter. The Brits call a license plate a "number plate" or just "vehicle registration." The payment machine will use these terms when you pay before exiting.

TAXIS AND UBER

Most British taxis are reliable and cheap. In many cities, couples can travel short distances by cab for little more than two bus or subway tickets. Taxis can be your best option for getting to the airport for an early morning flight or to connect two far-flung destinations. Ride-booking services like Uber usually work in Britain just like they do in the US: You request a car on your mobile device and the fare is automatically charged to your credit card. London's Uber is facing a legal challenge; check ahead to confirm it is operating.

FLIGHTS

The best comparison search engine for both international and intra-European flights is Kayak.com. An alternative is Google Flights, which has an easy-to-use system to track prices. For inexpensive flights within Europe, try Skyscanner.com.

Flying to Europe: Start looking for international flights about four to six months before your trip, especially for peak-season travel. Off-season tickets can usually be purchased a month or so in advance. Depending on your itinerary, it can be efficient to fly into one city and out of another. If your flight requires a connection in Europe, see my hints on navigating Europe's top hub airports at www.ricksteves.com/hub-airports.

Flying Within Europe: Several cheap, no-frills airlines affordably connect Britain with other destinations in the British Isles and throughout Europe. If you're considering a train ride that's more than five hours long, a flight may save you both time and money. When comparing your options, factor in the time it takes to get to the airport and how early you'll need to arrive to check in.

Well-known cheapo airlines include easyJet and Ryanair. **EasyJet** flies from London (Gatwick, Luton, Stansted, and Southend), Liverpool, Edinburgh, Glasgow, and Inverness. **Ryanair** flies from London (mostly from Stansted, as well as Gatwick and Luton), Liverpool, Edinburgh, and Glasgow. Other airlines to consider include **CityJet** (based at London City Airport), **TUI Airways, Flybe,** and **Brussels Airlines** (with frequent connections from Heathrow, Bristol, Birmingham, and Manchester to its Brussels hub).

But be aware of the potential drawbacks of flying with a discount airline: nonrefundable and nonchangeable tickets, minimal or nonexistent customer service, pricey and time-consuming treks to secondary airports, and stingy baggage allowances with steep overage fees. If you're traveling with lots of luggage, a cheap flight can quickly become a bad deal. To avoid unpleasant surprises, read the small print before you book. These days you can also fly within Europe on major airlines affordably—and without all the aggressive restrictions—for around $100 a flight.

Flying to the US and Canada: Because security is extra tight for flights to the US, be sure to give yourself plenty of time at the airport. It's also important to charge your electronic devices before you board because security checks may require you to turn them on (see www.tsa.gov for the latest rules).

Resources from Rick Steves

Begin your trip at www.ricksteves.com: My mobile-friendly **website** is *the* place to explore Europe. You'll find thousands of fun articles, videos, photos, and radio interviews organized by country; a wealth of money-saving tips for planning your dream trip; monthly travel news dispatches; a practical video library of my travel talks; my travel blog; and my latest guidebook updates (www.ricksteves.com/update).

Our **Travel Forum** is an immense, yet well-groomed collec-

PRACTICALITIES

tion of message boards, where our travel-savvy community answers questions and shares their personal travel experiences—and our well-traveled staff chimes in when they can be helpful (www.ricksteves.com/forums).

Our **online Travel Store** offers travel bags and accessories that I've designed specifically to help you travel smarter and lighter. These include my popular carry-on bags (which I live out of four months a year), money belts, totes, toiletries kits, adapters, other accessories, and a wide selection of guidebooks and planning maps (www.ricksteves.com/shop).

Choosing the right **rail pass** for your trip—amid hundreds of options—can drive you nutty. Our website will help you find the perfect fit for your itinerary and your budget: We offer easy, one-stop shopping for rail passes, seat reservations, and point-to-point tickets (www.ricksteves.com/rail).

Small Group Tours: Want to travel with greater efficiency and less stress? We offer more than 40 itineraries and have over 900 departures annually reaching the best destinations in this book...and beyond. We cover the best of Britain with our seven-day in-depth London city tour, our 14-day England tour, our 13-day South England tour, our 10-day Scotland tour, and our 13-day Family Europe: London to Florence tour. You'll enjoy great guides, a fun bunch of travel partners (with small groups of 24 to 28 travelers), and plenty of room to spread out in a big, comfy bus when touring between towns. You'll find European adventures to fit every vacation length. For all the details, and to get our Tour Catalog, visit www.ricksteves.com or call us at 425/608-4217.

Books: *Rick Steves Great Britain* is one of many books in my series on European travel, which includes country and regional guidebooks (including Scotland and England), city guidebooks, Snapshot guidebooks (excerpted chapters from my country guides), Pocket guidebooks (full-color little books on big cities, including London), "Best Of" guidebooks (condensed country guides in a full-color, easy-to-scan format), and my budget-travel skills handbook, *Rick Steves Europe Through the Back Door*. Most of my titles are available as ebooks.

My phrase books—for Italian, French, German, Spanish, and Portuguese—are practical and budget-oriented. My other books include *Europe 101* (a crash course on art and history designed for travelers); *Mediterranean Cruise Ports* and *Scandinavian & Northern European Cruise Ports* (how to make the most of your time in port); and *Travel as a Political Act* (a travelogue sprinkled with tips for bringing home a global perspective). A more complete list of my titles appears near the end of this book.

TV Shows: My public television series, *Rick Steves' Europe*, covers Europe from top to bottom with over 100 half-hour episodes, and we're working on new shows every year. We have 11 episodes on Britain—that's over five hours of vivid video coverage of one of my favorite countries. To watch full episodes online for free, see www.ricksteves.com/tv.

Travel Talks on Video: You can raise your travel I.Q. with video versions of our popular classes (including talks on travel skills, packing smart, cruising, tech for travelers, European art for travelers, travel as a political act, and individual talks covering most European countries). See www.ricksteves.com/travel-talks.

Radio: My weekly public radio show, *Travel with Rick Steves*, features interviews with travel experts from around the world. It airs on 400 public radio stations across the US, and you can also listen to it as a podcast on iTunes, iHeartRadio, Stitcher, Tune In, and other platforms. A complete archive of programs (over 400 in all) is available at www.soundcloud.com/rick-steves.

Audio Tours on My Free App: I've also produced dozens of free, self-guided audio tours of the top sights in Europe, including sights in London and Edinburgh. My audio tours and other audio content are available for free through my **Rick Steves Audio Europe app,** an extensive online library organized  into handy geographic playlists. For more on my app, see page 30.

APPENDIX

Useful Contacts

Emergency Needs

Police, Fire, and Ambulance: Tel. 112 (Europe-wide in English)

Police and Ambulance in UK: Tel. 999

US Consulate and Embassy in London: Tel. 020/7499-9000 (all services), no walk-in passport services; for emergency two-day passport service, schedule an appointment or fill out the online Emergency Passport Contact Form; 24 Grosvenor Square, Tube: Bond Street, https://uk.usembassy.gov

High Commission of Canada in London: Tel. 020/7004-6000, passport services available Mon-Fri 9:30-12:30, Canada House, Trafalgar Square, Tube: Charing Cross, www.unitedkingdom.gc.ca

US Consulate in Edinburgh: Tel. 0131/556-8315, after-hours tel. 020/7499-9000, no walk-in passport services; Mon-Fri 8:30-17:00, closed Sat-Sun; 3 Regent Terrace, https://uk.usembassy.gov/embassy-consulates/edinburgh

Canadian Consulate in Edinburgh: Mobile 0770-235-9916 (business hours); after hours call the High Commission of Canada in London (see earlier)

Holidays and Festivals

This list includes selected festivals in Britain plus national holidays observed throughout Britain. Many sights and banks close on national holidays—keep this in mind when planning your itinerary. Before planning a trip around a festival, verify the dates with the festival website, the Visit Britain website (www.visitbritain.com), local tourist office, or my "Upcoming European Holidays and Festivals" web page (www.ricksteves.com/europe/festivals).

Throughout Britain, hotels get booked up during Easter week; over Early May, Spring, and Summer Bank Holidays; and during Christmas, Boxing Day, and New Year's Day. On Christmas, virtually everything shuts down, even the Tube in London. Museums also generally close December 24 and 26.

Many British towns have holiday festivals in late November and early December, with markets, music, and entertainment in the Christmas spirit (for instance, Keswick's Victorian Fayre).

Throughout the summer, communities small and large across Scotland host their annual Highland Games (like a combination track meet/county fair)—a wonderful way to get in touch with local culture and traditions. For more on the Highland Games, see page 918.

Jan 1	New Year's Day
Jan 2	New Year's Holiday (closures)
Jan 25	Burns Night, Scotland (poetry readings, haggis)
Mid-Feb	London Fashion Week (www.londonfashionweek.co.uk)
Mid-Feb	Jorvik Viking Festival, York (costumed warriors, battles; www.jorvik-viking-festival.co.uk)
Late Feb-Early March	Literature Festival, Bath (www.bathlitfest.org.uk)
April	Easter Sunday-Monday: April 1-2 in 2018, April 21-22 in 2019
May	Early May Bank Holiday: May 7, 2018; May 6, 2019; Spring Bank Holiday: May 28, 2018; May 27, 2019
Early-mid-May	Jazz Festival, Keswick (www.keswickjazzfestival.co.uk)
Late May	Chelsea Flower Show, London (www.rhs.org.uk/chelsea)
Late May-early June	International Music Festival, Bath (www.bathmusicfest.org.uk)
Late May-early June	Fringe Festival, Bath (alternative music, dance, and theater; www.bathfringe.co.uk)

June	Edinburgh International Film Festival (www.edfilmfest.org.uk)
Early June	Beer Festival, Keswick (music, shows; www.keswickbeerfestival.co.uk)
Early-mid June	Trooping the Colour, London (military bands and pageantry, Queen's birthday parade; https://qbp.army.mod.uk)
Mid-June	Royal Highland Show, Edinburgh (Scottish-flavored county fair, www.royalhighlandshow.org)
Late June	Royal Ascot Horse Race, Ascot (near Windsor; www.ascot.co.uk)
Late June–mid-July	Wimbledon Tennis Championship, London (www.wimbledon.org)
July	Edinburgh Jazz and Blues Festival (www.edinburghjazzfestival.com)
Mid-July	Early Music Festival, York (www.ncem.co.uk)
Late July–early Aug	Cambridge Folk Festival (www.cambridgefolkfestival.co.uk)
Early Aug	Summer Bank Holiday (Scotland): August 6, 2018; August 5, 2019
Aug	Edinburgh Military Tattoo (massing of military bands, www.edintattoo.co.uk)
Aug	Edinburgh Fringe Festival (offbeat theater and comedy, www.edfringe.com)
Aug	Edinburgh International Festival (music, dance, shows; www.eif.co.uk)
Late Aug	Notting Hill Carnival, London (costumes, Caribbean music, www.thelondonnottinghillcarnival.com)
Late Aug	Bank Holiday (England and Wales): Aug 27 in 2018, Aug 26 in 2019
Mid-Sept	London Fashion Week (www.londonfashionweek.co.uk)
Mid-Late Sept	Jane Austen Festival, Bath (www.janeausten.co.uk)
Late Sept	York Food and Drink Festival (www.yorkfoodfestival.com)
Nov 5	Bonfire Night (fireworks, bonfires, effigy-burning of 1605 traitor Guy Fawkes)
Dec	St. Andrew's Day Bank Holiday (Scotland): Dec. 2, 2019 only
Dec 24-26	Christmas holidays

Books and Films

To learn more about Britain past and present, check out a few of these books and films.

Nonfiction

All Creatures Great and Small (James Herriot, 1972). Herriot's beloved semi-autobiographical tales of life as a Yorkshire veterinarian were made into a long-running BBC series (1978-1990).

The Anglo Files: A Field Guide to the British (Sarah Lyall, 2008). A *New York Times* reporter in London wittily recounts the eccentricities of life in the UK.

Cider with Rosie (Laurie Lee, 1959). This semi-autobiographical boyhood novel set in a Cotswolds village just after World War I has been adapted for TV three times, including by the BBC in 2015.

Crowded with Genius (James Buchan, 2003). This account of Edinburgh's role in the Scottish Enlightenment details the city's transformation from squalid backwater to marvelous European capital.

Dead Wake (Erik Larson, 2015). Larson gives an evocative account of the doomed 1915 voyage of British luxury liner *Lusitania,* sunk by a German U-boat during World War I.

Edinburgh: Picturesque Notes (Robert Louis Stevenson, 1879). One of the city's most famous residents takes readers on a tour of his hometown.

The Emperor's New Kilt (Jan-Andrew Henderson, 2000). Henderson deconstructs the myths surrounding the tartan-clad Scots.

England: 1000 Things You Need To Know (Nicolas Hobbes, 2009). Hobbes presents a fun peep into the facts, fables, and foibles of English life.

Fever Pitch (Nick Hornby, 1992). Hornby's memoir illuminates the British obsession with soccer.

A History of Britain (Simon Schama, 2000-2002). The respected historian presents a comprehensive, thoroughly-readable three-volume collection.

A History of Modern Britain (Andrew Marr, 2007). This searching look at the transformations in British life over the last few decades accompanies a BBC documentary series of the same name.

A History of Wales (John Davies, revised 2007). This insightful history tells the story of Wales from the Ice Age to the present.

How England Made the English: From Hedgerows to Heathrow (Harry Mount, 2012). Mount offers a witty, engaging look at the symbiotic relationship between the English landscape and English culture.

How the Scots Invented the Modern World (Arthur Herman, 2001). The author explains the disproportionately large influence the Scottish Enlightenment had on the rest of Europe.

The Kingdom by the Sea: A Journey Around the Coast of Great Britain (Paul Theroux, 1983). After 11 years as an American expatriate in London, travel writer Theroux takes a witty tour of his adopted homeland.

A Land (Jacquetta Hawkes, 1951). This postwar bestseller is a sweeping, poetic natural history of the British landscape and imagination.

The Last Lion (William Manchester, final book completed by Paul Reid; 1983, 1988, and 2012). This superb three-volume biography recounts the amazing life of Winston Churchill from 1874 to 1965.

Literary Trails (Christina Hardyment, 2000). Hardyment reunites famous authors with the environments that inspired them.

The Matter of Wales (Jan Morris, 1985). The half-English, half-Welsh author reveals the mysteries and joys of life in Wales.

My Love Affair with England (Susan Allen Toth, 1994). Toth brings England vividly to life in a captivating traveler's memoir recalling the country's charms and eccentricities.

Notes from a Small Island (Bill Bryson, 1995). In this irreverent and delightful memoir, US expat Bryson writes about his travels through Britain—his home for two decades.

This Little Britain: How One Small Country Changed the Modern World (Harry Bingham, 2007). Bingham offers an informative, entertaining review of Great Britain's contributions to world history.

A Traveller's History of England (Christopher Daniell, revised 2005). A British archaeologist and historian provides a comprehensive yet succinct overview of English history.

A Traveller's History of Scotland (Andrew Fisher, revised 2009). Fisher probes Scotland's turbulent history, beginning with the Celts.

With Wings Like Eagles (Michael Korda, 2009). An English-born writer gives a historical analysis of Britain's pivotal WWII air battles versus the German Luftwaffe.

Fiction

For the classics of British drama and fiction, read anything—and everything—by William Shakespeare, Charles Dickens, Jane Austen, and the Brontës.

Atonement (Ian McEwan, 2001). This disquieting family saga set in upper-class England at the start of World War II dramatizes the consequences of a childhood lie. The 2007 motion picture starring James McAvoy and Keira Knightley is also excellent.

Behind the Scenes at the Museum (Kate Atkinson, 1995). Starting at her conception, this book's quirky narrator recounts the highs and lows of life in a middle-class English family.

Brideshead Revisited (Evelyn Waugh, 1945). This celebrated novel examines the intense entanglement of a young man with an aristocratic family.

Bridget Jones's Diary (Helen Fielding, 1996). A year in the life of a single, 30-something woman in London is humorously chronicled in diary form (also a motion picture).

Complete Poems and Songs of Robert Burns (Robert Burns, 2012, featuring work from 1774–1796). This collection showcases the work of a Scottish icon who wrote in the Scots language, including that New Year's classic "Auld Lang Syne."

The Heart of Midlothian (Sir Walter Scott, 1818). This novel from one of Great Britain's most renowned authors showcases the life-and-death drama of lynchings and criminal justice in 1730s Scotland. Other great reads by Sir Walter include *Waverley* (1814, described later), *Rob Roy* (1818), and *Ivanhoe* (1819).

Here Be Dragons (Sharon Kay Penman, 1985). The author melds history and fiction to bring 13th-century Wales vividly to life (first in a trilogy).

High Fidelity (Nick Hornby, 1995). This humorous novel traces the romantic misadventures and musical musings of a 30-something record-store owner. Another good read is Hornby's 1998 coming-of-age story, *About a Boy.* (Both books were also made into films.)

Knots and Crosses (Ian Rankin, 1987). The Scottish writer's first Inspector Rebus mystery plumbs Edinburgh's seamy underbelly.

Macbeth (William Shakespeare, 1606). Shakespeare's "Scottish Play" depicts a guilt-wracked general who assassinates the king to take the throne.

Mapp and Lucia (E. F. Benson, 1931). A rural village in the 1930s becomes a social battlefield. In *Lucia in London* (1927), the protagonist attempts social climbing in the big city.

A Morbid Taste for Bones (Ellis Peters, 1977). Brother Cadfael, a Benedictine monk-detective, tries to solve a murder in 12th-century Shropshire (first book in a series; also adapted for British TV in 1996).

The Murder at the Vicarage (Agatha Christie, 1930). The prolific mystery writer's inquisitive Miss Marple character is first introduced in this book.

Outlander (Diana Gabaldon, 1991). This genre-defying series kicks off with the heroine time-traveling from the Scotland of 1945 to 1743. A popular TV adaptation began airing in 2014.

The Paying Guests (Sarah Waters, 2014). This realistic and suspenseful tale of love, obsession, and murder plays out amid the shifting culture of post-WWII upper-class London.

The Pillars of the Earth (Ken Follett, 1990). This epic set in a fictional town in 12th-century England chronicles the birth of Gothic architecture.

The Prime of Miss Jean Brodie (Muriel Spark, 1961). The story of an unconventional young teacher who plays favorites with her students is a modern classic of Scottish literature. (The film adaptation from 1969 stars Maggie Smith.)

Pygmalion (George Bernard Shaw, 1913). This stage play, on which the famous film *My Fair Lady* is based, tells the story of a young Cockney girl groomed for high society.

Rebecca (Daphne du Maurier, 1938). This mysterious tale set on the Cornish Coast examines upper-class English lives and their secrets.

Restoration (Rose Tremain, 1989). This evocative historical novel takes readers to the heights and depths of 17th-century English society.

The Strange Case of Dr. Jekyll and Mr. Hyde (Robert Louis Stevenson, 1886). This famous Gothic yarn by a Scottish author chronicles a fearful case of transformation in London, exploring Victorian ideas about conflict between good and evil.

SS-GB (Len Deighton, 1979). In a Nazi-occupied Great Britain, a Scotland Yard detective finds there's more to a murder than meets the eye.

A Study in Scarlet (Sir Arthur Conan Doyle, 1888). The mystery novel that introduced the world to detective Sherlock Holmes and his trusty sidekick, Dr. Watson.

The Sunne in Splendour (Sharon Kay Penman, 2008). Penman's big entertaining book paints King Richard III as a rather decent chap (one in a series of historical novels).

Sunset Song (Lewis Grassic Gibbon, 1932). Farm girl Chris Guthrie is rudely confronted by adolescence, modernity, and war in this lauded Scottish classic, the first book in the trilogy "A Scots Quair."

The Warden (Anthony Trollope, 1855). The first novel in the "Chronicles of Barsetshire" series addresses moral dilemmas in the 19th-century Anglican church.

Waverley (Sir Walter Scott, 1814). Idealistic young soldier Edward Waverley gets ensnared by the intrigues of the 1745 Jacobite uprising, which aimed to bring back the Stuart dynasty.

White Teeth (Zadie Smith, 2000). The postwar lives of two army buddies—a native Englishman and a Bengali Muslim—are chronicled in this acclaimed debut novel.

Wolf Hall (Hilary Mantel, 2010). At the intrigue-laced Tudor court of Henry VIII, Thomas Cromwell becomes the king's right-hand man. The story continues in *Bring Up the Bodies* (2012) and concludes in *The Mirror and the Light* (to be published in 2019).

Film and TV

Alfie (1966). In 1960s London, a womanizer (Michael Caine) eventually must face up to his boorish behavior (also a 2004 remake with Jude Law). Other "swinging London" films include *Blow-up* (1966) and *Georgy Girl* (1966).

Austin Powers: International Man of Mystery (1997). Mike Myers stars in this loony send-up of mid-century English culture and James Bond, the first film in a three-part series.

Battle of Britain (1969). An all-star cast and marvelous aerial combat scenes tell the story of Britain's "finest hour" of World War II.

Bend It Like Beckham (2003). A teenage girl of Punjabi descent plays soccer against her traditional parents' wishes in this lighthearted comedy-drama.

Billy Elliot (2000). A young boy pursues his dream to dance ballet amid a coal miners' strike in working-class northern England.

Blackadder (1983-1989). This wickedly funny BBC sitcom starring Rowan Atkinson skewers various periods of English history in the course of four series (also several TV specials).

Braveheart (1995). Mel Gibson stars in this Academy Award-winning adventure about the Scots overthrowing English rule in the 13th century.

Call the Midwife (2012-). London's poor East End comes to gritty, poignant life in this BBC drama tracing the lives of a team of nurse midwives in the late 1950s and early 1960s.

Chariots of Fire (1981). This Academy Award winner traces the lives of two British track stars competing in the 1924 Paris Olympics.

The Crown (2016-). Claire Foy stars as Elizabeth II in the Netflix biographical drama exploring the life of England's longest-reigning queen.

Doc Martin (2004-). A brilliant but socially inept London surgeon finds new challenges and opportunities when he opens a practice in a seaside village in Cornwall.

Downton Abbey (2010-2015). This popular aristocratic soap opera follows the travails of the Crawley family and their servants in early 20th-century Yorkshire (shot at Highclere Castle, about 70 miles west of London).

The Elephant Man (1980). A severely disfigured man reveals his sensitive soul in this stark portrayal of Victorian London.

Elizabeth (1998). Cate Blanchett portrays Queen Elizabeth I as she learns the royal ropes during the early years of her reign, and reprises her role in the sequel, *Elizabeth: The Golden Age* (2007).

Elizabeth I (2005). In this BBC/HBO miniseries, the inimitable Helen Mirren chronicles the queen's later years with a focus on her court's intrigue and her yearning for love.

The Englishman Who Went up a Hill but Came down a Mountain (1995). Starring Hugh Grant and scored with a Welsh choir, this heartwarming, somewhat-true tale of two cartographers who arrive in a Welsh village in 1917 focuses mainly on what makes the Welsh so different from the English.

Foyle's War (2002-2015). This fine BBC series follows detective Christopher Foyle as he solves crimes in southern England during and shortly after World War II.

Goodbye, Mr. Chips (1939). A long-serving schoolmaster at a boys' boarding school in Victorian-era England recalls his life in this romantic drama.

Gosford Park (2001). This intriguing film is part comedy, part murder mystery, and part critique of England's class stratification in the 1930s.

A Hard Day's Night (1964). The Beatles star in their debut film, a comedy depicting several days in the life of the band.

Highlander (1986). An immortal swordsman remembers his life in 16th-century Scotland while preparing for a pivotal battle in the present day.

A History of Scotland (2010). This BBC series presented by Neil Oliver offers a succinct, lightly dramatized retelling of Scottish history.

Hope and Glory (1987). John Boorman directed this semi-autobiographical story of a boy growing up during World War II's London blitz.

How Green Was My Valley (1941). Director John Ford's Academy Award winner chronicles the lives of a 19th-century Welsh coal-mining family.

Howards End (1992). This Academy Award winner, based on the E. M. Forster novel, captures the stifling societal pressure underneath the gracious manners in turn-of-the-century England.

The Imitation Game (2014). Cryptanalyst Alan Turing (Benedict Cumberbatch) is recruited by British intelligence agency MI6 to help crack the Nazis' Enigma code during World War II.

James Bond films (1962-). These classic films follow a dashing officer in Britain's Secret Intelligence Service, who likes his martinis "shaken, not stirred."

Jane Eyre (2011). Charlotte Brontë's 1847 gothic romance has been made into a movie at least nine times, most recently this one starring Mia Wasikowska and Michael Fassbender.

The King's Speech (2010). Colin Firth stars as the stuttering King George VI on the eve of World War II.

Lark Rise to Candleford (2008-2011). Based on Flora Thompson's memoirs, this evocative series chronicles life in a poor Victorian-era hamlet and its neighboring, more hoity market town.

A Man for All Seasons (1966). Lord Chancellor Sir Thomas More incurs the wrath of Henry VIII when he refuses to help annul the king's marriage to Catherine of Aragon.

Mary, Queen of Scots (2018). Saoirse Ronan stars in this portrayal of Mary upon her return to Scotland (from France) and her complicated relationship with cousin Elizabeth I. (A 1971 movie of the same name stars Vanessa Redgrave and Glenda Jackson.)

Mr. Bean (1990-1995). Rubber-faced comedian Rowan Atkinson's iconic character bumbles through life barely uttering a word in this zany sitcom (that also spawned two motion pictures).

Monarch of the Glen (2000). Set on Loch Laggan, this TV series features stunning Highland scenery and the eccentric family of a modern-day laird.

Monty Python and the Holy Grail (1975). This surreal take on Arthurian legend is a classic of British comedy.

Mrs. Brown (1997). A widowed Queen Victoria (Dame Judy Dench) forges a very close friendship with her Scottish servant, John Brown (Billy Connolly).

My Fair Lady (1964). Audrey Hepburn stars as a poor Cockney flower seller who is transformed into a lady of high society by an arrogant professor.

Notting Hill (1999). Hugh Grant and Julia Roberts star in this romantic comedy set in the London neighborhood of...you guessed it.

Persuasion (1995). Set in 19th-century England, this Jane Austen tale of status was partially filmed in Bath.

Poldark (2015-). In this hit BBC series, Ross Poldark returns to Cornwall after fighting in the Revolutionary War to find his estate, tin mines, and relationship in ruins.

Pride and Prejudice (1995). Of the many versions of Jane Austen's classic, this BBC miniseries starring Colin Firth is the winner.

The Queen (2006). Helen Mirren expertly channels Elizabeth II at her Scottish Balmoral estate in the days after Princess Diana's death. Its prequel, *The Deal* (2003), probes the relationship between Tony Blair and Gordon Brown.

The Remains of the Day (1993). Anthony Hopkins stars as a butler doggedly loyal to his misguided, politically-naive master in 1930s England.

Rob Roy (1995). The Scottish rebel struggles against feudal landlords in 18th-century Scotland.

Sammy and Rosie Get Laid (1987). An unconventional middle-class couple's promiscuous adventures expose racial tensions in multiethnic London.

Sense and Sensibility (1995). Star Emma Thompson wrote the screenplay for this adaptation of Jane Austen's 1811 novel of the Dashwood sisters, who seek financial security through marriage.

Shakespeare in Love (1999). Tudor-era London comes to life in this clever romantic film set in the original Globe Theatre.

Sherlock (2010-). Holmes (Benedict Cumberbatch) and Watson (Martin Freeman) are excellent in this BBC update of the detective's story, set in present-day London—but mainly filmed in Cardiff.

Sherlock Holmes (2009). Robert Downey Jr. tackles the role of the world's most famous detective.

Sweeney Todd (2007). Johnny Depp stars as a wrongfully imprisoned barber who seeks revenge in this gritty Victorian-era musical.

Tinker, Tailor, Soldier, Spy (2011). There's a Soviet mole inside Britain's MI6 and retired agent George Smiley is summoned to ferret him out in this adaptation of John le Carré's 1974 espionage thriller.

To Sir, with Love (1967). Sidney Poitier grapples with social and racial issues in an inner-city school in London's East End.

The Tudors (2007-2010). Showtime's racy, lavish series is a gripping loosely-accurate chronicle of the marriages of Henry VIII.

Upstairs, Downstairs (1971-1975). An aristocratic family and their servants make a new home at 165 Eaton Place in this TV series.

Waterloo Bridge (1940). This Academy Award-nominated romantic drama recalls the lost love between a ballerina (Vivien Leigh) and a WWI army officer.

Wolf Hall (2015). The exploits of Thomas Cromwell, the chief minister to King Henry VIII, are detailed in this excellent BBC historical miniseries.

Victoria (2017-). This PBS Masterpiece Theatre series chronicles the rise and reign of Queen Victoria (Jenna Coleman).

For Kids

A Bear Called Paddington (Michael Bond, 1958). A bear from Peru winds up in a London train station, where he's found and adopted by a human family. The 2014 *Paddington* film is also fun viewing.

An Illustrated Treasury of Scottish Folk and Fairy Tales (Theresa Breslin, 2012). Kelpies, dragons, brownies, and other inhabitants of the Scottish Isles come to life in this lovely volume of traditional lore.

Brave (2012). This Disney flick follows an independent young Scottish princess as she fights to take control of her own fate.

The Chronicles of Narnia books (C.S. Lewis, 1950-1956) and movies (2005-2010). Four siblings escape from WWII London into a magical world. The first of the seven novels, *The Lion, the Witch & the Wardrobe,* was also a BBC miniseries (1988).

Harry Potter books (J. K. Rowling, 1997-2007) and films (2001-2011). After discovering he's a wizard, a young boy in England gets whisked off to a magical world of witchcraft and wizardry. There he finds great friendships as well as grave evils, which he alone can destroy. (See page 1024 for a list of *Harry Potter* sights in Great Britain.)

Kidnapped (Robert Louis Stevenson, 1886). This fantastic adventure story is based on events in 18th-century Scotland.

A Little Princess (1995). In this film adaptation of the classic novel, a young girl's fortunes fall and rise again in a Victorian London boarding school.

Mary Poppins (1964). Though filmed on a set in California, this beloved musical starring Julie Andrews and Dick Van Dyke is set in Edwardian London. In the sequel, *Mary Poppins Returns* (2018), the kids are grown and revisited by Mary (Emily Blunt) and her friend Jack (Lin-Manuel Miranda).

Peter Pan (2003). The latest in a long line of films adapting the classic 1902 novel *Peter and Wendy,* this live-action version flies real English children to Neverland.

The Secret Garden (Frances Hodgson Burnett, 1911). Orphaned Mary discovers nature and love in a gloomy Yorkshire mansion on the edge of a moor in this beloved classic, which has been adapted for stage and screen.

The Story of Britain from the Norman Conquest to the European Union (Patrick Dillon, 2011). Studious older children will get a healthy dose of history from this elegant, illustrated volume.

This Is Britain (Miroslav Sasek, 1962, updated 2008). Vivid illustrations bring the British Isles to life in this classic picture book.

Wallace & Gromit TV series and films (1990-2012). Absent-minded inventor Wallace and his dog Gromit may live in northwest England, but these unique characters are beloved by children around Great Britain and the rest of the world.

Winnie-the-Pooh and *The House at Pooh Corner* (A. A. Milne, 1926-1928). This two-volume classic children's tale, set in England, revolves around a bear and his friends in the Hundred Acre Wood. The success of Milne's books has led to numerous book, film, and TV adaptations.

Young Sherlock Holmes (1985). A young Sherlock and his sidekick, Watson, work to solve the mystery of a series of nonsensical suicides (some scenes may be frightening for younger children).

Conversions and Climate

NUMBERS AND STUMBLERS
- Some British people write a few of their numbers differently than we do: 1 =1, 4 =4, 7 =7.
- In Europe, dates appear as day/month/year, so Christmas 2019 is 25/12/19.
- What Americans call the second floor of a building is the first floor in Britain.
- On escalators and moving sidewalks, Brits keep the left "lane" open for passing. Keep to the right.
- To avoid the British version of giving someone "the finger," don't hold up the first two fingers of your hand with your palm facing you. (It looks like a reversed victory sign.)
- And please...don't call your waist pack a "fanny" pack (see the British-Yankee Vocabulary list at the end of this appendix).

METRIC CONVERSIONS
Britain uses the metric system for nearly everything. Weight and volume are typically calculated in metric: A kilogram is 2.2 pounds, and one liter is about a quart (almost four to a gallon). Temperatures are generally given in Celsius.

1 foot = 0.3 meter	1 square yard = 0.8 square meter
1 yard = 0.9 meter	1 square mile = 2.6 square kilometers
1 mile = 1.6 kilometers	1 ounce = 28 grams
1 centimeter = 0.4 inch	1 quart = 0.95 liter
1 meter = 39.4 inches	1 kilogram = 2.2 pounds
1 kilometer = 0.62 mile	32°F = 0°C

IMPERIAL WEIGHTS AND MEASURES
Britain hasn't completely gone metric. Driving distances and speed limits are measured in miles. Beer is sold as pints (though milk can be measured in pints or liters), and a person's weight is measured in stone (a 168-pound person weighs 12 stone).

1 stone = 14 pounds
1 British pint = 1.2 US pints
1 imperial gallon = 1.2 US gallons or about 4.5 liters

CLOTHING SIZES

When shopping for clothing, use these US-to-Britain comparisons as general guidelines (but note that no conversion is perfect).

Women: For pants and dresses, add 4 (US 10 = UK 14). For blouses and sweaters, add 2. For shoes, subtract 2½ (US size 8 = UK size 5½)

Men: For clothing, US and UK sizes are the same. For shoes, subtract about ½ (US size 9 = UK size 8½)

BRITAIN'S CLIMATE

First line, average daily high; second line, average low; third line, average days without rain. For more detailed weather statistics for destinations in this book (and elsewhere), check www.wunderground.com.

	J	F	M	A	M	J	J	A	S	O	N	D
London												
	43°	44°	50°	56°	62°	69°	71°	71°	65°	58°	50°	45°
	36°	36°	38°	42°	47°	53°	56°	56°	52°	46°	42°	38°
	16	15	20	18	19	19	19	20	17	18	15	16
Cardiff (South Wales)												
	45°	45°	50°	56°	61°	68°	69°	69°	64°	58°	51°	46°
	35°	35°	38°	41°	46°	51°	54°	55°	51°	46°	41°	37°
	13	14	18	17	18	17	17	16	14	15	13	13
York												
	43°	44°	49°	55°	61°	67°	70°	69°	64°	57°	49°	45°
	33°	34°	36°	40°	44°	50°	54°	53°	50°	44°	39°	36°
	14	13	18	17	18	16	16	17	16	16	13	14
Edinburgh												
	42°	43°	46°	51°	56°	62°	65°	64°	60°	54°	48°	44°
	34°	34°	36°	39°	43°	49°	52°	52°	49°	44°	39°	36°
	14		13	16	16	17	15	14	15	14	14	13

Fahrenheit and Celsius Conversion

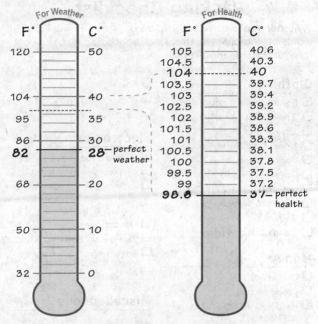

Europe takes its temperature using the Celsius scale, while we opt for Fahrenheit. For a rough conversion from Celsius to Fahrenheit, double the number and add 30. For weather, remember that 28°C is 82°F—perfect. For health, 37°C is just right. At a launderette, 30°C is cold, 40°C is warm (usually the default setting), 60°C is hot, and 95°C is boiling. Your air-conditioner should be set at about 20°C.

APPENDIX

Packing Checklist

Whether you're traveling for five days or five weeks, you won't need more than this. Pack light to enjoy the sweet freedom of true mobility.

Clothing

- ☐ 5 shirts: long- & short-sleeve
- ☐ 2 pairs pants (or skirts/capris)
- ☐ 1 pair shorts
- ☐ 5 pairs underwear & socks
- ☐ 1 pair walking shoes
- ☐ Sweater or warm layer
- ☐ Rainproof jacket with hood
- ☐ Tie, scarf, belt, and/or hat
- ☐ Swimsuit
- ☐ Sleepwear/loungewear

Money

- ☐ Debit card(s)
- ☐ Credit card(s)
- ☐ Hard cash ($100-200 in US dollars)
- ☐ Money belt

Documents

- ☐ Passport
- ☐ Tickets & confirmations: flights, hotels, trains, rail pass, car rental, sight entries
- ☐ Driver's license
- ☐ Student ID, hostel card, etc.
- ☐ Photocopies of important documents
- ☐ Insurance details
- ☐ Guidebooks & maps
- ☐ Notepad & pen
- ☐ Journal

Toiletries Kit

- ☐ Basics: soap, shampoo, toothbrush, toothpaste, floss, deodorant, sunscreen, brush/comb, etc.
- ☐ Medicines & vitamins
- ☐ First-aid kit
- ☐ Glasses/contacts/sunglasses

- ☐ Sewing kit
- ☐ Packet of tissues (for WC)
- ☐ Earplugs

Electronics

- ☐ Mobile phone
- ☐ Camera & related gear
- ☐ Tablet/ebook reader/media player
- ☐ Laptop & flash drive
- ☐ Headphones
- ☐ Chargers & batteries
- ☐ Smartphone car charger & mount (or GPS device)
- ☐ Plug adapters

Miscellaneous

- ☐ Daypack
- ☐ Sealable plastic baggies
- ☐ Laundry supplies: soap, laundry bag, clothesline, spot remover
- ☐ Small umbrella
- ☐ Travel alarm/watch

Optional Extras

- ☐ Second pair of shoes (flip-flops, sandals, tennis shoes, boots)
- ☐ Travel hairdryer
- ☐ Picnic supplies
- ☐ Water bottle
- ☐ Fold-up tote bag
- ☐ Small flashlight
- ☐ Mini binoculars
- ☐ Small towel or washcloth
- ☐ Inflatable pillow/neck rest
- ☐ Tiny lock
- ☐ Address list (to mail postcards)
- ☐ Extra passport photos

BRITISH-YANKEE VOCABULARY

For a longer list, plus a dry-witted primer on British culture, see *The Septic's Companion* (Chris Rae). Note that instead of asking, "Can I help you?" many Brits offer a more casual, "You alright?" or "You OK there?"

advert: advertisement

afters: dessert

Antipodean: an Australian or New Zealander

aubergine: eggplant

banger: sausage

bangers and mash: sausage and mashed potatoes

Bank Holiday: legal holiday

bap: small roll, roll sandwich

bespoke: custom-made

billion: a thousand of our billions (a million million)

biro: ballpoint pen

biscuit: cookie

black pudding: sausage made with onions, pork fat, oatmeal, and pig blood

bloody: damn

blow off: fart

bobby: policeman ("the Bill" is more common)

Bob's your uncle: there you go (with a shrug), naturally

boffin: nerd, geek

bollocks: all-purpose expletive (a figurative use of testicles)

bolshy: argumentative

bomb: success or failure

bonnet: car hood

boot: car trunk

braces: suspenders

bridle way: path for walkers, bikers, and horse riders

brilliant: cool

brolly: umbrella

bubble and squeak: cabbage and potatoes fried together

bum: butt

candy floss: cotton candy

caravan: trailer

car-boot sale: temporary flea market, often for charity

car park: parking lot

cashpoint: ATM

casualty: emergency room

cat's eyes: road reflectors

ceilidh (KAY-lee): informal evening of song and folk fun (Scottish and Irish)

cheap and cheerful: budget but adequate

cheap and nasty: cheap and bad quality

cheers: good-bye or thanks; also a toast

chemist: pharmacist

chicory: endive

Chinese whispers: playing "telephone"

chippy: fish-and-chips shop; carpenter

chips: French fries

chock-a-block: jam-packed

chuffed: pleased

chunter: mutter

clearway: road where you can't stop

coach: long-distance bus

concession: discounted admission (concs—pronounced "conks"—for short)

coronation chicken: curried chicken salad

cos: romaine lettuce

cot: baby crib

cotton buds: Q-tips

courgette: zucchini

craic (pronounced "crack"): fun, good conversation (Irish/Scottish and spreading to England)

crisps: potato chips

cuppa: cup of tea

dear: expensive

dicey: iffy, risky

digestives: round graham cookies

dinner: lunch or dinner

diversion: detour

dogsbody: menial worker

donkey's years: ages, long time

draughts: checkers

draw: marijuana

dual carriageway: divided highway (four lanes)

dummy: pacifier

elevenses: coffee-and-biscuits break before lunch

elvers: baby eels

face flannel: washcloth

fag: cigarette

fagged: exhausted

faggot: sausage

fancy: to like, to be attracted to (a person)

fanny: vagina

fell: hill or high plain (Lake District)

first floor: second floor

fiver: £5 bill

fizzy drink: pop or soda

flat: apartment

flutter: a bet

fly tipping: dumping garbage illegally

football: soccer

force: waterfall (Lake District)

fortnight: two weeks (shortened from "fourteen nights")

fringe: hair bangs

Frogs: French people

fruit machine: slot machine

full Monty: whole shebang, everything

gallery: balcony

gammon: ham

gangway: aisle

gaol: jail (same pronunciation)

gateau (or gateaux): cake

gear lever: stick shift

geezer: "dude"

give way: yield

goods wagon: freight truck

gormless: stupid

goujons: breaded and fried fish or chicken sticks

green fingers: green thumbs

grotty: unpleasant, lousy

half eight: 8:30 (not 7:30)

hard cheese: bad luck

heath: open treeless land

hen night (or **hen do**): bachelorette party

holiday: vacation

homely: homey or cozy

hoover: vacuum cleaner

ice lolly: Popsicle

interval: intermission

ironmonger: hardware store

ish: more or less

jacket potato: baked potato

jelly: Jell-O

jiggery-pokery: nonsense

Joe Bloggs: John Q. Public

jumble (sale): rummage sale

jumper: sweater

just a tick: just a second

kipper: smoked herring

kitchen roll: paper towels

knackered: exhausted (Cockney: cream crackered)

knickers: ladies' panties

knocking shop: brothel

knock up: wake up or visit (old-fashioned)

ladybird: ladybug

lady fingers: flat, spongy cookie

lady's finger: okra

lager: light, fizzy beer

lay-by: stopping place on road
left luggage: baggage check
lemonade: lemon-lime pop like 7-Up, fizzy
lemon squash: lemonade, not fizzy
let: rent
licensed: restaurant authorized to sell alcohol
lift: elevator
listed: protected historic building
loo: toilet or bathroom
lorry: truck
mack: mackintosh raincoat
made redundant: laid off
mangetout: snow peas
marrow: summer squash
mate: buddy (boy or girl)
mean: stingy
mental: wild, memorable
mews: former stables converted to two-story rowhouses
mobile (MOH-bile): cell phone
moggie: cat
motorway: freeway
naff: tacky or trashy
nappy: diaper
natter: talk on and on
newsagent: corner store
nought: zero
noughts & crosses: tic-tac-toe
off-licence: liquor store
on offer: for sale
on the pull: on the prowl
OTT: over the top, excessive
panto, pantomime: fairy-tale play performed at Christmas (silly but fun)
pants: (noun) underwear, briefs; (adj.) terrible, ridiculous
pasty (PASS-tee): crusted savory (usually meat) pastry from Cornwall

pavement: sidewalk
pear-shaped: messed up, gone wrong
petrol: gas
piccalilli: mustard-pickle relish
pillar box: mailbox
pissed (rude), **paralytic, bevvied, wellied, popped up, merry, trollied, ratted, rat-arsed, pissed as a newt:** drunk
pitch: playing field
plaster: Band-Aid
plonk: cheap, bad wine
plonker: one who drinks bad wine (a mild insult)
prat: idiot
press-on towel: panty liner
public school: private "prep" school (e.g., Eton)
publican: pub owner
pudding: dessert in general
pukka: first-class
punter: customer, especially in gambling
put a sock in it: shut up
queue (up): line (up)
quid: pound (£1)
randy: horny
rasher: slice of bacon
read: study, as a college major
Remembrance Day: Veterans' Day
return ticket: round trip
revising; doing revisions: studying for exams
ring up: call (telephone)
roundabout: traffic circle
rubber: eraser
rubbish: bad
satnav: satellite navigation, GPS
sausage roll: sausage wrapped in a flaky pastry

Scotch egg: hard-boiled egg wrapped in sausage meat

Scouser: a person from Liverpool

self-catering: accommodation with kitchen

Sellotape: Scotch tape

services: freeway rest area

serviette: napkin

setee: couch

shag: intercourse (cruder than in the US)

shambolic: chaotic

shandy: lager and 7-Up

silencer: car muffler

single ticket: one-way ticket

skip: dumpster

sleeping policeman: speed bumps

smalls: underwear

snap: photo (snapshot)

snogging: kissing, making out

sod: mildly offensive insult

sod it, sod off: screw it, screw off

sod's law: Murphy's law

soda: soda water (not pop)

soldiers (food): toast sticks for dipping

solicitor: lawyer

spanner: wrench

spend a penny: urinate

spotted dick: raisin cake with custard

stag night (or **stag do**): bachelor party

starkers: buck naked

starters: appetizers

state school: public school

sticking plaster: Band-Aid

sticky tape: Scotch tape

stone: 14 pounds (weight)

stroppy: bad-tempered

subway: underground walkway

sultanas: golden raisins

surgical spirit: rubbing alcohol

suspenders: garters

suss out: figure out

swede: rutabaga

ta: thank you

take the mickey/take the piss: tease

tatty: worn out or tacky

taxi rank: taxi stand

telly: TV

tenement: stone apartment house (not necessarily a slum)

tenner: £10 bill

theatre: live stage

throw shapes: dance to pop music

tick: check mark

tight as a fish's bum: cheapskate (watertight)

tights: panty hose

tin: can

tip: public dump

tipper lorry: dump truck

toad in the hole: sausage dipped in batter and fried

top hole: first rate

top up: refill (a drink, mobile-phone credit, petrol tank, etc.)

torch: flashlight

towpath: path along a river

trainers: sneakers

treacle: golden syrup

Tube: subway

twee: quaint, cutesy

twitcher: bird-watcher

Underground: subway

verge: grassy edge of road

verger: church official

way out: exit

wee (verb): urinate

Wellingtons, wellies: rubber boots

whacked: exhausted

whinge (rhymes with hinge): whine

wind up: tease, irritate
witter on: gab and gab
wonky: weird, askew
yob: hooligan

zebra crossing: crosswalk
zed: the letter Z

INDEX

INDEX

INDEX

INDEX

INDEX

MAP INDEX

Start your trip at

Our website enhances this book and turns

Explore Europe

At ricksteves.com you can browse through thousands of articles, videos, photos and radio interviews, plus find a wealth of money-saving travel tips for planning your dream trip. And with our mobile-friendly website, you can easily access all this great travel information anywhere you go.

TV Shows

Preview the places you'll visit by watching entire half-hour episodes of Rick Steves' Europe (choose from all 100 shows) on-demand, for free.

ricksteves.com

your travel dreams into affordable reality

Radio Interviews

Enjoy ready access to Rick's vast library of radio interviews covering travel

tips and cultural insights that relate specifically to your Europe travel plans.

Travel Forums

Learn, ask, share! Our online community of savvy travelers is a great resource for first-time travelers to Europe, as well as seasoned pros. You'll find forums on each country, plus travel tips and restaurant/hotel reviews. You can even ask one of our well-traveled staff to chime in with an opinion.

Travel News

Subscribe to our free Travel News e-newsletter, and get monthly updates from Rick on what's happening in Europe.

Audio Europe™

Rick's Free Travel App

Get your FREE **Rick Steves Audio Europe**™ app to enjoy...

- Dozens of self-guided tours of Europe's top museums, sights and historic walks
- Hundreds of tracks filled with cultural insights and sightseeing tips from Rick's radio interviews
- All organized into handy geographic playlists
- For Apple and Android

With Rick whispering in your ear, Europe gets even better.

Find out more at ricksteves.com

Rick Steves has

Experience maximum Europe

Save time and energy

This guidebook is your independent-travel toolkit. But for all it delivers, it's still up to you to devote the time and energy it takes to manage the preparation and logistics that are essential for a happy trip. If that's a hassle, there's a solution.

Rick Steves Tours

A Rick Steves tour takes you to Europe's most interesting places with great

great tours, too!

with minimum stress

guides and small groups of 28 or less. We follow Rick's favorite itineraries, ride in comfy buses, stay in family-run hotels, and bring you intimately close to the Europe you've traveled so far to see. Most importantly, we take away the logistical headaches so you can focus on the fun.

travelers—nearly half of them repeat customers— along with us on four dozen different itineraries, from Ireland to Italy to Athens. Is a Rick Steves tour the right fit for your travel dreams? Find out at ricksteves.com, where you can also request Rick's latest tour catalog. Europe is best experienced with happy travel partners. We hope you can join us.

Join the fun

This year we'll take thousands of free-spirited

See our itineraries at ricksteves.com

A Guide for Every Trip

BEST OF GUIDES

Full color easy-to-scan format, focusing on Europe's most popular destinations and sights.

Best of England
Best of Europe
Best of France
Best of Germany
Best of Ireland
Best of Italy
Best of Spain

COMPREHENSIVE GUIDES

City, country, and regional guides with detailed coverage for a multi-week trip exploring the most iconic sights and venturing off the beaten track.

Amsterdam & the Netherlands
Barcelona
Belgium: Bruges, Brussels,
  Antwerp & Ghent
Berlin
Budapest
Croatia & Slovenia
Eastern Europe
England
Florence & Tuscany
France
Germany
Great Britain
Greece: Athens & the Peloponnese
Iceland
Ireland
Istanbul
Italy
London
Paris
Portugal
Prague & the Czech Republic
Provence & the French Riviera
Rome
Scandinavia
Scotland
Spain
Switzerland
Venice
Vienna, Salzburg & Tirol

THE BEST OF ROME

me, Italy's capital, is studded with man remnants and floodlit-fountain ares. From the Vatican to the Colos-m, with crazy traffic in between, Rome onderful, huge, and exhausting. The ds, the heat, and the weighty history

of the Eternal City where Caesars walked can make tourists wilt. Recharge by taking siestas, gelato breaks, and after-dark walks, strolling from one atmospheric square to another in the refreshing evening air.

Rick Steves guidebooks are published by Avalon Travel, an imprint of Perseus Books, a Hachette Book Group company.

POCKET GUIDES

Compact, full color city guides with the essentials for shorter trips.

Amsterdam	Paris
Athens	Prague
Barcelona	Rome
Florence	Venice
Italy's Cinque Terre	Vienna
London	
Munich & Salzburg	

SNAPSHOT GUIDES

Focused single-destination coverage.

Basque Country: Spain & France
Copenhagen & the Best of Denmark
Dublin
Dubrovnik
Edinburgh
Hill Towns of Central Italy
Krakow, Warsaw & Gdansk
Lisbon
Loire Valley
Madrid & Toledo
Milan & the Italian Lakes District
Naples & the Amalfi Coast
Normandy
Northern Ireland
Norway
Reykjavík
Sevilla, Granada & Southern Spain
St. Petersburg, Helsinki & Tallinn
Stockholm

CRUISE PORTS GUIDES

Reference for cruise ports of call.

Mediterranean Cruise Ports
Scandinavian & Northern European
Cruise Ports

Complete your library with...

TRAVEL SKILLS & CULTURE

Study up on travel skills and gain insight on history and culture.

Europe 101
Europe Through the Back Door
European Christmas
European Easter
European Festivals
Postcards from Europe
Travel as a Political Act

PHRASE BOOKS & DICTIONARIES

French
French, Italian & German
German
Italian
Portuguese
Spanish

PLANNING MAPS

Britain, Ireland & London
Europe
France & Paris
Germany, Austria & Switzerland
Ireland
Italy
Spain & Portugal

Credits

RESEARCHERS
To help update this book, Rick relied on...

Ben Curtis

Ben is a native of the Pacific Northwest, but he's lived in the UK, Germany, Spain, Norway, Hungary, and a few other countries besides. He's worked as a professor of history and politics, a tour guide, and an advisor to the British government. These days, home is wherever he can go for a hike, listen to some Beethoven, and write.

Cameron Hewitt

Born in Denver and raised in central Ohio, Cameron settled in Seattle in 2000. Ever since, he has spent three months each year in Europe, contributing to guidebooks, tours, radio and television shows, and other media for Rick Steves' Europe, where he serves as content manager. Cameron married his high school sweetheart (and favorite travel partner), Shawna, and enjoys taking pictures, trying new restaurants, and planning his next trip.

Sandra Hundacker

Born and raised in Germany, Sandra developed a passion for travel when her parents took her to numerous countries throughout Europe. She later earned degrees in tourism and graphic design. Now living in Seattle, she works as a graphic content director for Rick Steves' Europe, and is happiest when she can share her travel experiences.

Cathy Lu

A researcher and editor at Rick Steves' Europe, Cathy feels very fortunate that she gets to travel and nitpick for a living. Originally from New Jersey, she now lives in Seattle, where she enjoys playing tennis, eating conveyor-belt sushi, engaging in late-night karaoke, and most of all, spending time outdoors with her (full-blooded Scottish) husband and daughter.

Carrie Shepherd

After a childhood spent traipsing around New England, Carrie's college semester in London spurred her to explore and travel as much as her budget and employers allowed. She's spent her career writing and editing arts and entertainment content, and now works as a guidebook editor and researcher for Rick Steves' Europe.

Robyn Stencil

Robyn credits the origin of her love affair with London to the Thames, supporting her motto "where there's a river, there's a run." Her ideal English adventure involves the call of gulls, plenty of flat whites, and friendly people from rocky coastline to green hills. When she's not researching, trapezing, or pursuing the perfect burger, Robyn calls Everett, Washington home and works as a tour product manager for Rick Steves' Europe.

CONTRIBUTOR
Gene Openshaw

Gene has co-authored a dozen *Rick Steves* books, specializing in writing walks and tours of Europe's cities, museums, and cultural sights. He also contributes to Rick's public television series, produces tours for Rick Steves Audio Europe, and is a regular guest on Rick's public radio show. Outside of the travel world, Gene has co-authored *The Seattle Joke Book.* As a composer, Gene has written a full-length opera called *Matter*, a violin sonata, and dozens of songs. He lives near Seattle with his daughter, enjoys giving presentations on art and history, and roots for the Mariners in good times and bad.

ACKNOWLEDGMENTS

Thanks to Roy and Jodi Nicholls for their research help, to Sarah Murdoch for writing the original version of the southern England chapters, to Jennifer Hauseman for the original version of the Glasgow chapter, to Colin Mairs for his help in Glasgow and throughout Scotland, and to friends listed in this book, who put the "Great" in Great Britain.

Avalon Travel
Hachette Book Group
1700 Fourth Street
Berkeley, CA 94710

Printed in Canada by Friesens
First printing May 2018

ISBN 978-1-63121-811-8

For the latest on Rick's talks, guidebooks, tours, public television series, and public radio show, contact Rick Steves' Europe, 130 Fourth Avenue North, Edmonds, WA 98020, 425/771-8303, www.ricksteves.com, rick@ricksteves.com.

Rick Steves' Europe
Managing Editor: Jennifer Madison Davis
Special Publications Manager: Risa Laib
Assistant Managing Editor: Cathy Lu
Editors: Glenn Eriksen, Julie Fanselow, Tom Griffin, Katherine Gustafson, Suzanne Kotz, Rosie Leutzinger, Carrie Shepherd
Editorial & Production Assistant: Jessica Shaw
Editorial Intern: Kevin Teeter
Contributors: Cameron Hewitt, Gene Openshaw
Researchers: Ben Curtis, Cameron Hewitt, Sandra Hundacker, Cathy Lu, Carrie Shepherd, Robyn Stencil
Graphic Content Director: Sandra Hundacker
Maps & Graphics: David C. Hoerlein, Lauren Mills, Mary Rostad

Avalon Travel
Senior Editor and Series Manager: Madhu Prasher
Editor: Jamie Andrade
Editor: Sierra Machado
Copy Editor: Kelly Lydick
Proofreader: Jamie Leigh Real
Indexer: Stephen Callahan
Cover Design: Kimberly Glyder Design
Maps & Graphics: Kat Bennett

Front Cover: Tintern Abbey, Wales © SIME/eStock Photo
Front Matter Color: Schoolboys © Dominic Arizona Bonuccelli
Additional Photography: Dominic Arizona Bonuccelli; p. 106, Lindisfarne Gospels © The British Library Board/CPA Media Co. Ltd; p. 124, Image State Alamy; p. 995, Horatio Nelson © The Granger Collection, New York; Cutty Sark Trust, Rich Earl, Barb Geisler, Tom Griffin, Jennifer Hauseman, Cameron Hewitt, David C. Hoerlein, Darbi Macy, Lauren Mills, Sarah Murdoch, Pat O'Connor, Gene Openshaw, Sarah Slauson, Rick Steves, Bruce VanDeventer, Wikimedia Commons (PD-Art/PD-US). Photos are used by permission and are the property of the original copyright owners.

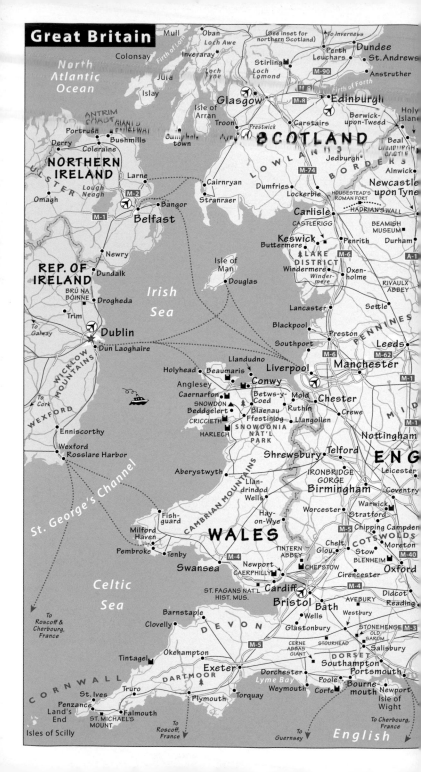

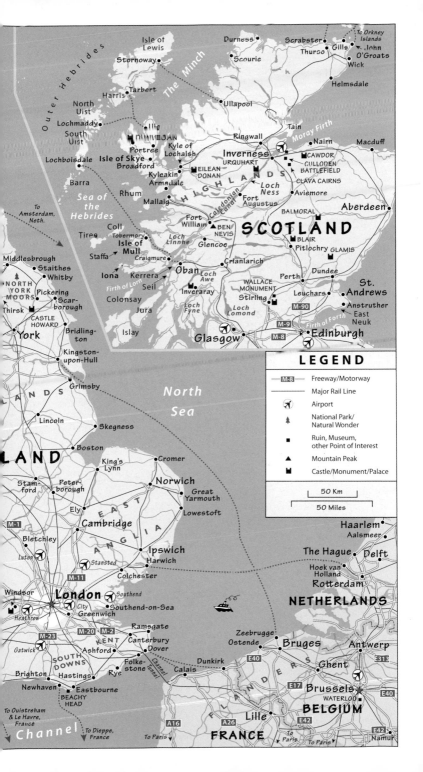

Isle of Lewis
Durness
Scrabster
To Orkney Islands
Gills · John O'Groats
Thurso
Stornoway
Scourie
Wick
Harris · Tarbert
The Minch
Helmsdale
North Uist
Ullapool
Lochmaddy
South Uist
Tain
Ringwall
Moray Firth
Nairn
Macduff
Isle of Skye
Portree
Kyle of Lochalsh
Inverness
CAWDOR
Lochboisdale
Broadford
URQUHART
CULLODEN BATTLEFIELD
Barra
Kyleakin
EILEAN DONAN
HIGHLANDS
CLAVA CAIRNS
Armadale
Loch Ness
Aviemore
Rhum
Sea of the Hebrides
Mallaig
Caledonian Canal
Fort Augustus
Aberdeen
To Amsterdam, Neth.
Fort William
BALMORAL
SCOTLAND
BEN NEVIS
Tiree
Coll
Tobermory
Loch Linnhe
Glencoe
BLAIR
Pitlochry
GLAMIS
Isle of Mull
Staffa
Craigmure
Crianlarich
Middlesbrough
Iona
Kerrera
Oban
Loch Awe
Perth
Dundee
Staithes
Whitby
NORTH YORK MOORS
Pickering
Seil
Inveraray
WALLACE MONUMENT
Leuchars
St. Andrews
Thirsk
Scarborough
Colonsay
Firth of Lorn
Stirling
Anstruther
East Neuk
CASTLE HOWARD
Jura
Loch Fyne
Loch Lomond
M-90
Firth of Forth
York
Bridlington
Islay
Glasgow
M-9
Edinburgh
Kingston-upon-Hull
M-8
Grimsby
North Sea
LANDS
Lincoln
Skegness
LEGEND
M-8 Freeway/Motorway
Major Rail Line
Airport
National Park/ Natural Wonder
Ruin, Museum, other Point of Interest
Mountain Peak
Castle/Monument/Palace
Boston
LAND
Cromer
King's Lynn
Stam-ford
Peter-borough
Norwich
50 Km
50 Miles
Great Yarmouth
Ely
Lowestoft
M-1
Cambridge
EAST ANGLIA
Haarlem
Aalsmeer
Bletchley
Ipswich
The Hague
Delft
Luton
Stansted
Harwich
Hoek van Holland
M-11
Colchester
Rotterdam
Windsor
London
Southend
City
Southend-on-Sea
NETHERLANDS
Heathrow
Greenwich
M-20 M-2
Ramsgate
Gatwick
KENT
Canterbury
Zeebrugge
Ostende
Bruges
Antwerp
M-23
Ashford
Dover
E40
E313
SOUTH DOWNS
Folke-stone
Dunkirk
Ghent
Brighton
Hastings
Rye
Channel Tunnel
Calais
E17
Brussels
Newhaven
Eastbourne
WATERLOO
BELGIUM
BEACHY HEAD
FLANDERS
E40
To Ouistreham & Le Havre, France
A16
Lille
E42
A26
To Dieppe, France
To Paris
FRANCE
To Paris
To Paris
E42
Namur
Channel

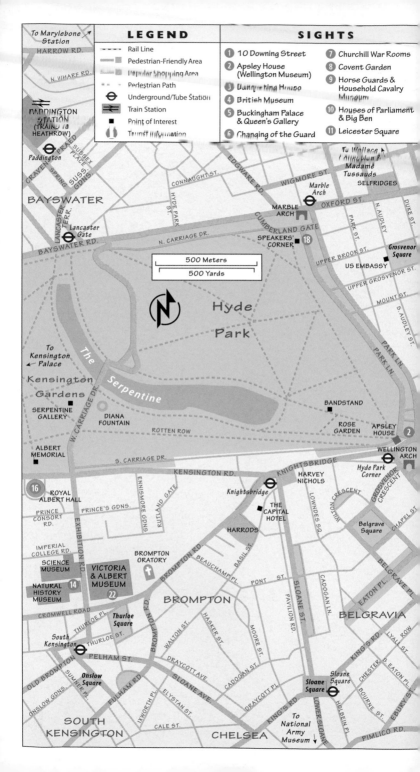

LEGEND

- ⋯⋯ Rail Line
- ▬ Pedestrian-Friendly Area
- ▬ Popular Shopping Area
- ▬ ▬ Pedestrian Path
- ⊖ Underground/Tube Station
- ⇄ Train Station
- ■ Point of Interest
- 𝗂 Tourist Information

SIGHTS

1. 10 Downing Street
2. Apsley House (Wellington Museum)
3. Banqueting House
4. British Museum
5. Buckingham Palace & Queen's Gallery
6. Changing of the Guard
7. Churchill War Rooms
8. Covent Garden
9. Horse Guards & Household Cavalry Museum
10. Houses of Parliament & Big Ben
11. Leicester Square

To Marylebone Station

HARROW RD.
N. WHARF RD.

PADDINGTON STATION (TRAINS TO HEATHROW)

Paddington

BAYSWATER

CRAVEN RD.
SPRING ST.
SUSSEX PLACE
SUSS. GDNS.
PRAED ST.
LANCASTER TERR.

Lancaster Gate

BAYSWATER RD.

CONNAUGHT ST.
EDGWARE RD.

HYDE PARK ST.
N. CARRIAGE DR.

CUMBERLAND GATE

SPEAKERS' CORNER ■ 18

WIGMORE ST.

Marble Arch

MARBLE ARCH

OXFORD ST.

SELFRIDGES

To Wallace Collection & Madame Tussauds

DUKE ST.
N. AUDLEY ST.
PARK ST.

Grosvenor Square

UPPER BROOK ST.

US EMBASSY

UPPER GROSVENOR ST.

MOUNT ST.
S. AUDLEY ST.

500 Meters

500 Yards

N

Hyde Park

To Kensington Palace

Kensington Gardens

The Serpentine

W. CARRIAGE DR.

SERPENTINE GALLERY ■

DIANA FOUNTAIN

ROTTEN ROW

ALBERT MEMORIAL ■

S. CARRIAGE DR.

KENSINGTON RD.

BANDSTAND ■

ROSE GARDEN

APSLEY HOUSE ■ 2

WELLINGTON ARCH

Hyde Park Corner

KNIGHTSBRIDGE

HARVEY NICHOLS

GROSVENOR CRESCENT

PARK LN.
PARK LN.

16 ROYAL ALBERT HALL

PRINCE CONSORT RD.

IMPERIAL COLLEGE RD.

SCIENCE MUSEUM

NATURAL HISTORY MUSEUM 14

CROMWELL ROAD

PRINCE'S GDNS.

ENNISMORE GDNS.

RUTLAND GATE

EXHIBITION RD.

BROMPTON ORATORY ✝

VICTORIA & ALBERT MUSEUM 22

Knightsbridge

THE CAPITAL HOTEL ■

HARRODS

BROMPTON RD.

BEAUCHAMP PL.

BASIL ST.

PONT ST.

CRESCENT

LOWNDES SQ.

LOWNDES ST.

SLOANE ST.

CADOGAN LN.

PAVILION RD.

Belgrave Square

BELGRAVE PL.

EATON PL.

BELGRAVIA

CHAPEL ST.

Thurloe Square

BROMPTON

WALTON ST.

HASKER ST.

MOORE ST.

CADOGAN PL.

South Kensington

THURLOE PL.
THURLOE ST.

PELHAM ST.

Onslow Square

OLD BROMPTON RD.

ONSLOW GDNS.
SUMNER PL.

FULHAM RD.

DRAYCOTT AVE.

SLOANE AVE.

IXWORTH PL.
ELYSTAN ST.

DRAYCOTT PL.

Sloane Square

Sloane Square

KING'S RD.

CHESTER ST.
EATON ST.

CALE ST.

SOUTH KENSINGTON

CHELSEA

To National Army Museum

LOWER SLOANE ST.

HOLBEIN PL.

PIMLICO RD.

EBURY ST.
BOURNE ST.

LYALL ST.
B. EATON PL.

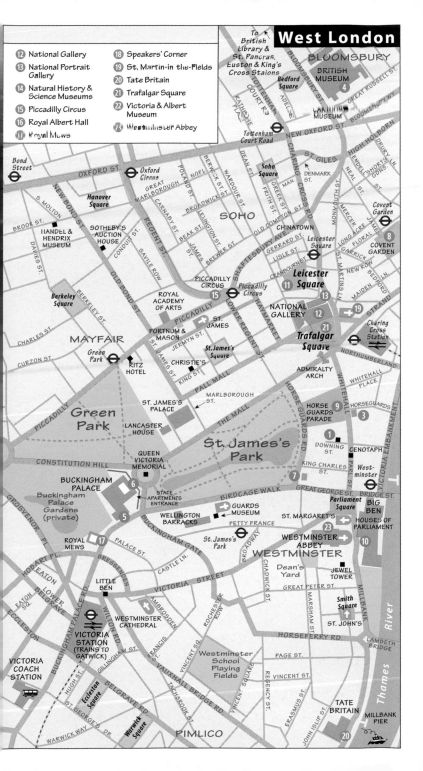

West London

To British Library & St. Pancras, Euston & King's Cross Stations

- 12 National Gallery
- 13 National Portrait Gallery
- 14 Natural History & Science Museums
- 15 Piccadilly Circus
- 16 Royal Albert Hall
- 17 Royal Mews
- 18 Speakers' Corner
- 19 St. Martin-in-the-Fields
- 20 Tate Britain
- 21 Trafalgar Square
- 22 Victoria & Albert Museum
- 23 Westminster Abbey

BLOOMSBURY

BRITISH MUSEUM 4

Bedford Square

TOTTENHAM COURT RD.

RATHBONE ST.

ADELINE

GREAT RUSSELL ST.

BLOOMSBURY WY.

CARTWRIGHT MUSEUM

NEW OXFORD ST.

HIGH HOLBORN

DRURY LN.

Tottenham Court Road

CHARING CROSS RD.

ST. GILES

SHORT'S GDNS.

ENDELL ST.

Bond Street

OXFORD ST.

Oxford Circus

HANOVER Square

S. MOLTON ST.

NEW BOND ST.

BROOK ST.

DAVIES ST.

HANDEL & HENDRIX MUSEUM

SOTHEBY'S AUCTION HOUSE

CONDUIT ST.

SAVILE ROW

REGENT ST.

CARNABY ST.

GREAT MARLBOROUGH

POLAND ST.

HOEL

BERWICK ST.

WARDOUR ST.

DEAN ST.

Soho Square

MAN.

DENMARK

BROADWICK ST.

LEXINGTON ST.

BEAK ST.

JAMES

BREWER ST.

SOHO

GREEK ST.

FRITH ST.

OLD COMPTON ST.

CHINATOWN

GERRARD ST.

LISLE ST.

SHAFTESBURY AVE.

CRANBOURN ST.

MERCER ST.

MONMOUTH

LONG ACRE

NEAL ST.

JAMES ST.

Covent Garden

FLORAL ST.

GARRICK ST.

NEW ROW

BEDFORD LN.

MAIDEN LN.

COVENT GARDEN 8

Berkeley Square

BERKELEY ST.

OLD BOND ST.

BRUTON ST.

ROYAL ACADEMY OF ARTS

PICCADILLY CIRCUS 15

Piccadilly Circus

Leicester Square 11

Leicester Square 13

MARTIN'S LN.

STRAND

19

CHARLES ST.

MAYFAIR

CURZON ST.

Green Park

PICCADILLY

ST. JAMES

FORTNUM & MASON

LOWER REGENT ST.

HAYMARKET

NATIONAL GALLERY 12

Trafalgar Square 21

Charing Cross Station

RITZ HOTEL

JERMYN ST.

St. James's Square

CHRISTIE'S

ST. JAMES ST.

KING ST.

PALL MALL

NORTHUMBERLAND

ADMIRALTY ARCH

WHITEHALL PLACE

HORSE GUARDS RD.

MARLBOROUGH ST.

ST. JAMES'S PALACE

THE MALL

LANCASTER HOUSE

Green Park

PICCADILLY

GROSVENOR PL.

CONSTITUTION HILL

St. James's Park

HORSE GUARDS PARADE 9

HORSEGUARDS

3

1

DOWNING ST.

CENOTAPH

KING CHARLES ST.

Westminster

WHITEHALL

VICTORIA EMBANKMENT

QUEEN VICTORIA MEMORIAL

BUCKINGHAM PALACE

Buckingham Palace Gardens (private)

6

5

STATE APARTMENTS ENTRANCE

BIRDCAGE WALK

7

GUARDS MUSEUM

PETTY FRANCE

GREAT GEORGE ST.

Parliament Square

ST. MARGARET'S

BRIDGE ST.

BIG BEN

HOUSES OF PARLIAMENT 10

WELLINGTON BARRACKS

BUCKINGHAM GATE

St. James's Park

BROADWAY

23

WESTMINSTER ABBEY

WESTMINSTER

ROYAL MEWS 17

PALACE ST.

CASTLE LN.

VICTORIA STREET

CHADWICK ST.

Dean's Yard

JEWEL TOWER

HOBART PL.

EATON

LOWER BELGRAVE

LITTLE BEN

BRESSENDEN PL.

WILTON RD.

AMBROSDEN AVE.

ROCHESTER ROW

GREAT PETER ST.

MARSHAM ST.

Smith Square

ST. JOHN'S

MILLBANK

EATON SQ.

ECCLESTON

VICTORIA STATION (TRAINS TO GATWICK)

WESTMINSTER CATHEDRAL

FRANCIS ST.

GILLINGHAM ST.

VINCENT SQ.

VAUXHALL BRIDGE RD.

Westminster School Playing Fields

VINCENT ST.

PAGE ST.

HORSEFERRY RD.

REGENCY ST.

LAMBETH BRIDGE

Thames River

VICTORIA COACH STATION

BUCKINGHAM PALACE RD.

HUGH ST.

BELGRAVE RD.

TACHBROOK ST.

ST. GEORGE'S DR.

Eccleston Square

Warwick Square

WARWICK WAY

PIMLICO

VINCENT SQUARE

REGENCY ST.

ERASMUS ST.

JOHN ISLIP ST.

TATE BRITAIN

20

MILLBANK PIER

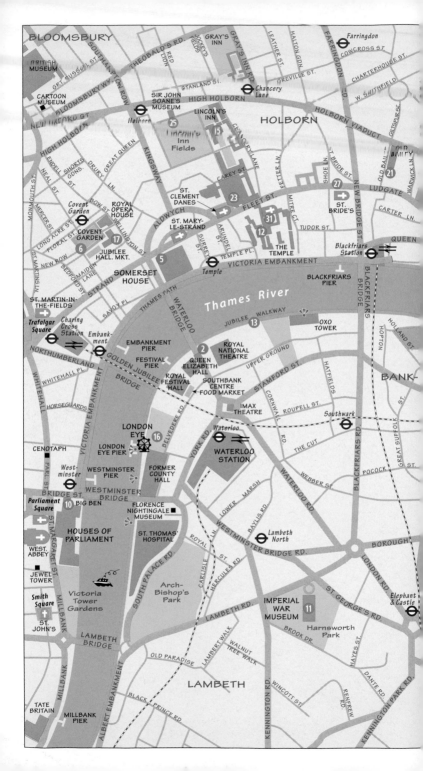

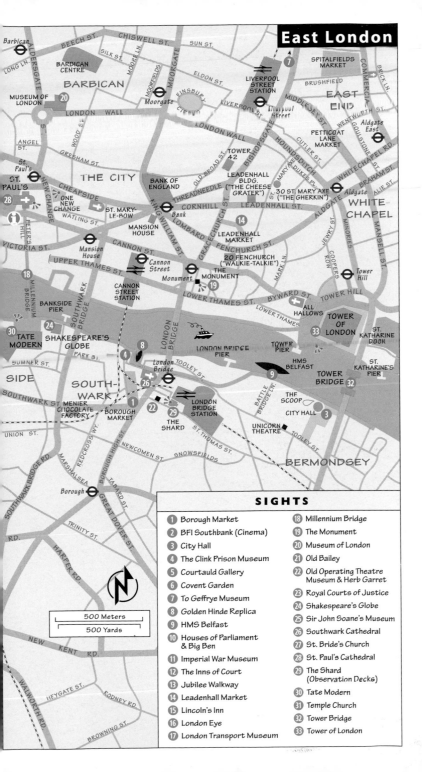

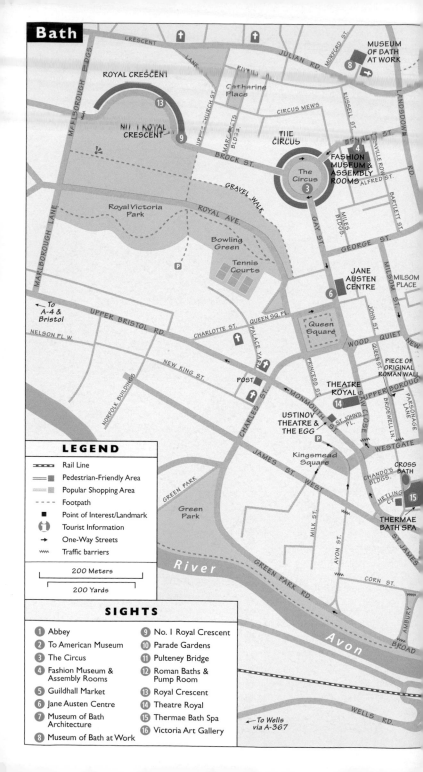

Bath

ROYAL CRESCENT

NO. I ROYAL CRESCENT

THE CIRCUS

The Circus

FASHION MUSEUM & ASSEMBLY ROOMS

MUSEUM OF BATH AT WORK

Catharine Place

CIRCUS MEWS

Royal Victoria Park

ROYAL AVE.

GRAVEL WALK

Bowling Green

Tennis Courts

JANE AUSTEN CENTRE

MILSOM PLACE

GEORGE ST.

Queen Square

PIECE OF ORIGINAL ROMAN WALL

THEATRE ROYAL

USTINOV THEATRE & THE EGG

Kingsmead Square

JAMES ST. WEST

WESTGATE

CROSS BATH

THERMAE BATH SPA

Green Park

River

Avon

To A-4 & Bristol

UPPER BRISTOL RD.

NELSON PL. W.

CHARLOTTE ST.

NEW KING ST.

NORFOLK BUILDINGS

POST

MARLBOROUGH LANE

MELBOROUGH BLDGS

JULIAN RD.

MORFORD ST.

RUSSELL ST.

GAY ST.

MILES BLDGS.

BARTLETT ST.

ALFRED ST.

MILSOM ST.

JOHN ST.

WOOD

QUIET

NEW

GREEN PARK RD.

MILK ST.

AVON ST.

CORN ST.

WELLS RD.

To Wells via A-367

LEGEND

- ▬▬▬ Rail Line
- ▬▬■ Pedestrian-Friendly Area
- ▬▬■ Popular Shopping Area
- ------ Footpath
- ■ Point of Interest/Landmark
- ⛨ Tourist Information
- → One-Way Streets
- ∿∿∿ Traffic barriers

200 Meters

200 Yards

SIGHTS

1. Abbey
2. To American Museum
3. The Circus
4. Fashion Museum & Assembly Rooms
5. Guildhall Market
6. Jane Austen Centre
7. Museum of Bath Architecture
8. Museum of Bath at Work
9. No. 1 Royal Crescent
10. Parade Gardens
11. Pulteney Bridge
12. Roman Baths & Pump Room
13. Royal Crescent
14. Theatre Royal
15. Thermae Bath Spa
16. Victoria Art Gallery

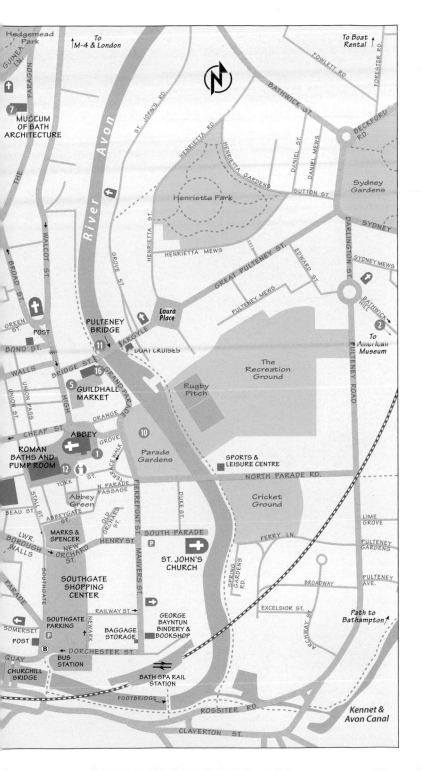

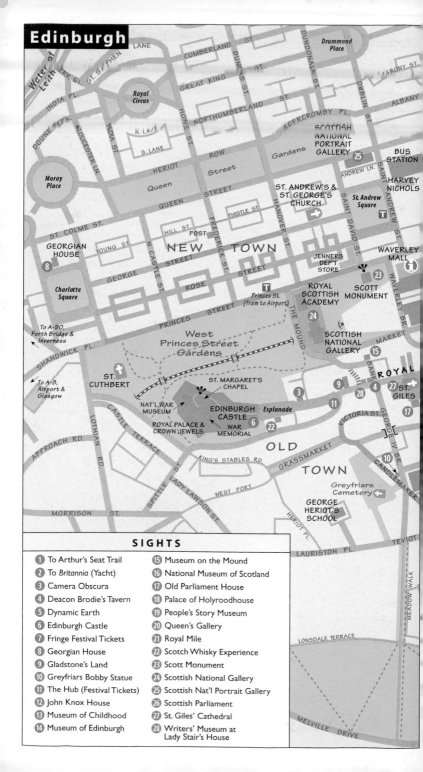

Edinburgh

SIGHTS

1. To Arthur's Seat Trail
2. To *Britannia* (Yacht)
3. Camera Obscura
4. Deacon Brodie's Tavern
5. Dynamic Earth
6. Edinburgh Castle
7. Fringe Festival Tickets
8. Georgian House
9. Gladstone's Land
10. Greyfriars Bobby Statue
11. The Hub (Festival Tickets)
12. John Knox House
13. Museum of Childhood
14. Museum of Edinburgh
15. Museum on the Mound
16. National Museum of Scotland
17. Old Parliament House
18. Palace of Holyroodhouse
19. People's Story Museum
20. Queen's Gallery
21. Royal Mile
22. Scotch Whisky Experience
23. Scott Monument
24. Scottish National Gallery
25. Scottish Nat'l Portrait Gallery
26. Scottish Parliament
27. St. Giles' Cathedral
28. Writers' Museum at Lady Stair's House